THE WORLD'S CLASSICS

THE WANDERER

FRANCES (FANNY) BURNEY (born 1752), the daughter of musicologist Charles Burney, published her highly successful novel *Evelina* in 1778. *Cecilia*, which sealed her mature reputation as a novelist, appeared in 1782. In 1786 Burney was unhappily thrust into a position at court as Second Keeper of the Robes to Queen Charlotte. Her journals and letters, particularly of the court period, have attracted attention from historians, but it is upon her work as a novelist that Burney staked her own claim to fame. After leaving court service in 1791, she met and married Alexandre d'Arblay, an aristocratic liberal, then a penniless émigré in England. Their son, Alexander, was born in 1794. Burney's third novel, the innovative *Camilla* (1796), put a roof over the heads of the new family. While living in France from 1802 to 1812 Burney wrote *The Wanderer*, a novel of the French Revolution, published in 1814. Her last published work was the *Memoirs of Doctor Burney* (1832), which contains much autobiographical material. Frances Burney (Mme d'Arblay) died in 1840.

MARGARET ANNE DOODY is Andrew W. Mellon Professor in the Humanities and Professor of English at Vanderbilt University. Her publications include *A Natural Passion: A Study of the Novels of Samuel Richardson*, *The Daring Muse: Augustan Poetry Reconsidered*, *Frances Burney: The Life in the Works*, as well as two novels, *Aristotle Detective* and *The Alchemists*.

ROBERT L. MACK is a Lecturer at Princeton University. He is currently editing a selection of *Oriental Tales*, and an edition of *The Thousand and One Nights*, for the World's Classics series.

PETER SABOR is a Professor of English at Queen's University, Ontario. His publications include *Horace Walpole: A Reference Guide*, *Horace Walpole: The Critical Heritage*, and editions of Richardson's *Pamela*, Cleland's *Memoirs of a Woman of Pleasure*, and (in collaboration) Burney's *Cecilia* and Carlyle's *Sartor Resartus*. He has co-edited, with Margaret Anne Doody, *Samuel Richardson: Tercentenary Essays*.

THE WORLD'S CLASSICS

THE WANDERER

FRANCES (FANNY) BURNEY, born 1752, the daughter of musicologist Charles Burney, published her highly successful novel *Evelina* in 1778. *Cecilia*, which sealed her mature reputation as a novelist, appeared in 1782. In 1786 Burney was reluctantly thrust into a position at court as Second Keeper of the Robes to Queen Charlotte. Her journals and letters, particularly of the court period, have attracted attention from historians, but it is upon her work as a novelist that Burney staked her own claim to fame. After leaving court service in 1791, she met and married Alexandre d'Arblay, an aristocratic officer, then a penniless émigré in England. Their son, Alexander, was born in 1794. Burney's third novel, the innovative *Camilla* (1796), put a roof over the heads of the new family. While living in France from 1802 to 1812 Burney wrote *The Wanderer*, a novel of the French Revolution, published in 1814. Her last published work was the *Memoirs of Doctor Burney* (1832), which contains much autobiographical material. Frances Burney (Mme d'Arblay) died in 1840.

MARGARET ANNE DOODY is Andrew W. Mellon Professor in the Humanities and Professor of English at Vanderbilt University. Her publications include: *A Natural Passion: A Study of the Novels of Samuel Richardson*, *The Daring Muse: Augustan Poetry Reconsidered*, *Frances Burney: The Life in the Works*, as well as two novels, *Aristotle Detective* and *The Alchemists*.

ROBERT L. MACK is a Lecturer at Princeton University. He is currently editing a selection of *Oriental Tales* and an edition of *The Thousand and One Days* for the World's Classics series.

PETER SABOR is a Professor of English at Queen's University, Ontario. His publications include *Horace Walpole: A Reference Guide*, *Horace Walpole: The Critical Heritage*, and editions of Richardson's *Pamela*, Cleland's *Memoirs of a Woman of Pleasure*, and (in collaboration) Burney's *Cecilia* and *Camilla*. He has co-edited, with Margaret Anne Doody, *Samuel Richardson: Tercentenary Essays*.

THE WORLD'S CLASSICS

FRANCES BURNEY

The Wanderer;

OR,

FEMALE DIFFICULTIES

Edited by

MARGARET ANNE DOODY,
ROBERT L. MACK,

and

PETER SABOR

with an introduction by

MARGARET ANNE DOODY

Oxford New York
OXFORD UNIVERSITY PRESS
1991

Oxford University Press, Walton Street, Oxford OX2 6DP

Oxford New York Toronto
Delhi Bombay Calcutta Madras Karachi
Petaling Jaya Singapore Hong Kong Tokyo
Nairobi Dar es Salaam Cape Town
Melbourne Auckland

and associated companies in
Berlin Ibadan

First published as a World's Classics paperback 1991

British Library Cataloguing in Publication Data
Burney, Fanny 1752–1840
The wanderer, or Female difficulties.
I. Title
823.6 [F]
ISBN 0–19–282133–4

Library of Congress Cataloging in Publication Data
Burney, Fanny, 1752–1840.
The wanderer, or, Female difficulties / Frances Burney; edited by Margaret Anne Doody, Robert L. Mack, and Peter Sabor: with an introduction by Margaret Anne Doody.
p. cm. — (The World's classics)
Includes bibliographical references.
1. France—History—Revolution, 1789–1799—Refugees—Fiction.
I. Doody, Margaret Anne. II. Mack, Robert L. III. Sabor, Peter.
IV. Title. V. Title: Wanderer. VI. Title: Female difficulties.
VII. Series.
PR3316.A4W36 1990 823'.6—dc20 90–31995
ISBN 0–19–282133–4

Typeset by B.P. Integraphics Ltd, Bath, Avon
Printed in Great Britain by
BPCC Hazell Books, Aylesbury, Bucks

CONTENTS

Acknowledgements vi
Introduction vii
Note on the Text xxxviii
Select Bibliography xl
A Chronology of Frances Burney xliii

THE WANDERER; OR, FEMALE DIFFICULTIES

To Doctor Burney 3
Volume I 11
Volume II 195
Volume III 383
Volume IV 563
Volume V 711

APPENDIX I: The French Revolution in *The Wanderer* 875
APPENDIX II: Burney and Race Relations 884
APPENDIX III: Geography 888
APPENDIX IV: Finance 893
APPENDIX V: Fashionable Amusements 897
APPENDIX VI: *The Provok'd Husband* 901

Explanatory Notes 906

ACKNOWLEDGEMENTS

WE are grateful to the Prado for permission to reproduce the cover painting by Goya. We thank the Bodleian Library for permission to reproduce the copy of the first edition of Burney's novel upon which text this edition is based. Thanks are due as well to the British Library, for permission to transcribe the Burney manuscripts included in Appendix VI. Particular thanks are due to the Henry W. and Albert A. Berg Collection of the New York Public Library and to the late curator, Dr Lola Szladits, for permitting us to read the Burney manuscripts in their possession. We are also grateful to the librarians of the Firestone Library of Princeton University, and Queen's University Library for their assistance. Welcome financial support was provided by Princeton University, and by the Advisory Research Committee of the School of Graduate Studies, Queen's University.

We should like to give personal thanks to the following individuals for their interest in and help with the project: Edward A. and Lillian D. Bloom, Tracy Brown, Grant Campbell, Marie Legroulx, F. P. Lock, George Logan, Emmi Sabor, James Sambrook, Florian Stuber, Frank Tompa, and Lars Troide.

INTRODUCTION

The Wanderer is a Romantic novel, declaring its Romanticism in its title, for wandering is a Romantic activity, and wanderers are favourite Romantic characters, from Rousseau's portrait of himself as a 'solitary walker'[1] through a host of female vagrants, gipsies, and old men travelling. One of Wordsworth's central characters is referred to as 'The Wanderer' and this character supplies the title of the first book of *The Excursion*, published in August 1814, a few months after Burney's novel. 'Wandering' is the quintessential Romantic activity, as it represents erratic and personal energy expended outside a structure, and without progressing to a set objective. Impelled either by the harshness of a rejecting society or by some inner spiritual quest, the Wanderer leaves the herd and moves to or through some form of symbolic wilderness or wildness, seeing a world very different from that perceived by those who think they are at the centre. Alien and alienated, yet potentially bearing a new compassion or a new wisdom, the Wanderer draws a different map.

Frances Burney has often been thought of as a cheerful Georgian satirist, but such a view of her has ignored some of the darker and stranger aspects of her earlier work. In *Evelina* (1778), the most overtly sunny of her novels, the orphaned heroine appears in the eyes of the world to be illegitimate; rejected by her father, she is horrified at the apparition of the matriarch in the form of her grandmother. The revelation of

[1] Jean-Jacques Rousseau wrote the autobiographical *Reveries du Promeneur solitaire*, after the *Confessions*, left unfinished at his death in 1778 and published at the end of the *Confessions*; cf. Mary Wollstonecraft to William Godwin: 'I—will become again a *Solitary Walker*.' *Collected Letters of Mary Wollstonecraft*, ed. Ralph M. Wardle (Ithaca, NY, 1979), p. 337. Wordsworth's wandering characters appear in poems such as 'The Female Vagrant' in *Lyrical Ballads* (1798), a volume reviewed by Burney's father, Dr Charles Burney. 'The Old Cumberland Beggar' (published 1800) offers another example, but Wordsworth's travellers are many. The Wanderer of *The Excursion* is a quintessentially wise observer: 'He could *afford* to suffer | With those whom he saw suffer. Hence it came | That in our best experience he was rich, | And in the wisdom of our daily life'. (Book I, ll. 370–3, in *Wordsworth Poetical Works*, Oxford Standard Authors (Oxford, 1969), p. 595.)

the maternal principle in the person who embodies the threat of the grotesque and powerless feminine heritage is quite a Gothic moment; 'amazed, frightened, and unspeakably shocked', Evelina sinks 'more dead than alive' into her friend's arms (i. 52). In *Cecilia* (1782) Burney produces not so much a light satirical analysis of individual defects and follies as an analysis of a whole society ridden by its false values of Class and Money; this is one of the first novels to introduce Gothic symbolism as a sort of running base to the more acceptable Augustan moral expression. *Cecilia* speaks a figurative language of castle, ruin, goal, gunshot, and hallucination—it prefigures and supports a new Romanticism. The novel also employs a vocabulary that endorses change, a language of 'reason', 'Prejudice', 'all-powerful Necessity', 'happiness'; *Cecilia* can be seen as one of the first of the Jacobin novels. *Camilla* (1796), in its five '*Udolphoish* volumes'[2] reflects the perturbation and the literary experiments of the revolutionary period of the 1790s, although the novel itself does not deal directly either with the French Revolution or with the Gothic novelists' enterprise.

Burney's *The Wanderer*, written over a period of about fourteen years, had the longest gestation period of any of her works. The novel was apparently begun in the later 1790s, after *Camilla*, but it was then put aside for some time. Burney wished and hoped to make money enough to keep herself and her husband, the French émigré Alexandre d'Arblay, and their child, little Alex. The proceeds of *Camilla* literally put a roof over the family's head (they built Camilla Cottage), but writing a novel always took Burney at least three years, and income from a novel was relatively low. More money was to be made in the theatre. Burney set to work to produce a theatrical comedy. The manager of Covent Garden Theatre offered her £400 for *Love and Fashion*, which was to be produced in the spring of 1800. The death of Burney's dearest sister and best friend, Susanna Phillips, in January 1800, a death which took place under particularly distressing circumstances, made such

[2] Frances Burney to brother Charles Burney, 15 July 1795, describing *Camilla*: 'we always meant to make 4 *Udolphoish* volumes', *The Journals and Letters of Fanny Burney (Madame d'Arblay)*, ed. Joyce Hemlow *et al.*, 12 vols. (Oxford, 1972–84) iii. 137.

a venture seem heartless, and Burney was the more vulnerable to persuasion from her father, Dr Charles Burney, who insisted she recall the play from production. Burney wrote two other comedies in this period: *A Busy Day* (1800–1) and *The Woman-Hater* (1801). But none was to be put on stage. The author's husband returned to France in 1801 and then called upon his wife and child to join him. General d'Arblay had been trying to regain his commission in the French army, but his stipulation that he not be required to bear arms against England was regarded as unacceptable by Napoleon, and he was advised that he could not leave France without incurring suspicion of some new disloyalty. His residence in France was thus indefinite. Frances Burney had been struggling to try to prevent just such an outcome of their lives; if only she had been able to make *enough* money quickly by her playwriting, d'Arblay might have been persuaded not to go to France nor to try to settle there. In April 1802 Burney moved to France, hurriedly, because no one could tell how long the brief peace between France and England would last. That tenuous peace was soon ruptured, and return to England was impossible. Frances Burney lived in exile in France for ten years. Only after that period did she give voice to her sense of the misery of living under a military dictatorship. In July 1815, writing to her old friend Mary Ann Waddington, who had professed admiration for Napoleon, Burney protested:

> How is it that my ever dear Mary can thus ... be a professed & ardent detester of Tyranny; yet an open & intrepid admirer of a Tyrant? O had you spent, like me, 10 years within the control of his unlimited power, & under the iron rod of its dread, how would you change your language! by a total reverse of sentiment! yet was I, because always innoffensive, never molested: as safe There, *another* would say, as in London; but *you* will not say so; the safety of deliberate prudence, or of retiring timidity, is not such as would satisfy a mind glowing for freedom like your's: it satisfies, indeed NO *mind*, it merely suffices for *bodily* security. It was the choice of my Companion, not of my Taste that drew ME to such a residence. PERSONALLY, for the reason I have assigned, I was always well-treated, & personally I was happy: but you know me, I am sure, better than to suppose me such an Egotist as to be really happy, or contented,

where Corporal Liberty could only be preserved by Mental forbearance—i.e. subjection.[3]

This is a rare and impressive political statement; particularly impressive in Burney's insistence that her personal and familial happiness is not an appropriate measure of the success of a government. Her statement also assumes that 'a mind glowing for freedom' is a good thing—and a good thing in a woman. Her language here seems entirely to call into question her own conduct and the conduct of others, male and female, who live successfully under tyrannies by pursuing a studied inoffensiveness. Such 'deliberate prudence' or 'retiring timidity' can satisfy no mind, and 'Mental forbearance' is merely an acquiescence in one's own subjection and the subjection of others. The principles expressed in this letter may profitably be kept in mind when reading *The Wanderer*—although the novel would have fared better with English reviewers had it dealt with the iniquities of Napoleon and let England alone.

Once the d'Arblays were in France, there was certainly no chance of Burney's making money by writing plays for the stage, and even publication of her novels now seemed a remote possibility, although she was still a known literary personality in France—to the extent that Napoleon referred to M. d'Arblay as 'the husband of Cecilia'.[4] Burney worked on the new novel that had been put aside for the plays. A diary section entitled 'Scribleration' shows that in 1806 she advanced in writing the first draft of *The Wanderer*; cryptic notes such as 'Humours of a Milliner's Shop' and 'Introduction to Toad Eating' show that she was working on the middle sections of the book in which the heroine tries to earn her own living. We do not, however, have any manuscript of this novel, as we do of *Evelina*, *Cecilia*, and *Camilla*; we cannot trace its progress or the changes she made in it.

[3] Frances Burney to Mary Ann Waddington, July 1815, *Journals and Letters*, viii. 282–3.

[4] Napoleon's words to M. de Lafayette as quoted by Lafayette to Alexandre d'Arblay (see *Journals and Letters*, v. 173), and translated by Burney for her account of this interview in her partly autobiographical *Memoirs of Doctor Burney*, 3 vols. (London, 1832), iii. 317–18.

The Wanderer was a novel completed under sharp intimations of mortality. The most startling event of Burney's residence in France was the operation that she underwent in 1811. She was diagnosed as having breast cancer; with a courage we can hardly even imagine, she decided to have the breast surgically removed, a momentous decision in the era before anaesthetics. She underwent a complete mastectomy in September.[5] This terrible experience itself seems to play a part in shaping some scenes in *The Wanderer*, while the event helped drive the novel to its conclusion. Under the stress of operation and recovery, Burney's desire to see her home and family again increased. The departure of Napoleon for Russia in 1812 led to some easing of bureaucratic restrictions and Mme d'Arblay and her son were given permission to depart, nominally for America. Actually the ship was intended to touch illegally at an English port and let off a number of passengers. In the event, the *Mary Anne* fell one of the first victims to the sudden renewal of active hostilities between France and England in 1812; the vessel was captured, and Burney returned to English shores nominally a prisoner.

Burney's crossing to England was nearly as adventurous as the heroine's crossing in the episode that begins *The Wanderer*. Surprisingly, it was not Burney's original intention to take the manuscript of the new novel with her. Only prolonged waiting at Dunkirk stimulated Burney to think of employing her time in writing; she sent to her husband a request for the manuscript, which d'Arblay lovingly packed up, having first obtained the necessary permission from the Police Office, assuring the officer 'upon his Honour, that the Work had nothing in it political, nor even National ... possibly offensive to the Government'. Burney records this episode in her Dedication, referring to the liberality of 'the Custom-house on either—alas!—hostile shore', since, at both, 'upon my given word that the papers contained neither letters, nor political writings; but simply a work of invention and observation; the voluminous

[5] See Burney's own account of this ordeal, *Journals and Letters*, vi. 596–615, and Julia Epstein's discussion of the event and Burney's account of it, 'Writing the Unspeakable: Fanny Burney's Mastectomy and the Fictive Body', *Representations*, 16 (Fall 1986), 131–66.

manuscript was suffered to pass, without demur, comment, or the smallest examination'.[6]

Whatever claims were made to the customs officials of both countries, *The Wanderer* is undoubtably political. Its 'invention' and 'observation' deal with political matters. Burney herself says in that same Dedication that no modern novel can really ignore the French Revolution:

> to attempt to delineate, in whatever form, any picture of actual human life, without reference to the French Revolution, would be as little possible, as to give an idea of the English government, without reference to our own: for not more unavoidably is the last blended with the history of our nation, than the first, with every intellectual survey of the present times (p. 6).

The English Revolution of 1688–9 had changed the English government and moulded a nation's constitution; yet, Burney says, the French Revolution is now more important as more pervasive. A contemporary writer must deal with it, not just when discussing government, or what is generally constructed as 'history', but when dealing with any picture of 'actual human life'. A novel is thus, by implication, an 'intellectual survey of the present times', and novel-writing is thus an historical and political activity. Burney had always in some manner understood this fact, at least since her second novel, *Cecilia*, which is an intellectual survey of its times, not only the 1780s but of an era of fully-developed capitalism meshing uneasily with a privileged aristocracy. It can be argued that most of the women writers of the eighteenth century understood that, as we say, 'the personal is the political'. But Burney offers the fullest articulation of this view in *Cecilia*. That novel was to influence the liberal and radical writers of the 1790s,

[6] Actually Burney in her Dedication gracefully elides over the real trouble she had with the customhouse officer at Dunkirk; the officer on seeing the little portmanteau full of the manuscript of *The Wanderer* flew into a rage and 'began a rant of indignation & amazement, at a sight so unexpected & prohibited ... He sputtered at the Mouth, & stamped with his feet'. He accused Burney of 'traiterous [*sic*] designs' and she believed at the time that, had she not had the timely assistance of an English merchant to vouch for her, 'this Fourth Child of my Brain had undoubtably been destroyed ere it was Born'; see *Journals and Letters*, vi. 716–17.

including Charlotte Smith, Mary Wollstonecraft, and William Godwin, all of whom register reactions in their writings to Burney's works. In her last novel Burney picks up various aspects of both radical 'Jacobin' and conservative discussions and offers a detailed exploration in her new 'intellectual survey' of the political nature of personal life.

By the time it was finished, *The Wanderer* was, indeed, ostensibly a historical novel, offering its own contribution to the new genre which had been largely produced by response to the French Revolution. In the 1790s and the early years of the new century, radical and conservative novelists alike wrote works exploring both the very recent past and the distant past. Charlotte Smith in *Desmond* (1792) and *The Banished Man* (1794) offered views of the Revolution; the first optimistic (and counter to Burke), set in 1790; the second, more pessimistic, as Smith was forced to come to terms with the new policies of terror, set in 1793–4—the execution of Louis XVI takes place in the middle of the latter novel. Jane Porter in *Thaddeus of Warsaw* (1803) explored the condition of Poland in 1794. Elizabeth Hamilton's conservative and lively *Memoirs of Modern Philosophers* (1800) mocks English enthusiasm for the Revolution in the early years of the 1790s; the villain of the piece sends others to the guillotine and at last perishes by it. There were also novels exploring historical events and conflicts of a more distant past, such as Jane West's *The Loyalists* (about the English civil war in the 1640s and the rule of Cromwell). Walter Scott came as a novelist upon a scene full of new works dealing with conflicts past and present; the first of his historical novels, *Waverley*, was published in the same year as Burney's *The Wanderer*.

The Wanderer when it was conceived must have seemed to its author another historical novel of the immediate past, like Charlotte Smith's *The Banished Man*; the long period of gestation meant that it became the more 'historical', as set in a period before the time of its completion and publication. The period in which the novel is set ('the dire reign of the terrific Robespierre') must be 1793–4. Yet Burney made the decision not to mention actual dates (save for months) and the number of overt specific historical references is very limited. 'Robespierre'—whose name is variously mispronounced and misinterpreted by the English characters the heroine meets—stands for whole sets of concepts of historicity and individualism. Both Frances Burney and M. d'Arblay had been greatly shaken and grieved by the execution of Louis XVI in January 1793. Burney also records her greater horror at the execution of Marie Antoinette (on 16 October 1793), 'this last act of savage hardness of Heart' as she wrote on 27 October.[7] It is startling to realize that there are no direct references at all to Louis XVI or to the late Queen in the whole of *The Wanderer*. In very noticeable contrast to Edmund Burke (whom Burney might be thought to have wished to follow), the novelist produces no propaganda for, or even references to, the pathos of suffering monarchy or the glory of the feudal state. There is no King Louis's head haunting the pages of *The Wanderer*.

The novel is in some sense 'haunted' by the Gothic novel and its forms and formulae as curious instruments with which to observe repression. The Gothic novelists such as Ann Radcliffe were Burney's own successors, but she, in turn, had learned from them—and also perhaps from the Godwin of *Caleb Williams* (1794), though she protested when she read *Caleb Williams* that she did not like the book. Mystery and concealment, spying and flight are important elements in both Godwin's novels and her own. But she had been thinking of such matters since the early 1790s, the period of gestation of *Camilla*. One of Burney's manuscript notes of that period suggests an idea picked up in *The Wanderer*: 'A carried on disguise, from virtuous motives, producing a mystery which the audience themselves cannot pierce. Exciting alternatively blame & pity'.[8] This describes the condition of 'Ellis' and also the condition of the readers (the audience). We are confronted in the heroine with a mystery which we cannot 'pierce'. The heroine steadily presents herself as ingenuous, but even more steadily adheres to forms of disguise and concealment. One of

[7] Frances Burney to Dr Charles Burney, 27 Oct. 1793, *Journals and Letters*, iii. 18.

[8] Among manuscript scraps in the Henry W. and Albert A. Berg Collection, The New York Public Library; see Doody, *Frances Burney: The Life in the Works* (New Brunswick, NJ, 1988), p. 251.

the important influences on this presentation appears to be Radcliffe's *The Romance of the Forest* (1791). Radcliffe's heroine also first appears to us as an unknown unnamed figure in immediate need of pity and succour; later, when we learn her first name and something of her story from her narrative to her hosts, we still do not know her last name or her whole story. Moreover, the mysterious manuscript, only intermittently legible, that Adeline finds in the ruined Abbey constantly conceals the name and identity of the distressed writer, thus redoubling the motifs presenting the unknowableness of identity.

Unlike Radcliffe's heroine, Burney's speaks up for herself; she is at first a voice and nothing else, speaking out of the darkness. Coming aboard the little boat that is setting off from the dangerous shore of France, she joins a group of English tourists for whom France has become too uncomfortable. The heroine is not like them. She is obviously no tourist, but none of her companions can say what she is. Is she a nun? Is she merely a lower-class woman, no better than a housemaid? How did she get her wounds for which she wears bandages? Is she French or English? As the morning light arrives, they see that she is apparently a black woman: is she West Indian? Is she African? The heroine thus arrives as a nameless Everywoman; both black and white, both Eastern and Western, both high and low, both English and French. She unites but does not resolve contradictions. Even when some elements of her disguise (her black colouring, the patches and bandages and floppy hat) are removed, she persists in being 'an Ænigma', the 'Incognita', or Unknown. She sustains her role of Everywoman throughout the novel, as is indicated by the name she adopts or has thrust upon her.

This nameless person tries to collect letters addressed to 'L.S.' (p. 63). She is then called by her English acquaintances 'Miss Ellis' or 'Ellis'. Thus, the name which the readers know her by is, we are well aware, a made-up affair. One may wonder why Burney chose those particular two letters of the alphabet for her heroine's mock name. One answer is to point out that 'L.S.' are the initials of Letitia Sourby, a character appearing in a paper of the reactionary periodical *The Anti-Jacobin* in December 1797, a paper perhaps written by Burney's father, Dr Charles Burney. Letitia Sourby writes a letter complaining that her father has accepted the new radical ideas—certainly not a problem in the Burney family. Frances Burney's 'L.S.' is not a Letitia Sourby, who would be happy to go back to some original state of conservative living. Once she has seen the world in which real lives are lived, no retreat is possible. Thus L.S. has to try to earn her own living, in a world hostile not just to herself in particular, but to women and to women's achievement of financial independence and self respect. L and S are the first letters of the sequence L.s.d.—livre, shilling, denarius—pounds, shillings, and pence. They represent a currency. To be a woman and to come upon the economic world, the world of exchange, is to realize that one is seen as a medium and means of exchange. Women do not command a currency—they *are* a currency. The hard initials are however transformed by various women into a name. Miss Bydel, the under-bred snob, hearing only the sound of the letters, calls the heroine 'Mrs. Elless', saying 'I see no reason why any body should be ashamed to own their name is Elless' (p. 81). But this is a name which means less—elle-less—less than a woman. It is Elinor the ardent champion of women's rights who transforms the name to 'Miss Ellis'—though 'Ellis' refers to the heroine as a first name or a last name, indifferently. That name, in a macaronic pun, signifies that elle is, i.e. 'she is'. Woman lives. (Emily Brontë, significantly, was to choose 'Ellis Bell' as her pen name.) Burney is very fond of names for her female characters that have that 'elle' or she built into them, and the similarity of 'Ellis' and 'Elinor' alerts us to the possibility that these two characters may be seen as aspects of each other.

Both 'Ellis' the refugee and Elinor the devotee of women's rights question and stir up the society around them. When Ellis first gets aboard the boat to cross the Channel, she joins a ship of fools, of whom Elinor is one; all of these characters recur, and all—save Elinor—are types presenting the stagnation of English life. We must sympathize with the nameless heroine, even while she antagonizes us with her mystery, because the English world in which she takes refuge proves so deadly dull, so limited. Proud that they are not cruel and disruptive like the

French, the English characters live in a stuffy middle-class aura of self-congratulation, ignoring the cruelty to the poor to which they themselves are contributing. The demands made upon ladies for acquiescence and propriety are quite evidently stultifying. The ladies have little better to do than to acquire accomplishments which have a sort of social currency, for the sake of status and show rather than of real pleasure or study. Ellis is an accomplished performer on the harp, who plays for herself rather than for display (she is first overheard). When she tries to make her living as a music teacher, she is absorbed into the system of ministering to the ladies, assisting their response to cultural demands that they do something pleasing. Ellis naïvely supposes that the basic reason for studying the harp must be a desire to play music. When she discovers that the fading beauty Miss Brinville has absolutely no ability, she feels honour-bound not to pursue the lessons, since 'the darkness of all musical apprehension was so impenetrable, that not a ray of instruction could make way through it'. As Ellis sees the matter, she would be dishonest in not saying so, since she herself, in taking more fees, would be 'the only one who could profit' from concealment of this truth (p. 236). She is of course wrong. Miss Brinville profits from the repute of taking the lessons, and has plans for displaying 'her attitudes and motions' to show off her figure to Sir Lyell. Ellis is in Miss Brinville's eyes depriving her of an important accessory of femininity, just as if she were a milliner who had refused to sell Miss Brinville a hat. She rapidly finds another 'professor' who understands the business better and ridicules—not stupid Miss Brinville but her former teacher. To make one's living as a woman ministering to ladies' wants is a difficult art, as the ladies' wants are so sophisticated and culturally distorted. The 'ladies' prove to want most of all someone they can patronize and boss around; to show off superiority is a need which many human beings are quick to gratify.

Women are not necessarily at all angelic to one another, nor are they devoid of the baser aspects of human nature that make repression and revolution (as well as other political developments) a perpetual possibility. Miss Arbe, desirous to get herself free lessons and even more anxious for the treat of acting the role of patroness, takes charge of Ellis's life both officiously and inefficiently. Miss Arbe regards herself as an *arbiter* (Burney's made-up names are full of puns) and sets going the plan that Ellis so much detests, of the ladies' concert. Miss Arbe takes over Aurora's gift of money (a gift which would have solved the immediate financial difficulties of the young harp player) and spends it on the cruelly brilliant rose-colour gown which is to mark the patronized girl as a being of another order. Miss Arbe heading the ladies' committee offers a comic spectacle of political life:

> She suggested all that was to be attempted; she directed all that was to be done. A committee of ladies was formed, nominally for consultation, but, in fact, only for applause ... the whole party was of opinion, that nothing less than utter ruin to the project could ensue from her defection.
>
> This helpless submission to ignorant dominion, so common in all committees where the leaders have no deeper science than the led, impeded not the progress of the preparations. Concentrated, or arbitrary government may be least just, but it is most effective. Unlimited in her powers, uncontrouled in their exertion, Miss Arbe saved as much time by the rapidity, as contention by the despotism of her proceedings (p. 305).

Burney satirically picks up a number of political terms, and generalizes at once about both small and large organizations. There is a succinct irony in the sentence which looks like a political aphorism: 'Concentrated, or arbitrary government may be least just, but it is most effective'. This is one of the truths universally acknowledged, as it were, and is in fact very close to the genuine sentiments of Burney's friend of the old days, elderly 'Daddy' Crisp, who wrote to her, in July 1779, during the American War of Independence, 'an arbitrary Government mildly administered ... is upon the whole the most permanent & eligible of all Forms'.[9] Arbitrary government is here represented in the truly *arbitrary* Miss Arbe, who exactly reflects in her small way the political management, rise, and decisiveness of Robespierre, that greater head of a com-

[9] Samuel Crisp to Frances Burney, 21 July 1779, British Library, Egerton MS 3694, fos. 104–5.

mittee and exponent of despotism whose name is so constantly invoked and so constantly mispronounced by the novel's characters. Neither Robespierre nor Miss Arbe is truly effective; the arrangements of both become swallowed in egotism, are highly disorganized if impetuously directed, and are bound to end in failure. Although the little ladies' committee (ostensibly founded for a charitable purpose) is not, apparently, at all like the Committee of Public Safety, the point is not to make fun of female ineffectuality in contrast to grand political movements, but to show how the same impulses may be found in various human constructions. Part of the trouble with Miss Arbe is that she has believed in an idea of 'leadership' which stimulates her desire to exert a masculine controlling power of a phallic nature that makes other resonances of her name (it is near to *arbre*, or tree) not inappropriate; she is a despotic tree. It is not merely the women's committee that reflects the tyranny and disorder to be found in England. A sort of tyranny much less susceptible of definition than Robespierre's is everywhere to be felt: an unthinking, settled but very powerful tyranny of received opinions, class distinctions, and social heartlessness.

The world of Brighton and Lewes that the novelist shows here is not, as the English think, a paradisal refuge from the disorders of France. The very kind of order that is sought by persons such as Mrs Howel, Mrs Maple, or Lady Kendover is a kind of diseased apathy. Nor is it the heroine only who is mistreated. Society runs along rigid class lines, and everyone takes it for granted that many people should be poor—even very poor—and yet should be despised for being poor. The tyranny exercised in England expresses itself in financial transactions and financial terms: the rich punish poor thieves and poachers with great show of indignation, and are very frightened at the thought that they might be taken in by a 'frenchified swindler'. Yet their regular practices are swindling. They think nothing of withholding or postponing the payment of money which a poor person (male or female) needs in order to eat, or to purchase some shelter. They may take music lessons from Ellis, but will not pay for them—and make up the excuse that after all, harp playing is mere 'luxury'. These attitudes Miss Arbe's odd cousin, Giles Arbe, tries to combat, in an important chapter dealing with economic relations where he seems to reflect the opinions of his author, Mme d'Arblay (ch. xxxiii). Burney here takes up the cause of all the actors, singers, musicians, dancers—so many of whom she had known in her youth in the house of Dr Burney, himself not only a musicologist but a performing musician, and also a music teacher.

Burney shrewdly picks out the sorts of excuses or rationales people invent in order not to have to regard other human beings as other human beings. Like her elder contemporary Immanuel Kant (1724–1804) (of whom it is unlikely that she had ever heard), Burney would have us believe that human beings belong to the kingdom of ends and cannot be treated instrumentally, as pertaining to the kingdom of means. For her as for Kant the doctrine of immortality is necessary as a God-given fulfilment of the moral life. Yet in the world of *The Wanderer*, the world her solitary wanderer encounters, human beings are everywhere treated as means. Women are expected to put up with the insulting posings of a Mr Scope, who myopically offers no scope at all. The general acquiescence in and perpetuation of an unexamined despotism manifested in constant injustice can be felt in the extreme sterility of the region the Wanderer enters. In Burney's version of the world of Brighton, that pleasant spot (by 1814 thoroughly associated with the Prince Regent and with the fantasy of the Brighton Pavilion) is a crazed cold place. Hardly anybody seems to be married; it is a region of old bachelors and widows and old maids, with a few young bachelors and some young and not so young women trying ineffectually to get husbands. It is an inturned world of lassitude and gossip; only Aurora, Elinor, and Harleigh seem to have any literary and intellectual resources. And only the poor *émigrées*, Ellis and Gabriella, look at the sea.

When Ellis arrives in the middle of this stale society, she is a catalytic force—a novelty, an amusement, and a presence that shakes the social assumptions. That is, she is all the things that Elinor tries to be. For all the oppression from which she suffers, and with all the mystery that surrounds her, she is still life-affirming—as can be felt when she is still the black girl, and in her joy at arriving at England gives 'a bright smile, that displayed a row of beautifully white and polished teeth' (p. 21). Such natural vivacity, combined with her solitary state, leads almost inevitably to the assumption that she must be a prostitute, or a cast-off mistress, which is the assumption that the old Admiral (actually her own relative) makes about the stranger (ch. iii). Admiral Powel lives in an innocent world that upholds his rights and beliefs. He believes in individual charity.

I can't consent to see you starve in a land of plenty; which would be a base ingratitude to our Creator, who, in dispensing the most to the upper class, grants us the pleasure of dispensing the overplus, ourselves, to the under class; which I take to be the true reason of Providence for ordering that difference between the rich and the poor ... (p. 35).

His belief in some duty of stewardship makes the Admiral better than most of the other middle-class people we meet, but his naïve interpretation of the class system is not really upheld by the experiences of the heroine, any more than is his very obviously naïve belief that the stranger must be a naughty woman or she wouldn't be put in such straits.

the devil himself never yet put it into a man's head, nor into the world's neither, to abandon, or leave, as you call it, desolate, a woman who has kept tight to her own duty, and taken a modest care of herself (p. 37).

This is arrant nonsense, as our knowledge of Ellis and later of Gabriella, the other *émigrée*, makes clear. Burney shows why we cannot believe that the system of male patronage and protection actually works justly and fairly for women. In fact, in order to save a man (her friend the bishop) from the guillotine, 'Ellis' in France has had in effect to prostitute herself in undergoing marriage to the Commissary. Blackmailed into a hated marriage, fortunately not consummated, she has kept to her duty by transcending in some sense the 'modest care of herself' which the world exhorts. She is always a woman on a cusp: neither French nor English, neither maid nor wife.

Ellis's very vitality as well as power to keep secrets about herself hidden—a power no one wishes or welcomes in a female—makes her a mysterious siren. She comes into Brighton as a seductive influence—at least, that is how some characters see her. Elinor, always trying to make some excitement in artificially and forever hankering after drama, has the scheme of producing a play—*The Provok'd Husband* (see Appendix VI). When her star actress Miss Arbe drops out of the leading role of Lady Townly, Elinor turns to the Incognita for help and Ellis, who has served as prompter and then as reader, is forced into participation. She demurs—but she acts very well. She starts off by being nervous, but gets more and more caught by the spirit of the activity: 'her performance ... seemed the essence of gay intelligence, of well bred animation, and of lively variety ... Her voice modulated into all the changes that vivacity, carelessness, pride, pleasure, indifference, or alarm demanded' (p. 94). She is that dangerous being, a fine female actress. She has already shown herself to be that equally dangerous creature, the harp-player and singer, producing alternately 'tones sweet, yet penetrating, of touching pathos or impassioned animation' (pp. 73–4). Ellis is a performer. She may have the modesty and timidity of Jane Austen's Fanny Price in *Mansfield Park* (another novel of 1814), yet Ellis can act where Austen's heroine Fanny cannot, and in many of her accoutrements and accomplishments she more resembles that other brilliant (and intelligent) actress and harp-player, Mary Crawford.

A being so animated placed in a world so dead is bound to awaken both interest and hostility. Both men and women try to use and dominate the Incognita. The exceptions are found among the novel's inner sisterhood: Aurora and Gabriella. Ellis is attracted at once to Aurora (a Romantic name; signifying dawn and new hope for women). Their friendship is mutual. For all her pride Ellis strangely does not shrink from taking benefits from the hand of Lady Aurora. 'Ellis', or 'Juliet', to use the real name that the heroine keeps secret, knows what Aurora does not know, that the two are literal sisters, if half-sisters. A similar kinship makes the courtship and propositions of Lord Melbury the more frightening, invoking that shadow of incest that would seem Shelleyan if we did not know that fraternal incest had figured in Burney's works as early as *Evelina.* The male relative poses a kind of threat, expressed as the sexual threat, whereas the sisterhood is free of all base designs. Gabriella, the sister in misfortune, is a reflection of Ellis incarnate as a Frenchwoman. Gabriella's name makes her a counterpart and a contrast to that false archangel, the bitter Gabriel Marchmont of *Camilla*, who is the heroine's sincerest enemy. This female archangel is the novel's true angel of annunciation. It is with the advent of Gabriella upon the scene that we learn at last the true name of Ellis: Juliet. But this Shakespearian name is in its French version 'Julie', a name that suggests Rousseau. Even the 'real' name is double.

Elinor is or ought to be the fourth member of the sisterhood, but she is not only a complement but an antagonist of Ellis-Juliet. The instrument that sets them at variance is the novel's hero, Harleigh—or rather he is the character who stands in stead of a 'hero'. As the two young women are both in love with the same man, they offer the conventional triangle, and, as it is customary for the heroine's rival to be a bad lady, the conventional reader may feel that this configuration makes certain the iniquity or wrongheadedness of Elinor's feminist views and impulsive behaviour. But Harleigh himself complicates this neat pattern, chiefly in being such a very passive and fussy person. He does not satisfy our ideas of the 'hero' of a love story—who ought to be handsome, dashing, strong, and courageous, if a trifle self-willed. Harleigh resembles only too much the other blighted and cranky bachelors who populate Burney's Sussex; he is correct, nervous, and anxious. The life of 'Ellis' means that she must take perpetual risks with propriety; Harleigh is there to enforce the proprieties, to remind the heroine of ladylike standards which she cannot honourably maintain. Harleigh himself is parodically ladylike. He is the last and least attractive of a series of Burney heroes, beginning with Lord Orville (who at least had some semblance of dash, though his male acquaintance call him an 'old woman'), progressing through Mortimer Delvile, the spoiled and depressed heir (whom saucy Lady Honoria Pemberton compares to a baby), to Edgar Mandlebert, the self-diffident and obsessively jealous orphan youth who causes so much misery to the heroine of *Camilla*. Albert Harleigh (how well that 'Albert' sounds in our ears as redolent of the later Prince Consort) is the weakest of this unpromising gallery, the least capable of emotional action. In the first debate with Elinor, aboard the little boat, one might expect him to take the side of Burke, as against her incipient Paine, but he never expresses anything with the enthusiasm of Burke, contenting himself with a cautious Whig meliorism. Elinor should have seen that the sight of any passion, let alone the kind she wants to offer, would frighten Harleigh severely. The sight of any woman doing anything seems to afflict him. But he cannot even express that affliction passionately, and in pretending to be disinterested and unselfish he is egotistical.

Harleigh wants to dissuade Ellis from performing at the public concert, for if she does so she will classify herself as a professional woman, a hired performer, thus rescinding her claim to be a lady, and making herself unfit for him to marry. Performing singers and instrumentalists were, like actresses, thought of as being on a level with workwomen but also as bearing about themselves, however personally innocent, the flavour of prostitution. Harleigh's attitude to public performance by women is not, it is hardly necessary to add, singular.[10] A woman's talents should be exerted only for the recreation of her husband and family—such was the belief. Such is certainly the belief of Harleigh, who explains that had he fallen in love with Ellis when she was already a public performer, he would have begged her to leave that way of life: 'must I not have made it my first petition, that your accomplishments should be reserved for the resources of your leisure, and the happiness of your friends, at your own time, and your own choice?' But only a husband could have dictated as much, and then the woman would sing at *his* time and choice. Ellis, as Harleigh insists, could not have called such desire 'pride' but must have 'allowed it to be called by that word, which your own every action, every speech, every look bring perpetually to mind, propriety'

[10] Burney was acquainted with the beautiful singer Elizabeth Linley and was impressed with her voice 'soft, sweet, clear & affecting', considering her 'superiour to *all* other English singers' except Giuseppe Millico; see *Early Journals and Letters*, ed. Lars E. Troide (Oxford, 1988), i. 249–50. Yet when Richard Brinsley Sheridan publicly married the young singer it was his boast and promise that she should never sing in public again.

(p. 338). *Propriety* means that the woman should not turn her talents into her own *property*.

The arguments here over the 'propriety' of Ellis-Juliet's performing in public must at some biographical level reflect the way Burney perceived the controversial nature of her writing novels at all—for to publish novels and get paid for them is definitely to engage in public performance. More recently, too, she had gone over the old controversial ground with her father, who could accept her novel-writing but was so opposed, in 'unaccountable ... displeasure' to her writing stage-comedies, as if, Burney exclaimed, she had been 'guilty of a crime'. Harleigh is an expert in 'disencouragement', and cumbers Ellis with delicate prohibitions and despondent anxieties. Ellis keeps modestly insisting there are reasons why she must decide for herself. On the plot level there are reasons why she cannot marry Harleigh, and only if he became formally engaged or married to her would accepting his help and advice be 'propriety'. But Harleigh (who does not know of her prior marriage) never exactly proposes. If we compare his delicate hints to Ellis with Elinor's full-blooded declarations to himself, we notice a decided difference. Harleigh hints at his likings: 'I have hinted that this plan might cloud my dearest hopes', he indicates cloudily to Ellis, intimating confusedly his fear of 'Relations' from which he cannot feel morally independent. The convolutions of this speech are reflected in the letter he writes to Ellis, beseeching her not be guilty of 'deviating, alone and unsupported as you appear, from the long-beaten track of female timidity' (p. 343). Ellis interprets 'timidity' as a coded word for 'delicacy', and one might add 'modesty'; she knows Harleigh is accusing her of being immodest. Yet he does seem to mean timidity also. He values timidity not only in women but also in himself. It is a bit shocking that Ellis should throw his letter into the fire—as the communication of such a phlegmatic unfiery character seems unsuited to an ardent fate.

Harleigh is a character with a context, who arises out of a novelistic tradition. He is a literary descendant and namesake of Henry Mackenzie's Harley, the original Man of Feeling. This hero of *The Man of Feeling* (1771) is nothing but sentiment and delicacy, a censor of the coarse world who applies to it standards of delicacy and sensibility that the world usually lacks. He is sensitive to women and to feminine attributes which confer charms: 'A blush, a phrase of affability to an inferior, a tear at a moving tale, were to him ... unequalled in conferring beauty.' Mackenzie's Harley feels love for the gentle pale Miss Walton of the soft voice, and he responds to her tact and politeness to his shy self: 'the most delicate consciousness of propriety often kindled that blush which marred the performance of it'. Towards the end of his short life this shy and exacting personage manages with much convolution and many broken sentences to stammer out something very like a declaration—if far from a proposal: 'To love Miss Walton could not be a crime;—if to declare it is one—the expiation will be made'.[11] Her statement of reciprocation leaves him with nothing to do but die, which he does at once.

The idea of a Man of Feeling was perpetually attractive and puzzling to women writers, as they tried to construct what a man of real feeling and sensitivity might be like, and found themselves usually faced with a point of impasse: the sensitive male becomes either extremely demanding and childlike, or else obstructive, an exponent of impossible delicacies or asexual proprieties. The name of Mackenzie's strange hero is used again by the radical feminist Mary Hays, whose heroine in *Emma Courtney* is in love with Augustus Harley. Emma Courtney rises to new heights of daring; if one believes in the equality between man and woman, then a woman has the right to declare her love to a man, and she makes the experiment (as Hays had done in real life in declaring her feelings to and for the philosopher William Frend). Emma Courtney declares her feelings in a series of letters to Harley, letters in which she acknowledges that those 'accustomed to consider mankind in masses' would censure her, regarding as 'romantic' any 'deviation of a solitary individual from *rules* sanctioned by usage, by prejudice, by expediency'. In successive letters she becomes increasingly outspoken:

Of what then, you may ask, do I complain?—Not of the laws of nature! But when mind has given dignity to natural affections; when reason,

[11] Henry Mackenzie, *The Man of Feeling*, ed. Brian Vickers (Oxford, 1967), pp. 14–15, 17, 130.

culture, taste and delicacy, have combined to chasten, to refine, to exalt (shall I say) to sanctify them—Is there, then, no cause to complain of rigor and severity, that such minds must either passively submit to a vile traffic, or be content to relinquish all the endearing sympathies of life?[12]

As matters are constituted, women are expected to be sexually passive, being exchanged either in marriage or prostitution, both of which rank as 'vile traffic'—or to be old maids, without sex and without love. Female powers of feeling and sexual feeling should not be put down and Emma regards herself as a pioneer in trying to free her sex from passivity, although she acknowledges to the full the pain of leaving the beaten track—such a beaten track as Burney's Harleigh advocates: 'Those who deviate from the beaten track', Emma Courtney acknowledges, 'must expect to be entangled in the thicket, and wounded by many a thorn—my wandering feet have already been deeply pierced'. Emma's powerful feelings are received with blank silence by Harley, and when the couple next meet he is diffident, stammering, and mysterious: '*I could not answer your letter.* What shall I say?—I am with-held from explaining myself further, by reasons, *by obligations*—'[13] Emma's beloved Harley impresses us not by rejecting the outspoken lady, but by the inadequacy of his response to the energy of the cause.

Elinor, a successor of Hays's Emma, employs similar phrases and many of the same arguments. She becomes, however, more violent than Emma Courtney, and in her disappointed love evidently takes the suicidal Mary Wollstonecraft as one of her models. (Mary Wollstonecraft's suicide attempts after Gilbert Imlay broke off with her had been fully brought to the public attention by William Godwin's over-frank biography included in Wollstonecraft's *Posthumous Works* in 1798.) Yet in her behaviour Elinor is forgetting those other principles preached in *A Vindication*—where Wollstonecraft emphasizes the advisability of women's giving up the notion of romantic love, which is often used to delude them; women are trained to

[12] Mary Hays, *Memoirs of Emma Courtney*, with an Introduction by Gina Luria, 2 vols. (New York, 1974), i. 156–7, 177.

[13] Ibid. i. 178–9; ii. 8–9.

think too much of love and sexual passion, and such ideas can draw them away from independence of mind and concern for others. Elinor's trouble is not that she falls in love with Harleigh. It is not even that she declares her love. Burney herself, in *Camilla*, had raised the question of whether there were any logical reason why women should not make the declaration, and the Reverend Mr Tyrold admits that there is no reason in nature or logic, but only in custom, why women should remain silent (*Camilla*, p. 358). Elinor's trouble is that she cannot take 'No' for an answer. Of course men have often been taught not to take 'No' for an answer, but to persist, so Elinor's persistence is understandable, but it becomes—not heroic, but mean-spirited. Flattering herself that she is a pioneer free spirit, she gives way to blackmail and confines her friends by her jealousy. And she idolizes her own obsession.

Frances Burney had reason to sympathize with Elinor's emotional plight. She herself had suffered acutely from love for George Cambridge, who had seemed to be courting her but proved to have no serious intentions; the obsession and pain of love unrequited but ever-hopeful can still be felt in the journal-letters to her sister Susanna for the years 1783–6—and beyond. The experience was repeated, to a slightly less intense degree, in Burney's briefer infatuation with Colonel Digby during her five-year incarceration at court (1786–91). During that same bitter time of trivial employment and irksome durance Burney had written her tragic plays, works unguardedly expressive of personal inner dissension (a state for which she consistently reserves the word 'conflicts', a word which occurs in that sense in *The Wanderer*, e.g. p. 348). In one of these (unpublished) tragedies, *Hubert De Vere*, there are distinct foreshadowings of the central situation of *The Wanderer*. The village maiden Cerulia falls in love with Hubert De Vere, but then finds he has become attached to the aristocratic stranger, Geralda. Cerulia has a vision of death, which commands her to seek out her grave:

> Then, with these Hands, I measur'd out the Ground
> And quick, from Head to foot, I mark'd my Grave.
> Next—so the vision bid—I cast me down

On the cold Earth, and there I bar'd my Breast,
And, with the fresh damp mould I strew'd it o'er.[14]

So Cerulia explains as she lies in the churchyard, waiting for a death which does indeed arrive. Cerulia is a reflection of Burney's own experience of being unloved and rejected, of suffering from helpless sexual longing, and the play reflects suicidal wishes. The scene of Cerulia's agony in the churchyard directly prefigures Elinor's passion in the churchyard and church, and her insistence on self-immolation (ch. lxi). Burney takes Cerulia seriously, but she renders Elinor's actions and exhibitionistic rhetoric suspect, and the upshot of the scene is farcical failure—Elinor does not succeed in killing herself. Yet the author of *Hubert De Vere* gives a lot of sympathy to Elinor's condition, and to her impulses.

Burney does not take the line adopted by Elizabeth Hamilton, who in *Memoirs of Modern Philosophers* (1800) ruthlessly satirized the sexually assertive exponents of women's rights, Wollstonecraft and Hays, particularly in her portrait of Bridgetina Botherhim, who pesters the hero, Henry Sydney, with her attentions, declarations of passion, and self-regarding epistles of proposal. When rejected, Bridgetina refuses to be downcast: 'You do not at present see my preferableness, but you may not be always blind to a truth so obvious . . . I shall talk, I shall write, I shall argue, I shall pursue you; and if I have the glory of becoming a moral martyr, I shall rejoice that it is in the cause of general utility'.[15] Reviewers of *The Wanderer* made it clear that they would have felt happier with such a clear satiric picture of female stupidity; they were not happy with Elinor. The reviewer for *The British Critic* pointed to Hamilton's work as preferable, and Bridgetina as more satisfactory: 'were we disposed to recommend a portrait of a female revolutionist, we should certainly advise them [female readers] to seek it in the chaste and animated pages of "Modern Philosophers",

[14] Act V of play, *Hubert De Vere*, in MS in the Berg Collection; see Doody, *Frances Burney: The Life in the Works*, pp. 188–91.

[15] Elizabeth Hamilton, *Memoirs of Modern Philosophers*, 4th edn., 3 vols. (Bath, 1805), iii. 103.

and not in the overdrawn caricature of Miss Elinor Joddrel'.[16] The reviewer has sensed the degree to which Burney subscribes to Elinor's views. Elinor's major points about women's rights are never rebutted by any other character, and Ellis seems implicitly to agree with many of them. In the scenes of debate between the two women, Ellis-Juliet's contribution is not retort, but amplification. She points out to middle-class Elinor the extent to which 'Female Difficulties' are not emotional but economic difficulties. Elinor has a private income, after all, on which to support her vagaries, and is so taken up with her emotional drama that she can ignore the suffering of others around her. She is making, in effect, the cardinal political error of confusing her own personal happiness with political justice. The achievement of her own personal happiness (supposing that such a thing is to be achievable with Albert Harleigh) would not be the all-sufficient matter she imagines. Burney was to make the distinction in her letter to Mary Ann Waddington: 'PERSONALLY ... I was happy but you know me, I am sure, better than to suppose me such an Egotist ...' The England displayed in *The Wanderer* is not a tyranny like Robespierre's or Napoleon's but it is a tyranny, and other women around Elinor are suffering in ways that she does not wish to see. Her main problem seems to be not her sexual energy, but her lack of true social direction.

In the middle of the novel, after the explosive event of the concert where Ellis (trying to earn her living) and Elinor (trying to be a flamboyant martyr to love) are both objects of spectators, the two characters diverge. Elinor is withdrawn into an obsession not untinged with self-irony; Ellis-Juliet is drawn into another sphere. The first part of the novel shows the heroine participating in Brighton's middle-class society as a marginal adherent to it, if not a member of it. Her course, however, is socially downhill. From being a kind of house-guest-cum-companion, Ellis becomes a music teacher, then a performer, then (without capital to keep renting a harp) a mere seamstress. Still, she is able to work at home for a while, but when Gabriella leaves she cannot support herself in this

[16] *The British Critic*, NS. 1 (Apr. 1814), 375–6.

manner. While Elinor recovers from her self-dramatizing suicide attempt, her former friend and protégée plunges abruptly downwards in the social scale. Ellis-Juliet loses all pretensions to gentility when she hires herself out as a milliner. In Burney's play *The Witlings*, which opens in a milliner's shop, working women figure in relation to the life of the heroine, Cecilia Stanley, but when she herself must find employment she thinks of becoming a governess or companion. In *Cecilia*, the heroine helps poor Mrs Hill find work in a haberdasher's shop; working women are conventionally the objects of the heroine's charity. But in *The Wanderer*, the heroine is herself a working woman. Ellis-Juliet finds that the milliners are treated as images of advertisement in a manner that savours of a genteel prostitution; the prettier girls are placed at the window to attract male customers and dalliers. The labour is treated as a frivolity, and the girls are being taught to sell themselves: the situation is dangerous not to Ellis so much as to her silly innocent colleague, Flora. When Ellis has to move to Mrs Hart's dressmaking establishment as a seamstress, she tries to prove her worth to her employer by labouring with great zeal, winning at first the approbation of her employer and the dislike of her co-workers. But then she finds she is expected to keep up this furious pace, and sees that the antagonism of the 'needle-sisterhood' was justifiable: 'she was soon taught to forgive the displeasure which, so inadvertently, she had excited, when she saw the claims to which she had made herself liable' (pp. 452–3).

Burney is the first novelist seriously to express sympathy for the working women in their normal conditions of work—and to see how the system of employment, not merely individual bad employers, creates conditions of impossible monotony. As Juliet wonders, 'what is the labour that never requires respite? What the mind, that never demands a few poor unshackled instants to itself?' (p. 453). Juliet finds herself unvalued save as a kind of machine; to her employer she is merely 'an odd hand' (p. 455) who can be dismissed when the extra business is completed. (Thus, by working too fast, the naïve Juliet had merely been forwarding her own dismissal.) It is astonishing that Burney could have so extrapolated from her own period of employment, as Second Keeper of the Robes to Queen Charlotte, an employment at the upper end of the scale, most certainly; Burney employed her imagination on women's work, and on work in general, with an intensity and disillusion not usually to be found until the social novels of the late 1830s and early 1840s. Burney was probably influenced by Wollstonecraft's unfinished novel, *The Wrongs of Woman, or Maria* (published posthumously in 1798). Wollstonecraft's novel shows in the experience of its heroine, the middle-class Maria, and in the experience of the lower-class Jemima a variety of problems afflicting women. Through the story of Jemima, as in the stories of some other females encountered, we get a cross-section of the female working world. In some ways Burney is more thorough than Wollstonecraft in examining both the upper end and the lower end of the scale, and she includes a low example of independence, in the keeper of the little dame-school, as well as the apparently luxurious but emotionally bruising employment of a 'humble companion'. In general, however, there is nothing to be said in favour of the lives of the poor; like Dr Johnson, Burney becomes infuriated with the literature that creates pastoral idylls by ignoring the pain, effort, and constriction of the lives of rural labourers.

Juliet in England finds that unjust oppression need not be manifested in heroic tyrant or bloody guillotine. Juliet wishes passionately that people would truly know what the poor go through:

> were ye to toil with them but one week! to rise as they rise, feed as they feed, and work as they work! like mine, then, your eyes would open ... (p. 701)

Like a female Lear, but much more rational and less egotistical, Juliet has exposed herself to feel what wretches feel, and has discovered not only that women are very badly treated in all ranks of English society, but that the complacent middle-class life such as she has seen at Brighton rests on injustice to both men and women. The very size of this injustice is horrific—and what can redeem the past? History is a terrible prospect. The only possible consolation is a belief in immortality and divine judgement:

who can examine and meditate upon the uncertain existence of thy creatures,—see failure without fault; success without virtue; sickness without relief; oppression in the very face of liberty; labour without sustenance; and suffering without crime,—and not see, and not feel that all call aloud for resurrection and retribution! that annihilation and injustice would be one! (pp. 701–2)

But England is perpetually guilty of committing injustice; it is a land of 'oppression in the very face of liberty'. No wonder, in 1814, when England was in such a self-congratulatory mood after the defeat of Napoleon, and when reactionary governmental controls and attitudes were still in place, that reviewers for the magazines (most of them right-wing) should rush to antagonistic judgement upon the novel.

The novel had been eagerly awaited. Lord Holland, laid up with the gout, asked Byron to ask John Murray the publisher to get him advance copies of Miss Edgeworth's or Madame d'Arblay's novels. Byron, complying, added in his letter to Murray, 'I need not say that when you are able or willing to confer the same favour on me I shall be obliged—I would almost fall sick myself to get at Me. D'Arblay's writings—'.[17] The novel sold out its first edition in advance, and about half the second printing. Then the reviewers got hold of it and in their attacks (particularly savage in the *Quarterly* and the *Edinburgh Review*) made sure that everyone knew it was a bad novel, written by a fading female of declining power and charm.[18]

[17] George Gordon, Lord Byron, to John Murray, 27 Dec. 1813, in 'Alas! The Love of Women', *Byron's Letters and Journals*, ed. Leslie A. Marchand (London, 1974), iii. 204.

[18] The hostile reviews were surprisingly quick in appearing, by contemporary standards. John Wilson Croker mounted a vitriolic attack in the April edition of the *Quarterly Review* a month after publication, and the *British Critic* made its negative pronouncement in the same month. There was a mildly favourable review in the *Gentleman's Magazine* for June, but the most favourable notice, the review in the *Monthly Review*, did not appear until a year later, in April 1815. By that time the world had read William Hazlitt's article in the *Edinburgh Review* for February 1815, an article condemning Burney and any other merely female writer who tried to go out of her sphere by judging the world; women writers are an inferior species and are deficient in imagination and reason. Hostile reviewers very visibly react against the interest in the position of women and the criticism of English life that appear in *The Wanderer*. See *Journals and Letters*, vii, Appendix IV, 564–6, and Doody, *The Life in the Works*, pp. 332–5, 338.

The reviewers were quite successful; the novel was not republished until 1988.

Juliet's anguished meditation on the human lot in England (quoted above) shows that she has reached a level of recognition of harsh truths and perpetual sorrows such that a 'happy ending' of the novel is in some sense not possible. Burney gives us the 'happy ending' of course, but not until after she has made sure that we see it is just a formality, and by no means a solution. Harley himself interests us so little that we cannot be particularly pleased at the heroine's marriage to him. The energy of the heroine has been much more devoted to escaping from marriage—in the form of the villainous figure of the French Commissary. In marrying him, Juliet becomes a medium of exchange; her ironic marriage is a civil ceremony undertaken to prop up the Church (in saving the life of the bishop) and a desperate response to blackmail—all of which one could see as a rather cynical or disillusioned reading of marriage in general. That the situation *is* closely related to marriage in general is made clear by Admiral Powel's disapproving comments on Juliet's joyous relief at hearing of the death of her husband (p. 856). The Commissary seems in some respects like a figure out of a Gothic novel—Radcliffe's Marquis of Monthalt, for instance, or Montoni, although Burney is obviously inspired too by the real-life accounts of émigrés, such as the story told by the chevalier de Beaumetz of his disguised wanderings through France; 'the next place of necessary rest was just threatened with a Commissioner. The general dread inspired by the visits of these bloody Dictators is not, he says, to be painted'.[19] Juliet was dragooned into marriage with one of these 'bloody Dictators'; the object that she threw overboard in the middle of the Channel was her hated wedding-ring. Such a presentation of marriage as that which is to be escaped and rejected casts an ironic shadow over the kind of 'happiness' the end of a novel can offer.

The deeper harmonies of the novel play under its surface, in a series of related and haunting images that make a fuller statement than could be carried out on the 'realistic' level, or

[19] Frances Burney to Dr Charles Burney, 8 Jan. 1794, *Journals and Letters*, iii. 28.

worked out in the 'romance' as the term is popularly understood to mean love-story. *The Wanderer* contains some of the deeper tropes of the Novel, in terms of its generic history that includes what we call Romance. In 1789 a new translator of Heliodorus' *Aethiopica* (a novel of *c*.300 AD) compared Heliodorus to both Samuel Richardson and Frances Burney: 'If his work abounds not with the striking and varied representations of character which we admire so much in the works of [Richardson], and in those of his great rival in this, as well as in many other of his excellencies, Miss Burney, several passages of his book lead one to imagine, that it might be rather owing to the different and more confined state of society and manners when he wrote, than to any deficiency of talent'.[20] Burney's novel, like that of Heliodorus, begins with a puzzling scene on a beach, offers the reader an odd point of view, and confronts the reader with an unknown, unnamed and mysterious heroine. Burney's heroine is also, like Heliodorus' striking and enigmatic Charicleia, multinational and polyglot, with an inheritance that must be reassembled or re-created. Most important, Ellis too bears the central riddle of the Aethiopica, the riddle of how to be at once both black and white, to be all things and reconcile antagonisms. This heroine Ellis-Juliet moves from black to white, and is found to have an interchangeable or indeterminate set of identities. Burney shows how a woman might rewrite the *Aethiopica*, that other novel of wandering, threat, and adventure, which had directly or indirectly inspired novels as rich and diverse as Sidney's *Arcadia* and Richardson's *Clarissa*. Like Heliodorus, Burney is fascinated with images of margins and incompleteness. The novel presents a series of circles that become more and more broken, from the round wedding-ring invisibly flung into the deeps, through the Temple of the Sun (a Heliodoran name!) to the strange circle of stone on Salisbury Plain. Juliet is rescued from her horrible husband not by the hero Harleigh (who is paralysed by the proprieties in a man-of-feeling manner, pp. 730–2) but by her elderly grotesque suitor Sir Jaspar Herrington. After her visit to Wilton, Juliet finds relief from the clutter of images in the severe

[20] 'Advertisement' to *The Adventures of Theagenes and Chariclea* [a new translation of Heliodorus' *Aethiopica*], 2 vols. (London, 1789) vol. i, pp. vi–vii.

loneliness of the Plain and the stark monument that confronts her (p. 765). Juliet flees into an open labyrinth; her entrance into this place of ruins symbolizes the momentary death of law, culture, names. Burney achieves the feat of describing Stonehenge for two pages without naming it. Lame Sir Jaspar, toiling after Juliet, tells her the name, and as 'nomenclator' begins to fill in the authority of the place, deciding its ritual and religious significance (p. 766). Sir Jaspar may try to define his stone circle in terms of male priesthood, hierarchy, and history, but *her* Stonehenge, the Stonehenge of Juliet's contemplation, will not bend to those meanings. The law and culture for which the place once stood are vanished. That which remains as purely phallic is, like Sir Jaspar, crippled and decayed. Burney makes Stonehenge, which might seem like a masculine symbol, into a feminine place. It is a circle, and the shape and nature of this broken circle has been anticipated in the earlier figure of the grave of Gabriella's infant. Juliet calls it a 'tombeau' but it is not at all the marble monument that word conventionally evokes. That seaside grave, unmarked by any monument save what the mother could contrive, was 'encircled by short sticks' (p. 385). The circle in *The Wanderer* is the place of the Mother. Stonehenge becomes another reflection of the woman-made inarticulate monument, which within the novel is a minute and ephemeral Stonehenge. The women's circles enshrine those who are written out of history. Not only women in general, but the poor altogether, have no real place in the privileged culture represented in the Earl of Pembroke's bewildering Wilton. Yet their unhistorical unofficial history is represented here. The stone circle testifies that it has been made by 'manual art and labour'—and manual art and labour are what Juliet and Gabriella have experienced themselves. They are part of that endless process of human work.

Human beings are always creating, yet what is human-made is incompletely known, not always survivable, always fragmentary, 'vast, irregular, strange, and in ruins'. Elinor Joddrel tries to resist the meaning of the deep sea, the grave, and the broken circle, by emphasizing individual desire and individual will. She wants fame through her suicide and designs her own tomb and inscription. She says that she wants to be forgotten

(p. 579) but her love of marble inscriptions shows otherwise. She wants the power-world of the 'tombeau', the solid marble wall. She resists the terror of the broken circle—the sense of what is incomplete, provisional, painful, and communal. The novel's true climax in many ways is in the scene at Stonehenge which interprets much that has gone before, and reminds us how many deeper levels there are to individual and social human life than those which either conservative or radical theory want to account for. There are levels of life which are not solved by either the reign or death of Robespierre, and which lie outside the capacity of novelistic 'endings'. The ending of *The Wanderer* is undone, demythologized, we might say, before we come upon it, as the novelist reminds us that we have sharper wants and need deeper myths than the idea of a novel or even a real-life happiness could satisfy, or supply. Happiness is not enough: 'PERSONALLY ... I was happy' is not a sufficient statement. How to contrive the happiness of Ellis-Juliet is not the riddle the novel poses. The images of the makeshift grave and the broken stones show us substitutions for something which will never be available. Officially, they are substitutes for something knowable: a temple, a monumental 'tombeau'. But the reality that they point to could not be satisfied by the edifying erection of the 'proper' object. Burney makes us aware of the unanswerable, the unrestorable—the gigantic absences which cannot be remedied or ignored. She is truly a Romantic here, showing us that we are not at home in the universe. The dream of eighteenth-century happiness depended vitally upon a belief that Virtue and Happiness are in accord. When we look at the world at last, we know this as an irony—as Stonehenge knows.

NOTE ON THE TEXT

This edition is based on the text of the first edition of *The Wanderer; or, Female Difficulties*, published in five volumes by Longman, Hurst, Rees, Orme and Brown on 28 March 1814. It has been set from the copy in the Bodleian Library, Oxford. Obvious misprints have been silently corrected and an occasional use of the old long 's' has been modernized, but idiosyncrasies of punctuation, spelling, and grammar have not been altered. Burney's notes, indicated here by daggers, are retained at the foot of the page; editorial notes, indicated by asterisks, are placed at the end of the text.

The first edition of *The Wanderer*, of which 3,000 copies were printed, was sold out two or three days before publication to booksellers securing copies for eager customers. The publishers had already distributed several advance copies of the first volume, printed without the dedication to Charles Burney. These copies, as Burney complained in a letter of 2 February 1814, were sent without her consent, some months before official publication, to a select group of readers, including Byron, Godwin, and Mme de Staël.

A second edition of *The Wanderer*, of which 1,000 copies were printed, was published by Longman and the same associates on 15 April 1814, less than three weeks after the first edition. Burney mistakenly assumed, in a letter of 29 April, that this edition too had been exhausted and that the novel had reached a third edition. In a diary entry of 30 May 1814, Henry Crabb Robinson noted that according to Martin Burney, Burney's nephew and agent in dealing with Longman, the publisher had received 800 advance orders for copies of the second edition; 'but in the three weeks while the second edition was preparing, 500 of the 800 copies were countermanded, and the second edition is still unsold'. Although 461 copies of the second edition had been bought by mid-1814, sales then slowed to a trickle. A mere 74 copies were sold over the next ten years, according to Burney's letter of February 1826 to the publishers. This letter also reveals that in 1824, with sales of the novel at a standstill, the publishers disposed of the remaining 465 copies of the second edition as 'waste'.

The second edition of *The Wanderer* contains no substantive variants. It frequently corrects the typographical errors of the first, especially in French accentuation, but adds many errors of its own. Its corrections have been incorporated into the present edition. That Burney herself was responsible for some of the corrections is suggested by her letter of 2 April 1814, in which she writes of the publishers begging her to 'prepare' the second edition. She was also, however, entreated 'to forbear seeing Revizes, or proofs; not to check the sail'.

A French translation of *The Wanderer*, *La Femme errante, ou les embarras d'une femme*, by J.-B.-J. Breton de la Martinière and A.-J. Lemierre d'Argy, was published in Paris in 1814. In a letter of 30 January 1815, Burney described it as 'abominable'. A three-volume American edition was published in New York, also in 1814. No further editions or translations of the novel appeared until 1988, when Pandora Press published an unannotated edition in London, apparently based on the first edition of 1814, with an introduction by Margaret Drabble.

In a letter to the publishers of *The Wanderer* of 30 August 1817, Burney announced her intention 'to prepare a corrected & revised Copy for some future—though perhaps posthumous Impression'. She began work on this revision in an interleaved copy of the first edition, now in the Berg Collection of the New York Public Library, but seems never to have completed the task. Her remarks—in pencil and extending through all five volumes of the novel—range from minor word changes (e.g. 'whispered' for 'said'), to annotations suggesting significant transpositions and omissions. Most of the contemplated changes entail a shortening and clarification of the text as it now stands. Burney frequently comments on the need to 'prune', 'compress', and 'curtail' sections of the novel. The commentary also suggests a number of projected structural changes. Burney notes in the first volume, for example, a need to 'bring forward the names of the party' in the boat to facilitate the introduction of the characters; later in the volume she reminds herself to 'mark Lewes from Brighton more clearly'.

SELECT BIBLIOGRAPHY

MODERN EDITIONS OF BURNEY'S WORKS

Camilla: or a Picture of Youth, ed. Edward A. Bloom and Lillian D. Bloom (Oxford, 1972).

Cecilia, or Memoirs of an Heiress, ed. Peter Sabor and Margaret Anne Doody, with an introduction by Margaret Anne Doody (Oxford, 1988).

Cecilia, or Memoirs of an Heiress, ed. Annie Raine Ellis, 2 vols. (London, 1882; reprinted with a new introduction by Judy Simons, London, 1986).

Evelina, or, The History of a Young Lady's Entrance into the World, ed. Edward A. Bloom with the assistance of Lillian D. Bloom (Oxford, 1968).

Evelina, or, The History of a Young Lady's Entrance into the World, ed. Frank D. Mackinnon (Oxford, 1930).

The Wanderer; or, Female Difficulties, introduction by Margaret Drabble (London, 1988).

A Busy Day, ed. Tara G. Wallace (New Brunswick, NJ, 1984).

Edwy and Elgiva, ed. Miriam J. Benkovitz (Hamden, Conn., 1957).

The Early Diary of Frances Burney, 1768–1778, ed. Annie Raine Ellis, 2 vols. (London, 1889; revised edn. 1907).

The Early Journals and Letters of Fanny Burney, ed. Lars E. Troide *et al.* (Oxford, 1988–).

Diary and Letters of Madame d'Arblay, ed. Charlotte Barrett, 7 vols. (London, 1842–6; revised by Austin Dobson, London, 6 vols., 1904–5).

The Journals and Letters of Fanny Burney (Madame d'Arblay), ed. Joyce Hemlow *et al.*, 12 vols. (Oxford, 1972–84).

Fanny Burney: Selected Letters and Journals, ed. Joyce Hemlow (Oxford, 1986).

BIOGRAPHICAL AND CRITICAL STUDIES

Michael E. Adelstein, *Fanny Burney* (New York, 1968).

Lillian D. Bloom and Edward A. Bloom, 'Fanny Burney's Novels: the Retreat from Wonder', *Novel: A Forum on Fiction*, 12 (1979), 215–35.

Martha G. Brown, 'Fanny Burney's "Feminism": Gender or Genre', in *Fetter'd or Free: British Women Novelists, 1670–1815*, ed. Mary Anne Schofield and Cecilia Macheski (Athens, Ohio, 1986), pp. 29–39.

Gabrielle Buffet, *Fanny Burney. Sa vie et ses romans*, 2 vols. (Paris, 1962).

S. Bugnot, '*The Wanderer* de Fanny Burney: Essai de réhabilitation', *Études anglaises*, 15 (1962), 225–32.

Edward W. Copeland, 'Money in the Novels of Fanny Burney', *Studies in the Novel*, 8 (1976), 24–37.

Rose-Marie Cutting, 'A Wreath for Fanny Burney's Last Novel: *The Wanderer*'s Contribution to Women's Studies', *Illinois Quarterly*, 37 (1975), 45–64.

——, 'Defiant Women: The Growth of Feminism in Fanny Burney's Novels', *Studies in English Literature*, 17 (1977), 519–30.

D. D. Devlin, *The Novels and Journals of Fanny Burney* (London, 1987).

Marjorie W. Dobbin, 'The Novel, Women's Awareness, and Fanny Burney', *English Language Notes*, 17 (1985), 42–52.

Austin Dobson, *Fanny Burney* (London, 1903).

Margaret Anne Doody, 'George Eliot and the Eighteenth-Century Novel', *Nineteenth-Century Fiction*, 35 (1980), 260–91.

——, 'Fanny Burney', in *Dictionary of Literary Biography 39: British Novelists 1660–1800*, ed. Martin C. Battestin (New York, 1985), pp. 90–101.

——, *Frances Burney: The Life in the Works* (New Brunswick, NJ, 1988).

Julia L. Epstein, 'Fanny Burney's Epistolary Voices': *The Eighteenth Century: Theory and Interpretation*, 27 (1986), 162–79.

——, 'Writing the Unspeakable: Fanny Burney's Mastectomy and the Fictive Body', *Representations*, 16 (1986), 131–66.

——, *The Iron Pen: Frances Burney and the Politics of Women's Writing* (Madison, Wisconsin, 1989).

Eva Figes, 'Fanny Burney', in *Sex and Subterfuge: Women Novelists to 1850* (London, 1982), pp. 33–55.

William B. Gates, 'An Unpublished Burney Letter', *Journal of English Literary History*, 5 (1938), 302–4.

Joseph A. Grau, *Fanny Burney: An Annotated Bibliography* (New York, 1981).

William Hazlitt, unsigned review of *The Wanderer*, *Edinburgh Review*, 24 (1815), 320–38.

Joyce Hemlow, 'Fanny Burney and the Courtesy Books', *PMLA*, 65 (1950), 732–61.

——, *The History of Fanny Burney* (Oxford, 1958).

——, 'Dr. Johnson and Fanny Burney—Some Additions to the Record', in *Johnsonian Studies*, ed. Magdi Wahba (Cairo, 1962), pp. 173–87.

Kathryn Kris, 'A 70-Year Follow-up of a Childhood Learning Disability: The Case of Fanny Burney', *Psychoanalytic Study of the Child*, 38 (1983), 637–53.

Thomas Babington Macaulay, unsigned review of *Diary and Letters of Madame d'Arblay*, *Edinburgh Review*, 76 (1843), 523–70.

Antoinette A. Overman, *An Investigation into the Character of Fanny Burney* (Amsterdam, 1933).

Katharine M. Rogers, 'Fanny Burney: the Private Self and the Public Self', *International Journal of Women's Studies*, 7 (1984), 110–17.

——, 'Burney, Fanny', in *A Dictionary of British and American Women Writers 1660–1800*, ed. Janet Todd (London, 1984), pp. 64–6.

Judy Simons, *Fanny Burney* (London, 1987).

Margaret M. Smith, 'Fanny Burney', in *English Literary Manuscripts, Volume III 1700–1800* (London, 1986), pp. 83–92.

Patricia M. Spacks, 'Dynamics of Fear: Fanny Burney', in *Imagining a Self: Autobiography and Novel in Eighteenth-Century England* (Cambridge, Mass., 1976), pp. 158–92.

Kristina Straub, *Divided Fictions: Fanny Burney and Feminine Strategy* (Lexington, Kentucky, 1987).

Janet Todd, 'Fanny Burney', in *Women's Friendship in Literature* (New York, 1980), pp. 312–19.

J. N. Waddell, 'Fanny Burney's Contribution to English Vocabulary', *Neuphilologische Mitteilungen*, 81 (1980), 260–3.

——, 'Additions to *O.E.D.* from the Writings of Fanny Burney', *Notes and Queries*, 225 (1980), 27–32.

Eugene White, *Fanny Burney, Novelist: A Study in Technique* (Hamden, Conn., 1960).

A CHRONOLOGY OF FRANCES BURNEY

1752 Born in King's Lynn, Norfolk, 13 June; baptized 7 July.

1760 Burney family moves to Poland Street, London.

1762 Death of mother, Esther Sleepe Burney (27 Sept.).

1763 or 1764 Samuel Crisp, gentleman and failed dramatist, becomes a friend of Burney family.

1767 Destroys all juvenilia, including diaries and ms. novel, *The History of Caroline Evelyn*, in bonfire on birthday (13 June). On second marriage of her father Charles Burney to Elizabeth Allen (2 Oct.), acquires stepmother, stepbrother Stephen, and two stepsisters, Maria (later Rishton), and Bessy (later Meeke).

1768 New journal (*Early Diary*) begun (27 Mar.); birth of half-brother Richard (20 Nov.).

1769 Charles Burney receives degree of Doctor of Music, Oxford (23 June).

1770 Marriage of sister Esther to cousin Charles Rousseau Burney.

1772 Secret marriage of Maria Allen to Martin Rishton in Ypres (May); birth of FB's half-sister Sarah Harriet (29 Aug.).

1774 Move to Newton's former house, St Martin's Street, Leicester Square.

1775 Badgered by marriage proposals from a Mr Barlow (May).

1777 Elopment of Bessy Allen with Samuel Meeke in Paris (summer); brother Charles Burney expelled from Caius College, Cambridge, for stealing books (Oct.).

1778 *Evelina, or, A Young Lady's Entrance into the World*, sold for 20 guineas, published (Jan.). Introduced to Thrales' circle at Streatham (July), begins friendship with Samuel Johnson and Hester Lynch Thrale.

1779 Dr Johnson tutors FB in Latin (summer), until her father puts a stop to the lessons. *The Witlings*, comic play, completed; after family play-reading (2 Aug.) Dr Burney and Crisp forbid production.

1780 Visit to Bath with Thrales (Apr.–June); Gordon Riots reach Bath; FB and Thrales escape to Brighton (10 June).

1781 Very ill with 'vile and irksome fever' and depression (Jan.–Mar.); work on new novel retarded; death of Hester Lynch Thrale's husband Henry Thrale (4 Apr.).

1782 Best-loved sister Susanna marries Molesworth Phillips (10 Jan.); *Cecilia, or Memoirs of an Heiress*, sold for £250, published (12 July).

1783 Begins friendship with Mary Delany (Jan.); death of Samuel Crisp (April); troubled by Hester Lynch Thrale's confidences over her suitor Gabriel Piozzi. Second and third editions of *Cecilia* appear, and serialized abridgements in magazines; French translation (abridged), and first part of German translation (completed 1785).

1784 Review of *Cecilia* by Choderlos de Laclos (Apr.–May). Rupture of friendship with Hester Lynch Thrale over marriage to Piozzi (23 July); death of Johnson (13 Dec.).

1783–6 Apparent courtship of George Owen Cambridge begins and fades; unrequited love causes FB acute misery.

1786 Largely through Mary Delany, given royal invitation to court service; becomes Second Keeper of the Robes to Queen Charlotte (17 July). Reluctantly agrees to join booksellers in protest against piracy of *Cecilia* (Dec.).

1788–9 King George III's madness forces virtual incarceration upon royal household; FB begins blank-verse tragedy, *Edwy and Elgiva.*

1789–91 Writes three other blank-verse tragedies, never printed or produced; *Hubert de Vere, The Siege of Pevensey*, and *Elberta* (draft); health declines.

1791 Leaves service of Queen (7 July), receiving pension of £100 p.a.; tour of West Country with Anna Ord (Aug.–Sept.).

1793 Meets Alexandre d'Arblay, exiled Adjutant-General of the Marquis de Lafayette (Jan.); secret courtship; marriage in Protestant ceremony (28 July) followed by Catholic rite (30 July); pamphlet, *Brief Reflections relative to the Emigrant French Clergy* (19 Nov.), proceeds to charity.

*c.*1792–4 Work on 'Clarinda' novel, to be redesigned and recast as *Camilla.*

1794 Birth of son, Alexander (18 Dec.).

1795 *Edwy and Elgiva* produced at Drury Lane for one night (21 Mar.); 'Proposals for Printing a New Work by the Author of *Evelina* and *Cecilia*' printed in newspapers (July–Aug.).

1796	*Camilla, or, A Picture of Youth* published (?12 July), copyright sold for £1,000. Stepmother dies (20 Oct.).
1797	'Camilla Cottage' in Surrey built with proceeds of *Camilla.*
1798	Writes comedy *Love and Fashion*; Rishtons separate; incestuous elopement of FB's brother James with his half-sister Sarah Harriet (2 Sept.).
1799	Manager of Covent Garden offers £400 to produce *Love and Fashion* in Mar. 1800; continued worry over health of Susanna in Ireland, mistreated by husband.
1800	Susanna dies upon arrival in England; FB keeps this date (6 Jan.) as day of mourning for rest of her life; *Love and Fashion* withdrawn from production (2 Feb.).
1800–2	Dramatic comedies *A Busy Day* and *The Woman-Hater* (not produced).
1802	Heavily revised second edition of *Camilla* published (Feb.); FB and son follow General d'Arblay to France (Apr.).
1811	Diagnosed as having breast cancer; at home in Paris undergoes mastectomy without anaesthetic (30 Sept.).
1812	Returns to England with son.
1814	*The Wanderer; or, Female Difficulties*, sold for £1,500 for first edition, published (28 Mar.); Dr Charles Burney dies (12 Apr.); second edition of *The Wanderer*, for which Burney receives £500, published (15 Apr.); hostile review by John Wilson Croker in the *Quarterly Review* (Apr.); American edition (New York) and French translation (Paris) published; FB returns to France, leaving son at Cambridge.
1815	Hostile review of *The Wanderer* by William Hazlitt in the *Edinburgh Review* (Feb.); FB moves to Belgium while d'Arblay fights in army opposing Napoleon; FB in Brussels during Battle of Waterloo, bandages the wounded (June); returns to England (Oct.) with wounded husband now Lieutenant-General, with title of *comte* conferred by Louis XVIII.
1817	Reconciliation with Hester Lynch Piozzi at Bath (17 Nov.); death of favourite brother, Charles (28 Dec.).
1818	Death of General d'Arblay (3 May) at home in Bath.
1819	Son Alexander ordained priest in Church of England (11 Apr.).
1821	Brother James appointed Rear-Admiral (July); death of James (Nov.).

1824	Remaining 465 copies of second edition of *The Wanderer* destroyed by the publishers as 'waste'.
1826	Introduced by the poet Samuel Rogers, Sir Walter Scott visits 'the celebrated authoress' at her home at 11 Bolton Street, Piccadilly, London (18 Nov.).
1832	Death of sister Esther (Feb.); *Memoirs of Doctor Burney* published (*c.*23 Nov.).
1837	Death of son Alexander, aged 43 (19 Jan.).
1838	Death of sister Charlotte (12 Sept.).
1840	Death of FB (Mme d'Arblay) in London, 6 Jan.; buried in Wolcot Churchyard, Bath, beside husband and son.
1842–6	Niece and literary executrix Charlotte Barrett publishes *Diary and Letters of Madame d'Arblay*, 7 volumes.
1889	*The Early Diary of Frances Burney 1768–1778*, ed. Annie Raine Ellis, published in 2 volumes.
1972 84	*The Journals and Letters of Fanny Burney (Madame d'Arblay) 1791–1840*, ed. Joyce Hemlow and others, published in 12 volumes.
1988–	*The Early Journals and Letters of Fanny Burney*, ed. Lars E. Troide and others.

THE

WANDERER;

OR,

FEMALE DIFFICULTIES

BY

THE AUTHOR OF

EVELINA; CECILIA; AND CAMILLA.

TO

DOCTOR BURNEY,

F.R.S.

AND CORRESPONDENT TO THE INSTITUTE OF FRANCE.[†]*

THE earliest pride of my heart was to inscribe to my much-loved Father the first public effort* of my pen; though the timid offering, unobtrusive and anonymous, was long unpresented; and, even at last, reached its destination through a zeal as secret as it was kind, by means which he would never reveal; and with which, till within these last few months, I have myself been unacquainted.*

With what grateful delight do I cast, now, at the same revered feet where I prostrated that first essay, this, my latest attempt!

Your name I did not dare then pronounce; and myself I believed to be "wrapt up in a mantle of impenetrable obscurity."[‡]* Little did I foresee the indulgence that would bring me forward! and that my dear father himself, whom, even while, urged by filial feelings, and yet nameless, I invoked,[§]* I thought would be foremost to aid, nay, charge me to shun the public eye; that He, whom I dreaded to see blush at my production, should be the first to tell me not to blush at it myself! The

† To which honour Dr. Burney was elected, by the wholly unsolicited votes of the members *des beaux arts*. His daughter brought over his diploma from Paris.

‡ Preface to Evelina.

§ Inscription of Evelina, "O Author of my being!" &c.

happy moment when he spoke to me those unexpected words, is ever present, and still gay to my memory.*

The early part of this immediate tribute has already twice traversed the ocean in manuscript: I had planned and begun it before the end of the last century! but the bitter, and ever to be deplored affliction with which this new era opened to our family, in depriving us of the darling of our hearts,[†]* at the very moment—when—after a grievous absence, we believed her restored to us, cast it from my thoughts, and even from my powers, for many years. I took with me, nevertheless, my prepared materials in the year 1802, to France; where, ultimately, though only at odd intervals, I sketched the whole work; which, in the year 1812, accompanied me back to my native land. And, to the honour and liberality of both nations, let me mention, that, at the Custom-house on either—alas!—hostile shore, upon my given word that the papers contained neither letters, nor political writings; but simply a work of invention and observation; the voluminous manuscript was suffered to pass, without demur, comment, or the smallest examination.*

A conduct so generous on one side, so trusting on the other, in time of war, even though its object be unimportant, cannot but be read with satisfaction by every friend of humanity, of either rival nation, into whose hands its narrative may chance to fall.

Such, therefore,—if any such there be,—who expect to find here materials for political controversy; or fresh food for national animosity; must turn elsewhere their disappointed eyes: for here, they will simply meet, what the Authour has thrice sought to present to them already, a composition upon general life, manners, and characters; without any species of personality, either in the form of foreign influence, or of national partiality. I have felt, indeed, no disposition,—I ought rather, perhaps, to say talent,—for venturing upon the stormy sea of politics; whose waves, for ever either receding or encroaching, with difficulty can be stemmed, and never can be trusted.

Even when I began,—how unconsciously you, dear Sir, well know,—what I may now, perhaps, venture to style my literary

[†] Susanna Elizabeth Phillips.

career, nothing can more clearly prove that I turned, instinctively, from that tempestuous course, than the equal favour with which I was immediately distinguished by those two celebrated, immortal authours, Dr. Johnson, and the Right Honourable Edmund Burke;* whose sentiments upon public affairs divided, almost separated them, at that epoch; yet who, then, and to their last hours, I had the pride, the delight, and the astonishment to find the warmest, as well as the most eminent supporters of my honoured essays.* Latterly, indeed, their political opinions assimilated; but when each, separately, though at the same time, condescended to stand forth the champion of my first small work; ere ever I had had the happiness of being presented to either; and ere they knew that I bore, my Father! your honoured name; that small work was nearly the only subject upon which they met without contestation†:—if I except the equally ingenious and ingenuous friend whom they vied with each other to praise, to appreciate, and to love; and whose name can never vibrate on our ears but to bring emotion to our hearts;—Sir Joshua Reynolds.*

If, therefore, then,—when every tie, whether public or mental, was single; and every wish had one direction; I held political topics to be without my sphere, or beyond my skill; who shall wonder that now,—united, alike by choice and by duty, to a member of a foreign nation,* yet adhering, with primæval enthusiasm, to the country of my birth, I should leave all discussions of national rights, and modes, or acts of government, to those whose wishes have no opposing calls; whose duties are undivided; and whose opinions are unbiassed by individual bosom feelings; which, where strongly impelled by dependant happiness, insidiously, unconsciously direct our views, colour our ideas, and entangle our partiality in our interests.

Nevertheless, to avoid disserting upon these topics as matter of speculation, implies not an observance of silence to the

† So strongly this coincidence of sentiment was felt by Mr. Burke himself, that, some years afterwards, at an assembly at Lady Galloway's,* where each, for a considerable time, had seemed to stimulate the other to a flow of partial praise on Evelina and—just then published—Cecilia; Mr. Burke, upon Dr. Johnson's endeavouring to detain me when I rose to depart, by calling out, "Don't go yet, little character-monger!" followed me, gaily, but impressively exclaiming, "Miss Burney, die to-night!"

events which they produce, as matter of fact: on the contrary, to attempt to delineate, in whatever form, any picture of actual human life, without reference to the French Revolution, would be as little possible, as to give an idea of the English government, without reference to our own:* for not more unavoidably is the last blended with the history of our nation, than the first, with every intellectual survey of the present times.

Anxious, however,—inexpressibly!—to steer clear, alike, of all animadversions that, to my adoptive country, may seem ungrateful, or, to the country of my birth unnatural; I have chosen, with respect to what, in these volumes, has any reference to the French Revolution, a period which, completely past, can excite no rival sentiments, nor awaken any party spirit; yet of which the stupendous iniquity and cruelty, though already historical, have left traces, that, handed down, even but traditionally, will be sought with curiosity, though reverted to with horrour, from generation to generation.

Every friend of humanity, of what soil or what persuasion soever he may be, must rejoice that those days, though still so recent, are over; and truth and justice call upon me to declare, that, during the ten eventful years, from 1802 to 1812, that I resided in the capital of France, I was neither startled by any species of investigation, nor distressed through any difficulties of conduct.* Perhaps unnoticed,—certainly unannoyed,—I passed my time either by my own small—but precious fire-side; or in select society; perfectly a stranger to all personal disturbance; save what sprang from the painful separation that absented me from you, my dearest Father, from my loved family, and native friends and country. To hear this fact thus publicly attested, you, dear Sir, will rejoice; and few, I trust, amongst its readers, will disdain to feel some little sympathy in your satisfaction.

With regard to the very serious subject treated upon, from time to time, in this work, some,—perhaps many,—may ask, Is a Novel the vehicle for such considerations? such discussions?

Permit me to answer; whatever, in illustrating the characters, manners, or opinions of the day, exhibits what is noxious or reprehensible, should scrupulously be accompanied by what is salubrious, or chastening. Not that poison ought to be infused merely to display the virtues of an antidote; but that, where errour and mischief bask in the broad light of day, truth ought not to be suffered to shrink timidly into the shade.

Divest, for a moment, the title of Novel* from its stationary standard of insignificance, and say! What is the species of writing that offers fairer opportunities for conveying useful precepts? It is, or it ought to be, a picture of supposed, but natural and probable human existence. It holds, therefore, in its hands our best affections; it exercises our imaginations; it points out the path of honour; and gives to juvenile credulity knowledge of the world, without ruin, or repentance; and the lessons of experience, without its tears.

And is not a Novel, permit me, also, to ask, in common with every other literary work, entitled to receive its stamp as useful, mischievous, or nugatory, from its execution? not necessarily, and in its changeless state, to be branded as a mere vehicle for frivolous, or seductive amusement? If many may turn aside from all but mere entertainment presented under this form, many, also, may, unconsciously, be allured by it into reading the severest truths, who would not even open any work of a graver denomination.

What is it that gives the universally acknowledged superiority to the epic poem? Its historic truth? No; the three poems, which, during so many centuries, and till Milton arose, stood unrivalled in celebrity, are, with respect to fact, of constantly disputed, or, rather, disproved authenticity. Nor is it even the sweet witchery of sound; the ode, the lyric, the elegiac, and other species of poetry, have risen to equal metrical beauty: —

'Tis the grandeur, yet singleness of the plan; the never broken, yet never obvious adherence to its execution; the delineation and support of character; the invention of incident; the contrast of situation; the grace of diction, and the beauty of imagery; joined to a judicious choice of combinations, and a living interest in every partial detail, that give to that sovereign species of the works of fiction, its glorious pre-eminence.

Will my dear Father smile at this seeming approximation of the compositions which stand foremost, with those which are sunk lowest in literary estimation? No; he will feel that it is not the futile presumption of a comparison that would be preposterous; but a fond desire to separate,—with a high hand!—falsehood, that would deceive to evil, from fiction, that would attract another way;—and to rescue from ill opinion the sort of production, call it by what name we may, that his daughter ventures to lay at his feet, through the alluring, but awful tribunal of the public.

He will recollect, also, how often their so mutually honoured Dr. Johnson has said to her, "Always aim at the eagle!—even though you expect but to reach a sparrow!"*

The power of prejudice annexed to nomenclature is universal: the same being who, unnamed, passes unnoticed, if preceded by the title of a hero, or a potentate, catches every eye, and is pursued with clamorous praise, or,—its common reverberator!—abuse: but in nothing is the force of denomination more striking than in the term Novel; a species of writing which, though never mentioned, even by its supporter, but with a look that fears contempt, is not more rigidly excommunicated, from its appellation, in theory, than sought and fostered, from its attractions, in practice.

So early was I impressed myself with ideas that fastened degradation to this class of composition, that at the age of adolescence, I struggled against the propensity which, even in childhood, even from the moment I could hold a pen, had impelled me into its toils; and on my fifteenth birth-day, I made so resolute a conquest over an inclination at which I blushed, and that I had always kept secret, that I committed to the flames whatever, up to that moment, I had committed to paper. And so enormous was the pile, that I thought it prudent to consume it in the garden.

You, dear Sir, knew nothing of its extinction, for you had never known of its existence. Our darling Susanna, to whom alone I had ever ventured to read its contents, alone witnessed the conflagration; and—well I remember!—wept, with tender partiality, over the imaginary ashes of Caroline Evelyn, the mother of Evelina.*

The passion, however, though resisted, was not annihilated: my bureau was cleared; but my head was not emptied; and, in defiance of every self-effort, Evelina struggled herself into life.

If then, even in the season of youth, I felt ashamed of appearing to be a votary to a species of writing that by you, Sir, liberal as I knew you to be, I thought condemned; since your large library, of which I was then the principal librarian, contained only one work of that class;[†]* how much deeper must now be my blush,—now, when that spring of existence has so long taken its flight,—transferring, I must hope, its genial vigour upon your grandson![‡]*—if the work which I here present to you, may not shew, in the observations which it contains upon various characters, ways, or excentricities of human life, that an exteriour the most frivolous may enwrap illustrations of conduct, that the most rigid preceptor need not deem dangerous to entrust to his pupils; for, if what is inculcated is right, it will not, I trust, be cast aside, merely because so conveyed as not to be received as a task. On the contrary, to make pleasant the path of propriety, is snatching from evil its most alluring mode of ascendency. And your fortunate daughter, though past the period of chusing to write, or desiring to read, a merely romantic love-tale, or a story of improbable wonders, may still hope to retain,—if she has ever possessed it,—the power of interesting the affections, while still awake to them herself, through the many much loved agents of sensibility, that still hold in their pristine energy her conjugal, maternal, fraternal, friendly, and,—dearest Sir!—her filial feelings.

Fiction, when animating the design of recommending right, has always been permitted and cultivated, not alone by the moral, but by the pious instructor; not alone, to embellish what is prophane, but to promulgate even what is sacred, from the first æra of tuition, to the present passing moment. Yet I am aware that all which, incidentally, is treated of in these volumes upon the most momentous of subjects, may HERE, in this favoured island, be deemed not merely superfluous, but, if indulgence be not shewn to its intention, impertinent; and HERE, had I always remained, the most solemn chapter of the work,*—I will not anticipate its number,—might never have been traced; for, since my return to this country, I have been forcibly struck in remarking, that all sacred themes, far from being either neglected, or derided, are become almost common

[†] Fielding's Amelia. [‡] Alexander Charles Lewis d'Arblay.

topics of common discourse; and rather, perhaps, from varying sects, and diversified opinions, too familiarly discussed, than defyingly set aside.

But what I observed in my long residence abroad, presented another picture; and its colours, not, indeed, with cementing harmony, but to produce a striking contrast, have forcibly, though not, I hope, glaringly tinted my pen.

Nevertheless, truth, and my own satisfaction, call upon me to mention, that, in the circle to which, in Paris, I had the honour, habitually, to belong, piety, generally, in practice as well as in theory, held its just pre-eminence; though almost every other society, however cultured, brilliant, and unaffectedly good, of which occasionally I heard, or in which, incidentally, I mixed, commonly considered belief and bigotry as synonimous terms.

They, however, amongst my adopted friends, for whose esteem I am most solicitous, will suffer my design to plead, I trust, in my favour; even where my essays, whether for their projection, or their execution, may most sarcastically be criticised.

Strange, indeed, must be my ingratitude, could I voluntarily give offence where, during ten unbroken years, I should, personally, have known nothing but felicity, had I quitted a country, or friends, I could have forgotten. For me, however, as for all mankind, concomitant circumstances took their usual charge of impeding any exception to the general laws of life.

And now, dear Sir, in leaving you to the perusal of these volumes, how many apprehensions would be hushed, might I hope that they would revive in your feelings the partial pleasure with which you cherished their predecessors!

Will the public be offended, if here, as in private, I conclude my letter with a prayer for my dearest Father's benediction and preservation? No! the public voice, and the voice of his family is one, in reverencing his virtues, admiring his attainments, and ardently desiring that health, peace of mind, and fulness of merited honours, may crown his length of days, and prolong them to the utmost verge of enjoyable mortality!*

F. B. D'ARBLAY.

March 14. 1814.

VOLUME I

BOOK I

CHAPTER I

DURING the dire reign of the terrific Robespierre, and in the dead of night, braving the cold, the darkness and the damps of December, some English passengers, in a small vessel, were preparing to glide silently from the coast of France, when a voice of keen distress resounded from the shore, imploring, in the French language, pity and admission.

The pilot quickened his arrangements for sailing; the passengers sought deeper concealment; but no answer was returned.

"O hear me!" cried the same voice, "for the love of Heaven, hear me!"

The pilot gruffly swore, and, repressing a young man who was rising, peremptorily ordered every one to keep still, at the hazard of discovery and destruction.

"Oh listen to my prayers!" was called out by the same voice, with increased, and even frightful energy; "Oh leave me not to be massacred!"

"Who's to pay for your safety?" muttered the pilot.

"I will!" cried the person whom he had already rebuffed, "I pledge myself for the cost and the consequence!"

"Be lured by no tricks;" said an elderly man, in English; "put off immediately, pilot."

The pilot was very ready to obey.

The supplications from the land were now sharpened into cries of agony, and the young man, catching the pilot by the arm, said eagerly, "'Tis the voice of a woman! where can be the danger? Take her in, pilot, at my demand, and my charge!"

"Take her in at your peril, pilot!" rejoined the elderly man.

Rage had elevated his voice; the petitioner heard it, and called—screamed, rather, for mercy.

"Nay, since she is but a woman, and in distress, save her, pilot, in God's name!" said an old sea officer. "A woman, a child, and a fallen enemy, are three persons that every true Briton should scorn to misuse."

The sea officer was looked upon as first in command; the young man, therefore, no longer opposed, separated himself from a young lady with whom he had been conversing, and, descending from the boat, gave his hand to the suppliant.

There was just light enough to shew him a female in the most ordinary attire, who was taking a whispering leave of a male companion, yet more meanly equipped.

With trembling eagerness, she sprang into the vessel, and sunk rather than sat upon a place that was next to the pilot, ejaculating fervent thanks, first to Heaven, and then to her assistant.

The pilot now, in deep hoarse accents, strictly enjoined that no one should speak or move till they were safely out at sea.

All obeyed; and, with mingled hope and dread, insensible to the weather, and dauntless to the hazards of the sea, watchful though mute, and joyful though filled with anxiety, they set sail.

In about half an hour, the grumbling of the pilot, who was despotic master of the boat, was changed into loud and vociferous oaths.

Alarmed, the passengers concluded that they were chaced. They looked around,—but to no purpose; the darkness impeded examination.

They were happily, however, mistaken; the lungs of the pilot had merely recovered their usual play, and his humour its customary vent, from a belief that all pursuit would now be vain.

This proved the signal to general liberty of speech; and the young lady already mentioned, addressing herself, in a low voice, to the gentleman who had aided the Incognita,* said, "I wonder what sort of a dulcinea* you have brought amongst us! though, I really believe, you are such a complete knight-errant, that you would just as willingly find her a tawny Hottentot as a fair Circassian. She affords us, however, the vivifying food of conjecture,—the only nourishment of which I never sicken!—I am glad, therefore, that 'tis dark, for discovery is almost always disappointment."

"She seems to be at prayers."

"At prayers? She's a nun, then, depend upon it. Make her tell us the history of her convent."

"Why what's all this, woman?" said the pilot, in French, "are you afraid of being drowned?"

"No!" answered she, in the same language, "I fear nothing now—it is therefore I am thankful!"

Retreating, then, from her rude neighbour, she gently approached an elderly lady, who was on her other side, but who, shrinking from her, called out, "Mr. Harleigh, I shall be obliged to you if you will change places with me."

"Willingly;" he answered; but the young lady with whom he had been conversing, holding his coat, exclaimed, "Now you want to have all the stories of those monks and abbesses to yourself! I won't let you stir, I am resolved!"

The stranger begged that she might not incommode any one; and drew back.

"You may sit still now, Mr Harleigh," said the elderly lady, shaking herself; "I do very well again."

Harleigh bit his lip, and, in a low voice, said to his companion, "It is strange that the facility of giving pain should not lessen its pleasure! How far better tempered should we all be to others, if we anticipated the mischief that ill humour does to ourselves!"

"Now are you such a very disciple of Cervantes," she replied, "that I have no doubt but your tattered dulcinea has secured your protection for the whole voyage, merely because old aunt Maple has been a little ill bred to her."

"I don't know but you are right, for nothing so uncontrollably excites resistance, as grossness to the unoffending."

He then, in French, enquired of the new passenger, whether she would not have some thicker covering, to shelter her from the chill of the night; offering her, at the same time, a large wrapping coat.*

She thanked him, but declared that she was perfectly warm.

"Are you so, faith?" cried the elderly man already mentioned,

"I wish, then, you would give me your receipt,* Mistress; for I verily think that my blood will take a month's thawing, before it will run again in my veins."

She made no answer, and, in a tone somewhat piqued, he added, "I believe in my conscience those out-landish* gentry have no more feeling without than they have within!"

Encreasing coldness and darkness repressed all further spirit of conversation, till the pilot proclaimed that they were half way over the straits.

A general exclamation of joy now broke forth from all, while the new comer, suddenly casting something into the sea, ejaculated, in French, "Sink, and be as nothing!" And then, clasping her hands, added, "Heaven be praised, 'tis gone for ever!"

The pilot scolded and swore; every one was surprized and curious; and the elderly man plumply* demanded, "Pray what have you thrown overboard, Mistress?"

Finding himself again unanswered, he rather angrily raised his voice, saying, "What, I suppose you don't understand English now? Though you were pretty quick at it when we were leaving you in the lurch! Faith, that's convenient enough!"

"For all I have been silent so long," cried the old sea officer, "it has not been for want of something to say; and I ask the favour that you won't any of you take it ill, if I make free to mention what has been passing, all this time, in my mind; though it may rather have the air of a hint than a compliment; but as I own to being as much in fault as yourselves, I hope you won't be affronted at a little plain dealing."

"You are mighty good to us, indeed, Sir!" cried Mrs. Maple, "but pray what fault have you to charge Me with, amongst the rest?"

"I speak of us in a body, Madam, and, I hope, with proper shame! To think that we should all get out of that loathsome captivity, with so little reverence, that not one amongst us should have fallen upon his knees, to give thanks, except just this poor outlandish gentlewoman; whose good example I recommend it to us all now to follow."

"What, and so overturn the boat," said the elderly man, "that we may all be drowned for joy, because we have escaped being beheaded?"

"I submit to your better judgment, Mr. Riley," replied the officer, "with regard to the attitude; and the more readily, because I don't think that the posture is the chief thing, half the people that kneel, even at church, as I have taken frequent note, being oftener in a doze than in a fit of devotion. But the fear of shaking the boat would be but a poor reason to fear shaking our gratitude, which seems to me to want it abundantly. So I, for one, give thanks to the Author of all things!"

"You are a fine fellow, noble Admiral!" cried Mr. Riley; "as fine a fellow as ever I knew! and I honour you, faith! for I don't believe there is a thing in the world that requires so much courage as to risk derision, even from fools."

A young man, wrapped up in flannels, who had been undisguisedly enjoying a little sneering laugh, now became suddenly grave, and pretended not to heed what was passing.

Mrs. Maple protested that she could not bear the parade of saying her prayers in public.

Another elderly lady, who had hitherto seemed too sick to speak, declared that she could not think of giving thanks, till she were sure of being out of danger.

And the young lady, laughing immoderately, vowed that she had never seen such a congress of quizzes* in her life; adding, "We want nothing, now, but a white foaming billow, or a shrill whistle from Boreas,* to bring us all to confession, and surprise out our histories."

"Aprôpos to quizzes," said Mr. Riley, addressing the hitherto silent young man, "how comes it, Mr. Ireton, that we have not had one word from you all this time?"

"What do you mean by aprôpos,* Sir?" demanded the young man, somewhat piqued.

"Faith, I don't very well know. I am no very good French dictionary. But I always say aprôpos, when I am at a loss how to introduce any thing. Let us hear, however, where you have been passing your thoughts all this time. Are you afraid the sea should be impregnated with informers, instead of salt, and so won't venture to give breath to an idea, lest it should be floated back to Signor Robespierre,* and hodge-podged* into a conspiracy?"

"Ay, your thoughts, your thoughts! give us your thoughts, Ireton!" cried the young lady, "I am tired to death of my own."

"Why, I have been reflecting, for this last hour or two, what a singular circumstance it is, that in all the domains that I have scampered over upon the continent, I have not met with one young person who could hit my fancy as a companion for life."

"And I, Sir, think," said the sea officer, turning to him with some severity, "that a man who could go out of old England to chuse himself a wife, never deserves to set foot on it again! If I knew any worse punishment, I should name it."

This silenced Mr. Ireton; and not another word was uttered, till the opening of day displayed the British shore.

The sea officer then gave a hearty huzza, which was echoed by Harleigh; while Riley, as the light gleamed upon the old and tattered garments of the stranger, burst into a loud laugh, exclaiming, "Faith, I should like to know what such a demoiselle as this should come away from her own country for? What could you be afraid of, hay! demoiselle?" —

She turned her head from him in silence. Harleigh enquired, in French, whether she had escaped the general contagion, from which almost all in the boat had suffered, of sickness.

She cheerfully replied, Yes! She had escaped every evil!

"The demoiselle is soon contented," said Riley; "but I cannot for my life make out who she is, nor what she wants. Why won't you tell us, demoiselle? I should like to know your history."

"Much obliged for the new fellow traveller you have given us, Mr. Harleigh!" said Mrs. Maple, contemptuously examining her; "I have really some curiosity myself, to be informed what could put it into such a body's mind as that, to want to come over to England."

"The desire of learning the language, I hope!" cried Harleigh, "for I should be sorry that she knew it already!"

"I wish, at least, she would tell us," said the young lady, "how she happened to find out our vessel just at the moment we were sailing."

"And I should be glad to discover," cried Riley, "why she understands English on and off at her pleasure, now so ready, and now answering one never a word."

The old sea officer, touching his hat as he addressed her, said, "For my part, Madam, I hope the compliment you make our country in coming to it, is that of preferring good people to bad; in which case every Englishman should honour and welcome you."

"And I hope," cried Harleigh, while the stranger seemed hesitating how to answer, "that this patriotic benevolence is comprehended; if not, I will attempt a translation."

"I speak French so indifferently, which, however, I don't much mind," cried the Admiral, "that I am afraid the gentlewoman would hardly understand me, or else I would translate for myself."

The stranger now, with a strong expression of gratitude, replied in English, but with a foreign accent, "It is only how to thank you I am at a loss, Sir; I understand you perfectly."

"So I could have sworn!" cried Riley, with a laugh, "I could have sworn that this would be the turn for understanding English again! And you can speak it, too, can you, Mistress?"

"And pray, good woman," demanded Mrs. Maple, staring at her, "how came you to learn English? Have you lived in any English family? If you have, I should be glad to know their names."

"Ay, their names! their names!" was echoed from Mrs. Maple by her niece.

The stranger looked down, and stammered, but said nothing that could distinctly be heard.

Riley, laughing again, though provoked, exclaimed, "There! now you asked her a question, she won't comprehend a word more! I was sure how 'twould be! They are clever beings, those French, they are, faith! always playing fools" tricks, like so many monkies, yet always lighting right upon their feet, like so many cats!"

"You must resign your demoiselle, as Mr. Riley calls her, for a heroine;" whispered the young lady to Mr. Harleigh. "Her dress is not merely shabby; 'tis vulgar. I have lost all hope of a pretty nun. She can be nothing above a house-maid."

"She is interesting by her solitary situation," he answered, "be she what she may by her rank: and her voice, I think, is singularly pleasing."

"Oh, you must fall in love with her, I suppose, as a thing of course. If, however, she has one atom that is native in her, how will she be choaked by our foggy atmosphere!"

"And has our atmosphere, Elinor, no purifying particles, that, in defiance of its occasional mists, render it salubrious?"

"Oh, I don't mean alone the foggy air that she must inhale; but the foggy souls whom she must see and hear. If she have no political bias, that sets natural feelings aside, she'll go off in a lethargy, from *ennui*, the very first week. For myself I confess, from my happiness in going forth into the world at this sublime juncture, of turning men into infants, in order to teach them better how to grow up, I feel as if I had never awaked into life, till I had opened my eyes on that side of the channel."

"And can you, Elinor, with a mind so powerful, however—pardon me!—wild, have witnessed. . . . ."

"Oh, I know what you mean!—but those excesses are only the first froth of the cauldron. When once 'tis skimmed, you will find the composition clear, sparkling, delicious!"

"Has, then, the large draught which, in a two years" residence amidst that combustion, you have, perforce, quaffed, of revolutionary beverage, left you, in defiance of its noxious qualities, still thus. . . . ." He hesitated.

"Inebriated, you would say, Albert," cried she, laughing, "if you blushed not for me at the idea. But, in this one point, your liberality, though matchless in every other, is terribly narrowed by adhesion to old tenets. You enjoy not, therefore, as you ought, this glorious epoch, that lifts our minds from slavery and from nothingness, into play and vigour; and leaves us no longer, as heretofore, merely making believe that we are thinking beings."

"Unbridled liberty, Elinor, cannot rush upon a state, without letting it loose to barbarism. Nothing, without danger, is suddenly unshackled: safety demands control from the baby to the despot."

"The opening essays here," she replied, "have certainly been calamitous: but, when all minor articles are progressive, in rising to perfection, must the world in a mass alone stand still, because its amelioration would be costly? Can any thing be so absurd, so preposterous, as to seek to improve mankind individually, yet bid it stand still collectively? What is education, but reversing propensities; making the idle industrious, the rude civil, and the ignorant learned? And do you not, for every student thus turned out of his likings, his vagaries, or his vices, to be new modelled, call this alteration improvement? Why, then, must you brand all similar efforts for new organizing states, nations, and bodies of society, by that word of unmeaning alarm, innovation?"

"To reverse, Elinor, is not to new model, but to destroy. This education, with which you illustrate your maxims, does it begin with the birth? Does it not, on the contrary, work its way by the gentlest gradations, one part almost imperceptibly preparing for another, throughout all the stages of childhood to adolescence, and of adolescence to manhood? If you give Homer before the Primer,* do you think that you shall make a man of learning? If you shew the planetary system to the child who has not yet trundled his hoop, do you believe that you will form a mathematician? And if you put a rapier into his hands before he has been exercised with foils,*—what is your guarantee for the safety of his professor?"

Just then the stranger, having taken off her gloves, to arrange an old shawl, in which she was wrapt, exhibited hands and arms of so dark a colour, that they might rather be styled black than brown.

Elinor exultingly drew upon them the eyes of Harleigh, and both taking, at the same instant, a closer view of the little that was visible of the muffled up face, perceived it to be of an equally dusky hue.

The look of triumph was now repeated.

"Pray, Mistress," exclaimed Mr. Riley, scoffingly fixing his eyes upon her arms, "what part of the world might you come from? The settlements in the West Indies? or somewhere off the coast of Africa?"

She drew on her gloves, without seeming to hear him.

"There!" said he, "now the demoiselle don't understand English again! Faith, I begin to be entertained with her. I did not like it at first."

"What say you to your dulcinea now, Harleigh?" whispered

Elinor; "you will not, at least, yclep her the Fair Maid of the Coast."*

"She has very fine eyes, however!" answered he, laughing.

The wind just then blowing back the prominent borders of a French night-cap, which had almost concealed all her features, displayed a large black patch, that covered half her left cheek, and a broad black ribbon, which bound a bandage of cloth over the right side of her forehead.

Before Elinor could utter her rallying congratulations to Harleigh, upon this sight, she was stopt by a loud shout from Mr. Riley; "Why I am afraid the demoiselle has been in the wars!" cried he. "Why, Mistress, have you been trying your skill at fisty cuffs for the good of your nation? or only playing with kittens for your private diversion?"

"Now, then, Harleigh," said Elinor, "what says your quixotism now? Are you to become enamoured with those plaisters* and patches, too?"

"Why she seems a little mangled, I confess; but it may be only by scrambling from some prison."

"Really, Mr. Harleigh," said Mrs. Maple, scarcely troubling herself to lower her voice as, incessantly, she continued surveying the stranger, "I don't think that we are much indebted to you for bringing us such company as this into our boat! We did not pay such a price to have it made a mere common hoy.* And without the least enquiry into her character, too! without considering what one must think of a person who could look out for a place, in a chance vessel, at midnight!"

"Let us hope," said Harleigh, perceiving, by the down-cast eyes of the stranger, that she understood what passed, "that we shall not make her repent her choice of an asylum."

"Ah! there is no fear!" cried she, with quickness.

"Your prepossession, then, is, happily, in our favour?"

"Not my prepossession, but my gratitude!"

"This is true practical philosophy, to let the sum total of good out-balance the detail, which little minds would dwell upon, of evil."

"Of evil! I think myself at this moment the most fortunate of human beings!"

This was uttered with a sort of transport that she seemed

unable to control, and accompanied with a bright smile, that displayed a row of beautifully white and polished teeth.

Riley now, again heartily laughing, exclaimed, "This demoiselle amuses me mightily! she does, faith! with hardly a rag to cover her this cold winter's night; and on the point of going to the bottom every moment, in this crazy little vessel; with never a friend to own her body if she's drowned, nor an acquaintance to say a word to before she sinks; not a countryman within leagues, except our surly pilot, who grudges her even life-room, because he's afraid he shan't be the better for her: going to a nation where she won't know a dog from a cat, and will be buffetted from pillar to post, if she don't pay for more than she wants; with all this, she is the most fortunate of human beings! Faith, the demoiselle is soon pleased! She is, faith! But why won't you give me your receipt, Mistress, for finding all things so agreeable?"

"You would be sorry, Sir, to take it!"

"I fear, then," said Harleigh, "it is only past suffering that bestows this character of bliss upon simple safety?"

"Pray, Mr. Riley," cried Mrs. Maple, "please to explain what you mean, by talking so freely of our all going to the bottom? I should be glad to know what right you had to make me come on board the vessel, if you think it so crazy?"

She then ordered the pilot to use all possible expedition for putting her on shore, at the very first jut of land; adding, "you may take the rest of the company round, wherever you chuse, but as to me, I desire to be landed directly."

She could not, however, prevail; but, in the panic which had seized her, she grew as incessant in reproach as in alarm, bitterly bewailing the moment that she had ever trusted herself to such an element, such a vessel, and such guides.

"See," said Harleigh, in a low voice to the stranger, "how little your philosophy has spread; and how soon every evil, however great, is forgotten when over, to aggravate the smallest discomfort that still remains! What recompence, or what exertion would any one of us have thought too great, for obtaining a place in this boat only a few hours ago! Yet you, alone, seem to have discovered, that the true art of supporting present inconvenience is to compare it with past calamity,—not with our disappointed wishes."

"Calamity!" repeated she with vivacity, "ah! if once I reach that shore,—that blessed shore! shall I have a sorrow left?"

"The belief that you will not," said he, smiling, "will almost suffice for your security, since, certainly, half our afflictions are those which we suffer through anticipation."

There was time for nothing more; the near approach to land seeming to fill every bosom, for the instant, with sensations equally enthusiastic.

CHAPTER II

Upon reaching the British shore,* while Mrs. Maple, her niece, the elderly lady, and two maid-servants, claimed and employed the aid of the gentlemen, the Incognita, disregarding an offer of Harleigh to return for her, darted forward with such eagerness, that she was the first to touch the land, where, with a fervour that seemed resistless, she rapturously ejaculated, "Heaven, Heaven be praised!"

The pilot, when he had safely disembarked his passengers, committed the charge of his vessel to a boy, and, abruptly accosting the stranger, demanded a recompence for the risk which he had run in saving her life.

She was readily opening her work bag* to seek for her purse, but the old sea officer, approaching, and holding her arm, gravely asked whether she meant to affront him; and, turning to the pilot, somewhat dictatorially said, "Harkee, my lad! we took this gentlewoman in ourselves; and I have seen no reason to be sorry for it: but she is our passenger, and not your's. Come to the inn, therefore, and you shall be satisfied, forthwith, for her and the rest of us, in a lump."

"You are infinitely good, Sir," cried the stranger, "but I have no claim—."

"That's your mistake, gentlewoman. An unprotected female, provided she's of a good behaviour, has always a claim to a man's care, whether she be born amongst our friends or our foes. I should be ashamed to be an Englishman, if I held it my duty to think narrower than that. And a man who could bring himself to be ashamed of being an Englishman, would find it a difficult solution, let me tell you, my good gentlewoman, to discover what he might glory in. However, don't think that I say this to affront you as a foreigner, for I hope I am a better Christian. I only drop it as a matter of fact."

"Worthy Admiral," said Mr. Harleigh, now joining them, "you are not, I trust, robbing me of my office? The pecuniary engagement with the pilot was mine."

"But the authority which made him act," returned the officer, "was mine."

A bright smile, which lightened up the countenance of the Incognita, again contrasted her white teeth with her dingy complexion; while dispersing the tears that started into her eyes, "Fie upon me!" she cried, "to be in England and surprised at generosity!"

"Gentlewoman," said the Admiral, emphatically, "if you want any help, command my services; for, to my seeming, you appear to be a person of as right a way of thinking, as if you had lisped English for your mother-tongue."

He then peremptorily insisted that the boat's company should discharge the pilot, without any interference on the part of the lone traveller, as soon as it had done with the custom-house officers.*

This latter business was short; there was nothing to examine: not a trunk, and scarcely a parcel, had the hurry and the dangers of escape hazarded.

They then proceeded to the principal inn, where the Admiral called all the crew, as he styled the party, to a spacious room, and a cheering fire, of which he undertook the discipline.

The sight of this meanly attired person, invited into the apartment both by the Admiral and Mr. Harleigh, with a civility that seemed blind to her shabby appearance, proved so miraculous a restorative to Mrs. Maple, that, rising from a great chair, into which, with a declaration that she was half dead from her late fright and sickness, she had thrown herself, she was endowed with sudden strength of body to stand stiffly upright, and of lungs to pronounce, in shrill but powerful accents, "Pray, Mr. Harleigh, are we to go on any farther as if we were to live all our lives in a stage coach? Why can't that body as well stay in the kitchen?"

The stranger would hastily have retired, but the Admiral, taking her softly by the shoulder, said, "I have been a commanding officer the best part of my life, Gentlewoman; and though a devil of a wound has put me upon the superannuated list, I am not sunk into quite such a fair weather chap, as to make over my authority, in such a little pitiful skiff's company* as this, to petticoat government;—though no man has a better respect for the sex, in its proper element; which, however, is not the sea. Therefore, Madam," turning to Mrs. Maple, "this gentlewoman being my own passenger, and having comported herself without any offence either to God or man, I shall take it kind if you will treat her in a more Christian-like manner."

While Mrs. Maple began an angry reply, the stranger forced herself out of the apartment. The Admiral followed.

"I hope, gentlewoman," he was beginning, "you won't be cast down, or angry, at a few vagaries—" when, looking in her face, he saw a countenance so gaily happy, that his condolence was changed into pleased astonishment. "Angry!" she repeated, "at a moment such as this!—a moment of so blessed an escape! —I should be the most graceless of wretches, if I had one sensation but of thankfulness and joy!"

"You are a very brave woman," said the Admiral, "and I am sorry," looking at her tattered clothing, "to see you in no better plight: though, perchance, if you had been born to more glitter without, you might have had less ore within. However, if you don't much like the vapouring* of that ancient lady, which I have no very extraordinary liking to myself, neither, why stay in another room till we have done with the pilot; and then, if I can be of any use in helping you to your friends, I shall be glad to be at your service. For I take it for granted, though you are not in your own country, you are too good a woman to be without friends, as I know no worse sign of a person's character."

He then joined his fellow-voyagers, and the stranger went on to enquire for the master of the house.

Sounds from without, that seemed to announce distress, catching, soon after, the attentive ear of Harleigh, he opened the door, and perceived that the stranger was returned to the passage, and in evident disorder.

The sea officer briskly advanced to her. "How now!" he cried, "disheartened at last? Well! a woman can be but a woman! However, unless you have a mind to see all my good opinion blown away—thus!—in a whiff, you won't think of drooping, now once you are upon British ground. For though I should scorn, I hope, to reproach you for not being a native born, still, not to be overjoyed that you can say, Here I am! would be a sure way to win my contempt. However, as I don't take upon me to be your governor, I'll send your own countryman to you, if you like him better,—the pilot?"

"Not for the universe! Not for the universe!" she eagerly cried, and, darting into an empty room, with a hasty apology, shut the door.

"Mighty well, indeed!" said Mrs. Maple, who, catching the contagion of curiosity, had deigned to listen; "so her own countryman, the only person that she ought to belong to, she shuts the door upon!"

She then protested, that if the woman were not brought forth, before the pilot, who was already paid and gone, had re-embarked, she should always be convinced that she had lost something, though she might not find out what had been taken from her, for a twelvemonth afterwards.

The landlord, coming forward, enquired whether there were any disturbance; and, upon the complaint and application of Mrs. Maple, would have opened the door of the closed apartment; but the Admiral and Harleigh, each taking him by an arm, declared the person in that room to be under their protection.

"Well, upon my word," cried Mrs. Maple, "this is more than I could have expected! We are in fine hands, indeed, for a sea officer, and an Admiral, that ought to be our safe-guard, to take part with our native enemy, that, I make no doubt, is sent amongst us as a spy for our destruction!"

"A lady, Madam," said the Admiral, looking down rather contemptuously, "must have liberty to say whatever she pleases, a man's tongue being as much tied as his hands, not to annoy the weaker vessel; so that, let her come out with what she will, she is amenable to no punishment; unless she take some account of a man's inward opinion; in which case she can't be said to escape quite so free as she may seem to do. This, Madam, is all the remark that I think fit to make to you. But as for you, Mr. Landlord, when the gentlewoman in this room has occasion to consult you, she speaks English, and can call you herself."

He would then have led the way to a general retreat, but Mrs. Maple angrily desired the landlord to take notice, that a foreigner, of a suspicious character, had come over with them by force, whom he ought to keep in custody, unless she would tell her name and business.

The door of the apartment was now abruptly opened by the stranger, who called out, "O no! no! no!—Ladies!—Gentlemen!—I claim your protection!"

"It is your's, Madam!" cried Harleigh, with emotion.

"Be sure of it, Gentlewoman!" cried the old officer; "We did not bring you from one bad shore to another. We'll take care of you. Be sure of it!"

The stranger wept. "I thought not," she cried, "to have shed a tear in England; but my heart can find no other vent."

"Very pretty! very pretty, indeed, Gentlemen!" said Mrs. Maple; "If you can answer all this to yourselves, well and good; but as I have not quite so easy a conscience, I think it no more than my duty to inform the magistrates myself, of my opinion of this foreigner."

She was moving off; but the stranger rushed forth, and with an expression of agonized affright, exclaimed, "Stay! Madam, stay! hear but one word! I am no foreigner,—I am English!"—

Equal astonishment now seized every one; but while they stared from her to each other, the Admiral said: "I am cordially glad to hear it! cordially! though why you should have kept secret a point that makes as much for your honour as for your safety, I am not deep enough to determine. However, I won't decide against you, while I am in the dark of your reasons; though I own I have rather a taste myself for things more above board. But for all that, Ma'am, if I can be of any use to you, make no scruple to call upon me."

He walked back to the parlour, where all now, except Harleigh, assembled to a general breakfast, of which, during this scene, Riley, for want of an associate, had been doing the honors to himself. The sick lady, Mrs. Ireton, was not yet sufficiently recovered to take any refreshment; and the young man, her son, had commanded a repast on a separate table.

Harleigh repeated to the stranger, as she returned, in trembling, to her room, his offer of services.

"If any lady of this party," she answered, "would permit me to say a few words to her not quite in public, I should thankfully acknowledge such a condescension. And if you, Sir, to whom already I owe an escape that calls for my eternal gratitude, if you, Sir, could procure me such an audience —— "

"What depends upon me shall surely not be left undone," he replied; and, returning to the parlour, "Ladies," he said, "this person whom we have brought over, begs to speak with one of you alone."

"Alone!" repeated Mrs. Maple, "How shocking! Who can tell what may be her designs?"

"She means that we should go out to hold a conference with her in the passage, I suppose?" said Mrs. Ireton, the sick lady, to whom the displeasure raised by this idea seemed to restore strength and speech; "or, perhaps, she would be so good as to receive us in the kitchen? Her condescension is really edifying! I am quite at a loss how I shall shew my sense of such affability."

"What, is that black insect buzzing about us still?" cried her son, "Why what the deuce can one make of such a grim thing?"

"O, it's my friend the demoiselle, is it?" said Riley; "Faith, I had almost forgotten her. I was so confoundedly numbed and gnawn, between cold and hunger, that I don't think I could have remembered my father, I don't, faith! before I had recruited.* But where's poor demoiselle? What's become of her? She wants a little bleaching, to be sure; but she has not bad eyes; nor a bad nose, neither."

"I am no great friend to the mystical," said the Admiral, "but I promised her my help while she stood in need of my protection, and I have no title to withdraw it, now that I presume she is only in need of my purse. If any of the ladies, therefore, mean to go to her, I beg to trouble them to carry this." He put a guinea upon the table.

"Now that she is so ready to tell her story," said Elinor, "I am confident that there is none to tell. While she was enveloped in the mystical, as the Admiral phrases it, I was dying with curiosity to make some discovery."

"O the poor demoiselle!" cried Riley, "why you can't think of leaving her in the lurch, at last, ladies, after bringing her so far? Come, lend me one of your bonnets and your fardingales,* or what is it you call your things? And twirl me a belt round my waist, and something proper about my neck, and I'll go to her myself, as one of your waiting maids: I will, faith!"

"I am glad, at least, niece Elinor, that this once," said Mrs. Maple, "you are reasonable enough to act a little like me and other people. If you had really been so wild as to sustain so glaring an impostor—."

"If, aunt?—dont you see how I am scalding my throat all this time to run to her?" replied Elinor, giving her hand to Harleigh.

As they re-entered the passage, the stranger, rushing from her room with a look the most scared and altered, exclaimed, that she had lost her purse.

"This is complete!" cried Elinor, laughing; "and will this, too, Harleigh, move your knight-errantry? If it does—look to your heart! for I won't lose a moment in becoming black, patched, and pennyless!"

She flew with this anecdote to the breakfast parlour; while the stranger, yet more rapidly, flew from the inn to the sea-side, where she carefully retraced the ground that she had passed; but all examination was vain, and she returned with an appearance of increased dismay.

Meeting Harleigh at the door, his expression of concern somewhat calmed her distress, and she conjured him to plead with one of the ladies, to have the charity to convey her to London, and thence to help her on to Brighthelmstone. "I have no means," she cried, "now, to proceed unaided; my purse, I imagine, dropt into the sea, when, so unguardedly! in the dark, I cast there—" She stopt, looked confused, and bent her eyes upon the ground.

"To Brighthelmstone?" repeated Harleigh; "some of these ladies reside not nine miles from that town. I will see what can be done."

She merely entreated, she said, to be allowed to travel in their suite, in any way, any capacity, as the lowest of attendants. She was so utterly reduced by this dreadful loss, that she must else beg her way on foot.

Harleigh hastened to execute this commission; but the moment he named it, Elinor called out, "Do, pray, Mr. Harleigh, tell me where you have been secreting your common sense?—Not that I mean to look for it!—'twould despoil me of all the dear freaks and vagaries that give zest to life!"

"Poor demoiselle!" cried Riley, throwing half a crown upon the table, "she shall not be without my mite, for old acquaintance sake."

"What! has she caught even you, Mr. Cynical* Riley?" cried Elinor; "you, who take as much pleasure in lowering or mortifying your fellow-creatures, as Mr. Harleigh does in elevating, or relieving them?"

"Every one after his own fashion, Miss Nelly. The best amongst us has as little taste for being thwarted as the worst. He has, faith! We all think our own way the only one that has any common sense. Mine, is that of a diver: I seek always for what is hidden. What is obvious soon surfeits me. If this demoiselle had named herself, I should never have thought of her again; but now, I'm all agog to find her out."

"Why does she not say who she is at once?" cried Mrs. Maple. "I give nothing to people that I know nothing of; and what had she to do in France? Why don't she tell us that?"

"Can such a skin, and such a garb, be worth so much breath?" demanded Ireton, taking up a news-paper.

Harleigh enquired of Mrs. Ireton, whether she had succeeded in her purposed search, of a young woman to replace the domestic whom she had left in France, and to attend her till she arrived at her house in town.

"No, Sir," she answered; "but you don't mean, I presume, to recommend this vagabond to be about my person? I should presume not; I should presume you don't mean that? Not but that I should be very sensible to such a mark of distinction. I hope Mr. Harleigh does not doubt that? I hope he does not suspect I should want a proper sensibility to such an honour?"

"If you think her a vagabond, Madam," replied Harleigh, "I

have not a word to offer: but neither her language nor her manners incline me to that opinion. You only want an attendant till you reach your family, and she merely desires and supplicates to travel free. Her object is to get to Brighthelmstone. And if, by waiting upon you, she could earn her journey to London, Mrs. Maple, perhaps, in compassion to her pennyless state, might thence let her share the conveyance of some of her people to Lewes, whence she might easily find means to proceed."

The two elderly ladies stared at each other, not so much as if exchanging enquiries how to decline, but in what degree to resent this proposition; while Elinor, making Harleigh follow her to a window, said, "Now, do inform me, seriously and candidly, what it is that urges you to take the pains to make so ridiculous an arrangement?"

"Her apparently desolate state."

"Now do put aside all those fine sort of sayings, which you know I laugh at, and give me, instead, a little of that judgment which you so often quarrel with me for not giving to you; and then honestly tell me, can you really credit that any thing but a female fortune-hunter, would travel so strangely alone, or be so oddly without resource?"

"Your doubts, Elinor, are certainly rational; and I can only reply to them, by saying, that there are now and then uncommon causes, which, when developed, shew the most extraordinary situations to be but their mere simple effect."

"And her miserable accoutrement?—And all those bruises, or sores, and patches, and bandages? —"

"The detail, I own, Elinor, is unaccountable and ill looking: I can defend no single particular, even to myself; but yet the whole, the all-together, carries with it an indescribable, but irresistible vindication. This is all I can say for befriending her."

"Nay, if you think her really distressed," cried Elinor, "I feel ready enough to be her handmaid; and, at all events, I shall make a point to discover whom and what she may be, that I may know how to value your judgment, in odd cases, for the future. Who knows, Harleigh, but I may have some to propose for your decision of my own?"

The Admiral, after some deliberation, said, that, as it was certainly possible that the poor woman might really have lost her purse, which he, for one, believed to be the simple truth, he could not refuse to help her on to her friends; and, ringing for the landlord, he ordered that a breakfast should be taken to the gentlewoman in the other room, and that a place should be secured for her in the next day's stage to London; for all which he would immediately deposit the money.

"And pray, Mr. Landlord," said Mrs. Maple, "let us know what it was that this body wanted, when she desired to speak with you?"

"She asked me to send and enquire at the Post-office if there were any letter directed for L.S., to be left till called for; and when she heard that there was none, I thought, verily, that she would have swooned."

Elinor now warmly united with Harleigh, in begging that Mrs. Maple would let her servants take charge of the young woman from London to Lewes, when, through the charity of the Admiral, she should arrive in town. Mrs. Maple pronounced an absolute negative; but when Elinor, not less absolutely, declared that, in that case, she would hire the traveller for her own maid; and the more readily because she was tired to death of Golding, her old one, Mrs. Maple, though with the utmost ill will, was frightened into compliance; and Elinor said that she would herself carry the good news to the Incognita.

The landlord desired to know in what name the place was to be taken.

This, also, Elinor undertook to enquire, and, accompanied by Harleigh, went to the room of the stranger.

They found her standing pensively by the window; the breakfast, which had been ordered for her by the Admiral, untouched.

"I understand you wish to go to Brighthelmstone?" said Elinor.

The stranger courtsied.

"I believe I know every soul in that place. Whom do you want to see there?—Where are you to go?"

She looked embarrassed, and with much hesitation, answered, "To ... the Post-office, Madam."

"O! what, you are something to the post-master, are you?"

"No, Madam ... I ... I ... go to the Post-office only for a letter!"

"A letter? Well! an hundred or two miles* is a good way to go for a letter!"

"I am not without hopes to find a friend.—The letter I had expected here was only to contain directions for the meeting."

"O! if your letter is to be personified, I have nothing more to say. A man, or a woman?—which is it?"

"A woman, Madam."

"Well, if you merely wish to go to Brighthelmstone, I'll get you conveyed within nine miles of that place, if you will come to me, at Mrs. Maple's, in Upper Brooke-street, when you get to town."

Surprise and pleasure now beamed brightly in the eyes of the stranger, who said that she should rejoice to pass through London, where, also, she particularly desired to make some enquiries.

"But we have no means for carrying you thither, except by the stage; and one of our gentlemen offers to take a place in it for you."

The stranger looked towards Harleigh, and confusion seemed added to her embarrassment.

Harleigh hastily spoke, "It is the old officer,—that truly benevolent veteran, who wishes to serve you, and whose services, from the nobleness of his character, confer still more honour than benefit."

Again she courtsied, and with an air in which Harleigh observed, with respect, not displeasure, her satisfaction in changing the object of this obligation.

"Well, that's settled," said Elinor; "but now the landlord wants your name, for taking your place."

"My place?—Is there no machine, Madam, that sets off immediately?"

"None sooner than to-morrow. What name am I to tell him?"

"None sooner than to-morrow?"

"No; and if you do not give in your name, and secure it, you may be detained till the next day."

"How very unfortunate!" cried she, walking about the room.

"Well, but what is your name?"

A crimson of the deepest hue forced its way through her dark complexion: her very eyes reddened with blushes, as she faintly answered, "I cannot tell my name!"

She turned suddenly away, with a look that seemed to expect resentment, and anticipate being abandoned.

Elinor, however, only laughed, but laughed "in such a sort"* as proclaimed triumph over Harleigh, and contempt for the stranger.

Harleigh drew Elinor apart, saying, "Can this, really, appear to you so ridiculous?"

"And can you, really, Harleigh, be allured by so glaring an adventurer? a Wanderer,—without even a name!"

"She is not, at least, without probity, since she prefers any risk, and any suspicion, to falsehood. How easily, otherwise, might she assume any appellation that she pleased!"

"You are certainly bewitched, Harleigh!"

"You are certainly mistaken, Elinor! yet I cannot desert her, till I am convinced that she does not merit to be protected."

Elinor returned to the stranger. "You do not chuse, then, to have your place secured?"

"O yes Madam!—if it is impossible for me to attend any lady to town."

"And what name shall you like for the book-keeper?* Or what initials?—What think you of L.S.?"

She started; and Harleigh, again taking Elinor aside, more gravely said, "Elinor, I am glad I am not—at this moment—my brother!—for certainly I could not forbear quarrelling with you!"

"I heartily wish, then," cried she, with quickness, "that,—at this moment!—you were your brother!"

Harleigh, now, addressing the stranger, in whose air and manner distress seemed palpably gaining ground, gently said, "To save you any further trouble, I will take a place in my own name, and settle with the landlord, that, if I do not appear to claim it, it is to be made over to the person who produces this card. The book-keeper shall have such another for a check."

He put into her hand a visiting ticket,* on which was engraven Mr. Harleigh, and, not waiting for her thanks, conducted Elinor back to the parlour, saying, "Pardon me, Elinor, that I have stopt any further enquiries. It is not from a romantic admiration of mystery, but merely from an opinion that, as her wish of concealment is open and confessed, we ought not, through the medium of serving her, to entangle her into the snares of our curiosity."

"Oh, you are decided to be always right, I know!" cried Elinor, laughing, though piqued; "and that is the very reason I always hate you! However, you excite my curiosity to fathom her; so let her come to me in town, and I'll take her under my own care, if only to judge your discernment, by finding out how she merits your quixotism."

Harleigh then returned to the young woman, and hesitatingly said, "Pardon my intrusion, but—permit me, as you have so unfortunately lost your purse—"

"If my place, Sir," hastily interrupted the stranger, "is taken, I can require nothing else."

"Yet—you have the day to pass here; and you will with difficulty exist merely upon air, even where so delightedly you inhale it; and Miss Joddrel, I fear, has forgotten to bring you the little offering of your veteran friend; therefore—"

"If he has the infinite goodness to intend me any, Sir, permit, at least, that he may be my only pecuniary creditor! I shall want no addition of that sort, to remember,—gratefully and for ever! to whom it is I owe the deepest obligation of my life!"

Is this a house-maid? thought Harleigh; and again he rejoiced in the perseverance with which he had supported her; and, too much respecting her refusal to dispute it, expressed his good wishes for her welfare, and took leave; yet would not set out upon his journey till he had again sought to interest the old officer in her favour.

The guinea was still upon the tea-table; but the Admiral, who, in the fear of double dealing, had conceived some ideas to the disadvantage of the Incognita, no sooner heard that she had declined receiving any succour except from himself, than, immediately softened, he said that he would take care to see her well treated.

Harleigh then drove after the carriage of Mrs. Maple and Elinor, who were already on their way to London.

CHAPTER III

THE Admiral immediately repaired to the stranger. "Young woman," he cried, "I hope you don't take it into your mind, that I was more disposed to serve you while I thought you of foreign culture, than now I know you to be of our own growth? If I came forwarder then, it was only because I was afraid that those who have had less occasion than I have had, to get the upper hand of their prejudices, would keep backwarder."

The stranger bowed her thanks.

"But as to me," he continued, "I have had the experience of what it is to be in a strange land; and, moreover, a prisoner: in which time I came to an agreement with myself—a person over whom I keep a pretty tight hand! because why? If I don't the devil will! So I came, I say, to an agreement with myself, to remember all the ill-usage I then met with, as a memento to forbear exciting in others, those black passions which sundry unhandsome tricks excited, in those days, in myself."

Observing her breakfast to be utterly neglected, he demanded, with an air of some displeasure, whether she had no longing to taste the food of her mother country again?

The fulness of her mind, she answered, had deprived her of appetite.

"Poor girl! poor woman!" cried he, compassionately, "for I hardly know which to call you, those cap-flounces* upon the cheeks making a young woman look no better than an old one. However, be you which you may, I can't consent to see you starve in a land of plenty; which would be a base ingratitude to our Creator, who, in dispensing the most to the upper class, grants us the pleasure of dispensing the overplus, ourselves, to the under class; which I take to be the true reason of Providence for ordering that difference between the rich and the poor; as, most like, we shall all find, when we come to give in our accounts in t'other world."

He then enquired what it was she intended to do; adding, "I don't mean as to your secrets, because they are what I have no right to meddle with; though I disapprove your having any, they being of little service, except to keep foul deeds from the light; for what is fair loves to be above board. Besides, as every thing is sure to come out, sooner or later, it only breeds suspicion and trouble for nothing, to procrastinate telling to-day with your own free will, what you may be certain will be known to-morrow, or next day, with or without it. Don't be discomposed, however, for I don't say this by way of a sift,* nor yet for a reproach; I merely drop it as a piece of advice."

"And I should be happy, Sir, to endeavour to deserve it, by frankly explaining my situation, but that the least mistake, the smallest imprudence, might betray me to insupportable wretchedness."

"Why then, if that's the case, you are very right to hold your tongue. If the law never makes a person condemn himself, much less ought a little civility. There are dangers enough in the world without running risks out of mere compliment."

Then putting his guinea before her, upon the table, he charged her to keep it unbroken till she set out, assuring her that he should himself order whatever she could require for her dinner, supper, and lodging, and settle for the whole with the landlord; as well as with the book-keeper for her journey to London.

The stranger seemed almost overpowered with gratitude; but interrupting what she attempted to say, "No thankings," he cried, "young woman! it's a bad sign when a good turn surprises a person. I have not escaped from such hard fare with my body, to leave my soul behind me; though, God knows, I may forget it all fast enough. There's no great fear of mortal man's being too good."

Then, wishing her farewell, he was quitting the room, but, thoughtfully turning back, "Before we part," he said, "it will be but Christian-like to give you a hint for your serious profit. In whatever guise you may have demeaned yourself, up to this present date, which is a solution I don't mean to meddle with, I hope you'll always conduct yourself in a becoming manner, for the rest of your days, in remembrance of your great good fortune, in landing safely upon this happy shore."

He was going, but the Incognita stopt him, and again the dark hue of her skin, was inadequate to disguise the deep blushes that were burning upon her cheeks, as she replied. "I see, Sir, through all your benevolence, that you believe me to be one of those unhappy persons, whose misfortunes have been the effect of their crimes: I have no way to prove my innocence; and assertion may but make it seem more doubtful; yet—"

"You are right! you are right!" interrupted he; "I am no abettor of assertions. They are but a sort of cheap coinage, to make right and wrong pass current together."

"I find I have been too quick," she answered, "in thinking myself happy! to receive bounty under so dreadful a suspicion, proves me to be in a desolate state indeed!"

"Young woman," said the Admiral, in a tone approaching to severity, "don't complain! We must all bear what we have earned. I can't but see what you are, though it's what I won't own to the rest of the crew, who think a flaw in the character excuse plenty for letting a poor weak female starve alive; for which, to my seeming, they deserve to want a crust of bread themselves. But I hope I know better than that where the main fault is apt to lie; for I am not ignorant how apt our sex is to misbehave to yours; especially in slighting you, if you don't slight them; a thing not to be defended, either to God or man. But for all that, young woman, I must make free to remark, that the devil himself never yet put it into a man's head, nor into the world's neither, to abandon, or leave, as you call it, desolate, a woman who has kept tight to her own duty, and taken a modest care of herself."

The eyes of the stranger were now no longer bright from their mere natural lustre, nor from the beams of quick surprize, or of sudden vivacity; 'twas with trembling emotion that they shone, and with indignation that they sparkled. She took up the guinea, from which her sight seemed averted with horror, and said, "Pardon me, Sir, but I must beg you to receive this again."

"Why, what now? do you think, because I make no scruple to give you an item that I don't fancy being imposed upon; do you think, I say, because of that, I have so little Christian charity, as not to know that you may be a very good sort of woman in the main, for all some flaunty* coxcomb may have played the scoundrel, and left you to the wide world, after teaching you to go so awry, that he knows the world will forsake you too? a thing for which, however, he'll pay well in time; as I make no doubt but the devil takes his own notes of all such actions."

She now cast the guinea upon the table. "I would rather, Sir," she cried, "beg alms of every passenger that I may meet, than owe succour to a species of pity that dishonours me!"

The Admiral looked at her with earnestness. "I don't well know," he said, "what class to put you in; but if you are really a virtuous woman, to be sure I ought to ask your pardon for that little hint I let drop; and, moreover, if I asked it upon my knees, I can't say I should think it would be overmuch, for affronting a virtuous woman, without cause. And, indeed, if I were free to confess the truth, I must own there's something about you, which I don't over-much know what to call, but that is so agreeable, that it goes against me to think ill of you."

"Ah, Sir! think well of me, then!—let your benevolence be as liberal as it is kind, and try, for once, to judge favourably of a stranger upon trust!"

"Well, I will! I will, then! if you have the complaisance to wish for my good opinion, I will!" cried he, nodding, while his eyes glistened; "though it's not my general method, I can tell you, young woman, to go the direct opposite road to my understanding. But, out of the way as things may look, you seem to me, in the main, to be an innocent person; so pray, Ma'am, don't refuse to accept this little token of my good will."

The countenance of the stranger exhibited strong indecision. He enjoined her, however, to keep the guinea, and, after struggling vainly to speak, she sighed, and seemed distressed, but complied.

He nodded again, saying, "Be of good cheer, my dear. Nothing comes of being faint-hearted. I give you my promise I'll see you in town. And, if I find that you turn out to be good; or, moreover, if you turn good, after having unluckily been t'other thing, I'll stand your friend. You may depend upon it."

With a look of mingled kindness and concern, he then left the room.

And here, shocked, yet relieved, and happy, however forlorn, she remained, till a waiter brought her a fowl, a tart, and a pint of white wine, according to commands issued by the Admiral. She then heard that the whole of the boat-party had set off for London, except Mrs. Ireton, the sick lady, who did not think herself sufficiently recovered to travel till the next day, and who had enquired for some genteel young lady to attend her to town; but she was so difficult, the waiter said, to please, that she had rejected half-a-dozen candidates who had been presented to her successively. She seemed very rich, he added, for she ordered things at a great rate, though she found fault with them as fast as they were carried to her; but what had put her the most out of humour of all, was that the young gentleman, her son, had set off without her, in a quarrel: which was not, however, so much to be wondered at, for the maids of the two other ladies said that the gentlewoman was of so aggravating a humour, that nobody could live with her; which had provoked her own woman to leave her short in France, and hire herself to a French lady.

The little repast of the stranger was scarcely over, when the waiter brought her word that the sick lady desired to see her up stairs.

Extremely surprised, she demanded for what purpose.

He answered, that a seventh young person whom he had taken into the lady's room, with an offer to serve her, upon being sharply treated, had as sharply replied; which had so affronted her, that she had ordered that no one else should be brought into her presence; though in two minutes more, she had rung the bell, said she was too ill to be left alone, and bid him fetch her the woman who came over from France.

The stranger, at first, refused to obey this imperious summons; but the wish of placing herself under female protection during her journey, presently conquered her repugnance, and she accompanied the messenger back.

Mrs. Ireton was reclining upon an easy chair, still somewhat disordered from her voyage, though by no means as much in need of assistance for her shattered frame, as of amusement for her restless mind.

"So!" she cried, "you are here still? Pray,—if I may ask so confidential a question,—what acquaintance may you have found in this inn?—The waiters?—or the grooms?"

"I was told, Madam, that you had some commands for me."

"O, you are in haste, are you? you want to be shewing off

those patches and bandages, perhaps? You won't forget a veil, I hope, to preserve your white skin? Not but 'twould be pity to make any sort of change in your dress, 'tis so prodigiously tasty!"*

The stranger, offended, was now moving off, but, calling her back, "Did not the waiter," Mrs. Ireton demanded, "give you to understand that I sent for you?"

"Yes, Madam; and therefore—"

"Well, and what do you suppose it was for? To let you open and shut the door, just to give me all the cold wind of the passages? You suppose it was for that, do you? You surmize that I have a passion for the tooth-ache? You conclude that I delight in sneezing?—coughing?—and a stuft-up nose?"

"I am sorry, Madam,—"

"Or perhaps you think me so robust, that it would be kind to give me a little indisposition, to prevent my growing too boisterous? You may deem my strength and health to be overbearing? and be so good as to intend making me more delicate? You may be of opinion that it would render me more interesting?"

"Indeed, Madam,—"

"Or, you may fancy that a friendly catarrh might be useful, in furnishing me with employment, from ordering water-gruel, and balm-tea, and barley-water,* and filling up my leisure in devising successive slops?"

The difficulty of being heard made the stranger now cease to attempt speaking; and Mrs. Ireton, after sundry similar interrogatories, angrily said, "So you really don't think fit to initiate me into your motives for coming to me, without troubling yourself to learn mine for admitting you into my presence?"

"On the contrary, Ma'am, I desire—"

"O! I am mistaken, am I? It's on the contrary, is it? You are vastly kind to set me right; vastly kind, indeed! Perhaps you purpose to give me a few lessons of behaviour?"

"I am so wholly at a loss, Madam, why I have been summoned, that I can divine no reason why I should stay. I beg, therefore, to take my leave."

Again she was retreating; but Mrs. Ireton, struck by her courage, began to conceive that the mystery of her birth and business, might possibly terminate in a discovery of her belonging to a less abject class than her appearance announced;

and therefore, though firmly persuaded that what might be diminished in poverty, would be augmented in disgrace, her desire was so inflamed to develop the secret, that, softening her tone, she asked the young person to take a chair, and then entered into discourse with some degree of civility.

Yet with all this restraint, inflicted upon a nature that, to the privilege of uttering whatever it suggested, claimed that of hearing only what it liked, she could gather no further intelligence, than that the stranger had received private information of the purposed sailing of the vessel, in which they all came over: but her birth, her name, her connexions, her actual situation, and her object in making the voyage, resisted enquiry, eluded insinuation, and baffled conjecture. Nevertheless, her manners were so strikingly elevated above her attire, that, notwithstanding the disdain with which, in the height of her curiosity, Mrs. Ireton surveyed her mean apparel, and shrunk from her dusky skin, she gave up her plan of seeking for any other person to wait upon her, during her journey to town, and told the Incognita that, if she could make her dress a little less shocking, she might relinquish her place in the stage-coach, to occupy one in a post-chaise.*

To avoid new and untried risks, in travelling wholly alone, the stranger acceded to this proposal; and immediately, by the assistance of the maid of the inn, appropriated the guinea of the Admiral to purchasing decent clothing, though of the cheapest and coarsest texture.

The next morning they set off together for London.

CHAPTER IV

THE good understanding with which the eagerness of curiosity on one side, and the subjection of caution on the other, made the travellers begin their journey, was of too frail a nature to be of long endurance. 'Tis only what is natural that flows without some stimulus; what is factitious prospers but while freshly supplied with such materials as gave it existence. Mrs. Ireton, when she found that neither questions, insinuations, nor petty artifices to surprise confessions, succeeded in drawing any forth, cast off a character of softness that so little paid the violence which its assumption did her humour; while the stranger, fatigued by finding that not one particle of benevolence, was mixed with the avidity for amusement which had given her a place in the chaise, ceased all efforts to please, and bestowed no further attentions, than such as were indispensably due to the mistress of the vehicle in which she travelled.

At a little distance from Rochester, the chaise broke down. No one was hurt; but Mrs. Ireton deemed the mere alarm an evil of the first magnitude; remarking that this event might have brought on her death; and remarking it with the resentment of one who had never yet considered herself as amenable to the payment of that general, though dread debt to nature. She sent on a man and horse for another carriage, and was forced to accept the arm of the stranger, to support her till it arrived. But so deeply was she impressed with her own ideas of the hardships that she endured, that she put up at the first inn, went to bed, sent for an apothecary,* and held it to be an indispensable tribute to the delicacy of her constitution, to take it for granted that she could not be removed for some days, without the most imminent hazard to her life.

Having now no other resource, she hung for comfort, as well as for assistance, upon her fellow-traveller, to whom she gave the interesting post of being the repository of all her complaints, whether against nature, for constructing her frame with such exquisite daintiness, or against fate, for it's total insensibility to the tenderness which that frame required. And though, from recently quitting objects of sorrow, and scenes of woe, in the dreadful apparel of awful reality, the Incognita had no superfluous pity in store for the distresses of offended self-importance, she yet felt relief from experiencing milder usage, and spared no assiduity that might purchase its continuance.

It was some days before Mrs. Ireton thought that she might venture to travel, without appearing too robust. And, in this period, one only circumstance called forth, with any acrimony, the ill humour of her disposition. This was a manifest alteration in the complexion of her attendant, which, from a regular and equally dark hue, appeared, on the second morning, to be smeared and streaked; and, on the third, to be of a dusky white. This failed not to produce sundry inquisitive comments; but they never succeeded in obtaining any explanatory replies. When, however, on the fourth day, the shutters of the chamber, which, to give it a more sickly character, had hitherto been closed, were suffered to admit the sunbeams of a cheerful winter's morning, Mrs. Ireton was directed, by their rays, to a full and marvellous view, of a skin changed from a tint nearly black, to the brightest, whitest, and most dazzling fairness. The band upon the forehead, and the patch upon the cheek, were all that remained of the original appearance.

The first stare at this unexpected metamorphosis, was of unmingled amazement; but it was soon succeeded by an expression of something between mockery and anger, evinced, without ceremony or reserve, by the following speech: "Upon my word, Ma'am, you are a very complete figure! Beyond what I could have conjectured! I own that! I can't but own that. I was quite too stupid to surmize so miraculous a change. And pray, Ma'am, if I may take the liberty to enquire,—who are you?"

The stranger looked down.

"Nay, I ought not to ask, I confess. It's very indelicate, I own; very rude, I acknowledge; but, I should imagine, it can hardly be the first time that you have been so good as to pardon a little rudeness. I don't know, I may be mistaken, to be sure, but I should imagine so."

The Incognita now raised her eyes. A sense of ill treatment seemed to endue her with courage; but her displeasure, which, though not uttered, was not disguised, no sooner reached the observation of Mrs. Ireton, than she conceived it to be an insolence to justify redoubling her own.

"You are affronted, I hope, Ma'am? Nay, you have reason enough, I acknowledge; I can't but acknowledge that! to see me impressed with so little awe by your wonderful powers; for 'twas but an hour or two since, that you were the blackest, dirtiest, raggedest wretch I ever beheld; and now—you are turned into an amazing beauty! Your cheeks are all bedaubed with *rouge*,* and you are quite a belle! and wondering, I suppose, that I don't beseech you to sit on the sofa by my side! And, to be sure, it's very ill bred of me: I can't deny that; only as it is one of the rudenesses that I conceive you to have had the goodness to submit to before, I hope you'll forgive it."

The young woman begged leave to retire, till she should be called for the journey.

"O! what, you have some other metamorphosis to prepare, perhaps? Those bandages and patches are to be converted into something else? And pray, if it will not be too great a liberty to enquire, what are they to exhibit? The order of Maria Theresa? or of the Empress of all the Russias?* If I did not fear being impertinent, I should be tempted to ask how many coats of white and red you were obliged to lay on, before you could cover over all that black."

The stranger, offended and tired, without deigning to make any answer, walked back to the chamber which she had just quitted.

The astonished Mrs. Ireton was in speechless rage at this unbidden retreat; yet anger was so inherently a part of her composition, that the sight she saw with the most lively sensation was whatever authorized its vent. She speedily, therefore, dispatched a messenger, to say that she was taken dangerously ill, and to desire that the young woman would return.

The Incognita, helpless for seeking any more genial mode of travelling, obeyed the call, but had scarcely entered the apartment, when Mrs. Ireton, starting, and forgetting her new illness, exclaimed, in a powerful voice, "Why, what is become of your black patch?"

The young woman, hastily putting her hand to her cheek, blushed extremely, while she answered, "Bless me, it must have dropt off!—I will run and look for it."

Mrs. Ireton peremptorily forbade her to move; and, staring at her with a mixture of curiosity and harshness, ordered her to draw away her hand. She resisted for some time, but, overpowered by authoritative commands, was reduced, at length, to submit; and Mrs. Ireton then perceived, that neither wound, scar, nor injury of any sort, had occasioned the patch to have been worn.

The excess of her surprize at this discovery, led her to apprehend some serious imposition. She fearfully, therefore, rose, to ring the bell, still fixing her eyes upon the face of the young woman, who, in her confusion, accidentally touching the bandage which crossed her forehead, displaced it, and shewed that feature, also, as free from any cause for having been bound up, as the cheek.

It was now rather consternation than amazement with which Mrs. Ireton was seized, till the augmenting disorder, and increasing colour of her new attendant, changed all fear of any trick into personal pique at having been duped; and she protested that if such beggar-stratagems were played upon her any more, she would turn over the impostor to the master of the inn.

The paleness of terror with which this menace overspread the complexion of the stranger, forced a certain, however unwilling conviction upon the mind of Mrs. Ireton, that *rouge*, at least, was not amongst the artifices of which she had to complain. But, though relieved from her own alarm, by the alarm which she inspired, she was rather irritated than appeased in finding something less to detect, and, scoffingly perusing her face, "You are a surprising person, indeed!" she cried, "as surprising a person as ever I had the honour to see! So you had disfigured yourself in that horrid manner, only to extort money from us upon false pretences? Very ingenious, indeed! mighty ingenious, I confess! Why that new skin must have cost you more than your new gown. Pray which did you get the best bargain?"

The stranger did not dare risk any sort of reply.

"O, you don't chuse to tell me? But how could I be so indiscreet as to ask such a thing? Will it be impertinent, too, if I enquire whether you always travel with that collection of bandages and patches? and of black and white outsides? or whether you sometimes change them for wooden legs and broken arms?"

Not a word of answer was returned.

"So you won't tell me that, neither? Nay, you are in the right, I own. What business is it of mine to confine your genius to only one or two methods of maiming or defacing yourself? as if you did not find it more amusing to be one day lame, and another blind; and, to-day, it should seem, dumb? The round must be entertaining enough. Pray do you make it methodically? or just as the humour strikes you?"

A fixed silence still resisted all attack.

"O, I am diving too deeply into the secrets of your trade, am I? Nay, I ought to be contented, I own, with the specimens with which I have already been indulged. You have not been niggardly in varying them. You have been bruised and beaten; and dirty and clean; and ragged and whole; and wounded and healed; and a European and a Creole, in less than a week. I suppose, next, you will dwindle into a dwarf; and then, perhaps, find some surprising contrivance to shoot up into a giantess. There is nothing that can be too much to expect from so great an adept in metamorphoses."

The pleasure of giving vent to spleen, disguised from Mrs. Ireton, that by rendering its malignancy so obvious, she blunted its effect. She continued, therefore, her interrogatories a considerable time, before she discovered, that the stillness with which they were heard was produced by resolution, not awe. Almost intolerably offended when a suspicion of this truth occurred, she assumed a tone yet more imperious. "So I am not worth an answer? You hold it beneath you to waste your breath upon me? And do you know whom it is you dare treat in this manner? Do you imagine that I am a fellow-adventurer?"

The hand of the young woman was now upon the lock of the door, but there, trembling, it stopt, withheld by a thousand terrors from following its first impulse; and the entrance of a waiter, with information that a chaise was at the door, interrupted any further discourse. The journey was resumed, and the rest of the way was only rendered supportable to the stranger, from the prospect that its conclusion would terminate all intercourse with one who, so wilfully and so wantonly, seemed to revel in her powers of mockery and derision.

CHAPTER V

UPON the entrance of the travellers into London, the curiosity of Mrs. Ireton was more than ever inflamed, to find that the journey, with all its delays, was at an end, before she had been able to gratify that insatiable passion in a single point. Yet every observation that she could make tended to redouble its keenness. Neither ill humour nor haughtiness, now the patches and bandages were removed, could prevent her from perceiving that the stranger was young and beautiful; nor from remarking that her air and manner were strikingly distinguished from the common class. One method, however, still remained for diving into this mystery; it was clear that the young woman was in want, whatever else might be doubtful. Mrs. Ireton, therefore, resolved to allow no recompense for her attendance, but in consideration of what she would communicate of her history.

At a large house in Grosvenor Square they stopt. Mrs. Ireton turned exultingly to the stranger: but her glance met no gratification. The young woman, instead of admiring the house, and counting the number of steps that led to the vestibule, or of windows that commanded a view of the square, only cast her eyes upwards, as if penetrated with thankfulness that her journey was ended.

Surprized that stupidity should thus be joined with cunning, Mrs. Ireton now intently watched the impression which, when her servants appeared, would be made by their rich liveries.

The stranger, however, without regarding them, followed their mistress into the hall, which that lady was passing through in stately silence, meaning to confound the proud vagrant more completely, by dismissing her from the best drawing-room; when the words, "Permit me, Madam, to wish you good morning," made her look round. She then saw that her late attendant, without waiting for any answer, was tranquilly preparing to be gone. Amazed and provoked, she deigned to call after her, and desired that she would come the next day to be paid.

"I am more than paid already, Madam," the Incognita replied, "if my little services may be accepted as cancelling my obligation for the journey."

She had no difficulty, now, to leave the house without further interruption, so astonished was Mrs. Ireton, at what she thought the effrontery of a speech, that seemed, in some measure, to level her with this adventurer; though, in her own despite, she was struck with the air of calm dignity with which it was uttered.

The Wanderer obtained a direction to the house of Mrs. Maple, from a servant; and demanded another to Titchfield Street. To the latter she rapidly bent her steps; but, there arrived, her haste ended in disappointment and perplexity. She discovered the apartment in which, with her husband and child, the lady whom she sought had resided; but it was no longer inhabited; and she could not trace whether her friend had set off for Brighthelmstone, or had only changed her lodging. After a melancholy and fruitless search, she repaired, though with feet and a mind far less eager, to Upper Brooke Street, where she soon read the name of Mrs. Maple upon the door of one of the capital houses. She enquired for Miss Joddrel, and begged that young lady might be told, that a person who came over in the same boat with her from France, requested the honour of admission.

To this message she presently heard the voice of Elinor, from the landing-place,* answer, "O, she's come at last! Bring her up Tomlinson, bring her up!"

"Yes, Ma'am; but I'll promise you she is none of the person you have been expecting."

"How can you tell that Tomlinson? What sort of figure is she?"

"As pretty as can be."

"As pretty as can be, is she? Go and ask her name."

The man obeyed.

The stranger, disconcerted, answered, "My name will not be known to Miss Joddrel, but if she will have the goodness to receive, I am sure she will recollect me."

Elinor, who was listening, knew her voice, and, calling Tomlinson up stairs, and heartily laughing, said, "You are the greatest fool in the whole world, Tomlinson! It is she! Bid her come to me directly."

Tomlinson did as he was ordered, but grinned, with no small satisfaction, at sight of the surprise with which, when they reached the landing-place, his young mistress looked at the stranger.

"Why, Tomlinson," she cried, "who have you brought me hither?"

Tomlinson smirked, and the Incognita could not herself refrain from smiling, but with a countenance so little calculated to excite distrust, that Elinor, crying, "Follow me," led the way into her dressing room.

The young woman, then, with an air that strongly supplicated for indulgence, said, "I am truly shocked at the strange appearance which I must make; but as I come now to throw myself upon your protection, I will briefly—though I can enter into no detail—state to you how I am circumstanced."

"O charming! charming!" cried Elinor, clapping her hands, "You are going, at last, to relate your adventures! Nay, no drawing back! I won't be disappointed! If you don't tell me every thing that ever you did in your life, and every thing that ever you said, and every thing that ever you thought,—I shall renounce you!"

"Alas!" answered the Incognita, "I am in so forlorn a situation, that I must not wonder if you conclude me to be some outcast of society, abandoned by my friends from meriting their desertion,—a poor destitute Wanderer, in search of any species of subsistence!"

"Don't be cast down, however," cried Elinor, "for I will help you on your way. And yet you have exactly spoken Aunt Maple's opinion of you."

"And I have no right, I acknowledge, to repine, at least, none for resentment: yet, believe me, Madam, such is not the case! and if, as you have given me leave to hope, you will have the benevolence to permit me to travel in your party, or in whatever way you please, to Brighthelmstone, I may there meet with a friend, under whose protection I may acquire courage to give a more intelligible account of myself."

A rap at the street door made Elinor ring the bell, and order, that when Mr. Harleigh came, he should be shewn immediately up stairs.

Harleigh, presently appearing, looked round the apartment, with striking eagerness, yet evident disappointment; and, slightly bowing to the scarcely noticed, yet marked courtsie of the stranger, said, "Tomlinson told me that our fellow-traveller was at last arrived?"

Elinor, taking the young woman apart, whispered a hasty injunction that she would not discover herself. Then, addressing Harleigh, "I believe," she said, "you dream of nothing but that dismal Incognita. However, do not fancy you have all the mysterious charmers to yourself. I have one of my own, now; and not such a dingy, dowdy heroine as your's!"

Harleigh turned with quickness to the stranger; but she looked down, and her complexion, and bloom, and changed apparel, made a momentary suspicion die away.

Elinor demanded what news he had gathered of their strayed voyager?

None, he answered; and uneasily added, that he feared she had either lost herself, or been misled, or betrayed, some other way.

"O, pray don't waste your anxiety!" cried Elinor; "she is in perfect safety, I make no doubt."

"I should be sorry," he gravely replied, "to think you in equal danger."

"Should you?" cried she in a softened tone; "should you, Harleigh, be sorry if any evil befel me?"

"But why," he asked, "has Tomlinson given me this misinformation?"

"And why, Mr. Harleigh, because Tomlinson told you that a stranger was here, should you conclude it could be no other than your black fugitive?"

Again Harleigh turned to the traveller, and fixed his eyes upon her face: the patch, the bandage, the large cap, had hitherto completely hidden its general form; and the beautiful outline he now saw, with so entire a contrast of complexion to what he remembered, again checked, or rather dissolved his rising surmizes.

Elinor begged him to be seated, and to quiet his perturbed spirit.

He took a chair, but, in passing by the young woman, her sex, her beauty, her modest air, gave him a sensation that repelled his using it, and he leant upon its back, looking expressively at Elinor; but Elinor either marked not the hint, or mocked it. "So you have really," she said, "taken the pains to go to that eternal inn again, to enquire after this maimed and defaced Dulcinea? What in the world can have inspired you with such an interest for this wandering Creole?

"'Tis not her face does love create,
For there no graces revel."—*

The bell of Mrs. Maple now ringing, Elinor made a sign to the Incognita not to avow herself, and flew down stairs to caution Tomlinson to silence.

The chair which Harleigh had rejected for himself, he then offered to the fair unknown. She declined it, but in a voice that made him start, and wish to hear her speak again. His offer then became a request, and she thanked him in a tone that vibrated certainty upon his ears, that it could be no other than the voice of his fellow-voyager.

He now looked at her with an earnest gaze, that seemed nearly to draw his eyes from their sockets. The embarrassment that he occasioned her brought him to his recollection, and, apologising for his behaviour, he added; "A person—a lady—who accompanied us, not long since, from abroad, had a voice so exactly resembling yours—that I find it rather impossible than difficult not to believe that I hear the same. Permit me to ask—have you any very near relation returned lately from France?"

She blushed, but without replying.

"I fancy," he cried, "I must have encountered two sisters?—yet you have some reason, I own, to be angry at such a supposition—such a comparison——"

He paused, and a smile, which she could not repress, forced her to speak; "By no means!" she cried; "I know well how good you have been to the person to whom you allude, and I beg you will allow me—in her name—to return you the most grateful acknowledgements."

Harleigh, now, yet more curiously examining her, said, "It would not have been easy to have forborne taking an interest in her fate. She was in evident distress, yet never suffered herself to forget that she had escaped from some yet greater. Her mind seemed fraught with strength and native dignity. There was something singular, indescribable, in her manner of supporting the most harassing circumstances. It was impossible not to admire her."

The blush of the stranger now grew deeper, but she remained silent, till Elinor, re-entering, cried, "Well, Harleigh, what say you to my new demoiselle? And where would you have looked for your heart, if such had seemed your Dulcinea?"

"I should, perhaps, have been but the safer!" answered he, laughing.

"Pho! you would not make me believe any thing so out of nature, as that, when you were in such a tindery* fit as to be kindled by that dowdy,* you could have resisted being blown into flames at once by a creature such as this?"

"Man is a perverse animal, Elinor; that which he regards as pointed for his destruction, frequently proves harmless. We are all—boys and libertines alone excepted—upon our guard against beauty; for, as every sense is up in arms to second its assault, our pride takes the alarm, and rises to oppose it. Our real danger is where we see no risk."

"You enchant me, Harleigh! I am never so delighted as when I hear beauty set at nought—for I always suspect, Harleigh, that you do not think me handsome?"

"If I think you better than handsome, Elinor——"

"Pho! you know there is no such better in nature; at least not in such nature as forms taste in the mind of man; which I certainly do not consider as the purest of its works; though you all hold it, yourselves, to be the noblest. Nevertheless, imagination is all-powerful; if, therefore, you have taken the twist to believe in such sublimity, you may, perhaps, be seriously persuaded, that your heart would have been more stubborn to this dainty new Wanderer, than to your own walnut-skinned* gypsey."

"Walnut-skinned?"

"Even so, noble knight-errand, even so! This person whom you now behold, and whom, if we believe our eyes, never met them till within this half hour, if we give credit to our ears, scrambled over with us in that crazy boat from France."

Harleigh was here summoned to Mrs. Maple, and Elinor returned to her interrogatories; but the stranger only reverted to her hopes, that she might still depend upon the promised conveyance to Brighthelmstone?

"Tell me, at least, what it was you flung into the sea?"

"Ah, Madam, that would tell every thing!"

"You are a most provoking little devil," cried Elinor, impatiently, "and I am half tempted to have nothing more to say to you. Give me, however, some account how you managed matters with that sweet tender dove Mrs. Ireton."

The recital that ensued of the disasters, difficulties, and choler of that lady, proved so entertaining to Elinor, that she soon not only renewed her engagement of taking her unknown guest free to Lewes, but joined the warmest assurances of protection. "Not that we must attempt," she cried, "to get rid of the spite of Aunt Maple, for if we do, 'tis so completely the basis of her composition, that she won't know how to stand upright."

"But now," she continued, "where are you to dine? Aunt Maple is too fusty* to let you sit at our table."

The stranger earnestly solicited permission to eat alone: Elinor consented; assigned her a chamber, and gave orders to Mrs. Golding, her own maid, to take care of the traveller.

The repast below stairs was no sooner finished, than Elinor flew back to summon the Incognita to descend for exhibition. "I have told them all," she said, "that you are arrived, though I have revealed nothing of your metamorphosis; and there is a sister of mine, a conceited little thing, who is just engaged to be married, and who is wild to see you; and it is a rule, you know, to deny nothing to a bride elect; probably, poor wretch, because every one knows what a fair way she is in to be soon denied every thing! That quiz, Harleigh, would not stay; and that nothingly* Ireton has nearly shrugged his shoulders out of joint, at the very idea of so great a bore as seeing you again. Come, nevertheless; I die to enjoy Aunt Maple's astonishment at your new phiz."*

The stranger sought to evade this request as a pleasantry; but finding that it was insisted upon seriously, protested that she had neither courage nor spirits for being produced as an object of sport.

Elinor now again felt a strong temptation to draw back from her promise; but while, between anger and generosity, she hung suspended, a message arrived from Mrs. Maple, to order that the woman from France should be sent to the kitchen.

Elinor, changing the object of her displeasure, now warmly repeated her resolution to support the stranger; and, hastening to the dining-parlour, declared to her aunt, and to the party, that the woman from France should not be treated with indignity; that she was evidently a person who had been too well brought up to be consigned to domestics; and that she herself admired, and would abet her spirit, in refusing to be stared at like a wild beast.

CHAPTER VI

THE affairs of Mrs. Maple kept her a week longer in London; but the impatience of the Wanderer to reach Brighthelmstone, was compelled to yield to an utter inability of getting thither unaided. During this period, she gathered, from various circumstances, that Elinor had been upon the point of marriage with the younger brother of Harleigh, a handsome and flourishing lawyer; but that repeated colds, ill treated, or neglected, had menaced her with a consumption, and she had been advised to try a change of climate. Mrs. Maple accompanied her to the south of France,* where she had resided till her health was completely re-established. Harleigh, then, in compliment to his brother, who was confined by his profession to the capital, crossed the Channel to attend the two ladies home. They had already arrived at ——— on their return, when an order of Robespierre cast them into prison, whence enormous bribes, successful stratagems, and humane, though concealed assistance from some compassionate inhabitants of the town, enabled them, in common with the Admiral, the Iretons, and Riley, to effect their escape to a prepared boat, in which, through the friendly darkness of night, they reached the harbour of their country and their wishes.

The stranger learnt also from Elinor, by whom secresy or discretion were as carelessly set aside, as by herself they were fearfully practised, that young Ireton, urged by a rich old uncle, and an entailed estate,* to an early marriage, after addressing and jilting half the women of England, Scotland, and Ireland, had run through France, Switzerland, and Italy, upon the same errand; yet was returned home heart-whole, and hand-unshackled; but that, she added, was not the extraordinary part of the business, male coquets being just as common, and only more impertinent than female; all that was worth remarking, was his conduct for the last few days. Some accounts which he had to settle with her aunt, had obliged him to call at their house, the morning after their arrival in London. He then saw Selina, Elinor's younger sister, a wild little girl, only fourteen years of age, who was wholly unformed, but with whom he had become so desperately enamoured, that, when Mrs. Maple, knowing his character, and alarmed by his assiduities, cautioned him not to make a fool of her young niece, he abruptly demanded her in marriage. As he was very rich, Mrs. Maple had, of course, Elinor added, given her consent, desiring only that he would wait till Selina reached her fifteenth birthday; and the little girl, when told of the plan, had considered it as a frolic, and danced with delight.

During this interval, the time of the stranger was spent in the tranquil employment of needle-work, for which she was liberally supplied with cast-off materials, to relieve her necessities, from the wardrobe of Elinor, through whose powerful influence she was permitted to reside entirely up stairs. Here she saw only her protectress, into whose apartment Mrs. Maple did not deign, and no one else dared, to intrude unbidden. The spirit of contradiction, which was termed by Elinor the love of independence, fixed her design of supporting the stranger, to whom she delighted to do every good office which Mrs. Maple deemed superfluous, and whom she exulted in thus exclusively possessing, as a hidden curiosity. But when she found that no enquiry produced any communication, and that nothing fresh offered for new defiance to Mrs. Maple, a total indifference to the whole business took place of its first energy, and the young woman, towards the end of the week, fell into such neglect that it was never mentioned, and hardly even remembered, that she was an inhabitant of the house.

When the morning, most anxiously desired by herself, for the journey to Lewes, arrived, she heard the family engaged in preparations to set off, yet received no intimation how she was to make one of the party. With great discomfort, though with tolerable patience, she awaited some tidings, till the sound of carriages driving up to the street door, alarmed her with apprehensions of being deserted, and, hastily running down stairs, she was drawn by the voice of Elinor to the door of the breakfast-parlour; but the sound of other voices took from her the courage to open it, though the baggage collected around her shewed the journey so near, that she deemed it unsafe to return to her chamber.

In a few minutes, Harleigh, loaded with large drawings, crossed the hall, and, observing her distress, enquired into it's cause.

She wished to speak to Miss Joddrel.

He entered the parlour, and sent out Elinor, who, exclaiming, "O, it's you, is it? Mercy on me! I had quite forgotten you!—" ran back, crying, "Aunt, here's your old friend, the grim French voyager! Shall she come in?"

"Come in? What for, Miss Joddrel? Because Mr. Harleigh was so kind as to make a hoy of my boat, does it follow that you are to make a booth* of my parlour?"

"She is at the door!" said Harleigh, in a low voice.

"Then she is at her proper place; where else should such a sort of body be?"

Harleigh took up a book.

"O, but do let her come in, Aunt, do let her come in!" cried the young Selina. "I was so provoked at not seeing her the other day, that I could have cried with pleasure! and sister Elinor has kept her shut up ever since, and refused me the least little peep at her."

The opposition of Mrs. Maple only the more strongly excited the curiosity of Selina, who, encouraged by the clamorous approbation of Elinor, flew to the door.

There, stopping short, she called out, "La! here's nothing but a young woman!—La! Aunt, I'm afraid she's run away!"

"And if she is, Niece, we shall not break our hearts, I hope! not but, if she's decamped, it's high time I should enquire whether all is safe in the house."

"Decamped?" cried Elinor, "Why she's at the door! Don't you know her, Aunt? Don't you see her, Ireton?"

The stranger, abashed, would have retreated. Harleigh, raising his eyes from his book, shook his head at Elinor, who, laughing and regardless, seized the hand of the young person, and dragged her into the parlour.

"Who is this?" said Mrs. Maple.

"Who, Aunt? Why your memory is shorter than ever! Don't you recollect our dingy French companion, that you took such a mighty fancy to?"

Mrs. Maple turned away with angry contempt; and the housekeeper, who had been summoned, appearing, orders were given for a strict examination whether the swarthy traveller, who followed them from France, were gone.

The stranger, changing colour, approached Elinor, and with an air that claimed her protection, said, "Will you not, Madam, have the goodness to explain who I am?"

"How can I," cried Elinor, laughing, "when I don't know it myself?"

Every one stared; Harleigh turned round; the young woman blushed, but was silent.

"If here is another of your Incognitas, Miss Joddrel," said Mrs. Maple, "I must beg the favour that you'll desire her to march off at once. I don't chuse to be beset by such sort of gentry quite so frequently. Pray, young woman, what is it you want here?"

"Protection, Madam, and compassion!" replied the stranger, in a tone of supplication.

"I protest," said Mrs. Maple, "she has just the same sort of voice that that black girl had! and the same sort of cant! And pray, young woman, what's your name?"

"That's right, Mrs. Maple, that's right!" cried Ireton; "make her tell her name!"

"To be sure I shall!" said Mrs. Maple, seating herself on a sofa, and taking out her snuff-box.* "I have a great right to know the name of a person that comes, in this manner, into my parlour. Why do you not answer, young woman?"

The stranger, looking at Elinor, clasped her hands in act of entreaty for pity.

"Very fine, truly!" said Mrs. Maple: "So here's just the second edition of the history of that frenchified swindler!"

"No, no, Aunt; it's only the sequel to the first part, for it's the same person, I assure you. Did not you come over with us from France, Mademoiselle? In the same boat? and with the same surly pilot?"

The stranger silently assented.

Mrs. Maple, now, doubly enraged, interrogated her upon the motives of her having been so disfigured, with the sternness and sharpness of addressing a convicted cheat.

The stranger, compelled to speak, said, with an air of extreme embarrassment, "I am conscious, Madam, how dreadfully all appearances are against me! Yet I have no means, with any prudence, to enter into an explanation: I dare not, therefore, solicit your good opinion, though my distress is so urgent, that I am forced to sue for your assistance,—I ought, perhaps, to say your charity!"

"I don't want," said Mrs. Maple, "to hear all that sort of stuff over again. Let me only know who you are, and I shall myself be the best judge what should be done for you. What is it, then, once for all, that you call yourself? No prevarications! Tell me your name, or go about your business."

"Yes, your name! your name!" repeated Elinor.

"Your name! your name!" echoed Selina.

"Your name! your name!" re-echoed Ireton.

The spirits and courage of the stranger seemed now to forsake her; and, with a faultering voice, she answered, "Alas! I hardly know it myself!"

Elinor laughed; Selina tittered; Ireton stared; the leaves of the book held by Harleigh were turned over with a speed that shewed how little their contents engaged him; and Mrs. Maple, indignantly swelling, exclaimed, "Not know your own name? Why I hope you don't come into my house from the Foundling Hospital?"*

Harleigh, throwing down his book, walked hastily to Mrs. Maple, and said, in a low voice, "Yet, if that should be the case, would she be less an object of compassion? of consideration?"

"What your notions may be upon such sort of heinous subjects, Mr. Harleigh," Mrs. Maple answered, with a look of high superiority, "I do not know; but as for mine, I think encouraging things of that kind, has a very immoral tendency."

Harleigh bowed, not as acquiescent in her opinion, but as declining to argue it, and was leaving the room, when Elinor, catching him by the arm, called out, "Why, Harleigh! what are you so sour for? Are you, also, angry, to see a clean face, and a clean gown? I'll make the demoiselle put on her plasters and patches again, if that will please you better."

This forced him to smile and to stay; and Elinor then ended the inquisition, by proposing that the stranger should go to Lewes in the chaise with Golding, her own maid, and Fenn, Mrs. Maple's housekeeper.

Mrs. Maple protested that she would not allow any such indulgence to an unknown pauper; and Mrs. Fenn declared, that there were so many hats, caps, and things of consequence to take care of, that it would be impossible to make room for a mouse.

Elinor, ever alert to carry a disputed point, felt her generosity doubly excited to support the stranger; and, after some further, but overpowered opposition from Mrs. Maple, the hats, caps, and things of consequence were forced to submit to inferior accommodation, and the young woman obtained her request, to set off for Sussex, with the housekeeper and Elinor's maid.

CHAPTER VII

THE house of Mrs. Maple was just without the town of Lewes, and the Wanderer, upon her arrival there, learnt that Brighthelmstone was still eight miles farther. She earnestly desired to go on immediately; but how undertake such a journey on foot, so late, and in the dark month of December, when the night appears to commence at four o'clock in the afternoon? Her travelling companions both left her in the courtyard, and she was fain, uninvited, to follow them to the apartment of the housekeeper; where she was beginning an apology upon the necessity that urged her intrusion, when Selina came skipping into the room.

The stranger, conceiving some hope of assistance from her extreme youth, and air of good humour, besought her interest with Mrs. Maple for permission to remain in the house till the next day. Selina carried the request with alacrity, and, almost instantly returning, gave orders to the housekeeper to prepare a bed for her fellow-traveller, in the little room upon the stairs.

The gratitude excited by this support was so pleasant to the young patronness, that she accompanied her *protegée* to the destined little apartment, superintended all the regulations for her accommodation and refreshments, and took so warm a fancy to her, that she made her a visit every other half-hour in the course of the evening; during which she related, with earnest injunctions to secresy, all the little incidents of her little life, finishing her narration by intimating, in a rapturous whisper, that she should very soon have a house of her own, in which her aunt Maple would have no sort of authority. "And then," added she, nodding, "perhaps I may ask you to come and see me!"

No one else appeared; and the stranger might tranquilly have passed the night, but from internal disturbance how she should reach Brighthelmstone the following morning, without carriage, friends, money, or knowledge of the road thither.

Before the tardy light invited her to rise the next day, her new young friend came flying into the room. "I could not sleep," she cried, "all last night, for the thought of a play that I am to have a very pretty dress for; and that we have fixed upon acting amongst ourselves; and so I got up on purpose to tell you of it, for fear you should be gone."

She then read through every word of her own part, without a syllable of any other.

They were both soon afterwards sent for into the parlour by Elinor, who was waiting breakfast for Mrs. Maple, with Harleigh and Ireton. "My dear demoiselle," she cried, "how fares it? We were all so engrossed last night, about a comedy that we have been settling* to massacre, that I protest I quite forgot you."

"I ought only, Madam," answered the stranger, with a sigh, "to wonder, and to be grateful that you have ever thought of me."

"Why what's the matter with you now? Why are you so solemn? Is your noble courage cast down? What are you projecting? What's your plan?"

"When I have been to Brighthelmstone, Madam, when I have seen who—or what may await me there—"

Mrs. Maple, now appearing, angrily demanded who had

invited her into the parlour? telling her to repair to the kitchen, and make known what she wanted through some of the servants.

The blood mounted into the cheeks of the Incognita, but she answered only by a distant courtsie, and turning to Elinor and Selina, besought them to accept her acknowledgements for their goodness, and retired.

Selina and Elinor, following her into the ante-room, asked how she meant to travel?

She had one way only in her power; she must walk.

"Walk?" exclaimed Harleigh, joining them, "in such a season? And by such roads?"

"Walk?" cried Ireton, advancing also, "eight miles? In December?"

"And why not, gentlemen?" called out Mrs. Maple, "How would you have such a body as that go, if she must not walk? What else has she got her feet for?"

"Are you sure," said Ireton, "that you know the way?"

"I was never in this part of the world till now."

"Ha! Ha! pleasant enough! And what are you to do about money? Did you ever find that purse of your's that you—lost, I think, at Dover?"

"Never!"

"Better and better!" cried Ireton, laughing again, yet feeling for his own purse, and sauntering towards the hall.

Harleigh was already out of sight.

"Poor soul!" said Selina, "I am sure, for one, I'll help her."

"Let us make a subscription," said Elinor, producing half a guinea, and looking round to Mrs. Maple.

Selina joined the same sum, full of glee to give, for the first time, as much as her sister.

Mrs. Maple clamorously ordered them to shut the parlour door.

With shame, yet joy, the stranger accepted the two half guineas, intimated her hopes that she should soon repay them, repeated her thanks, and took leave.

The sisters would still have detained her, but Mrs. Maple peremptorily insisted upon breakfasting without further delay.

The Incognita was proceeding to the housekeeper's room,

for a packet of the gifts of Elinor, but she was stopt in the hall by Ireton, who was loitering about, playing with his purse, and jerking and catching it from hand to hand.

"Here, my dear," he cried, "look at this, and take what you will from it."

She coldly thanked him, and, saying that the young ladies had amply supplied her, would have moved on: but he prevented her, repeating his offer, and adding, while with uncontrolled freedom he stared at her, "How the deuce, with such a pretty face as that, could you ever think of making yourself look such a fright?"

She told him that she was in haste.

"But what was the whim of it?"

She desired him to make way, every moment of day-light being precious to her.

"Hang day-light!" cried he, "I never liked it; and if you will but wait a few minutes—"

Selina, here, running to call him to breakfast, he finished in a whisper, "I'll convey you in my own chaise wherever you like to go;" and then, forced to put up his purse, he gallantly handed his fair bride-elect back to the parlour.

The stranger, entering the housekeeper's room, met Harleigh, who seriously remonstrated against her walking project, offering his servant to procure her a post-chaise. The sigh of her negative expressed its melancholy economy,* though she owned a wish that she could find some meaner vehicle that would be safe.

Harleigh then disappeared; but, a few minutes afterwards, when she was setting out from the garden-gate, she again met him, and he told her that he was going to order a parcel from a stationer's at Brighthelmstone; and that a sort of chaise-cart,* belonging to a farmer just by, would be sent for it, almost immediately. "I do not recommend," added he, smiling, "such a machine for its elegance; and, if you would permit me to offer you one more eligible—"

A grave motion of the head repressed him from finishing his phrase, and he acquainted her that he had just been to the farm, to bespeak a sober driver, with whom he had already settled for his morning's work.

This implied assurance, that he had no plan of following the machine, induced her to agree to the proposition; and, when the little carriage was in sight, he expressed his good wishes that she might find the letter, or the friend, that she desired, and returned to the breakfast parlour.

The length of the way, joined to the dirt of the roads, made her truly sensible of his consideration, in affording her this safe conveyance.

When she arrived at the Post-office, the words, "Oh, you are come at last!" struck her ear, from the street; but not conceiving herself to be addressed, they failed to catch her attention, till she saw, waiting to give her his hand, while exclaiming, "What the deuce can have made you so long in coming?" young Ireton.

Far less pleased than surprised, she disengaged herself from him with quickness, and enquired for the post-master.

He was not within.

She was extremely disturbed, and at a loss where to wait, or what to do.

"Why did not you stay for my chaise?" said Ireton. "When I found that you were gone, I mounted my steed, and came over by a short cut, to see what was become of you; and here you have kept me cooling my heels all this devil of a time. That booby of a driver must have had a taste for being out-crawled by a snail."

Without answering him, she asked whether there were any clerk at hand, to whom she could apply?

Oh, yes! and she was immediately shewn into an office, and followed, without any ceremony, by Ireton, though she replied not a word to any thing that he said.

A young man here received her, of whom, in a fearful voice, she demanded whether he had any letter directed for L. S., to be left till called for.

"You must make her tell you her name, Sir!" cried Ireton, with an air of importance. "I give you notice not to let her have her letter, without a receipt, signed by her own hand. She came over with Mrs. Maple of Lewes, and a party of us, and won't say who she is. 'T has a very ugly look, Sir!"

The eye of the stranger accused him, but vainly, of cruelty.

The clerk, who listened with great curiosity, soon produced a foreign letter, with the address demanded.

While eagerly advancing to receive it, she anxiously enquired, whether there were no inland letter with the same direction?

None, she was answered.

Ireton then, clapping his hand upon the shoulder of the clerk, positively declared, that he would lodge an information* against him, if he delivered any letter, under such circumstances, without a signed receipt.

An almost fainting distress was now visible in the face of the Incognita, as the clerk, surprised and perplexed, said, "Have you any objection, Ma'am, to giving me your name?"

She stammered, hesitated, and grew paler, while Ireton smiled triumphantly, when the party was suddenly joined by Harleigh.

Ireton ceased his clamour, and hung back, ashamed.

Harleigh, approaching the stranger, with an apology for his intrusion, was struck with her disordered look, and enquired whether she were ill?

"Ah, Sir!" she cried, reviving with hope at his sight, and walking towards the window, whither, wondering, he followed, "assist me in mercy!—you know, already, that some powerful motive deters me from naming myself—"

"Have I been making any indiscreet enquiry?" cried he, gently, yet in a tone of surprise.

"You? O no! You have been all generosity and consideration!"

Harleigh, much gratified, besought her to explain herself with openness.

"They insist upon my telling my name—or they detain my letter!"

"Is that all?" said he, and, going to the clerk, he demanded the letter, for which he gave his own address and receipt, with his word of honour that he was authorised to require it by the person to whom it was written.

He then delivered it into her hand.

The joy of its possession, joined to the relief from such persecution, filled her with a delight which, though beaming from all her features, she had not yet found words to express, when Ireton, whom Harleigh had not remarked, burst into a significant, though affected laugh.

"Why, Harleigh! why, what the deuce can have brought you hither?" cried he. Harleigh wished to retort the question; but would not hazard a raillery that might embarrass the stranger, who now, with modest grace, courtsied to him; while she passed Ireton without notice, and left the room.

Each wished to follow her, but each was restrained by the other. Ireton, who continued laughing maliciously, owned that his journey to Brighthelmstone had been solely to prevail with the clerk to demand the name of the stranger, before he gave up the letter; but Harleigh protested that he had merely ridden over to offer his mediation for her return to Lewes, if she should miss the friend, or letter, of which she came in search.

Ireton laughed still more; and hoped that, from such abundant charity, he would attribute his own ride, also, to motives of as pure benevolence. He then begged he might not interfere with the following up of so charitable a purpose: but Harleigh assured him that he had neither right, pretension, nor design to proceed any farther.

"If that's the case," cried Ireton, "since charity is the order of the day, I'll see what is become of her myself."

He ran out of the room.

Harleigh, following, soon joined him, and they saw the Incognita enter a milliner's shop. They then separated; Harleigh pleading business for not returning immediately to Lewes; while Ireton, mounting his horse, with an accusing shake of the head, rode off.

Harleigh strolled to the milliner's, and, enquiring for some gloves, perceived, through the glass-door of a small parlour, the stranger reading her letter.

He begged that the milliner would be so good as to tell the lady in the inner room, that Mr. Harleigh requested to speak to her.

A message thus open could neither startle nor embarrass her, and he was instantly admitted.

He found her pale and agitated. Her letter, which was in her hand, she hastily folded, but looked at nothing else, while she waited an explanation of his visit.

"I could not," he said, "go back to Lewes without knowing whether your expectations are answered in coming hither; or whether you will permit me to tell the Miss Joddrels that they may still have the pleasure to be of some use to you."

She appeared to be unable to speak.

"I fear to seem importunate," he continued, "yet I have no intention, believe me, to ask any officious questions. I respect what you have said of the nature of your situation, too much to desire any information beyond what may tend to alleviate its uneasiness."

She held her hands before her eyes, to hide her fresh gushing tears, but they trickled fast through her fingers, as she answered, "My situation is now deplorable indeed!—I have no letter, no direction from the person whom I had hoped to meet; and whose abode, whose address, I know not how to discover! I must not apply to any of my original friends: unknown, and in circumstances the most strange, if not suspicious, can I hope to make myself any new ones?—Can I even subsist, when, though thus involved in mystery, I am as indigent as I am friendless, yet dare not say who, nor what I am,—and hardly even know it myself!"

Touched with compassion, he drew nearer to her, meaning, from an almost unconscious impulse of kindness, to take her hand; but feeling, with equal quickness, the impropriety of allowing his pity such a manifestation, he retreated to his first place, and, in accents of gentle, but respectful commiseration, expressed his concern for her distress.

Somewhat soothed, yet heavily sighing, "To fail finding," she said, "either the friend, or her direction, that I expected, overwhelms me with difficulty and perplexity. And even this letter from abroad, though most welcome, has grievously disappointed me! I am promised, however, another, which may bring me, perhaps, happier tidings. I must wait for it patiently; but the person from whom it comes little imagines my destitute state! The unfortunate loss of my purse makes it, by this delay of all succour, almost desperate!"

The hand of Harleigh was involuntarily in his pocket, but before he could either draw out his purse, or speak, she tremulously added, colouring, and holding back, "I am ashamed to have mentioned a circumstance, which seems to call for a species of assistance, that it is impossible I should accept."

Harleigh bowed, acquiescent.

Her eyes thanked him for sparing her any contest, and she then gratefully acceded to his proposal, of soliciting for her the renewed aid and countenance of the Miss Joddrels, from whom some little notice might be highly advantageous, in securing her decent treatment, during the few days,—perhaps more,—that she might be kept waiting at Brighthelmstone for another letter.

He gently exhorted her to re-animate her courage, and hoped to convince her, by the next morning, that he had not intruded upon her retirement from motives of idle and useless curiosity.

As soon as he was gone, she treated with Miss Matson, the milliner, to whom Harleigh had considerately named her as a young person known to Mrs. Maple, for a small room in her house during a few days; and then, somewhat revived, she endeavoured, by recollecting the evils which she had escaped, to look forward, with better hopes of alleviation, to those which might yet remain to be encountered.

CHAPTER VIII

The next morning, the Wanderer had the happy surprise of seeing Elinor burst into her chamber. "We are all on fire," she cried, "at our house, so I am come hither to cool myself. Aunt Maple and I have fought a noble battle; but I have won the day."

She then related, that Harleigh had brought them an account of her disappointments, her letter, her design to wait for another, and her being at the milliner's. "Aunt Maple," she continued, "treated the whole as imposition; but I make it a rule never to let her pitiful system prevail in the house. And so, to cut the matter short, for I hate a long story, I gave her to understand, that, if she would not let you return to Lewes, and stay with us till your letter arrives, I should go to Brighthelmstone myself, and stay with you. This properly frightened her; for she knew I would keep my word."

"And would you, Madam?" said the stranger, smiling.

"Why not? Do you think I would not do a thing only because no one else would do it? I am never so happy as in ranging without a guide. However, we came to a compromise this morning; and she consents to permit your return, provided I don't let you enter her chaise, and engage for keeping you out of every body's way."

The stranger, evidently hurt and offended, declined admission upon such terms. Her obligations, she said, were already sufficiently heavy, and she would struggle to avoid adding to their weight, and to supply her own few wants herself, till some new resource might open to her assistance.

Elinor, surprised, hastily demanded whether she meant to live alone, that she might only be aided, and only be visited by Mr. Harleigh.

The stranger looked all astonishment.

"Nay, that will certainly be the most pleasant method; so I don't effect to wonder at it; nevertheless ——"

She hesitated, but her face was tinted with a glow of disturbance, and her voice announced strong rising emotion, as she presently added, "If you think of forming any attachment with that man—" She stopt abruptly.

The heightened amazement of the stranger kept her for a few instants speechless; but the troubled brow of Elinor soon made her with firmness and spirit answer, "Attachment? I protest to you, Madam, except at those periods when his benevolence or urbanity have excited my gratitude, my own difficulties have absorbed my every thought!"

"I heartily congratulate your apathy!" said Elinor, her features instantly dilating into a smile; "for he is so completely a non-descript, that he would else incontestably set you upon hunting out for some new Rosamund's Pond.* That is all I mean."

She then, but with gaiety and good humour, enquired whether or not the stranger would return to Lewes.

Nothing, to the stranger, could be less attractive at this moment; yet the fear of such another misinterpretation and rebuff, and the unspeakable dread of losing, in her helpless situation, all female countenance, conquered her repugnance.

Elinor then said that she would hurry home, and send off the same elegant machine from the farm, which, she found, had been made use of in her service the preceding day.

Far from exhilarated was the young person whom she left, who, thus treated, could scarcely brook the permission to return, which before she would have solicited. Small are the circumstances which reverse all our wishes! and one hour still less resembles another in our feelings, than in our actions.

Upon arriving again at the house of Mrs. Maple, she was met by Selina, who expressed the greatest pleasure at her return, and conducted her to the little room which she had before occupied; eagerly announcing that she had already learnt half her part, which she glibly repeated, crying, "How lucky it is that you are come back; for now I have got somebody to say it to!"

Mrs. Maple, she added, had refused her consent to the whole scheme, till Elinor threatened to carry it into execution in Farmer Gooch's barn, and to invite all the county.

She then entered into sundry details of family secrets, the principal of which was, that she often thought that she should be married before her sister Elinor, though Sister Elinor was twenty-two years old, and she herself was only fourteen: but Sister Elinor had had a violent quarrel with Mr. Dennis Harleigh, whom she had been engaged to marry before she went abroad, about the French Revolution, which Sister Elinor said was the finest thing in the world, but which Mr. Dennis said was the very worst. But, for all that, he loved her so, that he had made his brother fetch her home, and wanted the marriage to take place directly: and Aunt Maple wished it too, of all things, because Sister Elinor was so hard to manage; for, now she was of age, she did everything that she liked; and she protested that she would not give her consent, unless Mr. Dennis promised to change his opinion upon the French Revolution; so they quarrelled again the day before they left town; and Aunt Maple, quite frightened, invited Mr. Harleigh, the elder brother, to come and spend a week or two at Lewes, to try to bring matters round again.

These anecdotes were interrupted by the appearance of Elinor, of whom the Incognita entreated, and obtained, permission to reside, as in town, wholly in her own room.

"I wish you could hear," said Elinor, "how we all settle your history in the parlour. No two of us have the same idea of whom or what you are." She then entered upon the subject of the play, which was to be the Provoked Husband, in compliment to Miss Arbe, a young lady of celebrated talents, who, having frequently played the part of Lady Townly, with amazing applause, at private theatres, had offered her services for that character, but would study no other. This, Elinor complained, was singularly provoking, as Harleigh, who alone of the whole set was worth acting with, must necessarily be Lord Townly. However, since she could not try her own theatrical skill, by the magnetizing powers of reciprocated exertions, she determined, in relinquishing what was brilliant, to adopt at least what was diverting; for which reason she had taken the part of Lady Wronghead. Selina was to be Miss Jenny; Ireton, 'Squire Richard; and she had pitched upon Mr. Scope and Miss Bydel, two famous, formal quizzes, residing in Lewes, to compliment them with the fogrum* parts of Manly and Lady Grace; characters which always put the audience to sleep; but that, as they were both good sort of souls, who were never awake themselves, they would not find out. The other parts she had chiefly arranged for the pleasure of giving a lesson of democracy to Aunt Maple; for she had appointed Sir Francis Wronghead to Mr. Stubbs, an old steward belonging to Lord Rockton; Count Basset to young Gooch, a farmer's son; Myrtylla to Golding, her own maid, and John Moody to Tomlinson, the footman.

The air of attention with which the stranger listened, whether she answered or not, renewed again in Elinor the pleasure which she had first found in talking to her; and thus, between the two sisters, she had almost constantly a companion till near midnight.

To be left, then, alone was not to be left to unbroken slumbers. She had no dependence, nor hope, but in an expected second letter, yet had devised no means to secure its immediate reception, even if its quick arrival corresponded with her wishes. As soon, therefore, as she heard the family stirring the next morning, she descended, with an intention of going to the housekeeper's room, to make some arrangement for that purpose.

Ireton, who caught a glimpse of her upon the stairs, met and stopt her. "My dear," he cried, "don't think me such a prig as to do you any mischief; but take a hint! Don't see quite so much of a certain young lady, whom I don't wish should know the world quite so soon! You understand me, my dear?"

Inexpressibly offended, she was contemptuously shrinking from him, when they were joined by Harleigh, who asked, with an air of respect that was evidently meant to give a lesson to Ireton, whether she would permit him to call at the post-office, to order that her letters should be forwarded to Lewes.

This offer was irresistible, and, with looks of the brightest gratitude, she was uttering her acknowledgements, when the voice of Elinor, from a distance, sounding tremulous and agitated, checked her, and she hastily retreated.

But her room-door was only shut to be almost instantly thrown open by Elinor herself, who, entering with a large parcel in her hands, while her face shewed pain and disorder, said, "See how I have been labouring to assist and to serve you, at the very moment of your insidious duplicity!"

Thunderstruck by the harshness of an attack nearly as incomprehensible as it was vehement, the stranger fixed her eyes upon her accuser with a look that said, Are you mad?

The silent, yet speaking expression was caught by Elinor, who, struck with sudden shame, frankly begged her pardon; and, after a little reflexion, coolly added, "You must never mind what I say, nor what I do; for I sport all sort of things, and in all sort of manners. But it is merely to keep off stagnation: I dread nothing like a lethargy. But pray what were you all about just now?"

The Incognita related her intended purpose; its interruption; the offer of Mr. Harleigh; and its acceptance.

Elinor looked perturbed again, and said, "You seem mighty fond, methinks, of employing Mr. Harleigh for your Mercury!"*

"He is so good as to employ himself. I could never think of taking such a liberty."

Elinor put up her lip; but told her to make what use she could of the parcel, and, with an abrupt "Good morning," went down to breakfast.

The stranger, amazed and confounded, remained for some time absorbed by conjectures upon this scene.

The parcel contained cast-off clothes of almost every description; but, much as she required such aid, the manner in which it was offered determined her upon its rejection.

In a few hours, the maid who brought her meals, was desired by Mr. Harleigh to inform her, that he had executed her commission at the post-office.

This assurance revived her, and enabled her to pass the day in tolerable tranquillity, though perfectly alone, and without any species of employment to diversify her ruminations, or help to wear away the tediousness of expectation.

When the next day, however, and the next, passed without her seeing any of the family, she felt disconcerted and disturbed. To be abandoned by Elinor, and even by Selina, made her situation appear worse than forlorn; and her offended spirit deemed the succour thus afforded her, inadequate to compensate for the endurance of universal disesteem and avoidance. She determined, therefore, to quit the inhospitable mansion, persuaded that no efforts could be too difficult, no means too laborious, that might rescue her from an abode which she could no longer inhabit, without seeming to herself to be degraded.

But the idea of this project had a facility of which its execution did not partake. She had no money, save what she had received from the two sisters; even that, by a night and day spent at the milliner's, was much diminished. She could not quit the neighbourhood of Brighthelmstone, while still in expectation of a letter; and if, while awaiting it in any other house, the compassion, or the philanthropy of Harleigh should urge him to see her, might not Elinor conclude that she had only retreated to receive his visits alone?

Apprehensions such as these frightened her into forbearance: but in teaching her prudence, they did not endow her with contentment. Her hours lingered in depression and uncertainty; her time was not employed but consumed; her faculties were not enjoyed, but wasted.

Yet, upon more mature reflexion, she enquired by what right she expected kinder treatment. Unknown, unnamed, without any sort of recommendation, she applied for succour, and it was granted her: if she met with the humanity of being listened to, and the charity of being assisted, must she quarrel with her benefactors, because they gave not implicit credit to the word of a lonely Wanderer for her own character? or think herself ill used that their donations and their aid were not delicate as well as useful?

This sober style of reasoning soon chased away resentment, and, with quieter nerves, she awaited some termination to her suspence and solitude.

Meantime, most of the other inhabitants of the house, were engaged by studying their parts for the intended representation, which so completely occupied some by choice, and others by complaisance, or necessity, that no visit or excursion was made abroad, till several days after their arrival at Lewes. Mrs. Maple then, with her whole party, accepted an invitation to dine and spend the evening with the family of their principal actress, Miss Arbe; but a sudden indisposition with which that lady was seized after dinner, forced them home again early in the evening. Their return being unexpected, the servants were all out, or out of the way, but, entering by a door leading from the garden, which they found open, they were struck with the sound of music. They stopped, and distinctly heard a harp; they listened, and found that it was played with uncommon ability.

"'Tis my harp!" cried Selina, "I am sure of that!"

"Your harp?" said Mrs. Maple; "why who can be playing it?"

"Hist! dear ladies," said Harleigh; "'tis some exquisite performer."

"It must be Lady Kendover, then," said Mrs. Maple, "for nobody else comes to our house that plays the harp."

A new movement was now begun; it was slow and pathetic, and played with so much taste and expression, though mixed with bursts of rapid execution, that the whole auditory was equally charmed and surprized; and every one, Mrs. Maple herself not excepted, with uplifted finger seemed to beseech attention from the rest.

An Arpeggio* succeeded, followed by an air, which produced, alternately, tones sweet, yet penetrating, of touching pathos or impassioned animation; and announced a performer whom nature had gifted with her finest feelings, to second, or rather to meet the soul-pervading refinements of skilful art.

When the voice ceased, the harp was still heard; but some sounds made by an involuntary, though restrained tribute of general approbation, apparently found their way to the drawing-room, where it was played; for suddenly it stopped, the instrument seemed hastily to be put away, and some one was precipitately in motion.

Every body then hastened up stairs; but before they could reach the landing-place, a female figure, which they all instantly recognized for that of the unknown young woman, glided out of the drawing-room, and, with the quick motion of fear, ran up another flight of stairs.

"Amazing!" cried Mrs. Maple, stopping short; "could any body have credited assurance such as this? That bold young stroller* has been obtruding herself into my drawing-room, to hear Lady Kendover play!"

Harleigh, who had contrived to be the first to enter the apartment, now returned to the door, and, with a smile of the most animated pleasure, said, "No one is here!—Not a creature!"

His tone and air spoke more than his words, and, to the quick conceptions of Elinor, pronounced: This divine singer, whom you were all ready to worship, is no other than the lonely Wanderer whom you were all ready to condemn!

Mrs. Maple now, violently ringing the bell, ordered one of her servants to summon the woman who came from abroad.

The stranger obeyed, with the confused look of a person who expected a reprimand, to which she had not courage to reply.

"Be so good as to tell me," said Mrs. Maple, "what you have been into my drawing-room for? and whether you know who it is, that has taken the liberty to play upon my niece's harp?"

The Incognita begged a thousand pardons, but said that having learnt, from the housemaid, that the family was gone out for the day, she had ventured to descend, to take a little air and exercise in the garden.

"And what has that to do with my niece's harp?—And my drawing-room?"

"The door, Madam, was open.—It was long since I had seen an instrument—I thought no one would hear me—"

"Why you don't pretend that it was you who played?"

The young woman renewed her apology.

"You?—You play upon a harp?—And pray who was it that sung?"

The stranger looked down.

"Well, this is surprising indeed!—And pray where might such a body as you learn these things?—And what use can such a body want them for? Be so good as to tell me that; and who you are?"

The stranger, in the utmost disturbance, painfully answered, "I am truly ashamed, Madam, so often to press for your forbearance, but my silence is impelled by necessity! I am but too well aware how incomprehensible this must seem, but my situation is perilous—I cannot reveal it! I can only implore your compassion!—"

She retired hastily.

No one pursued nor tried to stop her. All, except Harleigh, remained nearly stupified by what had passed, for no one else had ever considered her but as a needy travelling adventurer. To him, her language, her air, and her manner, pervading every disadvantage of apparel, poverty, and subjection, had announced her, from the first, to have received the education, and to have lived the life of a gentlewoman; yet to him, also, it was as new, though not as wonderful, as to the rest, to find in her all the delicately acquired skill, joined to the happy natural talents, which constitute a refined artist.

Elinor seemed absorbed in mortification, not sooner to have divined what Harleigh had so immediately discovered; Selina, triumphant, felt enchanted with an idea that the stranger must be a disguised princess; Mrs. Maple, by a thousand crabbed grimaces, shewed her chagrin, that the frenchified stroller should not rather have been detected as a positive vagabond, than proved, by her possession of cultivated talents, to have been well brought up; and Ireton, who had thought her a mere female fortune-hunter, was utterly overset, till he comforted himself by observing, that many mere adventurers, from fortuitous circumstances, obtain accomplishments that may vie, in brilliancy, with those acquired by regular education and study.

Doubts, however, remained with all: they were varied, but not removed. The mystery that hung about her was rather thickened than cleared, and the less she appeared like an ordinary person, the more restless became conjecture, to dive into some probable motive, for the immoveable obstinacy of her concealment.

The pause was first broken by Elinor, who, addressing Harleigh, said, "Tell me honestly, now, what, all-together, you really and truly think of this extraordinary demoiselle?"

"I think her," answered he, with readiness, "an elegant and well bred young woman, under some extraordinary and inexplicable difficulties: for there is a modesty in her air which art, though it might attain, could not support; and a dignity in her conduct in refusing all succour but your's, that make it impossible for me to have any doubt upon the fairness of her character."

"And how do you know that she refuses all succour but mine? Have you offered her your's?"

"She will not let me go so far. If she perceive such an intention, she draws back, with a look that would make the very mentioning it insolent."

Elinor ran up stairs.

She found the stranger disturbed and alarmed, though she was easily revived upon seeing Elinor courteous, almost respectful; for, powerfully struck by a discovery, so completely accidental, of talents so superior, and satisfied by the assurance just received from Harleigh, that his pecuniary aid had never been accepted, she grew ashamed of the angry flippancy with which she had last quitted the room, and of the resolute neglect with which she had since kept aloof. She now apologized for having stayed away, professed a design to be frequent in her future visits, and presented, with generous importunity, the trifles which she blushed to have offered so abruptly.

Addressed thus nearly upon equal terms, the stranger gracefully accepted the donation, and, from the relief produced by this unexpected good treatment, her own manners acquired an ease, and her language a flow, that made her strikingly appear to be what Harleigh had called her, a well bred and elegant young woman; and the desire of Elinor to converse with her no longer hung, now, upon the mere stimulus of curiosity; it became flattering, exhilarating, and cordial.

The stranger, in return, upon nearer inspection, found in Elinor a solid goodness of heart, that compensated for the occasional roughness, and habitual strangeness of her manners. Her society was gay and original; and, to great quickness of parts, and liberality of feeling, she joined a frankness of character the most unbounded. But she was alarming and sarcastic, aiming rather to strike than to please, to startle than to conquer. Upon chosen and favourite subjects she was impressive, nay eloquent; upon all others she was careless, flighty, and indifferent, and constantly in search of matter for ridicule: yet, though severe, almost to ferocity, where she conceived herself to be offended, or injured, she became kind, gentle, and generously conceding, when convinced of any errour.

Selina, when her sister retired, tripped fleetly into the chamber, whisperingly revealing, that it was Mr. Ireton who had persuaded her to relinquish her visits; but that she would now make them as often as ever.

Thus supported and encouraged, the stranger, again desiring to stay in the house, earnestly wished to soften the ill will of Mrs. Maple; and having heard, from Selina, that the play occupied all hands, she begged Mrs. Fenn to accept her services at needle-work.

Mrs. Fenn conveyed the proposal to her mistress, who haughtily protested that she would have nothing done under her roof, by she did not know who; though she tacitly suffered Mrs. Fenn to try the skill of the proposer with some cambric handkerchiefs.

These she soon returned, executed with such admirable neatness, that Mrs. Fenn immediately found her other similar employment; which she presented to her with the air of conferring the most weighty of obligations.

And such, in the event, it proved; for she now continued to

receive daily more business of the same sort, without any hint relative to her departure; and heard, through Selina, that Mrs. Maple herself had remarked, that this was the first singer and player she had ever known, who had not been spoilt by those idle habits for a good huswife.*

The Incognita now thankfully rejoiced in the blessing bestowed upon her, by that part of her education, which gave to her the useful and appropriate female accomplishment of needle-work.

CHAPTER IX

MRS. MAPLE was of opinion, that every woman ought to live with a needle and thread in her hand; the stranger, therefore, had now ample occupation; but as labour, in common with all other evils, is relative, she submitted cheerfully to any manual toil, that could rescue her from the mental burthen of exciting ill will and reproach.

Two days afterwards, Elinor came to summon her to the drawing-room. They were all assembled, she said, to a rehearsal, and in the utmost confusion for want of a prompter, not a soul, except Miss Arbe, knowing a word, or a cue, of any part but his own; and Miss Arbe, who took upon her to regulate every thing, protested that she could not consent to go on any longer in so slovenly a manner.

In this dilemma it had occurred to Elinor to have recourse to the stranger; but the stranger desired to be excused: Mrs. Maple seemed now to be softened in her favour; and it would be both imprudent and improper to risk provoking fresh irritation, by coming forward in an enterprize that was a known subject of dissention.

Elinor, when she had formed a wish, never listened to an objection. "What an old fashioned style you prose* in!" she cried; "who could believe you came so lately from France? But example has no more force without sympathy, than precept has without opinion! However, I'll get you a licence from Aunt Maple in a minute."

She went down stairs, and, returning almost immediately,

cried, "Aunt Maple is quite contented. I told her I was going to send for Mr. Creek, a horrible little pettifogging* wretch, who lives in this neighbourhood, and whom she particularly detests, to be our prompter; and this so woefully tormented her, that she proposed you herself. I have ample business upon my hands, between my companions of the buskin,* and this pragmatical old aunt; for Harleigh himself refused to act against her approbation, till I threatened to make over Lord Townly to Sir Lyell Sycamore, a smart beau at Brighthelmstone, that all the mammas and aunts are afraid of. And then poor aunty was fain, herself, to request Harleigh to take the part. I could manage matters no other way."

Personal remonstrances were vain, and the stranger was forced down stairs to the theatrical group.

All that was known of her situation having been sketched by Elinor, and detailed by Selina, the mixt party there assembled, was prepared to survey her with a curiosity which she found extremely abashing. She requested to have the book of the play; but Elinor, engaged in arranging the entrances and exits, did not heed her. Harleigh, however, comprehending the relief which any occupation for the eyes and hands might afford her, presented it to her himself.

It preserved her not, nevertheless, from a volley of questions, with which she was instantly assailed from various quarters. "I find, Ma'am, you are lately come from abroad," said Mr. Scope, a gentleman self-dubbed a deep politician, and who, in the most sententious manner, uttered the most trivial observations: "I have no very high notion, I own, of the morals of those foreigners at this period. A man's wife and daughters belong to any man who has a taste to them, as I am informed. Nothing is very strict. Mr. Robertspierre, as I am told, is not very exact in his dealings."

"But I should like to know," cried Gooch, the young farmer, "whether it be true, of a reality, that they've got such numbers and numbers, and millions and millions of red-coats there, all made into generals,* in the twinkling, as one may say, of an eye?"

"Money must be a vast scarce commodity there," said Mr. Stubbs, the steward: "did you ever happen to hear, Ma'am, how they go to work to get in their rents?"

Before the stranger could attempt any reply to these several addresses, Miss Arbe, who was the principal person of the party, seating herself in the chair of honour, desired her to advance, saying, "I understand you sing and play amazingly well. Pray who were your masters?"

While the Incognita hesitated, Miss Bydel, a collateral and uneducated successor to a large and unexpected fortune, said, "Pray, first of all, young woman, what took you over to foreign parts? I should like to know that."

Elinor, now, being ready, cut short all further investigation by beginning the rehearsal.

During the first scenes, the voice of the Incognita was hardly audible. The constraint of her forced attendance, and the insurmountable awkwardness of her situation, made all exertion difficult, and her tones were so languid, and her pronunciation was so inarticulate, that Elinor began seriously to believe that she must still have recourse to Mr. Creek. But Harleigh, who reflected how much the faculties depend upon the mind's being disengaged, saw that she was too little at her ease to be yet judged.

Every one else, absorbed in his part and himself, in the hope of being best, or the shame of being worst; in the fear of being out, or the confusion of not understanding what next was to be done, was regardless of all else but his own fancied reputation of the hour.

Harleigh, however, as the play proceeded, and the inaccuracy of the performers demanded greater aid, found the patience of his judgment recompensed, and its appretiation of her talents just. Her voice, from seeming feeble and monotonous, became clear and penetrating: it was varied, with the nicest discrimination, for the expression of every character, changing its modulation from tones of softest sensibility, to those of archest humour; and from reasoning severity, to those of uncultured rusticity.

When the rehearsal was over, Miss Bydel, who had no other idea of the use of speech than that of asking questions, said, "I should be glad, before you go, to say a few words to you, young woman, myself."

The stranger stood still.

"In the first place, tell me, if you please, what's your name?"

The Incognita coloured at this abrupt demand, but remained silent.

"Nay," said Miss Bydel, "your name, at least, can be no such great secret, for you must be called something or other."

Ireton, who had hitherto appeared decided not to take any notice of her, now exclaimed, with a laugh, "I will tell you what her name is, Miss Bydel; 'tis L. S."

The stranger dropt her eyes, but Miss Bydel, not comprehending that Ireton meant two initial letters, said, "Elless? Well I see no reason why any body should be ashamed to own their name is Elless."

Selina, tittering, would have cleared up the mistake; but Ireton, laughing yet more heartily, made her a sign to let it pass.

Miss Bydel continued: "I don't want to ask any of your secrets, as I say, Mrs. Elless, for I understand you don't like to tell them; but it will be discovering no great matter, to let me know whether your friends are abroad, or in England? and what way you were maintained before you got your passage over in Mrs. Maple's boat."

"Don't let that young person go," cried Miss Arbe, who had now finished the labours of her theatrical presidency, "till I have heard her play and sing. If she is so clever, as you describe her, she shall perform between the acts."

The stranger declared her utter inability to comply with such a request. "When I believed myself unheard," she cried, "musick, I imagined, might make me, for a few moments, forget my distresses: but an expected performance—a prepared exhibition!—pardon me!—I have neither spirits nor powers for such an attempt!"

Her voice spoke grief, her look, apprehension; yet her manner so completely announced decision, that, unopposed even by a word, she remounted the stairs to her chamber.

She was, there, surprised by the sight of a sealed packet upon her table, directed, "For L. S. at her leisure."

She opened it, and found ten bank notes, of ten pounds each.

A momentary hope which she had indulged, that this letter, by some accidental conveyance, had reached her from abroad, was now changed into the most unpleasant perplexity: such a donation could not come from any of the females of the family; Mrs. Maple was miserly, and her enemy; and the Miss Joddrells knew, by experience, that she would not refuse their open assistance: Mr. Harleigh, therefore, or Mr. Ireton, must have conveyed this to her room.

If it were Mr. Ireton, she concluded he meant to ensnare her distress into an unguarded acceptance, for some latent purpose of mischief; if it were Mr. Harleigh, his whole behaviour inclined her to believe, that he was capable of such an action from motives of pure benevolence: but she could by no means accept pecuniary aid from either, and determined to keep the packet always ready for delivery, when she could discover to whom it belonged.

She was surprised, soon afterwards, by the sight of Selina. "I would not let Mr. Ireton hinder me from coming to you this once," she cried, "do what he could; for we are all in such a fidget, that there's only you, I really believe, can help us. Poor Miss Arbe, while she was teaching us all what we have to do, put her part into her muff,* and her favourite little dog, that she doats upon, not knowing it was there, poor thing, poked his nose into the muff to warm himself; and when Miss Arbe came to take her part, she found he had sucked it, and gnawed it, and nibbled it, all to tatters! And she says she can't write it out again if she was to have a diamond a word for it; and as to us, we have all of us got such immensities to do for ourselves, that you are the only person; for I dare say you know how to write. So will you, now, Ellis? for they have all settled, below, that your real name is Ellis."

The stranger answered that she should gladly be useful in any way that could be proposed. The book, therefore, was brought to her, with writing implements, and she dedicated herself so diligently to copying, that the following morning, when Miss Arbe was expected, the part was prepared.

Miss Arbe, however, came not; a note arrived in her stead, stating that she had been so exceedingly fatigued the preceding day, in giving so many directions, that she begged they would let somebody read her part, and rehearse without her; and she hoped that she should find them more advanced when she joined them on Monday.

The stranger was now summoned not only as prompter, but to read the part of Lady Townly. She could not refuse, but her compliance was without any sort of exertion, from a desire to avoid, not promote similar calls for exhibition.

Elinor remarked to Harleigh, how inadequate were her talents to such a character. Harleigh acquiesced in the remark; yet his good opinion, in another point of view, was as much heightened, as in this it was lowered: he saw the part which she had copied for Miss Arbe; and the beautiful clearness of the hand-writing, and the correctness of the punctuation and orthograpy, convinced him that her education had been as successfully cultivated for intellectual improvement, as for elegant accomplishments.

Elinor herself, now, would only call the stranger Miss Ellis, a name which, she said, she verily believed that Miss Bydel, with all her stupidity, had hit upon, and which therefore, henceforth, should be adopted.

CHAPTER X

THE Incognita continued to devote herself to needle-work till the morning of the next rehearsal. She was then again called to the double task of prompting, and of reading the part of Lady Townly, Miss Arbe having, unceremoniously, announced, that as she had already performed that character three several times, and to the most brilliant audiences, though at private theatres, any further practice for herself would be a work of supererogation; and if the company, she added, would but be so good as to remember her directions, she need only attend personally at the final rehearsal.

The whole party was much offended by this insinuation of its inferiority, as well as by so contemptuous an indifference to the prosperity of the enterprize. Nor was this the only difficulty caused by the breach of attendance in Miss Arbe. The entertainment was to conclude with a cotillon,* of which Ireton had brought the newest steps and method from France, but which, through this unexpected failure, the sett was incomplete for practising. Elinor was persuaded, that in keeping the whole group thus imperfect, both in the play and in the dance, it was the design of Miss Arbe to expose them all to ridicule, that her own fine acting and fine steps might be contrasted to the greater advantage. To obviate, as much as possible, this suspected malice, the stranger was now requested to stand up with them; for as she was so lately come from abroad, they concluded that she might know something of the matter.

They were not mistaken: the steps, the figure, the time, all were familiar to her; and she taught the young Selina, dropt hints to Elinor, endeavoured to set Miss Bydel right, and gave a general, though unpremeditated lesson to every one, by the measured grace and lightness of her motions, which, little as her attire was adapted to such a purpose, were equally striking for elegance and for modesty.

Harleigh, however, alone perceived her excellence: the rest had so much to learn, or were so anxious to shine, that if occasionally they remarked her, it was rather to be diverted by seeing any one dance so ill equipped, than to be struck with the elevated carriage which no such disadvantage could conceal.

Early on the morning preceding the intended representation, the stranger was summoned to the destined theatre, where, while she was aiding the general preparations, of dresses, decorations, and scenery, previous to the last grand rehearsal, which, in order to try the effect of the illuminations, was fixed to take place in the evening, Mrs. Maple, with derision marked in every feature of her face, stalked into the room, to announce to her niece, with unbridled satisfaction, that all her fine vagaries would now end in nothing, as Miss Arbe, at last, had the good sense to refuse affording them her countenance.

Elinor, though too much enraged to inquire what this meant, soon, perforce, learnt, that an old gentleman, a cousin of Miss Arbe's, had ridden over with an apology, importing, that the most momentous reasons, yet such as could not be divulged, obliged his relation to decline the pleasure of belonging to their dramatic party.

The offence given by this abrupt renunciation was so general, though Elinor, alone, allowed it free utterance, that Mr. Giles Arbe, the bearer of these evil tidings, conceived it to be more advisable to own the plump truth, he said, at once, than to see them all so affronted without knowing what for; though he begged them not to mention it, his cousin having peremptorily charged him not to speak out: but the fact was, that she had repented her engagement ever since the first rehearsal; for though she should always be ready to act with the Miss Joddrels, who were nieces to a baronet, and Mr. Harleigh, who was nephew to a peer, and Mr. Ireton, who was heir to a large entailed estate; she was yet apprehensive that it might let her down, in the opinion of the noble theatrical society to which she belonged, if she were seen exhibiting with such common persons as farmers and domestics; whom, however, for all his cousin's nicety, Mr. Giles said he thought to be full as good men as any other; and, sometimes, considerably better.

Mrs. Maple was elevated into the highest triumph by this explanation. "I told you how it would be!" she cried. "Young ladies acting with mere mob! I am truly rejoiced that Miss Arbe has given you the slip." *

Elinor heard this with a resentment, that determined her, more vehemently than ever, not to abandon her project; she proudly, therefore, returned thanks, by Mr. Giles, for the restoration of the part, which she had resigned in mere complaisance, as there was nothing in the world she so much desired as to act it herself, even though it must be now learnt in the course of a day; and she begged leave, as a mark that she was not offended at the desertion, to borrow the dress of the character, which she knew to be ready, and with which she would adorn herself the following night, at the performance.

This last clause, she was well aware, would prove the most provoking that she could devise, to Miss Arbe, who was renowned for being finically tenacious of her attire; but Elinor would neither add a word to her message, nor suffer one to be taken from it; and when Mr. Giles Arbe, frightened at the ill success of his confidence, would have offered some apology, she drove him from the house, directing a trusty person in the neighbourhood, to accompany him back, with positive orders not to return without the dress.

She then told the stranger to study the part of Lady Wronghead, to fill up the chasm.

The stranger began some earnest excuses, but they were lost in the louder exclamations of Mrs. Maple, whose disappointment in finding the scheme still supported, was aggravated into rage, by the unexpected proposition of admitting the stranger into the sett. "What, Miss Joddrel!" she cried, "is it not enough that you have made us a by-word in the neighbourhood, by wanting to act with farmers and servants? Must you also bring a foundling girl into your sett? an illegitimate stroller, who does not so much as know her own name?"

The stranger, deeply reddening, gravely answered, "Far from wishing to enter into any plan of amusement, I could not have given my consent to it, even if solicited."

"Nobody asks what you could have done, I hope!" Mrs. Maple began, when Elinor, pushing the stranger into a large light closet,* and throwing the part after her, shut the door, charging her not to lose a moment, in getting ready for the final rehearsal that very evening.

The Incognita, fixed not to look at the manuscript, now heard, perforce, a violent quarrel between the aunt and the niece, the former protesting that she would never agree to such a disgrace, as suffering a poor straggling pauper to mix herself publicly with their society; and the latter threatening, that, if forced to grant such a triumph to Miss Arbe, as that of tamely relinquishing the undertaking, she would leave the country and settle at once in France, and in the house of Robespierre himself.

Harleigh, who, in a hasty and dashing, but masterly manner, was colouring some scenery, had hitherto been silent; but now, advancing, he proposed, as a compromise, that the performance should be deferred for a week, in which time Miss Sycamore, a young lady at Brighthelmstone, whom they all knew, would learn, he doubted not, the part, and supply, with pleasure, the vacant place.

To this Mrs. Maple, finding no hope remained that she could abolish the whole project, was sullenly assenting, when Elinor reproachfully exclaimed, "What, Don Quixote! is your spirit of chivalry thus cooled? and are you, too, for rejecting, with all this scorn, the fellow-voyager you were so strenuous to support?"

"Scorn?" repeated Harleigh, "No! I regard her, rather, with reverence! 'Tis she herself that has declined the part, and with a dignity that does her honour. All she suffers to be discerned of her, announces distinguished merit; and yet, highly as I have conceived of her character, she is unknown to us; except by her distresses; and these, though they call loudly for our sympathy and assistance, and, through the propriety of her conduct, lay claim to our respect, may be thought insufficient by the world, to justify Mrs. Maple, who has two young ladies so immediately under her care, for engaging a perfect stranger, in a scheme which has no reference to humanity, or good offices."

"Ah ha, Mr. Harleigh!" cried Ireton, shaking his head, "you are afraid of what she may turn out! You think no better of her, at last, than I do."

"I think, on the contrary, so well of her," answered Harleigh, "that I am sincerely sorry to see her thus haughtily distanced. I often wish these ladies would as generously, as I doubt not that they might safely, invite her into their private society. Kindness such as that might produce a confidence, which revolts from public and abrupt enquiry; and which, I would nearly engage my life, would prove her innocence and worth, and vindicate every trust."

He then begged them to consider, that, should their curiosity and suspicions work upon her spirits, till she were urged to reveal, prematurely, the secret of her situation, they would themselves be the first to condemn her for folly and imprudence, if breaking up the mystery of her silence should affect either her happiness or her safety.

Mrs. Maple would have been inconsolable at a defence against which she had nothing positive to object, had she not reaped some comfort from finding that even Harleigh opposed including the stranger in the acting circle.

The delay of the performance, and an application to Miss Sycamore, seemed now settled, when Mrs. Fenn, the housekeeper, who was also aiding in the room, lamented the trouble to be renewed for the supper-preparations, as neither the fish, nor the pastry, nor sundry other articles, could keep.

This was a complaint to which Mrs. Maple was by no means deaf. The invitations, also, were made; the drawing-room was given up for the theatre; another apartment was appropriated for a green-room;* and there was not any chance that the house could be restored to order, nor the maids to their usual occupations, till this business were finally over.

Her rancour now suddenly relented, with regard to the stranger, and, to the astonishment of every one, she stopt Harleigh from riding over to Brighthelmstone, to apply to Miss Sycamore, by concedingly saying, that, since Mr. Harleigh had really so good an opinion of the young woman who came from France, she must confess that she had herself, of late, taken a much better notion of her, by finding that she was so excellent a needle-woman; and, therefore, she did not see why they should send for so finical a person as Miss Sycamore, who was full of airs and extravagance, to begin all over again, and disappoint so much company, when they had a body in the house who might do one of the parts, so as to pass amongst the rest, without being found out for what she was.

Harleigh expressed his doubts whether the young person herself, who was obviously in very unpleasant circumstances, might chuse to be brought forward in so public an amusement.

The gentleness of Mrs. Maple was now converted into choler; and she desired to know, whether a poor wretch such as that, who had her meat, drink, and lodging for nothing, should be allowed to chuse any thing for herself one way or another.

Elinor, dropping, though not quite distinctly, some sarcastical reflections upon the persistence of Harleigh in preferring Miss Sycamore to his Dulcinea, retired to her room to study the part of Lady Townly; saying that she should leave them full powers, to wrangle amongst themselves, for that of Lady Wronghead.

Harleigh, who had not seen the stranger turned into the closet, now entered it, in search of a pencil. Not a little was then his surprize to find her sketching, upon the back of a letter, a view of the hills, downs, cottages, and cattle, which formed the prospect from the window.

It was beautifully executed, and undoubtedly from nature. Harleigh, with mingled astonishment and admiration, clasped his hands, and energetically exclaimed, "Accomplished creature! who .... and what are you?"

Confused, she blushed, and folded up her little drawing. He seemed almost equally embarrassed himself, at the expression and the question which had escaped him. Mrs. Maple, following, paradingly told the stranger, that, as she had hemmed the last cambric-handkerchiefs so neatly, she might act, upon this particular occasion, with the Miss Joddrels; only first promising, that she must not own to a living soul her being such a poor forlorn creature; as the only way to avoid disgrace to themselves, amongst their acquaintance, for admitting her, would be to say that she was a young lady of family, who came over with them from France.

To the last clause, the stranger calmly answered that she could offer no objection, in a manner which, to the attentive Harleigh, clearly indicated that it was true; but that, with respect to performing, she was in a situation too melancholy, if not disastrous, to be capable of making any such attempt.

Mrs. Maple was so angry at this presumption, that she replied, "Do as you are ordered, or leave my house directly!" and then walked, in high wrath, away.

The stranger appeared confounded: she felt an almost resistless impulse to depart immediately; but something stronger than resentment told her to stay: it was distress! She paused a moment, and then, with a sigh, took up the part, and, without looking at Harleigh, who was too much shocked to offer any palliation for this grossness, walked pensively to her chamber.

She was soon joined by Elinor, who, in extreme ill humour, complained that the odious Lady Townly was so intolerably prolix, that there was no getting her endless babbling by heart, at such short notice: and that, but for the triumph which it would afford to Miss Arbe, to find out their embarrassment, and the spite that it would gratify in Aunt Maple, the whole business should be thrown up at once. Sooner, however, than be conquered, either by such impertinence, or such malignity, she would abandon Lady Townly to the prompter, whom Miss Arbe might have the surprise and amusement to dizen out in her fine attire.*

Then, declaring that she hated and would not act with Miss Sycamore, who was a creature of insolence and conceit, she flung the part of Lady Townly to the Incognita, saying, that she must abide herself by that of Lady Wronghead; a name which she well merited to keep for the rest of her life, from her inconceivable mismanagement of the whole affair.

The stranger earnestly entreated exemption from the undertaking, and solicited the intercession of Elinor with Mrs. Maple, to soften the hard sentence denounced against her refusal. To act such a character as that of Lady Townly, she should have thought formidable, if not impossible, even in her gayest moments: but now, in a situation the most helpless, and with every reason to wish for obscurity, the exertion would be the most cruel that could be exacted.

Elinor, however, listened only to herself: Miss Arbe must be mortified; Mrs. Maple must be thwarted; and Miss Sycamore must be omitted: these three things, she declared, were indispensable, and could only be accomplished by defying all obstacles, and performing the comedy upon the appointed day.

The stranger now saw no alternative between obsequiously submitting, or immediately relinquishing her asylum.

How might she find another? she knew not where even to seek her friend, and no letter was arrived from abroad.

There was no resource! She decided upon studying the part.

This was not difficult: she had read it at three rehearsals, and had carefully copied it; but she acquired it mechanically because unwillingly, and while she got the words by rote, scarcely took their meaning into consideration.

When called down, at night, to the grand final rehearsal, she gave equal surprise to Harleigh, from finding her already perfect in so long a part, and from hearing her repeat it with a tameness almost lifeless.

At the scene of the reconciliation, in the last act, he took her hand, and slightly kissed her glove. Ireton called out, "Embrace! embrace!—the peace-making is always decided, at the theatre, by an embrace. You must throw your arms lovingly over one another's shoulders."

Harleigh did not advance, but he looked at the stranger, and the blush upon her cheeks shewed her wholly unaccustomed even to the mention of any personal liberty; Ireton, however, still insisting, he laughingly excused himself, by declaring, that he must do by Lord Townly as he would do by himself; and he never meant, should he marry, to be tender to his wife before company.

Mrs. Maple now, extremely anxious for her own credit, told all the servants, that she had just discovered, that the stranger who came from France, was a young lady of consequence, and she desired that they would make a report to that effect throughout the neighbourhood; and, in the new play-bills which were now written, she suffered to see inserted, Lady Townly by Miss Ellis.

Harleigh was the first to address the stranger by this name, previously taking an opportunity, with an air of friendly regard, to advise that she would adopt it, till she thought right to declare her own. She thanked him gratefully for his counsel, confessing, that she had long felt the absurdity of seeming nameless; and adding, "but I had made no preparation for what I so little expected, as the length of time in which I have been kept in this almost unheard of situation! and the hourly hope of seeing it end, made me decide to spare myself, at least by silence, from deceit."

The look of Harleigh shewed his approbation of her motive, while his words strengthened her conviction, that it must now give way to the necessity of some denomination. "Be it Ellis, then," said she, smiling, "though evasion may, perhaps, be yet meaner than falsehood! Nevertheless, I am rather more contented to make use of this name, which accident has bestowed upon me, than positively to invent one for myself."

Ellis, therefore, which appellation, now, will be substituted for that of the Incognita, seeing no possibility of escaping this exhibition, comforted herself, that, however repugnant it might be to her inclinations, and her sense of propriety, it gave her, at least, some chance, during the remainder of her stay at Lewes, of being treated with less indignity.

CHAPTER XI

THE hope of meeting with more consideration in the family, inspirited Ellis with a wish, hitherto unfelt, of contributing to the purposed entertainment. The part which she had been obliged to undertake, was too prominent to be placed in the back ground; and the whole performance must be flat, if not ridiculous, unless Lady Townly were a principal person. She read over, therefore, repeated, and studied the character, with an attention more alive to its meaning, style, and diversities; and the desire which animated all that she attempted, of doing with her best means whatever unavoidably must be done, determined her to let no effort in her power be wanting, to enliven the representation.

The lateness of this resolution, made her application for its accomplishment so completely fill up her time, that not a moment remained for those fears of self-deficiency, with which diffidence and timidity enervate the faculties, and often, in sensitive minds, rob them of the powers of exertion.

When the hour of exhibition approached, and she was summoned to the apartment destined for the green-room, universal astonishment was produced by her appearance. It was not from her dress; they had seen, and already knew it to be fanciful and fashionable; nor was it the heightened beauty which her decorations displayed; this, as she was truly lovely, was an effect that they expected: but it was from the ease with which she wore her ornaments, the grace with which she set them off, the elegance of her deportment, and an air of dignified modesty, that spoke her not only accustomed to such attire, but also to the good breeding and refined manners, which announce the habits of life to have been formed in the superiour classes of society.

Selina, as she opened the door, exultingly called out, "Look! look! only look at Ellis! did you ever see any thing in the world so beautiful?"

Ireton, to whom dress, far more than feature or complexion, presented attraction, exclaimed, "By my soul, she's as handsome as an angel!"

Elinor, thus excited, came forward; but seemed struck speechless.

They now all flocked around her; and Mrs. Maple, staring, cried, "Why who did you get to put your things on for you?" when, suddenly recollecting the new account which she had herself given, and caused to be spread of this young person, she forced a laugh, and added, "Bless me, Miss Ellis, if I had not quite forgotten whom I was speaking to! Why should not Miss Ellis know how to dress herself as well as any other young lady?"

"Why, indeed," said Miss Bydel, "it makes a prodigious change, a young lady's turning out a young lady, instead of a common young woman. I've seen a good many of the Ellis's. Pray, Ma'am, does your part of the family come from Yorkshire? or Devonshire? for I should like to know."

"And, if there were any gentlemen of your family, with you, Ma'am, in foreign parts," said Mr. Scope, "I should be glad to have their opinion of this Convention, now set up in France: for as to ladies, though they are certainly very pleasing, they are but indifferent judges in the political line, not having, ordinarily, heads of that sort. I speak without offence, inferiority of understanding being no defect in a female."

"Well, I thought from the first," said young Gooch, "and I said it to sisters, that the young lady was a young lady, by her travelling, and that. But pray, Ma'am, did you ever look on, to see that Mr. Robert Speer mow down his hundreds, like to grass in a hay-field? We should not much like it if they were to do so in England. But the French have no spirit. They are but a poor set; except their generals, or the like of that. And, for them, they'll fight you like so many lions. They are afraid of nobody."

"By what I hear, Ma'am," said Mr. Stubbs, "a gentleman, in that country, may have rents due to the value of thousands, and hardly receive a frog,* as one may say, an acre."

While thus her fellow-performers surrounded the Incognita, Harleigh, alone, held back, absorbed in contemplating the fine form, which a remarkably light and pretty robe, now first displayed; and the beautiful features, and animated complexion, which were set off to their utmost lustre, by the waving feathers, and artificial flowers, which were woven into her soft, glossy, luxuriant brown hair. But though he forbore offering her any compliments, he no sooner observed that she was seized with a sudden panic, upon a servant's announcing, that the expected audience, consisting of some of the principal families of Sussex, was arrived, than he addressed, and endeavoured to encourage her.

"I am aware, Sir," she said, "that it may seem rather like vanity than diffidence, for one situated as I am to feel any alarm; for as I can have raised no expectations, what have I to fear from giving any disappointment? Nevertheless, now the time is come, the attempt grows formidable. It must seem so strange—so wond'rous strange,—to those who know not how little my choice has been consulted—"

She was interrupted, for all was ready; and Harleigh was summoned to open the piece, by the famous question, "Why did I marry?"*

The fright which now had found its way into the mind of the new Lady Townly, augmented every moment till she appeared; and it was then so great, as nearly to make her forget her part, and occasion what, hesitatingly, she was able to utter, to be hardly audible, even to her fellow-performers. The applause excited by her beauty, figure, and dress, only added to her embarrassment. She with difficulty kept to her post, and finished her first scene with complete self-discontent. Elinor, who watched her throughout it, lost all admiration of her exterior attractions, from contempt of her feeble performance.

But her second scene exhibited her in another point of view; her self-displeasure worked her up to exertions that brought forth the happiest effects; and her evident success produced ease, by inspiring courage. From this time, her performance acquired a wholly new character: it seemed the essence of gay intelligence, of well bred animation, and of lively variety. The grace of her motions made not only every step but every turn of her head remarkable. Her voice modulated into all the changes that vivacity, carelesness, pride, pleasure, indifference, or alarm demanded. Every feature of her face spoke her discrimination of every word; while the spirit which gave a charm to the whole, was chastened by a taste the most correct; and while though modest she was never aukward; though frightened, never ungraceful.

A performance such as this, in a person young, beautiful, and wholly new, created a surprize so powerful, and a delight so unexpected, that the play seemed soon to have no other object than Lady Townly, and the audience to think that no other were worth hearing or beholding; for though the politeness exacted by a private representation, secured to every one an apparent attention, all seemed vapid and without merit in which she was not concerned; while all wore an air of interest in which she bore the smallest part; and she soon never spoke, looked, nor moved, but to excite pleasure, admiration, and applause, amounting to rapture.

Whether this excellence were the result of practice and instruction, or a sudden emanation of general genius, accidentally directed to a particular point, was disputed by the critics amongst the audience; and disputed, as usual, with the greater vehemence, from the impossibility of obtaining documents to decide, or direct opinion. But that which was regarded as the highest refinement of her acting, was a certain air of inquietude, which was discernible through the utmost gaiety of her exertions, and which, with the occasional absence and sadness, that had their source in her own disturbance, was attributed to deep research into the latent subjects of uneasiness belonging to the situation of Lady Townly. This, however, was nature, which would not be repressed; not art, that strove to be displayed.

But no pleasure excited by her various powers, approached to the pleasure which they bestowed upon Harleigh, who could look at, could listen to her alone. To himself, he lost all power of doing justice; wrapt up in the contemplation of an object thus singular, thus excelling, thus mysterious, all ambition of personally shining was forgotten. He could not fail to speak his part with sense and feeling; he could not help appearing fashioned to represent a man of rank and understanding; but that address which gives life and meaning to every phrase; that ingenuity, which beguiles the audience into an illusion, which, for the current moment, inspires the sympathy due to reality; that skill which brings forth on the very instant, all the effect which, to the closet reader, an author can hope to produce from reflection; these, the attributes of good acting, and for which his taste, his spirit, and his judgment all fitted him, were now, from slackened self-attention, beyond his reach, though within his powers. At a public theatre, such an actress might have proved a spur to have urged the exertions of competition; in this private one, where success, except to vanity, was unimportant, her merit was, to Harleigh, an absorbent that occupied, exclusively, all his faculties.

In the last act, where Lady Townly becomes serious, penitent, and pathetic, the new actress appeared to yet greater advantage: the state of her mind accorded with distress, and her fine speaking eyes, her softly touching voice, her dejected air, and penetrating countenance, made quicker passage to the feelings of her auditors, even than the words of the author. All were moved, tears were shed from almost every eye, and Harleigh, affected and enchanted, at the moment of the peace-making, took her hand with so much eagerness, and pressed it to his lips with so much pleasure, that the rouge, put on for the occasion, was paler than the blushes which burnt through it on her cheeks. He saw this, and, checking his admiration, relinquished with respect the hand which he had taken nearly with rapture.

When the play was over, and the loudest applause had marked its successful representation, the company arose to pay their compliments to Mrs. Maple. Lady Townly, then, followed by every eye, was escaping from bearing her share in the bursts of general approbation; when a youth of the most engaging appearance, and evidently of high fashion, sprang over the forms, to impede her retreat; and to pour forth the highest encomiums upon her performance, in well-bred, though enthusiastic language, with all the eager vivacity of early youth, which looks upon moderation as insipidity, and measured commendation as want of feeling.

Though confused by being detained, Ellis could not be angry, for there was no impertinence in his fervour, no familiarity in his panegyric; and though his speech was rapid, his manners were gentle. His eulogy was free from any presumption of being uttered for her gratification; it seemed simply the uncontrollable ebullition of ingenuous gratitude.

Surprised still more than all around her, at the pleasure which she found she had communicated, some share of it now stole insensibly into her own bosom; and this was by no means lessened, by seeing her youthful new admirer soon followed by a lady still younger than himself, who called out, "Do you think, brother, to monopolize Miss Ellis?" And, with equal delight, and nearly equal ardour, she joined in the acknowledgements made by her brother, for the entertainment which they had received; and both united in declaring that they should never endure to see or hear any other Lady Townly.

There was a charm, for there seemed a sincerity in this youthful tribute of admiration, that was highly gratifying to the new actress; and Harleigh thought he read in her countenance, the soothing relief experienced by a delicate mind, from meeting with politeness and courtesie, after a long endurance of indignity or neglect.

Almost every body among the audience, one by one, joined this little set, all eager to take a nearer view of the lovely Lady Townly, and availing themselves of the opportunity afforded by this season of compliment, for examining more narrowly whom it was that they addressed.

Mrs. Maple, meanwhile, suffered the utmost perplexity: far from foreseeing an admiration which thus bore down all before it, she had conceived that, the piece once finished, the actress would vanish, and be thought of no more: nor was she without hope, in her utter disdain of the stranger, that the part thus given merely by necessity, would be so ill represented, as to disgust her niece from any such frolics in future. But when, on the contrary, she found that there was but one voice in favour of this unknown performer; when not all her own pride, nor all her prejudice,* could make her blind to that performer's truly elevated carriage and appearance; when every auditor flocked to her, with "Who is this charming Miss Ellis?"—"Present us to this incomparable Miss Ellis;" she felt covered with shame and regret; though compelled, for her own credit, to continue repeating, that she was a young lady of family who had passed over with her from the Continent.

Provoked, however, she now followed the crowd, meaning to give a hint to the Incognita to retire; but she had the mortification of hearing her gallant new enthusiast pressing for her hand, in a cotillon, which they were preparing to dance; and though the stranger gently, yet steadily, was declining his proposition, Mrs. Maple was so much frightened and irritated that such a choice should be in her power, that she called out impatiently, "My Lord, we must have some refreshments before the dance. Do pray, Lady Aurora Granville, beg Lord Melbury to come this way, and take something."

The young lord and lady, with civil but cold thanks, that spoke their dislike of this interference, both desired to be excused; but great was their concern, and universal, throughout the apartment, was the consternation, upon observing Miss Ellis change colour, and sink upon a chair, almost fainting. Harleigh, who had strongly marked the grace and dignity with which she had received so much praise, now cast a glance of the keenest indignation at Mrs. Maple, attributing to her rude interruption of the little civilities so evidently softening to the stranger, this sudden indisposition; but Mrs. Maple either saw it not, or did not understand it, and seized, with speed, the opportunity of saying, that Miss Ellis was exhausted by so much acting, and of desiring that some of the maids might help her to her chamber.

Elinor stood suspended, looking not at her, but at Harleigh. Every one else came forward with inquiry, fans, or sweet-scented vials; but Ellis, a little reviving, accepted the salts* of Lady Aurora Granville, and, leaning against her waist, which her arm involuntarily encircled, breathed hard and shed a torrent of tears.

"Why don't the maids come?" cried Mrs. Maple. "Selina, my dear, do call them. Lady Aurora, I am quite ashamed.—Miss Ellis, what are you thinking of, to lean so against Her Ladyship? Pray, Mr. Ireton, call the maids for me."

"Call no one, I beg!" cried Lady Aurora: "Why should I not have the pleasure of assisting Miss Ellis?" And, bending down, she tried better to accommodate herself to the ease and relief of her new acquaintance, who appeared the more deeply sensible of her kindness, from the ungenerous displeasure which it evidently excited in Mrs. Maple. And when, in some degree recovered, she rose to go, she returned her thanks to Lady Aurora with so touching a softness, with tearful eyes, and in a voice so plaintive, that Lady Aurora, affected by her manner, and charmed by her merit, desired still to support her, and, entreating that she would hold by her arm, begged permission of Mrs. Maple to accompany Miss Ellis to her chamber.

Mrs. Maple recollecting, with the utmost confusion, the

small and ordinary room allotted for Ellis, so unlike what she would have bestowed upon such a young lady as she had now described for her fellow-voyager, found no resource against exposing it to Lady Aurora, but that of detaining the object of her compassionate admiration; she stammered, therefore, out, that as Miss Ellis seemed so much better, there could be no reason why she should not stay below, and see the dance.

Ellis gladly courtsied her consent; and the watchful Harleigh, in the alacrity of her acceptance, rejoiced to see a revival to the sentiments of pleasure, which the acrimonious grossness of Mrs. Maple had interrupted.

Lord Melbury now took the hand of Selina, and Harleigh that of Lady Aurora. Elinor would not dance, but, seating herself, fixed her eyes upon Harleigh, whose own were almost perpetually wandering to watch those of his dramatic consort.

Since the first scene, in which the stranger had so ill entered into the spirit of Lady Townly's character, Elinor had ceased to deem her worthy of observation; and, giving herself up wholly to her own part, had not witnessed the gradations of the improvements of Ellis, her rising excellence, nor her final perfection. In her own representation of Lady Wronghead, she piqued herself upon producing new effects, and had the triumph, by her cleverness and eccentricities, her grotesque attitudes and attire, and an unexpected and burlesque manner of acting, to bring the part into a consequence of which it had never appeared susceptible. Happy in the surprise and diversion she occasioned, and constantly occupied how to augment it, she only learnt the high success of Lady Townly, by the bursts of applause, and the unbounded admiration and astonishment, which broke forth from nearly every mouth, the instant that the audience and the performers were united. Amazed, she turned to Harleigh, to examine the merits of such praise; but Harleigh, no longer silent, cautious, or cold, was himself one of the "admiring throng,"* and so openly, and with an air of so much pleasure, that she could not catch his attention for any critical discussion.

After two country dances, and two cotillons, the short ball was broken up, and Lady Aurora hastened to seat herself by Miss Ellis, and Lord Melbury to stand before and to converse with her, followed by all the youthful part of the company, to whom she seemed the sovereign of a little court which came to pay her homage. Harleigh grew every instant more enchanted; for as she discoursed with her two fervent new admirers, her countenance brightened into an animation so radiant, her eyes became so lustrous, and smiles of so much sweetness and pleasure embellished every feature, that he almost fancied he saw her now for the first time, though her welfare, or her distresses, had for more than a month chiefly occupied his mind. Who art thou? thought he, as incessantly he contemplated her; where hast thou thus been formed? And for what art thou designed?

Supper being now announced, Mrs. Maple commissioned Harleigh to lead Lady Aurora down stairs, adding, with a forced smile of civility, that Miss Ellis must consult her health in retiring.

"Yes, Ma'am; and Miss Ellis knows," cried Lady Aurora, offering her arm, "who is to be her chevalier."

Again embarrassed, Mrs. Maple saw no resource against exposing her shabby chamber, but that of admitting its occupier to the supper table. She hastily, therefore, asked whether Miss Ellis thought herself well enough to sit up a little longer; adding, "For my part, I think it will do you good."

"The greatest!" cried Ellis, with a look of delight; and, to the speechless consternation of Mrs. Maple, Lord Melbury, calling her the Queen of the night, took her hand, to conduct her to the supper-room. Ellis would have declined this distinction, but that the vivacity of her ardent new friend, precipitated her to the stair-case, ere she was aware that she was the first to lead the way thither. Gaily, then, he would have placed her in the seat of honour, as Lady President of the evening; but, more now upon her guard, she insisted upon standing till the visitors should be arranged, as she was herself a resident in the house.

Lord Melbury, however, quitted her not, and would talk to no one else; and finding that his seat was destined to be next to that of Mrs. Maple, who called him to her side, he said, that he never supped, and would therefore wait upon the ladies; and, drawing a chair behind that of Ellis, he devoted himself to conversing with her, upon her part, upon the whole play, and upon dramatic works, French and English, in general, with the eagerness with which such subjects warm the imagination of youth, and with a pleasure which made him monopolize her attention.

Harleigh listened to every word to which Ellis listened, or to which she answered; and scarcely knew whether most to admire her good sense, her intelligent quickness, her elegant language, or the meaning eyes, and varied smiles which spoke before she spoke, and shewed her entire conception of all to which she attended.

No one now could address her; she was completely engrossed by the young nobleman, who allowed her not time to turn from him a moment.

Such honours shewn to a pauper, a stroller, a vagabond; and all in the present instance, from her own unfortunate contrivance, Mrs. Maple considered as a personal disgrace; a sensation which was threefold encreased when the party broke up, and Lady Aurora, taking the chair of her brother, rallied him upon the envy which his situation had excited; while, in the most engaging manner, she hoped, during her sojourn at Brighthelmstone, to have frequently the good fortune of taking her revenge. Then, joining in their conversation, she became so pleased, so interested, so happy, that twice Mrs. Howel, the lady under whose care she had been brought to Lewes, reminded Her Ladyship that the horses were waiting in the cold, before she could prevail upon herself to depart. And, even then, that lady was forced to take her gently by the arm, to prevent her from renewing the conversation which she most unwillingly finished. "Pardon me, dear Madam," said Lady Aurora; "I am quite ashamed; but I hope, while I am so happy as to be with you, that you will yourself conceive a fellow feeling, how difficult it is to tear one's self away from Miss Ellis."

"What honour Your Ladyship does me!" cried Ellis, her eyes glistening: "and Oh!—how happy you have made me!" —

"How kind you are to say so!" returned Lady Aurora, taking her hand.

She felt a tear drop upon her own from the bent-down eyes of Ellis.

Startled, and astonished, she hoped that Miss Ellis was not again indisposed?

Smilingly, yet in a voice that denoted extreme agitation, "Lady Aurora alone," she answered, "can be surprised that so much goodness—so unlooked for—so unexpected—should be touching!"

"O Mrs. Maple," cried Lady Aurora, in taking leave of that lady, "what a sweet creature is this Miss Ellis!"

"Such talents and a sensibility so attractive," said Lord Melbury, "never met before!"

Ellis heard them, and with a pleasure that seemed exquisite, yet that died away the moment that they disappeared. All then crowded round her, who had hitherto abstained; but she drooped; tears flowed fast down her cheeks; she courtsied the acknowledgements which she could not pronounce to her complimenters and enquirers, and mounted to her chamber.

Mrs. Maple concluded her already so spoiled, by the praises of Lord Melbury and Lady Aurora Granville, that she held herself superior to all other; and the company in general imbibed the same notion. Many disdain, or affect to disdain, the notice of people of rank for themselves, but all are jealous of it for others.

Not such was the opinion of Harleigh; her pleasure in their society seemed to him no more than a renovation to feelings of happier days. Who, who, thought he again, can'st thou be? And why, thus evidently accustomed to grace society, why art thou thus strangely alone—thus friendless—thus desolate—thus mysterious?

BOOK II

CHAPTER XII

SELINA, regarding herself as a free agent, since Ireton professed a respect for Ellis that made him ashamed of his former doubts, flew, the next morning, to the chamber of that young person, to talk over the play, Lord Melbury, and Lady Aurora Granville: but found her *protegée* absorbed in deep thought, and neither able nor willing to converse.

When the family assembled to breakfast, Mrs. Maple declared that she had not closed her eyes the whole night, from the vexation of having admitted such an unknown Wanderer to sup at her table, and to mix with people of rank.

Elinor was wholly silent.

They were not yet separated, when Lady Aurora Granville and Mrs. Howel called to renew their thanks for the entertainment of the preceding evening.

"But Miss Ellis?" said Lady Aurora, looking around her, disappointed; "I hope she is not more indisposed?"

"By no means. She is quite well again," answered Mrs. Maple, in haste to destroy a disposition to pity, which she thought conferred undue honour upon the stranger.

"But shall we not have the pleasure to see her?"

"She. . . generally . . . . breakfasts in her own room," answered Mrs. Maple, with much hesitation.

"May I, then," said Lady Aurora, going to the bell, "beg that somebody will let her know how happy I should be to enquire after her health?"

"Your Ladyship is too good," cried Mrs. Maple, in great confusion, and preventing her from ringing; "but Miss Ellis—I don't know why—is so fond of keeping her chamber, that there is no getting her out of it . . . some how.—"

"Perhaps, then, she will permit me to go up stairs to her?"

"O no, not for the world! besides . . . . I believe she has walked out."

Lady Aurora now applied to Selina, who was scampering

away upon a commission of search; when Mrs. Maple, following her, privately insisted that she should bring back intelligence that Miss Ellis was taken suddenly ill.

Selina was forced to comply, and Lady Aurora with serious concern, to return to Brighthelmstone ungratified.

Mrs. Maple was so much disconcerted by this incident, and so nettled at her own perplexed situation, that nothing saved Ellis from an abrupt dismission, but the representations of Mrs. Fenn, that some fine work,* which the young woman had just begun, would not look of a piece if finished by another hand.

The next morning, the breakfast party was scarcely assembled, when Lord Melbury entered the parlour. He had ridden over, he said, to enquire after the health of Miss Ellis, in the name of his sister, who would do herself the pleasure to call upon her, as soon as she should be sufficiently recovered to receive a visit.

Elinor was struck with the glow of satisfaction which illumined the face of Harleigh, at this reiterated distinction. A glow of a far different sort flushed that of Mrs. Maple, who, after various ineffectual evasions, was constrained to say that she hoped Miss Ellis would be well enough to appear on the morrow. And, to complete her provocation, she was reduced, when Lord Melbury was gone, to propose, herself, that Selina should lend the girl a gown, and what else she might require, for being seen, once again, without involving them all in shame.

Ellis, informed by Selina of these particulars, shed a torrent of grateful tears at the interest which she had thus unexpectedly excited; then, reviving into a vivacity which seemed to renew all the pleasure that she had experienced on the night of the play, she diligently employed herself in appropriating the attire which Selina supplied for the occasion.

Mrs. Maple, now, had no consolation but that the stay of Lady Aurora in the neighbourhood would be short, as that young lady and her brother were only at Brighthelmstone upon a visit to the Honourable Mrs. Howel; who, having a capital mansion upon the Steyne, resided there the greatest part of the year.

Mrs. Howel accompanied her young guest to Lewes the following morning. Miss Ellis was enquired for without delay, and as Mrs. Maple would suffer no one to view her chamber, she was summoned into the drawing-room.

She entered it with a blush of bright pleasure upon her cheeks; yet with eyes that were glistening, and a bosom that seemed struggling with sighs. Lady Aurora hastened to meet her, uttering such kind expressions of concern for her indisposition, that Ellis, with charmed sensibility, involuntarily advanced to embrace her; but rapidly, and with timid shame, drew back, her eyes cast down, and her feelings repressed. Lady Aurora, perceiving the design, and its check, instantly held out her hand, and smilingly saying, "Would you cheat me of this kindness?" led her to a seat next to her own upon a sofa.

The eyes of the stranger were not now the only ones that glistened. Harleigh could not see her thus benignly treated, or rather, as he conceived, thus restored to the treatment to which she had been accustomed, and which he believed her to merit, without feeling tears moisten his own.

With marked civility, though not with the youthful enthusiasm of Lady Aurora, Mrs. Howel, also, made her compliments to Miss Ellis. Lord Melbury arrived soon afterwards, and, the first ceremonies over, devoted his whole attention to the same person.

O powerful prejudice! thought Harleigh; what is judgment, and where is perception in your hands? The ladies of this house, having first seen this charming Incognita in tattered garments, forlorn, desolate, and distressed; governed by the prepossession thus excited of her inferiority, even, to this moment, either neglect or treat her harshly; not moved by the varied excellencies that should create gentler ideas, nor open to the interesting attractions that might give them more pleasure than they could bestow! While these visitors, hearing that she is a young lady of family, and meeting her upon terms of equality, find, at once, that she is endowed with talents and accomplishments for the highest admiration, and with a sweetness of manners, and powers of conversation, irresistibly fascinating.

The visit lasted almost the whole morning, during which he observed, with extreme satisfaction, not only that the dejection of Ellis wore away, but that a delight in the intercourse seemed reciprocating between herself and her young friends, that gave new beauty to her countenance, and new spirit to her existence.

When the visitors rose to be gone, "I cannot tell you, Miss Ellis," said Lady Aurora, "how happy I shall be to cultivate your acquaintance. Will you give me leave to call upon you for half an hour to morrow?"

Ellis, with trembling pleasure, cast a fearful glance at Mrs. Maple, who hastily turned her head another way. Ellis then gratefully acceded to the proposal.

"Miss Ellis, I hope," said Mrs. Howel, in taking leave, "will permit me, also, to have some share of her society, when I have the honour to receive her at Brighthelmstone."

Ellis, touched, enchanted, could attempt no reply beyond a courtesy, and stole, with a full heart, and eyes overflowing, to her chamber, the instant that they left the house.

Mrs. Maple was now in a dilemma which she would have deemed terrible beyond all comparison, but from what she experienced the following minute, when the butler put upon the table a handful of cards, left by the groom of Mrs. Howel, amongst which Mrs. Maple perceived the name of Miss Ellis, mingled with her own, and that of the Miss Joddrels, in an invitation to a small dancing-party on the ensuing Thursday.

"This exceeds all!" she cried: "If I don't get rid of this wretch, she will bring me into universal disgrace! she shall not stay another day in my house."

"Has she, Madam, for a single moment," said Harleigh, with quickness, "given you cause to repent your kind assistance, or reason to harbour any suspicion that you have not bestowed it worthily?"

"Why, you go beyond Elinor herself, now, Mr. Harleigh! for even she, you see, does not ask me to keep her any longer."

"Miss Joddrel," answered Harleigh, turning with an air of gentleness to the mute Elinor, "is aware how little a single woman is allowed to act publicly for herself, without risk of censure."

"Censure?" interrupted Elinor, disdainfully, "you know I despise it!"

He affected not to hear her, and continued, "Miss Joddrel leaves, therefore, Madam, to your established situation in life, the protection of a young person whom circumstances have touchingly cast upon your compassion, and who seems as innocent as she is indigent, and as formed, nay elegant in her manners, as she is obscure and secret in her name and history. I make not any doubt but Miss Joddrel would be foremost to sustain her from the dangers of lonely penury, to which she seems exposed if deserted, were my brother already—" He approached Elinor, lowering his voice; she rose to quit the room, with a look of deep resentment; but could not first escape hearing him finish his speech with "as happy as I hope soon to see him!"

"Ah, Mr. Harleigh," said Mrs. Maple, "when shall we bring that to bear?"

"She never pronounces a positive rejection," answered Harleigh, "yet I make no progress in my peace-offerings."

He would then have entered more fully upon that subject, in the hope of escaping from the other: Mrs. Maple, however, never forgot her anger but for her interest; and Selina was forced to be the messenger of dismission.

She found Ellis so revived, that to destroy her rising tranquillity would have been a task nearly impossible, had Selina possessed as much consideration as good humour. But she was one amongst the many in whom reflection never precedes speech, and therefore, though sincerely sorry, she denounced, without hesitating, the sentence of Mrs. Maple.

Ellis was struck with the deepest dismay, to be robbed thus of all refuge, at the very moment when she flattered herself that new friends, perhaps a new asylum, were opening to her. Whither could she now wander? and how hope that others, to whom she was still less known, would escape the blasting contagion, and believe that distress might be guiltless though mysterious? A few shillings were all that she possessed; and she saw no prospect of any recruit. Elinor had not once spoken to her since the play; and the childish character, even more than the extreme youth of Selina, made it seem improper, in so discarded a state, to accept any succour from her clandestinely. Nevertheless, the awaited letter was not yet arrived; the expected friend had not yet appeared. How, then, quit the neighbourhood of Brighthelmstone, where alone any hope of receiving either still lingered? The only idea that occurred to her, was that of throwing herself upon the compassion of her new acquaintances, faithfully detailing to them her real situation at Mrs. Maple's, and appealing to their generosity to forbear, for the present, all enquiry into its original cause.

This determined, she anxiously desired, before her departure, to restore, if she could discover their owner, the anonymous bank-notes, which she was resolute not to use; and, hearing the step of Harleigh passing her door in descending the stairs, she hastened after him, with the little packet in her hand.

Turning round as he reached the hall, and observing, with pleased surprise, her intention to speak to him, he stopt.

"You have been so good to me, Sir," she said, "so humane and so considerate, by every possible occasion, that I think I may venture to beg yet one more favour of you, before I leave Lewes."

Her dejected tone extremely affected him, and he waited her explanation with looks that were powerfully expressive of his interest in her welfare.

"Some one, with great, but mistaken kindness," she continued, "has imagined my necessities stronger than my. . . . ." She stopt, as if at a loss for a word, and then, with a smile, added, "my pride, others, perhaps, will say; but to me it appears only a sense of right. If, however, my lengthened suspense forces me to require more assistance of this sort than I already owe to the Miss Joddrels, and to the benevolent Admiral, I shall have recourse to the most laborious personal exertions, rather than spread any further the list of my pecuniary creditors."

Harleigh did not, or seemed not to understand her, yet would not resist taking the little packet, which she put into his hands, saying, "I have some fear that this comes from Mr. Ireton; I shall hold myself inexpressibly obliged to you, Sir, if you will have the goodness to clear up that doubt for me; and, should it prove a fact, to return it to him with my thanks, but the most positive assurance that its acceptance is totally impossible."

Harleigh looked disturbed, yet promised to obey.

"And if," cried she, "you should not find Mr. Ireton to be my creditor, you may possibly discover him in a person to whom I owe far other services, and unmingled esteem. And should that be the case, say to him, I beg, Sir, that even from him I must decline an obligation of this sort, though my debts to him of every other, are nearly as innumerable as their remembrance will be indelible."

She then hastened away, leaving Harleigh impressed with such palpable concern, that she could no longer doubt that the packet was already deposited with its right owner.

He passed into the garden, and she was going back, when, at the entrance of the breakfast-parlour, she perceived Elinor, who seemed sternly occupied in observing them.

Ellis courtsied, and stood still. Elinor moved not, and was gloomily silent.

Struck with her mien, her stillness, and her manner, Ellis, in a fearful voice, enquired after her health; but received a look so indignant, yet wild, that, affrighted and astonished, she retreated to her chamber.

As she turned round upon entering it, to shut herself in, immediately before her stood Elinor.

She looked yet paler, and seemed in a sort of stupor. Ellis respectfully held open the door, but she did not advance: the fury, however, of her aspect was abated, and Ellis, in a voice condolingly soft, asked whether she might hope that Miss Joddrel would, once more, condescend to sit with her before her departure.

At these words Elinor seemed to shake herself, and presently, though in a hollow tone, pronounced, "Are you then going?"

Ellis plaintively answered Yes!

"And .... with whom?" cried Elinor, raising her eyes with a glance of fire.

"With no one, Madam. I go alone."

This answer was uttered with a firmness that annulled all suspicion of deceit.

Elinor appeared again to breathe.

"And whither?" she demanded, "whither is it you go?"

"I know not, alas!—but I mean to make an attempt at Howel Place."

The countenance of Elinor now lost its rigidity, and with a cry almost of extacy, she exclaimed, "Upon Lord Melbury?—

your new admirer? O go to him!—hasten to him!—dear, charming Ellis, away to him at once!—"

Ellis, half smiling, answered, "No, Madam; I go to Lady Aurora Granville."

Elinor, without replying, left the room; but, quick in action as in idea, returned, almost instantly, loaded with a packet of clothes.

"Here, most beautified Ophelia!"* she cried, "look over this trumpery. You know how skilfully you can arrange it. You must not appear to disadvantage before dear little Lord Melbury."

Ellis now, nearly offended, drew back.

"O, I know I ought to be excommunicated for giving such a hint," cried Elinor, whose spirits were rather exalted than recovered; "though every body sees how the poor boy is bewitched with you: but you delicate sentimentalists are never yourselves to suspect any danger, till the men are so crazy 'twould be murder to resist them; and then, you know, acceptance is an act of mere charity."

Ellis laughed at her raillery, yet declined her wardrobe, saying that she had resolved upon frankly stating to Lady Aurora, all that she was able to make known of her situation.

"Well, that's more romantic," returned Elinor, "and so 'twill be more touching; especially to the little peer; for as you won't say who you are, he can do no less than, like Selina, conclude you to be a princess in disguise; and that, as you know, will bring the match so properly forward, that parents, and uncles, and guardians, and all those supernumeraries* of the creation, will learn the business only just in time to drown themselves."

Ellis heard this with a calmness that shewed her superior to offering any vindication of her conduct; and Elinor more gently added, "Now don't construe all this into either a sneer or a reprimand. If you imagine me an enemy to what the old court call unequal connexions, you do me egregious injustice. I detest all aristocracy: I care for nothing upon earth but nature; and I hold no one thing in the world worth living for but liberty! and liberty, you know, has but two occupations,—plucking up and pulling down. To me, therefore, 'tis equally diverting, to see a beggar swell into a duchess, or a duchess dwindle into a beggar."

Ellis tried to smile, but felt shocked many ways; and Elinor, gay, now, as a lark, left her to get ready for Howel Place.

While thus employed, a soft tap called her to the door, where she perceived Harleigh.

"I will detain you," he said, "but a moment. I can find no owner for your little packet; you must suffer it, therefore, still to encumber you; and should any accident, or any transient convenience, make its contents even momentarily useful to you, do not let any idea of its having ever belonged to Mr. Ireton impede its employment: I have examined that point thoroughly, and I can positively assure you, that he has not the least knowledge even of its existence."

As she held back from taking it, he put it upon a step before the door, and descended the stairs without giving her time to answer.

She did not dare either to follow or to call him, lest Elinor should again appear; but she felt convinced that the bank-notes were his own, and became less uneasy at a short delay, though equally determined upon restitution.

She was depositing them in her work-bag, when Selina came jumping into the room. "O Ellis," she cried, "I have the best news in the world for you! Aunt Maple fell into the greatest passion you ever saw, at hearing you were going to Howel Place. 'What!' says she, 'shall I let her disgrace me for ever, by making known what a poor Wanderer I have taken into my house, and permitted to eat at my table? It would be a thing to ruin me in the opinion of the whole world.' So then, after the greatest fuss that ever you knew in your life, she said you should not be turned away till Lady Aurora was gone."

Ellis, however hurt by this recital, rejoiced in the reprieve.

The difficulties, nevertheless, of Mrs. Maple did not end here; the next morning she received a note from Mrs. Howel, with intelligence that Lady Aurora Granville was prevented from making her intended excursion, by a very violent cold; and to entreat that Mrs. Maple would use her interest with Miss Ellis, to soften Her Ladyship's disappointment, by spending the day at Howel Place; for which purpose Mrs. Howel begged leave to send her carriage, at an early hour, to Lewes.

Mrs. Maple read this with a choler indescribable. She would have sent word that Ellis was ill, but she foresaw an endless embarrassment from inquiring visits; and, after the most fretful, but fruitless lamentations, passionately declared that she would have nothing more to do with the business, and retired to her room; telling Elinor that she might answer Mrs. Howel as she pleased, only charging her to take upon herself all responsibility of consequences.

Elinor, enchanted, fixed upon two o'clock for the arrival of the carriage; and Ellis, who heard the tidings with even exquisite joy, spent the intermediate time in preparations, for which she no longer declined the assisting offers of Elinor, who, wild with renovated spirits, exhorted her, now in raillery, now in earnest, but always with agitated vehemence, to make no scruple of going off with Lord Melbury to Gretna Green.*

When the chaise arrived, Mrs. Maple restless and curious, suddenly descended; but was filled with double envy and malevolence, at sight of the look of pleasure which Ellis wore; but which gave to Harleigh a satisfaction that counterbalanced his regret at her quitting the house.

"I have only one thing to mention to you, Mrs. Ellis," said Mrs. Maple, with a gloomy scowl; "I insist upon it that you don't say one syllable to Mrs. Howel, nor to Lady Aurora, about your meanness, and low condition, and that ragged state that we found you in, patched, and blacked, and made up for an object to excite pity. Mind that! for if you go to Howel Place only to make out that I have been telling a parcel of stories, I shall be sure to discover it, and you shall repent it as long as you live."

Ellis seemed tempted to leave the room without condescending to make any reply; but she checked herself, and desired to understand more clearly what Mrs. Maple demanded.

"That there may be only one tale told between us, and that you will be steady to stand to what I have said, of your being a young lady of good family, who came over with me from France."

Ellis, without hesitation, consented; and Harleigh handed

her to the chaise, Mrs. Maple herself not knowing how to object to that civility, as the servants of Mrs. Howel were waiting to attend their lady's guest. "How happy, how relieved," cried he, in conducting her out, "will you feel in obtaining, at last, a little reprieve from the narrow prejudice which urges this cruel treatment!"

"You must not encourage me to resentment," cried she, smiling, "but rather bid me, as I bid myself, when I feel it rising, subdue it by recollecting my strange—indefinable situation in this family!"

CHAPTER XIII

THE presage of Harleigh proved as just as it was pleasant: the heart of Ellis bounded with delight as she drove off from the house; and the hope of transferring to Lady Aurora the obligation for succour which she was now compelled to owe to Mrs. Maple, seemed almost lifting her from earth to heaven.

Her fondest wishes were exceeded by her reception. Mrs. Howel came forward to meet her, and to beg permission not to order the carriage for her return, till late at night. She was then conducted to the apartment of Lady Aurora, by Lord Melbury, who assured her that his sister would have rejoiced in a far severer indisposition, which had procured her such a gratification. Lady Aurora welcomed her with an air of so much goodness, and with looks so soft, so pleased, so partial, that Ellis, in taking her held-out hand, overpowered by so sudden a transition from indignity to kindness, and agitated by the apprehensions that were attached to the hopes which it inspired, burst into tears, and, in defiance of her utmost struggles for serenity, wept even with violence.

Lady Aurora, shocked and alarmed, asked for her salts; and Lord Melbury flew for a glass of water; but Ellis, declining both, and reviving without either, wiped, though she could not dry her eyes, and smiled, while they still glistened, with such grateful sensibility, yet beaming happiness, that both the brother and the sister soon saw, that, greatly as she was affected, nothing was wanting to her restoration. "It is not sorrow," she cried, when able to speak; "'tis your goodness, your kindness, which thus touch me!"

"Can you ever have met with any thing else?" said Lord Melbury, warmly; "if you can—by what monsters you must have been beset!"

"No, my Lord, no," cried she: "I am far from meaning to complain; but you must not suppose the world made up of Lady Aurora Granvilles!"

Lady Aurora was much moved. It seemed evident to her that her new favourite was not happy; and she had conceived such high ideas of her perfections, that she was ready to weep herself, at the bare suggestion that they were not recompensed by felicity.

The rest of the morning passed in gentle, but interesting conversation, between the two young females; or in animated theatrical discussions, strictures, and declamation, with the young peer.

At dinner they joined Mrs. Howel, who was charmed to see her young guests thus delighted, and could not refuse her consent to a petition of Lady Aurora, that she would invite Miss Ellis to assist her again, the next day, to nurse her cold with the same prudence.

The expressive eyes of Ellis spoke enchantment. They parted, therefore, only for the night; but just before the carriage was driven from the door, the coachman discovered that an accident had happened to one of the wheels, which could not be rectified till the next morning.

After some deliberation, Mrs. Howel, at Lady Aurora's earnest desire, sent over a groom with a note to Mrs. Maple, informing her of the circumstance, and begging that she would not expect Miss Ellis till the following evening.

The tears of Ellis, at happiness so unlooked for, were again ready to flow, and with difficulty restrained. She wrote a few words to Elinor, entreating her kind assistance, in sending a packet of some things necessary for this new plan; and Elinor took care to provide her with materials for remaining a month, rather than a day.

A chamber was now prepared for Ellis, in which nothing was omitted that could afford either comfort or elegance; yet, from the fulness of her mind, she could not, even for a moment, close her eyes, when she retired.

Some drawback, however, to her happiness was experienced the next morning, when she found Mrs. Howel fearful that the cold of Lady Aurora menaced terminating in a violent cough. Dr. P— was immediately called in, and his principal prescription was, that Her Ladyship should avoid hot rooms, dancing, company, and talking. Mrs. Howel, easily made anxious for Lady Aurora, not only from personal attachment, but from the responsibility of having her in charge, besought Her Ladyship to give up the play for that night, an assembly for the following, and to permit that the intended ball of Thursday should be postponed, till Her Ladyship should be perfectly recovered.

Lady Aurora, with a grace that accompanied all her actions, unhesitatingly complied; but enquired whether it would not be possible to persuade Miss Ellis to remain with them during this confinement? Mrs. Howel repeated the request. The delight of Ellis was too deep for utterance. Joy of this tender sort always flung her into tears; and Lady Aurora, who saw that her heart was as oppressed as it was gentle, besought Mrs. Howel to write their desire to Lewes.

Mrs. Maple, however enraged and perplexed, had no choice how to act, without betraying the imposition which she had herself practised, and therefore offered no opposition.

Ellis now enjoyed a happiness, before which all her difficulties and disappointments seemed to sink forgotten, or but to be remembered as evils overpayed; so forcible was the effect upon her mind, of the contrast of her immediate situation with that so recently quitted. Mrs. Howel was all politeness to her; Lord Melbury appeared to have no study, but whether to shew her most admiration or respect; and Lady Aurora behaved to her with a sweetness that went straight to her heart.

It was now that they first became acquainted with her uncommon musical talents. Lady Aurora had a piano forte* in her room; and Mrs. Howel said, that if Miss Ellis could play Her Ladyship an air or two, it might help to amuse, yet keep her silent. Ellis instantly went to the instrument, and there performed, in so fine a style, a composition of Haydn,* that Mrs. Howel, who, though by no means a scientific judge of music, was sufficiently in the habit of going to concerts, to have acquired the skill of discriminating excellence from mediocrity, was struck with wonder, and congratulated both her young guest and herself, in so seasonable an acquisition of so accomplished a visitor.

Lord Melbury, who was himself a tolerable proficient upon the violoncello, was enraptured at this discovery; and Lady Aurora, whose whole soul was music, felt almost dissolved with tender pleasure.

Nor ended here either their surprise or their satisfaction; they soon learnt that she played also upon the harp; Lord Melbury instantly went forth in search of one; and it was then, as this was the instrument which she had most particularly studied, that Ellis completed her conquest of their admiration; for with the harp she was prevailed upon to sing; and the sweetness of her voice, the delicacy of its tones, her taste and expression, in which her soul seemed to harmonize with her accents, had an effect so delightful upon her auditors, that Mrs. Howel could scarcely find phrases for the compliments which she thought merited; Lord Melbury burst into the most rapturous applause; and Lady Aurora was enchanted, was fascinated: she caught the sweet sounds with almost extatic attention, hung on them with the most melting tenderness, entreated to hear the same air again and again, and felt a gratitude for the delight which she received, that was hardly inferior to that which her approbation bestowed.

Eager to improve these favourable sensations, Ellis, to vary the amusements of Lady Aurora, in this interval of retirement, proposed reading. And here again her powers gave the utmost pleasure; whether she took a French authour, or an English one; the accomplished Boileau, or the penetrating Pope; the tenderly-refined Racine, or the all-pervading Shakespeare,* her tones, her intelligence, her skilful modulations, gave force and meaning to every word, and proved alike her understanding and her feeling.

Brilliant, however, as were her talents, all the success which they obtained was short of that produced by her manners and conversation: in the former there was a gentleness, in the latter a spirit, that excited an interest for her in the whole house; but, while generally engaging to all by her general merit, to Lady Aurora she had peculiar attractions, from the excess of sensibility with which she received even the smallest attentions. She seemed impressed with a gratitude that struggled for words, without the power of obtaining such as could satisfy it. Pleasure shone lustrous in her fine eyes, every time that they met those of Lady Aurora; but if that young lady took her hand, or spoke to her with more than usual softness, tears, which she vainly strove to hide, rolled fast down her cheeks, but which, though momentarily overpowering, were no sooner dispersed, than every feature became re-animated with glowing vivacity.

Yet, that some latent sorrow hung upon her mind, Lady Aurora soon felt convinced; and that some solicitude or suspense oppressed her spirits, was equally evident: she was constantly watchful for the post, and always startled at sight of a letter. Lady Aurora was too delicate to endeavour to develope* the secret cause of this uneasiness; but the good breeding which repressed the manifestation of curiosity, made the interest thus excited sink so much the deeper into her mind; and, in a short time, her every feeling, and almost every thought, were absorbed in tender commiseration for unknown distresses, which she firmly believed to be undeserved; and which, however nobly supported, seemed too poignant for constant suppression.

Lady Aurora, who had just reached her sixteenth year, was now budding into life, with equal loveliness of mind and person. She was fair, but pale, with elegant features, a face perfectly oval, and soft expressive blue eyes, of which the "liquid lustre"* spoke a heart that was the seat of sensibility; yet not of that weak romantic cast, formed by early and futile love-sick reading, either in novels or poems;* but of compassionate feeling for woes which she did not suffer; and of anxious solicitude to lessen distress by kind offices, and affliction by tender sympathy.

With a character thus innately virtuous, joined to a disposition the most amiably affectionate, so attractive a young creature as the Incognita could not fail to be in unison. Without half her powers of pleasing, the most perfect good will of Lady Aurora would have been won, by the mere surmize that she was not happy: but when, to an idea so affecting to her gentle mind, were added the quick intelligence, the graceful manners, the touching sense of kindness, and the rare accomplishments of Ellis, so warm an interest was kindled in the generous bosom of Lady Aurora, that the desire to serve and to give comfort to her new favourite, became, in a short time, indispensable to her own peace.

Mrs. Howel, the lady with whom she was at present a guest, possessed none of the endearing qualities which could catch the affections of a mind of so delicate a texture as that of Lady Aurora. She was well bred, well born, and not ill educated; but her heart was cold, her manners were stiff, her opinions were austere, and her resolutions were immoveable. Yet this character, with the general esteem in which, for unimpeachable conduct, she was held by the world, was the inducement which led her cousin, Lord Denmeath, the uncle and guardian of Lady Aurora, to fix upon her as a proper person for taking his ward into public; the tender and facile nature of that young lady, demanding, he thought, all the guard which the firmness of Mrs. Howel could afford.

Lord Melbury was two years the senior of Lady Aurora: unassuming from his rank, and unspoiled by early independence, he was open, generous, kind-hearted and sincere; and though, from the ardour of juvenile freedom, and the credulity of youth, he was easily led astray, an instinctive love of right, and the acute self-reproaches which followed his least deviations, were conscious, and rarely erring guarantees, that his riper years would be happy in the wisdom of goodness.

In a house such as this, loved and compassionated by Lady Aurora, admired by Lord Melbury, and esteemed by Mrs. Howel, what felicity was enjoyed by its new guest! Her suspenses and difficulties, though never forgotten, were rather gratefully than patiently endured; and she felt as if she could scarcely desire their termination, if it should part her from such heart-soothing society.

Smoothly thus glided the hours, till nearly a fortnight elapsed, Lady Aurora, though recovered, saying, that she preferred this gentle social life, to the gayer or more splendid scenes offered to her abroad: yet neither with gaiety nor splendour had she quarrelled; it was Ellis whom she could not bear to quit; Ellis, whose attractions and sweetness charmed her heart, and whose secret disturbance occupied all her thoughts.

The admiration of Lord Melbury was wrought still higher; yet the constant respect attending it, satisfied Mrs. Howel, who would else have been alarmed, that his chief delight was derived from seeing that his sister, whom he adored, had a companion so peculiarly to her taste. Severely, however, Mrs. Howel watched and investigated every look, every speech, every turn of the head of Ellis, with regard to this young nobleman; well aware that, as he was younger than herself, though her beauty was in its prime, his safety might depend, more rationally, upon her own views, or her own honour, than upon his prudence or indifference: but all that she observed tended to raise Ellis yet more highly in her esteem. The behaviour of that young person was open, pleasing, good-humoured and unaffected. It was evident that she wished to be thought well of by Lord Melbury; but it appeared to be equally evident that she honourably deserved his good opinion. Her desire to give him pleasure was unmixt with any species of coquetry: it was as wide from the dangerous toil of tender languor, as from the fascinating snares of alluring playfulness. The whole of her demeanour had a decorum, and of her conduct a correctness, as striking to the taste of Mrs. Howel, as her conversation, her accomplishments, and her sentiments were to that of the youthful brother and sister. Mrs. Howel often begged Lady Aurora to remark, that this was the only young lady whom she had ever invited to her house upon so short an acquaintance; nor should she, even to oblige Her Ladyship, have made this exception to her established rules, but that she knew Mrs. Maple to be scrupulosity itself, with respect to the female friends whose intimacy she sanctioned with her nieces. It was well known, indeed, she observed, that Mrs. Maple was forced to be the more exact in these points on account of the extraordinary liberties taken by the eldest Miss Joddrel, who, being now entirely independent, frequently flung off the authority of her aunt, and did things so strange, and saw people so singular, that she continually distressed Mrs. Maple. Miss Ellis, therefore, having been brought back to her native land, by one so nice in these matters, must certainly be a young lady of good family; though there seemed reason to apprehend, that she was an orphan, and that she possessed little or no portion, by her never naming her friends nor her situation, notwithstanding they were subjects to which Mrs. Howel often tried to lead.

CHAPTER XIV

LADY Aurora being now perfectly well, and the period of her visit at Brighthelmstone nearly expired, Mrs. Howel could not dispense with repeating her dinner-invitation to Mrs. Maple; and, three days previously to the return of Lady Aurora to her uncle, it was accepted.

The whole Lewes party felt the most eager curiosity to see Ellis in her new dwelling; but not trifling was the effort required by Mrs. Maple to preserve any self-command, when she witnessed the high style in which that young person was treated throughout the house. Harleigh hastened to make his compliments to her, with an air of pleasure that spoke sympathising congratulation. Elinor was all eye, all scrutiny, but all silence. Ireton assumed, perforce, a tone of respect; and Selina, with such an example as Lady Aurora for her support, flew to embrace her *protegée*; and to relate, amongst sundry other little histories, that Mr. Harleigh had been going back to town, only Aunt Maple had begged him to stay, till something could be brought about with regard to his brother Dennis, who was grown quite affronted at sister Elinor's long delays.

Mrs. Maple, almost the whole dinner-time, had the mortification to hear, echoing from the sister to the brother, and re-echoed from Mrs. Howel, the praises of Miss Ellis; how delightfully the retirement of Lady Aurora had passed in her society; the sweetness of her disposition, the variety of her powers, and her amiable activity in seeking to make them useful. Not daring to dissent, Mrs. Maple, with forced smiles, gave a tacit concurrence; while the bright glow that animated the complexion, and every feature, of Harleigh, spoke that unequivocal approbation which comes warm from the heart.

Elinor, whose eyes constantly followed his, seemed sick during the whole repast, of which she scarcely at all partook. If Ellis offered to serve her, or enquired after her health, she darted at her an eye so piercing, that Ellis, shrinking and alarmed, determined to address her no more; though again, when any opportunity presented itself, for shewing some attention, the resolution was involuntarily set aside; but always with equal ill success, every attempt to soften, exciting looks the most terrific.

Lady Aurora surprised one of these glances, and saw its chilling effect. Astonished, at once, and grieved, she felt an impulse to rise, and to protect from such another shock her new and tenderly admired favourite. She now easily conceived why kindness was so touching to her; yet how any angry sensation could find its way in the breast of Miss Joddrel, or of any human being, against such sweetness and such excellence, her gentle mind, free from every feeling of envy, jealousy, or wrath, could form no conjecture. She sighed to withdraw her from a house where her merits were so ill appreciated; and could hardly persuade herself to speak to any one else at the table, from the eagerness with which she desired to dispel the gloom produced by Elinor's cloudy brow.

The looks of Elinor had struck Mrs. Howel also; but not with similar compassion for their object; it was with alarm for herself. A sudden, though vague idea, seized her, to the disadvantage of Ellis. With all her accomplishments, all her elegance, was she, at last, but a dependant? Might she be smiled or frowned upon at will? And had she herself admitted into her house, upon equal terms, a person of such a description?

Doubt soon gives birth to suspicion, and suspicion is the mother of surmise. It was now strange that she should have been told nothing of the family and condition of Miss Ellis; there must be some reason for silence; and the reason could not be a good one.

Yet, was it possible that Mrs. Maple could have been negligent upon such a subject? Mrs. Maple who, far from being dangerously facile, in forming any connexion, was proud, was even censorious about every person that she knew or saw?

Mrs. Howel now examined the behaviour of Mrs. Maple

herself to Ellis; and this scrutiny soon shewed her its entire constraint; the distance which she observed when not forced to notice her; the unwilling civility, where any attention was indispensable.

Something must certainly be wrong; and she determined, in the course of the evening, to find an opportunity for minutely, nay rigorously, questioning Mrs. Maple. Ellis, meanwhile, fearing no one but Elinor, and watching no one but Lady Aurora, found sufficient occupation in the alternate panic and consolation thus occasioned; or if any chasm occurred, Lord Melbury with warm assiduities, and Harleigh with delicate attentions, were always at hand to fill it up.

When, early in the evening, that the horses might rest, the carriage of Mrs. Maple arrived, the groom sent in a letter, which, he said, had just been brought to Lewes, according to order, by a messenger from the Brighthelmstone post-office. Ellis precipitately arose; but Mrs. Maple held out her hand to take it; though, upon perceiving the direction, 'For L. S., to be left at the post-office at Brighthelmstone till called for,' fearing that Mrs. Howel, who sat next to her, should perceive it also, she hastily said, "It is not for me; let the man take it back again;" and, turning the seal upwards, re-delivered it to the servant; anxious to avoid exhibiting an address, which might lead to a discovery that she now deemed personally ignominious.

Ellis, at this order, reseated herself, not daring to make a public claim, but resolving to follow the footman out, and to desire to look at the direction of the letter. Elinor, however, stopping him, took it herself, and, after a slight glance, threw it upon a table, saying, "Leave it for who will to own it."

Ellis, changing colour, again arose; and would have seized it for examination, had not Ireton, who was nearer to the table, taken it up, and read, aloud, 'For L. S.' Again Ellis dropt upon her chair, distressed and perplexed, between eagerness to receive her letter, and shame and fear at acknowledging so mysterious a direction.

Her dread of the consequence of disobeying Mrs. Maple, had made her, hitherto, defer relating her situation with regard to that lady; and she had always flattered herself, that the longer it was postponed, the greater would be her chance of inspiring such an interest as might cause an indulgent hearing.

Harleigh now took the letter himself, and, calmly saying that he would see it safely delivered, put it into his pocket.

Ellis, thus relieved from making an abrupt and unseasonable avowal, yet sure that her letter was in honourable custody, with difficulty refrained from thanking him. Lord Melbury and Mrs. Howel thought there was something odd and unintelligible in the business, but forbore any enquiry; Lady Aurora, observing distress in her amiable Miss Ellis, felt it herself; but revived with her revival; and the rest of the company, though better informed, were compulsatorily silenced by the frowns of Mrs. Maple.

Harleigh then, asking for a pen and some ink to write a letter, left the room. Ellis, tortured with impatience, and hoping to meet with him, soon followed. She was not mistaken: he had seated himself to write in an ante-room, which she must necessarily cross if she mounted to her chamber.

He softly arose, put the letter into her hand, bowed, and returned to his chair without speaking. She felt his delicacy as strongly as his kindness, but, breathless with eagerness, observed the silence of which he set the example, and, thanking him only by her looks, flew up stairs.

She was long absent, and, when she descended, it was with steps so slow, and with an air so altered, that Harleigh, who was still writing in the room through which she had to pass, saw instantly that her letter had brought disappointment and sorrow.

He had not, now, the same self-command as while he had hoped and thought that she was prosperous. He approached her, and, with a face of deep concern, enquired if there were any thing, of any sort, in which he could have the happiness to be of use to her? He stopt; but she felt his right to a curiosity which he did not avow, and immediately answered: "My letter brings me no consolation! on the contrary, it tells me that I must depend wholly upon myself, and expect no kind of aid, nor even any intelligence again, perhaps for a considerable time!"

"Is that possible?" cried he, "Does no one follow—or is no

one to meet you?—Is there no one whose duty it is to guard and protect you? to draw you from a situation thus precarious, thus unfitting, and to which I am convinced you are wholly unaccustomed?"

"It is fatally true, at this moment," answered Ellis, with a sigh, "that no one can follow or support me; yet I am not deserted—I am simply unfortunate. Neither can any one here meet me: the few to whom I have any right to apply, know not of my arrival—and must not know it!—How I am to exist till I dare make some claim, I cannot yet devise: but, indeed, had it not been under this kind, protecting roof, that I have received such a letter—I think I must have sunk from my own dismay:—but Lady Aurora—" Her voice failed, and she stopt.

"Lady Aurora," cried Harleigh, "is an angel. Her quick appreciation of your worth, shews her understanding to be as good as her soul is pure. I can wish you no better protection.—But pardon me, if I venture again to repeat my surprise—I had almost said my indignation—that those to whom you belong, can deem it right—safe—or decent, to commit you—young as you are, full of attractions, and evidently unused to struggle against the dangers of the world, and the hardships of life,—to commit you to strangers—to chance!—"

"I know not how," she cried, "to leave you under so false an impression of those to whom I belong. They are not to blame. They are more unhappy than I am myself at my loneliness and its mystery: and for my poverty and my difficulties, they are far, far from suspecting them! They are ignorant of my loss at Dover, and they cannot suppose that I have missed the friend whom I came over to join."

"Honour me," cried he, "with a commission, and I will engage to discover, at least, whether that friend be yet at Brighthelmstone."

"And without naming for whom you seek her?" cried Ellis, her eyes brightening with sudden hope.

"Naming?" repeated he, with an arch smile.

She blushed, deeply, in recollecting herself; but, seized with a sudden dread of Elinor, drew back from her inadvertant acceptance; and, though warmly thanking him, declined his services; adding that, by waiting at Brighthelmstone, she must, ultimately, meet her friend, since all her letters and directions were for that spot.

Harleigh was palpably disappointed; and Ellis, hurt herself, opened her letter, to lessen, she told him, his wonder, perhaps censure, of her secresy, by reading to him its injunction. This was the sentence: "Seek, then, unnamed and unknown, during this dread interval of separation, to reside with some worthy and happy family, whose social felicity may bring, at least, reflected happiness to your own breast."

"That family," she added, "I flatter myself I have found here! for this house, from the uniform politeness of Mrs. Howel, the ingenuous goodness of Lord Melbury, and the angelic sweetness of his sister, has been to me an earthly paradise."

She then proceeded, without waiting to receive his thanks for this communication; which he seemed hardly to know how to offer, from the fulness of his thoughts, his varying conjectures, his conviction that her friends, like herself, were educated, feeling, and elegant; and his increased wonder at the whole of her position. Charming, charming creature! he cried, what can have cast thee into this forlorn condition? And by what means—and by whom—art thou to be rescued?

Not chusing immediately to follow, he seated himself again to his pen.

Somewhat recovered by this conversation, Ellis, now, was able to command an air of tolerable composure, for re-entering the drawing-room, where she resolved to seek Elinor at once, and endeavour to deprecate her displeasure, by openly repeating to her all that she had entrusted to Mr. Harleigh.

As she approached the door, every voice seemed employed in eager talk; and, as she opened it, she observed earnest separate parties formed round the room; but the moment that she appeared, every one broke off abruptly from what he or she was saying, and a completely dead silence ensued.

Surprized by so sudden a pause, she seated herself on the first chair that was vacant, while she looked around her, to see whom she could most readily join. Mrs. Howel and Mrs. Maple had been, evidently, in the closest discourse, but now both fixed their eyes upon the ground, as if agreeing, at once, to say no more. Ireton was chatting, with lively volubility, to Lord Melbury, who attended to him with an air that seemed scared rather than curious; but neither of them now added another word. Elinor stood sullenly alone, leaning against the chimney-piece, with her eyes fastened upon the door, as if watching for its opening: but not all the previous resolution of Ellis, could inspire courage sufficient to address her, after viewing the increased sternness of her countenance. Selina was prattling busily to Lady Aurora; and Lady Aurora, who sat nearly behind her, and whom Ellis perceived the last, was listening in silence, and bathed in tears.

Terror and affliction seized upon Ellis at this sight. Her first impulse was to fly to Lady Aurora; but she felt discouraged, and even awed, by the strangeness of the general taciturnity, occasioned by her appearance. Her eyes next, anxiously, sought those of Lord Melbury, and instantly met them; but with a look of gravity so unusual, that her own were hastily withdrawn, and fixt, disappointed, upon the ground. Nor did he, as hitherto had been his constant custom, when he saw her disengaged, come to sit by her side. No one spoke; no one seemed to know how to begin a general or common conversation; no one could find a word to say.

What, cried she, to herself, can have happened? What can have been said or done, in this short absence, to make my sight thus petrifying? Have they told what they know of my circumstances? And has that been sufficient to deprive me of all consideration? to require even avoidance? And is Lord Melbury thus easily changed? And have I lost you—even you! Lady Aurora?

This last thought drew from her so deep a sigh, that, in the general silence which prevailed, it reached every ear. Lady Aurora started, and looked up; and, at the view of her evident dejection, hastily arose, and was crossing the room to join her; when Mrs. Howel, rising too, came between them, and taking herself the hand which Lady Aurora had extended for that of Ellis, led Her Ladyship to a seat on a sofa, where, in the lowest voice, she apparently addressed to her some remonstrance.

Ellis, who had risen to meet the evident approach of Lady Aurora, now stood suspended, and with an air so embarrassed, so perturbed, that Lord Melbury, touched by irresistible compassion, came forward, and would have handed her to a chair near the fire; but her heart, after so sudden an appearance of general estrangement, was too full for this mark of instinctive, not intentional kindness, and courtsying the thanks which she could not utter, she precipitately left the room.

She met Harleigh preparing to enter it, but passed him with too quick a motion to be stopt, and hurried to her chamber.

There her disturbance, as potent from positive distress, as it was poignant from mental disappointment, would nearly have amounted to despair, but for the visibly intended support of Lady Aurora; and for the view of that kind hand, which, though Mrs. Howel had impeded her receiving, she could not prevent her having seen stretched out for her comfort. The attention, too, of Lord Melbury, though its tardiness ill accorded with his hitherto warm demonstrations of respect and kindness, shewed that those feelings were not alienated, however they might be shaken.

These two ideas were all that now sustained her, till, in about an hour, she was followed by Selina, who came to express her concern, and to relate what had passed.

Ellis then heard, that the moment that she had left the room, Mrs. Howel, almost categorically, though with many formal apologies, demanded some information of Mrs. Maple, what account should be given to Lord Denmeath, of the family and condition in life, of the young lady introduced, by Mrs. Maple, into the society of Lady Aurora Granville, as Her Ladyship proposed intimately keeping up the acquaintance. Mrs. Maple had appeared to be thunderstruck, and tried every species of equivocation; but Mr. Ireton whispered something to Lord Melbury, upon which a general curiosity was raised; and Mr. Ireton's laughs kept up the enquiry, "till, bit by bit," continued Selina, "all came out, and you never saw such a fuss in your life! But when Mrs. Howel found that Aunt Maple did not take you in charge from your friends, because she did not know them; and when Mr. Ireton told of your patches, and black skin, and ragged dress, Mrs. Howel stared so at poor aunt, that I believe she thought that she had been out of her senses. And then, poor Lady Aurora fell a-crying, because Mrs. Howel said that she must break off the connexion. But Lady Aurora said that you might be just as good as ever, and only disguised to make your escape; but Mrs. Howel said, that, now you were got over, if there were not something bad, you would speak out. So then poor Lady Aurora cried again, and beckoned to me to come and tell her more particulars. Sister Elinor, all the time, never spoke one word. And this is what we were all doing when you came in."

Ellis, who, with pale cheeks, but without comment, had listened to this recital, now faintly enquired what had passed after she had retired.

"Why, just then, in came Mr. Harleigh, and Aunt Maple gave him a hundred reproaches, for beginning all the mischief, by his obstinacy in bringing you into the boat, against the will of every creature, except just the old Admiral, who knew nothing of the world, and could judge no better. He looked quite thunderstruck, not knowing a word of what had passed. However, he soon enough saw that all was found out; for Mrs. Howel said, 'I hope, Sir, you will advise us, how to get rid of this person, without letting the servants know the indiscretion we have been drawn into, by treating her like one of ourselves.'"

"Well? and Mr. Harleigh's answer?—" cried the trembling Ellis.

"Miss Joddrel, Madam, he said, knows as well as myself, all the circumstances which have softened this mystery, and rendered this young lady interesting in its defiance. She has generously, therefore, held out her protection; of which the young lady has shewn herself to be worthy, upon every occasion, since we have known her, by rectitude and dignity: yet she is, at this time, without friends, support, or asylum: in such a situation, thus young and helpless, and thus irreproachably conducting herself, who is the female—what is her age, what her rank, that ought not to assist and try to preserve so distressed a young person from evil? Lady Aurora, upon this, came forward, and said, 'How happy you make me, Mr. Harleigh, by thus reconciling me to my wishes!' And then she told Mrs. Howel that, as the affair no longer appeared to be so desperate, she hoped that there could be no objection to her coming up stairs, to invite you down herself. But Mrs. Howel would not consent."

"Sweet! sweet Lady Aurora!" broke forth from Ellis: "And Lord Melbury? what said he?"

"Nothing; for he and Mr. Ireton left the room together, to go on with their whispers, I believe. And Elinor was just like a person dumb. But Lady Aurora and Mr. Harleigh had a great deal of talk with one another, and they both seemed so pleased, that I could not help thinking, how droll it would be if their agreeing so about you should make them marry one another."

"Then indeed would two beings meet," said Ellis, "who would render that state all that can be perfect upon earth; for with active benevolence like his, with purity and sweetness like her's, what could be wanting?—And then, indeed, I might find an asylum!"

A servant came, now, to inform Selina that the carriage was at the door, and that Mrs. Maple was in haste.

What a change did this day produce for Ellis! What a blight to her hopes, what difficulties for her conduct, what agitation for her spirits!

CHAPTER XV

ELLIS, who soon heard the carriage drive off for Lewes, waited in terrour to learn the result of this scene; almost equally fearful of losing the supporting kindness of Lady Aurora through timid acquiescence, as of preserving it through efforts to which her temper and gentle habits were repugnant.

In about half an hour, Mrs. Howel's maid came to enquire whether Miss Ellis would have any thing brought up stairs for supper; Mrs. Howel having broken up the usual evening party, in order to induce Lady Aurora, who was extremely fatigued, to go to rest.

Not to rest went Ellis, after such a message, though to that bed which had brought to her, of late, the repose of peace and contentment, and the alertness of hope and pleasure. A thousand schemes crossed her imagination, for averting the desertion which she saw preparing, and which her augmenting attachment to Lady Aurora, made her consider as a misfortune that would rob her of every consolation. But no plan occurred that satisfied her feeling without wounding her dignity: the first prompted a call upon the tender heart of Lady Aurora, by unlimited confidence; the second, a manifestation how ill she thought she merited the change of treatment that she experienced, by resentfully quitting the house: but this was no season for the smallest voluntary hazard. All chance of security hung upon the exertion of good sense, and the right use of reason, which imperiously demanded active courage with patient forbearance.

She remitted, therefore, forming any resolution, till she should learn that of Mrs. Howel.

It was now the first week of February, and, before the break of day, a general movement in the house gave her cause to believe that the family was risen. She hastened to dress herself, unable to conjecture what she had to expect. The commotion continued; above and below the servants seemed employed, and in haste; and, in a little time, some accidental sounds reached her ears, from which she gathered that an immediate journey to London was preparing.

What could this mean? Was she thought so intruding, that by change of abode alone they could shake her off? or so dangerous, that flight, only, could preserve Lady Aurora from her snares? And was it thus, she was to be apprized that she must quit the house? Without a carriage, without money, and without a guide, was she to be turned over to the servants? and by them turned, perhaps, from the door?

Indignation now helped to sustain her; but it was succeeded by the extremest agitation, when she saw, from her window, Lord Melbury mounting his horse, upon which he presently rode off.

And is it thus, she cried, that all I thought so ingenuous in goodness, so open in benevolence, so sincere in partiality, subsides into neglect, perhaps forgetfulness?—And you, Lady Aurora, will you, also, give me up as lightly?

She wept. Indignation was gone: sorrow only remained; and she listened in sadness for every sound that might proclaim the departure which she dreaded.

At length, she heard a footstep advance slowly to her chamber, succeeded by a tapping at her door.

Her heart beat with hope. Was it Lady Aurora? had she still so much kindness, so much zeal?—She flew to meet her own idea—but saw only the lady of the house.

She sighed, cruelly disappointed; but the haughty distance of Mrs. Howel's air restored her courage; for courage, where there is any nobleness of mind, always rises highest, when oppressive pride seeks to crush it by studied humiliation.

Mrs. Howel fixed her eyes upon the face of Ellis, with an expression that said, Can you bear to encounter me after this discovery? Then, formally announcing that she had something important to communicate, she added, "You will be so good as to shut the door," and seated herself on an arm-chair, by the fire side; without taking any sort of notice that her guest was still standing.

Ellis could far better brook behaviour such as this from Mrs. Maple, from whom she had never experienced any of a superiour sort; but by Mrs. Howel she had been invited upon equal terms, and, hitherto, had been treated not only with equality but distinction: hard, therefore, she found it to endure such a change; yet her resentment was soon governed by her candour, when it brought to her mind the accusation of appearances.

Mrs. Howel then began an harangue palpably studied: "You cannot, I think, young woman—for you must excuse my not addressing you by a name I now know you to have assumed;—you cannot, I think, be surprised to find that your stay in this house is at an end. To avoid, however, giving any publicity to your disgrace, at the desire of Mrs. Maple, who thinks that its promulgation, in a town such as this, might expose her, as well as yourself, to impertinent lampoons,* I shall take no notice of what has passed to any of my people; except to my housekeeper, to whom it is necessary I should make over some authority, which you will not, I imagine, dispute. For myself, I am going to town immediately with Lady Aurora. I have given out that it is upon sudden business, with proper directions that my domestics may treat you with civility. You will still breakfast, therefore, in the parlour; and, at your own time, you will ask for a chaise, which I have bespoken to carry you back to Lewes. To prevent any suspicion in the neighbourhood, I shall leave commands that a man and horse may attend you, in the same manner as when you came hither. No remark, therefore, will follow your not having my own carriage again, as I make use of it myself. Lord Melbury is set off already. We shall none of us return till I hear, from Mrs. Maple, that you have left this part of the country; for, as I can neither receive you, nor notice you where I might happen to meet with you, such a difference of conduct, after this long visit, might excite animadversion. The sooner, therefore, you change your quarters, the better; for I coincide in the opinion of Mrs. Maple, that it is wisest, for all our sakes, that this transaction should not be spread in the world. And now, young woman, all I ask of you in return for the consideration I shew you, is this; that you will solemnly engage to hold no species of intercourse with Lady Aurora Granville, or with Lord Melbury, either by speech, or writing, or message. If you observe this, I shall do you no hurt; if not,—expect every punishment my resentment can inflict, and that of the noble family, involved in the indignity which you have made me suffer, by a surreptitious entrance into my house as a young lady of fashion."

No sort of answer was offered by Ellis. She stood motionless, her eyes fixed, and her air seeming to announce her almost incredulous of what she heard.

"Do you give me," said Mrs. Howel, "this promise? Will you bind yourself to it in writing?"

Ellis still was silent, and looked incapable of speaking.

"Young woman," said Mrs. Howel, with increased austerity, "I am not to be trifled with. Will you bind yourself to this agreement, or will you not?"

"What agreement, Madam?" she now faintly asked.

"Not to seek, and even to refuse, any sort of intercourse with Lady Aurora Granville, or with her brother, either by word of mouth, or letter, or messenger? Will you, I say, bind yourself, upon your oath, to this?"

'No, Madam!" answered Ellis, with returning recollection and courage; "no peril can be so tremendous as such a sacrifice!"

Mrs. Howel, rising, said, "Enough! abide by the consequence."

She was leaving the room; but Ellis, affrighted, exclaimed, "Ah, Madam, before you adopt any violent measures against me, deign to reflect that I may be innocent, and not merit them!"

"Innocent?" repeated Mrs. Howel, with an air of inexorable ire; "without a name, without a home, without a friend?—Innocent? presenting yourself under false appearances to one family, and under false pretences to another? No, I am not such a dupe. And if your bold resistance make it necessary, for the safety of my young friends, that I should lodge an information against you, you will find, that people who enter houses by names not their own, and who have no ostensible means of existence, will be considered only as swindlers; and as swindlers be disposed of as they deserve."

Ellis, turning pale, sunk upon a chair.

Mrs. Howel, stopping, with a voice as hard as her look was implacable, added; "This is your last moment for repentance. Will you give your promise, upon oath?"

"No, Madam! again no!" cried Ellis, starting up with sudden energy: "What I have suffered shall teach me to suffer more, and what I have escaped, shall give me hope for my support! But never will I plight myself, by willing promise, to avoid those whose virtuous goodness and compassion offer me the only consolation, that, in my desolate state, I can receive!"

"Tis well!" said Mrs. Howel, "You have yourself, then, only, to thank for what ensues."

She now steadily went on, opened the door, and left the room, though Ellis, mournfully following her, called out: "Ah, Madam!—ah, Mrs. Howel!—if ever you know more of me—which, at least, is not impossible,—you will look back to this period with no pleasure!—or with pleasure only to that part of it, in which you received me at your house with politeness, hospitality, and kindness!"

Mrs. Howel was not of a nature to relent in what she felt, or to retract from what she said: the distress, therefore, of Ellis, produced not the smallest effect upon her; and, with her head stiffly erect, and her countenance as unmoved as her heart, she descended the stairs, and issued, aloud, her commands that the horses should immediately be put to the chaise.

Ellis shut herself into her room, almost overpowered by the shock of this attack, so utterly unexpected, from a lady in whose character the leading feature seemed politeness, and who always appeared to hold that quality to be pre-eminent to all others. But the experience of Ellis had not yet taught her, how distinct is the politeness of manner, formed by the habits of high life, to that which springs spontaneously from benevolence of mind. The first, the product of studied combinations, is laid aside, like whatever is factitious, where there is no object for acting a part: the second, the child of sympathy, instructs us how to treat others, by suggesting the treatment we desire for ourselves; and this, as its feelings are personal, though its exertions are external, demands no effort, waits no call, and is never failingly at hand.

The gloomy sadness of Ellis was soon interrupted, by enquiries that reached her from the hall, whether the trunks of Lady Aurora were ready. Is she so nearly gone? Ellis cried; Ah! when may I see her again?—To the hall, to wait in the hall, she longed to go herself, to catch a last view, and to snatch, if possible, a kind parting word; but the tremendous Mrs. Howel!—she shrunk from the idea of ever seeing her again.

Soon afterwards, she heard the carriages drive up to the house. She now went to the window, to behold, at least, the loved form of Lady Aurora as she mounted the chaise. Perhaps, too, she might turn round, and look up. Fixt here, she was inattentive to the opening of her own room-door, concluding that the house-maid came to arrange her fire, till a soft voice gently articulated: "Miss Ellis!" She hastily looked round: it was Lady Aurora; who had entered, who had shut herself in, and who, while one hand covered her eyes, held out the other, in an attitude of the most inviting affection.

Ellis flew to seize it, with joy inexpressible, indescribable, and would have pressed it to her lips; but Lady Aurora, flinging both her arms round the neck of her new friend, fell upon her bosom, and wept, saying, "You are not, then, angry, though I, too, must have seemed to behave to you so cruelly?"

"Angry?" repeated Ellis, sobbing from the suddenness of a delight which broke into a sorrow nearly hopeless; "O Lady Aurora! if you could know how I prize your regard! your goodness!—what a balm it is to every evil I now experience, your gentle and generous heart would be recompensed for all the concern I occasion it, by the pleasure of doing so much good!"

"You can still, then, love me, my Miss Ellis?"

"Ah, Lady Aurora! if I dared say how much!—but, alas, in my helpless situation, the horror of being suspected of flattery—"

"What you will not say, then," cried Lady Aurora, smiling, "will you prove?"

"Will I?—Alas, that I could!"

"Will you let me take a liberty with you, and promise not to be offended?"

She put a letter into her hand, which Ellis fondly kissed, and lodged near her heart.

The words "Where is Lady Aurora?" now sounded from the stair-case.

"I must stay," she said, "no longer! Adieu, dear Miss Ellis! Think of me sometimes—for I shall think of you unceasingly!"

"Ah, Lady Aurora!" cried Ellis, clinging to her, "shall I see you, then, no more? And is this a last leave-taking?"

"O, far from it, far, far, I hope!" said Lady Aurora: "if I thought that we should meet no more, it would be impossible for me to tell you how unhappy this moment would make me!"

"Where is Lady Aurora?" would again have hurried her away; but Ellis, still holding by her, cried, "One moment! one moment!—I have not, then, lost your good opinion? Oh! if that wavers, my firmness wavers too! and I must unfold—at all risks—my unhappy situation!"

"Not for the world! not for the world!" cried Lady Aurora, earnestly: "I could not bear to seem to have any doubt to remove, when I have none, none, of your perfect innocence, goodness, excellence!"

Overpowered with grateful joy, "Angelic Lady Aurora!" was all that Ellis could utter, while tears rolled fast down her cheeks; and she tenderly, yet fervently, kissed the hand of the resisting Lady Aurora, who, extremely affected, leant upon her bosom, till she was startled by again hearing her name from without. "Go, then, amiable Lady Aurora!" Ellis cried; "I will no longer detain you! Go!—happy in the happiness that your sweetness, your humanity, your kindness bestow! I will dwell continually upon their recollection; I will say to myself, Lady Aurora believes me innocent, though she sees me forlorn; she will not think me unworthy, though she knows me to be unprotected; she will not conclude me to be an adventurer, though I dare not tell her even my name!"

"Do not talk thus, my dear, dear Miss Ellis! Oh! if I were my own mistress—with what delight I should supplicate you to live with me entirely! to let us share between us all that we possess; to read together, study our musick together, and never, never to part!"

Ellis could hardly breathe: her soul seemed bursting with emotions, which, though the most delicious, were nearly too mighty for her frame. But the melting kindness of Lady Aurora soon soothed her into more tranquil enjoyment; and when, at length, a message from Mrs. Howel irresistibly compelled a separation, the warm gratitude of her heart, for the consolation which she had received, enabled her to endure it with fortitude. But not without grief. All seemed gone when Lady Aurora was driven from the door; and she remained weeping at the window, whence she saw her depart, till she was roused by the entrance of Mrs. Greaves, the housekeeper.

Her familiar intrusion, without tapping at the door, quickly brought to the recollection of Ellis the authority which had been vested in her hands. This immediately restored her spirit; and as the housekeeper, seating herself, was beginning, very unceremoniously, to explain the motives of her visit, Ellis, without looking at her, calmly said, "I shall go down stairs now to breakfast; but if you have time to be so good as to make up my packages, you will find them in those drawers."

She then descended to the parlour, leaving the housekeeper stupified with amazement. But the forms of subordination, when once broken down, are rarely, with common characters, restored. Glad of the removal of a barrier which has kept them at a distance from those above them, they revel in the idea that the fall of a superiour is their own proper elevation. Following, therefore, Ellis to the breakfast-room, and seating herself upon a sofa, she began a discourse with the freedom of addressing a disgraced dependent; saying, "Mrs. Maple will be in a fine taking, Miss, to have you upon her hands, again, so all of the sudden."

This speech, notwithstanding its grossness, surprised from Ellis an exclamation, "Does not Mrs. Maple, then, expect me?"

"How should she, when my lady never settled what she should do about you herself, till after twelve o'clock last night? However, as to sending you back without notice, she has no notion, she says, of standing upon any ceremony with Mrs. Maple, who made so little of popping you upon her and Lady Aurora in that manner."

Ellis turned from her with disdain, and would reply to nothing more; but her pertinacious stay still kept the bosom letter unopened.

Grievously Ellis felt tormented with the prospect of what her reception might be from Mrs. Maple, after such a blight. The buoyant spirit of her first escape, which she had believed no after misfortune could subdue, had now so frequently been repressed, that it was nearly borne down to the common standard of mortal condition, whence we receive our daily fare of good and of evil, with the joy or the grief that they separately excite; independently of that wonderful power, believed in by the youthful and inexperienced, of hoarding up the felicity of our happy moments, as a counterpoise to future sorrows and disappointments. The past may revisit our hearts with renewed sufferings, or our spirits with gay recollections; but the interest of the time present, even upon points the most passing and trivial, will ever, from the pressure of our wants and our feelings, predominate.

Mrs. Greaves, unanswered and affronted, was for some minutes silenced; but, presently, rising and calling out, "Gemini!* something has happened to my Lady, or to Lady Aurora? Here's My Lord gallopped back!" she ran out of the room.

Affrighted by this suggestion, Ellis, who then perceived Lord Melbury from the window, ran herself, after the housekeeper, to the door, and eagerly exclaimed, as he dismounted, "O, My Lord, I hope no accident—"

"None!" cried he, flying to her, and taking and kissing both her hands, and drawing, rather than leading, her back to the parlour, "none!—or if any there were,—what could be the accident that concern so bewitching would not recompense?"

Ellis felt amazed. Lord Melbury had never addressed her before in any tone of gallantry; had never kissed, never touched her hand; yet now, he would scarcely suffer her to withdraw it from his ardent grasp.

"But, My Lord," said Mrs. Greaves, who followed them in, "pray let me ask Your Lordship about my Lady, and My Lady Aurora, and how—"

"They are perfectly well," cried he, hastily, "and gone on. I am ridden back myself merely for something which I forgot."

"I was fearful," said Ellis, anxious to clear up her eager reception, "that something might have happened to Lady Aurora; I am extremely happy to hear that all is safe."

"And you will have the charity, I hope, to make me a little breakfast? for I have tasted nothing yet this morning."

Again he took both her hands, and led her to the seat which she had just quitted at the table.

She was extremely embarrassed. She felt reluctant to refuse a request so natural; yet she was sure that Mrs. Howel would conclude that they met by appointment; and she saw in the face of the housekeeper the utmost provocation at the young Lord's behaviour: yet neither of these circumstances gave her equal disturbance, with observing a change, indefinable yet striking, in himself. After an instant's reflection, she deemed it most advisable not to stay with him; and, saying that she was in haste to return to Lewes, she begged that Mrs. Greaves would order the chaise that Mrs. Howel had mentioned.

"Ay, do, good Greaves!" cried he, hurrying her out, and, in his eagerness to get her away, shutting the door after her himself.

Ellis said that she would see whether her trunk were ready.

"No, no, no! don't think of the trunk," cried he: "We have but a few minutes to talk together, and to settle how we shall meet again."

Still more freely than before, he now rather seized than took her hand; and calling her his dear charming Ellis, pressed it to his lips, and to his breast, with rapturous fondness.

Ellis, struck, now, with terrour, had not sufficient force to withdraw her hand; but when she said, with great emotion, "Pray, pray, My Lord!—" he let it go.

It was only for a moment. snatching, it then, again, as she was rising to depart, he suddenly slipt upon one of her fingers a superb diamond ring, which he took off from one of his own.

"It is very beautiful, My Lord;" said she, deeply blushing; yet looking at it as if she supposed he meant merely to call for her admiration, and returning it to him immediately.

"What's this?" cried he: "Won't you wear such a bauble for my sake? Give me but a lock of your lovely hair, and I will make myself one to replace it."

He tried to put the ring again on her finger; but, forcibly breaking from him, she would have left the room: he intercepted her passage to the door. She turned round to ring the bell: he placed himself again in her way, with a flushed air of sportiveness, yet of determined opposition.

Confounded, speechless, she went to one of the windows, and standing with her back to it, looked at him with an undisguised amazement, that she hoped would lead him to some explanation of his behaviour, that might spare her any serious remonstrance upon its unwelcome singularity.

"Why, what's this?" cried he gaily, yet with a gaiety not perfectly easy; "do you want to run away from me?"

"No, my lord," answered she, gravely, yet forcing a smile, which she hoped would prove, at once, a hint, and an inducement to him to end the scene as an idle and ill-judged frolic; "No; I have only been afraid that your lordship was running away from yourself!"

"And why so?" cried he, with quickness, "Is Harleigh the only man who is ever to be honoured with your company tête-à-tête?"

"What can your lordship mean?"

"What can the lovely Ellis blush for? And what can Harleigh have to offer, that should obtain for him thus exclusively all favour? If it be adoration of your charms, who shall adore them more than I will? If it be in proofs of a more solid nature, who shall vie with me? All I possess shall be cast at your feet. I defy him to out-do me, in fortune or in love."

Ellis now turned pale and cold: horrour thrilled through her veins, and almost made her heart cease to beat. Lord Melbury saw the change, and, hastily drawing towards her a chair, besought her to be seated. She was unable to refuse, for she had not strength to stand; but, when again he would have taken her hand, she turned from him, with an air so severe of soul-felt repugnance, that, starting with surprise and alarm, he forbore the attempt.

He stood before her utterly silent, and with a complexion frequently varying, till she recovered; when, again raising her eyes, with an expression of mingled affliction and reproach, "And is it, then," she cried, "from a brother of the pure, the exemplary Lady Aurora Granville, that I am destined to receive the most heart-rending insult of my life?"

Lord Melbury seemed thunderstruck, and could not articulate what he tried to say; but, upon again half pronouncing the name of Harleigh, Ellis, standing up, with an air of dignity the most impressive, cried, "My lord, Mr. Harleigh rescued me from the most horrible of dangers, in assisting me to leave the Continent; and his good offices have befriended me upon every occasion since my arrival in England. This includes the whole of our intercourse! No calumny, I hope, will make him ashamed of his benevolence; and I have reaped from it such benefit, that the most cruel insinuations must not make me repent receiving it; for to whom else, except to Lady Aurora, do I owe gratitude without pain? He knows me to be indigent, my lord, yet does not conclude me open to corruption! He sees me friendless and unprotected,—yet offers me no indignity!"

Lord Melbury now, in his turn, looked pale. "Is it possible—" he cried, "Is it possible, that—" He stammered, and was in the utmost confusion.

She passed him, and was quitting the room.

"Good Heaven!" cried he, "you will not go?—you will not leave me in this manner?—not knowing what to think,—what to judge,—what to do?"

She made no answer but by hastening her footsteps, and wearing an aspect of the greatest severity; but, when her hand touched the lock, "I swear to you," he cried, "Miss Ellis, if you will not stay—I will follow you!"

Her eyes now shot forth a glance the most indignant, and she resolutely opened the door.

He spread out his arms to impede her passage.

Offended by his violence, and alarmed by this detention, she resentfully said, "If you compel me, my lord, to summon the servants—" when, upon looking at him again, she saw that his whole face was convulsed by the excess of his emotion.

She stopt.

"You must permit me," he cried, "to shut the door; and you must grant me two minutes audience."

She neither consented nor offered any opposition.

He closed the door, but she kept her place.

"Tell—speak to me, I beseech you!" he cried, "Oh clear the cruel doubts—"

"No more, my lord, no more!" interrupted Ellis, scorn taking possession of every feature; "I will neither give to myself the disgrace, nor to your lordship the shame, of permitting another word to be said!"

"What is it you mean?" cried he, planting himself against the door; "you would not—surely you would not brand me for a villain?"

She determined to have recourse to the bell, and, with the averted eyes of disdain, resolutely moved towards the chimney.

He saw her design, and cast himself upon his knees, calling out, in extreme agitation, "Miss Ellis! Miss Ellis! you will not assemble the servants to see me grovelling upon the earth?"

Greatly shocked, she desisted from her purpose. His look was aghast, his frame was in a universal tremour, and his eyes were wild and starting. Her wrath subsided at this sight, but the most conflicting emotions rent her heart.

"I see," he cried, in a tremulous voice, and almost gnashing his teeth, "I see that you have been defamed, and that I have incurred your abhorrence!—I have my own, too, completely! You cannot hate me more than I now hate—than I shrink from myself! And yet—believe me, Miss Ellis! I have no deliberate hardness of heart!—I have been led on by rash precipitance, and—and want of thought!—Believe me, Miss Ellis!—believe me, good Miss Ellis!—for I see, now, how good you are!—believe me—"

He could find no words for what he wished to say. He rose, but attempted not to approach her. Ellis leant against the wainscoat, still close to the bell, but without seeking to ring it.

Both were silent. His extreme youth, his visible inexperience, and her suspicious situation; joined to his quick repentance, and simple, but emphatic declaration, that he had no hardness of heart, began not only to offer some palliation for his conduct, but to soften her resentment into pity.

He no sooner perceived the touching melancholy which insensibly took place, in her countenance, of disgust and indignation, than, forcibly affected, he struck his forehead, exclaiming, "Oh, my poor Aurora!—when you know how ill I have acted, it will almost break your gentle heart!"

This was an apostrophe to come home quick to the bosom of Ellis: she burst into tears; and would instantly have held out to him her hand, as an offering of peace and forgiveness, had not her fear of the impetuosity of his feelings checked the impulse. She only, therefore, said, "Ah, my lord, how is it that with a sister so pure, so perfect, and whose virtues you so warmly appreciate, you should find it so difficult to believe that other females may be exempt, at least, from depravity? Alas! I had presumed, my lord, to think of you as indeed the brother of Lady Aurora; and, as such, I had even dared to consider you as a succour to me in distress, and a protector in danger!"

"Ah! consider me so again!" cried he, with sudden rapture; "good—excellent Miss Ellis! consider me so again, and you shall not repent your generous pardon!"

Ellis irresistibly wept, but, by a motion of her hand, forbad his approach.

"Fear, fear me not!" cried he, "I am a reclaimed man for the rest of my life! I have hitherto, Miss Ellis, been but a boy, and therefore so easily led wrong. But I will think and act, now, for myself.* I promise it you sincerely! Never, never more will I be the wretched tool of dishonourable impertinence! Not that I am so unmanly, as to seek any extenuation to my guilt, from its being excited by others;—no; it rather adds to its heinousness, that my own passions, violent as they sometimes are, did not give it birth. But your so visible purity, Miss Ellis, had kept them from any disrespect, believe me! And, struck as I have been with your attractions, and charmed with your conversation, it has always been without a single idea that I could not tell to Aurora herself; for as I thought of you always as of Aurora's favourite, Aurora's companion, Aurora's friend, I thought of you always together."

"Oh Lord Melbury!" interrupted Ellis, fresh tears, but of pleasure, not sorrow, gushing into her eyes; "what words are these! how penetrating to my very soul! Ah, my lord, let this unhappy morning be blotted from both our memories! and let me go back to the morning of yesterday! to a partiality that made,—and that makes me so happy! to a goodness, a kindness, that revive me with heart-consoling gratitude!"

"Oh, incomparable—Oh, best Miss Ellis!" cried Lord Melbury, in a transport of joy, and passionately advancing; but retreating nearly at the same instant, as if fearful of alarming her; and almost fastening himself against the opposite wainscoat; "how excessive is your goodness!"

A sigh from Ellis checked his rapture; and she entreated him to explain what he meant by his allusion to "others."

His complexion reddened, and he would have evaded any reply; but Ellis was too urgent to be resisted. Yet it was not without the utmost difficulty that she could prevail upon him to be explicit. Finally, however, she gathered, that Ireton, after the scene produced by the letter for L. S., had given vent to the most sneering calumnies, chiefly pointed at Harleigh, to excite the experiment of which he had himself so shamefully, yet foolishly, been the instrument. He vowed, however, that Ireton should publicly acknowledge his slanders, and beg her pardon.

Ellis earnestly besought his lordship to let the matter rest. "All public appeals," cried she, "are injurious to female fame. Generously inform Mr. Ireton, that you are convinced he has wronged me, and then leave the clearing of his own opinion to time and to truth. When they are trusted with innocence, Time and Truth never fail to do it justice."

Lord Melbury struggled to escape making any promise. His self-discontent could suggest no alleviation so satisfactory, as that of calling Mr. Ireton to account for defamation; an action which he thought would afford the most brilliant amends that could be offered to Miss Ellis, and the best proof that could blazon his own manliness. But when she solemnly assured him, that his compliance with her solicitation was the only peace-offering she could accept, for sinking into oblivion the whole morning's transaction, he forbore any further contestation.

Mrs. Greaves now brought information, that a chaise was at the door, and that a groom was in readiness. Lord Melbury timidly offered Ellis his hand, which she gracefully accepted; but neither of them spoke as he led her to the carriage.

CHAPTER XVI

FROM all the various sufferings of Ellis, through the scenes of this morning, the predominant remaining emotion, was that of pity for her penitent young offender; whom she saw so sorely wounded by a sense of his own misconduct, that he appeared to be almost impenetrable to comfort.

But all her attention was soon called to the letter of Lady Aurora.

"To Miss Ellis.

"I cannot express the grief with which I have learnt the difficulties that involve my dear Miss Ellis. Will she kindly mitigate it, by allowing me, from time to time, the consolation of offering her my sympathy? May I flatter myself that she has sufficient regard for me, to let the enclosed trifle lead the way to some little arrangement during her embarrassment? Oh! were I in similar distress, I would not hesitate to place in her a similar trust! Generously, then, sweet Miss Ellis, confide in my tender regard.

"AURORA GRANVILLE."

"At Lord Denmeath's,
Portman Square."

The "enclosed trifle" was a bank-note of twenty pounds.

Most welcome to the distress of Ellis was this kindness and this succour; and greatly she felt revived, that, severe as had been her late conflicts, they thus terminated in casting her, for all pecuniary perplexities, upon the delicate and amiable Lady Aurora.

Uncertain what might prove her reception, she desired,

upon approaching Lewes, that the groom would ride on, and enquire whether she could have the honour of seeing Mrs. Maple. The man then said, that he had a note for that lady, from Mrs. Howel.

After being detained at the gate a considerable time, a servant came to acquaint Miss Ellis, that the ladies were particularly engaged, but begged that she would walk up stairs to her room.

There, again established, she had soon a visit from Selina, who impatiently demanded, how she had parted from Lady Aurora; and, when satisfied that it had been with the extremest kindness, she warmly embraced her, before she related, that Aunt Maple had, at first, declared, that she would never, again, let so unknown a pauper into her house; but, when she had read the note of Mrs. Howel, she changed her tone. That lady had written word, that she was hastening to consign Lord Melbury and Lady Aurora to their uncle; in order to be acquitted of all responsibility, as to any continuance of this amazing acquaintance, now that, at last, she was apprized of its unfitness. She conceived that she had some claim, however, to desire, that Mrs. Maple would, for the present, receive the person as usual; since if any dismissal, or disgrace, were immediately to follow her return from Howel House, it might publish to the world what an improper character had been admitted there; a mortification from which she thought that she had some right to be exempted.

Mrs. Maple was by no means the less offended, by the pride and selfishness of this note, because those qualities were familiar to her own practice. It is the wise and good alone that make allowance for defects in others. Her resentment, however, endowed her with rancour, but not with courage; she complied, therefore, with the demand which she did not dare dispute; but her spleen against its helpless object was redoubled; and she sent her a message, by Selina, to order that she would complain of a sore throat, as an excuse for not quitting her room, nor expecting any of the ladies to visit her: yet charged her to be careful, at the same time, to say, that it was very slight, lest the people in the neighbourhood, or the servants themselves, should wonder at not seeing a physician.

Ellis could by no means repine at a separation, that saved her from the pride and malevolence of Mrs. Maple and of Ireton, and from the distressing incongruities of Elinor.

Her spirits being thus freed from immediate alarm, she was able to ruminate upon her situation, and upon what efforts she might make for its amelioration. Her letter from abroad enjoined her still to live in concealment, with respect to her name, circumstances, and story: all hope, therefore, of any speedy change was blown over; and many fears remained, that this helpless obscurity might be of long duration. It was necessary that she should form some plan, to accommodate her mode of life to her immediate condition; and to liberate, if possible, her feelings, from the continual caprices to which she was now subject.

To live upon charity, was hostile to all her notions, though the benefaction of Lady Aurora had soothed, not mortified, her proudest sensations. But Lady Aurora was not of an age to be supposed already free from controul, in the use of her income; and still less was she of a character, to resist the counsel, or even wishes of her friends. Ellis was determined not to induce her to do either: nor could she endure to give a mercenary character to a grateful affection, which languished to shew that its increase, as well as its origin, sprang from disinterested motives. All her thoughts, therefore, turned upon making the present offering suffice.

Yet she was aware how short a time she could exist upon twenty pounds; and while a residence at Mrs. Maple's would be now more than ever unpleasant, recent circumstances had rendered it, more than ever, also, unlikely.

To acquire that sort of independence, that belongs, physically, to sustaining life by her own means, was her most earnest desire. Her many accomplishments invited her industry, and promised it success; yet how to bring them into use was difficult. She had no one with whom she could consult. Elinor, though, at times, cordially her friend, seemed, in other minutes, her enraged foe. Selina was warmly good natured, but young in every sense of the word; and Mrs. Maple considered her always with such humiliating ideas, that to ask her advice would be to invite an affront.

The occupation for which she thought herself most qualified, and to which, from fondness for young people, she felt herself most inclined, was that of governess to some young lady, or ladies; and, finally, she settled, that she would endeavour to employ herself in that capacity.

This arrangement mentally made, she communicated it, in a letter of the tenderest and most grateful thanks, to Lady Aurora; entreating her ladyship's kind and valuable aid, to enable her to leave, in future, for other distressed objects, such marks of benevolence as she had last received; and to owe, personally, those, only, of esteem and regard; which she prized beyond all power of expression.

The next day, again, very unexpectedly, Selina skipt into her room. "We have had a most terrible fuss:" she cried; "Do you know Lord Melbury's come on purpose to see you!"

"Lord Melbury? Is he not gone to town?"

"Mrs. Howel wrote word so, and aunt thought so; but he only went a little way; and then came back to spend two or three days with Sir Lyell Sycamore, at Brighthelmstone. He asked after you, when he came in, and said that he begged leave to be allowed to speak with you, a few minutes, upon a commission from Lady Aurora. Aunt was quite shocked, and said, that she hoped his lordship would excuse her, but she really could not consent to any such acquaintance going on, in her house, now he knew so well what a nobody you were; if not worse. Upon which he said he did not doubt your being a well brought up young lady, for he was certain that you were modesty itself. And then he begged so hard, and said so many pretty and civil things to Aunt, that she was brought round; only it was upon condition, she said, that there should be a witness; and she proposed Mrs. Fenn. Lord Melbury was as red as fire, and said that would not be treating Miss Ellis with the respect which he was sure was her due; and he could not be so impertinent as to desire to see her, upon such terms. So, after a good deal more fuss, it was settled, at last, that Sister Elinor should be present. So now you are to come down to her dressing-room."

Ellis, though startled at the effect that might be produced by his remaining at Brighthelmstone, was sensibly touched by these public and resolute marks of his confirmed and undoubting esteem.

Elinor, presently, with restored good humour, and an air of

the most lively pleasure, came to fetch her. "Lord Melbury," she cried, "certainly adores you. You never saw a man's face of so many colours in your life, as when Aunt Maple speaks of you irreverently. If you manage well, you may be at Gretna Green in a week."

They descended, without any answer made by Ellis, to the dressing-room.

The air of Lord Melbury was far less dejected than when they had last parted; yet it had by no means regained its natural spring and vivacity; and he advanced to pay his compliments to Ellis, with a look of even studious deference. He would detain her, he said, but a few minutes; yet could not leave the country, without informing her of two visits, which he had made the day before: both of which had ended precisely with the amity that she had wished.

Elinor, enchanted in believing, from this opening, that a confidential intercourse was already arranged, declared, that her aunt must look elsewhere for a spy, as she would by no means play that part; and then ran into the adjoining room. Lord Melbury and Ellis would have detained, but could not follow her, as it was her bed-chamber.

Lord Melbury then, who saw that Ellis was uneasy, promised to be quick. "I demanded," said he, "yesterday, an interview with Mr. Harleigh. I told him, without reserve, all that had passed. I cannot paint to you the indignation he shewed at the aspersions of Ireton. He determined to go to him directly, and I resolved to accompany him.—Don't look pale, Miss Ellis: I repeated to Mr. Harleigh the promise you had exacted from me, and he confessed himself to be perfectly of your opinion, that all angry defence, or public resentment, must necessarily, in such a case, be injurious. Yet to let the matter drop, might expose you to fresh abominations. Ireton received us with a mixture of curiosity and carelessness; very inquisitive to know what had passed, but very indifferent whether it were good or bad. We both, by agreement, affected to treat the matter lightly, gravely as we both thought of it: I thanked him, therefore, for the salutary counsel, by which he had urged me to procure myself so confounded a rap of the knuckles, for my assurance; and Mr. Harleigh made his acknowledgements in the same tone, for the compliment paid to his liberality, of supposing that a person, who, in any manner, should be thought under his protection, could be in a state of penury. We both, I hope, made him ashamed. He had not, he owned, reflected deeply upon the subject; for which, Mr. Harleigh told me, afterwards, there was a very cogent reason, namely, that he did not know how! Mr. Harleigh, when we were coming away, forcibly said, 'Ireton, placing Lord Melbury and myself wholly apart in this business, ask your own sagacity, I beg, how a female, who is young, beautiful, and accomplished, can suffer from pecuniary distress, if her character be not unimpeachable?' Upon that, struck with the truth of the remark, he voluntarily protested that he would make you all the amends in his power. So ended our visit; and I cannot but hope that it will release you from all similar persecutions."

Ellis expressed her sincere and warm gratitude; and Lord Melbury, with an air of penetrated respect, took his leave; evidently much solaced, by the consciousness of serving one whom he had injured.

Ellis had every reason to be gratified by this attention, which set her mind wholly at rest upon the tenour of Lord Melbury's regard: while Elinor was so much delighted, to find the acquaintance advance so rapidly to confidence, that she embraced Ellis, wished her joy, mocked all replies of a disclaiming nature, and, accompanying her back to her room, made her a long, social, lively, and entertaining visit; hearing and talking over her project of becoming a governess, but laughing at it, as a ridiculous idea, for the decided wife elect of Earl Melbury.

She was succeeded by Selina, who exultingly came to acquaint Ellis, that Mr. Ireton had just made a formal renunciation of all ill opinion of her; and had told Mrs. Maple, that he had indubitable proofs that she was a person of the very strictest character. "So now," cried she, "Lady Aurora and I may vow our friendship to you for life."

This was a very solid satisfaction to Ellis, to whom the calumny of Ireton had been almost insupportable. She now hoped that Mrs. Maple would favour her new scheme, and that she might remain tranquilly in the house till it took place; and equip herself, from the donation of Lady Aurora, for her immediate appearance in the situation which she sought. She resolved to seize the first opportunity for returning Harleigh his bank notes, and the Miss Joddrels their half-guineas. She wished, also, to repay the guinea of the worthy Admiral, and to repeat to him her grateful acknowledgements: his name and address she concluded that she might learn from Harleigh; but she deferred this satisfaction till more secure of success.

The next day, Selina ran upstairs to her again. "Who do you think," she cried, "came into the parlour in the middle of breakfast? Mr. Dennis Harleigh! He arrived at Brighthelmstone last night. Sister Elinor turned quite white, and never spoke to him; she only just made a sort of bow to his asking how she did, and then swallowed her tea burning hot, and left the room. He can stay only one day, for he must be in London to-morrow night. He is come for his final answer; for he's quite out of patience."

Selina had hardly descended the stairs, when Elinor herself mounted them. She entered the chamber precipitately, her face colourless, and her eyes starting from her head. "Ellis!" she cried, "I must speak with you!"

She seated herself, made Ellis sit exactly opposite to her, and went on: "There are two things which I want to say to you; or, rather, to demand of you. Have you fortitude enough to tell truth, even though it should wound your self-love? and honour enough to be trusted with a commission a thousand times more important than life or death? and to execute it faithfully,—though at the risk of seeing the greatest idiot that ever existed, shew sufficient symptoms of sense to run mad?"

Alarmed by her ghastly look, and frightened at the abruptness of questions utterly incomprehensible, Ellis gently entreated to be spared any request with which she could not comply.

"I do not mean," cried Elinor, with quickness, "to make any call upon your confidence, or to put any fetters upon your conduct. You will be as free after you have spoken as before. I want merely to ascertain a fact, of which my ignorance distracts me! If you have to give me a negative, your vanity alone can suffer; if an affirmative——" She put her hand upon her forehead, and then rapidly added,—"the suffering will not be yours!—give it, therefore, boldly! 'Twill be heaven to me to end this suspense, be it how it may!"

Starting up, but preventing Ellis from rising, by laying a hand upon each of her shoulders, she gazed upon her eyes with a fixed stare, of almost frantic impatience, and said, "Speak! say Yes, or No, at once! Give me no phrase—Let me see no hesitation!—Kill me, or restore me to life!—Has Harleigh—" she gasped for breath—"ever made you any declaration?"

"None!" steadily, forcibly, and instantly Ellis answered.

"Enough!" cried she, recovering some composure.

She then walked up and down the room, involuntarily smiling, and her lips in a motion, that shewed that she was talking to herself. Then stopping, and taking Ellis by the hand, and half laughing, "You will think me," she cried, "crazy; but I assure you I had never a more exquisite enjoyment of my senses. I see every thing to urge, and nothing to oppose my following the bent of my own humour; or, in other words, throwing off the trammels of unmeaning custom, and acting, as well as thinking, for myself."

Again, then, walking up and down the chamber, she pursued her new train of ideas, with a glee which manifested that she found them delightful.

"My dear Ellis," she cried, presently, "have you ever chanced to hear of such a person as Dennis Harleigh?"

Ellis wished to avoid answering this question, on account of her informant, Selina; but her embarrassment was answer sufficient. "I see yes!" cried Elinor, "I see that you have heard of that old story. Don't be frightened," added she, laughing, "I am not going to ask who blabbed it. I had as lieve it were one impertinent fool as another. Only never imagine me of the tribe of sentimental pedants, who think it a disgrace to grow wiser; or who suppose that they must abide by their first opinions, for fear the world should know, that they think twice upon one subject. For what is changing one's mind, but taking the *pro* one time, and the *con* another?"

"But come," continued she, "this is no time for rattling. Two years I have existed upon speculation; I must now try how I shall fare upon practice. Is it not just, Ellis, that it should be you who should drag me out of the slough of despond,* since it was you who flung me into it?—However, now for your commission. Do you feel as if you could execute it with spirit?"

"With willingness, certainly, if I see any chance of success."

"No ifs, Ellis. I hate the whole tribe of dubiosity.* However, that you may not make any blunder, I shall tell you my story myself; for all that you have heard from others, you must set down to ignorance or prejudice. Nobody knows my feelings, and nobody understands my reasons. So every body is at war against me in the dark."

"Now hearken!"

"Just as I came of age, and ought to have shaken off the shackles of Aunt Maple, and to have enjoyed my independence and my fortune together, accident brought into my way a young lawyer—this Dennis Harleigh—of great promise in the only profession in the world that gives wit fair play. And I thought him, then,—mark me, Ellis, then!—of a noble appearance. He delighted to tell me his causes, state their merits, and ask my opinions. I always took the opposite side to that which he was employed to plead, in order to try his powers, and prove my own. The French Revolution had just then burst forth, into that noble flame that nearly consumed the old world, to raise a new one, phœnix like, from its ashes. Soon tired of our every day subjects and contests, I began canvassing with him the Rights of Man.* He had fallen desperately in love with me, either for my wit or my fortune, or both; and therefore all topics were sure to be approved. Enchanted with a warfare in which I was certain to be always victorious, I grew so fond of conquest, that I was never satisfied but when combating; and the joy I experienced in the display of my own talents, made me doat upon his sight. The truth is, our mutual vanity mutually deceived us: he saw my pleasure in his company, and concluded that it was personal regard: I found nothing to rouse the energies of my faculties in his absence, and imagined myself enamoured of my vanquished antagonist. Aunt Maple did her little best—for every thing she does is little—to forward the connexion; because, though his fortune is trifling, his proffessional expectations are high; and though he is a younger brother, he is born of a noble family: and that sort of mean old stuff is always in her head; for if the whole world were revolutionized, you could never make her conceive a new idea. And the great fact of all is, she cannot bear I should leave her house before I marry, because, she is sure, in one of my own, I shall adopt some new system of life. Thus, in the toils of my self-love, I became entangled; poor Dennis called himself the happiest of men; the settlements were all drawn up; and we were looking about us for a house to our fancy, and all that sort of stuff, when Dennis introduced his family to us.—Now the rest, I suppose, you can divine?"

This was, indeed, not difficult; but Ellis durst not risk any reply.

With a rapidity scarcely intelligible, and in a manner wholly incoherent, she then went on: "Ellis, I pretend not to any mystery. Why is one person adorable, and another detestable, but to call forth our love and our hatred? to give birth to all that snatches us from mere inert existence; to our passions, our energies, our noblest conceptions of all that is towering and sublime? Whether you have any idea of this mental enlargement I cannot tell; but with it I see human nature endowed with capabilities immeasurable of perfection; and without it, I regard and treat the whole of my race as the mere dramatis personæ of a farce; of which I am myself, when performing with such fellow-actors, a principal buffoon."

Nearly out of breath, she stopt a moment; then, looking earnestly at Ellis, said, "Do you understand me?"

Ellis, in a fearful accent, answered, "I ... I am not quite sure."

"Remove your doubts, then!" cried she, impatiently; "I despise what is obscure, still more than I hate what is false. Falsehood may at least approach to that degree of grandeur which belongs to crime; but obscurity is always mean, always seeking some subterfuge, always belonging to art."

Again she stopt; but Ellis, uncertain whether this remark were meant to introduce her confidence, or to censure her own secresy, waited an explanation in silence. Elinor was evidently, however, embarrassed, though anxious to persuade herself, as well as Ellis, that she was perfectly at her ease. She walked a quick pace up and down the room; then stopt, seemed pausing, hemmed to clear her voice for speech; and then walked backwards and forwards before the window, which she frequently opened and shut, without seeming to know that she touched it; till, at length, seized with sudden indignation against herself, for this failure of courage, she energetically exclaimed, "How paltry is shame where there can be no disgrace!—I disdain it!—disclaim it!—and am ready to avow to the whole world, that I dare speak and act, as well as think and feel for myself!"

Yet, even thus buoyed up, thus full fraught with defiance, something within involuntarily, invincibly checked her, and she hastily resumed her walks and her ruminations.

"What amazing, unaccountable fools," she cried, "have we all been for these quantities of centuries! Worlds seem to have a longer infancy taken out of the progress of their duration, even than the long imbecility of the childhood of poor mortals. But for the late glorious revolutionary shake given to the universe, I should, at this very moment, from mere cowardly conformity, be the wife of Dennis!—In spite of my repentance of the engagement, in spite of the aversion I have taken to him, and in spite of the contempt I have conceived—with one single exception—for the whole race of mankind, I must have been that poor man's despicable wife!—O despicable indeed! For with what sentiments could I have married him? Where would have been my soul while I had given him my hand? Had I not seen—known—adored—his brother!"

She stopt, and the deepest vermillion overspread her face; her effort was made; she had boasted of her new doctrine, lest she should seem impressed with confusion from the old one which she violated; but the struggle being over, the bravado and exultation subsided; female consciousness and native shame took their place; and abashed, and unable to meet the eyes of Ellis, she ran out of the room.

In the whole of this scene, Ellis observed, with mingled censure and pity, the strong conflict in the mind of Elinor, between ungoverned inclination, which sought new systems for its support; and an innate feeling of what was due to the sex that she was braving, and the customs that she was scorning.

She soon re-appeared, but with a wholly new air; lively, disengaged, almost sportive. Her heart was lightened by unburthening her secret; the feminine delicacies which opposed the discovery, once broken through, oppressed her no more; and the idea of passing, now, straight forward, to the purposes for which she had done herself this violence, re-animated her spirit, and gave new vigour to her faculties.

She laughed at herself for having run away, without explaining the meaning of her communication; and for charging Ellis with a commission, of which she had not made known even the nature. She then more clearly stated her situation.

From the time of her first interview with Albert, her whole mind had recoiled from all thought of union with his brother; yet the affair was so far advanced, and she saw herself so completely regarded by Albert as a sister, though treated by him with an openness, a frankness, and an affection the most captivating, that she had not courage to proclaim her change of sentiment.

The conflict of her mind, during this doubting state, threatened to cast her into a consumption. She was ordered to the south of France. And there, happily arrived, new scenes,—a new world, rather, opened to her a code of new ideas, that soon, she said, taught her to scoff at idle misery: and might even, from the occupation given to her feelings, by the glorious confusion, and mad wonders around her, have recovered her from the thraldom of an over-ruling propensity, had not Dennis, unable, from professional engagements, to quit his country, been so blind, upon hearing that her health was re-established, as to persuade his brother to cross the Channel, in order to escort the two travellers home. From the moment, the fated moment, that Albert arrived to be her guide and her guard, he became so irresistibly the master of her heart, that her destiny was determined. Whether good or ill, she knew not yet; but it was fixed. Ill had not occurred to her sanguine expectations, nor doubt, nor fear, till the eventful meeting with Ellis: till then, she had believed her happiness secure, for she had supposed that nothing stood in her way, save a little brotherly punctilio. But, since the junction of Ellis, the spontaneous interest which Albert had taken in her fate, and her affairs, had appeared to be so marvellous, that, at every new view of his pity, his respect, or his admiration, she was seized with the most uneasy feelings; which sometimes worked her up into pangs of excruciating jealousy; and, at others, seemed to be so ill founded, that, recollecting a thousand instances of his general benevolence, she laughed her own surmises to scorn. How the matter still stood, with regard to his heart, she confessed herself unable to form any permanent judgment. The time, however, was now, happily, arrived, to abolish suspense, for even Dennis, now, could bear it no longer. She expected, she said, a desperate scene, but, at least, it would be a final one. She had only, for many months past, been restrained from giving Dennis his dismission, lest Albert should drop all separate acquaintance, from the horrour of seeming treacherously to usurp the place of his brother. Nevertheless, she would frankly have ended her disturbance, by an avowal of the truth, had not Albert been the eldest brother, and, consequently, the richest; and the disgraceful supposition, that she might be influenced to desire the change from mercenary motives, would have had power to yoke her to Dennis, for the rest of her weary existence, had not her mind been so luminously opened to its own resources, and inherent right of choice, by her continental excursion.

"The grand effect," she continued, "of beholding so many millions of men, let loose from all ties, divine or human, gave such play to my fancy, such a range to my thoughts, and brought forth such new, unexpected, and untried combinations to my reason, that I frequently felt as if just created, and ushered into the world—not, perhaps, as wise as another Minerva,* but equally formed to view and to judge all around me, without the gradations of infancy, childhood, and youth, that hitherto have prepared for maturity. Every thing now is upon a new scale, and man appears to be worthy of his faculties; which, during all these past ages, he has set aside, as if he could do just as well without them; holding it to be his bounden duty, to be trampled to the dust, by old rules and forms, because all his papas and uncles were trampled so before him. However, I should not have troubled myself, probably, with any of these abstruse notions, had they not offered me a new road for life, when the old one was worn out. To find that all was novelty and regeneration throughout the finest country in the universe, soon infected me with the system-forming spirit; and it was then that I conceived the plan I am now going to execute; but I shall not tell it you in its full extent, as I am uncertain what may be your strength of mind for measures of force and character; and perhaps they may not be necessary. So now to your commission.

"I am fixed to cast wholly aside the dainty common barriers, which shut out from female practice all that is elevated, or even natural. Dennis, therefore, shall know that I hate him; Albert ... Ah, Ellis! that I hate him not!

"My operations are to commence thus: Act I. Scene I. Enter Ellis, seeking Albert. Don't stare so; I know perfectly well what I am about. Scene II. Albert and Ellis meet. Ellis informs him that she must hold a confabulation with him the next day; and desires that he will remain at Lewes to be at hand.—"

"Oh, Miss Joddrel!" interrupted Ellis, "you must, at least, give me leave to say, that it is by your command that I make a request so extraordinary!"

"By no means. He must not suspect that I have any knowledge of your intention. The truth, like an explosion of thunder, shall burst upon his head at once. So only shall I truly know whether it will shake him with dismay—or magnetize* him by its sublimity."

"Yet how, Madam, under what pretence, can I take such a liberty?"

"Pho, pho; this is no time for delicate demurs. If he be not engaged to stay before I turn his brother adrift, he will accompany him to town, as a thing of course, to console him in his willowed* state. The rest of my plot is not yet quite ripe for disclosure. But all is arranged. And though I know not whether the catastrophe will be tragic or comic, I am prepared in my part for either."

She then went away.

CHAPTER XVII

ELINOR returned almost instantly. "Hasten, hasten," she cried, "Ellis! There is no time to be lost. Scene the first is all prepared. Albert Harleigh, at this very moment, is poring over the county map in the hall. Run and tell him that you have something of deep importance to communicate to him to-morrow."

"But may he not—if he means to go—desire to hear it immediately?"

Elinor, without answering, forced her away. Harleigh, whose back was to the stair-entrance, seemed intently examining some route. The distress of Ellis was extreme how to call for his notice, and how to execute her commission when it should be obtained. Slowly and unwillingly approaching a little nearer, "I am afraid," she hesitatingly said, "that I must appear extremely importunate, but—"

The astonishment with which he turned round, at the sound of her voice, could only be equalled by the pleasure with which he met her eyes; and only surpassed, by the sudden burst of clashing ideas with which he saw her own instantly drop; while her voice, also, died away; her cheeks became the colour of crimson; and she was evidently and wholly at a loss what to say.

"Importunate?" he gently repeated, "impossible!" yet he waited her own explanation.

Her confusion now became deeper; any sort of interrogation would have encouraged and aided her; but his quiet, though attentive forbearance seemed the result of some suspension of opinion. Ashamed and grieved, she involuntarily looked away, as she indistinctly pronounced, "I must appear .... very strange .... but I am constrained .... Circumstances of which I am not the mistress, force me to .... desire—to request—that to-morrow morning—or any part of to-morrow .... it might be possible that I could .... or rather that you should be able to .... to hear something that .... that ...."

The total silence with which he listened, shewed so palpably his expectation of some competent reason for so singular an address, that her inability to clear herself, and her chagrin in the idea of forfeiting any part of an esteem which had proved so often her protection, grew almost insupportably painful, and she left her phrase unfinished: yet considered her commission to be fulfilled, and was moving away.

"To-morrow," he said, "I meant to have accompanied my brother, whose affairs—whatever may be his fate—oblige him to return to town: but if .... if to-morrow—"

He had now, to impede her retreat, stept softly between her and the stair-case, and perceived, in her blushes, the force which she had put upon her modesty; and read, in the expression of her glistening eyes, that an innate sense of delicacy was still more wounded, by the demand which she had made, even than her habits of life. With respect, therefore, redoubled, and an interest beyond all calculation increased, he went on; "If to-morrow .... or next day—or any part of the week, you have any commands for me, nothing shall hurry me hence till they are obeyed."

Comforted to find herself treated with unabated consideration, however shocked to have the air of detaining him purposely for her own concerns, she was courtsying her thanks, when she caught a glance of Elinor on the stairs, in whose face, every passion seemed with violence at work.

Ellis changed colour, not knowing how to proceed, or how to stop. The alteration in her countenance made Harleigh look round, and discern Elinor; yet so pre-occupied was his attention, that he was totally unmindful of her situation, and would have addressed her as usual, had she not abruptly remounted the stairs.

Harleigh would then have asked some directions, relative to the time and manner of the purposed communication; but Ellis instantly followed Elinor; leaving him in a state of wonder, expectation, yet pleasure indescribable; fully persuaded that she meant to reveal the secret of her name and her history; and forming conjectures that every moment varied, yet every moment grew more interesting, of her motives for such a confidence.

Ellis found Elinor already in her chamber, and, apparently, in the highest, though evidently most factitious spirits: not, however, feigned to deceive Ellis, but falsely and forcibly elated to deceive, or, at least, to animate herself. "This is enchanting!" she cried, "this is delectable! this is every thing that I could wish! I shall now know the truth! All the doubts, all the difficulties, that have been crazing me for some time past, will now be solved: I shall discover whether his long patience in waiting my determination, has been for your sake, or for mine. He will not go hence, till he has obeyed your commands!—Is he glad of a pretence to stay on my account? or impelled irresistibly upon yours? I shall now know all, all, all!"

The lengthened stay of Albert being thus, she said, ascertained, she should send Dennis about his business, without the smallest ceremony.

What she undertook, she performed. Early in the evening she again visited Ellis, exultingly to make known to her, that Dennis was finally dismissed. She had assigned no reason, she said, for her long procrastination, reserving that for his betters, alias Albert; but she had been so positive and clear in announcing her decision, and assuring him that it proceeded from a most sincere and unalterable dislike, both to his person and mind, that he had shewn spirit enough to be almost respectable, having immediately ordered his horse, taken his leave of Aunt Maple, and set off upon his journey. Albert, meanwhile, had said, that he had business to transact at Brighthelmstone, which might detain him some days; and had accepted an invitation to sleep at Lewes, during that period, from poor Aunt Maple; whose provocation and surprise at all that had passed were delightful.

"To-morrow morning, therefore," she continued, "will decide my fate. What, hitherto, Albert has thought of me, he is probably as ignorant as I am myself; for while he has considered me as the property of his brother, his pride is so scrupulous, and his scruples are so squeamish, that he would deem it a crime of the first magnitude, to whisper, even in his own ear, How should I like her for myself? He is suspicious of some sophistry in whatever is not established by antiquated rules; and, with all his wisdom, and all his superiority, he is constantly anxious not to offend that conceited old prejudice, that thinks it taking a liberty with human nature, to suppose that any man can be so indecent as to grow up wiser, or more knowing, than his grandpapa was before him.

"Trifling, however, apart, all my real alarm is to fathom what his feelings are for you! Are they but of compassion, playing upon a disengaged mind? If nothing further, the awakening a more potent sentiment will plant them in their proper line of subordination. This is what remains to be tried. He has not made you any declaration; he is free, therefore, from any entanglement: his brother is discharged, and for ever out of the question; he knows me, therefore, also, to be liberated from all engagement. When I said that you had given me life, I did not mean, that merely to hear that nothing had yet passed, was enough to secure my happiness:—Ah no!—but simply that it inspired me with a hope that gives me courage to resolve upon seeking certitude. And now, hear me!

"The second act of the comedy, tragedy, or farce, of my existence, is to be represented to-morrow. The first scene will be a conference between Ellis and Albert, in which Ellis will relate the history of Elinor."

Suddenly, then, looking at her, with an air the most authoritative, "Ellis!" she added, "there is one article to which you must answer this moment! Would you, should the choice be in your power, sacrifice Lord Melbury to Harleigh? No hesitation!"

"Miss Joddrel," answered Ellis, solemnly, "I have neither the hope, nor the fear, that belongs to what might be called sacrifice relative to either of them: I earnestly desire to preserve the esteem of Mr. Harleigh; and the urbanity—I can call it by no other name—of Lord Melbury; but I am as free from the thought as from the presumption, of expecting, or coveting, to engage any personal, or particular regard, from either."

Elinor, appeased, said, "You are such a compound of mystery, that one extraordinary thing is not more difficult to credit in you, than another. My design, as you will find, in making you speak instead of myself, is a stroke of Machievalian policy; for it will finish both suspences at once; since if, when you talk to him of me, he thinks only of my agent, how will he refrain, in answering your embassy, to betray himself? If, on the contrary, when he finds his scruples removed about his brother, he should feel his heart penetrated by the cause of that brother's dismission—Ah Ellis!—But let us not anticipate act the third. The second alone can decide, whether it will conclude the piece with an epithalamium—or a requiem!"*

She then disappeared.

Ellis saw her no more till the next morning, when, entering the chamber, breathless with haste and agitation, "The moment," she cried, "is come! I have sent out Aunt Maple, and Selina, upon visits for the whole morning; and I have called Harleigh into my dressing-room. There, wondering, he waits; I shall introduce you, and wait, in my turn, till, in ten minutes' time, you follow, to give me the argument of the third and last act of my drama."

Ellis, alarmed at what might be the result, would again have supplicated to be excused; but Elinor, proudly saying, "Fear no consequences for me! Those who know truly how to love, know how to die, as well as how to live!" forcibly dragged her down to the dressing-room; through which she instantly passed herself, with undisguised trepidation, to her inner apartment.

The astonishment of Harleigh was inexpressible; and Ellis, who had received no positive directions, felt wholly at a loss what she was to relate, how far she ought to go, and what she ought to require. Hastily, therefore, and affrighted at her task, she tapped at the bed-room door, and begged a moment's audience. Elinor opened it, in the greatest consternation. "What!" cried she, taking her to the window, "is all over, without a word uttered?"

No; Ellis answered; she merely wished for more precise commands what she should say.

"Say?" cried Elinor, reviving, "say that I adore him! That since the instant I have seen him, I have detested his brother; that he alone has given me any idea of what is perfection in human nature! And that, if the whole world were annihilated, and he remained ... I should think my existence divine!"

She then pushed her back, prohibiting any reply.

Harleigh, to whom all was incomprehensible, but whose expectations every moment grew higher, of the explanation he so much desired, perceiving the embarrassment of Ellis, gently advanced, and said, "Shall I be guilty of indiscretion, if I seize this hurried, yet perhaps only moment, to express my impatience for a communication of which I have thought, almost exclusively, from the moment I have had it in view? Must it be deferred? or—"

"No; it admits of no delay. I have much to say—and I am allowed but ten minutes—"

"You have much to say?" cried he, delighted; "ten minutes to-day may be followed by twenty, thirty, as many as you please, to-morrow,—and after to-morrow,—and whenever you command."

"You are very good, Sir, but my commission admits as little of extension as of procrastination. It must be as brief as it will be abrupt."

"Your commission?" he repeated, in a tone of disappointment.

"Yes; I am charged by ... by ... by a lady whom I need not name—to say that ... that your brother—"

She stopt, ashamed to proceed.

"I can have no doubt," said he, gravely, "that Miss Joddrel is concerned, for the length of time she has wasted in trifling with his feelings; but this is all the apology her conduct requires: the breach of the engagement, when once she was convinced, that her attachment was insufficient to make the union as desirable to herself as to him, was certainly rather a kindness than an injury."

"Yes,—but, her motives—her reasons—"

"I conceive them all! she wanted courage to be sooner decided; she apprehended reproach—and she gathered force to make her change of sentiments known, only when, otherwise, she must have concealed it for ever.—Pardon this presumptuous anticipation!" added he, smiling; "but when you talk to me of only ten minutes, how can I suffer them to be consumed in a commission?"

He spoke in a low tone, yet, Ellis, excessively alarmed, pointed expressively to the chamber-door. In a tone, then, still softer, he continued: "I have been anxious to speak to you of Lord Melbury, and to say something of the indignation with which I heard, from him, of the atrocious behaviour of Ireton. Nothing less than the respect I feel for you, could have deterred me from shewing him the resentment I feel for myself. I should not, however, have been your only champion; Lord Melbury was equally incensed; but we both acknowledged that our interests and our feelings ought to be secondary to yours, and by yours to be regulated. The matter, therefore, is at an end. Ireton is convinced that he has done you wrong; and, as he never meant to be your enemy, and has no study but his own amusement, we must pity his want of taste, and hope that the disgrace necessarily hanging upon detected false assertion, may be a lesson not lost upon him. Yet he deserves one far more severe. He is a pitiful egotist,* who seeks nothing but his own diversion; indifferent whose peace, comfort, or reputation pays its purchase."

"I am infinitely obliged," said Ellis, "that you will suffer the whole to drop; but I must not do the same by my commission!—You must let me, now, enter more particularly upon my charge, and tell you—"

"Forgive, forgive me!" cried he, eagerly; "I comprehend all that Miss Joddrel can have to say. But my impatience is irrepressible upon a far different subject; one that awakens the most lively interest, that occupies my thoughts, that nearly monopolizes my memory; and that exhausts—yet never wearies my conjectures.—That letter you were so good as to mention to me?—and the plan you may at length decide to pursue?—permit me to hope, that the communication you intend me, has some reference to those points?"

"I should be truly glad of your counsel, Sir, in my helpless situation: but I am not at this moment at liberty to speak of myself;—Miss Joddrel—"

Her embarrassment now announced something extraordinary; but it was avowedly not personal, and Harleigh eagerly besought her to be expeditious.

"You must make me so, then," cried she, "by divining what I have to reveal!"

"Does Miss Joddrel relent?—Will she give me leave to summon my brother back?"

"Oh no! no! no!—far otherwise. Your brother has been indifferent to her .... ever since she has known him as such!"

She thought she had now said enough; but Harleigh, whose faculties were otherwise engaged, waited for further explanation.

"Can you not," said Ellis, "or will you not, divine the reason of the change?"

"I have certainly," he answered, "long observed a growing insensibility; but still—"

"And have you never," said Ellis, deeply blushing, "seen, also,—its reverse?"

This question, and yet more the manner in which it was made, was too intelligible to admit of any doubt. Harleigh, however, was far from elated as the truth opened to his view: he looked grave and disturbed, and remained for some minutes profoundly silent. Ellis, already ashamed of the indelicacy of her office, could not press for any reply.

"I am hurt," he at length said, "beyond all measure, by what you intimate; but since Miss Joddrell has addressed you thus openly, there can be no impropriety in my claiming leave, also, to speak to you confidentially."

"Whatever you wish me to say to her, Sir,——"

"And much that I do not wish you to say to her," cried he, half smiling, "I hope you will hear yourself! and that then, you will have the goodness, according to what you know of her intentions and desire, to palliate what you may deem necessary to repeat."

"Ah, poor Miss Joddrell!" said Ellis, in a melancholy tone, "and is this the success of my embassy?"

"Did you, then, wish—" Harleigh began, with a quickness of which he instantly felt the impropriety, and changed his phrase into, "Did you, then, expect any other?"

"I was truly sorry to be entrusted with the commission."

"I easily conceive, that it is not such a one as you would have given! but there is a dangerous singularity in the character of Miss Joddrel, that makes her prone to devote herself to whatever is new, wild, or uncommon. Even now, perhaps, she conceives that she is the champion of her sex, in shewing it the road,—a dangerous road!—to a new walk in life. Yet,—these eccentricities set apart,—how rare are her qualities! how powerful is her mind! how sportive her fancy! and how noble is her superiority to every species of art or artifice!"

"Yet, with all this," said Ellis, looking at him expressively, "with all this . . ." she knew not how to proceed; but he saw her meaning. "With all this," he said, "you are surprised, perhaps, that I should look for other qualities, other virtues in her whom I should aspire to make the companion of my life? I beseech you, however, to believe, that neither insolence nor ingratitude makes me insensible to her worth; but, though it often meets my admiration, sometimes my esteem, and always my good will and regard, it is not of a texture to create that sympathy without which even friendship is cold. I have, indeed, ... till now . . . ."

He paused.

"Poor, poor Miss Joddrel!" exclaimed Ellis, "If you could but have heard,—or if I knew but how to repeat, even the millioneth part of what she thinks of you!—of the respect with which she is ready to yield to your opinions; of the enthusiasm with which she honours your character; of the devotion with which she nearly worships you—"

She stopt short, ashamed; and as fearful that she had been now too urgent, as before that she had been too cold.

Harleigh heard her with considerable emotion. "I hope," he said, "your feelings, like those of most minds gifted with strong sensibility, have taken the pencil, in this portrait, from your cooler judgment? I should be grieved, indeed, to suppose—but what can a man suppose, what say, upon a subject so delicate that may not appear offensive? Suffer me, therefore, to drop it; and have the goodness to let that same sensibility operate in terminating, in such a manner as may be least shocking to her, all view, and all thought, that I ever could, or ever can, entertain the most distant project of supplanting my brother."

"Will you not, at least, speak to her yourself?"

"I had far rather speak to you!—Yet certainly yes, if she desire it."

"Give me leave, then, to say," cried Ellis, moving towards the bed-room door, "that you request an audience."

"By no means! I merely do not object to it. You may easily conceive what pain I shall be spared, if it may be evaded. All I request, is a few moments with you! Hastily, therefore, let me ask, is your plan decided?"

"To the best of my power,—of my ideas, rather,—yes. But, indeed, I must not thus abandon my charge!"

"And will you not let me enquire what it is?"

"There is one thing, only, in which I have any hope that my exertions may turn to account; I wish to offer myself as a governess to some young lady, or ladies."

"I beseech you," cried he, with sudden fervour, "to confide to me the nature of your situation! I know well I have no claim; I seem to have even no pretext for such a request; yet there are sometimes circumstances that not only excuse, but imperiously demand extraordinary measures: perhaps mine, at this moment, are of that sort! perhaps I am at a loss what step to take, till I know to whom I address myself!"

"O Sir!" cried Ellis, holding up her hands in act of supplication, "you will be heard!"

Harleigh, conscious that he had been off all guard, silenced himself immediately, and walked hastily to the window.

Ellis knew not whether to retire, at once, to her own room; or to venture into that of Elinor; or to require any further answer. This last, however, Harleigh seemed in no state to give: he leant his forehead upon his hand, and remained wrapt in thought.

Ellis, struck by a manner which shewed that he felt, and, apparently, repented, the possible meaning that his last words might convey, was now as much ashamed for herself as for Elinor; and not wishing to meet his eyes, glided softly back to her chamber.

Here, whatever might be the fulness of her mind, she was not allowed an instant for reflection: Elinor followed her immediately.

She shut the door, and walked closely up to her. Ellis feared to behold her; yet saw, by a glance, that her eyes were sparkling, and that her face was dressed in smiles. "This is a glorious day for me!" she cried; "'tis the pride of my life to have brought such a one into the history of my existence!"

Ellis officiously got her a chair; arranged the fire; examined if the windows were well closed; and sought any occupation, to postpone the moment of speaking to, or looking at her.

She was not offended; she did not appear to be hurried; she seemed enchanted with her own ideas; yet she had a strangeness in her manner that Ellis thought extremely alarming.

"Well," she cried, when she had taken her seat, and saw that Ellis could find no further pretext for employing herself in the little apartment; "what garb do you bring me? How am I to be arrayed?"

Ellis begged to know what she meant.

"Is it a wedding-garment?" replied she, gaily; "or . . . ." abruptly changing her tone into a deep hoarse whisper, "a shroud?"*

Ellis, shuddering, durst not answer. Elinor, catching her hand, said, "Don't be frightened! I am at this moment equal to whatever may be my destiny: I am at a point of elevation, that makes my fate nearly indifferent to me. Speak, therefore! but only to the fact. I have neither time nor humour for narratory delays. I tried to hear you; but you both talked so whisperingly, that I could not make out a sentence."

"Indeed, Miss Joddrel," said Ellis, trembling violently, "Mr. Harleigh's regard—his affection—"

"Not a word of that trite class!" cried Elinor, with sudden severity, "if you would not again work all my passions into inflammation, involve me no more in doubt! Fear nothing else. I am no where else vulnerable. Set aside, then, all childish calculations, of giving me an inch or two more, or an inch or two less of pain,—and be brief and true!"

Ellis could not utter a word: every phrase she could suggest seemed to teem with danger; yet she felt that her silence could not but indicate the truth which it sought to hide; she hung her head, and sighed in disturbed perplexity. Elinor looked at her for some time with an examining eye, and then, hastily rising, emphatically exclaimed, "You are mute?—I see, then, my doom! And I shall meet it with glory!"

Smiles triumphant, but wild, now played about her face. "Ellis," she cried, "go to your work, or whatever you were about, and take no manner of heed of me. I have something of importance to arrange, and can brook no interruption."

Ellis acquiesced, returning to the employment of her needle, for which Mrs. Fenn took especial care that she should never lack materials.

Elinor spoke to her no more; but her ruminations, though undisturbed by her companion, were by no means quiet, or silent. She paced hastily up and down the room; sat, in turn, upon a chair, a window seat, and the bed; talked to herself, sometimes with a vehemence that made several detached words, though no sentences, intelligible; sometimes in softer accents, and with eyes and gestures of exultation; and, frequently, she went into a corner by the side of the window, where she looked, in secret, at something in a shagrin case* that she held in her hand, and had brought out of her chamber; and to which she occasionally addressed herself, with a fervency that shook her whole frame, and with expressions which, though broken, and half pronounced, denoted that she considered it as something sacred.

At length, with an air of transport, she exclaimed, "Yes! that will produce the best effect! what an ideot have I been to hesitate!" then, turning with quickness to Ellis: "Ellis," she cried, "I have withheld from any questions relative to yourself, because I abominate all subterfuge; but you will not suppose I am contented with my ignorance? You will not imagine it a matter of indifference to me, to know how I have failed?"

She reddened; passion took possession of every feature, and for a moment nearly choaked her voice: she again walked, with rapid motion, about the room, and then ejaculated, "Let me be patient! let me not take away all grandeur from my despair, and reduce it to mere common madness!— Let me wait the fated moment, and then—let the truth burst, blaze, and flame, till it devour me!"

"Ellis," she presently added, "find Harleigh; tell him I will wish him a good journey from the summer-house* in the garden. Not a soul ever enters it at this time of the year. Bid him go thither directly. I shall soon join him. I will wait in my room till you call me. Be quick!"

Ellis required not to have this order repeated: to place her under the care of Harleigh, and intimate to him the excess of her love, with the apprehensions which she now herself conceived of the dangerous state of her mind, was all that could be wished; and where so essential a service might be rendered, or a mischief be prevented, personal punctilio was out of the question.

He was not in the hall; but, from one of the windows, she perceived him walking near the house. A painful sensation, upon being obliged, again, to force herself upon his notice, disturbed, though she would not suffer it to check her. He was speaking with his groom. She stopt at the hall-door, with a view to catch his eye, and succeeded; but he bowed without approaching her, and continued to discourse with his groom.

To seem bent upon pursuing him, when he appeared himself to think that he had gone too far, and even to mean to shun her, dyed her cheeks of the deepest vermilion; though she compelled herself, from a terrour of the danger of delay, to run across the gravel-walk before the house, to address him. He saw her advance, with extreme surprise, but by no means with the same air of pleasure, that he had manifested in the morning. His look was embarrassed, and he seemed unwilling to meet her eyes. Yet he awaited her with a respect that made his groom, unbidden, retire to some distance; though to await her at all, when he might have met her, struck her, even in this hurried and terrified moment, as offering the strongest confirmation which she had yet received, that it was not a man of pleasure or of gallantry, but of feeling and of truth, into whose way she was thus singularly and frequently cast: and the impression which she had made upon his mind, had never, to her hitherto nearly absorbed faculties, appeared to be so serious or so sincere, as now, when he first evidently struggled to disguise a partiality, which he seemed persuaded that he had, now, first betrayed. The sensations which this discovery might produce in herself were unexamined: the misery with which it teemed for Elinor, and a desire to relieve his own delicacy, by appearing unconscious of his secret, predominated: and she assumed sufficient self-command, to deliver the message of Elinor, with a look, and in a voice, that seemed insensible and unobservant of every other subject.

He soon, now, recovered his usual tone, and disengaged manner. "She must certainly," he said, "be obeyed; though I so little expected such a summons, that I was giving directions for my departure."

"Ah, no!" cried Ellis, "rather again defer it."

"You would have me again defer it?" he repeated, with a vivacity he tried still more, though vainly, to subdue than to disguise.

The word again did not make the cheeks of Ellis paler; but she answered, with eagerness, "Yes, for the same purpose and same person!—I am forced to speak explicitly—and abruptly. Indeed, Sir, you know not, you conceive not, the dreadfully alarming state of her nerves, nor the violence of her attachment.—You could scarcely else—" she stopt, for he changed colour and looked hurt: she saw he comprehended that she meant to add, you could scarcely else resist her: she finished, therefore, her phrase, by "scarcely else plan leaving her, till you saw her more composed, and more reconciled to herself, and to the world."

"You may imagine," said he, pensively, "it is any thing rather than my inclination that carries me hence .... but I greatly fear 'tis the only prudent measure I can pursue."

"You can best judge by seeing her," said Ellis: "her situation is truly deplorable. Her faculties are all disordered; her very intellects,* I fear, are shaken; and there is no misfortune, no horrour, which her desperation, if not softened, does not menace."

Harleigh now seemed awakened to sudden alarm, and deep concern; and Ellis painfully, with encreasing embarrassment, from encreasing consciousness, added, "You will do, I am sure, what is possible to snatch her from despair!" and then returned to the house: satisfied that her meaning was perfectly comprehended, by the excess of consternation into which it obviously cast Harleigh.

CHAPTER XVIII

COMFORTED, at least, for Elinor, whose situation in being known, seemed to lose its greatest danger, Ellis, with less oppression upon her spirits, returned to the dressing-room.

Elinor was writing, and too intently occupied to heed the opening of the door. The motion of her hand was so rapid, that her pen seemed rather to skim over, than to touch her paper. Ellis gently approached her; but, finding that she did not raise her head, ventured not even to announce that her orders had been executed.

At length, her paper being filled, she looked up, and said, "Well! is he there?"

"I have delivered to him, Madam, your commands."

"Then," cried she, rising with an exulting air, "the moment of my triumph is come! Yes, Harleigh! if meanly I have offered you my person, nobly, at least, I will consecrate to you my soul!"

Hastily rolling up what she had been writing, and putting it into a desk, "Ellis!" she added, "mark me well! should any accident betide me, here will be found the last and unalterable codicil to my will. It is signed, but not witnessed: it is not, however, of a nature to be disputed; it is to desire only that Harleigh will take care that my bones shall be buried in the same charnel-house, in which he orders the interment of his own. All that remains, finally, of either of us, there, at least, may meet!"

Ellis turned cold with horrour. Her first idea was to send for Mrs. Maple; yet that lady was so completely without influence, that any interference on her part, might rather stimulate than impede what it was meant to oppose. It seemed, therefore, safest to trust wholly to Harleigh.

The eyes of Elinor were wild and fierce, her complexion was livid, her countenance was become haggard; and, while she talked of triumph, and fancied it was what she felt, every feature exhibited the most tortured marks of impetuous sorrow, and ungoverned disappointment.

She took from her bureau the shagreen case which she had so fondly caressed, and which Ellis concluded to contain some portrait, or cherished keep-sake of Harleigh; and hurried down stairs. Ellis fearfully followed her. No one happened to be in the way, and she was already in the garden, when, turning suddenly round, and perceiving Ellis, "Oh ho!" she cried, "you come unbidden? you are right; I shall want you."

She then precipitately entered the summer-house, in which Harleigh was awaiting her in the keenest anxiety.

His disturbance was augmented upon observing her extreme paleness, though she tried to meet him with a smile. She shut and bolted the door, and seated herself before she spoke.

Assuming then a mien of austerity, though her voice betrayed internal tremour, "Harleigh!" she cried, "be not alarmed. I have received your answer!—fear not that I shall ever expect—or would, now, even listen to another! 'Tis to vindicate, not to lower my character that I am here. I have given you, I am aware, a great surprise by what you conceive to be my weakness; prepare yourself for a yet greater, from an opposite cause. I come to explain to you the principles by which I am actuated, clearly and roundly; without false modesty, insipid affectation, or artful ambiguity. You will then know from what plan of reasoning I adopt my measures; which as yet, believing to be urged only by my feelings, you attribute, perhaps,—like that poor scared Ellis, to insanity."

Ellis forced a smile, and, seating herself at some distance, tried to wear the appearance of losing her apprehensions; while Harleigh, drawing a chair near Elinor, assured her that his whole mind was engaged in attention to what she might disclose.

Her voice now became more steady, and she proceeded.

"You think me, I know, tarnished by those very revolutionary ideas through which, in my own estimation, I am ennobled. I owe to them that I dare hold myself intellectually, as well as personally, an equal member of the community; not a poor, degraded, however necessary appendant* to it: I owe to them my enfranchisement from the mental slavery of subscribing to unexamined opinions, and being governed by prejudices that I despise: I owe to them the precious privilege, so shamefully new to mankind, of daring to think for myself. But for them—should I not, at this moment, be pining away my lingering existence, in silent consumption? They have rescued me from that slow poison!"

"In what manner," said Harleigh, "can I presume—"

She interrupted him. "Imagine not I am come to reproach you! or, still less, to soften you!" She stopt, confused, rose, and again seated herself, before she could go on. "No! littleness of that description belongs not to such energies as those which you have awakened! I come but, I repeat, to defend myself, from any injurious suspicion, of having lightly given way to a mere impulse of passion. I come to bring you conviction that reason has guided my conduct; and I come to solicit a boon from you,—a last boon, before we separate for ever!"

"I am charmed if you have anything to ask of me," said Harleigh, "that my zeal, my friendship, my attachment, may find some vent; but why speak of so solemn a separation?"

"You will grant, then, what I mean to request?"

"What can it be I could refuse?"

"Enough! You will soon know. Now to my justification. Hear me, Harleigh!"

She arose, and, clasping her hands, with strong, yet tender, emotion, exclaimed, "That I should love you—" She stopt. Shame crimsoned her skin. She covered her face with both her hands, and sunk again upon her chair.

Harleigh was strongly and painfully affected. "O Elinor!" he cried, and was going to take her hand; but the fear of misinterpretation made him draw back; and Elinor, almost instantly recovering, raised her head, and said, "How tenacious a tyrant is custom! how it clings to our practice! how it embarrasses our conduct! how it awes our very nature itself, and bewilders and confounds even our free will! We are slaves to its laws and its follies, till we forget its usurpation. Who should have told me, only five minutes ago, that, at an instant such as this; an instant of liberation from all shackles, of defiance to all forms; its antique prescriptions should still retain their power to confuse and torment me? Who should have told me, that, at an instant such as this, I should blush to pronounce the attachment in which I ought to glory? and hardly know how to articulate .... That I should love you, Harleigh, can surprise no one but yourself!"

Her cheeks were now in flames; and those of Harleigh were tinted with nearly as high a colour. Ellis fixed her eyes stedfastly upon the floor.

Shocked, in despite of her sunk expectations, that words such as these could be heard by Harleigh in silence, she resumed again the haughty air with which she had begun the conference.

"I ought not to detain you so long, for a defence so unimportant. What, to you, can it matter, that my valueless preference should be acknowledged from the spur of passion, or the dictates of reason?—And yet, to the receiver, as well as to the offerer, a sacrifice brings honour or disgrace, according to its motives. Listen, therefore, for both our sakes, to mine: though they may lead you to a subject which you have long since, in common with every man that breathes, wished exploded, the Rights of woman:* Rights, however, which all your sex, with all its arbitrary assumption of superiority, can never disprove, for they are the Rights of human nature; to which the two sexes equally and unalienably belong. But I must leave to abler casuists, and the slow, all-arranging ascendance of truth, to raise our oppressed half of the human species, to the equality and dignity for which equal Nature, that gives us Birth and Death alike, designs us. I must spend my remaining moments in egotism; for all that I have time to attempt is my personal vindication. Harleigh! from the first instant that I saw you—heard you—knew you—"

She breathed hard, and spoke with difficulty; but forced herself on.

"From that first instant, Harleigh! I have lived but to cherish your idea!"

Her features now regained their highest expression of vivacity; and, rising, and looking at him with a sort of wild rapture, "Oh Harleigh!" she continued, "have I attained, at last, this exquisite moment? What does it not pay of excruciating suspense, of hateful, laborious forbearance, and unnatural self-denial? Harleigh! dearest Harleigh! you are master of my soul! you are sovereign of my esteem, my admiration, my every feeling of tenderness, and every idea of perfection!—Accept, then, the warm homage of a glowing heart, that beats but for you; and that, beating in vain, will beat no more!"

The crimson hue now mounted to her forehead, and reddened her neck: her eyes became lustrous; and she was preparing, with an air of extacy, to open the shagreen case, which she had held folded to her bosom, when Harleigh, seizing her hand, dropt on one knee, and, hardly conscious of what he did, or what he felt, from the terrible impression made by a speech so full of love, despair, and menace, exclaimed, "Elinor! you crown me, then, with honours, but to kill me with torture?"

With a look of softness new to her features, new to her character, and emanating from sensations of delight new to her hopes, Elinor sunk gently upon her chair, yet left him full possession of her hand; and, for some instants, seemed silent from a luxury of inward enjoyment. "Is it Harleigh," she then cried, "Albert Harleigh, I see at my feet? Ah! what is the period, since I have known him, in which I would not joyfully have resigned all the rest of my life, for a sight, a moment such as this! Dear, dear, delicious poison! thrill, thrill through my veins! throb at my heart! new string every fibre of my frame! Is it, then, granted me, at last, to see thee thus? and thus dare speak to thee? to give sound to my feelings; to allow utterance to my love? to dare suffer my own breath to emit the purest flame that ever warmed a virgin heart?—Ah! Harleigh! proud Harleigh!—"

Harleigh, embarrassed, had risen, though without quitting her hand, and reseated himself.

"Proud, proud Harleigh!" she continued, angrily snatching away her hand; "you think even this little moment of sympathy, too long for love and Elinor! you fear, perhaps, that she should expect its duration, or repetition? Know me, Harleigh, better! I come not to sue for your compassion,—I would not accept it!—Elinor may fail to excite your regard, but she will never make you blush that you have excited her's. My choice itself speaks the purity of my passion, for are not Harleigh and Honour one?"

She paused to recover some composure, and then went on.

"You have attached neither a weak, giddy, unguarded fool, nor an idly wilful or romantic voluptuary. My defence is grafted upon your character as much as upon my own. I could divide it into many branches; but I will content myself with only striking at its root, namely, the Right of woman, if endowed with senses, to make use of them. O Harleigh! why have I seen you wiser and better than all your race; sounder in your judgment, more elegant in your manners, more spirited in your conduct;—lively though benevolent,—gentle, though brilliant,—Oh Albert! Albert! if I must listen to you with the same dull ears, look at you with the same unmarking eyes, and think of you with the same unmeaning coldness, with which I hear, see, and consider the time-wearing, spirit-consuming, soul-wasting tribe, that daily press upon my sight, and offend my understanding? Can you ask, can you expect, can you wish to doom half your species to so degraded a state? to look down upon the wife, who is meant for the companion of your existence; and upon the mother, of whose nature you must so largely partake; as upon mere sleepy, slavish, uninteresting automatons?* Say! speak! answer, Harleigh! can such be your lordly, yet most unmanly desire?"

"And is it seriously that Elinor would have me reply to such a question?"

"No, Harleigh! your noble, liberal nature answers it in every word, in every look! You accord, then,—you conceive, at least, all that constitutes my defence, in allowing me the use of my faculties; for how better can I employ them than in doing honour to excellence? Why, for so many centuries, has man, alone, been supposed to possess, not only force and power for action and defence, but even all the rights of taste; all the fine sensibilities which impel our happiest sympathies, in the choice of our life's partners? Why, not alone, is woman to be excluded from the exertions of courage, the field of glory, the immortal death of honour;—not alone to be denied deliberating upon the safety of the state of which she is a member, and the utility of the laws by which she must be governed:—must even her heart be circumscribed by boundaries as narrow as her sphere of action in life? Must she be taught to subdue all its native emotions? To hide them as sin, and to deny them as shame? Must her affections be bestowed but as the recompence of flattery received; not of merit discriminated? Must every thing that she does be prescribed by rule? Must every thing that she says, be limited to what has been said before? Must nothing that is spontaneous, generous, intuitive, spring from her soul to her lips?—And do you, even you, Harleigh, despise unbidden love!"

"No, Elinor, no!—if I durst tell you what I think of it—"

He stopt, embarrassed.

"I understand you, Harleigh; you know not how to find expressions that may not wound me? Well! let me not pain you. Let us hasten to conclude. I have spoken all that I am now capable to utter of my defence; nothing more remains but the boon I have to beg. Harleigh!—if there be a question you can resolve me, that may mitigate the horrour of my destiny, without diminishing its glory—for glory and horrour go hand in hand! would you refuse me—when I solicit it as a boon?—

would you refuse, Harleigh, to satisfy me, even though my demand should be perplexing? could you, Harleigh, refuse me?—And at such a moment as this?"

"No, certainly not!"

"Tell me, then, and fear not to be sincere. Is it to some other attachment—" a sort of shivering fit stopt her for a moment, but she recovered from it by a pride that seemed to burn through every vein, as she added, "or is it to innate repugnance that I owe your dislike?"

"Dislike? repugnance?" Harleigh repeated, with quickness, "can Elinor be, at once, so generous and so unjust? Can she delineate her own feelings with so touching and so glowing a pencil, yet so ill describe, or so wilfully fail in comprehending mine?"

"Dare, then, to be ingenuous, and save me, Harleigh,—if with truth you can, the depression, the shame, of being rejected from impenetrable apathy! I ought, I know, to be above such narrow punctilio, and to allow the independence of your liberty; but I did not fall into the refining hands of philosophy, early enough to eradicate wholly from my mind, all dregs of the clinging first impressions of habit and education. Say, then, Harleigh, if it be in your power so to say, that it is not a free heart which thus coldly disdains me; that it is not a disengaged mind which refuses me its sympathy! that it is not to personal aversion, but to some previous regard, that I owe your insensibility! To me the event will be the same, but the failure will be less ignoble."

"How difficult, O Elinor!—how next to impossible such a statement makes every species of answer!"

"At a period, Harleigh, awful and finite to our intercourse like this, fall not into what I have hitherto, with so much reverence, seen you, upon all occasions, superiour to, subterfuge and evasion! Be yourself, Harleigh!—what can you be more noble? and plainly, simply let me into the cause, since you cannot conceal from me the effect. Speak, then! Is it but in the sullen majesty of masculine superiority,

'Lord of yourself, uncumber'd by a wife,'†*

† Dryden.

that you fly all marriage-bonds, with insulated, haughty singleness? or is it that, deceived by my apparent engagement, your heart never asked itself the worth of mine, till already all its own pulsations beat for another object?"

Harleigh tried to smile, tried to rally, tried to divert the question; all in vain; Elinor became but more urgent, and more disordered. "O Harleigh!" she cried, "is it too much to ask this one mark of your confidence, for a creature who has cast her whole destiny at your feet? Speak!—if you would not devote me to distraction! Speak!—if you would not consign me to immediate delirium!"

"And what," cried he, trembling at her vehemence, "would you have me say?"

"That it is not Elinor whom you despise—but another whom you love."

"Elinor! are you mad?"

"No, Harleigh, no!—but I am wild with anguish to dive into the full depth of my disgrace; to learn whether it were inevitable, from the very nature of things,—from personal antipathy,—gloss it over as you will with esteem, regard, and professions;—or whether you had found that you, also, had a soul, before mine was laid open to you. No evasion! no delay!" continued she, with augmenting impetuosity; "you have promised to grant my boon,—speak, Harleigh, speak!—was it my direful fate, or your insuperable antipathy?"

"It was surely not antipathy!" cried he, in a tone the most soothing; yet with a look affrighted, and unconscious, till he had spoken, of the inference to which his words might be liable.

"I thank you!" cried she, fervently, "Harleigh, I thank you! This, at least, is noble; this is treating me with distinction, this is honouring me with trust. It abates the irritating tinglings of mortified pride; it persuades me I am the victim of misfortune, not of contempt."

Suddenly, then, turning to Ellis, whose eyes, during the whole scene, had seemed rivetted to the floor, she expressively added, "I ask not the object!"

Harleigh breathed hard, yet kept his face in an opposite direction, and endeavoured to look as if he did not understand her meaning. Ellis commanded her features to remain unmoved; but her complexion was not under the same controul: frequent blushes crossed her cheeks, which, though they died away almost as soon as they were born, vanished only to re-appear; evincing all the consciousness that she struggled to suppress.

A pause ensued, to Harleigh unspeakably painful, and to Ellis indiscribably distressing; during which Elinor fell into a profound reverie, from which, after a few minutes, wildly starting, "Harleigh," she cried, "is your wedding-day fixed?"

"My wedding-day?" he repeated, with a forced smile, "Must not my wedding itself be fixed first?"

"And is it not fixed?—Does it depend upon Ellis?"

He looked palpably disconcerted; while Ellis, hastily raising her head, exclaimed, "Upon me, Madam? no, indeed! I am completely and every way out of the question."

"Of you," said Elinor, with severity, "I mean not to make any enquiry! You are an adept in the occult sciences; and such I venture not to encounter. But you, Harleigh, will you, also, practise disguise? and fall so in love with mystery, as to lose your nobler nature, in a blind, infatuated admiration of the marvellous and obscure?"

Ellis resentfully reddened; but her cheeks were pale to those of Harleigh. Neither of them, however, spoke; and Elinor continued.

"I cannot, Harleigh, be deceived, and I will not be trifled with. When you came over to fetch me from France; when the fatal name of sister gave me a right to interrogate you, I frankly asked the state of your heart, and you unhesitatingly told me that it was wholly free. Since that period, whom have you seen, whom noticed, except Ellis! Ellis! Ellis! From the first moment that you have beheld her, she has seemed the mistress of your destiny, the arbitress of your will. My boon, then, Harleigh, my boon! without a moment's further delay! Appease the raging ferment in my veins; clear away every surmize; and generously, honestly say 'tis Ellis!—or it is another, and not Ellis, I prefer to you!"

"Elinor! Elinor!" cried Harleigh, in a universal tremour, "it is I that you will make mad!" while Ellis, not daring to draw upon herself, again, the rebuke which might follow a single disclaiming word, rose, and turning from them both, stood facing the window.

"It is surely then Ellis! what you will not, Harleigh, avow, is precisely what you proclaim—it is surely Ellis!"

Ellis opened the window, and leant out her head; Harleigh, clapping his hand upon his crimsoned forehead, walked with hasty steps round the little apartment.

Losing now all self-command, and wringing her hands, in a transport of ungovernable anguish, "Oh, Harleigh! Harleigh!" Elinor cried, "to what a chimera you have given your heart! to an existence unintelligible, a character unfathomable, a creature of imagination, though visible! O, can you believe she will ever love you as Elinor loves? with the warmth, with the truth, with the tenderness, with the choice? can she show herself as disinterested? can she prove herself as devoted?—"

"She aims, Madam, at no rivalry!" said Ellis, gravely, and returning to her seat: while Harleigh, tortured between resentment and pity, stood still; without venturing to look up or reply.

"Rivalry?" repeated Elinor, with high disdain: "No! upon what species of competition could rivalry be formed, between Elinor, and a compound of cold caution, and selfish prudence? Oh, Harleigh! how is it you thus can love all you were wont to scorn? double dealing, false appearances, and lurking disguise! without a family she dare claim, without a story she dare tell, without a name she dare avow!"

A deep sigh, which now burst from Ellis, terminated the conflict between indignation and compassion in Harleigh, who raised his eyes to meet those of Elinor, with an expression of undisguised displeasure.

"You are angry?" she cried, clasping her hands, with forced and terrible joy; "you are angry, and I am thankful for the lesson. I meant not to have lingered thus; my design was to have been abrupt and noble."

Looking at him, then, with uncontrolled emotion, "If ever man deserved the sacrifice of a pure heart," she continued, " 'tis you, Harleigh, you! and mine, from the period it first became conscious of its devotion to you, has felt that it could not survive the certitude of your union with another. All else, of slight, of failure, of inadequate pretensions, might be borne; for where neither party is happy, misery is not aggravated by contrast, nor mortification by comparison. But to become the object of insolent pity to the happy!—to make a part of a rival's blessings, by being offered up at the shrine of her superiority—No, Harleigh, no! such abasement is not for Elinor. And what is the charm of this wretched machine of clay, that can pay for sustaining its burthen under similar disgrace? Let those who prize support it. For me,—my glass is run,—my cup is full,—I die!"

"Die?" repeated Ellis, with a faint scream, while Harleigh looked petrified with horrour.

"Die, yes!" answered Elinor, with a smile triumphant though ghastly; "or sleep! call it which you will! so animation be over, so feeling be past, so my soul no longer linger under the leaden oppression of disappointment; under sickness of all mortal existence; under incurable, universal disgust:—call it what you please, sleep, rest, or death; termination is all I seek."

"And is there, Elinor, no other name for what follows our earthly dissolution?" cried Harleigh, with a shuddering frown: "What say you if we call it immortality?"

"Will you preach to me?" cried she, her eyes darting fire; "will you bid me look forward to yet another life, when this, short as it is deemed, I find insupportable? Ah, Harleigh! Harleigh!" her eyes suffusing with sudden tenderness; "were I your's—I might wish indeed to be immortal!"

Harleigh was extremely affected: he approached her, took her hand, and soothingly said, "My dear Elinor, compose your spirits, exert your strength of mind, and suffer us to discuss these subjects at some length."

"No, Harleigh; I must not trust myself to your fascinations! How do I know but they might bewitch me out of my reason, and entangle me, again, in those antique superstitions which make misery so cowardly? No, Harleigh! the star of Ellis has prevailed, and I sink beneath its influence. Else, only sometimes to see you, to hear of you, to watch you, and to think of you always, I would still live, nay, feel joy in life; for still my imagination would gift you, ultimately, with sensibility to my regard. But I anticipate the union which I see to be inevitable, and I spare my senses the shock which I feel would demolish them.—Harleigh!—dearest Harleigh, Adieu!"

A paleness like that of death overspread her face.

"What is it," cried Harleigh, inexpressibly alarmed, "what is it Elinor means?"

"To re-conquer, by the courage of my death, the esteem I may have forfeited by my jealousy, my envy, my littleness in life! You only could have corrected my errours; you, by your ascendance over my feelings, might have refined them into virtues. Oh, Harleigh! weigh not alone my imperfections when you recollect my attachment! but remember that I have loved you so as woman never loved!"

Her voice now faultered, and she shook so violently that she could not support herself. She put her hand gently upon the arm of Harleigh, and, gliding nearly behind him, leant upon his shoulder. He would have spoken words of comfort, but she seemed incapable of hearing him. "Farewell!" she cried, "Harleigh! Never will I live to see Ellis your's!—Farewell!—a long farewell!"

Precipitately she then opened the shagreen case, and was drawing out its contents, when Ellis, darting forward, caught her arm, and screamed, rather than articulated, "Ellis will never be his!—Forbear! forbear!—Ellis never will be his!"

The astonished Harleigh, who, hitherto, had rigorously avoided meeting the eyes of Ellis, now turned towards her, with an expression in which all that was not surprise was resentment; while Elinor, seeming suddenly suspended, faintly pronounced, "Ellis—deluding Ellis!—what is it you say?"

"I am no deluder!" cried Ellis, yet more eagerly: "Rely, rely upon my plighted honour!"

Harleigh now looked utterly confounded; but Ellis only saw, and seemed only to breathe for Elinor, who recovering, as if by miracle, her complexion, her voice, and the brightness of her eyes, rapturously exclaimed, "Oh Harleigh!—Is there, then, sympathy in our fate? Do you, too, love in vain?"—And, from a change of emotion, too sudden and too mighty for the shattered state of her nerves, she sunk senseless upon the floor.

The motive to the strange protestations of Ellis was now apparent: a poniard dropt from the hand of Elinor as she fell, of which, while she spoke her farewell, Ellis had caught a glance.

Harleigh seemed himself to require the aid that he was called upon to bestow. He looked at Elinor with a mixture of compassion and horrour, and, taking possession of the poniard, "Unhappy Elinor!" he cried, "into what a chaos of errour and of crime have these fatal new systems bewildered thee!"

The revival of Elinor was almost immediate; and though, at first, she seemed to have lost the remembrance of what had happened, the sight of Ellis and Harleigh soon brought it back. She looked from one to the other, as if searching her destiny; and then, with quick impatience, though somewhat checked by shame, cried, "Ellis! have you not mocked me?"

Ellis, covered with blushes and confusion, addressing herself to Harleigh, said, "Pardon, Mr. Harleigh, my seeming presumption, where no option has been offered me; and where such an option is as wide from my expectations as it would be from my desert. This terrible crisis must be my apology."

A shivering like that of an ague-fit* again shook the agitated Elinor, who, ejaculating, "What farce is this?—Fool! fool! shall I thus sleepily be duped?" looked keenly around for her lost weapon.

"Duped? no, Madam," cried Ellis, in a tone impressive of veracity: "if I had the honour to be better known to Miss Joddrel, one assertion, I flatter myself, would suffice: my word is given; it has never yet been broken!"

While this declaration, though softened by a sigh the most melancholy, struck cold to the heart of Harleigh, its effect upon Elinor was that of an extacy which seemed the offspring of frenzy. "Do I awake, then," she cried, "from agony and death—agony, impossible to support! death, willing and welcome! to renewed life? to an interesting, however deplorable, existence? is my fate in harmony with the fate of Harleigh? Has he, even he! given his soul,—his noble soul!—to one who esteems and admires him, yet who will not be his? Can Harleigh love in vain?"

Tears now rolled fast and unchecked down her cheeks, while, in tones of enthusiasm, she continued, "I hail thee once again, oh life! with all thy arrows! Welcome, welcome, every evil that associates my catastrophe with that of Harleigh!—Yet I blush, methinks, to live!—Blush, and feel little,—nearly in the same proportion that I should have gloried to die!"

With these words, and recoiling from a solemn, yet tender

exhortation, begun by Harleigh, she abruptly quitted the little building; and, her mind not more highly wrought by self-exaltation, than her body was weakened by successive emotions, she was compelled to accept the fearfully offered assistance of Ellis, to regain, with tottering steps, the house.

CHAPTER XIX

ELLIS entered into the chamber with Elinor; who, equally exhausted in body and in mind, flung herself upon her bed, where she remained some time totally mute: her eyes wide open, yet looking at nothing, apparently in a state of stupefaction; but from which, in a few minutes, suddenly starting, and taking Ellis by the hand, with a commanding air, she abruptly said, "Ellis, are you fixed to marry Lord Melbury?"

Ellis positively disclaimed any such idea.

"What am I to infer?" cried Elinor, with returning and frightful agitation; "Will you be firm to your engagement? Is it truly your decision to refuse the hand of Harleigh, though he were to offer it you?"

Ellis shuddered, and looked down; but answered, "I will surely, Madam, never forget my engagement!"

The most perfect calm now succeeded to the many storms which had both impelled and shattered Elinor; and, after swallowing a copious draught of cold water, she laid her head upon her pillow, and fell into a profound and heavy, though not tranquil sleep.

Ellis, unable to conjecture in what frame of mind she might awake, did not dare leave her. She sat watchfully by her side, amazed to see, that, with such energy of character, such quickness of parts, such strength of comprehension, she not only gave way to all her impulses like a child, but, like a child, also, when over-fatigued, could suddenly lose her sufferings and her remembrance in a sort of spontaneous slumber.

But the balmy rest of even spirits, and a composed mind, was far from Elinor; exhausted nature claimed some respite from frantic exertion, and obtained it; but no more. She awoke then; yet, though it was with a frightful start, even this short repose proved salutary, not only to her nerves, but to her intellects. Her passions became less inflamed, and her imagination less heated; and, though she remained unchanged in her plans, and impenitent in her opinions, she acknowledged herself sensible to the strangeness of her conduct; and not without shame for its violence. These, however, were transitory sensations: one regret alone hung upon her with any serious weight: this was, having suffered her dagger to be seen and seized. She feared being suspected of a mere puerile effort, to frighten from Harleigh an offer of his hand, in menacing what she had not courage, nor, perhaps, even intention to perform.

This suggestion was intolerable: she blushed with shame as it crossed her mind. She shook with passion, as she considered, that such might be the disgraceful opinion, that might tarnish the glory that she meant to acquire, by dying at the feet of the object of her adoration, at the very moment of yielding to the happier star of an acknowledged rival; a willing martyr to successless, but heroick love.

She was now tempted to prove her sincerity by her own immediate destruction. "And yet," she cried, "shall I not bear what Harleigh bears? Shall I not know the destiny of Harleigh?"

This idea again reconciled her to present life, though not to her actual situation; and she ruminated laboriously, for some time, in gloomy silence; from which, however, breaking with sudden vivacity, "No, no!" she cried: "I will not risk any aspersing doubt; I will shew him I have a soul that strenuously emulates the nobleness of his own. He shall see, he shall confess, that no meanness is mixt with the love of Elinor. He shall not suppose, because she glories in its undisguised avowal, that she waits in humble hope for a turn in her favour; that she is a candidate for his regard; a suppliant for his compassion! No! he shall see that she is frank without weakness, and free from every species of dissimulation or stratagem."

She then rushed out of the room, shutting the door after her, and commanding Ellis not to follow: but Ellis, fearing every moment some dreadful catastrophe, softly pursued her, till she saw her enter the servants' hall; whence, after giving some orders, in a low voice and hurried manner, to her own footman, she remounted to her chamber; into which, without opposition, or even notice, Ellis also glided.

Here, eagerly seizing a pen, with the utmost rapidity, though with many blots, and frequent erazures, she wrote a long letter, which she read and altered repeatedly before she folded; she then wrote a shorter one; then rang for her maid, to whom she gave some secret directions, which she finished by commanding that she would find out Mr. Harleigh, and desire that he would go immediately to the summer-house.

In about a quarter of an hour, which she spent in reading, revising, sealing, and directing her letters, the maid returned; and, after a long whisper, said, that she had given the message to Mr. Harleigh.

Turning now to Ellis, with a voice and air of decision, that seemed imperiously to forbid resistance, she put into her hand the long letter which she had just written, and said, "Take this to him immediately; and, while he reads it, mark every change of his countenance, so as to be able to deduce, and clearly to understand, the sensations which pass in his mind."

When Ellis expostulated upon the utter impropriety of her following Mr. Harleigh, she sternly said, "Give the letter, then, to whatever other person you judge most proper to become a third in my confidence!"

She then nearly forced her out of the room.

Ellis did not dare venture to keep the letter, as she wished, till some opportunity should offer for presenting it quietly, lest some high importance should be annexed to its quick delivery; yet she felt that it would be cruel and indelicate to make over such a commission to another; in opposition, therefore, to the extremest personal repugnance, she compelled herself, with fearful and unwilling, yet hasty steps, to proceed again to the summer-house.

She found Harleigh, with an air at once pensive and alarmed, waiting for Elinor; but at the unexpected sight of Ellis, and of Ellis alone, every feature brightened; though his countenance, his manner, his whole frame, evinced increased agitation.

Anxious to produce her excuse, for an intrusion of which she felt utterly ashamed, she instantly presented him the letter, saying, "Miss Joddrel would take no denial to my being its bearer. She has even charged me to remain with you while you read it."

"Were that," said he, expressively, "the severest pain she inflicts upon me, I should soon become her debtor for feelings that leave pain apart!—Urgent, indeed, was my desire to see you again, and without delay; for after what has passed this morning, silence and forbearance are no longer practicable."

"Yet, at this moment," said Ellis, striving, but ineffectually to speak without disturbance; "it will be impossible for me to defer returning to the house."

"Yet if not now, when?"

"I know not—but she will be very impatient for some account of her letter."

"She will, at least, not be desperate, since she expects, and therefore will wait for you; how, then, can I hope to find a more favourable opportunity, for obtaining a few instants of your time?"

"But, though she may not be desperate just now, is it not possible, Sir, that my staying may irritate, and make her so?"

"That, unhappily, is but too true! There is no relying upon the patience, or the fortitude, of one so completely governed by impulse; and who considers her passions as her guides to glory,—not as the subtlest enemies of every virtue! Nevertheless, what I feel for her is far beyond what, situated as I now am with her, I dare express.—Yet, at this moment—"

"Will you not read her letter?"

"That you may run away?" cried he, half smiling; "no; at this moment I will not read her letter, that you may be forced to stay!"

"You cannot wish me to make her angry?"

"Far, far from it! but what chance have I to meet you again, if I lose you now? Be not alarmed, I beg: she will naturally conclude that I am studying her letter; and, but for an insuperable necessity of—of some explanation, I could, indeed, think of no other subject: for dreadful is the impression which the scene that I have just had with her has made upon my nerves.—Ah! how could she imagine such a one calculated to engage my heart? How wide is it from all that, to me, appears attractive! Her spirit I admire; but where is the sweetness I could love? I respect her understanding; but where is the softness that should make it charm while it enlightens? I am grateful for her partiality; but where is the dignity that might ennoble it, or the delicacy that might make it as refined as it is flattering? Where—where the soul's fascination, that grows out of the mingled excellencies, the blended harmonies, of the understanding with the heart and the manners?"

Vainly Ellis strove to appear unconscious of the comparison, and the application, which the eyes of Harleigh, yet more pointedly than his words, marked for herself in this speech: her quickly rising blushes divulged all that her stillness, her unmoved features tried to disguise; and, to get rid of her confusion, she again desired that he would open the letter, and with an urgency which he could not resist. He merely stipulated that she would wait to hear his answer; and then read what follows.

"For Albert Harleigh.

"I am sick of the world, yet still I crawl upon its surface. I scorn and defy the whole human race, yet doom myself to be numbered in its community. While you, Albert Harleigh, you whom alone, of all that live and breath, I prize,—you, even your sight, I, from this moment, eternally renounce! Such is the mighty ascendance of the passion which you have inspired, that I will sooner forego that only blessing—though the universe without it is a hateful blank to my eyes—than risk opposing the sway of your opinion, or suffer you to think me ignoble, though you know me to be enslaved. O Harleigh! how far from all that is vile or debasing is the flame, the pure, though ardent flame that you have kindled! To its animating influence I am indebted for one precious moment of heavenly truth; and for having snatched from the grave, which in its own nothingness will soon moulder away my frame, the history of my feelings.

"I have conquered the tyrant false pride; I have mocked the puerilities of education; I have set at nought and defeated even the monster custom; but you, O Harleigh! you I obey, without waiting for a command; you, I seek to humour, without aspiring to please! To you, my free soul, my liberated mind, my new-born ideas, all yield, slaves, willing slaves, to what I only conceive to be your counsel, only conjecture to be your judgment; that since I have failed to touch your heart, after having opened to you my own, a total separation will be due to my fame for the world, due to delicacy for myself . . .

"Be it so, Albert . . . we will part!—Though my fame, in my own estimation, would be elevated to glory, by the publication of a choice that does me honour; though my delicacy would be gratified, would be sanctified, by shewing the purity of a passion as spotless as it is hopeless—yet will I hide myself in the remotest corner of the universe, rather than resist you even in thought. O Albert! how sovereign is your power!—more absolute than the tyranny of the controlling world; more arbitrary than prescription; more invincible than the prejudices of ages!—You, I cannot resist! you, I shall only breathe to adore!—to bear all you bear,—the tortures of disappointment, the abominations of incertitude; to say, Harleigh himself endures this! we suffer in unison! our woes are sympathetic!—O word to charm all the rigour of calamity! . . . . Harleigh, I exist but to know how your destiny will be fulfilled, and then to come from my concealment, and bid you a last farewell! to leave upon the record of your memory the woes of my passion; and then consign myself for ever to my native oblivion. Till when, adieu, Albert Harleigh, adieu!

"ELINOR JODDREL."

Harleigh read this letter with a disturbance that, for a while, wholly absorbed his mind in its contents. "Misguided, most unfortunate, yet admirable Elinor!" he cried, "what a terrible perversion is here of intellect! what a confusion of ideas! what an inextricable chaos of false principles, exaggerated feelings, and imaginary advancement in new doctrines of life!"

He paused, thoughtfully and sadly, till Ellis, though sorry to interrupt his meditations, begged his directions what to say upon returning to the house.

"What her present plan may be," he answered, "is by no means clear; but so boundless is the licence which the followers of the new systems allow themselves, that nothing is too dreadful to apprehend. Religion is, if possible, still less respected than law, prescriptive rights, or any of the hitherto acknowledged ties of society. There runs through her letter, as there ran through her discourse this morning, a continual intimation of her disbelief in a future state; of her defiance of all revealed religion; of her high approbation of suicide.—The fatal deed from which you rescued her, had no excuse to plead from sudden desperation; she came prepared, decided, either to disprove her suspicions, or to end her existence!—poor infatuated, yet highly gifted Elinor!—what can be done to save her; to recal her to the use of her reason, and the exercise of her duties?"

"Will you not, Sir, see her? Will you not converse with her upon these points, in which her mind and understanding are so direfully warped?"

"Certainly I will; and I beg you to entreat for my admission. I must seek to dissuade her from the wild and useless scheme of seclusion and concealment. But as time now presses, permit me to speak, first, upon subjects which press also,—press irresistibly, unconquerably!—Your plan of becoming a governess—"

"I dare not stay, now, to discuss any thing personal; yet I cannot refrain from seizing a moment that may not again offer, for making my sincerest apologies upon a subject—and a declaration—I shall never think of without confusion. I feel all its impertinence, its inutility, its presumption; but you will make, I hope, allowance for the excess of my alarm. I could devise no other expedient."

"Tell me," cried he, "I beg, was it for her . . . or for me that it was uttered? Tell me the extent of its purpose!"

"You cannot, surely, Sir, imagine—cannot for a moment suppose, that I was guided by such egregious vanity as to believe—" She stopt, extremely embarrassed.

"Vanity," said he, "is out of the question, after what has just passed; spare then, I beseech, your own candour, as well as my suspense, all unnecessary pain."

"I entreat, I conjure you, Sir," cried Ellis, now greatly agitated, "speak only of my commission!"

"Certainly," he answered, "this is not the period I should have chosen, for venturing upon so delicate—I had nearly said so perilous a subject; but, so imperiously called upon, I could neither be insincere, nor pusillanimous enough, to disavow a charge which every feeling rose to confess!—Otherwise—just now,—my judgment, my sense of propriety,—all in the dark as I am—would sedulously, scrupulously have constrained my forbearance, till I knew—" He stopt, paused, and then expressively, yet gently added, "to whom I addressed myself!"

Ellis coloured highly as she answered, "I beg you, Sir, to consider all that was drawn from you this morning, or all that might be inferred, as perfectly null—unpronounced and unthought."

"No!" cried he with energy, "no! To have postponed an explanation would have been prudent,—nay right:—but every sentiment of my mind, filled with trust in your worth, and reverence for your virtues, forbids, now, a recantation! Imperious circumstances precipitated me to your feet—but my heart was there already!"

So extreme was the emotion with which Harleigh uttered these words, that he perceived not their effect upon Ellis, till, gasping for breath, and nearly fainting, she sunk upon a chair; when so livid a paleness overspread her face, and so deadly a cold seemed to chill her blood, that, but for a friendly burst of tears, which ensued, her vital powers appeared to be threatened with immediate suspension.

Harleigh was instantly at her feet; grieved at her distress, yet charmed with a thousand nameless, but potent sensations, that whispered to every pulse of his frame, that a sensibility so powerful could spring only from too sudden a concussion of pleasure with surprise.

He had hardly time to breathe forth a protestation, when the sight of his posture brought back the blood to her cheeks, and force to her limbs; and, hastily rising, with looks of blushing confusion, yet with a sigh that spoke internal anguish, "I cannot attempt," she cried, "Mr. Harleigh,—I could not, indeed, attempt—to express my sense of your generous good opinion!—yet—if you would not destine me to eternal misery, you must fly me—till you can forget this scene—as you would wish me to fly perdition!"

She rose to be gone; but Harleigh stopt her, crying, in a tone of amazement, "Is it possible,—can it be possible, that with intellects such as yours, clear, penetrating, admirable, you can conceive eternal misery will be your portion, if you break a forced engagement made with a mad woman?—and made but to prevent her immediate self-destruction?"

Shaking her head, but averting her eyes, Ellis would neither speak nor be detained; and Harleigh, who durst not follow her, remained confounded.

END OF THE FIRST VOLUME

of amazement. 'Is it possible,—can it be possible, that with intellects such as yours, clear, [illegible] [illegible], you cannot perceive eternal misery will be your portion, if you break a sacred engagement made with a mad woman?—and made but to prevent her immediate self-destruction?'

Shaking her head, but averting her eyes, Juliet would neither speak nor be detained; and Harleigh, who durst not follow her, [illegible] confounded.

END OF THE FIRST VOLUME.

VOLUME II

BOOK III

CHAPTER XX

ELLIS hastened to the house; but her weeping eyes, and disordered state of mind, unfitted her for an immediate encounter with Elinor, and she went straight to her own chamber; where, in severe meditation upon her position, her duties, and her calls for exertion, she "communed with her own heart."* Although unable, while involved in uncertainties, to arrange any regular plan of general conduct, conscience, that unerring guide, where consulted with sincerity, pointed out to her, that, after what had passed, the first step demanded by honour, was to quit the house, the spot, and the connexions, in which she was liable to keep alive any intercourse with Harleigh. What strikes me to be right, she internally cried, I must do; I may then have some chance for peace, ... however little for happiness!

Her troubled spirits thus appeased, she descended to inform Elinor of the result of her commission. She had received, indeed, no direct message; but Harleigh meant to desire a conference, and that desire would quiet, she hoped, and occupy the ideas of Elinor, so as to divert her from any minute investigation into the circumstances by which it had been preceded.

The door of the dressing room was locked, and she tapped at it for admission in vain; she concluded that Elinor was in her bed-chamber, to which there was no separate entrance, and tapped louder, that she might be heard; but without any better success. She remained, most uneasily, in the landing-place, till the approaching foot-step of Harleigh forced her away.

Upon re-entering her own chamber, and taking up her needle-work, she found a letter in its folds.

The direction was merely To Ellis. This assured her

that it was from Elinor, and she broke the seal, and read the following lines.

"All that now remains for the ill-starred Elinor, is to fly the whole odious human race. What can it offer to me but disgust and aversion? Despoiled of the only scheme in which I ever gloried, that of sacrificing in death, to the man whom I adore, the existence I vainly wished to devote to him in life;—despoiled of this—By whom despoiled?—by you! Ellis,—by you!—Yet—Oh incomprehensible!—You, refuse Albert Harleigh!—Never, never could I have believed in so senseless an apathy, but for the changed countenance which shewed the belief in it of Harleigh.

"If your rejection, Ellis, is that you may marry Lord Melbury, which alone makes its truth probable—you have done what is natural and pardonable, though heartless and mercenary; and you will offer me an opportunity to see how Harleigh—Albert Harleigh, will conduct himself when—like me!—he lives without hope.

"If, on the contrary, you have uttered that rejection, from the weak folly of dreading to witness a sudden and a noble end, to a fragile being, sighing for extinction,—on your own head fall your perjury and its consequences!

"I go hence immediately. No matter whither.

"Should I be pursued, I am aware I may soon be traced: but to what purpose? I am independent alike in person, fortune, and mind; I cannot be brought back by force, and I will not be moved by idle persuasion, or hacknied remonstrance. No! blasted in all my worldly views, I will submit to worldly slavery no longer. My aunt, therefore, will do well not to demand one whom she cannot claim.

"Tell her this.

"Harleigh——

"But no,—Harleigh will not follow me! He would deem himself bound to me ever after, by all that men hold honourable amongst one another, if, through any voluntary measure of his own, the shadow of a censure could be cast upon Elinor.

"O, perfect Harleigh! I will not involve your generous delicacy—for not yours, not even yours would I be, by the foul constraint of worldly etiquette! I should disdain to owe your smallest care for me to any menace, or to any meanness.

"Let him, not, therefore, Ellis, follow me; and I here pledge myself to preserve my miserable existence, till I see him again, in defiance of every temptation to disburthen myself of its loathsome weight. By the love I bear to him, I pledge myself!

"Tell him this.

"ELINOR JODDREL."

Ellis read this letter in speechless consternation. To be the confident of so extraordinary a flight, seemed danger to her safety, while it was horrour to her mind.

The two commissions with which, so inconsiderately, she was charged, how could she execute? To seek Harleigh again, she thought utterly wrong: and how deliver any message to Mrs. Maple, without appearing to be an accomplice in the elopement? She could only prove her innocence by shewing the letter itself, which, in clearing her from that charge, left one equally heavy to fall upon her, of an apparently premeditated design to engage, or, as the world might deem it, inveigle, the young Lord Melbury into marriage. It was evident that upon that idea alone, rested the belief of Elinor in a faithful adherence to the promised rejection; and that the letter which she had addressed to Ellis, was but meant as a memorandum of terrour for its observance.

Not long afterwards, Selina came eagerly to relate, that the dinner-bell having been rung, and the family being assembled, and the butler having repeatedly tapt at the door of sister Elinor, to hurry her; Mrs. Maple, not alarmed, because accustomed to her inexactitude, had made every body dine: after which, Tomlinson was sent to ask whether sister Elinor chose to come down to the dessert; but he brought word that he could not make either her or Mrs. Golding speak. Selina was then desired to enquire the reason of such strange taciturnity; but could not obtain any answer.

Mrs. Maple, saying that there was no end to her vagaries, then returned to the drawing-room; concluding, from former similar instances, that, dark, late, and cold as it was, Elinor had walked out with her maid, at the very hour of dinner. But Mr.

Harleigh, who looked extremely uneasy, requested Selina to see if her sister were not with Miss Ellis.

To this Ellis, by being found alone, was spared any reply; and Selina skipt down stairs to coffee.

How to avoid, or how to sustain the examination which she expected to ensue, occupied the disturbed mind of Ellis, till Selina, in about two hours, returned, exclaiming, "Sister Elinor grows odder and odder! do you know she is gone out in the chariot? She ordered it herself, without saying a word to aunt, and got in, with Golding, close to the stables! Tomlinson has just owned it to Mr. Harleigh, who was grown quite frightened at her not coming home, now it's so pitch dark. Tomlinson says she went into the hall herself, and made him contrive it all. But we are no wiser still as to where she is gone."

The distress of Ellis what course to take, increased every moment as it grew later, and as the family became more seriously alarmed. Her consciousness that there was no chance of the return of Elinor, made her feel as if culpable in not putting an end to fruitless expectation; yet how produce a letter of which every word demanded secresy, when all avowal would be useless, since Elinor could not be forced back?

No one ascended again to her chamber till ten o'clock at night: the confusion in the house was then redoubled, and a footman came hastily up stairs to summon her to Mrs. Maple.

She descended with terrour, and found Mrs. Maple in the parlour, with Harleigh, Ireton, and Mrs. Fenn.

In a voice of the sharpest reprimand, Mrs. Maple began to interrogate her: while Harleigh, who could not endure to witness a haughty rudeness which he did not dare combat, taking the arm of Ireton, whom he could still less bear to leave a spectator to a scene of humiliation to Ellis, quitted the room.

Vain, however, was either enquiry or menace; and Mrs. Maple, when she found that she could not obtain any information, though she had heard, from Mrs. Fenn, that Ellis had passed the morning with her niece, declared that she would no longer keep so dangerous a pauper in the house; and ordered her to be gone with the first appearance of light.

Ellis, courtseying in silence, retired.

In re-passing through the hall, she met Harleigh and Ireton;

the former only bowed to her, impeded by his companion from speaking; but Ireton, stopping her, said, "O! I have caught you at last! I thought, on my faith, I was always to seek you where you were never to be found. If I had not wanted to do what was right, and proper, and all that, I should have met with you a hundred times; for I never desired to do something that I might just as well let alone, but opportunity offered itself directly."

Ellis tried to pass him, and he became more serious. "It's an age that I have wanted to see you, and to tell you how prodigiously ashamed I am of all that business. I don't know how the devil it was, but I went on, tumbling from blunder to blunder, till I got into such a bog, that I could neither stand still, nor make my way out:—"

Ellis, gratified that he would offer any sort of apology, and by no means wishing that he would make it more explicit, readily assured him, that she would think no more upon the subject; and hurried to her chamber: while Harleigh, who stood aloof, thought he observed as much of dignity as of good humour, in her flying any further explanation.

But Mrs. Maple, who only meant, by her threat, to intimidate Ellis into a confession of what she knew of the absence, and of the purposes, of Elinor, was so much enraged by her calmness, that she told Mrs. Fenn to follow her, with positive orders, that, unless she would own the truth, she should quit the house immediately, though it were in the dead of the night.

Violence so inhuman rather inspired than destroyed fortitude in Ellis, who quietly answered, that she would seek an asylum, till day-light, at the neighbouring farmer's.

Selina followed, and, embracing her, with many tears, vowed eternal friendship to her; and asked whether she did not think that Lady Aurora would be equally constant.

"I must hope so!" she answered, sighing, "for what else have I to hope?"

She now made her preparations; yet decided not to depart, unless again commanded; hoping that this gust of passion would pass away, and that she might remain till the morning.

While awaiting, with much inquietude, some new order, Selina, to her great surprise, came jumping into the room, to assure her that all was well, and more than well; for that her aunt not only ceased to desire to send her away directly, but had changed her whole plan, and was foremost now in wishing her to stay.

Ellis, begging for an explanation, then heard, that Ireton had told Mrs. Maple, that there was just arrived at Brighton M. Vinstreigle, a celebrated professor,* who taught the harp; and of whom he should be charmed that Selina should take some lessons.

Mrs. Maple answered, that it would be the height of extravagance, to send for a man of whom they knew nothing, when they had so fine a performer under their own roof. Ireton replied, that he should have mentioned that from the first, but for the objections which then seemed to be in the way of trusting Miss Ellis with such a charge: but when he again named the professor, Mrs. Maple hastily commissioned Selina to acquaint Ellis, that, to-morrow morning they were to begin a regular course of lessons together upon the harp.

Though relieved, by being spared the danger and disgrace of a nocturnal expulsion, Ellis shrunk from the project of remaining longer in a house in which Harleigh was admitted at pleasure; and over which Elinor might keep a constant watch. It was consolatory, nevertheless, to her feelings, that Ireton, hitherto her defamer, should acquiesce in this offer, which, at least, not to disoblige Mrs. Maple, she would accept for the moment. To give lessons, also, to a young lady of fashion, might make her own chosen scheme, of becoming a governess in some respectable family, more practicable.

About midnight, a horseman, whom Mrs. Maple had sent with enquiries to Brighthelmstone, returned, and informed her, that he could there gather no tidings; but that he had met with a friend of his own, who had told him that he had seen Miss Joddrel, in Mrs. Maple's carriage, upon the Portsmouth road.

Mrs. Maple, now, seeing all chance of her return, for the night, at an end, said, that if her niece had freaks of this inconsiderate and indecorous sort, she would not have the family disordered, by waiting for her any longer; and, wishing the two gentlemen good night, gave directions that all the servants should go to bed.

The next morning, during breakfast, the groom returned

with the empty carriage. Miss Joddrel, he said, had made him drive her and Mrs. Golding to an inn, about ten miles from Lewes, where she suddenly told him that she should pass the night; and bid him be ready for returning at eight o'clock the next morning. He obeyed her orders; but, the next morning, heard, that she had gone on, over night, in a hired chaise, towards Portsmouth; charging no one to let him know it. This was all the account that he was able to give; except that, when he had asked whether his mistress would not be angry at his staying out all night, Miss Joddrel had answered, "O, Ellis will let her know that she must not expect me back."

Selina, who related this, was told to fetch Ellis instantly.

Ellis descended with the severest pain, from the cruel want of reflection in Elinor, which exposed her to an examination that, though she felt herself bound to evade, it must seem inexcuseable not to satisfy.

Mrs. Maple and the two gentlemen were at the breakfast-table. Harleigh would not even try to command himself to sit still, when he found that Ellis was forced to stand: and even Ireton, though he did not move, kept not his place from any intentional disrespect; for he would have thought himself completely old-fashioned, had he put himself out of his way, though for a person of the highest distinction.

"How comes it, Mistress Ellis," said Mrs. Maple, "that you had a message for me last night, from my niece, and that you never delivered it?"

Ellis, confounded, tried vainly to offer some apology.

Mrs. Maple rose still more peremptorily in her demands, mingling the haughtiest menaces with the most imperious interrogations; attacking her as an accomplice in the clandestine scheme of Elinor; and accusing her of favouring disobedience and disorder, for some sinister purposes of her own.

Ireton scrupled not to speak in her favour; and Selina eagerly echoed all that he advanced: but, Harleigh, though trembling with indignant impatience to defend her, feared, in the present state of things, that to become her advocate might rather injure than support her; and constrained himself to be silent.

A succession of categorical enquiries, forced, at length, an avowal from Ellis, that her commission had been given to her in a letter. Mrs. Maple, then, in the most authoritative manner, insisted upon reading it immediately.

Against the justice of this desire there was no appeal; yet how comply with it? The secret of Harleigh, with regard to herself, was included in that of Elinor; and honour and delicacy exacted the most rigid silence from her for both. Yet the difficulty of the refusal increased, from the increased urgency, even to fury, of Mrs. Maple; till, shamed and persecuted beyond all power of resistance, she resolved upon committing the letter to the hands of Harleigh himself; who, to an interest like her own in its concealment, superadded courage and consequence for sustaining the refusal.

This, inevitably, must break into her design of avoiding him; but, hurried and harassed, she could devise no other expedient, to escape from an appearance of utter culpability to the whole house. When again, therefore, Mrs. Maple, repeated, "Will you please to let me see my niece's letter, or not?" She answered that there was a passage in it upon which Miss Joddrel had desired that Mr. Harleigh might be consulted.

It would be difficult to say, whether this reference caused greater surprise to Mrs. Maple or to Harleigh; but the feelings which accompanied it were as dissimilar as their characters: Mrs. Maple was highly offended, that there should be any competition, between herself and any other, relative to a communication that came from her niece; while Harleigh felt an enchantment that glowed through every vein, in the prospect of some confidence. But when Mrs. Maple found that all resistance was vain, and that through this channel only she could procure any information, her resentment gave way to her eagerness for hearing it, and she told Mr. Harleigh to take the letter.

This was as little what he wished, as what Ellis meant: his desire was to speak with her upon the important subject open between them; and her's, was to make an apology for shewing him the letter, and to offer some explanation of a part of its contents. He approached her, however, to receive it, and she could not hold it back.

"If you will allow me," said he, in taking it, "to give you my plain opinion, when I have read it, ... Where may I have the pleasure of seeing you?"

Revived by this question, she eagerly answered, "Wherever Mrs. Maple will permit."

Harleigh, who, in the scowl upon Mrs. Maple's face, read a direction that they should remain where they were, would not wait for her to give it utterance; but, taking the hand of Ellis, with a precipitation to which she yielded from surprise, though with blushing shame, said, "In this next room we shall be nearest to give the answer to Mrs. Maple;" and led her to the adjoining apartment.

He did not dare shut the door, but he conducted her to the most distant window; and, having expressed, by his eyes, far stronger thanks for her trust than he ventured to pronounce with his voice, was beginning to read the letter; but Ellis, gently stopping him, said, "Before you look at this, let me beg you, Sir, to believe, that the hard necessity of my strange situation, could alone have induced me to suffer you to see what is so every way unfit for your perusal. But Miss Joddrel has herself made known that she left a message with me for Mrs. Maple; what right, then, have I to withhold it? Yet how—advise me, I entreat,—how can I deliver it? And—with respect to what you will find relative to Lord Melbury—I need not, I trust, mortify myself by disclaiming, or vindicating——"

He interrupted her with warmth: "No!" he cried, "with me you can have nothing to vindicate! Of whatever would not be perfectly right, I believe you incapable."

Ellis thanked him expressively, and begged that he would now read the letter, and favour her with his counsel.

He complied, meaning to hurry it rapidly over, to gain time for a yet more interesting subject; but, struck, moved, and shocked by its contents, he was drawn from himself, drawn even from Ellis, to its writer. "Unhappy Elinor!" he cried, "this is yet more wild than I had believed you! this flight, where you can expect no pursuit! this concealment, where you can fear no persecution! But her intellects are under the controul of her feelings,—and judgment has no guide so dangerous."

Ellis gently enquired what she must say to Mrs. Maple.

He hastily put by the letter. "Let me rather ask," he cried, half smiling, "what you will say to Me?—Will you not let me know something of your history,—your situation,—your family,—

your name? The deepest interest occasions my demand, my inquietude.—Can it offend you?"

Ellis, trembling, looking down, and involuntarily sighing, in a faltering voice, answered, "Have I not besought you, Sir, to spare me upon this subject? Have I not conjured you, if you value my peace,—nay, my honour!—what can I say more solemn?—to drop it for ever more?"

"Why this dreadful language?" cried Harleigh, with mingled impatience and grief: "Can the impression of a cumpulsatory engagement—or what other may be the mystery that it envelopes? Will you not be generous enough to relieve a perplexity that now tortures me? Is it too much for a man lost to himself for your sake,—lost he knows not how,—knows not to whom,—to be indulged with some little explanation, where, and how, he has placed all his hopes?—Is this too much to ask?"

"Too much?" repeated Ellis, with quickness: "O no! no! Were my confidence to depend upon my sense of what I owe to your generous esteem, your noble trust in a helpless Wanderer,—known to you solely through your benevolence,—were my opinion—and my gratitude my guides,—it would be difficult, indeed, to say what enquiries you could make, that I could refuse to satisfy;—what you could ask, that I ought not to answer! but alas!——"

She hesitated: heightened blushes dyed her cheeks; and she visibly struggled to restrain herself from bursting into tears.

Touched, delighted, yet affrighted, Harleigh tenderly demanded, "O, why resist the generous impulse, that would plead for some little frankness, in favour of one who unreservedly devotes to you his whole existence?"

Suddenly now, as if self-alarmed, checking her sensibility, she gravely cried, "What would it avail that I should enter into any particulars of my situation, when what has so recently passed, makes all that has preceded immaterial? You have heard my promise to Miss Joddrel,—you see by this letter how direfully she meditates to watch its performance;——"

"And can you suffer the wild flights of a revolutionary enthusiast,* impelled by every extravagant new system of the moment;—however you may pity her feelings, respect her purity, and make allowance for her youth, to blight every fair prospect of a rational attachment? to supersede every right? and to annihilate all consideration, all humanity, but for herself?"

"Ah no!—if you believe me ungrateful for a partiality that contends with all that appearances can offer against me, and all that circumstance can do to injure me; if you think me insensible to the honour I receive from it, you do yet less justice to yourself than to me! But here, Sir, all ends!—We must utterly separate;—you must not any where seek me;—I must avoid you every where!—"

She stopt.—The sudden shock which every feature of Harleigh exhibited at these last words, evidently and forcibly affected her; and the big tears, till now forced back, rolled unrestrained, and almost unconsciously, down her cheeks, as she suffered herself, for a moment, in silence to look at him: she was then hastily retiring; but Harleigh, surprised and revived by the sight of her emotion, exclaimed, "O why this fatal sensibility, that captivates while it destroys? that gives fascination even to repulse?" He would have taken her hand; but, drawing back, and even shrinking from his touch, she emphatically cried, "Remember my engagement!—my solemn promise!"

"Was it extorted?" cried he, detaining her, "or had it your heart's approbation?"

"From whatever motive it was uttered," answered she, looking away from him, "it has been pronounced, and must be adhered to religiously!" She then broke from him, and escaping by a door that led to the hall, sought refuge from any further conflict by hastening to her chamber: not once, till she arrived there, recollecting that her letter was left in his hands; while the hundred pounds, which she meant to return to him, were still in her own.

CHAPTER XXI

PAINFULLY revolving a scene which had deeply affected her, Ellis, for some time, had remained uninterrupted, when, opening her door to a gentle tap, she was startled by the sight of Harleigh. The letter of Elinor was in his hand, which he immediately presented to her, and bowing without speaking, without looking at her, instantly disappeared.

Ellis was so confounded, first by his unexpected sight, and next by his so speedily vanishing, that she lost the opportunity of returning the bank notes. For some minutes she gazed pensively down the stair-case; slowly, then, she shut her door, internally uttering "all is over:—he is gone, and will pursue me no more." Then casting up her eyes, which filled with tears, "may he," she added, "be happy!"

From this sadness she was roused, by feeling, from the thickness of the packet, that it must contain some additional paper; eagerly opening it, she found the following letter:

"I have acquainted Mrs. Maple that Miss Joddrel has determined upon living, for a while, alone, and that her manner of announcing that determination, in her letter to you, is so peremptory, as to make you deem it improper to be produced. This, as a mark of personal respect, appeases her; and, upon this subject, I believe you will be tormented no more. With regard to the unfortunate secret of Elinor, I can but wish it as safe in her own discretion, as it will remain in your honour.

"For myself, I must now practise that hardest lesson to the stubborn mind of man, submission to undefined, and what appears to be unnecessary evil. I must fly from this spot, and wait, where and as I can, the restoration of Elinor to prudence and to common life. I must trust that the less she is opposed, the less tenaciously she will cling to the impracticable project, of ruling the mind and will of another, by letting loose her own. When she hears that I deny myself inhabiting the mansion which you inhabit, perhaps, relieved from the apprehension of being deceived by others, she may cease to deceive herself. She may then return to her friends, contented to exist by the general laws of established society; which, though they may be ameliorated, changed, or reformed, by experience, wisely reflecting upon the past; by observation, keenly marking the present; or by genius, creatively anticipating the future, can never be wholly reversed, without risking a rebound that simply restores them to their original condition.

"I depart, therefore, without one more effort to see you. I yield to the strange destiny that makes me adore in the dark; yet that blazons to my view and knowledge the rarest excellencies, the most resistless attractions: but to remain in the same house, yet scarcely ever to behold you; or, in seeing you but for a moment, to awaken a sensibility that electrifies every hope, only to inflict, with the greater severity, the shock that strikes me back to mystery and despondence—no, I will be gone! Her whom I cannot soften, I will at least forbear to persecute.

"In this retreat, my only consolation for your happiness is in the friendship, so honourable for both, that you have formed with Lady Aurora Granville; my only reliance for your safety, is in the interest of Mrs. Maple to detain you under her roof, for the improvement of Selina; and my only hope for myself, is, that when Elinor becomes reasonable, you will no longer let her exclusively occupy your humanity or your feeling.

"ALBERT HARLEIGH."

The tone of remonstrance, if not of reproach, which was blended with the serious attachment marked by Harleigh in this letter, deeply touched Ellis; who was anxiously re-perusing it, when she received information, through Selina, that Mr. Harleigh had set out for London; whence he meant to proceed to Bath, or, perhaps, to make the western tour.

The earnestness of Ireton that Selina should take some lessons upon the harp, joined to the equal earnestness of Mrs. Maple, to elude the expensive professor at Brighthelmstone, confirmed the new orders that Selina should begin a course of instruction with Ellis. The mistress and the scholar were mutually well disposed, and Ellis was endeavouring to give her pupil some idea of a beautiful Sonata, when Miss Arbe, entering the house upon a morning visit, and catching the sound of a harp from the dressing-room of Selina, so touched as Selina, she knew, could not touch it, nimbly ran up stairs. Happy, then, to have surprised Miss Ellis at the instrument, she would take no denial to hearing her play.

The elegance and feeling of her performance, engaged, alike, the ready envy, and the unwilling admiration of Miss Arbe; who, a self-conceived paragon in all the fine arts, thought superior merit in a *diletante** a species of personal affront. She had already felt as an injury to her theatrical fame, the praise which had reached her ears of Ellis as Lady Townly; and a new rivalry seemed now to menace her supremacy as chief of lady performers: but when she gathered, through Selina, who knew not even of the existence of such an art as that of holding the tongue, that they were now practising together, her supercilious air was changed into one of rapture, and she was seized with a strong desire to profit, also, from such striking talents. A profusion of compliments and civilities, ended, therefore, in an earnest invitation to cultivate so charming an acquaintance.

Mrs. Maple, while this was passing, came uneasily into the room, meaning to make a sign to Ellis to glide away unnoticed. But when she found that Ellis was become the principal object with the fastidious Miss Arbe, and heard this wish of intimacy, she was utterly confounded that another person of consequence should countenance, and through her means, this itinerant Incognita. Yet to obviate the mischief by an avowal similar to that which she had been forced to make to Mrs Howel, she thought an insupportable degradation; and Miss Arbe, with the politest declarations that she should call again the next day, purposely to entitle herself to a visit in return from Miss Ellis, was already gone, before Mrs. Maple had sufficiently recovered from her confusion, to devise any impediment to the proposal.

All then that occurred to her, was her usually violent, but short measure, of sending Ellis suddenly from the house, and excusing her disappearance, by asserting that her own friends had summoned her away: for Mrs. Maple, like at least half the world, though delicate with respect to her character for truth in public, had palliations always ready for any breach of it, in favour of convenience, in private.

Ellis attempted not any opposition. The sufferings annexed to an asylum thus perpetually embittered by reproach and suspicion, had long made her languish to change it for almost any other; and her whole thoughts turned once more upon a journey to London, and an interview with Lady Aurora Granville.

Selina warmly protested that this separation should only augment her attachment to her favourite; by whose side she stayed, prattling, weeping, or practising the harp, till she was called away to Mrs. Maple; from whom, however, she soon returned, relating, with uplifted hands, that all below was again in the utmost confusion, through a letter, just arrived, from Mrs. Howel, stating the following particulars. That upon her communicating to Lord Denmeath the strange transaction, in which she must forever blush to have been, however innocently, involved, his lordship, very properly, had forbidden Lady Aurora to keep any sort of correspondence with so palpable an adventurer. But the excess of grief produced by this prohibition, had astonished and concerned both his lordship and herself: and their joint alarm had been cruelly augmented, by a letter from Mrs. Greaves, the housekeeper, with intelligence that Lord Melbury had been shut up nearly two hours with this suspicious young woman, on the day that Mrs. Howel had quitted Brighthelmstone; during which time, his lordship had suffered no one to come into the room, though she, Greaves, in accidentally passing by one of the windows, saw his lordship demean himself so far as to be speaking to her upon his knees. Lord Denmeath, treating this account as an impertinent piece of scandal, requested to have it shewn to his nephew; but how unspeakable was their consternation when Lord Melbury undauntedly avowed, that the charge was true; and added, that he was glad of the opportunity thus afforded him, to declare that Miss Ellis was the most virtuous and dignified, as well as the most beautiful and amiable of her sex: she had rejected, he said, a suit which he should always take shame to himself for having made; and rejected it in a manner so impressive of real purity, that he should for ever hold it his duty to do her honour by every means in his power. The wrath expressed by Lord Denmeath, and the tears shed by Lady Aurora, during this scene, were dreadful. Lord Denmeath saw that there was no time to be lost in guarding against the most eminent danger: he desired, therefore, that the young woman might be induced, if possible, to quit the country without delay; and his lordship was willing not only to pay for her voyage back, but to give security that she should receive a very considerable sum of money, the instant that he should be assured of her safe landing upon the continent. Mrs. Howel begged that Mrs. Maple would endeavour to bring this plan to bear; and, at all events, not lose sight of the young person, till she should be, some how or other, secured from Lord Melbury. The rest of the letter contained injunctions, that Mrs. Maple would not let this disgraceful affair transpire in the neighbourhood; with sundry scornful admonitions, that she would herself be more guarded, in future, whom she recommended to her friends.

Mrs. Maple, now, peremptorily sent word to Ellis, that she must immediately make up her mind to leaving the kingdom. But Ellis, without hesitation, answered that she had no such design. Commands and menaces, though amply employed, were fruitless to obtain any change in her resolution. She was, therefore, positively ordered to seek for charity in some other house.

Ellis, no longer wishing to stay, occupied her mind almost exclusively with the thoughts of her young friends. The tender attachment shewn to her by Lady Aurora, and the honourable testimony borne her by Lord Melbury, cheared her spirits, and warmed her heart, with a trust in their regard, that, defying the inflexibility of Mrs. Howel, the authority of Lord Denmeath, and the violence of Mrs. Maple, filled her with soft, consolatory ideas, that sweetened her night's rest, even in her uncertainty where she should find, or where seek repose on the night that would follow.

But this brighter side of her prospects, which soothed her on its first view, lost its gay colouring upon farther examination: that Lady Aurora should be forbidden to see, forbidden to write to her, was shocking to her feelings, and blighting to her happiness: and even though the tender nature, and strong partiality, of that youthful friend, might privately yield to the pleadings of an oppressed and chosen favourite, Ellis, while glowing with the hope that the interest which she had excited would be lastingly cherished, revolted from every plan that was clandestine.

Mrs. Maple, who, in common with all those whose tempers are violent in the same proportion that their judgment is feeble, had issued forth her mandates, without examining whether they could be obeyed; and had uttered her threats, without considering whether she could put them into execution; no sooner learnt, from Selina, that Ellis was tranquilly preparing to depart, than she repented the step which she had taken, and passed the night in suggesting how it might be retrieved, to spare herself the discredit, in the neighbourhood, of a breach with Mrs. Howel.

The next morning, therefore, the willing Selina was instructed to hasten to Ellis, with a message from Mrs. Maple, graciously permitting one more lesson upon the harp.

Destitute as Ellis felt, she would have resisted such a mockery of benevolence, but from gratitude at the pleasure which it procured to Selina.

Again, according to her promise, arrived Miss Arbe, and again hearing the sound of the harp, tript lightly up stairs to the dressing-room of Selina; where she paid her compliments immediately to Ellis, whom she courteously solicited to take an airing with her to Brighthelmstone, and thence to accompany her home for the day.

Anxious to strengthen her weak resources, by forming some new connection, Ellis was listening to this proposal, when a footman brought her a letter.

Concluding that it came from abroad, she received it with strong emotion, and evident alarm; but no sooner had she looked at the direction, than the brightest bloom glowed upon her cheeks, her eyes were suffused with tears of pleasure, and she pressed, involuntarily, to her heart, the writing of Lady Aurora Granville.

The little coronet seal, with the cypher* A.G., had been observed not alone by Miss Arbe, but by Mrs. Maple, who, curiously, had followed the footman into the room.

Miss Arbe, now, renewed her invitation with redoubled earnestness; and Mrs. Maple felt almost insane, from excess of wrath and embarrassment, when, suddenly, and most unexpectedly, Ellis accepted the offer; gratefully embracing Selina, and taking of herself a grave, but respectful leave.

From the window Mrs. Maple, then, saw this unknown Wanderer enter the carriage first.

For some time, she remained almost stupified by so unlooked for an event; and she could only quiet her conscience, for having been accessary, though so unintentionally, to procuring this favour and popularity for such an adventurer, by devoutly resolving, that no entreaties, and no representation, should ever in future, dupe her out of her own good sense, into other people's fantastical conceits of charity.

CHAPTER XXII

IT was not the design of Ellis to return any more to Lewes. The gross treatment which she had experienced, and the daily menace of being dismissed, were become utterly insupportable; and she determined, in a letter from Brighthelmstone, to take a final leave of Mrs Maple.

From the high influence of Miss Arbe in what is called the polite world, she hoped that to engage her favour, would almost secure prosperity to her favourite wish and plan, of exchanging her helpless dependancy, for an honourable, however fatiguing, exertion of the talents and acquirements with which she had been endowed by her education; though nothing short of the courage of distress could have stimulated her to such an attempt.

As soon, therefore, as Miss Arbe renewed her eager invitations, Ellis expressively said, "Are you sure, Madam, that you will not repent your goodness, when you know that I want, as well as that I value it?"

A carriage, which they just then met, stopt the chaise, and the voice of Miss Bydel called out a lamentation, that she was obliged to go home, because her brother wanted the coach; though she had earnest business at Brighthelmstone, whither she entreated Miss Arbe to convey her. Miss Arbe seemed much chagrined, both by the interruption and the intrusion, yet was so obviously going that way, that she knew not how to form an excuse; and Miss Bydel entered the chaise.

Extremely pleased by the sight of Ellis, "What," she cried, "my sister actress? Why this is what I did not expect indeed! I was told you would go no where, Miss Ellis, but to Lady Aurora Granville, and the Honourable Mrs. Howel. Pray is it true? I should not ask if it were a secret, for I know nobody likes one's being curious; but as all the servants must know it, it's not a thing to be kept long in the dark. And I am told, too, since it's being found out that you are a young lady of fashion, that it's the high talk that you've made a conquest of Lord Melbury; and I can't but say but I should like to know if that's a report that has got any foundation. Pray will you be so kind as to tell me."

Ellis assured her that it had not the least.

"Well, how people do like to make strange stories! One piece of information, however, I should be really glad if you would give me; and that is, whether you are come over to settle here, or only upon a visit to Mrs. Maple? And whether she has the care of your fortune, as a sort of guardian; or whether it is all in your own hands?"

Ellis, disturbed by these most unseasonable questions, answered, in a dejected tone, that she was not happy enough to be able, at this moment, to give any circumstantial account of herself.

Miss Arbe, who only imperfectly understood the speech which had been made as the chaise was stopt, languished to hear it explained. Privately, therefore, by arch winks, and encouraging taps, she urged on the broad questions of Miss Bydel; though she was too expert an adept in the rules, at least, of good breeding, not to hold back herself from such interrogatories, as might level her elevated fame with that of the gross and homely* Miss Bydel; who to sordid friends owed a large fortune, left her late in life; but neither education nor manners, that might have taught her that its most hateful privilege is that of authorising unfeeling liberties.

They had arrived, nevertheless, within half a mile of Brighthelmstone, before any thing really explanatory had passed: Ellis, then, alarmed with reflecting that, if again dragged to Lewes, she must again have to quit it, with scarcely a chance of such another opportunity for endeavouring to bring forward her project, conquered her reluctance to opening upon her distress, and said, "You little suspect, Miss Arbe, how deep an obligation I owe to your kindness, in carrying me to-day to Brighthelmstone!"

"How so, Miss Ellis? How so, my dear?" cried Miss Bydel, before Miss Arbe could answer.

"My situation," she continued, "which seems so pleasant, is perhaps amongst the most painful that can be imagined. I feel myself, though in my native country, like a helpless foreigner; unknown, unprotected, and depending solely upon the benevolence of those by whom, accidentally, I am seen, for kindness,—or even for support!—"

The amazement of the two ladies, at this declaration, was equally great, though Miss Arbe, who never spoke and never acted, but through the medium of what she believed the world would most approve to hear her say, or to see her do, had no chance of manifesting her surprise as promptly as Miss Bydel; who made her own judgment the sole arbitrator of her speech and conduct, and who immediately called out, "Well, nobody shall ever try to persuade me I am in the wrong again! I said, the whole time, there was certainly something quite out of the common way in this young person. And it's plain I was right. For how, I said, can it be, that, first of all, a young person is brought out as nothing, and then is turned into a fine lady; when, all the time, nobody knows any thing about her? But pray tell me this one thing, child; what was the first motive of your going over the seas? And what might be the reason of your coming back again in such an untowardly sort of manner? without any money, or any one to be accountable for your character?"

Ellis made no answer. The obligations, however heavy of endurance, which led her to bear similar, and still more offensive examinations from Mrs. Maple, existed not here; and the compulsion of debts of that nature, could alone strengthen the patience, or harden the feelings of a generous spirit, to sustain so rude and unfeeling an inquisition.

Miss Arbe, though anxious to understand, before she uttered even a word, what sort of footing, independently of Mrs. Maple, this young person was upon in the world, failed not to remark, in her silence, a courage that unavoidably spoke in her favour.

Ellis saw, but too plainly, how little she had to expect from spontaneous pity, or liberality; and hesitated whether to plead more humbly, or to relinquish at once her plan.

"You are still, then," resumed Miss Bydel, "at your secret-keeping, I find, that we were told so much about at the beginning, before the discovery of your being a lady of family and fashion; which came out so, all of the sudden, at last, that I should never have believed a word of it, but for knowing Mrs. Maple to be so amazing particular as to those points.—"

"And Mrs. Howel!" here interrupted Miss Arbe, casting at Ellis, upon the recollection of such a confirmation of her birth and connections, a look of so much favour, that, again hoping for her aid, Ellis begged to alight at Miss Matson's, the milliner.

Miss Arbe said that she would attend her thither with pleasure. "And I, my dear," said Miss Bydel, "will go in with you, too; for I want a few odd matters for myself."

Ellis, finding how little she was understood, was forced to add: "It is not for any purchases that I go to Miss Matson;—it is to lodge in her house, till I can find some better asylum!—"

The first amazement of the two ladies sunk into nothing, when contrasted with that which they experienced at this moment. That she should acknowledge herself to be poor, was quite enough, be her other claims to notice what they might, to excite immediate contempt in Miss Bydel: while Miss Arbe, in that point, more liberal, but, in all that she conceived to belong to fashion, a very slave, was embarrassed how to treat her, till she could gain some information how she was likely to be treated by the world: but neither of them had entertained the most distant suspicion, that she was not settled under the roof, and the patronage, of Mrs. Maple. To hear, therefore, of her seeking a lodging, and wanting an asylum, presented her in so new, so altered, and so humiliated a point of view, that Miss Bydel herself was not immediately able to speak; and the two ladies stared at each other, as if reciprocally demanding how to behave.

Ellis perceived their dilemma, and again lost her hope.

"A lodging?" at length cried Miss Bydel. "Well, I am less surprised than any body else will be, for when things have an odd beginning, I always expect them to have an odd end. But how comes it,—for that can be no secret,—that you are looking out for a lodging? I should like to know what all that means. Pray what may be the reason that Mrs. Maple does not find you a lodging herself? And who is to take care of you? Does she lend you any of her own servants? These things, at least, can be no secrets, or else I should not ask; but the servants must needs know whether they are lent or not."

Ellis made no reply; and still Miss Arbe held back.

"Well," resumed Miss Bydel, "I don't like to judge any body, but certainly it is no good sign to be so close. Some things, however, must be known whether people will or not: so I hope at least I may ask, whether your friends are coming to you in your lodging?—and what you intend to do there?—and how long you think to live there?—and what is the true cause of your going there?—For there must certainly be some reason."

Ellis, who now found that she must either answer Miss Bydel or forego her whole scheme, from the determined backwardness of Miss Arbe to take any active part in her affairs, said, "My past history, Madam, it would be useless to hear—and impossible for me to relate: my present plan must depend upon a charitable construction of my unavoidable, indispensable silence; without which it would be madness to hope for any favour, any recommendation, that may give the smallest chance of success to my attempt."

"And what is your attempt?" cried Miss Bydel; "for if that's a secret too, I can't find out how you're to do it."

"On the contrary," she answered, "I am well aware that I must publish, or relinquish it; and immediately I would make it known, if I dared hope that I might appear qualified for the office I wish to undertake, in the eyes of—"

She looked at Miss Arbe, but did not venture to proceed.

Miss Arbe, understanding, and feeling the compliment, yet uneasy to have it equally understood by Miss Bydel, complacently broke her silence, by saying, "In whose eyes?—Lady Aurora Granville's?"

"Ah! Madam,—the condescending partiality of Lady

Aurora, might encourage every hope of the honour of her interest and zeal;—but she is peculiarly situated;—and perhaps the weight that must be attached to a recommendation of the sort which I require—"

She was going to say, might demand more experience than her ladyship's extreme youth allowed to have yet fallen to her share; but she stopt. She was aware that she stood upon dangerous ground. The vanity of Miss Arbe was, at least, as glaring as her talents; and to celebrate even her judgment in the fine arts, though it was the pride of her life, by an insinuation that, at one-and-thirty she was not in the first budding youth of fifteen, might offend, by an implication that added years contributed to a superiority, which she wished to have considered as due to brighter genius alone.

From what was said, Miss Arbe could not be without some suspicion of what was held back; and she as little desired to hear, as Ellis could to utter, a word that might derogate from the universal elevation and distinction at which she aspired; she was perfectly ready, therefore, to accept what would flatter, and to reject what would mortify her; forgetting, in common with all vain characters, that to shrink from the truth ourselves, saves one person only from hearing our defects.

"It is true," said Miss Arbe, smiling, "Lady Aurora cannot be supposed to have much weight with the world, amiable as she is. The world is not very easily led; and, certainly, only by those who acquire a certain ascendance over it, by some qualifications not entirely of the most common sort.—"

"But still I don't understand," cried Miss Bydel, "what it is Miss Ellis means. What is it you want to be recommended about, child?—What is this attempt you talk of?—Have you got your fortune with you?—or does Mrs. Maple keep it in her own hands?—or have not you got any left?—or perhaps you've had none from the beginning?"

Ellis briefly explained, that her wish was to be placed in some family, where there were children, as a governess.

Again, the two ladies were equally surprised, at the project of so steady and elaborate an undertaking; and Miss Bydel broke forth into the most abrupt enquiries, of how Mrs. Maple came to agree to such a scheme; whether it were approved of by Mrs. Howel; and what Ellis could teach, or do, if it took place.

Ellis, when compelled to speak, was compelled, also, to confess, that she had not mentioned her design to either of those ladies.

Miss Bydel now, stiffly drawing up, declared that she could not help taking the liberty to say, that for a young lady, who was under the care of two persons of so much consideration and fortune, to resolve upon disposing of herself, without consulting either of them, was a thing she never should countenance; and which she was sure all the world would be against.

These were alarming words for Miss Arbe, whose constant and predominant thought, was ever upon public opinion. All, too, seemed, now, at an end, that had led, or could lead, to conciliation, where there was so peculiar a rivalry in talents; joined to a superiority of beauty, visible even to her own eyes; for how, if the hours of Ellis were to be consigned to the care and improvement of young ladies, could either time or opportunity be found, to give, and in private, the musical instructions, for the hope of which alone Miss Arbe had been so earnest in her invitations, and so courteous in her manners?

Without offering, therefore, the smallest softening word to the bluff questions, or gross censures of Miss Bydel, she was silent till they entered Brighthelmstone; and then only spoke to order the postilion to stop at Miss Matson's. There arrived, the two ladies let her alight alone; Miss Bydel, with a proud nod, just uttering, "Good bye!" and Miss Arbe, with a forced smile, saying she was happy to have been of any use to her.

Ellis remained so confounded, when thus unexpectedly abandoned, that she stood still, a few minutes, at the door, unable to answer, or even to understand, the civil inquiries of a young woman, from the shop, whether she would not come in, to give her commands. When a little recovered, she entered, and, in the meek tone of apprehension, asked whether she could again hire, for a few nights, or a week, the little room in which she had slept some time since.

Miss Matson, recollecting her voice, came now from the back parlour, most courteously rejoicing at seeing her; and disguising her surprise, that she should again enquire for so cheap and ordinary a little lodging. For Miss Matson, and her family, had learnt, from various reports, that she was the same young lady who had given so much pleasure by her performance in the Provoked Husband; and who had, since, made a long visit at the Honourable Mrs. Howel's, near whose mansion was situated the shop. But, whatever might be the motive of her return, there could be none against her admission, since they knew her high connections, and since, even now, she was set down at the shop by Miss Arbe. The little room, therefore, was speedily prepared, and the first use that Ellis made of it, was to write to Selina.

She desired leave to present her thanks to Mrs. Maple, for the asylum which had been afforded to her distress; without any hints at the drawbacks to its comfort; and then briefly communicated her intention, to pass the rest of the time of her suspence and difficulties, in working at her needle; unless she could find means to place herself in some respectable family, as a governess to its children. She finished her letter by the warmest acknowledgements, for the kindness which she had experienced from Selina.

The person who took this note was desired to apply to Mrs. Fenn, for the ready prepared baggage of Ellis.

This, which she thought a respect demanded by decency to Mrs. Maple, was her first action: she then opened, as a balm to her wounded feelings, the letter of Lady Aurora Granville; but had the cruel disappointment to find in it only these words:

"Hate me not, sweet Miss Ellis—but I am forbidden to write to you!—forbidden to receive your letters!—

"A. G."

Deeply hurt, and deeply offended, Ellis, now, was filled with the heaviest grief; though neither offended nor hurt by Lady Aurora, whose trembling handwriting she kissed a thousand times; with a perfect conviction, that their sufferings were nearly reciprocal, from this terrible prohibition.

Her little baggage soon arrived, with a letter from Selina, containing a permission from Mrs. Maple, that Ellis might immediately return to Lewes, lest, which Mrs. Howel would never forgive, she should meet with Lord Melbury.

Ellis wrote a cold excuse, declaring her firm purpose to endeavour to depend, henceforth, upon her own exertions.

And, to strengthen this resolution, she re-read a passage in one of her letters from abroad, to which she had frequent recourse, when her spirits felt unequal to her embarrassments.

"Dans une position telle que la vôtre,*—"&c.

"In your present lonely, unprotected, unexampled situation, many and severe may be your trials; let not any of them shake your constancy, nor break your silence: while all is secret, all may be safe; by a single surmise, all may be lost. But chiefly bear in mind, what has been the principle of your education, and what I wish to be that of your conduct and character through life: That where occasion calls for female exertion, mental strength must combat bodily weakness; and intellectual vigour must supply the inherent deficiencies of personal courage; and that those, only, are fitted for the vicissitudes of human fortune, who, whether female or male, learn to suffice to themselves. Be this the motto of your story."

CHAPTER XXIII

THE hope of self-dependence, ever cheering to an upright mind, sweetened the rest of Ellis in her mean little apartment, though with no brighter prospect than that of procuring a laborious support, through the means of Miss Matson, should she fail to obtain a recommendation for the superiour office of a governess.*

The decision was yet pending, when a letter from Selina charged her, in the name of Mrs. Maple, to adopt, as yet, no positive measure, in order to put an end to the further circulation of wonder, that a young lady should go from under Mrs. Maple's protection, to a poor little lodging, without any attendant, and avowedly in search of a maintenance: and, further, Selina was bid to add, that, if she would be manageable, she might still persist in passing for a young gentlewoman; and Mrs.

Maple would say that she was reduced to such straights by a bankruptcy in her family; rather than shock all the ladies who had conversed with her as Mrs. Maple's guest, by telling the truth. Mrs. Howel, too, with the approbation of Lord Denmeath himself, to keep her out of the way of Lord Melbury, would try to get her the place of an humble companion* to some sick old lady, who would take up with her reading and singing, and ask no questions.

Ellis, with utter contempt, was still perusing this letter, when she was surprised by a visit from Miss Arbe and Miss Bydel.

Miss Arbe had just been calling upon Mrs. Maple, by whom she had been told the plan of Mrs. Howel, and the plausible tale of its sudden necessity. Finding Ellis still under a protection so respectable, the wish of a little musical intercourse revived in Miss Arbe; and she remarked to Miss Bydel, that it would be a real charity, to see what could be done for an accomplished young woman of family, in circumstances so lamentable.

The reception they met with from Ellis was extremely cold. The careless air with which Miss Arbe had heard, without entering into her distress; and the indifference with which she had suddenly dropt the invitations that, the minute before, had been urgent nearly to persecution, had left an impression of the littleness of her character upon the mind of Ellis, that made her present civilities, though offered with a look that implied an expectation of gratitude, received with the most distant reserve. And still less was she disposed to welcome Miss Bydel, whose behaviour, upon the same occasion, had been rude as well as unfeeling.

Neither of them, however, were rebuffed, though Miss Arbe was disappointed, and Miss Bydel was amazed: but Miss Arbe had a point to carry, and would not be put from her purpose; and Miss Bydel, though she thought it but odd not to be made of more consequence, could not be hurt from a feeling which she neither possessed nor understood,—delicacy.

"So I hear, Miss Ellis, you have met with misfortunes?" Miss Bydel began: "I am sorry for it, I assure you; though I am sure I don't know who escapes. But I want to know how it all first began. Pray, my dear, in what manner did you set out in life? A great deal of one's pity depends upon what people are used to."

"What most concerns me for poor Miss Ellis," said Miss Arbe, "is her having no instrument. I can't think how she can live without one. Why don't you hire a harp, Miss Ellis?"

Ellis quietly answered, that she was not very musically inclined.

"But you must not think how you are inclined," said Miss Bydel, "if you are to go out for a companion, as Mrs. Howel wants you to do; for I am sure I don't know who you will get to take you, if you do. I have known pretty many young women in that capacity, and not one among them ever had such a thought. How should they? People do not pay them for that."

"I only hope," said Miss Arbe, "that whoever has the good fortune to obtain the society of Miss Ellis, will have a taste for music. 'Twill be a thousand shames if her fine talents should be thrown away."

Ellis, as she suspected not her design, was much surprised by this return to fine speeches. Still, however, she sustained her own reserve, for the difficulty of devising to what the change might be owing, made her cast it upon mere caprice. To the enquiries, also, of Miss Bydel, she was equally immoveable, as they evidently sprang from coarse and general curiosity.

This distance, however, was not successful, either in stopping the questions of Miss Bydel, or the compliments of Miss Arbe. Each followed the bent of her humour, till Miss Arbe, at length, started an idea that caught the attention of Ellis: this was, that instead of becoming an humble companion, she should bring her musical acquirements into use, by giving lessons to young ladies.

Ellis readily owned that such a plan would be best adapted to her inclinations, if Mrs. Howel and Mrs. Maple could be prevailed upon to exert their influence in procuring her some scholars.

"But a good word or two from Miss Arbe," said Miss Bydel, "would do more for you, in that tuning way, than all their's put together. I should like to know how it was you got this musical turn, Miss Ellis? Were your own friends rich enough, my dear, before their bankruptcy, to give you such an education themselves? or did it all come, as one may say, from a sort of knack?"

Ellis earnestly asked whether she might hope for the powerful aid of Miss Arbe to forward such a plan.

Miss Arbe, now, resumed all her dignity, as an acknowledged judge of the fine arts, and a solicited patronness of their votaries. With smiles, therefore, of ineffable affability, she promised Ellis her protection; and glibly ran over the names of twenty or thirty families of distinction, every one of which, she said, in the choice of instructors to their children, was guided by her opinion.

"But then," added she, with an air that now mingled authority with condescension, "you must have a better room than this, you know. The house is well enough, and the milliner is fashionable: she is my own; but this little hole will never do: you must take the drawing room. And then you must buy immediately, or at least hire, a very fine instrument. There is a delightful one at Strode's now: one I long for myself, and then—" patting her shoulder, "you must dress, too, a little .... like other people, you know."

"But how is she to do it," said Miss Bydel, "if she has got no money?"

Ellis, however ashamed, felt rather assisted than displeased by this plump truth; but it produced no effect upon Miss Arbe, who lightly replied, "O, we must not be shabby. We must get things a little decent about us. A few scholars of my recommending will soon set all that to rights. Take my advice, Miss Ellis, and you won't find yourself vastly to be pitied."

"But what have you got to begin with?" said Miss Bydel. "How much have you in hand?"

"Nothing!" answered Ellis, precipitately: "I lost my purse at Dover, and I have been destitute ever since! Dependant wholly upon accidental benevolence."

Miss Bydel, now, was extremely gratified: this was the first time that she had surprized from Ellis any account of herself, and she admitted not a doubt that it would be followed by her whole history.

"That was unlucky enough," she said; "and pray what money might you have in it?"

Ellis, strongly affected herself, though she had not affected her auditors, by the retrospection of a misfortune which had been so eventful to her of distress, said no more; till she saw some alarm upon the countenance of Miss Arbe, at the idea of a *protegée* really pennyless; and then, fearing to forfeit her patronage, she mentioned the twenty pounds which she owed to the generous kindness of Lady Aurora Granville.

Miss Arbe now smiled more complacently than ever; and Miss Bydel, straining wide open her large dull eyes, repeated, "Twenty pounds? Good me!* has Lady Aurora given you twenty pounds?"

"The money," said Ellis, blushing, "I hope I may one day return: the goodness surpasses all requital."

"Well, if that is the case, we must all try to do something for you, my dear. I did not know of any body's having begun. And I am never for being the first in those sort of subscriptions; for I think them little better than picking people's pockets. Besides that I entirely disapprove bringing persons that are poor into habits of laziness. However, if Lady Aurora has given so handsomely, one does not know how to refuse a trifle. So, I tell you what; I'll pay you a month's hire of a harp."

Ellis, deeply colouring, begged to decline this offer; but Miss Arbe, with an air of self-approbation that said: I won't be excelled! cried, "And I, Miss Ellis, will go to the music shop, and chuse your instrument for you myself."

Both the ladies, now, equally elated by internal applause, resolved to set out instantly upon this errand; without regarding either refusal or objection from Ellis. Yet Miss Bydel, upon finding that neither Mrs. Howel nor Mrs. Maple had yet given any thing, would have retracted from her intended benefaction, had not Miss Arbe dragged her away; positively refusing to let her recant, from a conviction that no other method could be started, by which her own contribution could so cheaply be presented.

A very fine harp soon arrived, with a message from Miss Arbe, desiring that she might find Miss Ellis wholly disengaged the next morning, when she meant to come quite alone, and to settle every thing.

The total want of delicacy shewn in this transaction, made the wishes of Ellis send back the instrument to Miss Bydel, and refuse the purposed visit of Miss Arbe: but a little reflection taught her, that, in a situation so defenceless, pride must give way to prudence; and nicer feelings must submit to necessity.

She sat down, therefore, to her harp, resolved diligently to practise it as a business, which might lead her to the self-dependence at which she so earnestly languished to arrive; and of which she had only learnt the just appreciation, by her helplessness to resist any species of indignity, while accepting an unearned asylum.

Cheered, therefore, again, by this view of her new plan, she received Miss Arbe, the next morning, with a gratitude the most flattering to that lady, who voluntarily renewed her assurances of protection. "Very luckily for you," she added, "I shall stay here very late; for Papa says that he can't afford to begin his winter this year before May or June."*

Then, sending for a large packet of music from her carriage, she proposed trying the instrument; complacently saying, that she had chosen the very best which could be procured, though Miss Bydel had vehemently struggled to make her take a cheaper one. Miss Arbe, however, would not indulge her parsimony. "I can't bear," she cried, "any thing that is mean."

What Miss Arbe called trying the instrument, was selecting the most difficult passages, from the most difficult music which she attempted to play, and making Ellis teach her the fingering, the time, and the expression, in a lesson which lasted the whole morning.

Miss Arbe, who aspired at passing for an adept in every accomplishment, seized with great quickness whatever she began to learn; but her ambition was so universal, and her pursuits were so numerous, that one of them marred another; and while every thing was grasped at, nothing was attained. Yet the general aim passed with herself for general success; and because she had taken lessons in almost all the arts, she concluded that of all the arts she was completely mistress.

This persuasion made her come forward, in the circles to which she belonged, with a courage that she deemed to be the just attribute of superiour merit; and her family and friends, not less complaisant, and rarely less superficial, in their judgments than herself, sanctioned her claims by their applause; and spread their opinions around, till, hearing them reverberated, they believed them to be fame.

The present scheme for Ellis had another forcible consideration in its favour with Miss Arbe; a consideration not often accustomed to be treated with utter contempt, even by higher and wiser characters; the convenience of her purse. Her various accomplishments had already exhausted the scanty powers for extra-expences of her father; and it was long since she had received any instructions through the ordinary means of remuneration. But, ingenious in whatever could turn to her advantage, she contrived to learn more when she ceased to recompense her masters, than while the obligation between them and their pupil was reciprocated; for she sought no acquaintance but amongst the scholars of the most eminent professors, whether of music or painting: her visits were always made at the moment which she knew to be dedicated to practising, or drawing; and she regularly managed, by adroit questions, seasoned with compliments, to attract the attention of the master to herself, for an explanation of the difficulties which distressed her in her private practice.

Compliments, however, were by no means the only payment that she returned for such assistance: if a benefit* were in question, she had not an acquaintance upon whom she did not force tickets; if a composition were to be published, she claimed subscriptions for it from all her friends; if scholars were desired, not a parent had a child, not a guardian had a ward, whom she did not endeavour to convince, that to place his charge under such or such a professor, was the only method to draw forth his talents. She scarcely entered a house in which she had not some little scheme to effect; and seldom left it with her purpose unfulfilled.

The artists, also, were universally her humble servants; for though they could not, like the world at large, be the dupes of her unfounded pretensions to skill, they were sure, upon all occasions, to find her so active to serve and oblige them, so much more civil than those who had money, and so much more social than those who had power, that, from mingling gratitude with their personal interest, they suffered her claims to superiour knowledge to pass uncanvassed; and while they remarked that her influence supplied the place of wealth, they sought her favour, they solicited her recommendation, they dedicated to her their works. She charmed them by personal civilities; she won them by attentions to their wives, sisters, or daughters; and her zeal in return for their gratuitous services had no limit—except what might be attached to her purse.

To pay for the instructions of Ellis by patronage, was no sooner decided than effected. A young lady who had been educated abroad, who was brought forth into the world by Mrs. Maple, and protected by Mrs. Howel, and Lady Aurora Granville, was already an engaging object; but when she was reduced to support herself by her own talents, through the bankruptcy of her friends, she became equally interesting and respectable; and, as such, touched for her misfortunes, yet charmed to profit from her accomplishments, Lady Kendover, a leading *Diletante* in the highest circles, was the first to beg that Miss Arbe would arrange the terms, and fix a day and hour, for Miss Ellis to attend Lady Barbara Frankland, her ladyship's niece.

One pupil of this rank, thus readily offered, procured another before the day was over; and, before the evening was finished, a third.

Miss Arbe, enchanted with her success, hastened to have the pleasure of communicating it to Ellis, and of celebrating her own influence. The gratitude of Ellis was, however, by no means unruffled, when Miss Arbe insisted upon regulating the whole of her proceedings; and that with an expence which, however moderate for any other situation, was for hers alarming, if not ruinous. But Miss Arbe declared that she would not have her recommendation disgraced by any meanness: she engaged, therefore, at a high price, the best apartment in the house; she chose various articles of attire, lest Ellis should choose them, she said, too parsimoniously; and employed, in fitting her up, some tradespeople who were honoured, occasionally, by working for herself. In vain Ellis represented the insufficiency of her little store for such expences. Miss Arbe impatiently begged that they might not waste their time upon such narrow considerations; and, seizing the harp, devoted the rest of the visit to a long, though unacknowledged lesson; after which, in hastily nodding an adieu, she repeated her high disdain of whatever was wanting in spirit and generosity.

Mrs. Maple, with mingled choler and amazement, soon learnt the wonderful tidings, that the discarded Wanderer had hired the best drawing-room at the famous milliner's, Miss Matson, and was elegantly, though simply arrayed, and prepared and appointed to be received, in various houses of fashion, as a favoured and distinguished professor.

The fear of some ultimate responsibility, for having introduced such an impostor into high life, now urged Mrs. Maple to work upon the curiosity of Mrs. Ireton, to offer the unknown traveller the post of her humble companion: but Ellis retained a horrour of the disposition and manners of Mrs. Ireton, that made her decidedly refuse the proposition; and the incenced Mrs. Maple, and the imperious Mrs. Howel, alike ashamed to proclaim what they considered as their own dupery,* were alike, ultimately, reduced to leave the matter to take its course: Mrs. Howel finally comforting herself, that, in case of detection, she could cast the whole disgrace upon Mrs. Maple; who equally consoled herself by deciding, in that case, to throw the whole blame upon Mr. Harleigh.

CHAPTER XXIV

THUS equipped, and decided, the following week opened upon Ellis, with a fair prospect of fulfilling the injunctions of her correspondent, by learning to suffice to herself. This idea animated her with a courage which, in some measure, divested her of the painful timidity, that, to the inexperienced and modest, is often subversive of the use of the very talents which it is their business and interest to display. Courage, not only upon such occasions, but upon others of infinitely higher importance, is more frequently than the looker on suspects, the effect of secret reasoning, and cool calculation of consequences, than of fearless temperament, or inborn bravery.

Her first essay exceeded her best expectations in its success; a success the more important, as failure, there, might have fastened discredit upon her whole enterprize, since her first pupil was Lady Barbara Frankland.

Lady Kendover, the aunt of that young lady, to whom Miss

Arbe, for the honour of her own patronage, had adroitly dwelt upon the fortnight passed at Mrs. Howel's, and, in the society of Lady Aurora Granville, by her *protegée*; received and treated her with distinguished condescension, and even flattering kindness. For though her ladyship was too high in rank, to share in the anxious tenaciousness of Mrs. Howel, for manifesting the superiour judgment with which she knew how to select, and how to reject, persons qualified for her society; and though yet less liable to be controlled by the futile fears of the opinion of a neighbourhood, which awed Mrs. Maple; still she was more a woman of quality than a woman of the world; and the circle in which she moved, was bounded by the hereditary habits, and imitative customs, which had always limited the proceedings of her ladyship's, in common with those of almost every other noble family, of patronizing those who had already been elevated by patronage; and of lifting higher, by peculiar favour, those who were already mounting by the favour of others. To go further,—to draw forth talents from obscurity, to honour indigent virtue, were exertions that demanded a character of a superiour species; a character that had learnt to act for himself, by thinking for himself and feeling for others.

The joy of Lady Barbara, a lively and lovely young creature, just blooming into womanhood, in becoming the pupil of Ellis, was nearly extatic. Lady Aurora Granville, with whom she was particularly connected, had written to her in such rapture of the private play, that she was wild to see the celebrated Lady Townly. And though she was not quite simple, nor quite young enough, to believe that she should literally behold that personage, her ideas were, unconsciously, so bewildered, between the representation of nature and life, or nature and life themselves, that she had a certain undefined pleasure in the meeting which perplexed, yet bewitched her imagination. She regarded it as the happiest possible event, to be brought into such close intercourse, with a person whom she delighted herself with considering as the first actress of the age. She looked at her; watched her; listened to her; and prevailed upon Lady Kendover to engage that she should every day take a lesson; during which her whole mind was directed to imitating Miss Ellis in her manner of holding the harp; in the air of her head as she turned from it to look at the musical notes; in her way of curving, straightening, or elegantly spreading her fingers upon the strings; and in the general bend of her person, upon which depended the graceful effect of the whole. Not very singular, indeed, was Lady Barbara, in regarding these as the principal points to be attained, in acquiring the accomplishment of playing upon the harp; which, because it shews beauty and grace to advantage, is often erroneously chosen for exhibiting those who have neither; as if its powers extended to bestow the charms which it only displays.

The admiration of Lady Barbara for her instructress, lost some boundary of moderation every day; and Ellis, though ashamed of such excess of partiality, felt fostered by its warmth, and returned it with sincerity. Lady Barbara, who was gaily artless, and as full of kindness as of vivacity, had the strong recommendation of being wholly natural; a recommendation as rare in itself, as success is in its deviations.

Miss Arbe was all happy exultation, at a prosperity for which she repaid herself, without scruple, by perpetual, though private lessons; and Ellis, whose merit, while viewed with rivalry, she had sought to depreciate, she was now foremost to praise. The swellings of envy and jealously gave way to triumph in her own discernment; and all severities of hypercriticism subsided into the gentler vanity, and more humane parade, of patronage.

Another happy circumstance signalized, also, this professional commencement of Ellis; Miss Arbe secured to her the popular favour of Sir Marmaduke Crawley, a travelled fine gentleman, just summoned from Italy, to take possession of his title and estate; and to the guardianship of two hoyden* sisters, many years younger than himself. His character of a connoisseur, an admirer of *les beaux arts*; a person of so refined a conformation,* as to desire to be thought rather to vegetate than to live, when removed from the genial clime of the sole region of the muses, and of taste, Italy; made his approbation as useful to her fame, as the active influence of Miss Arbe was to her fortune. This gentleman, upon hearing her perform to Lady Kendover, declared, with a look of melancholy recollection, that The Ellis* was more divine than any thing that he had yet met with on this side the Alps. He requested Miss Arbe, therefore, to place his sisters under her elegant tuition, if he might hope that The Ellis could be prevailed upon to undertake two such Vandals.*

Born to a considerable fortune, though with a narrow capacity, Sir Marmaduke had persuaded himself, that to make the tour of Europe, and to become a connoisseur in all the arts, was the same thing; and, as he was rich, and, therefore, able to make himself friends, civil, and therefore never addicted to make enemies, no one felt tempted, either by sincerity or severity, to undeceive him; and, as all he essentially wanted, for the character to which he thought himself elevated, was "spirit, taste, and sense,"* he uttered his opinions upon whatever he saw, or heard, without the smallest suspicion, that the assiduity with which he visited, or the wealth with which he purchased, works of art, included not every requisite for their appreciation. Yet though, from never provoking, he never encountered, that foe to the happy feelings of inborn presumption, truth, he felt sometimes embarrassed, when suddenly called upon to pronounce an opinion on any abstruse point of taste. He was always, therefore, watchful to catch hints from the dashing Miss Arbe, since to whatever she gave her fearless sanction, he saw fashion attached.

Nothing could be more different than the reception given to Ellis by Lady Kendover, and that which she experienced from the Miss Crawleys. Without any superiority to their brother in understanding, they had a decided inferiority in education and manners. They had been brought up by a fond uncle, in the country, with every false indulgence which can lead to idle ease and pleasure, for the passing moment; but which teems with that weariness, that a dearth of all rational employment nurses up for the listless and uncultured, when folly and ignorance out-live mere thoughtless merriment. Accustomed to follow, in every thing, the uncontrolled bent of their own humours, they felt fatigued by the very word decorum; and thought themselves oppressed by any representation of what was due to propriety. Their brother, on the contrary, taking the opposite extreme, had neither care nor wish but what related to the opinion of the *virtuosi*:* because, though possessed of whatever could give pecuniary, he was destitute of all that could inspire mental independence.

"Oh ho! The Ellis!" cried Miss Crawley, mimicking her brother: "you are come to be our school-mistress, are you? Quick, quick, Di; put on your dumpish* face, and begin your task."

"Be quiet, be quiet!" cried Miss Di; "I shall like to learn of all things. The Ellis shall make me The Crawley. Come, what's to be done, The Ellis? Begin, begin!"

"And finish, finish!" cried the eldest: "I can't bear to be long about any thing: there's nothing so fogrum."

Their brother, now, ventured, gently, to caution them not to make use of the word fogrum,* which, he assured them, was by no means received in good company.

"O, I hate good company!" cried the eldest: "it always makes me fall asleep."

"So do I," cried the youngest; "except when I take upon myself to wake it. O! that's the delight of my life! to run wild upon a set of formals,* who think one brainless, only because one is not drowsy. Do you know any fogrums of that sort, brother?"

The merriment that this question, which they meant to be personal, occasioned, extremely confused Sir Marmaduke; and his evident consciousness flung them into such immoderate laughter, that the new mistress was forced to desist from all attempt at instruction, till it subsided; which was not till their brother, shrugging his shoulders, with shame and mortification, left the room.

Yawning, then, with exhausted spirits, they desired to be set to work.

Proficiency they had no chance, for they had no wish to make; but Ellis, from this time, attended them twice a week; and Sir Marmaduke was gratified by the assurances of Miss Arbe, that all the world praised his taste, for choosing them so accomplished an instructress.

The fourth scholar that the same patronage procured for Ellis, was a little girl of eleven years of age, whose mother, Lady Arramede, the nearly ruined widow of a gamester peer, sacrificed every comfort to retain the equipage, and the establishment, that she had enjoyed during the life of her luxurious lord.

Her table, except when she had company, was never quite sufficient for her family; her dress, except when she visited, was always old, mended, and out of fashion; and the education of her daughter, though destined to be of the first order, was extracted, in common with her gala dinners, and gala ornaments,* from these daily savings. Ellis, therefore, from the very moderate price at which Miss Arbe, for the purpose of obliging her own various friends, had fixed her instructions, was a treasure to Lady Arramede; who had never before so completely found, what she was always indefatigably seeking, a professor not more cheap than fashionable.

On the part of the professor, the satisfaction was not quite mutual. Lady Arramede, reduced by her great expences in public, to the most miserable parsimony in private, joined, to a lofty desire of high consideration in the world, a constant alarm lest her pecuniary difficulties should be perceived. The low terms, therefore, upon which Ellis taught, though the real inducement for her being employed, urged the most arrogant reception of the young instructress, in the apprehension that she might, else, suspect the motive to her admission; and the instant that she entered the room, her little pupil was hurried to the instrument, that she might not presume to imagine it possible, that she could remain in the presence of her ladyship, even for a moment, except to be professionally occupied.

Yet was she by no means more niggardly in bestowing favour, than rapacious in seeking advantage. Her thoughts were constantly employed in forming interrogatories for obtaining musical information, by which her daughter might profit in the absence of the mistress; though she made them without troubling herself to raise her eyes, except when she did not comprehend the answer; and then, her look was of so haughty a character, that she seemed rather to be demanding satisfaction than explication.

The same address, also, accompanied her desire to hear the pieces, which her daughter began learning, performed by the mistress: she never made this request till the given hour was more than passed; and made it then rather as if she were issuing a command, for the execution of some acknowledged duty, than calling forth talents, or occupying time, upon which she could only from courtesy have any claim.

Miss Brinville, the fifth pupil of Ellis, was a celebrated beauty, who had wasted her bloom in a perpetual search of admiration; and lost her prime, without suspecting that it was gone, in vain and ambitious difficulties of choice. Yet her charms, however faded and changed, still, by candle-light, or when adroitly shaded, through a becoming skill in the arrangement of her head-dress,* appeared nearly in their first lustre; and in this view it was that they were always present to herself; though, by the world, the altered complexion, sunk eyes, and enlarged features, exhibited by day-light, or by common attire, were all, except through impertinent retrospection, that were any more noticed.

She was just arrived at Brighthelmstone, with her mother, upon a visit to an acquaintance, whom that lady had engaged to invite them, with a design of meeting Sir Lyell Sycamore, a splendid young baronet, with whom Miss Brinville had lately danced at a private ball; where, as he saw her for the first time, and saw her to every advantage which well chosen attire, animated vanity, and propitious wax-light could give, he had fallen desperately enamoured of her beauty; and had so vehemently lamented having promised to join a party to Brighthelmstone, that both the mother and the daughter concluded, that they had only to find a decent pretence for following him, to secure the prostration of his title and fortune at their feet. And though similar expectations, from gentlemen of similar birth and estate, had already, at least fifty times, been disappointed, they were just as sanguine, in the present instance, as if, new to the world, and inexperienced in its ways, they were now receiving their first lessons, upon the fallaciousness of self-appreciation: so slight is the impression made, even where our false judgment is self-detected, by wounds to our vanity! and so elastic is the rebound of that hope, which originates in our personal estimation of our deserts!

The young Baronet, indeed, no sooner heard of the arrival at Brighthelmstone of the fair one who had enchanted him, than, wild with rapture, he devoted all his soul to expected extacies. But when, the next morning, fine and frosty, though severely cold, he met her upon the Steyn, her complexion and her features were so different to those yet resting, in full beauty, upon his memory, that he looked at her with a surprise mingled with a species of indignation, as at a caricature of herself.

Miss Brinville, though too unconscious of her own double appearance to develope what passed in his mind, was struck and mortified by his change of manner. The bleak winds which blew sharply from the sea, giving nearly its own blue-green hue to her skin, while all that it bestowed of the carnation's more vivid glow, visited the feature which they least become, but which seems always the favourite wintry hot-bed of the ruddy tints; in completing what to the young Baronet seemed an entire metamorphosis, drove him fairly from the field. The wondering heroine was left in a consternation that usefully, however disagreeably, might have whispered to her some of those cruel truths which are always buzzing around faded beauties,—missing no ears but their own!—had she not been hurried, by her mother, into a milliner's shop, to make some preparations for a ball to which she was invited for the evening. There, again, she saw the Baronet, to whose astonished sight she appeared with all her first allurements. Again he danced with her, again was captivated; and again the next morning recovered his liberty. Yet Miss Brinville made no progress in self-perception: his changes were attributed to caprice or fickleness; and her desire grew but more urgent to fix her wavering conquest.

At the dinner at Lady Kendover's, where Miss Arbe brought forward the talents and the plan of Ellis, such a spirit was raised, to procure scholars amongst the young ladies of fashion then at Brighthelmstone; and it seemed so youthful to become a pupil, that Miss Brinville feared, if left out, she might be considered as too old to enter such lists. Yet her total ignorance of music, and a native dull distaste to all the arts, save the millinery, damped her wishes with want of resolution; till an exclamation of Sir Lyell Sycamore's, that nothing added so much grace to beauty as playing upon the harp, gave her sudden strength and energy, to beg to be set down, by Miss Arbe, as one of the first scholars for her *protegée*.

Ellis was received by her with civility, but treated with the utmost coldness. The sight of beauty at its height, forced a self-comparison of no exhilarating nature; and, much as she built upon informing Sir Lyell of her lessons, she desired nothing less than shewing him from whom they were received. To sit at the harp so as to justify the assertion of the Baronet, became her principal study; and the glass before which she tried her attitudes and motions, told her such flattering tales, that she soon began to think the harp the sweetest instrument in the world, and that to practise it was the most delicious of occupations.

Ellis was too sincere to aid this delusion. Of all her pupils, no one was so utterly hopeless as Miss Brinville, whom she found equally destitute of ear, taste, intelligence, and application. The same direction twenty times repeated, was not better understood than the first moment that it was uttered. Naturally dull, she comprehended nothing that was not familiar to her; and habitually indolent, because brought up to believe that beauty would supply every accomplishment, she had no conception of energy, and not an idea of diligence.

Ellis, whose mind was ardent, and whose integrity was incorrupt, felt an honourable anxiety to fulfil the duties of her new profession, though she had entered upon them merely from motives of distress. She was earnest, therefore, for the improvement of her pupils; and conceived the laudable ambition, to merit what she might earn, by their advancement. And though one amongst them, alone, manifested any genius; in all of them, except Miss Brinville, she saw more of carelessness, or idleness, than of positive incapacity. But here, the darkness of all musical apprehension was so impenetrable, that not a ray of instruction could make way through it; and Ellis who, though she saw that to study her looks at the instrument was her principal object, had still imagined that to learn music came in for some share in taking lessons upon the harp, finding it utterly vain to try to make her distinguish one note from another, held her own probity called upon to avow her opinion; since she saw herself the only one who could profit from its concealment.

Gently, therefore, and in terms the most delicate that she could select, she communicated her fears to Mrs. Brinville, that the talents of Miss Brinville were not of a musical cast.

Mrs. Brinville, with a look that said, What infinite impertinence! declared herself extremely obliged by this sincerity; and summoned her daughter to the conference.

Miss Brinville, colouring with the deepest resentment, protested that she was never so well pleased as in hearing plain truth; but each made an inclination of her head, that intimated to Ellis that she might hasten her departure: and the first news that reached her the next morning was, that Miss Brinville had sent for a celebrated and expensive professor, then accidentally at Brighthelmstone, to give her lessons upon the harp.

Miss Arbe, from whom Ellis received this intelligence, was extremely angry with her for the strange, and what she called unheard-of measure that she had taken. "What had you," she cried, "to do with their manner of wasting their money? Every one chooses to throw it away according to his own taste. If rich people have not that privilege, I don't see how they are the better for not being poor."

The sixth scholar whom Ellis undertook, was sister to Sir Lyell Sycamore. She possessed a real genius for music, though it was so little seconded by industry, that whatever she could not perform without labour or time, she relinquished. Thus, though all she played was executed in a truly fine style, nothing being practised, nothing was finished; and though she could amuse herself, and charm her auditors, with almost every favourite passage that she heard, she could not go through a single piece; could play nothing by book; and hardly knew her notes.

Nevertheless, Ellis found her so far superiour, in musical capacity, to every other pupil that had fallen to her charge, that she conceived a strong desire to make her the fine player that her talents fitted her for becoming.

Her utmost exertions, however, and warmest wishes, were insufficient for this purpose. The genius with which Miss Sycamore was endowed for music, was unallied to any soft harmonies of temper, or of character: she was presumptuous, conceited, and gaily unfeeling. If Ellis pressed her to more attention, she hummed an air, without looking at her; if she remonstrated against her neglect, she suddenly stared at her, though without speaking. She had a haughty indifference about learning; but it was not from an indifference to excel; 'twas from a firm self-opinion, that she excelled already. If she could not deny, that Ellis executed whole pieces, in as masterly a manner as she could herself play only chosen passages, she deemed that a mere mechanical part of the art, which, as a professor, Ellis had been forced to study; and which she herself, therefore, rather held cheap than respected.

Ellis, at first, seriously lamented this wayward spirit, which wasted real talents; but all interest for her pupil soon subsided; and all regret concentrated in having such a scholar to attend; for the manners of Miss Sycamore had an excess of insolence, that rather demanded apathy than philosophy to be supported, by those who were in any degree within her power. Ellis was treated by her with a sort of sprightly defiance, that sometimes seemed to arise from gay derision; at others, from careless haughtiness. Miss Sycamore, who gave little attention to the rumours of her history, saw her but either as a Wanderer, of blighted fortune, and as such looked down upon her with contempt; or as an indigent young woman of singular beauty, and as such, with far less willingness, looked up to her with envy.

Twice a-week, also, Selina, with the connivance, though not with the avowed consent of Mrs. Maple, came from Lewes, to continue her musical lessons, at the house of Lady Kendover, or of Miss Arramede.

Such was the set which the powerful influence of Miss Arbe procured for the opening campaign of Ellis; and to this set its own celebrity soon added another name. It was not, indeed, one which Miss Arbe would have deigned to put upon her list; but Ellis, who had no pride to support in her present undertaking, save the virtuous and right pride of owing independence to her own industry, as readily accepted a proferred scholar from the daughter of a common tradesman, as she had accepted the daughter of an Earl, whom she taught at Lady Kendover's.

Mr. Tedman, a grocer, who had raised a very large fortune, was now at Brighthelmstone, with his only daughter and heiress, at whose desire he called at Miss Matson's, to enquire for the famous music-teacher.

Ellis, hearing that he was an elderly man, conceived what

might be his business, and admitted him. Much surprised by her youthful appearance, "Good now, my dear," he cried, "why to be sure it can't be you as pretends to learn young misses music? and even misses of quality, as I am told? It's more likely it's your mamma; put in case you've got one."

When Ellis had set him right, he took five guineas from his purse, and said, "Well, then, my dear, come to my darter, and give her as much of your tudeling* as will come to this. And I think, by then, she'll be able to twiddle* over them wires by herself."

The hours of attendance being then settled, he looked smirkingly in her face, and added, "Which of us two is to hold the stakes, you or I?" shaking the five guineas between his hands. But when she assured him that she had not the most distant desire to anticipate such an appropriation, he assumed an air of generous affluence, and assuring her, in return, that he was not afraid to trust her, counted two guineas and half a guinea, upon the table, and said, "So if you please, my dear, we'll split the difference."

Ellis found the daughter yet more innately, though less obviously, vulgar; and far more unpleasant, because uncivil, than the father. In a constant struggle to hide the disproportion of her origin, and early habits, with her present pretensions to fashion, she was tormented by an incessant fear of betraying, that she was as little bred as born to the riches which she now possessed. This made her always authoritative with her domestics, or inferiours, to keep them in awe; pert with gentlemen, by way of being genteel; and rude with ladies, to shew herself their equal.

Mr. Tedman conceived, immediately, a warm partiality for Ellis, whose elegant manners, which, had he met with her in high life, would have distanced him by their superiority, now attracted him irresistibly, in viewing them but as good nature. He called her his pretty tudeler,* and bid her make haste to earn her five guineas; significantly adding, that, if his daughter were not finished before they were gone, he was rich enough to make them ten.

CHAPTER XXV

WITH these seven pupils, Ellis, combating the various unpleasant feelings that were occasionally excited, prosperously began her new career.

Her spirits, from the fulness of her occupations, revived; and she soon grew a stranger to the depression of the ruminating leisure, which is wasted in regret, in repining, or in wavering meditation.

Miss Arbe reaped, also, the fruits of her successful manœuvres, by receiving long, and almost daily instructions, under the pretence of trying different compositions; though never under the appellation of lessons, nor with the smallest acknowledgement of any deficiency that might require improvement; always, when they separated, exclaiming, "What a delightful musical regale we have enjoyed this morning!"

So sincere, nevertheless, was the sense which Ellis entertained of the essential obligations which she owed to Miss Arbe, that she suffered this continual intrusion and fatigue without a murmur.

Miss Bydel, also, who was nearly as frequent in her visits as Miss Arbe, claimed constantly, however vainly, in return for paying the month's hire of the harp, the private history of the way of life, expences, domestics, and apparent income, of every family to which that instrument was the means of introduction. And but that these ladies had personal engagements for their evenings, Ellis could not have found time to keep herself in such practice as her new profession required; and her credit, if not her scholars, might have been lost, through the selfishness of the very patronesses by whom they had been obtained.

Another circumstance, also, somewhat disturbed, though she would not suffer it to interrupt what she now deemed to be her professional study: she no sooner touched her harp, than she heard a hurrying, though heavy step, descend the stairs; and never opened her door, after playing or singing, without perceiving a gentlemen standing against it, in an attitude of listening. He hastened away ashamed, upon her appearance;

yet did not the less fail to be in waiting at her next performance. Displeased, and nearly alarmed by the continual repetition of this curiosity, she complained of it to Miss Matson, desiring that she would find means to put an end to so strange a liberty.

Miss Matson said, that the person in question, who was a gentleman of very good character, though rather odd in his ways, had taken the little room which Ellis had just relinquished: she was sure, however, that he meant no harm, for he had often told her, as he passed through the shop, that he ought to pay double for his lodging, for the sake of hearing the harp, and the singing. Miss Matson remonstrated with him, nevertheless, upon his indiscretion; in consequence of which, he became more circumspect.

From Selina, whose communications continued to be as unabated in openness, as her friendship was in fondness, Ellis had the heartfelt satisfaction of receiving occasional intelligence, drawn from the letters of Mrs. Howel to Mrs. Maple, of the inviolable attachment of Lady Aurora Granville.

She heard, also, but nearly with indifference, that the two elder ladies had been furious with indignation, at the prosperity of the scheme of Miss Arbe, by which Ellis seemed to be naturalized at Brighthelmstone; where she was highly considered, and both visited and invited, by all who had elegance, sense, or taste to appreciate her merits.

Of Elinor nothing was positively known, though some indirect information reached her aunt, that she had found means to return to the continent.

About three weeks passed thus, in the diligent and successful practice of this new profession, when a morning concert was advertised at the New Rooms, for a blind Welsh harper,* who was travelling through the principal towns of England.

All the scholars of Ellis having upon this occasion, taken tickets of Lady Kendover, who patronized the harper, Ellis meant to dedicate the leisure thus left her to musical studies; but she was broken in upon by Miss Bydel, who, possessing an odd ticket, and having, through some accident, missed joining her party, desired Ellis would immediately get ready to go with her to the concert. Ellis, not sorry to hear the harper, consented.

The harper was in the midst of his last piece when they arrived. Miss Bydel, deaf to a general buz of "Hush!" at the loud voice with which, upon entering the room, she said, "Well, now I must look about for some acquaintance," straitly* strutted on to the upper end of the apartment. Ellis quietly glided after her, concluding it to be a matter of course that they should keep together. Here, however, Miss Bydel comfortably arranged herself, between Mrs. Maple and Selina, telling them that, having been too late for all her friends, and not liking to poke her way* alone, she had been forced to make the young music-mistress come along with her, for company.

Ellis, though both abashed and provoked, felt herself too justly under the protection of Miss Bydel, to submit to the mortification of turning back, as if she had been an unauthorised intruder; though the averted looks, and her consciousness of the yet more disdainful opinions of Mrs. Maple, left her no hope of countenance, but through the kindness of Selina. She sought, therefore, the eyes of her young friend, and did not seek them in vain; but great was her surprise to meet them not merely unaccompanied by any expression of regard, but even of remembrance; and to see them instantaneously withdrawn, to be fixed upon those of Lady Barbara Frankland, which were wholly occupied by the blind harper.

Disappointed and disconcerted, she was now obliged to seat herself, alone, upon a side form,* and to strive to parry the awkwardness of her situation, by an appearance of absorbed attention to the performance of the harper.

A gentleman, who was lounging upon a seat at some distance, struck by her beauty, and surprised by her lonely position, curiously loitered towards her, and dropt, as if accidentally, upon the same form. He was young, tall, handsome, and fashionable, but wore the air of a decided libertine; and her modest mien, and evident embarrassment, rendered her peculiarly attractive to a voluptuous man of pleasure. To discover, therefore, whether that modesty were artificial, or the remains of such original purity as he, and such as he, adore but to demolish, was his immediate determination.

It was impossible for Ellis to escape seeing how completely she engrossed his attention, sedulously as she sought to employ her own another way. But, having advanced too far into the room, by following Miss Bydel, to descend without being recognized by those whose good opinion it was now her serious concern to preserve, all her scholars being assembled upon this occasion; she resolved to sustain her credit, by openly joining, or, at least, closely following, Miss Bydel, when the concert should be over.

When the concert, however, was over, her difficulties were but increased, for no one retired. Lady Kendover ordered tea for herself and her party; and the rest of the assembly eagerly formed itself into groups for a similar purpose. A mixt society is always jealous of its rights of equality; and any measure taken by a person of superiour rank, or superiour fortune to the herd, soon becomes general; not humbly, from an imitative, but proudly, from a levelling spirit.

The little coteries thus every where arranging, made the forlorn situation of Ellis yet more conspicuous. All now, but herself, were either collected into setts to take tea, or dispersed for sauntering. She felt, therefore, so awkward, that, hoping by a fair explanation, to acquit herself to her scholars at their next lessons, she was rising to return alone to her lodging, when the gentleman already mentioned, planting himself abruptly before her, confidently enquired whether he could be of any service in seeing her out.

She gravely pronounced a negative, and re-seated herself. He made no attempt at conversation, but again took his place by her side.

In the hope of lessening, in some degree, her embarrassment, Ellis, once more, sought the notice of Selina, whose behaviour appeared so extraordinary, that she began to imagine herself mistaken in believing that she had yet been seen; but when, again, she caught the eye of that young lady, a low and respectful courtesy vainly solicited return, or notice. The eye looked another way, without seeming to have heeded the salutation.

She grew, now, seriously apprehensive, that some cruel calumny must have injured her in the opinion of her affectionate young friend.

Her ruminations upon this unpleasant idea were interrupted, by the approach of Mrs. and Miss Brinville, who, scornfully passing her, stopt before her lounging neighbour, to whom Mrs. Brinville said, "Do you take nothing Sir Lyell? We are just going to make a little tea."

Sir Lyell, looking negligently at Miss Brinville, and then, from her faded beauty, casting a glance of comparison at the blooming prime of the lovely unknown by his side, carelessly answered, that he took tea but once in a day.

Miss Brinville, though by no means aware of the full effect of such a contrast, had not failed to remark the direction of the wandering eye; nor to feel the waste and inadequacy of her best smiles to draw it back. She was compelled, however, to walk on, and Ellis now concluded that her bold and troublesome neighbour must be Sir Lyell Sycamore, who, seldom at home but to a given dinner,* had never been present at any lesson of his sister's.

The chagrin of being seen, and judged, so unfavourably, by a friend of Lord Melbury, was a little softened, by the hope that he would soon learn who she was from Miss Sycamore; and that accident, not choice, had placed her thus alone in a public room.

Miss Brinville had not more keenly observed the admiring looks of Sir Lyell, than the Baronet had remarked her own of haughty disdain, for the same object. This confirmed his idea of the fragile character of his solitary beauty; though, while it fixed his pursuit, it deterred him from manifesting his design. His quietness, however, did not deceive Ellis; the admiration conveyed by his eyes was so wholly unmixt with respect, that, embarrassed and comfortless, she knew not which way to turn her own.

Mr. Tedman, soon after, perceiving her to be alone, and unserved, came, with a good humoured smirk upon his countenance, to bring her a handful of cakes. It was in vain that she declined them; he placed them, one by one, till he had counted half a dozen, upon the form by her side, saying, "Don't be so coy, my dear, don't be so coy. Young girls have appetites as well as old men, for I don't find that that tudeling does much for one's stomach; and, I promise you, this cold February morning has served me for as good a whet, as if I was an errand boy up to this moment—put in case* I ever was one before;—

which, however, is neither here nor there; though you may as well," he added, lowering his voice, and looking cautiously around, "not mention my happening to drop that word to my darter; for she has so many fine Misses coming to see her, that she got acquainted with at the boarding-school,* where I was over-persuaded to put her—for I might have set up a good smart shop for the money it cost me; but she had a prodigious hankering after being teached dancing, and the like; and so now, when they come to see us, she wants to pass for as fine a toss up* as themselves! And, lauk adaisy!* put in case I was to let the cat out of the bag—."*

Steadily as Ellis endeavoured to avoid looking either to the right or to the left, she could not escape observing the surprise and diversion, which this visit and whisper afforded to Sir Lydell; yet the good humour of Mr. Tedman, and her conviction of the innocence of his kindness, made it impossible for her to repulse him with anger.

Advancing, next, his mouth close to her ear, he said, "I should have been glad enough to have had you come and drink a cup of tea with I and my darter; I can tell you that; only my darter's always in such a fuss about what the quality will think of her; else, we are dull enough together, only she and me; for, do what she will, the quality don't much mind her. So she's rather a bit in the sulks, poor dear. And, at best, she is but a so so hand at the agreeable.* Though indeed, for the matter of that, I am no rare one myself; except with my particulars;*—put in case I am then."

He now, good-humouredly nodding, begged her not to spare the cakes, and promising she should have more if she were hungry, returned to his daughter.

Sir Lyell, with a scarcely stifled laugh, and in a tone the most familiar, enquired whether she wished for any further refreshment.

Ellis, looking away from him, pronounced a repulsive negative.

An elderly gentleman, who was walking up and down the room, now bowed to her. Not knowing him, she let his salutation pass apparently disregarded; when, some of her cakes accidentally falling from the form, he eagerly picked them up, saying, as he grasped them in his hand, "Faith, Madam, you had better have eaten them at once. You had, faith! Few things are mended by delay. We are all at our best at first. These cakes are no more improved by being mottled with the dirt of the floor, than a pretty woman is by being marked with the small pox. I know nothing that i'n't the worse for a put-off, ... unless it be a quarrel."

Ellis then, through his voice and language, discovered her fellow voyager, Mr. Riley; though a considerable change in his appearance, from his travelling garb, had prevented a more immediate recollection.

Additional disturbance now seized her, lest he should recur to the suspicious circumstances of her voyage and arrival.

While he still stood before her, declaiming upon the squeezed cakes, which he held in his hand, Mr. Tedman, coming softly back, and gently pushing him aside, produced, with a self-pleased countenance, a small plate of bread and butter, saying, "Look, here, my dear, I've brought you a few nice slices; for I see the misfortune that befel my cakes, of their falling down; and I resolved you should not be the worse for it. But I advise you to eat this at once, for fear of accidents; only take care," with a smile, "that you don't grease your pretty fingers."

He did not smile singly; Sir Lyell more than bore him company, and Riley laughed aloud, saying,

"'Twould be pity, indeed, if she did not take care of her pretty fingers, 'twould, faith! when she can work them so cunningly. I can't imagine how the lady could sit so patiently, to hear that old Welsh man thrum the cords in that bang wang way,* when she can touch them herself, like a little Queen David,* to put all one's feelings in a fever. I have listened at her door, till I have tingled all over with heat, in the midst of the hard frost. And, sometimes, I have sat upon the stairs, to hear her, till I have been so bent double, and numbed, that my nose has almost joined my toes, and you might have rolled me down to the landing-place without uncurbing* me. You might, faith!"

Ellis now further discovered, that Mr. Riley was the listening new lodger. Her apprehensions, however, of his recollection subsided, when she found him wholly unsuspicious that he had ever seen her before; and called to mind her own personal disguise at their former meeting.

Sir Lyell, piqued to see her monopolized by two such fogrums as he thought Messieurs Riley and Tedman, was bending forward to address her more freely himself, when Lady Barbara Frankland, suddenly perceiving her, flew to take her hand, with the most cordial expressions of partial and affectionate regard.

Sir Lyell Sycamore, after a moment of extreme surprise, combining this condescension with what Riley had said of her performance, surmized that his suspicious beauty must be the harp-mistress, who had been recommended to him by Miss Arbe; who taught his sister; and whose various accomplishments had been extolled to him by Lord Melbury. That she should appear, and remain, thus strangely alone in public, marked her, nevertheless, in his opinion, as, at least, an easy prey; though her situation with regard to his sister, and a sense of decency with regard to her known protectors, made him instantly change his demeanour, and determine to desist from any obvious pursuit.

Lady Barbara had no sooner returned to her aunt, than Sir Marmaduke Crawley, in the name of that lady, advanced with a request, that Miss Ellis would be so obliging as to try the instrument of the Welsh harper.

Though this message was sent by Lady Kendover in terms of perfect politeness, and delivered by Sir Marmaduke with the most scrupulous courtesy, it caused Ellis extreme disturbance, from her unconquerable repugnance to complying with her ladyship's desire; but, while she was entreating him to soften her refusal, by the most respectful expressions, his two sisters came hoydening up* to her, charging him to take no denial, and protesting that they would either drag The Ellis to the harp, or the harp to The Ellis, if she stood dilly dallying any longer. And then, each seizing her by an arm, without any regard to her supplications, or to the shock which they inflicted upon the nerves of their brother, they would have put their threat into immediate execution, but for the weakness occasioned by their own immoderate laughter at their merry gambols; which gave time for Lady Kendover to perceive the embarrassment and the struggles of Ellis, and to suffer her partial young admirer, Lady Barbara, to be the bearer of a civil apology, and a recantation of the request.

To this commission of the well-bred aunt, the kind-hearted niece added a positive insistance, that Ellis should join their party; to which she rather drew than led her, seating her, almost forcibly, next to herself, with exulting delight at rescuing her from the turbulent Miss Crawleys.

Lady Kendover, to whom the exact gradations of *etiquette* were always present, sought, by a look, to intimate to her niece, that while the Hon. Miss Arramede was standing, this was not the place for Ellis: but the niece, natural, inconsiderate, and zealous, understood not the hint; and the timid embarrassment of Ellis shewed so total a freedom from all obtrusive intentions, that her ladyship could not but forgive, however little she had desired the junction; and, soon afterwards, encouragingly led her to join both in the conversation and the breakfast.

Selina, now, ran to shake hands with her dear Ellis, expressing the warmest pleasure at her sight. Ellis as much, though not as disagreeably surprised by her notice now, as she had been by the more than neglect which had preceded it, was hesitating what judgment to form of either, when Miss Sycamore, from some distance, scornfully called out to her, "Don't fail to stop at our house in your way back to your lodgings, Miss Ellis, to look at my harp. I believe it's out of order."

Lady Kendover, whose invariable politeness made her peculiarly sensible of any failure of that quality in another, perceiving Ellis extremely disconcerted, by the pointed malice of this humiliating command, at the moment that she was bearing her part in superiour society, redoubled her own civilities, by attentions as marked and public as they were obliging; and, pleased by the modest gratitude with which they were received, had again restored the serenity of Ellis; when a conversation, unavoidably overheard, produced new disturbance.

Mr. Riley, who had just recognized Ireton and Mrs. Maple, was loud in his satisfaction at again seeing two of his fellow-voyagers; and, in his usually unceremonious manner, began discoursing upon their late dangers and escape; notwithstanding all the efforts of Mrs. Maple, who knew nothing of his birth, situation in life, or fortune, to keep him at a distance.

"And pray," cried he, "how does Miss Nelly do? She is a prodigious clever girl; she is faith! I took to her mightily; though I did not much like that twist she had got to the wrong side of my politics. I longed prodigiously to give her a twitch back to the right. But how could you think, Ma'am, of taking over such a brisk, warm, young girl as that, at the very instant when the new-fangled doctrines were beginning to ferment in every corner of France? boiling over in one half of their pates, to scald t'other half."

Mrs. Maple, however unwilling to hold a public conference with a person of whom she had never seen the pedigree, nor the rent-roll,* could still less endure to let even a shadow of blame against herself pass unanswered: she therefore angrily said, that she had travelled for health, and not to trouble herself about politics.

"O, as to you, Ma'am, it's all one, at your years: but how you could fancy a skittish young girl, like that, could be put into such a hot bed of wild plants, and not shoot forth a few twigs herself, I can't make out. You might as well send her to a dance, and tell her not to wag a foot. And pray what's become of Mr. Harleigh? I've no where seen his fellow. He was the most of a manly gentleman that ever fell in my walk. And your poor ailing mamma, Squire Ireton? Has she got the better of her squeamish fits? She was duced bad aboard; and not much better ashore. And that Demoiselle, the black-skinned girl, with the fine eyes and nose? Where's she, too? Have you ever heard what became of her?"

Ellis, who every moment expected this question, had prepared herself to listen to it with apparent unconcern: but Selina, tittering, and again running up to her, and pinching her arm, asked whether it were not she, that that droll man meant by the black-skinned girl?

"She was a good funny girl, faith!" continued Riley. "I was prodigiously diverted with her. Yet we did nothing but quarrel. Though I don't know why. But I could never find out who she was. I believe the devil himself could not have made her speak."

The continual little laughs of Selina, whom no supplications of Ellis could keep quiet, now attracted the notice of Lady Kendover; which so palpably encreased the confusion of Ellis, that the attention of her ladyship was soon transferred to herself.

"She was but an odd fish, I believe, after all," Riley went on; "for, one day, when I was sauntering along Oxford Street, who should I meet but the noble Admiral? the only one of our sett I have seen, till this moment, since I left Dover. And when we talked over our adventures, and I asked him if he knew any thing of the Demoiselle, how do you think she had served him? She's a comical hand,* faith! Only guess!"

Ellis, now, apprehensive of some strange attack, involuntarily, looked at him, with as much amazement and attention, as he began to excite in all others who were near him; while Mrs. Maple, personally alarmed, demanded whether the Admiral had found out that any fraud had been practised upon him by that person?

"Fraud? ay, fraud enough!" cried Riley. "She choused* him neatly out of the hire of her place in the Diligence;* besides that guinea that we all saw him give her."

Ellis now coloured deeply; and Ireton, heartily laughing, repeated the word "choused?" while Mrs. Maple, off all guard, looked fiercely at Ellis, and exclaimed, "This is just what I have all along expected! And who can tell who else may have been pilfered? I protest I don't think myself safe yet."

This hasty speech raised a lively curiosity in all around; for all around had become listeners, from the loud voice of Riley; who now related that the Admiral, having paid the full fare for bringing the black-skinned girl to town, had called at the inn at which the stage puts up in London, to enquire, deeming her a stranger, whether she were safely arrived; and there he had been informed, that she had never made use of her place.

Ellis had no time to dwell upon the cruel, but natural misconstruction, from the change of her plan, which had thus lost her the good opinion of the benevolent Admiral; the speech which followed from Mrs. Maple was yet more terrific. "I have not the least doubt, then," said that lady, in a tone of mingled triumph and rage, "that she put the money for her place into her pocket, as well as the guinea, while she wheedled Mrs. Ireton into bringing her up to town gratis! for I was all along sure she was an adventurer and an impostor; with her blacks, and her whites, and her double face!"—.

She stopt abruptly, recollecting the censure to which anger and self-importance were leading her, of having introduced into society, a creature of whom, from the origin of any knowledge of her, she had conceived so ill an opinion.

But while the various changes of complexion, produced in Ellis by this oration, were silently marked by Lady Kendover; and drew from Lady Barbara the most affectionate enquiries whether she were indisposed; the Miss Crawleys, who heard all that passed with their customary search of mirth, whether flowing from the ridiculous, the singular, or the mischievous, now clamourously demanded what Mrs. Maple meant, by the double face, the blacks, and the whites.

"Oh, no matter," answered Mrs. Maple, stammering; "'tis not a thing worth talking of."

"But the blacks—and the whites—and the double face?" cried Miss Crawley.

"Ay, the double face, the blacks, and the whites?" cried Miss Di.

"The blacks," said Mr. Riley, "I understand well enough; but I remember nothing about the double face. Surely the Demoiselle could not hodge-podge herself into one of the whites? What do you mean by all that, Ma'am?"

"Pray ask me nothing about the matter," replied Mrs. Maple, impatiently. "I am not at all accustomed to talk of people of that sort."

"Why, how's all this?" cried Riley. "Have any of you met with the Demoiselle again?"

Mrs. Maple would not deign to make any further reply.

He addressed himself to Ireton, who only laughed.

"Well, this is droll enough! it is, faith! I begin to think the Demoiselle has appeared amongst you again. I wish you'd tell me, for I should like to see her of all things, for old acquaintance sake. She was but a dowdy piece of goods, to be sure; but she had fine eyes, and a fine nose; and she amused me prodigiously, she was so devilish shy."

"You believe, then," said Ireton, excited, not checked, by the palpable uneasiness of Ellis, "that if you saw her again, you should know her?"

"Know the Demoiselle? ay, from an hundred, with her beautiful black marks, and *insignia* of the order of fisty cuffs."*

"Look for her, then, man! Look for her!"

"I shall want small compulsion for that, I promise you; but where am I to look? Is she here?"

Ireton nodded.

"Nay, then, Master Ireton, since you bid me look, lend me, at least, some sort of spectacles, that may help me to see through a mask; for I am sure, if she be here, she must wear one."

"Are you sure that, if you should see her without one, you should not mistake her?"

"Yes, faith, am I!"

"What will you bet upon it?"

"What you will, 'Squire Ireton. A guinea to half a crown."*

Mrs. Maple, alarmed now, for her own credit, desired Ireton to enquire whether her carriage were ready; but Ireton, urged by an unmeaning love of mischief, which, ordinarily, forms a large portion of the common cast of no character, would not rest till he had engaged Riley in a wager, that he could make him look his Demoiselle full in the face, without recollecting her.

Riley said that he should examine every lady, now, one by one, and take special note that she wore her own natural visage.

He began with the jocund Miss Crawleys, whose familiar gaiety, which deemed nothing indecorous that afforded them sport, encouraged him, by its flippant enjoyment, to proceed to others. But he no sooner advanced to Ellis, than she turned from his investigation, in so much disorder, that her kind young friend, Lady Barbara, enquired what was the matter.

She endeavoured to controul her alarm, cheerfully answering, that she was well; but Riley no sooner caught the sound of her voice, than, riotously clapping his hands, he exclaimed, "'Tis the Demoiselle! Faith, 'tis the Demoiselle herself! That's her voice! And those are her eyes! And there's her nose! It's she, faith! And so here are the whites, and the double face!"

A laugh from Ireton confirmed his suggestion, while the change of countenance in Ellis, satisfied all who could see her, that some discovery was made, or impending, which she earnestly wished concealed.

Mrs. Maple, scarcely less disconcerted than herself, enquired again for her carriage.

"Faith, this is droll enough! it is, faith!" cried Riley, when his first transport of surprise subsided. "So the Demoiselle is a Beauty, after all! And the finest harp-player, to boot, on this side King David!"

Ellis, dreadfully distressed, silently bowed down her head.

"I should like to have a model of her face," continued Riley; "to find out how it's done. What a fine fortune she may raise, if she will take up a patent for beauty-making! I know many a dowager* that would give half she is worth for the secret. I should think you would not be sorry yourself, Mrs. Maple, to have a little touch of the art. It would not do you much harm, I can tell you, Ma'am."

The scornful looks of Mrs. Maple alone announced that she heard him; and the disturbed ones of Ellis made the same confession; but both were equally mute.

"You'll pay for your sport, I can tell you, Master Ireton!" Riley triumphantly went on; "for I shall claim my wager. But pray, Demoiselle, what's become of all those plaisters and patches, as well as of the black coat over the skin? One could see nothing but eyes and nose. And very handsome eyes and nose they are. I don't know that I ever saw finer; I don't, faith! However, ladies, you need none of you despair of turning out beauties, in the long run, if she'll lend you a hand; for the ugliest Signora among you i'n't so frightful as poor Demoiselle was, when we saw her first; with her bruises, and scars, and bandages."

Overwhelmed with shame at this disgraceful, and, in public, unanswerable attack, Ellis, utterly confounded, was painfully revolving in her mind, what vindication she might venture to offer; and whether it were better to speak at once, or afterwards, and individually; when, at the intimation of these deceits and disguises, the whole party turned towards her with alarmed and suspicious looks; and then abruptly arose to depart; Lady Kendover, taking the hand of her young niece, who still would have fondled Ellis, leading the way. Miss Arbe alone, of all the society to which Ellis was known, personally fearing to lose her useful mistress, ventured to whisper, "Good morning, Miss Ellis: I'll call upon you to-morrow." While all others, with cast-up eyes and hands, hurried off, as if contagion were in her vicinity.

Riley, claiming his wager, followed Ireton.

Petrified at her own situation, Ellis remained immovable, till she was roused from her consternation, by a familiar offer, from Sir Lyell Sycamore, to attend her home.

Fearful of fresh offence, she recovered from her dismay to rise; but, when she saw that the bold Baronet was fixed to accompany her, the dread of such an appearance to any one that she might meet, after the disastrous scene in which she had been engaged, frightened her into again sitting down.

Sir Lyell stood, or sauntered before her, meaning to mark her, to the gentlemen who still lingered, observant and curious, in the room, as his property; till Mr. Tedman, coming back from an inner apartment, begged, in the civilest manner, leave to pass, and carry a glass of white wine negus* to the young music-player, which he had saved out of a bowl that he had been making for himself.

"Oh, by all manner of means, Sir!" cried Sir Lyell, sneeringly giving way: "pray don't let me mar your generosity!"

Ellis declined the negus, but, rejoicing in any safe and honest protection, entreated that Mr. Tedman would have the goodness to order one of his servants to see her home.

Sir Lyell, sneeringly, and again placing himself before her, demanded to play the part of the domestic; and Mr. Tedman, extremely disconcerted, as well as disappointed by the rejection of his negus, hung back ashamed.

Ellis, now, feeling a call for the most spirited exertion to rescue herself from this impertinence, begged Mr. Tedman to stop; and then, addressing the young Baronet with dignity, said, "If, as I believe, I have the honour of speaking to Sir Lyell Sycamore, he will rather, I trust, thank me, than be offended, that I take the liberty to assure him, that he will gratify the sister of his friend,—gratify Lady Aurora Granville,—by securing me from being molested."

Had she named Lord Melbury, the ready suspicions of libertinism would but have added to the familiarity of the

Baronet's pursuit; but the mention of Lady Aurora Granville startled him into respect, and he involuntarily bowed, as he made way for her to proceed. She then eagerly followed Mr. Tedman out of the room; while Sir Lyell merely vented his spleen, by joining some of his remaining companions, in a hearty laugh, at the manners, the dress, the age, and the liberality of her chosen esquire.

CHAPTER XXVI

THE shock given to Ellis by this scene of apparent detection and disgrace, prevented not Mr. Tedman from exulting at a mark of preference, which he considered as a letting down to what he called the quality. He ordered his footman to see Miss safe to her lodging; and regretted that he could not take her to it in his own coach, "which I would certainly, my dear, do," he said, "but for the particularity of my darter, who will never consent to the most minimus* thing in the world, but what she thinks will be agreeable to the quality."

Ellis passed the rest of the day in the most severe inquietude, ruminating upon the ill effects that would probably result from an attack which she had been so little able to parry. Vainly she expected Miss Arbe, from whom alone she had any hope of support; and the apprehension of being forsaken even by her professed patroness, made the thought of appearing before Lady Kendover grow seriously formidable: but all fears were trifling compared to the consternation with which they terminated, when, the next day, while fancying that every sound would prove the chaise of Miss Arbe, hour after hour passed, without any carriage, any message; and, finally, the night closed in by the reception of a note from the steward of Lady Kendover, to demand the account of Miss Ellis, as Lady Barbara Frankland did not purpose to take any more lessons.

The abruptness of this dismission, and the indelicacy of sending it through a domestic, were not more offensive to the feelings of Ellis, than the consequences to be expected from such a measure of hostility, were menacing to her present plan of existence.

She was still deliberating in what manner to address some sort of self-justification to Lady Kendover, when a similar note arrived from the butler of Lady Arramede.

The indignant sensations which these testimonies of utter contempt excited in Ellis, were embittered by every kind of perplexity. She had not courage to present herself to any other of her scholars, while uncertain whether she might not meet with treatment equally scornful; and in this state of depression and panic, she rejoiced to receive a visit, the following morning, even from Miss Bydel, as some mark of female countenance and protection.

Yet the opening of this interview seemed not very propitious: Miss Bydel, instead of ascending the stairs, as usual, seated herself with Miss Matson, and sent for Ellis; who obeyed the call with extreme ill will, conscious how little fit for a milliner's shop, was either what she might be called upon to say, or what she might be constrained to hear.

Miss Bydel failed not to take this opportunity of making sundry enquiries into the manner in which Ellis passed her time; whom she saw; whither she went; what sort of table she kept; and what allowance she made for the trouble which she gave to the servants.

"Well, my dear," she cried, "this is but a bad affair, this business of the day before yesterday. I have been to Mrs. Maple, and I have worked out the truth, at last; though nobody would believe the pains it cost me before I could sift it to the bottom. However, the most extraordinary part is, that when all came to all, she did not tell me who you were! for she persists she don't so much as know it herself!"

The surprise of the milliners, and the disturbance of Ellis, were alike unheeded by Miss Bydel, whose sole solicitude was to come to the point.

"Now the thing I principally want to know, my dear, is whether this is true? for though I would not for ever so much doubt Mrs. Maple's word, this is such a prodigious odd thing, that I can't give it the least credit."

Ellis, in much confusion, besought that she would have the goodness to walk up stairs.

"No, no; we are very well here; only be so kind as to let me know why you make such a secret of who you are? Every body asks me the question, go where I will; and it's making me look no better than a fool; to think I should be at such an expence as to hire a harp for a person I know nothing of."

Affrighted at the effect which this display of her poverty, and detection of it's mystery, might produce upon her hostess, Ellis was again entreating for a *tête à tête*, when Mr. Riley, descending from his room to pass through the shop, exclaimed, "Ah ha! the Demoiselle? Why I had never the pleasure to meet you down here before, Ma'am?"

"Well, if this is not the gentleman who told us all those odd things about you at the concert!" cried Miss Bydel: "I should not be sorry to speak a word or two to him myself. You were one of the passengers, I think, Sir, who came over in the same boat with Mrs. Maple? And glad enough you must have been to have got back; though I suppose you were only there upon business, Sir?"

"Not a whit, Madam! not a whit, faith! I never make bad better. I make that a rule. I always state the worst, that is to say the truth, in my own case as well as in my neighbour's."

"Why then pray, Sir, if it's no secret,—what might be the reason of your going over to such a place?"

"Curiosity, Madam! Neither more nor less. I was agog to know what those famous Mounseers were about; and whether there were any Revolution really going forward amongst them, or not. For I used often to think they invented tales here in England, basking by their own fire-sides, that had not an atom of truth in them. I thought so, faith! But I paid for my scepticism! I was cast into prison, by Master Robertspierre, a demon of an attorney, that now rules the roast* in France, without knowing what the devil it was for; while I was only gaping about me, to see what sort of a figure Mounseer would make as a liberty boy!* But I shall be content to look after my own liberty in future! I shall, faith. So one's never too old to learn; as you may find yourself, Madam, if you'll take the trouble to cross the little canal, on a visit to Master Robertspierre. He'll teach you gratis, I give you my word, if you have a fancy to take a few lessons. He won't mind your age of a fig,* any more than he did mine; though I imagine you to be some years my senior."

"I don't know what you may imagine Sir," said Miss Bydel; "but you can't know much of the matter, I think, if you have not seen my register."*

"Nay, Ma'am, you may just as well be my junior, for any knowledge I have about it. Women look old so much sooner than men, that there is no judging by the exteriour."

"Well, Sir, and if they do, I don't know any great right you have to call them to account for it."

"Bless me, Sir!" cried Miss Matson, "if you knew Miss Ellis all this time, why did you ask us all so many questions about her, as if you had never seen her before in your life?"

"Why I never had! That's the very problem that wants solving! Though I had spent a good seven or eight hours as near to her as I am to you, I never had seen her before!"

"Oh! you mean because of her disguise, I take it, Sir?" said Miss Bydel; "but I heard all that at the very first, from Miss Selina Joddrel; but Miss Elinor told us it was only put on for escaping; so I thought no more about it; for Mrs. Maple assured us she was a young lady of family and fashion, for else she would never, she said, have let her act with us. And this we all believed easily enough, as Mrs. Maple's own nieces were such chief performers; so that who could have expected such a turn all at once, as fell out the day before yesterday, of her proving to be such a mere nothing?"

Ellis would now have retired, but Miss Bydel, holding her gown, desired her to wait.

"Faith, Madam, as to her being a mere nothing," said Riley, "I don't know that any of us are much better than nothing, when we sift ourselves to our origin. What are you yourself, Ma'am, for one?"

"I, Sir? I'm descended from a gentleman's family, I assure you! I don't know what you mean by such a question!"

"Why then you are descended from somebody who was rich without either trouble or merit; for that's all that your gentleman is, as far as belongs to birth. The man amongst your grand-dads* who first got the money, is the only one worth praising; and he, who was he? Why some one who baked sugar, or brewed beer, better than his neighbours; or who slashed and hewed his fellow-creatures with greater fury than they could slash and hew him in return; or who culled the daintiest herbs for the cure of gluttony; or filled his coffers with the best address, in emptying those of the knaves and fools who had been set together by the ears. Such, Ma'am, are the origins of your English gentlemen."

"That, Sir, is as people take things. But the most particular part of the affair here, is; that here is a person that we have got in the very midst of us, without so much as knowing her name! for, would you believe it, Miss Matson, they tell me she had no name at all, till I gave her one? For I was the very first person that called her Miss Ellis! And so here I have been a godmother, without going to a christening!"

Miss Matson expressed her surprise, with a look towards Ellis that visibly marked a diminution of respect; while one of the young women, who had fetched Ellis a chair, at the back of which she had been courteously standing, now freely dropt into it herself.

"But pray, Sir, as we are upon the subject," continued Miss Bydel, "give me leave to ask what you thought of this Miss we don't know who, at the beginning."

"Faith, Madam, I had less to do with her than any of them. The Demoiselle and I did not hit it off together at all. I could never get her to speak for the life of me. Ask what I would, she gave me no answer. I was in a devil of an ill humour with her sometimes; but I hope the Demoiselle will excuse that, I was so plaguy qualmish:* for when a man with an empty stomach can't eat but he turns sick, nor fast, but he feels his bowels nipt with hunger, he is in no very good temper of mind for being sociable. However, the Demoiselle must know but little of human nature, if she fancies she can judge before breakfast what a man may be after dinner."

They were here broken in upon by the appearance of Mr. Tedman, who, gently opening the shop-door, and carefully closing it again before he spoke or looked round, was beginning a whispering enquiry after the young music-maker; when, perceiving her, he exclaimed, "Mercy me, why, where were my eyes? Why, my dear, I never hapt to light upon you in the shop before! And I often pop in, to buy me a bit of ribbon for my pig-tail;* or some odd little matter or other. However, I have called now, on purpose to have a little bit of a chat with you, about that consort* of music that we was at the day before yesterday."

Miss Bydel, in a low voice, enquired the name of this gentleman; and, hearing that he was a man of large fortune, said to Ellis, "Why you seem to be intimate friends together, my dear! Pray, Sir, if one may ask such a thing, how long may you and this young person have known one another?"

"How long, Ma'am? Why I'd never sate eyes upon Miss a fortnight ago! But she's music-learner to my darter. And they tell me she's one of the best; which I think like enough to be true, for she tudles upon them wires the prettiest of any thing I ever heard."

"And pray, Sir, if you have no objection to telling it, how might she come to be recommended to you? for I never heard Miss Arbe mention having the pleasure of your acquaintance."

"Miss Arbe? I don't know that ever I heard the lady's name in my life, Ma'am. Though, if she's one of the quality, my darter has, I make small doubt, for she sets great store upon knowing the names of all the quality; put in case she can light upon any body that can count them over to her. But the way I heard of this music-miss was at the book-shop, where my darter always makes me go to subscribe,* that our names, she says, may come out in print, with the rest of the gentry. And there my darter was put upon buying one of those tudeling things herself; for she heard say as a young lady was come over from France, that learns all the quality. So that was enough for my darter; for there's nothing the mode like coming from France. It makes any thing go down. And 'twould be a remarkable cheap job, they said, for the young lady was in such prodigious want of cash, as one Miss Bydel, her particular friend, told us in the shop, that she'd jump at any price; put in case she could but get paid. So, upon that——"

The narration was here interrupted by Sir Lyell Sycamore, who, having caught a glimpse of Ellis through the glass-door, entered the shop with a smile of admiration and pleasure; though, at sight of Mr. Tedman, it was changed into one of insolence and derision. With a careless swing of his hat, and of his whole person, he negligently said, that he hoped she had caught no cold at the concert; or at least none beyond what the cakes, the bread and butter, or the negus, of her gallant and liberal admirer, had been able to cure.

Mr. Tedman, much affronted, mumbled* the gilt head of his cane;* Ellis gravely looked another way, without deigning to make any answer; and Riley exclaimed, "O, faith, if you expect a reply from the Demoiselle, except she's in a talking humour, you'll find yourself confoundedly out in your reckoning! You will, faith! Unless you light upon something that happens to hit her taste, you may sail from the north pole to the south, and return home by a voyage round the world, before she'll have been moved to squeeze out a syllable."

The young Baronet, disdaining the plain appearance, and rough dialect and manners of Riley, nearly as much as he despised the more civil garrulity and meanness of Tedman, was turning scoffingly upon his heel, when he overheard the latter say, in a low voice, to Ellis, "Suppose we two go up stairs to your room, to have our talk, my dear; for I don't see what we get by staying down with the quality, only to be made game of."

Highly provoked, yet haughtily smiling, "I see," said the Baronet, "for whose interest I am to apply, if I wish for the honour of a private audience!"

"Well, if you do," said Mr. Tedman, muttering between his teeth, "it's only a sign Miss knows I would not misbehave myself."

Sir Lyell now, not able to keep his countenance, went to the other end of the shop; and pitched upon the prettiest and youngest of Miss Matson's work-women, to ask some advice relative to his cravats.

Mr. Tedman, in doubt whether this retreat were the effect of contempt, or of being worsted, whispered to Ellis, "One knows nothing of life, as one may say, without coming among the quality! I should have thought, put in case any body had asked me my opinion, that that gentleman was quite behind hand as to his manners; for I'll warrant it would not be taken well from me, if I was to behave so! but any thing goes down from the quality, by way of politeness."

"Sir Lyell Sycamore," said Miss Bydel, who was as hard, though not as bold as himself, "if it won't be impertinent, I should be glad to know how you first got acquainted with this young person? for I can't make out how it is so many people happen to know her. Not that I mean in the least to dive into any body's private affairs; but I have a particular reason for what I ask; so I shall take it as a favour, Sir Lyell, if you'll tell me."

"Most willingly, Ma'am, upon condition you will be so kind as to tell me, in return, whether this young lady is under your care?"

"Under my care, Sir Lyell? Don't you know who I am, then?"

A supercilious smile said No.

"Well, that's really odd enough! Did not you see me with Mrs. Maple at that blind harper's concert?"

"Faith, Madam," cried Riley, "when a man has but one pair of eyes, you elderly ladies can't have much chance of getting a look, if a young lass is by. The Demoiselle deserves a full pair to herself."

"Why yes, Sir, that's true enough!" said Mr. Tedman, simpering, "the young lady deserves a pair of eyes to herself! She's well enough to look at, to be sure!"

"If she has your eyes to herself, Sir," said Sir Lyell, contemptuously, "she must be happy indeed!"

"She should have mine, if she would accept them, though I had an hundred!" cried Riley.

Ellis, now, was only restrained from forcing her way up stairs, through the apprehension of exciting fresh sneers, by an offered pursuit of Mr. Tedman.

"Don't mind them, my dear," cried Miss Bydel; "I'll soon set them right. If you have any naughty thoughts, gentlemen, relative to this young person, you must give me leave to inform you that you are mistaken; for though I don't know who she is, nor where she comes from, nor even so much as what is her name; except that I gave her myself, without in the least meaning it; still you may take my word for it she is a person of character; for Mrs. Maple herself, though she confessed how the young woman played upon her, with one contrivance after another, to ferret herself into the house; declared, for positive, that she was quite too particular about her acquaintances, to let her stay, if she had not been a person of virtue. And, besides, Sir Lyell, my young Lord Melbury—"

At this name Ellis started and changed colour.

"My young Lord Melbury, Sir Lyell, as young lords will do, offered to make her his mistress; and, I can give you my word for it, she positively refused him. This his young lordship told to Mr. Ireton, from whom I had it; that is from Mrs. Maple, which is the same thing. Is it not true Mrs. Ellis? or Mrs. something else, I don't know what?"

The most forcible emotions were now painted upon the countenance of Ellis, who, unable to endure any longer such offensive discourse, disengaged herself from Miss Bydel, and, no longer heeding Mr. Tedman, hurried up stairs.

Sir Lyell Sycamore stared after her, for a few minutes, with mingled surprise, curiosity, admiration, and pique; and then loitered out of the shop.

Riley, shouting aloud, said the Demoiselle always amused him; and followed.

Mr Tedman, not daring, after the insinuations of Sir Lyell, to attempt pursuing the young *music-maker*, produced a paper-packet, consisting of almonds, and raisins, and French plums;* saying, "I intended to pop these nice things upon that young Miss's table, unbeknown to her, for a surprise; for I did not like to come empty handed; for I know your young house-keepers never afford themselves little dainties of this kind; so I poked together all that was left, out of all the plates, after desert,* yesterday, when we happened to have a very handsome dinner, because of company. So you'll be sure to give her the whole, Mrs. Matson. Don't leave 'em about, now! They are but tempting things."

Miss Bydel remained last; unable to prevail upon herself to depart, while she could suggest a single interrogatory for the gratification of her curiosity.

CHAPTER XXVII

THE retreat sought by Ellis, from a recital as offensive to her ear as it was afflicting to her heart, was not long uninterrupted:

Miss Arbe, next, made her appearance. Gravely, but civilly, she lamented the disturbance at the concert; paradingly assuring Ellis that she should have called sooner, but that she had incessantly been occupied in endeavours to serve her. She had conversed with every one of her scholars; but nothing was yet quite decided, as to what would be the result of that strange attack. Poor Mrs. Maple, to whom, of course, she had made her first visit, seemed herself in the utmost distress; one moment repining, that she had suffered her charity to delude her into countenancing a person so unknown; and another, vindicating herself warmly from all possible imputation of indiscretion, by the most positive affirmations of the unblemished reputation of Miss Ellis; and these assertions, most fortunately, had, at length, determined Miss Bydel to support her, for how else, as she justly asked, should she get the money repaid that she had advanced for the harp?

"And Miss Bydel," continued Miss Arbe, "like all other old maids, is so precise about those sort of particulars, that, though she has not the smallest influence with any body of any consequence, as to any thing else, she is always depended upon for that sort of thing. We must not, therefore, shew her that we despise her, for she may be useful enough; especially in letting you have the harp, you know, that we may still enjoy a little music together. For I can make her do whatever I please for the sake of my company."

Ellis had long known that the civilities which she owed to Miss Arbe, had their sole motive in selfishness; but the total carelessness of giving them any other colour, became, now, so glaring, that she could with difficulty conceal the decrease either of her respect or of her gratitude.

Miss Arbe, however, was but little troubled with that species of delicacy which is solicitous to watch, that it may spare the feelings of others. She continued, therefore, what she had to offer, hurrying to come to a conclusion, as she had not, she declared, three minutes to stay.

If Lady Kendover, she said, could be brought over, every body would follow; not excepting Lady Arramede, who was obliged to be so great a niggard, in the midst of her splendid expences, that she would be quite enchanted to renew her daughter's lessons, with so economical a mistress, if once she could be satisfied that she would be sustained by other persons of fashion. But Lady Kendover, who did not wait to be led, protested that she could by no means place her niece again under the tuition of Miss Ellis, till the concert-scene should be explained.

Miss Arbe then asked whether Ellis would give it any explanation.

Ellis dejectedly answered, that she could offer no other, than that necessity had forced her to disguise herself, that she might make her escape.

"Well but, then, people say," cried Miss Arbe, "now that your escape is made, why don't you speak out? That's the cry every where."

Ellis looked down, distressed, ashamed; and Miss Arbe declared that she had not another moment at present, for discussion, but would call again, to settle what should be done on Monday. Meantime, she had brought some new music with her, which she wished to try; for the time was so unaccountable, that she could not make out a bar of it.

Ellis heartily felicitated herself upon every occasion, by which she could lessen obligations of which she now felt the full weight, and, with the utmost alacrity, took her harp.

Miss Arbe here had so much to study, so many passages to pick out, and such an eagerness to practise till she could conquer their difficulties, that she soon forgot that she had not a moment to spare; and two hours already had been consecrated to her improvement, when intelligence was brought that Mr. Tedman's carriage was come for Miss Ellis.

"You must not accept it for the world!" cried Miss Arbe. "If, at the moment people of distinction are shy of you, you are known to cultivate amongst mechanics,* and people of that sort, it's all over with you. Persons of fashion can't possibly notice you again."

She then added, that, after the scene of the preceding day, Miss Ellis must make it a point to let the first house that she entered be that of somebody of condition. She might go amongst trades-people as much as she pleased, when once she was established amongst persons of rank; for trades-people were so much the best paymasters, that nobody could be angry if artists were partial to them; but they must by no means take the lead; nor suppose that they were to have any hours but those that would not suit other people. As she could not, therefore, re-commence her career at Lady Kendover's, or at Lady Arramede's, she must try to get received at Miss Sycamore's;—or, if that should be too difficult, at the Miss Crawleys, who would object to nothing, as they cared for nobody's opinion, and made it a rule to follow nobody's advice. And this they took so little pains to hide from the world, that their countenance would not be of the least service, but for their living with Sir Marmaduke, who was scrupulosity itself. This being the case, joined to their extreme youth, they had not yet been set down, as they must necessarily be, in a few years, for persons of no weight, and rather detrimental than advantageous to people of no consequence. At present, therefore, Ellis might safely make her court to them, as she could always drop them when they became dangerous, or of no use. And just now she must snap at* whoever and whatever could help to bring her again into credit. And the Miss Crawleys, though each of them was as wilful as a spoiled child, as full of tricks as a school-boy, and of as boisterous mirth as a dairy-maid, were yet sisters of a baronet, and born of a very good family; and therefore they would be more serviceable to her than that vulgar Miss Tedman, even though she were an angel.

Ellis listened in silent, and scarcely concealed disdain, to these worldly precepts; yet Miss Tedman was so utterly disagreeable, and the sneers of Sir Lyell Sycamore had added such repugnance to her distaste of the civilities of Mr. Tedman, that she did not attempt opposing the dictatorial proceedings of Miss Arbe; who gave orders, that the coachman should be told that Miss Ellis was indisposed, and sent her compliments, but could not wait upon Miss Tedman till the next week.

She then again went on with her unacknowledged, but not less, to her tutress, laborious lesson, till she was obliged to hasten to her toilette, for her dinner-engagement; leaving Ellis in the utmost alarm for her whole scheme; and tormented with a thousand fears, because unable to fix upon any standard for the regulation of her conduct.

The next day was Sunday. Ellis had constantly on that day attended divine worship, during the month which she had spent at Brighthelmstone; and now, to a call stronger than usual for the consolation which it might afford her, she joined an opinion, that to stay away, in her present circumstances, might have an air of absconding, or of culpability.

She was placed, as usual, in a pew, with some other decent strangers, by a fee to the pew-opener;* but she had the mortification to find, when the service was over, that the dry clear frost, of the latter end of March, which had enabled her to walk to the church, was broken up by a heavy shower of rain. She had been amongst the first to hurry away, in the hope of escaping unnoticed, by hastening down the hill, on which the church is built, before the higher ranks of the congregation left their pews; but, arrived at the porch, she was compelled to stop: she was unprovided with an umbrella, and the rain was so violent that, without one, she must have been wet through in a minute.

She would have made way back to the pew which she had quitted, to wait for more moderate weather; but the whole congregation was coming forth, and there was no re-passing.

She was the more sensibly vexed at being thus impeded, from finding herself, almost immediately, joined by Sir Lyell Sycamore; whose eagerness to speak to her by no means concealed his embarrassment in what manner to address, or to think of her. He was making various offers of service; to find the pew-opener; to give her a seat to herself; to fetch her a chaise from the nearest inn; or an umbrella from his own carriage; when Mrs. and Miss Brinville, who hurried from their pew, the instant that they saw the Baronet depart, cast upon them looks of such suspicious disdain, that he deemed it necessary, though he smiled and appeared gratified by their undisguised pique, to walk on with them to their carriage; whispering, however, to Ellis, that he should return to take her under his care.

Ellis, extremely shocked, could not endure to remain on the

same spot, as if awaiting his services; she glided, therefore, into a corner, close to the door; hoping that the crowd, which incommoded, would at least protect her from being seen: but she had not been stationed there a moment, before she had the unwelcome surprise of hearing the words, "Why, Mr. Stubbs, if here is not Miss Ellis!" and finding that she had placed herself between young Gooch, the farmer's son, and Mr. Stubbs, the old steward.

"Good now, Ma'am," the young man cried, "why I have never seen you since that night of our all acting together in that play, when you out-topped* us all so to nothing! I never saw the like, not even at the real play. And some of the judges said, you were not much short of what they be at the grand London theatre itself. I suppose, Ma'am, you were pretty well used to acting in France? for they say all the French are actors or dancers, except just them that go to the wars. I should like to know, Ma'am, whether they pop off them players and fidlers at the same rate they do the rest? for, if they do, it's a wonder how they can get 'em to go on acting and piping, and jiggetting* about, and such like, if they know they are so soon to have their heads off, all the same. You could not get we English now to do so, just before being hanged, or shot. But the French a'n't very thoughtful. They're always ready for a jig."

"I am sorry I had no notice of seeing you here to day, Ma'am," said Mr. Stubbs, "for if I had, I would have brought my bit of paper with me, that I've writ down my queries upon, about raising the rents in those parts, and the price that land holds in general; and about a purchase that I am advised to make.—"

"But I should like much to know, Ma'am," resumed Gooch, "whether it's a truth, what I've been told at our club,* that your commonest soldier in France, when once he can bring proof he has killed you his dozen or so, with his own hand, is made a general upon the spot? If that's the case, to be sure it's no great wonder there's so much blood shed; for such encouragement as that's enough to make soldiers of the very women and children."

"Why, I am told, the French have no great head," said Mr. Stubbs, "except for the wars; and that's what makes the land so cheap; for, I am told, you may buy an estate, of a thousand or two acres, for an old song. And that's the reason I am thinking of making a purchase. The only point is, how to see the premises without the danger of crossing the seas; and how to strike the bargain."

Ellis, thus beset, was not sorry to be joined by Mr. Scope, who, though more formal and tedious than either of the others, was a gentleman, spoke in a lower tone of voice, and attracted less attention.

"I am happy, Ma'am," he said, "to have met with you again; for I have wished for some time to hold a little discourse with you, relative to the rites practised abroad, as to that Goddess of Reason,* that, as I am credibly informed, has been set up by Mr. Robert-Spierre. Now I should wish to enquire, what good they expect to accrue by proclaiming, one day, that there is no religion, and then, the next day, making a new one by the figure of a woman. It is hardly to be supposed that such sort of fickleness can serve to make a government respectable. And as to so many females being called Goddesses of Reason,—for I am assured there are some score of them,—one don't very well see what that means; the ladies in general,—I speak without offence, as it's out of their line,—not being particularly famous for their reason; at least not here; and I should suppose they can hardly be much more so in that light nation. The Pagans, it is true, though from what mode of thinking we are now at a loss to discover, thought proper to have Reason represented by a female; and that, perhaps, may be the cause of the French adopting the same notion, on account of their ancient character for politeness; though I cannot much commend their sagacity, taken in a political point of view, in putting the female head, which is very well in its proper sphere, upon coping,* if I may use such an expression, with the male."

This harangue, which Mr. Stubbs and young Gooch, though too respectful to interrupt, waited, impatiently, to hear finished, might have lasted unbroken for half an hour, if Miss Bydel, in passing by with her brother, to get to her carriage, had not called out, "Bless me, Mr. Scope, what are you talking of there, with that young person? Have you been asking her about that business at the blind harper's concert? I should be glad to know, myself, Miss Ellis, as I call you, what you intend to do next? Have any of your scholars let you go to them again? And what says Miss Arbe to all this? Does she think you'll ever get the better of it?"

Mr. Bydel, here, begged his sister to invite Mr. Scope to take a place in the carriage.

Young Gooch, then, would have renewed his questions relative to the generals, but that, upon pronouncing again her name, Mr. Tedman, who, with his daughter, was passing near the porch, to examine whether they could arrive safely at their carriage, called out, "Well, if you are not here, too, my dear! Why how will you do to get home? You'll be draggled up to your chin, if you walk; put in case you haven't got your umbrella, and your pattens.* But I suppose some of your quality friends will give you a lift; for I see one of 'em just coming. It's Miss Ellis, the music-maker, Ma'am," added he, to Lady Arramede, who just then came out with Miss Arramede; "the young girl as teaches our darters the musics; and she'll spoil all her things, poor thing, if somebody don't give her a lift home."

Lady Arramede, without moving a muscle of her face, or deigning to turn towards either the object or the agent of this implied request, walked on in silent contempt.

Mr. Tedman, extremely offended, said "The quality always think they may behave any how! and Lady Arrymud is not a bit to choose, from the worst among them. And even my own darter," he whispered, "is just as bad as the best; for she'd pout at me for a month to come, put in case I was to ride you home in our coach, now that the quality's taken miff* at you."

During this whisper, which Ellis strove vainly to avoid hearing, and which the familiar junction of young Gooch, who was related to Mr. Tedman, rendered more observable, she had the mortification of being evidently seen, though no longer, as heretofore, courteously acknowledged, by all her scholars and acquaintances. Miss Sycamore, the hardiest, passed, staring disdainfully in her face; Mrs. Maple, the most cowardly, and who was accidentally at Brighthelmstone, pretended to have hurt her foot, that she might look down: the Miss Crawleys screamed out, "The Ellis! The Ellis! look, The Marmaduke, 'tis The Ellis!" Sir Marmaduke, turning back to address Miss Arbe, said, with concern, "Is it possible, Madam, 'tis The Ellis, the elegant Ellis, that can join such low company?" Miss Arbe shrugged her shoulders, crying, "What can one do with such people?" Lady Kendover's eyes kept carefully a straightforward direction; while Lady Barbara, whom she held by one hand, incessantly kissed the other at Ellis, with ingenuous and undisguised warmth of kindness; an action which was eagerly repeated by Selina, who closely followed her ladyship.

Ireton, who brought up the rear, quitted the group, to approach Ellis, and say, "I am, positively, quite confounded, my dear Miss Ellis, at the mischief my confounded giddiness has brought about. I had not an idea of it, I assure you. I merely meant to play upon that confounded queer fellow, Riley. He's so cursed troublesome, and so confounded free, that I hate him horribly. That's all, I assure you."

Ellis would make no answer, and he was forced to run after Selina.

The rain being, now, much abated, the congregation began to disperse, and Mr. Tedman was compelled to attend his daughter; but he recommended the young music-maker to the care of his cousin Gooch; whose assistance she was declining, when she was again joined by Sir Lyell Sycamore, with a capacious umbrella, under which he begged to be her escort.

She decidedly refused his services; but he protested that, if she would not let him walk by her side, he would follow her, like an Indian slave,* holding the umbrella over her head, as if she were an Indian queen.

Vexed and displeased, and preferring any other protection, she addressed herself to old Mr. Stubbs, who still stood under the porch, and begged him to have the kindness to see her home.

Mr. Stubbs, extremely flattered, complied. The other candidates vainly opposed the decision: they found that her decree was irrevocable, and that, when once it was pronounced, her silence was resolute. Mr. Stubbs, nevertheless, had by no means the enjoyment that he expected from this distinction; for Ellis had as little inclination as she had spirit, to exert herself for answering the numerous enquiries, relative to land and rents, which he poured into her ears.

CHAPTER XXVIII

HARASSED and comfortless, Ellis passed the remainder of the day in painful recollections and apprehensive forebodings; though utterly unable, either by retrospection to avoid, or by anticipation to prepare for the evils that she might have to encounter.

The next morning, Miss Arbe came to her usual appointment. Though glad, in a situation so embarrassed, to see the only person whom she could look upon as a guide, her opinion of Miss Arbe, already lowered during that lady's last visit, had been so completely sunk, from her joining in the cry raised at the church, that she received her with undisguised coldness; and an open remonstrance against the cruel injustice of ascribing to choice, circumstances the most accidental, and a position as unavoidable, as it had been irksome and improper.

Miss Arbe, who came into the room with a gravely authoritative air, denoting that she expected not simply a welcome, but the humblest gratitude, for the condescension of her visit, was astonished by the courage, and disconcerted by the truth of this exhortation. She was by no means ignorant how unpleasantly Ellis might have been struck by her behaviour at the church; but she thought her in a condition too forlorn to feel, much less to express any resentment: and she meant, by entering the chamber with an wholly uncustomary importance, to awe her from hazarding any complaint. But the modesty of Ellis was a mixture of dignity with humility; if she thought herself oppressed or insulted, the former predominated; if she experienced consideration and kindness, she was all meek gratitude in return.

But when, by the steadiness of her representation, Miss Arbe found her own mistake, and saw what firmness could exist with indigence, what spirit could break through difficulty, she disguised her surprise, and changed, with alertness, the whole of her manner. She protested that some other voice must have been taken for her's; declared that she had always thought nobody so charming as Miss Ellis; railed against the abominable world for its prejudices; warmly renewed her professions of regard; and then rang the bell, to order her footman to bring up a little parcel of music from her coach, which she was sure would delight them both to try together.

Ellis suffered the music to be fetched; but, before she would play it, entreated Miss Arbe to spare a few minutes to discourse upon her affairs.

"What, Madam, am I now to do? 'Tis to your influence and exertions I am indebted for the attempt which I have made, to procure that self-dependence which I so earnestly covet. I shall always be most ready to acknowledge this obligation; but, permit me to solicit your directions, and, I hope, your aid, how I may try to allay the storm which accident has so cruelly raised around me; but which misconception alone can make dangerous or durable."

"Very true, my dear Miss Ellis, if every body judged you as justly as I do; but when people have enemies—"

"Enemies?" repeated Ellis, amazed, "surely, Madam, you are not serious?—Enemies? Can I possibly have any enemies? That, in a situation so little known, and so unlikely to be understood, I may have failed to create friends, I can easily, indeed, conceive,—but, offending no one, distressed, yet not importunate, and seeking to obviate my difficulties by my exertions; to supply my necessities by my labours,—surely I cannot have been so strangely, so unaccountably unfortunate as to have made myself any enemies?"

"Why you know, my dear Miss Ellis, how I blamed you, from the first, for that nonsense of telling Miss Brinville that she had no ear for music: what could it signify whether she had or not? She only wanted to learn that she might say she learnt; and you had no business to teach, but that you might be paid for teaching."

"And is it possible, Madam, that I can have made her really my enemy, merely by forbearing to take what I thought would be a dishonourable advantage, of her ignorance of that defect?"

"Nay, she has certainly no great reason to be thankful, for she would never have found it out; and I am sure nobody else would ever have told it her! She is firmly persuaded that you only wanted to give Sir Lyell Sycamore an ill opinion of her accomplishments; for she declares that she has seen you unceasingly pursuing him, with all the wiles imaginable. One time she surprised you sitting entirely aloof, at the Welshman's benefit, till he joined you; another time, she caught you waiting for him in the aisle of the church; and, in short—"

"Miss Arbe," cried Ellis, interrupting her, with undisguised resentment, "if Miss Brinville can be amused by inventing, as well as propagating, premeditated motives for accidental occurrences, you must permit me to decline being the auditress, if I cannot escape being the object of such fictitious censure!"

Miss Arbe, somewhat ashamed, repeated her assurances of personal good opinion; and then, with many pompous professions of regard and concern, owned that there had been a discussion at Lady Kendover's, after church-time on Sunday, which had concluded by a final decision, of her ladyship's, that it was utterly impossible to admit a young woman, so obscurely involved in strange circumstances, and so ready to fall into low company, to so confidential a kind of intercourse, as that of giving instructions to young persons of fashion. Every body else, of course, would abide by her ladyship's decision, "and therefore, my dear Miss Ellis," she continued, "I am excessively sorry, but our plan is quite overset. I am excessively sorry, I assure you; but what can be done? However, I have not above three minutes to stay, so do let us try that sweet adagio.* I want vastly to conquer the horrid long bars of that eternal cadenza."*

Ellis, for a few moments, stood almost stupified with amazement at so selfish a proposition, at the very instant of announcing so ruinous a sentence. But disdain soon supplied her with philosophy, and scorning to make an appeal for a consideration so unfeelingly with-held, she calmly went to her harp.

When Miss Arbe, however, rose to be gone, she begged some advice relative both to the debts which she had contracted, and those which she was entitled to claim; but Miss Arbe, looking at her watch, and hurrying on her gloves, declared that she had not a second to lose. "I shall see you, however," she cried, in quitting the chamber, "as often as possible: I can find a thousand pretences for coming to Miss Matson's without any body's knowing why; so we can still have our delightful little musical meetings."

The contempt inspired by this worldly patroness, so intent upon her own advantage, so insensible to the distress of the person whom she affected to protect, occupied the mind of Ellis only while she was present; the door was no sooner shut, than she felt wholly engrossed by her own situation, and her disappointment at large. This scheme, then, she cried, is already at an end! this plan for self-dependence is already abortive! And I have not my disappointment only to bear; it is accompanied with disgrace, and exposes me to indignity!

Deeply hurt and strongly affected, how insufficient, she exclaimed, is a FEMALE to herself! How utterly dependant upon situation—connexions—circumstance! how nameless, how for ever fresh-springing are her DIFFICULTIES,* when she would owe her existence to her own exertions! Her conduct is criticised, not scrutinized; her character is censured, not examined; her labours are unhonoured, and her qualifications are but lures to ill will! Calumny hovers over her head, and slander follows her footsteps!

Here she checked herself; candour, the reigning feature of her mind, repressed her murmurs. Involved as I am in darkness and obscurity, she cried, ought I to expect milder judgment? No! I have no right to complain. Appearances are against me; and to appearances are we not all either victims or dupes?

She now turned her thoughts to what measures she must next pursue; but felt no chance of equally satisfying herself in any other attempt. Music was her favourite study, and in the practice of that elegant, grateful, soul-soothing art, she found a softening to her cares, that momentarily, at least, lulled them to something like forgetfulness. And though this was a charm that could by no means extend to the dull and dry labour of teaching, it was a profession so preferable to all others, in her taste, that she bore patiently and cheerfully the minute, mechanical, and ear-wearing toil, of giving lessons to the unapt, the stupid, the idle, and the wilful; for such, unhappily are the epithets most ordinarily due to beginners in all sciences and studies.

The necessity, however, of adopting some plan that should

both be speedy and vigorous, was soon alarmingly enforced by a visit from Miss Matson; who civilly, but with evidently altered manners, told her that she had a little account to settle with some tradesmen, and that she should take it as a favour if her own account could be settled for her lodgings.

There are few attacks to which we are liable, that give a greater shock to upright and unhackneyed* minds, than a pecuniary demand which they know to be just, yet cannot satisfy. Pride and shame assault them at once. They are offended by a summons that seems to imply a doubt of their integrity; while they blush at appearing to have incurred it, by not having more scrupulously balanced their means with their expences.

She suffered, therefore, the most sensible mortification, from her inability to discharge, without delay, a debt contracted with a stranger, upon whose generosity she had no claim; upon whose forbearance she had no tie.

Far from having this power, she had other bills to expect which she as little could answer. The twenty pounds of Lady Aurora were already nearly gone, in articles which did not admit of trust;* and in the current necessaries which her situation indispensably and daily required. She feared that all the money which was due to her would be insufficient to pay what she owed; or, at least, would be wholly employed in that act of justice; which would leave her, therefore, in the same utter indigence as when she began her late attempt.

Her look of consternation served but to stimulate the demands of Miss Matson, which were now accompanied with allusions to the conversation that had been held in the shop, between Miss Bydel and Mr. Riley, relative to her poverty and disguise, that were designedly offensive.

Ellis, with an air grave and commanding, desired to be left alone; calmly saying that Miss Matson should very speedily be satisfied.

The impulse of her wishes was to have recourse to the deposit of Harleigh, that her answer to this affront might be an immediate change of lodging, as well as payment. But this was a thought that scarcely out-lived the moment of its formation: Alas! she cried, he who alone could serve me, whose generosity and benevolence would delight in aiding me, has put it out of my power to accept his smallest assistance! Had my friendship contented him, how essentially might I have been indebted to his good offices!

She was here broken in upon by one of the young apprentices, who, with many apologies, brought, from the several trades-people, all the little bills which had been incurred through the directions of Miss Arbe.

However severely she was shocked, she could not be surprised. She wrote immediately to communicate these demands to Miss Arbe, stating her distress, and entreating that her late scholars might be urged to settle their accounts with the utmost expedition. She felt her right to make this application to Miss Arbe, whose advice, or rather insistance, had impelled her into the measures which produced her present difficulties. Her request, therefore, though urged with deference and respect, had a tone which she was sure could not justly be disputed.

She wished earnestly to address a few words to Lady Kendover, of such a nature as might speak in her favour to her scholars at large; but so many obstacles were in the way, to her giving any satisfactory explanation, that she was obliged to be contented with silent acquiescence.

Miss Arbe sent word that she was engaged, and could not write. The rest of the day was passed in great anxiety. But when the following, also, wore away, without producing any reply, she wrote again, proposing, if Miss Arbe had not time to attend to her request, to submit it to Miss Bydel.

In about half an hour after she had sent this second note, Mr. Giles Arbe desired to be admitted, that he might deliver to her a message from his cousin.

She recollected having heard, from Selina, that he was a very absent, but worthy old man, and that he had the very best temper of any person breathing.

She did not hesitate, therefore, to receive him; and his appearance announced, at once, the latter quality, by a smile the most inartificial, which was evidently the emanation of a kind heart, opening to immediate good will at sight of a fellow-creature. It seemed the visible index of a good and innocent mind; and his manners had the most singular simplicity.

His cousin, he said, had desired him to acquaint her, that she could not call, because she was particularly engaged; and could not write, because, she was particularly hurried. "And whenever I have a commission from my cousin," he continued, "I always think it best to deliver it in her own words, for two or three reasons; one of which is that my own might not be half as good; for she is the most accomplished young lady living, I am told; and my other reasons you'll do me a favour by not asking me to mention."

"I may, at least infer, then, Sir, that, when less hurried, and less engaged, Miss Arbe means to have the goodness to come, or to write to me?"

" I don't doubt it: those ladies that she don't like should see her with you, can hardly keep watching her all day long."

"What ladies, Sir?"

"O, I must not mention names!" returned he, smiling; "my cousin charged me not. My fair cousin likes very well to be obeyed. But, may be, so do you, too? For they tell me it's not an uncommon thing among ladies. And if that's the case, I shall find myself in a dilemma; for my cousin has the best right; and yet, what have you done to me that I should deny you what you ask me?"

Then looking earnestly, but with an air so innocent, that it was impossible to give offence, in her face, he added, "My cousin has often told me a great many things about you; yet she never mentioned your being so pretty! But may be she thought I might find it out."

Ellis enquired whether he were acquainted with the nature of her application to Miss Arbe.

He nodded an assent, but checking himself from confirming it, cried, "My cousin bid me say nothing; for she will have it that I always mention things that should not be told; and that makes me very careful. So I hope you won't be angry if you find me rather upon my guard."

Ellis disclaimed all inquisitive designs, beyond desiring to know, whether Miss Arbe meant that she should discuss her situation with him, and receive his counsel how she should proceed.

"My cousin never asks my counsel," he answered: "she knows

every thing best herself. She is very clever, they tell me. She often recounts to me how she surprises people. So does her papa. I believe they think I should not discover it else. And I don't know but they are in the right, for I am a very indifferent judge. But I can't make out, with that gentle air of yours, and so pretty a face, how you can have made those ladies take such a dislike to you?"

"A dislike, Sir?"

"Yes; Lady Arramede talks of you with prodigious contempt, and—"

Ellis colouring at this word, hung back, evidently declining to hear another; but Mr. Giles, not remarking this, went on. "And Miss Brinville can't endure you, neither. It's a curious thing to see what an angry look comes over her features, when she talks of you. Do you know the reason?"

"I flatter myself it is not to be known, Sir! Certainly I am innocent of any design of offending her."

"Why then perhaps she does not know what she has taken amiss, herself, poor lady! She's only affronted, and can't tell why. It will happen so sometimes, to those pretty ladies, when they begin going a little down hill. And they can't help it. They don't know what to make of it themselves, poor things! But we can see how it is better, we lookers-on."

He then seated himself upon an arm-chair, and, leaning back at his ease, continued talking, but without looking at Ellis, or seeming to address her.

"I always pity them, the moment I see them, those pretty creatures, even when they are in their prime. I always think what they have got to go through. After seeing every body admire them, to see nobody look at them! And when they cast their eyes on a glass, to find themselves every day changing,—and always for the worse! It is but hard upon them, I really think, when they have done nothing to deserve it. It is but a short time ago that that Miss Brinville was almost as pretty as this young harp-player here."—

"Sir!" cried Ellis, surprised.

"Ma'am?" cried he, starting, and looking round; and then, smiling at himself, adding, "I protest I did not think of your being so near me! I had forgot that. But I hope you won't take it ill?"

"By no means," she answered; and asked whether she might write a few lines by him to Miss Arbe.

He willingly consented.

She then drew up an animated representation, to that lady, of the irksome situation into which she was cast, from the evident distrust manifested by Miss Matson; and the suspicious speed with which the other bills had been delivered. She meant to send her small accounts immediately to all her scholars, and entreated Miss Arbe to use her interest in hastening their discharge.

When she raised her head to give this, with an apology, to Mr. Giles, she saw him unfolding some small papers, which he began very earnestly to examine. Not to interrupt him, she took up some needle-work; but, upon looking, soon after, at the chimney-piece, she missed the packet which she had placed there, of her bills, and then with the utmost surprise, perceived that it was in his hands.

She waited a few instants, in expectation that he would either put it down, or make some excuse for his curiosity; but he seemed to think of nothing less.* He sorted and counted the bills, and began casting them up.

"Have you then the goodness, Sir," said Ellis, "to prepare yourself for acquainting Miss Arbe with the state of my affairs?"

He started again at this question, and looked a little scared; but, after a minute's perplexity, he suddenly arose, and hastily refolding, and placing them upon the chimney-piece, said, with a good deal of confusion, "I beg your pardon a thousand times! I don't well know how this happened; but the chimney-piece looks so like my own,—and the fire was so comfortable,—that I suppose I thought I was at home, and took that parcel for one that the servant had put there for me. And I was wondering to myself when I had ordered all those linens, and muslins, and the like: I could not recollect one article of them."

He then, after again begging her pardon, took leave.

While Ellis was ruminating whether this strange conduct were the effect of absence,* oddity, or curiosity, he abruptly returned, and said, "I protest I was going without my errand, at last! Did you bid me tell my cousin that all those bills were paid?"

"All paid?—alas, no!—not one of them!"

"And why not? You should always pay your bills, my dear."

Ellis looked at him in much perplexity, to see whether this were uttered as a sneer, or as a remonstrance; but soon perceived, by the earnestness of his countenance, that it was the latter; and then, with a sigh, answered, "You are undoubtedly right, Sir! I am the first to condemn all that appears against me! But I made my late attempt with a persuasion that I was as secure of repaying others, as of serving myself. I would not, else, have run any risk, where I should not have been the sole sufferer."

"But what," said he, staring, and shutting the door, and not seeming to comprehend her, "what is the reason that you can't pay your bills?"

"A very simple reason, Sir?—I have not the power!"

"Not the power?—what, are you very poor, then?"

Ellis could not forbear smiling, but seeing him put his hand in his pocket, hastened to answer, "Yes, Sir,—but very proud, too! I am sometimes, therefore, involved in the double distress, of being obliged to refuse the very assistance I require."

"But you would not refuse mine!"

"Without a moment's hesitation!"

"Would you, indeed? And from what motive?"

Again Ellis could scarcely keep her countenance, at a question so unexpected, while she answered, "From the customs, Sir, of the world, I have been brought up to avoid all obligations with strangers."

"How so? I don't at all see that. Have you not an obligation to that linen draper, and hosier, and I don't know who, there, upon your chimney-piece, if you take their things, and don't pay for them?"

Yet more struck with the sense of unbiassed equity manifested by this question, than by the simplicity shewn by that which had preceded it, Ellis felt her face suffused with shame, as she replied, "I blush to have incurred such a reprimand; but I hope to convince you, by the exertions which I shall not a moment delay making, how little it is my intention to practise any such injustice; and how wide it would be from my approbation."

She sat down, sensibly affected by the necessity of uttering this vindication.

"Well, then," said he, without observing her distress, "won't it be more honest to run in debt with an old bachelor, who has nobody but himself to take care of, than with a set of poor people who, perhaps, have got their houses full of children?"

The word honest, and the impossibility of disproving a charge of injuring those by whom she had been served, so powerfully shocked her feelings in arraigning her principles, that she could frame no answer.

Conceiving her silence to be assent, he returned to the chimney-piece, and, taking the little packet of bills, prepared to put it into his pocket-book; but, hastily, then, rising, she entreated him to restore it without delay.

Her manner was so earnest that he did not dare contest her will, though he looked nearly as angry as he was sorry. "I meant," he said, "to have given you the greatest pleasure in the world; that was what I meant. I thought your debts made you so unhappy, that you would love me all your life for getting them off your hands. I loved a person so myself, who paid for some tops for me, when I was a boy, that I had bought for some of my playmates; without recollecting that I had no money to pay for them. However, I beg your pardon for my blunder, if you like your debts better."

He now bowed to her, with an air of concern, and, wishing her health and happiness, retreated; but left her door wide open; and she heard him say to the milliners, "My dears, I've made a great mistake: I wanted to set that pretty lady's heart at rest, by paying her bills; but she says she had rather owe them; though she did not mention her reason. So I hope the poor people are in no great hurry. However, whether they be or not, don't let them torment her for the money, for she says she has none. So 'twould only be plaguing her for nothing. And I should be sorry for that, for she looks as if she were very good; besides being so pretty."

BOOK IV

CHAPTER XXIX

ELLIS, for some minutes, hardly knew whether to be most provoked or diverted by this singular visit. But all that approached to amusement was short lived. The most distant apprehension that her probity could be arraigned, was shocking; and she determined to dedicate the evening to calculating all that she had either to pay or to receive; and sooner to leave herself destitute of every means of support, but such as should arise from day to day, than hazard incurring any suspicion injurious to her integrity.

These estimates, which were easily drawn up, afforded her, at once, a view of her ability to satisfy her creditors, and of the helpless poverty in which she must then remain herself: her courage, nevertheless, rose higher, from the conviction that her honour would be cleared.

She was thus employed, when, late in the evening, Miss Arbe, full dressed, and holding her watch in her hand, ran up stairs. "I have but a quarter of an hour," she cried, "to stay, so don't let us lose a moment. I am just come from dining at Lady Kendover's, and I am going to an assembly at the Sycamore's. But I thought I would just steal a few minutes for our dear little lyre. You can give me your answer, you know, as I am going down stairs. Come, quick, my dear Miss Ellis!—'Tis such a delight to try our music together!"

"My answer, Madam?" cried Ellis, surprised: "I had hoped for yours! and, as you will, probably, meet all the ladies to whom you have had the goodness to mention me, at Miss Sycamore's, I entreat—"

"I am so dreadfully hurried," cried she, unrolling her music, "that I can't say a word of all that now. But we'll arrange it, and you can tell me how you like our plan, you know, as I am putting up my music, and going; but we can't possibly play the harp while I am drawing on my gloves, and scampering down stairs."

This logic, which she felt to be irrefutable, she uttered with the most perfect self-complacency, while spreading her music, and placing herself at the harp; but once there, she would neither say nor hear another word; and it was equally in vain that Ellis desired an explanation of the plan to which she alluded, or an answer to the petition which she had written herself. Miss Arbe could listen to no sounds but those produced by her own fingers; and could balance no interests, but those upon which she was speculating, of the advantages which she should herself reap from these continual, though unacknowledged lessons. And Ellis found all her painful difficulties, how to extricate herself from the distresses of penury, the horrour of creditors, and the fears of want, treated but as minor considerations, when put in competition with the importance of Miss Arbe's most trivial, and even stolen improvement.

She saw, however, no redress; displeasure was unnoticed, distaste was unheeded; and she had no choice but to put aside every feeling, and give her usual instructions; or to turn a professed protectress into a dangerous and resentful enemy.

She sat down, therefore, to her business.

The quarter of an hour was scarcely passed, before Miss Arbe started up to be gone; and, giving her music to Ellis to fold, while she drew on her gloves, cried, "Well, you can tell me, now, what I must say to Lady Kendover. I hope you like my scheme?"

Ellis protested herself utterly ignorant what scheme she meant.

"Bless me," she cried, "did not my cousin tell you what I've been doing for you? I've quite slaved in your service, I can assure you. I never made such exertions in my life. Every body had agreed to give you up. It's really shocking to see how people are governed by their prejudices! But I brought them all round; for, after Lady Aurora's letter, they none of them could tell what to resolve upon, till I gave them my advice. That, indeed, is no unusual thing to happen to me. So few people know what they had best do!"

This self-eulogium* having elated her spirits, her haste to depart sufficiently slackened, to give her time to make a farther demand, whether her cousin had executed her commission.

Ellis knew not even that he had had any to execute.

"Well," she cried, "that old soul grows more provoking every day! I have resolved a thousand times never to trust him again; only he is always at hand, and that's so convenient, one does not know how to resist making use of him. But he really torments me more than any thing existing. If he had literally no sense, one should not be so angry; but, when it's possible to make him listen, he understands what one says well enough: and sometimes, which you will scarcely believe, he'll suddenly utter something so keen and so neat, that you'd suppose him, all at once, metamorphosed into a wit. But the fact is, he is so tiresomely absent, that he never knows what he does, nor hears what one says. At breakfast, he asks whether there is nothing more coming for dinner; at dinner, he bids his servant get ready his night-cap and slippers, because he shall eat no supper; if any body applies to him for a pinch of snuff, he brings them an arm chair; if they ask him how he does, he fetches his hat and cane, buttons his great coat up to his chin, and says he is ready to attend them; if they enquire what it is o'clock, he thanks them for their kindness, and runs over a list of all his aches and pains; and the moment any body enters the room, the first word he commonly says to them is Good-bye!"

Ellis earnestly begged to know what was meant by the letter of Lady Aurora.

Miss Arbe again declared herself too much hurried to stay; and spent more time in censuring Mr. Giles, for not having spared her such a loss of it, than would have been required for even a minute recital of the business which he had forgotten. Ellis, however, at length learnt, that Miss Arbe had had the address to hit upon a plan which conciliated all interests, and to which she had prevailed upon Lady Kendover to consent. "Her la'ship's name," she continued, "with my extensive influence, will be quite enough to obtain that of every body else worth having at Brighthelmstone. And she was vastly kind, indeed; for though she did it, she said, with the extremest repugnance, which, to be sure, is natural enough, not being able to imagine who or what she serves; yet, in consideration of your being patronized by me, she would not refuse to give you her countenance once more. Nothing in the world could be kinder. You must go immediately to thank her."

"Unhappily, Madam," answered Ellis, colouring, "I have too many obligations of my own unrepaid, to have the presumption to suppose I can assist in the acknowledgements of others: and this plan, whatever it may be, has so evidently received the sanction of Lady Kendover solely to oblige Miss Arbe, that it would be folly, if not impertinence, on my part, to claim the honour of offering her ladyship my thanks."

Miss Arbe, whose watch was always in her hand, when her harp was not, had no time to mark this discrimination; she went on, therefore, rapidly, with her communication. "Lady Kendover," she said, "had asserted, that if Miss Ellis had been celebrated in any public line of life, there would be less difficulty about employing her; but as she had only been seen or noticed in private families, it was necessary to be much more particular as to her connexions and conduct; because, in that case, she must, of course, be received upon a more friendly footing; and with a consideration and confidence by no means necessary for a public artist. If, therefore, all were not clear and satisfactory—"

Ellis, with mingled spirit and dignity, here interrupted her: "Spare me, Madam, this preamble, for both our sakes! for though the pain it causes is only mine, the useless trouble,—pardon me!—will be yours. I do not desire—I could not even consent to enter any house, where to receive me would be deemed a disgrace."

"O, but you have not heard my plan! You don't know how well it has all been settled. The harp-professor now here, a proud, conceited old coxcomb, full of the most abominable airs, but a divine performer, wants to obtrude his daughter upon us, in your place; though she has got so cracked a voice, that she gives one the head-ache by her squeaks. Well, to make it his interest not to be your enemy, I have prevailed with Lady Kendover to desire him to take you in for one of his band, either to play or sing, at the great concert-room."

Ellis, amazed, exclaimed, "Can you mean, Madam,—can Lady Kendover mean—to propose my performing in public?"

"Precisely that. 'Tis the only way in the world to settle the business, and conquer all parties."

"If so, Madam, they can never be conquered! for never, most certainly never, can I perform in public!"

"And why not? You'll do vastly well, I dare say. Why should you be so timid? 'Tis the best way to gain you admission into great houses; and if your performance is applauded, you'll have as many scholars as you like; and you may be as impertinent as you will. Your humility, now, won't make you half so many friends, as a set of airs and graces, then, will make you partizans."

"I am much obliged to you for a recommendation so powerful, Madam," answered Ellis, dryly; "but I must entreat you to pardon my inability to avail myself of it; and my frank declaration, that my objections to this plan are insuperable."

Miss Arbe only treated this as an ignorant diffidence, scarcely worth even derision, till Ellis solemnly and positively repeated, that her resolution not to appear in public would be unalterable: she then became seriously offended, and, slightly wishing her good night, ran down stairs; without making any other answer to her enquiry, concerning the request in her note, than that she knew not what it meant, and could not stay another moment.

Ellis, now, was deeply disturbed. Her first impulse was to write to Lady Aurora, and implore her protection; but this wish was soon subdued by an invincible repugnance, to drawing so young a person into any clandestine correspondence.

Yet there was no one else to whom she could apply. Alas! she cried, how wretched a situation!—And yet,—compared with what it might have been!—Ah! let me dwell upon that contrast!—What, then, can make me miserable?

With revived vigour from this reflection, she resolved to assume courage to send in all her accounts, without waiting any longer for the precarious assistance of Miss Arbe. But what was to follow? When all difficulty should be over with respect to others, how was she to exist herself?

Music, though by no means her only accomplishment, was the only one which she dared flatter herself to possess with sufficient knowledge, for the arduous attempt of teaching what she had learnt. Even in this, she had been frequently embarrassed; all she knew upon the subject had been acquired as a *diletante*, not studied as an artist; and though she was an elegant and truly superiour performer, she was nearly as deficient in the theoretical, as she was skilful in the practical part of the science* of which she undertook to give lessons.

Wide is the difference between exhibiting that which we have attained only for that purpose, from the power of dispensing knowledge to others. Where only what is chosen is produced; only what is practised is performed; where one favourite piece, however laboriously acquired, however exclusively finished, gains a character of excellence, that, for the current day, and with the current throng, disputes the prize of fame, even with the solid rights of professional candidates; the young and nearly ignorant disciple, may seem upon a par with the experienced and learned master. But to disseminate knowledge, by clearing that which is obscure, and explaining that which is difficult; to make what is hard appear easy, by giving facility to the execution of what is abstruse to the conception; to lighten the fatigue of practice, by the address of method; to shorten what requires study, by anticipating its result; and, while demonstrating effects to expound their cause: by the rules of art, to hide the want of science; and to supply the dearth of genius, by divulging the secrets of embellishments;—these were labours that demanded not alone brilliant talents, which she amply possessed, but a fund of scientific knowledge, to which she formed no pretensions. Her modesty, however, aided her good sense, in confining her attempts at giving improvement within the limits of her ability; and rare indeed must have been her ill fortune, had a pupil fallen to her lot, sufficiently advanced to have surpassed her powers of instruction.

But this art, the favourite of her mind, and in which she had taste and talents to excel, must be now relinquished: and Drawing, in which she was also, though not equally, an adept, presented the same obstacles of recommendation for obtaining scholars, as music. Her theatrical abilities, though of the first cast, were useless; since from whatever demanded public representation, her mind revolted: and her original wish of procuring herself a safe and retired asylum, by becoming a governess to some young lady, was now more than ever remote from all chance of being gratified.

How few, she cried, how circumscribed, are the attainments of women! and how much fewer and more circumscribed still, are those which may, in their consequences, be useful as well as ornamental, to the higher, or educated class! those through which, in the reverses of fortune, a FEMALE may reap benefit without abasement! those which, while preserving her from pecuniary distress, will not aggravate the hardships or sorrows of her changed condition, either by immediate humiliation, or by what, eventually, her connexions may consider as disgrace!

Thus situated, she could have recourse only to the dull, monotonous, and cheerless plan, from which Miss Arbe had turned her aside; that of offering her services to Miss Matson as a needle-woman.

Her first step, upon this resolution, was to send back the harp to the music-shop. Since no further hope remained of recovering her scholars, she would not pay her court to Miss Arbe at the expence of Miss Bydel. She next dispatched her small accounts to Lady Kendover, Lady Arramede, Miss Sycamore, Miss Brinville, the Miss Crawleys, and Miss Tedman; but, notwithstanding her poverty, she desired to be allowed to have instructed Selina simply from motives of gratitude.

To give up her large apartment, was her next determination; and she desired to speak with Miss Matson, to whom she made known her intention; soliciting, at the same time, some employment in needle-work.

This was a measure not more essential than disagreeable. "Mercy, Ma'am!" Miss Matson cried, seating herself upon the sofa: "I hope, at least, you won't leave my first floor before you pay me for it? And as to work,—what is the premium* you mean to propose to me?"

Ellis answered that she could propose none: she desired only to receive and to return her work from day to day.

Looking at her, now, with an air extremely contemptuous, Miss Matson replied, that that was by no means her way; that all her young ladies came to her with handsome premiums; and that she had already eight or nine upon her list, more than she was able to admit into her shop.

Ellis, affrighted at the prospect before her, earnestly enquired whether Miss Matson would have the kindness to aid her in an application elsewhere, for some plain work.*

"That, Ma'am, is one of the things the most difficult in the world to obtain. Such loads of young women are out of employ, that one's quite teized* for recommendations. Besides which, your being known to have run up so many debts in the town,—you'll excuse me, Ma'am,—makes it not above half reputable to venture staking one's credit—after all those droll things that Mr. Riley, you know, Ma'am, said to Miss Bydel.—"

Ellis could bear no more: she promised to hasten her payment; and begged to be left alone.

CHAPTER XXX

ELLIS had but just cast herself, in deep disturbance, upon a chair, when her door was opened, without tapping, or any previous ceremony, by Mr. Giles Arbe; who smilingly enquired after her health, with the familiar kindness of an intimate old friend; but, receiving no immediate answer, gave her a nod, that said, don't mind me; and, sitting down by her side, began talking to himself.

Roused by this interruption, she begged to know his commands.

He finished his speech to himself, before he took any notice of her's, and then, very good humouredly, asked what she wanted.

"May I hope," she cried, "that you have the goodness to bring me some answer to my note?"

"What note, my pretty lady?"

"That which you were so obliging as to undertake delivering for me to Miss Arbe?"

He stared and looked amazed, repeating, "Note?—what note?" but when, at last, she succeeded in making him recollect the circumstance, his countenance fell, and leaning against the back of his chair, while his stick, and a parcel which he held under his arm, dropt to the ground: "I am frighted to death," he cried, "for fear it's that I tore last night, to light my little lamp!"

Then, emptying every thing out of his pockets; "I can soon tell, however," he continued, "because I put t'other half back, very carefully; determining to examine what it was in the morning; for I was surprised to find a folded note in my pocket: but I thought of it no more, afterwards, from that time to this."

Collecting, then, the fragments; "Here," he continued, "is what is left.—"

Ellis immediately recognized her hand-writing.

"I protest," cried he, in great confusion, "I have never above twice or thrice, perhaps, in my life, been more ashamed! And once was when I was so unfortunate as to burn a gentleman's stick; a mighty curious sort of cane, that I was unluckily holding in my hand, just as the fire wanted stirring; and not much thinking, at that moment, by great ill luck, of what I was about, I poked it into the middle of the grate; and not a soul happened to take notice of it, any more than myself, till it made a prodigious crackling; and all that was not consumed split into splinters. I never was so out of countenance in my life. I could not make a single apology. So they all thought I did not mind it! Don't you think so, too, now? For I am very sorry I tore your note, I assure you!"

Ellis readily accepted his excuse.

"Well, and another time," he continued, "I had a still worse accident. I was running after an ill-natured gnat, that had stung a lady, with my hand uplifted to knock him down, and, very unluckily, after he had led me a dance all over the room, he darted upon the lady's cheek; and, in my hurry to crush him, I gave her such a smart slap of the face, that it made her quite angry. I was never so shocked since I was born. I ran away as fast as I could; for I had not a word to say for myself."

He then began relating a third instance; but Ellis interrupted him; and again desired to know his business.

"Good! true!" cried he, "you do well to put me in mind, for talking of one thing makes a man sometimes forget another. It's what has happened to me before now. One i'n't always upon one's guard. I remember, once, my poor cousin was disappointed of a chaperon, to go with her to a ball, after being dressed out in all the best things that she had in the world, and looking better than ever she did before in her life, as she told me herself;

and she asked me to run to a particular friend, to beg that she would accompany her, instead of the one that had failed her; so I set off, as fast as possible, for I saw that she was in a prodigious fidget; not much caring, I suppose, to be dizened out, and to put on her best looks, to be seen by nobody but her papa and me; which is natural enough, for her papa always thinks her pretty; and as to me, I don't doubt but she may be so neither; though I never happened to take much notice of it."

"Well, Sir, to our business?" cried Ellis.

"Well, when I arrived at this friend of my cousin's, I met there a friend of my own, and one that I had not seen for fifteen years. I had so prodigious much to say to him, that it put all my poor cousin's fine clothes and best looks out of my head! and, I am quite ashamed to own it, but we never once ceased our confabulation, my old friend and I, till, to my great surprise, supper was brought upon the table! I was in extreme confusion, indeed, for, just then, somebody asked me how my cousin did; which made me recollect my commission. I told it, in all haste, to the lady, and begged, so urgently, that she would oblige my cousin, who would never forgive me for not delivering my message sooner, if I carried a refusal, that, at last, I persuaded her to comply; but I was so abashed by my forgetfulness, that I never thought of mentioning the ball. So that when she arrived, all in her common gear,* my poor cousin, who supposed that she had only waited, for her hair-dressers and shoe-makers, looked at her with as much amazement as if she had never seen her before in her life. And the lady was prodigiously piqued not to be received better; so that they were upon the very point of a quarrel, when they discovered that all the fault was mine! But by the time that they came to that part, I was so out of countenance, you would have judged that I had done it all on purpose! I was frightened out of my wits: and I made off as fast as possible; and when I got to my own room, there was not a chair nor a table that I did not put against the door, for fear of their bursting the lock; they were both of them in such prodigious passions, to know why I had served them so. And yet, the whole time, I was as innocent of it as you are; for I never once thought about either of them! never in my life!"

Again Ellis enquired what were his commands, frankly

avowing, that she was too much engrossed by the melancholy state of her own affairs, to attend to any other.

"What, then, I'm afraid those poor people a'n't paid yet?"

"A poorer person, Sir, as I believe, and hope," answered she, sighing, "than any amongst them, is unpaid also! They would not, else, have this claim upon your compassion."

"What, have you got any bad debts yourself?"

"Enquire, Sir, of Miss Arbe; and if you extend your benevolence to representing what is due to my creditors, it may urge her to consider what is due to me."

"Does any body owe you any money, then?"

"Yes, Sir; and as much as will acquit all I myself owe to others."

"What is the reason, then, that they don't pay you?"

"The want of knowing, Sir, the value of a little to the self-supported and distressed! The want, in short, of consideration."

"Bad! bad!—that i'n't right!" cried he: "I'll put an end to it, however;" rising hastily: "I'll make my cousin go to every one of them. They must be taught what they should do. They mean very well; but that's of no use if they don't act well too. And if my cousin don't go to them, I'll go myself."

He then quitted the house, in the greatest haste; leaving behind him his parcel and his stick, which were not perceived till his departure.

Ellis knew not whether to lament or to rejoice at this promised interference; but, wholly overset by these new and unexpected obstacles to providing for her immediate subsistence, she had no resource but to await with patience the effect of his efforts.

The following day, while anxiously expecting him, she was surprised by another visit from Miss Arbe; who, with an air as sprightly as her own was dejected, cried, "Well, I hope this new plan will make an end of all our difficulties. You have had time enough, now, to consider of it; for I have such a little minute always to stay, that I can never pretend to discuss an hundred *pros* and *cons*. Though, indeed, I flatter myself, 'tis impossible your scruples should still hold out. But where in the world have you hid your harp? I have been peeping about for it ever since I came in. And my music? Have you looked it over? Is it not delightful? I long to play it with you. I tried it twenty times by myself, but I could not manage it. But every thing's so much easier when one tries it together, that I dare say we shall conquer all those horrid hard passages at once. But where's your harp?—Tell me, however, first, what you decide about our plan; for when once we begin playing, there's no thinking of any thing else."

"If it be the concert you mean, Madam, I can only repeat my thanks; and that I can never, except to those ladies who are, or who would venture to become my pupils, consent to be a performer."

"What a thousand pities, my dear Miss Ellis, to throw away your charming talents, through that terrible diffidence! However, I can't give you up so easily. I must positively bring you round;—only if we stop now, we shan't have a moment for those horrid hard passages. So where's my music? And where have you conjured your harp?"

The music, she answered, she had neither seen nor heard of; the harp, useless since no longer necessary, she had sent home.

The smiles and sprightly airs of Miss Arbe now instantly vanished, and were succeeded by undisguised displeasure. To send back, without consulting her, an instrument that could never have been obtained but through her recommendation, she called an action the most extraordinary: she was too much hurried, however, to enter into any discussions; and must drive home immediately, to enquire what that eternal blunderer, her cousin Giles, had done, not only with her note, but with her music; which was of so much consequence, that his whole life could not make her amends, if it had met with any accident.

Ellis had been so far from purporting to cast herself into any dependence upon Miss Arbe, that, upon this unjust resentment, she suffered her to run down stairs, without offering any apology. Conceiving, however, that the parcel, left by Mr. Giles, might possibly contain the music in question, she followed her with it into the shop; where she had the mortification of hearing her say, "Miss Matson, as to your debts, you must judge for yourself. I can't pretend to be responsible for the credit of every body that solicits my patronage."

With the silent displeasure of contempt, Ellis put the parcel into her hands, and retreated.

"Why how's this? here is my note unopened," cried Miss Arbe.

Ellis, returning, said that she had not seen any note.

Miss Arbe declared that she had placed it, herself, within the pack-thread that was tied round the music; but it appeared that Mr. Giles had squeezed it under the brown paper cover, whence it had not been visible.

"And I wrote it," cried Miss Arbe, "purposely that you might be ready with your answer; and to beg that you would not fail to study the passages I marked with a pencil, that we might know how to finger them when we met. However, I shall certainly never trust that monstrous tiresome creature with another commission."

She then, accompanied by Miss Bydel, who now entered the shop, and invited herself to be of the party, followed Ellis up stairs, to read the note, and talk the subject over.

From this note, Ellis discovered that the plan was entirely altered: the professor was wholly omitted, and she was placed herself at the head of a new enterprize. It was to be conducted under the immediate and avowed patronage of Miss Arbe, upon a scheme of that lady's own suggestion and arrangement, which had long been projecting.

A subscription was to be raised amongst all the ladies of any fashion, or consequence, in or near Brighthelmstone, who, whether as mothers, aunts, guardians, or friends, had the care of any young ladies possessing musical talents. Lady Kendover had consented that her name should be placed at the head of the list, as soon as any other lady, of sufficient distinction to be named immediately after her ladyship, should come forward. The concert was to be held, alternately, at the houses of the principal subscribers, whose apartments, and inclinations, should best be suited to the purpose. The young ladies were to perform, by rotation or selection, according as the lady directress of the night, aided by Miss Arbe's counsel, should settle. A small band was to be engaged, that the concert might be opened with the dignity of an overture; that the concertos might be accompanied; and that the whole might conclude with the *eclat** of a full piece. Ellis, for whose advancement, and in whose name, the money was to be raised, that was to pay herself, the other artists, and all the concomitant expences, was to play upon the harp, and to sing an air, in the course of every act.

This plan was far less painful to her feelings than that which had preceded it, since the concert was to be held in private houses, and young ladies of fashion were themselves to be performers; but, though her thanks were grateful and sincere, her determination was immoveable. "It is not," she said, "believe me, Madam, from false notions of pride, that, because I, alone, am to be paid, I decline so honourable a method of extricating myself from my present difficulties: my pride, on the contrary, urges me to every exertion that may lead to self-dependence: but who is permitted to act by the sole guidance of their own perceptions and notions? who is so free,—I might better, perhaps, say so desolate,—as to consider themselves clear of all responsibility to the opinions of others?"

"Of others? Why do you belong, then, really, to any body, Mrs. Ellis?" cried Miss Bydel.

"They must be pretty extraordinary people," said Miss Arbe, contemptuously dropping her eyes, "if they can disapprove a scheme that will shew your talents to so much advantage; besides bringing you into the notice of so many people of distinction." Then, rising, she would forbear, she said, to trouble her any more; inform Lady Kendover of her refusal; and let Lady Aurora know that her farther interference would be unacceptable.

At the name of Lady Aurora, Ellis entreated some explanation; but Miss Arbe, without deigning to make any, hurried to her carriage.

Miss Bydel, pouring forth a volley of interrogatories upon the intentions of Ellis, her expectations, and her means, would have remained; but she reaped so little satisfaction that, tired, at length, herself, she retreated; though not till she had fully caught the attention of Ellis, by the following words: "I have been very ready, Mrs. Ellis, to serve you in your distress; but I hope you won't forget that I always intended to be disbursed by your music teaching: so, if you don't do that any more, I can't see why you won't do this; that you may pay me."

She then took leave.

Ellis was far more grieved than offended by this reprimand, which, however gross, did not seem unjust. To judge me, she cried, by my present appearance, my resisting this offer must be attributed to impertinence, ingratitude, or folly. And how can I expect to be judged but by what is seen, what is known? Who is willing to be so generous, who is capable to be so noble, as to believe, or even to conceive, that lonely distress, like mine, may call for respect and forbearance, as well as for pity and assistance?—Oh Lady Aurora!—sole charm, sole softener of my sufferings!—Oh liberal, high-minded Harleigh!—why are there so few to resemble you? And why must your virtues and your kindness, for me, be null? Why am I doomed to seek—so hardly*—the support that flies me,—yet to fly the consolation that offers?

CHAPTER XXXI

THE sole hope of Ellis for extrication from these difficulties hung now upon Mr. Giles Arbe; whom she had begun to apprehend had forgotten his promise, when, to her great relief, he appeared.

Nothing could be less exhilarating than his air and manner. He looked vexed and disconcerted; sat down without answering the civilities of her reception; sucked, for some minutes, the head of his stick; and then began talking to himself; from time to time ejaculating little broken phrases aloud, such as: "It i'n't right!—It can't be right!—I wish they would not do such things.—Fair young creatures, too, some of them.—Fie! fie!—They've no thought;—that's it!—they've no thought.—Mighty good hearts,—and very pretty faces, too, some of 'em;—but sad little empty heads,—except for their own pleasures;—no want of flappers†* there!—Fie! fie!"

†Swift's Laputa.

Then letting fall two guineas and a half upon the table, "There, my dear," he cried, in a tone of chagrin, "there's all I have been able to gather amongst all your scholars put together! What they do with their money I don't know; but they are all very poor, they tell me: except Lady Arramede; and she's so rich, that she can't possibly attend, she says, to such pitiful claims: though I said to her, If the sum, Ma'am, is too small for your ladyship's notice, the best way to shew your magnificence, is to make it greater; which will also be very acceptable to this young person. But she did not mind me. She only said that you might apply to her steward at Christmas, which was the time, she believed, when he settled her affairs; but as to herself, she never meddled with such insignificant matters."

"Christmas?" repeated Ellis; "and 'tis now but the beginning of April!"

"I went next to the Miss Crawleys; but they only fell a laughing. All I could say, and all I could do, and all I could represent, only set 'em a laughing. I never knew what at. Nor they, neither. But they did not laugh the less for that. One of them stretched her mouth so wide, that I was afraid she would have cut her cheeks through to her ears: and t'other frightened me still more, for she giggled herself so black in the face, that I thought she must have expired in a fit. And not one among us knew what it was all for! But the more I stared at them, the louder they laughed. They never stopt till they were so weak that they could not stand; and then they held their sides, and were quiet enough; till I happened to ask them, if they had done? and that set them off again. They are merry little souls; not very heavy, I believe, in the head: I don't suppose they have a thought above once in a twelvemonth."

He had then applied to their brother. Sir Marmaduke professed himself extremely shocked, at the circumstances which had prevented his sisters from profiting longer by the instructions of so fine a virtuosa* as The Ellis; but he hoped that something might yet be adjusted for the future, as he was utterly ashamed to offer such a trifle as this account, to so accomplished a young person as The Ellis. "I told him, then," continued Mr. Giles, "that it was no trifle to you, for you were so very poor that you could not pay for your clothes; but I could never obtain any other answer from him, than that he had too much consideration for you, to think of offering you a sum so unworthy your merit."

"This, indeed, is rather singular," cried Ellis, half smiling, "that the smallness of my demands should make one person decline paying me from contempt, and another, from respect!"

Next, he related, he went to Miss Brinville, who, with great displeasure, denied, at first, having ever been a scholar of Miss Ellis. The young woman had been with her, indeed, she said, to chuse her a harp, or tune it, or something of that sort; but she had found her so entirely unequal to giving any lessons; and the professor, her present master, had so completely convinced her of the poor young woman's ignorance, that it was quite ridiculous to suppose having seen any body, once or twice, for an odd hour or two, was sufficient for being considered as their scholar. "Upon this," continued Mr. Giles, "I told her that if she were not amongst your pupils, she must be amongst your friends; and, in that case, I doubted not, from your great good nature, you would dispense with her payment."

"Well, Sir?" cried Ellis laughing, "and what said my friend?"

"Good me! all was changed in a minute! she had never, she said, had such a thought as receiving you but as her music-mistress. So then, again, I demanded the money; for if she is not your friend, said I, you can't expect her to teach you for nothing. But she told me she was just quitting Brighthelmstone, and could not pay you till she got to London. I really can't find out what makes them all so poor; but they are prodigiously out of cash. Those operas and gauzes,* I believe, ruin them. They dress themselves so prettily, and go to hear those tunes so often, that they have not a shilling left for other expences. It i'n't right! It can't be right! And so I told her. I gave her some advice. 'There's a great concert to-night, Miss Brinville,' said I; 'if you take my counsel, you won't go to it; nor to ever another for a week or two to come: and then you can pay this young lady what you owe her, without putting yourself to any difficulty.' But she made me no reply. She only eyed me askance, as if she would have liked prodigiously to order me out of the room. I thought I never saw her nose look so thick! I never took so much notice of it before: but it spoils her beauty sadly. After this, I went to Miss Sycamore, and I surprized her playing upon her harp. 'This is lucky enough,' said I, 'Miss Sycamore! I find you in the act of reaping advantage from the very person who wants to reap advantage from you.' So then I demanded your money. But she told me that she had none to spare, and that she could not pay you yet. 'Why then,' said I, 'Miss Sycamore, you must give her back her instructions!' I thought this would have piqued her; but she won't easily be put out of her way. So she threw her arms round her harp, with the prettiest languishment you can imagine, making herself look just like a picture; and then she played me a whole set of airs and graces; quite ravishing, I protest. And when she had done, 'There!' she cried, 'there, Mr. Arbe, those were her instructions: carry them back!'—I declare I don't know how I could be angry with her, she did it with such an elegant toss!* But it was not right; it could not be right; so I was angry enough, after the first moment, 'Pray, Miss Sycamore,' said I, 'what have you done for this young lady, to expect that she should do all this for you? Have you got her any place?—Have you procured her any emolument?—Have you given her any pleasure?—Have you done her any honour?'—She had not a word to answer: so she twirled her fingers upon her harp, and sung and played till I was almost ravished again. But I would not give way; so I said, 'Miss Sycamore, if she owes you neither place, nor profit; neither pleasure, nor honour, I should be glad to know upon what pretence you lay claim to her Time, her Trouble, her Talents, and her Patience?' "

"O could such a question," cried Ellis, "be put more at large for all the harassed industrious, to all the unfeeling indolent!—what reflections might it not excite! what injustice might it not obviate!"

"Why I'll say it any where, my dear, if you think it will do any good. I always give my opinion; for I never see what a man has one for, if he must not utter it. However, I could make nothing of Miss Sycamore. Those young ladies who play and sing in public, at those private rooms, of four or five hundred people, have their poor little heads so taken up, between the compliments of the company when they are in the world, and their own when they are by themselves, that there i'n't a moment left them for a little thought."

His next visit was to Lady Kendover; by whom he was received, he said, with such politeness, and by whom Ellis was mentioned with so much consideration, that he thought he should quite oblige her ladyship, by giving her an opportunity to serve a young person of whom she spoke with so much civility. "Upon which," continued he, "I told her about your debts, and how much you would thank her to be as quick as possible in helping you to pay them. But then she put on quite a new face. She was surprised, she said, that you should begin your new career by running into debt; and much more at my supposing that she should sanctify such imprudence, by her name and encouragement. Still, however, she talked about her concern, and her admiration, in such elegant sentences, that, thinking she was coming round, 'Madam,' said I, 'as your ladyship honours this young lady with so generous a regard, I hold it but my duty to tell you how you may shew it the most to her benefit. Send for all her creditors, and let them know your ladyship's good opinion of her; and then, I don't doubt, they'll wait her own convenience for being paid.' Well! all at once her face turned of a deep brick red, as if I had offered her an affront in only naming such a thing! So then I grew very angry indeed; for, as she is neither young nor pretty, there is no one thing to excuse her. If she had been young, one might have hoped she would mend; and if she were pretty, one might suppose she was only thinking of her looking-glass. But her ladyship is plain enough, as well as old; so I felt no scruple to reprimand her. But I gained no ground; for just as I was beginning to cry down the uselessness of that complimentary language, if it meant nothing; she said that she was very sorry to have the honour to leave me, but that she must go and dress for dinner. But then, just as I was coming away, and upon the point of being in a passion, I was stopt by little Lady Barbara; that sweet fine child; who asked me a hundred kind questions about you, without paying any regard to the winking or blinking of her aunt Kendover. She is a mighty agreeable little soul. I have taken a great kindness to her. She let out all their secrets to me; and I should like nothing better than to tell them all to you; only Lady

Kendover charged me to hold my tongue. The ladies are very fond of giving that recommendation to us men! I don't know (smiling) whether they are as fond of giving the example! In particular, she enjoined me not to mention Lady Aurora's being your banker."

"Lady Aurora?"

"Yes, because my cousin would be quite affronted; for she arranges things, Lady Kendover says, so extremely well, that she deserves to have her own way. She likes to have it too, I believe, very well."

"Lady Aurora my banker?"

"Yes; they wrote to Lady Aurora about it, and she sent them word that, if the scheme were agreeable to you, she begged to be considered as responsible for any expences that you might incur in it's preparation."

"Lady Aurora, then, approves the plan?" cried Ellis in much disturbance.

"Yes, mightily, I believe; though I am not quite sure, for she desired you might not be pressed, nor hurried; for 'if,' says she, in a letter to Lady Barbara, 'it is not her own desire, don't let any body be so cruel as to urge her. We know not her history, and cannot judge her objections; but she is so gently mannered, so sweetly well bred, so inexpressibly amiable, that it is impossible she should not do every thing that is right.' "

"Sweet-trusting-generous Lady Aurora!" cried Ellis, while tears gushed fast into her eyes, with strong, but delighted emotion: "Mr. Giles, I see, now, what path I may pursue; and you, who are so benevolent, will aid me on my way."

She then entreated him, through the medium of Lady Barbara, to supplicate that the beneficence of Lady Aurora might be exerted in the payment of the debts already contracted; not in obviating new ones, which she felt no disposition to incur.

"I'll undertake that with all my heart, my dear; and you'll be sure to have the money for what you like best, because it's a man who is to be your paymaster."

"A man?"

"Yes; for Lady Aurora says, that though she shall pay the whole herself ultimately, the draft upon the banker, for the present, must be in the name of her brother."

Ellis changed colour, and, with far deeper emotion, now walked about her room, now seated herself, now hid her face with her hands, and now ejaculated, "How—how shall I decide!"

She then enquired from whom Mr. Giles had received the two guineas and the half guinea which he had put upon the table.

From Mr. Tedman.

Mr. Tedman, she said, was the only person of the whole set who owed her nothing; but to whom, on the contrary, she was herself indebted; not having yet had an opportunity to clear what he had advanced.

"So he told me," cried Mr. Giles; "for I don't believe he forgets things of that sort. But he said he had such a regard for you, that he would stand to trusting you with as much again, *put in case** you would give him your receipt for paying it off in lessons to his daughter. And for this much, in the mean while, as you were not by, he consented to take mine."

"You are very kind, Sir," said Ellis; "and Mr. Tedman himself, notwithstanding his deficiency in education and language, is, I believe, really good: nevertheless, I am too uncertain of my power to continue my musical project, to risk a new bankruptcy of this nature." She then begged him to take back the money; with a promise that she would speedily settle what yet remained undischarged of the former account.

He blamed her warmly. "Mr. Tedman," he said, "is rich and good natured, you are poor and helpless: he ought to give; it's only being just: you ought to accept, or you are only very foolish."

"Do not be hasty to blame me, my good Mr. Giles. There are certain points in which every one must judge for himself. With regard to me, I must resist all pecuniary obligations."

"Except to poor trades-people!" cried he, nodding a little reproachfully; "and those you will let work and toil for you gratis!"

Ellis, shocked, and struck to the quick, looked deeply distressed. "Perhaps," she said, "I may be wrong! Justice, certainly, should take place of whatever is personal, however dear or near its interest!—"

She paused, ruminated, irresolute, and dissatisfied; and then said, "Were I to consult only myself, my own feelings, whatever they may be, should surely and even instantly, give way, to what is due to others; but I must not imagine that I shall be doomed for ever to this deplorable condition; and those to whom I may yet belong, may blame—may resent any measures that may give publicity to my situation. Will not this objection have some weight, Sir, to lessen your censure of my seeming insensibility, to claims of which I acknowledge the right?"

"What, then, you think, I suppose, that when your friends come to you, they'll be quite pleased to find you have accepted goods and favours from your shoe-maker, and your hosier, and your linen-draper? though they would be too proud to let you receive money from the rich and idle? Better sing those songs, my dear! much better sing those songs! Then you'll have money for yourself and every body."

Ellis now breathed hard. "Alas!" she cried, "justice, reason, common sense, all seem against me! If, therefore, Lady Aurora approve this scheme,—my fears and my feelings must yield to such a tide!"

Again, painfully, she paused; and then, sighing bitterly, added, "Tell Miss Arbe, Sir,—acquaint Lady Kendover,—let Lady Aurora be informed,—that I submit to their opinions, and accept, upon their own terms, their benevolent assistance."

He held out his hand to her, now, with exulting approbation; but she seemed overwhelmed with grief, apprehension, and regret.

He looked at her with surprise. "Why now, my dear," he said, tenderly, "what's the matter with you? Now that you are going to do all that is right, you must be happy."

"What is right, alas!—for me, at least," she cried, "I know not!—I should not else be thus perplexed.— But I act in the dark!—The measure in which I acquiesce, I may for ever repent,—yet I know not how, else, to extricate myself from difficulties the most alarming, and remonstrances—if not menaces—the most shocking!"

Heavily she sighed; yet, definitively, she agreed, that, since, unhappily, the debts were incurred, and her want of credit made immediate payment necessary, she could not, herself, in combining the whole of her intricate situation, find any plan more eligible than that of performing at this subscription-concert.

CHAPTER XXXII

THIS resolution once made known, not an instant was allowed to retract, or even to deliberate: to let it reach Miss Arbe was to put it into execution. That lady appeared now in her chosen element. She suggested all that was to be attempted; she directed all that was to be done. A committee of ladies was formed, nominally for consultation, but, in fact, only for applause; since whoever ventured to start the smallest objection to an idea of Miss Arbe's, was overpowered with conceited insinuations of the incompetency of her judgment for deciding upon such matters; or, if any one, yet bolder, presumed to hint at some new arrangement, Miss Arbe looked either sick or angry, and declared that she could not possibly continue to offer her poor advice, if it were eternally to be contested. This annihilated rather than subdued interference; for the whole party was of opinion, that nothing less than utter ruin to the project could ensue from her defection.

This helpless submission to ignorant dominion, so common in all committees where the leaders have no deeper science than the led, impeded not the progress of the preparations. Concentrated, or arbitrary government may be least just, but it is most effective. Unlimited in her powers, uncontrouled in their exertion, Miss Arbe saved as much time by the rapidity, as contention by the despotism of her proceedings.

All seemed executed as soon as planned. The rooms were fitted up; the music was selected for the performance; the uniform for the lady-artists* was fixed upon; all succeeded, all flourished,—save, only, the subscription for the concert!

But this, the essential point, neither her authority nor her influence was sufficiently potent to accelerate. Nothing is so quick as the general circulation of money, yet nothing requires more address than turning it into new channels. Curiosity was amply awakened for one evening's entertainment; but the subscription, which amounted to ten guineas, was for three nights in the week. The scheme had no interest adequate to the expence either of time or of money thus demanded; except for matrons who had young ladies, or young ladies who had talents to display. And even these, in the uncertainty of individual success, were more anxious to see the sum raised from others, than alert to advance it themselves.

This slackness of generosity, and dearth of spirit, however offensive to the pride, rather animated than dampt the courage of Miss Arbe. She saw, she said, that the enterprize was arduous; but it's difficulties, and not the design, should be vanquished. Her preparations, therefore, were continued with unabated confidence, and, within a week, all the performers were summoned to a rehearsal.

Ellis was called upon with the rest; for in the name of Miss Ellis, and for the sake and benefit of Miss Ellis, all the orders were given, all the measures were taken, and all the money was to be raised: yet in no one point had Ellis been consulted; and she would hardly have known that a scheme which owed to her it's name, character, and even existence, was in agitation, but from the diligence with which Miss Arbe ordered the restoration of the harp; and from the leisure which that lady now found, in the midst of her hurries, for resuming her lessons.

Ellis, from the time that she had agreed to this scheme, devoted herself completely to musical studies; and the melodious sounds drawn forth from her harp, in playing the exquisite compositions of the great masters, with whose works her taste, industry, and talents had enriched her memory, softened her sorrows, and soothed her solitude. Her vocal powers, also, she cultivated with equal assiduity; and she arrived at the house of Miss Sycamore, where the first rehearsal was to be held, calmly prepared to combat every internal obstacle to exertion, and to strive, with her best ability, to obtain the consideration which she desired, from the satisfaction, rather than solely from the indulgence of her auditors.

But the serenity given, at least assumed, by this resolution, was suddenly shaken through a communication made to her by

Mr. Giles Arbe, who was watching for her upon the stair-case, that fifty pounds had been deposited, for her use, with his cousin, Miss Arbe, by Lady Aurora Granville.

Intelligence so important, and so touching, filled her with emotion. Why had not Miss Arbe transmitted to her a donation so seasonable, and so much in unison with her wishes? Instantly, and without scruple, she resolved to accept it; to adopt some private plan of maintenance, and to relinquish the concert-enterprise altogether.

This idea was enforced by all her feelings. Her original dislike to the scheme augmented into terrour, upon her entrance into the apartment destined for its opening execution, when she perceived her own harp placed in the most conspicuous part of the upper end of the room, which was arranged for an orchestra: while the numerous forms with which the floor was nearly covered, shewed her by how many auditors she was destined to be judged, and by how many spectators to be examined. Struck and affrighted, her new hope of deliverance was doubly welcomed, and she looked eagerly round for Miss Arbe, to realize it without delay.

Miss Arbe, however, was so encircled, that there seemed little chance of obtaining her attention. The situation of Ellis was awkward and painful; for while the offences by which she had so lately been wounded, made her most want encouragement, the suspicions which she had excited seemed to distance all her acquaintance. No mistress of the house deigned to receive, or notice her; and though, as a thing of course, she would herself have approached any other than Miss Sycamore, there was a lively, yet hardy insolence in that young lady, which she had not courage to encounter.

The company, at large, was divided into groups, to the matron part of which Miss Arbe was dictatorially haranguing, with very apparent self-applause. The younger sets were engaged in busy whispering trios or quartettos, in corners, or at the several windows.

Embarrassed, irresolute, Ellis stopt nearly upon her entrance, vainly seeking some kind eye to invite her on; but how advance, where no one addressed, or seemed to know her? Ah! ye proud, ye rich, ye high! thought she, why will you make your power, your wealth, your state, thus repulsive to all who cannot share them? How small a portion of attention, of time, of condescension, would make your honours, your luxuries, your enjoyments, the consolation, not the oppression, of your inferiours, or dependants?

While thus, sorrowingly, if not indignantly, looking round, and seeing herself unnoticed, if not avoided, even by those whose favour, whose kindness, whose rising friendship, had most eminently distinguished her, since the commencement of her professional career, she recollected the stories of her disguises, and of her surreptitious name, which were spread abroad: her justice, then, felt appeased; and she ceased to resent, though she could not to grieve, at the mortification which she experienced.

Catching, nevertheless, the eye of Selina, she ventured to courtesy and smile; but neither courtesy nor smile was returned: Selina looked away, and looked confused; but rapidly continued her prattling, though without seeming to know herself what she was uttering, to Miss Arramede.

Ellis, disconcerted, then proceeded, with no other interruption than an "Ah ha! are you there, The Ellis?" from Miss Crawley; and an "Oh ho! how do do, The Ellis?" from Miss Di.

At the sound, however, of her name, Lady Barbara Frankland, starting from a little group, of which she had been the orator, exclaimed, "Ellis?—Is Miss Ellis come?" And, skipping to the place where Ellis was seated, expressed the most lively pleasure at her sight, mixt with much affectionate regret at their long separation.

This was a kindness the most reviving to Ellis, who was now approached, also, by Lady Kendover; and, while respectfully courtesying to a cold salutation from that lady, one of her hands was suddenly seized, and warmly pressed by Selina.

Excited by the example of Lady Kendover, various ladies, who, from meeting Ellis at the houses of her several scholars, had been struck with her merit, and had conceived a regard for her person, flocked towards her, as if she had now first entered the room. Yet the notice of Lady Kendover was merely a civil vehicle, to draw from her attractions the young and partial Lady Barbara.

Miss Arbe no sooner saw her thus surrounded, than, alertly advancing, and assuming the character and state of a patroness, she complacently bowed around her, saying, "How kind you all are to my *Protegée*!"

Miss Sycamore ended this scene, by calling upon one of the young ladies to open the rehearsal.

She called, however, in vain; every one declared herself too much frightened to take the lead; and those whose eager eyes rolled incessantly round the room, in search of admirers; and whose little laughs, animated gestures, and smiling refusals, invited solicitation, were the most eloquent in talking of their timidity, and delaying their exhibition; each being of opinion that the nearer she could place her performance to the conclusion, the nearer she should approach to the post of honour.

To finish these difficulties, Miss Arbe desired Ellis to sing and play.

Ellis, whose hopes were all alive, that she might spare herself this hazardous experiment, demanded a previous conference; but Miss Arbe was deaf and blind to whatever interfered with the vivacity of her proceedings; and Ellis, not daring, without more certain authority than that of Mr. Giles Arbe, to proclaim her intended change of measures, was forced to give way; though with an unwillingness so palpable, that she inspired general pity.

Mr. Scope himself would have handed her to the orchestra, but that he apprehended such a step might be deemed an action of gallantry, and as such affect the public opinion of his morals; and Mr. Giles Arbe would have been enchanted to have shewn her his high regard, but that the possibility of so doing, occurred to him only when the opportunity was past. Sir Marmaduke Crawley, however, studiously devoted to the arts, set apart, alike, the rumours which, at one time, raised Ellis to a level with the rest of the company, and, at another, sunk her beneath their domestics; and, simply considering her claim to good breeding and attention, as an elegant artist, courteously offered her his hand.

Somewhat comforted by this little mark of respect, Ellis

accepted it with so much grace, and crossed the apartment with an air so distinguished, that the urbanity of Sir Marmaduke soon raised an almost general envy of his office.

Every one now was attentive: singing charms universally: no art, no accomplishment has such resistless attraction: it catches alike all conditions, all ages, and all dispositions: it subdues even those whose souls are least susceptible either to intellectual or mental harmony.

Foremost in the throng of listeners came Lady Barbara Frankland, attended by Selina; unopposed either by Lady Kendover or Mrs. Maple; those ladies not being less desirous that their nieces should reap every advantage from Ellis, than that Ellis should reap none in return.

But Ellis was seized with a faint panic that disordered her whole frame; terrour took from her fingers their elasticity, and robbed her mind and fancy of those powers, which, when free from alarm, gave grace and meaning to her performance: and, what to herself she had played with a taste and an expression, that the first masters would most have admired, because best have understood, had now neither mark, spirit, nor correctness: while her voice was almost too low to be heard, and quite too feeble and tremulous to give pleasure.

The assembly at large was now divided between sneerers and pitiers. The first insinuated, that Ellis thought it fine and lady-like to affect being frightened; the second saw, and compassionated, in her failure, the natural effect of distressed modesty, mingled with wounded pride.

Nevertheless, her fervent, but indiscriminating juvenile admirer, Lady Barbara, echoed by Selina, enthusiastically exclaimed, "How delightfully she plays and sings! How adorably!"

Miss Arbe, well aware that fear alone had thus "unstrung the lyre"* of Ellis, secretly exulted, that the *Dilettanti* would possess her name and services for their institution, without her superiority. The Miss Crawleys were laughing so immoderately, at Mr. Giles Arbe's requesting them to be quiet, that they did not find out that the rehearsal was begun: and the rest of the ladies had seized the moment of performance, for communicating to one another innumerable little secrets, which never so aptly occur as upon such occasions; Miss

Sycamore excepted, who, with a cold and cutting sneer, uttered a malicious "bravissima!"*

Inexpressibly hurt and chagrined, Ellis precipitately quitted the orchestra; and, addressing Miss Arbe, said, "Alas, Madam, I am unequal to this business! I must relinquish it altogether! and,—if I have not been misinformed, Lady Aurora Granville—"

Miss Arbe, reddening, and looking much displeased, repeated, "Lady Aurora?—who has been talking to you about Lady Aurora?"

Ellis would have declined giving her authority; but Miss Arbe, without scruple, named Mr. Giles. "That tiresome old creature," she cried, "is always doing some mischief. He's my cousin, to be sure; and he's a very good sort of man, and all that; but I don't believe it's possible for an old soul to be more troublesome. As to this little sum of Lord Melbury's—"

"Lord Melbury's?" repeated Ellis, much agitated, "If it be Lord Melbury's, I have, indeed, no claim to make! But I had hoped Lady Aurora—"

"Well, well, Lady Aurora, if you will. It's Lady Aurora, to be sure, who sends it for you; but still—"

"She has, indeed, then, sent it for me?" cried Ellis, rapturously; "sweet, amiable Lady Aurora!—Oh! when will the hour come—"

She checked her speech; but could not check the brilliant colour, the brightened countenance, which indicated the gay ideas that internally consoled her recent mortification.

"And why, Madam," she soon more composedly, yet with spirit, added, "might I not be indulged with the knowledge of her ladyship's goodness to me? Why is Mr. Giles Arbe to be blamed for so natural a communication? Had it, happily, reached me sooner, it might have spared me the distress and disgrace of this morning?"

She then earnestly requested to receive what was so kindly meant for her succour, upon milder terms than such as did violence to her disposition, and were utterly unfitting to her melancholy situation.

Somewhat embarrassed, and extremely piqued, Miss Arbe made no reply but a fretful "Pish!"

"Lady Aurora," continued Ellis, "is so eminently good, so feelingly delicate, that if any one would have the charity to name my petition to her ladyship, she would surely consent to let me change the destination of what she so generously assigns to me."

Her eyes here glanced anxiously towards Lady Barbara; who, unable to resist their appeal, sprang from Lady Kendover, into the little circle that was now curiously forming around Ellis; eagerly saying, "Miss Ellis, 'tis to me that Lady Aurora wrote that sweet letter, about the fifty pounds; and I'll send for it to shew you this moment."

"Do, little lady, do!" cried Mr. Giles, smiling and nodding, "you are the sweetest little soul amongst them all!"

Laughing and delighted, she was dancing away; but Lady Kendover, gently stopping her, said, "You are too young, yet, my dear, to be aware of the impropriety of making private letters public."

"Well, then, at least, Miss Ellis," she cried, "I will tell you that one paragraph, for I have read it so often and often that I have got it by heart, it's so very beautiful! 'You will entreat Miss Arbe, my dear Lady Barbara, since she is so good as to take the direction of this concert-enterprize, to employ this little loan to the best advantage for Miss Ellis, and the most to her satisfaction. Loan I call it, for Miss Ellis, I know, will pay it, if not in money, at least in a thousand sweetnesses, of a thousand times more value.'"

Ellis, touched with unspeakable pleasure, was forced to put her hand before her eyes.

"'Don't let her consult Miss Ellis about its acceptance. Miss Ellis will decline every thing that is personal; and every thing that is personal is what I most wish to present to her. I beg Miss Arbe will try to find out what she most requires, and endeavour to supply it unnamed.

"'Oh! could I but discover what would sooth, would console her! How often I think of her! How I love to recollect her enchanting talents, and to dwell upon every hour that I passed in her endearing society! Why did not Lady Kendover know her at that time? She could not, then, my dear Lady Barbara, have wished you a sweeter companion. Even Mrs. Howel was nearly as much captivated by her elegance and manners, as I was, and must ever remain, by her interesting qualities, and touching sensibility. O be kind to her, Lady Barbara! for my sake be kind to her: I am quite, quite unhappy that I have no power to be so myself!'"

Tears now rolled in resistless streams down the cheeks of Ellis, though from such heartfelt delight, that her eyes, swimming in liquid lustre, shone but more brightly.

Nevertheless, the respect which such a panegyric might have excited in the assembly at large, was nearly lost through the rapidity with which it was uttered by the eager Lady Barbara; and nothing short of the fascinated attention, and quick consciousness given by deep personal interest, could have made it completely intelligible even to Ellis: but to the sounds we wish to hear the heart beats responsive: it seizes them almost unpronounced.

Revived, re-animated, enchanted, Ellis now, with grace, with modesty, yet with firmness, renewed her request to Miss Arbe; who, assuming a lively air, though palpably provoked and embarrassed, answered, that Miss Ellis did not at all understand her own interest; and declared that she had taken the affair in hand herself, merely to regulate it to the best advantage; adding, "You shall see, now, the surprise I had prepared for you, if that blabbing old cousin of mine had not told you every thing before hand."

Then, in a tone of perfectly restored self-complacency, she produced a packet, and, with a parading look, that said, See what I bestow upon you! ostentatiously spread its contents upon a table.

"Now," she cried, "Miss Ellis, I hope I shall have the good fortune to please you! see what a beautiful gown* I have bought you!"

The gown was a sarcenet* of a bright rose-colour; but its hue, though the most vivid, was pale to the cheeks of Ellis, as she repeated, "A gown, Madam? Permit me to ask—for what purpose?"

"For what purpose?—To sing at our concert, you know! It's just the thing you want the most in the world. How could you possibly do without it, you know, when you come to appear before us all in public?"

While Ellis hesitated what to reply, to a measure which, thus conducted, and thus announced, seemed to her unequivocally impertinent, the packet itself was surrounded by an eager tribe of females, and five or six voices broke forth at once, with remarks, or animadversions, upon the silk.

"How vastly pretty it is!" cried Miss Arramede, addressing herself courteously to Miss Arbe.

"Yes, pretty enough, for what it is meant for," answered Miss Sycamore; glancing her eyes superciliously towards Ellis.

"Pray, Miss Arbe, what did you give a yard for it," demanded Miss Bydel; "and how much will the body-lining* come to? I hope you know of a cheap mantua-maker?"

"Bless me, how fine you are going to make The Ellis!" cried Miss Crawley: "why I shall take her for a rose!"

"Why then The Ellis will be The rose!" said Miss Di; "but I should sooner take her for my wax-doll,* when she's all so pinky winky."

"Why then The Ellis will be The doll!" cried Miss Crawley.

The two sisters now seated, or rather threw themselves upon a sofa, to recover from the excessive laughter with which they were seized at their own pleasantry; and which was exalted nearly to extacy, by the wide stare, and uplifted hands, of Mr. Giles Arbe.

"It's horridly provoking one can't wear that colour one's self," said Miss Arramede, "for it's monstrously pretty."

"Pretty?" repeated Miss Brinville: "I hope, Miss Arramede, you don't wish to wear such a frightful vulgar thing, because it's pretty?"

"Well, I think it's vastly well," said Miss Sycamore, yawning; "so don't abuse it. As our uniform is fixed to be white, with violet-ornaments, it was my thought to beg Miss Arbe would order something of this shewy sort for Miss Ellis; to distinguish us *Dilettanti* from the artists."

It was not Ellis alone who felt the contemptuous haughtiness of this speech; the men all dropt their eyes; and Lady Barbara expressively exclaimed, "Miss Ellis can't help looking as beautiful and as elegant as an angel, let her dress how she will!"

All obstacles being now removed for continuing the rehearsal, the willing Lady-artists flocked around Miss Arbe; and songs were sung, and lessons* upon the piano forte, or harp, were played; with a readiness of compliance, taken, by the fair performers, for facility of execution; and with a delight in themselves that elevated their spirits to rapture; since it was the criterion whence they calculated the pleasure that they imparted to others.

The pieces which they had severally selected were so long, and the compliments which the whole company united to pour forth after every performance, were so much longer, that the day was nearly closing, when Ellis was summoned to finish the act.

Ellis, who had spent this interval first in curious, next in civil, and lastly in forced attention, rose now with diminished timidity, to obey the call. It was not that she thought better of the scheme, but that it appeared to her less formidable; her original determination, therefore, to make her best exertions, returned with more effect, and she executed a little prelude with precision and brilliancy; and then accompanied herself in a slow and plaintive air, with a delicacy, skill, and expression, at once touching and masterly.

This concluded the first act; and the first act was so long, that it was unanimously agreed, that some new regulations must be adopted, before the second and third could be rehearsed.

Every piece which had followed the opening performance, or, rather, failure, of Ellis, had been crowned with plaudits. Every hand had clapped every movement; every mouth had burst forth with exclamations of praise: Ellis alone was heard in silence; for Ellis was unprotected, unsustained, unknown. Her situation was mysterious, and seemed open, at times, to the most alarming suspicions; though the unequivocal regularity and propriety of her conduct, snatched her from any positive calumny. Yet neither this, nor the most striking talents, could have brought her forward, even for exhibition, into such an assembly, but for the active influence of Miss Arbe; who, shrewd, adroit, and vigilant, never lost an opportunity to serve herself, while seeming to serve others.

The fortune of this young lady was nearly as limited as her

ambition and vanity were extensive; she found, therefore, nothing so commodious, as to repay the solid advantages which she enjoyed, gratuitously, from various artists, by patronage; and she saw, in the present case, an absolute necessity, either to relinquish her useful and elegant mistress, as an unknown adventurer, not proper to be presented to people of fashion; or to obviate the singular obstacles to supporting her, by making them become a party themselves in the cause of her *protegée*, through the personal interest of a subscription for their own amusement.

Nevertheless, Ellis, after a performance which, if fairly heard, and impartially judged, must have given that warm delight that excites "spirit-stirring praise,"* was heard in silence; though had a single voice been raised in her favour, nearly every voice would have joined in chorus. But her patroness was otherwise engaged, and Lady Barbara was gone; no one, therefore, deemed it prudent to begin. Neglect is still more contagious than admiration: it is more natural, perhaps, to man, from requiring less trouble, less candour, less discernment, and less generosity. The *Dilettanti*, also, already reciprocally fatigued, were perfectly disposed to be as parsimonious to all without their own line,* as they were prodigal to all within it, of those sweet draughts of flattery, which they had so liberally interchanged with one another.

Miss Arbe considered her own musical debts to be cancelled, from the moment that she had introduced her *protegée* into this assembly. She was wholly, therefore, indifferent to what might give her support, or mortification; and had taken the time of her performance, to demand a general consultation, whether the first harmonic meeting should be held in the apartment of Lady Arramede, which was the most magnificent; or in that of Miss Sycamore, which, though superb, was the least considerable* amongst the select subscribers.

This was a point of high importance, and of animated discussion. The larger apartment would best excite the expectations of the public, and open the business in the highest style; but the smaller would be the most crowded;—there would not be room to stir a step;—scarcely a soul could get a seat;—some of the company must stand upon the stairs;—"O charming!"—"O delightful!"—was echoed from mouth to mouth; and the motion in favour of Miss Sycamore was adopted by acclamation.

Ellis now, perceiving that the party was breaking up, advanced to Miss Arbe, and earnestly requested to be heard; but Miss Arbe, looking as if she did not know, and was too busy to enquire what this meant, protested herself quite bewildered with the variety of matters which she had to arrange; and, shaking hands with Miss Sycamore, was hurrying away, when the words "Must I address myself, then, Madam, to Lady Aurora!" startled her, and she impatiently answered, "By no means! Lady Aurora has put the money into my hands, and I have disposed of it to the very best advantage."

"Disposed of it?—I hope not!—I hope—I trust—that, knowing the generous wishes of Lady Aurora to indulge, as well as to relieve me, you have not disposed of so considerable a sum, without permitting me first to state to you, how and in what manner her ladyship's benevolence may most effectually be answered?"

Miss Arbe, evidently more disturbed though more civil, lowered her tone; and, taking Ellis apart, gently assured her, that the whole had been applied exclusively for her profit, in music, elegant desks, the hire of instruments, and innumerable things, requisite for opening the concert upon a grand scale; as well as for the prettiest gown in the world, which, she was sure, would become her of all things.

Ellis, with undisguised astonishment, asked by what arrangement it could justly be settled, that the expences of a subscription-concert should be drawn from the bounty of one lady; that lady absent, and avowedly sending her subscription merely for the service of an individual of the sett?

"That's the very thing!" cried Miss Arbe, with vivacity: "her ladyship's sending it for that one performer, has induced me to make this very arrangement; for, to tell you the truth, if Lady Aurora had not been so considerate for you, the whole scheme must have been demolished; and if so, poor Miss Ellis! what would become of you, you know?"

Then, with a volubility that shewed, at once, her fear of expostulation, and her haste to have done, she sought to explain that, without the necessary preparations, there could be no concert; without a concert Miss Ellis could not be known; without being known, how could she procure any more scholars? and without procuring scholars, how avoid being reduced again to the same pitiable state, as that from which Miss Arbe had had the pleasure to extricate her? And, in short, to save further loss of time, she owned that it was too late to make any change, as the whole fifty pounds was entirely spent.

It was not, now, chagrin alone, nor disappointment, nor anxiety, that the speaking features of Ellis exhibited; indignation had a strong portion of their expression; but Miss Arbe awaited not the remonstrance that they announced: more courteous, while more embarrassed, she took Ellis by the hand, and caressingly said, "Lady Aurora knows—for I have written to her ladyship myself,—that every shilling is laid out for your benefit;—only we must have a beginning, you know,—so you won't distress poor Lady Aurora, by seeming discontented, after all that she has done for you? It would be cruel, you know, to distress her."

With all it's selfishness, Ellis felt the truth of this observation with respect to Lady Aurora, as forcibly as it's injustice with regard to herself. She sighed from helplessness how to seek any redress; and Miss Arbe, still fawningly holding her hand, added, "But you don't think to steal away without giving us another air?—Miss Sycamore!—Sir Marmaduke!—Sir Lyell! pray help me to persuade Miss Ellis to favour us with one more air."

Disgusted and fatigued, Ellis would silently have retired; but the signal being given by Miss Arbe, all that remained of the assembly professed themselves to be dying for another piece; and Ellis, pressed to comply with an eagerness that turned solicitation into persecution, was led, once more, by Sir Marmaduke, to the orchestra.

Here, her melancholy and distressed feelings again marred her performance; she scarcely knew what she played, nor how she sung; her execution lost its brilliancy, and her expression its refined excellence: but Miss Arbe, conscious of the cause, and alarmed lest any appeal to Lady Aurora should sully her own character of patroness, hoped, by the seductive bribery of flattery, to stifle complaint. She was the first, therefore, to applaud; and her example animated all around, except the supercilious Miss Sycamore, and the jealous Miss Brinville, whom envy rendered inveterate. "How exquisite!"—"How sweet!"—"How incomparable!"—"What taste!"—"What sounds!" —"What expression!"—now accompanied almost every bar of the wavering, incorrect performance; though not even an encouraging buzz of approbation, had cheered the exertions of the same performer during the elegant and nearly finished piece, by which it had been preceded. The public at large is generally just, because too enormous to be individually canvassed;* but private circles are almost universally biassed by partial or prejudiced influence.

Miss Arbe chose now to conclude, that every objection was obviated; and Ellis strove vainly to obtain a moment's further attention, from the frivolous flutter, and fancied perplexities, of busy self-consequence. The party broke up: the company dispersed; and the poor, unconsidered, unaided *protegée*, dejectedly left the house, at the same moment that it was quitted triumphantly, by her vain, superficial, unprotecting patroness.

CHAPTER XXXIII

DISCOURAGED and disgusted as Ellis returned from this rehearsal, the sad result of her reflections, upon all that had passed, and upon her complicate difficulties, with her debtors and creditors, served but to convince her of the necessity of perseverance in what she had undertaken; and of patience in supporting whatever that undertaking might require her to endure.

From the effects of a hard shower of rain, in which she had been caught, while returning from the first rehearsal, she was seized with a hoarseness, that forced her to decline her own vocal performance at the second. This was immediately spread about the room, as an excess of impertinence; and the words, "What ridiculous affectation!"—"What intolerable airs!"—"So she must have a cold? Bless us! how fine!"—were repeated from mouth to mouth, with that contemptuous exultation, which springs from the narrow pleasure of envy, in fixing upon superiour merit the stigma of insolence, or caprice.

Ellis, who, unavoidably, heard these murmurs, was struck with fresh alarm, at the hardship of those professions which cast their votaries upon the mercy of superficial judges; who, without investigation, discernment, or candour, make their decisions from common place prejudice; or current, but unexamined opinions.

Having no means to obviate similar injustice for the future, but by chacing the subject of suspicion, the dread of public disapprobation, to which she was now first awakened, made her devote her whole attention to the cure of her little malady.

Hitherto, a desire to do well, that she might not displease or disappoint her few supporters, had been all her aim; but sarcasms, uttered with so little consideration, in this small party, represented to her the disgrace to which her purposed attempt made her liable, in cases of sickness, of nervous terrours, or of casual inability, from an audience by which she could be regarded only as an artist, who, paid to give pleasure, was accountable for fulfilling that engagement.

She trembled at this view of her now dependant condition; and her health which, hitherto, left to nature, and the genial vigour of youth, had disdained all aid, and required no care, became the first and most painful object of her solicitude. She durst not venture to walk out except in the sun-shine; she forbore to refresh herself near an open window; and retreated from every unclosed door, lest humidity, or the sharpness of the wind, or a sudden storm, should again affect her voice; and she guarded her whole person from the changing elements, as sedulously as if age, infirmity, or disease, had already made her health the slave of prudential forethought.

These precautions, though they answered in divesting her of a casual and transient complaint, were big with many and greater evils, which threatened to become habitual. The faint warmth of a constantly shut up apartment; the total deprivation of that spring which exercise gives to strength, and fresh air to existence, soon operated a change in her whole appearance. Her frame grew weaker; the roses faded from her cheeks; she was shaken by every sound, and menaced with becoming a victim to all the tremors, and all the languors of nervous disorders.

Alas! she cried, how little do we know either of the labours, or the privations, of those whose business it is to administer pleasure to the public! We receive it so lightly, that we imagine it to be lightly given!

Alarmed, now, for her future and general health, she relinquished this dangerous and enervating system; and, committing herself again to the chances of the weather, and the exertions of exercise, was soon, again, restored to the enjoyment of her excellent constitution.

Meanwhile, the reproaches of Mr. Giles Arbe, for her seeming neglect of her own creditors, who had applied for his interest, constrained her to avow to him the real and unfeeling neglect which was its cause.

Extremely angry at this intelligence, he declared that he should make it his especial business, to urge those naughty ladies to a better behaviour.

Accordingly, at the next rehearsal,—for, as the relation of Miss Arbe, he was admitted to every meeting,—he took an opportunity, upon observing two or three of the scholars of Ellis in a group, to bustle in amongst them; and, pointing to her, as she sat upon a form, in a distant corner, "Do but look," he said, "at that pretty creature, ladies! Why don't you pay her what you owe her? She wants the money very much, I assure you."

A forced little laugh, from the ladies whom this concerned, strove to turn the attack into a matter of pleasantry. Lady Kendover alone, and at the earnest desire of her niece, took out her purse; but when Mr. Giles, smiling and smirking, with a hand as open as his countenance, advanced to receive what she meant to offer, she drew back, and, saying that she could not, just then, recollect the amount of the little sum, walked to the other end of the room.

"Oh, I'll bring you word what it is directly, my lady!" cried Mr. Giles; "so don't get out of the way. And you, too, my Lady Arramede; and you, Miss Sycamore; and you, Miss Brinville; if you'll all stand together, here, in a cluster, I'll bring every one of you the total of your accounts from her own mouth. And I may as well call those two merry young souls, the Miss Crawleys, to come and pay, too. She has earned her money hardly enough, I'm sure, poor pretty lady!"

"O, very hardly, to be sure!" cried Lady Arramede; "to play and sing are vast hardships!"

"O, quite insupportable!" said Miss Sycamore: "I don't wonder she complains. Especially as she has so much else to do with her time."

"Do you think it very agreeable, then, ladies," cried Mr. Giles, "to teach all that thrim thrum?"*

"Why what harm can it do her?" said Miss Brinville: "I don't see how she can well do any thing that can give her less trouble. She has only just to point out one note, or one finger, instead of another."

"Why yes, that's all she does, sure enough," said Miss Bydel, "for I have seen her give her lessons."

"What, then, ladies," cried Mr. Giles, surprised; "do you count for nothing being obliged to go out when one had rather stay at home? and to dress when one has nothing to put on? as well as to be at the call of folks who don't know how to behave? and to fag at teaching people who are too dull to learn?"

Ellis, who was within hearing, alarmed to observe that, in these last two phrases, he looked full at Miss Sycamore and Miss Brinville, upon whose conduct towards herself she had confidentially entrusted him with her feelings, endeavoured to make him some sign to be upon his guard: though, as neither of those two ladies had the misfortune to possess sufficient modesty to be aware of their demerits, they might both have remained as secure from offence as from consciousness, if her own quick fears had as completely escaped notice. But, when Mr. Giles perceived her uneasiness, he called out, "Don't be frightened, my pretty lady! don't think I'll betray my trust! No, no. I can assure you, ladies, you can't be in better hands, with respect to any of your faults or oversights, for she never names them but with the greatest allowances. For as to telling them to me, that's nothing; because I can't help being naturally acquainted with them, from seeing you so often."

"She's vastly good!"—"Amazingly kind!" was now, with affected contempt, repeated from one to another.

"Goodness, Mr. Giles!" cried Miss Bydel, "why what are you thinking of? Why you are calling all the ladies to account for not paying this young music-mistress, just as if she were a butcher, or a baker; or some useful tradesman."

"Well, so she is, Ma'am! so she is, Mrs. Bydel! For if she does not feed your stomachs, she feeds your fancies; which are all no better than starved when you are left to yourselves."

"Nay, as to that, Mr. Giles," said Miss Bydel, "much as it's my interest that the young woman should have her money, for getting me back my own, I can't pretend to say I think she should be put upon the same footing with eating and drinking. We can all live well enough without music, and painting, and those things, I hope; but I don't know how we are to live without bread and meat."

"Nor she, neither, Mrs. Bydel! and that's the very reason that she wants to be paid."

"But, I presume, Sir," said Mr. Scope, "you do not hold it to be as essential to the morals of a state, to encourage luxuries, as to provide for necessaries? I don't speak in any disparagement to this young lady, for she seems to me a very pretty sort of person. I put her, therefore, aside; and beg to discuss the matter at large. Or, rather, if I may take the liberty, I will speak more closely to the point. Let me, therefore, Sir, ask, whether you opine, that the butcher, who gives us our richest nutriment, and the baker, to whom we owe the staff of life, as Solomon himself calls the loaf,* should barely be put upon a par with an artist of luxury, who can only turn a sonata, or figure* a minuet, or daub a picture?"

"Why, Mr. Scope, a person who pipes a tune, or dances a jig, or paints a face, may be called, if you will, an artist of luxury; but then 'tis of your luxury, not his."

"Mine, Sir?"

"Yes, yours, Sir! And Mrs. Maple's; and Mrs. Bydel's; and Miss Brinville's; and Miss Sycamore's; and Mrs. and Miss every body's;—except only his own."

"Well, this," said Miss Bydel, "is curious enough! So because there are such a heap of squallers, and fidlers, and daubers, I am to have the fault of it?"

"This I could not expect indeed," said Mrs. Maple, "that a

gentleman so amazingly fond of charity, and the poor, and all that, as Mr. Giles Arbe, should have so little principle, as to let our worthy farmers and trades-people languish for want, in order to pamper a set of lazy dancers, and players, and painters; who think of no one thing but idleness, and outward shew, and diversion."

"No, Mrs. Maple; I am not for neglecting the farmers and trades-people; quite the contrary; for I think you should neither eat your meat, nor drink your beer, nor sit upon your chairs, nor wear your clothes, till you have rewarded the industrious people who provide them. Till then, in my mind, every body should bear to be hungry, and dry, and tired, and ragged! For what right have we to be fed, and covered, and seated, at other folks" cost? What title to gormandize over the butcher's fat joints, and the baker's quartern loaves,* if they who furnish them are left to gnaw bones, and live upon crumbs? We ought all of us to be ashamed of being warmed, and dizened in silks and satins, if the poor weavers, who fabricate them, and all their wives and babies, are shivering in tatters; and to toss and tumble ourselves about, on couches and arm-chairs, if the poor carpenters, and upholsterers, and joiners, who have had all the labour of constructing them, can't find a seat for their weary limbs!"

"What you advance there, Sir," said Mr. Scope, "I can't dispute; but still, Sir, I presume, putting this young lady always out of the way; you will not controvert my position, that the morals of a state require, that a proper distinction should be kept up, between the instruments of subsistence, and those of amusement."

"You are right enough, Mr. Scope," cried Miss Bydel; "for if singing and dancing, and making images, are ever so pretty, one should not pay folks who follow such light callings, as one pays people that are useful."

"I hope not, truly!" said Mrs. Maple.

Mr. Scope, thus encouraged, went on to a formal dissertation, upon the morality of repressing luxury; which was so cordially applauded by Miss Bydel; and enforced by sneers so personal and pointed against Ellis, by Mrs. Maple, Miss Brinville, and Miss Sycamore, that Mr. Giles, provoked, at length, to serious anger, got into the middle of the little auditory, and, with animated gesticulation, stopping all the attempts of the slow and prosing Mr. Scope to proceed, exclaimed, 'Luxury? What is it you all of you mean by luxury? Is it your own going to hear singing and playing? and to see dancing and capering? and to loll at your ease, while a painter makes you look pretty, if you are ever so plain? If it be, do those things no more, and there will soon be an end to them! but don't excite people to such feats, and then starve them for their pains. Luxury? do you suppose, because such sights, and such sounds, and such flattery, are luxuries to you, they are luxuries to those who produce them? Because you are in extacies to behold yourselves grow younger and more blooming every moment, do you conclude that he who mixes your colours, and covers your defects, shares your transports? No; he is sick to death of you; and longing to set his pencil at liberty. And because you, at idle hours, and from mere love of dissipation, lounge in your box at operas and concerts, to hear a tune, or to look at a jump, do you imagine he who sings, or who dances, must be a voluptuary? No! all he does is pain and toil to himself; learnt with labour, and exhibited with difficulty. The better he performs, the harder he has worked. All the ease, and all the luxury are yours, Mrs. Maple, and yours, Miss Bydel, and yours, ladies all, that are the lookers on! for he does not pipe or skip at his own hours, but at yours; he does not adorn himself for his own warmth, or convenience, but to please your tastes and fancies; he does not execute what is easiest, and what he likes best, but what is hardest, and has most chance to force your applause. He sings, perhaps, when he may be ready to cry; he plays upon those harps and fiddles, when he is half dying with hunger; and he skips those gavots, and fandangos,* when he would rather go to bed! And all this, to gain himself a hard and fatiguing maintenance, in amusing your dainty idleness, and insufficiency to yourselves.'

This harangue, uttered with an energy which provocation alone could rouse in the placid, though probing Mr. Giles, soon broke up the party: Miss Sycamore, indeed, only hummed, rather louder than usual, a favourite passage of a favourite air; and the Miss Crawleys nearly laughed themselves sick; but Mrs. Maple, Miss Bydel, and Miss Brinville, were affronted;

and Miss Arbe, who had vainly made various signs to her cousin to be silent, was ashamed, and retreated: without Miss Arbe, nothing could go on; and the rehearsal was adjourned.

The attempt of Mr. Giles, however, produced no effect, save that of occasioning his own exclusion from all succeeding meetings.

CHAPTER XXXIV

THE *Diletanti*, in a short time, thought themselves perfect, yet the destined concert was not opened; the fifty pounds, which had been sent for Ellis, had been lavished improvidently, in ornamental preparations; and the funds otherwise raised, were inadequate for paying the little band, which was engaged to give effect in the orchestra.

Severely as Ellis dreaded the hour of exhibition, a delay that, in it's obvious consequences, could only render it more necessary, gave her no satisfaction.

A new subject for conjecture and reflexion speedily ensued: the visits of Miss Arbe, hitherto wearisome and oppressive, alike from their frequency and their selfishness, suddenly, and without any reason assigned, or any visible motive, ceased.

The relief which, in other circumstances, this defection might have given to her spirits, she was now incapable of enjoying; for though Miss Arbe rather abused than fulfilled the functions of a patroness, Ellis immediately experienced, that even the most superficial protection of a lady of fashion, could not, without danger, be withdrawn from the indigent and unsupported. Miss Matson began wondering, with a suspicious air, what was become of Miss Arbe; the young work-women, when Ellis passed them, spared even the civility of a little inclination of the head; and the maid of the house was sure to be engaged, on the very few occasions on which Ellis demanded her assistance.

Some days elapsed thus, in doubt and uneasiness, not even broken into by a summons to a rehearsal: another visit, then, from Mr. Giles Arbe, explained the cause of this sudden desertion. He brought a manuscript air, which Miss Arbe desired that Ellis would copy, and, immediately, though unintentionally, divulged, that his cousin had met with the newly-arrived professor at Miss Brinville's, and had instantly transferred to him the enthusiasm of her favour.

Ellis but too easily comprehended, that the ruin of her credit and consequence in private families, would follow the uselessness of her services to her patroness. The prosecution, therefore, of the concert-scheme, which she had so much disliked in its origin, became now her own desire, because her sole resource.

The next morning, while she was busy in copying the MS., the customary sound of the carriage and voice of Miss Arbe, struck her ears, and struck them, for the first time, with pleasure.

'I have not,' cried that lady, 'a moment to stay; but I have something of the greatest importance to tell you, and you have not an instant to lose in getting yourself ready. What do you think? You are to sing, next week, at Mr. Vinstreigle's benefit!'

'I, Madam!'

'Yes! for you must know, my dear Miss Ellis, he has asked it of me himself! So you see what a compliment that is! I am quite charmed to bring you such news. So be sure to be ready with one of your very best *scenas*.'*

She was then, with a lively air, decamping; but Ellis gently, yet positively, declined performing at any concert open to the public at large.

'Pho, pho! don't begin all those scruples again, pray! It must be so, I assure you. I'll tell you how the matter stands. Our funds are not yet rich enough for beginning our own snug scrip-concert,* without risk of being stopt short the first or second night. And that, you know would raise the laugh against us all horridly. I mean against us *Diletanti*. So that, if we don't hit upon some new measure, I am afraid we shall all go to town* before the concert can open. And that, you know, would quite ruin you, poor Miss Ellis! which would really give me great concern. So I consulted with Sir Marmaduke Crawley; and he said that you ought, by all means, to sing once or twice in public, to make yourself known; for that would raise the subscription directly; especially as it would soon be spread that you are a *protegée* of mine. So, you see, we must either take this method, or give the thing quite up; which will be your utter destruction, I am sorry to say. So now decide quick, for there is not a second to spare.'

Ellis was alarmed, yet persisted in her negative.

Piqued and offended, Miss Arbe hurried away; declaring aloud, in passing through the shop, that people who were so determined to be their own enemies, might take care of themselves: that, for her part, she should do nothing more in the affair; and only wished that Miss Ellis might find better means for paying her debts, and procuring herself a handsome maintenance.

However shocked by this petulant indelicacy, Ellis saw not without the most serious concern, that the patronage of Miss Arbe was clearly at an end. Personal interest which, it was equally clear, had excited it, now ran in another channel; for if, by flattery or good offices, she could obtain gratis, the instructions of an eminent professor, what could she want with Ellis, whom she had never sought, nor known, nor considered, but as a musical preceptress? And yet, far from elevating as was such patronage, its extinction menaced the most dangerous effects.

With little or no ceremony, Miss Matson, the next morning, came into her room, and begged leave to enquire when their small account could be settled. And, while Ellis hesitated how to answer, added, that the reason of her desiring a reply as quickly as possible, was an interview that she had just had with the other creditors, the preceding evening; because she could not but let them know what had passed with Miss Arbe. 'For, after what I heard the lady say, Miss Ellis, as she went through my shop, I thought it right to follow her, and ask what she meant; as it was entirely upon her account my giving you credit. And Miss Arbe replied to me, in so many words, 'Miss Ellis can pay you All, if she pleases: she has the means in her own power: apply to her, therefore, in whatever way you think proper; for you may do her a great service by a little severity: but, for my part, remember, I take no further responsibility." So upon this, I talked it all over with your other creditors; and we came to a determination to bring the matter to immediate issue.'

Seized with terrour, Ellis now hastily took, from a locked drawer, the little packet of Harleigh, and, breaking the seal, was precipitately resolving to discharge every account directly; when other conflicting emotions, as quick as those which had excited, checked her first impulse; and, casting down, with a trembling hand, the packet, O let me think!—she internally cried;—surrounded with perils of every sort, let me think, at least, before I incur new dangers!

She then begged that Miss Matson would grant her a few minutes for deliberation.

Certainly, Miss Matson said; but, instead of leaving the room, took possession of the sofa, and began a long harangue upon her own hardships in trade; Ellis, neither answering nor listening.

Presently, the door opened, and Mr. Giles Arbe, in his usually easy manner, made his appearance.

'You are busy, you are busy, I see,' he cried; 'but don't disturb yourselves. I'll look for a book, and wait.'

Ellis, absorbed in painful ruminations, scarcely perceived him; and Miss Matson loquaciously addressed to him her discourse upon her own affairs; too much interested in the subject herself, to mark whether or not it interested others, till Mr. Giles caught her attention, and awakened even that of Ellis, by saying aloud, though speaking to himself, 'Why now here's money enough!—Why should not all those poor people be paid?'

Ellis, turning round, saw then, that he had taken up Harleigh's packet; of which he was examining the contents, and spreading, one by one, the notes upon a table.

She hastily ran to him, and, with an air extremely displeased, seized those which she could reach; and begged him instantly to deliver to her those which were still in his hand.

Her discomposed manner brought him to the recollection of what he was doing; and, making abundant apologies, 'I protest,' he cried, 'I don't know how it happened that I should meddle with your papers, for I meant only to take up a book! But I suppose it was because I could not find one.'

Ellis, in much confusion, re-folded the notes, and put them away.

'I am quite ashamed to have done such a thing, I assure you,' he continued, 'though I am happy enough at the accident, too; for I thought you very poor, and I could hardly sleep, sometimes, for fretting about it. But I see, now, you are better off than I imagined; for there are ten of those ten pound bank-notes, if I have not miscounted; and your bills don't amount to more than two or three of them.'

Ellis, utterly confounded, retreated to the window.

Miss Matson, who, with the widest stare, had looked first at the bank-notes, and next at the embarrassed Ellis, began now to offer the most obsequious excuses for her importunity; declaring that she should never have thought of so rudely hurrying such a young lady as Miss Ellis, but that the other creditors, who were really in but indifferent circumstances, were so much in want of their money, that she had not been able to quiet them.

And then, begging that Miss Ellis would take her own time, she went, courtesying, down stairs.

'So you have got all this money, and would not own it?' said Mr. Giles, when she was gone. 'That's odd! very odd, I confess! I can't well understand it; but I hope, my pretty lady, you won't turn out a rogue? I beg you won't do that; for it would vex me prodigiously.'

Ellis, dropping upon a chair, ejaculated, with a heavy sigh, 'What step must I take!'

'What?—why pay them all, to be sure! What do other people do, when they have got debts, and got money? I shall go and tell them to come to you directly, every one of them.'

Ellis, starting, supplicated his forbearance.

'And why?—why?' cried he, looking a little angry: 'Do you really want to hide up all that money, and make those poor good people, who have served you at their own cost, believe that you have not gotten any?'

She assured him that the money was simply a deposit left in her hands.

This intelligence overset and disappointed him. He returned to his chair, and drawing it near the fire, gave himself up to considering what could be done; ejaculating from time to time, 'That's bad!—that's very bad!—being really so poor is but melancholy!—I am sorry for her, poor pretty thing!—very sorry!—But still, taking up goods one can't pay for?—Who has a right to do that?—How are trades-people to live by selling their wares gratis?—Will that feed their little ones?'

Then, turning to Ellis, who, in deep disturbance at these commentaries, had not spirits to speak; 'But why,' he cried, 'since you have gotten this money, should not you pay these poor people with it, rather than let it lie dead by your side? for as to the money's not being yours,—their's is not yours, neither.'

'Should I raise myself, Sir, in your good opinion, by contracting a new debt to pay an old one?'

'If you contract it with a friend to pay a stranger, Yes.—And these notes, I suppose, of course, belong to a friend?'

'Not to ..... an enemy, certainly!—' she answered, much embarrassed; 'but is that a reason that I should betray a trust?'

'What becomes of the trust of these poor people, then, that don't know you, and that you don't know? Don't you betray that? Do you think that they would have let you take their goods, if they had not expected your payment?'

'Oh heaven, Mr. Arbe!' cried Ellis, 'how you probe—perplex—entangle me!'

'Don't vex, don't vex!' said he, kindly, 'for that will fret me prodigiously. Only, another time, when you are in want, borrow from the rich, and not from the poor; for they are in want themselves. This friend of yours is rich, I take for granted?'

'I ..... I believe so!'

'Well, then, which is most equitable, to take openly from a rich friend, and say, 'I thank you;" or to take, under-hand, from a hard-working stranger, whom you scorn to own yourself obliged to, though you don't scruple to harass and plunder? Which, I say, is most equitable?'

Ellis shuddered, hesitated, and then said, 'The alternative, thus stated, admits of no contest! I must pay my debts—and extricate myself from the consequences as I can!'

'Why then you are as good as you are pretty!' cried he, delighted: 'Very good, and very pretty, indeed! And so I thought you at first! And so I shall think you to the end!'

He then hurried away, to give her no time to retract;

nodding and talking to himself in her praise, with abundant complacency; and saying, as he passed through the shop, "Miss Matson, you'll be all of you paid to-morrow morning at farthest. So be sure bid all the good people come; for the lady is a person of great honour, as well as prettiness; and there's money enough for every one of you,—and more, too."

CHAPTER XXXV

ELLIS remained in the deepest disturbance at the engagement into which she had entered. O cruel necessity! cruel, imperious necessity! she cried, to what a resource dost thou drive me! How unjust, how improper, how perilous!—Ah! rather let me cast myself upon Lady Aurora—Yet, angel as she is, can Lady Aurora act for herself? And Lord Melbury, guileless, like his nature, as may now be his intentions, what protection can he afford me that calumny may not sully? Alas! how may I attain that self-dependence which alone, at this critical period, suits my forlorn condition?

The horrour of a new debt, incurred under circumstances thus delicate, made the idea even of performing at the public benefit, present itself to her in colours less formidable, if such a measure, by restoring to her the patronage of Miss Arbe, would obviate the return of similar evils, while she was thus hanging, in solitary obscurity, upon herself. Vainly she would have turned her thoughts to other plans, and objects yet untried; she had no means to form any independent scheme; no friends to promote her interest; no counsellors to point out any pursuit, or direct any measures.

Her creditors failed not to call upon her early the next morning, guided and accompanied by Mr. Giles Arbe; who, bright with smiles and good humour, declared, that he could not refuse himself the pleasure of being a witness to her getting rid of such a bad business, as that of keeping other people's money, by doing such a good one as that of paying every one his due. "You are much obliged to this pretty lady, I can tell you," he said, to the creditors, "for she pays you with money that is not her own. However, as the person it belongs to is rich, and a friend, I advise you, as you are none of you rich yourselves, and nearly strangers to her, to take it without scruple."

To this counsel there was not one dissentient voice.

Can the same person, thought Ellis, be so innocent, yet so mischievous? so fraught with solid notions of right, yet so shallow in judgment, and knowledge of the world?

With a trembling hand, and revolting heart, she changed three of the notes, and discharged all the accounts at once; Mr. Giles, eagerly and unbidden, having called up Miss Matson to take her share.

Ellis now deliberated, whether she might not free herself from every demand, by paying, also, Miss Bydel; but the reluctance with which she had already broken into the fearful deposit, soon fixed her to seal up the remaining notes entire.

The shock of this transaction, and the earnestness of her desire to replace money which she deemed it unjustifiable to employ, completed the conquest of her repugnance to public exhibition; and she commissioned Mr. Giles to acquaint Miss Arbe, that she was ready to obey her commands.

This he undertook with the utmost pleasure; saying, "And it's lucky enough your consenting to sing those songs, because my cousin, not dreaming of any objection on your part, had already authorised Mr. Vinstreigle to put your name in his bills."

"My name?" cried Ellis, starting and changing colour: but the next moment adding, "No, no! my name will not appear!—Yet should any one who has ever seen me ...."

She shuddered; a nervous horrour took possession of her whole frame; but she soon forced herself to revive, and assume new courage, upon hearing Mr. Giles, from the landing-place, again call Miss Matson; and bid all her young women, one by one, and the two maid-servants, hurry up stairs directly, with water and burnt feathers.*

Ellis made every enquiry in her power, of who was at Brighthelmstone; and begged Mr. Giles to procure her a list of the company. When she had read it, she became more tranquil, though not less sad.

Miss Arbe received the concession with infinite satisfaction; and introduced Ellis, as her *protegée*, to her new favourite; who professed himself charmed, that the presentation of so promising a subject, to the public, should be made at his benefit.

"And now, Miss Ellis," said Miss Arbe, "you will very soon have more scholars than you can teach. If once you get a fame and a name, your embarrassments will be at an end; for all enquiries about who people are, and what they are, and those sort of niceties, will be over. We all learn of the celebrated, be they what they will. Nobody asks how they live, and those sort of things. What signifies? as Miss Sycamore says. We don't visit them, to be sure, if there is any thing awkward about them. But that's not the least in the way against their making whole oceans of riches."

This was not a species of reasoning to offer consolation to Ellis; but she suppressed the disdain which it inspired; and dwelt only upon the hoped accomplishment of her views, through the private teaching which it promised.

In five days' time, the benefit was to take place; and in three, Ellis was summoned to a rehearsal at the rooms.

She was putting on her hat, meaning to be particularly early in her attendance, that she might place herself in some obscure corner, before any company arrived; to avoid the pain of passing by those who knowing, might not notice, or noticing, might but mortify her; when one of the young work-women brought her intelligence, that a gentleman, just arrived in a post chaise, requested admittance.

"A gentleman?" she repeated, with anxiety:—"tell him, if you please, that I am engaged, and can see no company."

The young woman soon returned. "The gentleman says, Ma'am, that he comes upon affairs of great importance, which he can communicate only to yourself."

Ellis begged the young woman to request, that Miss Matson would desire him to leave his name and business in writing.

Miss Matson was gone to Lady Kendover's, with some new patterns,* just arrived from London.

The young woman, however, made the proposition, but without effect: the gentleman was in great haste, and would positively listen to no denial.

Strong and palpable affright, now seized Ellis; am I—Oh heaven!—she murmured to herself, pursued?—and then began, but checked an inquiry, whether there were any private door by which she could escape: yet, pressed by the necessity of appearing at the rehearsal, after painfully struggling for courage, she faintly articulated, "Let him come up stairs."

The young woman descended, and Ellis remained in breathless suspense, till she heard some one tap at her door.

She could not pronounce, Who's there? but she compelled herself to open it; though without lifting up her eyes, dreading to encounter the object that might meet them, till she was roused by the words, "Pardon, pardon my intrusion!" and perceived Harleigh gently entering her apartment.

She started,—but it was not with terrour; she came forward,—but it was not to escape! The colour which had forsaken her cheeks, returned to them with a crimson glow; the fear which had averted her eyes, was changed into an expression of even extatic welcome; and, clasping her hands, with sudden, impulsive, irresistible surprise and joy, she cried, "Is it you?—Mr. Harleigh! you!"

Surprise now was no longer her own, and her joy was participated in yet more strongly. Harleigh, who, though he had forced his way, was embarrassed and confused, expecting displeasure, and prepared for reproach; who had seen with horrour the dismay of her countenance; and attributed to the effect of his compulsatory entrance the terrified state in which he found her; Harleigh, at sight of this rapid transition from agony to delight; at the flattering ejaculation of "Is it you?" and the sound of his own name, pronounced with an expression of even exquisite satisfaction;—Harleigh in a sudden trance of irrepressible rapture, made a nearly forcible effort to seize her hand, exclaiming, "Can you receive me, then, thus sweetly? Can you forgive an intrusion that—" when Ellis recovering her self-command, drew back, and solemnly said, "Mr. Harleigh, forbear! or I must quit the room!"

Harleigh reluctantly, yet instantly desisted; but the pleasure of so unhoped a reception still beat at his heart, though it no longer sparkled in her eyes: and though the enchanting animation of her manner, was altered into the most repressing gravity, the blushes which still tingled, still dyed her cheeks, betrayed that all within was not chilled, however all without might seem cold.

Checked, therefore, but not subdued, he warmly solicited a few minutes conversation; but, gaining firmness and force every instant, she told him that she had an appointment which admitted not of procrastination.

"I know well your appointment," cried he, agitated in his turn, "too, too well!—'Tis that fatal—or, rather, let me hope, that happy, that seasonable information, which I received last night, in a letter containing a bill of the concert, from Ireton, that has brought me hither;—that impelled me, uncontrollably, to break through your hard injunctions; that pointed out the accumulating dangers to all my views, and told me that every gleam of future expectation—"

Ellis interrupted him at this word: he entreated her pardon, but went on.

"You cannot be offended at this effort: it is but the courage of despondence, I come to demand a final hearing!"

"Since you know, Sir," cried she, with quickness, "my appointment, you must be sensible I am no longer mistress of my time. This is all I can say. I must be gone,—and you will not, I trust,—if I judge you rightly,—you will not compel me to leave you in my apartment."

"Yes! you judge me rightly! for the universe I would not cause you just offence! Trust me, then, more generously! be somewhat less suspicious, somewhat more open, and take not this desperate step, without hearkening to its objections, without weighing its consequences!"

She could enter, she said, into no discussion; and prepared to depart.

"Impossible!" cried he, with energy; "I cannot let you go!—I cannot, without a struggle, resign myself to irremediable despair!"

Ellis, recovered now from the impression caused by his first appearance, with a steady voice, and sedate air, said, "This is a language, Sir,—you know it well,—to which I cannot, must not listen. It is as useless, therefore, as it is painful, to renew it. I beseech you to believe in the sincerity of what I have already been obliged to say, and to spare yourself—to spare, shall I add, me?—all further oppressive conflicts."*

A sigh burst from her heart, but she strove to look unmoved.

"If you are generous enough to share, even in the smallest degree," cried he, "the pain which you inflict; you will, at least, not refuse me this one satisfaction .... Is it for Elinor .... and for Elinor only .... that you deny me, thus, all confidence?"

"Oh no, no, no!" cried she, hastily: "if Miss Joddrel were not in existence,—" she checked herself, and sighed more deeply; but, presently added, "yet, surely, Miss Joddrel were cause sufficient!"

"You fill me," he cried, "with new alarm, new disturbance! —I supplicate you, nevertheless, to forego your present plan;—and to shew some little consideration to what I have to offer.—"

She interrupted him. "I must be unequivocally, Sir,—for both our sakes,—understood. You must call for no consideration from me! I can give you none! You must let me pursue the path that my affairs, that my own perceptions, that my necessities point out to me, without interference, and without expecting from me the smallest reference to your opinions, or feelings.—Why, why," continued she, in a tone less firm, "why will you force from me such ungrateful words?—Why leave me no alternative between impropriety, or arrogance?"

"Why,—let me rather ask,—why must I find you for ever thus impenetrable, thus incomprehensible?—I will not, however, waste your patience. I see your eagerness to be gone.—Yet, in defiance of all the rigour of your scruples, you must bear to hear me avow, in my total ignorance of their cause, that I feel it impossible utterly to renounce all distant hope of clearer prospects.—How, then, can I quietly submit to see you enter into a career of public life, subversive—perhaps—to me, of even any eventual amelioration?"

Ellis blushed deeply as she answered, "If I depended, Sir, upon you,—if you were responsible for my actions; or if your own fame, or name, or sentiments were involved in my conduct .... then you would do right, if such is your opinion, to stamp my project with the stigma of your disapprobation, and to warn me of the loss of your countenance:—but, till then, permit me to say, that the business which calls me away has the first claim to my time."

She opened the door.

"One moment," cried he, earnestly, "I conjure you!—The hurry of alarm, the certainty that delay would make every effort abortive; have precipitated me into the use of expressions that may have offended you. Forgive them, I entreat! and do not judge me to be so narrow minded; or so insensible to the enchantment of talents, and the witchery of genius; as not to feel as much respect for the character, where it is worthy, as admiration for the abilities, of those artists whose profession it is to give delight to the public. Had I first known you as a public performer, and seen you in the same situations which have shewn me your worth, I must have revered you as I do at this instant: I must have been devoted to you with the same unalterable attachment: but then, also,—if you would have indulged me with a hearing,—must I not have made it my first petition, that your accomplishments should be reserved for the resources of your leisure, and the happiness of your friends, at your own time, and your own choice? Would you have branded such a desire as pride? or would you not rather have allowed it to be called by that word, which your own every action, every speech, every look bring perpetually to mind, propriety?"

Ellis sighed: "Alas!" she said, "my own repugnance to this measure makes me but too easily conceive the objections to which it may be liable! and if you, so singularly liberal, if even you—"

She stopt; but Harleigh, not less encouraged by a phrase thus begun, than if she had proceeded, warmly continued.

"If then, in a case such as I have presumed to suppose, to have withdrawn you from the public would not have been wrong, how can it be faulty, upon the same principles, and with the same intentions, to endeavour, with all my might, to turn you aside from such a project?—I see you are preparing to tell me that I argue upon premises to which you have not concurred. Suffer me, nevertheless, to add a few words, in explanation of what else may seem presumption, or impertinence: I have hinted that this plan might cloud my dearest hopes; imagine not, thence, that my prejudices upon this subject are invincible: no! but I have Relations who have never deserved to forfeit my consideration;—and these—not won, like me, by the previous knowledge of your virtues.—"

Ellis would repeatedly have interrupted him, but he would not be stopped.

"Hear me on," he continued, "I beseech you! By my plainness only I can shew my sincerity. For these Relations, then, permit me to plead. It is true, I am independent: my actions are under no controul; but there are ties from which we are never emancipated; ties which cling to our nature, and which, though voluntary, are imperious, and cannot be broken or relinquished, without self-reproach; ties formed by the equitable laws of fellow-feeling; which bind us to our family, which unite us with our friends; and which, by our own expectations, teach us what is due to our connexions. Ah, then, if ever brighter prospects may open to my eyes, let me not see them sullied, by mists hovering over the approbation of those with whom I am allied!"

"How just," cried Ellis, trying to force a smile, "yet how useless is this reasoning! I cannot combat sentiments in which I concur; yet I can change nothing in a plan to which they must have no reference! I am sorry to appear ungrateful, where I am only steady; but I have nothing new to say; and must entreat you to dispense with fruitless repetitions. Already, I fear, I am beyond the hour of my engagement."

She was now departing.

"You distract me!" cried he, with vehemence, "you distract me!" He caught her gown, but, upon her stopping, instantly let it go. Pale and affrighted, "Mr. Harleigh," she cried, "is it to you I must owe a scene that may raise wonder and surmises in the house, and aggravate distresses and embarrassments which, already, I find nearly intolerable?"

Shocked and affected, he shut the door, and would impetuously, yet tenderly, have taken her hand; but, upon her shrinking back, with displeasure and alarm, he more quietly said, "Pardon! pardon! and before you condemn me inexorably to submit to such rigorous disdain and contempt—"

"Why will you use such words? Contempt?—Good heaven!" she began, with an emotion that almost instantly subsided, and she added, "Yet of what consequence to you ought to be my sensations, my opinions? They can avail you nothing! Let me go,—and let me conjure you to be gone!"

"You are then decided against me?" cried he, in a voice scarcely articulate.

"I am:" she answered, without looking at him, but calmly.

He bowed, with an air that relinquished all further attempt to detain her; but which shewed him too much wounded to speak.

Carefully still avoiding his eyes, she was moving off; but, when she touched the lock of the door, he exclaimed, "Will you not, at least, before you go, allow me to address a few words to you as a friend? simply,—undesignedly,—solely as a friend?"

"Ah! Mr. Harleigh!" cried Ellis, irresistibly softened, "as a friend could I, indeed, have trusted you, I might long since,—perhaps,—have confided in your liberality and benevolence: but now, 'tis wholly impossible!"

"No!" exclaimed he, warmly, and touched to the soul; "nothing is impossible that you wish to effect! Hear me, then, trust and speak to me as a friend; a faithful, a cordial, a disinterested friend! Confide to me your name—your situation—the motives to your concealment—the causes that can induce such mystery of appearance, in one whose mind is so evidently the seat of the clearest purity:—the reasons of such disguise—"

"Disguise, I acknowledge, Sir, you may charge me with; but not deceit! I give no false colouring. I am only not open."

"That, that is what first struck me as a mark of a distinguished character! That noble superiority to all petty artifices, even for your immediate safety; that undoubting innocence, that framed no precautions against evil constructions; that innate dignity, which supported without a murmur such difficulties, such trials;——"

"Ah, Mr. Harleigh! a friend and a flatterer—are they, then synonimous terms? If, indeed, you would persuade me you feel that they are distinct, you will not make me begin a new and distasteful career—since to begin it I think indispensable;—with the additional chagrin of appearing to be wanting in punctuality. No further opposition, I beg!"

"O yet one word, one fearful word must be uttered—and one

fatal—or blest reply must be granted!—The excess of my suspense, upon the most essential of all points, must be terminated! I will wait with inviolable patience the explanation of all others. Tell me, then, to what barbarous cause I must attribute this invincible, this unrelenting reserve?—How I may bear an abrupt answer I know not, but the horrour of uncertainty I experience, and can endure no longer. Is it, then, to the force of circumstances I may impute it?—or … is it …"

"Mr. Harleigh," interrupted Ellis, with strong emotion, "there is no medium, in a situation such as mine, between unlimited confidence, or unbroken taciturnity: my confidence I cannot give you; it is out of my power—ask me, then, nothing!"

"One word,—one little word,—and I will torment you no longer: is it to pre-engagement——"

Her face was averted, and her hand again was placed upon the lock of the door.

"Speak, I implore you, speak!— Is that heart, which I paint to myself the seat of every virtue ….. is it already gone?—given, dedicated to another?"

He now trembled himself, and durst not resist her effort to open the door, as she replied, "I have no heart!—I must have none!"

She uttered this in a tone of gaiety, that would utterly have confounded his dearest expectations, had not a glance, with difficulty caught, shewed him a tear starting into her eye; while a blush of fire, that defied constraint, dyed her cheeks; and kept no pace with the easy freedom from emotion, that her voice and manner seemed to indicate.

Flushed with tumultuous sensations of conflicting hopes and fears, he now tenderly said, "You are determined, then, to go?"

"I am; but you must first leave my room."

"Is there, then, no further appeal?"

"None! none!—We may be heard disputing down stairs: —persecute me no longer!"

Her voice grew tremulous, and spoke displeasure; but her eyes still sedulously shunned his, and still her cheeks were crimsoned. Harleigh paused a moment, looking at her with speechless anxiety; but, upon an impatient motion of her hand that he would depart, he mildly said, "As your friend, at least, you will permit me to see you again?" and, without risking a reply, slowly descended the stairs.

Ellis, shutting herself into her room, sunk upon a chair, and wept.

She was soon interrupted by a message from Mr. Vinstreigle, to acquaint her that the rehearsal was begun.

She felt unable to sing, play, or speak, and, sending an excuse that she was indisposed, desired that her attendance might be dispensed with for that morning.

CHAPTER XXXVI

ELLIS passed the rest of the day in solitary meditation upon the scene just related, her singular situation, and complicated difficulties. If, at times, her project yielded to the objections to which she had been forced to give ear, those objections were soon subdued, by the painful recollection of the unacknowledged, yet broken hundred pounds. To replace them, by whatever efforts, without giving to Harleigh the dangerous advantage of discovering what she owed to him, became now her predominant wish. Yet her distaste to the undertaking, her fears, her discomfort, were cruelly augmented; and she determined that her airs should be accompanied only by herself upon the harp, to obviate any indispensable necessity for appearing at the rehearsals.

To this effect, she sent, the next morning, a message that pleaded indisposition, to M. Vinstreigle; yet that included an assurance, that he might depend upon her performance, on the following evening, at his concert.

Once more, therefore, she consigned herself to practice; but vainly she attempted to sing; her voice was disobedient to her desires: she had recourse, however, to her harp; but she was soon interrupted, by receiving the following letter from Harleigh.

"To Miss Ellis.

"With a satisfaction which I dare not indulge—and yet, how curb?—I have learnt, from Ireton, that you have renounced the rehearsals. 'Tis hut, however, the trembling joy of a reprieve, that, while welcoming hope, sees danger and death still in view. For me and for my feelings you disclaim all consideration: I will not, therefore, intrude upon you, again, my wishes or my sufferings; yet as you do not, I trust, utterly reject me as a friend, permit me, in that capacity, to entreat you to deliberate, before you finally adopt a measure to which you confess your repugnance. Your situation I know not; but where information is with-held, conjecture is active; and while I see your accomplishments, while I am fascinated by your manners, I judge your education, and, thence, your connections, and original style of life. If, then, there be any family that you quit, yet that you may yourself desire should one day reclaim you; and if there be any family—leave mine alone!—to which you may hereafter be allied, and that you may wish should appreciate, should revere you, as you merit to be revered and appreciated—for such let me plead! Wound not the customs of their ancestors, the received notions of the world, the hitherto acknowledged boundaries of elegant life! Or, if your tenderness for the feelings—say the failings, if you please,—the prejudices, the weaknesses of others,—has no weight, let, at least, your own ideas of personal propriety, your just pride, your conscious worth, point out to you the path in society which you are so eminently formed to tread. Or, if, singularly independent, you deem that you are accountable only to yourself for your conduct, that notion, beyond any other, must shew you the high responsibility of all actions that are voluntary. Remember, then, that your example may be pleaded by those who are not gifted, like you, with extraordinary powers for sustaining its consequences; by those who have neither your virtues to bear them through the trials and vicissitudes of public enterprise; nor your motives for encountering dangers so manifest; nor your apologies—pardon the word!—for deviating, alone and unsupported as you appear, from the long-beaten track of female timidity. Your example may be pleaded by the rash, the thoughtless, and the wilful; and, therefore, may be pernicious. An angel, such as I think you, may run all risks with impunity, save those which may lead feeble minds to hazardous imitation.

"Is this language plain enough, this reasoning sufficiently sincere, to suit the character of a friend? And as such may I address you, without incurring displeasure? or, which is still, if possible, more painful to me, exciting alarm? O trust me, generously trust me, and be your ultimate decision what it may, you shall not repent your confidence!

"A. H."

This was not a letter to quiet the shaken nerves of Ellis, nor to restore to her the modulation of her voice. She read it with strong emotion, dwelling chiefly upon the phrase, "long-beaten track of female timidity."—Ah! she cried, delicacy is what he means, though he possesses too much himself to mark more strongly his opinion that I swerve from it! And in that shall I be wanting?—And what he thinks—he, the most liberal of men!—will surely be thought by all whose esteem, whose regard I most covet!—How dreadfully am I involved! in what misery of helplessness!—What is woman,—with the most upright designs, the most rigid circumspection,—what is woman unprotected? She is pronounced upon only from outward semblance:—and, indeed, what other criterion has the world? Can it read the heart?

Then, again perusing her letter, You, alone, O Harleigh! she cried, you, alone, escape the general contagion of superficial decision! Your own heart is the standard of your judgment; you consult that, and it tells you, that honour and purity may be in the breasts of others, however forlorn their condition, however mysterious their history, however dark, inexplicable, nay impervious, the latent motives of their conduct!—O generous Harleigh!—Abandoned as I seem—you alone—Tears rolled rapidly down her cheeks, and she lifted the letter up to her lips; but ere they touched it, started, shuddered, and cast it precipitately into the fire.

One of Miss Matson's young women now came to tell her, that Mr. Harleigh begged to know whether her commissions were prepared for London.

Hastily wiping her eyes, she answered that she had no commissions; but, upon raising her head, she saw the messenger descending the stairs, and Harleigh entering the room.

He apologised for hastening her, in a calm and formal style, palpably intended for the hearing of the young woman; but, upon shutting the door, and seeing the glistening eyes of Ellis, calmness and formality were at an end; and, approaching her with a tenderness which he could not resist, "You are afflicted?" he cried. "Why is it not permitted me to soothe the griefs it is impossible for me not to share? Why must I be denied offering even the most trivial assistance, where I would devote with eagerness my life?—You are unhappy,—you make me wretched, and you will neither bestow nor accept the consolation of sympathy? You see me resigned to sue only for your friendship:—why should you thus inflexibly withhold it? Is it—answer me sincerely!—is it my honour that you doubt?—"

He coloured, as if angry with himself even for the surmize; and Ellis raised her eyes, with a vivacity that reproached the question; but dropt them almost instantaneously.

"That generous look," he continued, "revives, re-assures me. From this moment, then, I will forego all pretensions beyond those of a friend. I am come to you completely with that intention. Madness, indeed,—but for the circumstances which robbed me of self-command,—madness alone could have formed any other, in an ignorance so profound as that in which I am held of all that belongs to propriety. Does not this confession shew you the reliance you may have upon the sincerity with which I mean to sustain my promised character? Will it not quiet your alarms? Will it not induce you to give me such a portion of your trust as may afford me some chance of being useful to you? Speak, I entreat; devise some service,—and you shall see, when a man is piqued upon being disinterested, how completely he can forget—seem to forget, at least!—all that would bring him back, exclusively, to himself.—Will you not, then, try me?"

Ellis, who had been silent to recover the steadiness of her voice, now quietly answered, "I am in no situation, Sir, for hazarding experiments. What you deem to be your own duties I have no doubt that you fulfil; you will the less, therefore, be surprised, that I decidedly adhere to what appear to me to be mine. Your visits, Sir, must cease: your letters I can never answer, and must not receive: we must have no intercourse whatever, partial nor general. Your friendship, nevertheless, if under that name you include good will and good wishes, I am far from desiring to relinquish:—but your kind offices—grateful to me, at this moment, as all kindness would be!"—she sighed, but hurried on; "those, in whatever form you can present them, I must utterly disclaim and repel. Pardon, Sir, this hard speech. I hold it right to be completely understood; and to be definitive."

Turning then, another way, she bid him good morning.

Harleigh, inexpressibly disappointed, stood, for some minutes, suspended whether resentfully to tear himself away, or importunately to solicit again her confidence. The hesitation, as usual where hesitation is indulged in matters of feeling, ended in directing him to follow his wishes; though he became more doubtful how to express them, and more fearful of offending or tormenting her. Yet in contrasting her desolate situation with her spirit and firmness, redoubled admiration took place of all displeasure. What, at first, appeared icy inflexibility, seemed, after a moment's pause, the pure effect of a noble disdain of trifling; a genuine superiority to coquetry. But doubly sad to him was the inference thence deduced. She cruelly wanted assistance; a sigh escaped her at the very thought of kindness; yet she rejected his most disinterested offers of aid; evidently in apprehension lest, at any future period, he might act, or think, as one who considered himself to be internally favoured.

Impressed with this idea, "I dare not," he gently began, "disobey commands so peremptory; yet—" He stopt abruptly, with a start that seemed the effect of sudden horrour. Ellis, again looking up, saw his colour changed, and that he was utterly disordered. His eyes directed her soon to the cause: the letter which she had cast into the fire, and from which, on his entrance, he had scrupulously turned his view, now accidentally caught it, by a fragment unburnt, which dropt from the stove upon the hearth. He immediately recognized his hand-writing.

This was a blow for which he was wholly unprepared. He had imagined that, whether she answered his letter or not, she would have weighed its contents, have guarded it for that purpose; perhaps have prized it! But, to see it condemned to annihilation; to find her inexorably resolute not to listen to his representations; nor, even in his absence, to endure in her sight what might bring either him or his opinions to her recollection; affected him so deeply, that, nearly unconscious what he was about, he threw himself upon a chair, exclaiming, "The illusion is past!"

Ellis, with gravity, but surprise, ejaculated, an interrogative, "Sir?"

"Pardon me," he cried, rising, and in great agitation; "pardon me that I have so long, and so frequently, intruded upon your patience! I begin, indeed, now, to perceive—but too well!—how I must have persecuted, have oppressed you. I feel my errour in its full force:—but that eternal enemy to our humility, our philosophy, our contentment in ill success, Hope,—or rather, perhaps, self-love,—had so dimmed my perceptions, so flattered my feelings, so loitered about my heart, that still I imagined, still I thought possible, that as a friend, at least, I might not find you unattainable; that my interest for your welfare, my concern for your difficulties, my irrepressible anxiety to diminish them, might have touched those cords whence esteem, whence good opinion vibrate; might have excited that confidence which, regulated by your own delicacy, your own scruples, might have formed the basis of that zealous, yet pure attachment, which is certainly the second blessing, and often the first balm of human existence,—permanent and blameless friendship!"

Ellis looked visibly touched and disturbed as she answered, "I am very sensible, Sir, of the honour you do me, and of the value of your approbation: it would not be easy to me, indeed, to say—unfriended, unsupported, nameless as I am!—how high a sense I feel of your generous judgment: but, as you pleaded to me just now," half smiling, "in one point, the customs of the world; you must not so far forget them in another, as not to acknowledge that a confidence, a friendship, such as you describe, with one so lonely, so unprotected, would oppose them utterly. I need only, I am sure, without comment, without argument, without insistance, call this idea to your recollection, to see you willingly relinquish an impracticable plan: to see you give up all visits; forego every species of correspondence, and hasten, yourself, to finish an intercourse which, in the eye of that world, and of those prejudices, those connections, to which you appeal, would be regarded as dangerous, if not injurious."

"What an inconceivable position!" cried Harleigh, passionately; "how incomprehensible a state of things! I must admire, must respect the decree that tortures me, though profoundly in the dark with regard to its motives, its purposes,—I had nearly said, its apologies! for not trifling must be the cause that can instigate such determined concealment, where an interest is excited so warm, so sincere, and, would you trust it, so honourable as mine!"

"You distress, you grieve me," cried Ellis, with an emotion which she could not repress, "by these affecting, yet fruitless conflicts! Could I speak .... can you think I would so perseveringly be silent?"

"I think, nay I am convinced, that you can do nothing but what is dictated by purity, what is intentionally right; yet here, I am persuaded, 'tis some right of exaggeration, some right stretched, by false reasoning, or undue influence, nearly to wrong. That the cause of the mystery which envelopes you is substantial, I have not any doubt; but surely the effects which you attribute to it must be chimerical. To reject the most trivial succour, to refuse the smallest communication—"

"You probe me, Sir, too painfully!—I appear, to you, I see, wilfully obstinate, and causelessly obscure: yet to be justified to you, I must incur a harsher censure from myself! Thus situated, we cannot separate too soon. Think over, I beg of you, when you are alone, all that has passed: your candour, I trust, will shew you, that my reserve has been too consistent in its practice, to be capricious in its motives. I can add nothing more. I entreat, I even supplicate you, to desist from all further enquiry; and to leave me!"

"In such utter, such impenetrable darkness?—With no period assigned?—not even any vague, any distant term in view, for letting in some little ray of light?—"

He spoke this in a tone so melancholy, yet so unopposingly respectful, that Ellis, resistlessly affected, put her hand to her head, and half, and almost unconsciously pronounced, "Were my destiny fixed ... known even to myself ..."

She stopt, but Harleigh, who, slowly, and by hard self-compulsion, had moved towards the door, sprang back, with a countenance wholly re-animated; and with eyes brightly sparkling, in the full lustre of hope and joy, exclaimed, "It is not, then, fixed?—your destiny—mine, rather! is still open to future events?—O say that again! tell me but that my condemnation is not irrevocable, and I will not ask another word!—I will not persecute you another minute!—I will be all patience, all endurance;—if there be barely some possibility that I have not seen and admired only to regret you!—that I have not known and appreciated—merely to lose you!"

"You astonish, you affright me, Sir!" cried Ellis, recovering a dignity that nearly amounted to severity: "if any thing has dropt from me that can have given rise to expressions—deductions of this nature, I beg leave, immediately, to explain that I have been utterly misunderstood. I see however, too clearly, the danger of such contests to risk their repetition. Permit me, therefore, unequivocally, to declare, that here they end! I have courage to act, though I have no power to command. You, Sir, must decide, whether you will have the kindness to quit my apartment immediately;—or whether you will force me to so unpleasant a measure as that of quitting it myself. The kindness, I say; for however ill my situation accords with the painful perseverance of your . . . . investigations . . . my memory must no longer 'hold its seat,'* when I lose the impression I have received of your humanity, your goodness, your generosity! . . . You will leave me, Mr. Harleigh, I am sure!"

Harleigh, as much soothed by these last words, as he was shocked by all that had preceded them, silently bowed; and, unable, with a good grace, to acquiesce in a determination which he was yet less entitled to resist, slowly, sadly, and speechless, with concentrated feelings, left the room.

"All good betide you, Sir!—and may every blessing be yours!"—in a voice of attempted cheerfulness, but involuntary tremour, was pronounced by Ellis, as, hastily rising, she herself shut the door.

CHAPTER XXXVII

THE few, but precious words, that marked, in parting, a sensibility that he had vainly sought to excite while remaining, bounded to the heart of Harleigh; but were denied all acknowledgement from his lips, by the sight of Miss Bydel and Mr. Giles Arbe, who were mounting the stairs.

Miss Bydel tapt at the door of Ellis; and Harleigh, ill as he felt fitted for joining any company, persuaded himself that immediately to retreat, might awaken yet more surmize, than, for a few passing minutes, to re-enter the room.

He looked at Ellis, in taking this measure, and saw that, while she struggled to receive her visitors with calm civility, her air of impatience for his departure was changed, by this surprize, into confusion at his presence.

He felt culpable for occasioning her so uneasy a sensation; and, to repair it as much as might be in his power, assumed a disengaged countenance, and treated as a mark of good fortune, having chanced to enquire whether Miss Ellis had any commands for town, at the same time that Miss Bydel and Mr. Giles Arbe made their visit.

"Why we are come, Mrs. Ellis," said Miss Bydel, "to know the real reason of your not being at the rehearsal this morning. Pray what is it? Not a soul could tell it me, though I asked every body all round. So I should be glad to hear the truth from yourself. Was it real illness, now? or only a pretext?"

"Illness," cried Mr. Giles, "with all those roses on her cheeks? No, no; she's very well; as well as very pretty. But you should not tell stories, my dear: though I am heartily glad to see that there's nothing the matter. But it's a bad habit. Though it's convenient enough, sometimes. But when you don't like to do a thing, why not say so at once? People mayn't be pleased, to be sure, when they are refused; but do you think them so ill natured, as to like better to hear that you are ill?"

Ellis, abashed, attempted no defence; and Harleigh addressed some discourse to Miss Bydel, upon the next day's concert; while Mr. Giles went on with his own idea.

"We should always honestly confess our likings and dislikings, for else what have we got them for? If every one of us had the same taste, half the things about us would be of no service; and we should scramble till we came to scratches for t'other half. But the world has no more business, my dear, lady, to be all of one mind, than all of one body."

"O now, pray Mr. Giles," cried Miss Bydel, "don't go beginning your comical talk; for if once you do that, one can't get in a word."

"But, for all that, we should all round try to help and be kind to one another; what else are we put all together for in this world? We might, just as well, each of us have been popt upon some separate bit of a planet, one by himself one. All I recommend, is, to tell truth, or to say nothing. We whip poor pretty children for telling stories, when they are little, and yet hardly speak a word, without some false turn or other, ourselves, when we grow big!"

"Well, but, Mr. Giles," said Miss Bydel, "where's the use of talking so long about all that, when I'm wanting to ask Mrs. Ellis why she did not come to the rehearsal?"

"For my own part, Ma'am," continued Mr. Giles, "if any body puts me to a difficulty, I do the best I can: but I'd rather do the worst than tell a fib. So when I am asked an awkward question, which some people can't cure themselves of doing, out of an over curiosity in their nature, as, Giles, how do you like Miss such a one? or Mr. such a one? or Mrs. such a one? as Miss Bydel, for instance, if she came into any body's head; or——"

"Nay, Mr. Giles," interrupted Miss Bydel, "I don't see why I should not come into a person's head as well as another; so I don't know what you say that for. But if that's your notion of being so kind one to another, Mr. Giles, I can't pretend to say it's mine; for I see no kindness in it."

"I protest, Ma'am, I did not think of you in the least!" cried Mr. Giles, much out of countenance: "I only took your name because happening to stand just before you put it, I suppose, at my tongue's end; but you were not once in my thoughts, I can assure you, Ma'am, upon my word of honour! No more than if you had never existed, I protest!"

Miss Bydel, neither accepting nor repelling this apology, said, that she did not come to talk of things of that sort, but to settle some business of more importance. Then, turning to Ellis, "I hear," she continued, "Mrs. Ellis, that all of the sudden, you are grown very rich. And I should be glad to know if it's true? and how it has happened?"

"I should be still more glad, Madam," answered Ellis, "to be able to give you the information!"

"Nay, Mrs. Ellis, I had it from your friend, Mr. Giles, who is always the person to be telling something or other to your advantage. So if there be any fault in the account, it's him you are to call upon, not me."

Mr. Giles, drawn by the silence of Ellis to a view of her embarrassment, became fearful that he had been indiscreet, and made signs to Miss Bydel to say no more upon the subject; but Miss Bydel, by no means disposed, at this moment, to oblige him, went on.

"Nay, Mr. Giles, you know, as well as I do, 'twas your own news. Did not you tell us all, just now, at the rehearsal, when Miss Brinville and Miss Sycamore were saying what a monstrous air they thought it, for a person that nobody knew any thing of, to send excuses about being indisposed; just as if she were a fine lady; or some famous singer, that might be as troublesome as she would; did you not tell us, I say, that Mrs. Ellis deserved as much respect as any of us, on account of her good character, and more than any of us on account of her prettiness and her poverty? Because her prettiness, says you, tempts others, and her poverty tempts herself; and yet she is just as virtuous as if she were as rich and as ordinary as any one of the greatest consequence amongst you. These were your own words, Mr. Giles."

Harleigh, who, conscious that he ought to go, had long held by the lock of the door, as if departing, could not now refrain from changing the position of his hand, by placing it, expressively, upon the arm of Mr. Giles.

"And if all this," Miss Bydel continued, "is not enough to make you respect her, says you, why respect her for the same thing that makes you respect one another, her money. And when we all asked how she could be poor, and have money too, you said that you had yourself seen ever so many bank-notes upon her table."

Ellis coloured; but not so painfully as Harleigh, at the sight of her blushes, unattended by any refutation; or any answer to this extraordinary assertion.

"And then, Mr. Giles, as you very well know, when I asked, If she has money, why don't she pay her debts? you replied, that she had paid them all. Upon which I said, I should be glad to know, then, why I was to be the only person left out, just only for my complaisance in waiting so long? and upon that I resolved to come myself, and see how the matter stood. For though I have served you with such good will, Mrs. Ellis, while I thought you poor, I must be a fool to be kept out of my money, when I know you have got it in plenty: and Mr. Giles says that he counted, with his own hands, ten ten-pound bank-notes. Now I should be glad, if you have no objection, to hear how you came by all that money, Mrs. Ellis; for ten ten-pound bank-notes make a hundred pounds."

Oh! absent—unguarded—dangerous Mr. Giles Arbe! thought Ellis, how much benevolence do you mar, by a distraction of mind that leads to so much mischief!

"I hope I have done nothing improper?" cried Mr. Giles, perceiving, with concern, the disturbance of Ellis, "in mentioning this; for I protest I never recollected, till this very minute, that the money is not your own. It slipt my memory, somehow, entirely."

"Nay, nay, how will you make that out, Mr. Giles?" cried Miss Bydel. "If it were not her own, how came she to pay her tradesmen with it, as you told us that she did, Mr. Giles?"

Ellis, in the deepest embarrassment, knew not which way to turn her head.

"She paid them, Miss Bydel," said Mr. Giles, "because she is too just, as well as too charitable, to let honest people want, only because they have the good nature to keep her from wanting herself; while she has such large sums, belonging to a rich friend, lying quite useless, in a bit of paper, by her side. For the money was left with her by a very rich friend, she told me herself."

"No, Sir,—no, Mr. Giles," cried Ellis, hastily, and looking every way to avoid the anxious, enquiring, quick-glancing eyes of Harleigh: "I did not . . . I could not say . . ." she stopt, scarcely knowing what she meant either to deny or to affirm.

"Yes, yes, 'twas a rich friend, my dear lady, you owned that. If you had not given me that assurance, I should not have urged you to make use of it. Besides, who but a rich friend would leave you money in such a way as that, neither locked, nor tied, nor in a box, nor in a parcel; but only in a little paper cover, directed For Miss Ellis, at her leisure?"

At these words, which could leave no doubt upon the mind of Harleigh, that the money in question was his own; and that that money, so often refused, had finally been employed in the payment of her debts, Ellis involuntarily, irresistibly, but most fearfully, stole a hasty glance at him; with a transient hope that they might have escaped his attention; but the hope died in its birth: the words, in their fullest meaning, had reached him, and the sensation which they produced filled her with poignant shame. A joy beamed in his countenance that irradiated every feature; a joy that flushed him into an excess of rapture, of which the consciousness seemed to abash himself; and his eyes bent instantly to the ground. But their checked vivacity checked not the feelings which illumined them, nor the alarm which they excited, when Ellis, urged by affright to snatch a second look, saw the brilliancy with which they had at first sought her own, terminate in a sensibility more touching; saw that they glistened with a tender pleasure, which, to her alarmed imagination, represented the potent and dangerous inferences that enchanted his mind, at a discovery that he had thus essentially succoured her; and that she had accepted, at last, however secretly, his succour.

This view of new danger to her sense of independence, called forth new courage, and restored an appearance of composure; and, addressing herself to Miss Bydel, "I entreat you," she cried, "Madam, to bear a little longer with my delay. To-morrow I shall enter upon a new career, from the result of which I hope speedily to acknowledge my obligation to your patience; and to acquit myself to all those to whom I am in any manner, pecuniarily obliged;—except of the lighter though far more lasting debt of gratitude."

Harleigh understood her determined perseverance with cruel disappointment, yet with augmented admiration of her spirited delicacy; and, sensible of the utter impropriety of even an apparent resistance to her resolution in public, he faintly expressed his concern that she had no letters prepared for town, and with a deep, but stifled sigh, took leave.

Miss Bydel continued her interrogations, but without effect; and soon, therefore, followed. Mr. Giles remained longer; not because he obtained more satisfaction, but because, when not answered, he was contented with talking to himself.

The rest of the day was passed free from outward disturbance to Ellis; and what she might experience internally was undivulged.

CHAPTER XXXVIII

THE day now arrived which Ellis reluctantly, yet firmly, destined for her new, and hazardous essay. Resolute in her plan, she felt the extreme importance of attaining courage and calmness for its execution. She shut herself up in her apartment, and gave the most positive injunctions to the milliners, that no one should be admitted. The looks of Harleigh, as he had quitted her room, had told her that this precaution would not be superfluous; and, accordingly, he came; but was refused entrance: he wrote; but his letters were returned unread. His efforts to break, served but to fix her purpose: she saw the expectations that he would feed from any concession; and potent as had hitherto been her objections to the scheme, they all subsided, in preference to exciting, or passively permitting, any doubts of the steadiness of her rejection.

Still, however, she could not practise: her voice and her fingers were infected by the agitation of her mind, and she could neither sing nor play. She could only hope that, at the moment of performance, the positive necessity of exertion, would bring with it, as so often is its effect, the powers which it requires.

The tardiness of her resolution caused, however, such an accumulation of business, not only for her thoughts, but for her time, from the indispensable arrangements of her attire, that scarcely a moment remained either for the relief or the anxieties of rumination. She set off, therefore, with tolerable though forced composure, for the rooms, in the carriage of Miss Arbe; that lady, once again, chusing to assume the character of her patroness, since as such she could claim the merit of introducing her to the public, through an obligation to her own new favourite, M. Vinstreigle.

Upon stopping at the hôtel,* in which the concert was to be held, a strange figure, with something foreign in his appearance, twice crossed before the chariot, with a menacing air, as if purposing to impede her passage. Easily startled, she feared descending from the carriage; when Harleigh, who was watching, though dreading her arrival, came in sight, and offered her his hand. She declined it; but, seeing the intruder retreat abruptly, into the surrounding crowd of spectators, she alighted and entered the hôtel.

Pained, at once, and charmed by the striking elegance of her appearance, and the air of gentle dignity which shewed such attire to be familiar to her, Harleigh felt irresistibly attracted to follow her, and once more plead his cause. "Hear, hear me!" he cried, in a low, but touching voice: "one moment hear me, I supplicate, I conjure you! still it is not too late to avert this blow! Indisposition cannot be disputed; or, if doubted, of what moment would be the suspicion, if once, generously, trustingly, you relinquish this cruel plan?"

He spoke in a whisper, yet with an impetuosity that alarmed, as much as his distress affected her; but when she turned towards him, to call upon his forbearance, she perceived immediately at his side, the person who had already disconcerted her. She drew hastily back, and he brushed quickly past, looking round, nevertheless, and evidently and anxiously marking her. Startled, uneasy, she involuntarily stopt; but was relieved by the approach of one of the door-keepers, to the person in question; who haughtily flung at him a ticket, and was passing on; but who was told that he could not enter the concert-room in a slouched hat.*

A sort of attendant, or humble friend, who accompanied him, then said, in broken English, That the poor gentleman only came to divert himself, by seeing the company, and would disturb nobody, for he was deaf and dumb, and very inoffensive.

Re-assured by this account, Ellis again advanced, and was met by Mr. Vinstreigle; who had given instructions to be called upon her arrival, and who, now, telling her that it was late, and that the concert was immediately to be opened, handed her to the orchestra. She insisted upon seating herself behind a violencello-player, and as much out of sight as possible, till necessity must, of course, bring her forward.

From her dislike to being seen, her eyes seemed rivetted upon the music-paper which she held in her hand, but of which, far from studying the characters, she could not read a note. She received, with silent civility, the compliments of M. Vinstreigle; and those of his band, who could approach her; but her calmness, and what she had thought her determined courage, had been so shaken by personal alarm, and by the agitated supplications of Harleigh, that she could recover them no more. His desponding look, when he found her inexorable, pursued her; and the foreign clothing, and foreign servant, of the man who, though deaf and dumb, had so marked and fixt her, rested upon her imagination, with a thousand vague fears and conjectures.

In this shattered state of nerves, the sound of many instruments, loud however harmonious, so immediately close to her ears, made her start, as if electrified, when the full band struck up the overture, and involuntarily raise her eyes. The strong lights dazzled them; yet prevented her not from perceiving, that the deaf and dumb man had planted himself exactly opposite to the place, which, by the disposition of the harp, was evidently prepared for her reception. Her alarm augmented: was he watching her from mere common curiosity? or had he any latent motive, or purpose? His dress and figure were equally remarkable. He was wrapt in a large scarlet coat, which hung loosely over his shoulders, and was open at the breast, to display a brilliant waistcoat of coloured and spangled embroidery.* He had a small, but slouched hat, which he had refused to take off, that covered his forehead and eye-brows, and shaded his eyes; and a cravat* of enormous bulk encircled his chin, and enveloped not alone his ears, but his mouth. Nothing was visible but his nose, which was singularly long and pointed. The whole of his habiliment seemed of foreign manufacture;* but his air had something in it that was wild, and uncouth; and his head was continually in motion.

To the trembling Ellis, it now seemed but a moment before she was summoned to her place, though four pieces were first performed. M. Vinstreigle would have handed her down the steps; she declined his aid, hoping to pass less observed alone; but the moment that she rose, and became visible, a violent clapping was begun by Sir Lyell Sycamore, and seconded by every man present.

What is new, of almost any description, is sure to be well received by the public; but when novelty is united with peculiar attractions, admiration becomes enthusiasm, and applause is nearly clamour. Such, upon the beholders, was the effect produced by the beauty, the youth, the elegance, and the timidity of Ellis. Even her attire, which, from the bright pink sarsenet, purchased by Miss Arbe, she had changed into plain white satin, with ornaments of which the simplicity shewed as much taste as modesty, contributed to the interest which she inspired. It was suited to the style of her beauty, which was Grecian;* and it seemed equally to assimilate with the character of her mind, to those who, judging it from the fine expression of her countenance, conceived it to be pure and noble. The assembly appeared with one opinion to admire her, and with one wish to give her encouragement.

But, unused to being an object of tumultuous delight, the effect produced by such transports was the reverse of their intention; and Ellis, ashamed, embarrassed, confused, lost the recollection, that custom demanded that she should postpone her acknowledgements till she arrived at her post. She stopt; but in raising her eyes, as she attempted to courtesy, she was struck with the sight of her deaf and dumb tormentor; who, in agitated watchfulness, was standing up to see her descend; and whose face, from the full light to which he was exposed, she now saw to be masked; while she discerned in his hand, the glitter of steel. An horrible surmise occurred, that it was Elinor disguised, and Elinor come to perpetrate the bloody deed of suicide. Agonized with terrour at the idea, she would have uttered a cry; but, shaken and dismayed, her voice refused to obey her; her eyes became dim; her tottering feet would no longer support her; her complexion wore the pallid hue of death, and she sunk motionless on the floor.

In an instant, all admiring acclamation subsided into tender pity, and not a sound was heard in the assembly; while in the orchestra all was commotion; for Harleigh no sooner saw the fall, and that the whole band was in movement, to offer aid, than, springing from his place, he overcame every obstacle, to force a passage to the spot where the pale Ellis was lying. There, with an air of command, that seemed the offspring of rightful authority, he charged every one to stand back, and give her air; desired M. Vinstreigle to summon some female to her aid; and, snatching from him a phial of salts,* which he was attempting to administer, was gently bending down with them himself, when he perceived that she was already reviving: but the instant that he had raised her, what was his consternation and horrour, to hear a voice, from the assembly, call out: "Turn, Harleigh, turn! and see thy willing martyr!—Behold, perfidious Ellis! behold thy victim!"

Instantly, though with agony, he quitted the sinking Ellis to dart forward.

The large wrapping coat, the half mask, the slouched hat, and embroidered waistcoat, had rapidly been thrown aside, and Elinor appeared in deep mourning; her long hair, wholly unornamented, hanging loosely down her shoulders. Her complexion was wan, her eyes were fierce rather than bright, and her air was wild and menacing.

"Oh Harleigh!—adored Harleigh!—" she cried, as he flew to catch her desperate hand;—but he was not in time; for, in uttering his name, she plunged a dagger into her breast.

The blood gushed out in torrents, while, with a smile of triumph, and eyes of idolizing love, she dropt into his arms, and clinging round him, feebly articulated, "Here let me end!—accept the oblation—the just tribute—of these dear, delicious, last moments!"

Almost petrified with horrour, he could with difficulty support either her or himself; yet his presence of mind was sooner useful than that of any of the company; the ladies of which were hiding their faces, or running away; and the men, though all eagerly crowding to the spot of this tremendous event, approaching rather as spectators of some public exhibition, than as actors in a scene of humanity. Harleigh called upon them to fly instantly for a surgeon;* demanded an arm-chair for the bleeding Elinor, and earnestly charged some of the ladies to come to her aid.

Selina, who had made one continued scream resound through the apartment, from the moment that her sister discovered herself, rapidly obeyed the summons, with Ireton, who, being unable to detain, accompanied her. Mrs. Maple, thunderstruck by the apparition of her niece, scandalized by her disguise, and wholly unsuspicious of her purpose, though sure of some extravagance, had pretended sudden indisposition, to escape the shame of witnessing her disgrace; but ere she could get away, the wound was inflicted, and the public voice, which alone she valued, forced her to return.

A surgeon of eminence, who was accidentally in the assembly, desired the company to make way; declaring no removal to be practicable, till he should have stopt the effusion of blood.

The concert was immediately broken up; the assembly, though curious and unwilling, dispersed; and the apparatus for dressing the wound, was speedily at hand:—but to no purpose. Elinor would not suffer the approach of the surgeon; would not hear of any operation, or examination; would not receive any assistance. Looks of fiery disdain were the only answers that she bestowed to the pleadings of Mrs. Maple, the shrieks of Selina, the remonstrances of the surgeon, and the entreaties of every other. Even to the supplications of Harleigh she was immovable; though still she fondly clung to him, uttering from time to time, "Long—long wished for moment! welcome, thrice welcome to my wearied soul!"

The shock of Harleigh was unspeakable; and it was aggravated by almost indignant exhortations, ejaculated from nearly every person present, that he would snatch the self-devoted enthusiast* from this untimely end, by returning her heroic tenderness.

Mrs. Maple was now covered with shame, from apprehension that this conduct might be imputed either to any precepts or any neglect of her own. "My poor niece is quite light-headed, Mr. Harleigh," she cried, "and knows not what she says."

Fury started into the eyes of Elinor as she caught these words, and neither prayers nor supplications could silence or quiet her. "No, Mrs. Maple, no!" she cried, "I am not light-headed! I never so perfectly knew what I said, for I never so perfectly spoke what I thought. Is it not time, even yet, to have done with the puerile trammels of prejudice?—Yes! I here cast them to the winds! And, in the dauntless hour of willing death, I proclaim my sovereign contempt of the whole race of mankind! of its cowardly subterfuges, its mean assimilations, its heartless subtleties! Here, in the sublime act of voluntary self-extinction, I exult to declare my adoration of thee,—of thee alone, Albert Harleigh! of thee and of thy haughty,—matchless virtues!"

Gasping for breath, she leant, half motionless, yet smiling, and with looks of transport, upon the shoulder of Harleigh; who, ashamed, in the midst of his concern, at his own situation, thus publicly avowed as the object of this desperate act; earnestly wished to retreat from the gazers and remarkers, with whom he shared the notice and the wonder excited by Elinor. But her danger was too eminent, and the scene was too critical, to suffer self to predominate. Gently, therefore, and with tenderness, he continued to support her; carefully forbearing either to irritate her enthusiasm, or to excite her spirit of controversy, by uttering, at such a crisis, the exhortations to which his mind and his principles pointed: or even to soothe her feelings too tenderly, lest misrepresentation should be mischievous, either with herself or with others.

The surgeon declared that, if the wound were not dressed without delay, no human efforts could save her life.

"My life? save my life?" cried Elinor, reviving from indignation: "Do you believe me so ignoble, as to come hither to display the ensigns of death, but as scare crows, to frighten lookers on to court me to life? No! for what should I live? To see the hand of scorn* point at me? No, no, no! I come to die: I bleed to die; and now, even now, I talk to die! to die—Oh Albert Harleigh! for thee!—Dost thou sigh, Harleigh?—Do I hear thee sigh?—Oh Harleigh! generous Harleigh!—for me is it thou sighest?—"

Deeply oppressed, "Elinor," he answered, "you make me indeed wretched!"

"Ebb out, then, oh life!" cried she, "in this extatic moment! Harleigh no longer is utterly insensible!—Well have I followed my heart's beating impulse!—Harleigh! Oh noble Harleigh!—"

Spent by speech and loss of blood, she fainted.

Harleigh eagerly whispered Mrs. Maple, to desire that the surgeon would snatch this opportunity for examining, and, if possible, dressing the wound.

This, accordingly, was done, all who were not of some use, retiring.

Harleigh himself, deeply interested in the event, only retreated to a distant corner; held back by discretion, honour, and delicacy, from approaching the spot to which his wishes tended.

The surgeon pronounced, that the wound was not in its nature mortal; though the exertions and emotions which had succeeded it, gave it a character of danger, that demanded the extremest attention, and most perfect tranquillity.

The satisfaction with which Harleigh heard the first part of this sentence, though it could not be counterbalanced, was cruelly checked by its conclusion. He severely felt the part that he seemed called upon to act; and had a consciousness, that was dreadful to himself, of his power, if upon her tranquillity alone depended her preservation.

She soon recovered from her fainting fit; though she was too much weakened and exhausted, both in body and spirits, to be as soon restored to her native energies. The moment, therefore, seemed favourable for her removal: but whither? Lewes was too distant; Mrs. Maple, therefore, was obliged to apply for a lodging in the hôtel; to which, with the assiduous aid of Harleigh, Elinor, after innumerable difficulties, and nearly by force, was conveyed.

The last to quit the apartment in which this bloody scene had been performed, was Ellis; who felt restored by fright for another, to the strength of which she had been robbed by affright for herself. Her sufferings, indeed, for Elinor, her grief, her horrour, had set self wholly aside, and made her forget all by which, but the moment before, she had been completely absorbed. She durst not approach, yet could not endure to retreat. She remained alone in the orchestra, from which all the band had been dismissed. She looked not once at Harleigh; nor did Harleigh once dare turn her way. In the shock of this scene, she thought it would be her duty to see him no more; for though she was unassailed by remorse, since unimpeached by self-reproach—for when had she wilfully, or even negligently, excited jealousy?—still she could not escape the inexpressible shock, of knowing herself the cause, though not, like Harleigh, the object of this dreadful deed.

When Elinor, however, was gone, she desired to hurry to her lodgings. Miss Arbe had forgotten, or neglected her, and she had no carriage ordered. But the terrific magnitude of the recent event, divested minor difficulties of their usual powers of giving disturbance. 'Tis only when we are spared great calamities, that we are deeply affected by small circumstances. The pressing around her, whether of avowed, or discreet admirers; the buzz of mingled compliments, propositions, interrogatories or entreaties; which, at another time, would have embarrassed and distressed her, now scarcely reached her ears, and found no place in her attention; and she quietly applied for a maid-servant of the hôtel; leaning upon whose arm she reached, sad, shaken, and agitated, the house of Miss Matson.

Before she would even attempt to go to rest, she sent a note of enquiry to Mr. Naird, the surgeon, whom she had seen at Mrs. Maple's: his answer was consonant to what he had already pronounced to Harleigh.

CHAPTER XXXIX

NOTHING now appeared so urgent to Ellis, as flying the fatal sight of Harleigh. To wander again alone, to seek strange succour, new faces, and unknown haunts; to expose her helplessness, plead her poverty, and confess her mysterious, nameless situation; even to risk delay in receiving the letter upon which hung all her ultimate expectations, seemed preferable to the danger of another interview, that might lead to the most horrible of catastrophes;—if, already, the danger were not removed by a termination the most tragic.

To escape privately from Brighthelmstone, and commit to accident, since she had no motive for choice, the way that she should go, was, therefore, her determination. Her debts were all paid, save what their discharge had made her incur with that very Harleigh from whom she must now escape; though to the resources which he had placed in her hands, she owed the liberation from her creditors, that gave her power to be gone; and must owe, also, the means for the very flight which she projected from himself. Severely she felt the almost culpability of an action, that risked implications of encouragement to a persevering though rejected man. But the horrour of instigating self-murder conquered every other; even the hard necessity of appearing to act wrong, at the very moment when she was braving every evil, in the belief that she was doing right.

She ordered a post-chaise, in which she resolved to go one stage;* and then to wait at some decent house upon the road, for the first passing public vehicle; in which, whithersoever it might be destined, she would proceed.

At an early hour the chaise was ready; and she was finishing her preparations for removal, when a tap at her chamber-door, to which, imagining it given by the maid, she answered, "Come in," presented Harleigh to her affrighted view.

"Ah heaven!" she cried, turning pale with dismay, "are you then fixed, Mr. Harleigh, to rob me of peace for life?"

"Be not," cried he, rapidly, "alarmed! I will not cost you a moment's danger, and hardly a moment's uneasiness. A few words will remove every fear; but I must speak them myself. Elinor is at this instant out of all but wilful danger; wilful danger, however, being all that she has had to encounter, it must be guarded against as sedulously as if it were inevitable. To this end, I must leave Brighthelmstone immediately—"

"No, Sir," interrupted Ellis; "it is I who must leave Brighthelmstone; your going would be the height of inhumanity."

"Pardon me, but it is to clear this mistake that, once more, I force myself into your sight. I divined your design when I saw an empty post-chaise drive up to your door; which else, at a time such as this, I should unobtrusively have passed."

"Quick! quick!" cried Ellis, "every moment affrights me!"

"I am gone. I cannot oppose, for I partake your fears. Elinor has demanded to see us together to-morrow morning."

"Terrible!" cried Ellis, trembling; "what may be her design? And what is there not to dread! Indeed I dare not encounter her!"

"There can be, unhappily, but one opinion of her purpose," he answered: "She is wretched, and from impatience of life, wishes to seek death. Nevertheless, the cause of her disgust to existence not being any intolerable calamity, though the most probing, perhaps, of disappointments, life, with all its evils, still clings to her; and she as little knows how to get rid of, as how to support it."

"You cannot, Sir, mean to doubt her sincerity?"

"Far from it. Her mind is as noble as her humour and taste are flighty; yet, where she has some great end in view, she studies, in common with all those with whom the love of fame is the ruling passion,* Effect, public Effect, rather than what she either thinks to be right, or feels to be desirable."

"Alas, poor Miss Joddrel! You are still, then, Sir, unmoved—" She stopt, and blushed, for the examining eyes of Harleigh said, "Do you wish to see me conquered?"

Pleased that she stopt, enchanted that she blushed, an expression of pleasure illumined his countenance, which instantly drew into that of Ellis a cold severity, that chilled, or rather that punished his rising transport. Ah! thought he, was it then but conscious modesty, not anxious doubt, that mantled in her cheek?

"Pity," he returned, "in a woman to a man, is grateful, is lenient, is consoling. It seems an attribute of her sex, and the haughtiest of ours accepts it from her without disdain or disgrace; but pity from a man—upon similar causes—must be confined to his own breast. It's expression always seems insolent. Who is the female that could wish, that could even bear to excite it? Not Elinor, certainly! with all her excentricities, she would consider it as an outrage."

"Give it her, then," cried Ellis, with involuntary vivacity, "the sooner to cure her!"

"Nay, who knows," he smilingly returned, "since extremes meet, that absconding may not produce the same effect? At all events, it will retard the execution of her terrible project; and to retard an act of voluntary violence, where the imagination is as ardent, the mind as restless, and the will as despotic as those of Elinor, is commonly to avert it. Some new idea ordinarily succeeds, and the old one, in losing its first moment of effervescence, generally evaporates in disgust."

"Do not, Sir, trust to this! do not be so cruel as to abandon her! Think of the desperation into which you will cast her; and if you scruple to avow your pity, act at least with humanity, in watching, soothing, and appeasing her, while you suffer me quietly to escape; that neither the sound, nor the thought, of my existing so near her, may produce fresh irritation."

"I see,—I feel,—" cried he, with emotion, "how amiable for her,—yet how barbarous for me,—is your recommendation of a conduct, that, if pursued, must almost inevitably involve my honour, from regard to her reputation, in a union to which every word that you utter, and every idea to which you give expression, make me more and more averse!—"

Ellis blushed and paused; but presently, with strengthened resolution, earnestly cried, "If this, Sir, is the sum of what you have to say, leave me, I entreat, without further procrastination! Every moment that you persist in staying presents to me the image of Miss Joddrel, breaking from her physicians, and darting, bloody and dying, into the room to surprize you!"

"Pardon, pardon me, that I should have given birth to so dreadful an apprehension! I will relieve you this instant: and omit no possible precaution to avert every danger. But the least reflexion, to a mind delicate as yours, will exculpate me from blame in not remaining at her side,—after the scene of last night,—unless I purposed to become her permanent guardian. The tattling world would instantly unite—or calumniate us. But you, who, if you retreat, will be doubted and suspected, You, must, at present, stay, and openly, clearly, and unsought, be seen. Elinor, who breathes but to spur her misery by despair, that she may end it, reserves for me, and for my presence,—to astonish, to shock, or to vanquish me,—every horrour she can devise. In my absence, rest assured, no evil will be perpetrated. 'Tis for her, then, for her sake, that you must remain, and that I must depart."

Ellis could not contest a statement which, thus explained, appeared to be just; and, gratified by her concurrence, he no longer resisted her urgent injunctions that he would be gone. He tried, in quitting her, to seize and kiss her hand; but she drew back, with an air not to be disputed; and a look of reproach, though not of displeasure. He submitted, with a look, also, of reproach; though expressive, at the same time, of reverence and admiration mixt with the deepest regret.

Mechanically, rather than intentionally, she went to the window, when he had left her, whence she saw him cross the way, and then wistfully look up. She felt the most painful blushes mount into her cheeks, upon observing that he perceived her. She retreated like lightning; yet could not escape remarking the animated pleasure that beamed from his countenance at this surprise.

She sat down, deeply confused, and wept.

The postilion sent in the maid for orders.

She satisfied and discharged him; and then, endeavouring to dismiss all rumination upon the past, deliberated upon the course which she ought immediately to pursue.

Her musical plan once more became utterly hopeless; for what chance had she now of any private scholars? what probability of obtaining any new protection, when, to the other mysterious disadvantages under which she laboured, would be added an accusation of perjury, denounced at the horrible moment of self-destruction?

While suggesting innumerable new schemes, which, presented by desperation, died in projection, she observed a small packet upon the ground, directed to herself. The inside was sealed, but upon the cover she found these words:

"This packet was prepared to reach you by an unknown messenger; but I see that you are departing, and I must not risk its missing you. As a friend only, a disinterested, though a zealous one, I have promised to address you. Repel not, then, my efforts towards acquiescence, by withholding the confidence, and rejecting the little offices, which should form the basis of that friendship. 'Tis as your banker, only, that I presume to enclose these notes. "A. H."

Ellis concluded that, upon seeing the chaise at the door, he had entered some shop to write these lines.

The silence which she had guarded, relative to his former packet, from terrour of the conflicts to which such a subject might lead, had made him now, she imagined, suppose it not partially but completely expended. And can he think, she cried, that not alone I have had recourse,—unacknowledged, yet essential recourse,—to his generosity in my distress, but that I am contented to continue his pensioner?

She blushed; but not in anger: she felt that it was from his view of her situation, not his notions of her character, that he pressed her thus to pecuniary obligation. She would not, however, even see the amount, or contents, of what he had sealed up, which she now enclosed, and sealed up herself, with the remaining notes of the first packet.

The lines which he had written in the cover, she read a second time. If, indeed, she cried, he could become a disinterested friend! . . . She was going to read them again, but checked by the suggested doubt,—the if,—she paused a moment, sighed, felt herself blush, and, with a quick motion that seemed the effect of sudden impulse, precipitately destroyed them; murmuring to herself, while brushing off with her hand a starting tear, that she would lose no time and spare no exertions, for replacing and returning the whole sum.

Yet she was forced, with whatever reluctance, to leave the development of her intentions to the chances of opportunity; for she knew not the address of Harleigh, and durst not risk the many dangers that might attend any enquiry.

A short time afterwards, she received a letter from Selina, containing a summons from Elinor for the next morning.

Mr. Naird, the surgeon, had induced Mrs. Maple to consent to this measure, which alone deterred Elinor from tearing open her wound; and which had extorted from her a promise, that she would remain quiet in the interval. She had positively refused to admit a clergyman; and had affronted away a physician.

Ellis could not hesitate to comply with this demand, however terrified she felt at the prospect of the storm which she might have to encounter.

The desperate state of her own affairs, called, nevertheless, for immediate attention; and she decided to begin a new arrangement, by relinquishing the far too expensive apartment which Miss Arbe had forced her to occupy.

In descending to the shop, to give notice of her intention, she heard the voice of Miss Matson, uttering some sharp reprimand; and presently, and precipitately, she was passed, upon the stairs, by a forlorn, ill-dressed, and weeping female; whose face was covered by her handkerchief, but whose air was so conspicuously superiour to her garb of poverty, that it was evidently a habit of casual distress, not of habitual indigence. Ellis looked after her with quick-awakened interest; but she hastily mounted, palpably anxious to escape remark.

Miss Matson, softened in her manners since she had been paid, expressed the most violent regret, at losing so genteel a lodger. Ellis knew well how to appreciate her interested* and wavering civility; yet availed herself of it to beg a recommendation to some decent house, where she might have a small and cheap chamber; and again, to solicit her assistance in procuring some needle-work.

A room, Miss Matson replied, with immediate abatement of complaisance, of so shabby a sort as that, might easily enough be found; but as to needle-work, all that she had had to dispose of for some time past, had been given to her new lodger up two pair of stairs, who had succeeded Mr. Riley; and who did it quicker and cheaper than any body; which, indeed, she had need do, for she was extremely troublesome, and always wanting her money.

"And for what else, Miss Matson," said Ellis, dryly, "can you imagine she gives you her work?"

"Nay, I don't say any thing as to that," answered Miss Matson, surprised by the question: "I only know it's sometimes very inconvenient."

Ah! thought Ellis, must we be creditors, and poor creditors, ourselves, to teach us justice to debtors? And must those who endure the toil be denied the reward, that those who reap its fruits may retain it?

Miss Matson accepted the warning, and Ellis resolved to seek a new lodging the next day.

CHAPTER XL

At five o'clock, on the following morning, the house of Miss Matson was disturbed, by a hurrying message from Elinor, demanding to see Miss Ellis without delay. Ellis arose, with the utmost trepidation: it was the beginning of May, and brightly light; and she accompanied the servant back to the house.

She found all the family in the greatest disorder, from the return of another messenger, who had been forwarded to Mr. Harleigh, with the unexpected news that that gentleman had quitted Brighthelmstone. The intelligence was conveyed in a letter, which he had left at the hôtel, for Mrs. Maple; and in which another was enclosed for Elinor. Mrs. Maple had positively refused to be the bearer of such unwelcome tidings to the sick room; protesting that she could not risk, before the surgeon and the nurse, the rude expressions which her poor niece might utter; and could still less hazard imparting such irritating information *tête à tête*.

"Why, then," said Ireton, "should not Miss Ellis undertake the job? Nobody has had a deeper share in the business."

This idea was no sooner started, than it was seized by Mrs. Maple; who was over-joyed to elude the unpleasant task imposed upon her by Harleigh; and almost equally gratified to mortify, or distress, a person whom she had been led, by numberless small circumstances, which upon little minds operate more forcibly than essential ones, to consider as a source of personal disgrace to her own dignity and judgment. Deaf, therefore, to the remonstrances of Ellis, upon whom she forced the letter, she sent for Mr. Naird, charged him to watch carefully by the side of her poor niece, desired to be called if any thing unhappy should take place; and, complaining of a violent head-ache, retired to lie down.

Ellis, terrified at this tremendous commission, and convinced that the feelings and situation of Elinor were too publicly known for any attempt at secresy, applied to Mr. Naird for counsel how to proceed.

Mr. Naird answered that, in cases where, as in the present

instance, the imagination was yet more diseased than the body, almost any certainty was less hurtful than suspense. "Neverthe-less, with so excentrical a genius," he added, "nothing must be risked abruptly: if, therefore, as I presume, this letter is to acquaint the young lady, with the proper modifications, that Mr. Harleigh will have nothing to say to her; you must first let her get some little inkling of the matter by circumstances and surmizes, that the fact may not rush upon her without warning: keep, therefore, wholly out of her way, till the tumult of her wonder and her doubts, will make any species of explication medicinal."

She had certainly, he added, some new project in contem-plation; for, after extorting from her, the preceding evening, a promise that she would try to sleep, he heard her, when she believed him gone, exclaim, from Cato's soliloquy:*

> "Sleep? Ay, yes,—This once I'll favour thee,
> That my awaken'd soul may take its flight
> Replete with all its pow'rs, and big with life,
> An offering fit for ... Glory, Love ... and Harleigh!"

"Our kind-hearted young ladies of Sussex," continued Mr. Naird, "are as much scandalized that Mr. Harleigh should have the insensibility to resist love so heroic, as their more prudent mammas that he should so publicly be made its object. No men, however,—at least none on this side the Channel,—can wonder that he should demur at venturing upon a treaty for life, with a lady so expert in foreign politics, as to make an experiment, in her own proper person, of the new atheistical and suicidical doctrines, that those ingenious gentlemen, on t'other side the water, are now so busily preaching, for their fellow-countrymen's destruction.† This mode of challenging one's existence for every quarrel with one's Will; and running one's self through the Body for every affront to one's Mind; used to be thought peculiar to the proud and unbending humour of John Bull;* but John did it rarely enough to make it a subject of gossipping, and news-paper squibs, for at least a week. Our merry neighbours, on the contrary, now once they have set about it, do the job with an air, and a grace, that shew us we are as drowsy in our desperation, as we are phlegmatic in

†During the dominion of Robespierre.

our amusements. They talk of it wherever they go; write of it whenever they hold a pen; and are so piqued to think that we got the start of them, in beginning the game first, that they pop off* more now in a month, than we do in a year: and I don't in the least doubt, that their intention is to go on with the same briskness, till they have made the balance even."

Looking then archly at Ellis, "However clever," he added, "this young lady may be; and she seems an adept in their school of turning the world upside down; she did not shew much skill in human nature, when she fired such a broadside* at the heart of the man she loved, at the very instant that he had forgotten all the world, in his hurry to fire one himself upon the heart of another woman."

Ellis blushed, but was silent; and Mrs. Golding, Elinor's maid, came, soon after, to hasten Mr. Naird to her mistress; who, persuaded, she said, by their non-appearance, that Mr. Harleigh had eloped with Miss Ellis, was preparing to dress herself; and was bent to pursue them to the utmost extremity of the earth.

Mr. Naird, then, entering the room, heard her in the agitated voice of feverish exultation, call out, "Joy! Joy and peace, to my soul! They are gone off together!—'Tis just what I required, to 'spur my almost blunted purpose!—' "*

Ellis, beckoned by Mr. Naird, now appeared.

Elinor was struck with astonishment; and her air lost something of its wildness. "Is Harleigh," she cried, "here too?"

Ellis durst not reply; nor, still less, deliver the letter; which she dropt unseen upon a table.

Amazed at this silence, Elinor repeated her enquiries: "Why does he not come to me? Why will he not answer me?"

"Nay, I should think it a little odd, myself," said Mr. Naird, "if I did not take into consideration, that our hearing requires an approximation* that our wishes can do without."

"Is he not yet arrived, then?—Impenetrable Harleigh! And can he sleep? O noble heart of marble! polished, white, exquisite—but unyielding!—Ellis, send to him yourself! Call him to me immediately! It is but for an instant! Tell him it is but for an instant."

Ellis tremblingly drew back. The impatience of Elinor was

redoubled, and Mr. Naird thought proper to confess that Mr. Harleigh could not be found.

Her vehemence was then converted into derision, and, with a contemptuous laugh, "You would make me believe, perhaps," she cried, "that he has left Brighthelmstone? Spare your ingenuity a labour so absurd, and my patience so useless a disgust. From me, indeed, he may be gone! for his soul shrinks from the triumph in which it ought to glory! 'Tis pity! Yet in him every thing seems right; every thing is becoming. Even the narrow feelings of prudence, that curb the expansions of greatness, in him seem graceful, nay noble! Ah! who is like him? The poor grovelling wretches that call themselves his fellow-creatures, sink into nothingness before him, as if beings of another order! Where is he? My soul sickens to see him once more, and then to be extinct!"

No one venturing to speak, she again resolved to seek him in person; convinced, she said, that, since Ellis remained, he could not be far off. This appeared to Mr. Naird the moment for producing the letter.

At sight of the hand-writing of Harleigh, addressed to herself, every other feeling gave way to rapturous joy. She snatched the letter from Mr. Naird, blew it all around, as if to disperse the contagion of any foreign touch, and then, in a transport of delight, pressed it to her lips, to her heart, and again to her lips, with devouring kisses. She would not read it, she declared, till night: all she experienced of pleasure was too precious and too rare, not to be lengthened and enjoyed to its utmost possible extent; yet, nearly at the same moment, she broke the seal, and ordered every one to quit the room; that the air which would vibrate with words of Harleigh, should be uncontaminated by any breath but her own. They all obeyed; though Mr. Naird, fearing what might ensue, stationed himself where, unsuspectedly, he could observe her motions. Eagerly, rapidly, and without taking breath till she came to the conclusion, she then read aloud the following lines:

"To Miss JODDREL.

"I fly you, O Elinor, not to irritate those feelings I dare not hope to soothe! My heart recoils, with prophetic terrour, from the summons which you have issued for this morning. I know you too noble to accept, as you have shewn yourself too sincere to present, a heartless hand; but will you, therefore, blight the rest of my existence, by making me the cause of your destruction? Will you only seek relief to your sufferings, by means that must fix indelible horrour on your survivors? Will you call for peace and rest to yourself, by an action that must nearly rob me of both?

"Where death is voluntary, without considering our ultimate responsibility, have we none that is immediate? For ourselves only do we exist? No, generous Elinor, such has not been your plan. For ourselves alone, then, should we die? Shall we seek to serve and to please merely when present, that we may be served and pleased again? Is there no disinterested attachment, that would suffer, to spare pain to others? that would endure sooner than inflict?

"If to die be, as you hold, though as I firmly disbelieve, eternal sleep, would you wish the traces that may remain of that period in which you thought yourself awake, to be marked, for others, by blessings, or by misfortunes? Would you desire those whom you have known and favoured whilst amongst them, gratefully to cherish your remembrance, or to shrink with horrour from its recollection? Would you bequeath to them the pleasing image of your liberal kindness, or the terrific one of your despairing vengeance?

"To you, to whom death seems the termination of all, the extinguisher, the absorber of unaccounted life, this airy way of meeting, of invoking it, may appear suitable:—to me, who look forward to corporeal dissolution but as to the opening to spiritual being, and the period of retribution for our past terrestrial existence; to me it seems essential to prepare for it with as much awe as hope, as much solicitude as confidence.

"Wonder not, then, that, with ideas so different, I should fly witnessing the crisis which so intrepidly you invite. Would you permit your cooler reason to take the governance of your too animated feelings, with what alacrity, and what delight, should I seek your generous friendship!

"The Grave, you say, is the end of All; of soul and of body alike!

"Pause, Elinor!—should you be mistaken!.....

"Pause!—The less you believe yourself immortal, the less you should deem yourself infallible.

"You call upon us all, in this enlightened age, to set aside our long, old, and hereditary prejudices. Give the example with the charge, in setting aside those that, new, wilful, and self-created, have not even the apology of time or habit to make them sacred; and listen, O Elinor, to the voice and dictates of religion! Harden not your heart against convictions that may pour balm into all its wounds!

"Consent to see some learned and pious divine.

"If, upon every science, every art, every profession, you respect the opinions of those who have made them their peculiar study; and prefer their authority, and the result of their researches, to the sallies, the loose reasoning, and accidental knowledge of those who dispute at large, from general, however brilliant conceptions; from partial, however ingenious investigations; why in theology alone must you distrust the fruits of experience? the proofs of examination? the judgment of habitual reflexion?

"Consent, then, to converse with some devout, yet enlightened clergyman. Hear him patiently, meditate upon his doctrine impartially; and you will yet, O Elinor, consent to live, and life again will find its reviving, however chequered, enjoyments.

"Youth, spirits, fortune, the liveliest parts, the warmest heart, are yours. You have only to look around you to see how rarely such gifts are thus concentrated; and, grateful for your lot, you will make it, by blessing others, become a blessing to yourself: and you will not, Elinor, harrow to the very soul, the man who flattered himself to have found in you the sincerest of friends, by a stroke more severe to his peace than he could owe to his bitterest enemy.

"ALBERT HARLEIGH."

The excess of the agitation of Elinor, when she came to the conclusion, forced Mr. Naird to return, but rendered her insensible to his re-appearance. She flung off her bandages, rent open her wound, and tore her hair; calling, screaming for death, with agonizing wrath. "Is it for this," she cried, "I have thus loved—for this I have thus adored the flintiest of human hearts? to see him fly me from the bed of death? Refuse to receive even my parting sigh? Make me over to a dissembling priest?"

Ellis, returning also, urged Mr. Naird, who stood aloof, stedfastly, yet quietly fixing his eyes upon his patient, to use his authority for checking this dangerous violence.

Without moving, or lowering his voice, though Ellis spoke in a whisper, he drily answered, "It is not very material."

"How so?" cried Ellis, extremely alarmed: "What is it you mean, Sir?"

"It cannot, now," he replied, "occasion much difference."

Ellis, shuddering, entreated him to make some speedy effort for her preservation.

He thoughtfully stroked his chin, but as Elinor seemed suddenly to attend to them, forbore making further reply.

"What have you been talking of together?" cried she impatiently, "What is that man's opinion of my situation?—When may I have done with you all? Say! When may I sleep and be at rest?—When, when shall I be no longer the only person in this supine* world, awake? He can sleep! Harleigh can sleep, while he yet lives!—He, and all of you! Death is not wanted to give repose to hearts of adamant!"*

Ellis, in a low voice, again applied to Mr. Naird; but Elinor, watchful and suspicious, insisted upon hearing the subject of their discourse.

Mr. Naird, advancing to the bed-side, said, "Is there any thing you wish, my good lady? Tell me if there is any thing we can do, that will procure you pleasure?"

In vain Ellis endeavoured to give him an hint, that such a question might lead her to surmise her danger: the perceptions of Elinor were too quick to allow time for retraction or after precaution: the deepest damask flushed her pallid cheeks; her eyes became wildly dazzling, and she impetuously exclaimed, "The time, then, is come! The struggle is over!—and I shall quaff no more this 'nauseous draught of life?'"†*

She clasped her hands in an extacy, and vehemently added,

† Dryden.

"When—when—tell me if possible, to a moment! when eternal stillness may quiet this throbbing breast?—when I may bid a final, glad adieu to this detestable world, to all its servile customs, and all its despicable inhabitants?—Why do you not speak?—Be brief, be brief!"

Mr. Naird, slowly approaching her, silently felt her pulse.

"Away with this burlesque dumb shew!" cried she, indignantly. "No more of these farcical forms! Speak! When may your successor close these professional mockeries? fit only for weak patients who fear your sentence: to me, who boldly, eagerly demand it, speak reason and truth. When may I become as insensible as Harleigh?—Colder, death itself has not power to make me!"

Again he felt her pulse, and, while her eyes, with fiery impatience, called for a prompt decision, hesitatingly pronounced, that if she had any thing to settle, she could not be too expeditious.

Her countenance, her tone, her whole appearance, underwent, now, a sudden change; and she seemed as powerfully struck as if the decree which so earnestly she had sought, had been internally unexpected. She sustained herself, nevertheless, with firmness; thanked him, though in a low and husky voice, for his sincerity; and crossing her arms, and shutting her eyes, to obviate any distraction to her ideas by surrounding objects, delivered herself up to rapt meditation: becoming, in a moment, as calm, and nearly as gentle, as if a stranger by nature to violent passions, or even to strong feelings.

An impression so potent, made by the no longer doubted, and quick approximation of that Death, which, in the vigour and pride of Life, and Health, she had so passionately invoked, forcibly and fearfully affected Ellis; who uttered a secret prayer, that her own preparations for an event, which though the most indispensably common, could never cease to be the most universally tremendous of mortality, might be frequent enough, and cheerful enough, to take off horrour from its approach, without substituting presumption.

After a long pause, Elinor opened her eyes; and, in a subdued voice and manner, that seemed to stifle a struggling sigh, softly said, "There is no time, then, it seems, to lose? My short race is already run,—yet already has been too long! O Harleigh! had I been able to touch your heart!—"

Tears gushed into her eyes: she dispersed them hastily with her fingers; and, looking around her with an air of inquietude and shame, said, with studied composure, "You have kindly, Mr. Naird, offered me your services. I thankfully accept them. Pursue and find, without delay, Mr. Harleigh; repeat to him what you have just pronounced, and tell him. . . . . ." She blushed deeply, sighed; checked herself, and mildly went on, "This is no season for pride! Tell him my situation, and that I beg, I entreat, I conjure, I even implore him to let me once more—" Again she stopt, almost choaked with repressed emotions; but presently, with a calmer accent, added, "Say to him, he will not merely soften, but delight my last moments, in being then the sole object I shall behold, as, from the instant that I first saw him, he has been the only one who has engaged my thoughts;—the imperious, constant master of my mind!"

Mr. Naird respectfully accepted the commission; demanding only, in return, that she would first permit him once more to dress her wound. This she opposed; though so faintly, that it was evident that she was more averse to being thought cowardly, or inconsistent, than to stopping the quicker progress of dissolution. When Mr. Naird, therefore represented, that it was sending him upon a fruitless errand, if she meant to bleed to death in his absence, she complied. He then enjoined her to be quiet, and went forth.

With the most perfect stillness she awaited his return; neither speaking nor moving; and holding her watch in her hand, upon which she fixed her eyes without intermission; except to observe, from time to time, whether Ellis were in sight.

When he re-appeared, she changed colour, and covered her face with her hand; but, soon removing it, and shewing a steady countenance, she raised her head. When, however, she perceived that he was alone; and, after looking vainly towards the door, found that no one followed, she tremulously said, "Will he not, then, come?"

Mr. Naird answered, that it had not been possible to overtake him; a note, however, had been left at his lodgings, containing an earnest request, that a daily written account of the patient, till the danger should be over, might be forwarded to Cavendish Square; where it would certainly find, or whence it would follow him with the utmost expedition.

Elinor now looked almost petrified. "Danger!" she repeated: "He knows me, then, to be in danger,—yet flies me! And for Him I have lived;—and for Him I die!"

This reflexion destroyed all her composure; and every strong passion, every turbulent emotion, resumed its empire over her mind. She commanded Mr. Naird from the room, forced Golding to dress her, and ordered a chaise and four horses* immediately to the door. She was desperate, she said, and careless alike of appearances and of consequences. She would seek Harleigh herself. His icy heart, with all its apathy, recoiled from the sound of her last groan; but she would not spare him that little pain, since its infliction was all that could make the end of her career less intolerable than its progress.

She was just ready, when Mrs. Maple, called up by Mr. Naird, to dissuade her niece from this enterprize, would have represented the impropriety of the intended measure. But Elinor protested that she had finally taken leave of all fatiguing formalities; and refused even to open the chamber-door.

She could not, however, save herself from hearing a warm debate between Mrs. Maple and Mr. Naird, in which the following words caught her ears: "Shocking, Madam, or not, it is indispensable, if go she will, that you should accompany her; for the motion of a carriage in her present inflamed, yet enfeebled state, may shorten the term of your solicitude from a few days to a few hours. I am sorry to pronounce such a sentence; but as I find myself perfectly useless, I think it right to put you upon your guard, before I take my leave."

Elinor changed colour, ceased her preparations, and sunk upon the bed. Presently, however, she arose, and commanded Golding to call Mr. Naird.

"I solemnly claim from you, Mr. Naird," she cried, "the same undisguised sincerity that you have just practised with Mrs. Maple." Then, fixing her eyes upon his face, with investigating severity, "Tell me," she continued, "in one word, whether you think I have strength yet left to reach Cavendish Square?"

"If you go in a litter,* Madam, and take a week to make the journey—"

"A week?—I would arrive there in a few hours!—Is that impossible?"

"To arrive?—no; to arrive is certainly—not impossible."

"Dead, you perhaps mean?—To arrive dead is not impossible?—Speak clearly!"

"A medical man, Madam, lives in a constant round of perplexity; for either he must risk killing his patients by telling them unpleasant truths; or letting them kill themselves by nourishing false hopes."

"Take some other time for bewailing your own difficulties, Sir! and speak to the point, without that hateful official cant."*

"Well, Madam, if nothing but rough honesty will satisfy you, bear it, at least, with fortitude. The motion of a carriage is so likely to open your wound, that, in all probability, before you could gain Cuckfield—or Riegate, at furthest,—"

He stopt. Elinor finished for him: "I should be no more?"

He was silent.

"I thank you, Sir!" she cried, in a firm voice, though with livid cheeks. "And pray, how long,—supposing I do just, and only, what you bid me,—how long do you think it likely I should linger?"

"O, some days, I have no doubt. Perhaps a week."

The storm, now, again kindled in her disordered mind: "How!" she cried, "have I done all this—dared, risked, braved all things human,—and not human—to die, at last, a common death?—to expire, in a fruitless journey, an unacknowledged, and unoffered sacrifice?—or to lie down tamely in my bed, till I am extinct by ordinary dissolution?—"

Wringing then her hands, with mingled anguish and resentment, "Mr. Naird," she cried, "if you have the smallest real skill; the most trivial knowledge or experience in your profession; bind up my wound so as to give me strength to speed to him! and then, though the lamp of life should be instantly extinguished; though the same moment that bless annihilate me, I shall be content—O more than content! I shall expire with transport!"

Mr. Naird making no reply, she went on yet more impetuously: "Oh snatch me," she cried, "snatch me from the despicable fate that threatens me!—With energies so pure, with affections so genuine, with feelings so unadulterated, as mine, let me not be swept from the earth, with the undistinguished herd of common broken-hearted, broken-spirited, love-sick fanatics! Let me but once more join Harleigh! once more see that countenance which is life, light, and joy to my soul! hear, once more, that voice which charms all my senses, which thrills every nerve!—and then, that parting breath which rapturously utters, Harleigh, I come to die in beholding thee! shall bless you, too, as my preserver, and bid him share with you all that Elinor has to bequeath!"

She uttered this with a rapidity and agitation that nearly exhausted her remnant strength; and, tamed by feeling her dependance upon medical skill, she listened patiently to the counsels and propositions of Mr. Naird; in consequence of which, an express was sent to Harleigh, explaining her situation, her inability to be removed, her request to see him, and her immediate danger, if not kept quiet both in body and mind.

This done, satisfied that Harleigh could not read such a letter without hastening back, she agreed to all the prescriptions that were proposed; and even suffered a physician to be called to the assistance of Mr. Naird, in her fear lest, if Harleigh should not be found in Cavendish Square, she might expire, before the sole instant for which she desired either to live or to die, should arrive.

END OF THE SECOND VOLUME

VOLUME III

BOOK V

CHAPTER XLI

FROM the time of this arrangement, the ascendance which Mr. Naird obtained over the mind of Elinor, by alternate assurances and alarms, relative to her chances of living to see Harleigh again, produced a quiet that gave time to the drafts, which were administered by the physician, to take effect, and she fell into a profound sleep. This, Mr. Naird said, might last till late the next day; Ellis, therefore, promising to be ready upon any summons, returned to her lodging.

Miss Matson, now, endeavoured to make some enquiries relative to the public suicide projected, if not accomplished, by Miss Joddrel, which was the universal subject of conversation at Brighthelmstone; but when she found it vain to hope for any details, she said, "Such accidents, Ma'am, make one really afraid of one's life with persons one knows nothing of. Pray, Ma'am, if it is not impertinent, do you still hold to your intention of giving up your pretty apartment?"

Ellis answered in the affirmative, desiring, with some surprise, to know, whether the question were in consequence of any apprehension of a similar event.

"By no means, Ma'am, from you," she replied; "you, Miss Ellis, who have been so strongly recommended; and protected by so many of our capital gentry; but what I mean is this. If you really intend to take a small lodging, why should not you have my little room again up stairs?"

"Is it not engaged to the lady I saw here this morning?"

"Why that, Ma'am, is precisely the person I have upon my mind to speak about. Why should I let her stay, when she's known to nobody, and is very bad pay, if I can have so genteel a young lady as you, Ma'am, that ladies in their own coaches come visiting?"

Ellis, recoiling from this preference, uttered words the most benevolent that she could suggest, of the unknown person who had excited her compassion: but Miss Matson gave them no attention. "When one has nothing better to do with one's rooms, Ma'am," she said, "it's sometimes as well, perhaps, to let them to almost one does not know who, as to keep them uninhabited; because living in them airs them; but that's no reason for letting them to one's own disadvantage, if one can do better. Now this person here, Ma'am, besides being poor, which, poor thing, may be she can't help; and being a foreigner, which, you know, Ma'am, is no great recommendation;—besides all this, Miss Ellis, she has some very suspicious ways with her, which I can't make out at all; she goes abroad in a morning, Ma'am, by five of the clock, without giving the least account of her haunts. And that, Ma'am, has but an odd look with it!"

"Why so, Miss Matson? If she takes time from her own sleep to enjoy a little air and exercise, where can be the blame?"

"Air and exercise, Ma'am? People that have their living to get, and that a'n't worth a farthing, have other things to think of than air and exercise! She does not, I hope, give herself quite such airs as those!"

Ellis, disgusted, bid her good night; and, filled with pity for a person who seemed still more helpless and destitute than herself, resolved to see her the next day, and endeavour to offer her some consolation, if not assistance.

Before, however, this pleasing project could be put into execution, she was again, nearly at day break, awakened by a summons from Selina to attend her sister, who, after quietly reposing many hours, had started, and demanded Harleigh and Ellis.

Ellis obeyed the call with the utmost expedition, but met the messenger returning to her a second time, as she was mounting the street which led to the lodging of Mrs. Maple, with intelligence that Elinor had almost immediately fallen into a new and sound sleep; and that Mr. Naird had ordered that no one should enter the room, till she again awoke.

Glad of this reprieve, Ellis was turning back, when she perceived, at some distance, Miss Matson's new lodger. The opportunity was inviting for her purposed offer of aid, and she determined to make some opening to an acquaintance.

This was not easy; for though the light feet of Ellis might soon have overtaken the quick, but staggering steps of the apparently distressed person whom she pursued, she observed her to be in a state of perturbation that intimidated approach, as much as it awakened concern. Her handkerchief was held to her face; though whether to conceal it, or because she was weeping, could not readily be discovered: but her form and air penetrated Ellis with a feeling and an interest far beyond common curiosity; and she anxiously studied how she might better behold, and how address her.

The foreigner went on her way, looking neither to the right nor to the left, till she had ascended to the church-yard upon the hill. There stopping, she extended her arms, seeming to hail the full view of the wide spreading ocean; or rather, Ellis imagined, the idea of her native land, which she knew, from that spot, to be its boundary. The beauty of the early morning from that height, the expansive view, impressive, though calm, of the sea, and the awful solitude of the place, would have sufficed to occupy the mind of Ellis, had it not been completely caught by the person whom she followed; and who now, in the persuasion of being wholly alone, gently murmured, "Oh ma chère patrie!—malheureuse, coupable,—mais toujours chère patrie!—ne te reverrai-je jamais!"†

Her voice thrilled to the very soul of Ellis, who, trembling, suspended, and almost breathless, stood watching her motions; fearing to startle her by an unexpected approach, and waiting to catch her eye.

But the mourner was evidently without suspicion that any one was in sight. Grief is an absorber: it neither seeks nor makes observation; except where it is joined with vanity, that always desires remark; or with guilt, by which remark is always feared.

Ellis, neither advancing nor receding, saw her next move solemnly forward, to bend over a small elevation of earth, encircled by short sticks, intersected with rushes. Some of these, which were displaced, she carefully arranged, while uttering, in a gentle murmur, which the profound stillness of all around alone enabled Ellis to catch, "Repose toi bien, mon

† "Oh my loved country!—unhappy, guilty—but for ever loved country!—shall I never see thee more!"

ange! mon enfant! le repos qui me fuit, le bonheur que j'ai perdu, la tranquilité précieuse de l'âme qui m'abandonne—que tout cela soit à toi, mon ange! mon enfant! Je ne te rappellerai plus ici! Je ne te rappellerais plus, même si je le pouvais. Loin de toi ma malheureuse destinée!* je priai Dieu pour ta conservation quand je te possedois encore; quelques cruelles que fussent tes souffrances, et toute impuissante que j'étois pour les soulager, je priai Dieu, dans l'angoisse de mon âme, pour ta conservation! Tu n'es plus pour moi—et je cesse de te réclamer. Je te vois une ange! Je te vois exempt à jamais de douleur, de crainte, de pauvreté et de regrets: te réclamerai-je, donc, pour partager encore mes malheurs? Non! ne reviens plus à moi! Que je te retrouve là—où ta félicité sera la mienne! Mais toi, prie pour ta malheureuse mère! que tes innocentes prières s'unissent à ses humbles supplications, pour que ta mère, ta pauvre mère, puisse se rendre digne de te rejoindre!"†

How long these soft addresses, which seemed to soothe the pious petitioner, might have lasted, had she not been disturbed, is uncertain: but she was startled by sounds of more tumultuous sorrow; by sobs, rather than sighs, that seemed bursting forth from more violent, at least, more sudden affliction. She looked round, astonished; and saw Ellis leaning over a monument, and bathed in tears.

She arose, and, advancing towards her, said, in an accent of pity, "Hélas, Madame, vous, aussi, pleurez vous* votre enfant?"‡

"Ah, mon amie! ma bien aimée!" cried Ellis, wiping her eyes,

† "Sleep on, sleep on, my angel child! May the repose that flies me, the happiness that I have lost, the precious tranquillity of soul that has forsaken me—be thine! for ever thine! my child! my angel! I cease to call thee back. Even were it in my power, I would not call thee back. I prayed for thy preservation, while yet I had the bliss of possessing thee;* cruel as were thy sufferings, and impotent as I found myself to relieve them, I prayed,—in the anguish of my soul,—I prayed for thy preservation! Thou art lost to me now!—yet I call thee back no more! I behold thee an angel! I see thee rescued for ever from sorrow, from alarm, from poverty, and from bitter recollections;—and shall I call thee back, to partake again my sufferings?—No! return to me no more! There, only, let me find thee, where thy felicity will be mine!—but thou! O pray for thy unhappy mother! Let thy innocent prayers be united to her humble supplications, that thy mother, thy hapless mother, may become worthy to join thee!"

‡ "Alas, Madam! are you, also, deploring the loss of a child?"

but vainly attempting to repress fresh tears; "t'ai-je cherchée t'ai-je attendue, t'ai-je si ardemment désirée, pour te retrouver ainsi? pleurant sur un tombeau? Et toi!—ne me rappelles tu pas? M'as tu oubliée?—Gabrielle! ma chère Gabrielle!"†

"Juste ciel!" exclaimed the other, "que vois-je? Ma Julie!* ma chère, ma tendre* amie? Est il bien vrai?—O! peut il être vrai, qu'il y ait encore du bonheur ici bas pour moi?"‡

Locked in each other's arms, pressed to each other's bosoms, they now remained many minutes in speechless agony of emotion, from nearly overpowering surprise, from gusts of ungovernable, irrepressible sorrow, and heart-piercing recollections; though blended with the tenderest sympathy of joy.

This touching silent eloquence, these unutterable conflicts between transport and pain, were succeeded by a reciprocation of enquiry, so earnest, so eager, so ardent, that neither of them seemed to have any sensation left of self, from excess of solicitude for the other; till Ellis, looking towards the little grave, said, "Ah! que ce ne soit plus question de moi?"§

"Ah, oui, mon amie," answered Gabriella, "ton histoire, tes malheurs, ne peuvent jamais être aussi terribles, aussi déchirants que les miens! tu n'as pas encore éprouvé le bonheur d'être mère—comment aurois-tu, donc, éprouvé, le plus accablant des malheurs? Oh! ce sont des souffrances qui n'ont point de nom; des douleurs qui rendent nulles toutes autres, que la perte d'un Etre pûr comme un ange,* et tout à soi!"¶

The fond embraces, and fast flowing tears of Ellis, evinced the keen sensibility with which she participated in the sorrows

† "Ah, my friend! my much loved friend! have I sought thee, have I awaited thee, have I so fervently desired thy restoration—to find thee thus? Weeping over a grave? And thou—dost thou not recollect me? Hast thou forgotten me?—Gabriella! my loved Gabriella!"

‡ "Gracious heaven! what do I behold? My Juliet! my tender friend? Can it be real?—O! can it, indeed, be true, that still any happiness is left on earth for me!"

§ "Ah!—upon me can you, yet, bestow a thought?"

¶ "True, my dear friend, true! thy history, thy misfortunes, can never be terrible, never be lacerating like mine! Thou hast not yet known the bliss of being a mother;—how, then, canst thou have experienced the most overwhelming of calamities! a suffering that admits of no description! a woe that makes all others seem null—the loss of a being pure, spotless as a cherub—and wholly our own!"

of this afflicted mother, whom she strove to draw away from the fatal spot; reiterating the most urgent enquiries upon every other subject, to attract her, if possible, to yet remaining, to living interests. But these efforts were utterly useless. "Restons, restons où nous sommes!" she cried: "c'est ici que je te parlerai; c'est ici que je t'écôuterai; ici, où je passe les seuls momens que j'arrache à la misère, et au travail. Ne crois pas que de pleurer est ce qu'il y a le plus à craindre! Oh! qu'il ne t'arrive jamais de savoir que de pleurer, même sur le tombeau de tout ce qui vous est le plus cher, est un soulagement, un délice, auprès du dur besoin de travailler, la mort dans le cœur, pour vivre, pour exister, lorsque la vie a perdu toutes ses charmes!"†

Seated then upon the monument which was nearest to the little grave, Gabriella related the principal events of her life, since the period of their separation. These, though frequently extraordinary, sometimes perilous, and always touchingly disastrous, she recounted with a rapidity almost inconceivable; distinctly, nevertheless, marking the several incidents, and the courage with which she had supported them: but when, these finished, she entered upon the history of the illness that had preceded the death of her little son, her voice tremblingly slackened its velocity, and unconsciously lowered its tones; and, far from continuing with the same quickness or precision, every circumstance was dwelt upon as momentous; every recollection brought forth long and endearing details; every misfortune seemed light, put in the scale with his loss; every regret seemed concentrated in his tomb!

Six o'clock, and seven, had tolled unheeded, during this afflicting, yet soothing recital; but the eighth hour striking, when the tumult of sorrow was subsiding into the sadness of grief, the sound caught the ear of Gabriella, who, hastily rising, exclaimed, "Ah, voilà que je suis encore susceptible de plaisir,

† "Here, here let us stay! 'tis here I can best speak to thee! 'tis here, I can best listen;—here, where I pass every moment that I can snatch from penury and labour! Think not that to weep is what is most to be dreaded; oh never mayst thou learn, that to weep—though upon the tomb of all that has been most dear to thee upon earth, is a solace, is a feeling of softness, nay of pleasure,* compared with the hard necessity of toiling, when death has seized upon the very heart, merely to breathe, to exist, after life has lost all its charms!"

puisque ta société m'a fait oublier les tristes et pénibles devoirs, qui m'appellent à des tâches qui—à peine—m'empêchent de mourir de faim!"[†]

At these words, all the fortitude hitherto sustained by Juliet,—for the borrowed name of Ellis will now be dropt,—utterly forsook her. Torrents of tears gushed from her eyes, and lamentations, the bitterest, broke from her lips. She could bear, she cried, all but this; all but beholding the friend of her heart, the daughter of her benefactress, torn from the heights of happiness and splendour; of merited happiness, of hereditary splendour; to be plunged into such depths of distress, and overpowered with anguish.

"Ah! que je te reconnois bien à ce trait!" cried Gabriella, while a tender smile tried to force its way through her tears: "cette âme si noble! si inébranlable pour elle-même, si douce, si compatissante pour tout autre! que de souvenirs chers et touchans ne se présentent, à cet instant, à mon cœur! Ma chère Julie! il est bien vrai, donc, que je te vois, que je te retrouve encore! et, en toi, tout ce qu'il y a de plus aimable, de plus pûr, et de plus digne! Comment ai-je pû te revoir, sans retrouver la félicité? Je me sens presque coupable de pouvoir t'embrasser,—et de pleurer encore!"[‡]

Forcing herself, then, from the fatal but cherished spot, she must hasten, she said, to her daily labour, lest night should surprise her, without a roof to shelter her head. But Juliet now detained her; clung and wept round her neck, and could not even endeavour to resign herself to the keen woes, and deplorable situation of her friend. She had come over, she said, buoyed up with the exquisite hope of joining the darling companion of her earliest youth; of sharing her fate, and of

[†] "See, if I am not still susceptible of pleasure! Thy society has made me forget the sad and painful duties that call me hence, to tasks that snatch me,—with difficulty,—from perishing by famine!"

[‡] "Ah, how I know thee by that trait! thy soul so noble! so firm in itself; so soft, so commiserating for every other! what tender, what touching recollections present themselves at this instant to my heart! Dearest Juliet! is it, then, indeed no dream, that I have found—that I behold thee again? and, in thee, all that is most exemplary, most amiable, and most worthy upon earth! How is it I can recover thee, and not recover happiness? I almost feel as if I were criminal, that I can embrace thee,—yet weep on!"

mitigating her hardships: but this softening expectation was changed into despondence, in discovering her, thus, a prey to unmixt calamity; not alone bowed down by the general evils of revolutionary events; punished for plans in which she had borne no part, and for crimes of which she had not even any knowledge;—not only driven, without offence, or even accusation, from prosperity and honours, to exile, to want, to misery, and to labour; but suffering, at the same time, the heaviest of personal afflictions, in the immediate loss of a darling child; the victim, in all probability, to a melancholy change of life, and to sudden privation of customary care and indulgence!

The task of consolation seemed now to devolve upon Gabriella: the feelings of Juliet, long checked by prudence, by fortitude, by imperious necessity; and kept in dignified but hard command; having once found a vent, bounded back to nature and to truth, with a vivacity of keen emotion that made them nearly uncontrollable. Nature and truth,—which invariably retain an elastic power, that no struggles can wholly subdue; and that always, however curbed, however oppressed,—lie in wait for opportunity to spring back to their rights. Her tears, permitted, therefore, at length, to flow, nearly deluged the sad bosom of her friend.

"Hélas, ma Julie! sœur de mon âme!" cried Gabriella, "ne t'abandonne pas à la douleur pour moi! mais parles moi, ma tendre amie, parles moi de ma mère! Où l'a tu quitté? Et comment? Et à quelle époque?—La plus digne, la plus chérie des mères! Hélas! éloignée de nous deux, comment saura-t-elle se résigner à tant de malheurs?"†

Juliet uttered the tenderest assurances, that she had left the Marchioness well; and had left her by her own injunctions, to join her darling daughter; to whom, by a conveyance that had been deemed secure, she had previously written the plan of the intended journey; with a desire that a few lines of direction, relative to their meeting, under cover to L. S., to be left till called

† "Alas, my Juliet! sister of my soul! abandon not thyself to sorrow for me! but speak to me, my tender friend, speak to me of my mother! where didst thou leave her? And how? And at what time? The most precious of mothers! Alas! separated from us both,—how will she be able to support such accumulation of misfortunes!"

for, might be sent to the post-offices both of Dover and Brighthelmstone; as it was not possible to fix at which spot Juliet might land. The initials L. S. had been fixed upon by accident.

Filial anxiety, now, took place of maternal sufferings, and Gabriella could only talk of her mother; demanding how she looked, and how she supported the long separation, the ruinous sacrifices, and the perpetual alarms, to which she must have been condemned since they had parted; expressing her own surprise, that she had borne to dwell upon any other subject than this, which now was the first interest of her heart; yet ceasing to wonder, when she contemplated the fatal spot where her meeting with Juliet had taken place.

Each, now, deeply lamented the time and consolation that had been lost, from their mutual ignorance of each other's abode. Juliet related her fruitless search upon arriving in London; and Gabriella explained, that, during three lingering, yet ever regretted months, she had watched over her dying boy, without writing a single line; to spare her absent friends the knowledge of her suspensive* wretchedness. Since the irreparable certainty which had followed, she had sent two letters to her beloved mother, with her address at Brighthelmstone; but both must have miscarried, as she had received no answer. That Juliet had not traced her in London was little wonderful, as, to elude the curiosity excited by a great name,* she had passed, in setting out for Brighthelmstone, by a common one. And to that change, joined to one so similar on the part of Juliet, it must have been owing that they had never heard of each other, though residents of the same place. Juliet, nevertheless, was astonished, in defiance of all alteration of attire and appearance, that she had not instantly recognized the air and form of her elegant and high bred Gabriella. But, equally unacquainted with her indigence, which was the effect of sundry cruel accidents, and with the loss of her child; no expectation was awakened of finding her either in so distressed or so solitary a condition. Now, however, Juliet continued, that fortunately, though, alas! not happily, they had met, they would part no more. Juliet was fully at liberty to go whithersoever her friend would lead, the hope of obtaining tidings of that beloved friend, having alone kept her stationary thus long at Brighthelmstone; where she could now leave the address of Gabriella, at the post-office, for their mutual letters: and, as insuperable obstacles impeded her writing herself, at present, to the Marchioness, Gabriella might make known, in a covert manner, that they were together, and were both safe.

And why, Gabriella demanded, could not Juliet write herself?

"Alas!" Juliet replied, "I must not even be named!"

"Eh, pour quoi?—n'as-tu pas vû tes parens?—Peut on te voir sans t'aimer? te connoître sans te chérir? Non, ma Julie, non! tu n'as qu'à te montrer."†

Juliet, changing colour, dejectedly, and not without confusion, besought her friend, though for reasons that could neither be assigned nor surmounted, to dispense, at present, with all personal narration. Yet, upon perceiving the anxious surprise occasioned by a request so little expected, she dissolved into tears, and offered every communication, in preference to causing even transitory pain to her best friend.

"O loin de moi cette exigeance!" cried Gabriella, with energy, "Ne sais-je pas bien que ton bon esprit, juste émule de ton excellent cœur, te fera parler lorsqu'il le faudra? Ne me confierai-je pas à toi, dont la seule étude est le bonheur des autres?"‡

Juliet, not more penetrated by this kindness, than affected by a facile resignation, that shewed the taming effect of misfortune upon the natural vivacity of her friend, could answer only by caresses and tears.

"Eh mon oncle?" continued Gabriella; "mon tout-aimable et si pieux oncle? où est il?"§

"Monseigneur l'Evêque?" cried Juliet, again changing colour; "Oh oui! tout-aimable! sans tâche et sans reproche!—Il

† "And why? Hast thou not seen thy relations?—Canst thou be seen, and not loved? —known, and not cherished? No, my Juliet, no! thou hast only to appear!"

‡ "Oh far from me be any such insistence! Know I not well that thy admirable judgment, just counterpart of thy excellent heart, will guide thee to speak when it is right? Shall I not entirely confide in thee?—In thee, whose sole study has been always the good and happiness of others?"

§ "And my uncle! My so amiable, so pious uncle? Where is he?"

sera bientôt, je crois, ici;—ou j'aurois de ses nouvelles; et alors—ma destinée me sera connue!"†

A deep sigh tried to swallow these last words. Gabriella looked at her, for a moment, with re-awakened earnestness, as if repentant of her own acquiescence; but the sight of encreasing disturbance in the countenance of Juliet, checked her rising impatience; and she quietly said, "Ah! s'il arrive ici!—si je le revois,—j'éprouverai encore, au milieu de tant de désolation, un mouvement de joie!—tel que toi, seule, jusqu'à ce moment, a su m'en inspirer!"‡

Juliet, with fond delight, promised to be governed wholly, in her future plans, occupations, and residence, by her beloved friend.

"C'est à Brighthelmstone, donc," cried Gabriella, returning to the little grave; "c'est ici que nous demeurions! ici, où il me semble que je n'ai pas encore tout à fait perdu mon fils!"

Then, tenderly embracing Juliet, "Ah, mon amie!" she cried, with a smile that blended pleasure with agony; "ah, mon amie! c'est à mon enfant que je te dois! c'est en pleurant sur* ses restes que je t'ai retrouvée! Ah, oui!" passionately bending over the grave; "c'est à toi, mon ange! mon enfant! que je dois mon amie! Ton tombeau, même, me porte bonheur! tes cendres veulent me bénir! tes restes, ton ombre veulent du bien à ta pauvre mère!"§

With difficulty, now, Juliet drew her away from the fond, fatal spot; and slowly, and silently, while clinging to each other with heartfelt affection, they returned together to their lodgings.

† "My lord the Bishop?—Oh yes! yes!—amiable indeed!—pure!—without blemish!—He will soon, I believe, be here; or I shall have some intelligence from him; and then—my fate will be known to me!"

‡ "Ah, should he come hither!—should I be blest again by his sight, I should feel, once more, even in the midst of my desolation, a sensation of joy—such as thou, only, as yet, hast been able to re-awaken!"

§ "'Tis at Brighthelmstone, then,—'tis here that we must dwell! Here, where I seem not yet, entirely, to have lost my darling boy!* Oh my friend! my dearest, best loved friend!* 'tis to him—to my child, that I am indebted for seeing thee again 'tis in visiting his remains that I have met my Juliet!—Oh thou! my child! my angel! 'tis to thee, to thee, I am indebted for my friend! Even thy grave offers me comfort! even thy ashes* desire to bless me! Thy remains, thy shadow, would do good, would bring peace to thy unhappy mother!"

CHAPTER XLII

ELINOR, kept in order by a continual expectation of seeing Harleigh, ceased to require the presence of Juliet; who, but for the sorrows of her friend, would have experienced a felicity to which she had long been a stranger, the felicity of being loved because known; esteemed and valued because tried and proved. The consideration that is the boon of even the most generous benevolence, however it may soothe the heart, cannot elevate the spirits: but here, good opinion was reciprocated, trust was interchanged, confidence was mutual.

The affliction of Gabriella, though of a more permanent nature, because from an irreparable cause, was yet highly susceptible of consolation from friendship; and when once the acute emotions, arising from the tale of woe which she had had to relate, at the meeting, were abated, the charm which the presence of Juliet dispensed, and the renewal of early ideas, pristine feelings, and first affections, soon reflected back their influence upon her own mind; which gradually strengthened, and insensibly revived.

Juliet immediately resigned her large apartment, and fixed herself in the small room of Gabriella. There they settled that they would live together, work together, share their little profits, and endure their failures, in common. There they hoped to recover their peace of mind, if not to re-animate their native spirits; and to be restored to the harmony of social sympathy, if not to that of happiness.

Yet, it was with difficulty that they learnt to enjoy each other's society, upon such terms as their altered condition now exacted; where the eye must never be spared from laborious business, to search, or to reciprocate a sentiment, in those precious moments of endearing converse, which, unconsciously, swell into hours, ere they are missed as minutes. Their intercourse was confined to oral language alone. The lively intelligence, the rapid conception, the arch remark, the cordial smile; which give grace to kindness, playfulness to counsel, gentleness to raillery, and softness even to reproach; these, the expressive sources of delight, and of comprehension, in social commerce, they were fain wholly to relinquish; from the hurry of unremitting diligence, and undivided attention to manual toil.

Nevertheless, to inhale the same air, and to feel the consoling certitude, that they were no longer cast wholly upon pity, or charity, for good opinion, were blessings that filled their thoughts with gratitude to Providence, and brought back calm and comfort to their minds.

Still, at every sun-rise, Gabriella visited the ashes of her little son; where she poured forth, in maternal enthusiasm, thanks and benedictions upon his departed spirit, that her earliest friend, the chosen sharer of her happier days, was restored to her in the hour of her desolation; and restored to her There,—on that fatal, yet adored spot, which contained the ever loved, though lifeless remains of her darling boy.

Juliet, in this peaceful interval, learnt, from the voluble Selina, all that had been gathered from Mrs. Golding relative to the seclusion of Elinor.

Elinor had travelled post to Portsmouth, whence she had sailed to the Isle of Wight. There, meeting with a foreign servant out of place, she engaged him in her service, and bid him purchase some clothes of an indigent emigrant. She then dressed herself grotesquely yet, as far as she could, decently, in man's attire; and, making her maid follow her example, returned to the neighbourhood of Brighthelmstone, and took lodgings, in the character of a foreigner, who was deaf and dumb, at Shoreham; where, uninterruptedly, and unsuspectedly, she resided. Here, by means of her new domestic, she obtained constant intelligence of the proceedings of Juliet; and she was no sooner informed of the musical benefit, in which an air, with an harp-accompaniment, was to be performed by Miss Ellis, then she sent her new attendant to the assembly-room, to purchase a ticket. Golding, who went thither with the lackey, met Harleigh in the street, as he was quitting the lodgings of Juliet.

The disguise of the maid saved her from being recognised; but her tidings set her mistress on fire. The moment seemed now arrived for the long-destined catastrophe; and the few days preceding the benefit, were spent in its preparation. Careless of what was thought, Elinor, had since, casually, though not confidentially, related, that her intention had been to mount suddenly into the orchestra, during the performance of Juliet; and thence to call upon Harleigh, whom she could not doubt would be amongst the audience; and, at the instant of his joining them, proclaim to the whole world her immortal passion, and expire between them. But the fainting fit of Juliet, and its uncontrollable effect upon Harleigh, had been so insupportable to her feelings, as to precipitate her design. She acknowledged that she had studied how to die without torture,* by inflicting a wound by which she might bleed gently to death, while indulging herself, to the last moment, in pouring forth to the idol of her heart, the fond effusions of her ardent, but exalted passion.

The tranquillity of Elinor, built upon false expectations, could not be long unshaken: impatience and suspicion soon took its place, and Mr. Naird was compelled to acknowledge, that Mr. Harleigh had set out upon a distant tour, without leaving his address, even at his own house; where he had merely given orders that his letters should be forwarded to a friend.

The rage, grief, and shame of the wretched Elinor, now nearly destroyed, in a moment, all the cares and the skill of Mr. Naird, and of her physician. She impetuously summoned Juliet, to be convinced that she was not a party in the elopement; and was only rescued from sinking into utter despair, by adroit exhortations from Mr. Naird, to yield patiently to his ordinances, lest she should yet die without a last view of Harleigh. This plea led her, once more, though with equal disgust to herself and to the whole world, to submit to every medical direction, that might give her sufficient strength to devise means for her ultimate project; and to put them into practice.

Mr. Naird archly confessed, in private, to Juliet, that the real danger or safety of Miss Joddrel, so completely hung upon giving the reins, or the curb, to her passions, that she might, without much difficulty, from her resolution to die no other death than that of heroic love, in the presence of its idol, be spurred on, while awaiting, or pursuing, its object, to the verge of a very comfortable old age.

He acknowledged himself, also, secretly entrusted with the abode of Mr. Harleigh.

Elinor, when somewhat calmed, demanded of Juliet when, and how, her meetings with Harleigh had been renewed.

Juliet recounted what had passed; sparing such details as might be hurtful, and solemnly protesting that all intercourse was now at an end.

With a view to draw Elinor from this agitating subject, she then related, at full length, her meeting, in the church-yard, with the friend whom she had so long vainly sought.

In a short time afterwards, feeling herself considerably advanced towards a recovery, Elinor, impetuously, again sent for Juliet, to say, "What is your plan? Tell it me sincerely! What is it you mean to do?"

Juliet answered, that her choice was small, and that her means were almost null: but when she lamented the severe DIFFICULTIES of a FEMALE, who, without fortune or protection, had her way to make in the world, Elinor, with strong derision, called out, "Debility and folly! Put aside your prejudices, and forget that you are a dawdling woman, to remember that you are an active human being, and your FEMALE DIFFICULTIES will vanish into the vapour of which they are formed. Misery has taught me to conquer mine! and I am now as ready to defy the world, as the world can be ready to hold me up to ridicule. To make people wise, you must make them indifferent; to give them courage, you must make them desperate. 'Tis then, only, that we throw aside affectation and hypocrisy, and act from impulse."

Laughing, now, though with bitterness, rather than gaiety, "What does the world say," she cried, "to find that I still live, after the pompous funeral orations, declaimed by myself, upon my death? Does it suspect that I found second thoughts best, and that I delayed my execution, thinking, like the man in the song,

> That for sure I could die whenever I would,
> But that I could live but as long as I could?*

"Well, ye that laugh, laugh on! for I, when not sick of myself, laugh too! But, to escape mockery, we must all be guided one by another; all do, and all say, the very same thing. Yet why? Are we alike in our thoughts? Are we alike in our faces? No. Happily, however, that soporiferous monotony is beginning to get obsolete. The sublimity of Revolution has given a greater shake to the minds of men, than to the kingdoms of the earth."

After pausing, then, a few minutes, "Ellis," she cried, "if you are really embarrassed, why should you not go upon the stage? You know how transcendently you act."

"That which might seem passable in a private representation," Juliet answered, "might, at a public theatre—"

"Pho, pho, you know perfectly well your powers. But you blight them, I suppose, yourself, with anathemas, from excommunicating scruples?* You are amongst the cold, the heartless, the ungifted, who, to discredit talents, and render them dangerous, leave their exercise to vice, by making virtue fear to exert, or even patronize them?"

"No, Madam, indeed," cried Juliet: "I admire, most feelingly, the noble art of declamation:—how, then, can I condemn the profession which gives to it life and soul? which personifies the most exalted virtues, which brings before us the noblest characters, and makes us witnesses to the sublimest actions? The stage, well regulated, would be the school of juvenile emulation; would soothe sorrow in the unhappy, and afford merited relaxation to the laborious. Reformed, indeed, I wish it, and purified; but not destroyed."

"Why, then, do you disdain to wear the buskins?"

"Disdain is by no means the word. Talents are a constant source to me of delight; and those who,—rare, but in existence,—unite, to their public exercise, private virtue and merit, I honour and esteem even more than I admire; and every mark I could shew, to such, of consideration,—were I so situated as to bestow, not require protection!—I should regard as reflecting credit not on them, but on myself."

"Pen and ink!" cried Elinor, impatiently: "I'll write for you to the manager this moment!—"

"Hold, Madam!" cried Juliet smiling: "Much as I am enchanted with the art, I am not going to profess it! On the contrary, I think it so replete with dangers and improprieties, however happily they may sometimes be combatted by fortitude and integrity, that, when a young female, not forced by peculiar circumstances, or impelled by resistless genius, exhibits herself a willing candidate for public applause;—she must have, I own, other notions, or other nerves, than mine!"

"Ellis, Ellis! you only fear to alarm, or offend the men—who would keep us from every office, but making puddings and pies* for their own precious palates!—Oh woman! poor, subdued woman! thou art as dependant, mentally, upon the arbitrary customs of man, as man is, corporally, upon the established laws of his country!"

She now grew disturbed, and went on warmly, though nearly to herself.

"By the oppressions of their own statutes and institutions, they render us insignificant; and then speak of us as if we were so born! But what have we tried, in which we have been foiled? They dare not trust us with their own education, and their own opportunities for distinction:—I except the article of fighting; against that, there may, perhaps, be some obstacles: but to be condemned, as weaker vessels in intellect, because, inferiour in bodily strength and stature, we cannot cope with them as boxers and wrestlers! They appreciate not the understandings of one another by such manual and muscular criterions. They assert not that one man has more brains than another, because he is taller; that he is endowed with more illustrious virtues, because he is stouter. They judge him not to be less ably formed for haranguing in the senate; for administering justice in the courts of law; for teaching science at the universities, because he could ill resist a bully, or conquer a footpad! No!—Woman is left out in the scales of human merit, only because they dare not weigh her!"

Then, turning suddenly to Ellis, "And you, Ellis, you!" she cried, "endowed with every power to set prejudice at defiance, and to shew and teach the world, that woman and man are fellow-creatures, you, too, are coward enough to bow down, unresisting, to this thraldom?"

Juliet hazarded not any reply.

"Yet what futile inconsistency dispenses this prejudice! This Woman, whom they estimate thus below, they elevate above themselves. They require from her, in defiance of their examples!—in defiance of their lures!—angelical perfection.

She must be mistress of her passions; she must never listen to her inclinations; she must not take a step of which the purport is not visible; she must not pursue a measure of which she cannot publish the motive; she must always be guided by reason, though they deny her understanding!—Frankness, the noblest of our qualities, is her disgrace;—sympathy, the most exquisite of our feelings, is her bane!—"

She stopt here, conscious, colouring, indignant, and dropt the subject, to say, "Tell me, I again demand, what is it you mean to do? Return to your concert-singing and harping?"

"Ah, Madam," cried Juliet, reproachfully, "can you believe me not yet satisfied with attempting any sort of public exhibition?"

"Nay, nay," cried Elinor, resuming her careless gaiety, "what passed that evening will only have served to render you more popular. You may make your own terms, now, with the managers, for the subscription will fill, merely to get a stare at you. If I were poor myself, I would engage to acquire a large fortune, in less than a week, by advertising, at two-pence a head, a sight of the lady that stabbed herself."

"What, however," she continued, "is your purpose? Will you go and live with Mrs. Ireton? She is just come hither to give her favourite lap-dog a six weeks" bathing. What say you to the place of her toad-eater?* It may be a very lucrative thing; and I can procure it for you with the utmost ease. It is commonly vacant every ten days. Besides, she has been dying to have you in her toils, ever since she has known that you spurned the proposition, when it was started by Mrs. Howel."

Juliet protested, that any species of fatigue would be preferable to subservience of such a sort.

"Perhaps you are afraid of seeing too much of Ireton? Be under no apprehension. He makes it a point not to visit her. He cannot endure her. Besides, 'tis so rustic,* he says, to have a mother!"

Juliet answered, that her sole plan, now, was to be guided by her friend.

"And who is this friend? Is she of the family of the Incognitas, also? What do you call her?—L. S.?"

Juliet only replied by stating their project of needle-work.

Elinor scoffed the notion; affirming that they would not obtain a morsel of bread to a glass of water, above once in three days. She felt, nevertheless, sufficient respect to the design of the noble fugitive, to send her a sealed note of what she called her approbation.

This note Juliet took in charge. It contained a draft for fifty pounds.

Ah, generous Elinor! thought Juliet, tears of gratitude glistening in her eyes: what a mixture of contrasting qualities sully, and ennoble your character in turn! Ah, why, to intellects so strong, a heart so liberal, a temper so gay, is there not joined a better portion of judgment, a larger one of diffidence, a sense of feminine propriety, and a mind rectified by religion,—not abandoned, uncontrolled, to imagination?

Gabriella, though truly touched by a generosity so unexpected, declined accepting its fruits; not being yet, she said, so helpless, however poor, as to prefer pecuniary obligation to industry. She would leave, therefore, the donation, for those who had lost the resources of independence which she yet possessed—youth and strength.

The tender admiration of Juliet forbade all remonstrance, and excluded any surprise. She well knew, and had long seen, that the distress which is the offspring of public calamity, not of private misfortune, however it may ruin prosperity, never humbles the mind.

Gabriella, in a letter of elegant acknowledgements, to obviate any accusation of undue pride, solicited the assistance of Elinor, in procuring orders for embroidery, amongst the ladies of her acquaintance.

Elinor, zealous to serve, and fearless to demand, instantly attacked, by note or by message, every rich female at Brighthelmstone; urging the generous, and shaming the niggardly, till there was scarcely a woman of fortune in the place, who had not given, or promised, a commission for some fine muslin-work.

The two friends, through this commanding protection, began their new plan of life under the most favourable auspices; and had soon more employment than time, though they limited themselves to five hours for sleep; though their meals were rather swallowed than eaten; and though they allowed not a moment for any kind of recreation, of rest, or of exercise; save the sacred visit, which they unfailingly made together, at break of day, to the little grave in the church-yard upon the hill.

Yet here first, since her arrival on the British shores, the immediate rapturous moment of landing, and the fortnight passed with Lady Aurora Granville excepted, here first sweet contentment, soft hopes, and gentle happiness visited the bosom of Juliet. No privation was hard, no toil was severe, no application was tedious, while the friend of her heart was by her side; whose sorrows she could mitigate, whose affections she could share, and whose tears she could sometimes chace.

But this relief was not more exquisite than it was transitory; a week only had passed in delicious repose, when Gabriella received intelligence that her husband was taken ill.

Whatever was her reluctance to quitting the spot, where her memory was every moment fed with cherished recollections, she could not hesitate to depart; but, when Juliet, in consonance with her inclination and her promise, prepared to accompany her, that hydra-headed* intruder upon human schemes and desires, Difficulty, arose, in as many shapes as she could form projects, to impede her wishes. Money they had none: even for the return to town of Gabriella, her husband was fain to have recourse for aid to certain admirable persons, whose benevolence had enabled her, upon the illness of her son, to quit it for Brighthelmstone: and, in a situation of indigence so obvious, could they propose carrying away with them the work with which they were entrusted? Juliet, indeed, had still Harleigh's bank notes in her possession; but she turned inflexibly from the temptation of adopting a mode of conduct, which she had always condemned as weak and degrading; that of investing circumstance with decision, in conscientious dilemmas.

These terrible obstacles broke into all their plans, their wishes, their happiness; involved them in new distress, deluged them in tears, and, after every effort with which ingenious friendship could combat them, ended in compelling a separation. Gabriella embraced, with pungent affliction, the sorrowing Juliet; shed her last bitter tears over the grave of her lost darling, and, by the assistance of the angelic beings† already hinted at, whose delicacy, whose feeling, whose respect for misfortune, made their beneficence as balsamic* to sensibility, as it was salutary to want, returned alone to the capital.

Juliet thus, perforce, remaining, and once again left to herself, was nearly overwhelmed with grief at a stroke so abrupt and unexpected; so ruinous to her lately acquired contentment, and dearly prized social enjoyment. Yet she suffered not regret and disappointment to consume her time, however cruelly they preyed upon her spirits, and demolished her comfort. Solitarily she continued the employment which she had socially begun; but without relaxing in diligence and application, without permitting herself the smallest intermission that could be avoided: urged not alone to maintain herself, and to replace what she had touched of the deposit of Harleigh, but excited, yet more forcibly, by the fond hope of rejoining her friend; to which she eagerly looked forward, as the result and reward of her activity and labour.

CHAPTER XLIII

LEFT thus to herself, and devoted to incessant work, Juliet next, had the vexation to learn, how inadequate for entering into any species of business was a mere knowledge of its theory.

She had concluded that, in consecrating her time and her labours to so simple an employment as needle-work, she secured herself a certain, though an hardly earned maintenance: but, as her orders became more extensive, she found that neither talents for what she undertook, nor even patronage to bring them into notice, was sufficient; a capital also was requisite, for the purchase of frames, patterns, silver and gold threads, spangles, and various other articles; to procure which, she was forced, in the very commencement of her new career, again to run in debt.

Alas! she cried, where business is not necessary to subsistence, how little do we know, believe, or even conceive, it's

† Residing in, and,—in 1795!—at the foot of Norbury Park.*

various difficulties! Imagination may paint enjoyments; but labours and hardships can be judged only from experience!

She was equally, also, unprepared for continual and vexatious delays of payment. Her work was frequently, when best executed, returned for capricious alterations; or set apart for some distant occasion, and forgotten; or received and worn, with no retribution but by promise. Even the few who possessed more consideration, seemed to estimate her time and her toil as nothing, because she was brought forward by recommendation; and to pay debts of common justice, with the parade of generosity.

Yet, vanity and false reasoning set apart, the ladies for whom she worked were neither hard of heart nor illiberal; but they had never known distress! and were too light and unreflecting to weigh the circumstances by which it might be produced, or prevented.

To save time, and obviate innumerable mortifications, Juliet, at first, employed a commissioner to carry home her work, and to deliver her bills; but he returned always with empty messages, that if Miss Ellis would call herself, she should be paid. Yet when, with whatever reluctance, she complied, she was ordinarily condemned to wait in passages, or anti-chambers, for whole hours, and even whole mornings; which were commonly ended by an excuse, through a footman, or lady's maid, that Lady or Miss such a one was too much engaged, or too much indisposed, to see her till the next day. The next day, when, with renewed expectation, she again presented herself, the same scene was re-acted; though the passing to and fro of various comers and goers, proved that it was only to herself her fair creditor was invisible.

Nevertheless, if she mentioned that she had some pattern, or some piece of work, finished for any other lady to exhibit, she was immediately admitted; though still, with regard to payment, she was desired to call again in the evening, or the next morning, with a new bill; her old one happening, unluckily, to be always lost or mislaid; and not seldom, while stopping in an anti-room, to arrange her packages, she heard exclamations of "How amazingly tiresome is that Miss Ellis! pestering one so, always, for her money!"

Is it possible, thought Juliet, that common humanity, nay, common sense, will not tell these careless triflers, that their complaint is a lampoon upon themselves? Will no reflexion, no feeling point out to them, that the time which they thus unmercifully waste in humiliating attendance, however to themselves it may be a play-thing, if not a drug,* is, to those who subsist but by their use of it, shelter, clothing, and nourishment?

If sometimes, in the hope of exciting more attention from this dissipated set, she ventured to drop a mournful hint, that she was a novice to this hard kind of life; the warm compassion that seemed rapidly kindled, raised expectations of immediate assistance; but the emotion, though good, took a direction that made it useless; it merely played about in exclamations of pity; then blazed into curiosity, vented itself in questions,—and evaporated.

She soon, therefore, ceased all attempt to obtain regard through personal representations; feeling yet more mortified to be left in passages, or recommended to domestics, after avowing that her lowly state was the effect of misfortune; than while she permitted it to be presumed, that she had nothing to brook but what she had been born and bred to bear.

Some, indeed, while leaving their own just debts unpaid and unnoticed, would have collected, from their friends, a few straggling half-crowns; but when Juliet, declining such aid, modestly solicited her right, they captiously disputed a bill which had been charged by the strictest necessity; or offered half what they would have dared propose to any ordinary and hired day-jobber.* And whatever admiration they bestowed upon the taste and execution of work prepared for others, all that she finished for themselves, was received with that wary precursor of under-valuing its price, contempt; and looked over with fault-finding eyes, and unmeaning criticism.

Yet, if the following day, or even the following hour, some sudden invitation to a brilliant assembly, made any of these ladies require her services, they would give their orders with caressing solicitations for speed; rush familiarly into her room, three or four times in a day, to see how she went on; supplicate her to touch nothing for any other human being; load her with professions of regard; confound her with hurrying entreaties;

shake her by the hand; tap her on the shoulder; call her the best of souls; assure her of their eternal gratitude; and torment her out of any time for sleep or food:—yet, the occasion past, and the work seen and worn, it was thought of no more! Her pains and exertions, their promises and fondness, sunk into the same oblivion; and the commonest and most inadequate pay was murmured at, if not contested.

Now and then, however, she was surprised by sudden starts of kindness, and hasty enquiries, eagerly made, though scarcely demanding any answer, into her situation and affairs; followed by drawing her, with an air of confidence, into a dressing-room or closet:—but there, when prepared for some mark of favour or esteem, she was only asked, in a mysterious whisper, whether she could procure any cheap foreign lace, or French gloves? or whether she could get over from France, any particularly delicate paste for the hands.*

To ladies and to behaviour of this cast, there were, however, exceptions; especially amongst the residents of the place and it's neighbourhood, who were not there, like the visitors, for dissipation or irregular extravagance, that, alternately, causes money to be loosely squandered, and meanly held back. But this better sort was rare, and sufficed not to supply employment to Juliet for her maintenance, though the most parsimonious. Nor were there any amongst them that had the leisure, or the discernment, to discover, that her mind both required and merited succour as much as her circumstances.

Yet there was the seat of what she had most to endure, and found hardest to sustain. Her short, but precious junction with her Gabriella, gave poignancy to every latent regret, and added disgust to her solitary toil. Thoughts uncommunicated, ideas unexchanged, fears unrevealed, and sorrows unparticipated, infused a heaviness into her existence, that not all her activity in business could conquer; while slackness of pay, by rendering the result of her labours distant and precarious, robbed her industry of cheerfulness, and her exertions of hope. With an ardent love of elegant social intercourse, she was doomed to pass her lonely days in a room that no sound of kindness ever cheered; with enthusiastic admiration of the beauties of Nature, she was denied all prospect, but of the coarse red tilings of opposite attics: with an innate taste for the fine arts, she was forced to exist as completely out of their view or knowledge, as if she had been an inhabitant of some uncivilized country: and fellow-feeling, that most powerful master of philanthropy! now taught her to pity the lamentations of seclusion from the world, that she had hitherto often contemned as weak and frivolous; since now, though with time always occupied, and a mind fully stored, she had the bitter self-experience of the weight of solitude without books, and of the gloom of retirement without a friend.

During this period, the only notice that she attracted, was that of a gouty old gentleman, whom she frequently met upon the stairs, when forced to mount or descend them in pursuit of her fair heedless creditors. She soon found, by the manner in which he entered, or quitted, at pleasure, the apartment that she had recently given up, that he was her successor. He was evidently struck by her beauty, and, upon their first meeting, looked earnestly after her till she was out of sight; and then, descended into the shop, to enquire who she was of Miss Matson. Miss Matson, always perplexed what to think of her, gave so indefinite, yet so extraordinary an account, that he eagerly awaited an opportunity of seeing her again. Added examination was less calculated to diminish curiosity, than to change it into pleasure and interest; and soon, during whole hours together, he perseveringly watched, upon the landing-places, for the moments of her going out, or coming back to the house; that, while smiling and bowing to her as she passed, he might obtain yet another, and another view of so singular and so lovely an Incognita.

As he annexed no fixed idea himself to this assiduity, he impressed none upon Juliet; who, though she could not but observe it, had a mind too much occupied within, for that mental listlessness that applies for thoughts, conjectures, or adventures from without.

Soon, however, becoming anxious to behold her nearer, and, soon after, to behold her longer, he contrived to place himself so as somewhat to obstruct, though not positively to impede, her passage. The modest courtesy, which she gave to his age, when, upon her approach, he made way for her, he pleased himself by attributing to his palpable admiration; and his bow, which had always been polite, became obsequious; and his smile, which had always spoken pleasure, displayed enchantment.

Still, however, there was nothing to alarm, and little to engage the attention of Juliet; for though ostentatiously gallant, he was scrupulously decorous. His manners and deportment were old-fashioned, but graceful and gentleman-like; and his eyes, though they had lost their brilliancy, were still quick, scrutinizing, and, where not softened by female attractions, severe.

One day, upon her return from a fruitless expedition, as fearfully, while ascending the stairs, she opened a paper that had just been delivered to her in the shop, her deeply absorbed and perplexed air, and the sigh with which she looked at its contents, induced him, with heightened interest, to attempt following her, that he might make some enquiry into her situation. He had discerned, as she passed, that what she held was a bill; he could not doubt her poverty from her change of apartment; and he wished to offer her some assistance: but finding that he had no chance of overtaking her, before she reached her chamber, he gently called, "Young lady!" and begged that she would stop.

With that alacrity of youthful purity, which is ever disposed to consider age and virtue as one, she not only complied, but, seeing the difficulty with which he mounted the stairs, respected his infirmities, and descended herself to meet him, and hear his business.

To a younger man, or to one less experienced, or less sagacious, this action might have appeared the effect of forwardness, of ignorance, or of levity; but to a man of the world, hackneyed in it's ways, and penetrating into the motives by which it is ordinarily influenced, it seemed the result of innocence without suspicion; yet of an innocence to which her air and manner gave a dignity that destroyed, in its birth, all interpretation to her disadvantage. His purse, therefore, which already he held in his hand, he felt must be offered with more delicacy than he had at first supposed to be necessary; and, though he was by no means a man apt to be embarrassed, he hesitated, for a moment, how to address a forlorn young stranger.

That moment, however, sufficed to determine him upon making an apology, with the most marked respect, for the liberty which he had taken in claiming her attention. The look with which she listened rewarded his judgment: it expressed the gratitude of feelings to which politeness was a pleasure; but not a novelty.

"I think—I understand, Ma'am," he then said, "you are the lady who inhabited the apartment to which, most unworthily, I have succeeded?"

Juliet bowed.

"I am truly concerned, Ma'am, at a mistake so preposterous in our destinies, so diametrically in opposition to our merits, as that which immures so much beauty and grace, which every one must wish to behold, in the attics; while so worn-out, and good-for-nothing an old fellow as I am, from whom every body must wish to turn their eyes, is perched, full in front, and precisely on the very spot so every way your superiour due. Whatever wicked Elf has done this deed, I confess myself heartily ashamed of my share in its operation; and humbly ready, should any better genius* come amongst us, with a view to putting things into their proper places, to agree, either that you should be lodged, in the face of day, in the drawing-room, and I be jammed, out of sight, in the garret; or—that you should become gouty and decrepit, and I grow suddenly young and beautiful."

Juliet could not but smile, yet waited some explanation without speaking.

Charmed with the smile, which his own rigid features immediately caught, "I have so frequently," he continued, "pondered and ruminated upon the good which those little aerial beings I speak of might do; and the wrongs which they might redress; were they permitted to visit us, now and then, as we read of their doing in days of yore; that, sometimes, I dream while wide awake, and fancy I see them; and feel myself at the mercy of their antic corrections; or receive courteous presents, or wholesome advice. Just this moment, as you were passing, methought one of them appeared to me!"

Juliet, surprised, involuntarily looked round.

"And it said to me, 'Whence happens it, my worthy antique, that you grow as covetous as you are rich? Bear, for your pains, the punishment due to a miser, of receiving money that you must not hoard; and of presenting, with your own avaricious hand, this purse to the fair young creature whose dwelling you have usurped; yet who resides nearest to those she most resembles, the gods and goddesses.'"

With these words, and a low bow, he would have put his purse into her hand; but upon her starting back, it dropt at her feet.

Surprized, yet touched, as well as amused, by a turn so unexpected to his pleasantry, Juliet, gracefully restoring, though firmly declining his offer, uttered her thanks for the kindness of his intentions, with a sweetness so unsuspicious of evil, that they separated with as strong an impression of wonder upon his part, as, upon her's, of gratitude.

Anxious to relieve the perplexity thus excited, and to settle his opinion, he continued to watch, but could not again address her; for aware, now, of his purpose, she fled down, or darted up stairs, with a swiftness that defied pursuit; yet with a passing courtesy, that marked respectful remembrance.

Thus, in a life of solitary hardship, with no intermission but for mortifying disappointment, passed nearly three weeks, when Juliet found, with affright and astonishment, that all orders for work seemed at an end. It was no longer the season for Brighthelmstone, whose visitors were only accidental stragglers, that, here to-day, and gone to-morrow, had neither care nor leisure but for rambling and amusement. The residents, though by no means inconsiderable, were soon served; for Elinor was removed to Lewes, and her influence was lost with her presence. Some new measure, therefore, for procuring employment, became necessary; and Juliet, once more, was reduced to make application to Miss Matson.

In passing, therefore, one morning, through the shop, with some work prepared for carrying home, she stopt to open upon the subject; but the appearance of Miss Bydel at the door, induced her, with an hasty apology, to make an abrupt retreat; that she might avoid an encounter which, with that lady, was always irksome, if not painful, from her unconstrained curiosity; joined to the grossness of her conceptions and remarks.

CHAPTER XLIV

JULIET, in remounting the stairs, was stopt, by her new acquaintance, before the door of his apartment.

"If you knew," he said, "how despitefully I have been treated, and how miserably black and blue I have been pinched, by the little Imp whose offer you have rejected, sleep would fly your eyes at night, from remorse for your hardness of heart. Its Impship* insists upon it, that the fault must all be mine. What! it cries, would you persuade me, that a young creature whose face beams with celestial sweetness, whose voice is the voice of melody, whose eyes have the softness of the Dove's*——"

Juliet, though she smiled, would have escaped; but he told her he must be heard.

"Would you persuade me, quoth my sprite, that such an angelic personage, would rather let my poor despised coin canker and rust in your miserly coffers, than disperse it about in the world, in kind, generous, or useful activity? No, my antique, continues my little elf, you have presented it in some clumsy, hunchy, awkward mode, that has made her deem you an unworthy bearer of fairy gifts; and she flies the downy wings of my gentle succour, from the fear of falling into your rough and uncooth claws."

Juliet, who now, through the ill-closed fingers of his gouty hand, discerned his prepared purse, seriously begged to decline this discussion.

"What malice you must bear me!" he cried. "You are surely in the pay of my evil genius! and I shall be whipt with nettles,* or scratched with thorns, all night, in revenge of my failure! And that parcel, too,—which strains the fine fibres of your fair hands,—cast it but down, and millions of my little elves will struggle to convey it safely to your chamber."

"I doubt not their dexterity," answered Juliet, "nor the

benevolence of their fabricator; but I assure you, Sir, I want no help."

"If you will not accept their aerial services, deign, at least, not to refuse mine!"

He endeavoured, now, to take the gown-packet into his own hands; laughingly saying, upon her grave resistance, "Beware, fair nymph, of the dormant sensations which you may awaken, if you should make me suppose you afraid of me! Many a long day is past, alas! and gone, since I could flatter myself with the idea of exciting fear in a young breast!"

Ceasing, however, the attempt, after some courteous apologies, he respectfully let her pass.

But, upon entering her room, she heard something chink as she deposited her parcel upon a table; and, upon examination, found that he had managed to slip into it, during the contest, a little green purse.

Vexed at this contrivance, and resolved not to lose an instant in returning what no distress could induce her to retain, she immediately descended; but the stair-case was vacant, and the door was closed. Fearful any delay might authorize a presumption of acceptance, she assumed courage to tap at the door.

A scampering, at the same moment, up the stairs, made her instantly regret this measure; and by no means the less, for finding herself recognized, and abruptly accosted by young Gooch, the farmer's son, at the very moment that her gouty admirer had hobbled to answer to her summons.

"Well, see if I a'n't a good marksman!" he cried; "for else, Ma'am, I might have passed you; for they told me, below, you were up there, at the very top of the house. But I'd warrant to pick you out from a hundred, Ma'am; as neat as my father would one of his stray sheep. But what I come for, Ma'am, is to ask the favour of your company, if it's agreeable to you, to a little junket* at our farm."

Then, rubbing his hands with great glee, unregarding the surprise look of Juliet, at such an invitation, or the amused watchfulness of the observant old beau, he went glibly on.

"Father's to give it, Ma'am. You never saw old dad, I believe, Ma'am? The old gentleman's a very good old chap; only he don't like our clubs: for he says they make me speak quite in the new manner;* so that the farmers, he says, don't know what I'd be at. He's rather in years, Ma'am, poor man. He don't know much how things go. However, he's a very well meaning old gentleman."

Juliet gravely enquired, to what unknown accident she might attribute an invitation so unexpected?

"Why, Ma'am," answered Gooch, delighted at the idea of having given her an agreeable surprize, "Why it's the 'Squire, Ma'am, that put it into my head. You know who I mean? our rich cousin, 'Squire Tedman. He's a great friend of yours, I can assure you, Ma'am. He wants you to take a little pleasure sadly. And he's sadly afraid, too, he says, that you'll miss him, now he's gone to town; for he used often, he says, to bring you one odd thing or another. He's got a fine fortune of his own, my cousin the 'Squire. And he's a widower.—And he's taken a vast liking to you, I can tell you, Ma'am;—so who knows. . . . ."

Juliet would have been perfectly unmoved by this ignorant forwardness, but for the presence of a stranger, to whose good opinion, after her experience of his benevolence, she could not be indifferent. With an air, therefore, that marked her little satisfaction at this familiar jocoseness, she declined the invitation; and begged the young man to acquaint Mr. Tedman, that, though obliged to his intentions, she should feel a yet higher obligation in his forbearance to forward to her, in future, any similar proposals.

"Why, Ma'am," cried young Gooch, astonished, "this i'n't a thing you can get at every day! We shall have all the main farmers of the neighbourhood! for it's given on account of a bargain that we've made, of a nice little slip of land,* just by our square hay-field. And I've leave to choose six of the company myself. But they won't be farmers, Ma'am, I can tell you! They'll be young fellows that know better how the world goes. And we shall have your good friend 'Squire Stubbs; for it's he that made our bargain."

Juliet, now, turning from him to the silent, remarking stranger, said, "I am extremely ashamed, Sir, to obtrude thus upon your time, but the person for whom you so generously destined this donation commissions me to return it, with many thanks, and an assurance that it is not at all wanted."

She held out her hand with the purse, but drawing back from receiving it, "Madam," he cried, "I would upon no account offend any one who has the honour of being known to you; but you will not, therefore, I hope, insist that I should quarrel with myself, by taking what does not belong to me?"

While Juliet, now, looked wistfully around, to discover some place where she might drop the purse, unseen by the young man, whose misinterpretations might be injurious, the youth volubly continued his own discourse.

"We shall give a pretty good entertainment in the way of supper, I assure you, Ma'am; for we shall have a goose at top, and a turkey at bottom, and as fine a fat pig as ever you saw in your life in the middle; with as much ale, and mead,* and punch, as you can desire to drink. And, as all my sisters are at home, and a brace or so of nice young lasses of their acquaintance, besides ever so many farmers, and us seven stout young fellows of my club, into the bargain, we intend to kick up a dance. It may keep you out a little late, to be sure, Ma'am, but you shall have our chay-cart* to bring you home. You know our chay-cart of old, Ma'am?"

"I, Sir?"

"Why, lauk!* have you forgot that, Ma'am? Why it's our chay-cart that brought you to Brighton, from Madam Maple's at Lewes, as good as half a year ago. Don't you remember little Jack, that drove you? and that went for you again the next day, to fetch you back?"

Juliet now found, that this was the carriage procured for her by Harleigh, upon her first arrival at Lewes; and, though chagrined at the air of former, or disguised intimacy, which such an incident might seem to convey to her new friend, she immediately acknowledged recollecting the circumstance.

"Well, I'm only sorry, Ma'am, I did not drive you myself; but I had not the pleasure of your acquaintance then, Ma'am; for 'twas before of our acting together."

The surprise of the listening old gentleman now altered its expression, from earnest curiosity to suppressed pleasantry; and he leant against his door, to take a pinch of snuff, with an air that denoted him to be rather waiting for some expected amusement, than watching, as heretofore, for some interesting explanation.

Juliet, in discerning the passing change in his ideas, became more than ever eager to return the purse; yet more than ever fearful of misconstruction from young Gooch; whom she now, with encreased dissatisfaction, begged to lose no time in acquainting Mr. Tedman, that business only ever took her from home.

"Why, that's but moping for you, neither, Ma'am," he answered, in a tone of pity. "You'd have double the spirits if you'd go a little abroad; for staying within doors gives one but a hippish* turn. It will go nigh to make you grow quite melancholick, Ma'am."

Hopeless to get rid either of him or of the purse, Juliet, now, was moving up stairs, when the voice of Miss Bydel called out from the passage, "Why, Mr. Gooch, have you forgot I told you to send Mrs. Ellis to me?"

"That I had clean!" he answered. "I ask your pardon, I'm sure, Ma'am.—Why, Ma'am, Miss Bydel told me to tell you, when I said I was coming up to ask you to our junket, that she wanted to say a word or two to you, down in the shop, upon business."

Juliet would have descended; but Miss Bydel, desiring her to wait, mounted herself, saying, "I have a mind to see your little new room:" stopping, however, when she came to the landing-place, which was square and large, "Well-a-day!" she exclaimed: "Sir Jaspar Herrington!—who'd have thought of seeing you, standing so quietly at your door? Why I did not know you could stand at all! Why how is your gout, my good Sir? And how do you like your new lodgings? I heard of your being here from Miss Matson. But pray, Mrs. Ellis, what has kept you both, you and young Mr. Gooch, in such close conference with Sir Jaspar? I can't think what you've been talking of so long. Pray how did you come to be so intimate together? I should like to know that."

Sir Jaspar courteously invited Miss Bydel to enter his apartment; but that lady, not aware that nothing is less delicate than professions of delicacy; which degrade a just perception, and strict practice of propriety, into a display of conscious caution, or a suspicion of evil interpretation; almost angrily answered, that she could not for the world do such a thing, for it would set every body a talking: "for, as I'm not married, Sir Jaspar, you know, and as you're a single gentleman, too, it might make Miss Matson and her young ladies think I don't know what. For, when once people's tongues are set a-going, it's soon too late to stop them. Besides, every body's always so prodigious curious to dive into other people's affairs, that one can't well be too prudent."

Sir Jaspar, with an arched brow, of which she was far from comprehending the meaning, said that he acquiesced in her better judgment; but, as she had announced that she came to speak with this young lady upon business, he enquired, whether there would be any incongruity in putting a couple of chairs upon the landing-place.

"Well," she cried, "that's a bright thought, I declare, Sir Jaspar! for it will save me the trouble of groping up stairs;" and then, seizing the opportunity to peep into his room, she broke forth into warm exclamations of pleasure, at the many nice and new things with which it had been furnished, since it had been vacated by Mrs. Ellis.

A look, highly commiserating, shewed him shocked by these observations; and the air, patiently calm, with which they were heard by Juliet, augmented his interest, as well as wonder, in her story and situation.

He ordered his valet to fetch an arm-chair for Miss Bydel; while, evidently meant for Juliet, he began to drag another forward himself.

"Bless me, Sir Jaspar!" cried Miss Bydel, looking, a little affronted, towards Juliet, "have you no common chairs?"

"Yes," he answered, still labouring on, "for common purposes!"

This civility was not lost upon Juliet, who declining, though thankful for his attention, darted forward, to take, for herself, a seat of less dignity; hastily, as she passed, dropping the purse upon a table.

A glance at Sir Jaspar sufficed to assure her, that this action had not escaped his notice; and though his look spoke disappointment, it shewed him sensible of the propriety of avoiding any contest.

Relieved, from this burthen, she now cheerfully waited to hear the orders of Miss Bydel: young Gooch waited to hear them also; seated, cross-legged, upon the balustrade; though Sir Jaspar sent his valet away, and retired, scrupulously, himself, to the further end of his apartment.

Miss Bydel, as little struck with the ill breeding of the young farmer, as with the good manners of the baronet, forgot her business, from recollecting that Mr. Scope was waiting for her in the shop. "For happening," said she, "to pass by, and see me, through the glass-door, he just stept in, on purpose to have a little chat."

"O ho, what, is 'Squire Scope here?" cried young Gooch; and, rapidly sliding down the banisters, seized upon the unwilling and precise Mr. Scope, whom he dragged up to the landing-place.

"Well, this is droll enough!" cried Miss Bydel, palpably enchanted, though trying to look displeased; "only I hope you have not told Mr. Scope 'twas I that sent you for him, Mr. Gooch? for, I assure you, Mr. Scope, I would not do such a thing for the world. I should think it quite improper. Besides, what will Miss Matson and the young milliners say? Who knows but you may have set them a prating, Mr. Gooch? It's no joke, I can assure you, doing things of this sort."

"I'm sure, Ma'am," said Gooch, "I thought you wanted to see the 'Squire; for I did not do it in the least to make game."

"There can be no doubt, Madam," said Mr. Scope, somewhat offended, "that all descriptions of sport are not, at all times, advisable. For, in small societies, as in great states, if I may be permitted to compare little things with great ones, danger often lurks unseen, and mischief breaks out from trifles. In like manner, for example, if one of those young milliners, misinterpreting my innocence, in obeying the supposed commands of the good Miss Bydel, should take the liberty to laugh at my expence, what, you might ask, could it signify that a young girl should laugh? Young persons, especially of the female gender, being naturally given to laughter, at very small provocatives; not to say sometimes without any whatsoever.

Whereupon, persons of an ordinary judgment, may conclude such an action, by which I mean laughing, to be of no consequence.—"

"But I think it very rude!" cried Miss Bydel, extremely nettled.

"Please to hear me, Madam!" said Mr. Scope. "Persons, I say, of deeper knowledge in the maxims and manners of the moral world, would look forward with watchfulness, on such an occasion, to its future effects; for one laugh breeds another, and another breeds another; for nothing is so catching as laughing; I mean among the vulgar; in which class I would be understood to include the main mass of a great nation. What, I ask, ensues?—"

"O, as to that, Mr. Scope," cried Miss Bydel, rather impatiently, "I assure you if I knew any body that took such a liberty as to laugh at me, I should let them know my thoughts of such airs without much ceremony!"

"My very good lady," said Mr. Scope, formally bowing, "if I may request such a favour, I beg you to be silent. The laugh, I observe, caught thus, from one to another, soon spreads abroad; and then, the more aged, or better informed, may be led to enquire into its origin: and the result of such investigation must needs be, that the worthy Miss Bydel, having sent her commands to her humble servant, Mr. Scope, to follow her up stairs—"

"But if they said that," cried Miss Bydel, looking very red, "it would be as great a fib as ever was told, for I did not send my commands, nor think of such a thing. It was Mr. Gooch's own doing, only for his own nonsense. And I am curious to know, Mr. Gooch, whether any body ever put such thoughts into your head? Pray did you ever hear any body talk, Mr. Gooch? For, if you have, I should be glad to know what they said."

Mr. Scope, waving his hand to demand attention, again begged leave to remark, that he had not finished what he purposed to advance.

"My argument, Madam," he resumed, "is a short, but, I hope, a clear one, for 'tis deduced from general principles and analogy; though, upon a merely cursory view, it may appear somewhat abstruse. But what I mean, in two words, is, that the laugh raised by Mr. Gooch, and those young milliners; taking it for granted that they laughed; which, indeed, I rather think I heard them do; may, in itself, perhaps, as only announcing incapacity, not be condemnable; but when it turns out that it promulgates false reports, and makes two worthy persons, if I may take the liberty to name myself with the excellent Miss Bydel, appear to be fit subjects for ridicule; then, indeed, the laugh is no longer innocent; and ought, in strict justice, to be punished, as seriously as any other mode of propagating false rumours."

Miss Bydel, after protesting that Mr. Scope talked so prodigiously sensible, that she was never tired of hearing him, for all his speeches were so long; abruptly told Juliet, that she had called to let her know, that she should be glad to be paid, out of hand, the money which she had advanced for the harp.

Sir Jaspar, who, during the harangue of Mr. Scope, which was uttered in too loud and important a manner, to leave any doubt of it's being intended for general hearing; had drawn his chair to join the party, listened to this demand with peculiar attention; and was struck with the evident distress which it caused to Juliet; who fearfully besought a little longer law,* to collect the debts of others, that she might be able to discharge her own.

Young Gooch, coming behind her, said, in a half whisper, "If you'll tell me how much it is you owe, Ma'am, I'll help you out in a trice; for I can have what credit I will in my father's name; and he'll never know but what 'twas for some frolic of my own; for I don't make much of a confidant of the old gentleman."

The most icy refusal was insufficient to get rid of this offer, or offerer; who assured her that, if the worst came to the worst, and his father, by ill luck, should find them out, he would not make a fuss for above a day or two; "because," he continued, "he has only me, as one may say, for the rest are nothing but girls; so he can't well help himself. He gave me my swing* too long from the first, to bind me down at this time of day. Besides, he likes to have me a little in the fashion, I know, though he won't own it; for he is a very good sort of an old gentleman, at bottom."

Sir Jaspar sought to discover, whether the colour which heightened the cheeks of Juliet at this proposal, which now ceased to be delivered in a whisper, was owing to confusion at its publicity, or to disdain at the idea of conspiring either at deceiving or braving the young man's father; while Miss Bydel, whose plump curiosity saved her from all species of speculative trouble, bluntly said, "Why should you hesitate at such an offer, my dear? I'm sure I don't see how you can do better than accept it. Mr. Gooch is a very worthy young man, and so are all his family. I'm sure I only wish he'd take to you more solidly, and make a match of it. That would put an end to your troubles at once; and I should get my money out of hand."

This was an opportunity not to be passed over by the argumentative but unerring Mr. Scope, for trite observations, self-evident truths, and hackneyed calculations, upon the mingled dangers and advantages of matrimony, "which, when weighed," said he, "in equal scales, and abstractedly considered, are of so puzzling a nature, that the wise and wary, fearing to risk them, remain single; but which, when looked upon in a more cursory way, or only lightly balanced, preponderate so much in favour of the state, that the great mass of the nation, having but small means of reflection, or forethought, ordinarily prefer matrimony. If, therefore, young Mr. Gooch should think proper to espouse this young person, there would be nothing in it very surprising; nevertheless, in summing up the expences of wedlock, and a growing family, it might seem, that to begin the married state with debts already contracted, on the female side, would appear but a shallow mark of prudence on the male, where the cares of that state reasonably devolve; he being naturally supposed to have the most sense."

"O, as to that, Mr. Scope," cried Miss Bydel, "if Mr. Gooch should take a liking to this young person, she has money enough to pay her debts, I can assure you: I should not have asked her for it else; but the thing is, she don't like to part with it."

Juliet solemnly protested, that the severest necessity could alone have brought her into the pecuniary difficulties under which she laboured; the money to which Miss Bydel alluded being merely a deposit which she held in her hands, and for which she was accountable.

"Well, that's droll enough," said Miss Bydel, "that a young person, not worth a penny in the world, should have the care of other people's money! I should like to know what sort of persons they must be, that can think of making such a person their steward!"

Young Gooch said that it would not be his father, for one, who would do it; and Mr. Scope was preparing an elaborate dissertation upon the nature of confidence, with regard to money-matters, in a great state; when Miss Bydel, charmed to have pronounced a sentence which seemed to accord with every one's opinion, ostentatiously added, "I should like, I say, Mrs. Ellis, to know what sort of person it could be, that would trust a person with one's cash, without enquiring into their circumstances? for though, upon hearing that a person has got nothing, one may give 'em something, one must be no better than a fool to make them one's banker."

Juliet, who could not enter into any explanation, stammered, coloured, and from the horrour of seeing that she was suspected, wore an air of seeming apprehensive of detection.

A short pause ensued, during which, every one fixed his eyes upon her face, save Sir Jaspar; who seemed studying a portrait upon his snuff-box.*

Her immediate wish, in this disturbance, was to clear herself from so terrible an aspersion, by paying Miss Bydel, as she had paid her other creditors, from the store of Harleigh; but her wishes, tamed now by misfortune and disappointment, were too submissively under the controul of fear and discretion, to suffer her to act from their first dictates: and a moment's reflection pointed out, that, joined to the impropriety of such a measure with respect to Harleigh himself, it would be liable, more than any other, to give her the air of an impostor, who possessed money that she could either employ, or disclaim all title to, at her pleasure. Calling, therefore, for composure from conscious integrity, she made known her project of applying once more to Miss Matson, for work; and earnestly supplicated for the influence of Miss Bydel, that this second application might not, also, be vain.

The eyes of the attentive Sir Jaspar, as he raised them from his snuff-box, now spoke respect mingled with pity.

"As to recommending you to Miss Matson, Mrs. Ellis," answered Miss Bydel, "it's out of all reason to demand such a thing, when I can't tell who you are myself; and only know that you have got money in your hands nobody knows how, nor what for."

An implication such as this, nearly overpowered the fortitude of Juliet; and, relinquishing all further effort, she rose, and, silently, almost gloomily, began ascending the stairs. Sir Jaspar caught the expression of her despair by a glance; and, in a tone of remonstrance, said to Miss Bydel, "In your debt, good Miss Bydel? Have you forgotten, then, that the young lady has paid you?"

"Paid me? good Me! Sir Jaspar," cried Miss Bydel, staring; "how can you say such a thing? Do you think I'd cheat the young woman?"

"I think it so little," answered he, calmly, "that I venture to remind you, thus publicly, of the circumstance; in full persuasion that I shall merit your gratitude, by aiding your memory."

"Good Me! Sir Jaspar, why I never heard such a thing in my life! Paid me? When? Why it can't be without my knowing it?"

"Certainly not; I beg you, therefore, to recollect yourself."

The stare of Miss Bydel was now caught by Mr. Scope; and her "Good Me!" was echoed by young Gooch; while the surprised Juliet, turning back, said, "Pardon me, Sir! I have never been so happy as to be able to discharge the debt. It remains in full force."

"Over you, too, then," cried Sir Jaspar, with quickness, "have I the advantage in memory? Have you forgotten that you delivered, to Miss Bydel, the full sum, not twenty minutes since?"

Miss Bydel now, reddening with anger, cried, "Sir Jaspar, I have long enough heard of your ill nature; but I never suspected your crossness would take such a turn against a person as this, to make people believe I demand what is not my own!"

Juliet again solemnly acknowledged the debt; and Mr. Scope opened an harangue upon the merits of exactitude between debtor and creditor, and the usefulness of settling no accounts, without, what were the only legal witnesses to obviate financial controversy, receipts in full; when Sir Jaspar, disregarding, alike, his rhetoric or Miss Bydel's choler, quietly patting his snuff-box, said, that it was possible that Miss Bydel had, inadvertently, put the sum into her work-bag, and forgotten that it had been refunded.

Exulting that means, now, were open for vindication and redress, Miss Bydel eagerly untied the strings of her work-bag; though Juliet entreated that she would spare herself the useless trouble. But Sir Jaspar protested, with great gravity, that his own honour was now as deeply engaged to prove an affirmative, as that of Miss Bydel to prove a negative: holding, however, her hand, he said that he could not be satisfied, unless the complete contents of the work-bag were openly and fairly emptied upon a table, in sight of the whole party.

Miss Bydel, though extremely affronted, consented to this proposal; which would clear her, she said, of so false a slander. A table was then brought upon the landing-place; as she still stiffly refused risking her reputation, by entering the apartment of a single gentleman; though he might not, as she observed, be one of the youngest.

Sir Jaspar demanded the precise amount of the sum owed. A guinea and a half.

He then fetched a curious little japan basket* from his chamber, into which he desired that Miss Bydel would put her work-bag; though he would not suffer her to empty it, till, with various formalities, he had himself placed it in the middle of the table; around which he made every one draw a chair.

Miss Bydel now triumphantly turned her work-bag inside out; but what was her consternation, what the shock of Mr. Scope, and how loud the shout of young Gooch, to see, from a small open green purse, fall a guinea and half!

Miss Bydel, utterly confounded, remained speechless; but Juliet, through whose sadness Sir Jaspar saw a smile force its way, that rendered her beauty dazzling, recollecting the purse, blushed, and would have relieved Miss Bydel, by confessing that she knew to whom it belonged; had she not been withheld by the fear of the strange appearance which so sudden a seeming intimacy with the Baronet might wear.

Sir Jaspar, again patting his snuff-box, composedly said, "I was persuaded Miss Bydel would find that her debt had been discharged."

Miss Bydel remained stupified; while Mr. Scope, with a look

concerned, and even abashed, condolingly began an harangue upon the frail tenure of the faculty of human memory.

Miss Bydel, at length, recovering her speech, exclaimed, "Well, here's the money, that's certain! but which way it has got into my work-bag, without my ever seeing or touching it, I can't pretend to say: but if Mrs. Ellis has done it to play me a trick—"

Juliet disavowed all share in the transaction.

"Then it's some joke of Sir Jaspar's! for I know he dearly loves to mortify; so I suppose he has given me false coin, or something that won't go, just to make me look like a fool."

"The money, I have the honour to assure you, is not mine," was all that, very tranquilly, Sir Jaspar replied: while Mr. Scope, after a careful examination of each piece, declared each to be good gold, and full weight.

Sundry "Good me's!" and other expressions of surprise, though all of a pleasurable sort, now broke forth from Miss Bydel, finishing with, "However, if nobody will own the money, as the debt is fairly my due, I don't see why I may not take it; though as to the purse, I won't touch it, because as that's a thing I have not lent to any body, I've no right to it."

Juliet here warmly interfered. The purse, she said, and the money belonged to the same proprietor; and, as neither of them were her's, both ought to be regarded as equally inadmissible for the payment of a debt which she alone had contracted. This disinterested sincerity made even Mr. Scope turn to her with an air of profound, though surprised respect; while Sir Jaspar fixed his eyes upon her face with encreased and the most lively wonder; young Gooch stared, not perfectly understanding her; but Miss Bydel, rolling up the purse, which she put back into the basket, said, "Well, if the money is not yours, Mrs. Ellis, my dear, it can be nobody's but Sir Jaspar's; and if he has a mind to pay your debt for you, I don't see why I should hinder him, when 'twould be so much to my disadvantage. He's rich enough, I assure you; for what has an old bachelor to do with his money? So I'll take my due, be it which way it will." And, unmoved by all that Juliet could urge, she put the guinea and the half-guinea carefully into her pocket.

Juliet declared, that a debt which she had not herself discharged, she should always consider as unpaid, though her creditor might be changed.

Confused then, ashamed, perplexed,—yet unavoidably pleased, she mounted to her chamber.

CHAPTER XLV

WITH whatever shame, whatever chagrin, Juliet saw herself again involved in a pecuniary obligation, with a stranger, and a gentleman, a support so efficacious, at a moment of such alarm, was sensibly and gratefully felt. Yet she was not less anxious to cancel a favour which still was unfitting to be received. She watched, therefore, for the departure of Miss Bydel, and the restoration of stillness to the stair-case, to descend, once more, in prosecution of her scheme with Miss Matson.

The anxious fear of rejection, and dread of rudeness, with which she then renewed her solicitation, soon happily subsided, from a readiness to listen, and a civility of manner, as welcome as they were unexpected, in her hostess; by whom she was engaged, without difficulty, to enter upon her new business the following morning.

Thus, and with cruel regret, concluded her fruitless effort to attain a self-dependence which, however subject to toil, might be free, at least, from controul. Every species of business, however narrow its cast, however limited its wants, however mean its materials; required, she now found, some capital to answer to its immediate calls, and some steady credit for encountering the unforeseen accidents, and unavoidable risks, to which all human undertakings, whether great or insignificant, are liable.

With this conviction upon her mind, she strove to bear the disappointment without murmuring; hoping to gain in security all that she lost in liberty. Little reason, indeed, had she for regretting what she gave up: she had been worn by solitary toil, and heavy rumination; by labour without interest, and loneliness without leisure.

Nevertheless, the beginning of her new career promised little amelioration from the change. She was summoned early to the shop to take her work; but, when she begged leave to return with it to her chamber, she was stared at as if she had made a demand the most preposterous, and told that, if she meant to enter into business, she must be at hand to receive directions, and to learn how it should be done.

To enter into business was far from the intention of Juliet; but the fear of dismission, should she proclaim how transitory were her views, silenced her into acquiescence; and she seated herself behind a distant counter.

And here, perforce, she was initiated into a new scene of life, that of the humours of a milliner's shop.* She found herself in a whirl of hurry, bustle, loquacity, and interruptions. Customers pressed upon customers; goods were taken down merely to be put up again; cheapened* but to be rejected; admired but to be looked at, and left; and only bought when, to all appearance, they were undervalued and despised.

It was here that she saw, in its unmasked futility, the selfishness of personal vanity. The good of a nation, the interest of society, the welfare of a family, could with difficulty have appeared of higher importance than the choice of a ribbon, or the set of a cap; and scarcely any calamity under heaven could excite looks of deeper horrour or despair, than any mistake committed in the arrangement of a feather or a flower. Every feature underwent a change, from chagrin and fretfulness, if any ornament, made by order, proved, upon trial, to be unbecoming; while the whole complexion glowed with the exquisite joy of triumph, if something new, devised for a superiour in the world of fashion, could be privately seized as a model by an inferiour.

The ladies whose practice it was to frequent the shop, thought the time and trouble of its mistress, and her assistants, amply paid by the honour of their presence; and though they tried on hats and caps, till they put them out of shape; examined and tossed about the choicest goods, till they were so injured that they could be sold only at half price; ordered sundry articles, which, when finished, they returned, because they had changed their minds; or discovered that they did not want them; still their consciences were at ease, their honour was self-acquitted, and their generosity was self-applauded, if, after two or three hours of lounging, rummaging, fault-finding and chaffering,* they purchased a yard or two of ribbon, or a few skanes of netting silk.*

The most callous disregard to all representations of the dearness of materials, or of the just price of labour, was accompanied by the most facile acquiescence even in demands that were exorbitant, if they were adroitly preceded by, "Lady ***, or the Duchess of ***, gave that sum for just such another cap, hat, &c., this very morning."

Here, too, as in many other situations into which accident had led, or distress had driven Juliet, she saw, with commiseration and shame for her fellow-creatures, the total absence of feeling and of equity, in the dissipated and idle, for the indigent and laborious. The goods which demanded most work, most ingenuity, and most hands, were last paid, because heaviest of expence; though, for that very reason, the many employed, and the charge of materials, made their payment the first required. Oh that the good Mr. Giles Arbe, thought Juliet, could arraign, in his simple but impressive style, the ladies who exhibit themselves with unpaid plumes, at assemblies and operas; and enquire whether they can flatter themselves, that to adorn them alone is sufficient to recompense those who work for, without seeing them; who ornament without knowing them; and who must necessarily, if unrequited, starve in rendering them more brilliant!

Upon further observation, nevertheless, her compassion for the milliner and the work-women somewhat diminished; for she found that their notions of probity were as lax as those of their customers were of justice; and saw that their own rudeness to those who had neither rank nor fortune, kept pace with the haughtiness which they were forced to support, from those by whom both were possessed. Every advantage was taken of inexperience and simplicity; every article was charged, not according to its value, but to the skill or ignorance of the purchaser; old goods were sold as if new; cheap goods as if dear; and ancient, or vulgar ornaments, were presented to the unpractised chafferer, as the very pink of the mode.

The rich and grand, who were capricious, difficult, and long in their examinations, because their time was their own; or rather, because it hung upon their hands; and whose utmost exertion, and sole practice of exercise consisted in strolling from a sofa to a carriage, were instantly, and with fulsome adulation, attended; while the meaner, or economical, whose time had its essential appropriations, and was therefore precious, were obliged to wait patiently for being served, till no coach was at the door, and every fine lady had sauntered away.* And even then, they were scarcely heard when they spoke; scarcely shewn what they demanded; and scarcely thanked for what they purchased.

In viewing conflicts such as these, between selfish vanity and cringing cunning, it soon became difficult to decide, which was least congenial to the upright mind and pure morality of Juliet, the insolent, vain, unfeeling buyer, or the subtle, plausible, over-reaching seller.

The companions of Juliet in this business, though devoted, of course, to its manual operations, left all its cares to its mistress. Their own wishes and hopes were caught by other objects. The town was filled with officers, whose military occupations were brief, whose acquaintances were few, and who could not, all day long, ride, or pursue the sports of the field. These gentlemen, for their idle moments, chose to deem all the unprotected young women whom they thought worth observance, their natural prey. And though, from race to race, and from time immemorial, the young female shop-keeper had been warned of the danger, the folly, and the fate of her predecessors; in listening to the itinerant admirer, who, here to-day and gone to-morrow, marches his adorations, from town to town with as much facility, and as little regret, as his regiment; still every new votary to the counter and the modes, was ready to go over the same ground that had been trodden before; with the fond persuasion of proving an exception to those who had ended in misery and disgrace, by finishing, herself, with marriage and promotion. Their minds, therefore, were engaged in airy projects; and their leisure, where they could elude the vigilance of Miss Matson, was devoted to clandestine coquetry, tittering whispers, and secret frolics.

"These," said Juliet, in a letter to Gabriella, "are now my destined associates! Ah, heaven! can these—can such as these,—setting aside pride, prejudice, propriety, or whatever word we use for the distinctions of society,—can these—can such as these, suffice as companions to her whose grateful heart has been honoured with the friendship of Gabriella? O hours of refined felicity past and gone, how severe is your contrast with those of heaviness and distaste now endured!"

The inexperience of Juliet in business, impeded not her acquiring almost immediate excellence in the millinery art, for which she was equally fitted by native taste, and by her remembrance of what she had seen abroad. The first time, therefore, that she was employed to arrange some ornaments, she adjusted them with an elegance so striking, that Miss Matson, with much parade, exhibited them to her best lady-customers, as a specimen of the very last new fashion, just brought her over by one of her young ladies from Paris.

In a town that subsists by the search of health for the sick, and of amusement for the idle, the smallest new circumstance is of sufficient weight to be related and canvassed; for there is ever most to say where there is least to do. The phrase, therefore, that went forth from Miss Matson, that one of her young ladies was just come from France, was soon spread through the neighbourhood; with the addition that the same person had brought over specimens of all the French *costume.**

Such a report could not fail to allure staring customers to the shop, where the attraction of the youth and beauty of the new work-woman, contrasted with her determined silence to all enquiry, gave birth to perpetually varying conjectures in her presence, which were followed by the most eccentric assertions where she was the subject of discourse in her absence. All that already had been spread abroad, of her acting, her teaching, her playing the harp, her needle-work, and, more than all, her having excited a suicide; was now in every mouth; and curiosity, baffled in successive attempts to penetrate into the truth, supplied, as usual, every chasm of fact by invention.

This species of commerce, always at hand, and always fertile, proved so highly amusing to the lassitude of the idle, and to the frivolousness of the dissipated, that, in a very few days, the shop of Miss Matson became the general rendezvous of the saunterers, male and female, of Brighthelmstone. The starers were happy to present themselves where there was something to see; the strollers, where there was any where to go; the loungers, where there was any pretence to stay; and the curious where there was any thing to develop in which they had no concern.

Juliet, at first, ignorant of the usual traffic of the shop, imagined this affluence of customers to be habitual; but she was soon undeceived, by finding herself the object of inquisitive examination; and by overhearing unrestrained inquiries made to Miss Matson, of "Pray, Ma'am, which is your famous French milliner?"

In the midst of these various distastes and discomforts, some interest was raised in the mind of Juliet, for one of her young fellow-work-women. It was not, indeed, that warm interest which is the precursor of friendship; its object had no qualities that could rise to such a height; it was simply a sensation of pity, abetted by a wish of doing good.

Flora Pierson, without either fine features or fine countenance, had strikingly the beauty of youth in a fair complexion, round, plump, rosy cheeks, bright, though unmeaning eyes, and an air of health, strength, and juvenile good humour, that was diffused copiously through her whole appearance. She was innocent and inoffensive, and, as far as she was able to think, well meaning, and ready to be at every body's command; though incapable to be at any body's service. Yet her simplicity was of that happy sort that never occasions self-distress, from being wholly unaccompanied by any consciousness of deficiency or inferiority. Accustomed to be laughed at almost whenever she spoke, she saw the smile that she raised without emotion; or participated in it without knowing why; and she heard the sneer that followed her simple merriment without displeasure; though sometimes she would a little wonder what it meant.

This young creature, who had but barely passed her sixteenth year, had already attracted the dangerous attention of various officers, from whose several attacks and manœuvres she had hitherto been rescued by the vigilance of Miss Matson. Each of these anecdotes she eagerly took, or rather made opportunities to communicate to Juliet; waiting for no other encouragement than the absence of Miss Matson, and using no other prelude than "Now I've got something else to tell you!"

Except for some slight mixture of contempt, Juliet heard

these tales with perfect indifference; till that ungenial feeling, or rather absence of feeling, was superceded by compassion, upon finding that she was the object, probably the dupe, of a new and unfinished adventure, with which Miss Matson was as yet unacquainted. "Now, Miss Ellis!" she cried, "I'll tell you the drollest part of all, shall I? Well, do you know I've got another admirer that's above all the rest? And yet he i'n't a captain, neither, nor an officer. But he's quite a gentleman of quality, for he's a knight baronight.* And he's very pretty, I assure you. As pretty as you, only his nose is a little shorter, and his mouth is a little bigger. And he has not got quite so much colour; for he is very pale. But he's prettier than I am, I believe. Yet I'm not very homely, people say. I'm sure I don't know. One can't judge one's self. But I believe I'm very well. At least, I am not very brown; I know that, by my looking-glass. I've a pretty good skin of my own."

Neither the giggling derision of her fellow-work-women, nor the total abstinence from enquiry or comment with which Juliet heard these insignificant details, checked the pleasure of Flora in her own prattle; which, whenever she could find some one to address,—for she waited not till any one would listen,—went on, with sleepy good humour, and pretty, but unintelligent smiles, from the moment that she rose, to the moment that she went to rest. But when, in great confidence, and declaring that nobody was in the secret, except just Miss Biddy, and Miss Jenny, and Miss Polly, and Miss Betsey, she made known who was this last and most striking admirer, the attention of Juliet was roused; it was Sir Lyell Sycamore.

Copiously, and with looks of triumph, Flora related her history with the young Baronet. First of all, she said, he had declared, in ever so many little whispers, that he was in love with her; and next, he had made her ever so many beautiful presents, of ear-rings, necklaces, and trinkets; always sending them by a porter, who pretended that they were just arrived by the Diligence; with a letter to shew to Miss Matson, importing that an uncle of Flora's, who resided in Northumberlandshire, begged her to accept these remembrances. "Though I'm sure I don't know how he found out that I've got an uncle there," she continued, "unless it was by my telling it him, when he asked me what relations I had."

Her gratitude and vanity thus at once excited, Sir Lyell told her that he had some important intelligence to communicate, which could not be revealed in a short whisper in the shop: he begged her, therefore, to meet him upon the Strand, a little way out of the town, one Sunday afternoon; while Miss Matson might suppose that she was taking her usual recreation with the rest of the young ladies. "So I could not refuse him, you may think," she said, "after being so much obliged to him; and so we walked together by the sea-side, and he was as agreeable as ever; and so was I, too, I believe, if I may judge without flattery. At least, he said I was, over and over; and he's a pretty good judge, I believe, a man of his quality. But I sha'n't tell you what he said to me; for he said I was as fresh as a violet, and as fair as jessamy,* and as sweet as a pink, and as rosy as a rose; but one must not over and above believe the gentlemen, mama says, for what they say is but half a compliment. However, what do you think, Miss Ellis? Only guess! For all his being so polite, do you know, he was upon the point of behaving rude? Only I told him I'd squall out, if he did. But he spoke so pretty when he saw I was vexed, that I could not be very angry with him about it; could I? Besides, men will be rude, naturally, mamma says."

"But does not your mama tell you, also, Miss Pierson, that you must not walk out alone with gentlemen?"

"O dear, yes! She's told me that ever so often. And I told it to Sir Lyell; and I said to him we had better not go. But he said that would kill him, poor gentleman! And he looked as sorrowful as ever you saw; just as if he was going to cry. I'm sure I'm glad he did not, poor gentleman! for if he had, it's ten to one but I should have cried too; unless, out of ill luck, I had happened to fall a laughing; for it's odds which I do, sometimes, when I'm put in a fidget. However, upon seeing his sister, along with some company of his acquaintance, not far off, he said I had better go back: but he promised me, if I would meet him again the next Sunday, he would have a post-chaise o'purpose for me, because of the pebbles being so hard for my feet; and he'd take me ever so pretty a ride, he said, upon the Downs. But he came the next morning to tell me he was forced, by ill luck, to go to London; but he'd soon be back: and he bid me, ever so often, not to say one word of what had passed to a living creature; for if his sister should get an inkling of his being in love with me, there would be fine work, he said! But he'd bring me ever so many pretty things, he said, from London."

Juliet listened to this history with the deepest indignation against the barbarous libertine, who, with egotism so inhuman, sought to rob, first of innocence, and next, for it would be the inevitable consequence, of all her fair prospects in life, a young creature whose simplicity disabled her from seeing her danger; whose credulity induced her to agree to whatever was proposed; and whose weakness of intellect rendered it as much a dishonour as a cruelty to make her a dupe.

Whatever could be suggested to awaken the simple maiden to a sense of her perilous situation, was instantly urged; but without any effect. Sir Lyell Sycamore, she answered, had owned that he was in love with her; and it was very hard if she must be ill natured to him in return; especially as, if she behaved agreeably, nobody could tell but he might mean to make her a lady. Where a vision so refulgent, which every speech of Sir Lyell's, couched in ambiguous terms, though adroitly evasive of promise, had been insidiously calculated to present, was sparkling full in sight, how unequal were the efforts of sober truth and reason, to substitute in its place cold, dull, disappointing reality! Juliet soon relinquished the attempt as hopeless. Where ignorance is united with vanity, advice, or reproof, combat it in vain. She addressed her remonstrances, therefore, to their fellow-work-women; every one of which, it was evident, was a confident of the dangerous secret. How was it, she demanded, that, aware of the ductility of temper of this poor young creature, they had suffered her to form so alarming a connexion, unknown either to her friends or to Miss Matson?

Pettishly affronted, they answered, that they were not a set of fusty duennas:* that if Miss Pierson were ever so young, that did not make them old; that she might as well take care of herself, therefore, as they of themselves. Besides, nobody could tell but Sir Lyell Sycamore meant to marry her; and indeed they none of them doubted that such was his design; because he was politeness itself to all of them round, though he was most particular, to be sure, to Miss Pierson. They could not think, therefore, of making such a gentleman their enemy, any more than of standing in the way of Miss Pierson's good fortune; for, to their certain knowledge, there were more grand matches spoilt by meddling and making, than by any thing else upon earth.

Here again, what were the chances of truth and reason against the semblance, at least the pretence of generosity, which thus covered folly and imprudence? Each aspiring damsel, too, had some similar secret, or correspondent hope of her own; and found it convenient to reject, as treachery, an appeal against a sister work-woman, that might operate as an example for a similar one against herself.

Juliet, therefore, could but determine to watch the weak, if not willing victim, while yet under the same roof; and openly, before she quitted it, to reveal the threatening danger to Miss Matson.

CHAPTER XLVI

THE first Sunday that Juliet passed in this new situation, nearly robbed her of the good will of the whole of the little community to which she belonged. It was the only day in the week in which the young work-women were allowed some hours for recreation; they considered it, therefore, as rightfully dedicated, after the church-service, to amusement with one another; and Juliet, in refusing to join in a custom which they held to be the basis of their freedom and happiness, appeared to them an unsocial and haughty innovator. Yet neither wearying remonstrances, nor persecuting persuasions, could prevail upon her to parade with them upon the Steyne; to stroll with them by the sea-side; to ramble upon the Downs; or to form a party for Shoreham, or Devil's Dyke.

Evil is so relative, that the same chamber, the lonely sadness of which, since her privation of Gabriella, had become nearly insupportable to her, was now, from a new contrast, almost all that she immediately coveted. The bustle, the fatigue, the obtrusion of new faces, the spirit of petty intrigue, and the eternal clang of tongues; which she had to endure in the shop, made quiet, even in its most uninteresting dulness, desirable and consoling.

To approach herself, as nearly as might be in her power, to the loved society which she had lost, she destined this only interval of peace and leisure, to her pen and Gabriella; and such was her employment, when the sound of slow steps, upon the stairs, followed by a gentle tap at her door, at once interrupted and surprised her. Miss Matson and her maids, as well as her work-women, were spending their Sabbath abroad; and a shopman was left to take care of the house. The tap, however, was repeated, and, obeying its call, Juliet beheld Sir Jaspar Herrington, the gouty old Baronet.

The expression of her countenance immediately demanded explanation, if not apology, as she stepped forward upon the landing-place, to make clear that she should not receive him in her apartment.

His keen eye read her meaning, though, affecting not to perceive it, he pleasantly said, "How? immured in your chamber? and of a gala day?"*

The recollection of the essential, however forced obligation, which she owed to him, for her deliverance from the persecution of Miss Bydel, soon dissipated her first impression in his disfavour, and she quietly answered that she went very little abroad: but when she would have enquired into his business, "You can refuse yourself, then," he cried, pretending not to hear her, "the honour—or pleasure, which shall we call it? of sharing in the gaieties of your fair fellow-votaries to the needle? I suspected you of this self-denial. I had a secret presentiment that you would be insensible to the fluttering joys of your sister spinsters. How did I divine you so well? What is it you have about you that sets one's imagination so to work?"

Juliet replied, that she would not presume to interfere with the business of his penetration, but that, as she was occupied, she must beg to know, at once, his commands.

"Not so hasty! not so hasty!" he cried: "You must shew me some little consideration, if only in excuse for the total want of it which you have caused in those little imps, that beset my slumbers by night, and my reveries by day. They have gotten so much the better of me now, that I am equally at a loss how to sleep or how to wake for them. 'Why don't you find out,' they cry, 'whether this syren likes her new situation? Why don't you discover whether any thing better can be done for her?' And then, all of one accord, they so pommel* and bemaul me, that you would pity me, I give you my word, if you could see the condition into which they put my poor conscience; however little so fair a young creature may be disposed to feel pity, for such a hobbling, gouty old fellow as I am!"

Softened by this benevolent solicitude, Juliet, thankfully, spoke of herself with all the cheerfulness that she could assume; and, encouraged by her lessened reserve, Sir Jaspar, to her unspeakable surprise, said, "There is one point, I own, which I have an extreme desire to know; how long may it be that you have left the stage, and from what latent cause?"

No explanation, however, could be attempted: the attention of Juliet was called into another channel, by the sound of a titter, which led her to perceive Flora Pierson; who, almost convulsed with delight at having surprised them, said that she had heard, from the shop-man, that Miss Ellis and Sir Jaspar were talking together upon the stairs, and she had stolen up the back way, and crept softly through one of the garrets, on purpose to come upon them unawares. "So now," added she, nodding, "we'll go into my room, if you please, Miss Ellis; for I have got something else to tell you! only you must not stay with me long."

"And not to tell me, too?" cried Sir Jaspar, chucking her under the chin: "How's this, my daffodil? my pink? my lilly? how's this? surely you have not any secrets for me?"

"O yes, I have, Sir Jaspar! because you're a gentleman, you know, Sir Jaspar. And one must not tell every thing to gentlemen, mamma says."

"Mamma says? but you are too much a woman to mind what mamma says, I hope, my rose, my daisy?" cried Sir Jaspar, chucking her again under the chin, while she smiled and courtsied in return.

Juliet would have re-entered her chamber; but Flora, catching her gown, said, "Why now, Miss Ellis, I bid you come to my room, if you please, Miss Ellis; 'cause then I can show you my presents; as well as tell you something.—Come, will you go? for it's something that's quite a secret, I assure you; for I have not told it to any body yet; not even to our young ladies; for it's but just happened. So you've got my first confidence this time: and you have a right to take that very kind of me, for it's what I've promised, upon my word and honour, and as true as true can be, not to tell to any body; not so much as to a living soul!"

To be freed quietly from the Baronet, Juliet consented to attend her; and Flora, with many smiles and nods at Sir Jaspar, begged that he would not be affronted that she did not tell all her secrets to gentlemen; and, shutting him out, began her tale.

"Now I'll tell you what it is I'm going to tell you, Miss Ellis. Do you know who I met, just now, upon the Steyne, while I was walking with our young ladies, not thinking of any thing? You can't guess, can you? Why Sir Lyell himself. I gave such a squeak! But he spoke to all our young ladies first. And I was half a mind to cry; only I happened to be in one of my laughing fits. And when once I am upon my gig,* papa says, if the world were all to tumble down, it would not hinder me of my smiling. Though I am sure I often don't know what it's for. If any body asked me, I could not tell, one time in twenty. But Sir Lyell's very clever; cleverer than I am, by half, I believe. For he got to speak to me, at last, so as nobody could hear a word he said, but just me. Nor I could not, either, but only he spoke quite in my ear."

"And do you think it right, Miss Pierson, to let gentlemen whisper you?"

"O, I could not bid him not, you know. I could not be rude to a Knight-Baronet! Besides, he said he was come down from London, on purpose for nothing else but to see me! A Knight-Baronet, Miss Ellis! That's very good natured, is it not? I dare say he means something by it. Don't you? However, I shall know more by and by, most likely; for he whispered me to make believe I'd got a head-ache, and to come home by myself, and wait for him in my own room: for he says he has brought me the prettiest present that ever I saw from London. So you see how generous he is; i'n't he? And he'll bring it me himself, to make me a little visit. So then, very likely, he'll speak out. Won't he? But he bid me tell it to nobody. So say nothing if you see him, for it will only be the way to make him angry. I must not put the shop-man in the secret, he says, for he shall only ask for old Sir Jaspar; and he shall go to him first, and make the shop-man think he is with him all the time. So I told our young ladies I'd got a head-ache, sure enough; but don't be uneasy, for it's only make believe; for I'm very well."

Filled with alarm for the simple, deluded maiden, Juliet now made an undisguised representation of her danger; earnestly charging her not to receive the dangerous visit.

But Flora, self-willed, though good natured, would not hear a word.

No ass so meek;—no mule so obstinate.*

She never contradicted, yet never listened; she never gave an opinion, yet never followed one. She was neither endowed with timidity to suspect her deficiencies, nor with sense to conceive how she might be better informed. She came to Juliet merely to talk; and when her prattle was over, or interrupted, she had no thought but to be gone.

"O yes, I must see him, Miss Ellis," she cried; "for you can't think how ill he'll take it, if I don't. But now we have stayed talking together so long, I can't shew you my presents till he is gone, for fear he should come. But don't mind, for then I shall have the new ones to shew you, too. But if I don't do what he bids me, he'll be as angry as can be, for all he's my lover, (smiling.) He makes very free with me sometimes; only I don't mind it; because I'm pretty much used to it, from one or another. Sometimes he'll say I am the greatest simpleton that ever he knew in his life; for all he calls me his angel! He don't make much ceremony with me, when I don't understand his signs. But it don't much signify, for the more he's angry, the more he's kind, when it's over, (smiling.) And then he brings me prettier things than ever. So I a'n't much a loser. I've no great need to cry about it. And he says I'm quite a little goddess,* often and often, if I'd believe him. Only one must not believe the men over much, when they are gentlemen, I believe."

Juliet, kindly taking her hand, would have drawn her into her own chamber; but they were no sooner in the passage, than Flora jumped back, and, shaking with laughter at her ingenuity, shut and locked herself into her room.

Juliet now renounced, perforce, all thought of serving her except through the medium of Miss Matson; and she was returning, much vexed, to her own small apartment, when she saw Sir Jaspar, who, leaning against the banisters, seemed to have been waiting for her, step curiously forward, as she opened her door, to take a view of her chamber. With quick impulse, to check this liberty, she hastily pushed to the door; not recollecting, till too late, that the key, by which alone it was opened, was on the inside.

Chagrined, she repaired to Flora, telling the accident, and begging admittance.

Flora, laughing with all her heart, positively refused to open the door; saying that she would rather be without company.

The shop-man now came up stairs, to see what was going forward, and to enquire whether Miss Pierson, who had told him that she was ill, found herself worse. Flora, hastily checking her mirth, answered that her head ached, and she would lie down; and then spoke no more.

The shop-man made an attempt to enter into conversation with Juliet; but she gravely requested that he would be so good as to order a smith to open the lock of her door.

He ought not, he said, to leave the house in the absence of Miss Matson; but he would run the risk for the pleasure of obliging her, if she would only step down into the shop, to answer to the bell or the knocker.

To this, in preference to being shut out of her room, she would immediately have consented, but that she feared the arrival of Sir Lyell Sycamore. She asked the shop-man, therefore, if there were any objection to her waiting in the little parlour.

None in the world, he answered; for he had Miss Matson's leave to use it when she was out of a Sunday; and he should be very glad if Miss Ellis would oblige him with her company.

Juliet declined this proposal with an air that repressed any further attempt at intimacy; and the shop-man returned to his post.

"I must not, I suppose," the Baronet, then advancing, said, "presume to offer you shelter under my roof from the inclemencies of the stair-case? And yet I think I may venture, without being indecorous, to mention, that I am going out for my usual airing; and that you may take possession of your old apartment, upon your own misanthropical terms. At all events, I shall leave you the door open, place some books upon the table, take out my servants, and order that no one shall molest you."

Extremely pleased by a kindness so much to her taste, Juliet would gratefully have accepted this offer, but for the visit that she knew to be designed for the same apartment; which the absence of its master was not likely to prevent, as the pretence of writing a note, or his name, would suffice with Sir Lyell for mounting the stairs. Who then could protect Flora? Could Juliet herself come forward, when no one else remained in the house, conscious, as she could not but be, of the dishonourable views of which she, also, had been the object? The departure of Sir Jaspar appeared, therefore, to be big with mischief; and, when he was making a leave-taking bow, she almost involuntarily said, "You are forced, then, Sir, to go out this morning?"

Surprised and pleased, he answered, "What! have my little fairy elves given you a lesson of humanity? Nay, if so, though they should pommel and maul me for a month to come, I shall yet be their obedient humble servant."

He then gave orders aloud that his carriage should be put up; saying, that he had letters to write, and that his servants might go and amuse themselves for an hour or two where they pleased.

Juliet, now, was crimsoned with shame and embarrassment. How account for thus palpably wishing him to remain in the house? or how suffer him, by silence, to suppose it was from a desire of his society? Her blushes astonished, yet, by heightening her beauty, charmed still more than they perplexed him. To settle what to think of her might be difficult and teazing; but to admire her was easy and pleasant. He approached her, therefore, with the most flattering looks and smiles; but, to avoid any mistake in his manner of addressing her, he kept his speech back, with his judgment, till he could learn her purpose.

This prudential circumspection redoubled her confusion, and she hesitatingly stammered her concern that she had prevented his airing.

More amazed still, but still more enchanted, to see her thus at a loss what to say, though evidently pleased that he had relinquished his little excursion, he was making a motion to take her hand, which she had scarcely perceived, when a violent ringing at the door-bell, checked him; and concentrated all her solicitude in the impending danger of Flora; and, in her eagerness to rescue the simple girl from ruin, she hastily said: "Can you, Sir Jaspar, forgive a liberty in the cause of humanity? May I appeal to your generosity? You will receive a visitor in a few minutes, whom I have earnest reasons for wishing you to detain in your apartment to the last moment that is possible. May I make so extraordinary a request?"

"Request?" repeated Sir Jaspar, charmed by what he considered as an opening to intimacy; "can you utter any thing but commands? The most benignant sprite of all Fairyland, has inspired you with this gracious disposition to dub me your knight."

Yet his eyes, still bright with intelligence, and now full of fanciful wonder, suddenly emitted an expression less rapturous, when he distinguished the voice of Sir Lyell Sycamore, in parley with the shop-man. Disappointment and chagrin soon took place of sportive playfulness in his countenance; and, muttering between his teeth, "O ho! Sir Lyell Sycamore!"—he fixed his keen eyes sharply upon Juliet; with a look in which she could not but read the ill construction to which her seeming knowledge of that young man's motions, and her apparent interest in them, made her liable; and how much his light opinion of Sir Lyell's character, affected his partial, though still fluctuating one of her own.

Sir Lyell, however, was upon the stairs, and she did not dare enter into any justification; Sir Jaspar, too, was silent; but the young baronet mounted, singing, in a loud voice,

> O my love, lov'st thou me?
> Then quickly come and see one who dies for thee!*

"Yes here I come, Sir Lyell!"—in a low, husky, laughing voice, cried Flora, peeping through her chamber-door; which was immediately at the head of the stairs, upon the second floor; and to which Sir Lyell looked up, softly whispering, "Be still, my little angel! and, in ten minutes—" He stopt abruptly, for

Sir Jaspar now caught his astonished sight, upon the landing-place of the attic story, with Juliet retreating behind him.

"O ho! you are there, are you?" he cried, in a tone of ludicrous accusation.

"And you, you are there, are you?" answered Sir Jaspar, in voice more seriously taunting.

Juliet, hurt and confounded, would have escaped through the garret to the back stairs; but that her hat and cloak, without which she could not leave the house, were shut into her room. She tried, therefore, to look unmoved; well aware that the best chance to escape impertinence, is by not appearing to suspect that any is intended.

Three strides now brought Sir Lyell before her. His amazement, vented by rattling exclamations, again perplexed Sir Jaspar; for how could Juliet have been apprized of his intended visit, but by himself?

Sir Lyell, mingling the most florid compliments upon her radiant beauty, and bright bloom, with his pleasure at her sight, said that, from the reports which had reached him, that she had given up her singing, and her teaching, and that Sir Jaspar had taken the room which she had inhabited, he had concluded that she had quitted Brighthelmstone. He was going rapidly on the same strain, the observant Sir Jaspar intently watching her looks, while curiously listening to his every word; when Juliet, without seeming to have attended to a syllable, related, with grave brevity, that she had unfortunately shut in the key of her room, and must therefore see Miss Matson, to demand another; and then, with steady steps, that studiously kept in order innumerable timid fears, she descended to the shop; leaving the two Baronets mutually struck by her superiour air and manner; and each, though equally desirous to follow her, involuntarily standing still, to wait the motions of the other; and thence to judge of his pretensions to her favour.

Juliet found the shop empty, but the street-door open, and the shop-man sauntering before it, to look at the passers by. Glad to be, for a while, at least, spared the distaste of his company, she shut herself into the little parlour, carefully drawing the curtain of the glass-door.

The two Baronets, as she expected, soon descended; the

younger one eager to take leave of the elder, and privately remount the stairs; and Sir Jaspar, fixed to obey the injunctions, however unaccountable, of Juliet, in detaining and keeping sight of him to the last moment.

"Decamped, I swear, the little vixen!" exclaimed Sr Lyell, striding in first; "but why the d—l do you come down, Sir Jaspar?"

"For exercise, not ceremony," he answered; though, little wanting further exertion, and heartily tired, he dropt down upon the first chair.

Sir Lyell vainly offered his arm, and pressed to aid him back to his apartment; he would not move.

After some time thus wasted, Sir Lyell, mortified and provoked, cast himself upon the counter, and whistled, to disguise his ill humour.

A pause now ensued, which Sir Jaspar broke, by hesitatingly, yet with earnestness, saying, "Sir Lyell Sycamore, I am not, you will do me the justice to believe, a sour old fellow, to delight in mischief; a surly old dog, to mar the pleasures of which I cannot partake; if, therefore, to answer what I mean to ask will thwart any of your projects, leave me and my curiosity in the lurch; if not, you will sensibly gratify me, by a little frank communication. I don't meddle with your affair with Flora; 'tis a blooming little wild rose-bud, but of too common a species to be worth analysing. This other young creature, however, whose wings your bird-lime seems also to have entangled—"

"How so?" interrupted Sir Lyell, jumping eagerly from the counter, "what the d—l do you mean by that?"

"Not to be indiscreet, I promise you," answered Sir Jaspar; "but as I see the interest she takes in you,—"

"The d—l you do?" exclaimed Sir Lyell, in an accent of surprize, yet of transport.

Sir Jaspar now, ironically smiling, said, "You don't know it, then, Sir Lyell? You are modest?—diffident? unconscious?—"

"My dear boy!" cried Sir Lyell, riotously, and approaching familiarly to embrace him, "what a devilish kind office I shall owe you, if you can put any good notions into my head of that delicious girl!"

New doubts now destroying his recent suspicions, Sir Jaspar

held back, positively refusing to clear up what had dropt from him, and laughingly saying, "Far be it from me to put any such notions into your head! I believe it amply stored! All my desire is to get some out of it. If, therefore, you can tell me, or, rather, will tell me, who or what this young creature is, you will do a kind office to my imagination, for which I shall be really thankful. Who is she, then? And what is she?"

"D—l take me if I either know or care!" cried Sir Lyell, "further than that she is a beauty of the first water; and that I should have adored her, exclusively, three months ago, if I had not believed her a thing of alabaster.* But if you think her——"

"Not I! not I!—I know nothing of her!" interrupted Sir Jaspar: "she is a rose planted in the snow, for aught I can tell! The more I see, the less I understand; the more I surmize, the further I seem from the mark. Honestly, then, whence does she come? How did you first see her? What does she do at Brighthelmstone?"

"May I go to old Nick* if I am better informed than yourself! except that she sings and plays like twenty angels, and that all the women are jealous of her, and won't suffer a word to be said to her. However, I made up to her, at first, and should certainly have found her out, but for Melbury, who annoyed me with a long history of her virtue, and character, and Lady Aurora's friendship, and the d—l knows what; that made me so cursed sheepish, I was afraid of embarking in any measures of spirit. My sister, also, took lessons of her; and other game came into chace; and I should never have thought of her again, but that, when I went to town, a week or two ago, I learnt, from that Queen of the Crabs,* Mrs. Howel, that Melbury, in fact, knows no more of her than we do. He had nobody's word but her own for all her fine sentiments; so that he and his platonics would have kept me at bay no longer, if I had not believed her decamped from Brighthelmstone, upon hearing that you had got her lodging. How came you to turn her into the garret, my dear boy? Is that *à la mode* of your *vieille cour?*"*

Sir Jaspar protested that, when he took the apartment, he knew not of her existence; and then enquired, whether Sir Lyell could tell in what name she had been upon the stage; and why she had quitted it.

"The stage? O the d—l!" he exclaimed, "has she been upon the stage?"

"Yes; I heard the fact mentioned to her, the other day, by a fellow-performer! some low player, who challenged her as a sister of the buskins."

"What a glorious Statira she must make!" cried Sir Lyell. "I am ready to be her Alexander* when she will. That hint you have dropt, my dear old boy, sha'n't be thrown away upon me. But how the d—l did you find the dear charmer out?"

Sir Jaspar again sought to draw back his information; but Sir Lyell swore that he would not so lightly be put aside from a view of success, now once it was fairly opened; and was vowing that he should begin a siege in form, and persevere to a surrender; when the conversation was interrupted, by the entrance of the shop-man, accompanied by a mantua-maker,* who called upon some business.

Juliet, who, from the beginning, had heard this discourse with the utmost uneasiness, and whom its conclusion had filled with indignant disgust; had no resource to avoid the yet greater evil of being joined by the interlocutors, but that of sitting motionless and unsuspected, till they should depart; or till Miss Matson should return. But her care and precaution proved vain: the shop-man invited Mrs. Hart, the mantua-maker, into the little parlour; and, upon opening the door, Juliet met their astonished view.

Sir Jaspar, not without evident anxiety, endeavoured to recollect what had dropt from him, that might hurt her; or how he might palliate what might have given her offence. But Sir Lyell, not at all disconcerted, and privately persuaded that half his difficulties were vanquished, by the accident that acquainted her with his design; was advancing, eagerly, with a volley of rapid compliments, upon his good fortune in again meeting with her; when Juliet, not deigning to seem conscious even of his presence, passed him without notice; and, addressing Mrs. Hart, entreated that she would go up stairs to the room of Miss Pierson, to examine whether it were necessary to send for any advice; as she had returned home alone, and complained of being ill. Mrs. Hart complied; and Juliet followed her to Flora's chamber-door.

CHAPTER XLVII

THE gentle tap that Mrs. Hart, fearing to disturb her, gave at the door of Flora, deceived the expecting girl into a belief that Sir Lyell was at length arrived; and crying, in a low voice, as she opened it, "O Sir! how long you have been coming!" she stared at sight of Mrs. Hart, with an amazement equal to her disappointment.

Presently, however, with a dejected look and tone, "Well, now!" she cried, "is it only you, Mrs. Hart?—I thought it had been somebody quite different!"

Mrs. Hart, entering, enquired, with surprize, why Miss Ellis had said that Miss Pierson was ill, when, on the contrary, she had never seen her look better.

"Well, now, Miss Ellis," cried Flora, whispering Juliet, "did not I tell you, as plain as could be, 'twas nothing but make believe?"

Juliet, without offering any apology, answered, that she had invited Mrs. Hart to make her a visit.

"Why, now, what can you be thinking of?" cried Flora, angrily: "Why, you know, as well as can be, that I want to see nobody! Why, have you forgot all I told you, already, about you know who? Why I never knew the like! Why he'll be fit to kill himself! I'll never tell you any thing again, if you beg me on your knees! so there's the end to your knowing any more of my secrets! and you've nobody but yourself to thank, if it vexes you never so!"

Mrs. Hart interrupted this murmuring, by enquiring who was the *Sir* that Miss Pierson expected; adding that, if it were the shop-man, it would be more proper Miss Pierson should go down stairs, than that she should let him come up to her room.

"The shop-man?" repeated Flora, simpering, and winking at Juliet; "no, indeed, Mrs. Hart; you have not made a very good guess there! Has she, Miss Ellis? I don't think a man of quality, and a baronet, is very like a shop-man! Do you, Miss Ellis?"

This blundering simplicity of vanity was not lost upon Mrs. Hart. "O ho!" she cried, "you expect a baronet, do you, then, Miss Pierson? Why there were no less than two Baronets in the shop as I came through, just now; and there's one of them this minute crossing the way, and turning the corner."

"O Me! is he gone, then?" cried Flora, looking out of the window. "O Me! what shall I do? O Miss Ellis! this is all your fault! And now, perhaps, he'll be so angry he'll never speak to me again! And if he don't, ten to one but it may break my heart! for that often happens when one's crossed in love. And if it does, I sha'n't thank you for it, I assure you! And it's just as likely as not!"

Juliet, though she sought to appease both her grief and her wrath, could not but rejoice that their unguarded redundance informed Mrs. Hart of the whole history: and Mrs. Hart, who, though a plain, appeared to be a very worthy woman, immediately endeavoured to save the poor young creature, from the snares into which she was rather wilfully jumping, than deludedly falling, by giving her a pressing invitation to her own house for the rest of the day. But to this, neither entreaty nor reproof could obtain consent. Flora, like many who seem gentle, was only simple; and had neither docility nor comprehension for being turned aside from the prosecution of her wishes. To be thwarted in any desire, she considered as cruelty, and resented as ill treatment. She refused, therefore, to leave the house, while hoping for the return of Sir Lyell; and continued her childish wailing and fretting, till accident led her eyes to a favourite little box; when, her tears suddenly stopping, and her face brightening, she started up, seized, opened it, and, displaying a very pretty pair of ear-rings, exclaimed, "Oh, I have never shewn you my presents, Miss Ellis! And now Mrs. Hart may have a peep at them, too. So she's in pretty good luck, I think!"

And then, with exulting pleasure, she produced all the costly trinkets that she had received from Sir Lyell; with some few, less valuable, which had been presented to her by Sir Jaspar; and all the baubles, however insignificant or babyish, that had been bestowed upon her by her friends and relatives, from her earliest youth. And these, with the important and separate history of each, occupied, unawares, her time, till the return of Miss Matson.

Mrs. Hart then descended, and, urged by Juliet, briefly and

plainly communicated the situation and the danger of the young apprentice.

Miss Matson, affrighted for the credit of her shop, determined to send for the mother of Flora, who resided at Lewes, the next day.

Relieved now from her troublesome and untoward charge, Juliet had her door opened, and re-took possession of her room.

And there, a new view of her own helpless and distressed condition, filled and dejected her with new alarm. The licentiously declared purpose of Sir Lyell had been shocking to her ears; and the consciousness that he knew that she was informed of his intention added to its horrour, from her inability to shew her resentment, in the only way that suited her character or her disposition, that of positively seeing him no more. But how avoid him while she had no other means of subsistence than working in an open shop?

The following morning but too clearly justified her apprehensive prognostics, of the improprieties to which her defenceless state made her liable. At an early hour, Sir Lyell, gay, courteous, gallant, entered the shop, under pretence of enquiring for Sir Jaspar; whom he knew to be invisible, from his infirmities, to all but his own nurses and servants, till noon. Miss Matson was taciturn and watchful, though still, from the fear of making an enemy, respectful; while Flora, simpering and blushing, was ready to jump into his arms, in her eagerness to apologize for not having waited alone for him, according to his directions: but he did not look at Miss Matson, though he addressed her; nor address Flora, though, by a side glance, he saw her expectations; his attention, from the moment that he had asked, without listening to any answer, whether he could see Sir Jaspar, was all, and even publicly devoted to Juliet; whom he approached with an air of homage, and accosted with the most flattering compliments upon her good looks and her beauty.

Juliet turned aside from him, with an indignant disgust, in which she hoped he would read her resentment of his scheme, and her abhorrence of his principles. But those who are deep in vice are commonly incredulous of virtue. Sir Lyell took her apparent displeasure, either for a timidity which flattery would banish, or an hypocrisy which boldness would conquer. He continued, therefore, his florid adulation to her charms; regarding the heightened colour of offended purity, but as an augmented attraction.

Juliet perceived her failure to repress his assurance, with a disturbance that was soon encreased, by the visible jealousy manifested in the pouting lips and frowning brow of Flora; who, the moment that Sir Lyell, saying that he would call upon Sir Jaspar again, thought it prudent to retire, began a convulsive sobbing; averring that she saw why she had been betrayed; for that it was only to inveigle away her sweetheart.

Pity for the ignorant accuser, might have subdued the disdain due to the accusation, and have induced Juliet to comfort her by a self-defence; but for a look, strongly expressing a suspicion to the same effect, from Miss Matson; which was succeeded by a general tossing up of the chins of the young work-women, and a murmur of, "I wonder how she would like to be served so herself!"

This was too offensive to be supported, and she retired to her chamber.

If, already, the mingled frivolity and publicity of the business into which she had entered, had proved fatiguing to her spirits, and ungenial to her disposition; surmises, such as she now saw raised, of a petty and base rivality, urged by a pursuit the most licentious, rendered all attempt at its continuance intolerable. Without, therefore, a moment's hesitation, she determined to relinquish her present enterprise.

The only, as well as immediate notion that occurred to her, in this new difficulty, was to apply to Mrs. Hart, who seemed kind as well as civil, for employment.

When she was summoned, therefore, by Miss Matson, with surprize and authority, back to the shop, she returned equipped for going abroad; and, after thanking her for the essay which she had permitted to be made in the millinery-business, declared that she found herself utterly unfit for so active and so public a line of life.

Leaving then Miss Matson, Flora, and the young journeywomen to their astonishment, she bent her course to the house of Mrs. Hart; where her application was happily successful.

Mrs. Hart had work of importance just ordered for a great wedding in the neighbourhood, and was glad to engage so expert a hand for the occasion; agreeing to allow, in return, bed, board, and a small stipend per day.

With infinite relief, Juliet went back to make her little preparations, and take leave of Miss Matson; by whom she was now followed to her room, with many earnest instances that she would relinquish her design. Miss Matson, in unison with the very common character to which she belonged, had appreciated Juliet not by her worth, her talents, or her labours, but by her avowed distress, and acknowledged poverty. Notwithstanding, therefore, her abilities and her industry, she had been uniformly considered as a dead weight to the business, and to the house. But now, when it appeared that the pennyless young woman had some other resource, the eyes of Miss Matson were suddenly opened to merits to which she had hitherto been blind. She felt all the advantages which the shop would lose by the departure of such an assistant; and recollected the many useful hints, in fashion and in elegance, which had been derived from her taste and fancy: her exemplary diligence in work; her gentle quietness of behaviour; and the numberless customers, which the various reports that were spread of her history, had drawn to the shop. All, now, however, was unavailing; the remembrance of what was over occurred too late to change the plan of Juliet; though a kinder appreciation of her character and services, while she was employed, might have engaged her to try some other method of getting rid of the libertine Baronet.

Miss Matson then admonished her not to lose, at least, the benefit of her premium.

"What premium?" cried Juliet.

"Why that Sir Jaspar paid down for you."

Juliet, astonished, now learnt, that her admission as an inmate of the shop, which she had imagined due to the gossipping verbal influence of Miss Bydel, was the result of the far more substantial money-mediation of Sir Jaspar.

She felt warmly grateful for his benevolence; yet wounded, in reflecting upon his doubts whether she deserved it; and confounded to owe another, and so heavy an obligation, to an utter stranger.

She was finishing her little package, when the loud sobbings of Flora, while mounting the stairs for a similar, though by no means as voluntary a purpose, induced her to go forth, with a view to offer some consolation; but Flora, not less resentful than disconsolate, said that her mother was arrived to take her from all her fine prospects; and loaded Juliet with the unqualified accusation, of having betrayed her secrets, and ruined her fortune.

Juliet had too strong a mind to suffer weak and unjust censure to breed any repentance that she had acted right. She could take one view only of the affair; and that brought only self-approvance of what she had done: if Sir Lyell meant honourably, Flora was easily followed; if not, she was happily rescued from earthly perdition.

Nevertheless, she had too much sweetness of disposition, and too much benovolence of character, to be indifferent to reproach; though her vain efforts, either to clear her own conduct, or to appease the angry sorrows of Flora, all ended by the indignantly blubbering damsel's turning from her in sulky silence.

Juliet then took a quick leave of Miss Matson, and of the young journey-women; and repaired to her new habitation.

CHAPTER XLVIII

EXPERIENCE, the mother of caution, now taught Juliet explicitly to make known to her new chief, that she had no view to learn the art of mantua-making as a future trade, or employment; but simply desired to work at it in such details, as a general knowledge of the use of the needle might make serviceable and expeditious: no premium, therefore, could be expected by the mistress; and the work-woman would be at liberty to continue, or to renounce her engagement, from day to day.

This agreement offered to her ideas something which seemed like an approach to the self-dependence, that she had so earnestly coveted: she entered, therefore, upon her new occupation with cheerfulness and alacrity, and with a diligence to which the hope, by being useful, to become necessary, gave no relaxation.

The business, by this scrupulous devotion to its interests, was forwarded with such industry and success, that she soon became the open and decided favourite of the mistress whom she served; and who repaid her exertions by the warmest praise, and proposed her as a pattern to the rest of the sewing sisterhood.

This approbation could not but cheer the toil of one whose mind, like that of Juliet, sought happiness, at this moment, only from upright and blameless conduct. She was mentally, also, relieved, by the local change of situation. She was now employed in a private apartment; and, though surrounded by still more fellow-work-women than at Miss Matson's, she was no longer constrained to remain in an open shop, in opposition alike to her inclinations and her wishes of concealment; no longer startled by the continual entrance and exit of strangers; nor exposed to curious enquirers, or hardy starers; and no longer fatigued by the perpetual revision of goods. She worked in perfect quietness, undisturbed and uninterrupted; her mistress was civil, and gave her encouragement; her fellow-sempstresses were unobservant, and left her to her own reflexions.

It is not, however, in courts alone that favour is perilous; in all circles, and all classes, from the most eminent to the most obscure, the "Favourite has no friend[†]!"* The praises and the comparisons, by which Mrs. Hart hoped to stimulate her little community to emulation, excited only jealousy, envy, and ill will; and a week had not elapsed, in this new and short tranquility, before Juliet found that her superiour diligence was regarded, by her needle-sisterhood, as a mean artifice "to set herself off to advantage at their cost." Sneers and hints to this effect followed every panegyric of Mrs. Hart; and robbed approbation of its pleasure, though they could not of its value.

Chagrined by a consequence so unpleasant, to an industry that demanded fortitude, not discouragement; Juliet now felt the excess of her activity relax; and soon experienced a desire, if not a necessity, to steal some moments from application, for retirement and for herself.

Here, again, she found the mischief to which ignorance of life

[†] Gray.

had laid her open. The unremitting diligence with which she had begun her new office, had advanced her work with a rapidity, that made the smallest relaxation cause a sensible difference in its progress: and Mrs. Hart, from first looking disappointed, asked next, whether nothing more were done? and then observed, how much quicker business had gone on the first week. In vain Juliet still executed more than all around her; the comparison was never made there, where it might have been to her advantage; all reference was to her own setting out; and she was soon taught to forgive the displeasure which, so inadvertently, she had excited, when she saw the claims to which she had made herself liable, by an incautious eagerness of zeal to reward, as well as earn, the maintenance which she owed to Mrs. Hart.

Alas, she thought, with what upright intentions may we be injudicious! I have thrown away the power of obliging, by too precipitate an eagerness to oblige! I retain merely that of avoiding to displease, by my most indefatigable application! All I can perform seems but a duty, and of course; all I leave undone, seems idleness and neglect. Yet what is the labour that never requires respite? What the mind, that never demands a few poor unshackled instants to itself?

From this time, the little pleasure which she had been able to create for herself, from the virtue of her exertions, was at an end: to toil beyond her fellow-labourers, was but to provoke ill will; to allow herself any repose, was but to excite disapprobation. Hopeless, therefore, either way, she gave, with diligence, her allotted time to her occupation, but no more: all that remained, she solaced, by devoting to her pen and Gabriella, with whom her correspondence,—her sole consolation,—was unremitting.

This unaffected conduct had its customary effect; it destroyed at once the too hardly earned favour of Mrs. Hart, and the illiberal, yet too natural enmity of her apprentices; and, in the course of a very few days, Juliet was neither more esteemed, nor more censured, than any of her sisters of the sewing tribe.

With the energy, however, of her original wishes and efforts, died all that could reconcile her to this sort of life. The hope of pleasing, which alone could soften its hardships, thus forcibly set aside, left nothing in its place, but calmness without contentment; dulness without serenity.

Experience is not more exclusively the guide of our judgment, than comparison is the mistress of our feelings. Juliet now, also, found, that, local publicity excepted, there was nothing to prefer in her new to her former situation; and something to like less. The employment itself was by no means equally agreeable for its disciples. The taste and fancy, requisite for the elegance and variety of the light work which she had quitted; however ineffectual to afford pleasure when called forth by necessity, rendered it, at least, less irksome, than the wearying sameness of perpetual basting, running,* and hemming. Her fellow-labourers, though less pert and less obtrusive than those which she had left, had the same spirit for secret cabal, and the same passion for frolic and disguise; and also, like those, were all prattle and confidential sociability, in the absence of the mistress; all sullenness and taciturnity, in her presence. What little difference, therefore, she found in her position, was, that there she had been disgusted by under-bred flippancy; here, she was deadened by uninteresting monotony; and that there, perpetual motion, and incessant change of orders, and of objects, affected her nerves; while here, the unvarying repetition of stitch after stitch, nearly closed in sleep her faculties, as well as her eyes.

The little stipend which, by agreement, she was paid every evening, though it occasioned her the most satisfactory, by no means gave her the most pleasant feeling, of the day. However respectable reason and justice render pecuniary emolument, where honourably earned; there is a something indefinable, which stands between spirit and delicacy, that makes the first reception of money in detail, by those not brought up to gain it, embarrassing and painful.

During this tedious and unvaried period, if some minutes were snatched from fatiguing uniformity, it was only by alarm and displeasure, through the intrusion of Sir Lyell Sycamore; who though always denied admission to herself, made frequent, bold, and frivolous pretences for bursting into the work-room. At one time, he came to enquire about a gown for his sister, of which Mrs. Hart had never heard; at another, to look at a trimming for which she had had no commission; and at a third, to hurry the finishing of a dress, which had already been sent home. The motive to these various mock messages, was too palpable to escape even the most ordinary observation; yet though the perfect conduct, and icy coldness of Juliet, rescued her from all evil imputation amongst her companions, she saw, with pique and even horrour, that they were insufficient to repress the daring and determined hopes and expectations of the licentious Baronet; with whom the unexplained hint of Sir Jaspar had left a firm persuasion, that the fair object of his views more than returned his admiration; and waited merely for a decent attack, or proper offers, to acknowledge her secret inclinations.

Juliet, however shocked, could only commit to time her cause, her consistency, her vindication.

Three weeks had, in this manner, elapsed, when the particular business for which Mrs. Hart had wanted an odd hand was finished; and Juliet, who had believed that her useful services would keep her employed at her own pleasure, abruptly found that her occupation was at an end.

Here again, the wisdom of experience was acquired only by distress. The pleasure with which she had considered herself free, because engaged but by the day, was changed into the alarm of finding herself, from that very circumstance, without employment or home; and she now acknowledged the providence of those ties, which, from only feeling their inconvenience, she had thought oppressive and unnecessary. The established combinations of society are not to be judged by the personal opinions, and varying feelings, of individuals; but by general proofs of reciprocated advantages. If the needy helper require regular protection, the recompensing employer must claim regular service; and Juliet now saw, that though in being contracted but by the day, she escaped all continued constraint, and was set freshly at liberty every evening; she was, a stranger to security, subject to dismission, at the mercy of accident, and at the will of caprice.

Thus perplexed and thus helpless, she applied to Mrs. Hart, for counsel how to obtain immediate support. Gratified by the application, Mrs. Hart again recommended her as a pattern to the young sisterhood; and then gave her advice, that she should bind herself, either to some milliner or some mantua-maker, as a journey-woman* for three years.

Painfully, again, Juliet attained further knowledge of the world, in learning the danger of asking counsel; except of the candid and wise, who know how to modify it by circumstances, and who will listen to opposing representations.

Mrs. Hart, from the moment that Juliet declined to be guided wholly by her judgment, lost all interest in her young work-woman's distresses. "If people won't follow advice," she said, "'tis a sign they are not much to be pitied."* Vainly Juliet affirmed, that reasons which she could not explain, put it out of her power to take any measure so decisive; that, far from fixing her own destiny for three years, she had no means to ascertain, or scarcely even to conjecture, what it might be in three days; or perhaps in three hours; although in the interval of suspense, she was not less an object for present humanity, from the incertitude of what either her wants or her abundance might be in future; vainly she reasoned, vainly she pleaded. Mrs. Hart always made the same reply: "If people won't follow advice, 'tis a sign they are not much to be pitied."

In consequence of this maxim, Juliet next heard, that the small room and bed which she occupied, were wanted for another person.

Alas! she thought, how long must we mingle with the world, ere we learn how to live in it! Must we demand no help from the understandings of others, unless we submit to renounce all use of our own?

These reflexions soon led her to hit upon the only true medium, for useful and safe general intercourse with the mass of mankind: that of avowing embarrassments, without demanding counsel; and of discussing difficulties, and gathering opinions, as matters of conversation; but always to keep in mind, that to ask advice, without a pre-determination to follow it, is to call for censure, and to risk resentment.

Thus died away in Juliet the short joy of freedom from the controul of positive engagements.*

Such freedom, she found, was but a source of perpetual difficulty and instability. She had the world to begin again; a new pursuit to fix upon; new recommendations to solicit; and a new dwelling to seek.

CHAPTER XLIX

JULIET was making enquiries of the young work-women, for a recommendation to some small lodging, when she was surprised by the receipt of a letter from Mrs. Pierson, soliciting her company immediately at Lewes; where poor Flora, she said, was taken dangerously ill of a high fever, and was raving, continually, for Miss Ellis. A return post-chaise,* to the postilion of which Mrs. Pierson had given directions to call at Mrs. Hart's at three o'clock in the afternoon, would bring her, for nearly nothing; if she would have so much charity as to come and comfort the poor girl; and Mrs. Pierson would find a safe conveyance back at night, if Miss Ellis could not oblige them by sleeping at the house: but she hoped that Mrs. Hart would not refuse to spare her from her work, for a few hours, as it might produce a favourable turn in the disorder.

Juliet read this letter with real concern. Had she rescued the poor, weak, and wilful Flora from immediate moral, only to devote her to immediate physical, destruction? And what now could be devised for her relief? Her intellects were too feeble for reason, her temper was too petulant for entreaty. Nevertheless, the benevolent are easily urged to exertion; and Juliet would not refuse the summons of the distressed mother, while she could flatter herself that any possible means might be suggested for serving the self-willed, and half-witted, but innocent daughter.

She set out, therefore, upon this plan, far from sanguine of success, but persuaded that the effort was a duty.

By her own calculations from memory, she was arrived within about a mile of Lewes, when the horses suddenly turned down a narrow lane.

She demanded of the postilion why he did not proceed straight forward. He answered, that he knew a short cut to the house of Mrs. Pierson. Uneasy, nevertheless, at quitting thus alone the high road, she begged him to go the common way, promising to reward him for the additional time which it might require. But he drove on without replying; though, growing now alarmed, she called, supplicated, and menaced in turn.

She looked from window to window to seek some object to

whom she might apply for aid; none appeared, save a man on horseback, whom she had already noticed from time to time, near the side of the chaise; and to whom she was beginning an appeal, when she surprised him making signs to hurry on the postilion.

She now believed the postilion himself to be leagued with some highwayman; and was filled with affright and dismay.

The horses galloped on with encreased swiftness, the horseman always keeping closely behind the chaise; till they were stopt by a small cart, from which Juliet had the joy to see two men alight, forced, by the narrowness of the road, to take off their horse, and drag back their vehicle.

She eagerly solicited their assistance, and made an effort to open the chaise door. This, however, was prevented by the pursuing horseman, who, dismounting, opened it himself; and, to her inexpressible terrour, sprung into the carriage.

What, then, was her mingled consternation and astonishment, when, instead of demanding her purse, he gaily exclaimed, "Why are you frightened, you beautiful little creature?" And she saw Sir Lyell Sycamore.

A change, but not a diminution of alarm, now took place; yet, assuming a firmness that sought to conceal her fears, "Quit the chaise, Sir Lyell," she cried, "instantly, or you will compel me to claim protection from those two men!"

"Protection? you pretty little vixen!" cried he, yet more familiarly, "who should protect you like your own adorer?"

Juliet, leaning out, as far as was in her power, from the chaise-window, called with energy for help.

"What do you mean?" cried he, striving to draw her back. "What are you afraid of? You don't imagine me such a blundering cavalier, as to intend to carry you off by force?"

The postilion was assisting the two men to fix their horse, for dragging back their cart; but her cries reached their ears, and one of them, advancing to the chaise, exclaimed, "Good now! if it is not Miss Ellis!" And, to her infinite relief and comfort, she beheld young Gooch.

She entreated him to open the door; but, lolling his arms over it, without attending to her, he said, "Well! to see but how things turn out! Here have I been twice this very morning, at your new lodgings, to let you know it's now or never, for our junket's to night; and the old gentlewoman that keeps the house, who's none of the good-naturedest, as I take it, would never let me get a sight of you, say what I would; and here, all of the sudden, when I was thinking of you no more than if you had never been born, I come pop upon you, as one may say, within cock-crow of our very door; all alone, with only the young Baronight!"

Nearly as much shocked, now, as, the moment before, she had been relieved, Juliet eagerly declared, that she was not with any body; she was simply going to Lewes upon business.

"Why then," cried he, "the Baronight must be out of his head, begging his pardon, to let you come this way; and the postilion as stupid as a post; for it's quite the contrary. It will lead you to you don't know where. We only turned down it ourselves, just to borrow a few glasses, of farmer Barnes, because we've more mouths than we have got of our own: for I've invited all our club; which poor dad don't much like. He says I am but a bungler at saving money, any more than at getting it; but I am as rare a hand as any you know, far or near, says the old gentleman, for spending it. The old gentleman likes to say his say. However, I must not leave my horse to his gambols."

Then nodding, still without listening to Juliet, he returned to his *chay-cart.*

Juliet now unhasped the chaise-door herself, and was springing from the carriage; when Sir Lyell, forcibly holding her, exclaimed, "What would you do, you lovely termagant? Would you make me pass for a devil of a ravisher? No, no, no! you handsome little fire-brand! name your terms, and command me! I know you love me,—and I adore you. Why then this idle cruelty to us both? to nature itself; and to beauty?"

More and more indignant, Juliet uttered a cry for help, that immediately brought back young Gooch, who was followed by an elderly companion.

Provoked and resentful, yet amazed and ashamed, the Baronet jumped out of the chaise, saying, with affected contempt, yet stronger pique, "Yes! help, gentlemen, help! come quick! quick! Miss Ellis is taken suddenly ill!"

The insolent boldness of this appeal, was felt only by

Juliet; whose scorn, however potent, was less prevalent than her satisfaction, upon beholding her old friend Mr. Tedman. She descended to meet him, with an energetic "Thank Heaven!" and an excess of gladness, not more tormenting to the Baronet, than unexpected by himself. "Well, this is very kind of you, indeed, my dear," cried he, heartily shaking hands with her; "to be so glad to see me; especially after the ungenteel way I was served in by your lodging-gentlewoman, making no more ceremony than refusing to let me up, under cover that you saw no gentlemen; though I told her what a good friend I had been to you; and how you learnt my darter the musics; and how I used to bring you things; and lend you money; and that; and how I was willing enough to do the like again, put in case you was in need: but I might just as well have talked to the post; which huffed* me a little, I own."

"O, those old gentlewomen," interrupted Gooch, "are always like that. One can never make any thing of 'em. I don't over like them myself, to tell you the truth."

Juliet assured them that, having no time but for business, her injunctions of non-admission had been uniform and universal; and ought not, therefore, to offend any one. She then requested Mr. Tedman to order that the postilion would return to the high road; which he had quitted against her positive direction; and to have the goodness to insist upon his driving her by the side of his own vehicle, till they reached Lewes.

Tedman, looking equally important and elated, again heartily shook hands with her, and said, "My dear, I'll do it with pleasure; or, I'll engage Tim to send off your chay, and I'll take you in his'n; put in case it will be more to your liking; for I am as little agreeable as you are, to letting them rascals of drivers get the better of me."

Juliet acceded to this proposal, in which she saw immediate safety, with the most lively readiness; entreating Mr. Tedman to complete his kindness, in extricating her from so suspicious a person, by paying him the half-crown, which she had promised him, for carrying her to Lewes.

"Half-a-crown?" repeated Mr. Tedman, angrily refusing to take it. "It's too much by half, for coming such a mere step; put in case he did not put to o'purpose. You're just like the quality;

and they're none of your sharpest; to throw away your money, and know neither the why nor the wherefore."

The Baronet, with a loud oath, said that the postilion was a scoundrel, for having offended the young lady; and menaced to inform against him, if he received a sixpence.

The postilion made no resistance; the horses were taken off, and the chaise was drawn back to the high road. The little carriage belonging to young Gooch followed, into which Juliet, refusing all aid but from Mr. Tedman, eagerly sprang; and her old friend placed himself at her side; while Gooch took the reins.

Sir Lyell looked on, visibly provoked; and when they were driving away, called out, in a tone between derision and indignation, "Bravo, Mr. Tedman! You are still, I see, the happy man!"

Young Gooch, laughing without scruple, smacked his horse; while Mr. Tedman angrily muttered, "The quality always allows themselves to say any thing! They think nothing of that! All's one to them whether one likes it or not."

The design of Juliet was, when safely arrived at the farm, which was within a very short walk of the town of Lewes, to beg a safe guide to accompany her to the house of Mrs. Pierson; where she resolved to pass the night; and whence she determined to write to Elinor, and solicit an interview; in which she meant to lay open her new difficulties, in the hope of reawakening some interest that might operate in her favour.

To save herself from the vulgar forwardness of ignorant importunity, she forbore to mention her plan, till she alighted from the little vehicle, at the gate of the farm-yard.

"Goodness! Ma'am," then cried young Gooch, "you won't think of such a thing as going away, I hope, before you've well come? Why our sport's all ready! why, if you'll step a little this way, you may see the three sacks, that three of our men are to run a race in! There'll be fine scrambling and tumbling, one o' top o' t'other. You'll laugh till you split your sides. And if you'll only come here, to the right, I'll shew you the stye where our pig is, that's to be caught by the tail. But it will be well soaped,* I can tell you; so it will be no such easy thing."

Slightly thanking him, Juliet applied for aid, in procuring

her a conductor, to Mr. Tedman; who, though at first he pressed her to stay, as she might get a little amusement so pure cheap, since it would cost nothing but looking on; no sooner heard her pronounce that she was called away by business, than he ceased all opposition; and promised to take care of her to Lewes himself, when he'd just spoken a word or two to his cousin Gooch: "For I can't go with you, my dear, only I and you, you know, without that," he said, "just upon coming; for fear it should put them upon joking; which I don't like; for all the quality's so fond of it. Besides which, I must give in my presents; for this little hamper's full of little odd things for the junket; and if I leave 'em out here, to the mercy of nobody knows who, somebody or other 'll be a pilfering, as sure as a gun; put in case they smoke* what I've got in my hamper. And they're pretty quick at mischief."

Juliet supplicated him to be speedy. Pleased to have his services accepted, he put his hamper under his arm, and walked on to the house; mindless of the impatient remonstrances of young Gooch, who exclaimed, "Why now, who'd have thought this of the 'Squire? it's doing just contrary; for he's the very person I thought would make you stay! for he's come, as one may say, half o' purpose for your sake; for he never plump accepted of our invitation till I told him, in my letter, of my having invited of you. And then he said he would come."

Then, lowering his voice into a whisper, he added, "Between ourselves, Ma'am, the poor 'Squire, my good cousin, don't get much for his money at home, I believe. His daughter's got quite the top end;* and she's none of your obligingests; she won't do one mortal thing he desires. She's been brought up at them fine boarding-schools, with misses that hold up their heads so high, that nothing's good enough for 'em. So she's always ashamed of her papa, because, she says, he's so mean; as he tells us. The poor 'Squire, my cousin, don't much like it; but he can't help himself. She's as exact like a fine lady as ever you see; and she won't speak a word to any of her poor relations, because they are so low, she says." He then added, "If you won't go while I'm gone, I'll give you as agreeable a surprize as ever you had in your life!"

He ran on to the house.

In a few minutes, Juliet felt something tickle the nape of her neck, and, imagining it to be an insect, she would have brushed it away with her hand, but received, between her fingers, a pink;* and, looking round, saw Flora Pierson, nearly breathless from her efforts to smother a laugh.

"Is it possible?" cried Juliet, in great amazement. "Miss Pierson! I thought you were ill in bed?"

No further efforts were necessary to repress the laugh; resentment, rather than gravity, took its place, and, with pouting lips, and a frowning brow, she answered, "Ill? Yes! I have had enough to make me ill, that's sure! It's more a wonder, by half, that I a'n't dead; for I cried so that my eyes grew quite little; and I looked quite a fright; and I grew so hoarse that nobody could tell a word I said; though I talked enough, I'm sure; for nothing can hinder me of my talking, if it was never so, papa says."

Juliet, now, upon closer enquiry, learnt that Flora had neither had a fever, nor desired a meeting; and that Mrs. Pierson had neither written the letter, nor given any orders about a return post-chaise.

The passing suspicions, which already had occurred to Juliet in disfavour of Sir Lyell Sycamore, returned, now, with redoubled force. That he had made signs to the driver to quit the high road, however dismaying, she had attributed to sudden impulse, upon meeting her alone in a post-chaise; and had not doubted that, upon seeing the sincerity of her resentment, he would have retired with shame and repentance: but a plan thus concerted to get her into his power, changed apprehension into certainty, and indignation into abhorrence.

The happy accident to which she owed her escape, even from the knowledge, till it was past, of her danger, she now blessed with rapture; and the junket, so disdained and rejected, she now felt that she could never recollect without grateful delight.

But how return to Brighthelmstone? What vehicle find? How trust herself to any even when procured?

She enquired of Flora whether it were possible that Mrs. Pierson could grant her one night's lodging?

The smiles, the dimples, and the good humour of the

simple girl, all revived, and played about her pretty face, at this request. "O yes!" she cried. "Miss Ellis, I shall be so glad to have you come! for mamma and I are so dull together that I'm quite moped.* I don't like it by half as well as I did the shop. So many smart gentlemen and ladies coming in and out every moment! dressed so nice, and speaking so polite! I'm obliged to wear all my worst things, now, to save my others, mamma says, for fear of the expence. And it makes me not look as well by half, as I did at Miss Matson's. I looked well enough there, I believe; as people told me; at least the gentlemen. But I go such a dowd,* here, that it's enough to frighten you. I'm sure when I go to the glass, and that's a hundred times a-day, for aught I know, if it were counted, to see what sort of a figure I make, I could break it with pleasure, for seeing me such a disguise; for I look quite ugly, unless I happen to be in my smilings."

This prattle was interrupted by a signal from Mr. Tedman, that made Juliet hope that he was now ready to depart; but, upon approaching him, he only said, "Come hither, my dear, and sit down a bit, upon this bench, for we can't go yet. I have not given all my presents. And I don't care to leave 'em!" winking significantly: "not that I mean to doubt any body; only it's as well have a sharp eye. We are all honestest with good looking after."

Juliet now was surrounded by young farmers, who offered her cakes, or ale, and asked her hand for the ensuing dance; while young Gooch collected around him an admiring audience, to listen to his account, how he and the young gentlewoman, who was so pretty, had acted together in a play.

Mr. Tedman then bid her divine how his cousin Gooch was employed, and why the presents were not yet delivered? and upon her declared inability to conjecture, "Would you believe it, my dear?" he cried, "For all Tim drove us such a good round trot, the quality got the start of us! And now he's in the kitchen, with cousin Gooch, taking a cup of ale!"

The disturbance of Juliet at this intelligence, he thought simply surprize, and continued, "Nay, it was not easy to guess, sure enough. He must have rid over every thing, hedge, ditch, and the like. But your quality's not over mindful of other people's property. He's come to buy some hay. He come o' purpose, he says. And he's a mortal good customer, for he says nothing but, 'Mighty well! That's very reasonable, indeed! I thought it had been twice the price!' Old coz* chuckles, I warrant him! Your quality's but a poor hand at a bargain. I would not employ 'em, between you and I. They never know what they are about."

They were now joined by Mr. Gooch, a hale, hearty, cherry-cheeked dapper farmer, fair in all his dealings, and upright in all his principles, except when they had immediate reference to his professional profits. "Well!" he cried, "'Squire!" rubbing his hands in great glee. "I've had a good chapman* enough here! I've often seen un at our races, but I little thought of having to chaffer with un. Howsever, one may have worse luck with one's money. A don't much understand business. But who's that pretty lass with ye, 'Squire? Some play-mate, I warrant, of cousin Molly? And why did no' cousin Molly come, too? A'd a have been heartily welcome. And perhaps a'd a picked up a sweetheart."

"Stop, father, stop!" cried young Gooch: "I've something to say to you. You know how you've always stood to it, that you would not believe a word about all those battles, and guiliotines,* and the like, of Mounseer Robert Speer, in foreign parts; though I told you, over and over, that I had it from our club? Well! here's a person now here, in your own grounds, that's seen it all with her own eyes! So if you don't believe it now, I'll bet what wager you will, you'll never believe it as long as you live."

"Like enough not, Tim," answered the father: "I do no" much give my mind to believing all them outlandish fibs, told by travellers. I can hear staring* stories eno" by my own fire-side. And I a'n't over friendly to believing 'em there. But, bless my heart! for a man for to come for to go for to pretend telling me, because it be a great ways off, and I can't find un out, that there be a place where there comes a man, who says, every morning of his life, to as many of his fellow-creatures as a can set eyes on, whether they be man, woman, or baby; here, mount me two or three dozen of you into that cart, and go and have your heads chopt off! And that they'll make no more ado, than go, only because they're bid! Why if one will believe such staring stuff as that be, one may as well believe that the moon be made of cream-cheese, and the like. There's no sense in such a set of lies; for life's life every where, even in France; thof* it be but a poor starving place, at best, without pasture, or cattle; or corn, either, fit for a man for to eat."

"Ay, father, ay; but Bob Spear, as we call him at our club—"

"Y're young, y're young, Tim," interrupted Mr. Gooch; "and your youngsters do believe every thing. When you've sold your wild oats, you'll know better. But we must n't all be calves at the same time. If there were none for to give milk, there'd be none for to suck. So it be all for the best. And that makes me for to take it the less to heart, when I do see you be such a gudgeon,* Tim, with no more sense than to swallow neat down every thing that do come in your way. But you'll never thrive, Tim, till you be like to what I be; people do tell such a peck* of staring lies, that I do no" believe, nor I wo" no" believe one mortal word by hearsay."

"For my part," said Mr. Tedman, "I never enquire into all that, whether it be true, or whether it be false; because it's nothing to me either way; and one wastes a deal of time in idle curiosity, about things that don't concern one; put in case one can't turn them to one's profit."

"That's true, coz," said Mr. Gooch; "for as to profit, there be none to come from foreign parts: for they be all main* poor thereabout; for, they do tell me, that there be not a man among un, as sets his eyes, above once in his life, or thereabout, upon a golden guinea! And as to roast beef and plum-pudding,* I do hear that they do no" know the taste of such a thing. So that they be but a poor stinted* race at best, for they can never come to their natural growth."

"What, then, you do believe what folks tell you sometimes, father?" cried the son, grinning.

"To be sure I do, Tim; when they do tell me somewhat that be worth a man's hearing."

They were now joined by Mr. Stubbs, who, seeing Juliet, was happy in the opportunity of renewing his favourite enquiries, relative to the agricultural state of the continent.

Mr. Gooch, extremely surprized, exclaimed, "Odds heart! Why sure such a young lass as that be, ha'n't been across seas already? Why a could n't make out their gibberish, I warrant me! for 't be such queer stuff that they do talk, all o'un, that there's no getting at what they'd be at; unless one larns to speak after the same guise, like to our boarding-school misses. I've seen one or two o'un myself, that passed here about; but their manner o" talk was so out of the way, I could no" make out a word they did say. T'might all be Dutch for me. And I found 'em vast ignorant. They knew no more than my horse when land ought for to be manured, from when it ought for to lie fallow. I did ask un a many questions; but a could no" answer me, for to be understood."

"But, for all that, Master Gooch," said Mr. Stubbs, "my late Lord has told me that France is sincerely a fine country, if they knew how to make the most of it; but the waste lands are quite out of reason; for they are such a boggling* set of farmers, that they grow nothing but what comes, as one may say, of itself."

"France a fine country, Maister Stubbs? Well, that be a word I did no" count to hear from a man of your sense. Why't be as poor a place as ye might wish to set eyes on, all overrun with weeds, and frogs, and the like. Why ye be as frenchified as Tim, making out them mounseers* to be a parcel of Jack the Giant-killers,* lopping off heads for mere play, as a body may say. However, here be one that's come to our hop,* that be a finer spark than there be in all France, I warrant me: for a makes a bow as like to a mounseer, as if a was twin-brother to un; and a was so ready to pay down his money handsomely, I could no" but say a'd be welcome to our junket; for a says a does like such a thing more than all them new fangled balls and concerts."

"Oh, and you believe that upon hear-say, do you, father?" cried Tim, sneeringly.

"Yes, to be sure, I do, Tim. When a man do say a thing that ha" got some sense in it, why should no" I believe un, Tim?"

Juliet, who from what had preceded, had concluded the Baronet to be gone, earnestly now pressed Mr. Tedman to fulfil his kind engagement; but in vain: Mr. Gooch brought his best silver tankard, to insist upon his cousin's drinking success to the new purchase, that occasioned the junket; and Tim was outrageous at the proposal of retiring, just as the feats were going to commence. "Before five minutes are over," said he, "the pig will begin!"

"Well," answered Mr. Tedman, "it is but a silly thing, to be sure, things of that sort; and I never give my mind to them; but still, as it's a thing I never saw, put in case you've no objections, we'll just stay for the pig, my dear."

Flora, having now gathered that *the quality* meant Sir Lyell Sycamore, began dancing and singing, in a childish extacy of delight, that shewed her already, in idea, Lady Sycamore; when, turning to Juliet with sudden and angry recollection, her smiles, gaiety, and capering gave way to a bitter fit of crying, and she exclaimed, "But if he is here, it will be nothing to me, I dare say, if Miss Ellis is here the while; for he won't look at me, almost, when she is by: will he? For some people play one so false, that one might as well be as ugly as the cat, almost, when they are in the way."

"Don't be fretted, Miss Flora," cried young Gooch, soothingly; "for I shall ask Miss Ellis to dance myself; for as I shall begin the hop, because of its being our own, I think I've a good right to chuse my partner; so don't be fretted, so, Miss Flora, for you'll have the Baronight left to you whether he will or no! But come; don't let's lose time: if you'll follow me, you won't want sport, I can tell you; for the beginning's to be a syllabub under the cow."*

Flora was not too proud to accept this consolation; but Juliet positively declared that she should not dance; and earnestly entreated that some one might be found to conduct her to Mrs. Pierson's.

Flora, recovering her spirits, with the hopes of getting rid of her rival, whispered, "If you're in real right earnest, Miss Ellis, and don't say you want to go, only to make a fool of me, which I shall take pretty unkind, I assure you; why I can shew you the way so as you can't miss it, if you'd never so. And I'm sure I shall be glad enough to have you go, if I must needs speak without a compliment. Only don't tell mamma who's here, for she don't like persons of quality, she says, because of their bad designs; but I'm sure if she was to hear 'em talk as I do, she'd think quite another opinion: wouldn't she?"

Fortunately for the intentions of Juliet, which were instantly to make known to Mrs. Pierson the new danger of her daughter, Flora waited not for any answer to this injunction; but set out, prattling incessantly as they went on, to put the willing Juliet on her way to Lewes.

The cry, however, from young Gooch, of "Come! Where are the young ladies? The pig's ready!" caught the ears of Flora, with a charm not to be resisted; and, hastily pointing out a style, to pass into a meadow, and another, to pass thence to the high road, she capered briskly back; fearing to miss some of the sport, if not a seat next to the Baronet.

CHAPTER L

JULIET, as earnest to avoid, as Flora felt eager to pursue, the opening feats, hurried from the destined spot, after charging the simple damsel not to make known her departure. Unavailing, however, was the caution; and immaterial alike the prudence or the indiscretion of Flora: Juliet had no sooner crossed the first style, than she perceived Sir Lyell Sycamore sauntering in the meadow.

She would promptly have returned to the farm, but a shout of noisy merriment reached her ears from the company that she was quitting, and pointed out the danger of passing the evening in the midst of such turbulent and vulgar revelry. She hastened, therefore, on; but neither the lightness of her step, nor the swiftness of her speed, could save her from the quick approach of the Baronet. "My angel!" he cried, "whither are you going? and why this prodigious haste? What is it my angel fears? Can she suppose me rascal enough, or fool enough, to make use of any violence? No, my angel, no! I only ask to be regaled, from your own sweet lips, with the delicious tale of divine partiality, that the quaint old knight began revealing. I sigh, I pant to hear confirmed——"

"Hold, Sir Lyell!" interrupted Juliet. "If Sir Jaspar is the author of this astonishing mistake, I trust he will have the honour to rectify it. When I named you to him, it was but with a view to rescue a credulous young creature from your pursuit, whom I feared it might injure; not to expose to it one whom it never can endanger; however deeply it may offend."

Struck and disappointed at the courage and coolness of this explanation, Sir Lyell looked mortified and amazed; but, upon seeing her reach the style, he sprang over it, and, recovering his usual effrontery, offered her his hand.

Juliet knew not whether her risk were greater to proceed or to return; but while she hesitated, a phaeton,* which was driving by, stopt, and an elderly lady, addressing the Baronet, in a tone of fawning courtesy, enquired after his health, and added, "So you are come to this famous junket, Sir Lyell?"

Sir Lyell forced a laugh, and bowed low; though he muttered, loud enough for Juliet to hear, "What cursed spies!"

Juliet now perceived Mrs. and Miss Brinville; and neither innocence, nor contempt of calumny, could suppress a rising blush, at being surprised, by persons already unfavourably disposed towards her, in a situation apparently so suspicious.

The countenance of the mother exhibited strong chagrin at sight of Juliet; while the daughter, in a tone of pique, said, "No doubt but you are well amused, Sir Lyell?"

They drove on; not, however, very fast, and with so little self-command, as frequently to allow themselves to look back. This indelicacy, however ill adapted to raise them in the esteem of the Baronet, at least rescued Juliet from his persecution. Disconcerted himself, he felt the necessity of decency; and, quitting her, with affected carelessness, he hummed an air, while grumbling curses, and, swinging his switch to and fro, walked off; not more careful that the ladies in the phaeton should see him depart, than assiduous to avoid with them any sort of junction.

The relief caused to Juliet by his retreat, was cruelly clouded by her terrour of the false suggestions to which this meeting made her liable. Neither mother nor daughter would believe it accidental; nor credit it to have been contrived without equal guilt in both parties. Is there no end, then, she cried, to the evils of defenceless female youth? And, even where actual danger is escaped, must slander lie in wait, to misconstrue the most simple actions, by surmising the most culpable designs?

Neither to follow the footsteps of Sir Lyell, nor to remain

where he might return, she was going back to the farm; when she was met by Flora, who, with a species of hysterical laughter, nearly of kin to crying, called out, "So Ma'am! so Miss Ellis! I've caught you at last! I've surprised you at last! a-courting with my sweet-heart!"

Pitying her credulous ignorance, Juliet would have cleared up this mistake; but the petulant Flora would not listen. "I'll speak to the gentleman myself!" she cried, running forward to the style; "for I have found out your design; so it's of no use to deny it! I saw you together all the way I came; so you may as well not try to make a ninny of me, Miss Ellis, for it i'n't so easy!"

Catching a glimpse of the Baronet as he descended the road, she jumped over the style to run after him; but seeing him look round, and, though he perceived her, quietly walk on, she stopt, crying bitterly: "Very well, Miss Ellis! very well! you've got your ends!* I see that! and, I don't thank you for it, I assure you, for I liked him very well; and it i'n't so easy to find a man of quality every day; so it i'n't doing as you'd be done by; for nobody likes much to be forsaken, no more than I, I believe, for it i'n't so agreeable. And I had rather you had not served me so by half! In particular for a man of quality!"

Juliet, though vainly, was endeavouring to appease and console her, when a young lady, bending eagerly from the window of a post chaise which was passing by, ejaculated, "Ellis!" and Juliet, with extreme satisfaction, perceived Elinor.

The chaise stopt, and Juliet advanced to it with alacrity; but before she could speak, the impatient Elinor, still looking pale, meagre, and wretched, burst forth, with rapid and trembling energy, into a string of disordered, incoherent, scarcely intelligible interrogatories. "Ellis! what brings you to this spot?—Whither is it you go?—What project are you forming?—What purpose are you fulfilling?—Whom are you flying?—Whom are you following?—What is it you design?—What is it you wish?—Why are you here alone?—Where—Where—"

Leaning, then, still further out of the window, she fixed her nearly hagard, yet piercing eyes upon those of Juliet, and, in a hollow voice, dictatorially added: "Where—tell me, I charge you! where—is Harleigh?"

Consternation at sight of her altered countenance, and

affright at the impetuosity of her questions, produced a hesitation in the answer of Juliet, that, to the agitated Elinor, seemed the effect of surprised guilt. Her pallid cheeks then burnt with the mixed feelings of triumph and indignation; yet her voice sought to disguise her wounded feelings, and in subdued, though broken accents, "'Tis well!" she cried, "You no longer, at least, seek to deceive me, and I thank you!" Deaf to explanation or representation, she then hurried her weak frame from the chaise, aided by her foreign lackey; and, directing Juliet to follow, crossed the road to a rising ground upon the Downs; seated herself; sent off her assistant, and made Juliet take a place by her side; while Flora returned, crying and alone, to the farm.

"Now, then," she said, "that you try no more to delude, to cajole, to blind me, tell me now, and in two words,—where is Harleigh?"

"Believe me, Madam,——" Juliet was tremblingly beginning, when Elinor, casting off the little she had assumed of self-command, passionately, cried, "Must I again be played upon by freezing caution and duplicity? Must I die without end the lingering death of cold inaction and uncertainty? breathe for ever without living? Where, I demand, is Harleigh? Where have you concealed him? Why will Harleigh, the noble Harleigh, degrade himself by any concealment? Why stoop to the subtilty of circumspection, to spare himself the appearance of destroying one whose head, heart, and vitals, all feel the reality of the destruction he inflicts? And yet not he! No, no! 'tis my own ruthless star! He loves me not! he is not responsible for my misery, though he is master of my fate! Where is he? where is he? You,—who are the tyrant of his! tell me, and at once!"

"I solemnly protest to you, Madam, with the singleness of the most scrupulous truth," cried Juliet, recovering her presence of mind, "I am entirely ignorant of his abode, his occupations, and his intentions." Ah why, she secretly added, am I not equally unacquainted with his feelings and his wishes!

Unable to discredit the candour with which this was pronounced, and filled with wonder, yet involuntarily consoled, the features of Elinor lost their rigidity, and her eyes their fierceness; and, in milder accents, she replied, "Strange! how strange! Where, then, can he be?—with whom?—how employed?—Does he fly the whole world as well as Elinor? Has no one his society?—no one his confidence?—his society, which, by contrast, makes all existence without it disgusting!—his confidence, which, to obtain, I would yet live, though doomed daily to the rack! O Harleigh! love like mine, who has felt?—love like mine, who but you, O matchless Harleigh! ever inspired!"

Tears now gushed into her eyes. Ashamed, and angry with herself, she hastily brushed them off with the back of her hand, and, with forced vivacity, continued, "He thinks, perchance, to sicken me into the pining end of a love-sick consumption? to avert the kindly bowl or dagger,* that cut short human misery, for the languors, the sufferings and despair of a loathsome natural death? And for what?—to restore, to preserve me? No! I have no share in the arrangement; no interest, no advantage from the plan. Appearances alone are considered; all else is regarded as immaterial; or sacrificed. And he, Harleigh, the noblest,—the only noble of men!—can level himself with the narrowest and most illiberal of his race, to pay coward obeisance to appearances!"

Again she then repeated her personal interrogatories to Juliet; and demanded whether she should set off immediately for Gretna Green, with Lord Melbury; or whether she must wait till he should be of age.

"Neither!" Juliet solemnly answered; and frankly recounted her recent difficulties; and entreated the advice of Elinor for adopting another plan of life.

Elinor, interrupting her, said, "Nay, 'twas your own choice, you know, to live in a garret, and hem pocket-handkerchiefs."

"Choice, Madam! Alas! deprived of all but personal resource, I fixed upon a mode of life that promised me, at least, my mental freedom. I was not then aware how imaginary is the independence, that hangs for support upon the uncertain fruits of daily exertions! Independent, indeed, such situations may be deemed from the oppressions of power, or the tyrannies of caprice and ill humour; but the difficulty of obtaining employment, the irregularity of pay, the dread of want,—ah! what is freedom but a name, for those who have not an hour at command from the subjection of fearful penury and distress?"

"If all this is so," said Elinor, "which, unless you wait for Lord Melbury's majority, is more than incomprehensible; what say you, now, to an asylum safe, at least, from torments of this sort;—will you commission me, at length, to apply to Mrs. Ireton?"

Juliet, instinctively, recoiled at the very name of that lady; yet a little reflection upon the dangers to which she was now exposed, through unprotected poverty; through the lawless pursuit of Sir Lyell Sycamore; and the vindictive calumnies of the Brinvilles, made the wish of solid safety repress the disgusts of offended sensibility; and, after a painful pause, she recommended herself to the support of Elinor: resolving to accept, for the moment, any proposition, that might secure her an honourable refuge from want and misconception.

Elinor, looking at her suspiciously, said, "And Harleigh?—Will he let you submit to such slavery?"

Mr. Harleigh, Juliet protested, could have no influence upon her determination.

"But you yourself, who a month or two ago, could so ill bear her tauntings, how is it you are thus suddenly endued with so much humility?"

"Alas, Madam, all choice, all taste, all obstacles sink before necessity! When I came over, I had expectations of immediate succour. I knew not that the friend I sought was herself ruined, as well as unhappy! I had hopes, too, of speedy intelligence that might have liberated me from all my difficulties . . ."

She stopt; Elinor exclaimed, "From whence?—From abroad?—"

Juliet was silent; and Elinor, after a few passing sallies against secrets and mystery, sarcastically bid her consider, before she adopted this new scheme, that Harleigh never visited at Mrs. Ireton's; having taken, in equal portions, a dose of aversion for the mother, and of contempt for the son.

Juliet calmly replied, that such a circumstance could be but an additional motive to seek the situation; and, hopeless, for the moment, of doing better, seriously begged that proper measures might be taken to accelerate the plan.

Elinor, now, from mingled wonder, satisfaction, and scorn, recovered all her wonted vivacity. "You are really, and bona fide, contented, then," she cried, "to be shut up as completely from Harleigh, through his horrour of that woman's irascible temper, as if you were separated by bolts, bars, dungeons, towers, and bastilles? I applaud your taste, and wish you the full enjoyment of its fruits! Yet what materials you can be made of, to see the first of men at your feet, and voluntarily to fly him, to be trampled under by those of the most odious of women, I cannot divine! 'Tis an exuberance of apathy that surpasses my comprehension. And can He, the spirited Harleigh, love, adore, such a composition of ice, of snow, of marble?"

She could not, however, disguise the elation with which she looked forward, to depositing Juliet where information might constantly be procured of her visitors and her actions. They went together to the carriage; and Elinor conveyed her submissive and contemned, yet agonizingly envied rival, to Brighthelmstone.

In her usually unguarded manner, Elinor, by the way, communicated the various, but successless efforts by which she had endeavoured to gain intelligence whither Harleigh had rambled. "If I pursued him," she cried, "with the vanity of hope; or with the meanness of flattery, he would do well to shun me; but the pure-minded Harleigh is capable of believing, that the moment is over for Elinor to desire to be his! And, to sustain at once and shew my principles, I never seek his sight, but in presence of her who has blasted even my wishes! Else, thus clamourously to invoke, thus pertinaciously to follow him, might, indeed, merit avoidance. But Elinor, now, would be as superiour to accepting, . . . as she is to forgetting him!"

"Yet his obdurate seclusion," she continued, "is the only mark I receive, that I escape his disdain. It shews me that he fears the event of a meeting. He does not, therefore, utterly deride the pusillanimity of my abortive attempt. O could I justify his good opinion!—All others, I doubt not, insult me by the most ludicrous suspicions; they are welcome. They judge me by their little-minded selves. But thou, O Harleigh! could I see thee once more!—in thy sight, thy loved sight, could I sink, at last, my sorrows and my disgrace to rest! to oblivion, to sleep eternal!"—

Vainly Juliet essayed to plead the cause of religion, and the duties of life; unanswered, unmarked, unheard, she talked but to the air. All that was uttered in return, began and ended alike with Harleigh, death, and annihilation.

BOOK VI

CHAPTER LI

JULIET could not but be gratified by a circumstance so important to her reputation, with the Brinvilles, and with those among the inhabitants of Brighthelmstone to whom she was known, as that of being brought home by Miss Joddrel, after an adventure that must unavoidably raise curiosity, and that threatened to excite slander. For with however just a pride wronged innocence may disdain injurious aspersions, female fame, like the wife of Cæsar, ought never to be suspected.*

The celerity of the motions of Elinor, nearly equalled the quickness of her ideas. Her lackey arrived the next morning, to help to convey Juliet, and her baggage, immediately to the dwelling of Mrs. Ireton; with a note from his mistress, indicating that Mrs. Ireton was already prepared to take her for a companion. "An humble companion," Elinor wrote, "I need not add; I had nearly said a pitiful one; for who would voluntarily live with such an antidote to all the comforts of life, that has spirit, sense, or soul? O envied Ellis! how potent must be the passion, the infatuation, that can make Harleigh view such meanness as grace, and adore it as dignity!—O icy Ellis!—but the human heart would want strength to support such pre-eminent honour, were it bestowed upon a mind gifted for its appreciation!"

Then again, wishing her joy of her taste, she assured her that it was reciprocated; for Mrs. Ireton was all impatience to display, to a new dependent, her fortune, her power, and her magnificence.

Juliet, with her answer of thanks for this service, wrote a few lines for Mrs. Pierson, which she begged the messenger to deliver. They were to warn the imprudent, or deceived mother of the dangerous state of mind in which her daughter still continued; and to give her notice that Sir Lyell Sycamore, who could not be guarded against too carefully, was still in the neighbourhood.

With a mind revolting from a measure which, while prudence, if not necessity, dictated, choice and feeling opposed, she now quitted her mantua-maker's abode, to set out for her new destination; seeking to cheer herself that, at least, by this step, she should be secured from the licentious pursuit of Sir Lyell Sycamore; the envenomed shafts of calumny of the enraged Brinvilles; the perpetual terrour of debts; and the cruel apprehension of want.

She had not far to go; but the mortifications, for which she prepared herself, began by the very sight of the dwelling into which she was to enter. Mrs. Ireton had taken the house of Mrs. Howel:—that house in which Juliet had first, after her arrival in England, received consolation in her distresses; been melted by kindness; or animated by approbation. There, too, indeed, she had experienced the pain which she had felt the most severely; for there all the soothing consideration, so precious to her sorrows, had abruptly been broken off, to give place to an assault the most shocking upon her intentions, her probity, her character.

Here, too, she had suffered the cruel affront, and heart-felt grief, of seeing the ingenuous, amiable Lord Melbury forget what was due to the rights of hospitality; to his own character; and to the respect due to his sister: and here she had witnessed his sincere and candid repentance; here had been softened, touched, and penetrated by the impressive anguish of his humiliation.

These remembrances, and the various affecting and interesting ideas by which they were accompanied, gave a dejection to her thoughts, and a sadness to her air, that would have awakened an interest in her favour, in any one whose heart had been open to the feelings of others: but the person under whose protection she was now to place herself, was a stranger to every species of sensation that was not personal. And where the calls of self upon sensibility are unremitting, what must be the stock that will gift us, also, with supply sufficient for our fellow-creatures?

She found Mrs. Ireton reclining upon a sofa; at the side of which, upon a green velvet cushion, lay a tiny old lap dog, whom a little boy, evidently too wanton to find pleasure but in mischief, was secretly tormenting, by displaying before him the breast bone of a chicken, which he had snatched from the platter of the animal; and which, the moment that he made it touch the mouth of the cur, he hid, with all its fat and its grease, in his own waistcoat pocket.

Near to these two almost equally indulged and spoilt animals, stood a nursery maid, with a duster and an hearth-broom in her hands, who was evidently incensed beyond her pittance of patience, from clearing away, repeatedly, their joint litter and dirt.

Scared, and keeping humbly aloof, near a window frame, stood, also, a little girl, of ten or twelve years of age, who, as Juliet afterwards heard from the angry nursery maid, was an orphan, that had been put to a charity school* by Mrs. Ireton, as her particular *protegée*; and who was now, for the eighth time, by the direction of her governess, come to solicit the arrears due from the very beginning of her school instruction.

Yet another trembler, though not one equally, at this moment, to be pitied, held the handle of the lock of the door; not having received intelligible orders to advance, or to depart. This was a young negro, who was the favourite, because the most submissive servant of Mrs. Ireton; and whose trembling was simply from the fear that his lady might remark a grin which he could not repress, as he looked at the child and the dog.

Mrs. Ireton herself, though her restless eye roved incessantly from object to object, in search of various food for her spleen, was ostensibly occupied in examining, and decrying, the goods of a Mercer:* but when Juliet, finding herself unnoticed, was retreating, she called out, "O, you are there, are you? I did not see you, I protest. But come this way, if you please. I can't possibly speak so far off."

The authoritative tone in which this was uttered, joined to what Juliet observed of the general tyranny exercised around her, intimidated and shocked her; and she stood still, and nearly confounded.

Mrs. Ireton, holding her hand above her eyes, as if to aid her sight, and stretching forward her head, said, "Who is that?—pray who's there?—I imagined it had been a person I had sent for; but I must certainly be mistaken, as she does not come to me. Pray has any body here a spying glass?* I really can't see so far off. I beg pardon for having such bad eyes! I hope you'll forgive it. Let me know, however, who it is, I beg."

Juliet tried to speak, but felt so confused and disturbed what to answer, that she could not clearly articulate a word.

"You won't tell me, then?" continued Mrs. Ireton, lowering her voice nearly to a whisper, "or is it that I am not heard? Has any body got a speaking trumpet?* or do you think my lungs so capacious and powerful, that they may take its place?"

Juliet, now, though most unwillingly, moved forward; and Mrs. Ireton, surveying her, said, "Yes, yes, I see who you are! I recollect you now, Mrs.... Mrs.... I forget your name, though, I protest. I can't recollect your name, I own. I'm quite ashamed, but I really cannot call it to mind. I must beg a little help. What is it? What is your name, Mrs.... Mrs.... Hay?—Mrs.... What?"

Colouring and stammering, Juliet answered, that she had hoped Miss Joddrel would have saved her this explanation, by mentioning that she was called Miss Ellis.

"Called?" repeated Mrs. Ireton; "what do you mean by called?—who calls you?—What are you called for?—Why do you wait to be called?—And where are you called from?"

The entire silence of Juliet to these interrogatories, gave a moment to the mercer to ask for orders.

"You are in haste, Sir, are you?" said Mrs. Ireton; "I have your pardon to beg, too, have I? I am really very unfortunate this morning. However, pray take your things away, Sir, if it's so immensely troublesome to you to exhibit them. Only be so good as to acquaint your chief, whoever he may be, that you had not time to wait for me to make any purchase."

The man offered the humblest apologies, which were all disdained; and self-defending excuses, which were all retorted; he was peremptorily ordered to be gone; with an assurance that he should answer for his disrespect to his master; who, she flattered herself, would give him a lesson of better behaviour, by the loss of his employment.

Harassed with apprehension of what she had to expect in this new residence, Juliet would silently have followed him.

"Stay, Ma'am, stay!" cried Mrs. Ireton; "give me leave to ask one question:—whither are you going, Mrs.... what's your name?"

"I ... I feared, Madam, that I had come too soon."

"O, that's it, is it? I have not paid you sufficient attention, perhaps?—Nay it's very likely. I did not run up to receive you, I confess. I did not open my arms to embrace you, I own! It was very wrong of me, certainly. But I am apt to forget myself. I want a flapper prodigiously. I know nothing of life,—nothing of manners. Perhaps you will be so good as to become my monitress? 'Twill be vastly kind of you. And who knows but, in time, you may form me? How happy it will be if you can make something of me!"

The maid, now, tired of wiping up splash after splash, and rubbing out spot after spot; finding her work always renewed by the mischievous little boy, was sullenly walking to the other end of the room.

"O, you're departing too, are you?" said Mrs. Ireton; "and pray who dismissed you? whose commands have you for going? Inform me, I beg, who it is that is so kind as to take the trouble off my hands, of ordering my servants? I ought at least to make them my humble acknowledgements. There's nothing so frightful as ingratitude."

The maid, not comprehending this irony, grumblingly answered, that she had wiped up the grease and the slops till her arms ached; for the little boy made more dirt and nastiness than the cur himself.

"The boy?—The cur?—What's all this?" cried Mrs. Ireton; "who, and what, is the woman talking of? The boy? Has the boy no name?—The cur? Have you no more respect for your lady's lap dog?—Grease too?—Nastiness!—you turn me sick! I am ready to faint! What horrible images you present to me! Has nobody any salts? any lavendar-water?* How unfortunate it is to have such nerves, such sensations, when one lives with such mere speaking machines!"

She then cast around her eyes, with a look of silent, but pathetic appeal to the sensibility of all who were within sight, against this unheard of indignity; but her speech was soon restored, from mingled wrath and surprise, upon perceiving her favourite young negro nearly suffocating with stifled laughter, though thrusting both his knuckles into his capacious mouth, to prevent its loud explosion.

"So this amuses you, does it, Sir? You think it very comical? You are so kind as to be entertained, are you? How happy I am to give you so much pleasure! How proud I ought to be to afford you such diversion! I shall make it my business to shew my sense of my good fortune; and, to give you a proof, Sir, of my desire to contribute to your gaiety, to-morrow morning I will have you shipped back to the West Indies. And there, that your joy may be complete, I shall issue orders that you may be striped till you jump, and that you may jump,—you little black imp!—between every stripe!"

The foolish mirth of poor Mungo* was now converted into the fearfulest dismay. He dropt upon his knees to implore forgiveness; but he was peremptorily ordered to depart, with an assurance that he should keep up his fine spirits upon bread and water for a fortnight.

If disgust, now, was painted upon every feature of the face of Juliet, at this mixture of forced derision with but too natural inhumanity, the feeling which excited that expression was by no means softened, by seeing Mrs. Ireton turn next to the timid young orphan, imperiously saying, "And you, Ma'am, what may you stand there for, with your hands before you? Have you nothing better to do with them? Can't you find out some way to make them more useful? or do you hold it more fitting to consider them as only ornamental? They are very pretty, to be sure. I say nothing to the contrary of that. But I should suppose you don't quite intend to reserve them for mere objects of admiration? You don't absolutely mean, I presume, to devote them to the painter's eye? or to destine them to the sculptor's chisel? I should think not, at least. I should imagine not. I beg you to set me right if I am wrong."

The poor little girl, staring, and looking every way around to find some meaning for what she did not comprehend, could only utter a faint "Ma'am!" in a tone of so much fear and distress, that Juliet, unable, silently, to witness oppression so wanton, came forward to say, "The poor child, Ma'am, only wishes to understand your commands, that she may obey them."

"O! they are not clear, I suppose? They are too abstruse, I imagine?" contemptuously replied Mrs. Ireton. "And you, who are kind enough to offer yourself for my companion; who think yourself sufficiently accomplished to amuse,—perhaps instruct me,—you, also, have not the wit to find out, what a little chit of an ordinary girl can do better with her hands, than to stand still, pulling her own fingers?"

Juliet, now, believing that she had discovered what was meant, kindly took the little girl by the arm, and pointed to the just overturned water-bason of the dog.

"But I don't know where to get a cloth, Ma'am?" said the child.

"A cloth?—In my wardrobe, to be sure!" cried Mrs. Ireton; "amongst my gowns, and caps, and hats. Where else should there be dirty cloths, and dusters, and dish-clouts?* Do you know of any other place where they are likely to be found? Why don't you answer?"

"Ma'am?"

"You never heard, perhaps, of such a place as a kitchen? You don't know where it is? nor what it means? You have only heard talk of drawing-rooms, dressing-rooms, boudoirs? or, perhaps, sometimes, of a corridor, or a vestibule, or an anti-chamber?* But nothing beyond!—A kitchen!—O, fie, fie!"

Juliet now hurried the little girl away, to demand a cloth of the house-maid; but the moment that she returned with it, Mrs. Ireton called out, "And what would you do, now, Ma'am? Make yourself all dirt and filth, that you may go back to your school, to shew the delicate state of my house? To make your mistress, and all her brats, believe that I live in a pig-stie? Or to spread abroad that I have not servants enough to do my work, and that I seize upon you to supply their place? But I beg your pardon; perhaps that may be your way to shew your gratitude? To manifest your sense of my saving you from the work-house?* to reward me for snatching you from beggary, and want, and starving?"

The poor little girl burst into tears, but courtsied, and quitted the room; while Mrs. Ireton called after her, to desire that she would acquaint her governess, that she should certainly be paid the following week.

Juliet now stood in scarcely less dismay than she had been witnessing all around her; panic-struck to find herself in the power of a person whose character was so wantonly tyrannic and irascible.

The fortunate entrance of some company enabled her, for the present, to retreat; and to demand, of one of the servants, the way to her chamber.

CHAPTER LII

FROM the heightened disgust which she now conceived against her new patroness, Juliet severely repented the step that she had taken. And if her entrance into the family contributed so little to her contentment, her subsequent introduction into her office was still less calculated to exhilarate her spirits. Her baggage was scarcely deposited in a handsome chamber, of which the hangings, and decorations, as of every part of the mansion, were sumptuous for the spectator; but in which there was a dearth of almost every thing that constitutes comfort to the immediate dweller; ere she was summoned back, by a hasty order to the drawing-room.

Mrs. Ireton, who was reading a newspaper, did not, for some time, raise her head; though a glance of her eye procured her the satisfaction of seeing that her call had been obeyed. Juliet, at first, stood modestly waiting for commands; but, receiving none, sat down, though at an humble distance; determined to abide by the consequences, be they what they might, of considering herself as, at least, above a common domestic.

This action shortened the term of neglect; Mrs. Ireton, letting the newspaper fall, exclaimed, in a tone of affected alarm, "Are you ill, Ma'am? Are you disordered? I hope you are not subject to fits?"

Juliet coldly answered No.

"I am very glad to hear it, indeed! Very happy, upon my word! I was afraid you were going to faint away! But I find that you are only delicate; only fatigued by descending the stairs. I ought, indeed, to have sent somebody to help you; somebody you could have leant upon as you came along. I was very stupid not to think of that. I hope you'll pardon me?"

Juliet looked down, but kept her place.

Mrs. Ireton, a little nettled, was silent a few minutes, and then said, "Pray,—if I may ask,—if it will not be too great a liberty to ask,—what have been your pursuits since I had the honour of accompanying you to London? How have you passed your time? I hope you have found something to amuse you?"

Juliet sighed a negative.

"You have been studying the fine arts, I am told. Painting?—Drawing?—Sculpture?—or what is it?—Something of that sort, I am informed. Pray what is it, Mrs. Thing-a-mi?—I am always forgetting your name. Yet you have certainly a name; but I don't know how it is, I can never remember it. I believe I must beg you to write it down."

Juliet again only sighed.

"Perhaps I am making a mistake as to your occupations? Very likely I may be quite in the wrong? Indeed I think I recollect, now, what it is you have been doing. Acting?—That's it. Is it not? Pray what stage did you come out upon first? Did you begin wearing your itinerant buskins in England, or abroad?"

"Where I began, Madam, I have ended; at Mrs. Maple's."

"And pray, have you kept that same face ever since I saw you in Grosvenor Square? or have you put it on again only now, to come back to me? I rather suppose you have made it last the whole time. It would be very expensive, I apprehend, to change it frequently: it can by no means be so costly to keep it only in repair. How do you put on your colours? I have heard of somebody who had learnt the art of enamelling their own skin:* is that your method?"

Waiting vainly for an answer, she went on.

"Pray, if I may presume so far, how old are you?—But I beg pardon for so indiscreet a question. I did not reflect upon what I was saying. Very possibly your age may be indefinable. You may be a person of another century. A wandering Jewess. I never heard that the old Jew* had a wife, or a mother, who partook of his longevity; but very likely I may now have the pleasure of seeing one of his family under my own roof? That red and white, that you lay on so happily, may just as well hide the wrinkles of two or three grand climacterics,* as of only a poor single sixty or seventy years of age. However, these are secrets that I don't presume to enquire into. Every trade has its mystery."

These splenetic witticisms producing no reply, Mrs. Ireton, more categorically, demanded, "Pray, Ma'am, pray Mrs. What's-your-name, will you give me leave to ask what brings you to my house?"

"Miss Joddrel, Madam, informed me that you desired my attendance."

"Yes; but with what view?"

Disconcerted by this interrogatory, Juliet stammered, but could devise no answer.

"To what end, what purpose, what intent, I say, may I owe the honour of your presence?"

The office pointed out by Elinor, of an humble companion, now died the cheeks of Juliet with shame; but resentment of the palpable desire to hear its mortifying acknowledgement, tied her tongue; and though each of the following interrogatories was succeeded by a pause that demanded a reply, she could not bring herself to utter a word.

"You are hardly come, I should imagine, without some motive: I may be mistaken, to be sure; but I should hardly imagine you would take the trouble to present yourself merely to afford me the pleasure of seeing you?—Not but that I ought to be extremely flattered by such a compliment. 'Twould be vastly amiable, certainly. A lady of your indescribable consequence! 'Twould be difficult to me to shew an adequate sense of so high an honour. I am distressed at the very thought of it.—But perhaps you may have some other design?—You may have the generosity to intend me some improvement?—You may come to favour me with some lessons of declamation?—Who knows but you may propose to make an actress of me?—Or perhaps to instruct me how to become an adept in your own favourite art of face-daubing?"

At least, thought Juliet, I need not give you any lessons in the *art of ingeniously tormenting!** There you are perfect!

"What! no answer yet?—Am I always so unfortunate as to hit upon improper subjects?—To ask questions that merit no reply?—I am quite confounded at my want of judgment! Excuse it, I entreat, and aid me out of this unprofitable labyrinth of conjecture, by telling me, at once, to what happy inspiration I am indebted for the pleasure of receiving you in my house?"

Juliet pleaded again the directions of Miss Joddrel.

"Miss Joddrel told you to come, then, only to come?—Only to shew yourself?—Well, you are worth looking at, I acknowledge, to those who have seen you formerly. The transformation must always be curious: I only hope you intend to renew it, from time to time, to keep admiration alive? That pretty face you exhibit at present, may lose its charms, if it should become familiar. When shall you put on the other again, that I had the pleasure to see you in first?"

Fatigued and spiritless, Juliet would have retired; but Mrs. Ireton called after her, "O! you are going, are you? Pray may I take the liberty to ask whither?"

Again Juliet was silent.

"You mean perhaps to repose yourself?—or, may be, to pursue your studies?—or, perhaps, you may have some visits upon your hands?—And you may only have done me the favour to enter my house to find time to follow your humour?—You may think it sufficient honour for me, that I may be at the expence of your board, and find you in lodging, and furniture, and fire, and candles, and servants?—you may hold this ample recompense for such an insignificant person as I am? I ought to be much obliged to Miss Joddrel, upon my word, for bringing me into such distinction! I had understood her, indeed, that you would come to me as my humble companion."

Juliet, cruelly shocked, turned away her head.

"And I was stupid enough to suppose, that that meant a person who could be of some use, and some agreeability; a person who could read to me when I was tired, and who, when I had nobody else, could talk to me; and find out a thousand little things for me all day long; coming and going; prating, or holding her tongue; doing every thing she was bid; and keeping always at hand."

Juliet, colouring at this true, however insulting description of what she had undertaken, secretly revolved in her mind, how to renounce, at once, an office which seemed to invite mortification, and license sarcasm.

"But I perceive I was mistaken! I perceive I knew nothing of the matter! It only means a fine lady! a lady that's so delicate it fatigues her to walk down stairs; a lady who is so independent, that she retires to her room at pleasure; a lady who disdains to speak but when she is disposed, for her own satisfaction, to talk; a lady——"

"A lady who, indeed, Madam," said the tired Juliet, "weighed too little what she attempted, when she hoped to find means of obtaining your favour; but who now sees her errour, and entreats at once your pardon and dismission."

She then courtsied respectfully, but, though called back even with vehemence, steadily left the room.

Not, however, with triumph did she return to her own. The justice of the sensibility which urged her retreat, could not obviate its imprudence, or avert its consequences. She was wholly without friends, without money, without protection, without succour; and the horrour of a licentious pursuit, and the mischiefs menaced by calumniating ill wishers, still made a lonely residence as unsafe as when her first terrour drove her to acquiesce in the proposition of Elinor. Yet, though she could not exult, she could not repent: how desire, how even support a situation so sordid? a situation not only distressing, but oppressive; not merely cruel, but degrading.

She was preparing, therefore, for immediate departure, when she was stopt by a footman, who informed her that Mrs. Ireton demanded to see her without delay.

The expectation of reproach made her hesitate whether to obey this order; but a desire not to have the air of meriting it, by the defiance of a refusal, led her again to the dressing-room.

Here, however, to her great surprise, instead of the haughty or taunting upbraidings for which she was prepared, she was received with a gracious inclination of the head; while the footman was told to give her a chair.

Mrs. Ireton, then, fixing her eyes upon a pamphlet which she held in her hand; that she might avoid taking any notice of the stiff and decided air with which Juliet stood still, though amazed, said, "My bookseller has just sent me something to look at, which may serve for a beginning of our readings."

Juliet now saw, that, however imperiously she had been treated, Mrs. Ireton had no intention to part with her. She saw, too, that that lady was amongst the many, though terrible characters, who think superiour rank or fortune authorises perverseness, and legitimates arrogance; who hold the display of ill humour to be the display and mark of power; and who set no other boundary to their pleasure in the art of tormenting, than that which, if passed, might endanger their losing its object. She wished, more than ever, to avoid all connexion with a nature so wilfully tyrannic; but Mrs. Ireton, who read in her dignified demeanour, that a spirit was awakened which threatened the escape of her prey, determined to shun any discussion. Suddenly, therefore, rising, and violently ringing the bell, she exclaimed, "I dare say those fools have not placed half the things you want in your chamber; but I shall make Whitly see immediately that all is arranged as it ought to be."

She then gave some parading directions, that Miss Ellis should want for nothing; and, affecting not to perceive the palpable design of Juliet to decline these tardy attentions, graciously nodded her head, and passed into another room.

Juliet, not absolutely softened, yet somewhat appeased, again hesitated. A road seemed open, by some exertion of spirit, for obtaining better treatment; and however ungenial to her feelings was a character whose humours submitted to no restraint, save to ensure their own lengthened indulgence, still, in appearing more contemptible, it became less tremendous.

She began, also, to see her office as less debasing. Why, she cried, should I exaggerate my torments, by blindly giving into received opinions, without examining whether here, as in all things else, there may not be exceptions to general rules? A sycophant must always be despicable; a parasite must eternally deserve scorn; but may there not be a possibility of uniting the affluent with the necessitous upon more equitable terms? May not some medium be hit upon, between oppression on one side, and servility on the other? If we are not worthless because indigent, why conclude ourselves abject because dependent?

Happiness, indeed, dwells not with undue subordination; but the exertion of talents in our own service can never in itself be vile. It can only become so, where it is mingled and contaminated with flattery, with unfitting obsequiousness, and unworthy submissions. They who simply repay being sustained and protected, by a desire to please, a readiness to serve, a wish to instruct; without falsehood in their counsels, without adulation in their civilities, without meanness in their manners and conduct; have at least as just a claim to respect and consideration, for their services and their labours, as those who, merely through pecuniary retribution, reap their fruits.

This idea better reconciled her with her condition; and she blessed her happy acquaintance with Mr. Giles Arbe, which had strengthened her naturally philosophical turn of mind, by leading her to this simple, yet useful style of reasoning.

The rest of the day was propitious to her new views. The storms with which it had begun subsided, and a calm ensued, in which Mrs. Ireton set apart her querulous irascibility, and forbore her contemptuous interrogatories.

The servants were ordered not to neglect Miss Ellis; and Miss Ellis received permission to carry to her own apartment, any books from off the piano-forte or tables, that might contribute to her amusement.

Juliet was not of a character to take advantage of a moment of concession, even in an enemy. The high and grave deportment, therefore, which had thus happily raised alarm, had no sooner answered its purpose, than she suffered it to give place to an air of gentleness, more congenial to her native feelings: and, the next morning, subduing her resentment, and submitting, with the best grace in her power, to the business of her office, she cheerfully proposed reading; complied with the first request that was made her to play upon the piano-forte and the harp; and even, to sing; though, not so promptly; for her voice and sensibility were less ductile than her manners. But she determined to leave nothing untried, that could prove, that it was not more easy to stimulate her pride by indignity, than to animate her desire to oblige by mild usage.

This resolution on her part, which the fear of losing her, on that of Mrs. Ireton, gave time to operate, brought into play so many brilliant accomplishments, and opened to her patroness such sources of amusement, that, while Juliet began to hope she had found a situation which she might sustain till her suspences should be over, Mrs. Ireton conceived that she had met with a treasure, which might rescue her unoccupied hours from weariness and spleen.

CHAPTER LIII

THIS delusion, unfortunately, was not of long duration on either side. Mrs. Ireton no sooner observed that Juliet appeared to be settled, than all zest for detaining her ceased; no sooner became accustomed to hearing at will the harp, or the piano-forte, than she found something to say, or to do, that interrupted the performance every four or five bars; and had no sooner secured a reader whose voice she could command at pleasure, than she either quarrelled with every book that was begun; or yawned, or fondled and talked aloud to her little lap dog, during the whole time that any work was read.

This quick abatement in the power of pleasing, was supported by Juliet with indifference rather than philosophy. Where interest alone is concerned, disappointment is rarely heavy with the young and generous. Age, or misfortune, must teach the value of pecuniary considerations, to give them force. Yet, though no tender affections, no cherished hopes, no favourite feelings were in the power of Mrs. Ireton, every moment of time, and consequently all means of comfort, were at her disposal. Juliet languished, therefore, though she would not repine; and though she was not afflicted at heart, she sickened with disgust.

The urgency of finding security from immediate insult and want, induced her, nevertheless, to persevere in her fortitude for supporting, and her efforts for ameliorating her situation. But, the novelty over, all labour was vain, all success was at an end; and, in a very short time, she would have contributed no more to the expulsion of spleen, than any other inmate of the house; had not her superiour acquirements opened a more extensive field for the exercise of tyranny and caprice. And in that exercise alone, Juliet soon saw, consisted every sensation of pleasure of which Mrs. Ireton was susceptible.

Of the many new tasks of Juliet, that which she found the most severe, was inventing amusement for another while sad and dispirited herself. It was her duty to be always at hand, early or late; it was her business to furnish entertainment, whether sick or well. Success, therefore, was unacknowledged, though failure was resented. There was no relaxation to her toil, no rest for her person, no recruit for her spirits. From her sleep alone she could purloin the few minutes that she dedicated to her pen and her Gabriella.

If a new novel excited interest, or a political pamphlet awakened curiosity, she was called upon to read whole hours, nay, whole days, without intermission; even a near extinction of voice did not authorize so great a liberty as that of requesting a few minutes for rest. Mrs. Ireton, who regarded all the world as robust, compared with herself, deemed it an impertinent rivalry of a delicacy which she held to be unexampled, ever to pronounce the word fatigue, ever to heave a sigh of lassitude, or ever even to allude to that part of the human frame which is called nerves, unless with some pointed reference to herself.

With the same despotic hardness, she ordered Juliet to the harp, or piano-forte, and made her play though she were suffering from the acutest head-ache; and sing when hoarse and short-breathed from the most violent cold. Yet these commands, however arbitrary and unfeeling, were more supportable than those with which, after every other source of tyrannic authority had been drained, the day was ordinarily concluded. Mrs. Ireton, at the hour of retiring, when weary alike of books and of music, listless, fretful, captious; too sleepy for any exertion, yet too wakeful or uneasy for repose; constantly brought forward the same enquiries which had so often been urged and repelled, in the week that they had spent together upon their arrival from France; repeated the same sneers, revived the same suspicions, and recurred to the same rude interrogatories or offensive insinuations.

At meals, the humble companion was always helped last; even when there were gentlemen, even when there were children at the table; and always to what was worst; to what was rejected, as ill-cooked, or left, as spoilt and bad. No question was ever asked of what she chose or what she disliked. Sometimes she was even utterly forgotten; and, as no one ventured to remind Mrs. Ireton of any omission, her helpless *protegée*, upon such occasions, rose half famished from the inhospitable board.

Upon the entrance of any visitors, not satisfied to let the humble companion glide gently away, the haughty patroness called out, in a tone of command, "You may go to your room now: I shall send for you when I am at leisure." Or, "You may stand at the window if you will. You won't be in the way, I believe; and I shall want you presently."

Or, if she feared that any one of the party had failed to remark this augmentation of her household and of her power, she would retard the willing departure by some frivolous and vexatious commission; as, "Stop, Miss Ellis; do pray tie this string a little tighter." Or, "Draw up my gloves a little higher: but be so good as not to pinch me; unless you have a particular fancy for it!"

If, drily, though respectfully, Juliet ever proposed to wait in her own room, the answer was, "In your own room? O,—ay—well,—that may be better! I beg your pardon for having proposed that you should wait in one of mine! I beg your pardon a thousand times! I really did not think of what I was saying! I hope you'll forgive my inattention!"

When then, silently, and with difficulty forbearing from shrugging her shoulders, Juliet walked away, she was again stopt by, "One moment, Miss Ellis! if it won't be requesting too great a favour. Pray, when I want you, where may I hear of your servants? For to be sure you don't mean that mine should scamper up and down all day long for you? You cannot mean that. You must have a lackey of your own, no doubt: some page, or spruce foot-boy at your command, to run upon your errands: only pray let some of my people know where he may be met with."

But if, when the purpose was answered of drawing the attention of her guests upon her new dependent, that attention were followed by any looks of approbation, or marks of civility, she hastily exclaimed, "O, pray don't disturb yourself, Sir!" or "Ma'am! 'tis only a young woman I have engaged to read to me;—a young person whom I have taken into my house out of compassion." And then, affably nodding, she would affect to be suddenly struck with something which she had already repeatedly seen, and cry, "Well, I declare, that gown is not ugly, Miss Ellis! How did you come by it?" or, "That ribbon's pretty enough: who gave it you?"

Ah, thought Juliet, 'tis conduct such as this that makes inequality of fortune baleful! Where superiour wealth falls into liberal hands,—where its possessor is an Aurora Granville, it proves a good still more to the surrounders than to the owners; "it blesses those that give, and those that take."*—But Oh! where it is misused for the purposes of bowing down the indigent, of oppressing the helpless, of triumphing over the dependent,—then, how baneful then is inequality of fortune!

With these thoughts, and deeply hurt, she was twenty times upon the point of retiring, during the first week of her distasteful office; but the sameness of the offences soon robbed the mortifications of their poignancy; and apathy, in a short time, taking place of sensibility, she learnt to bear them if not with indifference, at least with its precursor contempt.

Amongst the most irksome of the toils to which this subjection made her liable, was the care,—not of the education, nor mind, nor manners, but of the amusements,—of the little nephew of Mrs. Ireton; whom that lady rather exulted than blushed to see universally regarded as a spoilt child.

The temper of this young creature was grown so capricious, from incessant indulgence, that no compliance, no luxury, no diversion could afford him more than momentary pleasure; while his passions were become so ungovernable, that, upon every contrariety or disappointment, he vented his rage, to the utmost extent of his force, upon whomsoever, or whatsoever, animate or inanimate, he could reach.

All the mischief thus committed, the injuries thus sustained, the noise and disturbance thus raised, were to be borne throughout the house without a murmur. Whatever destruction he caused, Mrs. Ireton was always sure was through the fault of some one else; what he mutilated, or broke, she had equal certainty must have been merely by accident; and those he hurt or ill used, must have provoked his anger. If any one ventured to complain, 'twas the sufferer, not the inflictor who was treated as culpable.

It was the misfortune of Juliet to excite, by her novelty, the attention of this young tyrant; and by her powers of entertainment, exerted inadvertently, from a love of obliging, to become his favourite. The hope of softening his temper and manners, by amusing his mind, had blinded her, at first, to the trouble, the torment rather, of such pre-eminence, which soon proved one of the most serious evils of her situation. Mrs. Ireton, having raised in his young bosom expectations never to be realised, by passing the impossible decree, that nothing must be denied to her eldest brother's eldest son; had authorised demands from him, and licensed wishes, destructive both to his understanding and his happiness. When the difficulties which this decree occasioned, devolved upon a domestic, she left him to get rid of them as he could; only reserving to herself the right to blame the way that was taken, be it what it might: but when the embarrassment fell to her own lot; when the spoilt urchin claimed what was every way unattainable; she had been in the habit of sending him abroad, for the immediate relief of her nerves. The favour into which he took Juliet now offered a new and more convenient resource. Instead of "Order the carriage, and let the child go out:" Miss Ellis was called upon to play with him; to tell him stories; to shew him pictures; to build houses for him with cards; or to suffer herself to be dragged unmeaningly, yet wilfully and forcibly, from walk to walk in the garden, or from room to room in the house; till tired, and quarrelling even with her compliance, he recruited his wearied caprices with sleep.

Nor even here ended the encroachments upon her time, her attention, her liberty; not only the spoilt child, but the favourite dog was put under her superintendence; and she was instructed to take charge of the airings and exercise of Bijou;* and to carry him where the road was rough or miry, that he might not soil those paws, which had the exclusive privilege of touching the lady of the mansion; and even of pulling, patting, and scratching her robes and attire for his recreation.

To many, in the place of Juliet, the spoilt child and the spoilt cur would have been objects of detestation: but against the mere instruments of malice she harboured no resentment. The dog, though snarling and snapping at every one but his mistress, Juliet saw as vicious only from evil habits, which were imbibed, nay taught, rather than natural: the child, though wantonly revelling in mischief of every kind, she considered but as a little savage, who, while enjoying the splendour and luxury of civilized life, was as unformed, as rough, as untaught, and therefore as little responsible for his conduct, as if just caught, and brought, wild and untamed, from the woods. The animal, therefore, she exculpated; the child she pitied; it was the mistress of the mansion alone, who, wilful in all she did, and conscious of all she inflicted, provoked bitterer feelings. And to these, the severest poignancy was accidentally added to Juliet, by the cruel local circumstance of receiving continual indignity in the very house, nay the very room, where, in sweetest intercourse, she had been accustomed to be treated upon terms of generous equality by Lady Aurora Granville.

CHAPTER LIV

JULIET had passed but a short space, by the measure of time, in this new residence, though by that of suffering and disgust it had seemed as long as it was irksome, when, one morning, she was informed, by the nursery-maid, that a grand breakfast was to be given, about two o'clock,* to all the first gentry in and near Brighthelmstone.

Mrs. Ireton, herself, making no mention of any such purpose, issued her usual orders for the attendance of Juliet, with her implements of amusement; and went, at an early hour, to a light building, called the Temple of the Sun,* which overlooked the sea, from the end of the garden.

This Temple, like every place which Mrs. Ireton capriciously, and even for the shortest interval, inhabited, was now filled with materials for recreation, which, ingeniously employed, might have whiled away a winter; but which, from her fluctuating whims, were insufficient even for the fleet passage of a few hours. Books, that covered three window-seats; songs and sonatas that covered those books; various pieces of needle-work; a billiard-table; a chess-board; a backgammon-board; a cup and ball,* &c. &c.; all, in turn, were tried; all, in turn, rejected; and invectives the most impatient were uttered against each, as it ceased to afford her pleasure; as if each, with living malignity, had studied to cause her disappointment.

About noon, she took the arm of Juliet, to descend the steps of the Temple. Upon opening the door, Ireton appeared sauntering in the garden. Juliet vexed at his sight, which Elinor had assured her that she would never encounter, severely felt the mortification of being seen in her present situation, by one who had so repeatedly offended her by injurious suspicions, and familiar impertinence.

Mrs. Ireton, hastily relinquishing the arm of Juliet, from expecting that of her son, at whose sight she was evidently surprised; now resolved, with her most brilliant flourishes, to exhibit the new object of her power.

"Why don't you take care of the child, Miss Ellis?" she cried aloud. "Do you design to let him break his neck down the stone steps? I beg your pardon, though, for asking the question. It may be very *mal à propos*.* It may be necessary, perhaps, to some of your plans, to see a tragedy in real life? You may have some work in agitation, that may require that sort of study. I am sorry to have stood so unopportunely in your way: quite ashamed, upon my word, to have prevented your taking a few hints from the child's dislocating a limb, or two; or just fracturing his skull. 'Twould have been a pretty melancholy sight, enough, for an elegiac muse. I really beg your pardon, for being so uncooth, as to think of such a trumpery circumstance as saving the child's life."

Juliet, during this harangue, assiduously followed the young gentleman; who, with a shout of riotous rebellion, ran down the steps, and jumping into a parterre,* selected, by his eye, the most beautiful of the flowers for treading under his feet; and, at every representation of Juliet, flung at her as many pinks, carnations, and geraniums, as his merciless little fingers could grasp.

Ireton, approaching, looked smilingly on, negligently nodding, and calling out, "Well done, Loddard!* Bravo, my little Pickle!"

Loddard, determined to merit this honourable testimony of his prowess, continued his sport, with augmented boldness. His wantonness, however, though rude, was childish; Juliet, therefore, though tormented, gave it no serious resentment; but she was not equally indifferent to the more maturely malicious insolence of Ireton, who, while he openly enjoyed the scene, negligently said to Loddard, "What, my boy, hast got a new nurse?"

Mrs. Ireton, having stood some time leaning upon the balustrade of the steps which she was descending, in vain expectation of the arm of her son, who had only slightly bowed to her, with an "How do do, Ma'am?" to which he waited not for an answer; now indignantly called out, "So I am to be left to myself, am I? In this feeble and alarming state to which I am reduced, incapable to withstand a gust of wind, or to baffle the fall of a leaf, I may take care of myself, may I? I am too stout to require any attention? too robust, too obstreperous to need any help? If I fall down, I may get up again, I suppose? If I faint, I may come to myself again, I imagine? You will have the goodness to permit that, I presume? I may be mistaken, to be sure, but I should presume so. Don't you hear me, Mistress Ellis? But you are deaf, may be?—I am alarmed to the last degree!—You are suddenly seized, perhaps, with the loss of one of your senses?"

This attack, begun for her son, though, upon his romping with the little boy, in total disregard to its reproach, ending for Juliet, made Ireton now, throwing back his head, to stare, with a sneering half-laugh, at Juliet, exclaim, "Fie, Mrs. Betty! How can you leave Mrs. Ireton, unaided, in such peril? Fie, Mrs. Polly,* fie! Mrs. . . . . What is your new nurse's name, my boy?"

The boy, who never held his tongue but when he was desired to speak, would make no answer, but by running violently after Juliet, as she sought to escape from him; flinging flowers, leaves, grass, or whatever he could find, at her, with boisterous shouts of laughter, and with all his little might.

Mrs. Ireton, brought nearly to good humour by the sight of the perplexity and displeasure of Juliet, only uttered, "Pretty dear! how playful he is!" But when, made still more daring by this applause, the little urchin ventured to touch the hem of her own garments, she became suddenly sensible of his disobedience and wanton mischief, and commanded him from her presence.

As careless of her wrath as he was ungrateful for her favour, the young gentleman thought of nothing so little as of obedience. He jumped and skipped around her, in bold defiance of all authority; laughing loudly in her face; making a thousand rude grimaces; yet screaming, as if attacked by a murderer, when she attempted to catch him; though, the moment that he forced himself out of her reach, hallooing his joyous triumph in her ears, with vociferous exultation.

Juliet was ordered to take him in hand, and carry him off; an order which, to quit the scene, she prepared with pleasure to obey: but the young gentleman, though he pursued her with fatiguing fondness when she sought to avoid him, now ran wildly away.

Mrs. Ireton, enraged, menaced personal chastisement; but, upon his darting at Juliet, and tearing her gown, she turned abruptly aside, in the apprehension of being called upon for reparation; and, gently saying, "What a frisky little rogue it is!" affected to observe him no longer.

The torn robe proved a potent attraction to the little dog, who, yelping with unmeaning fury, flew at and began gnawing it, with as much vehemence, as if its destruction were essential to his well being.

A party of company was now announced, that begged to join Mrs. Ireton in the garden; and, tripping foremost from the advancing throng, came Selina.

Ireton, flapping his hat* over his eyes, leisurely sauntered away. Mrs. Ireton returned to the Temple, to receive her guests with more state; and Juliet hoping, though doubtfully, some relief and countenance, bent forward to greet her young friend.

Selina, with a look of vivacity and pleasure, eagerly approached; but while her hands were held out, in affectionate amity, and her eyes invited Juliet to meet her, she stopt, as if from some sudden recollection; and, after taking a hasty glance around her, picked a flower from a border of the parterre, and ran back with it to present to Lady Arramede.

Juliet, scarcely disappointed, retreated; and the party advanced in a body. She would fain have hidden herself, but had no power; the boy, with romping violence, forcibly detaining her, by loud shrieks, which rent the air, when she struggled to disengage herself from his hold. And, as every visitor, however stunned or annoyed, uttered, in approaching him, the admiring epithets of "Dear little creature!" "Sweet little love!" "Pretty little dear!" &c. the boy, in common with children of a larger growth,* concluding praise to be approbation, flung himself upon Juliet, with all his force; protesting that he would give her a green gown: while all the company,—upon Mrs. Ireton's appearing at an open window of the Temple,—unanimously joined in extolling his strength, his agility, and his spirited character.

The wearied and provoked Juliet now seriously and strenuously sought to disengage herself from the stubborn young athletic; but he clung round her waist, and was jumping up at her shoulders, to catch at the ribbon of her hat, when Lady Kendover and her niece, who were the last of the company that arrived, entered the garden.

Lady Barbara Frankland no sooner perceived Juliet, and her distress, than, swift as the wind, breaking from her aunt, she flew forward to give her succour; seizing the sturdy little assailant by his arms, when unprepared to defend himself, and twisting him, adroitly, from his prey; exclaiming, "You spoilt little wicked creature, beg pardon of that lovely Miss Ellis directly! this moment!"

"Ellis! Dear, if it is not Ellis!" cried Selina, now joining them. "How glad I am to see you, my dear Ellis! What an age it is since we met!"

Juliet, whose confidence was somewhat more than staggered in the regard of Selina, coldly courtsied to her; while, with the warmest gratitude, she began expressing her acknowledgements for the prompt and generous kindness of Lady Barbara; when the boy, recovering from his surprise, and furious at any controul, darted at her ladyship with vindictive violence; attempting, and intending, to practise upon her the same feats which had nearly subdued Juliet: but the situation was changed: the exclamations were reversed; and "O, you naughty little thing!" "How can you be so rude?" "Fie, child, fie!" were echoed from mouth to mouth; while every step bent forward to protect "poor Lady Barbara" from the troublesome little creature.

The boy was then seriously made over to his maid, to be new dressed; with a promise of peaches and sugar plums, if he would be so very good a child, as to submit to the repugnant operations of his toilette, without crying or fighting.

The butler now appeared, to announce that the breakfast was ready; and Juliet saw confirmed, that the party had been invited and expected; though Mrs. Ireton meant to impress her with the magnificent idea, that this was her common way of life.

The company all re-entered the house, and all without taking the smallest notice of Juliet; Lady Barbara excepted, who affectionately shook hands with her, and warmly regretted that she did not join the party.

Juliet, to whom the apparent mystery of her situation offered as much apology for others, as it brought distress to herself, went back, far more hurt than offended to the Temple.

Hence, presently, from under one of the windows, she heard a weak, but fretful and angry voice, morosely giving impatient reprimands to some servant, while imperiously refusing to listen to even the most respectful answer.

Looking from the window, she saw, and not without concern, from the contrast to the good humour which she had herself experienced, that this choleric reproacher was Sir Jaspar Herrington.

The nursery-maid, who came, soon afterwards, in search of some baubles, which her young master had left in the Temple; complained that her mistress's rich brother-in-law, Sir Jaspar, who never entered the house but upon grand invitations, had been at his usual game of scolding, and finding fault with all the servants, till they all wished him at Jericho;* sparing nobody but Nanny, whom the men called the Beauty. He was so particular, when he was in his tantarums, the maid added, that he was almost as cross as the old lady herself; except, indeed, to his favourites, and those he could never do enough for. But he commanded about him at such a rate, that Mrs. Ireton, she was sure, would never let him into the house, if it were not in the hope of wheedling him into leaving the great fortune, that had fallen to him with the name of Herrington, to the young 'Squire; though the young 'Squire was well enough off without it; being certain of the Ireton estate, because it was entailed upon him, if his uncle, Sir Jaspar, should die without children.

Juliet did not hear this history of the ill temper of her generous old beau, without chagrin; but the prating nursery-maid ceased not recording what she called his tantarums, till the well known sound of his crutches announced his approach, when she hastily made her exit.

With the awkward feeling of uncertain opinion, softened off, nevertheless, by the remembrance of strong personal obligation, Juliet presented herself at the door, to shew her intention of descending.

Occupied by the pain of labouring up the steps, he did not raise his head, or perceive her, till he had reached the threshold of the little building. His still brilliant eyes became then brighter, and the air of harsh asperity which, while mounting, his countenance still retained, from recent anger, was suddenly converted into a look of the most lively pleasure, and perfect good humour. After touching his hat, and waving his hand, with an old fashioned, but well bred air of gallantry, he laughingly confessed, that he had ascended with the view of recruiting his strength and spirits, by a private visit to the god Morpheus;* to enable him to get through the weighty enterprize, of encountering a throng of frivolous females, without affronting them by his yawns. "How little," he continued, "did I imagine myself coming to Sleep's most resistless conqueror, Delight! If I rouse not now, I must have more soporiferous qualities than the Seven Sleepers!* or even than the Sleeping Beauty in the Wood, who took a nap of forty years."*

Then entreating her to be seated, he dropt upon the easy chair, which had been prepared for Mrs. Ireton; and crossed his crutches, as if by accident, in a manner that prevented her from retreating. She was the less, however, impatient of this delay, as she saw that the windows looking from the house into the garden, were filled with company, which she desired nothing so little as to pass in review.

Taking, therefore, a place as far from him as was in her power, she made herself an occupation, in arranging some mulberry leaves for silk-worms.*

The Baronet, whose face expressed encreasing satisfaction at his situation, courteously sought to draw her into discourse. "My little friends," cried he, smiling, "who are always at work, have continually been tormenting me of late, with pinches and twitches, upon my utter neglect of my sister-in-law, Mrs. Ireton. I could not for my life imagine why they took so prodigious an interest in my visiting her; but they nipt, and squeezed, and worried me, without intermission; accusing me of misbehaviour; saying she was my sister-in-law; and ill, and hypochondriac; and that it was by no means pretty behaved in me, not to shew her more respect. It was in vain I represented, that she was rich, and did not want me; or that she was disagreeable, and that I did not want her; 'twas all one; they insisted I should go: and this morning, when I would have excused myself from coming to her fine breakfast, they beset me in so many ways, that I was forced to comply. And now I see why! Poor, earthly, mundane mortal that I was! I took them for envious sprites, jealous of my repose! But I see, now, they were only recreative* little sylphs, amusing themselves with whipping and spurring me on to my own good!"

And is this, thought Juliet, the man who bears a character of impatience and ill humour? this man, whose imagination is so playful, and whose desire to please can only be equalled by his desire to serve?

"And where," he continued, "have you all this time been eclipsed? From sundry circumstances, that perversely obtruded themselves upon my knowledge, in defiance of the ill reception I gave them, I was led, at first, to conclude, that you had been spirited away by Sir Lyell Sycamore."

He fixed his eyes upon her curiously; but the colour that rose in her cheeks betrayed no secret consciousness; it shewed open resentment.

"O! I soon saw," he resumed, as if he had been answered, though she had not deigned to disclaim an idea that she deemed fitted simply for contempt; "by the mortified silence of my young gallant, that the fates had not been propitious to his wishes. In characters of his description, success never courts the shade. It basks in the sunshine, and seeks the broadest day. How is it that you have thus piqued the vain spark? He came to me in such a flame, to upbraid me for what he called the cursed ridiculous dance that I had led him, that I fairly thought he meant to call me out! I began, directly, to look about me for the stoutest of my crutches, to parry, for a last minute or two, his broad sword; and to deliberate which might be the thickest of my leather cushions, to hold up in my defence, for reverberating the ball,* in case he should prefer pistols. But he deigned, most fortunately, to content himself with only abusing me: hinting, that such superannuated old geese, as those who had passed their grand climacteric, ought not to meddle with affairs of which they must have lost even the memory. I let him bounce off without any answer; very thankful to the "Sisters three"* to feel myself in a whole skin."

Looking at her, then, with an expression of humorous reproach, "You will permit me, I hope, at least," he added, "to flatter myself, that, when your indulgence to the garrulity of age has induced you to bear with my loquacity till I am a little hoarser, your consideration for sore throats and heated lungs, will prevail upon you to utter a little word or two in your turn?"

Juliet, laughing, answered that she had been too well amused, to be aware how little she had seemed to merit his exertions.

"Tell me, then," cried he, with looks that spoke him enchanted by this reply; "through what extraordinary mechanism, in the wheel of fortune, you have been rolled to this spot? The benevolent sprites, who have urged me hither, have not given me a jot of information how you became known to Mrs. Ireton? By what strange spell have you been drawn in, to seem an inmate of her mansion? and what philters and potions have you swallowed, to make you endure her never-ending vagaries?"

Half smiling, half sighing, Juliet looked down; not willing to accept, though hardly able to resist, the offered licence for complaint.

"Make no stranger," the old Baronet laughingly added, "of me, I beg! She is my sister-in-law, to be sure; but the law, with all its subtleties, has not yet entailed our affections, with our estates, to our relations; nor articled our tastes, with our jointures, to our dowagers.* Use, therefore, no manner of ceremony! How do you bear with her freaks and fancies? or rather,—for that is the essential point, why do you bear with them?"

"Can that," said Juliet, "be a question?"

"Not a wise one, I confess!" he returned; "for what but Necessity could link together two creatures who seem formed to give a view of human nature diametrically opposite the one from the other? These indeed must be imps,—and imps of darkness,—who, busy, busy still! delight

To join the gentle to the rude![†]*

that can have coupled so unharmonizing a pair. Hymen,* with all the little active sinister devils in his train, that yoke together, pell mell, for life, hobbling age with bounding youth; choleric violence with trembling timidity; haggard care with thoughtless merriment;—Hymen himself, that marrying little lawyer, who takes upon him to unite what is most discordant, and to tie together all that is most heterogeneous; even he, though provided with what is, so justly, called a licence, for binding together what nature itself seems to sunder; he, even he, I assert, never buckled in the same noose, two beings so completely and equally dissimilar, both without and within. Since such, however, has been the ordinance of these fantastic workers of wonders, will you let me ask, in what capacity it has pleased their impships to conjure you hither?"

Juliet hesitated, and looked ashamed to answer.

"You are not, I hope," cried he, fixing upon her his keen eyes, "one of those ill starred damsels, whose task, in the words of Madame de Maintenon, is to 'amuse the unamuseable?'* You are not, I hope, ..." he stopt, as if seeking a phrase, and then, rather faintly, added, "her companion?"

"Her humble servant, Sir!" with a forced smile, said Juliet; "and yet, humbled as I feel myself in that capacity, not humble enough for its calls!"

† Thomson.

The smiles of the old Baronet vanished in a moment, and an expression of extreme severity took their place. "She uses you ill, then?" he indignantly cried, and, grasping the knobs of his two crutches, he struck their points against the floor, with a heaviness that made the little building shake, ejaculating, in a hoarse inward voice, "Curse her!"

Juliet stared at him, affrighted by his violence.

"Can it be possible," he cried, "that so execrable a fate should be reserved for so exquisite a piece of workmanship? Sweet witch! were I but ten years younger, I would snatch you from her infernal claws!—or rather, could I cut off twenty;—yet even then the disparity would be too great!—thirty years younger,—or perhaps forty,—my hand and fortune should teach that Fury her distance!"

Juliet, surprised, and doubting whether what dropt from him were escaped sincerity, or purposed irony, looked with so serious a perplexity, that, struck and ashamed, he checked himself; and recovering his usually polite equanimity, smiled at his own warmth, saying, "Don't be alarmed, I beg! Don't imagine that I shall forget myself; nor want to hurry away, lest my animation should be dangerous! The heat that, at five-and-twenty, might have fired me into a fever, now raises but a kindly glow, that stops, or keeps off stagnation. The little sprites, who hover around me, though they often mischievously spur my poor fruitless wishes, always take care, by seasonable twitches, in some vulnerable gouty part, to twirl me from the regions of hope and romance, to very sober real life!"

Fearful of appearing distrustful, Juliet looked satisfied, and again he went on.

"Since, then, 'tis clear that there can be no danger in so simple an intercourse, why should I not give myself the gratification of telling you, that every sight of you does me good? renovates my spirits; purifies my humours; sweetens my blood; and braces my nerves? Never talk to me with mockery of fairyism, witchcraft, and sylphs; the real influence of lovely youth, is a thousand times more wonderful, more potent, and more incredible! When I have seen you only an instant, I feel in charity with all mankind for the rest of the day; and, at night, my kind little friends present you to me again; renew every pleasing idea; revive the most delightful images; and paint you to me—just such as I see you at this moment!"

Juliet, embarrassed, talked of returning to the house.

"Do you blush?" cried he, with quickness, and evidently increasing admiration; "is it possible that you are not enough habituated to praise, to hear it without modest confusion? I have seen 'full many a lady—but you—O you!—so perfect and so peerless are created, of every creature best!'†*

"My whole life has been spent in worshipping beauty, till within these very few years, when I have gotten something like a surfeit, and meant to give it over. For I have watched and followed Beauties, till I have grown sick of them. I have admired fine features, only to be disgusted with vapid vanity. A face with a little meaning, though as ugly as sin and satan, I have lately thought worth forty of them! But you! fair sorceress! you have conjured me round again to my old work! I have found the spell irresistible. You have such intelligence of countenance; such spirit with such sweetness; smiles so delicious, though rare! looks so speaking; grace so silent;—that I forget you are a beauty; and fasten my eyes upon you, only to understand what you say when you don't utter a word! That's all! Don't be uneasy, therefore, at my staring. Though, to be candid, we know ourselves so little, that, 'tis possible, had you not first caught my eye as a beauty, I might never have looked at you long enough to find out your wit!"

A footman now came to acquaint Sir Jaspar, that the rice-soup, which he had ordered, was ready; and that the ladies were waiting for the honour of his company to breakfast.

"I heartily wish they would wait for my company, till I desire to have theirs!" Sir Jaspar muttered: but, sensible of the impropriety of a refusal, arose, and, taking off his hat, with a studied formality, which he hoped would impress the footman with respect for its object, followed his messenger: whispering, nevertheless, as he quitted the building, "Leave you for a breakfast!—I would almost as willingly be immersed in the witches' cauldron, and boiled into morsels, to become a breakfast myself, for the amusement of the audience at a theatre!"

† Shakespeare.

CHAPTER LV

JULIET, who perceived that the windows were still crowded with company, contentedly kept her place; and, taking up the second volume of the Guardian, found, in the lively instruction, the chaste morality, and the exquisite humour of Addison,* an enjoyment which no repetition can cloy.

In a short time, to her great discomposure, she was broken in upon by Ireton; who, drawing before the door, which he shut, an easy chair, cast himself indolently upon it, and, stretching out his arms, said, "Ah ha! the fair Ellis! How art thee, my dear?"

Far more offended than surprised by this freedom, Juliet, perceiving that she could not escape, affected to go on with her reading, as if he had not entered the building.

"Don't be angry, my dear," he continued, "that I did not speak to you before all those people. There's no noticing a pretty girl, in public, without raising such a devil of a clamour, that it's enough to put a man out of countenance. Besides, Mrs. Ireton is such a very particular quiz, that she would be sure to contrive I should never have a peep at you again, if once she suspected the pleasure I take in seeing you. However, I am going to turn a dutiful son, and spend some days here. And, by that means, we can squeeze an opportunity, now and then, of getting a little chat together."

Juliet could no longer refrain from raising her head, with amazement, at this familiar assurance: but he went on, totally disregarding the rebuke of her indignant eye.

"How do you like your place here, my dear? Mrs. Ireton's rather qualmish, I am afraid. I never can bear to stay with her myself; except when I have some point to carry. I can't devise what the devil could urge you to come into such a business. And where's Harleigh? What's he about? Gone to old Nick I hope with all my heart! But you,—why are you separated? What's the reason you are not with him?"

Yet more provoked, though determined not to look up again, Juliet fixed her eyes upon the book.

Ireton continued: "What a sly dog he is, that Harleigh! But what the deuce could provoke him to make me cut such a silly figure before Lord Melbury, with my apologies, and all that? He took me in, poz!* I thought he'd nothing to do with you. And if you had not had that fainting fit, at the concert; which I suppose you forgot to give him notice of, that put him so off his guard, I should have believed all he vowed and swore, of having no connection with you, and all that, to this very moment."

This was too much. Juliet gravely arose, put down her book, and said, with severity, "Mr. Ireton, you will be so good as to let me pass!"

"No, not I! No, not I! my dear!" he answered, still lolling at his ease. "We must have a little chat together first. 'Tis an age since I have been able to speak with you. I have been confounded discreet, I promise you. I have not told your secret to a soul."

"What secret, Sir?" cried Juliet, hastily.

"Why who you are, and all that."

"If you knew, Sir," recovering her calmness, she replied, "I should not have to defend myself from the insults of a son, while under the protection of his mother!"

"Ha! ha! ha!" cried he. "What a droll piece of dainty delicacy thee art! I'd give a cool hundred, this moment, only to know what the deuce puts it into thy little head, to play this farce such a confounded length of time, before one comes to the catastrophe."

Juliet, with a disdainful gesture, again took her book.

"Why won't you trust me, my dear? You sha'n't repent it, I promise you. Tell me frankly, now, who are you?—Hay?"

Juliet only turned over a new leaf of her book.

"How can you be so silly, child?—Why won't you let me serve you? You don't know what use I may be of to you. Come, make me your friend! only trust me, and I'll go to the very devil for you with pleasure."

Juliet read on.

"Come, my love, don't be cross! Speak out! Put aside these dainty airs. Surely you a'n't such a little fool, as to think to take me in, as you have done Melbury and Harleigh?"

Juliet felt her cheeks now heated with increased indignation.

"As to Melbury,—'tis a mere school-boy, ready to swallow any thing; and as to Harleigh, he's such a queer, out of the way genius, that he's like nobody: but as to me, my dear, I'm a man of the world. Not so easily played upon, I promise you! I have known you from the very beginning! Found you out at first sight! Only I did not think it worth while telling you so, while you appeared so confounded ugly. But now that I see you are such a pretty creature, I feel quite an interest for you. So tell me who you are? Will you?"

Somewhat piqued, at length, by her resolute silence, "Nay," he added, with affected scorn, "don't imagine I have any view! Don't disturb yourself with any freaks and qualms of that sort. You are a fine girl, to be sure. Devilish handsome, I own; but still too—too—grave,—grim,—What the deuce is the word I mean? for my taste. I like something more buckish.* So pray make yourself easy. I sha'n't interfere with your two sparks. I am perfectly aware I should have but a bad chance. I know I am neither as good a pigeon to pluck as Melbury, nor as marvellous a wight* to overcome as Harleigh. But I can't for my life make out why you don't take to one or t'other of them, and put yourself at your ease. I'm deadly curious to know what keeps you from coming to a finish. Melbury would be managed the easiest; but I strongly suspect you like Harleigh best. What do you turn your back for? That I mayn't see you blush? Come, come, don't play the baby with a man of the world like me."

To the infinite relief of the disgusted Juliet, she now heard the approach of some foot-step. Ireton, who heard it also, nimbly arose, and, softly moving his chair from the door, cast half his body out of the window, and, lolling upon his elbows, began humming an air; as if totally occupied in regarding the sea.

A footman, who entered, told Juliet that his lady desired that she would come to the parlour, to play and sing to the company, while they breakfasted.

Juliet, colouring at this unqualified order, hesitated what to answer; while Ireton, turning round, and pretending not to have heard what was said, maliciously made the man repeat, "My lady, Sir, bid me tell Miss Ellis, that she must come to play and sing to the company."

"Play and sing?" repeated Ireton. "O the devil! Must we be

bored with playing and singing too? But I did not know breakfast was ready, and I am half starved."

He then sauntered from the building; but the moment that the footman was out of sight, turned back, to say, "How devilish provoking to be interrupted in this manner! How can we contrive to meet again, my dear?"

The answer of Juliet was shutting and bolting the door.

His impertinence, however, occupied her mind only while she was under its influence; the insignificance of his character, notwithstanding the malice of his temper, made it sink into nothing, to give way to the new rising difficulty, how she might bear to obey, or how risk to refuse, the rude and peremptory summons which she had just received. Ought I, she cried, to submit to treatment so mortifying? Are there no boundaries to the exactions of prudence upon feeling? or, rather, is there not a mental necessity, a call of character, a cry of propriety, that should supersede, occasionally, all prudential considerations, however urgent?—Oh! if those who receive, from the unequal conditions of life, the fruits of the toils of others, could,—only for a few days,—experience, personally, how cruelly those toils are embittered by arrogance, or how sweetly they may be softened by kindness,—the race of the Mrs. Iretons would become rare,—and Lady Aurora Granville might, perhaps, be paralleled!

Yet, with civility, with good manners, had Mrs. Ireton made this request; not issued it as a command by a footman; Juliet felt that, in her present dependent condition, however ill she might be disposed for music, or for public exhibition, she ought to yield: and even now, the horrour of having another asylum to seek; the disgrace of seeming driven, thus continually, from house to house; though they could not lessen her repugnance to indelicacy and haughtiness, cooled all ardour of desire for trying yet another change; till she should have raised a sufficient sum for joining Gabriella; and softening, nay delighting, the future toils to which she might be destined, by the society of that cherished friend.

In a few minutes, she was visited by Selina, who, rapturously embracing her, declared that she could not stay away from her any longer; and volubly began her usual babble of news and tales; to all which Juliet gave scarcely the coldest attention; till she had the satisfaction of hearing that the health of Elinor was re-established.

Selina then owned that she had been sent by Mrs. Ireton, to desire that Miss Ellis would make more haste.

Juliet worded a civil excuse; which Selina, with hands uplifted, from amazement, carried back to the breakfast-room.

Soon afterwards, peals of laughter announced the vicinity of the Miss Crawleys; who merrily called aloud upon Ireton, to come and help them to haul The Ellis, Will ye, nill ye?* to the piano-forte, to play and sing.

Happy in this intimation of their purpose, Juliet bolted the door; and would not be prevailed upon to open it, either by their vociferous prayers, or their squalls of disappointment.

But, in another minute, a slight rustling sound drawing her eyes to a window, she saw Ireton preparing to make a forced entry.

She darted, now, to the door, and, finding the passage clear, as the Miss Crawleys had gone softly round, to witness the exploit of Ireton, seized the favourable moment for eluding observation; and was nearly arrived at the house, before the besiegers of the cage perceived that the bird was flown.

CHAPTER LVI

THE two sisters no sooner discovered the escape of their prey, than, screaming with violent laughter, they began a romping race in its pursuit.

Near the entrance into the hall, Juliet was met by Selina, with commands from Mrs. Ireton, that she would either present herself, immediately, to the company; or seek another abode.

In minds of strong sensibility, arrogance rouses resentment more quickly even than injury: a message so gross, an affront so public, required, therefore, no deliberation on the part of Juliet; and she was answering that she would make her preparations to depart; when the Miss Crawleys, rushing suddenly upon her, exclaimed, with clamourous joy, "She's caught!

She's caught! The Ellis is caught!" and, each of them seizing a hand, they dragged her, with merry violence, into the breakfast-room.

Her hoydening conductors failed not to excite the attention of the whole assembly; though it fell not, after the first glance, upon themselves. Juliet, to whom exercise and confusion gave added beauty; and whom no disorder of attire could rob of an air of decency, which, inherent in her nature, was always striking in her demeanour; was no sooner seen, than, whether with censure or applause, she monopolized all remark.

Mrs. Ireton haughtily bid her approach.

Averse, yet unwilling to risk the consequences of a public breach, she slowly advanced.

"I am afraid, Ma'am," said Mrs. Ireton, with a smile of derision; "I am afraid, Ma'am, you have hurried yourself? It is not much above an hour, I believe, since I did myself the honour of sending for you. I have no conception how you have been able to arrive so soon! Pray how far do you think it may be from hence to the Temple? ten or twelve yards, I verily believe! You must really be ready to expire!"

Having constrained herself to hear thus much, Juliet conceived that the duty even of her humble station could require no more; she made, therefore, a slight reverence, with intention to withdraw. But Mrs. Ireton, offended, cried, "Whither may you be going, Ma'am?—And pray, Ma'am,—if I may take the liberty to ask such a question,—who told you to go?—Was it I?—Did any body hear me?—Did you, Lady Arramede?—or you, Miss Brinville?—or only Miss Ellis herself? For, to be sure I must have done it: I take that for granted: she would not, certainly, think of going without leave, after I have sent for her. So I make no doubt but I did it. Though I can't think how it happened, I own. 'Twas perfectly without knowing it, I confess. In some fit of absence—perhaps in my sleep;—for I have slept, too, perhaps, without knowing it!"

Sarcasms so witty, uttered by a lady at an assembly in her own house, could not fail of being received with applause; and Mrs. Ireton, looking around her triumphantly, regarded the disconcerted Juliet as a completely vanquished vassal. In a tone, therefore, that marked the most perfect self-satisfaction,

"Pray, Ma'am," she continued, "for what might you suppose I did myself the favour to want you? was it only to take a view of your new *costume*? 'Tis very careless and picturesque, to be sure, to rove abroad in that agreeable dishabille, just like the 'maiden all forlorn;' or rather, to speak with more exactitude, like the 'man all tattered and torn,'* for 'tis more properly his *costume* you adopt, than the neat, tidy maiden's."

The warm-hearted young Lady Barbara, all pity and feeling for Juliet, here broke from her quiet and cautious aunt, and, with irrepressible eagerness, exclaimed, "Mrs. Ireton, 'twas Mr. Loddard, your own little naughty nephew, who deranged in that manner the dress of that elegant Miss Ellis."

The Miss Crawleys, now, running to the little boy, called out, "The Loddard! the Loddard! 'tis the Loddard has set up the new *costume*!"

Mrs. Ireton, though affecting to laugh, had now done with the subject; and, while she was taking a pinch of snuff, to gain time to suggest some other, Sir Jaspar Herrington, advancing to Juliet, said, "Has this young lady no place?" and, gallantly taking her hand, he led her to his own chair, and walked to another part of the room.

A civility such as this from Sir Jaspar, made all the elders of the company stare, and all the younger titter; but the person the most surprized was Mrs. Ireton, who hastily called out, "Miss Ellis would not do such a thing! Take Sir Jaspar's own seat! That has his own particular cushions! She could not do such a thing! I should think not, at least! I may judge ill, but I should think not. A seat prepared for Sir Jaspar by my own order! Miss Ellis can dispense with having an easy chair, and three cushions, I should presume! I may be wrong, to be sure, but I should presume so!"

"Madam," answered Sir Jaspar, "in days of old, I never could bear to sit, when I saw a lady standing; and though those days are past, alas! and gone,—still I cannot, even to escape a twitch of the gout, see a fair female neglected, without feeling a twitch of another kind, that gives me yet greater pain."

"Your politeness, Sir Jaspar," replied Mrs. Ireton, "we all know; and, if it were for one of my guests,—but Miss Ellis can hardly desire, I should suppose, to see you drop down with fatigue, while she is reposing upon your arm-chair. Not that I pretend to know her way of thinking! I don't mean that. I don't mean to have it imagined I have the honour of her confidence; but I should rather suppose she could not insist upon turning you out of your seat, only to give you a paroxysm of the gout."

However internally moved, Juliet endured this harangue in total silence; convinced that where all authority is on the side of the aggressor, resistance only provokes added triumph. Her looks, therefore, though they shewed her to be hurt and offended, evinced a dignified forbearance, superiour to the useless reproach, and vain retaliation, of unequal contention.

She rose, nevertheless, from the seat which she had only momentarily, and from surprise occupied, and would have quitted the room, but that she saw she should again be publicly called back; and hers was not a situation for braving open enmity. She thankfully, however, accepted a chair which was brought to her by Sir Marmaduke Crawley, and placed next to that which had been vacated by the old Baronet; who then returned to his own.

She now hoped to find some support from his countenance; as his powerful situation in the house, joined to his age, would make his smallest attention prove to her a kind of protection. Her expectation, however, was disappointed: he did not address to her a word; or appear to have ever beheld her before; and his late act of politeness seemed exerted for a perfect stranger, from habitual good breeding.

And is it you, thought the pensive Juliet, who, but a few minutes since, spoke to me with such flattery, such preference? with an even impassioned regard? And shall this so little assembly guide and awe you? There, where I wished to escape your notice, you obtruded upon me your compliments;—while here, where a smile would be encouragement, where notice would be charity, you affect to have forgotten, or appear never to have seen me! Ah! mentally continued the silent moralist, if we reflected upon the difficulty of gaining esteem; upon the chances against exciting affection; upon the union of time and circumstance necessary for obtaining sincere regard; we should require courage to withhold, not to follow, the movement of kindness, that, where distress sighs for succour, where helplessness solicits support, gives power to the smallest exertion, to a single word, to a passing smile,—to bestow a favour, and to do a service, that catch, in the brief space of a little moment, a gratitude that never dies!

But, while thus to be situated, was pain and dejection to Juliet, to see her seated, however unnoticed, in the midst of this society, was almost equally irksome to Mrs. Ireton; who, after some vain internal fretting, ordered the butler to carry about refreshments; consoled with the certainty, that he would as little dare present any to Juliet, as omit to present them to every one else.

The smiles and best humour of Mrs. Ireton now soon returned; for the dependent state of Juliet became more than ever conspicuous, when thus decidedly she was marked as the sole person, in a large assembly, that the servants were permitted, if not instructed to neglect.

Juliet endeavoured to sit tranquil, and seem unconcerned; but her fingers were in continual motion; her eyes, meaning to look no where, looked every where; and Mrs. Ireton had the gratification to perceive, that, however she struggled for indifference, she was fully sensible of the awkwardness of her situation.

But this was no sooner remarked by Lady Barbara Frankland, than, starting with vivacity from her vainly watchful aunt, she flew to her former instructress, crying, "Have you taken nothing yet, Miss Ellis? O pray, then, let me chuse your ice for you?"

She ran to a side-board, and selecting the colour most pleasing to her eyes, hastened with it to the blushing, but relieved and grateful Juliet; to whom this benevolent attention seemed instantly to restore the self-command, that pointed indignities, and triumphant derision, were sinking into abashed depression.

The sensation produced by this action in Mrs. Ireton, was as ungenial as that which it caused to Juliet was consolatory. She could not for a moment endure to see the creature of her power, whom she looked upon as destined for the indulgence of her will, and the play of her authority, receive a mark of consideration which, if shewn even to herself, would have been accepted as a condescension. Abruptly, therefore, while they were standing together, and conversing, she called out, "Is it possible, Miss Ellis, that you can see the child in such imminent danger, and stay there amusing yourself?"

Lady Kendover hastily called off her young niece; and Juliet, sighing, crossed over the room, to take charge of the little boy, who was sitting a straddle out of one of the windows.

"But I had flattered myself," cried Sir Marmaduke Crawley, addressing Mrs. Ireton, "that we should have a little music?"

Mrs. Ireton, to whom the talents of Juliet gave pleasure in proportion only to her own repugnance to bringing them into play, had relinquished the projected performance, when she perceived the general interest which was excited by the mere appearance of the intended performer. She declared herself, therefore, so extremely fearful lest some mischief should befal her little nephew, that she could not possibly trust him from the care of Miss Ellis.

Half the company, now, urged by the thirst of fresh amusement, professed the most passionate fondness for children, and offered their services to watch the dear, sweet little boy, while Miss Ellis should play or sing; but the averseness of Ellis remained uncombated by Mrs. Ireton, and, therefore, unconquered.

The party was preparing to break up, when Mr. Giles Arbe entered the room, to apologize for the non-appearance of Miss Arbe, his cousin, who had bid him bring word, he said, that she was taken ill.

Ireton, by a few crafty questions, soon drew from him, that Miss Arbe was only gone to a little private music-meeting at Miss Sycamore's: though, affrighted when he had made the confession, he entreated Mrs. Ireton not to take it amiss; protesting that it was not done in any disrespect to her, but merely because his cousin was more amused at Miss Sycamore's.

Mrs. Ireton, extremely piqued, answered, that she should be very careful, in future, not to presume to make an invitation to Miss Arbe, but in a total dearth of other entertainment; in a famine; or public fast.

But, the moment he sauntered into another room, to partake of some refreshments, "That old savage," she cried, "is a perfect horrour! He has not a single atom of common sense; and if he were not Miss Arbe's cousin, one must tell one's butler to shew him the door. At least, such is my poor opinion. I don't pretend to be a judge; but such is my notion!"

"O! I adore him!" cried Miss Crawley. "He makes me laugh till I am ready to die! He has never a guess what he is about; and he never hears a word one says. And he stares so when one laughs at him! O! he's the delightfullest, stupidest, dear wretch that breathes!"

"O! I can't look at him without laughing!" exclaimed Miss Di. "He's the best thing in nature! He's delicious! enchanting! delightful! O! so dear a fool!"

"He is quite unfit," said Mrs. Maple, "for society; for he says every thing that comes uppermost, and has not the least idea of what is due to people."

"O! he is the sweetest-tempered, kindest-hearted creature in the world!" exclaimed Lady Barbara. "My aunt's woman has heard, from Miss Arbe's maid, all his history. He has quite ruined himself by serving poor people in distress. He is so generous, he can never pronounce a refusal."

"But he dresses so meanly," said Miss Brinville, "that mamma and I have begged Miss Arbe not to bring him any more to see us. Besides,—he tells every thing in the world to every body."

"Poor Miss Arbe a'n't to blame, I assure you, Miss Brinville," said Selina; "for she dislikes him as much as you do; only when her papa invited him to live with them, he was very rich; and it was thought he would leave all his fortune to them. But, since then, Miss Arbe says, he is grown quite poor; for he has dawdled away almost all his money, in one way or another; letting folks out of prison, setting people up in business, and all that."

"O! he's the very king of quizzes!" cried Ireton. "He drags me out of the spleen, when I feel as if there were no possibility I could yawn on another half hour."

Sir Jaspar now, looking with an air of authority towards Ireton, said, "It would have been your good star, not your evil genius, by which you would have been guided, Mr. Ireton, had you been attracted to this old gentleman as to an example, rather than as a butt for your wit. He has very good parts, if he knew how to make use of them; though he has a simplicity of manners, that induces common observers to conclude him to be nearly an ideot. And, indeed, an absent man seems always in a state of childhood; for as he is never occupied with what is present, those who think of nothing else, naturally take it for granted that what passes is above his comprehension; when, perhaps, it is only below his attention. But with Mr. Arbe, though his temper is incomparably good and placid, absence is neither want of understanding, nor of powers of observation; for, when once he is awakened to what is passing, by any thing that touches his feelings of humanity, or his sense of justice, his seeming stupor turns to energy; his silence is superseded by eloquence; and his gentle diffidence is supplanted by a mental courage, which electrifies with surprize, from its contrast with his general docility; and which strikes, and even awes, from an apparent dignity of defying consequences;—though, in fact, it is but the effect of never weighing them. Such, however, as he is, Mr. Ireton, with the singularities of his courage, or the oddities of his passiveness, he is a man who is useful to the world, from his love of doing good; and happy in himself, from the serenity of a temper unruffled by any species of malignity."

Ireton ventured not to manifest any resentment at this conclusion; but when, by his embarrassed air, Sir Jaspar saw that it was understood, he smiled, and more gaily added, "If the fates, the sisters three, and such little branches of learning,* had had the benevolence to have fixed my own birth under the influence of the same planet with that of Mr. Giles Arbe, how many twitches, goadings, and worries should I have been spared, from impatience, ambition, envy, discontent, and ill will!"

The subject was here dropt, by the re-entrance of Mr. Arbe; who, observing Selina, said that he wanted prodigiously to enquire about her poor aunt, whom, lately, he had met with no where; though she used to be every where.

"My aunt, Sir?—She's there!" said Selina, pointing to Mrs. Maple.

"No, no, I don't mean that aunt; I mean your young aunt, that used to be so all alive and clever. What's become of her?"

"O, I dare say it's my sister you are thinking of?"

"Ay, it's like enough; for she's young enough, to be sure; only you look such a mere child. Pray how is she now? I was very sorry to hear of her cutting her throat."

A titter, which was immediately exalted into a hearty laugh by the Miss Crawleys, was all the answer.

"It was not right to do such a thing," he continued; "very wrong indeed. There's no need to be afraid of not dying soon enough, for we only come to be gone! I pitied her, however, with all my heart, for love is but a dangerous thing; it makes older persons than she is go astray, one way or other. And it was but unkind of Mr. Harleigh not to marry her, whether he liked or not, to save her from such a naughty action. And pray what is become of that pretty creature that used to teach you all music? I have enquired for her at Miss Matson's, often; but I always forgot where they said she was gone. Indeed they made me a little angry about her, which, probably, was the reason that I could never recollect what they told me of her direction."

"Angry, Mr. Giles?" repeated Mrs. Ireton, with an air of restored complacency; "What was it, then, they said of her? Not that I am very curious to hear it, as I presume you will believe! You won't imagine it, I presume, a matter of the first interest to me!"

"O, what they said of her was very bad! very bad, indeed; and that's the reason I give no credit to it."

"Well, well, but what was it?" cried Ireton.

"Why they told me that she was turned toad-eater."

Universal and irresistible smiles throughout the whole company, to the exception of Lady Barbara and Sir Jaspar, now heightened the embarrassment of Juliet into pain and distress: but young Loddard every moment struggled to escape into the garden, through the window; and she did not dare quit her post.

"So I asked them what they meant," Mr. Giles continued; "for I never heard of any body's eating toads; though I am assured our neighbours, on t'other bank, are so fond of frogs. But they made it out, that it only meant a person who would swallow any thing, bad or good; and do whatever he was bid, right or wrong; for the sake of a little pay."

This definition by no means brought the assembly back to

its gravity; but while Juliet, ashamed and indignant, kept her face turned constantly towards the garden, Ireton called out, "Why you don't speak to your little friend, Loddard, Mr. Giles. There he is, at the window."

Mr. Giles now, notwithstanding her utmost efforts to avoid his eyes, perceived the blushing Juliet; though, doubting his sight, he stared and exclaimed, "Good la! that lady's very like Miss Ellis! And, I protest, 'tis she herself! And just as pretty as ever! And with the same innocent face that not a soul can either buy or make, but God Almighty himself!"

He then enquired after her health and welfare, with a cordiality that somewhat lessened the pain caused by the general remark that was produced by his address: but the relief was at an end upon his adding, "I wanted to see you prodigiously, for I have never forgotten your paying your debts so prettily, against your will, that morning. It fixed you in my good opinion. I hope, however, it is a mistake, what they tell me, that you are turned what they call toad-eater? and have let yourself out, at so much a year, to say nothing that you think; and to do nothing that you like; and to beg pardon when you are not in fault; and to eat all the offals; and to be beat by the little gentleman; and worried by the little dog? I hope all that's mere misapprehension, my dear; for it would be but a very mean way of getting money."

The calmness of conscious superiority, with which Juliet heard the beginning of these interrogatories, was converted into extreme confusion, by their termination, from the appearance of justice which the incidents of the morning had given to the attack.

"For now," continued he, "that you have paid all your debts, you ought to hold up your head; for, where nothing is owing, we are all of us equal, rich and poor; another man's riches no more making him my superiour, or benefactor, if I do not partake of them, than my poverty makes me his servant, or dependent, if I neither work for, nor am benefited by him. And I am your witness that you gave every one his due. So don't let any body put you out of your proper place."

The mortification of Juliet, at this public exhortation, upon a point so delicate, was not all that she had to endure: the little dog, who, though incessantly tormented by the little boy, always followed him; kept scratching her gown, to be helped up to the window, that he might play with, or snarl at him, more at his ease; and the boy, making a whip of his pocket-handkerchief, continually attracted, though merely to repulse him; while Juliet, seeking alternately to quiet both, had not a moment's rest.

"Why now, what's all this my pretty lady?" cried Mr. Giles, perceiving her situation. "Why do you let those two plagueful things torment you so? Why don't you teach them to be better behaved."

"Miss Ellis would be vastly obliging, certainly," with a supercilious brow, said Mrs. Ireton, "to correct my nephew! I don't in the least mean to contest her abilities for superintending his chastisement; not in the least, I assure you! But only, as I never heard of my brother's giving her such a *carte blanche*; and as I don't recollect having given it myself,—though I may have done it, again, perhaps, in my sleep!—I should be happy to learn by what authority she would be invested with such powers of discipline?"

"By what authority? That of humanity, Ma'am! Not to spoil a poor ignorant little fellow-creature; nor a poor innocent little beast."

"It would be immensely amiable of her, Sir, no doubt," said Mrs. Ireton, reddening, "to take charge of the morals of my household; immensely! I only hope you will be kind enough to instruct the young person, at the same time, how she may hold her situation? That's all! I only hope that!"

"How? Why by doing her duty! If she can't hold it by that, 'tis her duty to quit it. Nobody is born to be trampled upon."

"I hope, too, soon," said Mrs. Ireton, scoffingly, "nobody will be born to be poor!"

"Good! true!" returned he, nodding his head. "Nobody should be poor! That is very well said. However, if you think her so poor, I can give you the satisfaction to shew you your mistake. She mayn't, indeed, be very rich, poor lady, at bottom; but still—"

"No, indeed, am I not!" hastily cried Juliet, frightened at the communication which she saw impending.

"But still," continued he, "if she is poor, it is not for want of money; nor for want of credit, neither; for she has bank-notes in abundance in one of her work-bags; and not a penny of them is her own! which shews her to be a person of great honour."

Every one now looked awakened to a new curiosity; and Selina exclaimed, "O la! have you got a fortune, then, my dear Ellis? O! I dare say, then, my guess will prove true at last! for I dare say you are a princess in disguise?"

"As far as disguise goes Selina," answered Mrs. Maple, "we have never, I think, disputed! but as to a princess . . . . .!"

"A princess?" repeated Mrs. Ireton. "Upon my word, this is an honour I had not imagined! I own my stupidity! I can't but own my stupidity; but I really had never imagined myself so much honoured, as to suspect that I had a princess under my roof, who was so complaisant as to sing, and play, and read to me, at my pleasure; and to study how to amuse and divert me! I confess, I had never suspected it! I am quite ashamed of my total want of sagacity; but it had never occurred to me!"

"And why not, Ma'am?" cried Mr. Giles. "Why may not a princess be pretty, and complaisant, and know how to sing and play, and read, as well as another lady? She is just as able to learn as you, or any common person. I never heard that a princess took her rank in the place of her faculties. I know no difference; except that, if she does the things with good nature, you ought to love and honour her the double, in consideration of the great temptation she has to be proud and idle, and to do nothing. We all envy the great, when we ought only to revere them if they are good, and to pity them if they are bad; for they have the same infirmities that we have; and nobody that dares put them in mind of them: so that they often go to the grave, before they find out that they are nothing but poor little men and women, like the rest of us. For my part, when I see them worthy, and amiable, I look up to them as prodigies! Whereas, a common person, such as you, or I, Ma'am,—"

Mrs. Ireton, unable to bear this phrase, endeavoured to turn the attention of the company into another channel, by abruptly calling upon Juliet to go to the piano-forte.

Juliet entreated to be excused.

"Excused? And why, Ma'am? What else have you got to do?

What are your avocations? I shall really take it as a favour to be informed."

"Don't teize her, pretty lady; don't teize her," cried Mr. Giles. "If she likes to sing, it's very agreeable; but if not, don't make a point of it, for it's not a thing at all essential."

"Likes it?" repeated Mrs. Ireton, superciliously; "We must do nothing, then, but what we like? Even when we are in other people's houses? Even when we exist only through the goodness of some of our superiours? Still we are to do only what we like? I am quite happy in the information! Extremely obliged for it, indeed! It will enable me, I hope, to rectify the gross errour of which I have been guilty; for I really did not know I had a young lady in my house, who was to make her will and taste the rule for mine! and, as I suppose, to have the goodness to direct my servants; as well as to take the trouble to manage me. I knew nothing of all this, I protest. I thought, on the contrary, I had engaged a young person, who would never think of taking such a liberty as to give her opinion; but who would do, as she ought, with respect and submission, whatever I should indicate."—

"Good la, Ma'am," interrupted Mr. Giles: "Why that would be leading the life of a slave! And that, I suppose, is what they meant, all this time, by a toad-eater. However, don't look so ashamed, my pretty dear, for a toad-eater-maker is still worse! Fie, fie! What can rich people be thinking of, to lay out their money in buying their fellow-creatures' liberty of speech and thought! and then paying them for a bargain which they ought to despise them for selling?"

This unexpected retort turning the smiles of the assembly irresistibly against the lady of the mansion, she hastily renewed her desire that Juliet would sing.

"Sing, Ma'am?" cried Mr. Giles. "Why a merry-andrew* could not do it, after being so affronted! Bless my heart! Tell a human being that she must only move to and fro, like a machine? Only say what she is bid, like a parrot? Employ her time, call forth her talents, exact her services, yet not let her make any use of her understanding? Neither say what she approves, nor object to what she dislikes? Poor, pretty young thing! You were never so much to be pitied, in the midst of your worst distresses, as when you were relieved upon such terms! Fie upon it, fie!—How can great people be so little?"

The mingled shame and resentment of Mrs. Ireton, at a remonstrance so extraordinary and so unqualified, were with difficulty kept within the bounds of decorum; for though she laughed, and affected to be extremely diverted, her laugh was so sharp, and forced, that it wounded every ear; and, through the amusement that she pretended to receive, it was obvious that she suffered torture, in restraining herself from ordering her servants to turn the orator out of the room.

With looks much softened, though in a manner scarcely less fervent, Mr. Giles then, approaching Juliet, repeated, "Don't be cast down, I say, my pretty lady! You are none the worse for all this. The thing is but equal, at last; so we must not always look at the bad side of our fate. State every thing fairly; you have got your talents, your prettiness, and your winning ways,—but you want these ladies' wealth: they, have got their wealth, their grandeur, and their luxuries; but they want your powers of amusing. You can't well do without one another. So it's best be friends on both sides."

Mrs. Ireton, now, dying to give some vent to her spleen, darted the full venom of her angry eyes upon Juliet, and called out, "You don't see, I presume, Miss Ellis, what a condition Bijou has put that chair in? 'Twould be too great a condescension for you, I suppose, just to give it a little pat of the hand, to shake off the crumbs? Though it is not your business, I confess! I confess that it is not your business! Perhaps, therefore, I am guilty of an indiscretion in giving you such a hint. Perhaps I had better let Lady Kendover, or Lady Arramede, or Mrs. Brinville, or any other of the ladies, sit upon the dirt, and soil their clothes? You may think, perhaps, that it will be for the advantage of the mercer, or the linen-draper? You may be considering the good of trade? or perhaps you may think I may do such sort of menial offices for myself?"

However generally power may cause timidity, arrogance, in every generous mind, awakens spirit; Juliet, therefore, raising her head, and, clearing her countenance, with a modest, but firm step, moved silently towards the door.

Astonished and offended, "Permit me, Madam," cried Mrs.

Ireton; "permit me, Miss Ellis,—if it is not taking too great a liberty with a person of your vast consequence,—permit me to enquire who told you to go?"

Juliet turned back her head, and quietly answered, "A person, Madam, who has not the honour to be known to you,—myself!" And then steadily left the room.

CHAPTER LVII

AN answer so little expected, from one whose dependent state had been so freely discussed, caused a general surprize, and an almost universal demand of who the young person might be, and what she could mean. The few words that had dropt from her had as many commentators as hearers. Some thought their inference important; others, their mystery suspicious; and others mocked their assumption of dignity. Tears started into the eyes of Lady Barbara; while those of Sir Jaspar were fixed, meditatively, upon the head of his crutch; but the complacent smile of admiration, exhibited by Mr. Giles, attracted the notice of the whole assembly, by the peals of laughter which it excited in the Miss Crawleys.

With rage difficultly disguised without, but wholly ungovernable within, Mrs. Ireton would instantly have revenged what she considered as the most heinous affront that she had ever received, by expelling its author ignominiously from her house, but for the still sharpened curiosity with which her pretentions to penetration became piqued, from the general cry of, "How very extraordinary that Mrs. Ireton has never been able to discover who she is!"

When Juliet, therefore, conceiving her removal from this mansion to be as inevitable, as her release from its tyranny was desirable, made known, as soon as the company was dispersed, that she was ready to depart; she was surprised by a request, from Mrs. Ireton, to stay a day or two longer; for the purpose of taking care of Mr. Loddard the following morning; as Mrs. Ireton, who had no one with whom she could trust such a charge, had engaged herself to join a party to see Arundel Castle.

Little as Juliet felt disposed to renew her melancholy wanderings, her situation in this house appeared to her so humiliating, nay degrading, that neither this message, nor the fawning civilities with which, at their next meeting, Mrs. Ireton sought to mitigate her late asperity, could prevail with her to consent to any delay beyond that which was necessary for obtaining the counsel of Gabriella; to whom she wrote a detailed account of what had passed; adding, "How long must I thus waste my time and my existence, separated from all that can render them valuable, while fastened upon by constant discomfort and disgust? O friend of my heart, friend of my earliest years, earliest feelings, juvenile happiness,—and, alas! maturer sorrows! why must we thus be sundered in adversity? Oh how,—with three-fold toil, should I revive by the side of my beloved Gabriella!—Dear to me by every tie of tender recollection; dear to me by the truest compassion for her sufferings, and reverence for her resignation; and dear to me,—thrice dear! by the sacred ties of gratitude, which bind me for ever to her honoured mother, and to her venerated, saint-like uncle, my pious benefactor!"

She then tenderly proposed their immediate re-union, at whatever cost of fatigue, or risk, it might be obtained; and besought Gabriella to seek some small room, and to enquire for some needle-work; determining to appropriate to a journey to town, the little sum which she might have to receive for the long and laborious fortnight, which she had consigned to the terrible enterprize of aiming at amusing, serving, or interesting, one whose sole taste of pleasure consisted in seeking, like Strife, in Spenser's Fairy Queen,* occasion for dissension.

With the apprehension, however, of losing, the desire of retaining her always revived; and now, as usual, proved some check to the recreations of spleen, in which Mrs. Ireton ordinarily indulged herself. Yet, even in the midst of intended concession, the love of tormenting was so predominant, that, had the resolution of Juliet still wavered, whether to seek some new retreat, or still to support her present irksome situation, all indecision would have ceased from fresh disgust, at the sneers which insidiously found their way through every effort at civility. What had dropt from Mr. Giles Arbe, relative to the bank-notes, had excited curiosity in all; tinted, in some, with suspicion, and, in Mrs. Ireton, blended with malignity and wrath, that a creature whom she pleased herself to consider, and yet more to represent, as dependent upon her bounty for sustinence, should have any resources of her own. Nor was this displeasure wholly free from surmises the most disgraceful; though to those she forbore to give vent, conscious that to suggest them would stamp with impropriety all further intercourse with their object. And a moment that offered new food for inquisition, was the last to induce Mrs. Ireton to relinquish her *protegée.* She confined her sarcasms, therefore, when she could not wholly repress them, to oblique remarks upon the happiness of those who were able to lay by private stores for secret purposes; lamenting that such was not her fate; yet congratulating herself that she might now sleep in peace, with respect to any creditors; since, should she be threatened with an execution,* her house had a rich inmate, by whom she flattered herself that she should be assisted to give bail.

Already, the next morning, her resolution with regard to her nephew was reversed; and, the child desiring the change of scene, she gave directions that Miss Ellis should prepare herself to take him in charge during the excursion.

But Juliet was now initiated in the services and the endurance of an humble companion in public; she offered, therefore, to amuse and to watch him at home, but decidedly refused to attend him abroad; and her evident indifference whether to stay or begone herself, forced Mrs. Ireton to deny the humoured boy his intended frolic.

Little accustomed to any privation, and totally unused to disappointment, the young gentleman, when his aunt was preparing to depart, had recourse to his usual appeals against restraint or authority, clamourous cries and unappeasable blubbering. Juliet, to whose room he refused to mount, was called upon to endeavour to quiet him, and to entice him into the garden; that he might not hear the carriage of his aunt draw up to the door.

But this commission the refractory spirit of the young heir made it impossible to execute, till he overheard a whisper to

Juliet, that she would take care, should Mr. Loddard chuse to go to the Temple, to place the silk-worms above his reach.

Suddenly, then, he sprang from his consolers and attendants, to run forward to the forbidden fruit; and, with a celerity that made it difficult for Juliet, even with her utmost speed, and longer limbs, to arrive at the spot, in time to prevent the mischief for which she saw him preparing. She had just, however, succeeded, in depositing the menaced insects upon a high bracket, when a footman came to whisper to her the commands of his lady, that she would detain Mr. Loddard till the party should be set off.

Before the man had shut himself out, Ireton, holding up his finger to him in token of secresy, slipt past him into the little building; and, having turned the key on the inside, and put it into his pocket, said, "I'll stand centinel for little Pickle!" and flung himself, loungingly, upon an arm-chair.

Confounded by this action, yet feeling it necessary to appear unintimidated, Juliet affected to occupy herself with the silk-worms; of which the young gentleman now, eager to romp with Ireton, thought no more.

"At last, then, I have caught you, my skittish dear!" cried Ireton, while jumping about the little boy, to keep him in good humour. "I have had the devil of a difficulty to contrive it. However, I shall make myself amends now, for they are all going to Arundel Castle, and you and I can pass the morning together."

The indignant look which this boldness excited, he pretended not to observe, and went on.

"I can't possibly be easy without having a little private chat with you. I must consult you about my affairs. I want devilishly to make you my friend. You might be capitally useful to me. And you would find your account in it, I promise you. What sayst thee, my pretty one?"

Juliet, not appearing to hear him, changed the leaves of the silk-worms.

"Can you guess what it is brings me hither to old madam my mother's? It is not you, with all your beauty, you arch prude; though I have a great enjoyment in looking at you and your blushes, which are devilishly handsome, I own; yet, to say the truth, you are not—all together—I don't know how it is—but you are not—upon the whole—quite exactly to my taste. Don't take it ill, my love, for you are a devilish fine girl. I own that. But I want something more skittish, more wild, more eccentric. If I were to fix my fancy upon such symmetry as you, I should be put out of my way every moment. I should always be thinking I had some Minerva tutoring, or some Juno* awing me. It would not do at all. I want something of another cast; something that will urge me when I am hippish, without keeping me in order when I am whimsical. Something frisky, flighty, fantastic,—yet panting, blushing, dying with love for me!—"

Neither contempt nor indignation were of sufficient force to preserve the gravity of Juliet, at this unexpected ingenuousness of vanity.

"You smile?" he cried; "but if you knew what a deuced difficult thing it is, for a man who has got a little money, to please himself, you would find it a very serious affair. How the deuce can he be sure whether a woman, when once he has married her, would not, if her settlement be to her liking, dance at his funeral? The very thought of that would either carry me off in a fright within a month, or make me want to live for ever, merely to punish her. It's a hard thing having money! a deuced hard thing! One does not know who to trust. A poor man may find a wife in a moment, for if he sees any one that likes him, he knows it is for himself; but a rich man,—as Sir Jaspar says,—can never be sure whether the woman who marries him, would not, for the same pin-money,* just as willingly follow him to the outside of the church, as to the inside!"

At the name of Sir Jaspar, Juliet involuntarily gave some attention, though she would make no reply.

"From the time," continued Ireton, "that I heard him pronounce those words, I have never been able to satisfy myself; nor to find out what would satisfy me. At least not till lately; and now that I know what I want, the difficulty of the business is to get it! And this is what I wish to consult with you about; for you must know, my dear, I can never be happy without being adored."

Juliet, now, was surprised into suddenly looking at him, to see whether he were serious.

"Yes, adored! loved to distraction! I must be idolized for myself, myself alone; yet publicly worshiped, that all mankind may see,—and envy,—the passion I have been able to inspire!"

Suspecting that he meant some satire upon Elinor, Juliet again fixed her eyes upon her silk-worms.

"So you don't ask me what it is that makes me so devilish dutiful all of a sudden, in visiting my mamma? You think, perhaps, I have some debts to pay? No; I have no taste for gaming. It's the cursedest fatiguing thing in the world. If one don't mind what one's about, one is blown up in a moment; and to be always upon one's guard, is worse than ruin itself. So I am upon no coaxing expedition, I give you my word. What do you think it is, then, that brings me hither? Cannot you guess?—Hay?—Why it is to arrange something, somehow or other, for getting myself from under this terrible yoke, that seems upon the point of enslaving me. My neck feels galled by it already! I have naturally no taste for matrimony. And now that the business seems to be drawing to a point, and I am called upon to name my lawyer, and cavilled with to declare, to the uttermost sixpence, what I will do, and what I will give, to make my wife merry and comfortable upon my going out of the world,—I protest I shudder with horrour! I think there is nothing upon earth so mercenary, as a young nymph upon the point of becoming a bride!"

"Except,—" Juliet here could not resist saying, "except the man,—young or old,—who is her bridegroom!"

"O, that's another thing! quite another thing! A man must needs take care of his house, and his table, and all that: but the horridest thing I know, is the condition tied to a man's obtaining the hand of a young woman; he can never solicit it, but by giving her a prospect of his death-bed! And she never consents to live with him, till she knows what she may gain by his dying! 'Tis the most shocking style of making love that can be imagined. I don't like it, I swear! What, now, would you advise me to do?"

"I?"

"Yes; you know the scrape I am in, don't you? Sir Jaspar's estate, in case he should have no children, is entailed upon me; and, in case I should have none neither, is entailed upon a cousin; the heaviest dog you ever saw in your life, whom he hates and despises; and whom I wish at old Nick with all my heart, because I know he, and all his family, will wish me at the devil myself, if I marry; and, if I have children, will wish them and my wife there. I hate them all so heartily, that, whenever I think of them, I am ready, in pure spite, to be tied to the first girl that comes in my way: but, when I think of myself, I am taken with a fit of fright, and in a plaguey hurry to cut the knot off short. And this is the way I have got the character of a male jilt. But I don't deserve it, I assure you; for of all the females with whom I have had these little engagements, there is not one whom I have seriously thought of marrying, after the first half hour. They none of them hit my fancy further than to kill a little time."

The countenance of Juliet, though she neither deigned to speak nor to turn to him, marked such strong disapprobation, that he thought proper to add, "Don't be affronted for little Selina Joddrel: I really meant to marry her at the time; and I should really have gone on, and "buckled to,"* if the thing had been any way possible: but she turns out such a confounded little fool, that I can't think of her any longer."

"And was it necessary,—" Juliet could not refrain from saying, "to engage her first, and examine whether she could make you happy afterwards?"

"Why that seems a little awkward, I confess; but it's a way I have adopted. Though I took the decision, I own, rather in a hurry, with regard to little Selina; for it was merely to free myself from the reproaches of Sir Jaspar, who, because he is seventy-five, and does not know what to do with himself, is always regretting that he did not take a wife when he was a stripling; and always at work to get me into the yoke. But, the truth is, I promised, when I went abroad, to bring him home a niece from France, or Italy; unless I went further east; and then I would look him out a fair Circassian. Now as he has a great taste for any thing out of the common way, and retains a constant hankering after Beauty, he was delighted with the scheme. But I saw nothing that would do! Nothing I could take to! The pretty ones were all too buckish; and the steady ones, a set of the yellowest frights I ever beheld."

"Alas for the poor ladies!"

"O, you are a mocker, are you?—So to lighten the disappointment to Sir Jaspar, I hit upon the expedient of taking up with little Selina, who was the first young thing that fell in my way. And I was too tired to be difficult. Besides, what made her the more convenient, was her extreme youth, which gave me a year to look about me, and see if I could do any better. But she's a poor creature; a sad poor creature indeed! quite too bad. So I must make an end of the business as fast as possible. Besides, another thing that puts me in a hurry is,—the very devil would have it so!—but I have fallen in love with her sister!—"

Juliet, at a loss how to understand him, now raised her eyes; and, not without astonishment, perceived that he was speaking with a grave face.

"O that noble stroke! That inimitable girl! Happy, happy, Harleigh! That fellow fascinates the girls the more the less notice he takes of them! I take but little notice of them, neither; but, some how or other, they never do that sort of thing for me! If I could meet with one who would take such a measure for my sake, and before such an assembly,—I really think I should worship her!"

Then, lowering his voice, "You may be amazingly useful to me, my angel," he cried, "in this new affair. I know you are very well with Harleigh, though I don't know exactly how; but if,—nay, hear me before you look so proud! if you'll help me, a little, how to go to work with the divine Elinor, I'll bind myself down to make over to you,—in case of success,—mark that!—as round* a sum as you may be pleased to name!"

The disdain of Juliet at this proposition was so powerful, that, though she heard it as the deepest of insults, indignation was but a secondary feeling; and a look of utter scorn, with a determined silence to whatever else he might say, was the only notice it received.

He continued, nevertheless, to address her, demanding her advice how to manage Harleigh, and her assistance how to conquer Elinor, with an air of as much intimacy and confidence, as if he received the most cordial replies. He purposed, he said, unless she could counsel him to something better, making an immediate overture to Elinor; by which means, whether he should obtain, or not, the only girl in the world who knew how to love, and what love meant, he should, at least, in a very summary way, get rid of the little Selina.

Juliet knew too well the slightness of the texture of the regard of Selina for Ireton, to be really hurt at this defection; yet she was not less offended at being selected for the confidant of so dishonourable a proceeding; nor less disgusted at the unfeeling insolence by which it was dictated.

An attempt at opening the door at length silenced him, while the voice of Mrs. Ireton's woman called out, "Goodness! Miss Ellis, what do you lock yourself in for? My lady has sent me to you."

Juliet cast up her eyes, foreseeing the many disagreeable attacks and surmises to which she was made liable by this incident; yet immediately said aloud, "Since you have thought proper, Mr. Ireton, to lock the door, for your own pleasure, you will, at least, I imagine, think proper to open it for that of Mrs. Ireton."

"Deuce take me if I do!" cried he, in a low voice: "manage the matter as you will! I have naturally no taste for a prude; so I always leave her to work her way out of a scrape as well as she can. But I'll see you again when they are all off." Then, throwing the key upon her lap, he softly and laughingly escaped out of the window.

Provoked and vexed, yet helpless, and without any means of redress, Juliet opened the door.

"Goodness! Miss Ellis," cried the Abigail,* peeping curiously around, "how droll for you to shut yourself in! My lady sent me to ask whether you have seen any thing of Mr. Ireton in the garden, or about; for she has been ready to go ever so long, and he said he was setting off first on horseback; but his groom is come, and is waiting for orders, and none of us can tell where he is."

"Mr. Ireton," Juliet quietly answered, "was here just now; and I doubt not but you will find him in the garden."

"Yes," cried the boy, "he slid out of the window."

"Goodness! was he in here, then, Master Loddard? Well! my lady'll be in a fine passion, if she should hear of it!"

This was enough to give the tidings a messenger: the boy darted forward, and reached the house in a moment.

The Abigail ran after him; Juliet, too, followed, dreading the impending storm, yet still more averse to remaining within the reach and power of Ireton. And the knowledge, that he would now, for the rest of the morning, be sole master of the house, filled her with such horrour, of the wanton calumny to which his unprincipled egotism might expose her, that, rather than continue under the same roof with a character so unfeelingly audacious, she preferred risking all the mortifications to which she might be liable in the excursion to Arundel Castle.

Advanced already into the hall, dragged thither by her turbulent little nephew, and the hope of detecting the hiding-place of Ireton, stood the patroness whom she now felt compelled to soothe into accepting her attendance. Not aware of this purposed concession, and nearly as much frightened as enraged, to find with whom her son had been shut up, Mrs. Ireton, in a tone equally querulous and piqued, cried, "I beg you a thousand pardons, Ma'am, for the indiscretion of which I have been guilty, in asking for the honour of your company to Arundel Castle this morning! I ought to make a million of apologies for supposing that a young lady,—for you are a lady, no doubt! every body is a lady, now!—of your extraordinary turn and talents, could endure the insupportable insipidity of a tête à tête with a female; or the dull care of a bantling;* when a splendid, flashy, rich, young travelled gentleman, chusing, also, to remain behind, may be tired, and want some amusement! 'Twas grossly stupid of me, I own, to expect such a sacrifice. You, who, besides these prodigious talents, that make us all appear like a set of vulgar, uneducated beings by your side; you, who revel also, in the luxury of wealth; who wanton in the stores of Plutus;* who are accustomed to the magnificence of unaccounted hoards!—How must the whole detail of our existence appear penurious, pitiful to you!—I am surprised how you can forbear falling into fits at the very sight of us! But I presume you reserve the brilliancy of an action of that *eclat*, for objects better worth your while to dazzle by a stroke of that grand description? I must have lost my senses, certainly, to so ill appreciate my own insignificance! I hope you'll pity me! that's all! I hope you will have so much unction as to pity me!"

If, at the opening of this harangue, the patience of Juliet nearly yielded to resentment, its length gave power to reflection,—which usually wants but time for checking impulse,—to point out the many and nameless mischiefs, to which quitting the house under similar suspicions might give rise. She quietly, therefore, answered, that though to herself it must precisely be the same thing, whether Mr. Ireton were at home or abroad, if that circumstance gave any choice to Mrs. Ireton, she would change her own plans, either to go or to stay, according to the directions which she might receive.

A superiority to accusation or surmize thus cool and decided, no sooner relieved the apprehensions of Mrs. Ireton by its evident innocence, than it excited her wrath by its deliberate indifference, if not contempt: and she would now disdainfully have rejected the attendance which, the moment before, she had anxiously desired, had not the little master of the house, who had seized the opportunity of this harangue to make his escape, caught a glimpse of the carriage at the door; and put an end to all contest, by stunning all ears, with an unremitting scream till he forced himself into it; when, overpowering every obstacle, he obliged his aunt and Juliet to follow; while he issued his own orders to the postilion to drive to Arundel Castle.

Even the terrour of calumny, that most dangerous and baneful foe to unprotected woman! would scarcely have frightened Juliet into this expedition, had she been aware that, as soon as she was seated in the landau,* with orders to take the whole charge of Mr. Loddard, the little dog, also, would have been given to her management. "Bijou will like to take the air," cried Mrs. Ireton, languidly; "and he will serve to entertain Loddard by the way. He can go very well on Miss Ellis's lap. Pretty little creature! 'Twould be cruel to leave him at home alone!"

This terrible humanity, which, in a hot day, in the middle of July, cast upon the knees of Juliet a fat, round, well furred, and over-fed little animal, accustomed to snarl, scratch, stretch, and roll himself about at his pleasure, produced fatigue the most pitiless, and inconvenience the most comfortless. The little tyrant of the party, whose will was law to the company, found no diversion so much to his taste, during the short journey, as exciting the churlish humour of his fellow-favourite, by pinching his ears, pulling his nose, filliping* his claws, squeezing his throat, and twisting round his tail. And all these feats, far from incurring any reprimand, were laughed at and applauded. For whom did they incommode? No one but Miss Ellis;—and for what else was Miss Ellis there?

Yet this fatigue and disgust might have been passed over, as local evils, had they ceased with the journey; and had she then been at liberty to look at what remains of the venerable old castle; to visit its ancient chapel; to examine the genealogical records of the long gallery; to climb up to the antique citadel, and to enjoy the spacious view thence presented of the sea: but she immediately received orders to give exercise to Bijou, and to watch that he ran into no danger: though Selina, who assiduously came forward to meet Mrs. Ireton, without appearing even to perceive Juliet, officiously took young Loddard in charge, and conducted him, with his aunt, to a large expecting party, long arrived, and now viewing the citadel.

CHAPTER LVIII

RELIEVED, nevertheless, through whatever means effected, by a separation, Juliet, with her speechless, though far from mute companion, went forth to seek some obscure walk. But her purpose was defeated by the junction of a little spaniel, to which Bijou attached himself, with a fondness so tenacious, that her utmost efforts either to disengage them, or to excite both to follow her, were fruitless; Bijou would not quit the spaniel; nor the spaniel his post near the mansion.

Not daring to go on without her troublesome little charge, the approach of a carriage made her hasten to a garden-seat, upon which, though she could not be hidden, she might be less conspicuous.

The carriage, familiar to her from having frequently seen it at Miss Matson's, was that of Sir Jaspar Herrington. Not satisfied, though she had no right to be angry, at the so measured politeness which he had shewn her the preceding day, when further notice would have softened her mortifying embarrassment, she was glad that he had not remarked her in passing.

She heard him enquire for Mrs. Ireton's party, which he had promised to join; but, affrighted at the sound of the citadel, he said that he would alight, and wait upon some warm seat in the grounds.

In descending from his chaise, one of his crutches fell, and a bonbonniere,* of which the contents were dispersed upon the ground, slipt from the hand of his valet. It was then, and not without chagrin, that Juliet began further to comprehend the defects of a character which she had thought an entire composition of philanthropy and courtesy. He reviled rather than scolded the servant to whom the accident had happened; and treated the circumstance as an event of the first importance. He cast an equal share of blame, and with added sharpness, upon the postilion, for not having advanced an inch nearer to the stone-steps; and uttered invectives even virulent against the groom, that he had not come forward to help. Angry, because vexed, with all around, he used as little moderation in his wrath, as reason in his reproaches.

How superficially, thought Juliet, can we judge of dispositions, where nothing is seen but what is meant to be shewn! where nothing is pronounced but what is prepared for being heard! Had I fixed my opinion of this gentleman only upon what he intended that I should witness, I should have concluded that he had as much urbanity of humour as of manners. I could never have imagined, that the most trifling of accidents could, in a moment, destroy the whole harmony of his temper!

In the midst of the choleric harangue of the Baronet, against which no one ventured to remonstrate, the little dogs came sporting before him; and, recollecting Bijou, he hastily turned his head towards the person upon the garden-seat, whom he had passed without any attention, and discerned Juliet.

He hobbled towards her without delay, warmly expressing his delight at so auspicious a meeting: but the air and look, reserved and grave, with which, involuntarily, she heard him, brought to his consciousness, what the pleasure of her sight had driven from it, his enraged attack upon his servants; which she must unavoidably have witnessed, and of which her countenance shewed her opinion.

He stood some moments silent, leaning upon his crutches, and palpably disconcerted. Then, shrugging his shoulders, with a half smile, but a piteous look, "Many," he cried, "are the tricks which my quaint little imps have played me! many, the quirks and villainous wiles I owe them!—but never yet, with all the ingenuity of their malice, have they put me to shame and confusion such as this!"

Rising to be gone, yet sorry for him, and softened, the disapprobation of Juliet was mingled with a concern, from her disposition to like him, that made its expression, in the eyes of her old admirer, seem something nearly divine. He looked at her with reverence and with regret, but made no attempt to prevent her departure. To separate, however, the dogs, or induce the spaniel to go further, she still found impossible; and, not daring to abandon Bijou, was fain quietly to seat herself again, upon a garden-chair, nearer to the house.

Sir Jaspar, for some minutes, remained, pensively, upon the spot where she had left him; then, again shrugging his shoulders, as if bemoaning his ill luck, and again hobbling after her, "There is nothing," he cried, "that makes a man look so small, as a sudden self-conviction that he merits ridicule or disgrace! what intemperance would be averted, could we believe ourselves always,—not only from above, but by one another, overheard! Don't take an aversion to me, however! nor suppose me worse than I am; nor worse than the herd of mankind. You have but seen an old bachelor in his true colours! Not with the gay tints, not with the spruce smiles, not with the gallant bows, the courteous homage, the flowery flourishes, with which he makes himself up for shew; but with the grim colouring of factious age, and suspicious egotism!"

The countenance of Juliet shewing her now to be shocked that she had given rise to these apologies, that of Sir Jaspar brightened; and, dragging a chair to her side, "I came hither," he cried, "in the fair hope to seize one of those happy moments, that the fates, now and then, accord to favoured mortals, for holding interesting and dulcet discourse, with the most fascinating enchantress that a long life, filled up with fastidious, perhaps fantastic researches after female excellence, has cast in my way. Would not one have thought 'twas some indulgent sylph that directed me? that inspired me with the idea, and then seconded the inspiration, by contriving that my arrival should take place at the critical instant, when that syren was to be found alone? Who could have suspected 'twas but the envious stratagem of some imp of darkness and spite, devised purely to expose a poor antiquated soul, with all his infirmities, physical and moral, to your contempt and antipathy?"

Peering now under her hat, his penetrating eyes discerned so entire a change in his favour, that he completely recovered his pleasantry, his quaint archness, and his gallantry.

"If betrayed," he continued, "by these perfidious elves, where may a poor forlorn solitary wight, such as I am, find a counsellor? He has no bosom friend, like the happy mortal, whose kindly star has guided him to seek, in lively, all-attractive youth, an equal partner for melancholy, all revolting age! He has no rising progeny, that, inheritors of his interests, naturally share his difficulties. He has nothing at hand but mercenary dependents. Nothing at heart but jealous suspicion of others, or secret repining for himself! Such, fair censurer! such is the natural state of that unnatural character, an old bachelor! How, then, when not upon his guard, or, in other words, when not urged by some outward object, some passing pleasure, or some fairy hope,—how,—tell me, in the candour of your gentle conscience! how can you expect from so decrepit and unwilling a hermit, the spontaneous benevolence of youth?"

"But what is it I have said, Sir," cried Juliet smiling, "that makes you denounce me as a censurer?"

"What is it you have said? ask, rather, what is it you have not said, with those eyes that speak with an eloquence that a thousand tongues might emulate in vain? They administered to me a lesson so severe, because just, that, had not a little pity, which just now beamed from them, revived me, the malignant goblins, who delight in drawing me into these scrapes, might have paid for their sport by losing their prey! But what invidious little devils ensnare me even now, into this superannuated folly, of prating about so worn out an old subject, when I meant only to name a being bright, blooming, and juvenile?"

The recollection of his nearly complete neglect, the preceding day, in presence of Mrs. Ireton, and her society, again began to cloud the countenance of Juliet, as she listened to compliments thus reserved for private delivery. Sir Jaspar soon penetrated into what passed in her mind, and, yet again shrugging his shoulders, and resuming the sorrowful air of a self-convicted culprit, "Alas!" he cried, "under what pitiful star did I first begin limping upon this nether sphere? And what foul fiend is it, that, taking upon him the name of worldly cunning, has fashioned my conduct, since here I have been hopping and hobbling? I burned, yesterday, with desire to make public my admiration of the fair flower, that I saw nearly trampled under foot; and I should have considered as the most propitious moment of my life, that in which I had raised its drooping head, by withering, with a blast, all the sickly, noxious surrounding weeds: but those little devils, that never leave me quiet, kept twitching and tweaking me every instant, with representations of prudence and procrastination; with the danger of exciting observation; and the better judgment of obtaining a little private discourse, previous to any public display."

Not able to divine to what this might be the intended prelude, Juliet was silent. Sir Jaspar, after some hesitation, continued.

"In that motley assembly, you had two antique friends, equally cordial, and almost equally admiring and desirous to serve you; but by different means,—perhaps with different views! one of them, stimulated by the little fairy elves, that alternately enlighten and mislead him, not seeing yet his way, and embarrassed in his choice of measures, was lying in wait, cautiously to avail himself of the first favourable moment, for soliciting your fair leave to dub himself your knight-errant; the other, urged solely, perhaps, by good-nature and humanity, with an happy absence of mind, that precludes circumspection; coming forward in your defence, and for your honour, with unsuspecting, unfearing, untemporising zeal. Alas! in my conscience, which these tormenting little imps are for ever goading on, to inflict upon me some disagreeable compliment, I cannot, all simple as he is, but blush to view the intrinsic superiority of the unsophisticated man of nature, over the artificial man of the world! How much more truly a male character."

Looking at her then with examining earnestness, "To which of these antediluvian wights," he continued, "you will commit the gauntlet, that must be flung in your defence, I know not; either of us,—alas!—might be your great grandfather! But, helpless old captives as we are in your chains, we each feel a most sincere, nay, inordinate desire, to break those fetters with which, at this moment, you seem yourself to be shackled. And for this I am not wholly without a scheme, though it is one that demands a little previous parleying."

Juliet positively declined his services; but gratefully acknowledged those from which she had already, though involuntarily, profited.

"You cannot, surely," he cried, "have a predilection for your present species of existence? and, least of all, under the galling yoke of this spirit-breaking dame, into whose ungentle power I cannot see you fallen without losing sleep, appetite, and pleasure. How may I conjure you into better hands? How release you from such bondage? And yet, this pale, withered, stiff, meagre hag, so odious, so tyrannical, so irascible, but a few years,—in my calculation!—but a few years since,—had all the enchantment of blithe, blooming loveliness! You, who see her only in her decline, can never believe it; but she was eminently fair, gay, and charming!"

Juliet looked at him, astonished.

"Her story," he continued, "already envelopes the memoirs of a Beauty, in her four stages of existence. During childhood, indulged in every wish; admired where she should have been chidden, caressed where she should have been corrected; coaxed into pettishness, and spoilt into tyranny. In youth, adored, followed, and applauded till, involuntarily, rather than vainly, she believed herself a goddess. In maturity,—ah! there's the test of sense and temper in the waning beauty!—in maturity, shocked and amazed to see herself supplanted by the rising bloomers; to find that she might be forgotten, or left out, if not assiduous herself to come forward; to be consulted only upon grave and dull matters, out of the reach of her knowledge and resources; alternately mortified by involuntary negligence, and affronted by reverential respect! Such has been her maturity; such, amongst faded beauties, is the maturity of thousands. In old age,—if a lady may be ever supposed to suffer the little loves and graces to leave her so woefully in the lurch, as to permit her to know such a state;—in old age, without stores to amuse, or powers to instruct, though with a full persuasion that she is endowed with wit, because she cuts, wounds, and slashes from unbridled, though pent-up resentment, at her loss of adorers; and from a certain perverseness, rather than quickness of parts, that gifts her with the sublime art of ingeniously tormenting; with no consciousness of her own infirmities, or patience for those of others; she is dreaded by the gay, despised by the wise, pitied by the good, and shunned by all."

Then, looking at Juliet with a strong expression of surprise, "What Will o'the Wisp,"* he cried, "has misled you into this briery thicket of brambles, nettles, and thorns? where you cannot open your mouth but you must be scratched; nor your ears, but you must be wounded; nor stir a word but you must be pricked and worried? How is it that, with the most elegant ideas, the most just perceptions upon every subject that presents itself, you have a taste so whimsical?"

"A taste? Can you, then, Sir, believe a fate like mine to have any connexion with choice?"

"What would you have me believe, fair Ænigma?* Tell me, and I will fashion my credulity to your commands. But I only hear of you with Mrs. Maple; I only see you with Mrs. Ireton! Mrs. Maple, having weaker parts, may have less power, scientifically, to torment than Mrs. Ireton; but nature has been as active in personifying ill will with the one, as art in embellishing spite with the other. They are equally egotists, equally wrapt up in themselves, and convinced that self alone is worth living for in this nether world. What a fate! To pass from Maple to Ireton, was to fall from Scylla to Charybdis!"*

The blush of Juliet manifested extreme confusion, to see herself represented, even though it might be in sport, as a professional parasite. Reading, with concern, in her countenance, the pain which he had caused her, he exclaimed, "Sweet witch! loveliest syren!—let me hasten to develope a project, inspired, I must hope, by my better genius! Tell me but, frankly, who and what you are, and then—"

Juliet shook her head.

"Nay, nay, should your origin be the most obscure, I shall but think you more nearly allied to the gods! Jupiter, Apollo, and such like personages, delighted in a secret progeny.* If, on the contrary, in sparkling correspondence with your eyes, it is brilliant, but has been clouded by fortune, how ravished shall I be to twirl round the wheels of that capricious deity,* till they reach those dulcet regions, where beauty and merit are in harmony with wealth and ease! Tell me, then, what country first saw you bloom; what family originally reared you; by what name you made your first entrance into the world;—and I will turn your champion against all the spirits of the air, all the fiends of the earth, and all the monsters of the "vast abyss!"* Leave, then, to such as need those goaders, the magnetism of mystery and wonder, and trust, openly and securely, to the charm of youth, the fascination of intelligence, the enchantment of grace, and the witchery of beauty!"

Juliet was still silent.

"I see you take me for a vain, curious old caitiff,* peeping, peering and prying into business in which I have no concern. Charges such as these are ill cleared by professions; let me plead, therefore, by facts. Should there be a person,—young, rich, *à la mode*, and not ugly; whose expectations are splendid, who moves in the sphere of high life, who could terminate your difficulties with honour, by casting at your feet that vile dross, which, in fairy hands, such as yours, may be transmuted into benevolence, generosity, humanity,—if such a person there should be, who in return for these grosser and more substantial services, should need the gentler and more refined ones of soft society, mild hints, guidance unseen, admonition unpronounced;—would you, and could you, in such a case, condescend to reciprocate advantages, and their reverse? Would you,—and could you,—if snatched from unmerited embarrassments, to partake of luxuries which your acceptance would honour, bear with a little coxcomical nonsense, and with a larger portion, still, of unmeaning perverseness, and malicious nothingness? I need not, I think, say that the happy mortal whom I wish to see thus charmed and thus formed, is my nephew Ireton."

Uncertain whether he meant to mock or to elevate her, Juliet simply answered, that she had long, though without knowing why, found Mr. Ireton her enemy; but had never foreseen that an ill will as unaccountable as it was unprovoked, would have extended so far, and so wide, as to spread all around her the influence of irony and derision.

"Hold, hold! fair infidel,"—cried Sir Jaspar, "unless you mean to give me a fit of the gout."

He then solemnly assured her, that he was so persuaded that her excellent understanding, and uncommon intelligence, united, in rare junction, with such youth and beauty, would make her a treasure to a rich and idle young man, whose character, fluctuating between good and bad, or rather between something and nothing, was yet unformed; that, if she would candidly acknowledge her real name, story, and situation, he should merely have to utter a mysterious injunction to Ireton, that he must see her no more, in order to bring him to her feet. "He acts but a part," continued the Baronet, "in judging you ill. He piques himself upon being a man of the world, which, he persuades himself, he manifests to all observers, by a hardy, however vague spirit of detraction and censoriousness; deeming, like all those whose natures have not a kindlier bent, suspicion to be sagacity."

Juliet was entertained by this singular plan, yet frankly acknowledged, after repeating her thanks, that it offered her no temptation; and continued immoveable, to either address or persuasion, for any sort of personal communication.

A pause of some minutes ensued, during which Sir Jaspar seemed deliberating how next to proceed. He then said, "You are decided not to hear of my nephew? He is not, I confess, deserving you; but who is? Yet,—a situation such as this,—a companion such as Mrs. Ireton,—any change must surely be preferable to a fixture of such a sort? What, then, must be done? Where youth, youth itself, even when joined to figure and to riches, is rejected, how may it be hoped that age,—age and infirmity!—even though joined with all that is gentlest in kindness, all that is most disinterested in devotion, may be rendered more acceptable?"

Confused, and perplexed how to understand him, Juliet was rising, under pretence of following Bijou; but Sir Jaspar, fastening her gown to the grass by his two crutches, laughingly said, "Which will you resist most stoutly? your own cruelty, or the kindness of my little fairy friends? who, at this moment, with a thousand active gambols, are pinning, gluing, plaistering, in sylphick mosaic-work, your robe between the ground and my sticks; so that you cannot tear it away without leaving me, at least, some little memorial that I have had the happiness of seeing you!"

Forced either to struggle or to remain in her place, she sat still, and he continued.

"Don't be alarmed, for I shall certainly not offend you. Listen, then, with indulgence, to what I am tempted to propose, and, whether I am impelled by my evil genius, or inspired by my guardian angel——"

Juliet earnestly entreated him to spare her any proposition whatever; but vainly; and he was beginning, with a fervour almost devout, an address to all the sylphs, elves, and aeriel beings of his fanciful idolatry, when a sudden barking from Bijou making him look round, he perceived that Mrs. Ireton, advancing on tiptoe, was creeping behind his garden-chair.

Confounded by an apparition so unwished, he leant upon his crutches, gasping and oppressed for breath; while Juliet, to avoid the attack of which the malevolence of Mrs. Ireton's look was the sure precursor, would have retreated, had not her gown been so entangled in the crutches of Sir Jaspar, that she could not rise without leaving him the fragment that he had coveted. In vain she appealed with her eyes for release; his consternation was such, that he saw only, what least he wished to see, the scowling brow of Mrs. Ireton; who, to his active imagination, appeared to be Megara herself, just mounted from the lower regions.*

"Well! this is really charming! Quite edifying, I protest!" burst forth Mrs. Ireton, when she found that she was discovered. "This is a sort of intercourse I should never have divined! You'll pardon my want of discernment! I know *I* am quite behind hand in observation and remark; but I hope, in time, and with so much good instruction, I may become more sagacious. I am glad, however, to see that I don't disturb you Miss Ellis! Extremely glad to find that you treat me in so friendly a way, and keep your place so amiably without ceremony. I am quite enchanted to be upon terms so familiar and agreeable with you. I may sit down myself, I suppose, upon the grass, meanwhile! 'Twill be really very rural! very rural and pretty!"

Juliet now could no longer conceal her confined situation, for, pinioned to her place, she was compelled to petition the Baronet to set her at liberty.

The real astonishment of Mrs. Ireton, upon discovering the cause and means of her detention, was far less amusing to herself, than that which she had affected, while concluding her presumptuous *protegée* to be a voluntary intruder upon the time, and encroacher upon the politeness of the Baronet. Her eyes now opened, with alarm, to a confusion so unusual in her severe and authoritative brother-in-law; whom she was accustomed to view awing others, not himself awed. Suggestions of the most unpleasant nature occurred to her suspicious mind; and she stood as if thunderstruck in her turn, in silent suspension how to act, or what next to say; till Selina came running forward, to announce that all the company was gone to look at the Roman Catholic chapel; and to enquire whether Mrs. Ireton did not mean to make it a visit.

If Sir Jaspar, Mrs. Ireton hesitatingly answered, would join the party, she would attend him with pleasure.

Sir Jaspar heard not this invitation. In his haste to give Juliet her freedom, his feeble hands, disobedient to his will, and unable to second the alacrity of his wishes, struck his crutches through her gown; and they were now both, and in equal confusion, employed in disentangling it; and ashamed to look up, or to speak.

Selina, perceiving their position, with the unmeaning glee of a childish love of communication, ran, tittering, away, to tell it to Miss Brinville; who, saying that there was nothing worth seeing in the Roman Catholic chapel, was sauntering after Mrs. Ireton, in hopes of finding entertainment more congenial to her mind.

The sight of this lady, restored to Mrs. Ireton the scoffing powers which amazement, mingled with alarm, had momentarily chilled; and, as Miss Brinville peeringly approached, to verify the whisper of Selina, exclaiming, "Dear! what makes poor Sir Jaspar stoop so?" his loving sister-in-law answered, "Sir Jaspar, Miss Brinville? What can Sir Jaspar do? I beg pardon for the question, but what can a gentleman do, when a young woman happens to take a fancy to place herself so near him, that he can't turn round without incommoding her? Not that I mean to blame Miss Ellis. I hope I know better. I hope I shall never be guilty of such injustice; for how can Miss Ellis help it? What could she do? Where could she turn herself in so confined a place as this? in so narrow a piece of ground? How could she possibly find any other spot for repose?"

A contemptuous smile at Juliet from Miss Brinville, shewed that lady's approbation of this witty sally; and the junction of Mrs. Maple, whose participation in this kind of enjoyment was known to be lively and sincere, exalted still more highly the spirit of poignant sarcasm in Mrs. Ireton; who, with smiles of ineffable self-complacency, went on, "There are people, indeed,—I am afraid,—I don't know, but I am afraid so,—there are people who may have the ill nature to think, that the charge of walking out a little delicate animal in the grounds, did not imply an absolute injunction to recline, with lounging elegance, upon an easy chair. There are people, I say, who may have so little intelligence as to be of that way of thinking. 'Tis being abominably stupid, I own, but there's no enlightening vulgar minds! There is no making them see the merit of quitting an animal for a gentleman; especially for a gentleman in such penury; who has no means to recompense any attentions with which he may be indulged."

Juliet, more offended, now, even than confused, would willingly have torn her gown to hasten her release; but she was still sore, from the taunts of Mrs. Ireton, upon a recent similar mischief.

They were presently joined by the Arramedes; and Mrs. Ireton, secure of new admirers, felt her powers of pleasantry encrease every moment.

"I hope I shall never fail to acknowledge," she continued, "how supremely I am indebted to those ladies who have had the goodness to recommend this young person to me. I can never repay such kindness, certainly; that would be vastly beyond my poor abilities; for she has the generosity to take an attachment to all that belong to me! It was only this morning that she had the goodness to hold a private conference with my son. Nobody could tell where to find him. He seemed to have disappeared from the whole house. But no! he had only, as Mr. Loddard afterwards informed me, stept into the Temple, with Miss Ellis."

Sir Jaspar now, surprised and shocked, lifted up his eyes; but their quick penetration instantly read innocence in the indignation expressed in those of Juliet.

Mrs. Ireton, however, saw only her own triumph, in the malicious simpers of Miss Brinville, the spiteful sneers of Mrs. Maple, and the haughty scorn of Lady Arramede.

Charmed, therefore, with her brilliant success, she went on. "How I may be able to reward kindness so extraordinary, I can't pretend to say. I am so stupid, I am quite at a loss what to devize that may be adequate to such services; for the attentions bestowed upon my son in the morning, I see equally displayed to his uncle at noon. Though there is some partiality, I think, too, shewn to Ireton. I won't affirm it; but I am rather afraid there is some partiality shewn to Ireton; for though the conference has been equally interesting, I make no doubt, with Sir Jaspar, it has not had quite so friendly an appearance. The open air is very delightful, to be sure; and a beautiful prospect helps to enliven one's ideas; but still, there is something in complete retirement that seems yet more romantic and amicable. Ireton was so impressed with this idea, as I am told; for I don't pretend to speak from my own personal knowledge upon subjects of so much importance; but I am told,—Mr. Loddard informs me, that Ireton was so sensible to the advantage of having the honours of an exclusive conference, that he not only chose that retired spot, but had the precaution, also, to lock the door. I don't mean to assert this! it may be all a mistake, perhaps. Miss Ellis can tell best."

Neither the steadiness of innate dignity, nor the fearlessness of conscious innocence, could preserve Juliet from a sensation of horrour, at a charge which she could not deny, though its implications were false and even atrocious. She saw, too, that, at the words "lock the door," Sir Jaspar again raised his investigating eyes, in which there was visibly a look of disturbance. She would not, however, deign to make a vindication, lest she should seem to acknowledge it possible that she might be thought culpable; but, being now disengaged, she silently, and uncontrollably hurt, walked away.

"And pray, Ma'am," said Mrs. Ireton, "if the question is not too impertinent, don't you see Mr. Loddard coming? And who is to take care of Bijou? And where is his basket? And I don't see his cushion?"

Juliet turned round to answer, "I will send them Madam, immediately."

"Amazing condescension!" exclaimed Mrs. Ireton, in a rage that she no longer aimed at disguising: "I shall never be able to shew my sense of such affability! Never! I am vastly too obtuse, vastly too obtuse and impenetrable to find any adequate means of expressing my gratitude. However, since you really intend me the astonishing favour of sending one of my people upon your own errand, permit me to entreat,—if it is not too great a liberty to take with a person of your unspeakable rank,—permit me to entreat that you will make use of the same vehicle for conveying to me your account; for you are vastly too fine a lady for a person so ordinary as I am to keep under her roof. I have no such ambition, I assure you; not an intention of the kind. So pray let me know what retribution I am to make for your trouble. You have taken vast pains, I imagine, to serve me and please me. I imagine so! I must be prodigiously your debtor, I make no doubt!"

"What an excess of impertinence!" cried Lady Arramede.

"She'll never know her place," said Mrs. Maple: "'tis quite in vain to try to serve such a body."

"I never saw such airs in my life!" exclaimed Miss Brinville.

Juliet could endure no more. The most urgent distress seemed light and immaterial, when balanced against submission to treatment so injurious. She walked, therefore, straight forward to the castle, for shelter, immediate shelter, from this insupportable attack; disengaging herself from the spoilt little boy, who strove, nay cried to drag her back; forcing away from her the snarling cur, who would have followed her; and decidedly mute to the fresh commands of Mrs. Ireton, uttered in tones of peremptory, but vain authority.

CHAPTER LIX

OFFENDED, indignant; escaped, yet without safety; free, yet without refuge; Juliet, hurried into the noble mansion, with no view but to find an immediate hiding-place, where, unseen, she might allow some vent to her wounded feelings, and, unmarked, remain till the haughty party should be gone, and she could seek some humble conveyance for her own return.

Concluding her in haste for some commission of Mrs. Ireton's, the servants let her pass nearly unobserved; and she soon came to a long gallery, hung with genealogical tables of the Arundel family, and with various religious reliques, and historical curiosities.

Believing herself alone, and in a place of which the stillness suited her desire of solitude and concealment, she had already shut the door before she saw her mistake. What, then, was her astonishment, what her emotion, when she discerned, seated, and examining a part of the hangings, at the further end of the gallery, the gentle form of Lady Aurora Granville!

Sudden transport, though mingled with a thousand apprehensions, instantly converted every dread that could depress into every hope that could revive her. A start evinced that she was seen. She endeavoured to courtesy, and would have advanced; but, the first moment over, fear, uncertainty, and conflicting doubts took place of its joy, and robbed her of force. Her dimmed eyes perceived not the smiling pleasure with which Lady Aurora had risen at her approach; her breast heaved quick; her heart swelled almost to suffocation; and, wholly disordered, she leaned against a window-frame cut in the immensely thick walls of the castle.

Lady Aurora now ran fleetly forward, exclaiming, in a voice of which the tender melody spoke the softness of her soul, "Miss Ellis! My dear Miss Ellis! have I, indeed, the happiness to meet with you again? O! if you could know how I have desired, have pined for it!—But,—are you ill?—You cannot be angry? Miss Ellis! sweet Miss Ellis! Can you ever have believed that it has been my fault that I have appeared so unkind, so hard, so cruel?"

With a fulness of joy that, in conquering doubt, overpowered timidity, Juliet now, with rapturous tears, and resistless tenderness, flung herself upon the neck of Lady Aurora, whom she encircled with her arms, and strained fondly to her bosom.

But the same vent that gave relief to internal oppression brought her to a sense of external impropriety: she felt that it was rather her part to receive than to bestow such marks of affection. She drew back; and her cheeks were suffused with the most vivid scarlet, when she observed the deep colour which died those of Lady Aurora at this action; though evidently with the blushes of surprise, not of pride.

Ashamed, and hanging her head, Juliet would have attempted some apology; but Lady Aurora, warmly returning her embrace, cried, "How happy, and how singular a chance that we should have fixed upon this day for visiting Arundel Castle! We have been making a tour to the Isle of Wight and to Portsmouth; and we did not intend to go to Brighthelmstone; so that I had no hope, none upon earth, of such a felicity as that of seeing my dear Miss Ellis. I need not, I think, say it was not I who formed our plan, when I own that we had no design to visit Brighthelmstone, though I knew, from Lady Barbara Frankland, that Miss Ellis was there?"

"Alas! I fear," answered Juliet, "the design was to avoid Brighthelmstone! and to avoid it lest a blessing such as I now experience should fall to my lot! Ah, Lady Aurora! by the pleasure,—the transport, rather, with which your sudden sight has made me appear to forget myself, judge my anguish, my desolation, to be banished from your society, and banished as a criminal!"

Lady Aurora shuddered and hid her face. "O Miss Ellis!" she cried, "what a word! never may I hear it,—so applied,—again, lest it should alienate me from those I ought to respect and esteem! and you so good, so excellent, would be sorry to see me estrange myself, even though it were for your own sake, from those to whom I owe gratitude and attachment. I must try to shew my admiration of Miss Ellis in a manner that Miss Ellis herself will not condemn. And will not that be by speaking to her without any disguise? And will she not have the goodness to encourage me to do it? For the world I would not take a liberty with her;—for the universe I would not hurt her!—but if it were possible she could condescend to give, ... however slightly, however imperfectly, some little explanation to .... to .... Mrs. Howel ....."

Juliet here, with a strong expression of horrour, interrupted her: "Mrs. Howel?—O no! I cannot speak with Mrs. Howel!—I had nearly said I can see Mrs. Howel no more! But happier days would soon subdue resentment. And, indeed, what I feel even now, may more justly be called terrour. Appearances have so cruelly misrepresented me, that I have no right to be indignant, nor even surprised that they should give rise to false judgments. I have no right to expect,—in a second instance,—unknown, friendless, lonely as I am! a trusting angel! a Lady Aurora!"

The tears of Lady Aurora now flowed as fast as her own. "If I have been so fortunate," she cried, "as to inspire such sweet kindness in so noble a mind, even in the midst of its unhappiness, I shall always prize it as the greatest of honours, and try to use it so as to make me become better; that you may never wound me by retracting it, nor be wounded yourself by being ashamed of your partiality."

With difficulty Juliet now forbore casting herself at the feet of Lady Aurora, the hem of whose garment she would have kissed with extacy, had not her own pecuniary distresses, and the rank of her young friend, made her recoil from what might have the semblance of flattery. She attempted not to speak; conscious of the inadequacy of all that she could utter for expressing what she felt, she left to the silent eloquence of her streaming, yet transport-glittering eyes, the happy task of demonstrating her gratitude and delight.

With calmer, though extreme pleasure, Lady Aurora perceived the impression which she had made. "See," she cried, again embracing her; "see whether I trust in your kindness, when I venture, once more, to renew my earnest request, my entreaty, my petition—"

"O! Lady Aurora! Who can resist you? Not I! I am vanquished! I will tell you all! I will unbosom myself to you entirely!"

"No, my Miss Ellis, no! not to me! I will not even hear you! Have I not said so? And what should make me change? All I have been told by Lady Barbara Frankland of your exertions, has but increased my admiration; all she has written of your sufferings, your disappointments, and the patient courage with which you have borne them, has but more endeared you to my heart. No explanation can make you fairer, clearer, more perfect in my eyes. I take, indeed, the deepest interest in your welfare; but it is an interest that makes me proud to wait, not curious to hear; proud, my Miss Ellis, to shew my confidence, my trust in your excellencies! If, therefore, you will have the goodness to speak, it must be to others, not to me! I should blush to be of the number of those who want documents, certificates, to love and honour you!"

Again Juliet was speechless; again all words seemed poor, heartless, unworthy to describe the sensibility of her soul, at this touching proof of a tenderness so consonant to her wishes, yet so far surpassing her dearest expectations. She hung over her ingenuous young friend; she sighed, she even sobbed with unutterable delight; while tears of rapture rolled down her glowing cheeks, and while her eyes were lustrous with a radiance of felicity that no tears could dim.

Charmed, and encouraged, Lady Aurora continued: "To those, then, who have not had the happiness to see you so justly; who dwell only upon the singularity of your being so .... alone, and so .... young,—O how often have I told them that I was sure you as little knew as merited their evil constructions! How often have I wished to write to you! how certain have I felt that all your motives to concealment, even the most respectable, would yield to so urgent a necessity, as that of clearing away every injurious surmise! Speak, therefore, my Miss Ellis, though not to me! Even from them, when you have trusted them, I will hear nothing till the time of your secresy is over; that I may give them an example of the discretion they must observe with others. Yet speak! have the goodness to speak, that every body,—my uncle Denmeath himself,—and even Mrs. Howel,—may acknowledge and respect your excellencies and your virtues as I do! And then, my Miss Ellis, who shall prevent,—who will even desire to prevent my shewing to the whole world my sense of your worth, and my pride in your friendship?"

The struggles that now heaved the breast of Juliet were nearly too potent for her strength. She gasped for breath; she held her hand to her heart; and when, at length, the kind caresses and gentle pleadings of Lady Aurora, brought back her speech, she painfully pronounced, "Shall I repay goodness so exquisite, by filling with regret the sweet mind that intends me only honour and consolation? Must the charm of such unexpected kindness, even while it penetrates my heart with almost piercing delight, entail, from its resistless persuasion, a misery upon the rest of my days, that may render them a burthen from which I may hourly sigh,—nay pray, to be delivered?"

Seized with horrour and astonishment, Lady Aurora exclaimed, "Oh heaven, no! I must be a monster if I would not rather die, immediately die, than cause you any evil! Miss Ellis, my dear Miss Ellis! forget I have made such a request, and forgive my indiscretion! With all your misfortunes, Miss Ellis, all your so undeserved griefs, you are yet quite a stranger to sorrow, compared to that which I should experience, if, through me, through my means, you should be exposed to any fresh injury!"

"Angelic goodness!" cried Juliet, deeply affected: "I blush, I blush to hear you without casting myself entirely into your power, without making you immediate arbitress of my fate! Yet,—since you demand not my confidence for your own, satisfaction,—can I know that to spread it beyond yourself,—your generous self!—might involve me in instantaneous earthly destruction, and, voluntarily, suffer your very benevolence to become its instrument? With regard to Lord Denmeath,—to your uncle,—I must say nothing; but with regard to Mrs. Howel,—let me conjure your ladyship to consent to my utterly avoiding her, that I may escape the dreadful accusations and reproaches that my cruel situation forbids me to repel. I have no words to paint the terrible impression she has left upon my mind. All that I have borne from others is short of what I have suffered from that lady! The debasing suspicions of Mrs. Maple, the taunting tyranny of Mrs. Ireton, though they make me blush to owe,—or rather, to earn from them the subsistence without which I know not how to exist; have yet never smote so rudely and so acutely to my inmost heart, as the attack I endured from Mrs. Howel! They rob me, indeed, of comfort, of rest, and of liberty—but they do not sever me from Lady Aurora!"

"Alas, my Miss Ellis! and have I, too, joined in the general persecution against such afflicted innocence? I feel myself the most unpardonable of all not to have acquiesced, without one ungenerous question, or even conjecture; in full reliance upon the right and the necessity of your silence. I ought to have forseen that if it were not improper you should comply, your own noble way of thinking would have made all entreaty as useless as it has been impertinent. Yet when prejudice alone parts us, how could I help trying to overcome it? And even my brother, though he would forfeit, I believe, his life in your defence; and though he says he is sure you are all purity and virtue; and though he thinks that there is nothing upon earth that can be compared with you;—even he has been brought to agree to the cruel resolution, that I should defer knitting myself closer to my Miss Ellis, till she is able to have the goodness to let us know—"

She stopt, alarmed, for the cheeks of Juliet were suddenly dyed with the deepest crimson; though the transient tint faded away as she pronounced, "Lord Melbury!—even Lord Melbury!—" and they became pale as death, while, in a faint voice, and with stifled emotion, she added, "He is right! He acts as a brother; and as a brother to a sister whom he can never sufficiently appreciate.—And yet, the more I esteem his circumspection, the more deeply I must be wounded that calumny,—that mystery,—that dire circumstance, should make me seem dangerous, where, otherwise—"

Unable longer to constrain her feelings, she sunk upon a seat and wept.

"O Miss Ellis? What have I done?" cried Lady Aurora. "How have I been so barbarous, so inconsiderate, so unwise? If my poor brother had caused you this pain, how should I have blamed him? And how grievously would he have repented! How severely, then, ought I to be reproached! I who have done it myself, without his generous precipitancy of temper to palliate such want of reflection!—"

The sudden entrance of Selina here interrupted the conversation. She came tripping forward, to acquaint Lady Aurora that the party had just discerned a magnificent vessel; and that every body said if her ladyship did not come directly, it would be sailed away.

At sight of Juliet, she ran to embrace her, with the warmest expressions of friendship; unchecked by a coldness which she did not observe, though now, from the dissatisfaction excited by so unseasonable an intrusion, it was far more marked, than while it had been under the qualifying influence of contempt.

But when she found that neither caresses, nor kind words, could make her share with Lady Aurora, even for a moment, the attention of Juliet, she became a little confused; and, drawing her apart, asked what was the matter? consciously, without waiting for any answer, running into a string of simple apologies, for not speaking to her in public; which she should always, she said, do with the greatest pleasure; for she thought her the most agreeable person in the whole world; if it were not, that, nobody knowing her, it would look so odd.

All answer, save a smile half disdainful, half pitying, was precluded by the appearance of the Arramedes, Mrs. Ireton, and Miss Brinville; who announced to Lady Aurora that the ship was already out of sight.

Upon perceiving Juliet, they were nearly as much embarrassed as herself; for though she instantly retreated, it was evident that she had been sitting by the side of Lady Aurora, in close and amicable conference.

An awkward general silence ensued, when Juliet, hearing other steps, was moving off; but Lady Aurora, following, and holding out her hand, affectionately said, "Are you going, Miss Ellis? Must you go? And will you not bid me adieu?"

Touched to the soul at this public mark of kindness, Juliet was gratefully returning, when the voice of Lord Melbury spoke his near approach. Trembling and changing colour, her folded hands demanded excuse of Lady Aurora for a precipitate yet reluctant flight; but she had still found neither time nor means to escape, when Lord Melbury, who was playing with young Loddard, entered the gallery, saying, "Aurora, your genealogical studies have lost you a most beautiful sea-view."

The boy, spying Juliet, whom he was more than ever eager to join when he saw that she strove to avoid notice; darted from his lordship, calling out, "Ellis! Ellis! look! look! here's Ellis!"

Lord Melbury, with an air of the most animated surprize and delight, darted forward also, exclaiming, "Miss Ellis! How unexpected a pleasure! The moment I saw Mrs. Ireton I had some hope I might see, also, Miss Ellis—but I had already given it up as delusory."*

Again the fallen countenance of Juliet brightened into sparkling beauty. The idea that even Lord Melbury had been infected by the opinions which had been circulated to her disadvantage, had wounded, had stung her to the quick: but to find that, notwithstanding he had been prevailed upon to acquiesce that his sister, while so much mystery remained, should keep personally aloof, his own sentiments of esteem remained unshaken; and to find it by so open, and so prompt a testimony of respect and regard, displayed before the very witnesses who had sought to destroy, or invalidate, every impression that might be made in her favour, was a relief the most exquisitely welcome to her disturbed and fearful mind.

Eager and rapid enquiries concerning her health, uttered with the ardour of juvenile vivacity, succeeded this first address. The party standing by, looked astonished, even abashed; while the face of Lady Aurora recovered its wonted expression of sweet serenity.

Mrs. Ireton, now, was seized with a desire the most violent, to repossess a *protegée* whose history and situation seemed daily to grow more wonderful. With a courtesy, therefore, as foreign from her usual manners, as from her real feelings, she said, "Miss Ellis, I am sure, will have the goodness to help me home with my two little companions? I am sure of that. She could not be so unkind as to leave the poor little things in the lurch?"

Indignant as Juliet had felt at the treatment which she had

received, resentment at this moment found no place in her mind; she was beginning, therefore, a civil, however decided excuse; when Mrs. Ireton, suspicious of her purpose, flung herself languishingly upon a seat, and complained that she was seized with such an immoderate pain in her side, that, if somebody would not take care of the two *little souls*, she should arrive at Brighthelmstone a corpse.

The Arramedes, Miss Brinville, and Selina, all declared that it was impossible to refuse so essential a service to a health so delicate.

The fear, now, of a second public scene, with the dread lest Lord Melbury might be excited to speak or act in her favour, forced the judgment of Juliet to conquer her inclination, in leading her to defer the so often given dismission till her return to Brighthelmstone; she acceded, therefore, though with cruel unwillingness, to what was required.

Mrs. Ireton instantly recovered; and with the more alacrity, from observing that Lady Barbara Frankland joined the group, at this moment of victory. "Take the trouble, then, if you please, Ma'am," she replied, in her usual tone of irony; "if it will not be too great a condescension, take the trouble to carry Bijou to the coach. And bid Simon keep him safe while you come back,—if it is not asking quite too great a favour,—for Mr. Loddard. And pray bring my wrapping cloak with you, Ma'am. You'll be so good, I hope, as to excuse all these liberties? I hope so, at least! I flatter myself you'll excuse them. And, if the cloak should be heavy, I dare say Simon will give you his arm. Simon is a man of gallantry, I make no doubt. Not that I pretend to know; but I take it for granted he is a man of gallantry."

Juliet looked down, repentant to have placed herself, even for another moment, in a power so merciless. Lord Melbury and Lady Aurora, each hurt and indignant, advanced, uttering kind speeches: while Lady Barbara, still younger and more unguarded, seizing the little dog, exclaimed "No, I'll carry Bijou myself, Mrs. Ireton. Poor Miss Ellis looks so tired! I'll take care of him all the way to Brighthelmstone myself. Dear, pretty little creature!" Then, skipping behind Lady Aurora, "Nasty whelp!" she whispered, "how I'll pinch him for being such a plague to that sweet Miss Ellis! Perhaps that will mend him!"

The satisfaction of Lady Aurora at this trait glistened in her soft eyes; while Lord Melbury, enchanted, caught the hand of the spirited little lady, and pressed it to his lips; though, ashamed of his own vivacity, he let it go before she had time to withdraw it. She coloured deeply, but visibly with no unpleasant sensation; and, grasping the little dog, hid her blushes, by uttering a precipitate farewell upon the bosom of Lady Aurora; who smilingly, though tenderly, kissed her forehead.

An idea that teemed with joy and happiness rose high in the breast of Juliet, as she looked from Lord Melbury to Lady Barbara. Ah! there, indeed, she thought, felicity might find a residence! there, in the rare union of equal worth, equal attractions, sympathising feelings, and similar condition!

"And I, too," cried Lord Melbury, "must have the honour to make myself of some use; if Mrs. Ireton, therefore, will trust Mr. Loddard to my care, I will convey him safely to Brighthelmstone, and overtake my sister in the evening. And by this means we shall lighten the fatigue of Mrs. Ireton, without increasing that of Miss Ellis."

He then took the little boy in his arms; playfully dancing him before the little dog in those of Lady Barbara.

The heart of Juliet panted to give utterance to the warm acknowledgments with which it was fondly beating; but mingled fear and discretion forced her to silence.

All the evil tendencies of malice, envy, and ill will, pent up in the breast of Mrs. Ireton, now struggled irresistibly for vent; yet to insist that Juliet should take charge of Mr. Loddard, for whom Lord Melbury had offered his services; or even to force upon her the care of the little dog, since Lady Barbara had proposed carrying him herself, appeared no longer to exhibit dependency: Mrs. Ireton, therefore, found it expedient to be again taken ill; and, after a little fretful moaning, "I feel quite shaken," she cried, "quite in a tremour. My feet are absolutely numbed. Do get me my furred clogs,* Miss Ellis; if I may venture to ask such a favour. I would not be troublesome, but you will probably find them in the carriage. Though perhaps I have left them in the hall. You will have the condescension to help the coachman and Simon to make a search. And then pray run back, if it won't fatigue you too much, and tie them on for me."

If Juliet now coloured, at least it was not singly; the cheeks of Lady Aurora, of Lady Barbara, and of Lord Melbury were equally crimsoned.

"Let me, Mrs. Ireton," eagerly cried Lord Melbury "have the honour to be Miss Ellis's deputy."

"No, my lord," said Juliet, with spirit: "grateful and proud as I should feel to be honoured with your lordship's assistance, it must not be in a business that does not belong to me. I will deliver the orders to Simon. And as Mrs. Ireton is now relieved from her anxiety concerning Mr. Loddard, I beg permission, once more, and finally, to take my leave."

Gravely then courtsying to Mrs. Ireton, and bowing her head with an expression of the most touching sensibility to her three young supporters, she quitted the gallery.

END OF THE THIRD VOLUME

VOLUME IV

BOOK VII

CHAPTER LX

JULIET was precipitately followed by Lord Melbury.

"It is not, then," he cried, "your intention to return to Mrs. Ireton?"

"No, my lord, never!"

She had but just uttered these words, when, immediately facing her, she beheld Mrs. Howel.

A spectre could not have made her start more affrighted, could not have appeared to her more horrible. And Lord Melbury, who earnestly, at the same moment, had pronounced, "Tell me whither, then,—" stopping abruptly, looked confounded.

"May I ask your lordship to take me to Lady Aurora?" Mrs. Howel coldly demanded.

"Aurora?—Yes;—she is there, Ma'am;—still in the gallery."

Mrs. Howel presented him her hand, palpably to force him on with her; and stalked past Juliet, without any other demonstration of perceiving her than what was unavoidably manifested by an heightened air of haughty disdain.

Lord Melbury, distressed, would still have hung back; but Mrs. Howel, taking his arm, proceeded, as if without observing his repugnance.

Juliet, in trembling dismay, glided on till she entered a vacant apartment, of which the door was open. To avoid intrusion, she was shutting herself in; but, upon some one's applying, nearly the next minute, for admittance, the fear of new misconstruction forced her to open the door. What, then, was her shock at again viewing Mrs. Howel! She started back involuntarily, and her countenance depicted undisguised horrour.

With a brow of almost petrifying severity, sternly fixing her eyes upon Juliet, Mrs. Howel, for a dreadful moment, seemed internally suspended, not between hardness and mercy, but between accusation and punishment. At length, in a tone, from the deep sounds of which Juliet shrunk, but had no means to retire, she slowly pronounced, while her head rose more loftily at every word, "You abscond from Mrs. Ireton, though she would permit you to remain with her? 'Tis to Lord Melbury that you reveal your purpose; and the inexperienced youth whom you would seduce, is the only person that can fail to discover your ultimate design, in taking the moment of meeting with him, for quitting the honourable protection which snatches you from want, if not from disgrace: at the same time that it offers security to a noble family, justly alarmed for the morals, if not for the honour of its youthful and credulous chief."

The terrour which, in shaking the nerves, seemed to have clouded even the faculties of Juliet, now suddenly subsided, superseded by yet more potent sensations of quick resentment. "Hold, Madam!" she cried: "I may bear with cruelty and injustice, for I am helpless! but not with insult, for I am innocent!"

Mrs. Howel, surprised, paused an instant; but then harshly went on, "This cant, young woman, can only delude those who are ignorant of the world. Whatever you may chuse to utter to me of that sort will be perfectly null. What I have to say is simple; what you have to offer must, of course, be complicate. But I have no time to throw away upon rants and rodomontades, and I have no patience to waste upon impostors. Hear me then without reply."

"Not to reply, Madam, will cost me little," indignantly cried Juliet: "but to hear you,—pardon me, Madam,—force only can exact from me so dreadful a compliance."

She looked round, but not having courage to open a further door, nor power to pass by Mrs. Howel, walked to a window.

Not heeding her resistance, and disdaining her emotion, Mrs. Howel continued: "My Lord Melbury is not, it is true, like his sister, under my immediate care; but he is here only to join her ladyship, whom my Lord Denmeath has entrusted to my protection. And, therefore, though he is as noble in mind as in rank, since he is still, in years, but a boy, I must, in honour, consider myself to be equally responsible to my Lord Denmeath for the brother as for the sister. This being the case, I must not leave him to the machinations of an adventurer. In two words, therefore,—Declare yourself for what you are; or return with Mrs. Ireton to Brighthelmstone, and remain under her roof, since she deigns to permit it, till I have restored my young friends, safe and uninjured, to their uncle. Otherwise—"

Juliet, casting up her eyes, as if calling upon heaven for patience, would have opened the window, to seek refuge in the air from sounds of which the shock was insupportable: but Mrs. Howel, offended into yet deeper wrath, advanced with a mien of such rigid austerity, that she lost her purpose in her consternation, and listened irresistibly to what follows: "Otherwise,—mark me, young woman! the still unexplained mystery with which you have made your way into the kingdom, will authorise an application which you will vainly try to elude, and with which you will not dare to prevaricate. You will take your choice, and, in five minutes, you will be summoned to make it known."

With this menace she left the room.

In an agony of terrour, that again absorbed even resentment, Juliet remained motionless, confounded, and incapable of deliberation, till the groom of Mrs. Ireton came to inform her that his lady was ready to set out.

Juliet, scarcely herself knowing her own intentions, precipitately ejaculated, "The crisis is arrived!—I must cast myself upon Lady Aurora!"

The servant said he did not understand her.

"Tell Lady Aurora—;" she cried, "or Lord Melbury,—no, Lady Aurora,—" she stopt, fearfully balancing upon which to fix.

The groom asked what he was to say.

"You will say,—I must beg you to say,—" cried Juliet, endeavouring to recollect herself, "that I desire,—that I wish,—that I take the liberty to request that Lady Aurora will have the goodness to honour me,—that I shall be eternally obliged if her ladyship will honour me with a few moment's conversation!"

The groom went; and almost the next instant, she heard the fleet step of Lady Aurora approaching, and her soft voice, with unusual emphasis, pronounce, "Pardon me, dear Madam, but I could not refuse her for a thousand worlds!"

"She ought not to refuse her, Mrs. Howel!" added, with fervency, the voice of Lord Melbury; "in humanity, in justice, in decency, Aurora ought not to refuse her! Whatever may be your fears or objections to an intimacy, there can be none to common civility; for though we know not what Miss Ellis has been, we see what she now is;—a pattern of elegance, sweetness, and delicacy."

"A moment, my lord!—one moment, Lady Aurora!" answered Mrs. Howel; "we may be overheard here;—honour me with a moment's attention in another room." She seemed drawing them away, and not a word more reached Juliet.

A dreadful ten minutes preceded any farther information: a quick step, then, followed by a tap at the door, reawakened at once terrour and hope. She awaited, motionless, its opening, but then saw neither the object she desired, nor that which she dreaded; neither Lady Aurora nor Mrs. Howel, but Lord Melbury.

Affrighted by the threatened vengeance of Mrs. Howel, but irresistibly charmed by his generous defence, and trusting esteem, Juliet looked so disturbed, yet through her disturbance so gratified, that Lord Melbury, evidently much agitated himself, approached her with a vivacity of pleasure that he did not seek to repress, and could not have disguised.

"Miss Ellis will, I am sure, forgive my intrusion," he cried, "when I tell her that it is made in the name of my sister. Aurora is grieved past all expression not to wait upon you herself; but Mrs. Howel is in such haste to depart, from her fear of travelling after sun-set, that it is not possible to detain her. Poor Aurora sends you a thousand apologies, and entreats you not to think ill of her for appearing thus unfeeling—"

"Think ill of Lady Aurora?" interrupted Juliet, "I think her an angel!—"

"She is very near it, indeed!" cried Lord Melbury, ardently; "as near it, I own, as I wish her; for I don't see, without wings, and flying up to heaven, how she can well be nearer! However, since you are so kind, so liberal, as to do her that justice, would it be possible that you could communicate, through me, what you had the goodness to intend saying to her? She is quite broken-hearted at going away with an appearance of such unkindness. Can you give her this consolation?"

"Oh, my lord!" answered Juliet, with an energy that shewed her off all guard, "if I might hope for Lady Aurora's support—for your lordship's protection,—with what transport would my o'er-burthened heart,—" Seized with sudden dread of Mrs. Howel, she stopt abruptly, and fearfully looked around.

Enchanted by a prospect of some communication, Lord Melbury warmly exclaimed, "Miss Ellis, I swear to you, by all that I hold most sacred, that if you will do me so great an honour as to trust me to be the bearer of your confidence to my sister, no creature upon earth, besides, shall ever, without your permission, hear what you may unfold! and it shall be my whole study to merit your good opinion, and to shew you my respect."

"O my lord! O Lord Melbury," cried Juliet, "what hopes, what sweet balsamic hopes you pour into my wounded bosom! after sufferings by which I have been nearly,—nay, through which I have even wished myself demolished!—"

Lord Melbury, inexpressibly touched, eagerly, yet tenderly, answered, "Name, name what there is I can be so happy as to do! Your wishes shall be my entire direction. And if I can offer you any services, I shall console Aurora, and, permit me to say, myself, still more than you."

"I will venture, then, my lord,—I must venture!—to lay open my perilous situation!—And yet I may put your feelings,—alas!—to a test,—alas, my lord!—that not all your virtues, nor even your compassion may withstand!"

Trembling almost as violently as she trembled herself, from impatience, from curiosity, from charmed interest, and indescribable wonder, Lord Melbury bent forward, so irresistibly and so palpably to take her hand, that Juliet, alarmed, drew back; and calling forth the self-command of which her sorrows, her terrours, and her hopes had conjointly bereft her, "If I have been guilty," she cried, "of any indiscretion, my lord, in this hasty, almost involuntary disposition to confidence,—excuse,—and do not punish an errour that has its source only in a—perhaps—too high wrought esteem!—"

Starting with a look nearly of horrour, "You kill me," he

cried, "Miss Ellis, if you suspect me to be capable, a second time, of dishonouring the purest of sisters by forgetting the respect due to her friend!—"

"No, my lord, no!" warmly interrupted Juliet; "whatever you think dishonourable I am persuaded your lordship would find impracticable: but the stake is so great,—the risk so tremendous,—and failure would be so fatal!—"

Her perturbation now became nearly overpowering; and, notwithstanding she was prepared, and resolved, to disclose herself, her ability seemed unequal to her will, and her breast heaved with sighs so oppressive, that though she frequently began with—"I will now,—I must now,—" she strove vainly to finish her sentence.

After anxiously and with astonishment waiting some minutes, "Why does Miss Ellis thus hesitate?" cried Lord Melbury. "What can I say or do to remove her scruples?"

"I have none, my lord, none! but I have so solemnly been bound to silence! and ..."

"Oh, but you are bound, now, to speech!" cried he, with spirit; "and, to lessen your inquietude, and satisfy your delicacy, I will shew you the way to openness and confidence, by making a disclosure first. Will you, then, have more reliance upon my discretion?"

"You are too,—too good, my lord!" cried Juliet, again brightening up; "but I dream not of such indulgence: 'tis to your benevolence only I apply."

"Oh, but I have a fancy to trust you! Aurora will be delighted that I should have found such a confidant. Yet I have nothing positive,—nothing fixed,—to say, it is but an idea,—a thought,—a kind of distant perspective ..."

He coloured, and looked embarrassed, yet evidently with feelings of pleasure.

A radiant smile now illumined the face of Juliet, "Ah! my lord," she cried, "if I might utter a conjecture,—I had almost said a wish—"

"Why not?" cried he, laughing.

"Your lordship permits me?—Well, then, let me name—Lady Barbara Frankland?—"

"Is it possible?" cried he, while the blood mantled in his

cheeks, and pleasure sparkled in his eyes; "what can have led you to such a thought? How can you possibly have suspected ... She is still so nearly a child...."

"It is true, my lord, but, also, how amiable a child! how richly endowed with similar qualities to those which, at this instant, engage my gratitude!—"

He bowed, with smiling delight. "I will not deny," he cried, "that you have penetrated into my secret; though as yet, in fact, it is hardly even a secret; for we have not,—hitherto,—you will easily believe, conversed together upon the subject! Nor shall we say a word about it, together, till I have made the tour.* But I will frankly own, that we have been brought up from our very cradles, with this notion, mutually. It was the wish of my father even in our infancy.—"

"Hold it then sacred!" cried Juliet, with strong emotion. "Happy, thrice happy, in such a wish for your guide!"

She burst into tears.

"How your sorrows," said he, tenderly, "affect me! and how they interest me more deeply every moment! Tell me, then, sweet Miss Ellis!—amiable friend of my sister!—tell me why you are thus afflicted? and how, and in what manner, there is the least possibility that I may offer you my services, or procure you any consolation?"

The door here was abruptly opened by Mrs. Howel.

Red with constrained rage, yet assuming a courteous demeanour, "Your lordship will pardon," she cried, "my intrusion; but Lady Aurora is so delicate, that I am always uneasy at keeping her ladyship out late."

Highly provoked, yet deeply confused, Lord Melbury stammered that he was extremely sorry to have detained them, and begged that they would set out; promising to follow immediately.

Civilly smiling, though fixing her eyes upon his face in a manner that doubled his embarrassment, she entreated him to use his own influence with Lady Aurora, to prevail upon her ladyship to proceed.

Too much perturbed to resist, he ran out of the room; casting a glance at Juliet, as he passed, expressive of his chagrin at this interruption, and full of sensibility and respect.

Juliet dreadfully affrighted, and utterly confounded, had hid her streaming eyes, and conscious blushes, with her handkerchief, upon the entrance of Mrs. Howel; but, when left alone with that tremendous lady, mingled terrour and indignation would have urged immediate flight, had she not been apprehensive of seeming to follow, and clandestinely, Lord Melbury.

Benign had been as yet the countenance, and melody itself the voice of Mrs. Howel, compared with the expression of the one, or the sound of the other, while she now pronounced the following words: "The terms, young woman, that I would keep with a person of name and character; the honour and delicacy due to myself in any intercourse with such a one, I set wholly aside in treating with an adventurer. I know all that has passed! I have heard every syllable! Convinced, therefore, of your deep laid scheme, to captivate to his disgrace a youth of an illustrious house, by revealing to him a pretended tale, which you craftily refuse to trust to all who may better judge, or try, its truth; I shall take, without delay, such measures as it behoves should be taken, by a friend of his family, and of himself, to effectually open his eyes to your arts, and to his own danger. In one word, therefore, Will you, and this instant, return to Brighthelmstone under the superintendence of Mrs. Ireton?"

"No, Madam!" Juliet, without hesitation, replied.

"Enough! I shall myself take in charge, then, that you do not quit the castle, till the arrival of a peace-officer;* who may conduct you where you may make your confession with rather more propriety than to a young nobleman!"

Neither native courage, nor resentment of hard usage, could support Juliet against a menace such as this. She changed colour, and sunk, terrified, upon a chair.

Mrs. Howel, after a moment's pause, magisterially moved to the door; whence she took the key, which was within side, and was leaving the room; but Juliet, struck with horrour at such a preparation for confinement, started up, exclaiming, "If you reduce me, Madam, to cry for help, I must cast myself at once upon the protection of Lord Melbury;—and then assure yourself,—be very sure! he will not suffer this outrage!"

"This affrontery exceeds all credibility! Assure yourself, however, young woman, and be very sure, in return! that I shall not be intimidated by an impostor, from detecting imposition; nor from consigning it to infamy!"

With a scoffing smile of power, she then left the room, locking the door without.

Consternation alone had prevented Juliet from rushing past her, and forcing a passage; though such violence was as opposite to her nature, as to propriety, and to the habits of her sex.

Alone, and a prisoner, the first reflexion that found way through her disturbance, served less to diminish her terrour than to awaken new alarm. It represented to her all the blighting horrours of calumny, in being known to place her confidence in Lord Melbury, while forced to exact that he himself should guard her secret. She felt as if cast upon a precipice, from which, though a kind hand might save, the least imprudence might precipitate her downfall. She struggled for fortitude, she prayed for patience. What, indeed, she cried, are any sufferings that Mrs. Ireton can inflict, compared with those I am flying? If I must submit to transient tyranny, or hazard incurring misery as durable as my existence,—can I hesitate to which I shall yield?

Hastily, now, she looked for the bell, and rang it repeatedly, till some one through the door demanded her orders.

"Acquaint Mrs. Ireton," she answered, "that I am ready to attend her to Brighthelmstone."

The door was almost instantly unlocked, and Mrs. Howel again appeared. "I deign not, young woman," she sternly said, "to enquire into the reasons, the arts, or the apprehensions that may have induced your repentance: I am aware that whatever you would tell me is precisely what I ought not to believe. I come merely to give you notice that, if you venture to attempt keeping up any sort of correspondence with Lady Aurora Granville, or with Lord Melbury, nothing can save you from detection and punishment. Mark me well! You will be properly watched."

She then retired, shutting, but no longer locking the door.

All of philosophy, of judgment, or of forbearance that the indignant Juliet possessed, was nearly insufficient to keep her firm to her concession upon an harangue thus insulting. Necessity, however, inculcated prudence. I will await, she cried, better days! I will learn my ultimate doom ere I seek any mitigation to my passing sorrows. If all end well,—this will be as nothing!—forgiven and forgotten at once! If ill,—in so overwhelming a weight of woe, 'twill be still less material!

CHAPTER LXI

JULIET was aroused from this species of patient despondency by the groom of Mrs. Ireton, who broke in upon her with orders to enquire, whether it were her intention to detain his lady at the castle all night? adding, that all the rest of the party had been gone some time.

Juliet followed him to the hall, where she was greeted, as usual, with sharp reproaches, conveyed through ironical compliments.

Upon reaching the portico, she perceived, hastily returned, and dismounting his horse, Lord Melbury.

He held back, with an air of irresolution, till Mrs. Ireton, to whom he distantly bowed, was seated; and then, suddenly springing forward, offered his hand to her depressed and neglected dependent.

Blushingly, yet gratefully she accepted his assistance; and, having placed her in the coach, and made a slight compliment to Mrs. Ireton, the carriage drove off; and, the first amazement over, the envenomed taunts of that lady were indulged in a full scope of unrestrained malignity during the whole little journey.

Juliet scarcely heard them; new perplexity, though mingled with hope and pleasure, affected and occupied her. Lord Melbury, in aiding her into the carriage, had said, "I am afraid you will lose your shawl;" and, snatching at it, as if to prevent its falling, he enveloped a small packet in the folds which he put into her hands, of which, in her first confusion, she was scarcely conscious; though she felt it the instant that he disappeared.

Was it money? Nothing, in her helpless state, could be more welcome; yet to what construction, even from himself, might not its acceptance be liable? Nevertheless, with so suspicious and ill-judging a witness by her side, to call him back, might seem accusing him of intentions of which she sincerely believed him guiltless.

The moment that she could disengage herself from her troublesome charges, she stole to her chamber, where she read the following words, written with a pencil upon the cover of a letter.

"How shall I ever endure myself again, should Miss Ellis withdraw her kind promise of communication, in resentment of an acquiescence in quitting her, for which already I begin almost to disdain myself? Yet my consent was granted to two of the purest of her admirers and well wishers. I could not have been biassed an instant by those who know not how to appreciate her. Hold, therefore, amiable Miss Ellis, your condescending promise sacred, though I make a momentary cession of my claim upon it, to the pleadings of those who are every way better entitled to judge than I am, of what will best demonstrate the high and true respect felt for Miss Ellis, by

"Her most obedient,

"humble servant,

"MELBURY.

"P. S. Aurora had no time to entreat for your permission to lodge the enclosed trifle in your hands. She is ashamed of its insignificance; but she has a plan, which I shall unfold when I have next the honour of seeing you, to solicit, as a mark of your confidence, becoming, through me, your banker till your affairs are arranged.

"Pardon this paper. I write on horseback, to catch you flying."

Soft were the tears of Juliet, and radiant the eyes whence they flowed, as she perused these words. Nor could she hesitate in accepting the offering, though the little gold-purse,* which contained it, was marked with the cypher of Lord Melbury. It was presented in the name of his sister; a sister whom he revered as truly as he loved; such a name, therefore, sanctioned both the loan and the kindness. And the intimation, given by the young peer himself, of the equal influence over his mind possessed by Lady Barbara Frankland, proclaimed and proved the purity of his regard, and the innocence of his intentions.

An idea now struck her, that bounded to her heart with rapture. Might not the sum of which she permitted herself to take the disposal, prove the means of re-union with Gabriella? A very small part of it would suffice for the journey; and the rest might enable them, when once together, to make some arrangement for being parted no more.

A plan so soothing could not, even for a moment, present itself to her imagination, unaccompanied by some effort to put it into execution, and she instantly wrote a few lines to her beloved friend; stating the present possibility of their junction, and demanding her opinion, her consent, and her directions, for the immediate accomplishment of so delicious a scheme.

Cheered by a hope so dear to her wishes, so promising to her happiness, Juliet, now, was perfectly contented to continue at Brighthelmstone, till she should receive an answer to her proposal.

But, before its arrival was yet possible, she was called to a messenger, who would deliver his commission only to herself.

She descended, not without perturbation, into the hall; where a countryman told her, that he had been ordered to beg that she would go, at the usual time, the next morning, to the usual place, to meet her old friend.

He was then walking off; but Juliet stopt him, to demand whence he came, and who sent him.

A lady, he answered, who spoke broken English, and who had named five of the clock in the morning.

"Oh yes! Oh yes!" cried Juliet: "I will not fail!" whilst a soft murmur finished with 'Tis herself!—'tis my Gabriella!

What brought her back to Brighthelmstone, now occupied all the thoughts of her friend. Was it a design to fix her abode where her maternal enthusiasm might daily be cherished by visiting the grave of her child? Or, was it for the single indulgence of bathing that melancholy spot once more with her tears?

It was already night, or Juliet would have sought to anticipate the meeting, by some enquiry at their former lodgings: the morning, however, soon arrived, and, nearly with its dawn, she arose, and, by a previous arrangement made with the gardener, quitted the house, to hasten to the church-yard upon the hill.

In her way thither, she was seized, from time to time, with

something like an apprehension that she was pursued; for, though no one came in sight, the stillness of the early morning enabled her to hear, distinctly, a footstep that now seemed to follow her own, now to stop till she had proceeded some yards.

It might merely be some workman;—yet would not a workman overtake her, and pass on? It was more probably some traveller. Nevertheless, she would not ascend the hill without making some examination; and, casting a hasty glance behind her, she perceived a tall man, muffled up, whose air denoted him to be a gentleman; but who instantly hung back.

A thousand anxious doubts were now awakened. Was it possible that she had been summoned upon any false pretence? Gabriella had not written; and though that omission had, at first, appeared the natural result of haste upon her arrival; joined to the difficulty of immediately procuring writing implements, it left an opening to uncertainty upon reflection, by no means satisfactory. That she should not personally have presented herself at the house of Mrs. Ireton, could excite no surprize, for she well knew that Juliet had neither time nor a room at her own command; and to revisit the grave of her child had always been the purpose of Gabriella.

With a slackened and irresolute step, she now went on, till, wistfully looking towards the church-yard, she descried a female, with arms uplifted, that seemed inviting her approach. Relieved and delighted, she then quickened her pace; though, as she advanced, the form retreated, till, gradually, it was wholly out of sight.

This affected and saddened her. The little grave was on the other side of the church. It is there, then, only, she cried, there, where our melancholy meeting took place, that my ever wretched Gabriella will suffer me to rejoin her!

With an aching heart she proceeded, though no Gabriella came forward to give her welcome; but when, upon crossing over to the other side of the church, in full sight of the little grave, no Gabriella was there; and not a human being was visible, she felt again impressed with a fear of imposition, and was turning back to hurry home; when she observed, just mounting the hill, the person by whose pursuit she had already been startled.

Terrour now began to take possession of her mind. She had surely been deluded, and she was evidently followed. She had neither time nor composure for divining why; but she was instantly certain that she could be no object for premeditated robbery; and the unprincipled Sir Lyell Sycamore alone occurred to her, as capable of so cruel a stratagem to enveigle her to a lonely spot. The height of the man was similar: his face was carefully concealed; but, transient as had been her glance, it was obvious to her that he was no labourer, nor countryman.

To descend the hill, would be to meet him: to go on yet further, when not a cottage, perhaps, might be open, would almost seem to expect being overtaken: yet to remain and await him, was out of all question. She saw, therefore, no hope of security, but by endeavouring to regain the street, through a circuitous path, by sudden rapidity of flight.

But, upon gliding, with this design, to the other side of the church, she was struck with amazement to see that the church-door was ajar; and to perceive, at the same instant, a passing shadow, reflected through a window, of some one within the building.

Was this accident? or had it any connection with the tall unknown who followed her?

Filled with wonder and alarm, though a stranger to every species of superstition, her feet staggered, and her presence of mind threatened to play her false; when again a fleeting shadow, of she knew not whom nor what, gleamed athwart a monument.

Summoning now her utmost force, though shaking with nameless apprehensions, she crossed, with celerity, a grave-stone, to gain what appeared to be the quickest route for descending; when the sound of a hasty step, immediately behind her, gave her the fearful intelligence that escape was impossible.

Nevertheless, though nearly overcome with dread, she was pressing on; but some one, rushing abruptly past her, and turning short round, stopt her passage.

Horrour thrilled through her every vein, in the persuasion that she was the destined victim of deliberate delusion, when the words, "It is, indeed, then, you!" uttered in an accent of astonishment, yet with softness, made her hastily raise her eyes,—and raise them upon Harleigh.

Bereft of prudence, in the suddenness of her joy; forgetting self-command, and casting off all guard, all reserve, she rapturously held out to him her willing hands, exclaiming, "Oh, Mr. Harleigh!—are you, then, my destined protector?—my guardian angel!"

Speechless from transported surprize, Harleigh pressed to his lips and to his heart each unresisting hand; while Juliet, whose eyes beamed lustrous with buoyant felicity, was unconscious of the happiness that she bestowed, from the absorption of the delight that she experienced.

"Precious, for ever precious moment!" cried Harleigh, when the power of utterance returned; "Here, on this spot, where first the tortures of the most deadly suspense give way to the most exquisite hopes,—"

The countenance of Juliet now again underwent a change the most sudden; its brilliancy was overclouded; its smiles vanished; its joy died away; not, indeed, to return to its look of horrour and affright, but to convey an expression of the deepest shame and regret; and, with cheeks tingling with burning blushes, she strove to regain her hands; to recover her composure; and to account to him, by relating what had been her dread, and her mistake, for her flattering reception.

But she strove in vain: her efforts to disengage herself had no more that frozen severity which Harleigh had not dared resist; and though her earnestness and distress shewed their sincerity, her varying blushes, her inability to find words, and her uncontroulable emotion, demonstrated, to his quick perception, that to govern her own conflicting feelings, at this critical moment, was as difficult as to resume over his her accustomed dominion.

"Here on this spot," he continued, "this blessed, sacred, hallowed spot! clear, and eternally dismiss, every torturing doubt by which I have so long been martyrized! Here let all baneful mystery, all heart-wounding distrust, be for ever exiled; and here—"

A faint, but earnest, "Oh no! no! no!" now quivered from the lips of Juliet; but Harleigh would not be silenced.

"And here, where you have condescended to call me your

protector,—your destined protector!—a title which gives me claims that never while I live shall be relinquished!—claims which not even yourself, now, can have power to recall—"

"Hear me! hear me!—" interrupted, but vainly, the pleading Juliet; Harleigh, uncontrouled, went on.

"Initiate me, without delay, in the duties of my office. Against whom, and against what may I be your protector? You have called me, too, your guardian-angel; Oh suffer me to call you mine! Consent to that sweet reciprocation, which blends felicity with every care of life! which animates our virtues by our happiness! which secures the performance of every duty, by making every duty an enjoyment!"

A frequent "Alas! alas!" was all that Juliet could gain time to utter, from the rapid energy with which Harleigh overpowered all attempt at remonstrance.

"Why, why," he then cried, with redoubled vivacity; "why not exile now, and repudiate for ever, that terrible rigour of reserve that has so long been at war with your humanity?—Listen to your softer self! It will plead, it will surely plead for gentler measures!"

"Oh no, no, no!" reiterated the agitated Juliet, with a vehemence that would have startled, if not discouraged him, had not another incautious "Alas! alas!" stole its way into the midst of her tremulous negatives; and revealed that her heart, her wishes, her feelings, bore no part in the refusals which her tongue pronounced.

This was not a circumstance to escape Harleigh, who, indescribably touched, fervently exclaimed, "And what, now, shall sunder us? Pardon my presumption if I say us! What is the power,—the earthly power,—while yet I live, and breathe, and feel, that can now compel me to give up the rights with which, from this decisive moment, I hold myself invested? No! our destinies are indissolubly united!—All procrastination,—all concealment must be over! They would now be literally distracting. Why, then, that start?—Why that look?—Can you regret having shewn a little feeling?—a trait of sensibility?—O put a period to this unequalled, unexampled mystery! I am yours! faithfully, honourably yours! Yours to the end of my mortal existence; yours, by my most sacred hopes, far, far longer!—You weep?—not from grief, I trust,—I hope,—not from grief flow those touching tears? Open to me your situation,—your heart! Here, on this sacred, and henceforth happiest spot, where first you have accorded me a ray of hope, let our mutual vows be plighted to all eternity!"

Juliet, whose whole soul seemed dissolved in poignant yet tender distress, cast up to heaven, as if imploring for aid, her irresistibly streaming eyes; when, caught by some shadowy motion to turn them towards the church, she fancied that she beheld again the female, whose appearance and vanishing had been forgotten from the excess of her own emotions.

Startled, she looked more earnestly, and then clearly perceived, though half hidden behind a monument, a form in white; whose dress appeared to be made in the shape, and of the materials, used for our last mortal covering, a shroud. A veil of the same stuff fell over the face of the figure, of which the hands hung down strait at each lank side.

Struck with awe and consternation, Juliet involuntarily ceased her struggles for freedom; and Harleigh, who saw her strangely moved, pursuing the direction of her eyes, discerned the object by which they had been caught; who now, slowly raising her right hand, waved to them to follow; while, with her left, she pointed to the church, and, uttering a wild shriek, flitted out of sight.

Could it be Elinor? Each felt at the same instant the same terrible apprehension. Harleigh sprang after her; Juliet, almost petrified with affright, was immovable.

The fugitive entered the church, and darted towards the altar; where she threw her left hand over a tablet of white stone, cut in the shape of a coffin, with the action of embracing it; yet in a position to leave evident the following inscription:

"This Stone
Is destined by herself to be the last kind covering
of all that remains of
ELINOR JODDREL:
Who, sick of Life, of Love, and of Despair,
Dies to moulder, and be forgotten."

Casting off her veil when she perceived Harleigh, "Here! Harleigh, here!" she cried, in a tone authoritative, though tremulous, "'tis here you must reciprocate your vows! Here is the spot! Here stands the altar for the happy;—here, the tomb for the hopeless!"

Suspicious of some sinister purpose, Harleigh was at her side with the swiftness of lightening; but not till her fingers were upon the trigger of a pistol, which she had pointed to her temple; though in time, by attaining her arm, and forcibly giving it a new direction, to make her fire the deadly weapon in the air.

Her own design, nevertheless, seconded by the loud din of a pistol, so close to her ear, and let off by her own hand, operated upon her deranged imagination with a belief that her purpose was fulfilled; and she sunk upon the ground, uttering, with a deep groan, "Oh Harleigh! bless the dying Elinor,—and be happy!—"

Harleigh, terrified and shocked, though thankfully perceiving her mistake, dropped down at her side, and supported her head; while his congratulating eyes stole a glance at Juliet; who, at the sound of the pistol, had hastened, aghast, to the spot; but who now, dreading to be seen, retreated.

"Oh Elinor!" he then cried, "what direful infatuation of wrong is this!—What have you done with your nobler, better self?—How have you thus warped your reason and your religion alike, to an equal and terrible defiance of here and hereafter?"

Recovering, at these interrogatories, to conscious failure, and conscious existence, she hastily arose, indignantly spurned at the tablet, looked around for Juliet with every mark of irritation, and, casting a glance of suffering, yet investigating shame at Harleigh, "'Tis again, then," she cried, "abortive!—and, a third time, I am food, for fools,—when I meant to be food only for worms!"*

She then peremptorily demanded Juliet; who, affrighted, was absconding, till shrieks rather than calls forced her forward.

With an exaltation so violent that it seemed incipient frenzy, Elinor hailed her. "Approach, Ellis, approach!" she cried. "Oh chosen of the chosen! Oh born to shew, and prove the perfectibility of earthly happiness, and the falsehood and sophistry of the ignorance and superstition that deny it! Approach! and let me sanction your nuptial contract! I here solemnly give you back your promise. I renounce all tie over your actions, your engagements, your choice. Approach, then, that I may join your hands, while I quaff my last draught of tender poison from the grateful eyes of Harleigh, whose happiness,—my own donation!—will cast a glory upon my exit!"

Juliet stood motionless, pale, almost livid, and appearing nearly as unable to think as to speak. But the feelings of Harleigh were as much too actively alive, as her's seemed morbid. Agitation beat in every pulse, flowed in every vein, throbbed even visibly in his heart, which bounded with tumultuous triumph, that Juliet, now, was liberated from all adverse engagements: and though he sought, and meant, to turn his eyes, with tender pity, upon Elinor, they stole involuntarily, impulsively, glances of extatic felicity at the mute and appalled Juliet.

The watchful Elinor discerned the distraction, which he imagined to be as impenetrable as it was irresistible. Shame, mingled with despondence, superseded her exaltation; and disdainfully, and even wrathfully, she disengaged herself from his hold; but, suspicious of some new violence, he hovered over her with extended arms; and presently caught a glimpse of a second pistol, placed behind the tablet, and, as nearly as possible, out of sight. Her intention could not be doubted; but, forcibly anticipating her movement, he seized the destined instrument of death, and, flying to the porch, fired it also into the air.

Elinor now was confounded; she reddened with confusion, trembled with ire, and seemed nearly fainting with excess of emotion; but, after holding her hands a minute or two crossed over her face, she forced a smile, and said, "Harleigh, our tragi-comedy has a long last act! But you can never, now, believe me dead, till you see me buried. That, next, must follow!" And abruptly she was rushing out of the church, when she was encountered, in the porch, by her foreign servant, accompanied by the whole house of Mrs. Maple.

Juliet, satisfied that this victim to her own passions and delusions, would now fall into proper hands, eagerly glided past them all; and, finding the streets no longer empty, fled back to the mansion of Mrs. Ireton.

CHAPTER LXII

JULIET re-entered her chamber without having been missed, but in a perturbation of mind indescribable; affrighted, confused, overpowered with various and varying sensations; wretched for Elinor; dissatisfied with herself; and yet more at war with what seemed to be her destiny; ejaculating, from time to time, Oh Gabriella! receive, console, strengthen, and direct your terrified,—bewildered friend!—

Unusual sounds from the hall soon announced some disturbance; but, wholly without courage to go forth upon any enquiry, she remained, in trembling ignorance of what was passing; till she was relieved by a visit from Selina, which gave her the extreme satisfaction of hearing that Elinor was actually in the house.

Grief, however, though unmixt with surprize, followed the information, when she heard, also, that Elinor was in so disordered a state, that she had been forced from the church only by the interference of Mr. Naird; for whom Mr. Harleigh had sent; and who had positively told her, that, if she would not submit to be conveyed to some house, and try to repose, he should hold it his duty to send for proper persons to controul and take care of her, as one unfit to be trusted to herself.

Even then, though evidently startled, she would not consent to go back to Lewes, which she had quitted, she loudly declared, for ever: but, after wildly enquiring for Ellis, and being assured that she was returned to Mrs. Ireton's, she was, at length, wrought upon to accept an invitation, which, through measures that were taken by the active Harleigh, Mrs. Ireton had been prevailed with to send to her; and which included her sister and Mrs. Maple.

What else of the history of this transaction was known to Selina, was speedily revealed.

The whole house of Mrs. Maple had been awakened at daylight, by the foreign servant of Elinor; who came to bid Tomlinson call up Mrs. Maple, and acquaint her, that he believed that her niece was determined to make away with herself. She had found means, he said, over night, to induce the clerk of the church at Brighthelmstone to let her have the key of the church, to begin a drawing, of one of the monuments, at sunrise, when no idle loungers would interrupt her: and the clerk, knowing her for a lady of property and fashion, in the neighbourhood, had not had the thought to refuse her. She had made him, the lackey, come for her at Mrs. Maple's, with a post chaise, and wait near the house at three o'clock in the morning: she and Mrs. Golding then got into it, while he attended, as usual, on horseback. They stopt at a place, by the way, to receive a heap of things, that he did not take much notice of, as it was not well light; and then they all gallopped to Brighthelmstone. He thought no harm, all the time, as his lady so often went about oddly, nobody knowing why. She made the chaise stop at the church-yard, and told him, and Golding, to help up with all the things, into the church. She then said she was going to begin her drawing; and bid the postilion wait at some inn, till she sent for him. But she told the lackey to stay in the church-yard. She and Golding were then shut up together a quarter of an hour; when Golding came out, crying. Her lady, she said, had put a white trimmed stuff dress over her cloaths, that made her look as if she were buried alive, and just the same as a ghost; and she was afraid all was not right; for she had made her help to place what she had called a pallet,* for her drawing, upon the altar-table, and it looked just like a coffin; only it was covered over with paper. She had ordered that they should both go to an inn, and return for her, with the chaise, at eight o'clock. Neither of them knew what to make of all this; but so many out of the way things had passed, and nothing had come of them, that, still, they should have done only as they were bid, but that the lackey recollected two loaded pistols, which his lady had made him charge, upon the route, to frighten away robbers, by firing one of them off, she said, if they saw any suspicious persons dodging* them: and these, which had been put carefully into the chaise, Golding had seen, in the hand of her mistress, in the church. This gave him such a panic, that he thought it safest to ride back to Madame Maple's, and tell the whole at once. All the family, upon this alarming news, set out for Brighthelmstone, the moment that the horses could be got ready: and, just as they arrived at the church, Elinor herself, had appeared, bursting from it into the porch.

Her indignation at thus being followed and detected, had been terrible: Who, she asked, had any right to controul her? But that was nothing to her disturbance, when she found that Ellis had vanished. She grew so agitated, that it was frightful, Selina continued, to see her; and looked franticly about her, as if for means to destroy herself: and nothing could urge her to quit the church, or church-yard, whence she eagerly tried to command away all others; till Mr. Harleigh had recourse to Mr. Naird, who had alarmed her into submission. They had then brought her in a chaise, between Mrs. Maple and the surgeon, to Mrs. Ireton's; where, to hide herself, she said, from light and life, she had gloomily consented to go to bed; but she raved, sighed, groaned, started, and was in a state of shame and despair, the most deplorable.

Juliet heard this narration with equal pity and terrour; but no sooner understood that Mrs. Maple had entreated Mr. Harleigh to remain at Brighthelmstone, for a day or two, than she determined to quit the place herself; persuaded that these bloody enterprizes were always reserved for their joint presence.

The nearly exhausted Elinor passed the rest of the day without effort, without speech, and almost without sign of life. But, early on the following morning, Juliet received from her a hasty summons.

Juliet essayed, by every means that she could devise, to avoid obeying it; but every effort of resistance was ineffectual. By compulsion, therefore, and slowly, she mounted the stairs; secretly determining that, should Harleigh also be called upon, she would seize the first instant in which she could elude observation, to escape, not alone from the room, nor from the house, but from Brighthelmstone; whence she would set off, by the quickest conveyance that she could find, for London and Gabriella.

Elinor, muffled up, and looking pale, haggard, and altered, was reclining upon a sofa; not in compliance with the request of her friends, but from an indispensable necessity of repose, after the violent exertions which had recently shaken her already weakened frame. At the entrance of Juliet she lifted up her head, with an air of eager satisfaction, and exclaimed, "You are really, then, here? And you come, at length, to my call? Harleigh is less courteous! Triumphant Harleigh! he leaves me, he says, to take some rest:—rest?—"

She paused, and her under lip shewed her contempt of the idea; and presently, with a sarcastic smile, she added, "Yes, yes, I shall certainly take rest! I mean no less. He, too, will take some rest! There, at least, ultimately, our destinies will approximate. And you, even you, victorious Ellis! will sink to vapid rest, like those who have never known happiness!"

With a laugh, then, but expressive of scorn, not gaiety, she exclaimed, "Am I, too, preaching? Can we never be tired, and good for nothing, but we must take to moralizing? Summon him, however, Ellis, yourself. Tell him to come without delay. I am sick;—and he is sick; and you are sick;—we are all round sick of this loathsome procrastination."

Alert to seize any pretence to be gone, Juliet was already at the door; when Elinor, suddenly seeming to penetrate into her intentions, called her back; and demanded a solemn promise that she would not fail to return with Harleigh.

To the quick perceptions of Elinor, hesitation was alarm; she no sooner, therefore, observed it, than she peremptorily ordered Selina and Mrs. Golding out of the room, and then, yet more positively, commanded Juliet to approach the sofa.

"I see," she cried, "your collusion! You imagine, by coming to me alternately, that you shall keep me in order? You conclude that I only present myself a bowl and a dagger, like a Tragedy Queen, to have them dashed from my hands, that I may be ready for a similar exhibition another day?—And can Harleigh, the noble Harleigh! judge me thus pitifully? No! no! Full of great and expansive ideas himself, he can better comprehend the exaltation of which a high, uncurbed, independent spirit is capable. But little minds deem all that is not common, all that has not been practised from father to son, and from generation to generation, to be trick, or to be impossible. You, Ellis, and such as you, who act always by rule, who never utter a word of which you have not weighed the consequence; never indulge a wish of which you have not canvassed the effects: who listen to no generous feeling; who shrink from every liberal impulse; who know nothing of nature, and care for nothing but opinion

—you, and such as you, tame animals of custom, wearied and wearying plodders on of beaten tracks, may conclude me a mere vapouring impostor, and believe it as safe to brave as to despise me! You, Ellis—But no!—"

She stopt, and her look and manner suddenly lost their fierceness, as she added: "Oh no!—You! You are not of that cast! Harleigh can only admire what alone is admirable. He would soon see through littleness or hypocrisy; you must be good and great at once—eminently good, unaffectedly great!—or how could Harleigh, the punctilious, discriminating Harleigh, adore you? Oh! I have known, and secretly appreciated you long; though I have been too little myself to acknowledge it! I have not been calm enough—perhaps not blind enough for justice! for if I saw your beauty less clearly—O happy Ellis! how do I admire, envy, revere,—and hate you!"

Shocked, yet filled with pity, Juliet would have sought to deprecate her enmity, and soften her feelings; but her fiery eye shewed that any attempt at offering her consolation would be regarded as insult. "I disdain," she cried, "all expedient, all pretence. However the abortion of my purpose may have made me appear a mere female mountebank, I have meant all that I have seemed to mean: though, by waiting for the moment of most *eclat*, opportunity has been past by, and action has been frustrated. But I can die only once. That over,—all is ended. 'Tis therefore I have studied how to finish my career with most effect. Let Harleigh, however, beware how he doubt my sincerity! doubt from him would drive me mad indeed! To the torpid formalities of every-day customs; the drowsy thoughts of every-day thinkers; he may believe me insensible, and I shall thank him; but, indifferent to my own principles of honour!—lost to my own definitions of pride, of shame, of heroism!—Oh! if he touch me there!—if he can judge of me so degradingly ..... my senses will still go before my life!"

She held her forehead, with a look of fearful pain; but, soon recovering, laughed, and said, "There are fools, I know, in the world, who suppose me mad already! only because I go my own way; while they, poor cowards, yoked one to another, always follow the path of their forefathers; without even venturing to mend the road, however it may have been broken up by time, accident, or mischief. I have full as much contempt of their imbecility, as they can have of my insanity. But hear me, Ellis! approach and mark me. I must have a conference with Harleigh. You must be present. A last conference! Whatever be its event, I have bound myself to Elinor Joddrel never to demand another! But do not therefore imagine my life or death to be in your power. No! My resolution is taken. Take yours. Let the interview which I demand pass quietly in this room; or be responsible for the consequences of the public desperation to which I may be urged!"

Gloomily, she then added, "Harleigh has refused to come; I will send him word that you are here; will he still refuse?"

Juliet blushed; but could not answer. Elinor paused a moment, and then said, "If he knows that he can see you elsewhere, he will be firm; if not .... he will return with my messenger! By that I can judge the present state of your connexion."

She rang the bell, and told Mrs. Golding to go instantly to Mr. Harleigh, and acquaint him that Elinor Joddrel and Miss Ellis desired to speak with him immediately.

Vainly Juliet remonstrated against the strange appearance of such a message, not only to himself, but to the family and the world: "Appearance?" she cried; "after what I have done, what I have dared,—have I any terms to keep with the world? with appearances? Miserable, contemptible, servile appearances, to which sense, happiness, and feeling are for ever to be sacrificed! And what will the world do in return? How recompense the victims to its arbitrary prejudices? By letting them quietly sink into nothing; by suffering them to die with as little notice and distinction as they have lived; and with as little choice."

Mrs. Golding returned, bringing the respects of Mr. Harleigh, but saying that he was forced, by an indispensable engagement, to refuse himself the honour of waiting upon Miss Joddrel.

"Run to him again!—" cried Elinor, with vehemence; "run, or he will be gone! Make him enter the first empty room, and tell him 'tis Miss Ellis alone who desires to speak with him. Fly!"

Yet more earnestly, now, Juliet would have interfered; but the peremptory Elinor insisted upon immediate obedience. "If still," she cried "he come not .... I shall conclude you to be already married!"

She laughed, yet wore a face of horrour at this idea; and spoke no more till Mrs. Golding returned, with intelligence that Mr. Harleigh was waiting in the parlour.

The bosom of Juliet now swelled and heaved high, with tumultuous distress and alarm, and her cheeks were dyed with the crimson tint of conscious shame; while Elinor, turning pale, dropt her head upon the pillow of the sofa, and sighed deeply for a moment in silence. Recovering then, "This, at least," she said, "is explicit; let it be final! Your influence is not disguised; use it, Ellis, to snatch me from the deplorable buffoonery of running about the world—not like death after the lady, but the lady after death! Assure yourselves that you will never devise any stratagem that will turn me from my purpose; though you may render ridiculous in its execution, what in its conception was sublime. Happiness such as yours, Ellis, ought to be above all narrow malignity. You ought to be proud, Ellis, voluntarily to serve her whom involuntarily you have ruined!"

Juliet was beginning some protestations of kindness; but Elinor, interrupting her, said, "I can give credit only to action. I must have a conference; but it is not to talk of myself;—nor of you; nor even of Harleigh. No! the soft moment of indulgence to my feelings is at an end! When I allowed my heart that delicious expansion; when I abandoned it to nature, and permitted it those open effusions of tenderness, I thought my dissolution at hand, and meant but to snatch a few last precious minutes of extacy from everlasting annihilation! but these endless delays, these eternal procrastinations, make me appear so unmeaning an idiot, even to myself, that, for the remnant of my doleful ditty, I must resist every natural wish; and plod on, till I plod off, with the stiff and stupid decorum of a starched old maid of half a century. Procure me, however, this definitive conference. It is upon no point of the old story, I promise you. You cannot be more tired of that than I am ashamed. 'Tis simply an earnest curiosity to know the pure, unadulterate thoughts of Harleigh upon death and immortality. I have applied to him, fruitlessly, myself; he inexorably refers me to some old canonicals;* without considering that it is vain to ask for guides to shew us a road, before we are convinced, or at least persuaded, that it will lead us to some given spot. Let him but make clear, that 'tis his own opinion that death does not sink us to nothing; let him but satisfy me, that he does not turn me over to others, only because he thinks as I think himself, and has not the courage to avow it;—and then, in return, I may suffer him to send to me some one of his black robed tribe, to harangue me about here and hereafter."

All contestation on the part of Juliet, was but irritating; she was forced upon her commission, and compelled solemnly to promise, that she would return with Harleigh, and be present at the conference.

CHAPTER LXIII*

WITH unsteady footsteps, and covered with blushes, Juliet repaired to the parlour, where Harleigh, with delighted, yet trembling impatience, was awaiting her arrival.

The door was half open, and he had placed himself at a distant window, to force her entire entrance into the room, before she could see him, or speak; but, that point gained, he hastened to shut it, exclaiming, "How happy for me is this incident, whatever may have been its origin! Let me instantly avail myself of it, to entreat—"

"Give me leave," interrupted Juliet, looking every way to avoid his eyes; "to deliver my message. Miss Joddrel—"

"When we begin," cried Harleigh, eagerly, "upon the unhappy Elinor, she must absorb us; let me, then, first—"

"I must be heard, Sir," said Juliet, with more firmness, "or I must be gone!—"

"You must be heard, then, undoubtedly!" he cried, with a smile, and offering her a chair, "for you must not be gone!"

Juliet declined being seated, but delivered, nearly in the words that she had received it, her message.

Harleigh looked pained and distressed, yet impatient, as he listened. "How," he cried, "can I argue with her? The false exaltation of her ideas, the effervescence of her restless imagination, place her above, or below, whatever argument, or reason can offer to her consideration. Her own creed is settled—not by investigation into its merits, not by reflection upon its justice, but by an impulsive preference, in the persuasion that such a creed leaves her mistress of her destiny."

"Ah, do not resist her!" cried Juliet. "If there is any good to be done—do it! and without delay!"

"It is not you I can resist!" he tenderly answered, "if deliberately it is your opinion I should comply. But her peculiar character, her extraordinary principles, and the strange situation into which she has cast herself, give her, for the moment, advantages difficult, nay dangerous to combat. Unawed by religion, of which she is ignorant; unmoved by appearances, to which she is indifferent; she utters all that occurs to an imagination inflamed by passion, disordered by disappointment, and fearless because hopeless, with a courage from which she has banished every species of restraint: and with a spirit of ridicule, that so largely pervades her whole character, as to burst forth through all her sufferings, to mix derision with all her sorrows, and to preponderate even over her passions! Reason and argument appear to her but as marks for dashing eloquence or sportive mockery. Nevertheless, if, by striking at every thing, daringly, impetuously, unthinkingly, she start some sudden doubt; demand some impossible explanation; or ask some humanly unanswerable question; she will conclude herself victorious; and be more lost than ever to all that is right, from added false confidence in all that is wrong."

"If so, the conference were, indeed, better avoided," said Juliet with sadness; "yet—as it is not the sacred truth of revealed religion that she means to canvass; as it is merely the previous question, of the possibility, or impossibility, according to her notions, of a future state for mankind, which she desires to discuss; I do not quite see the danger of answering the doubts, or refuting the assertions, that may lead her afterwards, to an investigation so important to her future welfare. If she would consult with a clergyman, it were certainly preferable; but that will be a point no longer difficult to gain, when once you have convinced her, upon her own terms of controversy, that you yourself have a firm belief in immortality."

"The attempt shall surely be made," said Harleigh, "if you

think such a result, as casting her into more reverend hands, may ensue. If I have fled all controversy with her, from the time that she has publicly proclaimed her religious infidelity, it has by no means been from disgust; an unbeliever is simply an object of pity; for who is so deplorably without resource in sickness or calamity?—those two common occupiers of half our existence! No; if I have fled all voluntary intercourse with her, it has only been that her total contempt of the world, has forced me to take upon myself the charge of public opinion for us both. While I considered her as the future wife of my brother, I frankly contested whatever I thought wrong in her notions. The wildness of her character, the eccentricity of her ideas, and the violence of all her feelings; with her extraordinary understanding—parts, I ought to say; for understanding implies rather what is solid than brilliant;—joined to the goodness of her heart, and the generosity, frankness, and openness of her nature, excited at once an anxiety for my brother, and an interest for herself, that gave occasion to the most affectionate animadversion on my part, and produced alternate defence or concession on hers. But her disdain of flattery, or even of civil acquiescence, made my freedom, opposed to the courteous complaisance which my brother deemed due to his situation of her humble servant, strike her in a point of view ... that has been unhappy for us all three! Yet this was a circumstance which I had never suspected,—for, where no wish is met, remark often sleeps;—and I had been wholly unobservant, till you—"

Called from the deep interest with which she had involuntarily listened to the relation of his connection with Elinor, by this sudden transition to herself, Juliet started; but he went on.

"Till you were an inmate of the same house! till I saw her strange consternation, when she found me conversing with you; her rising injustice when, with the respect and admiration which you inspired, I mentioned you; her restless vigilance to interrupt whatever communication I attempted to have with you; her sudden fits of profound, yet watchful taciturnity, when I saw you in her presence;—"

"I may tell her," interrupted Juliet, disturbed, "that you will wait upon her according to her request?"

"When you," cried he, smiling, "are her messenger, she must not expect quite so quick, quite so categorical an answer! I must first—"

"On the contrary, her impatience will be insupportable if I do not relieve it immediately."

She would have opened the door, but, preventing her, "Can you indeed believe," he cried, with vivacity; "is it possible you can believe, that, having once caught a ray of light, to illumine and cheer the dread and nearly impervious darkness, that so long and so blackly over-clouded all my prospects, I can consent, can endure to be cast again into desolate obscurity?"

Juliet, blushing, and conscious of his allusion to her reception of him in the church-yard, for which, without naming Sir Lyell Sycamore, she knew not how to account, again protested that she must not be detained.

Still, however, half reproachfully, half laughingly, stopping her, "And is it thus," he cried, "that you summon me to Brighthelmstone,—only to mock my obedience, and disdain to hear me?"

"I, Sir?—I, summon you?"

"Nay, see my credentials!"

He presented to her the following note, written in an evidently feigned hand:

"If Mr. Harleigh will take a ramble to the church-yard upon the Hill, at Brighthelmstone, next Thursday morning, at five o'clock, he will there meet a female fellow-traveller, now in the greatest distress, who solicits his advice and assistance, to extricate her from her present intolerable abode."

Deeply colouring, "And could Mr. Harleigh," she cried, "even for a moment believe,—suppose,—"

He interrupted her, with an air of tender respect. "No; I did not, indeed, dare believe, dare suppose that an honour, a trust such as might be implied by an appeal like this, came from you! Yet for you I was sure it was meant to pass; and to discover by whom it was devised, and for what purpose, irresistibly drew me hither, though with full conviction of imposition. I came, however, pre-determined to watch around your dwelling, at the appointed hour, ere I repaired to the bidden place. But what was my agitation when I thought I saw you! I doubted my senses. I retreated; I hung back; your face was shaded by your head-dress;—yet your air,—your walk,—was it possible I could be deceived? Nevertheless, I resolved not to speak, nor to approach you, till I saw whether you proceeded to the church-yard. I was by no means free from suspicion of some new stratagem of Elinor; for, fatigued with concealment, I was then publicly at my house upon Bagshot-Heath, where the note had reached me. Yet her distance from Brighthelmstone for so early an hour, joined to intelligence which I had received some time ago,—for you will not imagine that the period which I spend without seeing, I spend also without hearing of you?—that you had been observed,—and more than once,—at that early hour, in the church-yard—"

"True!" cried Juliet, eagerly, "at that hour I have frequently met, or accompanied, a friend, a beloved friend! thither; and, in her name, I had even then, when I saw you, been deluded: not for a walk; a ramble; not upon any party of pleasure; but to visit a little tomb, which holds the regretted remains of the darling and only child of that dear, unhappy friend!"

She wept. Harleigh, extremely touched, said, "You have, then, a friend here?—Is it,—may I ask?—is it the person you so earnestly sought upon your arrival?—Is your anxiety relieved?—your embarrassment?—your suspence?—your cruel distress?—Will you not give me, at length, some little satisfaction? Can you wonder that my forbearance is worn out?—Can my impatience offend you?—If I press to know your situation, it is but with the desire to partake it!—If I solicit to hear your name—it is but with the hope ... that you will suffer me to change it!"

He would have taken her hand, but, drawing back, and wiping her eyes, though irresistibly touched, "Offend?" she repeated; "Oh far,—far! ... but why will you recur to a subject that ought so long since to have been exploded?—while another,—an essential one, calls for all my attention?—The last packet which you left with me, you must suffer me instantly to return; the first,—the first—" She stammered, coloured, and then added, "The first,—I am shocked to own,—I must defer returning yet a little longer!"

"Defer?" ardently repeated Harleigh. "Ah! why not condescend to think, at least, another language, if not to speak it? Why not anticipate, in kind idea, at least, the happy period,—for me! when I may be permitted to consider as included, and mutual in our destinies, whatever hitherto——"

"Oh hold!—Oh Mr. Harleigh!" interrupted Juliet, in a voice of anguish. "Let no errour, no misconstruction, of this terrible sort,—no inference, no expectation, thus wide from all possible reality, add to my various misfortunes the misery of remorse!"

"Remorse?—Gracious powers! What can you mean?"

"That I have committed the most dreadful of mistakes,—a mistake that I ought never to forgive myself, if, in the relief from immediate perplexity, which I ventured to owe to a momentary, and, I own, an intentionally unacknowledged, usage of some of the notes which you forced into my possession, I have given rise to a belief,—to an idea,—to—"

She hesitated, and blushed so violently, that she could not finish her phrase; but Harleigh appeared thunderstruck, and was wholly silent. She looked down, abashed, and added, "The instant, by any possible means,—by work, by toil, by labour,—nothing will be too severe,—all will be light and easy,—that can rectify,—that—"

She could not proceed; and Harleigh, somewhat recovered by the view of her confusion, gently, though reproachfully, said, "All, then, will be preferable to the slightest, smallest trust in me?—And is this from abhorrence?—or do you deem me so ungenerous as to believe that I should take unworthy advantage of being permitted to offer you even the most trivial service?"

"No, no, oh, no!" with quickness cried Juliet; "but the more generous you may be, the more readily you may imagine——"

She stopt, at a loss how to finish.

"That you would be generous, too?" cried Harleigh, revived and smiling.

She could not refrain from a smile herself, but hastily added, "My conduct must be liable to no inference of any sort. Adieu, Sir. I will deliver you the packet in Miss Joddrel's room."

Her hand was upon the lock, but his foot, fixed firmly against the door, impeded its being opened, while he exclaimed, "I cannot part with you thus! You must clear this terrific obscurity, that threatens to involve me, once more, in the horrours of excruciating suspense!—Why that cruel expression of displeasure? Can you think that the moment of hope,—however brief, however unintentional, however accidental,—can ever be obliterated from my thoughts? that my existence, to whatever term it may be lengthened, will ever out-live the precious remembrance that you have called me your destined protector?—your guardian angel?"

He could add no more; a mortal paleness overspread the face of Juliet, who, letting go the lock of the door, sunk upon a chair, faintly ejaculating, "Was I not yet sufficiently miserable?"

Penetrated with sorrow, and struck with alarm, Harleigh looked at her in silence; but when again he sought to take her hand, shrinking from his touch, though regarding him with an expression that supplicated rather than commanded forbearance; "If you would not kill me, Mr. Harleigh," she cried, "you will relinquish this terrible perseverance!"

"Relinquish?" he repeated, "What now? Now, that all delicacy for this wild, eccentric, though so generous Elinor is at an end? that she has, herself, annulled your engagement? Relinquish, now, the hopes so long pursued,—so difficultly caught? No, I swear to you—"

Juliet arose. "Oh hold, Mr. Harleigh!" she cried; "recollect yourself a moment! I lament if I have, involuntarily, caused you any transient mistake; yet, do me the justice to reflect, that I have never cast my destiny upon that of Miss Joddrel. No decision, therefore, of her's can make any change in mine."

She again put her hand upon the lock of the door.

Harleigh fixt upon her his eyes, which spoke the severest disturbance, while, in tremulous accents, he uttered, "And can you leave me thus, to wasting despondence?—and with this cold, chilling, blighting composure?—Is it from pitiless apathy, which incapacitates for judging of torments which it does not experience?—O no! Those eyes that so often glisten with the most touching sensibility,—those cheeks that so beautifully mantle with the varying dies of quick transition of sentiment,—

that mouth, which so expressively plays in harmony with every word,—nay, every thought,—all, all announce a heart where every virtue is seconded and softened by every feeling!—a mind alive to the quickest sensations, yet invigorated with the ablest understanding! a soul of angelic purity!—"

Some sound from the passage made him suddenly stop, and remove his foot; while the hand of Juliet dropt from the lock. They were both silent, and both, affrighted, stood suspended; till Juliet, shocked at the impropriety of such a situation, forced herself to open the door,—at the other side of which, looking more dead than alive, stood Elinor, leaning upon her sister.

"I began to think," she cried, in a hollow tone, "that you were eloped!—and determining to trust to no messenger, I came myself." She then endeavoured to call forth a smile; but it visited so unwillingly features nearly distorted by internal agony, that it gave a cast almost ghastly to her countenance.

"Why, Harleigh," she cried, "should you thus shun me? Have I not given back her plighted faith to Ellis? Yet I am not ignorant how tired you must be of those old thread-bare topics, bowls, daggers, poignards, and bodkins: but they have had their reign, and are now dethroned. What remains is plain, common, stupid rationality. I wish to converse with you, Albert, only as a casuist; and upon a point of conscience which you alone can settle. For this world, and for all that belongs to it, all, with me, is utterly over! I have neither care nor interest left in it; and I have no belief that there is any other. I am very composedly ready, therefore, to take my last nap. I merely wish to learn, before I return to my torpid ignorance, whether it can be a fact, that you, Harleigh, you! believe in a future state for mortal man? And I engage you by your friendship,—which I still prize above all things! and by your honour, which you, I know, prize in the same manner, to answer me this question, instantly and categorically."

"Most faithfully, then, Elinor, yes! All the happiness of my present life is founded upon my belief of a life to come!"

Elinor held up her hands. "Astonishing!" she cried. "Can judgment and credulity, wisdom and superstition, thus jumble themselves together! And in a head so clear, so even oracular! Give me, at least, your reasons; and see that they are your own!"

Harleigh looked disturbed, but made not any answer.

The wan face of Elinor was now lighted up with hues of scarlet. "I feel," she cried, "the impropriety of this intrusion;—for who, if not I,—since we all prize most what we know least,—should respect happiness? When you have finished, however, your present conference, honour me, both of you, if you please,—that the period so employed may be less wearisome to either,—with a final one up stairs. Harleigh! A final one!"

Harleigh was still silent.

A yet deeper red now dyed the whole complexion of Elinor, and she added, "If, to-day, you are too much engaged,—to-morrow will suffice. To-day, indeed, your solemn protestation of belief, upon a subject which to me, is a chaos,—dark,—impervious, impenetrable! has given ample employment to my ideas."

Repulsing, then, his silently offered arm, she returned, with Selina, to the chamber consigned to her by Mrs. Ireton.

CHAPTER LXIV

HARLEIGH, confused, disconcerted, remained motionless; but when the conscious Juliet would have glided silently past him, he entreated for a moment's audience.

"Oh no, Mr. Harleigh, no!" she cried: "these are scenes and alarms, that must be risked no more!—"

She was hurrying away; but, upon his saying, "Hear me, at least, for Elinor!" she turned back.

His eye, now reproached even her compliance; but he rapidly communicated his opinion, that the conference demanded by Elinor ought, in prudence, for the present, to be avoided; since, while she had still some favourite object in view, life, would, unconsciously, be still supported. Time, thus, might insensibly be gained, not only for eluding her fatal project, but happily, perhaps, for taming the dauntless wildness that made her, now, seem to stand scoffingly at bay, between life and death.

Juliet saw nothing to oppose to this statement, and thanking him that, at least, it liberated her, was again hastening away.

"Hold, hold!" cried he, stopping her: "it is not from me that it must liberate you! Elinor has ratified the restoration of your word—"

"Oh, were that all!—" she cried, hastily; but, stopping short, deeply blushing, "Mr. Harleigh," she added, "compel me not to repeat declarations that cannot vary!—Aid me rather, generously,—kindly, shall I say?—aid me,—to fly, to avoid you,—lest you become yourself . . ." her voice faltered as she pronounced, "the most fatal of my enemies!"

The penetrated Harleigh, charmed, though tortured, saw her eyes glittering with tears; but she forced her way past him, and took refuge in her chamber.

There, in deep anguish, she was sinking upon a chair, when she received the gentle balm of a letter from Gabriella, written with extatic joy at the prospect of their re-union.

This decided her plan of immediate escape to London, under a full conviction that Harleigh, to obviate any calumnious surmizes from her disappearance, would studiously shew himself in the world; however cautiously he might avoid any interview with Elinor.

The shock of Juliet, at this unfortunate intrusion, somewhat abated, when she reflected that confirmed hopelessness might, perchance, lead Elinor to acquiescence in disappointment; for hopelessness, equally with resignation,—though not so respectably,—terminates all struggles against misfortune.

She now, therefore, seized an opportunity, when she knew Mrs. Ireton to be engaged with Mrs. Maple, for going forth to secure a place in some machine, for a journey to London on the following morning.

This office performed, she thought, while returning home, that she perceived, though at a considerable distance, Harleigh.

In the dread of some new conflict, she was planning to seek another way back, when recollecting that she had his banknotes in her work-bag, she judged that she might more promptly return them at this accidental meeting, than in the house of Mrs. Ireton.

She slackened, therefore, her pace, and, taking out her ever ready packet, turned round, as the footstep approached, gravely and calmly to deliver it; when, to her utter surprize, she faced Lord Melbury.

Pleasure emitted its brightest hues in the tints of her cheeks, at sight of the marked respect that chastened the visible delight with which she was looked at and accosted by the young peer. "How fortunate," he cried, "am I to meet with you thus directly! This moment only I dismount from my horse. I have a million of things to say to you from Aurora, if you will have the goodness to hear them; and I have more at heart still my own claim upon your patience. When may I see you for a little conversation?"

The pleasure of Juliet was now severely checked by perplexity, how either to fulfil or to break her engagement. Observing the change in her countenance, and her hesitation and difficulty to answer, Lord Melbury, whose look and air changed also, said, in a tone of concern, "Miss Ellis has not forgotten her kind promise?"

"Your lordship is extremely good, to remember either that or me; yet I hope——"

"What does Miss Ellis hope? I would not counteract her hopes for the world; but surely she cannot be so cruel as to disappoint mine? to make me fear that she has changed her opinion? to withdraw her amiable trust?"

"No, my lord, no! not a moment could I hesitate were trust alone in question! but the hurry of this instant,—the impossibility of detailing so briefly, and by an imperfect account—"

"And why an imperfect account? Why, dear Miss Ellis, since you have the kindness to believe I may be trusted, not confide to me the whole truth?"

"Alas, my lord! how?—where?"

"In some parlour,—in the garden,—any where.—"

"Ah, my lord, what I have to say must be uninterrupted; unheard but by yourself; and—I can command neither a place nor a moment free from intrusion!"—

"Sweet Miss Ellis!—sweet injured Miss Ellis! I know, I have witnessed the unworthiness of your treatment. Even Aurora, with all her gentleness, has been as indignant at it, nearly, as myself. All our wonder is how you bear it!—We burn, we expire to learn what can urge so undue a subjection. But I have not obtruded myself upon you only for myself; I have galloped hither to prepare you,—and to entreat you not to be uneasy,—and to save you from any surprize, by acquainting you that my uncle Denmeath—"

He stopt short, as if thunderstruck. Juliet, alarmed, looked at him, and saw that, in bending over her, to name, in a lower voice, his uncle, his eyes had caught the direction of her packet, "For Albert Harleigh, Esq."

Shocked at the evidently unpleasant effect which this sight produced, and covered with blushes at the suspicions to which it might give rise, Juliet hastily exclaimed, "Oh my lord! I must no longer defer my explanation! any, every risk will be preferable to the loss of your esteem!"

Delight, enchantment again were depicted on the countenance, as they seized the faculties of the young peer; and, involuntarily, his eager hands were stretching forwards to seize hers, when he perceived, just approached to them, pale, agitated, and with the look of some one taken suddenly ill, Harleigh.

The colour of Juliet now rose and died away alternately, from varying sensations of shame and apprehension; to which the deepest confusion soon succeeded, as she discerned the contrast of the cheeks, whitened by pale jealousy, of Harleigh; with those of Lord Melbury, which were crimsoned with the reddest hues of sudden suspicion, and painful mistrust.

Harleigh, with a faint and forced smile, bowed, but stood aloof: Lord Melbury seemed to have not alone his sentiments, but his faculties held in suspension.

Juliet, with cruel consciousness, perceived that each surmized something clandestine of the other; and the immense importance which she annexed to their joint good opinion; and the imminent danger which she saw of the double forfeiture, soon re-invigorated her powers, and, addressing herself with dignity, though in a tone of softness, to Lord Melbury, "If you judge me, my lord, from partial circumstances," she cried, "I have every thing to apprehend for what I value more than words can express, your lordship's approbation of the favour with which I am honoured by Lady Aurora Granville; but let me rather hope,—suffer me, my lord, to hope, that by the opinion I have formed of the honour of your own character, you will judge,—though at present in the dark,—of the integrity of mine!"

Turning then from him, as, touched, electrified, he was beginning, "I have always judged you to be an angel!"—she would have presented her packet to Harleigh; though without raising her eyes, saying, "Mr. Harleigh has so long,—and upon so many occasions, honoured me with marks of his esteem,—and benevolence,—that I flatter myself,—I think,—I trust—"

She stammered, confused; and Harleigh, who, from the moment that Lady Aurora had been mentioned, had recovered his complexion, his respiration, and his strength; recovered, also, his hopes and his energy, at sight of the embarrassment of Juliet. Not doubting, however, what were the contents of the packet, he held back from receiving it; though with a smile that conveyed the most lively expression of grateful delight, at her palpable anxiety to preserve his esteem.

"Nay, you must take your property!" she resumed, with attempted cheerfulness; yet blushing more deeply every moment, at thus betraying to Lord Melbury that she had any property of Mr. Harleigh's to return.

"I will take your commands in every shape in which they can be framed," cried Harleigh, gaily; "but you must not refuse to grant me, at the same time, directions for their execution."

The interest with which Lord Melbury listened to what passed, was now mingled with undisguised impatience: but Juliet could not endure to satisfy him; could not support letting him know, that she retained money of Harleigh's in her hands; nor yet bear to suffer Harleigh, now the address had been seen, to leave it still in her possession: hesitating, abashed, she turned from one to the other, with looks at Lord Melbury that seemed appealing for forbearance; and to Harleigh with downcast eyes, that had not force to encounter his, but that were expressive of distress, timidity, and fear of misconstruction.

This pause, while it astonished and perplexed Lord Melbury, gave rise, in Harleigh, to the most flattering emotions. Her disturbance was, indeed, visible, and cruelly painful to him; but, since their meeting in the church-yard, the severity of her reserve had seemed shaken, beyond her power, evident as were her struggles, to call back its original firmness. The more exquisitely he felt himself bewitched by this observation, the more fondly he desired to spare her delicacy, by concealing, though not repressing his hopes; but his eyes, less under his controul than his words, air, or address, spoke a language not to be doubted of tenderness, and sparkled with lustrous happiness. Juliet felt their beams too powerfully to mistake, or even to sustain them. Her head dropt, her eyelids nearly closed; blushing shame tingled in her cheeks, and apprehension and perturbation trembled in every limb.

Perceiving, and adoring, her inability to find utterance, Harleigh, with subdued rapture, yet in a tone that spoke all his feelings to be, at length, in harmony with all his wishes, was gently beginning an entreaty that she would adjourn this little dispute to another day, when the words, "Well! if here i'n't the very person we were talking off!" striking his ears, he looked round, and saw Miss Bydel, accompanied by Mr. Giles Arbe; whose approach had been unheeded by them all, from the deep interest which had concentrated their attention to themselves.

"Why, Mrs. Ellis," she continued, "why what are you doing here? I should like to know that. I've just had a smart battle about you with my good friend, Mr. Giles. He will needs have it, that you paid all your debts from a hoard that you had by you, of your own; though I have told him I dare say an hundred times, at the least, I must needs be a better judge, having been paid myself, for my own share, by that cross-grained Baronet, who's been such a good friend to you."

The sensations of Juliet underwent now another change, though shame was still predominant; her fears of exciting the expectations she sought to annul in Harleigh, were superseded by a terrour yet more momentous, of giving ground for suspicion, not alone to himself, but to Lord Melbury, that, while fashioning a thousand difficulties, to accepting the assistance that was generously and delicately offered by themselves, she had suffered a third person, that person, also, a gentleman, to supply her pecuniary necessities. She breathed hard, and looked disordered, but could suggest nothing to say; while Harleigh and Lord Melbury stood as if transfixed by disturbed astonishment.

"Well! I protest," resumed Miss Bydel, "if here i'n't another of the people that we were talking of, Mr. Giles! for I declare it's Mr. Harleigh, that I was telling you, you know, my good friend, was the person that made poor Miss Joddrel make away with herself, because of his skimper-scampering after Mrs. Ellis, when she had that swoon! which, to be sure, had but an out of the way look; for the music* would have taken care of her. Don't you think so yourself, my dear?"

The most painful confusion again took possession of Juliet; who would silently have walked away, had not Miss Bydel caught hold of her arm, saying, "Don't be in a hurry, my dear, for you shan't be chid; for I'll speak for you myself to Mrs. Ireton."

"I am mighty glad to hear that Sir Jaspar is your friend, my pretty lady," said the smiling Mr. Giles; "and I am mighty glad, too, that you have persuaded him to help to pay your debts. He's a very good sort of man, where he takes;* and very witty and clever. Though he is crabbed, too; rather crabbed and waspish, when he i'n't pleased. He always scolds all the men: and, indeed, the maids, too, when they a'n't pretty, poor things! And they can't help that: else, I dare say, they would. Yet, I am afraid, I don't like them quite so well myself, neither, in my heart, when they are ugly; which is but hard upon them; so I always do them double the good, to punish myself. But I'm prodigiously sorry you should have taken to that turn of running in debt, my dear, for it's the only thing I know to your disadvantage; for which reason I have never named it to a single soul; only it just dropt out, before I was aware, to Miss Bydel; which I am sorry enough for; for I am afraid it will be but hard to her, poor lady, to keep it to herself."

"What do you mean by that Mr. Giles?" cried Miss Bydel, angrily. "Do you want to insinuate that I don't know how to keep a secret? I should be glad to know what right you have to fleer* at a person about that, when you blab out every thing in such a manner yourself! and before these two gentlemen, too; who don't lose a word of what passes, I can tell you!"

"True! Good! You are right there, Mrs. Bydel! I did not

think of that, I protest. However, these two gentlemen have too much kindness about them, to repeat a thing that may hurt a young person just coming, as one may say, into the world; for she is but a chicken; and my lord, here, who looks younger still, is scarcely more than an egg. So you may be sure he has no guile in him, for he seems almost as innocent as herself. However, my pretty lady, if you have still any more debts, new or old, only tell me who you owe them to, and I'll run and fetch all the people here; and we'll join together to discharge them at once; for Mr. Harleigh is always at home when he is doing good; and this young nobleman can't begin too soon to learn what he is rich for: so you can never be in better hands for taking up a little money. When we settled the last batch, you had no debt left but to Mrs. Bydel; and, as the Baronet has paid her, she's off our hands. So tell me whether there is any new one that you have been running up since?"

Wounded, and nearly indignant at this demand, "None!" Juliet spontaneously answered; when catching a glance at Lord Melbury, who involuntarily looked down, his purse and the fifteen guineas of Lady Aurora, rushed upon her memory, and filled her again with visible embarrassment.

"Good! good!" cried the pleased Mr. Giles: "you could not tell me better news. But are there any poor souls, then, that you forgot to mention in our last reckoning? Are there any old debts that you did not count?"

Inexpressibly hurt at a supposition so offensive to her sense of probity, Juliet hastily repeated, "No, Sir, there are none!" but, in raising her head, and encountering the penetrating eyes of Harleigh, the terrible recollection of the capital into which she had broken, and of the large sum so long his due, struck cold to her heart; though it burnt her cheeks with a dye of crimson.

Yet were these sensations nearly nugatory, compared with those which she suffered the next instant, when Miss Bydel, suddenly perceiving the direction upon the packet, read aloud "For Albert Harleigh, Esq."

Her exclamations, her blunt, unqualified interrogatories, and the wonder, and simple ejaculations of Mr. Giles Arbe, filled Juliet with a confusion so intolerable, that she forced her arm from Miss Bydel, with intention to insist upon publicly restoring the packet to Harleigh; but Harleigh, confounded himself, had advanced towards the house, which, frequently as they had stopt, they now insensibly reached; but from which he would most willingly have retrograded,* upon seeing Ireton issue, laughing, into the portico.

The laugh of Ireton, whose gaiety was always derision, and whose derision was always scandal, though it was innocently echoed by the unsuspicious Mr. Giles, was as alarming to the two gentlemen and to Juliet, as it was offensive to Miss Bydel; who pettishly demanded, "Pray what are you laughing at, Mr. Ireton? I should like to know that. If it is at me, you may as well tell me at once, for I shall be sure to find it out; because I always make a point of doing that."

Ireton, seizing upon Harleigh, exclaimed "What, Monsieur le Moniteur!* still hankering after our mysterious fair one?" when, perceiving the wishes of Juliet, to pass on, he wantonly filled up the door-way.

Harleigh, who, also, could not but guess them, though he dared not look at her, hoped, by delaying her entrance, to catch a moment's discourse: but the youthful Lord Melbury, deeming all caution to be degrading, that interfered with protection to a lovely female, openly desired that Ireton would stand aside, and let the ladies enter the house.

"Most undoubtedly, my lord!" answered Ireton, making way, with an air of significant acquiescence.

Miss Bydel, with a warm address of thanks to his lordship, whose interference she received as a personal civility, said, "This is like a gentleman, indeed, my lord, and quite fit for a lord to do, to take the part of us poor weak women, against people that keep one standing out in the street, because they think of nothing but joking;" and then, telling Juliet to follow her, "I can do no less," she added, as she entered the hall, "than be as good as my word to this poor young music-maker, to save her a chiding, poor creature, for staying, dawdling, out so long; when ten to one but poor Mrs. Ireton has wanted her a hundred times, for one odd thing or another. But I shall take all the fault upon myself for the last part of the job, because I can't deny but I held her a minute or two by her arm. But what she was gossipping about before we came up to her, my good friend

Mr. Giles and I, is what I don't pretend to say; though I should like to know very well; for it had but an odd appearance, I must own; both you gentlemen having been talked of so much, in the town, about this young person."

The most pointed darts of wit, and even the poisoned shafts of malice, are less disconcerting to delicacy, than the unqualified bluntness of the curious under-bred; for that which cannot be imputed to a spirit of sarcasm, or a desire of shining, passes, to the bye-standers, for unvarnished truth. As such, the intimation of Miss Bydel was palpably received by Ireton, and by Mr. Giles; though with malevolent wilfulness by the one, and, by the other, with the simplest credulity; while Lord Melbury, Harleigh and Juliet, were too much ashamed to look up, and too much confounded to attempt parrying so gross an attack.

Yet both Lord Melbury and Harleigh, urged invincibly by a desire of knowing in what manner Juliet was to be patronized by her loquacious mediatrix, and how they might themselves fare in the account, irresistibly entered the mansion; though marvelling, each, at the curiosity, and blaming the indiscretion of the other.

To avoid the aspersion of making a clandestine retreat, Juliet had decided, however painful to her might be such an exertion, openly to relinquish her situation with Mrs. Ireton; but she by no means felt equal to risking the irascibility of that lady before so many witnesses. Nevertheless, when she would have glided from the party, Miss Bydel, again seizing her arm, called out, "Come, don't be afraid, Mrs. Ellis: I've promised to take your part, and I am always as good as my word;" and then dragged, rather than drew her into the drawing-room; closely attended by Lord Melbury, Harleigh, Mr. Giles Arbe, and Ireton.

CHAPTER LXV

UNWEARIEDLY concerting means of detection relative to the stranger, which no failure of success could discourage, Mrs. Ireton and Mrs. Maple sate whispering upon the same sofa in the drawing-room; while Selina and Miss Arramede were tittering at a window.

"How do you do, ladies?" cried Miss Bydel. "In close chat, I see. However, I don't want to know what it's about. I'm only come to speak a word about this poor thing here, for fear you should think she has been all this time gossipping about her own affairs; which, I assure you, Mrs. Ireton, I can bear witness for her i'n't the case."

The supercilious silence of Mrs. Ireton to this address, would have authorised the immediate retreat of Juliet, but that Ireton maliciously placed himself against the door, and impeded its being opened; while Lord Melbury and Harleigh were obliged to approach the sofa, to pay their compliments to the lady of the mansion; who, giving them her whole attention, left Miss Bydel to finish her harangue to Mrs. Maple.

"Right! True!" cried Mr. Giles, eager to abet what he thought the good nature of Miss Bydel. "What you say is just and fair, Mrs. Bydel; for this pretty young lady here wanted to go from these two gentlemen the minute we came up to her; only Mrs. Bydel's arm being rather, I conceive, heavy, she could not so soon break away. But I did not catch one of her pretty dimples all the time. So pray, Mrs. Ireton, don't be angry with her; and the less because she's so sweet tempered, that, if you are, she won't complain; for she never did of Mrs. Maple."

"I hope this is curious enough!" cried Mrs. Maple. "A body to come and live upon me, for months together, upon charity, and then not to complain of me! I think if this is not enough to cure people of charity, I wonder what is! For my part, I am heartily sick of it, for the rest of my life."

Juliet having again, but vainly, tried to pass by Ireton, retired to an unoccupied window. Harleigh, though engaged in discourse with Mrs. Ireton, reddened indignantly; and Lord Melbury nearly mashed the nails of his fingers between his teeth; while Mr. Giles, staring, demanded, "Why what can there be, Ma'am, in charity, to turn you so sick? A poor helpless young creature, like that, can't make you her toad-eater."

Alarmed at an address which she looked upon as a prognostic to an exhortation, of which she dreaded, from experience, the plainness and severity, Mrs. Maple hastily changed her place: while Mrs. Ireton, startled, also, by the word toad-eater, unremittingly continued speaking to the two gentlemen; whose attention, nevertheless, she could not for a moment engage, though their looks and persons were her prisoners.

"I don't know why you ladies who are so rich and gay," continued Mr. Giles, composedly, and, to the great annoyance of Mrs. Ireton, taking possession of the seat which Mrs. Maple had abdicated; "should not try to make yourselves pleasing to those who are poor and sad. You, that have got every thing you can wish for, should take as much pains not to be distasteful, as a poor young thing like that, who has got nothing but what she works for, should take pains not to be starved."

Mrs. Ireton, extremely incensed, though affecting to be unconcerned, haughtily summoned Ellis.

Ellis, forced to obey, went to the back of the sofa, to avoid standing by the side of the two gentlemen; and determined to make use of this opportunity for announcing her project of retreat.

"Pray, Ma'am," Mrs. Ireton cried, "permit me to enquire—" her eye angrily, yet cautiously, glancing at Mr. Giles, "to what extraordinary circumstance I am indebted, for having the honour of receiving your visitors? Not that I am insensible to such a distinction; you won't imagine me such an Hottentot, I hope, as to be insensible to so honourable a distinction! Nevertheless, you'll pardon me, I trust, if I take the liberty to intimate, that, for the future, when any of your friends are to be indulged in waiting upon you, you will have the goodness to receive them in your own apartments. You'll excuse the hint, I flatter myself!"

"I shall intrude no apologies upon your time, Madam," said Ellis, calmly, "for relinquishing a situation in which I have acquitted myself so little to your satisfaction: to-morrow, therefore—"

Anticipating, and eager to convert a resignation which she

regarded as a disgrace, into a dismission which she considered as a triumph, Mrs. Ireton impatiently interrupted her, crying, "To-morrow? And why are we to wait for to-morrow? What has to-day done? Permit me to ask that. And pray don't take ill. Pray don't let me offend you: only—what has poor to-day done, that to-morrow must have such a preference?"

Juliet, frightened at the idea of being reduced to pass a night alone at an inn, now hesitated; and Mrs. Ireton, smiling complacently around her, went on.

"Suffer me, I beg, to speak a little word for poor, neglected to-day! Have we not long enough been slaves to to-morrow? Let the pleasures of dear expectation be superseded, this once, for those of actual enjoyment. Not but 'twill be very severe upon me to lose you. I don't dissemble that. So gay a companion! I shall certainly expire an hypochondriac upon first missing your amusing sallies. I can never survive such a deprivation. No! it's all over with me! You pity me, I am sure, my good friends?"

She now looked around, with an expression of ineffable satisfaction at her own wit: but it met no applause, save in the ever ready giggle of Selina, and the broad admiration of the round-eyed Miss Bydel.

Juliet silently courtsied, with a gravity that implied a leave-taking, and, approaching the door, desired that Ireton would let her pass.

Ireton, laughing, declared that he should not suffer her to decamp, till she gave him a direction where he could find her the next day.

Offended, she returned again to her window.

"O, now, pray, Mrs. Ireton," cried Miss Bydel, "don't turn her away, poor thing! don't turn her away, Ma'am, for such a mere little fault. I dare say she'll do her best to please you, if you'll only try her again. Besides, if she's turned off in this manner, just as young Lord Melbury is here, he may try to make her his kept mistress again. At least naughty people will say so."

"Who will say so, Ma'am?" cried Lord Melbury, starting up, in a rage to which he was happy to find so laudable a vent: "Who will dare say so? Name me a single human being!"

"Lord, my lord," answered Miss Bydel, a little frightened;

"nobody, very likely! only it's best to be upon one's guard against evil speakers; for young lords at your time of life, a'n't apt to be quite so good as they are when they are more stricken in years. That's all I mean, my lord; for I don't mean to affront your lordship, I'm sure."

Mrs. Ireton, again beckoning to Ellis, said, "Pray, Mrs. Thing-a-mi, have you done me so much honour as to make out your bill?" And, ostentatiously, she produced her purse. "What is the amount, Ma'am, of my debt?"

Juliet paused a moment, and then answered, "'Tis an amount, Madam, much too difficult and complicate for me, just now, to calculate!"

Mr. Giles, alertly rising, cried, "Let me help you, then, my pretty lady, to cast it up. What have you given her upon account, Mrs. Ireton?"

"I am not her book-keeper, Sir!" returned Mrs. Ireton, extremely nettled. "I don't pretend to the honour of acting as her steward! But I trust she will be good enough to take what is her due. 'Tis very much beneath her, I own; extremely beneath her, I confess; yet I hope, this once, she will let herself down so far." And, ten guineas, which she had held in her hand, were augmented to twenty, which she paradingly flung upon the table.

Mrs. Maple and Miss Bydel poured forth the warmest exclamations of admiration at this magnificence; but Juliet, quietly saying, "Let me hope, Madam, that my successor may merit your generosity," again courtsied, and was going: when Mr. Giles, eagerly picking up the money, and following her with it, spread upon his open hand, said, "What do you go without your cash for, my pretty lady? Why don't you take your guineas?"

"Excuse, excuse me, Sir!" cried Juliet, hastily, and trying to be gone.

"And why?" cried he, a little angrily. "Are they not your own? What have you been singing for, and playing, and reading, and walking? and humouring the little naughty boy? and coddling the cross little dog? Take your guineas, I say! Would you be so proud as to leave the obligation all on the side of Mrs. Ireton?"

A smile at this statement, in defiance of her distress, irresistibly stole its way upon the features of Juliet; while Mrs. Ireton, stung to the quick, though forcing a contemptuous laugh, exclaimed, "This is really the height of the marvellous! It transcends all my poor ideas! I own that! I can't deny that! However, I must drop my acquaintance entirely with Miss Arbe, if it is to subject me to intrusions of every sort, on pretence of visiting that Miss what's her name! I have had quite enough of all this! I really desire no more."

Harleigh, to hide his acute interest in the situation of Juliet, pretended to be examining a portrait that was hung over the chimney-piece; but Lord Melbury, less capable of self-restraint, applaudingly seized the hand of Mr. Giles, and grasping it warmly, cried, "Where may I have the pleasure of waiting upon you, Sir? I desire infinitely to cultivate your acquaintance."

"And I shall like it too, my good young nobleman," said Mr. Giles, with a look of great satisfaction; and was beginning, at very full length, to give his direction, when Selina called out from the window, as a carriage drove up to the door, "Mrs. Ireton, it's Lord Denmeath's livery."

Lord Melbury, abruptly breaking from Mr. Giles, hurried out of the room; which alone prevented the same action from Juliet, whose face suddenly exhibited horrour rather than affright. But she felt that to fly the uncle, at a moment when she might seem to pursue the nephew, might be big with suspicious mischief; and, though shaking with terrour, she placed herself as if she were examining a small landscape, behind an immense screen, which in summer, as well as in winter,* nearly surrounded the sofa of Mrs. Ireton. And hence she hoped, when his lordship should be entered, to steal unnoticed from the room.

"This is a stroke that surpasses all the rest!" faintly cried Mrs. Ireton; "that Lord Denmeath, whom I have not seen these seven ages, should renew his acquaintance at an epoch of such strange disorder in my house! He will never believe this apartment to be mine! it will not be possible for him to believe it. He'll conclude me in some lodging. He'll imagine me the victim of some dreadful reverse of fortune. He is so little accustomed to see me in any motley group! He can so little figure me to himself as a person in a general herd!"

"Well, I, for one, am here by mere accident, to be sure," said

Miss Bydel; "but, however, I did not come in from mere curiosity, I assure you, Mrs. Ireton; for I knew nothing of Lord Denmeath's being to come. However, as I happen to be here, I sha'n't be sorry to see his lordship, if I sha'n't be in any body's way, for I never happened to be where he was before. Only I can't think what Lord Melbury went off so quick for; unless it was to shew his uncle the way up stairs. And if it was for that, it was pretty enough of him."

"No, no, you'll be in nobody's way, Mrs. Bydel," said Mr. Giles; "don't be afraid of that. Here's abundance of room for us all. The apartment's a very good apartment for that."

Mrs. Ireton now, impatiently ringing the bell, demanded, of a servant, what he had done with Lord Denmeath; adding, "I should be glad, Sir, to be informed! very glad, I must confess; for, perhaps, as you have been so good as to shew a visitor of one of my people into the drawing-room, you may have thought proper to usher a visitor of mine into the kitchen?"

His lordship, the servant answered, had been met by Lord Melbury, upon alighting from the coach, and had stept with him into the dining-parlour.

Mrs. Maple exulted that she should now, at last, have an opportunity to clear herself to his lordship, about the many odd appearances which had so long stood against her: while Ireton, who had espied the effort of Juliet to escape notice, called out, "I don't know where the devil I have put my hat;" and suddenly rushing towards her, with a blustrous appearance of search, gave her a mischievous nod, as she started back from his bold approach, and encircled her completely within the broad leaves of the screen.

She suffered this malicious sport in preference to attempting any resistance; though vexed at the noise which she must now unavoidably make in removing.

She was scarcely thus enclosed, when Lord Denmeath was announced.

Her heart now beat so violently with terrour, that her shaking hand could scarcely grasp a leaf of the screen, as she tried to make an opening for letting herself out, while his lordship was returning a reception of fawning courtesy, by some embarrassed and ambiguous apologies, relative to the motives of his visit. And when, at length, she succeeded, she was deterred from endeavouring to abscond, by seeing Harleigh, with his hand upon the door, making his bow.

Mrs. Maple, interfering, would not permit him to depart; clamorously declaring, that he was the properest person to give an account to his lordship of this adventurer, as he must best know why he had forced them to take such a body into their boat.

With deep agitation, and blushing anxiety, Juliet now unavoidably heard Harleigh answer, "I can but repeat to his lordship what I have a thousand times assured these ladies, that I have not the smallest knowledge whence this young lady comes, nor whom she may be. I can only, therefore, reply to these enquiries from my mental perceptions. These convince me, through progressive observations, that she is a person of honour, well educated, accustomed to good society, highly principled, and noble minded. You smile, my lord! But those only who judge without conversing with her, or converse without drawing forth her sentiments, can annex any disparaging doubt to the mystery of her situation. Her conduct has rather been exemplary than irreproachable from the moment that she has been cast upon our knowledge; though she has suffered, during that short interval, distress of almost every description. Her language is always that of polished life; her manners, even when her occupations are nearly servile, are invariably of distinguished elegance; yet, with all their softness, all their gentleness, she has a courage that, upon the most trying occasions, is superiour to difficulty; and a soul that, even in the midst of injury or misfortune, depends upon itself, and is above complaint. Such, my lord, I think her! not, indeed, from any certain documents; but from a self-conviction, founded, I repeat, upon progressive observations; which have the weight with me, now, of mathematical demonstration."

Tears resistless, yet benign, flowed down the cheeks of Juliet in listening to this defence; and, while she endeavoured to disperse them, before she ventured from her retreat, Lord Denmeath began an enquiry, whether this young person had regularly refused to say who she was; or whether she had occasionally made any partial communication; or given any hints relative to her family or connexions.

Juliet was now in an agony of mind indescribable. She had hoped to glide away with the general party unobserved; but Harleigh had kept constantly at the door till he made his exit; which, now, was so crowdingly followed by that of every one, except Mrs. Ireton and his lordship, that the delay ended in making her, individually, more conspicuous. Yet, to overhear, unsuspectedly, a conversation believed to be private, even though she knew herself to be its subject, was dishonour: hastily, therefore, though shaking in every limb, she forced herself from without the screen.

Mrs. Ireton shrieked and sunk back upon the sofa, crying out, "Oh, my lord, she's here!—Concealed to listen to us!—What a shock!—I shall feel it these three years!"

Juliet fleetly crossed the drawing-room, without daring to raise her head; but Lord Denmeath, passing quickly before her, as if intending to open the door, held the handle of the lock, while, steadily examining her as he spoke, he said, "Will you give me leave, Ma'am, to see you for a few minutes to-morrow?"

Juliet made not, nor even attempted to make any answer: terrour was painted in every line of her face, and she trembled so violently, that she was forced to catch by the back of a chair, to save herself from falling.

"I hope, Ma'am," said Lord Denmeath, "you are not ill?" and, approaching her with a look of compassion, added, in a whisper, "I know you!—but be not frightened. I will not hurt you. I will speak to you to-morrow alone, and arrange something to your advantage."

Juliet seemed utterly overcome, and remained motionless.

"Compose yourself," continued Lord Denmeath, speaking louder, and turning towards the wondering Mrs. Ireton; "I will see you when, and where you please to-morrow."

Mrs. Ireton, whose own curiosity knew not how to brook any delay, now recovered sufficient strength to rise; and, begging that his lordship would not postpone his business, she passed into her boudoir; the door of which, however, Lord Denmeath failed not to remark, was shut without much vigour.

Lowering, therefore, his tone till, even to Juliet, it was

scarcely audible, "We cannot," he said, "converse here with any openness; but, if you are not your own enemy, you may make me your friend; though I cannot but take ill your coming over against my advice and injunctions, and thus insidiously introducing yourself to my nephew and niece."

Juliet here looked up, with an air of self-vindication; but Lord Denmeath steadily went on.

"I have for some time suspected who you were, though but vaguely; yet, attributing your voyage to the officious counsel of the Bishop, I contented myself, for the moment, with putting a stop to your intercourse with my credulous young relations. But other information has reached me; and reached me at the very moment when Mrs. Howel,—when, indeed, my nephew and niece themselves had acquainted me with the meeting at Arundel Castle. I will talk upon all these matters in detail to-morrow morning. I have only to demand, in the interval, that you will neither speak nor write to Lord Melbury. I have already obtained his promise to be quiet till our conference is over. But I know that there are ways and means to induce a young man to forget his engagements. I hope you will try none such. Where can we have our conversation?"

"No where, my lord!" to the utter astonishment of Lord Denmeath, and even to her own, Juliet now, with sudden spirit, answered: but the courage which had been subdued by apprehension, was revived, during the preceding harangue, by strong glowing indignation.

"What is it," when amazement would give him leave to speak, "what is it," Lord Denmeath said, "that you mean?"

"That I will not trouble your lordship to offer me directions that I may not be at liberty to follow. I have already, my lord, a guide; and one to whose judgment I shall submit implicitly. That Bishop, whom your lordship is pleased to call officious, is my first, best, and nearly only friend; and if ever again I should be so blest as to meet with him, his opinion shall be my law,—as his benediction will be my happiness!"

In great emotion, yet with unappalled dignity, she was departing; but Lord Denmeath, with an air of surprize, stopping her, said, "You are then a Papist?"

"No, my lord! I am firmly a Protestant! But, as such, I am a

Christian; so, and most piously, yet not illiberally, is the Bishop."

"What is it,—tell me, if you please, that this Bishop purposes? To renew those old claims so long ago vainly canvassed? Can he imagine he will now have more influence than when possessed of his episcopal rank and fortune? Set him right in that point. You will do him a friendly turn. And permit me to do a similar one by yourself. I know the whole of your situation!"

Juliet started.

"I have just had information, which I meant to communicate to you, accompanied with offers of mediation and assistance; but you are sufficient to yourself! or your champion, the Bishop, makes all other aid superfluous! Suffer me, nevertheless, to intimate to you, that you will do well to return, quietly and expeditiously, to the spot whence you came. You may else make the voyage less pleasantly!"

The colour which resentment and exertion had just raised in the cheeks of Juliet, now faded away, and left them nearly as white as snow. Lord Denmeath, softening his voice and manner, and changing the haughty air of his countenance into something that approached kindness, went on more gently.

"I did not mean to alarm, but to befriend you. I allow not only for your youth and inexperience, but for the false ideas with which you have been brought up. If it had not pleased the Bishop to interfere, all would have been amicably arranged from the first. Take, however, a little time for reflection. Think upon the enormous risk which you run!—a fine young woman, like you,—and you are, indeed, a very fine young woman; flying from her house and home——"

Juliet, shaking, shuddering, hid her face, and burst into tears.

"I see that it is not impossible to work upon you," he continued; "I will beg Mrs. Ireton, therefore, to let us converse to-morrow where we may canvass the matter at leisure. The road is still open for you to affluence and credit. It will make me very happy to be your conductor. You will find I am authorized so to be. Make yourself, therefore, as easy as you can, and depend upon my best offices. We will certainly meet to-morrow morning."

He then bowed to her, and moved towards the boudoir; which Mrs. Ireton, appearing accidentally to open the door that had never been shut, quitted, to receive him; while Juliet, in speechless disorder, retired.

CHAPTER LXVI

UPON quitting the drawing-room, to mount to her chamber, Juliet caught a glance of Ireton, ascending the stair-case to the second story.

Apprehensive that he was watching for an opportunity to again torment her, she turned into a small apartment called the Print Closet, of which the door was open; purposing there to wait till he should have passed on.

There, however, she had no sooner entered, than, examining the beautiful engravings of Sir Robert Strange,* she perceived Harleigh.

Eagerly and with delight he advanced, and sought, once more, to take her hand. A look of solemnity repressed him; but 'twas a solemnity mixt with sorrow, not anger.

"Generous Mr. Harleigh!" she faintly articulated, while endeavouring to disperse the tears that again strove to find their way down her cheeks; "can you then, thus unabatedly preserve your good opinion of an unknown Wanderer, ... who seems the sport of insult and misfortune?"

Almost dissolved with tender feelings at this question, Harleigh, gently over-powering her opposition, irresistibly seized her hand, repeating, "My good opinion? my reverence, rather!—my veneration is yours!—and a confidence in your worth that has no limits!"

Ashamed of the situation into which a sudded impulse of gratitude had involuntarily betrayed her, the varying hues of her now white, now crimson cheeks manifested alternate distress and confusion; while she struggled incessantly to disengage her hand; but the happy heart of Harleigh felt so delightedly its possession, that she struggled in vain.

"Yet, let not that confidence," he continued, "be always the offspring of fascination! Give it, at length, some other food than conjecture! not to remove doubts; I have none! but to solve difficulties that rob me of rest.—"

"I am sorry, Sir, very sorry, if I cause you any uneasiness," said Juliet, resuming her usual calmness of manner; yet with bent down eyes, that neither ventured to meet his, nor to cast a glance at the hand which she still fruitlessly strove to withdraw; "but indeed you must not detain me;—no, not a minute!"

Enchanted by the mildness of this remonstrance, little as its injunction met his wishes; "Half a minute, then!" he gaily replied, "accord me only half a minute, and I will try to be contented. Suffer me but to ask,—"

"No, Sir, you must ask me nothing! There is no question whatever I can answer!—"

"I will not make one, then! I will only offer an observation. There is a something—I know not what; nor can I divine; but something there is strange, singular,—very unusual, and very striking, between you and Lord Melbury! Pardon, pardon my abruptness! You allow me no time to be scrupulous. You promise him your confidence,—that confidence so long, so fervently solicited by another!—so inexorably withheld!—"

"I earnestly desire," cried Juliet, recovering her look of openness, and raising her eyes; "the sanction of Lord Melbury to the countenance and kindness of Lady Aurora."

"Thanks! thanks!" cried Harleigh; who in this short, but expressive explanation, flattered himself that some concern was included for his peace; "'Tis to that, then, that cause,—a cause the most lovely,—he owes this envied pre-eminence?—And yet,—pardon me!—while apparently only a mediator—may not such a charge,—such an intercourse,—so intimate and so interesting a commission,—may it not,—nay, must it not inevitably make him from an agent become a principal?—Will not his heart pay the tribute—"

"Heaven forbid!" interrupting him, cried Juliet.

"Thanks! thanks, again! You do not, then, wish it? You are generous, noble enough not to wish it? And frank, sweet, ingenuous enough to acknowledge that you do not wish it? Ah! tell me but—"

"Mr. Harleigh," again interrupting him, cried Juliet, "I know not what you are saying!—I fear I have been misunderstood.—You must let me be gone!"—

"No!" answered he, passionately; "I can live no longer, breathe no longer, in this merciless solicitude of uncertainty and obscurity! You must give me some glimmering of light, some opening to comprehension,—or content yourself to be my captive!—"

"You terrify me, Mr. Harleigh! Let me go!—instantly! instantly!—Would you make me hate—" She had begun with a precipitance nearly vehement; but stopt abruptly.

"Hate me?" cried Harleigh, with a look appalled: "Good Heaven!"

"Hate you?—No,—not you! . . . I did not say you!—"

"Who, then? who then, should I make you hate?—Lord Melbury?—"

"O no, never!—'tis impossible!—Let me be gone!—let me be gone!—"

"Not till you tell me whom I should make you hate! I cannot part with you in this new ignorance! Clear, at least, this one little point. Whom should I make hate you?—"

"Myself, Sir, myself!" cried she, trembling and struggling. "If you persist in thus punishing my not having fled from you, at once, as I would have fled from an enemy!"

He immediately let go her hand; but, finding that, though her look was instantly appeased, nay grateful, she was hastily retreating, he glided between her and the door, crying, "Where,—at least deign to tell me!—Where may I see,—may I speak to you again?"

"Any where, any where!"—replied she, with quickness; but presently, with a sudden check of vivacity, added, "No where, I mean!—no where, Sir, no where!"—

"Is this possible!" exclaimed he. "Can you,—even in your wishes,—can you be so hard of heart?"—

"It is you," said she reproachfully, "who are hard of heart, to detain me thus!—Think but where I am!—where you are!—This house—Miss Joddrel—What may not be the consequence?—Is it Mr. Harleigh who would deliver me over to calumny?

Harleigh now held open the door for her himself, without venturing to reply, as he heard footsteps upon the stairs; but he permitted his lips to touch her arm, for he could not again seize her hand, as she passed him, eagerly, and with her face averted. She fled on to the stairs, and rapidly ascended them. Harleigh durst not follow; but he pursued her with his eyes. He could not, however, catch a glance, could not even view her profile, so sedulously her head was turned another way. Disappointment and mortification were again seizing him; till he considered, that that countenance thus hidden, had she been wholly unfearful of shewing some little emotion, had probably, nay, even purposely, been displayed.

Fleetly gaining her room, and dropping upon a chair, "I must fly!—I must fly!" she exclaimed. "Danger, here, attacks me in every quarter,—assails me in every shape! I must fly!—I must fly!"

This project, which had its origin in her terrour of Elinor, was now confirmed by the most profound, however troubled meditation. To difficulties of discussion which she deemed insurmountable with Harleigh; to claims of a confidence which she now considered to be deeply dangerous with Lord Melbury; and to indignities daily, nay, hourly, more insufferable from Mrs. Ireton, were joined, at this moment, the horrour of another interview with Lord Denmeath, still more repugnant to her thoughts, and formidable to her fears.

She refused to descend to the evening summons of Mrs. Ireton; determining to avoid all further offences from that lady, to whom she had already announced her intended departure; yet she sighed, she even wept at quitting with the same unexplained abruptness Lord Melbury and Harleigh; and the cruel disappointment, mingled with strange surmizes, of the ingenuous Lord Melbury; the nameless consternation, blended with resentful suspence, of the impassioned Harleigh; presented scenes of distress and confusion to her imagination, that occupied her thoughts the whole night, with varying schemes and incessant regret.

When the glimmering of light shewed her that she must soon

be gone, she mounted to a garret, which she knew to be inhabited by a young house-maid, whom she called up; and prevailed upon to go forth, and seek a boy who would carry a parcel to a distant part of the town.

Having thus gotten the street-door open, she guided the boy herself to the inn; where she arrived in time to save her place; and whence she set off for London.

CHAPTER LXVII

ESCAPE and immediate safety thus secured, her tender friendship for Gabriella, superseding all fear, and leaving behind all solicitude, made Juliet nearly pronounce aloud, what internally she repeated without intermission, "I come to you, then, at last, my beloved Gabriella!" Cheerful, therefore, was her heart, in defiance of her various distresses: she was quitting Mrs. Ireton, to join Gabriella!—What could be the circumstances that could make such a change severe to Juliet? Juliet, who felt ill treatment more terribly than misfortune; and to whom kindness was more essential than prosperity?

Her journey was free from accident, and void of event. Absorbed in her own ruminations, she listened not to what was said, and scarcely saw by whom she was surrounded; though her fellow-travellers surveyed her with curiosity, and, from time to time, assailed her with questions.

Arrived at London, she put herself into a hackney-coach; and, almost before her fluttered spirits suffered her to perceive that she had left the inn-yard, she found herself in a haberdasher's shop, in Frith Street, Soho; and in the arms of her Gabriella.

It was long ere either of them could speak; their swelling hearts denied all verbal utterance to their big emotions; though tears of poignant grief at the numerous woes by which they had been separated, were mingled with feelings of the softest felicity at their re-union.

Yet vaguely only Juliet gave the history of her recent difficulties; the history which had preceded them, and upon which hung the mystery of her situation, still remained unrevealed.

Gabriella forbore any investigation, but her look shewed disappointment. Juliet perceived it, and changed colour. Tears gushed into her eyes, and her head dropt upon the neck of her friend. "Oh my Gabriella!" she cried, "if my silence wounds, or offends you,—it is at an end!"

Gabriella, instantly repressing every symptom of impatience, warmly protested that she would await, without a murmur, the moment of communication; well satisfied that it could be withheld from motives only that would render its anticipation dangerous, if not censurable.

With grateful tears, and tenderest embraces, Juliet expressed her thanks for this acquiescence.

Of Gabriella, the history was brief and gloomy. She had entered into business with as little comprehension of its attributes, as taste for its pursuit; her mind, therefore, bore no part in its details, though she sacrificed to them the whole of her time. Of her son alone she could speak or think. From her husband she reaped little consolation. Married before the Revolution, from a convent, and while yet a child; according to the general custom of her country, which rarely permits any choice even to the man; and to the female allows not even a negative; chance had not, as sometimes is kindly the case, played the part of election, in assorting the new married couple. Gabriella was generous, noble, and dignified: exalted in her opinions, and full of sensibility: Mr. * * * was many years older than herself, haughty and austere, though brave and honourable; but so cold in his nature, that he was neither struck with her virtues nor her graces, save in considering them as appendages to their mutual rank; nor much moved even by the death of his little son, but from repining that he had lost the heir to his illustrious name. He was now set off, *incognito,* to an appointed meeting with a part of his family, upon the continent.

Again a new scene of life opened to Juliet. The petty frauds, the over-reaching tricks, the plausible address, of the crafty shop-keeper in retail, she had already witnessed: but the difficulties of honest trade she had neither seen nor imagined. The utter inexperience of Gabriella, joined to the delicacy of her probity, made her not more frequently the dupe of the artifices of those with whom she had to deal, than the victim to her own scruples. New to the mighty difference between buying and selling; to the necessity of having at hand more stores than may probably be wanted, for avoiding the risk of losing customers from having fewer; and to the usage of rating at an imaginary value whatever is in vogue, in order to repair the losses incurred from the failure of obtaining the intrinsic worth of what is old-fashioned or faulty;—new to all this, the wary shop-keeper's code, she was perpetually mistaken, or duped, through ignorance of ignorance, which leads to hazards, unsuspected to be hazards.

Repairs for the little shop were continually wanted, yet always unforeseen; taxes were claimed when she was least prepared to discharge them; and stores of merchandize accidentally injured, were obliged to be sold under prime cost, if not to be utterly thrown away.

Unpractised in every species of business, she had no criterion whence to calculate its chances, or be aware of its changes, either from varying seasons or varying modes; and to all her other intricacies, there was added a perpetual horrour of bankruptcy, from the difficulty of accelerating payment for what she sold, or of procrastinating it for what she bought.

Every embarrassment, however, at this period, was accommodated by Juliet; who had the exquisite satisfaction not only to bring to her beloved friend personal consolation, but solid and effectual comfort. The purse of Lord Melbury, which Juliet would only consider as the loan of Lady Aurora, was but little lightened by the small expences of the short journey from Brighthelmstone; and all that remained of its contents were instantly assigned to relieving the most painful of the distresses of Gabriella, those in which others were involved through her means.

Gabriella, with a grace familiar, if not peculiar, to her nation, of sharing, without the confusion of false pride, the offerings of tender friendship, or generous sympathy, accepted with noble frankness the assistance thus proposed; though Juliet again was obliged to hide her face from the enquiring eye, that seemed strangely to wonder whence this resource arose, and why its spring was concealed.

Juliet now became a partner in all the occupations and cares of her friend: together they prepared the shop for their customers every morning, and decked it out to attract passers bye; together they examined and re-arranged their goods every night; cast up their accounts, deposited sums for their creditors, and entered claims into their books for their debtors: together they sat in the shop, where one served and waited upon customers, and the other aided the household economy by the industry of her needle. Yet, laborious as might seem this existence to those who had known "other times,"* Juliet, by the side of Gabriella, thought every employment delightful; Gabriella, in the society of Juliet, felt every exertion lightened, and every sorrow softened.

CHAPTER LXVIII

THUS, in manual toil, yet mental comfort, had passed a week, when one morning, while the usual commissioner for carrying about goods happened to be out of the way, a lady from Soho Square sent, in great haste, an order for some ribbons. Juliet, to save a customer to her friend, proposed supplying the commissioner's place; and set forth for that purpose, with a little band-box* in her hands, and a large black bonnet drawn over her eyes. But before she reached the square, she overtook two men who were loitering on, as leisurely as she was tripping diligently, and the words, "You'll never know her again, I promise you; she's turned out quite a beauty!" struck her ears, from a voice which she recollected to be that of Mr. Riley.

Anxious to avoid being recognized by him, she crossed to the other side of the street, with a precipitance that caused the cover of her band-box, which she had neglected to fasten, to slip aside, and most of her stores to roll in the dust.

While, with great dismay, she sought to recover them, a feeble, but eager voice, from a carriage, which suddenly stopt, ordered a footman to descend and assist the young lady.

Not without confusion, Juliet perceived to whom she owed so uncommon a civility; it was to her old friend and admirer Sir Jaspar Herrington. She collected her merchandize, courtsied her thanks, but looked another way, and hurried back to her new home.

She related her adventure to Gabriella, with whom she bemoaned the mischief that had befallen the ribbons; and who now determined to spare her friend any further hazard of unwelcome encounters, by carrying herself what yet remained unsoiled of the pieces, to Soho Square.

Juliet had barely time to install herself as mistress of the small warehouse, when she saw, through the window, the carriage of Sir Jaspar; at the same time, that a young woman opened the shop-door, and demanded a drachm* of black sewing silk, and a yard of tape.

While Juliet with difficulty found, and with embarrassment prepared to weigh the first, and to measure the second, the Baronet, with a curious, but respectful air, entering, and hobbling towards the counter, desired to look at some ribbons.

Juliet, however vexed, could not refrain from smiling; but, through confusion, joined to the novelty of her office, she doubled the weight of her silk, and the measure of her tape, yet forgot to ask to be paid for either; and her customer, whether from similar forgetfulness, or from reluctance to mark the new shop-keeper's ignorance of business, walked off without seeming to notice this inattention.

Sir Jaspar, then, gravely repeated his request to be shewn some ribbons.

Juliet began now to hope that she had not been recollected by the Baronet. Shading her face, therefore, still lower with her large bonnet, she produced a drawer of black ribbons; concluding that what he required must be for his queue, or for his shoe-strings.*

No, he said, black would not do: the colour that he wanted was brown.

In a low voice that strove to disguise itself, she answered that she had no other colour at home.

He would stay till some other were returned, then, he said; and, composedly seating himself, and taking out his snuff-box, he added, that he did not want plain brown ribbons, but ribbons speckled, spotted, or splashed with brown.

Juliet who could now no longer doubt being known to him, made no reply; though again, irresistibly, she smiled.

To the Baronet her smile was always enchantment; setting aside, therefore, any further pretence to strangeness, he leant his hands upon the counter, and peering archly under her bonnet, said, "'Tis you, indeed, then, sweet sorceress? And what sylph is it,—or what imp?—dulcet, or malignant!—that has drawn me again into the witchery of your charms?"

He then poured forth countless enquiries into her situation, her projects, and her sentiments; but, all proving fruitless, he pathetically lamented the luckless meeting; and frankly owned, that he had brought himself to a resolution of seeing her no more. "The rude assault," said he, "made upon my feelings by those mundane harpies at Arundel Castle, removed a bandage from 'my mind's eye'* that had veiled me to myself, and shewed me that I was an old fool caught in the delusions of love and beauty! I could parry no raillery, I could brave no suspicion, I could retort no sneer! Panic-struck and disordered, I stole away, like a gentle Philander of Arcadia,* my head drooping upon my left shoulder, my eyes cast down upon the ground, with every love-lorn symptom,—except youth, which alone offers their apology! I spent the rest of the day in character with this opening; mute with my servants; loquacious in soliloquy; quarrelling with my books; and neglecting my dinner! Sleepless and sighing, I repaired to my solitary couch; lost to every idea of existence, but what pointed out to me how, when, and where I might again behold my lovely enchantress. Shall I tell you how it was I recovered, at last, my senses?"

"If you think the lesson may be useful to me, Sir Jaspar!—"

"Ah, cruel! 'He jests at scars who never felt a wound.'* Mark, however, the visions by which I have been tutored. The servants gone, the lights removed, and the world's bustle superseded by stillness, darkness, and solitude,—then, when my fancy meant to revel in smiles, dimples, sweet looks, and recreative wiles, then,—what a transformation from hope and enjoyment, to shame and derision! I no sooner closed my poor eyes, than an hundred little imps of darkness scrambled up my pillow. How was I tweaked, jirked, and jolted! Mumbled, jumbled, and pinched! Some of them encircled my eye-balls, holding mirrours in each hand. They spoke not; the mirrours were all eloquent! You think, they expressed, of a young girl? Behold here what a young girl must think of you! Others jammed my lean, lank arms into a machine of whale-bone, to strengthen and invigorate them for offering support, in cases of difficulty or danger, to my fair one: others fastened elastic strings to my withered neck and shoulders, to enable me, by little pulleys, to raise my head, after every obsequious reverence to my goddess. Crowds of the nimblest footed dived their little forked fingers into my heart, plucking up by the root sober contentment and propriety; and pummelling into their places restlessness, jealousy, and suspicion: mocking me when they had done, by peeping into my ears, and squeaking out, with merry tittering, See! see! see! what sickly rubbish the old dotard has got in his crazy noddle!"

Juliet again smiled, but so faintly, from uncertainty to what this fantastic gallantry might tend, that Sir Jaspar, looking at her with concern, said, "How's this, my dainty Ariel?* Why so serious a brow? Have some of my nocturnal visitants whisked themselves through the key-hole of your chamber-door, also? And have they tormented your fancy with waking visions of fearful omens? Spurn them all! sweet syren! What can the tricks and malice of hobgoblins, or even the freaks and vagaries of fortune itself, enact against youth, beauty, and health such as yours? Give me but such arms, and I will brave the wayward sisters* themselves."

More seriously, then, "Alas!" he cried, "what is it, thus mystic, yet thus attractive, that allures me whether I will or not into your chains?—Could I but tell who, or what you are,—besides being an angel,—it is possible there might occur some idea,—some—some little notion of means to exorcise the wicked familiars that severally annoy us. Tell me but under what semblance the pigmy enemies invade you? Whether, as usual, with the darts of Master Cupid, shot, furiously, into your snowy bosom, or—"

"No, no, no!"

"Or whether by the bags of Plutus, emptied, furtively, from your strong box? In the first case,—little as my bosom is snowy!—I should but too well know how to pity; in the second,

I should be proud and honoured to serve you. Tell me, then, who you are, resistless paragon! and you shall wander no more in this nameless state, an exquisite, but nearly visionary being! Tell me but who you are, and I will protect you, myself, with my life and fortune!"

Alarmed by this warmth, and doubtful whether it demanded gratitude or resentment, Juliet was silent.

"If you will not reveal to me your history," he resumed, "you will, at least, not refuse to let me divine it? I am a famous star-gazer; and, if once I can discover your ruling planet, I shall prognosticate your destiny in a second. Let me, then, read the lines of your face. Nay! you must not hide it! You must give me fair play. Or, shall I examine the palm of your hand?"

Juliet laughed, but drew on her gloves.

"O you little Tyrant! I must only, then, catch, as I can, a glimpse of your countenance. A nauseous task, enough, to dwell on any thing so ugly! All I can make out from it, just now, is the figure of a coronet."

"A coronet?"

"Yes; under which I perceive the cypher D. Do you know any thing of any nobleman whose name begins with a D? I cannot decipher the rest of the letters, except that the last is—I think,—an h."

Juliet started.

"My art, I must, however, own, is at a stand, to discover whether this nobleman may be a lover or a kinsman. To discern that, the general lines of the face are inadequate. I must investigate the eyes."

Juliet pertinaciously looked down.

"How now, my dainty Ariel? Will you give me no answer? neither verbal nor visual? Will you not even tell me whether I must try to make the old peer my advocate, or whether I must run him through the body? Surely you won't let me court him as of kin if he be a rival? nor pink* him as a rival if he be of kin?"

"He is neither, I can assure you, Sir: he is nothing to me whatsoever."

"You know, at least, then, it seems, whom I mean?"

"Sir?"

"My tiny elves have not here deluded me? I am always afraid

lest those merry little wags should be playing me some prank. But it is you who are the wicked Will o" the Wisp, that lures all others, yet never can be lured yourself! Lord Denmeath has really, then, and in sober truth, the happiness of some way belonging to you?"

"No, Sir;—you mistake me;—I never—" She left her phrase unfinished.

"Shall I relate what the prattling tell-tales have blabbed to me further? They pretend that Lord Denmeath ought himself to be your protector; but that he is so void of taste, so empty of sentiment, that he seeks to disguise, if not disown, an affinity that, with more liberal ideas, he would exult in as an honour."

"Who talked of affinity, Sir?" cried Juliet, with quickness irrepressible.—"Was it Lord Denmeath?—Did he name me to you?"

"Name you? Has any one named you? Indefinable, unconquerable, unfathomable Incognita! Has any one presumed to give you a human genealogy? Are you not straight descended from the clouds? without even taking the time to change yourself first into a mortal? Explain, expound, unravel to me, in soft pity—"

Juliet solemnly entreated him to forbear any further interrogatory, assuring him that all enquiry gave her pain.

"Then shall 'the stars,'" cried he, "'fade away, the sun grow dim, and nature,'—like my poor old carcass!—'sink in years,'* ere one grain more of the favourite attribute of our general mother* shall be sown in my discourse! But you, in all things marvellous! You! have you really, and *bona fide*, so little in your composition of our naughty mamma, as not even to desire to know in what shape appeared to me the tattling little elf, that talked to me of Lord Denmeath?"

"You have not then, Sir, seen him?"

"Or if I had?—twenty interviews would not have initiated me into his affairs with so much promptitude, as twenty minutes sufficed for doing with my elfin fay."

"I conjecture, then, Sir, your informant: Miss Selina Joddrel?"

"Even so. Upon determining to quit Brighthelmstone, three or four days ago, I drove over to Lewes, to offer what apologies I could suggest to Mrs. Maple, for the vagaries of my hopeful nephew and heir,—who is suddenly set out for Constantinople in search, as he writes me word, of a fair Circassian! The last of my designs, in so delicate a case, you will easily believe, was to embarrass the injured and deserted fair one by my sight. But she had a fortitude far above my precautions. She flew to me herself; and her own plaintive tale had no sooner been bemoaned, than she hastened to favour me with the history of the whole house. I then learnt your sudden disappearance; and heard, with extreme satisfaction, from the indignation I had felt in seeing your ill treatment, that my meek sister-in-law had fallen into fits, from the first shock of finding that you were no longer under her dominion. My Lord Denmeath, who had already gone through the ceremonial of demanding Mrs. Maple's permission to obtain a private audience with you, seemed thunderstruck at the news, that the bird he so much wished to sing to him was flown. The whole house was in disorder; running, enquiring, asserting, denying;—the wild Elinor alone was tame and tranquil,—for Mr. Harleigh has kept constantly in sight."

Delicate, and ever feeling Harleigh! thought Juliet; Her life, and My reputation, hang suspended upon the same guardian care!

"That eccentric and most original personage," continued Sir Jaspar, "has now wholly made over her mind to the study of controversial theology. Every chair is covered with polemical tracts, to prove one side of an argument, that every table is covered to disprove on the other. If she settle her opinions one way, she will probably become the foundress of some new-fangled monastery; if on the other, she will be discovered, some star-light night, seeking truth at the bottom of a well."

Juliet then anxiously enquired into the state of her health.

"She seems to me," answered the Baronet, "quite as well as it is possible for a person to be, who is afflicted with the restless malady of struggling for occasion to exhibit character; instead of leaving its display to the jumble of nature and of accident. But these new systemers do not break out of bounds more wildly from whim, than they afterwards seek retreat within them, tamely, from experience. The little Selina, on the contrary, who has escaped the trouble of supporting a character, by not having an idea that could form one, had the kindness to make me the most liberal communication of every thing that she has either seen or heard, since she has been skipping about in this nether world; and, in her scampers from room to room, and from person to person, she had gathered sundry interesting particulars of a certain fair unknown.——"

He paused; looked anxious, and then went on.

"I would not be officious,—impertinent, nor importunate,—yet, could I but ascertain some points.—If, however, you will not unfold to me your history, will you, at least,—syren of syrens!—to develop why I demand it, hear me divulge my own?"

Juliet, surprised and amused, gratefully assented.

"Know, then, my fair torment! it pleased my wise progenitors to entail my estate upon my next of kin, in case I should have no lineal heir. Brought up with the knowledge of this restriction to the fantasies of my future will, I conceived an early suspicion that my younger brother built sundry vain-glorious castles upon my celibacy; and I determined not to reach my twentieth year before I put an end to his presumption. The first idea, therefore, that fastened upon my mind was that of marriage. But as I entertained a general belief, that I should every where be accepted from mercenary motives, I viewed all females with the scrutiny of a bargain-maker. Thankless for any mark of partiality, difficult even to absurdity, I sought new faces with restless impatience; modestly persuaded that I ought to find a companion without a blot! yet, whatever was my success, regularly making off from every fair charmer, after the second interview, through the fear of being taken in."

"And were none of your little sylphs, Sir, at hand, to point out to you some one who was disinterested in her nature, however inferiour in her fortune?"

"No! alas! no; my sylphs all reserved themselves for my meeting with you! The wicked little imps who then guided and goaded me, incited me to suspect and to watch every thing that seemed lovely or amiable; and the pranks that they played me were endless. They urged me to pursue the glowing Beauty, whose vivid cheeks, crimsoned by the dance, had warmed all my senses at a ball, to her alighting from her carriage, at her return home, with the livid hue of fatigue and moonlight! They instigated me to surprize, when ill-dressed, negligent, and spiritless, the charming face and form that, skilfully adorned, had appeared to me Venus attired by the Graces.* They twitched me on to dart upon another, whose bloom had seemed the opening of the rose-bud, just as an untoward accident had rubbed off, from one cheek, the sweet pink which remained undiminished upon the other! And when, tired of the deceptions of beauty, I would only follow merit, the wanton little sprites suggested detections still more mischievous. They led me to overhear the softest of maidens insult a poor dependent; they shewed me a pattern of discretion, secretly involved in debt; and the frankest of human lasses, engaged in a clandestine affair! They whisked me, in short, into every crevice of female subtlety. They exhibited all as a drama, and gave me a peep behind the curtain to see the gayest damsel the sulkiest; the most pleasing one, the most spiteful; the delicate one, obstreperous; the bashful one, bold; the generous one, niggardly; and the humble one, a tyrant!"

"Oh wicked imps, indeed, Sir Jaspar! What a view of poor human nature have they deformed for you! And how have you preserved such a stock of philanthropy, while instigated by so much malignity?"

"Alas, my fair love, my history is but that of half the old bachelors existing! We pay, by our aged facility and good humour, for our youthful severity and impertinence! and, after having wasted our early life in conceiving that no one is good enough for us, we consume our latter days in envy of every married man! Now—all too late! I never see a lovely young creature, but my heart calls out what a delicious wife she would make me! were I younger, without reflection, without enquiry, were I younger, I would marry her! THEN—when such precipitation might have been pardonable, some difficulty instantly followed the sight of whatever was attractive: one had not fortune enough for my expectations; another, had beauty to make me eternally jealous; another, though charming, was too old to be formed to my taste; another, though lovelier still, was too young to be judged. One was too wise, and might hold me cheap; another was too simple, and might expose me to seeing her held cheap herself. THEN—I was so plaguely nice! Now, alas! I am so cursedly easy!"

"Your sylphs, elves, and imps, Sir, or in other words, your humour and imagination, must seek some counterpoise, and not always, you see, be trusted uncontrouled."

"You are right, my wise charmer! but we never arrive at judgment, the only counterpoise to our fancies, till we cease to want it! When we are young, in the midst of the world, and in pursuit of beauty, riches, honours, power, fame, or knowledge, then, when judgment would either guide us to success, or demolish our senseless expectations, it keeps aloof from us like a stern stranger: and will only hail us as an intimate, when we have no longer any occasion for its services! Of what value is judgment to a gouty old codger, who sits just as snugly over his fire-side, whether his opinions are erroneous or oracular? who wraps himself just as warmly in flannel, whether the world go ill or go well? and who, if, by ignorance or mismanagement, he be cheated, loses only what he cannot enjoy! I first became aware of my folly, by the folly of my nephew. When he was sent forth into the world, my decided—alas!—heir, I told him my case; and urged him to a rational but quick choice, to obviate a similar punishment to fantastical difficulties. He listened, according to the usage of youth, to half what I said; and, adopting only my mistrust, was inattentive to its result; and thus so caricatured my researches, suspicions, and irresolutions, that he has rendered them and myself, even in my own eyes, completely ridiculous. 'Tis a most piteous circumstance that a man can be young only once in his life! Could I but, with my present experience, lop off thirty or forty years of my age,—ah! fair seducer!—how would the desire of giving you pleasure, the fear of causing you pain, the wish to see your face always beaming with smiles——"

Juliet arose to interrupt him; but whither could she go? She again sat down.

The Baronet also rose; and stood for some minutes, covering his eyes with one hand, in deep rumination. Re-seating himself, then, with an air of the most lively satisfaction, "I have told you," he cried, "now, my history. You see in me a whimsical, but contrite old bachelor; whose entailed estate has lost to him his youth, by ungenerous mistrust: but who would gladly devote the large possessions which have fallen to him collaterally,* to making the rest of his existence companionable. Shrink not, sweet flower! I mean nothing that can offend you. Tell me but who you are, and, be you whom you may, if you will accept an old protector; if you will deign to become his friend; to give him your conversation, your society, your lovely presence; he will despise the mocking world—and decorate himself for your bridegroom, by a marriage settlement of the whole of his unintailed estate."

Astonished, and uncertain whether he were serious, Juliet was beginning a playful attack upon his fairy elves; but, stopping her with perturbed earnestness, "Will you," he cried, "accept me? Your beauty, your difficulties, your distresses; your exquisite looks, and witching manners; with my solitude, my repugnance to mercenary watchers, my deep regrets, and my desire of domestic commerce; unite to devote me to you for ever; provided, only I can catch a grain, a single grain, of gentle good will! Give me, then, but this one satisfaction—I ask no more! tell me but whence it comes that, thus formed, thus accomplished, thus wise, thus lovely,—you are helpless, dependent, indigent, and a Wanderer?"

Juliet, though no longer able to doubt his meaning, and though not disposed to suspect his sincerity, felt, nevertheless, shocked by such an investigation; though grateful, and even touched by his singular and romantic proposal. Delicacy, however, which keeps back acknowledged belief in unrequited partiality, as scrupulously as it is withheld by timid consciousness, where the partiality is returned; made her again have recourse to his visionary friends, in order to parry a serious reply; but, too much in earnest to submit to any delay, the Baronet, ejaculating, "Paragon of the world!" was bending over the counter, in an attempt to take her hand; when the sudden opening of the shop-door, which he had himself carefully closed, previous to his declaration, made him draw back, in the utmost confusion; to recover his seat and his crutches, and again demand to look at some ribbons.

CHAPTER LXIX

GABRIELLA, who had thus long been detained from her business, because the lady, whose orders she had obeyed, had either forgotten that those orders had been issued, or deemed that to wait in an anti-room was the natural fate of an haberdasher; now, entering the shop, saw, with no little surprize, Juliet in close conference with an old beau, who was evidently disconcerted, and embarrassed by the interruption. Remitting, however, all enquiry, and gracefully declining a chair, which was respectfully offered to her by Sir Jaspar, who imagined her to be some customer; she silently employed herself in examining and arranging her unpinned, unrolled, and tumbled ribbons.

The surprize of the Baronet, now, became greater than her own. No plainness of attire could hide, from his scrutinizing eye, a certain native taste with which her habiliments, however simple, were put on; nor could even the band-box which she held in her hand, and which he had supposed to be there from some accident, disguise the elegance of her motions, or conceal her lofty mien. When, therefore, he discovered that she was at home, and that she was an haberdasher, he looked from one lovely companion to the other, with reverential wonder, and uplifted hands. Long profoundly impressed by the beauty of Juliet, by her merit, her youth, her modest yet dignified demeanour, in the midst of all the difficulties of distressed poverty; he was now as powerfully affected by the appearance of Gabriella; whose noble, yet never haughty manners, joined to a tragic expression of constant woe in her countenance, rendered her if not as attractive, at least as interesting as her friend.

A general pause ensued, till Gabriella, fearing that she was obtrusive, retired to the inner room.

Sir Jaspar, wide opening his eyes, and again leaning forward, to hear more distinctly, exclaimed, "Who is that fine creature? What a majestic port! Yet how sweet a look! She awes while she invites! Who is she?"

Juliet felt enchanted; she even felt exalted by a testimony so impartial and so honourable, to the merit of her friend, and she eagerly answered, "Your admiration, Sir, does honour to your discernment. Her excellencies, her high qualities, and spotless conduct, might make the proudest Englishman exult to own her for his country-woman; though the lowest Frenchman would dispute, even at the risk of his life, the honour of her birth. Sprung from one of the first houses of Europe, a house not more ancient in its origin, than renowned for its virtues; allied to a family the most illustrious, whose military glory has raised it to the highest ranks in the state; herself an ornament to that birth, an honour to that alliance; she sustains a reverse of fortune, which reduces her from every indulgence to every privation, with a calm courage that keeps her always mistress of herself, and enables her to combat evil by labour, misery by industry! And which never has failed her, but in a personal, bosom affliction, that would equally have shaken her fortitude, in the brightest splendour of prosperity!—"

"Hold! hold, you little torment!" interrupted Sir Jaspar. "You don't consider what an artillery my wanton sprites are bringing upon me! My poor gouty fingers are so mumbled and pinched, and tweaked, to hurry me to get at my purse, that I cannot catch hold of it for very tremour!—"

"Oh no, Sir Jaspar, no! What she earns, however hardly and however humbly, she thankfully reaps; but she could only submit to accept alms, if bowed down by age, by malady, or by incapacity for work. Yet this spirit is not pride; 'tis but a strong and refined sense of propriety; since from a friend, in the tender persuasion, that participation of fortune ought to be leagued with participation of sentiment, she would candidly receive whatever would not injure that friend to bestow"

"Divinest of little mortals!" cried Sir Jaspar. "What whimsey is it, what astonishing whimsey of 'the sisters three,' that can have nailed to a counter two such delectable beings, to weigh pins and needles, and measure tapes and bobbins? And how,—beautiful witch! with charms, graces, accomplishments, talents such as yours, how is it you submit to such base drudgery in 'durance vile,'* without even making a wry face? without a scowl upon your eye-brow, or a grumble from your throat?"

"Can you look, Sir, at her whom you call my partner, and think of me? She has lost her country; she wastes in exile; she sinks in obscurity; she has no communication with her friends;

she knows not even whether they yet breathe the vital air!—nevertheless she works, she sustains herself by her industry and ingenuity; and repines only that she has not still another, has not her loved and lovely infant to sustain also!—and I, shall I complain?—Offspring of a race the most dignified, she toils manually, not to degrade it mentally;—and I, shall I blush to owe my subsistence to my exertions?"

Tears now flowed fast down her cheeks, while the crutches dropt from the feeble hands of the penetrated Baronet, whose eyes, dimmed by compassion, were fastened upon the face of the lovely mourner, when Gabriella re-appeared.

In deep amazement and concern, she hesitated whether she should come forward, to offer comfort; or whether, as she now concluded the old gentleman to be some intimate friend, she ought not again to retire; but Juliet entreated her to return to her place. She resumed, therefore, her business of restoring her ribbons to order; dejectedly announcing, that nothing had been bought; though every thing had been examined, deranged, and tossed about.

Sir Jaspar now, courteously waving his hand, smilingly addressed himself to Gabriella, saying, "'Tis my good Genius, Ma'am, make no doubt of it, that has run away with the feeling of those people you mention! For my good Genius, I must beg you to observe, has frequently taken lessons of the god Mercury,* and is nearly as adroit in petty larceny as his godship himself. I should not, therefore, wonder, if, in his eagerness to serve me, he had pilfered from those poor souls, who have used you so ill, every grain he could pick up of decency! For, knowing that ribbons are a commodity of which I want a prodigious stock, he would not suffer your assortment to be diminished, till I had had the pleasure of making my bargains."

He then selected the piece of ribbon which seemed the most considerable, and desired to have it measured.

Gabriella obeyed, not more amazed than Juliet felt amused.

But, when a similar order was given, for ascertaining the quantity of a second piece, and then of a third; Juliet, though delighted at the pleased looks of Gabriella, and charmed with the generosity of the Baronet, began to apprehend, that she might herself be supposed to incur some debt of gratitude for this liberality. She retreated, therefore, with her needle-work, to the adjoining little room.

In a few minutes, she was followed by Gabriella; who, uneasily, asked what she must do with this magnificent old beau, who still while she measured one piece of ribbon, employed himself in selecting another; and who, though so gallant that he never spoke without a compliment, was so respectful, that it was not possible to check him by any serious reproof.

Juliet disclaimed taking any share in his present munificence; yet owned that she had an ancient obligation to him that she was unable, at this moment, to repay; and which, from the delicacy with which it had been conferred, and the seasonable relief which it had procured her, would merit her lasting gratitude. He was brother-in-law, she added, to the lady with whom she had lately resided; and he was as rich as he was benevolent.

Her scruples, then, Gabriella said, were at an end. Juliet, therefore, begged that she would endeavour to enter into conversation with him concerning Brighthelmstone; and try to obtain some particulars relative to the party at Mrs. Ireton's.

"I began to fear you had flown away, Ma'am," said Sir Jaspar, upon Gabriella's re-entrance into the shop; "and I was much less surprised than concerned; for I had already surmized that you were an angel; though I had failed to remark your wings."

He then put into her hand three more pieces of ribbon, which he had chosen during her absence.

Gabriella, who understood English well, though she spoke it imperfectly, made her answers in French.

Having now given her ample employment, he sat down to examine, or, rather, to admire at his ease, the lightness and grace with which she executed her office; saying, "You are not, perhaps, aware, Madam, that there are certain little beings, nameless and invisible, yet active and penetrating, perpetually hovering around us, who have let me a little into your history; and have taken upon them to assure me that you were not precisely brought up to be a shop-keeper? How, then, is it that you have jumbled thus together such heterogeneous materials of existence? leaguing high birth with low life? superiour rank with vulgar employment; and grace, taste, and politeness with common drudgery? How, in short, born and bred to be dangled after by your vassals, and to lollop, the live-long-day, upon sofas and arm-chairs, have you acquired the necessary ingredients for being metamorphosed into a tidy little haberdasher?"

Gabriella, concluding that her situation had been made known to him by Juliet, answered, in a melancholy tone, "Is this a period, Sir, to consider punctilio? Alas! whence I come, all that are greatest, most ancient, and most noble,[†] have learnt, that self-exertion can alone mark nobility of soul; and that self-dependence can only sustain honour in adversity. Alas! whence I come, the first youth is initiated in the view, if not in the endurance of misfortune! There can be no understanding, or there must be early reflection; there can be no heart, or there must be commiserating sympathy!"

"I protest, Ma'am," cried Sir Jaspar, looking at her with astonishment, "I begin to suspect that I came into the world only this morning! Where I may have been rambling, all these years, in the persuasion I was in it already, I have by no means any clear notion! But to see two such instances of wisdom and resignation, united with youth and beauty, makes me believe myself in some new region, never yet visited by vice or folly."

"Ah, Sir, the French Revolution has opened our eyes to a species of equality more rational, because more feasible, than that of lands or of rank; an equality not alone of mental sufferings, but of manual exertions. No state of life, however low, or however hard, has been left untried, either by the highest, or by the most delicate, in the various dispersions and desolation of the ancient French nobility. And to see,—as I, alas! have seen,—the willing efforts, the even glad toil, of the remnants of the first families of Europe, to procure,—not luxuries, not elegancies, not even comforts,—but maintenance! mean, laborious maintenance!—to preserve,—not state, not fortune, not rank,—but life itself! but simple existence!"—

"Very wonderful personage!" cried Sir Jaspar, his air mingling reverence with amazement; "and what,—unfold to me, I beg, what is the necromancy through which you support, under such toils, your intellectual dignity? and strangle, in its birth, every struggle of false shame?"

[†] The period is the reign of Robespierre.

"Alas, Sir, I have seen guilt!—Since then, I have thought that shame belonged to nothing else!"

The eyes of Sir Jaspar were now suffused with tender admiration. "Fair deity of the counter!" he cried, "you are sublime! And she, too,—your witching little hand-maid; by what kind, dulcet chance,—new in the annals of misfortune,—have two such wonders met?—"

"Ah, rather, Sir,—since you couple us so kindly,—rather ask by what adverse chance we have so long been separated?"

"You have known her, then, some time?"

"We were brought up together!—the same convent, the same governess, the same instructors, were common to both till my marriage. And now, again,—as before that period,—I have not the most distant idea of any possible happiness, that is not annexed to her presence."

Touched to hear the word happiness once again, even though with such sadness, pronounced by Gabriella; yet alarmed at a discourse that might lead, inadvertently, to some secret history, Juliet was returning, to stop any further detail; when, upon Sir Jaspar's answering, "Sweet couple! Lord Denmeath, who ought at least, if I understand right,—to take care of one of you, will surely make it his business that you should coo together in the same cage?"—she again retreated, anxious to learn what this meant, and hoping that he would become more explicit.

"Lord Denmeath?" repeated Gabriella, "If you know Lord Denmeath, you may be better informed upon this subject than I am myself. Was it at Brighthelmstone that you met with his lordship?"

"It was at Brighthelmstone that I heard of him; and heard that, though wary of speech, he has been incautious in manner, and left little doubt upon the minds of his observers, that this fair flower springs from the same stock as some part of his own family; though she may be one of those sweet, but hapless buds, whose innocence pays for the guilt of its planter.—"

"No, Sir, no!" Gabriella precipitately interrupted him; "the birth of my friend is unstained, though unequal; the marriage of her parents was legal, though secret. Her mother came not, indeed, from an ancient race; but she was a pattern of virtue, as well as a model of beauty. Could it, indeed, be believed, that a young nobleman of such expectations, in every way, as those of the Earl of Melbury's only son, Lord Granville, would have given his hand to the orphan and destitute daughter of an insolvent man of business, had she not possessed every advantage, nay, every perfection to which human nature can rise?"

Affrighted by this so open relation, drawn forth involuntarily from the nobly ingenuous Gabriella, in the persuasion that Sir Jaspar was already a confidential, and might become a useful friend; Juliet, in the first moment, was advancing to stop it; but her heart, yet more than her ear, was so fascinated by the generous eulogy of her virtuous, though lowly mother, from the offspring of a house whose height, and natal prejudices, might have palliated, upon this subject, the language even of disdain; that she could not prevail with herself to break into what she considered as sacred praise.

"'Tis even so, then!" cried Sir Jaspar, with smiling delight; "this forlorn, but most beautiful Wanderer,—this so long concealed, and mysterious, but most lovely *incognita*, is the daughter of the late Lord Granville, and the grand-daughter of the late Earl of Melbury!"

Utterly confounded, to hear the secret history of her birth and family thus casually, yet irretrievably discovered, Juliet, trembling, again shrunk back; yet would not, now, and unavailingly, check the ardent zeal of her high-minded friend, since without any added danger, it might procure some useful intelligence.

The willing Baronet, whose sole desire was to keep up the conversation, wanted no urging to relate all that he had gathered from the loquacious Selina. Lord Denmeath, upon the sudden disappearance of Miss Ellis, had been surprised into confessing, that he had a faint notion that he knew something of that young person; that there had been, once, an odd story,—a report—that a young woman was existing in France, who was some way belonging to the late Lord Granville, his sister's husband;* though without ever having been acknowledged by the family. He let fall, also, sundry obscure hints of information, of the most serious import, which he had recently received, relating to this young woman; but which he would not divulge, till he had investigated; as he began to surmise, that it had been conveyed to him for some fraudulent and mercenary purpose. Mrs. Ireton, to all this, had answered, that she had suspected, from the beginning, that the creature was an adventurer; and that she was now fully convinced that they had been played upon by a supposititious person. Lord Denmeath, though he forbore confirming this assertion, listened to it with a smile of concurrence.

Juliet here felt shocked and confounded; but Gabriella, animated by generous resentment, warmly repeated her asseverations, of the validity of the marriage of Lord Granville with Miss Powel, her friend's mother; though an excess of fear of the inflexible character of the old Earl Melbury had prevented its early avowal; and the death of the concealed wife, while Juliet was yet in arms, had afterwards decided the young widower to guard the secret, till his child should be grown up; or till he should become his own master.

"But where, during this interval," said Sir Jaspar, "where,—and what was the hiding-place of that seraphic offspring?"

Till her seventh year, Gabriella answered, she had been consigned to the care of Mrs. Powel, her maternal grandmother; who, satisfied of the legality, had herself aided the secresy of the marriage. They had dwelt, during that period, in the same picturesque, but no longer loved retreat, upon the banks of the Tyne, in which Lady Granville, under a feigned name, had been concealed, for the short space of time between her marriage and her death.

Juliet, whose intention had been to gather, not to bestow intelligence, now came forward, and made signs to Gabriella to drop the subject. But this was no longer practicable. Urged by the idea of doing honour to her friend, and incited by adroit interrogatories, or piquant observations, from Sir Jaspar, Gabriella, having insensibly begun the tale, felt irresistibly impelled to make clear the birth and family of Juliet, beyond all doubt or cavil. She continued, therefore, the narration; and Juliet, much agitated, retreated wholly to the inner room.

Under pretence of change of air for his health, Lord Granville, to hide his grief from his father and friends, spent the first year of his widowhood at Montpellier;* then the residence of the Bishop of * * *, the maternal uncle of Gabriella; with whom he formed a friendship that neither time nor absence, nor even death itself, had had power to dissolve; and to whom he confided the history and punishment of his clandestine juvenile engagement. Called home, the following year, by the Earl, his father, he had been prevailed upon to marry a lady of quality and large fortune. But, previous to these new nuptials, to secure justice to his eldest born, though he had not the courage to own her; as well as to tranquillize Mrs. Powel; he deposited in the hands of that worthy old lady, the certificate of his first marriage; to which he added a deed, that he called the codicil to whatever will he might have made, or might hereafter make; and in which he declared Juliet Granville, born near——, in Yorkshire, to be his lawful daughter, by his first marriage, with Juliet Powel, in Flanders;* and, as such, he bequeathed to her the same portion, at his death, that should be settled upon any other daughter, or daughters, that he might have, hereafter, by any subsequent marriage.

The impossibility of obtaining, in the Yorkshire retirement, such means of improvement, as were suitable to the future expectations and lot in life of his little girl, determined Lord Granville to have her conveyed to France for her education. Mrs. Powel, who had no other remaining tie upon earth, but a son who was settled in the East Indies, preferred accompanying her little darling to a separation; the fear of which, with the possession of the marriage-certificate, and the codicil to the will, had always counteracted her impatience for the discovery ultimately promised. The uncle of Gabriella, the Bishop, consented to take the child under his immediate care; and to place her in the convent in which his sister, the Marchioness of * * *, had placed his niece. And here the children had been brought up together, with the same opportunities of improvement; except that the little Juliet had the advantage of speaking English with her grandmother; who knew no other language; and who entered the convent as a pensioner. By this means, and by books, Juliet had perfectly retained her native tongue, though she had acquired something of a foreign accent. She was known only as a young English lady of fortune, for whom no expence was to be spared;

and the remittances for her board and education were constant, and even splendid. She had been called simply by the name of Mademoiselle Juliette, which had generally been supposed to be the name of her family. Here, from the facility with which she caught instruction, and the ability with which she appropriated its result, she became the most accomplished pupil of the convent; and was not more generally, from her appearance, called *la belle*, than from her acquirements and conduct *la sage petite Anglaise*.* And here, still more united by the same sentiments than by the same studies, Gabriella had formed with her the tender, confiding, and unalterable friendship, that had bound them to each other with an even sisterly love.

The Bishop frequently pressed the young lord to avow the birth of Juliet, and to legitimate her claims upon his family: but he always answered, that since she, whose reputation, happiness, and spirits might have paid the avowal, was gone, he could not support the fruitless pain of offending his sickly, but imperious father, by such a discovery, till the necessity of receiving his daughter should make it indispensable.

Previous to this period, Gabriella was taken from the convent, to prepare for her marriage with the Comte de——; and Juliet, who had then lost her tender grandmother, was invited to the wedding-ceremony, and to remain with her friend till she should be called to her own country. Lord Granville, with that spirit of procrastination which always grows with indulgence, joyfully acceded to this invitation; and remitted to the ensuing summer the public acknowledgment of his daughter. But, ere the ensuing summer arrived, all these projects were rendered abortive! The Bishop, through a news-paper, received the fatal intelligence, that Lord Granville had been killed by a fall from his horse.

While the deeply disappointed and afflicted Juliet was the prey of heavy grief at this event, the Bishop, to whom the grandmother, in dying, had consigned the marriage-certificate, the codicil, and every letter or paper that authenticated the legitimacy of her grandchild, constituted himself guardian and protector of the young orphan.

Convinced that no time should be lost in making known her

rights, yet unwilling to risk shocking the old peer by an abrupt address, he stated the affair to Lord Denmeath, brother to Lord Granville's second lady, and guardian of two children by the second marriage. To this communication he received no answer. But, upon writing again, with more energy, and hinting at sending over an agent, Lord Denmeath thought proper to reply. His style was extremely cold. His brother-in-law, he said, had expired, after his fall, without uttering a word. Having, therefore, no knowledge of any secret business, he begged to be excused from entering into a discussion of the obscure affair to which the Bishop seemed to allude.

The Bishop grew but warmer in the interests of his Ward, from the difficulty of serving her. He sent over, to Lord Denmeath, copies of the codicil, of the certificate, and of every letter upon the subject, that had been written to the grandmother, or to himself, by the late lord.

The answer now was more civil, but evidently embarrassed, though professing much respect for the motives which guided the charitable Bishop; and a willingness to enter into some compromise for the young person in question; provided she could be settled abroad, that so strange a tale might not disturb his sister; nor involve his nephew and niece, by coming before the public.

All compromise was declined by the Bishop, who now made known the whole history to the old peer.

The answer, nevertheless, was again from Lord Denmeath, though written by the desire, and in the name of the Earl; briefly saying, Let the young woman marry and settle in France; and, upon the delivery of the original documents relative to her birth, she shall be portioned; but she shall never be received nor owned in England; the Earl being determined not to countenance such a disgrace to his family, and to the memory of his son, as the acknowledgment of so unsuitable a marriage.

The Bishop held his honour engaged to his departed friend, to sustain the birth-right of the innocent orphan; he menaced, therefore, accompanying her over to England himself, and putting all the documents, with the direction of the affair, into the hands of some celebrated lawyer.

Alarmed at this intimation, milder letters passed: but the result of all that the Bishop could obtain, was a promissory-note of six thousand pounds sterling, for the portion of a young person brought up at the convent of * * *, and known by the name of Mademoiselle Juliette; to be paid by Messieurs * * *, bankers, on the day of her marriage with a native of France, resident in that country.

The conditions annexed to the payment were then detailed, of delivering to the bankers the originals of all the MSS. of which copies had been sent over; with an acquittal, signed by the new married couple, and by the Bishop, to all future right or claim upon the Melbury family. The whole to be properly witnessed, &c. This promissory-note had the joint seal and signature of the old Earl and of Lord Denmeath.

But the Bishop inflexibly insisted, that his ward should be recognized as the Honourable Miss Granville; and share an equal portion with her half-sister, Aurora; for whom, upon the premature death of Lord Granville, the old peer had solicited and obtained the title and honours of an earl's daughter.*

All representation proving fruitless, the Bishop was preparing to attend Miss Granville to England, when the French Revolution broke out. The general confusion first stopt his voyage, and next destroyed even the materials of his agency. The family-chateau was burnt by the populace; and all the papers of Juliet, which had been carefully hoarded up with the records of the house, were consumed! The promissory-note alone, and accidentally, had been saved; the Bishop chancing to have it in his pocket-book, for the purpose of consulting upon it with some lawyer.

With the nobleness of unsuspicious integrity, the Bishop wrote an account of this disaster to Lord Denmeath; whose answer contained tidings of the death of the old Earl, and re-claimed the promissory-note for revisal. But the Bishop, who possessed no other proof or document of the identity of Juliet, would by no means part with a paper that became of the utmost importance.

Juliet, pitied and sustained, loved and esteemed by all, had been prevailed upon to continue with her cherished and cherishing friends, till some political calm should enable the

Bishop to conduct her to England, and there to struggle for her rights. At the opening, however, of the dreadful reign of Robespierre, sudden and immediate danger had compelled Gabriella, with her husband and her child, to emigrate: but Juliet, hopeless of making herself acknowledged by her family without the support of the Bishop, had preferred, till she could obtain the sanction of his presence, to remain with the Marchioness.

"And what," Sir Jaspar cried, "what is become of this Bishop? this man of peace, this worthiest wight that breathes the vital air?"

Gabriella herself knew not; nor what change of plan had induced her friend to venture over alone: she knew only that what was counselled by the Bishop must be wise; that what was executed by Juliet must be right.

Juliet, who had heard this recital with melting tenderness, was now with difficulty restrained, even by the presence of Sir Jaspar, from casting herself rather at the feet than into the arms, of her generous, noble, and confiding, though untrusted friend.

CHAPTER LXX

VARIOUS customers, though for small purchases, had, from time to time, interrupted, but not broken this narration. The Baronet respectfully made way for whoever came, but resumed his place the instant that it was vacated; spending the interval in selecting new pieces of ribbon; till, ere the history was finished, not a remnant of that article remained unsold. It was his purpose, he gallantly said, to present a top-knot,* for a twelvemonth to come, to every fair syren who, either by face, voice, shape, feature, complexion, size, air, or manner, should afford him so much pleasure as to remind him, however transiently, of the adorable haberdasher, whose taper* fingers had put it into his possession.

Gabriella interrupted these compliments, to observe, with some anxiety, two strange men, who were sauntering up and down the street, and who, from time to time, peeped in at the window.

"And how can they do any better?" said the Baronet; "unless you invite them into your apartments? 'Tis precisely what I shall enact myself, if you turn me out of doors! Do you fancy you are to dart yourselves, you and your mischievous partner, into as many hearts as you can find spectators, and then bid your poor wounded gazers go lie down and bleed, in the kennel,* like so many puppies; without allowing them even a lamenting yell, or friendly barking, to call themselves into notice before they give up the ghost? I pity the poor caitiffs with all my heart.

"A fellow-feeling makes one wond'rous kind!"†*

"Let me, however, hope, that the seductive tale which I have been quaffing, has not intoxicated all my senses only to my own destruction! that my poor nerves have not been pierced and pinched; that my feelings have not been twitched and tweaked, and my senses scared and confounded, only to drag my own crazy folly into fuller view!"

He paused a few minutes, during which Gabriella began making out the account of her ribbons; and then, with a mild voice, but an arch brow, "Hear me," he resumed, "my dulcet frog! for such, you know, is your destined classification in this country; hear, and under your auspices let me proceed. If this fair marvellous Wanderer,—in her birth no longer an Incognita, yet an Incognita still in her history; will venture to put herself under my protection,—honourably I mean; so don't frown! for nothing so spoils the forehead! Besides, who can look at you, and not mean honourably? With all your sweetness, there is a fire in your eye, that, if I harboured a naughty idea, only for a moment, would, I see plainly, consume me. Let us, however, talk the matter over with becoming seriousness. It may, perchance, be less difficult than you may imagine, to establish your fair journeywoman's rights."

"O make the attempt, then," cried Gabriella; "exert yourself in so noble a trial!"

"A little activity," he continued, "and a great deal of menacing, adroitly put in play, will now and then do wonders. A little money, too, dexterously handled, rarely does much

† Garrick.

harm. When Lord Denmeath sees all these at work, take my word for it, he will think twice, before he will let them operate upon the public. We like mighty well to reap the fruits of our address in the world; but we have a sagacious tendency to keeping our ways and means to ourselves. Lord Denmeath, after all, as a worldly man, does but his office, in putting to sleep his conscience for the better keeping awake his interest. This is simply in the ordinary course of things: but, when the blood that is youthful is not generous; when life is begun with the crafty hardness that years, experience, and disappointment have given to those who are ending it; when we see even striplings, who ought to be made up of wild romance, and credulous enthusiasm, meanly, basely, heartlessly, for a few pitiful thousands, suffer an orphan to be cheated, despoiled of her rank in life, and made an alien to her country, as well as to her family;—then it is, that I curse Vanity as an imp of darkness, and Pride as a demon of hell! When a boy like Lord Melbury, a young girl such as Lady Aurora—"

"They are innocent, Sir Jaspar! they are noble! they are faultless!" called out Juliet, eagerly returning to the shop; "they dream not of my claims; they have not the most distant idea that I have the honour to belong to their house. Innocent? they are meritorious! Conceiving me simply a helpless, unpatronized, and indigent Wanderer, they have treated me with a kindness, a consideration, an heavenly benevolence, that, towards a stranger so forlorn, could have been dictated only by the most angelic of natures!"

"Astonishing! incredible!" exclaimed Sir Jaspar. "What! do they not know your story? Have you made no appeal to their justice, their affections?"

"You will cease, Sir, to wonder, and cease also, I hope, to question me, when I tell you that here, even here, I have not made my situation known! here, even here,—to the friend of my heart, the confident of my life, the loved and honoured descendant of the house by which I have been preserved, and from which alone I hope for protection! Judge then, how powerful must be my motives for secresy! And she,—she submits to my silence! Too high-minded for distrust, too nobly mistress of herself for impatience; and conscious that even a wish, expressed, would to me have the force of a command, she waits my time! She knows the most dire and barbarous obstacles could alone lead me to reserve and concealment, where my softest consolation would be openness and sympathy!"

Gabriella could offer no answer but by wide extended arms, with which Juliet, gushing into tears, was fondly encircled; while the Baronet, touched, amazed, and enchanted, repeatedly wiped his eyes; when Gabriella, observing, again, at the window, one of the men of whom she had spoken, whispered Juliet to compose herself, or to retire.

There was not time: Riley, who had seen her, bounced into the shop.

"Ah, ha, I have caught you at last, have I Demoiselle?" he cried, rubbing his hands with joy. "I could not devise where the deuce you had hidden yourself. I only knew you were in some shabby little bit of a shop in this street. And who do you think is my author for this intelligence?—Won't you guess?—Why Surly! your old friend, Surly!"

Apprehensive of some attack similar to that which she had endured at Brighthelmstone, Juliet ventured not to speak, though she felt too anxious to withdraw: while Sir Jaspar, extremely curious, repeated, "Old Surly?" in a tone that invited explanation.

"The same, faith! He's come over o' purpose to hunt you out, Demoiselle."

"Me?" cried Juliet, changing colour, "and why?—And who is he?"

"Who is he? Well! that's droll, faith! Why you have not forgotten your old crony, the pilot?"

Juliet looked down, to conceal the alarm with which she was seized.

"Why, I'll tell you how it all happened," continued Riley, mounting upon the counter, as he might have mounted upon his horse; "I'll tell you how it all happened. About a month ago, in one of my rambles, I met Master Surly; and, for old acquaintance sake, I was prodigiously glad to see him: for I like, as a curiosity, to shew John Bull a Mounseer that i'n't a milksop. So we talked over our voyage; but when I told him that I had met with the Demoiselle at Brighthelmstone; and that she had cast off her slough, and was grown a beauty; he asked me a hundred questions, and said that, most likely, she was a person of whom he was in search; and after whom there had been a great hue and cry."

Juliet now opened various small drawers, shutting them almost at the same moment; but always with her face turned from Riley.

"Well, we parted, and I saw no more of him, and thought no more of him neither, faith! till this very morning, when I popt upon him, all at once, in Piccadilly. And then, he told me that he was just come from Brighthelmstone, where he had been looking for you."

Juliet though in a tremour that shook her whole frame, faintly said, "And why?"

"Because, by my account of you, he was satisfied you must be the very person that he was commissioned to find."

Juliet now seemed scarcely able to sustain herself. Gabriella and Sir Jaspar saw, with deep concern, her emotion; but Riley, unobservant, went on.

"At Brighton, he had discovered that you had journied up to town, in the stage. And he came up after you, in the very same carriage, only yesterday. And, by means of a boy at the inn, who had called your hackney-coach, he had just found out coachy; who informed him, that he had set down a pretty young damsel, that had arrived from Brighton about a week ago, at a small shop in Frith street, Soho. Upon that, I offered to help him in his search; and we jogged on to these quarters together: for I always liked you, Demoiselle, and always had a prodigious mind to know who you were. But the deuce a bit would you ever tell me. So we have been sauntering and maundering* up and down the street, one on one side, and t'other on t'other, in search of you; peeping and peering into every shop, and lounging and squinting at every window. We have had the devil of a job of it to find you, Demoiselle; we have, faith!—But my best sport will be to make Monsieur Surly look you full in the face, as I did myself, without knowing you! though he pretends that that's all one. The French always say that to every thing that they don't like; *c'est egal!** cries Monsieur, whenever he's put out of his way. However, old Surly stands to it, that he shall discover you in a twinkling; for he's got your description."

"My description?" Juliet repeated; in a tone of terrour.

"Ay; and there he is, faith! on t'other side the way! An old owl!" cried Riley; striding to the door, and calling aloud, "Surly! old Surly! Come over, Mounseer Surly!"

Juliet was now precipitately gliding into the little room; but Sir Jaspar, intercepting her flight, warmly entreated, whatever might be her fears or her difficulties, to be accepted as her protector: and, while she was struggling, with speechless impatience, to pass him, the pilot, pulled into the shop by Riley, stood full before her; stared hardily in her face; looked at a paper which he held in his hand, and, grinning horribly a scoffing smile, walked away, without speaking.

Juliet, who seemed nearly fainting, was drawn tenderly into the adjoining room by Gabriella; who was herself in almost equal consternation.

"A pretty feat you have performed here, Sir! An admirable exploit!" said Sir Jaspar, angrily, to Riley; who, laughing heartily at the savage satisfaction of the pilot, had re-mounted the counter. "And what sort of man must you be to find it so dulcet and recreative, to give chace to a timid, defenceless lamb?"

"What sort of man?" returned Riley; "faith, I don't know! I don't, faith! But who does? If you can tell me the man who knows himself, you'll do more than has been done yet since the days of old Adam. I never trouble myself with vain researches, and combinations, and developments, and metaphysical analysings. What do they do for us, beside cracking our skulls? They only leave us where they found us; forced to eat and drink, and sleep and wake, and live and die, just the same, since all the discoveries of Newton, as we did before we knew a square from an angle."*

"O ho, you are a philosopher, Sir, then, are you?" said Sir Jaspar; "a Cynic? guided by contempt of mankind?"

"Not a whit! I only follow my humour. If that happens to please my friends, so much the better; if not, I am but little 'of the melting mood;'* I go on all the same. I never stop to weigh opinion in the scale of my proceedings."

"And do you never weigh humanity, neither, Sir? the feelings of others? the good or ill of society?"

"No! I never think of all that. I let the world take its own course, as I take mine. I have long had a craving desire to know who this girl is; and she would never tell me. Her obstinacy doubles my curiosity; and when my curiosity gets at the helm, it does just what it will with me. It does, faith!"

Gabriella, now returning, demanded of Riley what business detained him in the shop, with an air of dignity that surprised him into making something like an apology; to which he added, that he only stayed to have a little further parley with the demoiselle.

That young lady was indisposed, and could be spoken to no more.

"Indisposed?" he repeated; "I am sorry for that! I am, faith! Poor demoiselle! she has been liberal enough of diversion to me, one way or another. However, I shall soon discover who she is; for I know where to catch Master Surly; and he says he is promised a thumping reward, if he finds that she is the right person. He is but an agent, poor Surly: but he expects his principal, with the cash, over every hour; if he i'n't landed already."

Gabriella, who had returned to the little parlour, perceived, now, that the face of Juliet looked convulsed with horrour. She procured her a glass of hartshorn and water; and entreated the Baronet, who seemed transfixed with concern, to force Riley away; and to be gone, also, himself.

Sir Jaspar could not refuse compliance; but neither could he deny himself advancing, for an instant, to say, in a low voice, to Juliet, "Bow not down your lovely head, sweet lilly! I have friends who will find means to succour and protect you, be who will your assaulter!"

Offering Riley, then, a place in his chariot, and dropping, as he passed, his purse into the till-box, he drove off, with his new acquaintance.

For some minutes, excess of terrour robbed Juliet of speech, and of all power of exertion; but when, by the cares and soothings of Gabriella, she was, in some degree, restored, "Oh my beloved friend!" she cried, "we must part again,—immediately part!"

A tear stole down the cheek of Gabriella as she heard this annunciation; but she offered no remonstrance; she permitted herself no enquiry; her eye alone said, "Why, why this!"

Juliet saw, but shrunk from this mute eloquence, hastily arranging herself for going out; making up a packet of linen to carry in her hand, and hanging a loaded work-bag upon her arm.

Casting herself, then, into the arms of her friend, "Oh my Gabriella," she cried, "I must fly,—instantly fly!—or entail a misery upon the rest of my existence too horrible for description! Whither,—which way to go, I know not,—but I must be hidden from all mankind!—To-morrow I will write to you;—constantly I will write to you,—dear, generous, noblest of friends, farewell, farewell!"

They embraced, mingled their tears, embraced again, and separated.

BOOK VIII

CHAPTER LXXI

HER head bowed low; her bonnet drawn over her eyes; ignorant what course she took, and earnest only to discover any inlet into the country by which she might immediately quit the town; Juliet, with hurried footsteps, and trembling apprehensions, became again a Wanderer.

She passed through various streets, but, unacquainted with London, read, without any aid to her purpose, their names, till, printed in large characters, her eyes were struck with the word Piccadilly; and, presently, she was accosted by an ordinary man, who had a long whip in his hand, and who, holding open the door of a carriage, asked whether she would have a cast;* saying that he was ready to set off immediately.

Finding that the vehicle was a stage-coach, she eagerly accepted the proposal, and seated herself next to an elderly woman.

The man demanded whether she meant to go all the way.

She answered in the affirmative; and, to her inexpressible satisfaction, was driven out of London.

Not to risk discovering to her fellow-travellers so extraordinary a circumstance, as that of beginning an excursion in utter ignorance where it might end, she forbore asking any questions; and left to the time of her alighting at the spot to which the stage was destined, her own acquaintance with her local situation.

It was not, therefore, till she descended from the coach, that she found that she had taken the road to Bagshot.

The immediate plan which, in her way, she had formed, was to enter the first shop that she saw open; thence to write to Gabriella; and then to stroll on to the nearest village, and lodge herself in the first clean cottage which could afford her a room.

The sight, however, of the Salisbury stage, gave her a desire to travel instantly further from London; and she asked whether there were a vacant place. She was immediately accommodated; and her journey thither, though long, and passed in dreadful apprehension, was without accident or event.

Arrived at Salisbury, she quitted the machine, and her fellow travellers, with whom she had scarcely exchanged a word; and, hoping that she was now out of the way of pursuit, she put her plan into execution, by writing a tranquillizing line to Gabriella, from a stationer's shop; and then, set forth in search of a dwelling.

This was by no means easy to find. A solitary stranger, bearing her own small baggage, after travelling all night, was not very likely to be seen but with eyes of scrutiny and suspicion. Yet her air, her manner, and her language made her application always best received by the upper class of tradespeople, who were most able to discern, that such belonged not to any vulgar or ordinary person: but, when they found that she enquired for a lodging, without giving any name, or any reference, they held back, alike, from granting her admission, or forwarding her wish by any recommendation.

The evident caution with which she hid as much as possible of her face, made the beauty of what was still necessarily visible, create as much ill opinion as admiration; though the perfect modesty of her deportment rescued her from receiving any offence.

In the smaller shops, and by the meaner and poorer sort of people, her carrying her parcel herself, levelled her, instantly, to their own rank; while her demand of assistance, her loneliness and even her loveliness, sunk her far beneath it, in their opinion; and, almost with one accord, they bluntly told her that she might find a lodging at an inn.

Helpless, distressed, she wandered some time in this fruitless research; too much self-occupied to remark the buildings, the neatness, the antiquities, or the singularities of the city which she was patrolling; till her eyes were caught by the little rivulets which, in most of the streets, separate the foot-path from the high-road, by perceiving two ruddy-cheeked, smiling little cherubs, attempting to paddle over one of them, and playing so incautiously, that they seemed every moment in danger of falling into the water.

She hastened towards them, to point out a bridge, somewhat higher up, by which they might more safely pass; but the elder child, a rosy boy, careless and sportive, heeded her not; till, finding the stream deeper than he expected, his little feet slipt, and he would inevitably have been under water, had not Juliet, with dextrous speed, caught him by the coat.

She aided him to scramble out, though with much difficulty, for he was wet through, and covered with mud. Frightened out of his little senses, he set up an unappeaseable cry; in which the other child, a pretty little girl, impelled by babyish though unconscious sympathy, joined, with all the vociferation which her feeble lungs were capable of emitting.

Juliet, with that kindness which childish helplessness ought always to inspire, soothed them with gentle words, and persuaded the boy to hasten to his home, that he might take off his wet cloaths before he caught cold. But they both sat down to cry at their leisure; though rather as if they did not understand, than as if they resisted her counsel.

Pitying their simple sufferings, she offered the boy a penny, to buy a gingerbread cake, if he would rise.

Quick, or rather immediate, now, was the transition from despondence to transport. The boy not merely wiped his eyes, and ceased his sobs, but, all smiles and delight, began a rapid prattling of where he should buy, and of what sort should be, his cake; while every word, rapturously, though indistinctly, was echoed by the little girl, not less slack in reviving.

The elasticity, however, of their little persons, kept not entirely pace with that of their spirits. The wet attire of the boy, which his seat on the dust had rendered as heavy as it was uncomfortable, nearly disabled him from rising; and his little sister, who had lost one of her shoes in the rivulet, had run a thorn into her foot, and could not stand without crying.

The children were not able to give any account of who they were that was intelligible; nor of whence they came, save that it was from a great, great way off. Unwilling to leave them in so pitiable a plight, Juliet, observing that the street, which led out of the town, was empty, looked for a clean spot, and, bending upon one knee, had just drawn out the splinter from the foot of the little girl, when the sound of the voice of a female, who was approaching, calling out, "Here I be, my loveys! here comes mammy!" so miraculously electrified the little creatures, that, forgetting all impediment to motion, they bounded up, delighted; the boy no longer sensible to the weight of his wet garments, nor the girl to the tenderness of her hurt foot: and both capered to embrace the knees of their mammy; whose eyes alone could return their caresses; her hands being engaged in holding a heavy basket upon her head.

But when she perceived their condition, she anxiously demanded what had happened.

They both again began grievously to cry, while the boy related that he had been drowned, but that the *dood ady* (good lady) had come and saved his life: and the little girl, interrupting him every moment, kept presenting her foot, in telling a similar story of the kindness of the *dood ady*.

To Juliet scarcely a word of their narrations was intelligible; but, to the ears of their mother, accustomed to their dialect, their lisping and their imperfect speech, these prattling details were as potent in eloquence, as the most polished orations of Cicero or Demosthenes,* are to those of the classical scholar.

The gratitude of the good woman for the services rendered to her little ones, was so warm and cordial, that she cried for joy, in pouring forth blessings upon the head of Juliet, for having lent so friendly a hand, she said, to her poor boy; and having done what she called so neighbourly a kindness by her dear little girl.

She had directed her children, she said, to go straight to Dame Goss's, beyond the turnpike; having had business to transact at a house which they could not enter; but the little dearys were not yet come to their memory; and, but for so good a friend, the poor loveys might have lain in the wet and the mud, till they had been half choaked.

Seeing the children thus safely restored to their best friend, Juliet meant to continue her solitary search; but the good woman, judging from her kind offices, that there was nothing to fear from her disdain; and concluding from her parcel, that there was nothing to respect in her rank, frankly demanded her assistance, for helping on the children as far as to the turnpike;

simply adding, that she would do as good a turn for her, in requital, another time; but that her basket was heavily laden, and the poor little things, one without its shoe, and the other in wet cloaths, would be but troublesome, in such a broiling sun, to pull all the way by her petticoat.*

Cruelly experiencing want of succour herself, Juliet, always open to charity, was now more than usually ready to serve or oblige. With the utmost alacrity, therefore, complying with the request, she deposited her packet in the poor woman's basket; bound her pocket-handkerchief round the foot and ancle of the little girl; and then, taking a hand of each of the children, and gently alluring them on, by lively and playful talk, she conducted them to the turnpike; without any other difficulty than some fatigue to herself; which was amply compensated by the pleasure of helping the little innocents, and their affectionate mother; joined to the relief to her own feelings, afforded by a social exercise, that drew her, for a while, from her fearful reflections.

The woman, charmed by such kindness, begged to have the direction of Juliet, that she might call to thank her, when next she came to Salisbury; whither some business commonly brought her every four or five months.

Juliet was obliged to confess herself a mere passenger; but asked, in return, the name and address of her new acquaintance.

Margery Fairfield, she answered, was her name, and she lived a far off in the New Forest. She was going, in a friend's cart, to Romsey, and there her husband would meet her, and carry her little girl. She could never come out without her children, if she were ever so heavily laden, for her husband was at work all day, and there was nobody to take care of them in her absence.

A ray of pleasure now broke through the gloomy forebodings of Juliet; there seemed to her an opening to an asylum, during the period of her concealment, fortunate beyond her hopes; to lodge with a rustic family of this simple description, in so retired and remote a spot, promising all the security and privacy that she required, with fine air, pleasant country, and worthy hosts.

A very few enquiries sufficed to satisfy her, that she might find a small room, in which she could sleep; and a little further discourse procured her all the details necessary for learning the route to the dame's cottage. She forbore, nevertheless, hinting at her design, that neither trouble, expence, nor preparation might precede her arrival.

She regretted her inability to accompany these new friends, at once, to their home; but her letter to Gabriella had desired that the answer might be directed to be left at the post office at Salisbury, till called for; and she was too uncertain what her position might be in the New Forest, to hazard any change of address. She was deeply anxious to hear from Gabriella; and to learn whether she had herself been sought since her flight.

When they reached the small, mean house of Dame Goss, beyond the turnpike, the expected cart was not yet arrived; and Juliet, being kindly invited to take a little rest, ventured to solicit, from her new friend, a recommendation to a cheap lodging, with some honest hostess.

Enchanted to be able to serve her, the poor woman immediately said, that she could no where be better than in that very house: and when its mistress made various objections; first, that she had not a room unoccupied; next, that she had no spare bed; and then, that her husband would be angry; the zealous Dame Fairfield obviated them all. The room, she said, with a significant nod, where they kept their boxes, would be never the worse for being slept in a few nights, now all the boxes were empty; and the bed she had had for herself the last winter, could be easily carried up stairs, for she would stop to carry it with her own hands: and as to Master Goss, he was so fond of her little dearys, that he could not have so bad a heart as to be off doing a service to a gentlewoman who had been so kind to them.

This eloquence was all-sufficient; the real obstacle, that of aiding an unknown traveller, occurring neither to the advocate nor to the opponent. Free from the niceties of custom in higher life, and unembarrassed by the perplexities of discriminating scruples, the good women, often lonely travellers themselves, saw nothing in such a situation to excite distrust; and regarded it therefore simply as a claim upon hospitality. To have manifested good nature, was sufficient to procure credit for good character; and to have done kind offices, was to secure their return.

Dame Fairfield busily set about putting into order a little apartment, that was encumbered with trunks and boxes, which she piled one upon another, to make a place for a small bed. She would suffer no one to give her any help; sweeping, dusting, rubbing, and arranging all the lumber herself; with an alacrity of pleasure, a gaiety of good will, that charmed away, for a while, the misery of Juliet, by the consoling picture thus presented to her view, of untaught benevolence and generosity: a picture which must always be pleasing to the friend of human nature, however less exalting, than when those qualities, as the cultured fruits of religion and of principle, are purified into virtues.

In this mean little lodging, to avoid being seen or heard of, Juliet passed three days, self-inclosed; with no employment but that of writing long letters to Gabriella, which, eventually, were to be sent by the post, or delivered by herself. This, however, not filling up her time, the wish of obliging, joined to a constant desire of acquiring, in every situation, the art of being useful,—that art which, more than wealth, or state, or power, preserves its cultivator from wearying either himself or those around him;—led her to bestow the rest of the day in aiding the woman of the house, in sundry occupations.

To have seen and examined the famous cathedral; to have found out the walks; to have informed herself of the manufactures; and to have visited the antiquities and curiosities of this celebrated city, and its neighbourhood, might have solaced the anxiety of this moment; but discretion baffled curiosity, and fear took place of all desire of amusement. She could only regale her confinement by the hope of soon obtaining her freedom in an innocent and beautiful retreat; and remained, therefore, perfectly stationary, till she conceived that an answer might be returned from Gabriella.

On the evening of that day, she prevailed upon Dame Goss, whose mornings were all engaged, but whose good will she had now completely secured, to be her messenger to the post-office.

Without any letter, however, the messenger returned, though with an acknowledgement that one was arrived; but that it could only be delivered to Miss Ellis herself; or to a written order with a receipt.

Juliet was immediately preparing to write one, when Dame Goss said, "They do tell me that you be a person advertised in the London news-papers?* It ben't true; be it?"

"Good Heaven, no!" Juliet ejaculated.

"Pray, be you the person called, 'Commonly known by the name of Miss Ellis?'"

Juliet, changing colour, asked why she made that enquiry.

The woman, instead of answering, looked earnestly in her face, with an air of stedfast examination.

In the greatest dismay, Juliet turned from her, without hazarding another question, and was going up stairs; but Dame Goss begged that she would just stop a bit, because two persons were a coming, that she had promised should have a peep at her.

Shocked and terrified, Juliet would still have passed on; but an instant sufficed to tell her, that, in such an emergency, not to make some immediate attempt to escape, was to be lost.

Turning, therefore, back, "Dame Goss," she cried, slipping a crown-piece into her hands, with an apology for giving her so much trouble, "hasten again to the post-office, and say that I shall come for my letter myself."

The woman, without question or demur, received the money and set off. And she was no sooner out of sight, than Juliet, taking her own small packet, unnoticed by Master Goss, who was at work in his little garden, went forth by the opposite way; turning, as quickly as possible, from the high road, where she might most naturally be pursued; and, for all else, committing her footsteps to chance and to hope,—those last, and not seldom, best friends of distress and difficulty.

Wandering on, by paths unknown to herself, with feet not more swift than trembling; fearing she was followed, yet not daring, by a glance around, to ascertain either danger or safety, she overtook a young village-girl, who was hoydening with a smart footman; but who caught her attention, by representing to him, that, if he detained her any longer, she should miss the return-chaise, and not know how to get back to Romsey; for her mother would be too angry to wait for her even a moment.

The sound of Romsey revived the spirits of Juliet. If she could join this young person, she might find a conveyance, equally unsuspected and expeditious, to within a mile or two of the very spot where she hoped for concealment. She loitered, therefore, in sight, till the footman retreated, and then, following the girl, though with affright, by returning to the town, she soon found herself in the church-yard of the cathedral; where the damsel encountered her waiting mother, with whom, boldly defying her wrath, she began, sturdily, to wrangle.

Juliet stood aloof, during the altercation, still hoping to accompany them in their route. The beautiful Gothic structure before her, the latest and finest remains of ancient elegance, lightness, and taste, was nearly lost to her sight, from the misery and pre-occupation of her mind; though appearing now with peculiar effect, from the shadows cast upon it by the rising moon. Yet soon, in defiance of all absorption, the magnetic affinity, in a mind natively pious, of religious solemnity with sorrow, made the antique grace of this wonderful edifice, catch, even in this instant of terrour and agitation, the admiring eye of Juliet; whose mind was always open to excellence, even when most incapable of receiving any species of pleasure.

She leaned, for a moment's repose, in a recess of the building, which the shade rendered dark, nearly sinking under the horrour of pursuit, and the shame of eluding it. To find herself advertised in a news-paper!—the blood mounted indignantly into her cheeks.—Perhaps to be described!—perhaps, named! and with a reward for her discovery!—cold from them, at this surmise, the blood again descended to her heart: yet every feeling was transient, that led not to immediate escape; every reflection was momentary, that turned, not to personal safety.

The dispute between the mother and daughter was interrupted,—not finished,—by the re-appearance of the footman, who told them that the postilion was just going off.

They scampered instantly to an inn, from the gateway of which a post-chaise was issuing.

Juliet, who had pursued, now joined them, and proposed making one in their party.

The women neither refused nor consented; they renewed their contention, and heard only one another: but the postilion, to whom Juliet held out half-a-crown, gave her a place with readiness,—and she was driven to Romsey.

CHAPTER LXXII

THE affrighted Juliet, every instant in expectation of being stopt, was silent the whole way; but the loquacity of her companions, to whom the journey was an uninterrupted opportunity for wrangling, secured her from any remark; and they arrived, and were separating, at Romsey, nearly without having taken notice that they had ever been together, when Juliet, having descended from the chaise, turned fearfully round, to examine whether she were pursued.

She saw no one; and blest Heaven.

Nevertheless, it was night; she was alone, in the suburbs of a strange town; and wholly ignorant of the way to the New Forest. It was too late to go on without a guide; yet, to demand one, or to order a chaise, at such an hour, would be risking to leave documents behind her, that might facilitate her being discovered. She addressed herself, therefore, to her fellow-travellers, and besought them to afford, or to procure her, a safe lodging for the night.

The mother, coarsely, demanded immediate payment; which being accorded, she said that she had some spare bedding, which could be put upon the floor, in the sleeping-room of Debby.

Juliet, accompanied them to their homely habitation, at the further extremity of a narrow lane, in the busy and prosperous town of Romsey; and though nothing could be more ordinary than the dwelling, or the accommodations which she there found, neither splendour, nor wealth, nor luxury, nor pleasure, could have devised for her, at that moment, a sojourn more acceptable; since, to all but safety, distress and affright made her insensible.

But, this first moment of solid satisfaction passed, her whole mind became absorbed in fearful ruminations upon the various risks that she was running, and in gloomy apprehensions of what might be their result.

Her taciturnity and dejection were as little imitated as they were little happy: her companion, almost equally self-occupied, though by no means equally incommoded by foresight, or burthened with discretion, broke forth immediately into the history of her own affairs and situation; bitterly inveighing against the ill nature of her mother, which was always thwarting every thing that was agreeable; and boldly declaring her fixed determination, to go to the fair with Mr. Thomas.

The humanity of Juliet here conquered her silence; but her representations, whether of danger or of duty, were scouted* with rude merriment; and she found again as wilful a victim to pleasure as Flora Pierson; though without the simplicity, the good humour, or the beauty of that credulous maiden.

Nearly with the light, Juliet arose, resolved, with whatever fatigue, to travel on foot, that she might not hazard being recognized, through the advertisement, by any coachman or postilion; and, to be less liable to detection from passing observers, she changed, over night, her bonnet, which was of white chip,* for one the most coarse and ordinary of straw, with her young hostess; of whom, also, she bought a blue striped apron.*

Shocking to all her feelings was this attempt at disguise, so imitative of guilt, so full of semblance to conscious imposture. But there are sometimes circumstances, great and critical, that call for all the energy of our courage, and demand all the resources of our faculties, for warding off impending and substantial evil, at whatever risk of transitory misconstruction.

Her account being already settled, she wished to depart unobserved, that she might less easily be traced. Her young hostess, sleeping late and tired, slept soundly, and was not disturbed by her rising, dressing, or opening the room-door; and she glided down stairs without being missed, or noticed. The door of the house was fastened only by a bolt, and she gained the street without noise or interruption.

Here all yet was still as night; the houses were shut up, and nothing was in view, nor in hearing, but a solitary cart, driven by a young carter, who amused his toil by the alternate pleasure of smacking his horse, and whistling to the winds.

This vehicle, which was probably travelling to the high road, she determined to follow.

The general stillness made the slightest motion heard, and the carter, though at a considerable distance, turned round, and called out, "Why you be up betimes, my lovey! come and Ize give you a cast."

Startled, she looked down, crossing the way, and appearing not to suppose herself to be the person thus addressed: but the carter, standing still, repeated his invitation; assuring her that he had plenty of room.

Uncertain how to act, she stopt.

Terms of coarse endearment, then, accompanied a more pressing desire that she would advance.

Frightened, she drew back; but the carter, throwing his whip upon his carriage, vowed that she should be caught, and ran after her, shouting aloud, till she regained the house. He then scoffingly exclaimed, "Why a be plaguy shy o'the sudden, Mistress Debby!" and, composedly turning upon his heel, began again to smack his horse, and whistle to the winds.

Juliet, who in finding herself taken for her young hostess, found, also, how light a character that young hostess bore, was struck to see danger thus every way surrounding her; and alarmed at the risk, to which impatience had blinded her, of travelling, at so early an hour, alone. Alas! she cried, is it only under the domestic roof,—that roof to me denied!—that woman can know safety, respect, and honour?

She now strolled to the vicinity of a capital mansion, at the door of which, if again put in fear, she could knock and make herself heard.

But the higgler* went on; and another cart soon appeared, in which she had the pleasure to see a woman, driven by a boy. Unannoyed, then, she walked by its side till she came to the long middle street; when she found that, from solitude, at least, she had nothing more to apprehend. Carts, waggons, and diligences, were wheeling through the town; market-women were arriving with butter, eggs, and poultry; workmen and manufacturers were trudging to their daily occupations; all was alive and in motion; and commerce, with its hundred hands, was every where opening and spreading its sources of wealth, through its active sisters, ingenuity and industry.

No difficulty now remained for finding the route; travellers of every kind led the way. Her coarse bonnet, and blue apron saved her from peculiar remark; and her appearance of decency, with the deep care in her countenance, which, to the common observer, seemed but an air of business, kept aloof all intrusive impertinence.

Thus, for the first early hours of the morning, she journeyed on, nearly unnoticed, and wholly unmolested. Every one, like herself, alert to proceed, and impressed with the value of time, because using it to advantage, pursued his own purpose, without leisure or thought to trouble himself with that of his neighbour.

Five times she had already counted the friendly mile-stone, since she had quitted Romsey: one mile only remained to be trodden, ere she reached the New Forest; but that mile was replete with obstacles, to which its five sisters had been strangers.

It was now noon; and a gentle breeze, which hitherto had fanned her passage, and wafted to her refreshment, suddenly ceased its playful benignity; chaced to a distance by the burning rays of a vertical sun, just bursting forth with meridianal fire and splendour; and dispersing the flying clouds which, in obstructing its refulgence, had softened its intenseness.

This quick change of temperature, operating, materially, like an effective change of climate, annihilated, for the moment, all the strength of Juliet; who, as yet, from the freshness of the morning air, and the vivacity of mental courage, had been a stranger to fatigue.

Upon looking around, to seek a spot where she might obtain a few instants" rest, and some passing succour; she observed that the road, but just before so busily peopled, appeared to be abruptly forsaken. The labourers were no longer working at the high ways, or at the hedges; the harvest-men were vanished; the market-women were gone; the road retained merely here and there an idle straggler; and the fields exhibited only a solitary boy, left to frighten away the birds.

A sensation nearly of famine with which next, from long fasting, joined to vigorous exercise in the open air, she felt assailed, soon pointed out to her that the cause of this general desertion was the rural hour of repast.

Initiated, now, by her own exertions, in the necessity both of support, and of rest, she, too, felt that this was the hour of nature for recruit. But where stop? and how procure sustenance with safety and prudence?

She looked about for some cottage, and was not long ere she found one; but, upon begging for a glass of water from a husbandman, who was standing upon the threshold, he answered that she should have it, if she would pay him with a kiss.

She walked on to another; but some men were smoaking at the door, and she had not courage to make her demand.

At a third, she was disconcerted, by a familiar invitation to partake of a cup of cyder.

She now resolved to make no further application but to females; since countrymen, even those who are freest from any evil designs, are almost all either gross or facetious.

Women, however, at this hour, were not easily met with; they were within, preparing their meals, or cleaning their platters, and feeding their poultry, rabbits, or pigs.

She now drooped, scarcely able to breathe from the oppression of the heat; or to sustain herself from the enfeebling effects of emptiness, joined to over-powering fatigue. With pain and difficulty she dragged on her wearied limbs; while a furious thirst parched her mouth, and seemed consuming her inside.

Now, too, her distress received the tormenting augmentation of intrusive interruption; for, in losing the elasticity of her motions, she lost, to the vulgar observer, her appearance of innocence. Her eye, eagerly cast around in search of an asylum, appeared to be courting attention; her languor seemed but loitering; and her slow unequal pace, wore the air of inviting a companion.

Nor was the character of chaste diligence, and vivacious business, any longer predominant in those whom she now casually encountered. The noon-tide heat, in impairing their bodily strength, caused a mental lassitude, that made them ready for any dissipation that might divert their weariness; and

Juliet, young, rosy, and alone, seemed exactly fashioned for awakening their drowsy faculties. No one, therefore, passed, without remarking her; and scarcely any one without making her some address. The inconsistency of her attire, which her slackened pace allowed time for developing, gave rise to much comment, and some mockery. Her ordinary bonnet and blue apron, ill accorded with the other part of her dress; and she was now assailed with coarse compliments upon her pretty face; now by jocose propositions to join company; and now by free solicitations for a salute.*

Painfully she forced herself on, till, at length, she discerned an ancient dame, in a field by the side of the road, who sat spinning at the door of a cottage.

She crossed a style, and, presenting herself to the old woman, craved a draught of water, and permission to take a little rest.

The good old dame, who was surrounded by little boys and girls, to whom she was singing the antique ballad of the children of the wood,* in a tone so dolorous, and with such heavy sighs, that the elder of her hearers, who were five and six years old, were dissolved in tears; while the younger ones clung to her knees, pale and scared, finished her stanza, before she would answer, or look at the suppliant stranger. She then raised her eyes, with evident vexation at the interruption: but, when she perceived the weak state, and listened to the faint accents of her petitioner, the expression of her countenance became all benevolence; and, good humouredly nodding her head, she disengaged herself from the children, arose, fetched a horn of water, added to it a cup of milk, and then, presenting to the weary traveller her own chair, which was large and low, she got a smaller, and less commodious one, from the kitchen for herself.

The nearly exhausted Juliet gratefully accepted this hospitality; and, in quaffing her milk and water, believed herself initiated in the knowledge of the flavour, and of all the occult qualities, of Nectar.*

It is thus, then, she thought, that the poor and laborious, also, learn, even from their toils and sufferings, what is luxury and enjoyment! for where is the regale, and what is the libation, which the most sumptuous table of refined elegance can offer, that can be more exquisite to the taste, than this simple beverage of milk and water, received thus at the moment of parching thirst, and deadly fatigue?

Meanwhile, the little ones, impatient at the interruption of a tale which engaged all their tenderest feelings; and of which no repetition could diminish the interest; looked with clouded brows, and unchecked ill humour, upon the intruder; and, while the elder ones vented their chagrin by crying, some of the younger ones, yet more completely in the rough hands of untutored nature, rushed forward to beat the cause of their vexation; while others, indignantly, struggled to pull her out of the chair of their grandame.

Juliet, whom their fat little hands could not hurt, and who approved their fondness both for their grandmother and for the ballad, forgave their petulance in favour of its motive: but the grandame, putting aside her spinning wheel, called them all around her, and calmly enquired what was the matter?

They vociferously answered that they wanted to push away the naughty person who was come to take granny's chair.

And what, she asked, would they do themselves, should they be obliged to walk a great way off, till they were tired to death, and as dry as dust, if nobody would give them a little drink, nor a seat to sit down?

But they would never walk a great way off, they answered; never as long as they lived! They would always stay at home with dad and mam and grandam.

But dad and mam, she resumed, were often obliged to walk a great way off themselves; and if nobody would let them have a seat, nor any thing to drink, what would become of them? whereas, if they should hap to light on this young gentlewoman in any trouble, she would remember what had been done for herself, and get them fresh water, and sweet milk, and the easiest chair she could find: and would not they be glad of such good luck to dad and mam? Besides that, by doing good, they would be loved by all good boys and girls; and even by God himself, who was the Father of them all.

This was speaking at once to their sensations and their understandings; dad and mam in distress and relieved seemed present to their view; and they all flew to do something for their guest, as if their gratitude were already indebted. One brought her half an apple, another, a quarter of a pear; one, a bunch of red currants; another, of white; the youngest of the little girls presented her with an old broken rattle; and the smallest of the little boys, waddled to her with a hoop.

Amused by this infantine scene of filial piety, and revived by rest and refreshment, Juliet soon recompensed their endearing innocence, by dancing the smaller ones in her arms, and prattling playfully with those who were less babyish.

Then, putting a shilling into one of their hands, she requested to have a couple of eggs and a crust of bread.

The eggs were immediately baked in the cinders; the crust was cut from a loaf of sweet and fresh brown bread. And if her drink had seemed nectar, what was more substantial appeared to her to be ambrosia!* and her little waiters became Hebes and Ganymedes.*

Refreshment thus salubrious, rest thus restorative, and security thus serene, after fatigue, fasting, and alarm, made her deem this one of the most felicitous moments of her life. Her sole immediate desire was to lengthen it, and to spend, in this tranquil retreat, a part, at least, of the period destined to concealment and obscurity. She had not forgotten her first little *protegés*, nor lost her wish to join them and their worthy mother; but she had severely experienced how little fitted to the female character, to female safety, and female propriety, was this hazardous plan of lonely wandering. She begged, therefore, permission, as a weary traveller, to pass the night in the cottage.

The good dame readily consented; saying, that she could not offer very handsome bedding; but that it should be clean and wholesome, for it had belonged to her youngest daughter, who was just gone out to service.

This arranged, the ballad was again begun, so exquisitely to the delight of the young audience, that though, at the stanza

> Their little lips with blackberries
> Were all besmear'd and dyed;
> And when they saw the darksome night
> They sat them down and cried,*

they all sobbed aloud; they were yet so grieved when it was over, that they clung round their grandame, saying, with one voice, "Aden, granny, aden!"

Granny, however, was too much tired to comply, and the repetition was deferred to another day.

In the evening, the mother of the children came home, and heard what had been settled with her new and unknown guest, without objection or interference. The father appeared soon after, and was equally passive. The grandame was mistress of the cottage, and in her own room, which was that, also, of the elder children, Juliet was lodged. The younger branches of the family slept, with their father and mother, in the kitchen; which, like the apartment of the cobler, served them equally for parlour and hall.*

Juliet found the man and his wife perfectly good sort of people, simply, but usefully employed in earning their living; while their aged mother took charge of their dwelling, their nourishment, and their children.

Thus safely and tranquilly situated, Juliet, without meeting any difficulty, proposed to sojourn with them for some days. She gave, also, a commission, to the younger mistress of the house, to purchase her some ready-made linen at Romsey; and she was soon more consistently equipped, in new, but homely apparel.

This interval was most seasonably passed, in recruiting her strength, and calming her spirits. She took pleasant walks, accompanied by the tallest boy and girl; she worked for the grandmother; taught a part of the catechism to some of the children; played with them all, and made herself at once so useful and so agreeable in the rustic dwelling, that she won the heart and good will of all its inhabitants.

Yet, three times only the sun had set thus serenely, when her host, returning half an hour later in the evening than usual, appeared so altered and ill humoured, that Juliet thought it advisable to leave him with his family: but the slightness of the small building made as inevitable as it was alarming, her learning that she was herself the subject of his discontent.

He told his mother that she must be more cautious how she harboured travellers, or she might come to trouble; for there was a young female-swindler, in or about Salisbury, who was advertised in the news-papers; and who, upon being found out in her tricks, had made off from Dame Goss's, without so much as paying for her lodging. She had been traced as far as Romsey, by means of a postilion; but there, too, she had left her lodging by stealth, in the very middle of the night. All the coachmen and postilions and inn-keepers were looking out for her; a handsome reward being offered, for sending tidings where she might be met with, to an attorney in London. "And now, mother," he continued, "suppose, by hap, this young gentlewoman be she? why you'll be fit to hong yourself, mother! for as to her being so koind to the children, that be no sign; for the bad ones be oftentimes the koindest."

He then enquired whether she had arrived in a white muslin gown, and a white chip-hat.

Her gown might be white muslin, the mother answered, for aught she could say to the contrary, for it was covered almost all round by a blue striped apron; but as to her hat, it was nothing but a straw-bonnet as coarse and ordinary as he might wish to set eyes on.

O then, he said, it was clear it could not be she, for she was not a person to wear a blue apron; she had been seen, the very night she made off, dressed quite genteel.

What now was the consternation of Juliet, to find herself thus pursued as a run-away, and stigmatized as a swindler and an impostor! Astonishing destiny! she cried; for what am I reserved? O when may I cast off this veil of humiliating concealment? when meet unappalled the fair eye of open day? when appear,—when alas!—even know what I am!

This, however, was not the end: it soon seemed scarcely the beginning of new distress, so far more deeply terrible to her was the intelligence by which it was followed. When the women demanded where he had heard this news, he answered, at the public-house; where he was told that all Salisbury was in an uproar; a rich outlandish Mounseer, in a post-chaise, having just come to the great inn, with the advertisement in his hand, pointing to the reward, and promising, in pretty good English, to double it, if the person should be found.

Not another word could Juliet hear; not an instant, not a

thought could she bestow to learn further what was past, or even to gather what was passing; the future, the dread of what was to come, took sole possession of her feelings and her faculties, and again to fly, more rapidly, more eagerly, more affrighted than ever, to fly, was her immediate act, rather than resolution.

She accoutred herself, therefore, in all that was most homely of her new apparel; made a packet of what remained of her genuine attire; left half-a-guinea open upon a little table, to avoid again the accusation of being a swindler; and then, descending the ladder, and contriving to hide her bundle with her blue apron, as she passed, said that she was going to walk in the neighbouring fields, but that it was too late to take out the children; and, giving to each of them a penny, to buy cakes, she quitted the cottage.

Without an instant, without even any powers for reflection, she darted across the fields, gained the road, and, within twenty minutes, arrived at an entrance into the New Forest; to which she had already learnt the way in her rambles with the children.

CHAPTER LXXIII

THE terrified eagerness with which Juliet sought personal security, made her enter the New Forest as unmoved by its beauties, as unobservant of its prospects, as the "Dull Incurious,"[†]* who pursue their course but to gain the place of their destination; unheeding all they meet on their way, deaf to the songsters of the wood, and blind to the pictures of "God's Gallery,"[‡]* the country.

Her steps had no guide but fear, which winged their flight; she sought no route but that which seemed most private. She flew past, across, away from the high road, without daring to raise her eyes, lest her sight should be blasted by the view of her dreaded pursuer.

But speed which surpasses strength must necessarily be transitory. Her feet soon failed; she panted for breath, and was

[†] Thomson. [‡] Twining.

compelled to stop. Fearfully, then, she glanced her eyes around. Nothing met them but trees and verdure. Again she blessed Heaven, and ventured to seat herself upon the "wild fantastic roots"* of an aged beech-tree.

Here, far removed from the "busy hum of man,"* from all public roads; not even a beaten path within view; not a sheep walk, nor a hamlet, nor a cottage to be discerned; nor a single domestic animal to announce the vicinity of mortal habitation; here, she began to hope that she had parried danger, escaped detection, and reached a spot so secluded, that all probability of pursuit was at an end.

With this flattering idea the freedom of her respiration returned: they will go on, she thought, from stage to stage, from mile-stone to mile-stone; they will never imagine I should dare thus to turn aside from the public way; or, should any unfortunate circumstance lead them to such a surmise, how many chances, how many thousand chances are in my favour, that they may not fix upon exactly the same direction, as that to which accident, alone, had been my guide into the mazes of this intricate forest!

This belief sufficed to attract back to her willing welcome, that invincible foe to helpless despondency, Hope; whose magic elasticity waits not for reason, consults not with probability; weighs not contending arguments for settling its expectations, or regulating its desires; but, airy, blyth, and bright, bounds over every obstacle that it cannot conquer.

To find some humble dwelling, by travelling on still further from the towns in which she had been seen, was her immediate project; but prudence forbade her seeking the asylum with Dame Fairfield which she had pleased herself with thinking secured, lest her arrival should be preceded by an accusing, or followed by a dangerous report from her hostess of Salisbury. She determined, therefore, to hide herself under some obscure roof, where she might be utterly unknown; and there to abide, till the fury of the storm by which she feared to be overtaken, should be passed.

No sooner were her spirits, in some degree, calmed, than, with the happy promptitude of youth to set aside evil, all personal fatigue was insensibly forgotten; her eyes began to recover their functions; and the moment that she cast them around with abated anxiety, she was so irresistibly struck with the prospect, and invigorated by the purity of the ambient air, which exhaled odoriferous salubrity, that, rising fresh as from the balmy restoration of undisturbed repose, she mounted a hillock to take a general survey of the spot, and thought all paradise was opened to her view.

The evening was still but little advanced; the atmosphere was as serenely clear, as the beauties which met her sight were sublimely picturesque; and the gay luxuriance of the scenery, though chastened by loneliness and silence, invited smiling admiration. Chiefly she was struck with the noble aspect of the richly variegated woods, whose aged oaks appeared to be spreading their venerable branches to offer shelter from the storms of life, as well as of the elements, charming her imagination by their lofty grandeur; while the zephyrs, which agitated their verdant foliage, seemed but their animation. Soon, however, all observation was seized and absorbed by the benignant west, where the sun, with glory indescribable and ever new, appeared to be concentrating its refulgence, to irradiate the world with its parting blessing: while the extatic wild notes, and warbling, intuitive harmony of the feathered race, struck her ear as sounds celestial, issuing from the abode of angels; or to that abode chanting invitation.

Here, for the first time, she ceased to sigh for social intercourse: she had no void, no want; her mind was sufficient to itself; Nature, Reflection, and Heaven seemed her own! Oh Gracious Providence! she cried, supreme in goodness as in power! What lesson can all the eloquence of rhetoric, science, erudition, or philosophy produce, to restore tranquillity to the troubled, to preserve it in the wise, to make it cheerful to the innocent,—like the simple view of beautiful nature? so divine in its harmony, in its variety so exquisite! Oh great Creator! beneficent! omnipotent! thy works and religion are one! Religion! source and parent of resignation! under thy influence how supportable is every earthly calamity! how supportable, because how transitory becomes all human woe, where heaven and eternity seem full in view!

Thus, in soul-expanding contemplation, Juliet composed

her spirits and recruited her strength, while she awaited the dusky hue of twilight to discover some retreat; and not without reluctance she then quitted the delicious spot, where her weary mind and body had been alike refreshed with repose and consolation.

Though too much occupied by the certain and cruel danger from which she was running, to bestow much attention upon the uncertain, yet immediate and local risks to which she might be liable, she was not, now, sorry to regain a beaten track, of which the rugged ruts shewed the recent passage of a rural vehicle.

In a few minutes, she descried a small cart, directed by a man on foot, who was jovially talking with some companion.

While seeking to discover whether their appearance were such as might encourage her to ask their assistance upon her way, she was startled with a cry of "Why if there ben't Deb. Dyson! O the jeade! if I ben't venged of un! a would no" know me this very blessed morning!"

"Deb. Dyson?" answered the other; "no, a be too slim for Debby. Debby'd outweigh the double o' un."

"O, belike I do no' know Deb. Dyson?" cried the carter, "Why I zee her, at five of the clock, at her own door, in that seame bonnet. And I do know her bonnet of old, for t' be none so new; for I was by when Johnny Ascot gin it her, at our fair, two years agone. I know un well enough, I va'nt* me! A can make herself fat or lean as a wull,* can Debby. A be a funny wench, be Debby. But a shall peay me for this trick, I van't me, a jeade!"

Juliet, in the utmost alarm to find herself thus recognised by the carter, though still supposed to be another, hastily glided back to the wood; cruelly vexed that the very disguise which had hitherto saved her from personal discovery, exposed her but additionally to another species of peril. She might easily, indeed, by speaking, or by suffering herself to be looked at, shew the carter his mistake in conceiving her to be of his acquaintance; but there would still remain a dangerous appearance of intimacy with a young woman who was evidently held in light estimation. She quickened, therefore, her pace, and determined to relinquish her suspicious bonnet by the first opportunity.

In a short time the cackling of fowls, and other sounds of rural animation, announced the vicinity of some inhabited spot. She pursued this unerring direction, and soon saw, and entered, a small hut; in which, though the whole dimensions might have stood in a corner of any large hall, without being in the way, she found a father, mother, and seven young children at supper.

Their looks, upon her entrance, were by no means auspicious; the woman scowled at her with an eye of ill will; the man harshly asked what she wanted; the children, who seemed ravenous, squalled and squabbled for food; and a fierce dog, quitting a half-gnawn bone, to bark vociferously, seemed panting for a sign to leap at and bite her; as a species of order to which he was accustomed upon the intrusion of a stranger.

Juliet told them that she was going to a neighbouring village; but that she had missed her road, and, as it was growing dark, had stopt to beg a night's lodging.

They answered morosely that they had neither bed nor room for travellers.

Was there any house in the neighbourhood where she could be accommodated?

Aye, there was one, they answered, not afar off, where an old man and his wife had a spare bed, belonging to their son: but the direction which they gave was so intricate that, in the fear of losing her way, or again encountering the carter, she entreated permission to sit up in the kitchen.

They went on with their supper, now helping, and now scolding their children, and one another, without taking any notice of this request.

To quicken their attention she put half-a-crown upon the table.

The man and woman both rose, bowing and courtsying, and each offering her their place, and their repast; saying it should go hard but they would find something upon which she might take a little rest.

She felt mortified that so mercenary a spirit could have found entrance in a spot which seemed fitted to the virtuous innocence of our yet untainted first parents; or to the guileless hospitality of the poet's golden age. She was thankful, however, for their consent, and partook of their fare; which she found, with great surprize, required not either air or exercise to give it zest: it consisted of scraps of pheasant and partridge, which the children called *chicky biddy*;* and slices of such fine-grained mutton, that she could with difficulty persuade herself that she was not eating venison.

All else that belonged to this rustic regale gave a surprize of an entirely different nature; the nourishment was not more strikingly above, than the discourse and general commerce of her new hosts were below her expectations. They were rough to their children, and gross to each other; the woman looked all care and ill humour; the man, all moroseness and brutality.

Safety, at this moment, was the only search of Juliet; yet, little as she was difficult with respect to the manner of procuring it, she did not feel quite at ease, when she observed that the man and his wife spoke to each other frequently apart, in significant whispers, which evidently, by their looks, had reference to their guest.

Nevertheless, this created but a vague uneasiness, till the children were put to bed; when the man and woman, having given Juliet some clothing, and an old rug for a mattrass, demanded whether she were a sound sleeper.

She answered in the affirmative.

They then mounted, by a stair-case ladder to their chamber; but, while they were shutting a trap-door, which separated the attic-story from the kitchen, Juliet caught the words, "You've only to turn the darkside of your lanthorn, as you pass, mon, and what can a zee then?"

She was now in a consternation of a sort yet new to her. What was there to be seen?—What ought to be hidden?—Where, she cried, have I cast myself! Have I fallen into a den of thieves?

Her first impulse was to escape; and the moment that all was still over her head, she stept softly to the door, guided by the light of the moon, which gleamed through sundry apertures of an old board, that was placed against the casement as a shutter: but the door was locked, and no key was hung up; nor was any where in sight.

This extraordinary caution in cottagers augmented her alarm. She had, however, no resource but to await the dark lanthorn with steadiness, and to collect all her courage for what might ensue.

She sat upright and watchful, till, by the calculations of probability, she conceived it to be about three o'clock in the morning. Lulled, then, by a hope that her fears were groundless, she was falling insensibly into a gentle slumber; when she was aroused by a step without, followed by three taps against the window, and a voice that uttered, in low accents, "Make heaste, or 'twull be light o'er we be back."

The upper casement was then opened, and the host, in a gruff whisper, answered, "Be still a moment, will ye? There be one in the kitchen."

Great as was now the affright of Juliet, she had the presence of mind to consider, that, whatever was the motive of this nocturnal rendezvous, it was undoubtedly designed to be secret; and that her own safety might hang upon her apparent ignorance of what might be going forward.

To obviate, therefore, more effectually any surmize of her alarm, she dropt softly upon the rug, and covered herself with the clothing provided by her hostess.

She had barely time for this operation before the trap-door was uplifted, and gently, and without shoes, the man descended. He crossed the room cautiously, unbolted and unlocked the door, and shut himself out. Immediately afterwards, the woman, with no other drapery than that in which she had slept, quickly, though with soft steps, came to the side of the rug, and bent over it for about a minute; she then rebolted and locked the door, returned up the ladder, and closed the trap-opening.

Juliet, though dismayed as much as astonished, forbore to rise, from ignorance, even could she effect her escape, by what course to avoid encountering the persons whom she meant to fly, in a manner still more dangerous than that of awaiting their return to their own abode; whence she hoped she might proceed quietly on her way the next morning, as an object not worth detention or examination; her homely attire, and laborious manner of travelling alike announcing profitless poverty.

Her doubts of the nature of what she had to apprehend, were as full of perplexity as of inquietude. Would robbers thus eagerly have caught at half-a-crown? Would they be residents in a fixed abode, with a family of children? Surely not. Yet the whispers, the cautions, the examination whether she slept, evinced clearly something clandestine; and their looks and appearance were so darkly in their disfavour, that, ultimately, she could only judge, that, if they were not actual robbers, they were the occasional harbourers, and miserable accomplices of those who, to similar want of principle, joined the necessary hardiness for following that brief mode of obtaining a livelihood; brief not alone in its success, but in its retribution!

In a state of disturbance so singular, there was not much danger that she should find herself surprised by

"Kind nature's soft restorer, balmy sleep."[†]*

In less than an hour, three taps again struck her ear, though not upon her own casement; taps so gentle, that had she been less watchful, they would not have been heard.

The woman instantly descended the ladder, and approached the bedding; over which she leant as before; and, as before, concluded stillness to be sleep. Cautiously, then, she unbolted and unlocked the door; when, low as were the whispers that ensued, Juliet distinguished three different tones of voice, though she caught not a word that was uttered.

The woman next, gliding across the room, opened a low door, which Juliet had not remarked. The man followed slowly, and as if heavily loaded; the woman shut him out by this private door, and returned to fasten that of public entrance; whispering "Good bye!" to some one who seemed to be departing. Juliet, at the same time, heard something fall, or thrown down, from within, weighty, and bearing a lumpish sound that made her start with horrour.

This involuntary and irresistible movement was immediately perceived by the hostess, who was re-crossing the room; but who, then, precipitately advanced to the bedding, and roughly demanded whether she slept?

Juliet struggled vainly to resume her serene appearance of

[†] Young.

repose; the shock of her nerves had mounted to her features; she felt her lips quiver, and her bosom heave; but she had still sufficient presence of mind to conceal her face by rubbing her eyes, while she asked whether it were time to breakfast?

Satisfied by this enquiry, the woman answered No; and that she had only gotten up to let in her husband, who had been abroad upon a little job, for which he had not found leisure in the day: she recommended to her, therefore, to lie still, and fall asleep.

Still, she remained; but sleep was as far from her eyes, as, in such a situation, from her wishes. She sought, however, again to wear its semblance, while the woman followed her husband through the small door, and shut herself, also, out.

They continued together about half an hour, when, re-entering, they both re-mounted the ladder; without further examination whether or not they were observed.

What might this imply? Was it simply that, concluding her to be awake, they deemed caution to be unavailing? or, that their secret business being finished, caution was no longer necessary?

Strange, also, it appeared to her, their rustic life and residence considered, that they should take such a season for rest, when she saw the vivid rays of the early sun piercing, through various crevices, into the apartment.

Raising her head, next, to view the door, which, the preceding night, had escaped her notice, she espied, close to its edge, a large clot of blood.

Struck with terrour, she started up; and then perceived that the passage from door to door was traced with bloody spots.

She remained for some minutes immovable, incapable either to think of her danger, or to form any plan for her preservation; and wholly absorbed by the image which this sight presented to her fears, of some victim to murderous rapacity.

Soon, however, rousing to a sense of her own situation, she determined upon making a new attempt to escape. She listened beneath the trap-door, to ascertain that all was quiet, and received the most unequivocal assurances, that fatigue and watchfulness had ended in sound sleep. Still, however, she could find no key; but, while fearfully examining every corner, she remarked that the low door was merely latched.

Should she here seek some out-let? She recoiled from the sight of the blood; yet it was a sight that redoubled her earnestness to fly. Whatever had been deposited would certainly be concealed: she resolved, therefore, to make the experiment, though her hand shook so violently, that, more than once, it dropt from the latch ere she could open the door.

Tremblingly she then crossed the threshold, and found herself in a miserable outer-building, without casements, and encumbered with old utensils and lumber. She observed a large cupboard which was locked, but of which, from the darkness of the place, she could take no survey. To the outward door there was no lock, but it was doubly bolted. She opened it, though not without difficulty, and saw that it led to a small disorderly garden, which was hedged round, half planted with potatoes, and half wasted with rubbish. She examined whether there were any opening by which she might enter the Forest; and discerned a small gate, over which, though it was covered with briars, she believed that she could scramble.

Nevertheless, she hesitated; she might be heard, or presently missed and pursued; and the vengeance incurred by such a detection of her suspicions and ill opinion, might provoke her immediate destruction. It might be better, therefore, to return; to rise only when called; to pay them another half-crown; and then publicly depart.

Accidentally, while thus deliberating, she touched the handle of a large wicker-basket, and found that it was wet: she held out her hand to the light, and saw that it was besmeared with blood.

She turned sick; she nearly fainted; she shrunk from her hand with horrour; yet strove to recover her courage, by ejaculating a fervent prayer.

To re-enter the house voluntarily, was now impossible; she shuddered at the idea of again encountering her dreaded hosts, and resolved upon a flight, at all risks, from so fearful a dwelling.

She made her way through the enclosure; crossed the briery gate, and, rushing past whatever had the appearance of already trodden ground, dived into a wood; where, trampling down thorns, brambles, and nettles, now braving, now unconscious of their stings, she continued her rapid course, till she came within view of a small cottage. There she stopt; not for repose; her troubled mind kept her body still insensible to weariness; but to ponder upon her dreadful suspicions.

Not a moment was requisite to satisfy her upright reason, that to discover what she had seen, and what she surmised, was an immediate duty to the community, if, by such a discovery, the community might be served; however repugnant the measure might be to female delicacy; however cruel to the pleadings of compassion for the children of the house; and however adverse to her feelings, to denounce what she could not have detected, but from seeking, and finding, a personal asylum in distress.

Yet who was she who must give such information? Anonymous accusation might be neglected as calumnious; yet how name herself as belonging to the noble family from which she sprung, but by which she was unacknowledged? How, too, at a moment when concealment appeared to her to be existence, come forward, a volunteer to public notice? Small as ought to be the weight given to a consideration merely selfish, if opposing the rights of general security; neither law, she thought, nor equity, demanded the sacrifice of private and bosom feelings, for an evil already irremediable, where, while the denunciation would be unavailing, the denunciator must be undone.

Appeased thus for the moment, though not satisfied in her scruples, she walked on towards the dwelling; but, seeing that it was still shut up, she seated herself upon the stump of a large tree, where deaf, from mental occupation, to the wild melody of innumerable surrounding singing birds, she shudderingly, and without intermission, bathed her bloody hand in the dew.

Rest, however, to her person, served but to quicken the energy of her faculties; and the less her fears, the more her judgment prevailed. Her reasoning, upon examination, she found to be plausible but fallacious. The evil already committed, it was, indeed, too late to obviate; but if the wretched hut, from which she had just escaped, were the receptacle of nocturnal culprits, or of their victims, there might not be a moment to lose to prevent some new and horrible catastrophe.

In a dilemma thus severe, between the terrour of exposing

herself to the personal discovery which she was flying to avoid, or the horrour of omitting the performance of a public duty; she had fixed upon no positive measure, decided upon nothing that was satisfactory, before the casements of the cottage were opened.

Not to lose, then, another moment in unprofitable deliberation, she resolved to communicate to the inhabitants her suspicions, and to urge their being made known to the nearest Justice of the Peace. She might then, with less scruple, continue her flight; and hereafter, if, unhappily, there should be no other alternative, give her assistance in following up the investigation.

She tapped at the cottage-door, and demanded admittance and rest, as a weary traveller.

She was let in, without difficulty, by an old woman, who was breakfasting with an old man, upon a rasher of bacon.

It now, with much alarm, occurred to her, that this might be the house to which she had been directed from the terrible hut. She fearfully enquired whether they had a spare bed? and, upon receiving an answer in the affirmative, with the history of their son's absence, not a doubt remained that she had sought refuge with the friends, perhaps the accomplices, of the very persons from whom she was escaping; and who, should they, through vengeful apprehension, pursue her, would probably begin their search at this spot.

Affrighted at the idea, yet not daring abruptly to abscond, she forced herself to sit still while they breakfasted; though unable to converse, and turning with disgust from the sight of food.

The old man and woman, meanwhile, intent solely upon their meal, which, now too hot for their mouths, now too cold for their taste, now too hard for their teeth, occupied all their discourse; heeded not her uneasiness, and, when she arose and took leave, saw her departure with as little remark as they had seen her entrance.

With a complication of fears she now went forth again; to seek,—not an asylum in the Forest, the beautiful Forest!—but the road by which she might quit it with the greatest expedition. Where, now, was the enchantment of its prospects?

Where, the witchery of its scenery? All was lost to her for pleasure, all was thrown away upon her as enjoyment; she saw nothing but her danger, she could make no observation but how to escape what it menaced.

She flew, therefore, from the vicinity of the hut, though with a celerity better adapted to her wishes than to her powers; for, in less than half an hour, she was compelled, from utterly exhausted strength, to seat herself upon the turf.

Not yet was she risen, and scarcely was she rested, when she was startled by a whistling in the wood, which was presently followed by the sound of two youthful male voices, in merry converse.

To escape notice, she, at first, thought it safest to sit still; but the nearer and nearer approach of feet, made her reflect, that to be surprised, in so unfrequented a spot, at so early an hour in the morning, might be yet more unfavourable to opinion, than being discerned to pace her lonely way, with the quick steps of busy haste, or timid caution. She moved, therefore, on; carefully taking a contrary direction to that whence the voices issued.

She soon found herself bewildered in a thicket, where she could trace no path, and whence she could see no opening. She was felicitating herself, however, that she had out-run the sounds by which she had been affrighted; when she first heard, and next perceived, an immense dog, who, after beating about the bushes at some distance, suddenly made a point at her, and sprang forward.

Terrour, which puts us into any state but that which is natural, bestows, occasionally, what, in common, it robs us of, presence of mind. Juliet knew that flight, to the intelligent, though dumb friend of man, was well seen to be cowardice, and instinctively judged to be guilt. Aware, therefore, that if she could not appease his fury, it were vain to attempt escaping it, she compelled herself to turn round and face him; holding out her hand in a caressing attitude, that seemed inviting his approach; though with difficulty sustaining herself upon her feet, from a dread of being torn to pieces.

The rage, unprovoked, but not inexorable, of the animal, withstood not this manifestation of kindness: from a pace so rapid, that it seemed menacing to level her with the earth by a single bound, he abruptly stopt, to look at and consider his imagined enemy; and from a barking, of which the stormy loudness resounded through the forest, his tone changed to a low though surly growl, in which he seemed to be debating with himself, whether to attack a foe, or accept a friend.

The hesitation sufficed to ensure to Juliet the victory. Encouraged by a view of success, her address supplanted her timidity, and, bending forwards, she called to him with endearing expressions. The dog, caught by her confidence, made a grumbling but short resistance; and, having first fiercely, and next attentively, surveyed her, wagged his tail in sign of accommodation, and, gently advancing, stretched himself at her feet.

Juliet repaid his trust with the most playful caresses. Good and excellent animal, she cried, what a lesson of mild philanthropy do you offer to your masters! The kindness of an instant gains you to a stranger, though no unkindness, nor even the hardest usage, can alienate you from an old friend!

She now flattered herself that, by following as he led, she might have a guide, as well as a protector, to the habitation to which he belonged. She sate by his side, determined to wait his movements, and to pursue his course. Perfectly contented himself, he basked in the sun-beams that broke through the thicket, and was evidently soothed, nay, charmed, by the fond accents with which she solicited his friendship.

This nearly silent, but expressive intercourse, was soon interrupted by a vociferous Haloo! from a distant part of the wood.

Up started the new companion of Juliet, who arose, also, to accompany, or, at least, to trace his steps. Neither were possible. He darted from her with the same rapidity, though wide from the same ferocity, as that with which he had at first approached her: vain was every soft appeal, lost was every gentle blandishment; in an instant he was out of sight, out of hearing,—she scarcely saw him go ere he was gone. Faithful creature! she cried, 'tis surely his master who calls! A new tie may excite his benevolence; none can shake his fidelity, nor slacken his services.

Alone and unaided, she had now to pierce a passage through the thicket, uncertain whither it might lead, and filled with apprehensions.

But, in a few minutes, greatly to her satisfaction, her new friend re-appeared; wagging his tail, rubbing himself against her gown, and meeting and returning her caresses.

Her project of obtaining a conductor was now recurring, when again an Haloo! followed by the whistling of two voices, called off her hope; and shewed her that her intended protector belonged to the young men whom she had been endeavouring to avoid.

She knew not whether it were better, under the auspices of her new ally, to risk begging a direction from these youths, to some house or village; or still to seek her desolate way alone.

She had time only to start, not to solve this doubt; the dog, again returning, as if unwilling to relinquish his new alliance, began to excite the curiosity of his masters; who, following, exclaimed, "Dash a vound zomething, zure!" and presently, through the trees, she descried two wood-cutters.

She was seen, also, by them; they scrambled faster on; and one of them said,

"Why t'be a girl!"

"Be it?" answered the other; "why then I'll have a kiss."

"Not a fore me, mon!" cried his companion, "vor I did zee her virzt!"

"Belike you did," the other replied; "but I zpoke virzt; zo you mun come after!"

Juliet now saw herself in a danger more dreadful than any to which either misfortune or accident had hitherto exposed her,—the danger of personal and brutal insult. She looked around vainly for succour or redress; the woods and the heavens were alone within view or within hearing.

The first terrible moment of this alarm was an agony of affright, that made her believe herself a devoted victim to outrage: but the moment after, observing that the young men were beginning to combat for precedence, a sudden hope of escape revived her courage, and gave wings to her feet; and, defying every obstacle, she pushed on a passage, through the intricate thicket, almost with the swiftness that she might have crossed the smoothest plain, till she arrived at an open spot of ground.

The fear of losing her now ended, though without deciding, the dispute; and the youths ran on together, mutually and loudly shouting familiar appeals, after the fugitive, upon their rights, with entreaties that she would stop.

Juliet again felt her strength expiring; but where courage is the result of understanding, if its operation is less immediate than that which springs from physical bravery, it is not less certain. The despair, therefore, of saving herself by bodily exertion, presently gave rise to a mental effort, which instigated her to turn round upon her persecutors, and await and face them; with the same assumed firmness, though not with the offered caresses, with which she had just encountered her four-footed pursuer.

Their surprize at this unexpected action put an end to their dissention; and, each believing her to be alike at the service of either, or of both, they laughed coarsely, and came on, arm in arm, and leisurely, together.

Juliet, calling to her assistance her utmost presence of mind. and dignity of manner, stept forward to meet them; and, with an air that disguised her apprehensions, said, "Gentlemen, I have business of great importance with the farmer who lives near this place; but I do not know the shortest way to his farm. If you will be so obliging as to shew it to me, you may depend upon his handsomely rewarding any trouble that you may take."

Their astonishment, now, was encreased; but although, at the word business, they leered at one another with an air of mockery, her air and mien, with her grave civility and apparent trust, caused, involuntarily, a suspension of their facetious design; and they enquired the name of the farmer, whom she was seeking.

She could not immediately, she said, recollect it; but he lived at the nearest farm.

"Why 't-ben't Master Zimmers?" They cried.

"The very same!"

"What, that do live yinder, across the copse?"

"Without any doubt."

They now ogled one another, with a consciousness that persuaded Juliet that this Simmers was their own master; or, perhaps, their father; and she repeated her request, with reiterated assurances, that a considerable recompence would be bestowed upon her conductor.

They looked irresolute, and extremely foolish; Dash, however, was firmly her friend, and, while they were whispering and hesitating, jumped and capered from his masters to his new associate, from his new associate to his masters, with an intelligent delight, that seemed manifesting his enjoyment of a junction which he had himself brought about.

Juliet shewed so much pleasure in his kindness, that the young men, proud of their dog, and glad, in their embarrassment, to be occupied rather than to reply, fondled him, in their rough manner, themselves; making him fetch, carry, stand on his hinder legs, leap over their hats, caper, bark, point, and display his various accomplishments.

Juliet encouraged this diversion, by patting the dog, applauding his teachers, and stimulating a repetition of every feat; till the youths, charmed by her good fellowship, were insensibly turned aside from their evil intentions; and soon, and in perfect harmony, they all arrived at a considerable farm, upon the borders of the New Forest.

CHAPTER LXXIV

JULIET, thus escaped from the eminent and terrific dangers to which she had been exposed, entered the farm-house with a glowing delight diffused over her countenance, that instinctively communicated a participating pleasure to the people of the farm; and caused her to be received with an hospitality that might have contented the expectations of an old friend.

Nothing so unfailingly ensures, or rather creates a welcome, as cheerfulness; cheerfulness! so beautifully, by Addison, called an Hymn to the Divinity!* Whether it be, that the view of sprightliness seems the fore-runner of pleasure to ourselves; or whether we judge all within to be innocent, where all without is serene; various, according to sentiment, or circumstance, as may be the motive, the result is nearly universal; that those who approach us with cheerfulness, are sure to be met with kindness. Cheerfulness is as distinct from insipid placidity as from buoyant spirits; it seems to indicate a disposition of thankful enjoyment for all that can be attained of good, blended with resignation upon principle to all that must be endured of evil.

Her first care was to satisfy her two still wondering conductors, who proved to be sons to the master of the farm, by giving to each half-a-crown; that they might not lose their time, she told them, by waiting till she had settled her business with their father: and, after doubling her caresses to her protector, Dash, she sent them back to their work; manifestly glad that they had not affronted a young woman, who knew how to behave herself, they said, so handsomely.

She now begged an audience of the farmer, to whom she resolved to communicate her alarming adventure at the hut.

The farmer, who was surrounded by his family and his labourers, to whom he was issuing orders, desired her to speak out at once.

Juliet could by no means consent to publish so dark and uncertain a history to so many hearers; she again, therefore, entreated to address him in private.

He had come home, he answered, only to take a mug of beer; for the plough was in the field: however, she might call again, if she would, at dinner-time; but he had no time to give to talk in a morning.

And forth he went, whistling, and hallooing after his labourers, as he jogged his way.

She then applied to his bustling, sturdy wife; but with no better success; Who was to feed the poultry? who was to give the wash* to the pigs? who was to churn the butter? if she threw away her time by gossipping in the morning?

The rest of the family consisted of three grown up daughters, and four or five children. The daughters, though more civil, because less voluntarily busy, and, as yet, less interested than their parents, were too inexperienced to give any assistance, or form any judgment upon such an affair; Juliet, therefore, who was sinking with fatigue and emptiness, and who desired nothing so much as to remain for some time under any safe roof, begged, of the young women, a bason of bread and milk for her breakfast; and permission to stay at the farm till the hour of dinner.

These requests were granted without the smallest demur, even before she produced her purse; which they viewed with no small surprize, saying that they hoped they were not so near,* as to take money for a little bread and milk of a traveller; but that, if she must needs do it, she might give a small matter to the children.

Recollecting, now, her rustic and ordinary garb, and fearing to awaken suspicion, or curiosity, she put a penny a-piece into the hands of two little boys and a girl.

It was then that she saw how far she was removed from the capital; in the precincts of which the poor and the labourer are almost constantly rapacious, or necessitous. The high price to be obtained, there, for whatever is marketable, makes generosity demand too great a sacrifice, save from the exalted few; who, still in all places, and in all classes, are, by the candid observer, occasionally, to be found. But in this obscure hamlet, where plenty was not bribed away to sale, this little donation was received with as much amazement as joy; and the children scampered to the dairy, and to the plough-field, to shew it first to mammy, and then to dad.

Juliet, having taken her simple repast, strolled into a small meadow, just without the farm-yard; where she seated herself upon a style, to enjoy, at once, the fragrant air, and personal repose.

The prospect here, though less sublime in itself, and less exalting in the ideas which it inspired, than that of the lonely and majestic beauty, which had so powerfully charmed her, visually and intellectually, in the midst of the New Forest; was yet gay, varied, verdant and lovely. On the opposite side of a winding and picturesque road, by which the greater part of the hedge around the meadow was skirted, was situated a small Gothic church; of which the steeple was nearly over-run with ivy, and the porch, half sunk into the ground, from the ravages of time and of neglect; wearing, all together, the air of a venerable ruin. Further on, and built upon a gentle acclivity, stood a clean white cottage, evidently appropriated to the instruction of youth, or rather childhood; to which sundry little boys and girls, each with a book, or with needle-work, in his hand, were trudging with anxious speed. Juliet spoke to each of them as they passed; pleased with their innocent prattle, and gathering alternately, from their native intelligence, or gaping stupidity, food to amuse her mind, with predictions of their future characters. Sheep were browsing upon a distant heath; cows were watering in a neighbouring stream; and two beautiful colts were prancing and skipping, with all the bounding vigour of untamed liberty, in the meadow. Geese, turkies, cocks and hens, ducks and pigs, peopled the farm-yard; keeping up an almost constant chorus of rural noises; which, at first, stunned her ears, but which, afterwards, entertained her fancy, by drawing her observation to their various habits and ways. The children came, jumping, to play around her; and her friend Dash, discovering her retreat, frequently left the wood-cutters to bound forwards, and court her caresses.

The young women of the house, to divert their several labours of weeding, churning, or washing, occasionally, also, joined her, for the pleasure of a little chat; which they by no means, like their father or mother, held in contempt. Juliet received them with an urbanity that gave such a zest to their little visits, that it served to quicken their work, that they might quicken their return; and, with the eldest, she changed the bonnet of Debby Dyson, for one that was plainer, and yet more coarse.

There was nothing in these young persons of sufficient "mark or likelihood"* to make them attractive to Juliet; but she was glad to earn their good will; and not sorry to learn what were their occupations; conscious that a dearth of useful resources, was a principal cause, in adversity, of FEMALE DIFFICULTIES.

Here, then, Juliet formed a project to rest, till her own should be removed; or, at least, till she could obtain some intelligence, that might guide her uncertain steps: this seemed the spot upon which she might find repose; this seemed the juncture for enjoying quiet and tranquillity in the country life; to which she desired to devote the residue of the time that might still be destined to suspense.—Here, retirement would be soothing, and even seclusion supportable, from the charm of the scenery, the beauty of the walks, the guileless characters, and vivifying activity of the inhabitants of the farm-house; and the fragrant serenity of all around. Here, peace and plenty were the result of industry; and primitive, though not polite hospitality, was the offspring of natural trust. If there was no cultivation, there was no art; if there was no refinement, there were integrity and good will.

She applied, therefore, to her new young acquaintances, to promote her plan with their parents. They lost not a moment in making the arrangement; and Juliet was immediately installed in a small chamber, upon the attic-story. She settled that she should eat from their table, but alone; for she dreaded remark or discovery. No terms were fixed; a little matter, they said, would suffice; and Juliet saw that she had nothing to fear from imposition; every face in the family bearing the mark, or the promise, of steady honesty.

Nor, indeed, could any price be exorbitant to Juliet, that could procure some relief to her fears, and some respite from her toils. Her first care was to obtain, through her new friends, implements for writing; and then to transmit, in detail, assurances of her present safety, and even comfort, to Gabriella; from whom she entreated intelligence, whether pursuit and enquiry were still active.

As fearful, now, of the name of Ellis, as, heretofore, she had been of that of Granville, she desired that the answer might be directed, under cover to "Master Simmers, Farmer, at——, near the New Forest;" and that the enclosed letter might have no other address than, "For the young Woman who lodges at the Farm."

Again, then, she returned to the meadow, which, now her mind was more at ease, seemed adorned with added verdure, freshness, and beauty. Here, pensive, yet not without consolation, she past the day.

The next, she rambled a few paces further, and found out a cottage, in a situation of the most romantic loveliness, in which two labourers, and their wives, resided with their mother; a cheerful, pleasing old woman, with whom Juliet was immediately in amity.

She visited, also, the school; made acquaintance with its mistress, who appeared to be a sensible and worthy woman; and captivated the easy hearts of the little scholars, by the playful manner in which she noticed their occupations, encouraged their diligence, and assisted them to learn their lessons.

She aided, also, the young women of the farm, in various of the lighter domestic offices that fell to their share; and amused, at once, and instructed her own mind, by opening a new road for admiration of the wondrous works of the Great Creator, in observing and studying the various animals abounding in and about the farm. The remark and attention of a few days, sufficed to shew her, not only as much difference in the interiour nature of the four-footed and of the plumaged race, as there is in their hides or their feathers; but nearly, or, perhaps, quite as much diversity, in their dispositions, as in those of their haughty human masters; though the means of manifestation bore no comparison. In fixing her attention upon them, in following their motions, and considering their actions; she found that though the same happy instinct guided them all alike to self-preservation, the degrees of skill with which they discovered the shortest and best method for attaining what they coveted, were infinite; yet not more striking than the variety of their humours; kind, complying, generous; or fierce, selfish, and gloomy, in their intercourse with one another. *Le droit du plus fort*, (the right of strength,)* though the most ordinary, was by no means the only, or the universal basis of animal legislation. Dexterity and sagacity find ascendance wherever there is animation: and propensities benign and social, or malignant and savage, as palpably distinguish beast from beast, and bird from bird, as man from his fellow.

What an inexhaustible source was here, to a thinking being, both for information and entertainment! Oh Providence Divine! she cried, how minute is the perfection, yet how grand the harmony of thy works!

Still, however, she sought vainly to obtain the requested conference. The farmer, whose thoughts were absorbed exclusively in the interests of his farm, was always too busy to afford her any time, and too indifferent to give her any attention. As she lodged in the house, he could hear her, he said, when he should be more at leisure; and all her eloquence was ineffectual, either to awaken his curiosity, or to excite his benevolence, by intimations of the importance, or of the haste, of the business which she wished to communicate. "Ay, girl, ay," he would reply; "by and by will do just as well."

But by and by came not! When she endeavoured to catch a moment, at the hour of breakfast, the whole day, he would cry, was as good as thrown away, if a man lost a moment of his morning: yet if she solicited his hearing in the evening, he would cordially offer her some bread and cheese, and beer; but rise from them himself, heavy and sleepy, to go to bed; saying, "Hark y', my girl; when you've worked as hard as a farmer, you'll be as glad of your night's rest."

If she sought him in the middle of the day, he was always surrounded by his family, and by labourers, from whom he would never step apart; telling her to speak out what she had to say, and to fear nothing and nobody.

Farming, she soon found, he regarded as the only art of life worth cultivation, or even worth attention; every other seemed to him superfluous or silly. A woman, therefore, as she could neither plough the field, nor mow the corn, he considered as every way an inferiour being: and, like the savages of uncivilised nature, he would scarcely have allowed a female a place at his board, but for the mitigation given to his contempt, from regarding her as the mother of man.

The sex, therefore, of Juliet, was here wholly against her; and youth and beauty, those powerful combatants of misanthropy! were necessarily without influence, where they were never looked at: Could they ripen his corn? or make his hay? No; What then, was their value?

Nevertheless, he treated neither his wife nor his daughters ill; he only considered them as his servants: and when they were diligent and useful, he praised them and gave them presents; and, when their work was done, suffered them to seek what diversion they pleased, without interference or controul. The females were indifferent, and therefore contented; though neither confidential nor affectionate.

The sons, on the contrary, were open, boisterous, and

daring; domineering over their sisters, and mocking their mother; while they nearly shared, with their partial father, both his authority and his profits.

In a family such as this, Juliet had no chance of softening the languor of her suspense by society; and books, its best substitute, had never found their way into the farm-house; save an odd volume or two of trials, sundry tracts upon farriery, and various dismal old ballads.*

The first charm of this rural residence, consisting in its views and its walks, soon lost something of its animation to Juliet, through the restriction of fear, which impeded her from roving beyond the neighbourhood of the farm. And though the beautiful prospect from the meadow, and the air and exercise of mounting to the school, might permanently have afforded her delight, if shared with some loved friend, or enjoyed with some good author; she became, in a short time, through the total deprivation of either, nearly as languid from monotony without, as she was wearied by ungenial intercourse within.

On Sunday, after they had all been to church, the young women proposed to accompany her in a stroll; and the hope of a romantic ramble without danger, induced her acceptance of the invitation. This, however, was an essay which she did not feel tempted to repeat. She found that their only idea of taking a stroll, was to get away from home; and their only object of pursuit, was to encounter their several sweethearts. They walked not for exercise; they had more than enough in their daily occupations. They walked not for air; they rarely spent an hour of the day under shelter. They walked still less in search of rural views, or picturesque beauties; they saw them not; or, rather, they saw them too constantly to heed them. Their chosen scene was the high road; along which they leisurely, but merrily sauntered, to enjoy,—not the verdure of the adjacent fields, or wood; not the freshness of the salubrious breeze; not the charm, here and there occasionally bursting upon the sight, of sloping hills, or flowery dales; but to watch for every distant cloud of rising dust, that announced, or that promised the approach of a horse, cart, or waggon.

What, to these, was the pleasure of situation? Juliet saw, with concern, that all which, to herself, would have solaced a similar way of life, to them was null. Accustomed from their infancy to beautiful scenery, they looked at it as a thing of course, without pleasure or admiration; because without that which fixes all worldly acceptation of happiness,—comparison.

The mother, whose existence, from the fear and from the commands of her husband, was laborious; and, from her own love of saving, penurious; had scarcely even any idea of pleasure, beyond what accrued from feeding her rabbits, fattening her hogs, and carrying her eggs and poultry to a good market.

The farmer, whose will had no controul, either from himself or his family; and who indulged his own humours in the same proportion that he kept theirs in awe, had yet a master; and a master more despotic and ungovernable than himself,—the Weather! to whose power, however, he by no means submitted tamely. The whole house rang with the violence of his rage, if the rain fell while his hay were cutting or stacking; and he could scarcely swallow his dinner for chagrin, if it failed to fall when his peas wanted filling: his imprecations were those of a man provoked by the grossest personal injury, if a sharp wind came not at his bidding, when he perceived insects crawling upon the leaves of his fruit-trees in the orchard; and his whole family trembled, as if immediate ruin, or an earthquake were impending, when he claimed, and claimed in vain, the sun to ripen his corn.

Juliet now found, that a farmer is sensible to no happiness, that a gust of wind, a shower of rain, or the beams of the sun; as they meet, or oppose, his wishes; does not confirm, or may not destroy.

The storms, nevertheless, raised by this man of the elements, were from causes too obvious to create surprize; and they were known to be too harmless in their operations, to occasion any other movement in his household, than that of a general struggle which should first get out of his way till they were blown over: but, to a stranger, to Juliet, they were more tremendous, because as foreign to the habits of her life, as they were ungenial to her nature. To change therefore, a scene so continually overcast, she took leave of the family, thankfully repaying the services which she had received; and left the farm, to lodge herself with the pleasing old woman, who had won her favour, in the beautifully picturesque cottage in the neighbourhood.

CHAPTER LXXV

IN this cottage, Juliet, again, witnessed another scene of life; and one which, serene and soothing, appeared, upon its opening, to exclude all evil.

The dwelling of the shepherd, or husbandman, had already in its favour the imagery of poesy, and the ardent predilection of juvenile ideas; and, with the vivacity of a heart always open to hope, Juliet hailed in it, at once, tranquillity and contentment.

Paid for his work by the day, the labourer had no anxiety for the morrow; the ground he was to plough, or till, or sow, was not his own; the goodness, badness, and variations of the weather touched not his property, nor endangered his subsistence. Be the seasons, therefore, what they might, he was not to be pitied.

Yet though his sound repose, the fruit of his toil, was undisturbed by elemental strife, he waked not to active hope; he looked not forward to sanguine expectation: the changes which could do him no mischief, could not bring him any advantage. No view of amelioration to his destiny enlivened his prospect; no opening to better days spurred his industry; and, as all action is debased, or exalted, by its motive; and all labour, by its object; those who struggle but to eat and sleep, may be saved from solicitude, but cannot be elevated to prosperity. He could not, therefore, be envied.

Two of the young men were married, and their wives, strong and healthy like themselves, worked almost as laboriously. Juliet found them as worthy as they were industrious; and hoped, by exciting their kindness, to add the interest of gentle amity to peace and rural enjoyment. But, though pleased and satisfied with their characters, and honouring their active and useful lives, she sought vainly to content herself with their uncultured society; and soon saw, with regret, how much the charm, though not the worth, of innocence depends upon manners; of goodness, upon refinement; and of honesty upon elevation. There was much to merit her approbation; but not a point to engage her sympathy; and, where the dominion of the character falls chiefly upon the heart, life, without sympathy, is a blank. The unsatisfied soul sighs for communion; its affections demand an expansion, its ideas, a development, that, instinctively, call for interchange; and point out, that solitude, sought only by misery, remorse, or misanthropy, is as ungenial to our natural feelings, as retirement is salubrious.

She had here time and opportunity to see the fallacy, alike in authors and in the world, of judging solely by theory. Those who are born and bred in a capital; who first revel in its dissipations and vanities, next, sicken of its tumults and disappointments, write or exclaim for ever, how happy is the country peasant's lot! They reflect not that, to make it such, the peasant must be so much more philosophic than the rest of mankind, as to see and feel only his advantages, while he is blind and insensible to his hardships. Then, indeed, the lot of the peasant might merit envy!

But who is it that gives it celebrity? Is it himself? Does he write of his own joys? Does he boast of his own contentment? Does he praise his own lot? No! 'tis the writer, who has never tried it, and the man of the world who, however murmuring at his own, would not change with it, that give it celebrity.

Though natively endowed with that first, perhaps of worldly blessings, high animal spirits, Juliet, from an early experience of the vicissitudes of fortune, was become meditative. She looked with an intelligent desire of information, upon every new scene of life, that was presented to her view; and every class of society, that came within her knowledge: she now, therefore, with equal clearness and concern, saw how false an idea is conceived, at a distance, not only of the shepherd's paradise, but of the general happiness of the country life;—save to those who enjoy it with a large family to bring up; or with means not alone competent to necessity, but to benevolence; which not alone give leisure for the indulgence of contemplation, and the cultivation of rural taste, of literature, and of the fine arts; but which supply means for lightening the labours, and softening the hardships of the surrounding poor and needy. Then, indeed, the country life is the nearest upon earth, to what we may conceive of joys celestial!

The verdure of the flower-motleyed meadow; the variegated foliage of the wood; the fragrance and purity of the air, and the wide spreading beauties of the landscape, charm not the labourer. They charm only the enlightened rambler, or affluent possessor. Those who toil, heed them not. Their eyes are upon their plough; their attention is fixed upon the harvest; their sight follows the pruning hook. If the vivid field catches their view, it is but to present to them the image of the scythe, with which their labour must mow it; if they look at the shady tree, it is only with the foresight of the ax, with which their strength must fell it; and, while the body pants but for rest, which of the senses can surrounding scenery, ambient perfumes, or vocal warblers, enchant or enliven?

Juliet now, herself an inhabitant of the cottage, which, hitherto, she had only beheld in perspective, smiled, yet sighed at her mistake, in having considered shepherds and peasants as objects of envy. O ye, she cried, who view them through your imaginations! were ye to toil with them but one week! to rise as they rise, feed as they feed, and work as they work! like mine, then, your eyes would open; you would no longer judge of their pleasures and luxuries, by those of which they are the instruments for yourselves! you would feel and remark, that yours are all prepared for you; and that they, the preparers, are sufferers, not partakers! You would see then, as I see now, that the most delightful view which the horizon can bound, affords not to the poor labourer the joy that is excited by the view of the twilight through which it is excluded; but which sends him home to the mat of straw, that rests, for the night, his spent and weary limbs.

Then, as she looked around, from the summit of the hill upon which stood the small seminary for children, which she frequently visited, Oh that Elinor, she cried, escaping from the pressure of her passions, would expand her feelings by contemplating the works of God! Oh Father of All!—Who can reflect, yet doubt, that Man, placed at the head of these stupenduous operations, lord of the earthly sphere, can fail to be destined for Immortality? Yet more, who can examine and meditate upon the uncertain existence of thy creatures,—see failure without fault; success without virtue; sickness without relief; oppression in the very face of liberty; labour without sustenance; and suffering without crime;—and not see, and not feel that all call aloud for resurrection and retribution! that annihilation and injustice would be one! and that Man, from the very nature of his precarious earthly being, must necessarily be destined, by the All Wise, and All Just, for regions that we see not; for purposes that we know not;—for Immortality!

CHAPTER LXXVI

THUS, in beautiful scenery, and meditative resignation, with outward quiet, though by no means with internal tranquillity, Juliet had passed about a week, when the wife of the farmer broke rudely into the cottage; bearing in her hand the bonnet of Debby Dyson, which she flung scornfully upon a table.

Angrily, then, reproaching Juliet that she had caused Bet to be taken for that bold hussy, by the higler, she demanded back the exchanged bonnet; declaring, that the girl should never wear one again, to the longest day that she had to live, rather than dress herself up in any thing of Debby Dysons's.

Turning next to the old cottager, she added, that a good mother would do well not to keep a person used to such light company under her roof; unless she had a mind to bring her daughters-in-law to ruin.

Then, snatching up her girl's bonnet, she bustled away to look after her evening's milking; roughly refusing to hearken to any sort of explanation from Juliet, and saying that she never knew any good come of listening to talking; which was no better than idling away time.

Juliet remained confounded; while the tender old cottager shed tears, saying that she had never before had so pretty a companion in her life. But Juliet would not tempt the good woman to defy the persons upon whom her children chiefly depended; and, once more, therefore, she was reduced to make up her little packet.

She entreated of the cottager that, if a letter came for her to the farm, it might be kept till she sent her direction; then doubled the pay of all that she owed for board and lodging; and, kindly taking leave of the old dame, who wept bitterly at the parting, quitted the cottage; and again, in search of a new asylum, became a Wanderer.

Which way to turn, she made no enquiry, wholly ignorant what choice might bring security.

It was the end of August, and still not more than six o'clock in the afternoon. She avoided the high road, in the fear of some unfortunate encounter, and went down a pleasant looking lane; purposing to proceed as far, and as fast, as she could go, while it was yet light; and then to enter some new humble dwelling.

The evening was serene and warm, and occasional openings, through the hedges on either side, presented views so picturesque, that, had her mind been more at ease, they would have rendered her walk delightful.

She crossed various corn-fields, and beautiful meadows; but met with no cottage from which some lounging labourer did not frighten her; till, at length, overtaken by the dusk of the evening, she was fain to turn back, and seek, with whatever apprehension, some lodging, for the night, upon the public road.

But to do this was no longer easy. She mistook what she thought was her direction, and, instead of arriving at the road, found herself upon a broad, open, dreary heath.

She endeavoured to discover the track of some carriage, and succeeded; and followed the mark, till she thought that she perceived a cottage.

She hastened towards it, with all the speed that her wearied limbs would permit; but the expected habitation proved merely a group of Pollards.*

She would then have recovered the wheel-track; but the moon became suddenly clouded, a general darkness overspread the face of the country around, and she could discover no kind of path.

She now grew apprehensive that she should pass the night in the open air; with not a human being within hearing, nor any house, nor any succour within reach. What she might have to dread she knew not; but, in a situation so wildly solitary, the very ignorance of what there might be to fear, was intimidating, nay, awful.

The darkness encreased; cautiously and slowly she went on, starting at every breeze, and in continual terrour of meeting some unknown mischief.

She wandered thus for some hours, now sinking into marshy ground, now wounded by rude stones, now upon a soft, smooth plain, and now stung or torn by bushes, nettles, and briars; till she concluded it to be about midnight. A light wind then arose, the clouds were dispersed; and the moon, which, though upon the wane, afforded a gentle, melancholy light, shewed her that she was once again in the midst of the New Forest.

Few sights could have been less welcome; what already she had suffered, and, far more, what she had apprehended, filled her with terrour; and her imagination was fearfully at work, now to bring her to the hut which she had so suspiciously fled; now to the encounter of disorderly young assailants, with no Dash for her protection; now to the attack of lurking thieves, and strolling vagabonds; and now to the danger of being bewildered and lost in the mazes of the Forest.

The last of these evils soon ceased to be a mere phantasm of fear; the wind no sooner was calmed than the moon again was obscured, and all around her was darker, and therefore more tremendous than ever.

She continued to move on, though without knowing whether she were advancing or retrograding. But, ere long, her walk became embarrassed and difficult; her progress was every way obstructed; and her retreat at the same time impeded; and she found herself in a thick wood, of which the deep hanging boughs continually annoyed her face and her limbs; while the unscythed grass, the growth of ages, entangled her feet, and made every step a labour.

Wearied and dejected, she leaned against a tree, and determined to make no further attempt to proceed, till some gleam of dawn should direct her way.

She had not remained long in this position of despondence, ere she discerned, through the trees, at a considerable distance, a dim light.

She concluded that this must proceed from some dwelling; and, feeling instantly revived, re-commenced her journey: yet, presently, she stopt and hesitated,—it might emit from the hut!

In the dead of the night there was little probability that any common cottagers would require a light.

Discomfited, discouraged, she again leaned against a tree.

Yet some one might be ill; and the chamber of sickness and danger could no more, in the cottage, than in the palace, be consigned to darkness. She determined, therefore, to approach the spot, and, at break of day, to examine the premises; certain she could not ever mistake, or ever forget, the situation of the hut.

She went forward.

The light, in a few moments, disappeared; but she was not, therefore, led to consider it as a Will with the Wisp, to beguile her to some illusion; for, ere it vanished, it displayed, in passing sideways, a view of a cottage double or treble the length of the dreaded hut.

This was a sight truly consoling; yet, though it happily removed the most terrible of her fears, it awakened new perplexity. The light had been evidently without doors: the suggestion, therefore, of a sick chamber proved unfounded. Yet what, in the middle of the night, could replace it, that was natural, and free from suspicion of evil?

Nevertheless, she moved on; seeking to guide herself by the recollection of the spot which she had transiently seen; till she was startled by a murmuring of human voices.

But for the alarm left upon her mind, by the adventure of the hut, and the pursuit of the wood-cutters, this would have been a sound in which her ears would have rejoiced, as the forerunner of succour and of safety; for, till then, she had always connected the idea of rusticity with innocence, and of rural life with felicity. But now, she had fatally learnt, that no class, and no station, appropriatively merit trust; and that the poor, like the rich, the humble, like the proud, can only by principle be worthy of confidence: whether that principle be the happy inherent growth of favouring Providence; or the fruit of religion, and cultivated virtue.

But fear and incertitude, though they slackened, did not long stop her progress: the terrour of her lonely situation pointed out to her, indeed, the danger of falling into evil hands; yet peremptorily, at the same time, urged her to seek almost any protection, that might rescue her from the vague horrours of this dark and tremendous solitude. It was, at least, possible that these might be the voices of some unfortunate travellers, belated, or lost, like herself, in the Forest. On, therefore, she glided, till she distinguished three different tones, all of which were male, but none of which sounded either youthful or gay. They spoke so low, that not a word reached her ears; nor could she have caught even a sound, but for the total stillness of the air. That they spoke in whispers, therefore, was certain: Was it from fear? Was it from guilt?

The doubt sufficed to check all project of addressing them; but, as she meant to retreat, she trod upon a broken bough of a tree, which made a crackling noise under her feet, that, she had reason to believe, was heard by the interlocutors, as it was followed by profound silence.

She was now forced to remain immovable; for she felt herself entangled in some of the branches of the bough, and feared that any attempt to dissembarrass herself might cause a new commotion, and point out her position.

She soon became but too certain that she had been heard; for the light reappeared, and she was sufficiently near to observe, that it had been produced by a dark lanthorn, which she now saw turned round, by a man who was evidently seeking to discover whence the noise made by the bough had issued: she saw, also, that he had two companions; but what was her shock when, presently, in one of them, she perceived the master of the hut!

She now gave herself up as lost! Lost alike from his fear of detection, and his vengeance for her escape. To run away was impossible; she could find no path; she could not even venture to stir a step, lest she should betray her concealment.

They searched, for some time, in different directions; two of them then approached so nearly to the spot upon which she was standing, saying, to each other, that they were sure the sound came from that quarter, that she almost fainted with excess of terrour. But they soon turned off another way; one of them averring that the noise was only from some windfall; and the hut-man replying, in a coarse bass voice, that, if any body were watching, 'twas well they had come no sooner; for he'd defy the sharpest eye living to give a guess, now, at what they had been about.

In this terrible interval, the door of the habitation, of which she had already had a glimpse, was opened by a female; who, depositing a candle upon the threshold, ran up to one of the men, with whom she conversed for a few minutes; after which, saying "Good night!" she re-entered the house; while the men, all three repeating "Good night!" trudged away, and were soon out of hearing.

Juliet now conceived a hope, that a female, left, probably, alone, might, either through kindness or through interest, be made a friend. She disengaged herself, therefore, from her impediments, and gently tapped at the door.

It was immediately opened by the woman, who said, "Why now, dear me, what have a forgot?" but who no sooner saw a stranger, than she screamed aloud, "La be good unto me! what been ye come for here, at such an untoward time o' night as this be?" while some children who were in bed, and suddenly awakened, jumping upon the ground, clang round their mother, and began crying piteously.

Juliet, more affrighted than themselves, uttered the softest petition, for a few hours' refuge from the dreariness of travelling by night. The woman, then, casting up her hands in wonder, exclaimed, "Good la! be you only no other but the good gentlewoman that was so koind to my little dearies?"

The children, recollecting her at the same moment, loosened their mother to throw their little arms around their guest; skipping and rejoicing, and crying, "O dood ady! dood ady! it's dood ady!"

This, indeed, was a moment of joy to Juliet, such as life, even at its best periods, can but rarely afford. From fears the most horrible of unknown dangers; and from fatigue nearly insupportable, she found herself suddenly welcomed by trusting kindness. All her dread and scruples, with respect to the Salisbury turnpike hostess, or to any previous reports, were, she now saw, groundless; and she delightedly felt herself in the bosom of security, while encircled in the arms of affectionate and unsuspicious innocence.

The good woman uncovered her hot embers, and put on

some fresh wood, to restore the weary traveller from the chill of the night: and brought out of her cupboard a slice of bacon, and the end of a brown loaf of bread: not mingling, with the warmth of her genuine hospitality, one mistrustful enquiry into the reason of her guest's late wandering, or the cause of her lonely difficulties.

The children with, instinctively, the same sensations, ran about, nearly naked, in search of their homely play-things; persuaded that the "dood ady" would be as pleased as they were themselves, by the sight of the several pieces of broken platter, which they called their tea-things; and a small truss of straw, rolled round with rags, which they denominated their doll. Nor would they return to rest, till Juliet sat down by their side, to tell them some simple stories, of other good boys and girls; while their mother prepared, for the "dood ady," a bed above stairs.

The thankful happiness of Juliet, at a deliverance so unexpected, so sweet, so soothing, induced her cordially to partake of a repast of which she stood greatly in need; but, before she could mount to the offered chamber, officious doubts and apprehensions broke into the fulness of her contentment, with enquiries: Who might be the men whom she had seen hovering about the house? What might be their business without doors during the dead of the night? What had the man of the hut to do away from his dwelling at such an hour? And why, and for whom, was the good dame herself up so late, without giving any reason for what must necessarily appear so extraordinary?

Bewildered in her ideas, uncertain in her judgment, and fearful how to act, she could not resolve to inhabit a lonely chamber up stairs, at the risk of some fatal surprize, or new danger. She complained of cold, and entreated for leave to sit over the embers; while she begged them, without heeding her, to take their usual repose.

The good woman started not the smallest difficulty; and, placing herself by the side of the children, in less than three minutes, was visited, like themselves, with the soundest sleep.

This woman, thought Juliet, must be as guileless as she is benevolent, unaccountable as are all the circumstances that hang about her; could she, else, with trust thus facile, taste rest thus undisturbed, in presence of a wandering stranger, known to her only by a small and accidental kindness shewn to her children?

Quieted by this example, Juliet herself, leaning her head against the wall, partook of that common, but ever wonderful oblivion, by which life is recruited, sorrow supported, and care assuaged.

With the first sun-beam they all awoke, and Juliet besought her hostess to accompany her to the nearest town. The good woman cheerfully complied with this request, making no other condition than that of demanding the time to dress and breakfast her bantlings, as she never went any where without them.

Juliet then officiated as nurse to the children: and here, again, the wish of obliging, with the talent of being serviceable, so endeared her to the little ones, and made her so agreeable to their parent, that she was earnestly solicited to remain with them a little longer.

"But, your husband?" Juliet then ventured to ask; "may I not be in his way?"

"O no," the woman answered; "a be gone his rounds; and 't be odds but they do take un, God willing, a week."

This was sufficient encouragement for the harassed Juliet joyfully to accept the invitation for remaining with them a few days. She deposited, therefore, her baggage in the no longer rejected up stairs chamber; and, after a few hours of quiet repose, took the entire charge of the children for the rest of the day; not merely to play with and amuse them, but to work for them. And her industry and adroitness soon put their whole little wardrobe in order; and she fashioned their clothing to their little shapes, in a manner so neat and commodious, that all that they possessed appeared to them to be new.

The day following, with the same happy skill, she dedicated her time to the service of the mother; whose entreaties grew more and more urgent, that she would prolong her stay at the cottage.

Far was she from desirous to quit it. With repose so much required, she here found comfort, peace, and affection,—three principal ingredients in the composition of happiness!

which her mind, in her uncertainty of the fate awaiting her, was delighted to seize, and eager to requite.

For whomsoever, therefore, and at whatsoever she worked, she sung simple songs, or told simple stories, with invariable good humour and pleasantry, to her little friends, who clung to her with passionate fondness; while their enchanted mother thought that some angel was descended amongst them, in guise of a traveller, to charm and to serve them at once.

To the unhackneyed observation of this good woman, the change of attire in Juliet, since their meeting at Salisbury, offered no sort of food to conjecture; she concluded that to walk about that fine city, had well deserved the best clothes; and that the worst had naturally been put on, afterwards, for economy, upon the road. Juliet found her wholly ignorant of the Salisbury adventure; and filled with innocent gratitude, in concluding that she had been benighted in the Forest, while seeking to find the little dearys whom she had thought so pretty upon the high road.

END OF THE FOURTH VOLUME

VOLUME V

BOOK IX

CHAPTER LXXVII

THE final purposes for which man is ordained to move in this nether sphere, will for ever remain disputable, while the doubts to which it gives rise can be answered only by fellow-doubters: but that the basis of his social comfort is confidence, is an axiom that waits no revelation, requires no logic, and dispenses with mathematical accuracy for proof: it is an axiom that comes home, straight forward and intuitively, to our "business and bosoms;"*—there, with life, to lodge.

Juliet, therefore, in this rustic abode, surrounded by the clinging affection of instinctive partiality, felt a sense of security, more potent in its simplicity, than she could have owed to any engagement, even of honour, even of law, even of duty. And, while to the fond mother and her little ones, she was every moment newly endeared, she experienced herself, in their favour, an increase of regard, that excited in her an ardent desire to make this her permanent dwelling, till she could procure tidings from Gabriella.

The night-scene, nevertheless, hung upon her with perplexity. The good dame never reverted to it, evidently not imagining that it had been observed; and persuaded that the entrance, at that moment, of her guest, had been accidental. She constantly evaded to speak of her husband, or of his affairs; while all her happiness, and almost her very existence, seemed wrapt up in her children.

Unable to devise any better method of arriving at the subject, Juliet, at length, determined upon relating the story of the hut. She watched for an opportunity, when the little boy and girl, whom she would not risk frightening, were asleep; and then, while occupied at her needle, began detailing every circumstance of that affair.

The narrative of the place, and of the family, sufficed to draw, at once, from the dame the exclamation, "O, you been gone, then, to Nat Mixon's? That be just he; and her, too. They be none o' the koindest, that be sure, poor folk!"

But at the history of the calling up in the night; the rising, passing, and precautions; the dame changed colour, and, with palpable disturbance, enquired upon what day of the week this had happened: she revived, however, upon being answered that it was Thursday, simply saying, "Mercy be proised! that be a day as can do me no harm."

But, at the description of the sack, the lumpish sound, and the subsequent appearance of a clot of blood, the poor woman turned pale; and, blessing herself, said, "The La be good unto me!* Nat Mixon wull be paid, at last, for all his bad ways! for, sure and sure, the devil do owe un a grudge, or a would no ha' let a straunger in, to bear eye sight to's goings on! 'T be a mercy 't be no worse, for an if 't had bin a Friday—"

She checked herself, but looked much troubled. Juliet, affrighted by her own conjectures, would have stopt; the dame, however, begged her to go on: but when she mentioned the cupboard, and the door smeared with blood, the poor woman, unable to contain her feelings, caught her guest by the arm, and exclaimed, "You wull no' inform against un, wull you?"

"Indeed, I should be most reluctant," answered Juliet, "to inform against people who, be they what they may, admitted me to a night's lodging, when I was in distress: nevertheless—what am I to think of these appearances? Meetings in the dead of the night, so dark, private, and clandestine?"

"But, who could 't be as did call up Nat?" interrupted Dame Fairfield; "for my husband do go only o' the Friday.—" and then, giving a loud scream, "La be good unto me!" she continued, "if an't be last month, 't be my husband for sure! for a could no' go o' the Friday, being the great fair!"

The expression of horrour now depicted upon the countenance of Juliet, told the dame the mischief done by her unguarded speech; and, in a panic uncontroulable, she flung her apron over her face, and sobbed out, "'T be all blown, then,* and we be all no better than ondone!"

Shocked, grieved, and appalled at this detection, and uncertain whither it might lead, or what might be its extent, the thoughts of Juliet were now all engrossed in considering how immediately to abscond from a situation so alarming and perilous.

In a few minutes, Dame Fairfield, starting up, ran precipitately to the bed, calling out, "Come, my pretty ones, come, my dearys! come and down o' your knees to the good gentlewoman, and praoy her to ha' mercy o' poor daddy; for if so be a come to be honged and transported, you can never show your poor innocent pretty faces agen! Come, little dearys, come! down o' your marrow-bones; and praoy her to be so good as not to be hard-hearted; for if a do be so onkoind as to inform against us, we be all ondone!"

Juliet would have stopt this scene, but it was not possible; the children, though comprehending nothing that was said, and crying at being awaked, obeyed; and, falling at her feet, and supporting themselves by her gown, said, "Pay, dood ady, don't hurt daddy! pay don't, dood ady!"

Touched, yet filled with augmented dismay by their prayers, Juliet, tenderly embracing, carried them back to bed; and, with words of comfort, and kind promises, soon hushed them again to sleep.

But the mother was not to be appeased; she had flung herself upon her knees, and upon her knees she pertinaciously kept; sobbing as if her heart were bursting, and lamenting that her husband never would listen to her, or things would not have come to such a pass.

Juliet, full of compassion, yet shuddering, attempted to console her, but would enter into no engagement. Pity, in such a case, however sincerely felt, could not take the lead; humanity itself invoked justice; and she determined to let no personal consideration whatsoever, interfere any longer with her causing an immediate investigation to be made into this fearful business.

The poor woman would not quit the floor, even when, in despondence, she gave over her kneeling importunity. Juliet, from the instant that she discovered how deeply the husband was involved, forbore all enquiry that might make the wife an informer against him; and sate by her side, trying to revive her, with offers of friendship and assistance.

But when, anxious to escape from this eventful Forest, and still confiding in the simplicity and goodness of her hostess, she begged a clear direction to the shortest way for getting to the high road; saying, "Alas! how little had I imagined that there had been any spot in England, where travellers were thus dreadfully waylaid to their destruction!" Dame Fairfield, suddenly ceasing her outcries, demanded what she meant; saying, "Why sure, and sure, there be no daunger to nobody in our Forest! We do go up it and down it, noight and day, without no manner of fear; and though I do come from afar off myself, being but a straunger in these parts, till I was married; my feather-in-law, who has lived in them, mon and boy, better than ninety and odd years,—for, thof a be still as fresh as a rose, a be a'most a hondred; he do tell me that a would carry his gold watch, if a had one, in his open hand, from top to bottom of our nine walks, in the pitch of the night; and a should aunswer to come to no harm; for a had never heard of a traveller as had had so much as a hair of his head hurt in the New Forest."

"What is it you tell me, my good dame?" cried Juliet amazed: "What are these alarming scenes that I have witnessed? And why are your apprehensions for your husband so direful?"

"The La be good unto me!" exclaimed the dame: "why sure and sure you do no' go to think the poor mon be a murderer?"

"I am disposed to think whatever you will bid me," replied Juliet; "for I see in you such perfect truth and candour, that I cannot hesitate in giving you my belief."

"Why the La be good unto me, my good gentlewoman, there be but small need to make bad worse! What the poor mon ha' done, may bring un to be honged and transported; but if so be a had killed a mon, a might go to old Nick besoides; and no one could say a deserved ony better."

Juliet earnestly begged an explanation; and Dame Fairfield then confessed, that her husband and Nat Mixon were deer-stealers.

After the tremendous sensations to which the mistake of Juliet, from her ignorance of this species of traffic, had given rise, so unexpected a solution of her perplexity, made this crime, contrasted with the assassination of a fellow-creature, appear venial. But though relieved from personal terrours, she would not hazard weakening the morality, in lessening the fears of the good, but uncultivated Dame Fairfield, by making her participate in the comparative view taken by herself, of the greater with the less offence. She represented, therefore, warmly and clearly, the turpitude of all failure of probity; dwelling most especially upon the heinousness of a breach of trust.

The good woman readily said, that she knew, well enough, that the deer were as much the King's Majesty's as the Forest; and that she had told it over and over to her husband; and bid him prepare for his latter end, if he would follow such courses: "But the main bleame, it do all lie in Nat Mixon; for a be as bad a mon as a body might wish to set eyes on. And a does always say a likes ony thing better than work. It be he has led my poor husband astray: for, thof a be but a bad mon, at best, to my mishap! a was a good sort of a husband enough, poor mon, till a took to these courses. But a knows I do no' like un for that; and that makes it, that a does no' much like me. But I would no' ha' un come to be honged or transported, if so be a was as onkoind agen! I would sooner go with un to prison; thof it be but a dismal life to be shut up by dark walls, and iron bars for to see out of! but I'd do it for sure and sure, not to forsake un, poor mon! in his need; if so be I could get wherewithal to keep my little dearys."

Touched by such genuine and virtuous simplicity, Juliet now promised to apply to some powerful gentleman, to take her husband from the temptation of his present situation; and to settle them all at a distance from the Forest.

The good woman, at this idea, started up in an extacy, and jumped about the room, to give some vent to her joy; kissing her little ones till she nearly suffocated them; and telling them, for sure and certain, that they had gotten an angel come amongst them, to save them all from shame. "For now," she continued, "if we do but get un away from Nat Mixon and his wife, who be the worst mon in all the Forest, a wull think no more of selling unlawful goods than unlawful geame."

Juliet, though delighted at her happiness, was struck with the words "unlawful goods;" which she involuntarily repeated. Dame Fairfield, unable, at this moment, to practise any restraint upon her feelings, plumply, then, acknowledged that Nat Mixon was a smuggler, as well as a deer-stealer: and that three of them were gone, even now, about the country, selling laces, and cambrics, and gloves, just brought to land.

This additional misdemeanour, considerably abated the hopes of reformation which had been conceived by Juliet; and every word that, inadvertently, escaped from the unguarded dame, brought conviction that the man was thoroughly worthless. To give him, nevertheless, if possible, the means to amend; and, at all events, to succour his good wife, and lovely children, occupied as much of the thoughts of Juliet as could be drawn, by humanity, from the danger of her own situation, and her solicitude to escape from the Forest.

More fearful than ever of losing her way, and falling into new evil, she again entreated Dame Fairfield to accompany her to the next town on the morrow. The dame agreed to every thing; and then, light of heart, though heavy with fatigue, went to rest; and was instantly visited by the best physician to all our cares.

Juliet, also, courted repose; and not utterly in vain; though it came not to the relief of her anxious spirits, agitated by all the anticipating inquietude of foresight, with the same salutary facility with which it instantly hushed the fears and the griefs of the unreflecting, though feeling Dame Fairfield.

The moment that the babbling little voices of the children reached, the next morning, the ear of Juliet, she descended from her small chamber, to hasten the breakfast, and to quicken her departure. Dame Fairfield, during the preparations and the repast, happy in new hope, and solaced by unburthening her heart, conversed, without reserve, upon her affairs; and the picture which her ingenuous avowals, and simple details, offered to the mental view of Juliet, presented to her a new sight of human life; but a sight from which she turned with equal sadness and amazement.

The wretched man of the hut, of whom the poor dame's husband was the servile accomplice, was the leader in all the illicit adventures of the New Forest. Another cottager, also, was entirely under his direction; though the difficulty and danger attendant upon their principal traffic, great search being always made after a lost deer, caused it to be rarely repeated; but smaller game; hares, pheasants, and partridges, were easily inveigled, by an adroit dispersion of grain, to a place proper for their seizure; and it required not much skill to frame stories for satisfying purchasers, who were generally too eager for possession, to be scrupulous in investigating the means by which their luxury was so cheaply indulged.

The fixed day of rendezvous was every Friday month, that each might be ready for his part of the enterprize.

Juliet, the dame imagined, had been admitted because it was Thursday, and that her husband had not given notice that he should change his day, on account of the fair; besides which, neither Mixon, she said, nor his wife, ever refused money, be it ever so dangerous. He and his family nearly subsisted upon the game which could not be got off in time; or the refuse; or parts that were too suspicious for sale, of the deer. But Dame Fairfield, though at the expence of the most terrible quarrels, and even ill usage from her husband, never would consent to touch, nor suffer her children to eat, what was not their own; "for I do tell un," she continued, "it might strangle us down our throats; for it be all his King's Majesty's; and I do no' know why we should take hisn goods, when a do never come to take none of ours! for we be never mislested,* night nor day. And a do deserve well of us all; for a be as good a gentlemon as ever broke bread! which we did all see, when a was in these parts; as well as his good lady, the Queen, who had a smile for the lowest of us, God bless un! and all their pretty ones!* for they were made up of good nature and charity; and had no more pride than the new-born baby. And we did all love 'em, when they were in these parts, so as the like never was seen before."

With regard to the smuggling, there were three men, she said, who came over, alternately, from beyond seas, with counterband merchandize.* They landed where they could, and, if they were surprised, they knew how to hide their goods, and pass for poor fishermen, blown over by foul winds: for they had always fishing tackle ready to shew. They had agents all round the coast, prepared to deal with them; but when they came to the Forest, they always treated with Mixon.

Her friend near the turnpike, at Salisbury, commonly kept a

good store of articles; which she carried about, occasionally, to the ladies of the town. "And I ha' had sums and sums of goods," she added, "here, oftentimes, myself; and then I do no dare to leave the house for one yearthly moment: for we be all no better than slaves when the smugglers be here, for fear of some informer. And I do tell my poor husband, we should be mainly happier to work our hands to the bone, ony day of the year, so we did but live by the King's Majesty's laws, than to make money by being always in a quandary. And a might see the truth of what I do say, if a would no' blind his poor eyes; for Nat Mixon, thof a do get a power of money, do live the most pitiful of us all, for the fear of being found out: a does no' dare get un a hat, nor a waistcoat like to another mon. And his wife be the dirtiest beast in all the Forest. And their house and garden be no better than a piggery. So that they've no joy of life. They be but bad people at best, poor folk! And Nat be main cross-grained; for, with all his care, a do look to be took up every blessed day; and that don't much mend a mon's humour."

Ah, thought Juliet, were the wilful, but unreflecting purchaser, amenable to sharing the public punishment of the tempted and needy instrument,—how soon would this traffic die away; and every country live by its own means; or by its own fair commerce!

They had all, the dame said, been hard at work, to cover some goods under ground, the very night of Juliet's arrival: and they had put what was for immediate sale into hods, spread over with potatoes, to convey to different places. When Juliet had tapped at the door, the dame had concluded it to be her husband, returned for something that had been forgotten; but the sight of a stranger, she said, though it were but a woman, made her think that they were all undone; for the changed dress of Juliet impeded any recollection of her, till she spoke.

In the communication to which this discourse gave rise, Juliet, with surprize, and even with consternation, learnt, how pernicious were the ravages of dishonest cupidity; how subversive alike of fair prosperity, and genial happiness, even in the bosom of retired and beautiful rusticity. For those who were employed in poaching, purloining wood, or concealing illicit merchandize by night, were as incapable of the arts and vigour of industry by day, as they were torpid to the charms and animation of the surrounding beauties of nature. Their severest labour received no pay, but from fearful, accidental, and perilous dexterity; their best success was blighted by constant apprehension of detection. Reproachful with each other, suspicious of their neighbours, and gloomy in themselves, they were still greater strangers to civilized manners than to social morality.

In the midst, however, of the dejection excited by such a view of human frailty, Juliet, whose heart always panted to love, and prided in esteeming her fellow-creatures, had the consolation to gather, that the houses which contained these unworthy members of the community were few, in comparison with those which were inhabited by persons of unsullied probity; that several of the cottagers were even exemplary for assiduous laboriousness and good conduct; and that many of the farmers and their families were universally respected.

CHAPTER LXXVIII

WHEN Dame Fairfield was nearly ready, Juliet, to forward the march, set out with the two children; but had scarcely quitted the house, when the sight of a man, advancing towards the habitation, made her plant herself behind a tree, to examine him before she ventured to proceed.

She observed that he stopt, every two or three minutes, himself, to take an inquisitive view all around him; frequently bending upon the ground, and appearing to be upon some eager search.

As he approached, she thought that his air was familiar to her; she regarded him more earnestly as he drew nearer; what, then, was her horrour to recognize the pilot!

She glided back, instantaneously, to the house, beckoning to the children to follow; and, rushing upon Dame Fairfield, and, taking both her hands, she faintly ejaculated, "Oh my good dame!—hide, conceal me, I entreat!—I am pursued by a cruel enemy, and lost if you are not my friend!—Serve, save me, now, and I will be yours to the end of my life!"

"That I wull!" answered the dame, delighted; "if you wull but be so koind as to save my poor husband the sheame of being honged or transported, I wull go through fire and water to serve you, to the longest day I have to live upon the feace of God's yearth!"

Then, making the children play without doors, that they might not observe what passed, she told Juliet to bolt herself into the upper chamber.

In a few minutes, the children, running into the house, called out, "Mam, mam, yonder be dad!"

The dame went forth to meet him; and Juliet spent nearly half an hour in the most cruel suspense.

Dame Fairfield then came to her; and, by the discourse that ensued, she found that the pilot was one of the smugglers who brought merchandize to Mixon; and heard that he and Fairfield had thus unexpectedly returned, in search of a piece of fine broad French lace, of great value, which was missing; and which Fairfield suspected to have dropt from one of his parcels, while he was making his assortments, by the light of the lanthorn. She had been, she said, helping them to look for it, high and low; but had stolen away, for an instant, to bring this account; and to beg Juliet not to be frightened, because though, if Fairfield would go up stairs, she could not hinder him, she would take care that the smuggler should not follow.

Juliet was now seized with a panic that nearly bereft her of all hope; and Dame Fairfield was so much touched by the sight of her sufferings, that she descended, unbidden, to endeavour to discover some means to facilitate an escape.

That the pilot should prove to be a smuggler, caused no surprize to Juliet; but that accident should so cruelly be her foe, as to lead her to the spot where he deposited and negociated his merchandize, at the very period when his affairs brought him thither himself; that she should find her chosen retreat her bane; and that, even where she was unpursued, she should be overtaken; was a stroke of misfortune as severe as it was unexpected.

And, soon after, she found her situation still more terrible than she had imagined it. Fairfield, presently entering the kitchen, to take some food, accused his wife, in a loud and angry tone, of having abetted an impostor. Mounseer, the smuggler, he said, had not come to these parts, this time, merely for his own private business. He had been offered a great reward for discovering a young gentlewoman who had run away; and who turned out to be no other than the very same that she had been such a ninny as to impose upon Dame Goss, at Salisbury; and who had made off without paying for her board and lodging.

The Dame warmly declared, that this could not be possible; that it must be some other gentlewoman; for that a person who could be so kind to her children could not have so black a heart.

Fairfield, with bitter reproaches against her folly, persisted in the accusation: stating, that, upon Dame Goss's going to the post-office for a letter, it had been refused to her, because of its being directed to a person advertised in the public newspapers; and Dame Goss had been sent back, with an excuse, to while away the time, till somebody should follow, to confront the gentlewoman with the advertisement. But Dame Goss, instead of keeping a sharp watch, had been over-persuaded to go of an errand; and she had no sooner turned her back, than the gentlewoman made off. However, they had written to the newspapers that she was somewhere in those parts; and they could do no more; for there was no right to seize her; for the advertisement only desired to know where she might be heard of, and found. It had made a rare hue and cry in the town; and Mounseer, the smuggler, who had come down to Salisbury along with another outlandish man, had traced the gentlewoman as far as to Romsey; but could not find out what had become of her afterwards. The other outlandish man, who was as rich as a Duke, and was to pay the reward, had stopt at Salisbury, for tidings: upon which Mounseer, the smuggler, thought he might as well come on, and see a bit after his own business by the way; for it would not lose much time; and he might not get to these parts again for months.

The silence that ensued, gave Juliet an afflicting presentiment that she had lost, by this history, her friend and advocate: and accordingly, when, upon her husband's returning to his search, the dame remounted the stairs, her air was so changed, that Juliet, again clasping her hands, cried, "Oh! Dame

Fairfield!—Kind, good Dame Fairfield! judge me not till you know me better! Aid me still, my good dame, in pity, in charity aid me!—for, believe me, I am innocent!"

"Why then so I wull!" cried the dame, resuming her looks of mild good will; "I wull believe you! And I'll holp you too, for sure: for now you be under my own poor roof, 'twould be like unto a false heart to give you up to your enemies. Besoides, I do think in my conscience you wull pay every one his own, when you've got wherewithal. And it be but hard to expect it before. And I do say, that a person that could be so koind to my little Jacky and Jenny, in their need, must have a good heart of her own; and would no' wrong no yearthly creature, unless a could no' holp it."

She then promised to watch the moment of the smuggler's turning round to the garden-side of the house, to assist her flight; and, once a few yards distant, all would be safe; for her change of clothes from what she had worn at Salisbury, would secure her from any body's recollection.

This, in a few minutes, was performed; and, without daring to see the children, who would have cried at her departure, Juliet took a hasty leave, silent but full of gratitude, of the good dame; into whose bosom, as her hand refused it, she slipt a guinea for the little ones; and, having received full directions, set forward, by the shortest cut, to the nearest high road.

She reached it unannoyed, but breathless; and seated herself upon a bank by its side; not to hesitate which way to turn; the right and the left were alike unknown to her, and alike liable to danger; but to recover respiration, and force to proceed.

She could now form no plan, save to hasten to some other part of the country; certain that here she was sought all around; and conscious that the disguise of her habiliment, if not already betrayed, must shortly, from a thousand accidents, prove nugatory.

In her ignorance what course the pilot might take, upon quitting the cottage of Fairfield, she determined upon seeking, immediately, some decent lodging for the rest of the day; hoping thus, should he pursue the same route, to escape being overtaken.

She had soon the satisfaction to come to a small habitation, a little out of the high road, where she was accommodated, by a man and his wife, with a room that precisely answered her purpose: and here she spent the night.

Thankful in obtaining any sort of tranquillity, she would fain have remained longer; but she durst not continue in the neighbourhood of Fairfield; and, the following morning, she re-commenced her wanderings.

She asked the way to Salisbury, though merely that she might take an opposite direction. She ventured not to raise her eyes from the earth, nor to cast even a glance at any one whom she passed. She held her handkerchief to her face at the sound of every carriage; and trembled at the approach of every horseman. Her steps were quick and eager; though not more precipitate to fly from those by whom she was followed, than fearful of being observed by those whom she met.

In a short time, the sight of several hostlers, helpers, and postilions, before a large house, which appeared to be a capital inn, made her cross the way. She wished to turn wholly from the high road; but low brick-walls had now, on either side, taken place of hedges, and she searched in vain for an opening. Her earnestness to press onward, joined to her fear of looking up, made her soon follow, unconsciously, an ordinary man, till she was so close behind him, as suddenly to perceive, by his now well known coat, that he was the pilot! A scream struggled to escape her, in the surprize of her affright; but she stifled it, and, turning short back, speeded her retrograde way with all her force.

She had reason, however, to fear that her uncontrollable first emotion had caught his notice, for she heard footsteps following. Hopeless of saving herself, if watched or suspected, by flight; as she knew that there was no turning for at least half a mile; she darted precipitately into the inn; which seemed alone to offer her even a shadow of any chance of concealment. She rushed past ostlers, helpers, postilions, and waiters; seized the hand of the first female that she met; and hastily begged to be shewn to a room.

The chamber-maid, astonished at such a request from a person no better equipped, pertly asked what she meant.

Juliet, whose apprehensive eyes roved every where, now saw the pilot at the door.

She held the maid by the arm, and, in a voice scarcely audible, entreated to be taken any where that she might be alone; and had the presence of mind to hint at a recompence.

This instantly prevailed. The maid said, "Well, come along!" and led her to a small apartment up stairs.

Juliet put a shilling into her hand, and was then left to herself.

In an agony of suffering that disordered her whole frame, What a life, she cried, is this that I lead! How tremendous, and how degrading! Is it possible that even what I fly can be more dreadful?

This question restored her fortitude. Ah yes! ah yes! she cried, all passing evil is preferable to such a termination!

She now composed her spirits, and, while deliberating how she might make a friend of the maid, to aid her escape, perceived, from the window, the pilot, in a stable-yard, examining an horse, for which he seemed to be bartering.

This determined her to attempt to regain the cottage which she had last quitted, and thence to try some opposite route.

Swiftly she descended the stairs; a general bustle from some new arrival enabled her to pass unnoticed; but a chaise was at the door, and she was forced to make way for a gentleman, who had just quitted it, to enter the house. Unavoidably, by this movement, she saw the gentleman also; the colour instantly forsook her cheeks and lips; her feet tottered, and she fell.

She was immediately surrounded by waiters; but the gentleman, who, observing only her dress, concluded her to belong to the house, walked on into the kitchen, and asked, in broken English, for the landlord or landlady.

Juliet, whose fall had been the effect of a sudden deprivation of strength, from an abrupt sensation of horrour, had not fainted. She heard, therefore, what passed, and was easily helped to rise; and, shaded by her packet, which, even in her first terrour, she had instinctively held to her face, she made a motion to walk into the air. One of the men, good-naturedly, placed her a chair without doors; she sat upon it thankfully, and almost as quickly recovered as she had lost her force, by a reviving idea, that, even yet, thus situated, she might make her escape.

She had just risen with this view, when the voice of the pilot, who was coming round the house, from the stable-yard, forced her hastily to re-enter the passage; but not before she heard him enquire, whether a French gentleman were arrived in that chaise?

Again, now, she glided on towards the stairs; hearing, as she passed, the answer made by the French gentleman himself: "*Oui, oui; me voici. Quelles sont tes nouvelles?*"†

The voices of both proved each to be advancing to the passage, to meet the other. Juliet was no longer sensible of bodily weakness; nor scarcely of bodily existence. She seemed to herself a mere composition of terrour. She flew up the stairs, meaning to regain her little chamber; but, mistaking her way, found herself in a gallery, leading to the best apartments. Glad, however, rather than sorry, in the hope she might here be less liable to be sought, she opened the first door; and, entering a large vast room, locked and bolted herself in, with such extreme precipitance, that already she had sunk upon her knees, in fervent prayer, before a shadow, which caught her eyes, made her look round; when she perceived, at a distant window, a gentleman who was writing.

In the deepest consternation, she arose, hurrying to find the key; which, in her perturbation, she had taken out, and let drop she knew not where.

While earnestly searching it, the gentleman, mildly, yet in a tone of some surprize, enquired what she wanted.

Startled at the sound of his voice, she looked up, and saw Harleigh.

Her conflicting emotions now exceeded all that she had hitherto experienced. To seem to follow, even to his room, the man whom she had adjured, as he valued her preservation, to quit and avoid her; joined sensations of shame so poignant, to those of horrour and anguish, with which she was already overwhelmed, that, almost, she wished her last hour to arrive; that, while finishing her wretchedness, she might clear her integrity and honour.

† "Yes, yes; here I am. What's your news?"

Harleigh, to whom her dress, as he had not caught a view of her face, proved a complete disguise of her person, concluded her to be some light nymph of the inn, and suffered her to search for the key, without even repeating his question: but when, upon her finding it, he observed that her shaking hand could not, for some time, fix it in the lock, he was struck with something in her general form that urged him to rise, and offer his assistance.

Still more her hand shook, but she opened the door, and, without answering, and with a head carefully averted, eagerly quitted the room; shutting herself out, with trembling precipitation.

Harleigh hesitated whether to follow; but it was only for a moment: the next, a shriek of agony reached his ears, and, hastily rushing forth, he saw the female who had just quitted him, standing in an attitude of despair; her face bowed down upon her hands; while an ill-looking man, whom he presently recollected for the pilot, grinning in triumph, and with arms wide extended, to prevent her passing, loudly called out, "*Citoyen! Citoyen! venez voir! c'est Elle! Je la tiens!*"[†]

Harleigh would have remonstrated against this rude detention; but he had no sooner begun speaking, than Juliet, finding that she could not advance, retreated; and had just put her hand upon the lock of a door, higher up in the gallery; when another man, dressed with disgusting negligence, and of an hideous countenance, yet wearing an air of ferocious authority; advancing by large strides, roughly seized her arm, with one hand, while, with the other, he rudely lifted up her bonnet, to examine her face.

"*C'est bien!*" he cried, with a look of exultation, that gave to his horrible features an air of infernal joy; "*viens, citoyenne, viens; suis moi.*"[‡]

Harleigh, who, when the bonnet was raised, saw, what as yet he had feared to surmize,—that it was Juliet; sprang forward, exclaiming, "Daring ruffian! quit your hold!"

"*Oses tu nier mes droits?*" cried the man, addressing Juliet; whose arm he still griped;—"*Dis!—parles!—l'oses tu?*"[§]

[†] "'Tis she, citizen! come and see! I have her safe!"

[‡] "'Tis well! come, citizen, come along! follow me."

[§] "Darest thou deny my rights?—say!—speak! darest thou?"

Juliet was mute; but Harleigh saw that she was sinking, and bent towards her to save her fall; what, then, was his astonishment, to perceive that it was voluntary! and that she cast herself at the feet of her assailant!

Thunderstruck, he held back.

The man, with an expression of diabolical delight at this posture, cast his eyes now upon her, now upon her appalled defendant; and then, in French, gave orders to the pilot, to see four fresh horses put to the chaise: and, in a tone of somewhat abated rage, bid Juliet arise, and accompany him down stairs.

"Ah, no!—ah, spare—ah, leave me yet!—" in broken accents, and in French, cried the still prostrate Juliet.

The man, who was large made, tall, and strong, seized, then, both her arms, with a motion that indicated his intention to drag her along.

A piercing shriek forced its way from her at his touch: but she arose, and made no appeal, no remonstrance.

"*Si tu peus te conduire toute seule,*" said the man, sneeringly, "*soit! Mais vas en avant! Je ne te perdrai plus de vue.*"[†]

Juliet again hid her face, but stood still.

The man roughly gave her a push; seeming to enjoy, with a coarse laugh, the pleasure of driving her on before him.

Harleigh, who saw that her face was convulsed with horrour, fiercely planted himself in the midst of the passage, vehemently exclaiming, "Infernal monster! by what right do you act."

"*De quel droit me le demandez vous?*"[‡] cried the man; who appeared perfectly to understand English.

"By the rights of humanity!" replied Harleigh; "and you shall answer me by the rights of justice! One claim alone can annul my interference. Are you her father?"

"*Non!*" he answered, with a laugh of scorn; "*mais il y a d'autres droits!*"[§]

"There are none!" cried Harleigh, "to which you can pretend; none!"

"*Comment cela? n'est-ce pas ma femme? Ne suis-je pas son mari?*"[¶]

† "If you can walk alone, well and good; but go on first. I shall lose sight of you no more."

‡ "By what right do you enquire?" § "No; but there are other rights!"

¶ "How so? Is she not my wife? Am I not her husband?"

"No!" cried Harleigh, "no!" with the fury of a man seized with sudden delirium; "I deny it!—'tis false! and neither you nor all the fiends of hell shall make me believe it!"

Juliet again fell prostrate; but, though her form turned towards her assailant, her eyes, and supplicating hands, that begged forbearance, were lifted up, in speechless agony, to Harleigh.

Repressed by this look and action, though only to be overpowered by the blackest surmizes, Harleigh again stood suspended.

Finding the people of the inn were now filling the stair-case, to see what was the matter, the foreigner, in tolerable English, told them all to be gone, for he was only recovering an eloped wife. Then, addressing Juliet, "If you dare assert," he said, "that you are not my wife, your perjury may cost you dear! If you have not that hardiness, hold your tongue and welcome. Who else will dare dispute my claims?"

"I will!" cried Harleigh, furiously. "Walk this way, Sir, and give me an account of yourself! I will defend that lady from your inhuman grasp, to the last drop of my blood!"

"Ah, no! ah, no!" Juliet now faintly uttered; but the man, interrupting her, said, "Dare you assert, I demand, that you are not my wife? Speak! Dare you?"

Again she bowed down her face upon her hands,—her face that seemed bloodless with despair;* but she was mute.

"I put you to the test;" continued the man, striding to the end of the gallery, and opening the last door: "Go into that chamber!"

She shrieked aloud with agony uncontrollable; and Harleigh, with an emotion irrepressible, cast his arms around her, exclaiming, "Place yourself under my protection! and no violence, no power upon earth shall tear you away!"

At these words, all the force of her character came again to her aid; and she disengaged herself from him, with a reviving dignity in her air, that shewed a decided resolution to resist his services: but she was still utterly silent; and he saw that she was obliged to sustain her tottering frame against the wall, to save herself from again sinking upon the floor.

The foreigner seemed with difficulty to restrain his rage

from some act of brutality; but, after a moment's pause, fixing his hands fiercely in his sides, he ferociously confronted the shaking Juliet, and said, "I have informed your family of my rights. Lord Denmeath has promised me his assistance and your portion."

"Lord Denmeath!" repeated the astonished Harleigh.

"He has promised me, also," the foreigner, without heeding him, continued, "the support of your half-brother, Lord Melbury,—"

"Lord Melbury!" again exclaimed Harleigh; with an expression that spoke of a sudden delight, thrilling, in defiance of agony, through his burning veins.

"Who, he assures me, is a young man of honour, who will never abet a wife in eloping from her husband. I shall take you, therefore, at first, and at once, to Lord Denmeath, who will only pay your portion to your own signature. Go, therefore, quietly into that room, till the chaise is ready, and I promise that I won't follow you: though, if you resist, I shall assert my rights by force."

He held the door open. She wrung her hands with agonizing horrour. He took hold of her shoulder; she shrunk from his touch; but, in shrinking, involuntarily entered the room. He would have pushed her on; but Harleigh, who now looked wild with the violence of contending emotions; with rage, astonishment, grief, and despair; furiously caught him by the arm, calling out, "Hold, villain, hold!—Speak, Madam, speak! Utter but a syllable!—Deign only to turn towards me!—Pronounce but with your eyes that he has no legal claim, and I will instantly secure your liberty,—even from myself!—even from all mankind!—Speak!—turn!—look but a moment this way!—One word! one single word!—"

She clapped her hands upon her forehead, in an action of despair; but the word was not spoken,—not a syllable was uttered! A look, however, escaped her, expressive of a soul in torture, yet supplicating his retreat. She then stepped further into the room, and the foreigner shut and double-locked the door.

Triumphantly brandishing the key, as he eyed, sidelong, the now passive Harleigh, he went into the adjoining apartment; where, seating himself in the middle of the room, he left the door wide open, to watch all egress and regress in the passage.

Harleigh now appeared to be lost! The violence of his agitation, while he concluded her to be wrongfully claimed, was transformed into the blackest and most indignant despondence, at her unresisting, however wretched acquiescence, to commands thus brutal; emanating from an authority of which, however evidently it was deplored, she attempted not to controvert the legality. The dreadful mystery, more direful than it had been depicted, even by the most cruel of his apprehensions, was now revealed: she is married! he internally cried; married to the vilest of wretches, whom she flies and abhors,—yet she is married! indisputably married! and can never, never,—even in my wishes, now, be mine!

A sudden sensation, kindred even to hatred, took possession of his feelings. Altered she appeared to him, and delusive. She had always, indeed, discouraged his hopes, always forbidden his expectations; yet she must have seen that they subsisted, and were cherished; and could not but have been conscious, that a single word, bitter, but essentially just, might have demolished, have annihilated them in a moment.

He dragged himself back to his apartment, and resolutely shut his door; gloomily bent to nourish every unfavourable impression, that might sicken regret by resentment. But no indignation could curb his grief at her loss; nor his horrour at her situation: and the look that had compelled his retreat; the look that so expressively had concentrated and conveyed her so often reiterated sentence, of "leave, or you destroy me!" seemed rivetted to his very brain, so as to take despotic and exclusive hold of all his faculties.

In a few minutes, the sound of a carriage almost mechanically drew him to the window. He saw there an empty chaise and four horses. It was surely to convey her away!—and with the man whom she loathed,—and from one who, so often! had awakened in her symptoms the most impressive of the most flattering sensibility!—

The transitory calm of smothered, but not crushed

emotions, was now succeeded by a storm of the most violent and tragic passions. To lose her for ever, yet irresistibly to believe himself beloved!—to see her nearly lifeless with misery, yet to feel that to demand a conference, or the smallest explanation, or even a parting word, might expose her to the jealousy of a brute, who seemed capable of enjoying, rather than deprecating, any opportunity to treat her ill; to be convinced that she must be the victim of a forced marriage; yet to feel every sentiment of honour, and if of honour of happiness! rise to oppose all violation of a rite, that, once performed, must be held sacred: —thoughts, reflections, ideas thus dreadful, and sensations thus excruciating, almost deprived him of reason, and he cast himself upon the ground in wild agony.

But he was soon roused thence by the gruff voice, well recollected, of the pilot, who, from the bottom of the stairs, called out, "*Viens, citoyen! tout est pret.*"†

With horrour, now, he heard the heavy step of the foreigner again in the passage; he listened, and the sound reached his ear of the key fixing—the door unlocking.—Excess of torture then caused a short suspension of his faculties, and he heard no more.

Soon, however, reviving, the stillness startled him. He opened his door. No one was in the passage; but he caught a plaintive sound, from the room in which Juliet was a prisoner: and soon gathered that Juliet herself was imploring for leave to travel to Lord Denmeath's alone.

What an aggravation to the sufferings of Harleigh, to learn that she was thus allied, at the moment that he knew her to be another's! for however the violence of his admiration had conquered every obstacle, he had always thought, with reluctance and concern, of the supposed obscurity of her family and connections.

Juliet pleaded in vain. A harsh refusal was followed by the grossest menace, if she hesitated to accompany him at once.

The pilot, repeating his call, now mounted the stairs; and Harleigh felt compelled to return to his room; but, looking back in re-entering it, he saw Juliet forced into the passage; her face not merely pale, but ghastly; her eyes nearly starting from her head.

† "Come, citizen; all is ready."

To rescue, to protect her, Harleigh now thought was all that could render life desirable; but, while adoring her almost to madness, he respected her situation and her fame, and re-passed into his chamber, unseen by the foreigner.

Yet he could not forbear placing himself so that he might catch a glance of her as she went by; he held the door, therefore, in his hand, as if, accidentally, at that moment, opening it. She did not turn her head, but assumed an air of resignation, and walked straight on; yet though she did not meet his eye, she evidently felt it; a pale pink suffusion shot across her cheeks; taking place of the death-like hue they had exhibited as she quitted her room; but which, fading away almost in the same moment, left her again a seeming spectre.

A nervous dimness took from Harleigh even the faculty of observing the foreigner. She loves me! was his thought; she surely loves me! And the idea which, not many minutes sooner, would have chaced from his mind every feeling but of felicity, now rent his heart with torture, from painting their mutual unhappiness. It was not a sigh that he stifled, nor a sigh that escaped him; but a groan, a piercing groan, which broke from his sorrows, as he heard her tottering step reach the stairs, while internally he uttered, She is gone from me for ever!

When he thought she would no longer be in sight, he followed to the first landing-place; to catch, once more, even the most distant sound of her feet: but the passage to and fro of waiters, forced him again to mount to his chamber. There, he hastened to the window, to take a view, a last view! of her loved form; but thence, shuddering, retreated, at sight of the chaise and four; destined to whirl her everlastingly away from him, with a companion so undisguisedly dreaded!—so evidently abhorred!.

Yet, at the first sound, he returned to the window; whence he perceived Juliet just arrived upon the threshold; looking like a picture of death, and leaning upon a chamber-maid, to whom she clung as to a bosom friend; yet not attempting to resist the foreigner; who, on her other side, dragged her by the arm, in open triumph. But, when she came to the chaise-step, she staggered, her vital powers seemed forsaking her; she heaved a hard and painful sigh, and, but for the chambermaid, who knelt down to catch her, had fallen upon the ground.

Harleigh was already half way down the stairs, almost frantic to save her; before he had sufficient recollection to remind him, that any effort on his part might cause her yet grosser insult. He was then again at his window; where he saw a second chambermaid administering burnt feathers, which had already recovered her from the fainting fit; while the mistress of the house was presenting her with hartshorn and water.

She refused no assistance; but the foreigner, who was loudly enraged at the delay, said that he would lift her into the chaise; and bid the pilot get in first, to help the operation.

She now again looked so sick and disordered, that all the women called upon the foreigner to let her re-enter the house, and take a little rest, before her journey. Her eyes, turned up at heaven with thankfulness, even at the proposal, encouraged them to grow clamorous in their demand; but the man, with a scornful sneer, replied that her journey would be her cure; and told the pilot, who was finishing a bottle of wine, to make haste.

The wretched Juliet, resuming her resolution, though with an air of despair, faintly pronounced, that she would get into the carriage herself; and, leaning upon the woman, ascended the steps, and dropt upon the seat of the chaise.

CHAPTER LXXIX

AT this moment, a horseman, who had advanced full gallop, hastily dismounting, enquired aloud, whether any French gentleman had lately arrived.

All who were present, pointed to the foreigner; who, not hearing, or affecting not to hear the demand, began pushing away the women, that he might follow Juliet.

The horseman, approaching, asked the foreigner his name.

"*Qu'est ce que cela vous fait?*"[†] he answered.

"You must come with me into the inn," the horseman replied, after stedfastly examining his face.

[†] "What is that to you?"

The foreigner, with a loud oath, refused to stir.

The horseman, holding out a paper, clapped him upon the shoulder, saying, that he was a person who had been looked for some time, in consequence of information which had been lodged against him; and that he was to be sent out of the kingdom.

This declaration made, he called upon the master of the house to lend his assistance, for keeping the arrested person in custody, till the arrival of the proper officers of justice.

The man, at first, could find no vent for his rage, except horrid oaths, and tremendous imprecations; but, when he was positively seized, with a menace of being bound hand and foot, if he offered any opposition, he swore that his wife, at least, should accompany him; and put forth his hand towards the chaise, to drag out Juliet.

But Juliet was saved from his grasp by the landlady; who humanely, upon seeing her almost expiring condition, had entered the carriage, during the dispute, with a viol of sal volatile.*

The horseman, who was a peace-officer, said that he had no orders to arrest any woman. She might come, or stay, as she pleased.

The foreigner vociferously claimed her; uttering execrations against all who unlawfully withheld her; or would abet her elopement. He would then have passed round to the other door of the chaise, to seize her by force; but the peace-officer, who was habitually deaf to any appeal, and resolute against any resistance; compelled him, though storming, raging, and swearing, his face distorted with fury, his under-jaw dropt, and his mouth foaming, to re-enter the inn.

Juliet received neither relief nor fresh pain from what passed. Though no longer fainting, terrour and excess of misery operated so powerfully upon her nerves, that his cries assailed her ears but as outrage upon outrage; and, though clinging to the landlady, with instinctive entreaty for support, she was so disordered by her recent fainting, and so absorbed in the belief that she was lost, that she knew not what had happened; nor suspected any impediment to her forced journey; till the landlady, now quitting her, advised her to have a room and lie down; saying that no wife could be expected to follow such a brute of a husband to jail.

Amazed, she enquired what was meant; and was answered, that her husband was in the hands of justice.

The violence of the changed, yet mixed sensations, with which she was now assailed, made every pulse throb with so palpitating a rapidity, that she felt as if life itself was seeking a vent through every swelling vein. But, when again she was pressed to enter the house, and not to accompany her husband to prison; she shuddered, her head was bowed down with shame; and, making a motion that supplicated for silence, she seemed internally torn asunder with torturing incertitude how to act.

During this instant,—it was scarcely more,—of irresolution, the landlady alighted, and the chaise was driven abruptly from the door. But Juliet had scarcely had time for new alarm, ere she found that she had only been removed to make way for another carriage; from the window of which she caught a glimpse of Sir Jaspar Herrington.

Nor had she escaped his eye; her straw-bonnet having fallen off, without being missed, while she fainted, her head was wholly without shade.

With all of speed in his power, the Baronet hobbled to the chaise. She covered her face, sinking with every species of confusion and distress. "Have I the honour," he cried, "to address Miss Granville? the Honourable Miss Granville?"—

"Good Heaven!—" Juliet astonished, and raising her head, exclaimed.

"If so, I have the dulcet commission," he continued, "to escort her to her brother and sister, Lord Melbury, and Lady Aurora Granville."

"Is it possible? Is it possible?" cried Juliet, in an ecstacy that seemed to renovate her whole being: "I dare not believe it!—Oh Sir Jaspar! dear, good, kind, generous Sir Jaspar! delude me not, in pity!"

"No, fairest syren!" answered Sir Jaspar, in a rapture nearly equal to her own; "if there be any delusion to fear, 'tis poor I must be its victim!"

"Oh take me, then, at once,—this instant,—this moment,— take me to them, my benevolent, my noble friend! If, indeed, I have a brother, a sister,—give me the heaven of their protection!—"

Sir Jaspar, enchanted, invited her to honour him by accepting a seat in his chaise. With glowing gratitude she complied; though the just returning roses faded from her cheeks, as she alighted, upon perceiving Harleigh, aloof and disconsolate, fixed like a statue, upon a small planted eminence. Yet but momentarily was the whiter hue prevalent, and her skin, the next instant, burned with blushes of the deepest dye.

This transition was not lost upon Harleigh: his eye caught, and his heart received it, with equal avidity and anguish. Ah why, thought he, so sensitive! why, at this period of despair, must I awaken to a consciousness of the full extent of my calamity! Yet, all his resentment subsided; to believe that she participated in his sentiments, had a charm so softening, so all-subduing, that, even in this crisis of torture and hopelessness, it dissolved his whole soul into tenderness.

Juliet, faintly articulating, "Oh, let us be gone!" moved, with cast down eyes, to the carriage of the Baronet; forced, from remaining weakness, to accept the assistance of his groom; Sir Jaspar not having strength, nor Harleigh courage, to offer aid.

Sir Jaspar demanded her permission to stop at Salisbury, for his valet and baggage.

"Any where! any where!" answered the shaking Juliet, "so I go but to Lady Aurora!"

Astonished, and thrilled to the soul by these words, Harleigh, who, unconsciously, had advanced, involuntarily repeated, "Lady Aurora?—Lady Aurora Granville?"—

Unable to answer, or to look at him, the trembling Juliet, eagerly laying both her hands upon the arm of the Baronet, as, cautiously, he was mounting into the carriage, supplicated that they might be gone.

A petition thus seconded, from so adored a suppliant, was irresistible; he kissed each fair hand that thus honoured him; and had just accepted the offer of Harleigh, to aid his arrangements; when the furious prisoner, struggling with the peace-officers, and loudly swearing, re-appeared at the inn-door, clamorously demanding his wife.

The tortured Juliet, with an impulse of agony, cast, now,

the hands that were just withdrawn from the Baronet, upon the shoulder of Harleigh, who was himself fastening the chaise-door; tremulously, and in a tone scarcely audible, pronouncing, "Oh! hurry us away, Mr. Harleigh!—in mercy!—in compassion!"

Harleigh, bowing upon the hands which he ventured not to touch, but of which he felt the impression with a pang indescribable, called to the postilion to drive off full gallop.

With a low and sad inclination of the head, Juliet, in a faultering voice, thanked him; involuntarily adding, "My prayers, Mr. Harleigh,—my every wish for happiness,—will for ever be yours!"

The chaise drove off; but his groan, rather than sigh, reached her agonized ear; and, in an emotion too violent for concealment, yet to which she durst allow no vent, she held her almost bursting forehead with her hand; breathing only by smothered sighs, and scarcely sensible to the happiness of an uncertain escape, while bowed down by the sight of the misery that she had inflicted, where all that she owed was benevolence, sympathy, and generosity.

Not even the delight of thus victoriously carrying off a disputed prize, could immediately reconcile Sir Jaspar to the fear of even the smallest disorder in the economy of his medicines, anodynes, sweetmeats, and various whims; which, from long habits of self-indulgence, he now conceived to be necessaries, not luxuries.

But when, after having examined, in detail, that his travelling apparatus was in order, he turned smilingly to the fair mede of his exertions; and saw the deep absorption of all her faculties in her own evident affliction, he was struck with surprise and disappointment; and, after a short and mortified pause, "Can it be, fair ænigma!" he cried, "that it is with compunction you abandon this Gallic Goliah?"*

Surprised, through this question, from the keen anguish of speechless suffering; retrospection and anticipation alike gave way to gratitude, and she poured forth her thanks, her praises, and her wondering delight, at this unexpected, and marvellous rescue, with so much vivacity of transport, and so much softness of sensibility for his kindness, that the enchanted Sir

Jaspar, losing all forbearance, in the interest with which he languished to learn, more positively, her history and her situation, renewed his entreaties for communication, with an urgency that she now, for many reasons, no longer thought right to resist: anxious herself, since concealment was at an end, to clear away the dark appearances by which she was surrounded; and to remove a mystery that, for so long a period, had made her owe all good opinion to trust and generosity.

She pondered, nevertheless, and sighed, ere she could comply. It was strange to her, she said, and sad, to lift up the veil of secresy to a new, however interesting and respectable acquaintance; while to her brother, her sister, and her earliest friend, she still appeared to be inveloped in impenetrable concealment. Yet, if to communicate the circumstances which had brought her into this deplorable situation, could shew her sense of the benevolence of Sir Jaspar, she would set apart her repugnance, and gather courage to retrace the cruel scenes of which he had witnessed the direful result. Her inestimable friend had already related the singular history of all that had preceded their separation; but, uninformed herself of the dreadful events by which it had been followed, she could go no further: otherwise, from a noble openness of heart, which made all disguise painful, if not disgusting to her, Sir Jaspar would already have been satisfied.

The Baronet, ashamed, would now have withdrawn his petition; but Juliet no longer wished to retract from her engagement.

CHAPTER LXXX

THE first months after the departure of Gabriella, were passed, Juliet narrated, quietly, though far from gaily, in complete retirement. To lighten, through her cares and services, the terrible change of condition experienced by her benefactress, the Marchioness, and by her guardian, the Bishop, was her unremitting, and not successless endeavour: but even this sad tranquillity was soon broken in upon, by an accidental interview with a returned emigrant, who brought news of the dangerous state of health into which the young son of Gabriella had fallen. Too well knowing that this cherished little creature was the sole consolation and support of its exiled mother, the Marchioness earnestly desired that her daughter should possess again her early companion; who best could aid to nurse the child; or, should its illness prove fatal, to render its loss supportable. It was, therefore, settled, that, guarded and accompanied by a faithful ancient servant, upon whose prudence and attachment the Marchioness had the firmest reliance, Juliet should follow her friend: and the benevolent Bishop promised to join them both, as soon as his affairs would permit him to make the voyage.

To obtain a passport being then impossible, Ambroise, this worthy domestic, was employed to discover means for secretly crossing the channel: and, as adroit as he was trusty, he found out a pilot, who, though ostensibly but a fisherman, was a noted smuggler; and who passed frequently to the opposite shore; now with goods, now with letters, now with passengers. By this man the Marchioness wrote to prepare Gabriella for the reception of her friend, who was to join her at Brighthelmstone; whither, in her last letter, written, as Juliet now knew, in the anguish of discovering symptoms of danger in the illness of her darling boy, Gabriella had mentioned her intended excursion for sea-bathing. The diligent Ambroise soon obtained information that the pilot was preparing to sail with a select party. The Marchioness would rather have postponed the voyage, till an answer could have been received from her daughter; yet this was not an opportunity to be neglected.

The light baggage, therefore, was packed, and they were waiting the word of command from the pilot, when a commissary, from the Convention, arrived, to purify, he said, and new-organize the town, near which, in a villa that had been a part of her marriage-portion, the Marchioness and her brother then resided. To this villa the commissary made his first visit. The Bishop, by this agent of the inhuman Robespierre, was immediately seized; and, while his unhappy sister, and nearly adoring ward, were vainly kneeling at the feet of his condemner,—not accuser! to supplicate mercy for innocence,—not for guilt! the persons who were rifling the

Bishop, shouted out, with savage joy, that they had found a proof of his being a traitor, in a note in his pocket-book, which was clearly a bribe from the enemy to betray the country. The commissary, who, having often been employed as a spy, had a competent knowledge of modern languages, which he spoke intelligibly, though with vulgar phraseology and accent; took the paper, and read it without difficulty. It was the promissory note of the old Earl Melbury.

He eagerly demanded the Citoyenne Julie; swearing that, if six thousand pounds were to be got by marrying, he would marry without delay. He ordered her, therefore, to accompany him forthwith to the mayoralty. At her indignant refusal, he scoffingly laughed; but, upon her positive resistance, ordered her into custody. This, also, moved her not; she only begged to be confined in the same prison with the Bishop. Coarsely mocking her attachment for the priest, and holding her by the chin, he swore that he would marry her, and her six thousand pounds.

A million of deaths, could she die them, she resolutely replied, she would suffer in preference.

Her priest, then, he said, should away to the guillotine; though she had only to marry, and sign the promissory-note for the dower, to set the parson at liberty. Filled with horrour, she wrung her hands, and stood suspended; while the Marchioness, with anguish indescribable, and a look that made a supplication that no voice could pronounce, fell upon her neck, gasping for breath, and almost fainting.

"Ah, Madam!" Juliet cried, "what is your will? I am yours,—entirely yours! command me!"—

The Marchioness could not speak; but her sighs, her groans, rather, were more eloquent than any words.

"Bind the priest!" the commissary cried. "His trial is over; bind the traitor, and take him to the cell for execution."

The Marchioness sunk to the floor.

"No!" cried Juliet, "bind him not! Touch not his reverend and revered person!—Give me the paper! I will sign what you please! I will go whither you will!"

"Come, then," cried the commissary, "to the mayoralty."

Juliet covered her face, but moved towards the door.

The Bishop, hitherto passive and meekly resigned, now, with a sudden effort of strength, repulsing his gaolers, while fire darted from his eyes, and a spirit of command animated all his features, exclaimed, "No, generous Juliet! my own excellent child, no! Are a few years more or less,—perhaps but a few minutes,—worth purchasing by the sacrifice of truth, and the violation of every feeling? I will not be saved upon such terms!"

"No preaching," cried the commissary; "off with him at once."

The men now bound his hands and arms; while, returning to his natural state of calmness, he lifted up his eyes towards heaven, and, in a loud and sonorous voice, ejaculated, in Latin, a fervent prayer; with an air so absorbed in mental and pious abstraction, that he seemed unconscious what became of his person.

Juliet, who had shrunk back at his speech, again advanced, and, with agony unspeakable, held out her hand, in token of consent. The commissary received it triumphantly, at the moment that the Bishop, upon reaching the door, turned round to take a last view of his unhappy sister; who, torn with conflicting emotions, seemed a statue of horrour. But no sooner did he perceive the hand of his ward unresistingly grasped by the commissary, than again the expression of his face shewed his soul brought back from its heavenly absorption; and, stopping short, with an air which, helpless and shackled as he was, overawed his fierce conductors, "Hold yet a moment," he cried. "Oh Juliet! Think,—know what you are about! 'Tis not to this world alone you are responsible for vows offered up at the altar of God! My child! my more than daughter! sacrifice not your purity to your affections! Drag me not back from a virtuous death to a miserable existence, by the foul crime of wilful perjury!"

Juliet affrighted, again snatched away her hand, with a look at the commissary which pronounced an abhorrent refusal.

The commissary, stamping with fury, ordered the Bishop instantly to the cell of death. Where guilt, he said, had been proved, there was no need of any tribunal; and the execution should take place with the speed called for by his dangerous crimes.

Juliet, cold, trembling, and again irresolute, was involuntarily turning to the commissary; but the Bishop, charging her to be firm, pronounced a pious blessing upon her head; faintly spoke a last adieu to his miserable sister, and, with commanding solemnity, accompanied his gaolers away.

The horrour of that moment Juliet attempted not to describe; nor could she recur to it, without sighs and emotions that, for a while, stopt her narration.

Sir Jaspar would have spared her the resumption of the history; but she would not, having thus raised, trifle with his curiosity.

The commissary, she continued, then took possession of all the money, plate, and jewels he could find, and pursued what he called his rounds of purification.

How the Marchioness or herself outlived that torturing day, Juliet declared she could with difficulty, now, conceive. She was again willing to become a victim to the safety of her guardian; but even the Marchioness ceased to desire his preservation upon terms from which he himself recoiled as culpable. Early the next morning they were both conducted to a large house upon the market-place, where, in the most direful suspense, they were kept waiting for more than two hours; in which interval, such was the oppression of terrour, neither of them opened their lips.

The commissary, at length, broke into the room, and, seating himself in an arm-chair, while, humbly and tremblingly, they stood at the door, demanded of Juliet whether she were become more reasonable. Her head drooped, but she would not answer. "Follow me," he cried, "to this balcony." He opened a door leading to a large apartment that looked upon the market-place. She suspected some sinister design, and would not obey. "Come you, then!" he cried, to the Marchioness; and, taking her by the shoulder, rudely and grossly, he pushed her before him, till she entered upon the balcony. A dreadful scream, which then broke from her, brought Juliet to her side.

Here, again, overpowered by the violence of bitter recollections, which operated, for the moment, with nearly the force of immediate suffering, Juliet was obliged to take breath before she could proceed.

"Oh Sir Jaspar!" she then cried, "upon approaching the wretched Marchioness, what a distracting scene met my eyes! A scaffolding,—a guillotine,—an executioner,—were immediately opposite me! and in the hand of that hardened executioner, was held up to the view of the senseless multitude, the ghastly, bleeding head of a victim that moment offered up at the shrine of unmeaning though ferocious cruelty! Four other destined victims, kneeling and devoutly at prayers, their hands tied behind them, and their heads bald, were prepared for sacrifice; and amidst them, eminently conspicuous, from his dignified mien, and pious calmness, I distinguished my revered guardian! the Marchioness had distinguished her beloved brother!—Oh moment of horrour exceeding all description! I cast myself, nearly frantic, at the feet of the commissary; I embraced his knees, as if with the fervour of affection; wildly and passionately I conjured him to accept my hand and fortune, and save the Bishop!—He laughed aloud with triumphant derision; but gave an immediate order to postpone the execution of the priest. I blest him,—yes, with all his crimes upon his head!—and even again I should bless him, to save a life so precious!

"The Marchioness, recovering her strength with her hopes, seized the arm of the messenger of this heavenly news, hurrying him along with a force nearly supernatural, and calling out aloud herself, from the instant that she entered the market place, '*Un sursit! Un sursit!*'†

" 'Now, then,' cried the commissary, 'come with me to the mayoralty;' and was taking my no longer withheld, but shaking hand, when some soldiers abruptly informed him that an insurrection had broken out at * * *, which demanded his immediate presence.

"I caught this moment of his engaged attention to find my way down stairs, and into the market-place: but not with a view to escape; every feeling of my soul was concentrated in the safety of the Bishop. I rushed forward, I forced my way through the throng, which, though at first it opposed my steps, no sooner looked at me than, intimidated by my desperation, or affected by my agony, it facilitated my passage. Rapidly I

† "A Reprieve! a reprieve!"

overtook the Marchioness, whose age, whose dignified energy, and loud cries of Reprieve! made way for her through every impediment, whether of crowd or of guards, to the scaffolding. How we accomplished it, nevertheless, I now wonder! But a sense of right, when asserted with courage, is lodged in the lowest, the vilest of mankind;—a sense of right, an awe of justice, and a propensity to sympathize with acute distress! The reprieve which our cries had anticipated, and which the man whom we accompanied confirmed, was received by the multitude, from an ardent and universal respect to the well known excellencies of the Bishop, with shouts of applause that exalted our joy at his deliverance into a felicity which we thought celestial! At his venerable feet we prostrated ourselves, as if he had been a martyr to religion, and already was sainted. He was greatly affected; though perhaps only by our emotion; for he looked too uncertain how this event had been brought to bear, to partake of our happiness; and at me he cast an eye so full of compassion, yet so interrogative, that mine sunk under it; and, far from exulting that I had thus devoted myself to his preservation, I was already trembling at the acknowledgement I had to make, when I was suddenly seized by a soldier, who forced me, from all the tenderest interests of my heart, back to the stormy commissary. Oh! what a change of scene! He roughly took me by the arm, which felt as if it were withered, and no longer a part of my frame at his touch; and, with accusations of the grossest nature, and vows the most tremendous of vengeance, compelled me to attend him to the mayor alty; deaf to my prayers, my entreaties, my kneeling supplications that he would first suffer me to see the Bishop at liberty.

"At the mayoralty he was accosted by a messenger sent from the Convention. Ah! it seemed to me, at that moment, that a whole age of suffering could not counterbalance the delight I experienced, when, to read an order thus presented to him, he was constrained to relinquish his hard grasp! Still greater was my relief, when I learnt, by what passed, that he had received commands to proceed directly to * * *, where the insurrection was become dangerous.

"Such a multiplicity of business now crowded upon him, that I conceived a hope I might be forgotten; or, at least, set apart as a future prey: but alas! the promissory-note was still in his hand, and,—if heart he has any,—if heart be not left out in his composition, there, past all doubt, the six thousand pounds were already lodged. All my hopes, therefore, faded away, when he had given some new directions; for, seizing me again, by the wrist, he dragged me to the place,—I had nearly said of execution!—There, by his previous orders, all were in waiting,—all was ready!—Oh, Sir Jaspar! how is it that life still holds, in those periods when all our earthly hopes, and even our faculties of happiness, seem for ever entombed."

The bitterest sighs again interrupted her narration; but neither the humanity nor the politeness of Sir Jaspar could combat any longer his curiosity, and he conjured her to proceed.

"The civil ceremony, dreadful, dreadful! however little awful compared with that of the church, was instantly begun; in the midst of the buz of business, the clamour of many tongues, the sneers of contempt, and the laughter of derision; with an irreverence that might have suited a theatre, and with a mockery of which the grossest buffoons would have been ashamed. Scared and disordered, I understood not,—I heard not a word; and my parched lips, and burning mouth, could not attempt any articulation.

"In a minute or two, this pretended formality was interrupted, by information that a new messenger from the Convention demanded immediate admittance. The commissary swore furiously that he should wait till the six thousand pounds were secured; and vociferously ordered that the ceremony should be hurried on. He was obeyed! and though my quivering lips were never opened to pronounce an assenting syllable, the ceremony, the direful ceremony, was finished, and I was called,—Oh heaven and earth!—his wife! his married wife!—The Marchioness, at the same terrible moment, broke into the apartment. The conflict between horrour and tenderness was too violent, and, as she encircled me, with tortured pity, in her arms, I sunk senseless at her feet.

"Upon recovering, the first words that I heard were, 'Look up, my child, look up! we are alone!' and I beheld the unhappy Marchioness, whose face seemed a living picture of commiserating woe. The commissary had been forced away by a new express; but he had left a charge that I should be ready to give my signature upon his return. The Marchioness then, with expressions melting, at once, and exalting, condescended to pour forth the most soothing acknowledgements; yet conjured me not to leave my own purpose unanswered, by signing the promissory-note, till the Bishop should be restored to liberty, with a passport, by which he might instantly quit this spot of persecution. To find something was yet to be done, and to be done for the Bishop, once more revived me; and when the commissary re-entered the apartment, neither order nor menace could intimidate me to take the pen, till my conditions were fulfilled. My life, indeed, at that horrible period, had lost all value but what was attached to the Bishop, the Marchioness, and my beloved Gabriella; for myself, it seemed, thenceforth, reserved not for wretchedness, but despair!

"The passport was soon prepared; but when the Bishop was brought in to receive it in my presence, he rejected it, even with severity, till he heard,—from myself heard!—that the marriage-ceremony, as it was called! was already over. Into what a consternation was he then flung! Pale grew his reverend visage, and his eyes glistened with tears. He would not, however, render abortive the sacrifice which he could no longer impede, and I signed the promissory-note; while the Marchioness wept floods of tears upon my neck; and the Bishop, with a look of anguish that rent my heart, waved, with speechless sorrow, his venerable hand, in token of a blessing, over my head; and, deeply sighing, silently departed.

"The commissary, forced immediately away, to transact some business with his successor at this place, committed me to the charge of the mayor. I was shewn to a sumptuous apartment; which I entered with a shuddering dread that the gloomiest prison could scarcely have excited. The Marchioness followed her brother; and I remained alone, trembling, shaking, almost fainting at every sound, in a state of terrour and misery indescribable. The commissary, however, returned not; and the mayor, to whom my title of horrour was a title of respect, paid me attentions of every sort.

"In the afternoon, the Marchioness brought me the reviving

tidings that the Bishop was departed. He had promised to endeavour to join Gabriella. The rest of this direful day passed, and no commissary appeared: but the anguish of unremitting expectation kept aloof all joy at his absence, for, in idea, he appeared every moment! Nevertheless, after sitting up together the whole fearful night, we saw the sun rise the next morning without any new horrour. I then received a visit from the mayor, with information that the insurrection at * * * had obliged the commissary to repair thither, and that he had just sent orders that I should join him in the evening. Resistance was out of the question. The tender Marchioness demanded leave to accompany me; but the mayor interposed, and forced her home, to prepare and deliver my wardrobe for the journey. It was so long ere she returned, that the patience of the mayor was almost exhausted; but when, at last, she arrived, what a change was there in her air! Her noble aspect had recovered more than its usual serenity; it was radiant with benevolence and pleasure; and, when we were left an instant together, 'My Juliet!' she cried, while beaming smiles illumined her fine face, 'my Juliet! my other child! blessed be Heaven, I can now rescue our rescuer! I have found means to snatch her from this horrific thraldom, in the very journey destined for its accomplishment!'

"She then briefly prepared me for meeting and seconding the scheme of deliverance that she had devised with the excellent Ambroise; and we separated,—with what tears, what regret,—yet what perturbation of rising hope!

"All that the Marchioness had arranged was executed. Ambroise, disguised as an old waggoner, preceded me to the small town of * * *, where the postilion, he knew, must stop to water the horses. Here I obtained leave to alight for some refreshment, of which an old municipal officer, who had me in charge, was not sorry, in idea, to partake; as he could not entertain the most distant notion that I had formed any plan of escape. As soon, however, as I was able to disengage myself from his sight, a chambermaid, who had previously been gained by Ambroise, wrapt me in a man's great coat, put on me a black wig, and a round hat, and, pointing to a back door, went out another way; speaking aloud, as if called; to give herself the power of asserting, afterwards, that the evasion had been effected in her absence. The pretended waggoner then took me under his arm, and flew with me across a narrow passage, where we met, by appointment, an ancient domestic of the Bishop's; who conveyed me to a small house, and secreted me in a dark closet, of which the entrance was not discernible. He then went forth upon his own affairs, into such streets and places as were most public; and my good waggoner found means to abscond.

"Here, while rigidly retaining the same posture, and scarcely daring to breathe any more than to move, I heard the house entered by sundry police-officers, who were pursuing me with execrations. They came into the very room in which I was concealed; and beat round the wainscot in their search; touching even the board which covered the small aperture, not door, by which I was hidden from their view! I was not, however, discovered; nor was the search, there, renewed; from the adroitness of the domestic by whom I had been saved, in having shewn himself in the public streets before I had yet been missed.

"In this close recess, nearly without air, wholly without motion, and incapable of taking any rest; but most kindly treated by the wife of the good domestic, I passed a week. All search in that neighbourhood being then over, I changed my clothing for some tattered old garments; stained my face, throat, and arms; and, in the dead of the night, quitted my place of confinement, and was conducted by my protector to a spot about half a mile from the town. There I found Ambroise awaiting me, with a little cart; in which he drove me to a small mean house, in the vicinity of the sea-coast. He introduced me to the landlord and landlady as his relation, and then left me to take some repose; while he went forth to discover whether the pilot were yet sailed.

"He had delivered to me my work-bag, in which was my purse, generously stored by the Marchioness, with all the ready money that she could spare, for my journey. For herself, she held it essential to remain stationary, lest a general emigration should alienate the family-fortune from every branch of her house. Excellent lady! At the moment she thus studied the prosperity of her descendants, she lived upon roots, while deprived of all she most valued in life, the society of her only child!

"To repose the good Ambroise left me; but far from my pillow was repose! the dreadful idea of flying one who might lay claim to the honoured title of husband for pursuing me; the consciousness of being held by an engagement which I would not fulfil, yet could not deny; the uncertainty whether my revered Bishop had effected his escape; and the necessity of abandoning my generous benefactress when surrounded by danger; joined to the affliction of returning to my native country,—the country of my birth, my heart, and my pride!—without name, without fortune, without friends! no parents to receive me, no protector to counsel me; unacknowledged by my family,—unknown even to the children of my father!—Oh! bitter, bitter were my feelings!—Yet when I considered that no action of my life had offended society, or forfeited my rights to benevolence, I felt my courage revive, for I trusted in Providence. Sleep then visited my eye-lids, though hard was the bed upon which I sought it; hard and cold! the month was December. Happy but short respite of forgetfulness! Four days and nights followed, of the most terrible anxiety, ere Ambroise returned. He then brought me the dismaying intelligence, that circumstances had intervened, in his own affairs, that made it impossible for him, at that moment, to quit his country. Yet less than ever could my voyage be delayed, the commissary having, in his fury, advertised a description of my person, and set a price upon my head; publicly vowing that I should be made over to the guillotine, when found, for an example. Oh reign so justly called of terrour! How lawless is its cruelty! How blest by all mankind will be its termination.

"It now became necessary to my safety, that Ambroise, who was known to be a domestic of the Marchioness, should not appear to belong to me; and that, to avoid any suspicion that I was the person advertised by the commissary, I should present myself to the pilot as an accidental passenger.

"Ambroise had found means, during his absence, to communicate with the Marchioness; from whom he brought me a letter of the sweetest kindness; and intelligence and injunctions of the utmost importance.

"The commissary, she informed me, immediately upon my disappearance, had presented the promissory-note to the bankers; but they had declared it not to be valid, till it were either signed by the heir of the late Earl Melbury, or re-signed, with a fresh date, by Lord Denmeath. The commissary, therefore, had sent over an agent to Lord Denmeath, to claim, as my husband, the six thousand pounds, before my evasion should be known. The Marchioness conjured me, nevertheless, to forbear applying to my family; or avowing my name, or my return to my native land, till I should be assured of the safety of the Bishop; whom the commissary had now ordered to be pursued, and upon whom the most horrible vengeance might be wreaked, should my escape to this happy land transpire, before his own should be effected: though, while I was still supposed to be within reach of our cruel persecutor, the Bishop, even if he were seized, might merely be detained as an hostage for my future concession; till happier days, or partial accident, might work his deliverance.

"Inviolably I have adhered to these injunctions. In a note which I left for the Marchioness, with Ambroise, I solemnly assured her, that no hardships of adversity, nor even any temptation to happiness, should make me waver in my given faith; or tear from me the secret of my name and story, till I again saw, or received tidings of the Bishop. And Oh how light, how even blissful,—in remembrance, at least,—will prove every sacrifice, should the result be the preservation of the most pious and exemplary of men! But, alas! I have been discovered, while still in the dark as to his destiny, by means which no self-denial could preclude, no fortitude avert!

"The indefatigable Ambroise had learned that the pilot was to sail the next evening for Dover. I now added patches and bandages to my stained skin, and garb of poverty; and stole, with Ambroise, to the sea-side; where we wandered till past mid-night; when Ambroise descried a little vessel, and the pilot; and, soon afterwards, sundry passengers, who, in dead silence, followed each other into the boat. I then approached, and called out to beg admission. I desired Ambroise to be gone; but he was too anxious to leave me. Faithful, excellent creature! how he suffered while I pleaded in vain! how he rejoiced when one of the passengers, open to heavenly pity, humanely returned to the shore to assist me into the boat! Ambroise took my last adieu to the Marchioness; and I set sail for my loved, long lost, and fearfully recovered native land.

"The effect upon my spirits of this rescue from an existence of unmingled horrour, was so exhilarating, so exquisite, that no sooner was my escape assured, than, from an impulse irresistible, I cast my ring, which I had not yet dared throw away, into the sea; and felt as if my freedom were from that moment restored! And, though innumerable circumstances were unpleasant in the way, I was insensible to all but my release; and believed that only to touch the British shore would be liberty and felicity!

"Little did I then conceive, impossible was it I should foresee, the difficulties, dangers, disgraces, and distresses towards which I was plunging! Too, too soon was I drawn from my illusion of perfect happiness! and my first misfortune was the precursor of every evil by which I have since been pursued;—I lost my purse; and, with it, away flew my fancied independence, my ability to live as I pleased, and to devote all my thoughts and my cares to consoling my beloved friend!

"Vainly in London, and vainly at Brighthelmstone I sought that friend. I would have returned to the capital, to attempt tracing her by minuter enquiry; but I was deterred by poverty, and the fear of personal discovery. I could only, therefore, continue on the spot named by the Marchioness for our general rendezvous, where the opening of every day gave me the chance of some direction how to proceed. But alas! from that respected Marchioness two letters only have ever reached me! The first assured me that she was safe and well, and that the Bishop, though forced to take a distant route, had escaped his pursuers: but that the commissary was in hourly augmenting rage, from Lord Denmeath's refusing to honour the promissory-note, till the marriage should be authenticated by the bride, with the signature and acquittal of the Bishop. The second letter,—second and last from this honoured lady!—said that all was well; but bid me wait with patience, perhaps to a long period, for further intelligence, and console and seek to dwell with her Gabriella: or, should any unforeseen circumstances inevitably separate us, endeavour to fix myself in some respectable and happy family, whose social felicity might bring, during this dread interval of suspense, reflected happiness to my own heart: but still to remain wholly unknown, till I should be joined by the Bishop.

"Cast thus upon myself, and for a time indefinite, how hardly, and how variously have I existed! But for the dreadful fear of worse, darkly and continually hovering over my head, I could scarcely have summoned courage for my unremitting trials. But whatever I endured was constantly light in comparison with what I had escaped! Yet how was I tried,—Oh Sir Jaspar! how cruelly! in resisting to present myself to my family! in forbearing to pronounce the kind appellation of brother! the soft, tender title of sister! Oh! in their sight, when witnessing their goodness, when blest by their kindness, and urged by the most generous sweetness to confidence, how violent, how indescribable have been my struggles, to withhold from throwing myself into their arms, with the fair, natural openness of sisterly affection! But Lord Denmeath, who disputed, or denied, my relation to their family, was their uncle and guardian. To him to make myself known, would have been to blight every hope of concealment from the commissary, whose claims were precisely in unison with the plan of his lordship, for making me an alien to my country. What, against their joint interests and authority, would be the power of a sister or a brother under age? Often, indeed, I was tempted to trust them in secret; and oh how consolatory to my afflicted heart would have been such a trust! but they had yet no establishment, and they were wards of my declared enemy. How unavailing, therefore, to excite their generous zeal, while necessarily forced to exact that our ties of kindred should remain unacknowledged? Upon their honour I could rely; but by their feelings, their kind, genuine, ardent feelings, I must almost unavoidably have been betrayed.

"To my Gabriella, also, I have forborne to unbosom my sorrows, and reveal my alarms, that I might spare her already so deeply wounded soul, the restless solicitude of fresh and cruel uncertainties. She concludes, that though her letters have miscarried, or been lost, her honoured mother and uncle still reside safely together, in the villa of the Marchioness, in which she had bidden them adieu. And that noble mother charged me to hide, if it should be possible, from her unhappy child, the terrible history in which I had borne so considerable a part, till she could give assurances to us both of her own and the Bishop's safety. Alas! nine months have now worn away since our separation, yet no news arrives!—no Bishop appears!

"And now, Sir Jaspar, you have fully before you the cause and history of my long concealment, my strange wanderings, and the apparently impenetrable mystery in which I have been involved: why I could not claim my family; why I could not avow my situation; why I dared not even bear my name; all, all is before you! Oh! could I equally display to you the events in store! tell you whether my revered Bishop is safe!—or whether his safety, his precious life, can only be secured by my perpetual captivity! One thing alone, in the midst of my complicate suspenses, one thing alone is certain; no consideration that this world can offer, will deter me from going back, voluntarily, to every evil from which I have hitherto been flying, should the Bishop again be seized, and should his release hang upon my final self-devotion!"

CHAPTER LXXXI

SIR JASPAR had listened to this narrative with trembling interest, and a species of emotion that was indefinable; his head bent forward, and his mouth nearly as wide open, from the fear of losing a word, as his eyes, from eagerness not to lose a look: but, when it was finished, he exclaimed, in a sort of transport, "Is this all? Joy, then, to great Caesar!* Why 'tis nothing! My little fairies are all skipping in ecstacy; while the wickeder imps are making faces and wry mouths, not to see mischief enough in the wind to afford them a supper! This a marriage? Why you are free as air!

"The little birds that fly,
With careless ease, from tree to tree,"*

are not more at liberty. Ah! fair enslaver! were I as unshackled!"—

The smiles that, momentarily, broke their way through the tears and sadness of Juliet, shewed how much this declaration was in unison with her wishes; but, exhausted by relating a history so deeply affecting to her, she could enter into no discussion; and remained ceaselessly weeping, till the Baronet, with an expression of surprize, asked whether the meeting that would now ensue with her own family, could offer her no consolation?

Rousing, then, from her sorrow, to a grateful though forced exertion, "Oh yes!" she cried, "yes! Your generous goodness has given me new existence! But horrour and distress have pursued me with such accumulating severity, that the shock is still nearly overpowering. Yet,—let me not diminish the satisfaction of your beneficence. I am going now to be happy!—How big a word!—how new to my feelings!—A sister!—a brother!—Have I, indeed, such relations?" smiling even brightly through her tears. "And will Lady Aurora,—the sweetest of human beings!—condescend to acknowledge me? Will the amiable Lord Melbury deign to support, to protect me? Oh Sir Jaspar, how have you brought all this to bear? Where are these dearest persons? And when, and by what means, am I to be blest with their sight, and honoured with their sanction to my claim of consanguinity?"

Sir Jaspar begged her to compose her spirits, promising to satisfy her when she should become more calm. But, her thoughts having once turned into this channel, all her tenderest affections gushed forth to oppose their being diverted into any other; and the sound, the soul-penetrating sound of sister!—of brother! once allowed utterance, vibrated through her frame with a thousand soft emotions, now first welcomed without checking her heart.

Urgently, therefore, she desired an explanation of the manner in which this commission had been given; of the tone of voice in which she had been named; and of the time and place destined for the precious meeting.

Sir Jaspar, though enchanted to see her revived, and enraptured to give ear to her thanks, and to suck in her praises, was palpably embarrassed how to answer her enquiries; which he suffered her to continue so long without interruption or reply, that, her eagerness giving way to anxiety, she solemnly required to know, whether it were by accident, or through his own information, that Lord Melbury and Lady Aurora had been made acquainted with her rights, or, more properly, with her hopes and her fears in regard to their kindness and support.

Still no answer was returned, but smiling looks, and encouraging assurances.

The most alarming doubts now disturbed the just opening views of Juliet. "Ah! Sir Jaspar!" she cried, "why this procrastination? Practise no deception, I conjure you!—Alas, you make me fear you have acted without commission?"—

He protested, upon his honour, that that was not the case; yet asked why she had settled that his commission came from Lady Aurora, or Lord Melbury?

"Good Heaven!"—exclaimed Juliet, astonished and affrighted.

He had only, he said, affirmed, that his commission was to take her to those noble personages; not that it had been from themselves that it had emanated.

Again every feature of Juliet seemed changed by disappointment; and the accent of reproach was mingled with that of grief, as she pronounced, "Oh Sir Jaspar! can you, then, have played with my happiness? have trifled with my hopes?"—

"Not to be master of the whole planetary system," he cried, "with Venus, in her choicest wiles, at its head!* I have honourably had my commission; but it has been for, not from your honourable relations. Those little invisible, but active beings, who have taken my conscience in charge, have spurred and goaded me on to this deed, ever since I saw your distress at the fair Gallic needle-monger's. Night and day have they pinched me and jirked me, to seek you, to find you, and to rescue you from that brawny caitiff."—

"Alas! to what purpose? If I have no asylum, what is my security?"—

"If I have erred, my beauteous fugitive," said Sir Jaspar, archly, "I must order the horses to turn about! We shall still, probably, be in time to accompany the happy captive to his cell."

Juliet involuntarily screamed, but besought, at least, to know how she had been traced; and what had induced the other pursuit; or caused the seizure, which she had so unexpectedly witnessed, of her persecutor?

He answered, that, restless to fathom a mystery, the profundity of which left, to his active imagination, as much space for distant hope as for present despair, he had invited Riley to dinner, upon quitting Frith Street; and, through his means, had discovered the pilot; whose friendship and services were secured, without scruple, by a few guineas. By this man, Sir Jaspar was shewn the advertisement, which he now produced; and which Juliet, though nearly overcome with shame, begged to read.

"ELOPED from her HUSBAND,

"A young woman, tall, fair, blue-eyed; her face oval; her nose Grecian; her mouth small; her cheeks high coloured; her chin dimpled; and her hair of a glossy light brown.

"She goes commonly by the name of Miss Ellis.

"Whoever will send an account where she may be met with, or where she has been seen, to *** Attorney, in *** Street London, shall receive a very handsome reward."

The pilot further acknowledged to Sir Jaspar, that his employer had, formerly, been at the head of a gang of smugglers and swindlers; though, latterly, he had been engaged in business of a much more serious nature.

This intelligence, with an internal conviction that the marriage must have been forced, decided Sir Jaspar to denounce the criminal to justice; and then to take every possible measure, to have him either imprisoned for trial, or sent out of the country, by the alien-bill,* before he should overtake the fair fugitive. His offences were, it seems, notorious, and the warrant for his seizure was readily granted; with an order for his being embarked by the first opportunity: nevertheless, the difficulty to discover him had almost demolished the scheme: though the Baronet had aided the search in person, to enjoy the bliss of being the first to announce freedom to the lovely Runaway; and to offer her immediate protection.

But the pilot, who, after being well paid for his information, had himself absconded, delayed all proceedings till he was found out, by Riley, upon the Salisbury-road. He evaded giving any further intelligence, till the glitter of a few guineas restored his spirit of communication, when he was brought to confess, that his master was in that neighbourhood; where they had received assurances that the fugitive herself was lodged. Sir Jaspar instantly, then, took the measures of which the result, seconded by sundry happy accidents, had been so seasonable and prosperous. "And never," said he, in conclusion, "did my delectable little friends serve me so cogently, as in suggesting my stratagem at your sight. If you do not directly name, they squeaked in my ear, her brother and sister, she may demur at accompanying you: if her brother and sister honour your assertion, you will fix the matchless Wanderer in her proper sphere; if they protest against it,—what giant stands in the way to your rearing and protecting the lovely flower yourself?—This was the manner in which these hovering little beings egged me on; but whether, with the playful philanthropy of courteous sylphs, to win me your gentle smiles; or whether, with the wanton malignity of little devils, to annihilate me with your frowns, is still locked up in the womb of your countenance!"

He then farther added, that Riley had accompanied him throughout the expedition; but that, always exhilarated by scenes which excited curiosity, or which produced commotion; he had scampered into the inn, to witness the culprit's being secured, while Sir Jaspar had paid his respects at the chaise.

With a disappointed heart, and with affrighted spirits, Juliet now saw that she must again, and immediately, renew her melancholy flight, in search of a solitary hiding-place; till she could be assured of the positive embarkation of the commissary.

In vain Sir Jaspar pressed to pursue his design of conveying her to her family; the dread of Lord Denmeath, who was in actual communication and league with her persecutor, decided her refusal; though, while she had believed in Sir Jaspar's commission for seeking her, neither risk nor doubt had had power to check the ardour of her impatience, to cast herself upon the protection of Lord Melbury and Lady Aurora: but she felt no courage,—however generously they had succoured and distinguished her as a distressed individual,—to rush upon them, uncalled and unexpected, as a near relation; and one who had so large a claim, could her kindred be proved, upon their inheritance.

Her most earnest wish was to rejoin her Gabriella; but there, where she had been discovered, she could least hope to lie concealed. She must still, therefore, fly, in lonely silence. But she besought Sir Jaspar to take her any whither rather than to Salisbury, where she had had the horrour of being examined by the advertisement.

Proud to receive her commands, he recommended to her a farm-house about three miles from the city, of which the proprietor and his wife, who were worthy and honest people, had belonged, formerly, to his family.

She thankfully agreed to this proposal: but, when they arrived at the farm, they heard that the master and mistress were gone to a neighbouring fair, whence they were not expected back for an hour or two; and that they had locked up the parlour. Some labourers being in the kitchen, Sir Jaspar proposed driving about in the interval; and ordered the postilion to Wilton.

CHAPTER LXXXII

ABSORBED in grief, and unable to converse, though endeavouring to listen to the Baronet, Juliet was only drawn from her melancholy reverie, by the rattling of the carriage upon a pavement, as it passed, through a spacious gate, into the court-yard of a magnificent country seat.

She demanded what this meant.

Where better, he demanded in return, could she while away the interval of waiting, than in viewing the finest works of art, displayed in a temple consecrated to their service?

This was a scheme to force back all her consideration. In hearing him pronounce the word Wilton, she had merely thought of the town; not of the mansion of the Earl of Pembroke; which she now positively refused entering; earnestly representing the necessity, as well as propriety, in a situation so perilous, of the most entire obscurity.

He assured her that she would be less liable to observation in a repository of the *beaux arts*, at the villa of a nobleman, than by waiting in a post-chaise, before the door of an inn; as he must indispensably change horses; and grant a little repose to his old groom, who had been out with him all day.

This she could not dispute, convinced, herself, that her greatest danger lay in being recognized, or remarked, within the precincts of an inn.

Nevertheless, how enter into such a mansion in a garb so unfit for admission? She besought him to ask leave that she might remain in some empty apartment, as an humble dependent, while he viewed the house.

Extremely pleased by an idea so consonant to his fantastic taste, he answered her aloud, in alighting, "Yes, yes, Mrs. Betty! if you wish to see the rooms, that you may give an account of all the pretty images to my little ones, there can be no objection."

She descended from the chaise, meaning to remonstrate upon this misconstruction of her request; but, not allowing her the opportunity, he gaily represented, to the person who shewed him the mansion, that he was convoying a young nursery-maid, the daughter of a worthy old tenant, to his grand-children; and that she had a fancy to see all the finery, that she might make out some pretty stories, to tell the little dears, when she wanted to put them to sleep.

Juliet, whose deep distress made her as little desire to see as to be seen, repeated that she wished to sit still in some spare room: he walked on, pretending not to hear her, addressing himself to his *Cicerone*,* whom he kept at his side; and therefore, as there was no female in view, to whom she could apply, she was compelled to follow.

Not as Juliet she followed; Juliet whose soul was delightedly "awake to tender strokes of art,"* whether in painting, music, or poetry; who never saw excellence without emotion; and whose skill and taste would have heightened her pleasure into rapture, her approbation into enthusiasm, in viewing the delicious assemblage of painting, statuary, antiques, natural curiosities, and artificial rarities, of Wilton;—not as Juliet, she followed; but as one to whom every thing was indifferent; whose discernment was gone, whose eyes were dimmed, whose powers of perception were asleep, and whose spirit of enjoyment was annihilated. Figures of the noblest sculpture; busts of historical interest; *alto* and *basso relievos** of antique elegance; marbles, alabasters, spars, and lavers of all colours,* and in all forms; pictures glowing into life, and statues appearing to command their beholders;—all that, at another period, would have made her forget every thing but themselves, now vainly solicited a moment of her attention.

It was by no means the fault of the Baronet, that this nearly morbid insensibility was not conquered, by the revivyfying objects which surrounded her. He suffered her not to pass an Æsculapius, without demanding a prescription for her health; a Mercury, without supplicating an ordonnance for her spirits; a Minerva, without claiming an exhortation to courage; nor a Venus,* without pointing out, that perpetual beauty beams but through perpetual smiles: couching every phrase under emblematical recommendations of story-subjects for the nursery.

When the guide stood somewhat aloof, "What say you, now," he exultingly whispered, "to my famous little friends? Did they ever devise a more ingenious gambol? From your slave, by a mere wave of their wand, they have transformed me into your master! Ah, wicked syren! a dimple of yours demolishes all their work, and again totters me down to your feet!"

Nevertheless, even in this nearly torpid state, accident having raised her eyes to Vandyke's children of Charles the First,* the extraordinary attraction of that fascinating picture, was exciting, unconsciously, some pleasure, when the sound of a carriage announcing a party to see the house, she petitioned Sir Jaspar to avoid, if possible, being known.

All compliance with whatever she could wish, the Baronet promised to nail his eyes to the lowest picture in the room, should they be joined by any stragglers; and then, relinquishing all further examination, he begged permission to wait for his horses, in an apartment which is presided by a noble picture of Salvator Rosa;* to which, never discouraged, he strove to call the attention of Juliet.

Nothing could more aptly harmonize, not only with his enthusiastic eulogiums, but with his quaint fancy, than that exquisite effusion of the painter's imagination, "where, surely," said the rapturous Baronet, "his pencil has been guided, if not impelled, in every stroke, by my dear little cronies the fairies! And that variety of vivifying objects; that rich, yet so elegant scenery, of airy gaiety, and ideal felicity, is palpably a representation of fairy land itself! Is it thither my dear little friends will, some day, convey me? And shall I be metamorphosed into one of those youthful swains, that are twining their garlands with such bewitching grace? And shall I myself elect the fair one, around whom I shall entwine mine?"

This harangue was interrupted, by the appearance of a newly arrived party; but vainly Sir Jaspar kept his word, in reclining upon his crutches, till he was nearly prostrate upon the ground; he was immediately challenged by a lady; and that lady was Mrs. Ireton.

Juliet, inexpressibly shocked, hastily glided from the room, striving to cover her face with her luxuriously curling hair. She rambled about the mansion, till she met with a chamber-maid, from whom she entreated permission to wait in some private apartment, till the carriage to which she belonged should be ready.

The maid, obligingly, took her to a small room; and Juliet, taught by her cruel confusion at the sight of Mrs. Ireton, the censure, if not slander, to which travelling alone with a man, however old, might make her liable; determined, at whatever hazard, to hang, henceforth, solely upon herself.* She resolved, therefore, to beg the assistance of this maid-servant, to direct her to some safe rural lodging.

But how great was her consternation, when, requiring, now, her purse, she suddenly missed,—what, in her late misery, she had neither guarded nor thought of, her packet and her work-bag!

Every pecuniary resource was now sunk at a blow! even the deposit, which she had held as sacred, of Harleigh, was lost!

At what period of her disturbances this misfortune had happened, she had no knowledge; nor whether her property had been dropt in her distress, or purloined; or simply left at the inn; the consequence, every way, was equally dreadful: and but for Sir Jaspar, whom all sense of propriety had told her, the moment before, to shun, yet to whom, now, she became tied, by absolute necessity, her Difficulties, at this conjuncture, would have been nearly distracting.

When the carriage was returned, with fresh horses, Sir Jaspar found her in a situation of augmented dismay, that filled him with concern; though he also saw, that it was tempered by a grateful softness to himself, that he thought more than ever bewitching.

He assured her that Mrs. Ireton, whom he had adroitly shaken off, had not perceived her; but the moment that they were re-seated in the chaise, she communicated to him, with the most painful suffering, the new, and terrible stroke, by which she was oppressed.

Viewing this as a mere pecuniary embarrassment, the joy of becoming again useful, if not necessary, to her, sparkled in his eyes with almost youthful vivacity; though he engaged to send his valet immediately to the inn, to make enquiries, and offer rewards, for recovering the strayed goods.

This second loss of her purse, she suffered Sir Jaspar, without any attempt at justification, to call an active epigram upon modern female drapery; which prefers continual inconvenience, innumerable privations, and the most distressing untidiness, to the antique habit of modesty and good housewifery, which, erst, left the public display of the human figure to the statuary; deeming that to support the female character was more essential than to exhibit the female form.

This second loss, also, by carrying back her reflections to the first, brought to her mind several circumstances, which cast a new light upon that origin of the various misfortunes and adventures which had followed her arrival; and all her recollections, now she knew the rapacity and worthlessness of the pilot, pointed out to her that she had probably been robbed, at the moment when, impulsively, she was pouring forth, upon her knees, her thanks for her deliverance. Her work-bag, which, upon that occasion, she had deposited upon her seat, she remembered, though she had then attributed it to his vigilance and care, seeing in his hands, when she arose.

Arrived at the farm-house, they found themselves expected by the farmer and his wife, who paid the utmost respect to Sir Jaspar; but who saw, with an air of evidently suspicious surprize, the respect which he himself paid to Mrs. Betty, the nurse-maid; whose beauty, with her rustic attire, and disordered hair, would have made them instantly conclude her to be a lost young creature, had not the decency of her look, the dignity of her manner, and the grief visible in her countenance, spoken irresistibly in favour of her innocence. They spoke not, however, in favour of that of Sir Jaspar, whose old character of gallantry was well known to them; and induced their belief, that he was inveigling this young woman from her friends, for her moral destruction. They accommodated her, nevertheless, for the night; but, whatever might be their pity, determined, should the Baronet visit her the next day, to invent some other occupation for their spare bed-room.

Unenviable was that night, as passed by their lodger, however acceptable to her was any asylum. She spent it in continual alarm; now shaking with the terrour of pursuit; now affrighted with the prospect of being pennyless; now shocked to find herself cast completely into the power of a man, who, however aged, was her professed admirer; and now distracted by varying resolutions upon the measures which she ought immediately to take. And when, for a few minutes, her eyes, from extreme fatigue, insensibly closed, her dreams, short and horrible, renewed the dreadful event of the preceding day; again she saw herself pursued; again felt herself seized; and she blessed the piercing shrieks with which she awoke, though they brought to her but the transient relief that she was safe for the passing moment.

CHAPTER LXXXIII

SIR JASPAR arrived late the next morning, in wrath, he said, with his valet, who was not yet returned with the result of his enquiries from the inn; but before Juliet could express any uneasiness at the delay, the farmer and his wife, in evident confusion, though with professions of great respect, humbly besought that his honour would excuse their mentioning, that they expected a relation, to pass some days with them, who would want the spare apartment.

The Baronet, however displeased, humourously answered that their relation was mightily welcome to pass his days with them, provided he would be so kind as to go to the neighbouring public-house to take his dreams: but Juliet, much hurt, though with an air of dignity that made her hosts look more abashed than herself, desired that she might not incommode the family; and entreated Sir Jaspar to convey her to the nearest town.

Sir Jaspar, rather to confound than to gratify the farmer, flung down a guinea, which the man vainly sought to decline; and then led the way to the carriage; at the door of which, stopping, he said, with an arch smile, that he was not yet superannuated enough to take place of a fair female; and desired that Mrs. Betty would get in first.

Shocked as Juliet felt to find herself thus suspiciously situated, the affront was soon absorbed in the dread of greater evil; in the affright of pursuit, and the dismay of being exposed to improper pecuniary obligations.

Not knowing the country, and not heeding the way that she went, she concluded that they were driving to some neighbouring village, in search of a new lodging; till she perceived that the carriage, which was drawn by four horses, was laboriously mounting a steep acclivity.

Looking then around her, she found herself upon a vast plain; nor house, nor human being, nor tree, nor cattle within view.

Surprised, "Where are we?" she cried, "Sir Jaspar? and whither are we going?"

To a quick meeting with his valet, he answered, by a difficult road, rarely passed, because out of the common track.

They then quietly proceeded; Juliet, wrapt up in her own fears and affairs, making no comment upon the looks of enjoyment, and contented taciturnity of her companion; till the groom, riding up to the window, said that the horses could go no further.

Sir Jaspar ordered them a feed; and enquired of Juliet whether she would chuse, while they took a little rest, to mount on foot to the summit of the ascent, and examine whether any horsemen were yet within sight.

Glad to breathe a few minutes alone, she alighted and walked forward; though slowly, and with eyes bent upon the turf; till she was struck by the appearance of a wide ditch between a circular double bank; and perceived that she was approaching the scattered remains of some ancient building, vast, irregular, strange, and in ruins.

Excited by sympathy in what seemed lonely and undone, rather than by curiosity, she now went on more willingly, though not less sadly; till she arrived at a stupendous assemblage of enormous stones, of which the magnitude demanded ocular demonstration to be entitled to credibility. Yet, though each of them, taken separately, might seem, from its astonishing height and breadth, there, like some rock, to have been placed from "the beginning of things;"* and though not even the rudest sculpture denoted any vestige of human art, still the whole was clearly no phenomenon of nature. The form, that might still be traced, of an antique structure, was evidently circular and artificial; and here and there, supported by gigantic posts, or pillars, immense slabs of flat stone were raised horizontally, that could only by manual art and labour have been elevated to such a height. Many were fallen; many, with grim menace, looked nodding; but many, still sustaining their upright direction, were so ponderous that they appeared to have resisted all the wars of the elements, in this high and bleak situation, for ages.

Struck with solemn wonder, Juliet for some time wandered amidst these massy ruins, grand and awful, though terrific rather than attractive. Mounting, then, upon a fragment of the pile, she saw that the view all around was in perfect local harmony with the wild edifice, or rather remains of an edifice, into which she had pierced. She discerned, to a vast extent, a boundless plain, that, like the ocean, seemed to have no term but the horizon; but which, also like the ocean, looked as desert as it was unlimited. Here and there flew a bustard, or a wheat-ear;* all else seemed unpeopled air, and uncultivated waste.

In a state of mind so utterly deplorable as that of Juliet, this grand, uncouth monument of ancient days had a certain sad, indefinable attraction, more congenial to her distress, than all the polish, taste, and delicacy of modern skill. The beauties of

Wilton seemed appendages of luxury, as well as of refinement; and appeared to require not only sentiment, but happiness for their complete enjoyment: while the nearly savage, however wonderful work of antiquity, in which she was now rambling; placed in this abandoned spot, far from the intercourse, or even view of mankind, with no prospect but of heath and sky; blunted, for the moment, her sensibility, by removing her wide from all the objects with which it was in contact; and insensibly calmed her spirits; though not by dissipating her reverie. Here, on the contrary, was room for "meditation even to madness;"* nothing distracted the sight, nothing broke in upon attention, nor varied the ideas. Thought, uninterrupted and uncontrouled, was master of the mind.

Here, in deep and melancholy rumination, she remained, till she was joined by the Baronet; who toiled after his fair charge with an eager will, though with slack and discourteous feet.

"Do you divine, my beauteous Wanderer," he cried, "what part of the globe you now brighten? Have you developed my stratagem to surprize you by a view of what, perhaps, you thought impossible, something curious, and worthy of attention, though more antique than myself?"

Juliet tried, but vainly, to make a civil speech; and Sir Jaspar, after having vainly awaited it, went on.

"You picture yourself, perhaps, in the original temple of Gog and Magog?* for what less than giants could have heaved stones such as these? but 'tis not so; and you, who are pious, must view this spot, with bended knees and new ideas. Dart, then, around, the 'liquid lustre of those eyes,—so brightly mutable, so sweetly wild!'†*—and behold in each stony spectre, now staring you in the face, a petrified old Druid! for learn, fair fugitive, you ramble now within the holy precincts of that rude wonder of other days, and disgrace of modern geometry, Stonehenge."

In almost any other frame of mind, Juliet, from various descriptions, joined to the vicinity of Salisbury, would not have required any nomenclator to have told her where she was: but she could now make no reflections, save upon her own misery;

† Mason's Lady Coventry.

and no combinations, that were not relative to her own dangers.

Sir Jaspar apologized that he had not more roughly handled the farmer and his wife, for their inhospitality; and frankly owned that it was not from the milkiness of his nature that he had been so docile, but from an ardent eagerness to visit Stonehenge with so fair a companion.

Juliet, alarmed, demanded whether he had not taken the route by which they were to meet his valet?

"I have all my life," continued he, "fostered, as the wish next my heart, the idea of being the object of some marvellous adventure: but fortune, more deaf, if possible, than blind! has hitherto famished all my elevated desires, by keeping me to the strict regimen of mere common life. Nevertheless, to die like a brute, without leaving behind me one staring anecdote, to be recounted by my successors to my little nephews and nieces;—no! I cannot resolve upon so hum-drum an exit. Late, therefore, last night, I counselled with my tiny friends; and the rogues told me that those whom adventures would not seek, must seek adventures. They then suggested to me, that to visit some romantic spot, far removed from all living ken, on a vast unfrequented plain; where no leering eye, with deriding scrutiny, no envious ear, with prepared impertinence, could peep, or overhear;—where not even a bird could find a twig for the sole of his paw;—there to encounter a lovely nymph; to dally with her in dulcet discourse; to feast upon the sweet notes of her melodious voice;—while obedient fays, and sprightly elves, should accoutre some chosen fragment with offerings appropriate to the place and the occasion—"

One of his grooms, here, demanded of him a private audience.

He retired to some distance, and the heart-oppressed Juliet relieved her struggling feelings by weeping without controul.

While pondering upon her precarious destiny, she perceived, through an opening between two large stones, that Sir Jaspar had placed himself upon an eminence, where, apparently, by his gestures, he was engaged in an animated discourse.

She concluded that the valet de chambre was arrived from the inn; but, soon afterwards, she was struck with motions so extraordinary, and by an appearance of a vivacity so extravagant, that she almost feared the imagination of the Baronet had played him false, and was superseding his reason. She arose, and softly approaching, endeavoured to discover with whom he was conversing; but could discern no one, and was the more alarmed; though the nearer she advanced, the less he seemed to be an object of pity; his countenance being as bright with glee, as his hands and arms were busy with action.

After some time, she caught his eye; when, ceasing all gesticulation, he kissed his hand, with a motion that invited her approach; and, gallantly resigning his seat, begged her permission to take one by her side.

He was all smiling good humour; and his features, in defiance of his age, expressed the most playful archness. "It is not," he cried, "for nothing, permit me to assure you, that I have prowled over this druidical spot; for though the Druids have not been so debonnaire as to reanimate themselves to address me, they have suffered a flat surface of their petrifaction to be covered over with a whole army of my little frequenters; who have dragged thither a parcel, and the Lord knows what besides, that they have displayed, as you see, full before me; after which, with their usual familiarity, up they have been mounting to my shoulders, my throat, my ears, and my wig; and lolling all about me, in mockery of my remonstrances; saying, Harkee, old Sir!—for they use very little ceremony with me;—didst thou really fancy we would suffer the loveliest lily of the valley to droop without any gentle shade, under the blazing glare of this full light, while thy aukward clown of a valet trots to the inn for her bonnet? or let her wait his plodding return, for what other drapery her fair form may require? or permit her to be famished in the open air, whilst thou art hopping and hobbling, and hobbling and hopping, about these ruins, which thou art so fast ossifying to resemble? No, old Sir! look what our wands have brought hither for her! look!—but touch nothing for thy life! her own lily hands alone must develop our fairy gifts."

Juliet, who, already, had observed, upon the nearest flat stone, a large band-box, and a square new trunk, placed as supporters to an elegant Japan basket, in which were arranged various refreshments; could not, however disconcerted by attentions that she knew not how to acknowledge, prevail upon herself to damp the exaltation of his spirits, by resisting his entreaty that she would herself lift up the lid of the trunk and open the band-box.

The first of these machines presented to her sight a complete small assortment of the finest linen; the second contained a white chip bonnet of the most beautiful texture.

This last excited a transient feeling of pleasure, in offering some shade for her face, now exposed to every eye. She looked at it, wistfully, a few minutes, anticipating its umbrageous succour; yet irresolute, and fearing to give encouragement to the too evident admiration of the Baronet. Her deliberation, nevertheless, seconded by her wishes, was in his favour. She passed over, in her mind, that he knew her origin, and high natural, however disputed expectations; and that, with all his gallantry, he was not only aged and sickly, but a gentleman in manners and sentiments, as much as in birth and rank of life. He could not mean her dishonour; and to shew, since thus cast into his hands, and loaded with obligations of long standing, as well as recent, a voluntary confidence in his character and intentions, might, happily, from mingling a sense of honour with a sense of shame, turn aside what was wrong in his regard, and give pride and pleasure to a nobler attachment, that might fix him her solid and disinterested friend for life.

Decided by this view of things, she thankfully consented to receive his offerings, upon condition that he would permit her to consider him as the banker of Lord Melbury and of Lady Aurora Granville.

Enchanted by her acceptance, and enraptured by its manner, the first sensation of the melted Baronet was to cast himself at her feet: but the movement was checked by certain aches and pains; while the necessity of picking up one of his crutches, which, in his transport, had fallen from his hands, mournfully called him back from his gallantry to his infirmities.

At this moment, an "Ah ha! here's the Demoiselle!—Here she is, faith!" suddenly presented before them Riley, mounted upon a fragment of the pile, to take a view around him.

Starting, and in dread of some new horrour, Juliet looked at him aghast; while, clapping his hands, and turbently* approaching her, he exclaimed, "Yes! here she is, *in propria persona!* I was afraid that she had slipped through our fingers again! Monsieur *le cher Epoux** will have a pretty tight job of it to get her into conjugal trammels! he will, faith!"

To the other, and yet more horrible sensations of Juliet, this speech added a depth of shame nearly overwhelming, from the implied obloquy hanging upon the character of a wife eloping from her husband.

Presently, however, all within was changed; re-invigourated, new strung! and joy, irresistibly, beamed from her eyes, and hope glowed upon her cheeks, as Riley related that, before he had left the inn upon the road, he had himself seen the new Mounseer, with poor Surly, who had been seized as an accomplice, packed off together for the sea-coast, whence they were both, with all speed, to be embarked for their own dear country.

The Baronet waved his hand, in act of congratulation to Juliet, but forbore speaking; and Riley went on.

"They made confounded wry faces, and grimaces, both of them. I never saw a grimmer couple! They amused me mightily; they did, faith! But I can't compliment you, Demoiselle, upon your choice of a loving partner. He has as hang-dog a physiognomy as a Bow Street prowler* might wish to light upon on a summer's day. A most fiend-like aspect, I confess. I don't well make out what you took to him for, Demoiselle? His Cupid's arrows must have been handsomely tipt with gold, to blind you to all that brass of his brow and his port."

Sir Jaspar, distressed for Juliet, and much annoyed by this interruption, however happy in the intelligence to which it was the vehicle, enquired what chance had brought Mr. Riley to Stonehenge?

The chance, he answered, that generally ruled his actions, namely, his own will and pleasure. He had found out, in his prowls about Salisbury, that Sir Jaspar was to be followed to Stonehenge by a dainty repast; and, deeming his news well worth a bumper to the loving sea-voyagers, he had borrowed a horse of one of Master Baronet's grooms, to take his share in the feast.

The Baronet, at this hint, instantly, and with scrupulous politeness, did the honours of his stores; though he was ready to gnash his teeth with ire, at so mundane an appropriation of his fairy purposes.

"What a rare hand you are, Demoiselle," cried Riley, "at hocus pocus work!* Who the deuce, with that Hebe* face of yours, could have thought of your being a married woman! Why, when I saw you at that old Bang'em's concert,* at Brighthelmstone, I should have taken you for a boarding-school Miss. But you metamorphose yourself about so, one does not know which way to look for you. Ovid was a mere fool to you. His nymphs, turned into trees, and rivers, and flowers, and beasts, and fishes, make such a staring chaos of lies, that one reads them without a ray of reference to truth; like the tales of the Genii, or of old Mother Goose.* He makes such a comical hodge podge of animal, vegetable, and mineral choppings and changes, that we should shout over them, as our brats do at a puppet-shew, when old Nick teaches punchinello the devil's dance down to hell; or pummels his wife to a mummy;* if it were not for the sly rogue's tickling one's ears so cajolingly with the jingle of metre. But Demoiselle, here, scorns all that namby pamby work."

Sir Jaspar tried vainly to call him to order; the embarrassment of Juliet operated but as a stimulus to his caustic humour.

"I have met with nothing like her, Master Baronet," he continued, "all the globe over. Neither juggler nor conjuror is a match for her. She can make herself as ugly as a witch, and as handsome as an angel. She'll answer what one only murmurs in a whisper; and she won't hear a word, when one bawls as loud as a speaking-trumpet. Now she turns herself into a vagrant, not worth sixpence; and now, into a fine player and singer that ravishes all ears, and might make, if it suited her fancy, a thousand pounds at her benefit: and now, again, as you see, you can't tell whether she's a house-maid, or a country girl! yet a devilish fine creature, faith! as fine a creature as ever I beheld,—when she's in that humour! Look but what a beautiful head of hair she's displaying to us now! It becomes her mightily. But I won't swear that she does not change it, in a minute or two, for a skull-cap!* She's a droll girl, faith! I like her prodigiously!"

Utterly disconcerted, Juliet, expressively bowing to the Baronet, lifted up the lid of the band-box, and, encircling her head in his bonnet, begged his permission to re-seat herself in the chaise.

Charmed with the prospect of another tête à tête, Sir Jaspar, with alacrity, accompanied her to the carriage; leaving Riley to enjoy, at his leisure, the cynical satisfaction, of having worried a timid deer from the field.

Still, however, Juliet, while uncertain whether the embarkation might not be eluded, desired to adhere to her plan of privacy and obscurity; and the Baronet would not struggle against a resolution from which he hoped to reap the fruit of lengthened intercourse. Pleased and willingly, therefore, he told his postilion to drive across the plain to * * *, whence they proceeded post to Blandford.

Great was the relief afforded to the feelings of Juliet, by a removal so expeditious from the immediate vicinity of the scene of her sufferings; but she considered it, at the same time, to be a circumstance to obviate all necessity, and, consequently, all propriety of further attendance from the Baronet: here, therefore, to his utter dismay, with firmness, though with the gentlest acknowledgements, she begged that they might separate.

Cruelly disappointed, Sir Jaspar warmly remonstrated against the danger of her being left alone; but the possible hazards which might be annexed to acting right, could not deter her from the certain evil of acting wrong. Her greatest repugnance was that of being again forced to accept pecuniary aid; yet that, which, however disagreeable, might be refunded, was at least preferable to the increase and continuance of obligations, which, besides their perilous tendency, could never be repaid. Already, upon opening the band-box, she had seen a well furnished purse; and though her first movement had prompted its rejection, the decision of necessity was that of acceptance.

When Sir Jaspar found it utterly impossible to prevail with his fair companion still to bear that title, he expostulated against leaving her, at least, in a public town; and she was not sorry to accept his offer of conveying her to some neighbouring village.

It was still day-light, when they arrived within the picturesque view of a villa, which Juliet, upon enquiry, heard was Milton-abbey. She soon discovered, that the scheme of the Baronet, to lengthen their sojourn with each other, was to carry her to see the house: but this she absolutely refused; and her seriousness compelled him to drive to a neighbouring cottage; where she had the good fortune to meet with a clean elderly woman, who was able to accommodate her with a small chamber.

Here, not without sincere concern, she saw the reluctance, even to sadness, with which her old admirer felt himself forced to leave his too lovely young friend: and what she owed to him was so important, so momentous, that she parted from him, herself, with real regret, and with expressions of the most lively esteem and regard.

CHAPTER LXXXIV

RESTLESS, again, was the night of Juliet; bewildered with varying visions of hope, of despair, of bliss, of horrour; now presenting a fair prospect that opened sweetly to her best affections; now shewing every blossom blighted, by a dark, overwhelming storm.

To engage the good will of her new hostess, she bestowed upon her nearly every thing that she had worn upon entering the cottage. What she had been seen and discovered in, could no longer serve any purpose of concealment; and all disguise was disgusting to her, if not induced by the most imperious necessity. She clothed herself, therefore, from the fairy stores of her munificent old sylph; with whom her debts were so multiplied and so considerable, that she meant, at all events, to call upon her family for their disbursement.

The quietness of this residence, induced her to propose remaining here: and her new hostess, who was one of the many who, where interest preaches passiveness, make it a point not to be troublesome, consented, without objection or enquiry.

Hence, again, she wrote to Gabriella, from whom she languished for intelligence.

In this perfect retirement, she passed her time in deep-rumination; her thoughts for ever hovering around the Bishop, upon whose fate her own invariably depended.

Her little apartment was close and hot; unshaded by blinds, unsheltered by shutters; she went forth, therefore, early every morning, to enjoy fresh air in the cool of a neighbouring wood, which, once having entered, she knew not how to quit. Solitude there, had not the character of seclusion; it bore not, as in her room, the air of banishment, if not of imprisonment; and the beautiful prospects around her, though her sole, were a never-failing source of recreation.

She permitted not, however, her love of the country to beguile her into danger by the love of variety; she wandered not far from her new habitation, in the vicinity of Milton-abbey; of which she never lost sight from distance, though frequently from intervening hills and trees.

But no answer arrived from Gabriella; and, in a few days, her own letter was returned, with a line written by the post-man upon the cover, to say, No.—Frith-street, Soho, was empty.

New sorrow, now, and fearful distress assailed every feeling of Juliet: What could have occasioned this sudden measure? Whither was Gabriella gone? Might it be happiness?—or was it some new evil that had caused this change of abode? The letter sent to Salisbury had never been claimed; nor did Juliet dare demand it: but Gabriella might, perhaps, have written her new plan by the address sent from the farm-house.

It was now that she blessed the munificent Sir Jaspar, to whose purse she had immediate recourse for sending a man and horse to the cottage; with written instructions to enquire for a letter, concerning which she had left directions with the good old cottager.

While, to wear away the hours devoted to anxious waiting, she wandered, as usual, in the view of Milton-abbey, from a rich valley, bounded by rising hills, whose circling slopes bore the form of undulating waves, she perceived, from a small distance, a horseman gallopping towards her cottage.

It could not already be her messenger. She felt uneasy, and, gliding to the brow of an eminence, sat down upon the turf, as much as possible out of sight.

In a short time, she heard the quick pacing step of a man in haste. She tried to place herself still more obscurely; but, by moving, caught the eye of the object she meant to avoid. He approached her rapidly, but when near enough to distinguish her, abruptly stopt, as if to recollect himself; and Juliet, at the same moment that she was herself discerned, recognized Harleigh.

With difficulty restraining an exclamation, from surprize and painful emotion, she looked round to discover if it would be possible to elude him; but she could only walk towards Milton-abbey, in full view herself from that noble seat; or immediately face him by returning to her home. She stood still, therefore, though bending her eyes to the ground; hurt and offended that, at such a juncture, Harleigh could break into her retreat; and grieved yet more deeply, that Harleigh could excite in her even transitory displeasure.

Harleigh stept forward, but his voice, husky and nervous, so inarticulately pronounced something relative to a packet and a work-bag, that Juliet, losing her displeasure in a sudden hope of hearing some news of her property, raised her head, with a look that demanded an explanation.

Still he strove in vain for sufficient calmness to speak distinctly; yet his answer gave Juliet to understand, that he had conveyed her packet and work-bag to the cottage which he had been told she inhabited.

"And where, Sir," cried Juliet, surprized into vivacity and pleasure at this unexpected hearing, "how, and where have they been recovered?"

Harleigh now blushed himself, at the blushes which he knew he must raise in her cheeks, as he replied, that the packet and the work-bag which he had brought, had been dropt in his room at the inn.

Crimson is pale to the depth of red with which shame and confusion dyed her face; while Harleigh, recovering his voice, sought to relieve her embarrassment, by more rapidly continuing his discourse.

"I should sooner have endeavoured to deliver these articles, but that I knew not, till yesterday, that they had fallen to my care. I had left the inn, to follow, and seek Sir Jaspar

Herrington; but having various papers and letters in my room, that I had not had time to collect, I obtained leave to take away the key with me, of the landlady, to whom I was well known,—for there, or in that neighbourhood, an irresistible interest has kept me, from the time that, through my groom, I had heard ... who had been seen ... at Bagshot ... entering the Salisbury stage!—Yesterday, when I returned to the inn, I first perceived these parcels."—

He stopt; but Juliet could not speak, could not look up; could pronounce no apology, nor enter into any explanation.

"Sir Jaspar Herrington," he continued, "whom I have just left, is still at Salisbury; but setting out for town. From him I learnt your immediate direction; but not knowing what might be the value of the packets, nor,—" He hesitated a moment, and then, with a sigh, added, "nor how to direct them! I determined upon venturing to deliver them myself."

The tingling cheeks of Juliet, at the inference of the words "nor how to direct them," seemed on fire; but she was totally silent.

"I have carefully sealed them," he resumed, "and I have delivered them to the woman of the cottage, for the young lady who at present sleeps there; and, hearing that the young lady was walking in the neighbourhood, I ventured to follow, with this intelligence."

"You are very good, Sir," Juliet strove to answer; but her lips were parched, and no words could find their way.

This excess of timidity brought back the courage of Harleigh, who, advancing a step or two, said, "You will not be angry that Sir Jaspar, moved by my uncontrollable urgency, has had the charity to reveal to me some particulars ..."

"Oh! make way for me to pass, Mr. Harleigh!" now interrupted Juliet, forcing her voice, and striving to force a passage.

"Did you wish, then," said Harleigh, in a tone the most melancholy, "could you wish that I should still languish in harrowing suspense? or burst with ignorance?"

"Oh no!" cried she, raising her eyes, which glistened with tears, "no! If the mystery that so long has hung about me, by occupying your ..." She sought a word, and then continued; "your imagination, ... impedes the oblivion that ought to bury me and my misfortunes from further thought, then, indeed, I ought to be thankful to Sir Jaspar,—and I am thankful that he has let you know, . . . that he has informed you . . ."

She could not finish the sentence.

"Yes!" cried Harleigh with energy, "I have heard the dreadful history of your wrongs! of the violences by which you have suffered, of the inhuman attempts upon your liberty, your safety, your honour!—But since you have thus happily ——"

"Mr. Harleigh," cried Juliet, struggling to recover her presence of mind, "I need no longer, I trust, now, beg your absence! All I can have to say you must, now, understand . . . anticipate . . . acknowledge . . . since you are aware . . ."

"Ah!" cried Harleigh, in a tone not quite free from reproach;—"had you but, from the beginning, condescended to inform me of your situation! a situation so impossible to divine! so replete with horrour, with injury, with unheard of suffering,—had you, from the first, instead of avoiding, flying me, deigned to treat me with some trust——"

"Mr. Harleigh," said Juliet, with eagerness, "whatever may be your surprize that such should be my situation, . . . my fate, . . . you can, at least, require, now, no explanation why I have fled you!"

The word why, vibrated instantly to the heart of Harleigh, where it condolingly said: It was duty, then, not averseness, not indifference, that urged that flight! she had not fled, had she not deemed herself engaged!—Juliet, who had hastily uttered the why in the solicitude of self-vindication, shewed, by a change of complexion, the moment that it had passed her lips, that she felt the possible inference of which it was susceptible, and dropt her eyes; fearful to risk discovering the consciousness that they might indicate.

Harleigh, however, now brightened, glowed with revived sensations: "Ah! be not," he cried, "be not the victim to your scruples! let not your too delicate fears of doing wrong by others, urge you to inflict wrong, irreparable wrong, upon yourself! Your real dangers are past; none now remain but from a fancied,—pardon, pardon me!—a fancied refinement, unfounded in reason, or in right! Suffer, therefore—"

"Hold, Sir, hold!—we must not even talk upon this subject: —nor, at this moment, upon any other!—"

Her brow shewed rising displeasure; but Harleigh was intractable. "Pronounce not," he cried, "an interdiction! I make no claim, no plea, no condition. I will speak wholly as an impartial man;—and have you not condescended to tell me, that as a friend, if to that title,—so limited, yet so honourable,— I would confine myself,—you would not disdain to consult with me? As such, I am now here. I feel, I respect, I revere the delicacy of all your ideas, the perfection of your conduct! I will put, therefore, aside, all that relates not simply to yourself, and to your position; I will speak to you, for the moment, and in his absence,—as—as Lord Melbury!—as your brother!—"

An involuntary smile here unbent the knitting brow of Juliet, who could not feel offended, or sorry, that Sir Jaspar had revealed the history of her birth.

She desired, nevertheless, to pass, refusing every species of discussion.

"If you will not answer, will not speak," cried Harleigh, still obstructing her way, "fear not, at least, to hear! Are you not at liberty? Is not your persecutor gone?—Can he ever return?"

"Gone?" repeated Juliet.

"I have myself seen him embark! I rode after his chaise, I pursued it to the sea-coast, I saw him under sail."

Juliet, with uplifted eyes, clasped her hands, from an emotion of ungovernable joy; which a thousand blushes betrayed her vain struggles to suppress.

Harleigh observed not this unmoved: "Ah, Madam!" he cried, "since, thus critically, you have escaped;—since, thus happily, you are released;—since no church ritual has ever sanctioned the sacrilegious violence—"

"Spare all ineffectual controversy!" cried Juliet, assuming an air and tone of composure, with which her quick heaving bosom was ill in harmony; "I can neither talk nor listen upon this subject. You know, now, my story: dread and atrocious as is my connection, my faith to it must be unbroken, till I have seen the Bishop! and till the iniquity of my chains may be proved, and my restoration to my violated freedom may be legalized. Do not look so shocked; so angry, must I say?—Remember, that a point of conscience can be settled only internally! I will speak, therefore, but one word more; and I must hear no reply: little as I feel to belong to the person in question, I cannot consider myself to be my own! 'Tis a tie which, whether or not it binds me to him, excludes me, while thus circumstanced, from all others!—This, Sir, is my last word!—Adieu!"

Harleigh, though looking nearly petrified, still stood before her. "You fly us, then," he cried, resentfully, though mournfully, "both alike? You put us upon a par?—"

"No!" answered Juliet, hastily, "him I fly because I hate;—You——"

The deep scarlet which mounted into her whole face finished the sentence; in defiance of a sudden and abrupt breaking off, that meant and hoped to snatch the unguarded phrase from comprehension.

But Harleigh felt its fullest contrast; his hopes, his wishes, his whole soul completed it by You, because I love!—Not that he could persuade himself that Juliet would have used those words; he knew the contrary; knew that she would sooner thus situated expire; but such, he felt, was the impulse of her thoughts; such the consciousness that broke off her speech.

He durst not venture at any acknowledgement; but, once appeased in his doubts, and satisfied in his feelings, he respected her opinions, and, yielding to her increased, yet speechless eagerness to be gone, he silently, but with eyes of expressive tenderness, ceased to obstruct her passage.

Utterly confounded herself, at the half-pronounced thought, thus inadvertently surprised from her, and thus palpably seized and interpreted, she strove to devize some term that might obviate dangerous consequences; but she felt her cheeks so hot, so cold, and again so hot, that she durst not trust her face to his observation; and, accepting the opening which he made for her, she was returning to her cottage, tortured,—and yet soothed,—by indescribable emotions; when an energetic cry of "Ellis!—Harleigh!—Ellis!" made her raise her eyes to the adjacent hill, and perceive Elinor.

CHAPTER LXXXV

WITH arms extended, and a commanding air, Elinor, having made signs to the dismayed Harleigh not to move, awaited, where she stood, the terrified, but obedient Juliet.

"Avoid me not!" she cried, "Ellis! why should you avoid me? I have given you back your plighted word; and the pride of Harleigh has saved him from all bonds. Why, then, should you fly?"

Juliet attempted not to make any answer.

"The conference, the last conference," continued Elinor, "which so ardently I have demanded, is still unaccorded. Repeatedly I could have surprized it, singly, from Harleigh; but—"

She stopt, coloured, looked indignant, yet ashamed, and then haughtily went on: "Imagine not my courage tarnished by cowardly apprehensions of misinterpretation,—suspicion,—censoriousness; ... No! let the world sneer at its pleasure! Its spleen will never keep pace with my contempt. But Harleigh!—I brave not the censure of Harleigh! even though prepared, and resolved, to quit him for evermore! And, with ideas punctilious such as his of feminine delicacy, he might blame, perhaps,—should I seek him alone—"

She blushed more deeply, and, with extreme agitation, added, "Harleigh, when we shall meet no more, will always honourably say, Her passion for me might be tinctured with madness, but its purity was without alloy!"

She now turned away, to hide a starting tear; but, soon resuming her usually lively manner, said, "I have traced you, at last, together; and by means of our caustick, bilious fellow-traveller, Riley; whom I encountered by accident; and who runs, snarling, yet curious, after his fellow-creatures, working at making himself enemies, as if enmity were a pleasing, or lucrative profession! From him I learnt, that he had just seen you,—and together!—near Salisbury. I discovered you, Ellis, two days ago; but Harleigh, though I have been roving some time in your vicinity, only this moment."

A sudden shriek now broke from her, and Juliet, affrighted and looking around, perceived Harleigh pacing hastily away.

The shriek reached him, and he stopt.

"Fly, fly, to him," she cried, "Ellis; assure him, I have no present personal project; none! I solemnly promise, none! But I have an opinion to gather from him, of which my ignorance burns, devours me, and will not let me rest, alive nor dead!"

Juliet, distressed, irresolute, ventured not to move.

"'Tis his duty," continued Elinor, "after his solemn declaration, to initiate me into his motives for believing in a future state. I have been distracting my burthened senses over theological works; but my head is in no condition to comprehend them. They treat, also, of belief in a future state, as of a thing not to be proved, but to be taken for granted. Let him penetrate me with his own notions; or frankly acknowledge their insufficiency. But let him mark that they are indeed his own! Let them be neither fanatical, illusory, nor traditional."

Juliet was compelled to obey; but while she was repeating her message, Elinor descended the hill, and they all met at its foot.

"Harleigh," she cried, "fear me not! Do not imagine I shall again go over the same ground;—at least, not with the monotonous stupidity of again going over it in the same manner. Yet believe not my resolution to be shaken! But I have some doubts, relative to your own principles and opinions, of which I demand a solution."

She then seated herself upon the turf, and made Harleigh seat himself before her, while Juliet remained by her side.

"Can you feign, Harleigh? Can you endure to act a part, in defiance of your nobler nature, merely to prolong my detested life? Do you join in the popular cry against suicide, merely to arrest my impatient hand? If not, initiate me, I beseech, in the series of pretended reasoning, by which honour, honesty, and understanding such as yours, have been duped into bigotry? How is it, explain! that you can have been worked upon to believe in an existence after death? Ah, Harleigh! could you, indeed, give so sublime a resting-place to my labouring ideas!—I would consent to enter the ecclesiastical court myself, to sing the recantation* of what you deem my errours. And then, Albert, I might learn,—with all my wretchedness!—to bear to live,—for then, I might seek and foster some hope in dying!"

"Dear Elinor!" cried Harleigh, gently, almost tenderly, "let me send for some divine!"

"How conscious is this retreat," she cried, "of the weakness of your cause! Ah! why thus try to bewilder a poor forlorn traveller, who is dropping with fatigue upon her road? and to fret and goad her on, when the poor tortured wretch languishes to give up the journey altogether? Why not rather, more generously, more like yourself, aid her to attain repose? to open her burning veins, and bid her pent up blood flow freely to her relief? or kindly point the steel to her agonized heart, whose last sigh would be ecstacy if it owed its liberation to your pitying hand! Oh Harleigh! what vain prejudice, what superstitious sophistry, robs me of the only solace that could soothe my parting breath?"

"What is it Elinor means?" cried Harleigh, alarmed, yet affecting to speak lightly: "Has she no compunction for the labour she causes my blood in thus perpetually accelerating its circulation."

"Pardon me, dear Harleigh, I have inadvertently run from my purpose to my wishes. To the point, then. Make me, if it be possible, conceive how your reason has thus been played upon, and your discernment been set asleep. I have studied this matter abroad, with the ablest casuists I have met with; and though I may not retain, or detail their reasoning, well enough to make a convert of any other, they have fixed for ever in my own mind, a conviction that death and annihilation are one. Why do you knit your brow?—And see how Ellis starts!—And why do you both look at me as if I were mad? Mad? because I would rather crush misery than endure it? Mad? because I would rather, at my own time, die the death of reason, than by compulsion, and when least disposed, that of nature? Of reason, that appreciates life but by enjoyment; not of nature, that would make misery linger, till malady or old age dissolve the worn out fabric. To indulge our little miserable fears and propensities, we give flattering epithets to all our meannesses; for what is endurance of worldly pain and affliction but folly? what patience, but insipidity? what suffering, but cowardice?

Oh suicide! triumphant antidote to woe! straight forward, unerring route to rest, to repose! I call upon thy aid! I invoke—"

"Repose?—rest?" interrupted Harleigh, "how earned? By deserting our duties? By quitting our posts? By forsaking and wounding all by whom we are cherished?"

"One word, Harleigh, answers all that: Did we ask for our being? Why was it given us if doomed to be wretched? To whom are we accountable for renouncing a donation, made without our consent or knowledge? O, if ever that wretched thing called life has a noble moment, it must surely be that of its voluntary sacrifice! lopping off, at a blow, that hydra-headed monster of evil upon evil, called time; bounding over the imps of superstition; dancing upon the pangs of disease; and boldly, hardily mocking the senseless legends, that would frighten us with eternity!—Eternity? to poor, little, frail, finite beings like us! Oh Albert! worldly considerations, monkish inventions, and superstitious reveries set apart;—reason called forth, truth developed, probabilities canvassed,—say! is it not clear that death is an end to all? an abyss eternal? a conclusion? Nature comes but for succession; though the pride of man would give her resurrection. Mouldering all together we go, to form new earth for burying our successors."

"Horrible, Elinor, most horrible! yet if, indeed, it is your opinion that you are doomed to sink to nothing; if your soul, in the full tide of its energies, and in the pride of intellect, seems to you a mere appendant to the body; if you believe it to be of the same fragile materials; how can you wish to shorten the so short period of consciousness? to abridge the so brief moment of sensibility? Is it not always time enough to think, feel, see, hear,—love and be loved no more?"

"Yes! 'tis always too soon to lose happiness; but misery,—ah Albert!—why should misery, when it can so easily be stilled, be endured?"

"Stilled, Elinor?—What mean you? By annihilation?—How an infidel assumes fortitude to wish for death, is my constant astonishment! To believe in the eternal loss of all he holds, or knows, or feels; to be persuaded that 'this sensible, warm being,' will 'melt, thaw, and resolve itself into a dew,'*—and to believe that there all ends! Surely every species of existence must be preferable to such an expectation from its cessation! Dust!—literal dust!—Food for worms!—to be trod upon;—crushed;—dug up;—battered down;—is that our termination? That,—and nothing more?"

"'Tis shocking, Albert, no doubt; shocking and disgusting. Yet why disguise the fact? Reason, philosophy, analogy, all prove our materialism. Even common observation, even daily experience, in viewing our natural end, where neither sickness nor accident impede, nor shorten its progress, prove it by superannuation; shew clearly that mind and body, when they die the long death of nature, gradually decline together."

"Were that double decay constant, Elinor, in its junction, you might thence, perhaps, draw that inference; but does not the body wither as completely by decay, in the very prime, and pride, and bloom of youth, where the death is consumption, as in the most worn-out decrepitude of age? Yet the capacity is often, even to the last minute, as perfect as in the vigour of health. Were all within, as well as all without, material, would not the blight to one involve, uniformly, the blight to the other? How often, too, does age, even the oldest, escape any previous decay of intellect! There are records extant, of those who, after attaining their hundredth year, have been capable of bearing testimony in trials; but are there any of those, who, at half that age, have preserved their external appearance? No. It is the body, therefore, not the soul, that, in a natural state, and free from the accelerations of accident, seems first to degenerate. The grace of symmetry, the charm of expression, may last with our existence, and delight to its latest date; but that which we understand exclusively, as personal perfection,—how soon is it over! Not only before the intellects are impaired, but even, and not rarely, before they are arrived at their full completion. Can mind, then, and body be but one and the same thing, when they neither flourish nor wither together?"

"Ah, Harleigh! is it not your willing mind, that here frames its sentiments from its exaltation? not your deeper understanding, that defines your future expectations from your rational belief?"

"No, Elinor; my belief in the immortality of the soul may be strengthened, but it is not framed by my wishes. Let me, however, ask you a question in return. Your disbelief of the immortality of the soul, is founded on your inability to have it, visually, or orally, demonstrated: Let me, then, ask, can the nature, use, and destination of the soul, however darkly hidden from our analysing powers, be more impervious to our limited foresight, than the narrower, yet equally, to us, invisible, destiny of our days to come upon earth? But does any one, therefore, from not knowing its purposes, disbelieve that his life may be lengthened? Yet which of us can divine what his fate will be from year to year? What his actions, from hour to hour? his thoughts, from moment to moment?"

"Oh Harleigh! how fatally is that true! how little did I foresee, when I so delighted in your society, that that very delight would but impel me to burn for the moment of bidding you an eternal farewell!"

Harleigh sighed; but with earnestness continued: "We conceive the soul to influence, if not to direct our whole construction, yet we have no sensible proof of its being in any part of it: how, then, shall we determine that to be destroyed or departed, which we have never known to be created? never seen to exist? O bow we down! for all is inexplicable! We can but say, the body is obvious in its perfection, and still obvious in its decay; the soul is always unsearchable! were we sure it were only our understanding, we might, perhaps, develop it; or only our feeling, we might catch it; but it is a something indefinable, of which the consciousness tells us not the qualities, nor the possession the attributes; and of which the end leaves no trace! We follow it not to its dissolution like the body; which, after what we call death, is still as evident, as when our conceptions of what is soul were yet lent to it: if the soul, then, be equally material, say, is it still there also? though as unseen and hidden as when breath and motion were yet perceptible?"

"Body and soul, Albert, come together with existence, and together are nullified by death."

"And are you, Elinor, aware whither such reasoning may lead? If the body instead of being the tenement of the soul, is but one and the same with it;—how are you certain, if they are not sundered by death, that they do not in death, though by means, and with effects to us unknown, still exist together? That with the body, whether animated or inert, the soul may not always be adherent? who shall assure you, who, at least, shall demonstrate, that if the soul be but a part of the body, it may not think, though no utterance can be given to its thoughts; and may not feel, though all expression is at an end, and motion is no more? Whither may such reasoning lead? to what strange suggestions may it not conduct us? to what vain fantasies, what useless horrours? May we not apprehend that the insects, the worms which are formed from the human frame, may partake of and retain human consciousness? May we not imagine those wretched reptiles, which creep from our remains, to be sensible of their fallen state, and tortured by their degradation? to resent, as well as seek to elude the ill usage, the blows, the oppressions to which they are exposed?—"

"Fie! Albert, fie!"

"Nay, what proof, if for proof you wait, have you to the contrary? Is it their writhing? their sensitive shrink from your touch? their agonizing efforts to save their miserable existence from your gripe?"

"Harleigh! Harleigh!"

"And this dust, Elinor, to which you settle that, finally, all will be mouldered or crumbled;—fear you not that its every particle may possess some sensitive quality? When we cease to speak, to move, to breathe, you assert the soul to be annihilated: But why? Is it only because you lose sight of its operations? In chemistry are there not sundry substances which, by certain processes, become invisible, and are sought in vain by the spectator; but which, by other processes, are again brought to view? And shall the chemist have this faculty to produce, and to withdraw, from our sight, and the Creator of All be denied any occult powers?"

"Nay, Albert, 'how can we reason but from what we know?'*—Will you compare a fact which experiment can prove, which reason may discuss, and which the senses may witness, with a bare possibility? a vague conjecture?"

"Is nothing, then, credible, Elinor, that is out of the province of demonstration? nothing probable, that surpasses our understanding?—nothing sacred that is beyond our view? Are we so perfect in our knowledge, even of what we behold, or possess, as to draw such presumptuous conclusions, of the self-sufficiency and omnipotence of our faculties, for judging what is every way out of our sight, or reach? Do we know one radical point of our existence, here, where 'we live, and move, and have our being?'* Do we comprehend, unequivocally, our immediate attributes and powers? Can we tell even how our hands obey our will? how our desires suffice to guide our feet from place to place? to roll our eyes from object to object? If all were clear, save the existence and the extinction of the soul, then, indeed, we might pronounce all faith, but in self-evidence, to be folly!"

"Faith! Harleigh, faith? the very word scents of monkish subtleties! 'Tis to faith, to that absurd idea of lulling to sleep our reason, of setting aside our senses, our observation, our knowledge; and giving our ignorant, unmeaning trust, and blind confidence to religious quacks; 'tis to that, precisely that, you owe what you term our infidelity; for 'tis that which has provoked the spirit of investigation, which has shewn us the pusillanimity and the imbecility of consigning the short period in which we possess our poor fleeting existence, to other men's uses, deliberations, schemes, fancies, and ordinances. For what else can you call submission to unproved assertions, and concurrence in unfounded belief?"

"And yet, this faith, Elinor, which, in religion, you renounce, despise, or defy, because in religion you would think, feel, and believe by demonstration alone, you insensibly admit in nearly all things else! Have you it not in morals? Does society exist but by faith? Does friendship,—I will not name what is so open to controversy as love,—but say! has friendship any other tie? has honour any other bond than faith? We have no proofs, no demonstrations of worth that can reach the regions of the heart: we judge but by effects; we believe but by analogies; we love, we esteem, we trust but by credulity, by faith! For where is the mathematician who can calculate what may be pronounced of the mind; from what is seen in the countenance, or uttered by speech? yet is any one therefore so wretched, as not to feel any social reliance beyond what he can mathematically demonstrate to be merited?"

"And to what but that, Albert, precisely that, do we owe being so perpetually duped and betrayed? to what but building upon false trust upon appearance, and not certainty?"

"Certainty, Elinor! Where, and in what is certainty to be found? If you disclaim belief in immortality upon faith, as insufficient to satisfy reason, what is the basis even of your disbelief? Is it not faith also? When you demand the proofs of immortality, let me demand, in return, what are your proofs of materialism? And, till you can bring to demonstration the operations of the soul while we live, presume not to decide upon its extinction when we die! Of the corporeal machine, on the contrary, speak at pleasure; you have before you all your documents for ratiocination and decision; but, life once over,—when you have placed the limbs, closed the eyes, arranged the form,—can you arrange the mind?—the soul?"

"Excite no doubts in me, Harleigh!—my creed is fixed."

"When sleep overtakes us," he continued, "and all, to the beholder, looks the picture of death, save that the breath still heaves the bosom;—what is it that guards entire, uninjured, the mind? the faculties? It is not our consciousness,—we have none! Where is the soul in that period? Gone it is not, for we are sensible to all that had preceded its suspension, the moment that we awake. Yet, in that state of periodical insensibility, what, but experience, could make those who view us believe that we could ever rise, speak, move, or think again? How inert is the body! How helpless, how useless, how incapable? Do we see who is near us? Do we hear who addresses us? Do we know when the most frightful crimes are committed by our sides? What, I demand, is our consciousness? We have not the most distant of any thing that passes around us: yet we open our eyes,—and all is known, all is familiar again. We hear, we see, we feel, we understand!"

"Yes; but in that sleep, Harleigh, that mere mechanical repose of the animal, we still breathe; we are capable, therefore, of being restored to all our sensibilities, by a single touch, by a single start; 'tis but a separation that parts us from ourselves, as absence parts us from our friends. We yet live,—we yet, therefore, may meet again."

"And why, when we live no longer, may we not also, Elinor, meet again?"

"Why?—Do you ask why?—Look round the old church-yards! See you not there the dispersion of our poor mouldered beings? Is not every bone the prey,—or the disgust,—of every animal? How, when scattered, commixed, broken, battered, how shall they ever again be collected, united, arranged, covered and coloured so as to appear regenerated?"

"But what, Elinor, is the fragility, or the dispersion of the body, to the solidity and the durability of the soul? Why are we to decide, that to see ourselves again, and again to view each other, such as we seem here, substance, or what we understand by it, is essential to our reunion hereafter? Do we not meet, act, talk, move, think with one another in our dreams? What is it which, then, embodies our ideas? which gives to our sight, in perfect form and likeness, those with whom we converse? which makes us conceive that we move, act, speak, and look, ourselves, with the same gesture, mien, and voice as when awake?"

"Dreams? pho!—they are but the nocturnal vagaries of the imagination."

"And what, Elinor, is imagination? You will not call it a part of your body?"

"No; but the blood which still circulates in our veins, Harleigh, gives imagination its power."

"But does the blood circulate in the veins of our parents? of our friends? of our acquaintances? and of strangers whom we equally meet? yet we see them all; we converse with them all; we utter our opinions; we listen to their answers. And how ably we sometimes argue! how characteristically those with whom we dispute reply! yet we do not imagine we guide them. We wait their opinions and decisions, in the same uncertainty and suspense, that we await them in our waking intercourse. We have the same fears of ill fortune; the same horrour of ill usage; the same ardour for success; the same feelings of sorrow, of joy, of hope, or of remorse, that animate or that torture us, in our daily occurrences. What new countries we visit! what strange sights we see! what delight, what anguish, what alarms, what pleasures, and what pains we experience! Yet in all this variety of incident, conversation, motion, feeling,—we seem, to those who look at us, but unintelligent and senseless, though still breathing clay."

"Ay; but after all those scenes, we awake, Albert, we awake! But when do we awake from death? Death, the same experience tells us, is sleep eternal!"

"But in that sleep, also, are there no dreams? Are you sure of that? If, in our common sleep, there still subsists an active principle, that feels, speaks, invents, and only by awaking finds that the mind alone, and not the body has been working;—how are you so sure that no such active principle subsists in that sleep which you call eternal? Who has told you what passes where experience is at an end? Who has talked to you of 'that bourne whence no traveller returns?'* With the cessation, indeed, of warmth; with the stillness of those pulses which beat from circulating blood, all seems to end; but seems it not also to end when we fall into apoplexies? when we faint away? when we appear to be drowned? or when, by any means, life is casually suspended? Yet when those arts, that skill, of which even the success teaches not the principle, even the process discovers not the secret resources, draw back, by means intelligible and visible, but through causes indefinable, the fleeting breath to its corporeal habitation; animation instantly returns, and the soul, with all its powers, revives!"

"Ay, there, there, Albert, is the very point! If the soul were distinct from the body, why should not those who are recovered from drowning, suffocation, or other apparent death, be able to give some account of what passed in those periods when they seemed to be no more? And who has done it? No one, Harleigh! not a single renovated being, has explained away the doubts to which those suspensions of animation give rise."

"And has any one explained, Elinor, why, though sometimes we have such wonders to relate of the scenes in which we have borne a part in our dreams,—we open our eyes, at other times, with no consciousness whatever, that we have any way existed from the moment of closing them? The wants of refreshment and recruit of our corporeal machine, we all feel, and know; those of that part which is intellectual,—who is able to calculate? What, except the powers, can be more distinct than the exercises of the mind and of the body? Yet, though we see not the workings of what is intellectual; though they are known only by their effects,—does the student by the midnight oil require less rest from his mental fatigues,—whether he take it or not,—than the ploughman from his corporal labour? Is he not as wearied, as exhausted, after a day consigned to serious and unremitting study and reflection, as the labourer who has spent it in digging, paving, hewing, and sawing? Yet his body has been perfectly at peace; has not moved, has not made the smallest exertion."

"And why, Harleigh? Why is that, but because—"

"Hasten not, Elinor, thence, to your favourite conclusion, that soul and body, if wearied or rested together, are, therefore, one and the same thing: observation, and reflection, turned to other points of view, will shew you fresh reasons, and objects, every day, to disprove that identity: shew you, on one side, corporal force for supporting the bitterest grief of heart, with uninjured health; and, mental force, on the other side, for bearing the acutest bodily disorders with unimpaired intellectual vigour. How often do the most fragile machines, enwrap the stoutest minds? how often do the halest frames, encircle the feeblest intellects? All proves that the connexion between mind and body, however intimate, is not blended;—though where its limits begin, or where they end,—who can tell? But, who, also, I repeat, can explain the phenomenon, by which, in the dead of the night, when we are completely insulated, and left in utter darkness, we firmly believe, nay, feel ourselves shone upon by the broad beams of day; and surrounded by society, with which we act, think, and reciprocate ideas?"

"Dreams, I must own, Albert, are strangely incomprehensible. How bodies can seem to appear, and voices to be heard, where all around is empty space, it is not easy to conceive!"

"Let this insolvable, and acknowledged difficulty, then, Elinor, in a circumstance which, though daily recurring, remains inexplicable, check any hardy decision of the cause why, after certain suspensions, the soul may resume its functions to our evident knowledge; yet why we can neither ascertain its departure, its continuance, nor its return, after others. Oh Elinor! mock not, but revere the impenetrable mystery of eternity! Ignorance is here our lot; presumption is our most useless infirmity. The mind and body after death must either be separate, or together. If together, as you assert, there is no proof attainable, that the soul partakes not of all the changes, all the dispersions, all the sufferings, and all the poor enjoyments, of what to us seems the lifeless, but which, in that case, is only the speechless carcase: if separate, as I believe,—whither goest thou, Oh soul! to what regions of bliss?—or what abysses of woe?"

"Harleigh, you electrify me! you convulse the whole train of my principles, my systems, my long cherished conviction!"

"Say, rather, Elinor, of your faith!—your faith in infidelity! Oh Elinor! why call you not, rather, upon faith to aid your belief? Faith, and revealed religion! The limited state of our positive perceptions, grants us no means for comparison, for judgment, or even for thought, but by analogy: ask yourself, then, Elinor,—What is there, even in immortality, more difficult of comprehension, than that indescribable daily occurrence, which all mankind equally, though unreflectingly experience, of a total suspension of every species of living knowledge, of every faculty, of every sense,—called sleep? A suspension as big with matter for speculation and wonder, though its cessation is visible to us, as that last sleep, of which we view not the period."

"Albert!—should you shake my creed,—shall I be better contented? or but yet more wretched?"

"Can Elinor think,—yet ask such a question? Can a prospect of a future state fail to offer a possibility of future happiness? Why wilfully reject a consolation that you have no means to disprove? What know you of this soul which you settle to be so easily annihilated? By what criterion do you judge it? You have none! save a general consciousness, that a something there is within us that mocks all search, yet that always is uppermost; that anticipates good or evil; that outruns all events; that feels the blow ere the flesh is touched; that expects the sound before the ear receives it; that, unseen, untraced, unknown, pervades, rules, animates all! that harbours thoughts, feelings, designs which no human force can controul; which no mortal, unaided by our own will, can discover; and which no aid whatever, either of our own or of others, can bring forward to any possible manifestation!"

"Alas, Harleigh! You shew me nonentity itself to be as

doubtful as immortality! Of what wretched stuff are we composed! Which way must I now turn,—

'Lost and bewildered in my fruitless search,'[†]*—

which way must I turn to develop truth? to comprehend my own existence! Oh Albert!—you almost make me wish to rest my perturbed mind where fools alone, I thought, found rest, or hypocrites have seemed to find it,—on Religion!"

"The feeling mind, dear Elinor, has no other serious serenity; no other hold from the black, cheerless, petrifying expectation of nullity. If, then, even a wish of light break through your dark despondence, read, study the Evangelists!—and truth will blaze upon you, with the means to find consolation."

"Albert, I know not where I am!—You open to me possibilities that overwhelm me! My head seems bursting with fulness of struggling ideas!"

"Give them, Elinor, fair play, and they will soon, in return, give you tranquillity. Reflect only,—that that quality, that faculty, be its nature, its durability, and its purpose what they may, which the world at large agrees to call soul, has its universal comprehension from something that is felt; not that is proved! Yet who, and where is the Atheist, the Deist, the Infidel of any description, gifted with means to demonstrate, that, in quitting the body with the parting breath, it is necessarily extinct? that it may not, on the contrary, still BE, when speech and motion are no more? when our flesh is mingled with the dust, and our bones are dispersed by the winds? and BE, as while we yet exist, no part of our body, no single of our senses; never, while we seem to live, visible, yet never, when we seem to die, perishable? May it not, when, with its last sigh, it leaves the body, mingle with that vast expanse of air, which no instrument can completely analyse, and which our imperfect sight views but as empty space? May it not mount to upper regions, and enjoy purified bliss? May not all air be peopled with our departed friends, hovering around us, as sensible as we are unconscious? May not the uncumbered soul watch over those it loves? find again those it had lost? be received in the Heaven of

[†] Addison.

Heavens, where it is destined,—not, Oh wretched idea!—to eternal sleep, inertness, annihilating dust;—but to life, to joy, to sweetest reminiscence, to tenderest re-unions, to grateful adoration, to intelligence never ending! Oh! Elinor! keep for ever in mind, that if no mortal is gifted to prove that this is true,—neither is any one empowered to prove that it is false!"

"Oh delicious idea!" cried Elinor, rising: "Oh image of perfection! Oh Albert! conquering Albert! I hope,—I hope;—my soul may be immortal!—Pray for me, Albert! Pray that I may dare offer up prayers for myself!—Send me your Christian divine to guide me on my way; and may your own heaven bless you, peerless Albert! for ever!—Adieu! adieu! adieu!"—

Fervently, then, clasping her hands, she sunk, with overpowering feelings, upon her knees.

Juliet came forward to support her; and Harleigh, deeply gratified, though full of commiseration, eagerly undertook the commission; and, echoing back her blessing, without daring to utter a word to Juliet, slowly quitted the spot.

BOOK X

CHAPTER LXXXVI

ELINOR, for a considerable time, remained in the same posture, ruminating, in silent abstraction; yet giving, from time to time, emphatic, though involuntary utterance, to short and incoherent sentences. "A spirit immortal!—" "Resurrection of the Dead!—" "A life to come!—" "Oh Albert! is there, then, a region where I may hope to see thee again!"

Suddenly, at length, seeming to recollect herself, "Pardon," she cried, "Albert, my strangeness,—queerness,—oddity,—what will you call it? I am not the less,—O no! O no! penetrated by your impressive reasoning.—Albert!—"

She lifted up her head, and, looking around, exclaimed, with an air of consternation, "Is he gone?"

She arose, and with more firmness, said, "He is right! I meant not,—and I ought not to see him any more;—though dearer to my eyes is his sight, than life or light!—"

Looking, then, earnestly forwards, as if seeking him, "Farewell, Oh Albert!" she cried: "We now, indeed, are parted for ever! To see thee again, would sink me into the lowest abyss of contempt,—and I would far rather bear thy hatred!—Yet hatred?—from that soul of humanity!—what violence must be put upon its nature! And how cruel to reverse such ineffable philanthropy!—No!—hate me not, my Albert!—It shall be my own care that thou shalt not despise me!"

Slowly she then walked away, followed silently by Juliet, who durst not address her. Anxiously she looked around, till, at some distance, she descried a horseman. It was Harleigh. She stopped, deeply moved, and seemed inwardly to bless him. But, when he was no longer in sight, she no longer restrained her anguish, and, casting herself upon the turf, groaned rather than wept, exclaiming, "Must I live—yet behold thee no more!—Will neither sorrow, nor despair, nor even madness kill me?—Must nature, in her decrepitude, alone bring death to Elinor?"

Rising, then, and vainly trying again to descry the horse, "All, all is gone!" she cried, "and I dare not even die!—All, all is gone, from the lost, unhappy Elinor, but life and misery!"

Turning, then, with quickness to Juliet, while pride and shame dried her eyes, "Ellis," she said, "let him not know I murmur!—Let not his last hearing of Elinor be disgrace! Tell him, on the contrary, that his friendship shall not be thrown away; nor his arguments be forgotten, or unavailing: no! I will weigh every opinion, every sentiment that has fallen from him, as if every word, unpolluted by human ignorance or infirmity, had dropt straight from heaven! I will meditate upon religion: I will humble myself to court resignation. I will fly hence, to avoid all temptation of ever seeing him more!—and to distract my wretchedness by new scenes. Oh Albert!—I will earn thy esteem by acquiescence in my lot, that here,—even here,—I may taste the paradise of alluring thee to include me in thy view of happiness hereafter!"

Her foreign servant, then, came in view, and she made a motion to him with her hand for her carriage. She awaited it in profound mental absorption, and, when it arrived, placed herself in it without speaking.

Juliet, full of tender pity, could no longer forbear saying, "Adieu, Madam! and may peace re-visit your generous heart!"

Elinor, surprized and softened, looked at her with an expression of involuntary admiration, as she answered, "I believe you to be good, Ellis!—I exonerate you from all delusory arts; and, internally, I never thought you guilty,—or I had never feared you! Fool! mad fool, that I have been, I am my own executioner! my distracting impatience to learn the depth of my danger, was what put you together! taught you to know, to appreciate one another! With my own precipitate hand, I have dug the gulph into which I am fallen! Your dignified patience, your noble modesty—Oh fatal Ellis!—presented a contrast that plunged a dagger into all my efforts! Rash, eager ideot! I conceived suspense to be my greatest bane!—Oh fool! eternal fool!—self-willed, and self-destroying!—for the single thrill of one poor moment's returning doubt—I would now suffer martyrdom!"

She wept, and hid her face within the carriage; but, holding out her hand to Juliet, "Adieu, Ellis!" she cried, "I struggle hardly not to wish you any ill; and I have never given you my malediction: yet Oh!—that you had never been born!"—

She snatched away her hand, and precipitately drew up all the blinds, to hide her emotion; but, presently, letting one of them down, called out, with resumed vivacity, and an air of gay defiance, "Marry him, Ellis!—marry him at once! I have always felt that I should be less mad, if my honour called upon me for reason!—my honour and my pride!"

The groom demanded orders.

"Drive to the end of the world!" she answered, impatiently, "so you ask me no questions!" and, forcibly adding, "Farewell, too happy Ellis!" she again drew up all the blinds, and, in a minute, was out of sight.

Juliet deplored her fate with the sincerest concern; and ruminated upon her virtues, and attractive qualities, till their drawbacks diminished from her view, and left nothing but unaffected wonder, that Harleigh could resist them: 'twas a wonder, nevertheless, that every feeling of her heart, in defiance of every conflict, rose, imperiously, to separate from regret.

At the cottage, she found her recovered property, which she now concluded,—for her recollection was gone,—that she had dropt upon her entrance into the room occupied by Harleigh, before she had perceived that it was not empty.

Here, too, almost immediately afterwards, her messenger returned with a letter, which had remained more than a week at the post-office; whither it had been sent back by the farmer, who had refused to risk advancing the postage.*

The letter was from Gabriella, and sad, but full of business. She had just received a hurrying summons from Mr. de * * *, her husband, to join him at Teignmouth, in Devonshire; and, for family-reasons, which ought not to be resisted, to accompany him abroad. Mr. de * * * had been brought by an accidental conveyance to Torbay; whence, through a peculiarly favourable opportunity, he was to sail to his place of destination. He charged her to use the utmost expedition; and, to spare the expence of a double journey, and the difficulties of a double passport, for and from London,* he should procure permission to meet her at Teignmouth; where they might remain till their vessel should be ready; the town of Brixham, within Torbay, being filled with sailors, and unfit for female residence.

Gabriella owned, that she had nothing substantial, nor even rational, to oppose to this plan; though her heart would be left in the grave, the English grave of her adored child. She had relinquished, therefore, her shop, and paid the rent, and her debts; and obtained money for the journey by the sale of all her commodities. She then tenderly entreated, if no insurmountable obstacles forbid it, that Juliet would be of their party; and gave the direction of Mr. de * * * at Teignmouth.

Not a moment could Juliet hesitate upon joining her friend; though whether or not she should accompany her abroad, she left for decision at their meeting. She greatly feared the delay in receiving the letter might make her arrive too late; but the experiment was well worth trial; and she reached the beautifully situated small town of Teignmouth the next morning.

She drove to the lodging of which Gabriella had given the direction; where she had the affliction to learn, that the lady whom she described, and her husband, had quitted Teignmouth the preceding evening for Torbay.

She instantly demanded fresh horses, for following them; but the postilion said, that he must return directly to Exeter, with his chaise; and enquired where she would alight. Where she might most speedily, she answered, find means to proceed.

The postilion drove her, then, to a large lodging-house; but the town was so full of company, as it was the season for bathing, that there was no chaise immediately ready; and she was obliged to take possession of a room, till some horses returned.

As soon as she had deposited her baggage, she resolved upon walking back to the late lodging of Gabriella, to seek some further information.

In re-passing a gallery, which led from her chamber to the stairs, she perceived, upon a band-box, left at the half-closed door of what appeared to be the capital apartment, the loved name of Lady Aurora Granville.

Joy, hope, fondness, and every pleasurable emotion, danced

suddenly in her breast; and, chacing away, by surprize, all fearful caution, irresistibly impelled her to push open the door.

All possibility of concealment was, she knew, now at an end; and, with it, finished her long forbearance. How sweet to cast herself, at length, under so benign a protection! to build upon the unalterable sweetness of Lady Aurora for a consolatory reception, and openly to claim her support!

Filled with these delighting ideas, she gently entered the room. It was empty; but, the door to an inner apartment being open, she heard the soft voice of Lady Aurora giving directions to some servant.

While she hesitated whether, at once, to venture on, or to send in some message, a chambermaid, coming out with another band-box, shut the inner door.

The dress of Juliet was no longer such as to make her appearance in a capital apartment suspicious; and the chambermaid civily enquired whom she was pleased to want.

"Lady Aurora Granville," she hesitatingly answered; adding that she would tap at her ladyship's door herself, and begging that the maid would not wait.

The maid, busy and active, hurried off. Quickly, then, though softly, Juliet stept forward; but at the door, trembling and full of fears, she stopt short; and the sight of pen, ink, and paper upon a table, determined her to commit her attempt to writing.

Seizing a sheet of paper, without sitting down, and in a hand scarcely legible, she began,

"Is Lady Aurora Granville still the same Lady Aurora, the kind, the benignant, the indulgent Lady Aurora,—" when the sound of another voice, a voice more discordant, if possible, than that of Lady Aurora had been melodious, reached her ear from under the window: it was that of Mrs. Howel.

As shaking now with terrour as before she had been trembling with hope, she rolled up her paper; and was hurrying it into her work-bag, which had been returned to her by Harleigh; when the chambermaid, re-entering the room, stared at her with some surprize, demanding whether she had seen her ladyship.

"No; ... I believe ... she is occupied," Juliet, stammering, answered; and flew along the gallery back to her chamber.

That Lady Aurora should be under the care of Mrs. Howel, who was the nearest female relation of Lord Denmeath, could give no surprize to Juliet; but the impulse which had urged her forward, had only painted to her a previous interview with Lady Aurora alone: for how venture to reveal herself in presence of so hard, so inimical a witness? The very idea, joined to the terrible apprehension of irritating Lord Denmeath, to aid some new attack from her legal persecutor; so damped her rising joy, so repressed her buoyant hopes, that, to avoid the insupportable repetition of injurious interrogatories, painful explanations, and insulting incredulity, she decided, if she could join Gabriella at Torbay, to accompany her to her purposed retreat; and there to await either intelligence of the Bishop, or an open summons from her own family.

She hastened, therefore, to the late lodging of Gabriella; where, upon a more minute investigation, she found, that a message had been left, in case a lady should call to enquire for Madame de * * *, to say, that the small vessel in which M. de * * * and herself were humanely to be received as passengers, was ready to sail; and to promise to write upon their landing; and to endeavour to fix upon some means of re-union. The lady, the lodging-people said, had lost all hope of her friend's arrival, but had left that message in case of accidents.

More eagerly than ever, Juliet now enquired for any kind of carriage; but the town was full, and every vehicle was engaged till the next morning.

The next morning opened with a new and cruel disappointment: the chambermaid came with excuses, that no chaise could be had till towards evening, as the Honourable Mrs. Howel had engaged all the horses, to carry herself and her people to Chudleigh-park.

Dreadful to the impatience of Juliet was such a loss of time; yet she shrunk from all appeal, upon her prior rights, with Mrs. Howel.

Still, not to render impossible, before her departure, an interview, after which her heart was sighing, with Lady Aurora, she addressed to her a few lines.

"To the Right Honourable
Lady Aurora Granville.

"Brought hither in search of the friend of my earliest youth, what have been my perturbation, my hope, my fear, at the sound of the voice of her whom, proudly and fondly, it is my first wish to be permitted to love, and to claim as the friend of my future days! Ah, Lady Aurora! my inmost soul is touched and moved!—nevertheless, not to press upon the difficulties of your delicacy, nor to take advantage of the softness of your sensibility, I go hence without imploring your support or countenance. I quit again this loved land, scarcely known, though devoutly revered, to watch and wait,—far, far off!—for tidings of my future lot: I go to join the generous guardian of my orphan life,—till I know whether I may hope to be acknowledged by a brother! I go to dwell with my noble adopted sister,—till I learn whether I may be recalled, to be owned by one still nearer,—and who alone can be still dearer!"

She gave this paper sealed, for delivery, to the chambermaid; saying that she was going to take a long walk; and desiring, should there be any answer, that it might carefully be kept for her return.

This measure was to give Lady Aurora time to reflect, whether or not she should demand an explanation of the note; rather than to surprize the first eager impulse of her kindness.

She then bent her steps towards the sea-side; but, though it was still very early, there was so much company upon the sands, taking exercise before, or after bathing, that she soon turned another way; and, invited by the verdant freshness of the prospects, rambled on for a considerable time: at first, with no other design than to while away a few hours; but, afterwards, to give to those hours the pleasure ever new, ever instructive, of viewing and studying the works of nature; which, on this charming spot, now awfully noble, now elegantly simple; where the sea and the land, the one sublime in its sameness, the other, exhilarating in its variety, seem to be presented, as if in primeval lustre, to the admiring eye of a meditative being.

She clambered up various rocks, nearly to their summit, to

enjoy, in one grand perspective, the stupendous expansion of the ocean, glittering with the brilliant rays of a bright and cloudless sky: dazzled, she descended to their base, to repose her sight upon the soft, yet lively tint of the green turf, and the rich, yet mild hue of the downy moss. Almost sinking, now, from the scorching beams of a nearly vertical sun, she looked round for some umbrageous retreat; but, refreshed the next moment, by salubrious sea-breezes, by the coolness of the rocks, or by the shade of the trees, she remained stationary, and charmed; a devoutly adoring spectatress of the lovely, yet magnificent scenery encircling her; so vast in its glory, so impressive in its details, of wild, varied nature, apparently in its original state.

When, at length, she judged it to be right to return, upon coming within sight of the lodging-house, she saw a carriage at the door, into which some lady was mounting.

Could it be Lady Aurora?—could she so depart, after reading her letter? She retreated till the carriage drove off; and then, at the foot of the stairs, met the chambermaid; of whom she eagerly asked, whether there were any letter, or message, for her, from Lady Aurora.

The maid answered No; her ladyship was gone away without saying any thing.

The words "gone away" extremely affected Juliet, who, in ascending to her room, wept bitterly at such a desertion; even while concluding it to have been exacted by Mrs. Howel.

She rang her bell, to enquire whether she might now have a chaise.

The chambermaid told her that she must come that very moment to speak to a lady.

"What lady?" cried Juliet, ever awake to hope; "Is Lady Aurora Granville come back?"

No, no; Lady Aurora was gone to Chudleigh.

"What lady then?"

Mrs. Howel, the maid answered, who ordered her to come that instant.

"'Tis a mistake," said Juliet, with spirit; "you must seek some other person to whom to deliver such a message!"

The maid would have asserted her exactitude in executing

her commission; but Juliet, declining to hear her, insisted upon being left.

Extremely disturbed, she could suggest no reason why Mrs. Howel should remain, when Lady Aurora was gone; nor divine whether her letter were voluntarily unanswered; or whether it had even been delivered; nor what might still instigate the unrestrained arrogance of Mrs. Howel.

In a few minutes, the chambermaid returned, to acquaint her, that, if she did not come immediately, Mrs. Howel would send for her in another manner.

Too indignant, now, for fear, Juliet, said that she had no answer to give to such a message; and charged the maid not to bring her any other.

Another, nevertheless, and ere she had a moment to breathe, followed; which was still more peremptory, and to which the chambermaid sneeringly added,

"You wonna let me look into youore work-bag, wull y?"

"Why should you look into my work-bag?"

"Nay, it ben't I as do want it; it be Maddam Howel."

"And for what purpose?"

"Nay, I can't zay; but a do zay a ha' lost a bank-note."

"And what have I, or my work-bag, to do with that?"

"Nay I don't know; but it ben't I ha' ta'en it. And it ben't I——"

She stopt, grinning significantly; but, finding that Juliet deigned not to ask an explanation, went on: "It ben't I as husselled zomat into my work-bag, in zuch a peck o' troubles, vor to hide it; it ben't I, vor there be no mortul mon, nor womon neither, I be afeard of; vor I do teake no mon's goods but my own."

Juliet now was thunderstruck. If a bank-note were missing, appearances, from her silently entering and quitting the room, were certainly against her; and though it could not be difficult to clear away such a suspicion, it was shocking, past endurance, to have such a suspicion to clear.

While she hesitated what to reply, the maid, not doubting but that her embarrassment was guilt, triumphantly continued her own defence; saying, whoever might be suspected, it could not be she, for she did not go into other people's rooms, not she!

to peer about, and see what was to be seen; nor say she was going to call upon grand gentlefolks, when she was not going to do any such thing; not she! nor tear paper upon other people's tables, to roll things up, and poke them into her work-bag; not she! she had nothing to hide, for there was nothing she took, so there was nothing she had to be ashamed of, not she!

She then mutteringly walked off; but almost instantly returned, desiring to know, in the name of Mrs. Howel, whether Miss Ellis preferred that the business of her examination should be terminated, before proper witnesses, in her own room.

Juliet, thus assailed, urged by judgment, and a sense of propriety, struggled against personal feelings and fears; and resolved to rescue not only herself, but her family, from the disgrace of a public interrogatory. She walked, therefore, straight forward to the apartment of Mrs. Howel; determined to own, without delay, her birth and situation, rather than submit to any indignity.

At the entrance, she made way for the chambermaid to announce her; but when she heard that voice, which, to her shocked ears, sounded far more hoarse, more harsh, and more coarse than the raven's croak, her spirits nearly forsook her. To cast herself thus upon the powerful enmity of Lord Denmeath, with no kind Lady Aurora at hand, to soften the hazardous tale, by her benignant pity; no generous Lord Melbury within call, to resist perverse incredulity, by spontaneous support, and promised protection:—'twas dreadful!—Yet no choice now remained, no possible resource; she must meet her fate, or run away as a culprit.

The latter she utterly disdained; and, at the words, loudly spoken, from the inner room, "Order her to appear!" she summoned to her aid all that she possessed of pride or of dignity, to disguise her apprehensions; and obeyed the imperious mandate.

Mrs. Howel, seated upon an easy chair, received her with an air of prepared scorn; in which, nevertheless, was mixed some surprize at the elegance, yet propriety, of her attire. "Young woman," she sternly said, "what part is this you are acting? And what is it you suppose will be its result? Can you imagine that you are to brave people of condition with impunity? You have again dared to address, clandestinely, and by letter, a young lady of quality, whom you know to be forbidden to afford you any countenance. You have entered my apartment under false pretences; you have been detected precipitately quitting it, thrusting something into your work-bag, evidently taken from my table."—

Juliet now felt her speech restored by contempt. "I by no means intended, Madam," she drily answered, "to have intruded upon your benevolence. The sheet of paper which I took was to write to Lady Aurora Granville; and I imagined,—mistakenly, it seems,—that it was already her ladyship's."

The calmness of Juliet operated to produce a storm in Mrs. Howel that fired all her features; though, deeming it unbecoming her rank in life, to shew anger to a person beneath her, she subdued her passion into sarcasm, and said, "Her ladyship, then, it seems, is to provide the paper with which you write to her, as well as the clothes with which you wait upon her? That she refuses herself whatever is not indispensable, in order to make up a secret purse, has long been clear to me; and I now, in your assumed garments, behold the application of her privations!"

"Oh Lady Aurora! lovely and loved Lady Aurora! have you indeed this kindness for me! this heavenly goodness!"—interrupted, from a sensibility that she would not seek to repress, the penetrated Juliet.

"Unparalleled assurance!" exclaimed Mrs. Howel. "And do you think thus triumphantly to gain your sinister ends? No! Lady Aurora will never see your letter! I have already dispatched it to my Lord Denmeath."

The spirit of Juliet now instantly sunk: she felt herself again betrayed into the power of her persecutor; again seized; and trembled so exceedingly, that she with difficulty kept upon her feet.

Mrs. Howel exultingly perceived her advantage. "What," she haughtily demanded, "has brought you hither? And why are you here? If, indeed, you approach the sea-side with a view to embark, and return whence you came, I am far from offering any impediment to so befitting a measure. My Lord Denmeath, I have reason to believe, would even assist it. Speak, young woman! have you sense enough of the unbecoming situation in which you now stand, to take so proper a course for getting to your home?"

"My home!" repeated Juliet, casting up her eyes, which, bedewed with tears at the word, she then covered with her handkerchief.

"If to go thither be your intention," said Mrs. Howel, "the matter may be accommodated; speak, then."

"The little, Madam, that I mean to say," cried Juliet, "I must beg leave to address to you when you are alone." For the waiting-woman still remained at the side of the toilette-table.

"At length, then," said Mrs. Howel, much gratified, though always scornful; "you mean to confess?" And she told her woman to hasten the packing up, and then to step into the next room.

"Think, however;" she continued; "deliberate, in this interval, upon what you are going to do. I have already heard the tale which I have seen, by your letter, you hint at propagating; heard it from my Lord Denmeath himself. But so idle a fabrication, without a single proof, or document, in its support, will only be considered as despicable. If that, therefore, is the subject upon which you purpose to entertain me in this *tête à tête*, be advised to change it, untried. Such stale tricks are only to be played upon the inexperienced. You may well blush, young woman! I am willing to hope it is with shame."

"You force me, Madam, to speak!" indignantly cried Juliet; "though you will not, thus publicly, force me to an explanation. For your own sake, Madam, for decency's, if not for humanity's sake, press me no further, till we are alone! or the blush with which you upbraid me, now, may hereafter be yours! And not a blush like mine, from the indignation of innocence injured—yet unsullied; but the blush of confusion and shame; latent, yet irrepressible!"

Rage, now, is a word inadequate to express the violent feelings of Mrs. Howel, which, nevertheless, she still strove to curb under an appearance of disdain. "You would spare me, then," she cried, "this humiliation? And you suppose I can listen to such arrogance? Undeceive yourself, young woman; and produce the contents of your work-bag at once, or expect its immediate seizure for examination, by an officer of justice."

"What, Madam, do you mean?" cried Juliet, endeavouring, but not very successfully, to speak with unconcern.

"To allow you the choice of more, or fewer witnesses to your boasted innocence!"

"If your curiosity, Madam," said Juliet, more calmly, yet not daring any longer to resist, "is excited to take an inventory of my small property, I must endeavour to indulge it."

She was preparing to untie the strings of her work-bag; when a sudden recollection of the bank-notes of Harleigh, for the possession of which she could give no possible account, checked her hand, and changed her countenance.

Mrs. Howel, perceiving her embarrassment, yet more haughtily said, "Will you deliver your work-bag, young woman, to Rawlins?"

"No, Madam!" answered Juliet, reviving with conscious dignity; "I will neither so far offend myself at this moment,—nor you for every moment that shall follow! I can deliver it only into your own hands."

"Enough!" cried Mrs. Howel. 'Rawlins, order Hilson to enquire out the magistrate of this village, and to desire that he will send to me some peace-officer immediately."

She then opened the door of a small inner room, into which she shut herself, with an air of deadly vengeance.

Mrs. Rawlins, at the same time, passed to the outer room, to summon Hilson.

Juliet, confounded, remained alone. She looked from one side to the other; expecting either that Mrs. Howel would call upon her, or that Mrs. Rawlins would return for further orders. Neither of them re-appeared, or spoke.

Alarmed, now, yet more powerfully than disgusted, she compelled herself to tap at the door of Mrs. Howel, and to beg admission.

She received no answer. A second and a third attempt failed equally. Affrighted more seriously, she hastened to the outer room; where a man, Hilson, she supposed, was just quitting Mrs. Rawlins.

"Mrs. Rawlins," she cried; "I beseech you not to send any one off, till you have received fresh directions."

Mrs. Rawlins desired to know whether this were the command of her lady.

"It will be," Juliet replied, "when I have spoken to her again."

Mrs. Rawlins answered, that her lady was always accustomed to be obeyed at once; and told Hilson to make haste.

Juliet entreated for only a moment's delay; but the man would not listen.

Though from justice Juliet could have nothing to fear, the idea of being forced to own herself, when a peace-officer was sent for, to avoid being examined as a criminal, filled her with such horrour and affright, that, calling out, "Stop! stop! I beseech you stop!—" she ran after the man, with a precipitate eagerness, that made her nearly rush into the arms of a gentleman, who, at that moment, having just passed by Hilson, filled up the way.

Without looking at him, she sought to hurry on; but, upon his saying, "I ask pardon, Ma'am, for barricading your passage in this sort;" she recognized the voice of her first patron, the Admiral.

Charmed with the hope of succour, "Is it you, Sir?" she cried. "Oh Sir, stop that person!—Call to him! Bid him return! I implore you!—"

"To be sure I will, ma'am!" answered he, courteously taking off his hat, though appearing much amazed; and hallooing after Hilson, "Hark'ee, my lad! be so kind to veer about a bit."

Hilson, not venturing to shew disrespect to the uniform of the Admiral, stood still.

The Admiral then, putting on his hat, and conceiving his business to be done, was passing on; and Hilson grinning at the short-lived impediment, was continuing his route; but the calls and pleadings of Juliet made the Admiral turn back, and, in a tone of authority, and with the voice of a speaking trumpet, angrily cry, "Halloo, there! Tack about and come hither, my lad! What do you go t'other way for, when a lady calls you? By George, if they had you aboard, they'd soon teach you better manners!"

Juliet, again addressing him, said, "Oh Sir! how good you are! how truly benevolent!—Detain him but till I speak with his lady, and I shall be obliged to you eternally!"

"To be sure I will, Ma'am!" answered the wondering Admiral. "He sha'n't pass me. You may depend upon that."

Juliet, meaning now to make her sad and forced confession, re-entered the first apartment; and was soliciting, through Mrs. Rawlins, for an audience with Mrs. Howel; when Hilson, surlily returning, preceded the petitioner to his lady; and complained that he had been set upon by a bully of the young woman's.

Mrs. Howel, coming forth, with a wrath that was deaf to prayer or representation, gave orders that the master of the house should be called to account for such an insult to one of her people.

The master of the house appearing, made a thousand excuses for what had happened; but said that he could not be answerable for people's falling to words upon the stairs.

Mrs. Howel insisted upon reparation; and that those who had affronted her people should be told to go out of the house; or she herself would never enter it again.

The landlord declared that he did not know how to do such a thing, for the gentleman was his honour the Admiral; who was come to spend two or three days there, from the shipping at Torbay.

If it were a general-officer* who had acted thus, she said, he could certainly give some reason for his conduct; and she desired the landlord to ask it of him in her name.

In vain, during this debate, Juliet made every concession, save that of delivering her work-bag to the scrutiny of Mrs. Rawlins; nothing less would satisfy the enraged Mrs. Howel, who resisted all overtures for a *tête à tête*; determined publicly to humble the object of her wrath.

The Admiral, who was found standing centinel at the door, desired an audience of the lady himself.

Mrs. Howel accorded it with readiness; ordering Hilson, Mrs. Rawlins, and the landlord, to remain in the room.

CHAPTER LXXXVII

MRS. HOWEL received the Admiral, seated, with an air of state, upon her arm-chair; at one side of which stood Mrs. Rawlins, and at the other Hilson. The landlord was stationed near the door; and Juliet, indignant, though trembling, placed herself at a window; determining rather, with whatever mortification, to seek the protection of the Admiral, than to avow who she was thus publicly, thus disgracefully, and thus compulsorily.

The Admiral entered with the martial air of a man used to command; and whose mind was made up not to be put out of his way. He bestowed, nevertheless, three low bows, with great formality, to the sex of Mrs. Howel; to the first of which she arose and courtsied, returning the two others by an inclination of the head, and bidding Hilson bring the Admiral a chair.

The Admiral, having adjusted himself, his hat, and his sword to his liking, said, "I wish you good morning, Ma'am. You won't take it amiss, I hope, that I make free to wait upon you myself, for the sake of having a small matter of discourse with you, about a certain chap that I understand to be one of your domestics; a place whereof, if I may judge by what I have seen of him, he is not over and above worthy."

"If any of my people, Sir," answered Mrs. Howel, "have forgotten what is due to an officer of your rank, I shall take care to make them sensible of my displeasure."

The Admiral, much gratified, made her a low bow, saying, "A lady, Ma'am, such as I suppose you to be, can't fail having a right way of thinking. But that sort of gentry, as I have taken frequent note, have an ugly kind of a knack, of treating people rather short that have got a favour to ask; the which I don't uphold. And this is the main reason that I think it right to give you an item of my opinion upon this matter, respecting that lad; who just now, in my proper view, let a young gentlewoman call and squall after him, till she was black in the face, without so much as once veering round, to say, Pray, Ma'am, what do you please to want?"

Hilson, now, triumphant that he could plead his haste to obey the commands of his lady, was beginning an affronted self-defence; when the Admiral, accidentally perceiving Juliet, hastily arose; and, in a fit of unrestrained choler, clinching his double fist at Hilson, cried, "Why what sort of a fellow are you, Sir? to bring me a chair while you see a lady standing? Which do you take to be strongest? An old weather beaten tar, such as I am; or a poor weak female, that could not lend a hand to the pump, thof the vessel were going to the bottom?"

Approaching Juliet, then with his own arm-chair, he begged her to be seated; saying, "The lad will take care to bring another to me, I warrant him! A person who has got a scrap of gold-lace sewed upon his jacket, is seldom overlooked by that kind of gentry; for which reason I make no great account of complaisance, when I am dizened in my full dress uniform,—which, by the way, is a greater ceremony-monger than this, by thus much (measuring with his finger) more of tinsel!"

Juliet, gratefully thanking him, but declining his offer, thought this an opportunity not to be missed, to attempt, under his courageous auspice, to escape. She courtsied to him, therefore, and was walking away: but Mrs. Howel, swelling with ire, already, at such civility to a creature whom she had condemned to scorn, now flamed with passion, and openly told the landlord, to let that young woman pass at his peril.

Juliet, who saw in the anger which was mixed with the amazement of the Admiral, that she had a decided defender at hand, collected her utmost presence of mind, and, advancing to Mrs. Howel, said, "I have offered to you, Madam, any explanation you may require alone; but in public I offer you none!"

"If you think yourself still dealing with a novice of the inexperience of sixteen," answered Mrs. Howel, "you will find yourself mistaken. I will neither trust to the arts of a private recital, nor save your pride from a public examination."

Then, addressing the Admiral, "All yesterday morning, Sir," she continued, "I had sundry articles, such as rings, bank-notes, and letters of value, dispersed in my apartment, from a security that it was sacred; but the chambermaid informs me, that she caught this young woman entering it, under pretence of waiting upon a young lady, then in the inner room; and the same chambermaid, an hour after, found that she was still here; and endeavouring to conceal, in her work-bag something that she had wrapt into a sheet of paper, that was confessedly pilfered from my table."—

The Admiral, observing, in the midst of the disturbance of Juliet at this attack, an air of offended dignity, which urged him to believe that she was innocent, unhesitatingly answered, "'Tis an old saying, Madam, and a wise one, that standers-by see the most of the game;* and I have taken frequent note, that we are all of one mind, till we have heard two sides of the question: for which reason I hold it but fair, that the young gentlewoman should be asked what she has to say for herself."

"Can you suppose, Sir," said Mrs. Howel, the veins of whose face and throat now looked bursting, "that I mean to canvass this matter upon terms of equality? that I intend to be my own pleader against a pauper and an impostor?"—

Juliet here held her hand upon her forehead, as if scarcely able to sustain the indignant pain with which she was seized; and the fierce frown of the Admiral, showed his gauntlet not merely ready to be flung on the ground, but almost in the face of her adversary; Mrs. Howel, however, went on.

"I do not pretend to affirm that any thing has been purloined; but the circumstances of the case are certainly extraordinary; and I should be sorry to run the risk of wrongfully suspecting,—should something hereafter be missing,—any of my own people. I demand, therefore, immediately, an explanation of this transaction."

The Admiral, full of angry feelings as he looked at the panting Juliet, replied, himself; "To my seeming, Madam, the short cut to the truth in this business, would be for you to cast an eye upon your own affairs; which I doubt not but you will find in very good trim; and if you should like to know what passes in my mind, I must needs make bold to remark, that I think the so doing would be more good natured, by a fellow-creature, than putting a young gentlewoman out of countenance by talking so high: which, moreover, proves no fact."

"I am infinitely indebted to you, Sir, for the honour of your reprimand," Mrs. Howel, affectedly bowing, answered; "which I should not have incurred, had it not appeared to me, that it would be far more troublesome to my people, to take an exact review of my various and numerous trinkets and affairs, than for an innocent person to display the contents of a small work-bag."

"Nay, that is but reasonable," said the Admiral; "I won't say to the contrary. And I make small doubt, but that the young gentlewoman desires, in like manner with ourselves, that all should be fair and above board. The work-bag, I'll bet you all I am worth, has not a gimcrack in it that is not her own."

Juliet, to whom the consciousness was ever uppermost of the suspicious bank-notes, felt by no means inclined to submit to an examination. Again, therefore, and with firmness, she declined giving any communication, but in a private interview with Mrs. Howel.

Mrs. Howel, now, had not a doubt remaining, that something had been stolen; and, still more desirous to disgrace the culprit, than to recover her property, she declared, that she was perfectly ready to add to the number of witnesses, but resolutely fixed not to diminish it: public shame being the best antidote that could be offered, against those arts by which youth and credulity had been duped.

Juliet now looked down; embarrassed, distressed, yet colouring with resentment. The Admiral, not conceiving her situation; nor being able to comprehend the difficulty of displaying the contents of a work-bag, approached her, and strove to give her courage.

"Come! he cried, "young gentlewoman! don't be faint-hearted. Let the lady have her way. I always like to have my own, which makes me speak up for others. Besides which, I have no great opinion of quarrelling for straws. We are none of us the nearer the mark for falling to loggerheads:* for which reason I make it a rule never to lose my temper myself; except when I am provoked; so untie your work-bag, young gentlewoman. I'll engage that it will do you no discredit, by the very turn of your eye; for I don't know that, to my seeming, I ever saw a modester look of a face."

This harangue was uttered in a tone of good-humoured benevolence, that seemed seeking to raise her spirits; yet with an expression of compassion, that indicated a tender feeling for her disturbance; while the marked integrity, and honest frankness of his own character, with a high sense of honour, and a sincere love of virtue, beamed benignly, as he looked at her, in every feature of his kind, though furrowed face.

Juliet was sensibly touched by his goodness and liberality, which surprized from her all precaution; and the concession which she had refused to arrogant menace, she spontaneously granted, to secure the good will of her ancient, though unconscious friend. Raising, therefore, her eyes, in which an expression of gratitude took place of that of sadness, "I will not, Sir," she said, "resist your counsel; though I have in nothing forfeited my inherent right to the inviolability of my property."

She then put her work-bag into his own hands.

He received it with a bow down to the ground; while joy almost capered in his old eyes; and, exultingly turning to Mrs. Howel, "To my seeming, Madam," he said, "this young gentlewoman is as well-behaved a girl, as a man might wish to meet with, from one side the globe to the t'other; and I respect her accordingly. And, if I were to do so unhandsome a thing, as to poke and peer into her baggage, after seeing her comport herself so genteelly, I won't deny but I should merit a cat-o'-nine-tails,* better than many an honest tar that receives them. And, therefore, I hope, now, Madam, you will give back to the young gentlewoman your good opinion, in like manner as I, here, give her back her work-bag."

And then, with another profound bow, and a flourish of his hand, that shewed his pleasure in the part which he was taking, he was returning to Juliet her property; when he was startled by an ungovernable gust of wrath, from the utterly enraged Mrs. Howel, who exclaimed, "If you dare take it, young woman, unexamined, 'tis to a justice of the peace, and not to a sea-officer, that you will deliver it another time!"

Juliet, certain, whatever might be her ultimate fate, that her birth and family must, inevitably, be soon discovered, revolted from this menace; and determined, rather than submit to any further indignity, to risk casting herself, at once, upon the gentleman-like humanity of the Admiral. Unintimidated, therefore, by the alarming threat, which, heretofore, had appalled her, she steadily held out her hand, and received, from the old officer, in graceful silence, the proffered work-bag.

There is nothing which so effectually oversets an accusing

adversary, as self-possession; self-possession, which, if unaffected, is the highest attribute of fearless innocence; if assumed, the most consummate address of skilful art. Called, therefore, from rage to shame, by the calmness of Juliet, Mrs. Howel constrained herself to resume her air of solemn importance; and, perceiving the piqued look of the Admiral, at her slighting manner of naming sea-officers, she courteously said, "Permit me, Sir, as you are so good as to enter into this affair, to state to you that this young woman comes from abroad; and has no ostensible method of living in this country: will it not, then, be more consonant to prudence and decorum, that she should hasten to return whence she came?"

"Madam," answered the Admiral, coldly, "I never give advice upon the onset of a question; that is to say, never till I see that one thing had better be done than another. I have no great taste for groping in the dark; wherefore, when I don't rightly make out what a person would be at, I think the best mode to keep clear of a dispute, is to sheer off; whereby one avoids, in like manner, either to give or take an affront: two things not much more to my mind the one than the t'other. And so, Madam, I wish you good day."

He then, with a formal bow, left the room, Juliet gliding out by his side; while Mrs. Howel, powerless to detain her, wreaked her pent-up wrath upon the bell, which she rang, till every waiter in the house came to hear, that she was now ready to set off for Chudleigh-park.

CHAPTER LXXXVIII

THE kind looks, and determined approbation of the Admiral, gave Juliet, now, courage to address him, with a petition for his advice, how she might arrive most expeditiously at Torbay.

"Torbay?" he repeated; "why I could send you in my boat. But what,—" his brow overclouding, "what has a modest girl to do at Torbay?"

Juliet answered, that she should join, there, a friend whom she meant to accompany to the continent.

Every mark of favour was now changed into disdainful

displeasure; and, turning abruptly away from her, he muttered to himself, though aloud, that women's going abroad, to outlandish places, whereby they learnt more how to dizen themselves, and cut capers, than how to become good wives and mothers, was what he could not uphold; and would not lend a hand to; and then, without looking at her, he sullenly entered his own apartment.

The disappointed Juliet, utterly overset, was still dejectedly ruminating in the corridor, when she heard the servants of Mrs. Howel announce, that their lady's carriage was ready.

She then recovered her feet, to escape any fresh offence by regaining her apartment.

Her situation appeared to her now to be as extraordinary, as it was sad and difficult. Entitled to an ample fortune, yet pennyless; indebted for her sole preservation from insult and from famine, to pecuniary obligations from accidental acquaintances, and those acquaintances, men! pursued, with documents of legal right, by one whom she shuddered to behold, and to whom she was so irreligiously tied, that she could not, even if she wished it, regard herself as his lawful wife; though so entangled, that her fetters seemed to be linked with duty and honour; unacknowledged,—perhaps disowned by her family; and, though born to a noble and yet untouched fortune, consigned to disguise, to debt, to indigence, and to flight!

While mournfully taking this review of her condition, and seeking, but vainly, to form some plan for its amelioration, she heard the potent voice of the Admiral call out, "To Powderham Castle," as a carriage drove from the house; but ere she had time to lament the mortifying errour of her benevolent, though ill judging friend, the approach to the door of some other vehicle, announced a fresh arrival; and, presently, all difficulties were absorbed in immediate terrour, as again she heard that sound, which, of all others, most severely shocked her nerves, the voice of Mrs. Howel.

What could cause this abrupt return? Had she received the directions of Lord Denmeath? Was a new persecution arranged? or,—more horrible than all,—had means been devized, for casting again the most wretched of victims into the hands of the most terrific of her foes?

Tremblingly she listened to every noise. A general commotion, with quick pacing feet, spoke the entrance into the house of sundry servants; and, presently, she distinctly heard the apartment of Mrs. Howel taken possession of by that lady, and by some person with whom she was discoursing.

All now, for about a quarter of an hour, was still. She was then alarmed by a rustling sound, and a single footstep in the corridor: it approached, stopt, seemed turning back; approached again; and, after a few minutes, she was startled by a tapping at her door.

She shook, she was all dismay and apprehension: she hesitated whether to bolt herself in, or to accord admission; but a second tap bringing to her reflection how short, how futile, how ineffectual would be any resistance, she turned the key, opened her door, and her room was instantly entered.

Often, in the course of her long struggles and difficulties, had Juliet been struck with astonishment; but never had she known surprize that could bear any comparison with that which she experienced at this moment; when, expecting to see Mrs. Howel, or Lord Denmeath; when, prepared for reproach, for menace, and for insult; she saw, as fearfully she raised her eyes, instead of all that she dreaded and loathed, all that she thought most sweet, most lovely, most perfect upon earth, in the elegant form, and softly expressive face of Lady Aurora Granville, who, with eyes glistening, and arms opening, gently ejaculated, "My sister!" and fell, weeping, upon her neck.

Juliet nearly ceased to breathe: wonder, yet incredulity, took possession of her faculties, and she knew not whether it were possible that this could be reality, till the big surprize, mingled with the almost too powerful delight of her bosom, found some vent in a violent burst of tears.

Tender embraces, fond and open on the part of Lady Aurora, transported, yet fearful and doubtful, on that of Juliet, kept them for some minutes weeping in each other's arms. "Can you, then,—" cried the penetrated Juliet,—"may I believe in such felicity?—Can you condescend so far as not to disdain,—disclaim,—and turn away from so unhappy a relation? so distressed,—so helpless,—so desolate an object?"

"Oh! hush! hush! hush!" cried Lady Aurora, putting her

hand upon the mouth of Juliet; "you must not break my heart by such an idea,—such a profanation! by making me apprehend that you could ever think me such a monster! Did I wait till I knew your rights to my affection before I loved you? Did I not divine them from the moment I first conversed with you?"

Folding, then, her white arms around Juliet, with redoubled tenderness, "Oh my sweet Miss Ellis!" she cried. "Let me call you still a little while by that dear name! I have loved it so fondly that I can hardly love more even to call you my dearest sister! How you have engaged my thoughts; rested upon my imagination; occupied my ideas; been ever uppermost in my memory; and always highest,—Oh! higher than any one in my esteem and admiration! long, long before this loved moment, when Sir Jaspar Herrington's letter makes my enthusiasm but a tender duty!"

"Ah! Lady Aurora!" cried Juliet, "what sufferings are not repaid by a moment such as this! by a blessing so superlative, as thus to be acknowledged, thus to be received, by the person whose virtues and whose sweetness would have made me delight in her favour, had I never wanted protection! had my lot in life been the most brilliant!"

"Oh hush! sweet sister, hush!" interrupted Lady Aurora, again stopping her mouth; "what words are these? You would not make your blessing be my shame? What words are these? favour!—Lady Aurora!—Ah! never let me hear them more, if you love me! What have we to do with such phrases? Are we not sisters? Shall I use such to you? Would you love me if I did? Would you not rather chide me?"

Juliet could only shed tears, though tears so delicious, that it was luxury to shed them. Lady Aurora would have kissed them from her cheeks; but her own mingled with them so copiously, that it was not possible; and though the smiles of expressive joy that brightened each countenance, shewed their sensibility to be but fulness of happiness, the meeting, the acknowledgement, with the throbbing recollection of all that was passed, so touched each gentle heart, that they could but weep and embrace, embrace and weep, alternately.

"I have coveted," at length cried Juliet, "almost beyond light or life, I have coveted this precious moment! When first I heard you named,—you and Lord Melbury,—on the evening of the play, at Mrs. Maple's, Oh! what were my emotions! my satisfaction, my apprehensions, my hopes, and my solicitude! When I saw two beings so sweet, so formed to create esteem and love, so innocent, so unassuming, so attractive,—and whispered to myself, Are these my nearest relations? Is this my sister? Is this my brother?—how did my heart expand with joy and pride! How did I long to cast off all disguise, all reserve, and cry Own me, amiable beings! sweet sister! loved brother! pure, kind, and good! own your unhappy sister! take to your pitying protection the distressed, persecuted, insulated* daughter of your father!"

"Ah why," cried Lady Aurora, "did you not speak? why not indulge the impulse of nature, and of kindness? Your talents, your acquirements, your manners, won, instantly, all our admiration; enchanted, bewitched us; but how wide were we from thinking, at that first moment, that we had any tie to a mutual regard with the accomplished Miss Ellis! Our first notion of that happiness, though still far from the truth,—was after that cruel scene, which must for ever be blotted from all our memories;—when my poor brother was urged on,—so unhappily! to forget himself. The knowledge of that disgrace, from some listening servants, reached Mrs. Howel; she communicated it to my uncle Denmeath: no wonder he was alarmed! Still, however, he told us not the story; though, to stop the progress of what he feared, he acquainted us, that a report had formerly been spread, that we had a distant relation abroad; not, he said,—forgive him, if possible!—not in a right line related, and never, by my father, meant to be any way acknowledged.—Oh how little he knew my father! or, let me say, either of his daughters!—But, having put my brother upon his guard, by suggesting that it was possible that you might be this distant and unhonoured relation.—Ah, my Miss Ellis! if you had seen our indignant looks, when we heard such phrases!—He promised to seek you himself, and to examine into the affair; and exacted, forced from us both a promise, in return, that we would never either meet or write to you, till he had ascertained what was the truth. The unfortunate scene at Mrs. Howel's alone made my brother submit; for he feared misconstruction: and his submission of course included mine. Ah! had you spoken at that time! had you revealed——"

"Alas! my distresses were so complicate! What most I wished upon earth, was constantly counteracted by what most I dreaded! I could not make myself known to my friends,—in the soothing supposition that such I should find!—without betraying myself to my enemy; for Lord Denmeath would assuredly have made me over to my persecutor. How, then, in a situation so critical, yet so helpless, could I selfishly involve in my wretchedness, my perplexity and my concealment, the kindest and tenderest of human hearts?"

"Frequently," said Lady Aurora, "we have considered, and consulted together, what steps we ought to take; but the fear of some mistake, some imprudence, some offence, in a point so doubtful, so delicate, made us always decide that it was for you to speak first. And when I pressed so earnestly for your confidence, it was in the hope, the flattering hope, that I should prove my title to taking such a liberty. I had not, else, been so importunate, so inconsiderate. My brother, too, actuated by the same hope, urged you, perhaps, even more precipitately; but in all honour, with all respect; with no view, no thought, but to cement our regard by the ties of kindred. My brother can scarcely yet know our beloved acquisition; but Sir Jaspar tells me that he has sent a duplicate-letter to him, with the same precious history that he has written to me. Oh, how fervent will be his delight!"

She then related, to the grateful, but joy over-powered Juliet, that she had herself but just acquired this information, through the letter of which she had spoken; and which had been put into her hands as she was setting out for Chudleigh-park; to which place Mrs. Howel had, hastily, asked her to set off first, with her maid; promising to overtake her by the way.

The letter from Sir Jaspar, Lady Aurora continued, changed the whole system of her conduct. When she learnt that Miss Ellis, instead of being either an adventurer, or a distant and unhonoured relation, was the daughter of her own father; by a first, a lawful, though a secret marriage; all difficulty and irresolution vanished. Her first duty, she now thought, was the duty of a daughter, in the acknowledgement of a sister.

She gave orders that her chaise should be driven back instantly to Teignmouth; but, before she reached that village, she met Mrs. Howel; with whose woman she immediately changed place; and then communicated the interesting intelligence that she had just received. Mrs. Howel was utterly confounded; having either never conceived the truth, or been of opinion, with Lord Denmeath, that the interest, and the dignity of his lordship's nephew and niece, demanded its disavowal, or concealment. But when Lady Aurora openly protested, that she must instantly address her sister, through the medium of Sir Jaspar Herrington; Mrs. Howel, to stop any written acknowledgement, confessed that the young person was at Teignmouth; earnestly, however, insisting that no measure should be adopted, till the arrival of Lord Denmeath, to whom she had already sent an express. But Lady Aurora no sooner heard this welcome news, than, stimulated by conceiving, that her inclinations and her sense of right, were now one, she grew inflexible in her turn; and resolved to acknowledge and embrace her sister, without any other permission than the law of nature. Mrs. Howel, conscious, Lady Aurora thought, that, should the business take a new turn, from the interference of Sir Jaspar Herrington, she might, already, have gone too far, was fain to accompany her back to the lodging house; and, after giving many admonitions, to submit to the irrepressible impatience which sunk the niece in the sister.

Lady Aurora solicited, now, to know for what reason the name of Ellis had been taken; and learnt that, in the terrible perturbation in which Juliet had parted from the Marchioness, they had hastily agreed upon two initial letters for their correspondence; reserving some better adoption to a consultation with Gabriella. To have used the name of Granville, would have been courting danger and pursuit. But the embarrassed avowal of Juliet, that had been surprized from her at Dover, by the abrupt interrogatory of Elinor, that she knew not, herself, what she ought to be called; stood, ever after, in the way of any regulation upon that difficult point. She had been glad, therefore, to subscribe to the blunder of Miss Bydell, which seemed, in some measure, retaining an appellation, at least a sound, designed for her by the Marchioness; and which could not be called a deception, since all who then knew her, knew, also, its origin.

Lady Aurora acknowledged, that, even from their childhood, both Lord Melbury and herself had heard, though secretly and vaguely, of a suspected elder born; but not of a prior marriage; and they had often wished to meet with Miss Powel; for calumny and mystery, while they had hidden the truth, had not concealed the attachment of Lord Granville, nor the suspicious disappearance of its object, and her mother.

Innumerable plans, now, varying and short lived, because unsanctioned by any authority, succeeded to one another, of what measures might be adopted for their living together immediately. "For how," cried Juliet, "could I, henceforth, sustain an insulated life? How bear to look around me, again, and see no one whose kindness I could claim? Oh, how support so forlorn a state, after feeling every sorrow subside on the bosom,—may I, indeed, say so?—on the loved bosom of a sister?"

Thus, in the grateful transports of sensations as exquisite as they were sudden and unexpected, Juliet, acknowledged as her sister by Lady Aurora Granville; and with hopes all alive of the tender protection of a brother, felt every pulse, once again, beat to happiness; while every fear and foreboding, though not annihilated, was set aside.

CHAPTER LXXXIX

WHILE time was yet a stranger to regulation, and ere the dial* shewed its passage; when it had no computation but by our feelings, our weariness, our occupations, or our passions; the sun which arose splendid upon felicity, must have excited, by its quick parting rays, a surprize nearly incredulous; while that which gave light but to sorrow, may have appeared, at its evening setting, to have revolved the whole year. This period, so long past, seemed now present to Lady Aurora and to Juliet; so uncounted flew the minutes; so unconscious were they that they had more than met, more than embraced, more than reciprocated their joy in acknowledged kindred; that each felt amazed as well as shocked, when a summons from Mrs. Howel to Lady Aurora, told them that the day was fast wearing, away.

Lady Aurora reluctantly obeyed the call; and in thanksgiving, pious and delighted, Juliet spent the interval of her absence.

It was not long; she returned precipitately; but colourless, trembling, and altered, though making an effort to smile: but the struggle against her feelings ended in a burst of tears; and, again falling upon the neck of Juliet; "Oh my sweet sister!" she cried, "is your persecution never to end?"

Juliet, though quickly alarmed, fondly answered, "It is over already! While that precious appellation comes from your lips,—sweet title of tenderness and affection!—I feel above every danger!"

Lady Aurora, bitterly weeping, was compelled, then, to acknowledge that she had been hurried away by Mrs. Howel, to be told that a foreigner, ill dressed, and just arrived from the Continent, was demanding, in broken English, of every one that he met, some news of a young person called Miss Ellis.

The exaltation of Juliet was instantly at an end; and, in an accent of despair, she uttered, "Is it so soon, then, over!—my transient felicity!"

Whether this foreigner were her persecutor himself, escaped and disguised; or some emissary employed to claim or to entrap her, was all of doubt by which she was momentarily supported; for she felt as determined to resist an agent, as she thought herself incapable to withstand the principal.

Mrs. Howel, who had heard of the search, represented to Lady Aurora, the extreme impropriety of her ladyship's intercourse with a person thus suspiciously pursued; at least till the opinion of Lord Denmeath could be known. But Lady Aurora, fully satisfied that this helpless fugitive was her half-sister, was now as firm as she had hitherto been facile; and declared that, though her personal inclinations should still yield to her respect for her uncle, her sense of filial duty to the memory of her father, must bind her, openly and unreservedly, to sustain his undoubted daughter.

A waiter now interrupted them, to demand admission to Miss Ellis for a foreigner.

"She is not here!—There is no Miss Ellis here! No such person!"—precipitately cried Lady Aurora; but the foreigner himself, who stood behind the waiter, glided into the room.

Lady Aurora nearly fainted; Juliet screamed and hid her face; the foreigner called out, "Ah, Mademoiselle Juliette! c'est, donc, vous! et vous ne me reconnoissez pas?"†

"Ah heaven!" cried Juliet, uncovering her face; "Ambroise! my good, my excellent Ambroise! is it you?—and you only?"—Turning then, enraptured, to Lady Aurora, "Kindest," she cried, "and tenderest of human beings! condescend to receive, and to aid me to thank, the valuable person to whom I owe my first deliverance!"

Lady Aurora, revived and charmed, poured forth the warmest praises; while Juliet, eagerly demanding news of the Marchioness; and whether he could give any intelligence of the Bishop; saw his head droop, and seized with terrour, exclaimed, "Oh Ambroise! am I miserable for ever!"

He hastened to assure her that they were both alive, and well; and, in the ecstacy of her gratitude, upon the cessation of her first direful surmise, she promised to receive all other information with courage.

He shook his head, with an air the most sorrowful; and then related that the Bishop, after delays, dangers, fruitless journies, and disasters innumerable, which had detained him many months in the interiour, had, at last, and most unfortunately, reached a port, whence he was privately to embark for joining his niece, just as the commissary, upon returning from his abortive expedition, was re-landed. By some cruel accident, the voice of the prelate reached his ear: immediate imprisonment, accompanied by treatment the most ignominious, ensued. Ambroise, who, for the satisfaction of the Marchioness, had attended the Bishop to the coast, was seized also; and both would inevitably have been executed, had not a project occurred to the commissary, of employing Ambroise to demand and recover his prey, and her dowry.

Ambroise stopt and wept.

† "Ah, Miss Juliet! it is you then! and you do not know me?"

Bloodless now became the face of Juliet, though with forced, yet decided courage, "I understand you!" she cried; "and Oh! if I can save him,—by any sacrifice, any devotion,—I am contented! and I ought to be happy!"

"Ah, cruel sister!" cried Lady Aurora; "would you kill me?"—

Juliet, shedding a torrent of tears, tenderly embraced her.

"The Bishop," Ambroise continued, "no sooner comprehended than he forbade the attempt; but he was consigned, unheard, to a loathsome cell; and Ambroise was almost instantly embarked; with peremptory orders to acquaint *la citoyenne Julie* that unless she returned immediately to her husband, in order to sign and seal, by his side, and as his wife, their joint claim to her portion, upon the terms that Lord Denmeath had dictated; the most tremendous vengeance should fall upon the hypocritical old priest, by every means the most terrible that could be devised."

"I am ready! quite ready!" cried the pale Juliet, with energy; "I do not sacrifice, I save myself by preserving my honoured guardian!"

This eagerness to rescue her revered benefactor, which made her feel gloriously, though transiently, the exaltation of willing martyrdom, soon subsided into the deepest grief, upon seeing Lady Aurora, shivering, speechless, and nearly lifeless, sink despondingly upon the ground.

Juliet, kneeling by her side, and pressing her nearly cold face to her bosom, bathed her cheeks, throat, and shoulders with fast falling tears; but felt incapable of changing her plan. Yet all her own anguish was almost intolerably embittered, by thus proving the fervour of an affection, in which almost all her wishes might have been concentrated, but that honour, conscience, and religion united to snatch her from its enjoyment.

The news that Lady Aurora was taken ill, spread quickly to Mrs. Howel; and brought that lady to the apartment of Juliet in person. Lady Aurora was already recovered, and seated in the folding arms of Juliet, with whom her tears were bitterly, but silently mingling.

Mrs. Howel, shocked and alarmed, summoned the female attendants to conduct her ladyship to her own apartment.

Lady Aurora would accept no aid save from Juliet; fondly leaning upon whose arm she reached a sofa in her bed-chamber; where she assumed, though with cruel struggles against her yielding nature, voice and courage to pronounce, "My dear Mrs. Howel, you have always been so singularly good to me,—you have always done me so much honour, that you must not, will not refuse to be kinder to me still, and to permit me to introduce to you . . . Miss Granville! . . . For this young lady, Mrs. Howel, is my sister! . . . my very dear sister!"

Utterly confounded, Mrs. Howel made a silent inclination of the head, with eyes superciliously cast down. The letter of Sir Jaspar Herrington had not failed to convince her that this was the real offspring of Lord Granville; whose existence had never been doubted in the world, but whose legitimacy had never been believed. Still, however, Mrs. Howel, who was now, from her own hard conduct, become the young orphan's personal enemy, flattered herself that means might be found to prevent the publication of such a story; and determined to run no risk by appearing to give it credit; at the same time that, in her uncertainty of the event, she softened the austerity of her manner; and gave orders to the servants to shew every possible respect to a person who had the honour to be admitted to Lady Aurora Granville.

Juliet was in too desperate a state for any thought, or care, relative to Mrs. Howel; and, having soothed Lady Aurora by promises of a speedy return, she hastened back to Ambroise.

She earnestly besought him, since her decision would be immutable, to make immediate enquiries whence they might embark with the greatest expedition.

Sadly, yet, so circumstanced, not unwillingly he agreed; and gave to her aching heart nearly the only joy of which it was susceptible, in the news that the Marchioness was already at the sea-side, awaiting the expected arrival of her darling daughter.

Ambroise had been entrusted, he said, by the commissary, with this cruel office, from his well known fidelity to the Marchioness and to the Bishop, which, where the alternative was so dreadful, would urge him, whatever might be his repugnance, to its faithful discharge. His orders had been to proceed straight to Salisbury, whence, under the name of Miss Ellis, he was to seek Juliet in every direction. And her various adventures had made so much noise in that neighbourhood, that she had been traced, with very little difficulty to Teignmouth.

Her terrible compliance being thus solemnly fixed, she left him to prepare for their departure the next morning, and returned to the afflicted Lady Aurora; by whose side she remained till midnight; struggling to sink her own sufferings, and to hide her shuddering disgust and horrour, in administering words of comfort, and exhibiting an example of fortitude, to her weeping sister.

But when, early the next morning, with the dire idea of leave-taking, she revisited the gentle mourner, she found her nourishing a hope that her Juliet might yet be melted to a change of plan. "Oh my sister!" she cried, "my whole heart cannot thus have been opened to affection, to confidence, to fondest friendship, only to be broken by this dreadful separation! Our souls cannot have been knit together by ties of the sweetest trust, only to be rent for ever asunder! You will surely reflect before you destroy us both? for do you think you can now be a single victim?"

Dissolved with tenderness, yet agonized with grief, Juliet could but weep, and ejaculate half-pronounced blessings; while Lady Aurora, with renovating courage, said, "Ah! think, sweet Juliet, think, if our father,—was he not our's alike?—had lived to know the proud day of receiving his long lost, and so accomplished daughter, such as I see her now!—would he not have said to me, 'Aurora! this is your sister! You are equally my children; love her, then, tenderly, and let there be but one heart between you!'—And will you, then, Juliet, deliver us both up to wretchedness? Must I see you no more? And only have seen you, now, to embitter all the rest of my life?"

"Oh resistless Aurora!" cried the miserable Juliet, "rend not thus my heart!—Think for me, my Aurora;—Think, as well as feel for me,—and then—dispose of me as you will!"

"I accept being the umpire, my Juliet! my tenderest sister! I accept it, and you are saved!—We are both saved!—for this would be a sacrifice beyond any call of duty!"—cried Lady

Aurora, instantly reviving, not simply to serenity, but to felicity, to rapture. Her tears were dried up, her eyes shone with delight, and smiles the softest and most expressive dimpled her chin, and played about her cheeks and mouth, while, with a transport new to her serene temperament, she embraced the appalled Juliet. "'Tis now, indeed," she continued, "I feel I have a sister! 'Tis now I feel the force of kindred fondness! If you had not loved me with a sister's affection, you would not have listened to my solicitations; and if you had not listened, such a disappointment, and your loss together,—do you think I should have been strong enough to survive them?"

But this enchantment lasted not long; she soon perceived it was without participation, and her joy vanished, "like the baseless fabric of a vision."* Anguish sat upon the brow of Juliet; fits of shuddering horrour shook every limb; and her only answer to these tender endearments was by tears and embraces; while she strove to hide her altered and nearly distorted face upon Lady Aurora's shoulder.

"Speak to me, my sister!" cried Lady Aurora. "Tell me that your pity for the good Bishop is not stronger than all your love for me? than all your value for your own security from barbarous brutality? than your trust in Providence, that will surely protect so pious and exemplary a person?"

"No, Heaven forbid!" answered Juliet; "but, when Providence permits us to see a way,—when it opens a path to us by which evil may be avoided, by which duty may be exerted,—ought the difficulties of that way, the perils of that path, to make us recoil from the attempt? When the natural means are obvious, ought we to wait for some miracle?"

"Ah, my sister!" cried Lady Aurora, "would you, then, still go? Have you yielded in mere transient compassion?"

"No, sweet Aurora, no! To ruin your peace would every way destroy mine! Yet—what a fatality! to fear the very enjoyment of the family-protection for which I have been sighing my whole life, lest I can enjoy it but by a crime! I abandon the post of honour, in leaving the benefactor, the supporter, the preserver of my orphan existence, to perpetual chains, if not to massacre!—Or I break the tender heart of the gentlest, purest, and most beloved of sisters!"

Lady Aurora, now, looked all consternation; and, after a disturbed pause, "If you think it wrong," she cried, "not to sacrifice yourself,—Oh my sister! let not mere commiseration for my weakness lead you astray! We all know there is another world, in which we yet may meet again!"

"Angel! angel!" cried Juliet, pressing Lady Aurora to her bosom. "You will aid me, then, to do right? by nobly supporting yourself, you will help to keep me from sinking? Religion will give you strength of mind to submit to our worldly separation, and all my sufferings will be endurable, while they open to me the hope of a final re-union with my angel sister!"

They now mutually sought to re-animate each other. Piety strengthened the fortitude of Juliet, and supplied its place to Lady Aurora; and, in soft pity to each other, each strove to look away from, and beyond, all present and actual evil; and to work up their minds, by religious hopes and reflections, to an enthusiastic foretaste of the joys of futurity.

CHAPTER XC

THIS tenderly touching intercourse was broken in upon by a summons to Ambroise, whom Juliet found waiting for her in the corridor; where he was beginning to recount to her, that he had met with a sea-officer, who had promised him a letter of recommendation for procuring a passport, if he could bring proof that he was a proper person for having one; when the Admiral issued abruptly from his apartment.

He took off his hat, though with a severe air, to Juliet, who, abashed, passed on to her chamber; but stopping and bluffly accosting Ambroise, "Harkee!" he cried, "my lad! a word with you!—Pray, what business have you with that girl! I have, I know, as good as promised to help you off; but let all be fair and above board. I don't pretend to have much taste for any person who would go out of old England when once he has got footing into it; thoff if I had had the misfortune to be born in France, there's no being sure that I might not have liked it myself; from knowing no better: for which reason I think nothing narrower than holding a man cheap for loving his country, be it ever so bad a one. Therefore, if you have a mind, my lad, as far as yourself goes, to sheer off; as you are neither a sailor nor a soldier, nor, moreover, a prisoner, I will lend you a hand and welcome. But no foul play! If there's any person of your acquaintance, that, after being born in old England, wants to go flaunting and jiggetting to outlandish countries, you'll do well to give her a hint to keep astern of me; for I shall never uphold a person who behaves o' that sort."

Ambroise, in broken English, earnestly entreated him not to withdraw his promised protection; and Juliet, desirous to obtain his counsel for the execution of her perilous enterprize, ventured back, and joined to petition for instructions where she might embark most expeditiously; endeavouring to make her peace with him, by solemnly avowing, that necessity, not inclination, urged her to undertake this voyage; and claiming assistance, a second time, from his tried benevolence.

The words tried benevolence, and a second time, which inadvertently escaped her, from eagerness to interest his attention, struck him forcibly with ire. "Avast!" he cried, "none of your flummery!* You think, belike, because you've got a pretty face, to make a fool of me? but that's sooner thought than done! You'll excuse me for speaking my mind a little plainly; for how the devil, asking your pardon for such a word, should I do any thing for you a second time, when I have never seen or thought of you, up to this moment, a first? Please to tell me that!"

Juliet, looking round, and seeing that no witnesses were by, gently enquired whether he had no remembrance of a poor voyager, whom he had had the charity to save, the preceding winter, from immediate destruction, by admitting into a boat?

"What! a swarthy minx? with a sooty sort of skin, and all over rags and jags? Yes, yes, I remember her well enough: I thank her! but I don't much advise her to come in my way! She turned out a mere impostor. She was probably French. I gave her a guinea, and paid for her place to town, and her entertainment. She took my guinea, and eat and drank; and then made off by some other way! and has never been heard of since. I described her at all the Dover stages and diligences; for I intended to give her a trifle more, to help her to find her friends, for fear of her falling into bad hands. But I could never get any tidings of her; she was a mere cheat. How did you come to know the jade?"

Juliet blushed violently, and, with some difficulty stammered out, "Kind as you are, Sir, good and charitable,—you have not well judged that young person!"—

"By all that's sacred," cried he, striking his cane upon the ground, "if it were possible for a girl to be painted to such a pitch of nicety, I should swear you were that very mamselle yourself!—though, if you are, I should take it as a favour if you would tell me, how the devil it came into your head to let me pay for your stage-coach, when you never made use of your place? Where the fun of that was I can't make out!"

"I am but too sensible, Sir, that every thing seems against me!" said Juliet, in a melancholy tone; "yet the time, probably, is not very far off, when I may be able sufficiently to explain myself, to cause you much regret,—so generous seems your nature;—should you refuse me your services in my very great distress!"

The Admiral now looked deeply perplexed, yet evidently touched. "I should be loath, Madam," he said, "very loath, indeed, for the matter of that, there's something so agreeable in you,—to think you no better than you should be. Not that one ought to expect perfection; for a woman is but a woman; which a man, as her native superiour, ought always to keep in mind; however, don't take it amiss that I throw out that remark; for I don't mean it to dash you."

Juliet, too much shocked to reply, cast up her eyes in silent appeal to heaven, and, entering her room, resolved to fold two guineas in a small packet, and to send them to the Admiral by Ambroise, for an immediate acquittal of her double pecuniary debt.

But the Admiral, struck by her manner, looked thoughtful, and dissatisfied with himself; and, again calling to Ambroise, said, "Harkee, my lad! I should not be sorry to know who that young gentlewoman is?—I am afraid she thinks me rather unmannerly. And the truth is, I don't know that I have been over and above polite: which I take shame to myself for, I give you my word; for I am always devilish bad company with myself when I have misbehaved to a female; because why? She has no means to right herself. So I beg you to make my excuse to the gentlewoman. And please to tell her that, though I am no great friend to ceremony, I am very sorry if I have affronted her."

Ambroise said, that he was sure the young lady would think no more of it, if his honour would but be kind enough to give the recommendatory letter.

"Why, with regard to that," said the Admiral, after some deliberation, "I would do her any service, whereby I might shew my good will; after having been rather over-rough, be her class what it may, considering she's a female; and, moreover, seems somewhat in jeopardy; if I were not so cursedly afraid of being put upon! You, that are but an outlandish man,—though I can't say but you've as good a look as another man;—a very honest look, if one might judge by the face;—which made me take to you, without much thinking what I was about, I can tell you!—"

Ambroise, bowing low, hoped that he would not repent his goodness.

"You, I say, being more in the use of being juggled,* begging your pardon, from its being more the custom of foreign parts; can have no great notion, naturally, how little a British tar,—a person you don't know over-much about, I believe!" smiling, "there not being a great many such, as I am told, off our own shores!—You, as I was remarking, can't be expected to have much notion how little a British tar relishes being over-reached. But the truth, Sir, is, we are set afloat upon the wide ocean, before we have well done with our slabbering bibs;* which makes us the men we are! But, then, all we know of the world is only by bits and scraps; except, mayhap, what we can pick out of books. And that's no great matter; for the chief of a seaman's library is most commonly the history of cheats and rogues; so that we are always upon the look out, d'ye see, for fear of false colours."

Ambroise began a warm protestation of his honesty.

"Not but that, let me tell you, Sir!" the Admiral went on, "we have as many good scholars upon quarter-deck, counting such as could pay for their learning when they were younkers,* as in any other calling. But this was not the case with myself, who owe nothing to birth nor favour; whereof I am proud to be thankful; for, from ten years old, when I was turned adrift by my family, I have had little or no schooling,—except by the buffets of the world."

Then, after ruminating for some minutes, he told Ambroise that he should not be sorry to make his apologies to the gentlewoman himself; adding, "For I could have sworn, when I first met her in the gallery, I had seen her some where before; though I could not make out how nor when. But if she's only that black madmysell washed white, I should like to have a little parley with her. She may possibly do me the service of helping me to find a friend; and if she does, I sha'n't be backward, God willing, to requite her. And harkee, my lad! I should be glad to know the gentlewoman's name. What's she called?"

"She's called Mademoiselle Juliette, Monsieur."

"Juliet?—Are you sure of that?" cried the Admiral, starting. "Juliet?—Are you very sure, Sir?"

"Oui, oui, Monsieur."

"Harkee, sirrah! if you impose upon me, I'll trounce you within an inch of your life! Juliet, do you say? Are you sure it's Juliet?"

"Oui, Monsieur; Mademoiselle Juliette."

"Why then, as I am a living man, and on this side t'other world, I must speak to her directly! Tell her so this instant."

Ambroise tapped, and Juliet opened the door; but, when he would have spoken, the Admiral, taking him by the shoulders, and turning him round, bid him go about his business; and, entering the room, shut the door, and flung himself upon a chair.

Rising, however, almost at the same instant, though much agitated, he made sundry bows, but tried vainly to speak; while the astonished Juliet waited gravely for some explanation of so strange an intrusion.

"Madam," he at length said, "that Frenchman there, who, it's like enough, don't know what he says,—pretends your name is Juliet?"

"Sir!"—

"If it be so, Ma'am,—you'll do me a remarkable piece of

service, if you will be so complaisant as to let me know how you came by that name?"

Juliet now felt alarmed.

"It's rather making free, Ma'am, I confess, but I shall take it as a special favour, if you'll be pleased to tell me what part of the world you come from?"

"Sir, I—I—"

"If you think my inquisitiveness impertinent, Ma'am; which it's like enough you may, I shall beg leave to give you an item of my reason for it; and then it's odds but you'll make less scruple to give me the reply. Not that I mean to make conditions; for binding people down only hampers good will. But when you have heard me, you may be glad, perchance, to speak of your own accord; for I don't know, I give you my solemn word, but that at this very moment you are talking to one of your own kin!"

He fixed his eyes upon her, then, with great earnestness.

"My own kin?—What, Sir, do you mean?"

"I'll tell you out of hand, Ma'am,—if I may be so bold as to sit down; for whether we happen to be relations or no', there can be no law against our being friends."

Juliet hastily presented him a chair, and scarcely breathed from eagerness to reciprocate the enquiry. She had never heard the Admiral mentioned but by his military title.

Seated now by her side, he looked at her for some instants, smilingly, though with glistening eyes; "Madam," he said, "I had a sister whose name was Juliet!—and the name is dear to my soul for her sake! And it's no common name; so that I never hear it without being moved. She left a child, Ma'am, who for some unnatural reasons, that I sha'n't enter upon just now, was brought up in foreign parts. This child had her own sweet name; and her own sweet character, too, I make small doubt; as well as her own sweet face."—

He stopt, and again more earnestly looked at Juliet; but, seeing her strongly affected, begged her pardon, and, brushing a tear from his eye, went on.

"When I came home from my last station in the East Indies, I crossed over the channel to see after her; a great proof of my good will, I can tell you! for no little thing would have carried me to that lawless place; and from the best land upon God's earth! but I got nothing for my pains, except a cursed bad piece of news, which turned me upside down; for I was told that she was married to a French monsieur! Upon which I swore, God willing, never to see her face to the longest day I had to live! And I came away with that resolution. However, a Christian is never so perfect himself, as not to look over a flaw in his neighbour. Wherefore, if I could get any item of the poor girl's repentance, I don't think, for my dear sister's sake, but I could still take her to my bosom,—yea, to my very heart of hearts!"

"Tell me, Sir," cried Juliet, rising, with clasped hands, and eyes fast filling with tears; "tell me,—for I have never heard it,—your name?"

"By all that's holy!" cried he, rising too, and trembling, "you make my heart beat all over my body!—My name is Powel! In the name, then, of the Most High,—are you not my niece yourself?"

Juliet dropt at his feet; "Oh heavenly Providence!" she ejaculated, "you are then my poor mother's brother!"

Speech now, for a considerable time, was denied to both; strong emotions, though of joy, nearly suffocated Juliet, while the Admiral sobbed over her as he pressed her in his arms.

"My girl!" he cried, when a little recovered, "my sister's daughter!—daughter of the dearest of sisters!—I have found, then, at last, something appertaining to my poor sister! You shall be dear to my soul for her sake, whatever you may be for your own. And, moreover, as to what you may have done up to this time, whereof I don't mean to judge uncharitably, every one of us being but frail, I shall let it all pass by. So hold up your head, and take comfort, my girl, and don't be shy of your old uncle; for whatever may have slipt from him in a moment of choler, he'll protect you, God willing, to his last hour; and never come out with another unkind word upon what is past and gone."

The heart of Juliet was too full to let her offer any immediate vindication: she could but pronounce, "My uncle, when I can be explicit,—you will not—I hope, and trust,—have cause to blush for me!"—

"Why then you are a very good girl!" cried he, well pleased, "an excellent girl, in the main, I make small doubt." He then demanded, though not, he protested, to find fault with what was past; what had brought her over to her native land in such a ragged, mauled, and black condition; which had prevented the least guess of who she was; "for if, when I saw you off the coast," he continued, "you had shewn yourself such as you are now, you have so strong a look of my dear sister, that I should have hailed you out of hand. Though when I saw you Here it never came into my head; because why? I believed you to be There. And yet, instinct is main powerful, whereof I am a proof; for I took a fancy to you, even when I thought you an old woman; and, which is worse, a French woman. Coming away from those shores gave me a good opinion of you at once."

He then made many tender enquiries concerning the last illness, and the death of Mrs. Powel, his mother; whom it was now, he said, one-and-twenty years since he had seen; as, upon his poor father's insolvency, he had been taken from the royal navy, and sent out, in the company's service, to the East Indies.*

Juliet, after satisfying his filial solicitude, ventured to express her own, upon every circumstance of her mother's life, which had fallen to his knowledge.

The insolvency, the Admiral replied, had soon been succeeded by the death of his father; and then his poor mother and sister had been driven to a cheap country residence, in the neighbourhood of Melbury-Hall. There, before he set out for the East Indies, he had passed a few days to take leave; in which time Lord Granville, the Earl of Melbury's only son, who had met them, it seems, in their rural strolls, had got such a footing in their house, that he called in both morning and evening; and stayed sometimes for hours, without knowing how time went. Uneasy upon remarking this, he counselled his sister to keep out of the young nobleman's way; and advised his mother to change her house. They both promised so to do; but, for all that, before he set sail, he determined to wait upon his lordship himself; which he did accordingly; and made free to tell him, that he should take it but kind of his lordship, if he would not be quite so sweet upon his sister. His lordship made fair promises, with such a genteelness, that there was no help but to give him credit; and, this being done, he went off with an easy heart. He remained in the Company's service some time; during which, the letters of his mother brought him the sorrowful tidings of his sister's death; followed up, afterwards, by an account that, for her own health's sake, she was gone over to reside in France.

"This was a bit of news," he continued, "which I did not take quite so kindly as I ought, mayhap, to have done, it not appertaining to a son to have the upper hand of his mother. But, having been, from the first, somewhat of a spoilt child, whereby my poor mother made herself plenty of trouble; I was always rather over choleric when I was contradicted. Taking it, therefore, rather amiss her going out of old England, no great matter of letter-writing passed between us from that time, to my return to my native land.

"It was then I was told the worst tidings that ever I wish to hear! one came, and t'other came, and all had some fuel to make the fire burn fiercer, to give me an item that Lord Granville had over-persuaded my sister to elope with him; and that she died of a broken heart; leaving a child, that my mother, for my sister's reputation's sake, had gone to bring up in foreign parts. My blood boiled so, then, in my veins, that how it ever got cool enough not to burn me to a cinder is a main wonder. But I vowed revenge, and that, I take it, sustained me; revenge being, to my seeming, a noble passion, when it is not to spite those who have done an ill turn to ourselves, but to punish those who have oppressed the helpless. What aggravated me the more, was hearing that he was married; and had two fine children, who were dawdled about every day in his coach; while the child of my poor sister was shut up, immured, no body knew where, in an outlandish country. I called him, therefore, to account, and bid him meet me, at five o'clock in the morning, at a coffee-house. We went into a private room. I used no great matter of ceremony in coming to the point. You have betrayed, I cried, the unprotected! You have seduced the forlorn! You have sold yourself to the devil!—and as you have given him, of your own accord, your soul, I am come to lend a hand to your giving him your body."—

"Shocking!—Shocking!" interrupted Juliet. "O my uncle!"—

"Why it was not over mannerly, I own; but I was too much aggrieved to stand upon complimenting. I loved her, said I, with all my heart and soul; but I bore patiently with her death, because I am a Christian; and I know that life and death come from God; but I scorn to bear with her dishonour, for that comes from a man. For the sake of your wife and children, as they are not in fault, I would conceal your unmanly baseness; but for the sake of my much injured sister, who was dearer to me than all your kin and kind, I intend, by the grace, and with the help of the Most High, to take a proper vengeance for her wrongs, by blowing out your brains; unless, by the law of chance, you should blow out mine; which, however, I should hold myself the most pitiful of cowards to expect in so just a cause.

"I then presented him my pistols, and gave him his choice which he would have."

"Oh my poor father!" cried Juliet. "Go on, my uncle, go on!"

"He heard me to the finish without a word; and with a countenance so sad, yet so firm, and which had so little the hue of guilt, that I have thought since, many a time and often, that, if choler had not blinded me, I should have stopt half way, and said, This is surely an innocent man!"

"Oh blessed be that word!" cried Juliet, clasping her hands, "and blessed, blessed be my uncle for so kindly pronouncing it!"

"With what temper he answered me! If I insisted, he said, upon satisfaction, he would not deny it me; 'And I ought, indeed,' he said, 'after an attack so insulting, to demand it for myself. But you are in an errour; and your cause seems so completely the cause of justice and virtue, that I cannot defend, till I have cleared myself. The sister whom you would avenge was the beloved of my soul! Never will you mourn for her as I have mourned! I neither betrayed nor seduced her. The love that I bore her was as untainted as her own honour. The immoveable views of my father to another alliance, kept our connexion secret; but your sister, your unspotted sister, was my wedded wife!'—The joy of my heart, at that moment, my dear girl, made me forget all my mishaps. I jumped,—for I was but a boy, then, to what I am now; and I flung my arms about his neck, and kissed him; which his lordship did not seem to take at all unkindly. Since she is not dishonoured, I cried, I can bear all else like a man. She is gone, indeed, my poor sister!—but 'tis to heaven she is gone! and I can but pray that we may both, in our due time, go there after her!—And upon that,—if I were to tell you the honest truth,—we both fell a blubbering.—But she was no common person, my dear sister!"

Juliet wept with varying emotions.

"His lordship," the Admiral continued, "then recorded the whole history of his marriage, the birth of his child, and the loss of his poor wife. That the child, accompanied by her grandmother, who scarcely breathed out of its sight, was gone to be brought up in a convent, under the care of a family of quality, that had a grand castle in its neighbourhood; and under the immediate guidance of a worthy old parson; that, as soon as she was educated, he should go over to fetch her, and write a letter to his father to own his first marriage. But he begged me, for family-reasons, to agree to the concealment, till I returned home for good; and had a house of my own in which I could receive the child, in the case his second lady and his father should behave unhandsomely. I had no great taste for a hiding scheme; but I was so overcome with joy to think my sister had been always a woman of honour, that I was in no cue for squabbling: and, moreover, I gave way with the greater complaisance, from the fear of seeing the child fall into the hands of people who would be ashamed of her, whereby her spirit might be broken; and, moreover, I can't say but I took it kind of his lordship the thought of letting her come to a house of mine; for I had already returned to his majesty's service; which, God willing, the devil himself shall never draw me from again; and I was a post-captain,* and in pretty good circumstances. So I thought I had as well not meddle, nor do mischief. And the more, as his lordship was so honourable as to entrust to me a copy of a codicil to his will; written all in his own hand, and duly signed and sealed;

wherein he owns his lawful marriage with my poor sister; and leaves her child the same fortune that he leaves to his daughter by his wife of quality."

"Is it possible!—How fortunate! And have you, still, my dear uncle, this codicil?"

"Have I? Aye, my girl! I would sooner part with my right hand! It's the proof and declaration of my sister's honour! and I would not change it against all the diamonds, and all the pearls, and all the shawls of all the nabobs of all Asia! It has been my whole comfort in all my difficult voyages and hard services."

Ah! thought Juliet, were my revered Bishop safe, I might now be every way happy!

"What passed in my mind at that time, was to cross over the Channel, to get my dear mother's blessing, and to give my own to my little niece. But it's of no great consequence what we plan, if it is not upheld by the Most High. I was all prepared, but I wrote never a word over, for the sake of giving my mother a surprize; when, all at once, I had a sudden promotion, with orders to return to the East Indies. And there I was stationed, on and off, in and out, till t'other day, as one may say. And when, at last, I got home again; meaning to marry Jenny Barker,—as pretty a girl as ever came into the world; and to set her at the head of my house, and equip her handsomely,—I found every thing turned upside down! Lord Granville had been dead five months, and his father about as many weeks. I had already heard, in the Indies, that my poor mother was dead; and when I went to get a little comfort with Jenny Barker, and to give her the baubles I had got together for her in the Indies,—always priding myself in thinking how smart she'd look in this! and how pretty her face would peep out of that!—I found her so mortally changed, that I took her for her own mother! who I had left to the full as well looking twenty years before; for, after my first voyage, by ill luck, I had not seen Jenny, who was down in the country."

"But if she is amiable, uncle, and worthy—"

"You have a right way of thinking, my dear; and I honour your for it: but the disappointment came upon me so slap-dash, as one may say, for want of a little fore-thought, that I let out what passed in my mind with too little ceremony for making up again. However, I gave her the baubles; which she accepted out of hand; and made free to ask me to add something more, to make her amends for waiting for nothing; which was but fair; though it showed me that when she had lost her pretty face, she had no great matter to boast of in point of a noble way of thinking. I hope, else, I should have been above playing her false; without which I should be little to chuse from a scoundrel. But she was in such a main hurry to secure herself the rhino,* that it's my belief that her inside, if I could have got a look at it, was but little short, in point of ugliness, to her outside. Howbeit, I used her handsomely, and we parted friends."

The Admiral here walked about the room, a little disturbed, and then continued his narrative.

He crossed the Straits, having always preserved the direction of the lady of the castle near the convent; but the Revolution was then flaming; the castle had been burnt; all the family was dispersed; and he was warned not to make any enquiry even after the parson. But he grew sick of the whole business, and not sorry to cut it short, upon hearing that his niece, who was known by the appellation of Mademoiselle Juliette, was married to a French monsieur. He was coming away, in deep disgust, and burning wrath, when he was seized himself, and put into prison by order of Mr. Robespierre. But this durance did not last long; for he joined a party that was just getting off, and returned to Great Britain; and moreover, though little enough to his knowledge, in the very same vessel that brought over his niece. "And here, my dear girl, is the finish* of all I have to recount. But what I observe, with no great pleasure, if I should tell you my remark, is, that, while, for so many years, I have given up my head to nothing but thinking of my niece,—to the exception of poor Jenny Barker,—she does not seem so much as ever to have heard, or thought about her uncle?"

Juliet assured him, on the contrary, that her grandmother Powel had talked unceasingly of her son; but that, tender-hearted, timid, and devoted to Lord Granville, she had never ventured to trust to a letter a secret that demanded so much discretion; and had therefore postponed all communication to their meeting; of which she had lived in the constant hope. And Juliet herself, since the afflicting loss of that excellent lady, always believing him to be in the East Indies, had never dared claim his parentage, nor solicit his favour; her peculiar and unhappy situation making all written accounts, not only of her affairs, but of her name and her residence, dangerous.

This brought the conversation back to herself. "'Tis remarkable enough," said the Admiral, "that, in all this long parley, we have not yet said an item about the worst part of the job,—your marriage! How came you here without your husband? For all I have no great goust* to your marrying in that sort, God forbid I should uphold a wife in running away from her lawful spouse, even though he be a Frenchman! We should always do right, for the sake of shaming wrong. A man, being the higher vessel, may marry all over the globe, and take his wife to his home; but a woman, as she is only given him for his help-mate, must tack about after him, and come to the same anchorage."

Sadness now clouded the skin, and dimmed the eyes of Juliet. The story which she had to reveal, the hard necessity of separating herself from so near a relation, and so kind a protector, at the very moment of an apparent union; joined to the obstacles which his prejudices and feelings might put in the way of her decided sacrifice; made the avowal of her intention seem almost as difficult as its execution.

"Don't be cast down, however, my girl," continued the Admiral; "for when things are come to the worst, as I have taken frequent note, they often veer about, nobody knows how, and turn out for the best. I should as lieve you had not tied such an ugly knot,* I won't say to the contrary; howbeit, as the thing is done, we may as well make the best of it. The man may be a tolerable good Christian, mayhap, for a Papist. And indeed, to tell you the truth, though it is a thing I am not over fond of speaking about, I have seen some Frenchmen I could have liked mightily myself, if I had not known where they came from. I had some prisoners once aboard, that were as likely men, and as much of gentlemen, and as agreeable behaved, and had as good sense, too, of their own, as if they had been Englishmen. Perhaps your husband may be one of them? If so, let him come over here, and he shall want for nothing. I am always proud to shew old England; so invite him, my dear, to come."

"Alas!—alas!—" cried Juliet, weeping.

"What! he is but a sorry dog, then? Well, I can't pretend to be surprized at that. However, I'll tie up your fortune, and won't let him touch a penny of it, but upon condition that you come over for it yourself once a year. And now I have you safe and sure, I shall carry my codicil to Lord Denmeath,—a fellow of steel, they say!—and get you your thirty thousand pounds; for that, I am told, is the portion of the lady of quality's daughter. But all I shall give you myself shall only be bit by bit, till I know how that sorry fellow uses you. It's a main pity you threw yourself away in such a hurry! But I suppose he's a fine likely young dog?"

"Hideous! hideous!" off all guard, exclaimed the shuddering Juliet.

"Why, then, most like, you only married him for the sake of a little palaver? Poor girl! However, it's done, and a husband's a husband; so I'll ask no more questions."

Kissing her then very kindly, he said he would go and suck in a little fresh breeze upon the beach, to calm his spirits; for he felt as if he had been steering his vessel in a hurricane.

He asked her to accompany him; but she desired a little stillness and rest. He shook hands with her, and, with a look of concern, said, "My sister did but a foolish thing, after all, in marrying that young lord, however the world may judge it to have been an ambitious one. You would never have been smuggled out of your native land, in that fashion, if she had taken up with a man in her own rank of life: some honest tar, for example! for, to my seeming, there is not an honester person in the whole world, nor a person of more honour, than a British tar! And yet,—see the difference of those topsy-turvy marriages!—a worthy tar would have been proud of my sister for his wife; while your lord was only ashamed of her! for that's the bottom of the story, put what dust you will in your eyes for the top!"

CHAPTER XCI

JULIET, left alone, again vented her full heart by tears. Happiness never seemed within her reach, but to make her feel more severely the hard necessity that it must be resigned. All her tenderest affections had been delighted, and her most ardent wishes surpassed, in being recognized as his niece by a man of so much worth, honour, and benevolence as the Admiral; and her heart had been yet more exquisitely touched, by acknowledged affinity with so sweet a character as that of Lady Aurora; her portion, by the duplicate-codicil, flattered, and gave dignity to her softest feelings;—nevertheless, the cruelty of her situation was in nothing altered; the danger of the Bishop was still the same; the same, therefore, was her duty. Even for deliberation she allowed herself no choice, save whether to confess to the Admiral the dreadful nature of her call to the Continent; or to go thither simply as a thing of course, to join her husband.

For the latter, his approvance was declared; for the former, even his consent might be withdrawn: to spare, therefore, to his kind heart the unavailing knowledge of her misery; and to herself the useless conflicts that might ensue from the discovery; she ultimately decided to set out upon her voyage, with her story and misfortunes unrevealed.

This plan determined upon, she struggled to fortify her mind for its execution, by endeavouring to consider as her husband the man to whom, in any manner, she had given her hand; since so, only, she could seek to check the disgust with which she shrunk from him as her deadliest foe. She remembered, and even sought to call back, the terrific scruples with which she had been seized, when, while striving to escape, she heard him assert that she was his wife, and felt powerless to disavow his claim. Triumphant, menacing, and ferocious, she had fled him without hesitation, though not completely without doubt; but when she beheld him seized, in custody,—and heard him called her husband! and saw herself considered as his wife! duty, for that horrible instant, seemed in his favour; and, had not Sir Jaspar summoned her by her maiden name, to attend her own nearest relations, all her resistance had been subdued, by an overwhelming dread that to resist might possibly be wrong.

Recollection, also, told her that, at the epoch when, with whatever misery, she had suffered him to take her hand, no mental reservation had prepared for future flight and disavowal: she laboured therefore, now, to plead to herself the vows which she had listened to, though she had not pronounced; and to animate her sacrifice by the terrour of perjury.

Nevertheless, all these virtuous arguments against her own freedom, were insufficient to convince her that her marriage was valid. The violent constraint, the forced rites, the interrupted ceremony, the omission of every religious form;—no priest, no church to sanctify even appearances;—No! she cried, no! I am not his wife! even were it my wish, even were he all I prize upon earth, still I should fly him till we were joined by holier bands! Nevertheless, for the Bishop I meant the sacrifice, and, since so, only, he can be preserved;—for the Bishop I must myself invite its more solemn ratification!

Satisfied that this line of conduct, while dictated by tender gratitude, was confirmed by severer justice; she would not trust herself again with the sight of Lady Aurora, till measures were irreversibly taken for her departure; and, upon the return of the Admiral from his walk, she communicated to him, though without any explanation, her urgent desire to make the voyage with all possible expedition.

The Admiral, persuaded that her haste was to soften the harsh treatment of a husband who had inveigled her into marriage by flattery and falsehood, forbore either questions or comments; though he looked at her with commiseration; often shaking his head, with an expression that implied: What pity to have thrown yourself thus away! His high notions, nevertheless, of conjugal prerogative, made him approve and second her design; and, saying that he saw nothing gained by delay, but breeding more bad blood, he told her that he would conduct her to * * * himself, the next morning; and stay with her till he could procure her a proper passage; engaging to present her wherewithal to ascertain for her a good and hearty reception; with an assurance to her husband, that she should, at any time, have the same sum, only for fetching it in person.

This promising opening to occasional re-unions, gave her, now, more fortitude for announcing to her gentle sister the fixed approaching separation. But, though these were softening circumstances to their parting, Lady Aurora heard the decision with despair; and though the discovery of an uncle, a protector, in so excellent a man as the Admiral, offered a prospect of solid comfort; still she could dwell only upon the forced ties, the unnatural connexion, and the brutal character to which her unhappy sister must be the victim.

Each seeking, nevertheless, to console the other, though each, herself, was inconsolable, they passed together the rest of the melancholy, yet precious day; uninterrupted by the Admiral; who was engaged to dine out in the neighbourhood; or even by Mrs. Howel; who acquiesced, perforce, to the pleadings of Lady Aurora; in suffering her ladyship to remain in her own room with Juliet.

They engaged to meet again by day-break, the next morning, though to meet but to part. The next morning, however, when summoned to a post-chaise by the Admiral, the courage of Juliet, for so dreadful a leave-taking, failed; and, committing to paper a few piercingly tender words, she determined to write, more at length, all the consolation that she could suggest from the first stage.

But when, in speechless grief, she would have left her little billet in the anti-room, she found Lady Aurora's woman already in attendance; and heard that Lady Aurora, also, was risen and dressed. She feared, therefore, now, that an evasion might rather aggravate than spare affliction to her beloved sister; and, repressing her own feelings, entered the chamber.

Lady Aurora, who had scarcely closed her eyes all night, had now, in the fancied security of a meeting, from having placed her maid as a sentinel, just dropt asleep. Her pale cheeks, and the movement of sorrow still quivering upon her lips, shewed that she had been weeping, when overpowering fatigue had induced a short slumber. Juliet, in looking at her, thought she contemplated an angel. The touching innocence of her countenance; the sweetness which no sadness could destroy; the grief exempt from impatience; and the air of purity that overspread her whole face, and seemed breathing round her whole form, inspired Juliet, for a few moments, with ideas too sublime for mere sublunary sorrow. She knelt, with tender reverence, by her side, inwardly ejaculating, Sleep on, my angel sister! Recruit your harassed spirits, and wake not yet to the woes of your hapless Juliet! Then, placing gently upon her bosom the written farewell, she softly kissed the hem of her garments, and glided from the room.

She made a sign to the maid, for she had no power of utterance, not to awaken her lady; and hurried down stairs to join the Admiral, attended by the faithful Ambroise.

She was spared offering any apologies for detaining her uncle, by finding him preparing to step down to the beach, with a spying glass, without which he never stirred a step; to take a view, before they set off, of a sail, which his servant, an old seaman, had just brought him word was in sight. He helped her, therefore, into the chaise, begging her patience for a few minutes.

Juliet was not sorry to seize this interval for returning to the anti-room, to learn whether Lady Aurora were awake; and, by her resignation or emotion, to judge whether a parting embrace would prove baneful or soothing.

As she was re-entering the house, a vociferous cry of "Stop! stop!" issued from a carriage that was driving past. She went on, desiring Ambroise to give her notice when the Admiral came back; but had not yet reached the gallery, when the stairs were rapidly ascended by two, or more persons, one of which encircled her in his arms.

She shrieked with sudden horrour and despair, strenuously striving to disengage herself; though persuaded that the only person who would dare thus to assail her, was him to whom she was intentionally resigning her destiny; but her instinctive resistance was short; a voice that spoke love and sweetness exclaimed, "Miss Ellis! sweet, lovely Miss Ellis! you are, then, my sister!"

"Ah heaven! kind heaven!" cried the delighted Juliet, "is it you, Lord Melbury? and do you,—will you,—and thus kindly, own me?"

"Own? I am proud of you! My other sister alone can be as dear to me! what two incomparable creatures has heaven bestowed upon me for my sisters! How hard I must work not to disgrace them! And I will work hard, too! I will not see two such treasures, so near to me, and so dear to me, hold down their sweet heads with shame for their brother. Come with me, then, my new sister!—you need not fear to trust yourself with me now! Come, for I have something to say that we must talk over together alone!"

Putting, then, her willing arm within his, he eagerly conducted her down stairs; made her pass by the astonished Ambroise, at whom she nodded and smiled in the fulness of her contentment, and led her towards the beach; her heart exulting, and her eyes glistening with tender joy; even while every nerve was affected, and all her feelings were tortured, by a dread of quick approaching separation and misery.

"I am come," cried he, when they were at a little distance from the houses, "to take the most prompt advantage of my brotherly character. I have travelled all night, not to lose a moment in laying my scheme before you."

"What kindness!—Oh my lord!—and where did you hear,—where did Sir Jaspar's letter reach you?"

"Sir Jaspar?—I have received no letter from Sir Jaspar. I have seen no Sir Jaspar!"

"How, then, is it possible you can know—"

"Oh ho! you think you have no friend, then, but Sir Jaspar? And you suppose, perhaps, that you have no admirer but Sir Jaspar?"

"I am sure, at least, there is no other person to whom I have revealed my name."

"Then he must have betrayed it to some other himself, my sweet sister! for 'tis not from him I have had my intelligence. Be less sure, therefore, for the future, of an old man, and trust a younger one more willingly! However, there is no time now for raillery; a messenger is waiting the result of our conference. I am fully informed, my precious sister, of your terrible situation; I will not stop now to execrate your infernal pursuer, though he will not lose my execrations by the delay! I know, too, your sublime resolution to save our dear guardian,—for yours is ours!—that good and reverend Bishop; and to look upon yourself to be tied up, as a bond-woman,* till you are formally released from those foul shackles. Do I state the case right?"

"Oh far, far too accurately! And even now, at a moment so blest! I must tear myself away,—by my own will, with whatever horrour!—from the sweetest of sisters,—from you, my kindest brother!—and from the most benevolent of uncles, by a separation a thousand times more dreadful than any death!"

"Take comfort, sweet sister! take comfort, loveliest Miss Ellis!—for I can't help calling you Miss Ellis, now and then, a little while longer:—I have a plan to make you free! to set you completely at liberty, and yet save that excellent Bishop!"—

"Oh my lord! how heavenly an idea!—but how impossible!"

"Not at all! 'tis the easiest thing in the world! only hear me. That wretch who claims you, shall have the portion he demands; the six thousand pounds; immediately upon signing your release, sending over the promissory-note of Lord Denmeath, and delivering your noble Bishop into the hands of the person who shall carry over the money; which, however, shall only be paid at some frontier town, whence the Bishop may come instantly hither."

Struck with rapturous surprize, Juliet scarcely restrained herself from falling at his feet. She pressed his arm, she kissed the edge of his coat, and, while striving, inarticulately, to call for blessings upon his head, burst into a passion of tears,— though tears of ecstatic joy,—that nearly deprived her of respiration.

"My sister! my dear sister!" tenderly cried Lord Melbury, "how ashamed you make me? Could you, then, expect less? What a poor opinion you have entertained of your poor brother! I give you nothing! I merely agree that you shall possess what is your due. Know you not that you are entitled to thirty thousand pounds from our estate? To the same fortune that has been settled upon Aurora? 'Tis from your own portion, only, my poor sister, that this six thousand will be sunk."

"Can you, then, generous, generous, Lord Melbury!—can you see thus, without regret, without murmur, so capital a sum suddenly and unexpectedly torn from you?"

"I have not yet enjoyed it, my dear sister; I shall not, therefore, miss it. But if I had possessed it always, should I not be paid, ten million of times paid, by finding such a new sister? I shall be proud to shew the whole world I know how to prize such a relation. And I will not have them think me such a mere boy, because I am still rather young, as to be at a loss how to act by myself. I shall not, therefore, consult my uncle, for I am determined not to be ruled by him. I will solemnly bind myself to pay your whole fortune the moment I am of age. It is my duty, and my pride, and, at the same time, my delight, to spare your delicacy, as well as my own character, and our dear father's memory, any process, or any dispute."

Then, opening his arms, with design to embrace her, but checking himself upon recollecting that he might be observed, he animatedly added, "Yes, my dear father! I will shew how I cherish your memory, by my care of your eldest born! by my care of her interests, her safety, and her happiness!—As to her honour," he added, with a conscious smile, "she has shewn me that she knows how to be its guardian herself!"

The grateful Juliet frankly acknowledged, that both the thought and the wish had frequently occurred to her, of rescuing the Bishop, through her portion, without herself: but she had been utterly powerless to raise it. She was under age, and uncertain whether her rights might ever be proved: and the six thousand pounds proffered by Lord Denmeath, she was well aware, would never be accorded but to establish her as an alien. Her generous brother, by anticipating, as well as confirming her claims, alone could realize such a project. With sensations, then, of unmixed felicity, that seemed lifting her, while yet on earth, into heaven, she was flying to call for the participation of Lady Aurora, and of her uncle, in her joy; when Lord Melbury, stopping her, said, that all was not yet prepared for communication.

"You clearly," he continued, "agree to the scheme?"

"With transport!" she cried; "and with eternal thankfulness!"

Without delay, then, he said, they must appoint a person of trust, who knew the French language well, and to whom the whole history might be confided; to carry over the offer, and the money, and to bring back the Bishop. "And I have a friend," he continued, "now ready for the enterprize. One equally able and willing to claim the Bishop, and to give undoubted security for the six thousand pounds. Can you form any notion who such a man may be?"

He looked at her gaily, yet with a scrutiny that made her blush. One person only could occur to her; but occurred with an alarming sense of impropriety in allowing him such an employment, that instantly damped her high delight. She dropt her eyes; an unrepressed sigh broke from her heart; but secret consciousness hushed all enquiry into the truth of her conjecture.

In silence, too, for a moment, Lord Melbury contemplated her; struck with her sudden sadness, and uncertain to what it might be attributed. Affectionately, then, taking her hand, "I must come," he cried, "to the point, or my messenger will lose his patience. Proposals of marriage the most honourable have been made to me; such, my dear sister, as merit my best interest with you. The person is unexceptionable, high in mind, manners, and family, and has long been attached to you——"

Juliet here, with dignity, interrupted him, "My lord, I will not ask who this may be; I even beg not to be told. I can listen to no one! Till the Bishop is released and safe, I hold myself merely to be his hostage; and, till my freedom, atrociously as it has been violated, shall be legally restored to me, I cannot but feel hurt,—for I will not say offended where the intention is so kind, and so pure,—that any proposals of any sort, and from any person, should be addressed to me!"

Lord Melbury, prepared for expostulation, was beginning to reply; but she solemnly besought him not to involve her in any new conflicts.

She then asked his permission to introduce him to her uncle, Admiral Powel; whom she desired to join upon the beach.

No, no; he answered; other business, still more urgent, must have precedence. And, holding both her hands, he insisted upon acquainting her, that it was Mr. Harleigh who had been his informant of her history and situation; and that she was the undoubted and legitimate daughter of Lord Granville; all which he had learnt from Sir Jaspar Herrington. "And Mr. Harleigh has begged my leave," continued his lordship, smiling, "though I am not, you may think, perhaps, very old for judging of such matters; to make his addresses to you.—Now don't put yourself into that flutter till you hear how he arranged it; for he knows all your scruples, and reveres them,—or, rather, and reveres you, my sweet sister! for your scruples we both think a little chimerical: don't be angry at that; we honour you all the same for having them: and Mr. Harleigh seems to adore you only the more. So, I make no doubt does Aurora. And I, too, my dear sister! only I can't see you sacrificed to them. But Mr. Harleigh has found a way to reconcile all perplexities. He will save you, he says, in honour as well as in person; for the wretch shall still have the wife whom he married, if he will restore the Bishop!"

"What can you mean?"—

"His six thousand pounds, my dear sister! That sum, in full, he shall have; for that, as Harleigh says, is the wife that he married!"

Smiles now again, irresistibly, forced their way back to the face of Juliet, as she bowed her full concurrence to this observation.

"Harleigh, therefore," continued Lord Melbury, "for this very reason, will go himself to make the arrangement; to the end that, if the wretch refuses to take the six thousand without you, he may offer a thousand, or two, over: for, enraged as he is to enrich such a scoundrel, he would rather endow him with your whole thirty thousand, and, for aught I know, with as much more of his own, than let you fall into his clutches."

The eyes of Juliet again swam in tears. "Noble, incomparable Harleigh!" she irresistibly ejaculated; but, checking herself, "My lord," she said, "my thanks are still all that I can return to Mr. Harleigh,—yet I will not deny how much I am touched by his generosity. But I have insurmountable objections to this proposition; nor, indeed, ought I to cast upon any other, the risks of an engagement which honour and conscience make sacred to myself."

"Poor Harleigh!" said Lord Melbury, "I have been but a bad advocate, he will think! You will at least see him?"

"See him?"

"Yes; he came with me hither. 'Twas he descried you first, as you got out of the post-chaise. He was accompanying me up the stairs: but he retreated. You will surely see him?"

"No, my lord, no!—certainly not!"

"What! not for a moment? Oh, that would be too barbarous!"

With these words, he ran back to the town.

Juliet called after him; but in vain.

Her heart now beat high; it seemed throbbing through her bosom; but she bent her way towards the beach, to secure her safety by joining her uncle.

She perceived him at some distance, in the midst of a small group; conspicuous from his height, his naval air and equipment, and his long spying glass; which he occasionally brandished, as he seemed questioning, or haranguing the people around him.

In a minute, she was accosted by the old sailor, who was sent by his master to the chaise, in which he supposed his niece to be still waiting; to beg that she would not be impatient, because a boat being just come in, with a small handful of the enemy, his honour was giving a look at the vessel, to see to its being wind and weather proof, to the end that her ladyship might take a sail in it.

Juliet, though she answered, "Certainly; tell my uncle certainly;" knew not what she heard, nor what she said; confused by fast approaching footsteps, which told her that she could not, now, either by going on or by turning back, escape meeting Harleigh.

Lord Melbury advanced first; and, willing to give Harleigh a moment to press his suit, good humouredly addressed the sailor, with enquiries of what was going forward upon the beach. Harleigh, having made a bow, which her averted eyes had not seen, drew back, distressed and irresolute, waiting to catch a look that might be his guide. But when, from the discourse of the sailor with Lord Melbury, he learnt the arrival of a small vessel from the Continent, which was destined immediately to return thither; he precipitately took his lordship by the arm, spoke to him a few words apart, and then flew forward to the strand.

Juliet, disturbed by new fears, permitted her countenance to make enquiries which her tongue durst not pronounce; and Lord Melbury, who understood her, frankly said, "He is a man, sister, of ten thousand! He will sail a race with you, and strive which shall get in first to save the Bishop!"

Juliet felt thunderstruck; Harleigh seeking a passage in the very vessel which seemed pitched upon by her uncle for her own voyage! That they should go together was not to be thought of; but to suffer him to risk becoming the victim to her promise and her duties, was grief and shame and terrour united! Her eyes affrightedly pursued him, till he entered into the group upon the strand; and her perturbation then was so extreme, that she felt inclined to forfeit, by one dauntless stroke, the delicacy which, as yet, had, through life, been the prominent feature of her character, by darting on, openly to conjure him to return. But habits which have been formed upon principle, and embellished by self-approbation, withstand, upon the smallest reflection, every wish, and every feeling that would excite their violation. The idea, therefore, died in its birth; and she sought to compose her disordered spirits, by silent prayers for courage and resignation.

With the most fraternal participation in her palpable distress, Lord Melbury endeavoured to offer her consolation; till the sailor, who had returned to the Admiral, came from him, a second time, to desire that she would hasten upon the beach, "to help his honour, please your ladyship," said the merry tar, with a significant nod, "to a little French lingo; these mounseers and their wives,—if, behaps, they be'n't only their sweethearts; not over and above understanding his honour."

Juliet moved slowly on: the Admiral, used to more prompt obedience, came forward to hasten her, calling out, as soon as she was within hearing, "Please to wag* a little nimbler, niece; for here are some outlandish gentry come over, that speak so fast, one after t'other; or else all at a time; each telling his own story; or, for aught I can make out, each telling the same thing one as t'other; that, though I try my best to understand them, not being willing to dash them, I can't make out above one word in a dozen, if you take it upon an average, of what they say. However, though it is our duty to hold them all as our native enemies; and I shall never, God willing, see them in any other light; yet it would be but unchristian not to lend them an hand, when they are chopfallen* and sorrowful; and, moreover, consumedly out of cash. So if I can help them, I see no reason to the contrary; for my enemy in distress is my friend: because why? I was only his enemy to get the upper hand of him."

Then, turning to Lord Melbury and Harleigh, "I hope," he added, "you won't think me wanting to my country, if, for the honour of old England, I give these poor half-starved souls a hearty meal of good roast beef, with a bumper of Dorchester ale, and Devonshire cyder?* things which I conclude they have never yet tasted from their birth to this hour; their own washy diet of soup meagre* and sallad, with which I would not fatten a sparrow, being what they are more naturally born to. And I sha'n't be sorry, I confess, to shew the French we have a little politeness of our own; which, by what I have often taken note, I rather surmize they hold to be a merchandize of their own monopoly. And so, if you all think well of it, we'll tack about, and give them an handsome invitation out of hand; for when a person stops to ponder before he does a good office, 'tis a sign he had full as lieve let it alone."

Juliet readily complied, though she could not readily speak; but what was her perturbation, the next moment, to see Harleigh vehemently break from the group by which he had been surrounded, rush precipitately forward to meet them, and, singling out Lord Melbury, encircle his lordship in his arms, exclaiming, "My lord! my dear lord! your sister is free!—I claim, now, your suffrage!—Her brutal persecutor, convicted of heading a treasonable conspiracy in his own country, has paid the forfeit of his crimes! These passengers bring the tidings! My lord! my dear lord! your sister is free!"—

Juliet, who heard, as it was meant that she should hear, this passionate address, felt suspended in all her faculties. Joy, in the first instant, sought precedence; but it was supplanted, in another moment, by fearful incredulity; and she stood motionless, speechless, scarcely conscious whether she were alive.

An exclamation of "What's all this?" from the astonished Admiral; and a juvenile jump of unrestrained rapture from the transported Lord Melbury, brought Harleigh to himself. He felt confounded at the publicity and the abruptness of an address into which his ecstacy had surprized him; yet his satisfaction was too high for repentance, though he forced it to submit to some controul.

Suspension of sensibility could not, while there was life, be long allowed to Juliet; and the violence of her emotions, at its return, almost burst her bosom. What a change! her feet tottered; she sustained her shaking frame against the Admiral; she believed herself in some new existence! yet it was not unmixed joy that she experienced; there was something in the nature of her deliverance repulsive to joy; and the perturbed and tumultuous sensations which rushed into her breast, seemed overpowering her strength, and almost shattering even her comprehension; till she was brought back painfully to herself, by an abrupt recollection of the uncertainty of the fate of the Bishop; and, shudderingly, she exclaimed, "Oh if my revered guardian be not safe!"—

The wondering Admiral now, addressing Harleigh, gravely begged to be made acquainted, in plainer words, with the news that he reported.

Not sorry to repeat what he wished should be fully comprehended, Harleigh, more composedly, recounted his intelligence; dwelling upon details which brought conviction of the seizure, the trial, and the execution of the execrable commissary.

Juliet listened with rapt attention; but in proportion as her security in her own safety became confirmed, her poignant solicitude for that of the Bishop increased; and again she exclaimed, "Oh! if my guardian has not escaped!"

The Admiral, turning towards her rather austerely, said, "You must have had but a sad dog of a husband, Niece Granville, to think only of an old priest, when you hear of his demise! However, to my seeming, though he might be but a rogue, a husband's a husband; and I don't much uphold a wife's not thinking of that; for, if a woman may mutiny against her husband, there's an end of all discipline."

Overwhelmed with shame, Juliet could attempt no self defence; but Lord Melbury warmly assured the Admiral, that his niece, Miss Granville, had never really been married; that a forced, interrupted, and unfinished lay-ceremony, had mockingly been celebrated; accompanied by circumstances atrocious, infamous, and cruel: and that the marriage could never have been valid, either in sight of the church, or of her own conscience.

The Admiral, with avidity and rising delight, sucked in this vindication; and then whispered to Juliet, "Pray, if I may make so free, who is this pretty boy, that's got so much more insight into your affairs than I have? He's a very pretty boy; but I have no great taste to being put in the rear by him!"

Juliet was beginning to reply, when the Admiral called out, in a tone of some chagrin, "Now we are put off from doing the handsome thing! for here's the outlandish gentry coming among us before we have invited them! And now, you'll see, they'll always stand to it that they have the upper hand of us English in politeness! And I had rather have seen them all at the devil!"

Juliet, looking forward, perceived that they were approached by some strangers of a foreign appearance; but they detained not her attention; at one side, and somewhat aloof from them, a form caught her eye, reverend, aged, infirm. She started, and with almost agonized earnestness, advanced rapidly a few steps; then stopt abruptly to renew her examination; but presently, advancing again, called out, "Merciful Heaven!" and, rushing on, with extended arms, and uncontrolled rapture, threw herself at the feet of the ancient traveller; and, embracing his knees, sobbed rather than articulated, in French, "My guardian! my preserver! my more than father!—I have not then lost you!"

Deeply affected, the man of years bent over, and blessed her; mildly, yet fondly, uttering, in the same language, "My child! my Juliet!—Do I then behold you again, my excellent child!"

Then, helping her to rise, he added, "Your willing martyrdom is spared, my dear, my adopted daughter! and I, most mercifully! am spared its bitter infliction. Thanksgiving are all we have to offer, thanksgiving and humble prayers for UNIVERSAL PEACE!"

With anxious tenderness Juliet enquired for her benefactress, the Marchioness; and the Bishop for his niece Gabriella. The Marchioness was safe and well, awaiting a general reunion with her family; Gabriella, therefore, Juliet assured the Bishop, was now, probably in her revered mother's arms.

All further detail, whether of her own difficulties and sufferings, or of the perils and escapes of the Bishop, during their long separation, they mutually set apart for future communication; every evil, for the present, being sunk in gratitude at their meeting.

Harleigh, who witnessed this scene with looks of love and joy, though not wholly unmixed with suffering impatience, forced himself to stand aloof. Lord Melbury, who had no feeling to hide, nor result to fear, gaily capered with unrestrained delight; and the Admiral, impressed with wonder, yet reverence, his hat in his hand, and his head high up in the air, waited patiently for a pause; and then, bowing to the ground, solemnly said, "Mr. Bishop, you are welcome to old England! heartily welcome, Mr. Bishop! I ought to beg your pardon, perhaps, for speaking to you in English; but I have partly forgot my French; which, not to mince the matter, I never thought it much worth while to study; little enough devizing* I should ever meet with a native-born Frenchman who was so honest a man! For it's pretty much our creed, aboard, though I don't over and above uphold it myself, except as far as may belong to the sea-service,—to look upon your nation as little better than a cluster of rogues. However, we of the upper class, knowing that we are all alike, in the main, of God's workmanship, don't account it our duty to hold you so cheap. Therefore, Mr. Bishop, you are heartily welcome to old England."

The Bishop smiled; too wise to be offended, where he saw that no offence was meant.

"But, for all that," the Admiral continued, "I can't deny but I had as lieve, to the full, if I had had my choice, that my niece should not have been brought up by the enemy; yet I have always had a proper respect for a parson, whether he be of the true religion, or only a Papist. I hold nothing narrower than despising a man for his ignorance; especially when it's only of the apparatus, and not of the solid part. My niece, Mr. Bishop, will tell you the heads of what I say in your own proper dialect."

The Bishop answered, that he perfectly understood English.

"I am cordially glad to hear it!" cried the Admiral, holding out his hand to him; "for that's an item that gives me at once a good opinion of you! A man can be no common person who has a taste for our sterling sense, after being brought up to frothy compliments; and therefore, Mr. Bishop, I beg you to favour me with your company to eat a bit of roast beef with us at our lodging-house; after our plain old English fashion: which, if I should make free to tell you what passes in my mind, I hold to be far wholesomer than your ragouts and fricandos, made up of oil and grease.* But I only drop that as a matter of opinion; every nation having a right to like best what it can get cheapest. And if the rest of the passengers are people of a right way of thinking, I beg you to tell them I shall be glad of the favour of their company too."

The Bishop bowed, with an air of mild satisfaction.

"And I heartily wish you would give me an item, Monsieur the Bishop, how I might behave more handsomely; for, by what I can make out, you have been as kind to my niece, as if you had been born on this side the Channel; which is no small compliment to make to one born on t'other side; and if ever I forget it, I wish I may go to the bottom! a thing we seamen, who understand something of those matters, (smiling,) had full as lief leave alone."

He then recommended to them all to stroll upon the sands for a further whet to their appetite; while he went himself to the lodging-house, to see what could be had for a repast.

CHAPTER XCII

HAPPY to second the benevolent scheme of the kind-hearted Admiral, the Bishop hastened to his fellow-voyagers with the hospitable invitation. Juliet, in whom every feeling was awake to meet, to embrace, and to share her delight with Lady Aurora, would have followed; but Lord Melbury, to avoid, upon so interesting an occasion, any interruption from Mrs. Howel, objected to returning to the hotel; and proposed being the messenger to fetch their sister. Juliet joyfully consented, and went to await them in the beautiful verdant recess, between two rocks, overlooking the vast ocean, with which she had already been so much charmed.

No sooner, at this favourite spot, was Juliet alone, than, according to her wonted custom, she vented the fulness of her heart in pious acknowledgements. She had scarcely risen, when again,—though without Lady Aurora,—she saw Lord Melbury; yet not alone; he was arm in arm with Harleigh. "My dear new sister," he gaily cried, "I go now for Aurora. We shall be here presently; but Mr. Harleigh is so kind as to promise that he will stand without, as sentinel, to see that no one approaches nor disturbs you."

He was gone while yet speaking.

The immediate impulse of Juliet urged her to remonstrance, or flight; but it was the impulse of habit, not of reason; an instant, and a look of Harleigh, represented that the total change of her situation, authorized, on all sides, a total change of conduct.

Every part of her frame partook of the emotion with which this sudden consciousness beat at her heart; while her silence, her unresisting stay, and the sight of her varying complexion, thrilled to the soul of Harleigh, with an encouragement that he trembled with impatience to exchange for certainty. "At last,—at last,—may I," he cried, "under the sanction of a brother, presume upon obtaining a hearing with some little remittance of reserve? of mistrust?"

Juliet dropt her head.

"Will not Miss Granville be more gracious than Miss Ellis has been? Miss Granville can have no tie but what is voluntary: no hovering doubts, no chilling scruples, no fancied engagements—"

A half sigh, of too recent recollection, heaved the breast of Juliet.

"To plead," he continued, "against all confidence; to freeze every avenue to sympathy; to repel, or wound every rising hope! Miss Granville is wholly independent; mistress of her heart, mistress of herself—"

"No, Mr. Harleigh, no!" with quickness, though with gentleness, interrupted Juliet.

Harleigh, momentarily startled, ventured to bend his head below her bonnet; and saw, then, that the blush which had visited, flown, and re-visited her face, had fixed itself in the deepest tint upon her cheek. He gazed upon her in ecstatic silence, till, looking up, and, for the first time, suffering her eyes willingly to meet his, "No, Mr. Harleigh, no!" she softly repeated, "I am not so independent!" A smile then beamed over her features, so radiant, so embellishing, that Harleigh wondered he had ever thought her beautiful before, as she added, "Had I an hundred hearts,—ten thousand times you must have conquered them all!"

Rapture itself, now, is too cold a word,—or too common a one,—to give an adequate idea of the bliss of Harleigh. He took her no longer reluctant hand, and she felt upon it a burning tear as he pressed it to his lips; but his joy was unutterable. The change was so great, so sudden, and so exquisite, from all he most dreaded to all he most desired, that language seemed futile for its expression: and to look at her without fearing to alarm or offend her; to meet, with the softest assurance of partial favour, those eyes hitherto so coldly averted; to hold, unresisted, the fair hand that, but the moment before, it seemed sacrilege even to wish to touch; so, only, could he demonstrate the fulness of his transport, the fervour of his gratitude, the perfection of his felicity.

In Juliet, though happiness was not less exalted, pleasure wore the chastened garb of moderation, even in the midst of a frankness that laid open her heart. Yet, seeing his suit thus authorized by her brother, and certain of the approbation of the Bishop, and of her uncle, to so equal and honourable an alliance; she indulged her soft propensities in his favour, by gently conceding avowals, that rewarded not alone his persevering constancy, but her own long and difficult forbearance. "Many efforts, many conflicts," she cried, "in my cruel trials, I have certainly found harder; but none, none so distasteful, as the unremitting necessity of seeming always impenetrable—where most I was sensitive!"

"By sweetness such as this," cried Harleigh, "you would almost persuade me to rejoice at a suspense that has nearly maddened me! Yet,—could you have conceived the agony, the despair of my mind, at your icy, relentless silence! not once to trust me as a friend! not one moment to confide in my integrity! never to consult, to commune, to speak, nor to hear!—You smile?—Can it be at the pain you have inflicted?"—

"Oh no, no, no! If I smile, 'tis at the greater pain I have, I trust, averted! While conscious that I might, eventually, be chained to another, every duty admonished me to resist every feeling!—Yet with hope always, ultimately, before me, I had not the force to utter a word,—a baneful word!—that might teach you to renounce me!—even though I deemed it indispensable to my honour to exact a total separation. Had I confided to you my fearful secret,—had you yourself aided the abolition of my shackles, should I not, in a situation so delicate, so critical, have fixed an eternal barrier between us,—or have sacrificed the fame of both to the most wounding of calumnies? Ah no! from the instant that my heart interfered,—that I was conscious of a new motive that urged my wish of liberation,—I have held it my duty, I have felt it my future happiness, to avoid,—to fear,—to fly you!—"

"I was most favoured, then, it seems," replied Harleigh, with a smile of rapture, "when I thought you most inexorable? I must thank you for your rejections, your avoidance, your implacable, immoveable coldness?"

"Reverse, else, the medal," cried she, gaily, "and see whether the impression will be more to your taste!"

"Loveliest Miss Ellis! most beloved Miss Granville! My own,—at length! at length! my own sweet Juliet! that, and that only can be to my taste which has brought me to the bliss of this moment!"

With blushing tenderness, Juliet then confessed, that at the moment of his first generous declaration, following the summer-house scene with Elinor, she had felt pierced with an aggravated horrour of her nameless ties, that had nearly burst her heart asunder.

With minute retrospection, then, enjoying even every evil, and finding motives of congratulation from every pain that was past, they mutually recapitulated their feelings, their conjectures, their rising and progressive partiality, since the opening of their acquaintance. One circumstance alone was tinted with regret,—"Elinor?" cried Juliet, "Oh! how will Elinor bear to hear of this event!"

"Fear her not!" he returned. "She has a noble, though, perhaps, a masculine spirit, and she will soon, probably, think of this affair only with pique and wonder—not against me, for she is truly generous; but against herself, for she is candid and just. She has always internally believed, that perseverance in the honour that she has meant to shew me, must ultimately be victorious; but, where partiality is not desired, it can only be repaid, by man to woman as by woman to man, from weakness, or vanity. Gratitude is all-powerful in friendship, for friendship may be earned; but love, more wilful, more difficult, more capricious,—love must be inspired, or must be caught. When Elinor, who possesses many of the finest qualities of the mind, sees the fallacy of her new system; when she finds how vainly she would tread down the barriers of custom and experience, raised by the wisdom of foresight, and established, after trial, for public utility; she will return to the habits of society and common life, as one awakening from a dream in which she has acted some strange and improbable part.—"

A sound quick, but light, of feet here interrupted the *tête à tête*, followed by the words, "My sister! my sister!" and, in less than a minute, Lady Aurora was in the arms of Juliet. "Ah!" she cried, "You are not, then, gone! dear—cruel sister!—yet you could quit me, and quit me without even a last adieu!"

"Sweetest, most amiable of sisters!" cried the happy Juliet; "can you wonder I could not take leave of you, when that leave was, I feared, to sunder us for life? when I thought myself destined to exile, slavery, and misery? Could I dare imagine I was so soon to be restored to you? Could I presume to hope that from anguish so nearly insupportable, I was destined to be elevated,—every way!—to the summit of all I can conceive of terrestrial happiness!"

The grateful Harleigh, at these words, came forward to present himself to Lady Aurora; who learnt with enchantment the purposed alliance; not alone from the prospect of permanent happiness which it opened to her sister, but also as a means to overcome all possible opposition, on the part of Lord Denmeath, to a public acknowledgement of relationship.

Juliet, who, in the indulgence of sentiments so long and so imperiously curbed, found a charm nearly as fascinating as that which their avowal communicated to Harleigh, began now, with blushing animation, to recount to her delightedly listening Aurora, the various events, the unceasing obligations, which had formed and fixed her attachment.

A tale which, like this, had equal attraction to the speaker and to the hearers, had little chance to be brief: it was not, therefore, far advanced, when they were joined by Lord Melbury; who, gathering from Lady Aurora the situation of affairs, bounded, wild as a young colt, with joy.

The minutes, now, were lengthening unconsciously to hours, when the various narratives and congratulations were interrupted by a loud "Halloo!" followed by the appearance of the old sailor.

"Please your honours," said the worthy tar, "master begins to be afeard you've as good as forgot him: he's been walking upon the beach, alongside the old French parson, till one foot is plaguely put to it to wag afore t'other. Howsomever, he'd scorn to give up to a Frenchman, to the longest day he has to live; more especialsome to a parson; you may take Jack's word for that!"

The happy party now hastened to the strand; but there perceived neither the Bishop nor the Admiral. The sailor, slily grinning at their surprize, told them, with a merry nod, and a significant leer, that he would shew them a sight that would make them stare amain; which was no other than an honest Englishman, sitting, cheek by jowl, beside a Frenchman; as lovingly as if they were both a couple of Christians, coming off the same shore.

He then led them to a bathing-machine;* in which the Admiral was civilly, though with great perplexity, labouring to hold discourse with the Bishop.

The impatient Harleigh besought Lord Melbury to be his agent, with the guardian and the uncle of his lovely sister. Lord Melbury joyfully complied. The affair, however momentous, was neither long nor difficult to arrange. The Bishop felt an implicit trust in the known judgment and tried discretion of his ward; and the Admiral held that a female, as the weaker vessel, could never properly, nor even honourably, make the voyage of life, but under the safe convoy of a good husband.

Harleigh, therefore, was speedily summoned into the machine; his proposals were so munificent, that they were applauded rather than approved; and, All descending to the beach, the Bishop took one hand, and the Admiral another, of the blushing Juliet, to present, with tenderest blessings, to the happy, indescribably happy Harleigh.

Juliet, then, had the unspeakable delight of presenting her brother and her sister to her uncle, and to the Bishop. The Admiral, nevertheless, could not resist taking his niece apart, to tell her, that, if he had but had an insight into her being in such a hurry for a husband, he should have made free to speak a good word for a young sea-captain of his acquaintance; a lad for whom he had a great goust, and who would be sure to make his way to the very top; since, already, he had had the luck, while bravely fighting, in two different engagements, to see his two senior officers drop by his side: by which means he had arrived at his promotion of first lieutenant, and of captain. And if, which was likely enough, God willing, he should meet with such another good turn in a third future engagement, he bid fair for being a Commodore* in the prime of his days. "And then, my dear," he continued, "when he had been upon a long distant station; or when contrary winds, or the enemy, had stopt his letters, so that you could not guess whether the poor lad were alive or dead; think what would have been your pride to have read, all o' the sudden, news of him in the Gazette!"*

This regret, nevertheless, operated not against his affection, nor his beneficence, for, returning with her to the company, he solemnly announced her to be his heiress.

"One thing, however, pertaining to this business," he cried, "devilishly works me still, whether I will or no'. That oldish gentlewoman, who was taking upon her to send my Niece Granville before the justice! Who is she, pray? I should not be sorry to know her calling; nor, moreover, what 'tis puts her upon acting in such a sort."

Lord Melbury and Lady Aurora endeavoured to offer some excuse, saying, that she was a relation of their uncle Denmeath.

"Oh, if that be the case," cried he, holding his head high up in the air, "I shall make no scruple to let her a little into my way of thinking! It's a general rule with me, throughout life, to tell people their faults; because why? There are plenty of people to tell them their good qualities; in the proviso they have got any; or, in the t'other case, to vamp up some, out of their own heads, that serve just as well for ground-work to a few compliments; but as to their faults, not a soul will give 'em a hint of one of them. They'll leave them to be 'ticed strait to the devil, sooner than call out Jack Robinson!* to save them."

Lady Aurora was now advancing with a gentle supplication; but, taking off his hat, and making her a low bow, he declined hearing her; saying, "Though it may rather pass for a hint than a compliment, to come out with the plain truth to a young lady, I must make free to observe, that I never let my complaisance get the upper hand of my sincerity; because why? My sincerity is for myself; 'tis my honour! and whereby I keep my own good opinion; but my complaisance is for my neighbours; serving only to coax over the good opinion of others. For which reason, though I am as glad as another man of a good word, I don't much fancy turning out of my way for it. I hold it, therefore, my bounden duty, to demand a parley with that oldish gentlewoman; and the more so, abundantly, for her being a person of quality; for if she's better born, and better bred than her neighbours, she should be better mannered. For who the devil's the better for her birth and breeding, if they only serve to make her fancy she has a right to be impudent? If we don't take care to drop a word or two of advice, now and then, to persons of that sort, you'll see, before long, they won't let a man sit down in their company, under a lord!"

Then, enquiring her name, he sent his honest sailor to request an audience of her for the uncle of the Honourable Miss Granville; adding, with a significant smile, "Harkee, my boy! if she says she don't know such a person, tell her, one Admiral Powel will have the honour to introduce him to her! And if she says she does not know Admiral Powel neither, tell her to cast an eye upon the Gazette of the month of September this very day twelve years!"

To tranquillize Lady Aurora, Lord Melbury preceded the sailor to prepare Mrs. Howel for the interview; but he did not return, till a summons to the repast was assembling the whole company in the lodging-house. He then related that he had found his uncle Denmeath already arrived, and that he had acquainted both him and Mrs. Howel with the situation of affairs.

The Admiral now ordered the dinner to be kept warm, while he whetted, he said, his goust for it; and then sped to the combat; bent upon fighting as valiantly for the parental fortune of his niece with one antagonist, as for what was due to her wounded dignity with the other.

The party, however, was not long separated; Lord Denmeath, confounded by intelligence so easily authenticated, of the duplicate codicil, protested that he had never designed that the portion should be withheld; and Mrs. Howel, stung with rage and shame at this positive discovery of the family, the fortune, and the protection to which the young woman, whom she had used so ignominiously, was entitled, received the reprimands and admonitions of the Admiral in mortified silence.

Nothing, when once 'tis understood, is so quickly settled as business. Lord Denmeath, having given the name of his lawyer, broke up the conference, and quitted Teignmouth; Mrs. Howel, confused, offended, and gloomy, was not less eager to be gone; though the Admiral would gladly have detained her, to listen to a few more items of his opinions. Lady Aurora, forced to accompany her uncle, softly whispered Juliet, in an affectionate parting embrace, "My dearest sister, ere long, will give a new and sweet home to her Aurora!"

This, indeed, was a powerful plea to favour the impatience of Harleigh; a plea far more weighty than one urged by the Admiral; that she would be married without further parleying, lest people should be pleased to take it into their heads, that she had been the real wife of that scoundrel commissary, and was forced, therefore, to go through the ceremony of being his widow.

Called, now, to the kind and splendid repast, the Admiral insisted that Juliet should preside at his hospitable board; where, seated between her revered Bishop and beloved brother, and facing her generous uncle, and the man of her heart, she did the honours of the table to the enchanted strangers, with glowing happiness, though blended with modest confusion.

When the desert was served, the joyous Admiral, filling up a bumper of ale, and rising, said, "Ladies and gentlemen, I shall now make free to propose two toasts to you: the first, as in duty bound, is to the King and the Royal Navy. I always put them together; because why? I hold our King to be our pilot, without whom we might soon be all aground; and, in like manner, I hold us tars to be the best part of his majesty's ship's company; for though old England, to my seeming, is at the top of the world, if we tars were to play it false, it would soon pop to the bottom. So here goes to the King and the Royal Navy!"

This ceremony past; "And now, gentlemen and ladies," he resumed, "as I mortally hate a secret; having taken frequent note that what ought not to be said is commonly something that ought not to be done; I shall make bold to propose a second bumper, to the happy espousals of the Honourable Miss Granville; who, you are to know, is my niece; with a very honest gentleman, who is at my elbow; and who had the kindness to take a liking to her before he knew that she had a Lord on one side, and, moreover, an Admiral on t'other for her relations; nor yet that she would have been a lady in her own right, if her father had not taken the long journey before her grandfather."*

This toast being gaily drunk by every one, save the blushing Juliet, the Admiral sent out his grinning sailor, with a bottle of port, to repeat it with the postilions.

"Monsieur the Bishop," continued the Admiral, "there's one remark which I must beg leave to make, that I hope you won't think unchristian; though I confess it to be not over and above charitable; but I have always, in my heart, owed a grudge to my Lord Granville, though his lordship was my brother-in-law, for bringing up his daughter in foreign parts; whereby he risked the ruin of her morals both in body and soul. Not that I would condemn a dead man, who cannot speak up in his own defence, for I hold nothing to be narrower than that; therefore, Mr. Bishop, if you have any thing to offer in his behalf, it will look very well in you, as a parson, to make the most of it: and, moreover, give great satisfaction both to my niece, the Honourable Miss Granville, and to this young Lord, who is her half brother. And I, also, I hope, as a good Christian, shall sincerely take my share thereof."

"An irresistible, or rather, an unresisted disposition to procrastinate whatever was painful," answered the Bishop, in French, "was the origin and cause of all that you blame. Lord Granville always persuaded himself that the morrow would offer opportunity, or inspire courage, for a confession of his marriage that the day never presented, nor excited; and to avow his daughter while that was concealed, would have been a disgrace indelible to his deserving departed lady. This from year to year, kept Miss Granville abroad. With the most exalted sentiments, the nicest honour, and the quickest feelings, my noble, however irresolute friend, had an unfortunate indecision of character, that made him waste in weighing what should be done, the time and occasion of action. Could he have foreseen the innumerable hardships, the endless distresses, from which neither prudence nor innocence could guard the helpless offspring of an unacknowledged union, he would either, at once and nobly, have conquered his early passion; or courageously have sustained and avowed its object."

"It must also be considered," said Harleigh, while tears of filial tenderness rolled down the cheeks of Juliet, and started into the eyes of Lord Melbury, "that, when my Lord Granville trusted his daughter to a foreign country, his own premature death was not less foreseen, than the political event in which her property and safety, in common with those of the natives, were involved. That event has not operated more wonderfully upon the fate and fortune, than upon the minds and characters of those individuals who have borne in it any share; and who, according to their temperaments and dispositions, have received its new doctrines as lessons, or as warnings. Its undistinguishing admirers, it has emancipated from all rule and order; while its unwilling, yet observant and suffering witnesses, have been formed by it to fortitude, prudence, and philosophy; it has taught them to strengthen the mind with the body; it has animated the exercise of reason, the exertion of the faculties, activity in labour, resignation in endurance, and cheerfulness under every privation; it has formed, my Lord Melbury, in the school of refining adversity, your firm, yet tender sister! it has formed, noble Admiral, in the trials, perils, and hardships of a struggling existence, your courageous, though so gentle niece!—And for me, may I not hope that it has formed—"

He stopt; the penetrated Juliet cast upon him a look that supplicated silence. He obeyed its expression; and her mantling cheek, dimpling with grateful smiles, amply recompensed his forbearance.

"Gentlemen, both," said the Admiral, "I return you my hearty thanks for letting me into this insight of the case. And if I were to give you, in return, a little smattering of what passed in my own mind in those days, I can't deny but I should have been tempted, often enough, to out with the whole business, if I had not been afraid of being jeer'd for my pains; a thing for which I had never much taste. Many and many a time I used to muse upon it, and say to myself, My sister was married; honourably married! And I,—for I was but a young man then to what I am now,—a mere boy; and I, says I to myself, am brother-in-law to a lord! Yet I was too proud to publish it of my own accord, because of his being a lord! for, if I had, the whole ship's company, in those days, might have thought me little better than a puppy."

The repast finished, the pleased and grateful guests separated. Harleigh set off post for London and his lawyer; and the Bishop and Lord Melbury, gladly accepted an invitation from the Admiral to his country-seat near Richmond, of which, with the greatest delight, he proclaimed his niece mistress.

But short, here, was her reign. Harleigh was speedily ready; and his cause, seconded by Lady Aurora and the Admiral, could not be pleaded in vain to Juliet; who, in giving her hand where she had given her whole heart; in partaking the name, the mansion, the fortune, and the fate of Harleigh; bestowed and enjoyed such rare felicity, that all she had endured seemed light, all she had performed appeared easy, and even every woe became dear to her remembrance, that gradually and progressively, though painfully and unsuspectedly, had contributed to so exquisite and heart-felt a union.

Her own happiness thus fixed, her first solicitude was for her guardian and preserver the Bishop; whom, with her sympathizing Harleigh, she attended to the Continent. There she was embraced and blessed by her honoured benefactress, the

Marchioness; there, and not vainly, she strove to console her beloved Gabriella; and there, in the elegant society to which she had owed all her early enjoyments, she prevailed upon Harleigh to remain, till it became necessary to return to their home, to present, upon his birth, a new heir to the enchanted Admiral.

A rising family, then, put an end to foreign excursions; but the dearest delight of Harleigh was seeking to assemble around his Juliet her first friends.

Lady Aurora had hardly any other home than that of her almost adored sister, till she was installed in one, with an equal and amiable partner, upon the same day that Lord Melbury obtained the willing hand of the lively, natural, and feeling Lady Barbara Frankland.

Sir Jaspar Herrington, to whom Juliet had such essential obligations, became, now that all false hopes or fanciful wishes were annihilated, her favourite guest. He still saw her with a tenderness which he secretly, though no longer banefully nourished; but transferred to her rapturously attentive children, the histories of his nocturnal intercourse with sylphs, fairies, and the destinies; while, ever awake to the wishes of Juliet, he rescued the simple Flora from impending destruction, by portioning her in marriage with an honest vigilant farmer.

Scarcely less welcome than the whimsical Baronet to Juliet, nor less happy under her roof, was the guileless and benevolent Mr. Giles Arbe; who there enjoyed, unbroken by his restless, adroit, and worldly cousin, his innocent serenity.

Juliet sought, too, with her first power, the intuitively virtuous Dame Fairfield; whose incorrigible husband had briefly,* with the man of the hut, paid the dread earthly penalty of increased and detected crimes.

Harleigh placed a considerable annuity upon the faithful, excellent Ambroise; to whose care, soon afterwards, he committed the meritorious widow, and her lovely little ones, by a marriage which ensured to them the protection and endearments of a kind husband, and an affectionate father.

Even Mr. Tedman, when Harleigh paid him, with high interest, his three half-guineas, was invited to Harleigh Hall;

where, with no small pride, he received thanks for the first liberality he had ever prevailed with himself to practise.

No one to whom Juliet had ever owed any good office, was by her forgotten, or by Harleigh neglected. They visited, with gifts and praise, every cottage in which the Wanderer had been harboured; and Harleigh bought of the young woodcutters, at a high price, their dog Dash; who became his new master's inseparable companion in his garden, fields, and rides.

But Riley, whose spirit of tormenting, springing from bilious ill humour, operated in producing pain and mischief like the most confirmed malevolence; Ireton, whose unmeaning pursuits, futile changes, and careless insolence, were every where productive of disorder, save in his own unfeeling breast; and Selina, who, in presence of a higher or richer acquaintance, ventured not to bestow even a smile upon the person whom, in her closet, she treated, trusted, and caressed as her bosom friend; these, were excluded from the happy Hall, as persons of minds uncongenial to confidence; that basis of peace and cordiality in social intercourse.

But while, for these, simple non-admission was deemed a sufficient mark of disapprobation, the Admiral himself, when apprized of the adventures of his niece, insisted upon being the messenger of positive exile to three ladies, whom he nominated the three Furies;* Mrs. Howel, Mrs. Ireton, and Mrs. Maple; that he might give them, he said, a hint, as it behoved a good Christian to do, for their future amendment, of the reasons of their exclusion. All mankind, he affirmed, would behave better, if the good were not as cowardly as the bad are audacious.

To spare at least the pride, though he could not the softer feelings of Elinor, Harleigh thought it right to communicate to her himself, by letter, the news of his marriage. She received it with a consternation that cruelly opened her eyes to the false hopes which, however disclaimed and disowned, had still duped her wishes, and played upon her fancy, with visions that had brought Harleigh, ultimately, to her feet. Despair, with its grimmest horrour, grasped her heart at this self-detection; but pride supported her spirit; and Time, the healer of woe, though the destroyer of life, moderated her passions, in annihilating her expectations; and, when her better qualities found opportunity for exertion, her excentricities, though always what were most conspicuous in her character, ceased to absorb her whole being. Yet in the anguish of her disappointment, "Alas! alas!" she cried, "must Elinor too,—must even Elinor!—like the element to which, with the common herd, she owes, chiefly, her support, find,—with that herd!—her own level?—find that she has strayed from the beaten road, only to discover that all others are pathless!"

Here, and thus felicitously, ended, with the acknowledgement of her name, and her family, the DIFFICULTIES of the WANDERER;—a being who had been cast upon herself; a female Robinson Crusoe,* as unaided and unprotected, though in the midst of the world, as that imaginary hero in his uninhabited island; and reduced either to sink, through inanition, to non-entity, or to be rescued from famine and death by such resources as she could find, independently, in herself.

How mighty, thus circumstanced, are the DIFFICULTIES with which a FEMALE has to struggle! Her honour always in danger of being assailed, her delicacy of being offended, her strength of being exhausted, and her virtue of being calumniated!

Yet even DIFFICULTIES such as these are not insurmountable, where mental courage, operating through patience, prudence, and principle, supply physical force, combat disappointment, and keep the untamed spirits superiour to failure, and ever alive to hope.

FINIS

[illegible] the Nation, her eccentricities, though always [illegible] her character seemed to [illegible] of her [illegible]ment. [illegible] that [illegible] discover that all other is [illegible]

Here, and thus [illegible], with the solemn settlement of her hands and her fortune, the DIFFICULTIES of the WANDERER;—a being who had been cast upon herself; a female Robinson Crusoe, as unaided and unprotected, though in the midst of the world, as that imaginary hero in his uninhabited island; and reduced either to sink, through inanition, to non-entity, or to be rescued from famine and death by such resources as she could find, independently, in herself.

How few, [illegible] may have experienced any of the difficulties with which a FEMALE has struggled! Her honour always in danger of being assailed, her delicacy of being offended, her strength of being exhausted, and her virtue of being calumniated.

Yet even over these difficulties, mental courage, operating through patience, prudence, and principle, supplies physical force, combats disappointment, and keeps the mind, sometimes superiour to misfortune, and ever alive to hope.

FINIS

APPENDIX I

THE FRENCH REVOLUTION IN *THE WANDERER*

The French Revolution is powerfully if economically presented in *The Wanderer*. There are no large set-piece historical disquisitions by the author, and little elaborate historical scene-setting. We are not given a chronological ordering of events. The story begins amidst the confusion caused by the Terror, and only through the later narrative, and principally in the delayed stories of Gabriella and Juliet, do we hear about various earlier stages of the Revolution. Elinor Joddrel, the Englishwoman intoxicated by revolutionary ideas, alludes to 'bastilles' (p. 475), metaphorically introducing the major symbol of the tyranny of the *ancien régime*. That metaphor becomes literalized in the description of Arundel Castle (p. 537). The visit to Arundel Castle (chs. lvii–lx) offers an ironic view of the life of 'the old court' or 'vieille cour' (p. 444). This English château, property of the Howards, the family of the most ancient aristocratic lineage in England, promises a refuge for the heroine, but she is insulted by Lord Denmeath's surrogate Mrs Howel, and even temporarily locked up, or bastilled (pp. 570–1).

The use of the word 'bastilles' by the revolutionary Elinor reminds us of the storming of the Bastille on 14 July 1789. Elinor is the most likely of all the characters to recall the blissful dawn. She was not yet engaged to Dennis Harleigh when the Revolution began (i.e. in 1789): 'The French Revolution had just then burst forth, into that noble flame that nearly consumed the old world, to raise a new one, phoenix like, from its ashes' (p. 152). Elinor 'began canvassing with him [Dennis Harleigh] the Rights of Man'. The Declaration of the Rights of Man and Citizen, adopted by the National Assembly in August 1789, declared that 'men are born and remain free and equal in rights'. Elinor, like Mary Wollstonecraft, Mary Hays, and other women, proceeded to think of the possibilities of the Rights of Woman. Burney may not be a revolutionary enthusiast like Elinor, but she does not ignore the iniquities of the *ancien régime*, describing the compulsion exercised upon the unhappy Gabriella, an *aristocrate* whose marriage was a matter of family convenience. Gabriella was 'married, before the Revolution, from a convent, and while yet a child; according to the general custom of the country, which rarely permits any choice even to the man; and to the female allows not even a negative' (p. 622). The English Lord Denmeath in his corrupt and cruel haughtiness also exhibits the negative effects of aristocratic power. Gabriella's husband is likewise, we are told, cold and haughty, valuing his wife's qualities only 'as appendages to their mutual rank', and regretting in the death of his infant son chiefly 'that he had lost the heir to his illustrious name' (ibid). Frances Burney, like her husband Alexandre d'Arblay, believed that France had been in need of reform in 1789. The aristocratic d'Arblay, like his friend Lafayette, had been—and remained—'constitutionel', one of those who wished for a new written constitution limiting the power of king and nobles. Constitutionalists such as d'Arblay, Lafayette, and Mme de Staël were not among the émigrés who fled in 1789. But changes of direction in 1792 ended the hopes and even the safety of these constitutionalists, and they became emigrants and 'wanderers'. The list of political definitions drawn up by M. d'Arblay in 1793 for the Burneys' benefit offers a useful guide to the education in the new French politics received by Frances Burney during her courtship: see *Journal and Letters*, vol. ii. pp. xii–xiv. Like her husband, Burney is concerned about—and antipathetic to—the later phases of the Revolution, after the late summer of 1792. None of her emigrant characters—even Gabriella's unsympathetic husband, whom we never meet—leaves France before that period.

Burney treats events of the later phases of the Revolution, but there are a number of references to events of the earlier years. Elinor thinks the unknown heroine might be a 'pretty nun' (p. 17), reminding us of the dissolution of the religious orders declared in 1790. Convents were invaded, and monks and nuns forcibly evicted; the possible fate of pretty young nuns was a matter of (often lubricious) speculation during the early 1790s. Juliet, like Gabriella, was educated in a convent, and (though she assures us she remains a Protestant), the heroine respects the Roman Catholics who are undergoing trials on both sides of the Channel. Juliet's friend and guardian the Bishop would have been a conspicuous target for revolutionary hatred since 1790, when it was ordered that bishops and priests were to be selected by active (male) citizens. Not surprisingly the Pope, Pius VI, did not approve the new arrangements. On 27 November 1790 the Constituent Assembly ordered every priest and bishop to swear an oath of loyalty to the new constitution; only seven bishops signed. All bishops and priests who did not take the oath were considered by the new government as counter-revolutionary agents, while a papal bull of April 1791 condemned the individual clerics who took the oath and thus agreed to the elected clergy. After the abolition of monarchy, anti-clericalism mounted, and many Catholic clergy fled to other countries, including Protestant England. Frances Burney's only published work of nonfiction during her novel-writing years is her tract of 1793, *Brief*

Reflections Relative to the Emigrant French Clergy: Earnestly Submitted to the Humane Consideration of the Ladies of Britain. As Burney knew then, she was appealing to a public which included many who retained ancient prejudices against Roman Catholics. Such prejudices (as well as prejudices against the French) are reflected in the portraits of English characters in *The Wanderer.* 'You are then a Papist?' Lord Denmeath asks of Juliet in wondering disgust (p. 615). During a visit to Arundel Castle, the English touring party go to look at 'the Roman Catholic chapel' (p. 547), evidently in the vague expectation of seeing something remarkable or horrid, though Miss Brinville announces that there is 'nothing worth seeing in the Roman Catholic chapel' (ibid). Such touches remind us of the prejudices and legal disabilities which the co-religionists of Burney's own maternal family as well as of her husband had to combat, even in an England which thought of itself as free.

The novel's plot demands that Juliet in effect rescue the Bishop by both self-sacrifice and silence; the French Bishop himself, once a powerful and revered father, is now an object of hostility, and powerless. As Lord Denmeath knows, the Bishop is by 1794 inconsiderable, dispossessed 'of his episcopal rank and fortune' (p. 616). His status is not recognized by the state in which he lives, and his authority is entirely denied. The Bishop in the time of his power had been intending to accompany Juliet to England to claim her rightful inheritance when 'the French Revolution broke out' (p. 646), making travel difficult. 'The family-chateau was burnt by the populace', and the papers proving Juliet's claim were then destroyed. Some time probably elapsed between these two events, that is, the beginning of the Revolution in July 1789, and the burning of the château.

In 1789 many liberals had been optimistic about the outcome of the movement towards change. In October 1789 the King and Queen were forcibly removed from Versailles and lodged in the Tuileries, but the constitution to be drawn up by the Assembly was expected to provide for a limited monarchy and an elective legislature. The Constitution of 1791 set up a new Legislative Assembly, which became increasingly taken over by the more advanced and radical revolutionaries; certain formulae of compromise became less practicable. The declaration of war on Austria, accompanied by food shortages and riots, created a dangerous mood in the spring of 1792. In August, after losses in the war, members of the new Revolutionary Commune in Paris, accompanied by troops from Brittany and Marseilles, marched on the Tuileries. The Legislative Assembly was effectually destroyed, and the monarchical constitution with it. September 1792 saw new violence, with the unprecedented September massacres; nobles and priests in the prisons, as well as numbers of common criminals unfortunate enough to be incarcerated with them, were taken out and executed by mobs without trial. In this period attacks on the châteaux of the wealthy and noble, as well as threats to their lives, became more common. We may take it that the château of Juliet's guardians was destroyed about that time.

September 1792 also saw the elections for a new legislature, the National Convention, whose first act on its first day was to abolish monarchy. That day (22 September 1792) was declared the first day of the year One of the Republic. Louis XVI was executed on 21 January 1793. War was shortly after declared on England, Holland, and Spain. The Convention had many problems to contend with, including the war, inflation and shortages, and insurrections, as well as many factions within its own body. In *The Wanderer*, pompous Mr Scope tells the heroine 'if there were any gentlemen of your family, with you, Ma'am, in foreign parts ... I should be glad to have their opinion of this Convention, now set up in France' (p. 93). He is not only stupidly misogynistic, but also somewhat behind the times. The Convention had already had a long while in which to display its problems as well as it powers, and to set up new institutions, notably the Revolutionary Tribunal (10 March 1793) and the Committee of Public Safety (26 March 1793). These two bodies became the effective political executive. March 1793 also saw the beginning of an extensive revolt against the new government, principally in La Vendée, although as the anti-republican forces gained momentum what was in effect civil war raged in sixty departments of the nation. The Convention ordered representatives *en mission*, or commissioners of the Convention, to go into the provinces, taking goods in forced loan to help the war effort and putting down rebellions. The machinery for the Terror was already in place when Robespierre joined the Committee of Public Safety on 27 July 1793.

Robespierre is the central historical figure constantly alluded to in *The Wanderer*. He never appears in person, nor does any other named historical figure (and according to some criteria that fact is sufficient to deny to the novel the label of 'historical novel'). But if he does not appear, he is a looming presence, everywhere spoken of by the characters, and alluded to emphatically by the narrator (he appears in two footnotes as well as in the narrative text: pp. 371, 639). Burney is remarkably sparing of references to other known historical figures, or to particular events; it is surprising that she nowhere refers to the death of King Louis XVI, since she, like her husband-to-be, had experienced such shock upon hearing of his execution. But in *The Wanderer* there is no nostalgic monarchism. Robespierre alone stands for political power, and for such power manifested as brutality. He represents not only the force of the French Revolution, but also the human capacity for destruction and tyranny which is so apparent throughout even civilly ordered society. Maximilien Robespierre (b. 1758) was a lawyer from Arras, the son and grandson of lawyers (Mr Riley in the novel calls him 'a demon of an attorney', p. 257). Robespierre had an academic bent; he was fastidious, austere, and moralistic. A representative to the Estates General in 1789, he attached himself to the most radical wings of the new movements, and fanned the revolutionary ardour of the intelligentsia through the influence of the Jacobin Club, of which he became President in 1790. He had impeccable revolutionary credentials, and was known for the simplicity of his life and the purity of his revolutionary beliefs. Robespierre is the first truly modern despot—the despot as ideologue. As leading light of the Committee on Public Safety he prosecuted the war with zeal, and carried out, with conspicuous lack of remorse, the work of cleansing the new Republic of counter-revolutionaries. He authorized the trial and thus the execution of Marie Antoinette (executed 16 October 1793), and supported the pitiless devastation of La Vendée. Robespierre also authorized the arrest of all enemy aliens in France who had not resided there before 14 July 1789. Travellers such as Mrs Maple and Elinor, the Iretons and Riley, were thus immediately endangered. Some travellers had still attempted to come to France, as Elinor did, in search of health (p. 54; cf. *Cecilia*, p. 806). Some like Mr Riley (and in real life Mary Wollstonecraft) had come out of curiosity, a desire to see the Revolution at first hand. As Riley complains, 'I was cast into prison, by Master Robertspierre ... [who] now rules the roast in France ... while I was only gaping about me, to see what sort of a figure Mounseer would make as a liberty boy!' (p. 257). 'Liberty boy' seems a phrase left over from the American War of Independence; many English people hoped the French would have the same success as the Americans had had in their revolution, while not a few English maintained the old disdain of France and its 'mounseers'. Yet Robespierre is an exciting and disturbing object of regard for the English in *The Wanderer*, though few of the English characters can pronounce his name correctly. 'Bob Spear, as we call him at our club', says young Gooch (p. 466).

Robespierre dominates the political–historical time scheme of the novel. The novel's opening words are 'during the dire reign of the terrific Robespierre', and this phrase, rather than the statement of a date, sets the historical time. We hear of the cold of December, so we know the date must be December 1793. If we take Robespierre's entry into the Committee of Public Safety as the beginning of his 'reign', then that 'reign' is half over, although the characters have no way of foreseeing the ending of the chaos and terror about them. 'Terror' is indeed the operative political word, the creation of terror an announced and deliberate policy of the Committee of Public Safety under Robespierre, who was thus literally 'terrific', that is, creative of terror. During the Terror in Paris the tumbrils regularly took new passengers from prisons to the guillotine in the Place de la Revolution (now Place de la Concorde). These are places and events made vivid to us in numerous films and historical novels, chiefly Charles Dickens's *A Tale of Two Cities* (1859), a work which may well have been influenced by a reading of Burney's novel. The Terror was really a policy directed to subduing not only Paris but the nation, and the worst killings took place away from the capital, in provincial towns where the commissioners set the guillotines to work, or even cut down unarmed people with gunfire. At Nantes 2,000 people were towed in barges into the middle of the Loire, where they were forcibly drowned until the river choked with corpses.

It is this period, the autumn of 1793, which Burney has in mind—and expects her readers to have in mind—as the heroine's tale is unfolded. Juliet's friend Gabriella and Gabriella's husband the Comte, we are told, had been sufficiently frightened to try to make their escape as soon as they saw Robespierre ascend to power; presumably they fled in August 1793 'at the opening . . . of the dreadful reign of Robespierre' (p. 647). Gabriella's mother the Marchioness, the Bishop, and Juliet are left to face the horrors of the visit of the 'commissary', or Conventional commissioner who comes 'to purify . . . and new-organize the town' (p. 739). We may take it that his direful visit happens in October, when the Terror really began in earnest. October saw the execution of the Girondins and the accelerated de-Christianizing campaign.

The commissary *en mission* presides over the operation of the guillotine in the public square. The Bishop is a logical choice as one of the town's inhabitants to be duly sacrificed; personal greed, however, stimulates the commissary who hears of Juliet's potential dowry (or pay-off) from Lord Denmeath. He demands Juliet's hand in marriage in return for the Bishop's life; Juliet sees the guillotine in operation (p. 743), and consents. She is dragged to the *mairie* where a civil ceremony is quickly gone through. The French government had made marriage a civil matter only (see p. 745), desacramentalizing it and endeavouring to take it entirely out of the hands of the Church (laws changing the basis of marriage had also eased divorce). The horrible travesty-marriage under duress is Juliet's worst moment; we may believe that the monstrous sacrifice takes place around or shortly after the date of the Queen's execution. The commissary is fortunately called away immediately to put down an insurrection in another town. Juliet manages to hide and to escape in disguise, evidently making her way north, and at length crossing the Channel, as we see her doing in the first chapter. The horrible 'husband', Robespierre's representative, a representative tyrant in himself, comes searching for Juliet in the summer of 1794. He briefly catches up with her in late August (pp. 726–35). This 'Commissary'—who is never named—addresses Juliet in proper revolutionary language as '*citoyenne*' and as '*tu* ', but rather inappropriately speaks to Harleigh as '*vous*', although revolutionary usage proscribed the polite form. Burney of course could count on her original readers knowing that the commissioner came to England fresh from putting down insurrections, presumably after engaging in terrible brutalities. As the Commissary is away from France at a crucial point during the summer of 1794, he does not realize how gravely the situation has altered at the end of July; he returns to France in late summer to fall victim to new changes.

Throughout *The Wanderer*, we come upon the Revolution through the experience of the characters. The Revolution is mediated to the reader through two groups of characters: those (French or English) who have had some direct experience of revolutionary France, and those (all English) who have only heard about the Revolution. Those stay-at-home English who bother to notice events in France at all are often very muddled about what has actually happened, and are incapable of analysis. Mr Scope remarks disapprovingly on the loss of property, including the property a man has in his womenfolk; there is a nice irony in his considering Robespierre as not 'very strict', and 'not very exact in his dealings', since 'strict', 'exact', and 'exacting' would really describe the meticulous and fanatical leader. Mr Stubbs the steward comments on the financial situation of France where money is 'a vast scarce commodity' (p. 79). Money was indeed scarce; the first revolutionary government in 1789 had created paper money based on the value of church lands appropriated by the state, but the paper bills, called *assignats*, had sunk to half of their nominal value by February 1793. Rents indeed cannot be collected by landowners who have been burnt out and proscribed, but it is no use for an Englishman like Stubbs to think of picking up land cheaply (see pp. 268–9), at a time when any foreigner is liable to arrest.

Mr Scope complains of the institution of the Goddess of Reason, on the grounds that reason is what women lack. The Festival of the Goddess of Reason had been artificially created in the autumn of 1792, as a stimulus to the de-Christianization campaign. A young actress dressed in white and blue (as a parody of the Virgin Mary) wearing a red cap of liberty, was carried in triumph into the cathedral of Notre Dame. Similar ceremonies were conducted outside Paris, and a number of churches were converted into temples of Reason. 'Reason' had to be a female because grammatically the noun in Latin (*ratio*) and in French ('la raison') is feminine, but of course the revolutionaries felt the need of replacing the Virgin Mary with another female symbol. Robespierre became uneasy about the promulgation of atheism, and promoted the Festival of the Supreme Being, held on 8 June 1794. This event must have been taking place around the time of the Gooches' rural festivity with the pig-race and the syllabub, a festivity at which Flora appears, like a goddess, as the rustic girl herself notes, but certainly not like a goddess of reason (p. 438). Mr Scope is typically somewhat out of date in his reference to the Goddess of Reason. Indeed, the knowledge of provincial England about what is going on in France seems, throughout *The Wanderer*, to exhibit a time-lag. Really fresh news is hard to come by. Juliet seems very much cut off from developments in France, but we may recognize—and probably should—in the quiet references to months as 1794 advances a background of revolutionary upheaval and activity which Juliet does not know about. The difficult time she is having trying to collect fees from her creditors in 'the beginning of April' (p. 298) for instance, coincides with the conflict between Robespierre and Danton, which ended in the execution of Danton (with Desmoulins and others) on 5 April 1794. There is an active history going on in France; part of Juliet's pain is that she cannot know about it, cannot know if the Bishop is alive or dead. The English around her know little and pay little attention to current events, although they have indeed heard of Robespierre. Most of the English characters (the stay-at-homes and the travellers) are fascinated by the figure of Robespierre—save for Elinor, who ignores the figure of unpleasantly phallic power created by 'Bob Spear'. Young Gooch becomes slightly politicized by attending his 'club', but it is not the sort of radical 'club' that gave landowners in England sleepless nights. Gooch and his friends evidently discuss newspapers in an ill-informed manner. Young Gooch's father, Farmer Gooch, cannot believe that any man can say to others, 'here, mount me two or three dozen of you into that cart, and go and have your heads chopt off!' (p. 465). Unwilling to share the simple interest in sensation, this practical man rejects the news coming out of France as all lies, 'staring stories'—and his stout realism is also mistaken. If any of it is true, Gooch can add comfortably, it only proves that the French are poor folk, as the English have always thought. Mr Naird the surgeon, better educated, has similar opinions, seeing humorously in the French orgy of killing only an attempt to outdo the English in suicide (p. 371).

Juliet is forced to listen to a great deal of absurdity about the country of her adoption and affection. The novel well captures the frustration of the emigrant who must listen to misinformation, and misinterpretations of important or even tragic events at home, as well as suffering the opprobrium and suspicion customarily visited on refugees. The larger political issues of the unhappy social arrangements of the most prosperous Western societies, and the amount of tyranny that can go forward even without bloodbaths, are delineated so forcefully that we must recognize that the novel's ending does not entail an absolute end of all causes of pain and oppression. The most violent phases of the French Revolution, however, are over. Juliet does not know it, but the Terror is approaching its end at the time of her unhappy visit to Arundel Castle on 'a hot day in the middle of July' (p. 536). Robespierre himself went to the guillotine on 28 July 1794. During Juliet's terrified flight from her '*mari*' in her wanderings through the New Forest in August, the power authorizing the Commissary has already subsided. The weeks after the death of Robespierre saw the execution of his followers, and after that convulsion a subsiding into relative peace. The news of the death of Juliet's terrible 'husband' stands in for the tidings of the death of Robespierre and all his works—but the death of the much-emphasized tyrant is never directly mentioned in the novel; Burney expects her reader to work it out with a memory of the chronology of the French Revolution. The time of the novel's major action extends from early December 1793 to the end of August 1794; that is, it coincides with the peak of the Terror to its end and the aftermath of that end. That ending does not include the restoration of either the Bishop or Gabriella to their former position, or to the prosperity of their vanished lives.

APPENDIX II

BURNEY AND RACE RELATIONS

Burney lived in a period when both England and France were great colonial powers, engaged in the slave trade and supporting slave-owning in their colonies. The decree of Lord Mansfield in the Somerset case in 1772, in which he decided that a master did not have the right forcibly to remove his slave back to the West Indies, could be interpreted to mean that a slave ceased to be a slave once he set foot on English soil, though this was not Mansfield's intention. During the latter years of the eighteenth century, there was increasing agitation for an end to the slave trade, and many who shared the views of William Wilberforce looked for an end to slavery altogether. The Abolitionists seemed to be gaining ground in 1792. 'Antisaccharites' called for abstention from slave-produced sugar, tobacco, and rum; this, perhaps the first ideological boycott, was apparently supported by the King and Queen, to judge from the caricatures of James Gillray, who presents George III, Queen Charlotte, and Mrs Schwellenberg as merely motivated by avarice. (Four of the Princes were later to side with the slave-owners, but the Duke of Gloucester was to remain with the Abolitionists.) In April 1792 Charles James Fox succeeded in persuading the House of Commons to approve a motion to consider the measures necessary for the abolition of the slave trade, but nothing was to come of it. The new developments in France in late 1792 were frightening to a number of English people, and encouraged slave-owners and slave-traders to associate abolition with sinister revolutionary designs against property. The English did not declare an end to the slave trade until March 1807, and slavery itself was not abolished until 1833.

Meanwhile, England had greatly expanded her territories in India, a colony which had been largely under the control of the East India Company, but was to be administered by the English government with English judges. Warren Hastings had in effect been employed to put a check on the East India Company's licence; his trial for abuse of his position and of native people in India attracted widespread attention. Frances Burney records the early stages of his trial very vividly in her Diary; her sympathy for Hastings in 1788 was based not on sympathy for the actions he was accused of, but on a belief that he was not guilty of the atrocities attributed to him. (See *Diary and Letters*, ii. 45–106.) Later, Frances Burney's sister Charlotte's marriage (in 1798) to Ralph Broome brought an Indian into the family in Broome's natural daughter Miriam, his child by an Indian mistress.

France, the great colonial rival in both East and West, had seen a slave uprising in its colony in Saint Domingue (Haiti) in 1791, an episode which abolitionists and slave-owners on both sides of the Channel referred to in support of their views. Many who supported the French Revolution were anxious to see France liberate itself from the odium of slavery. The Convention legislated against slavery in 1794, but Napoleon re-established it, provoking the uprising led by Toussaint L'Ouverture in 1802; he was arrested and sent to Paris where he died in prison in 1803. It must be admitted that General d'Arblay, Burney's husband, was willing in March 1802 to join Napoleon's forces in putting down the insurrection in Saint Domingue (see *Journal and Letters*, v. 171–3). In 1802 a decree of the French government under Napoleon expelled all blacks from France, as Wordsworth was to explain in later reprintings of his sonnet 'We had a female Passenger who came / From Calais with us' (composed September 1802, first published 1803).

All these events which happened before the composition of *The Wanderer*, including events which happened after the period in which the novel is set, can be seen as having their effect on the book. Burney certainly knew about the anti-slavery movement and the controversies around it. She apparently supported William Wilberforce, although she did not have the pleasure of meeting him until 1813. She wrote of him in her Diary with great appreciation, describing the 'mixture of simplicity & Vivacity in his manner that I . . . found really Captivating'. She and Wilberforce, like Gabriella and Juliet, gazed together from the English coast towards France: 'In contemplating the Opposite—& alas hostile shore, which to our Fancy's Eye, at least was visible,—I could not forbear wafting over to it a partial blessing—' (*Journal and Letters*, vii. 182). In 1816 she was to tell Wilberforce of her hearing in France of the historic event of March 1807: even a letter from him has not 'electrified me with as striking a pleasure as that which I received from incidentally acquiring intelligence, during my Buonapartian seclusion, of the abolition of the slave trade' (*Journals and Letters*, ix. 163).

Burney's later works show a new awareness of the evils of slavery, and of the evils of prejudice against black or brown-skinned people. In *A Busy Day, or An Arrival from India* (written *c.*1800), an arrogant waiter at a London inn refuses to offer Eliza's servant the assistance she asks him to give, merely repeating unbelievingly 'What, the Black?' (I. 32). Eliza's white servant Deborah, who is returning from India with her mistress, speaks disparagingly of all people of colour: 'A Black's but a

Black; and let him hurt himself never so much, it won't shew. It in't like hurting us whites, with our fine skins' (I. 32–3). Eliza's vulgar sister Peg Watts exhibits disgusted horror at the mere idea of living among Indians: 'La, nasty black things! I can't abide the Indins [*sic*]. I'm sure I should do nothing but squeal if I was among 'em' (I. 47).

If *A Busy Day* seems still to approve implicitly a benevolent colonialism, *The Wanderer* exhibits more dissatisfaction with all forms of coercive power. The heroine of this novel, so strangely nameless at first, so impossible to identify, first rises upon our view, and upon that of the other characters, as a black. She seems very like Wordsworth's patient female passenger, a refugee with an unknown past and an unreadable future. In the first night view, she may be a 'tawny Hottentot' or a 'fair Circassian'. 'Hottentot' was the contemptuous name given by Europeans to black inhabitants of what is now South Africa, while Circassia in the Caucasus was a source of white concubines for the harems of Sultans. When the passengers find the 'demoiselle' is black, they presume that she has come from one of 'the settlements in the West Indies' (p. 19), that is from one of the French settlements such as Guadeloupe, Saint Domingue, or Martinique. If she is from the West Indies she is likely to be of a mixed race, hence 'Creole' (p. 46); if she is truly a black African, she would be from 'somewhere off the coast of Africa' (p. 19), i.e. the West of Africa, the Gold Coast where the French had a trade settlement at Accra, or perhaps from Gambia, further to the north-west. Making a jest of the strange woman's colour, Elinor tells Harleigh 'you will not ... yclep her the Fair Maid of the Coast' (see note to p. 20). Characters complain about 'her blacks, and her whites, and her double face!' (p. 251). As Riley complains, 'you metamorphose yourself about so' (p. 771).

When the heroine arrives on England's shore, in her disguise as a black woman, the Admiral says to her 'you won't think of drooping, now once you are upon British ground' (p. 25), a comment probably incited by his confused belief that she is a French slave (or a black in danger of being such) who is now free upon British soil. The novel shows us, however, that slavery still exists in Britain. When Juliet seeks employment with Mrs Ireton, she finds among the trembling dependents in that lady's room 'a young negro ... the favourite, because the most submissive servant of Mrs. Ireton' (p. 479). He commits the unforgivable error of laughing at his mistress, calling down upon himself a storm of terrifying vituperation. Mrs Ireton threatens 'tomorrow morning I will have you shipped back to the West Indies. And there, that your joy may be complete, I shall issue orders that you may be striped till you jump'. The threat of re-exporting the boy to the West Indies is against the spirit of Mansfield's judgement of 1772, and the cruelty of Mrs Ireton's imaginings ('you may jump,—you little black imp!—between every stripe!') illustrates the dangers inherent in allowing one person complete possession of another human being. Mr Arbe protests against Mrs Ireton's notion of the complete abjectness required of a 'humble companion': 'that would be leading the life of a slave!' (p. 524). But slavery is no mere metaphor.

References

Burney, Frances, *A Busy Day, or An Arrival from India*, ed. Tara Ghoshal Wallace (New Brunswick, NJ, 1984).

Fladeland, Betty, *Men and Brothers: Anglo-American Antislavery Cooperation* (Urbana, Ill., 1972).

George, M. Dorothy, *Catalogue of Prints and Drawings in the British Museum: Political and Personal Satires* (London, 1870–1954).

Walvin, James, *England, Slaves and Freedom, 1776–1838* (London, 1986).

APPENDIX III

GEOGRAPHY

The following list provides brief descriptions of the various towns, country seats, and physical features of England mentioned in *The Wanderer*, with page references to their first appearance in the novel. London streets and squares mentioned in the novel are listed together, at the end.

22 *Dover*: in Kent, 70 miles south-east of London; the closest English port to the Continent, and since the middle ages the most popular route to France. Burney left England from Dover in 1802, and was supposed to land there on her return in 1812; her vessel was seized by a British ship and brought instead to Deal.

28 *Brighthelmstone*: the old name for Brighton (Burney uses both names in her journals); on the Sussex coast, 50 miles south of London. Burney spent several months there with the Thrales in 1779, enjoying the fashionable shops along the Steine. See also Appendix V below.

30 *Lewes*: 8 miles north-east of Brighton; a fashionable town, but quieter than the bustling seaside resort.

42 *Rochester*: 33 miles south-east of London, and thus just over half-way on the Dover–London road.

200 *Portsmouth*: a large port on the South coast, west of Brighton; the closest town to the Isle of Wight.

207 *Bath ... western tour*: the most fashionable spa in England throughout the eighteenth century, Bath is 105 miles west of London. Burney was a frequent visitor, and was to settle in Bath with her husband, who died there in 1818. The western tour would follow a course similar to that taken by Burney in her tour of August 1791, taking in such attractions as Winchester, Salisbury, and Stonehenge. It might also include a visit to Bristol Hotwells, another popular spa, which features prominently in *Camilla* (pp. 268 ff.) and is mentioned in *Cecilia* (p. 487).

380 *Cuckfield*: a small town 14 miles north of Brighton, about a third of the way on the Brighton–London road. Burney admired it on her way to Brighton with the Thrales in May 1779.

Riegate: i.e. Reigate; a town 27 miles north of Brighton, just over half-way on the Brighton–London road. Burney found it unattractive when she visited it on her way to Brighton in May 1779.

395 *Isle of Wight*: part of Hampshire, separated from the mainland by the Solent and Spithead. Burney visited the island in June 1780, the month of the Gordon riots, when she accompanied the Thrales (suspected of being Roman Catholics) on their journey from Bath to Brighton.

Shoreham: a seaport, 6 miles west of Brighton; an important port in the late eighteenth century.

431 *Northumberlandshire*: the northernmost English county, adjacent to the Scottish border.

432 *The Downs*: a range of grass-covered hills north of Brighton in Sussex. Burney admired the view over the Downs from Cuckfield during her journey to Brighton in 1779.

434 *Devil's Dyke*: a hill close to Brighton, popular for walking excursions.

526 *Arundel Castle*: a medieval castle in the town of Arundel, Sussex, 21 miles west of Brighton. Greatly damaged during the seventeenth-century civil war, it was restored to splendour by Charles, 11th Duke of Norfolk, a friend of Burney's brother Charles. The Roman Catholic Chapel dates from 1380; the Arundels are among the oldest English Catholic families.

593 *Bagshot-Heath*: an open tract of ground in north-west Surrey.

642 *the Tyne*: a river flowing into the North sea at Tynemouth, Northumberland. Juliet spends her early childhood somewhere 'upon the banks of the Tyne', which Burney seems mistakenly to have supposed was in Yorkshire. The southernmost part of the Tyne is in Cross Fell, Cumberland, some miles from the Yorkshire border.

655 *Bagshot*: a town in Surrey, 30 miles south-west of London, on the Exeter road. Burney spent a night there in August 1791, on her way to the west of England. At the end of *Camilla*, the heroine suffers a mental breakdown at a small inn in Bagshot.

Salisbury: a Cathedral town in Wiltshire, 90 miles south-west of London. Burney travelled there with the Thrales in June 1780, with the Royal family in June 1789, and on her western tour in August 1791.

659 *New Forest*: a forest in south-west Hampshire, so named after its appropriation by William the Conqueror in 1079. Its ancient popularity as a hunting ground continued in the eighteenth century. Burney admired its beauty during her travels with the

Royal family in June 1789 and on her western tour in August 1791. It is the scene of parts of *Camilla*; see *Camilla*, p. 8 and note.

Romsey: a market town in the New Forest, 7 miles north-west of Southampton, which Burney visited with the Royal family in June 1789, and on her western tour in August 1791.

758 *Wilton*: Wilton House, in the town of Wilton, Wiltshire, occupies the site of an abbey first built in 1544. It was largely rebuilt by Inigo Jones in 1648–53; see note to p. 760 below. Its owner at the time of Juliet's visit was George Augustus Herbert, 11th Earl of Pembroke; the 10th Earl had died in January 1794.

766 *Stonehenge*: the origins and significance of this ancient circular setting of huge standing stones, 8 miles north of Salisbury, were the subject of much discussion in the eighteenth century. Burney records her reactions on first seeing the monument, changing from disappointment to wonder, in her journal for 5 August 1791 (*Journals and Letters*, i. 21–2).

772 *Blandford*: a town in Dorset, south-east of Salisbury, destroyed by fire and then rebuilt in 1731. Burney visited the town in June 1789 and in August 1791.

773 *Milton-abbey*: the seat of the Earl of Dorchester, who rebuilt the house and surrounding village in the 1770s. Burney gives a detailed description of the Abbey and the village in her journal for 7 August 1791. The village houses, rebuilt in uniform style, were 'meant to resemble a Gentleman's abode'; the Abbey was 'spacious & superb' (*Journals and Letters*, i. 24).

797 *Teignmouth*: a coastal resort in Devon, 16 miles south of Exeter. Burney spent two months there, from July to September 1778, visiting her stepsister Maria Rishton and her husband, who had rented a cottage for the summer. Burney described Teignmouth as 'situated the most beautifully of any Town I ever saw' (*Early Journals*, i. 275).

Torbay: Tor Bay; a bay 10 miles south of Teignmouth, in Devon. When Burney sailed there during her stay in Teignmouth, her boat nearly capsized in stormy seas.

798 *Brixham*: the town in Tor Bay, described by Burney as 'a most excellent fishing Town, but very dirty & disagreeable' (*Early Journals*, i. 281).

800 *Chudleigh-park*: the grounds of Ugbrooke Hall, the seat of Lord Clifford of Chudleigh, 5 miles from Teignmouth. Burney

admired the 'delightful Park, filled with Deer' during her stay in Teignmouth (*Early Journals*, i. 298).

816 *Powderham Castle*: in Devon, north-east of Teignmouth. Burney contrasts its 'noble & antique' exterior with the 'french finery' within in her journal for 16 August 1791 (*Journals and Letters*, i. 29).

870 *Richmond*: on the banks of the Thames in Surrey, 9 miles from London. Now a suburb of London, in the late eighteenth century it was an elegant and very fashionable village. In *Cecilia*, the impertinent Lady Honoria Pemberton suggests that Mortimer Delvile should leave his ancient family seat for a country house 'somewhere near Richmond' (p. 505).

LONDON

32 *Upper Brooke-street*: a highly fashionable street, running from Grosvenor Square to Park Lane, completed in 1759.

47 *Grosvenor Square*: in Mayfair; the second largest square in London. A suitably splendid address for Mrs Ireton, it was still more stately than Upper Brooke Street. Over half its residents were titled, and many of the houses were very large and well appointed.

Titchfield Street: in Marylebone, running off Oxford Street. In the 1790s it was the home of Burney's sister Esther, and Esther's husband (and cousin) Charles Rousseau Burney. Frances spent a month there in July 1792.

144 *Portman Square*: a new, large, fashionable square on the western outskirts of London, begun in 1764 and completed in 1784. Among its residents was Burney's acquaintance, the bluestocking Elizabeth Montagu. It is the home of the Harrels in *Cecilia*.

250 *Oxford Street*: with Piccadilly, one of the two principal routes leading westward out of London. Not yet a shopping street in the late eighteenth century, it was known instead for its places of entertainment.

379 *Cavendish Square*: a fashionable early Georgian square, close to Regent Street; the home of Sir Robert Floyer in *Cecilia*.

621 *Frith Street, Soho*: many French émigrés in London lived and worked in Soho in the eighteenth century, gradually displacing the English aristocratic families who had formerly resided there.

624 *Soho Square*: although no longer fashionable in the 1790s, there were still some wealthy residents. In *Cecilia*, Lady Margaret Monckton has her town house there.

651 *Piccadilly*: extending from the Haymarket to Hyde Park Corner, this and Oxford Street were the two principal routes leading westward out of London. The western part of Piccadilly became highly fashionable in the late eighteenth century.

APPENDIX IV

FINANCE

Prepared with the assistance of Grant Campbell

Much of the coinage of late eighteenth-century England is mentioned in *The Wanderer*: in gold the guinea and half-guinea; in silver the crown, half-crown, shilling, sixpence, threepence, twopence, and penny; in copper the halfpenny and farthing. There were four farthings to a penny, twelve pence to a shilling, five shillings to a crown, and twenty-one shillings to a guinea. For very approximate modern equivalents (in 1990), amounts should be multiplied by at least sixty; a pound was thus a considerable sum, and more than many workers earned in a week. England was truly on the gold standard, and the golden guinea was a handsome and valuable coin. Economic expansion and the high price of metals overseas, however, led to an acute shortage of coin and a general debasement of the currency, both by wear and by the illegal practice of clipping the edges of coins for metal which could be melted into bullion and exported. Since much of the coin in circulation was lighter than standard weight, monetary transactions were often impeded by arguments, and coins were examined suspiciously by people like Mr Scope, to ensure that they were true metals and of full weight (p. 424).

Payments for large sums were usually made in pounds, worth twenty shillings, for which there was no coin. Such payments were generally made through either banknotes or bank drafts, both of which appear in *The Wanderer*. Banknotes were issued by a bank, promising to pay the named bearer a certain amount on demand. In the late seventeenth century these notes were payable only to the depositor; by the early eighteenth century they could be made payable to a named 'payee'; by the late eighteenth century notes payable simply to a 'bearer' began to appear. The bank draft, on the other hand, functioned much like a modern cheque: a party with funds in a bank drew a specified amount in writing, and gave the draft to the payee. Bank drafts were used extensively by members of society such as Lord Melbury in *The Wanderer*, whose signatures carried acknowledged credibility.

Juliet's finances in *The Wanderer* follow a complex progress. Juliet's father, Lord Granville, remarries after the death of Juliet's mother; he leaves a certificate of his first marriage with Mrs Powel, Juliet's maternal grandmother, along with a codicil to any ensuing wills he might make, declaring Juliet to be his lawful daughter, and thereby entitled to a portion of his estate upon his death equal to that of any of his subsequent daughters. Juliet is therefore entitled to £30,000 upon Lord Granville's death, the same sum bequeathed to her half-sister, Lady Aurora, daughter of Lord Granville and his second wife.

Lord Granville sends Juliet to France when she is seven years old; Juliet resides in a convent with her friend Gabriella, her needs supplied by 'constant, and even splendid' payments (p. 644). Intimidated by his father, the Earl of Melbury, Lord Granville delays acknowledging Juliet's legitimacy. After Lord Granville's unexpected death, Juliet's guardian, the Bishop, appeals on Juliet's behalf, both to Lord Denmeath, the brother of the second Lady Granville, and to the Earl of Melbury himself. Both men refuse to receive or acknowledge Juliet as a legitimate daughter of the late Lord Granville. None the less, they agree to portion her if she remains in France. Lord Denmeath sends the Bishop a promissory note of £6,000, co-signed by himself and the earl, to be paid when Juliet marries a native resident of France. This amount is much smaller than Juliet's rightful inheritance; the Bishop continues to demand that Juliet receive a portion equal to that of Lady Aurora, and that she be recognized as 'the Honourable Miss Granville' (p. 646).

The promissory note alone escapes the fire that destroys all documents proving Juliet's legitimacy, and the commissary finds it when he arrests the Bishop. The commissary forces Juliet to marry him; she signs the promissory note only after he frees the Bishop. The Earl of Melbury has now died, and the bankers refuse to honour the note until it receives either the signature of his heir, the current Lord Melbury (Lord Granville's son and Juliet's half-brother), or a fresh signature from Lord Denmeath. Meanwhile, Juliet escapes from the commissary and crosses secretly to England, supplied with all of the ready money which Gabriella's mother, the Marchioness, can spare (p. 750). On the way across the Channel, the pilot steals her money.

Having arrived in England with no money, Juliet receives a guinea from Admiral Powel, in addition to breakfast and a place in the London coach, which she gives up to travel with Mrs Ireton. Juliet spends the Admiral's guinea on suitable clothes (p. 41). Elinor and Selina each give her a half-guinea, which she spends for a night and day's lodging at Brighthelmstone, waiting for her letter (p. 61). Harleigh gives her ten £10 banknotes, which she refuses to spend, and after Juliet is forced to return to Lewes, Lady Aurora Granville gives her a £20 banknote (pp. 81, 144). After Juliet leaves Mrs Maple, she sets out to teach music under the patronage of Miss Arbe. She spends Lady Aurora's £20, and goes further into debt, setting up her chambers and buying daily necessities. Miss Bydel advances 1 ½ guineas for a month's rental of the harp, while Mr Tedman advances her 2 ½ guineas for his daughter's lessons, and later advances an additional 2 ½ guineas, which she apparently refuses (pp. 224, 239, 303). Juliet receives no payments from any of her other students.

Burney does not specify the fees Juliet charges for lessons. Fees for music instructors in the late eighteenth century were highly subject to seasonal fluctuations, particularly in the provinces, ranging from one guinea per lesson (which Haydn received in London) to 5 shillings for less fortunate, ageing, or ailing musicians. Since Juliet teaches for three weeks, and since 1 ½ guineas remain from the money which Mr Tedman originally advanced for Miss Tedman's lessons (which presumably occur, like Selina's, twice a week), we can estimate Juliet's fee at about 3 ½ shillings per lesson. Lady Aurora pays the expenses for Miss Arbe's subscription concert with a bank draft of £50, which Miss Arbe spends entirely upon music, desks, instruments, and Juliet's gown (pp. 312, 317). Juliet is eventually forced to use £30 of Harleigh's money to pay debts to Miss Matson and various other creditors (p. 333); she carries on with the concert scheme in the hope of paying the money back. After the disastrous concert, Harleigh offers her an additional, unspecified sum of money (p. 367). Juliet and Gabriella go into business together doing needlework, refusing Elinor's bank draft of £50. When Gabriella leaves and the business drops off, Miss Bydel demands her 1 ½ guineas, which Sir Jaspar Herrington pays (p. 423); Sir Jaspar also secretly pays Miss Matson the premium for Juliet's place in the milliner's shop (p. 450).

Juliet leaves Miss Matson to do day work for Mrs Hart, a mantua-maker, and receives a daily stipend for three weeks, until she is abruptly dismissed. She then works as a companion for Mrs Ireton, who eventually offers her 20 guineas, which she refuses (p. 610). Lady Aurora gives her a further 15 guineas at Arundel Castle, which she spends on a trip to London and on relieving Gabriella's debts (p. 623). The two set up in business once again, receiving sums through various purchases from Sir Jaspar Herrington, as well as a purse dropped into the till (p. 653). After being discovered by the pilot, Juliet leaves London, still carrying Harleigh's banknotes and coins which she spends in various ways; she gives a penny to the Fairfield children, a crown to Dame Goss, and a half-crown for the post-chaise to Romsey (pp. 657, 662, 664). She gives a shilling for food and a half-guinea for lodging to the family on the edge of the forest (pp. 671, 674). She offers a half-crown to Nat Mixon, two half-crowns and three pennies to the farmer's children, and a shilling to the chambermaid of the hotel where she meets her husband (pp. 678, 691, 724). In addition, Sir Jaspar offers still more assistance; he finds and rescues Juliet by bribing the pilot with guineas; after Juliet loses her work-bag he pays a guinea for her night's lodging, and at Stonehenge he supplies her with 'a well furnished purse' (pp. 756, 764, 772). Harleigh later restores her work-bag (p. 775).

At Teignmouth, Juliet is accused by Mrs Howel of stealing a banknote from Lady Aurora's room, and later acquitted. Lord Melbury offers to obtain Juliet's release from the French commissary by paying him £6,000 out of the £30,000 portion to which Juliet is now entitled, as an acknowledged daughter of Lord Granville. This offer is rendered unnecessary by the death of the commissary and the safe arrival of the Bishop. Juliet comes into her portion of the Granville estate and marries Harleigh, thereby also partaking of his fortune. In the flush of wealth, she and Harleigh repay everyone to whom she 'ever owed any good office', including Mr Tedman, who receives three half-guineas with interest (p. 871).

APPENDIX V

FASHIONABLE AMUSEMENTS

The Wanderer was completed in the England of the Regency, although it is set in the early years of the 1790s. England in both periods was menaced by war and by the fear of both revolution and invasion. At times expenditure might be prudently curtailed, especially in years of inflation and scarcity, yet the fashionable world went its rounds and elaborate entertainments could be produced in public and in private. Brighton, the major setting of the novel, was one of the towns to profit most from the new age. Even before the period of the French Revolution, it had become a centre of holiday-making and luxury, partly owing to the favour the place found in the eyes of George, Prince of Wales, later Prince Regent (after 1811), and at length King George IV (1820). The Prince of Wales indulged, in a manner approved by Brighton shopkeepers, in conspicuous expenditure on himself and his entourage; he and his friends raced their chariots upon the sands. In 1789 the Prince had his Brighton house rebuilt; the new building, the Marine Pavilion, was a large Palladian house overlooking the Steine. Building in Brighton was further stimulated by the growing popularity of the resort during a period when the traditional jaunts to Paris or to the South of France or to Italy were becoming hazardous or impossible. By the late 1790s Brighton was more expensive than London: 'In 1785 a single room could be had for a guinea a week and a house on the Steine for eight or ten guineas, the charge in 1796 ranged from 2*s.* 6*d.* a night for a stable to £20 a week for a house' (Howell, p. 37). Brighton lacked a real harbour, and passengers had to be rowed from ship to shore, but before the war between France and Britain, declared in 1793, the Brighton–Dieppe passage was a common route of travel between the two countries. By the 1760s visitors commented on the number of French people to be found in Brighton, from milliners to visiting nobles, and the period of the French Revolution was to see an increase in such foreign visitors.

Brighton, like other seaside resorts, had risen in popularity with the rise of sea-bathing as a therapeutic and pleasurable exercise; seaside towns began to replace the old spas such as Bath. Jane Austen in *Sanditon*, the novel left unfinished at her death in 1817, describes the development of a small town into a watering-place. Burney's Brighton is less resort-like, nor is it a place of foolish fashion and excess so much as a seaside town of marked provinciality. We do see some glimpses of its status as a resort for cure and pleasure. Gabriella brought her sick child to Brighton for 'sea-bathing' (p. 739), a curative measure that failed. Elinor jokes that Mrs Ireton has come to Brighton 'to give her favourite lap-dog a six weeks' bathing' (p. 400). Only one scene in the novel involves a bathing machine, but the scene does not involve bathing (p. 864); the machine is used rather as the venue for a conference. Another seaside town, Teignmouth, is the scene of the novel's closing, where we are given a beach as setting, and a reminder that people often 'stroll upon the sands for a . . . whet to their appetite' (p. 859). The Brighton season is referred to (p. 410) as an earlier season than that of London; fashionable people or the semi-fashionable apparently came to Brighton about Easter time, when the London theatres were closed. We might expect Brighton's 'season' to be the warmer summer months, but the advent of warmer weather in *The Wanderer* sees the end of the season for wealthier visitors, who usually intend to spend winter or spring in the warmer seaside climate; there is a new influx of people, presumably often of the lower-middle class, who are in effect mere tourists, visiting for 'rambling and amusement' (p. 410) and taking no part in the settled life of the place. Residents and tourists alike try to ignore the émigrés who add to the population of the South coast.

The lower-class rural folk in the Brighton area have their own amusements, including the 'hop' for the young folk and the syllabub under the cow, as well as the rural sports so enthusiastically described by young Gooch, including sack races and the pursuit of a greased pig, sports for men only (p. 461). The upper-class characters do not participate in outdoor activities; only Gabriella and 'Ellis' seem to enjoy the sea air, or taking walks about the cliffs. Elinor, the Brinvilles, and Mrs Ireton go about in chariots and phaetons. Parties of pleasure go in coaches to visit historic sites, such as Arundel Castle and Wilton. The gentlemen do not seem given to hunting or to riding. This provincial world is a much less rural one than the provincial world of *Camilla*, and middle-class and upper-middle-class people, like the lower gentry, seem to live a sedentary life.

The inhabitants of Burney's Brighton and Lewes are governed only distantly by the manners and attraction of London. Some, like Miss Arbe, may hope to go to London for part of the season, which lasted from Easter to the celebration of the King's birthday on 4 June, although Miss Arbe's father is economizing, and will not 'begin his winter . . . before May or June' (p. 225). *The Wanderer* exhibits Brighton and its inland neighbour Lewes as an enclosed world whose residents are on the look-out for such amusements as can be afforded by the occasional concert. Burney, as a musician's daughter, was very aware of various aspects of the musical world, and presents in Mr

Vinstreigle the sort of musician who may eke out a living as a teacher and performer in a country town, with a professional expertise that falls short of quite meeting London demands. 'Ellis' as a newcomer has the value of novelty in her performance. There are no references to real performers popular at the time, as there are in *Cecilia.*

Young ladies are presumed to require instruction in music in order to amuse others—really to help them in the marriage market; 'Ellis' with her genuine love of music does not quite grasp what the ladies want. She herself is a superior performer on the newly fashionable instrument, the harp, which seems to have replaced the harpsichord and the new pianoforte in favour as a drawing-room instrument for young ladies. It is an instrument associated with ladies of the Regency rather than with the 1790s. Sir Walter Scott in the introductory first chapter of *Waverley* (1814), mocking various styles of narrative, remarks, 'if I had rather chosen to call my work a "Sentimental Tale", would it not have been a sufficient presage of a heroine with a profusion of auburn hair, and a harp, the soft solace of her solitary hours, which she fortunately finds always the means of transporting from castle to cottage...?' Mary Crawford, the enchantress of Austen's *Mansfield Park* (1814), plays beautifully upon the harp. Mary Crawford may have problems with the transport of her harp, but Burney's heroine finds most disconcertingly that she cannot afford the hire of the instrument when the ladies postpone paying her for their lessons (p. 289).

Parties in private homes involve cards and sometimes dances, and a great deal of eating (pp. 87, 97–8, 233, 263). Meal hours here are like those that applied in Cecilia's London a decade earlier, with breakfast at 9 or 10, dinner at 3 or 4, and tea after dinner, with a supper late in the evening. It typifies the provinciality of the place that the concert given by the harpist attended by Ellis should so decidedly feature refreshments—emphasized in the cakes with which Tedman plies the heroine (p. 244). Ladies occupy themselves in taking the air in carriages, in paying calls, and in shopping, a pointless amusement, here regarded from the viewpoint of the harassed milliners (p. 426); Burney had also emphasized the annoyance of shoppers to shopkeepers in her unproduced play *The Witlings*, written in 1779. In the play, as in this last novel, gentlemen may use shopping too as pastime and opportunity for gossip—but in the novel, we see gentlemen using the milliner's shop as a place to pick up girls. All ladies are expected to be able to do fancy needlework in the eighteenth century and throughout the nineteenth century, but most of the ladies in *The Wanderer* are unproductive and rely heavily on purchased materials and ornaments, thus giving employment to émigrées like Gabriella and Ellis, and to the sisterhood of Mrs Hart the mantua-maker.

The boredom of Brighton life is alleviated by the private theatricals planned by Elinor, which offer an interest to both performers and spectators. Miss Arbe is accustomed to appearing in such performances. There is a felt want of regular professional theatre. Nobody in the novel evinces the disapproval of the amateur production that we find in Austen's *Mansfield Park*; even the virtuous Harleigh is found rather dashingly painting scenery (p. 86). Private theatrical productions had become an increasingly common amusement. In Frances Brooke's *The Excursion* (1777) the heroine, a would-be playwright, is consoled for the failure of her London expedition by her future husband's promise to build a private theatre for her, and in reality some such theatres were constructed. The Austens, less expensively, fitted up an old barn, where the young people performed their plays, including *The Rivals* in 1784. Burney had engaged in private theatricals when visiting her uncle and cousins at Worcester in 1777, playing roles in both Murphy's *The Way to Keep Him*, and in Fielding's *Tom Thumb* (see Burney's *Early Diary*, ii. 164–79). Dramatic performance could be defended as educational; Burney's niece, the other Frances Burney, who worked as a governess, was to write some very violent plays (*Tragic Dramas*, 1818), for presentation by children. Evidently Burney was fascinated by the business of putting on a play, and by the relationships of actors to each other and to their characters.

References

Honan, Park, *Jane Austen Her Life* (London, 1987).
Howell, Sarah, *The Seaside* (London, 1974).
Lane, Maggie, *Jane Austen's England* (Bury St Edmunds, 1986).

APPENDIX VI

THE PROVOK'D HUSBAND

The Provok'd Husband, or A Journey to London, a comedy begun by Sir John Vanbrugh, was completed after his death by Colley Cibber and first produced in 1728. In this popular piece Lord Townly is tormented by the extravagance and gambling of his dissipated if sexually chaste wife, Lady Townly, whose conduct is in complete contrast to that of his sober sister, Lady Grace, beloved by the correct Manly. In contrast and counterpart to these town folk is the family of Sir Francis Wronghead, a foolish country knight who comes to town as member of parliament; not realizing he is destined to be thrown out of his seat in a week's time, Wronghead hopes to mend his family's fortunes, and nearly ruins them. His silly wife Lady Wronghead is soon caught up in the extravagances of gaming and shopping, and seems capable of sustaining an adulterous liaison. Their daughter Jenny is a hoyden who is rescued in the nick of time from running off to marry Count Basset, a cheat who assumed a title to which he has no right. Basset is abjectly cudgelled into good behaviour, and promises to marry the ruined if pert Myrtilla, niece of the milliner Mrs Motherly, who is the Wrongheads' landlady and a freelance bawd. Richard Wronghead, the hopeful son and heir, is a greedy booby who is nearly drawn into marriage with Basset's cast-off mistress, Myrtilla. The Wrongheads are shamed into behaviour more suited to their circumstances, and Lady Townly, once her husband plans a separation, is brought to repentance and promise of amendment. The play offers an audience the opportunity to laugh at the country idiocy of blunderers like the Wrongheads, as they encounter city manners while maintaining theoretical devotion to a simpler, older style of life. The vitality and wit of Lady Townly make her an attractive character, even while the audience knows throughout that she must repent and reform. Burney seems to have been perpetually attracted to this play, perhaps because it clearly sets out the orthodoxies of proper behaviour while allowing a place for libidinous questioning of them. It is a play in which the female roles are stronger than the male roles (with the exception of Sir Francis); even the good Lady Grace has some liveliness, as well as a sisterly disposition that forbids her finding fault with Lady Townly in front of the men.

Burney alludes to *The Provok'd Husband* in *Cecilia* (p. 275), and in *Camilla* (p. 265). One of her original plans for the novel that became *Camilla* entailed the inclusion of a quite detailed account of putting on this play, but the sequence of the play production was ultimately scrapped for the deliberately shapeless theatricals in the chapter entitled 'Attic Adventures' in *Camilla*. Evidence for this is the manuscript now in the British Library, a discontinuous collection of material pertaining to the novel that became *Camilla*, largely material that did not become part of the novel in its final form; the heroine is variously 'Ariella', 'Cleora', or 'Clarinda'.[†] The manuscript is much cut about, and pieces of individual pages are missing, as well as links to sequences, but enough remains of the 'play-giving' sequence to give us an idea both of what was once intended for a section of *Camilla*, and of the extent to which *The Wanderer* may be connected with the earlier novel. In the manuscript, the hostess who acts as director and producer is 'Mrs Solea', a prototype for the Mrs Arlbery of *Camilla*; her resemblance also to Elinor as director and producer hints at interesting connections between Elinor and Mrs Arlbery. In the sequence here quoted from the manuscript, 'Miss Hasty' is a prototype of Miss Dennel in *Camilla*, and 'Tybalt' of Lionel; Ensign Shelden is obviously the same type of character as Macdersey in the published *Camilla*, and 'Cyrill' is an Edgar Mandlebert. 'Ariella' the heroine resembles Camilla but also has some resemblance to Juliet. Much is made of the power that 'Mrs Solea' takes upon herself in casting her acquaintance in the various roles, as much is made of Elinor's power (and insight) in such casting in *The Wanderer*. Evidently Elinor thinks Mr Stubbs the steward will sound unconsciously ignorant and rural, like Sir Francis, and she looks forward to playing the vulgar Lady Wronghead herself. Miss Arbe fancies herself in the brilliant role of Lady Townly, but when she lets the company down the role devolves upon 'Ellis', who thus will do what Elinor wishes she herself could do, in acting opposite Harleigh's Lord Townly. Elinor does not think much of the roles of the models Manly and Lady Grace, giving them to Mr Scope and Miss Bydel; she mischievously casts the educated Ireton as the ignorant rural Richard, and the ignorant booby Gooch as the suave duplicitous Count Basset. She apparently thinks Myrtilla's part unimportant, giving the lower-class girl's role to her own maid—Elinor is never really free of class distinction and consciousness, however great a 'lesson of democracy' she supposes herself to be giving to her aunt (p. 70). There is no reference to a Mrs Motherly in Elinor's production; presumably the bawd's role was omitted as too broad. Myrtilla will be both milliner and whore, an anticipation of 'the humours of the milliner's shop' that Ellis discovers in chapters xlv and xlvi. There is no cross-dressing in *The Wanderer*'s production.

[†] See Doody, *Frances Burney*, pp. 205–15.

Here is a portion of the manuscript section, British Library Egerton MS 3696 33[r]–36[r]:

[*lacuna*] to Miss Hasty Myrtilla, & to Tybalt, as the Company was much in want of Women, Lady Wronghead.

Tybalt, to whom the greater the metamorphosis the greater the Zest, most merrily consented, upon condition he might be allowed the free ransacking of the wardrobe of Mrs. Solea for his attire.

The Colonel was now made sensible of the displeasure he had excited by his attentions to Ariella, in receiving, with a sarcastic dryness, the part of the exact & serious Manly. But as he concluded Lady Grace to be the only Female that could be appropriated to Ariella, he was far from murmuring, in secret, at his lot.

To the General she gave Sir Francis Wronghead, assuring him he might blunder all his life of his own accord, without ever doing it so amusingly.

To the Major she presented 'Squire Richard, telling him to rejoice in an opportunity of being, for once, a party, not merely a Spectator and Auditor, in society.

The Ensign, who, with the most energetic impatience, had supplicated for every Character as it passed in distribution, now received that of Count Basset.

Offended beyond his powers of restraint or forbearance, he vehemently whisked his Hat to the other end of the Room, & exclaimed "Madam, I don't know if you mean to affront me, but though I would go to the furthest corner of the Earth for a fair lady, I won't play the part of a scoundrel & a Coward for the prettiest Girl under the Sun!"

"You are in the wrong, there, Shelden, said Mrs. Solea calmly; if I had desired you to perform a Man of Honour you would have had reason to take it ill, for it might seem as if I had not thought it your real character: but when I tell you to perform a Cheat & a Poltroon, I pay you the compliment of supposing you are naturally neither."

"Dearest Madam! cried the Ensign, running to pick up his Hat, & then casting himself at her feet, if you were so kind & condescending as to be paying me a compliment, I shall never forgive myself for falling into a passion, before I knew if I had reason on my side or not. And now that I find I had not, I am ready to blow out my Brains for being in such a hurry. But indeed it's my particular misfortune, whenever I am in a choler, not to know well whether I am right or wrong till I get out of it."

Mrs. Solea gave him her Hand to Kiss, & bid him rise & compose himself.

He complied; but immediately after, said, "I beg pardon of all the company if I take the liberty to mention something to this fair lady in a whisper; which I should not be so rude as to do, if I had not particular objections to its being heard."

Every one desired him to be quite at his ease; & then, lowering his voice, he said to Mrs. Solea "My dearest Madam, I hope your good-nature will the sooner overlook my being a little heated upon this occasion, on account of the tremor that seizes me at the sight of that Gentleman, [looking at Cyrill] who, if I mistake not, is the very same who supplanted me with the fair young Angel that won my Heart, before ever I had the fortunate good luck to behold her."

Mrs. Solea adroitly appeasing him with a few kind words, made him promise to enter into no enquiries or explanations at present; and then, taking up the Comedy, appointed the part of Myrtilla to Miss Hasty.

"O, I shall like to do it of all things, cried Miss Hasty for I long to act of all things in the World. I hope it's a pretty part. Pray does she marry at the end?"

"Are you afraid, ma'am, said the General, smiling, to enter into so grave a State, even in a comedy?"

"O no! not for that; answered she; but pray tell me if she Marries?"

[*lacuna*]

This resolution being found unanswerable, Mrs. Solea then gave the part of Miss Jenny to Ariella: saying "'Tis by no means worthy of you, but you will give it an interest and effect perfectly new."

Ariella, earnest only to belong to a scheme she thought so delightful, accepted it without hesitation; but Cyrill who, like the Colonel, had concluded Lady Grace, however ill suited from its seriousness, was nevertheless the only character that could be proposed to Ariella, felt hurt & indignant; & secretly determined that if Ariella, after his intended remonstrance, persisted to degrade herself by consenting to such a performance, he would think of her no more.

The Colonel, equally surprised & disappointed, exclaimed "I had imagined Miss Elwin [?] would have been Lady Grace?"

"So she should, said Mrs. Solea if she wanted to go to school, or to take a lesson. In the mean while, I shall recommend her Ladyship to my Chamber Maid, who has a very pretty notion of acting. Or, rather, which will be infinitely to the advantage of our performance, I shall adroitly contrive to omit her entirely: for though it may be very flattering to we who have gayer parts to awaken our audience, it may be still more agreeable to themselves not to be lulled asleep."

The Colonel vainly contested this plan; Mrs. Solea neither answered nor listened to him: she rang for her Butler, to whom she gave orders to engage the journeyman of the circulating Library at . . . . . . to write out the parts without delay, & to be sure to have the two first Acts, at least, ready by the next Morning: at which time she desired the party to again assemble, for receiving what was copied, & such instructions as might, mean while, occur to her.

Cyrill attended to this arrangement with the extremest uneasiness . . . .

[After a little more of the impetuous humours of the Ensign, we come back to the play in an interesting if sadly incomplete section (fos.

41^r–42^r) in which the heroine, mortified, whether by fears of the sneers of a rival over her lost love or by graver worries about her poverty, determines to cover her feelings by acting well—presumably if not certainly in the same play, if not role, mentioned above.]

"Yes, indeed! cried Ariella, proudly, to herself, well will it be worth every exertion, & none will I leave untried to rescue me from this mortifying situation!"

[*four lines blacked out*]

She then, in an infinite flutter of spirits, determined to occupy herself wholly upon her appearance and performance for the Evening, that the Person she considered as her bitter, though only persecuter, might be convinced her Heart was at rest, by her ease, good looks, & gaiety.

She now examined the dress, prepared for her by Mrs. Solea which, hitherto, she had cast, with distaste, from her Sight. She fitted it on

[*lacuna*]

She next took her part, which she read, for the first time, with a desire to render interesting; & she soon found, both in that & in herself, powers of which she had formed no idea. She studied every speech attentively, tried various modes both of delivery & of action, & gave effect to every word.

The success which she could not feel but attended her labours, imperceptibly rendered them less irksome, & what at first she undertook in mere desperation, from the terror of being exposed to poverty,* she soon continued to put in force from that pleasure which arises from the first discovery & first use of faculties which, uncalled upon, had been unknown.

[*lacuna*]

She had no time to sink again, either from reflexion or from repentance; every one called for her opinion, & every call demanded a compliment; all had something to propose, to alter, or to relate; the company was fast arriving, & Tilson [Tybalt scratched out] repeated, or invented their observations as they passed by to the Theatre; while a thousand ludicrous little accidents or mistakes were continually occurring, which not merely engaged her attention from her own concerns, but insensibly, yet irresistibly, awakened from its late slumber the natural gaiety of her imagination. She encouraged its return with joy, though a Sigh from time to time refused to be repressed, & told the difference between amusement and contentment.

General note on MS: specific names are often hard to make out, as they are scrawled in lightly; it was Burney's custom to think of general or type names for characters, and then to apply more specific or more realistic names once she had written the novel or a large part of it. She often changes names in the writing of a sequence. Some of the lacunae here are the result of the bottom of the pages having been cut.

* *poverty:* substituted for 'the sneers of Miss [?] Solea'.

EXPLANATORY NOTES

We have attempted to supply information about places, customs, activities, and language not necessarily familiar to today's reader, as well as give complete references to literary quotations. Material covered in the Appendices (see 'French Revolution', 'Race Relations', 'Geography', 'Finance', 'Fashionable Amusements', and '*The Provok'd Husband*') is not included in the notes. The following works are cited in the Notes by short titles:

Burney, *Camilla*	Frances Burney, *Camilla: or, A Picture of Youth*, ed. Edward A. Bloom and Lillian D. Bloom (Oxford, 1972).
Burney, *Cecilia*	Frances Burney, *Cecilia, or Memoirs of an Heiress*, ed. Peter Sabor and Margaret Anne Doody, with an introduction by Margaret Anne Doody (Oxford, 1988).
Burney, *Diary and Letters*	*Diary and Letters of Madame d'Arblay*, ed. Charlotte Barrett, 7 vols. (London, 1842–6).
Burney, *Early Diary*	*The Early Diary of Frances Burney*, ed. Annie Raine Ellis, 2 vols. (London, 1889).
Burney, *Early Journals*	*The Early Journals and Letters of Frances Burney*, ed. Lars E. Troide (Oxford, 1988–).
Burney, *Journals and Letters*	*The Journals and Letters of Fanny Burney (Madame d'Arblay)*, ed. Joyce Hemlow *et al.*, 12 vols. (Oxford, 1972–84).
Burney, *Evelina*	Frances Burney, *Evelina: or, the History of a Young Lady's Entrance into the World*, ed. Edward A. Bloom with the assistance of Lillian D. Bloom (Oxford, 1968).
Cunnington, *Handbook*	C. Willett and Phillis Cunnington, *Handbook of English Costume in the Eighteenth Century* (London, 1957).
Dictionary of Proverbs	*Oxford Dictionary of English Proverbs*, ed. F. P. Wilson (3rd edn., Oxford, 1970).
Doody, *Frances Burney*	*Frances Burney: The Life in the Works* (New Brunswick, New Jersey, 1988).

OED	*A New English Dictionary on Historical Principles*, 2nd edn. (Oxford, 1989).
Opie, *Classic Fairy Tales*	Iona and Peter Opie, *The Classic Fairy Tales* (Oxford, 1974).

TO DOCTOR BURNEY

3 *F.R.S. ... Institute of France*: Charles Burney became a member of the Royal Society by invitation in 1774. In 1806 Frances told him that the Institut de France was considering making him an honorary correspondent of its 'Classe des Beaux Arts', in recognition of his achievement in his *History of Music* (1776–89). She feared her father, with his antagonism to the new regime in France, would be displeased, but he owned himself 'as much astonished as flattered even by the report, if that shd be all the notice bestowed on a man who has been all his life abusing the music in France...' (see Roger Lonsdale, *Dr Charles Burney: A Literary Biography* (Oxford, 1965), p. 459). The honour was not, however, actually bestowed until April 1810, when Dr Burney was sent a silver medal and a diploma. Frances Burney of course emphasizes the harmony achieved by the two warring nations in their recognition of her father's achievement.

first public effort: Frances Burney wrote and published her first novel, *Evelina* (1778), without her father's knowledge. Yet the book was dedicated to him, in being cryptically dedicated 'To—— ———', with a set of verses beginning 'Oh author of my being!' (*Evelina*, p. 1). Both 'filial feelings' and a desire to remain nameless were satisfied in this device; the author's father will never know about the book if it does not succeed ('Obscure be still the unsuccessful Muse, | Who cannot raise, but would not sink, your fame'). By the time of publication of *The Wanderer*, Burney could assume that she had vindicated her work as a writer; at last she felt free openly to dedicate a novel to her father.

unacquainted: according to Charles Burney's recollection in his own *Memoirs*, it was his daughter Susanna who confessed her sister's authorship of *Evelina*, six months after the publication of the novel, which had already proved a signal success.

wrapt ... obscurity: see 'Preface' to *Evelina*, p. 7.

dear father ... invoked: in verses 'Oh author of my being!', etc.; see above.

4 *gay to my memory*: according to Dr Charles Burney's recollection he 'perused the first Vol. with fear & trembling', but was favourably

impressed; when he next saw her, he wrote, 'I hasten'd to take her by the hand, & tell her that ... instead of being angry, I congratulated her on being able to write so well; this kindness affected her so much that she threw herself in my arms, & cried *à chaudes larmes* ...' (see Doody, *Frances Burney*, p. 39). Frances herself recollects the scene and recounts how 'she sobbed upon his shoulder; so moved was she by his precious approbation. But she soon recovered to a gayer pleasure—a pleasure more like his own' (*Memoirs of Doctor Burney*, 3 vols. (1832), ii. 145).

darling of our hearts: Susanna Phillips, née Burney, Dr Burney's favourite daughter and Frances's favourite sister, who had been suffering in an unhappy marriage in far-off Ireland. When her husband at last allowed her to return to see her family, Susanna died on the journey, at Chester, on 6 January 1800, a date that Frances Burney was to observe as a date of mourning for the rest of her life. The terrible grief of this bereavement had not, however, prevented Burney from writing plays, even if it interrupted the progress of the novel.

demur ... examination: Burney here glosses over the real difficulties she had in getting the manuscript of *The Wanderer* out of France. At first she had not intended to take the work with her; she sent for it while waiting at Dunkirk for a ship. M. d'Arblay packed up the manuscript, already 'nearly 3 Volumes', in a small portmanteau. When the officer at the Custom House in Dunkirk opened it he was enraged at the sight of the papers, 'a sight so unexpected & prohibited'. He erupted in a frenzy of rage, and 'this fourth Child of my Brain had undoubtedly been destroyed ere it was born, had I not recourse to an English Merchant ...' The merchant vouched for her, and Burney was able to produce a licence that allowed her papers and goods to pass. But Burney was convinced that neither she nor her papers would have been given such permission to depart if Napoleon had still been in Paris instead of advancing into Russia. See *Journals and Letters*, vi. 716–17.

5 *Johnson ... Burke*: Samuel Johnson (1709–84), lexicographer, essayist, and moralist; Edmund Burke (1729–97), statesman and writer. An influential public figure, Burke had been an MP since 1765, and, at the time of the publication of *Cecilia* in 1782, had just retired from the ministry. Johnson was a Tory in politics, and Burke a progressive Whig who had favoured the cause of the colonists in the American Revolution, although he was to turn heartily against the French Revolution (and thus, Burney thinks,

to sound 'latterly' more like Johnson). Burney again wishes to emphasize the possibilities of harmonizing opposites, and to plead that if her earlier novel, *Cecilia*, could please two such personages so notably on opposites sides, then she herself is not a 'political' writer. Some particular pleading is involved in the careful definitions of 'political' in these paragraphs.

honoured essays: literary attempts honoured by approbation.

Lady Galloway's: more properly Lady Galway's. The assembly was held by the Honourable Miss Monckton, at the home of her mother, the dowager Lady Galway, in Charles Street, Berkeley Square, on 8 December 1782. A partial account of the evening appears in *Diary and Letters*, ii. 154–63; the compliments recorded here were not printed by Barrett. Mary Monckton, daughter of John Monckton, first Viscount Galway, was known as a bluestocking; she married the Earl of Cork and Orrery in 1786 and became a noted hostess, perhaps satirized as Mrs Leo Hunter in Dickens's *Pickwick Papers*.

Sir Joshua Reynolds: Reynolds (1723–92), England's most celebrated artist of the late eighteenth century, was noted for his portraits. In 1764 he founded the Literary Club to give Johnson opportunities for talking; Burke and Dr Charles Burney were members. Reynolds was an old and dear friend of the Burney family, and a complimentary reader of Burney's fiction; he was also at the party at Lady Galway's, alluded to above.

member of a foreign nation: M. Alexandre Jean-Baptiste Piochard d'Arblay (1752–1818), whom Burney had married in July 1793, at Mickleham, in Surrey; M. d'Arblay was then a penniless émigré, and it had seemed not improbable that he would live the rest of his life in England. In 1801, during the Napoleonic era, he returned to France, and summoned his wife and son to join him; Frances and her son Alexander travelled to France in April 1802. Renewed hostilities between England and France made her return to England impossible for many years.

6 *our own*: that is the English Revolution (sometimes called the 'Glorious Revolution') of 1688, which changed the constitution of England and gave birth to political and social attitudes which prevailed throughout the eighteenth century.

during ... conduct: the d'Arblays lived very humbly in France, and had reason not to draw much attention to themselves, since many disapproved of those who had been aristocratic émigrés. M. d'Arblay tried to return to military service, but wished to stipulate that he never be required to fight againt his wife's country;

Napoleon refused to entertain any such agreement. Yet Napoleon, like many other educated French people, was an admirer of *Evelina* and *Cecilia*, and Burney's own literary reputation may have contributed to the d'Arblays' freedom from annoyance. Burney was, however, as she says in her letter to Mrs Waddington (quoted in the Introduction to this edition) always conscious of oppression in living under Napoleon's dictatorship, 'within the control of his unlimited power, & under the iron rod of its dread', *Journals and Letters*, viii. 282.

7 *title of Novel*: a number of eighteenth-century writers of fiction discuss fiction and the terms used for it in their prefatory material or within the fiction itself. Burney resembles Fielding in taking up the matter, but unlike Richardson or Fielding she does not repudiate the term 'Novel'. Her definition owes something to Johnson's *Rambler*, No. 4 (see *Camilla*, p. 7 and note), and more to Tobias Smollett's Dedication to *Ferdinand Count Fathom* (1753): 'A Novel is a large diffused picture, comprehending the characters of life, disposed in different groupes, and exhibited in various attitudes, for the purposes of an uniform plan ...' (*Ferdinand Count Fathom*, Oxford World's Classics, 1980, p. 2). In her spirited defence of the novel as a genre, Burney very closely resembles Jane Austen, whose *Northanger Abbey* contains a memorable protest in favour of the form: 'only some work in which the greatest powers of the mind are displayed, in which the most thorough knowledge of human nature, the happiest delineation of its varieties, the liveliest effusions of wit and humour are conveyed to the world in the best chosen language' (*Northanger Abbey*, Oxford World's Classics, p. 22). Austen singles out *Cecilia* and *Camilla* for praise here, but, since she revised *Northanger Abbey* as late as 1816, some parts of its fifth chapter may have been influenced by the Dedication of *The Wanderer*.

8 *Johnson ... sparrow*: in her diary for September 1778, Burney records Johnson's urging her 'always fly at the eagle' (*Diary and Letters*, i. 120). There is, however, no reference here to the sparrow.

imaginary ashes ... Evelina: this may be the first occasion on which Frances Burney told her father of the bonfire of 1767, when, according to her recollection, on her birthday (13 June) she and her sister Susanna burnt all her early works, including the manuscript of a complete novel, 'The History of Caroline Evelyn' (the contents of which are effectively summarized in the first letters of *Evelina*). Evelina's mother died at the end of that novel;

hence Susanna could weep at her 'imaginary ashes' as well as weeping over the real ashes of Burney's juvenilia.

9 *large library . . . of that class*: Frances Burney was indeed her father's 'librarian' and amanuensis for many years, but she is disingenuous in indicating that her father was not a novel reader. Gentlemen and men of letters do not read light fiction—that is the polite fiction. In fact, Charles Burney's letters are full of references to novels by Fielding, Smollett, Sterne, and others, and Frances Burney was reading a variety of novels in her teens. *Amelia* (1751) might be considered the most respectable and moral of Fielding's novels.

grandson: Alexandre Charles Louis (or Lewis) Piochard d'Arblay (1794–1837), who at the age of twenty was enjoying the spring-like season of youth, and of whom both his parents had insistently high hopes. Burney here gives the most English version of her son's name, anglicizing 'Louis' and omitting 'Piochard'.

the most solemn chapter of the work: chapter lxxxv, in Volume V (pp. 780–94).

10 *the utmost verge of enjoyable mortality*: Burney's wish that her father's life might be prolonged to the oldest age at which life can be enjoyable was not fulfilled; he died, just before his eighty-ninth birthday, on 12 April 1814, a very few days after the publication of the novel.

VOLUME I

12 *Incognita*: the unknown (female), perhaps with reference to William Congreve's novel *Incognita* (1692). Mrs Berlinton, in *Camilla*, is also introduced into the novel as a mysterious, 'fair Incognita'; see *Camilla*, p. 390.

dulcinea: from Dulcinea del Toboso, object of Don Quixote's imaginative love in Miguel de Cervantes' *Don Quixote* (1605; 1615). Quixote in his determinedly idealizing love attributes all sorts of beauty, accomplishments, and glamour to a rough peasant girl. Elinor accuses Harleigh of being quixotically ready to idealize a commonplace female; cf. 'disciple of Cervantes' p. 13. References to Cervantes' novel abound in Burney's works; see especially *Cecilia*, pp. 108–13, 127, 147.

13 *wrapping coat*: a large, loose, enveloping outer garment or greatcoat.

14 *receipt*: recipe. *out-landish*: foreign. *plumply*: bluntly.

15 *quizzes*: eccentric or odd-looking persons; connotes someone worthy of being teased or mocked who will not himself see the joke. *OED* gives first use as 1782.

Boreas: the North Wind.

What ... by aprôpos: there was a fashion for gallicisms in the cant of polite society at the end of the eighteenth century; silly Captain Aresby in *Cecilia* speaks a sort of macaronic English mixed with French phrases.

Signor Robespierre: characters seem incapable of pronouncing Robespierre's name properly; even Mr Ireton, with education enough to know better, gives the Frenchman's name an Italian prefix, probably in jest.

hodge-podged: a coinage from 'hodge-podge', a noun from 'hotchpotch', meaning a mixture of ingredients; 'hodge-podge' means a clumsy mixture of incongruous elements, and 'hodge-podged' means mixed up.

19 *Primer*: the first school-book, teaching a child to read, or also the Latin primer containing the first Latin vocabulary and rules of grammar.

rapier ... foils: a light, sharp pointed sword contrasted to fencing foils with blunted tips, used for practising swordsmanship.

20 *yclep ... the Fair Maid of the Coast*: 'yclep' is mock-archaic for 'call', with a dig at Harleigh's out-of-date, quixotically romantic notions. The 'Fair Maid' is from the title of Thomas Heywood's *The Fair Maid of the West* (1631), a play about fighting the Spanish for settlements and possessions, in which Bessie Bridges, the fair maid of Plymouth, rigs out a privateer to rescue her lover, wounded in the Azores. If the 'demoiselle' encountered on the French Coast is from the West Indies or West Africa, she is a maid of the West, but if she is a black woman she cannot be 'fair' in the sense of white-skinned.

plaisters: or plasters; a plaster is a piece of cloth, skin, or paper with some soothing substance spread upon it to cover and soothe a wound.

hoy: a small vessel rigged to carry passengers and goods for short distances along a sea coast.

22 *British Shore*: they apparently land at Dover; see p. 61.

work bag: a bag in which a woman carried her constantly present work, i.e. sewing, here used in the manner of a handbag or small carry-all, in which the purse, or small bag of money, is kept.

23 *custom-house officers*: these examined luggage, and could charge heavy duty on imported goods; they were also likely to examine persons suspected of trade with or espionage for France. Burney herself had had trouble with the French custom-house officers on departing from France, but no difficulty when landing at Deal. See note to p. 4 above, and note to *Cecilia*, p. 45.

24 *skiff's company*: a very small crew required to operate a skiff, or light boat fitted with oars and a sail, primarily used for going between ship and shore.

vapouring: getting into hysteria or depression (the vapours); also to become indecently exalted, to strut, swagger, and bluster.

27 *recruited*: been restored to bodily vigour and health by refreshment; *OED* quotes this as an example.

28 *fardingales*: or farthingales; frame-works of hoops extending ladies' dresses to the side in the fashion of the late sixteenth or early seventeenth century, long obsolete by the 1790s.

29 *Cynical*: sharing the beliefs of the Cynics, who got their name from the Greek word for 'dog', because they were rough and snappish, condemning ambition, ease, and pleasure. Diogenes was the most famous of the Cynics.

32 *an hundred or two miles*: an exaggerated estimate; the distance from Dover to Brighton is approximately 70 miles.

33 *"in such a sort"*: in such a way or manner.

book-keeper: the man who keeps accounts of reservations of places in the coach.

visiting ticket: a personal card, used in making formal calls.

35 *cap-flounces*: ruffled edging of a lady's cap; the 'demoiselle' is wearing a 'French night-cap' with prominent borders that conceal her face (see p. 20). Her head-gear is unusual, but all women wore head covering, indoors as well as out.

36 *a sift*: to sift someone is to subject the person to close questioning, to try to get at a concealed truth. This use of the noun is Burney's (*OED* quotes this as the example).

37 *flaunty*: flaunting (a nonce word).

40 *tasty*: tasteful, elegant.

water-gruel, and balm-tea, and barley-water: food for invalids, including thin porridge made with oatmeal, or other meal and water; herbal tea, especially tea made with balm mint (*melissa officinalis*); a drink made from simmering barley in water, drawing off the liquid and flavouring with sugar and (sometimes) fruit such as lemon. All of these might be employed in curing and soothing a cold and drawing off the discharge (catarrh); such watery home remedies are summed up under the title of 'slops'.

41 *stage-coach ... post-chaise*: stage-coaches went on particular routes between major towns at specified times, and took up various passengers; a post-chaise was privately hired at the traveller's pleasure, although, as with stage-coaches, the horses had to be changed at regular stops or posts. Post-chaise was the most rapid, convenient, and expensive mode of travel.

42 *apothecary*: apothocaries, who merely prepared and kept medicines for sale, were subordinate to physicians, who were general practitioners and qualified to practise surgery. See *Cecilia*, p. 768 and note.

43 *rouge*: fine red powder prepared from safflower, used as a cosmetic; young ladies were not supposed to employ such paint. Evelina and Cecilia are similarly insulted: see *Evelina* p. 79, and *Cecilia* p. 23.

44 *order of Maria Theresa ... Russias*: Maria Theresa became Empress of Austria after the leading powers of Europe agreed in the Pragmatic Sanction to permit a female's succession to the Hapsburg throne. Catherine, Czarina of all the Russias ('Catherine the Great'), deposed her husband Paul in 1762 and ruled Russia until her death in 1796. Mrs Ireton sarcastically imagines the mysterious lady being given 'an order' or honourable decoration by one of these powerful women.

48 *landing-place*: the landing on the stairs.

50 *"Tis not her face does love create, | For there no graces revel"*: slightly misquoted from William Whitehead's poem 'The Je Ne Scai Quoi' (1748), ll. 5–6.

52 *tindery*: resembling tinder in catching fire easily; inflammable; *OED* quotes this as an example.

dowdy: a woman or girl poorly dressed and unattractive.

walnut-skinned: coloured by being dyed with walnut-juice.

53 *fusty*: stale-smelling, mouldy; figuratively, out of date.

nothingly: a nonce word.

phiz: a jocular colloquial term for face, countenance, from 'physiognomy'.

54 *the south of France*: already a well-known resort for wealthy invalids; in *Cecilia* the hero's mother, Mrs Delvile, travels to Nice to recover her health after a stroke (see *Cecilia*, p. 806 and note).

an entailed estate: an estate secured to a predetermined line of successors by a legal entail; customarily used to provide for the estate's transmission only in the male line.

56 *booth*: a covered stall at a market or fair; hence a place open to all comers.

57 *snuff-box*: despite her disdain at being forced into vulgar company, Mrs Maple displays some vulgarity herself in taking snuff. The most delicate ladies did not do so, although in the Regency there were fine scented mixtures of snuff for ladies.

58 *the Foundling Hospital*: England's first institutional orphanage, founded by the philanthropist Thomas Coram, who obtained a charter in 1739 and opened the new building in 1745. The hospital was maintained by charitable subscriptions and donations. Foundlings had no parental name and thus could not know their own names, but each was given a name by the institution.

60 *settling*: deciding upon a plan of action; *OED* quotes this as an example.

62 *economy*: frugality.

chaise-cart: a one-horse vehicle capable of taking a passenger.

64 *lodge an information*: make a complaint against the clerk, either to his superiors in the Post Office organization or to the local magistrates; it is more likely that Ireton threatens the latter, as the clerk is being accused of having dealings with a suspicious character or foreign agent. Several characters set themselves up as spies or counter-spies; Ireton is pretending to be a patriotic citizen engaged in counter-espionage.

68 *new Rosamund's Pond*: Rosamund's pond in St James's Park, popularly associated with Fair Rosamund, mistress of Henry II, was a place of lovers' assignations as well as proverbially of the suicide of persons crossed in love. Cf. the young Frances Burney's response when, in 1768, her friend Dorothy Young teased her that if she persisted in diary keeping and then fell in love, she would be in danger of 'the object of your passion' reading the

Journal and getting sight of some part which related to himself. In that embarrassment of unrequited love displayed, Burney replied, 'Why then, Miss Young, I must make a little trip to Rosamond's Pond' (*Early Journals*, i. 22; cf. *Early Diary*, i. 20). Perhaps to discourage suicides, the pond was filled in 1770; hence Ellis, disappointed in Harleigh, would have to find a new site for suicide. Elinor's mind runs consistently upon suicide.

70 *fogrum*: formal, antiquated, old-fogeyish, a favourite word of Charles Burney and Samuel Crisp. *OED* records as first use an entry in Burney's *Early Diary* for 1772. Cf. *Cecilia*, p. 544 and note; *Camilla*, p. 46 and note.

71 *Mercury*: messenger; Mercury the god was also a messenger of the gods.

73 *Arpeggio*: the notes of a chord played in rapid succession, instead of simultaneously; an effect used chiefly in keyboard and harp music. Players of eighteenth-century music would extemporize arpeggios when the word was written beside a chordal sequence.

74 *stroller*: strolling actor or other kind of entertainer; strolling players, jugglers, musicians, etc. could be treated as vagabonds and subjected to legal penalties.

78 *huswife*: or 'hussy'; housewife, meaning not a married woman or a houseowner but a woman skilled in womanly work.

prose: to speak in a verbose, monotonous, and moralizing fashion.

79 *pettifogging*: practising law in inferior petty cases, or using petty and base devices as a legal practitioner, indulging in chicanery. Elinor means that Creek is a low lawyer, an attorney in a small way; cf. *Cecilia*, p. 173 and note.

buskin: high, thick-soled boot worn by actors of Athenian tragedy; hence generically of the stage; 'companions of the buskin' are companions in the theatrical venture, as fellow actors.

millions of red-coats ... generals: since English soldiers wore red coats, young Gooch takes that as the generic sign of a soldier, although the French army did not wear red coats at any point. He may well be impressed by accounts of promotion on merit within the post-Revolutionary French army, since in England commissions were bought. Fielding was not the only author to complain that able officers were not advanced in the service (see *Tom Jones*, Book VII, ch. 12, and *Amelia*, *passim*). Napoleon boasted that every private had a field marshal's baton in his knapsack—that is, that any soldier of distinguished merit could be promoted to even the highest office. The French army was being new-modelled, and officers still loyal to the King, though sympathetic to the first moves towards reform, had been forced to emigrate. Among such refugees were Lafayette and Alexandre d'Arblay.

82 *muff*: large muffs, which could be worn on all occasions, were fashionable at the end of the eighteenth century; they could be made of fur, velvet, satin, and even feathers.

83 *cotillon*: an elaborate dance with a variety of figures, developed from a French dance of the court of Louis XIV. Cf. *Camilla*, pp. 444–6 and note.

85 *mob ... the slip*: mob is a slang word (to which Swift, among others, strongly objected) abbreviating *mobile vulgus*; Mrs Maple does not mean that the demoiselle is a throng, but that she is vulgar, and that she is glad that another lady has escaped from Elinor. Mrs Maple's language is slangy, and itself savours of vulgarity.

86 *light closet*: a private room, with a window.

88 *green-room*: a room backstage in a theatre, set aside for actors between stage appearances.

89 *dizen out ... attire*: to bedizen, or deck out, her attire with fine ornaments.

93 *frog*: harking back to the old belief that the French were so poor they had to eat frogs, whereas the British enjoyed Roast Beef from British cows. Stubbs believes French land will not produce anything, which means the landlords cannot collect their rents, though this may just be his way of saying that rightful landlords under the Revolutionary system are deprived of their rents.

94 *"Why did I marry?"*: The opening words of *The Provok'd Husband*, spoken by Lord Townly in his soliloquy beginning: 'Why did I marry!—Was it not evident, my plain, rational Scheme of Life, was impracticable, with a Woman of so different a Way of thinking?'

97 *her own pride ... her prejudice*: echoing a celebrated passage of *Cecilia* which gave Jane Austen the title of her novel *Pride and Prejudice* (1813); see *Cecilia*, p. 930 and note.

98 *sweet-scented vials ... salts*: the ladies offer cologne or scented smelling salts; the salts Ellis accepts are presumably of hartshorn, or carbonate of ammonia, a common remedy for faintness.

99 *"admiring throng"*: Cf. John Dryden's *Mac Flecknoe*, l. 132: 'Th'admiring throng loud acclamations make'.

104 *fine work*: fine sewing, such as embroidery, in contrast to plain work such as hemming or stitching seams.

110 *most beautified Ophelia*: *Hamlet*, II. ii. 109, from Hamlet's letter 'to the celestial, and my soul's idol, the most beautified Ophelia'. Polonius says 'That's an ill phrase, a vile phrase, "beautified" is a vile phrase'.

supernumeraries: from theatrical usage, persons employed in addition to the regular company who appear on stage but do not have speaking parts.

112 *Gretna Green*: a village close to the Scottish border between Carlisle and Edinburgh. Almost as soon as Lord Hardwicke's 'Marriage Act' became law in England in 1753, Gretna Green became a refuge from the stiffened marriage laws of England. Marriages performed at Gretna Green (or elsewhere in Scotland) required no church setting nor previous calling of bans. Nevertheless, marriages contracted in Scotland were legally binding. In Burney's *Camilla*, Eugenia Tyrold elopes with the false Alphonso Bellamy and is married at Gretna Green; see *Camilla*, p. 800 and note; cf. *Cecilia*, p. 545 and note.

115 *piano forte*: the piano forte, resembling the modern piano, was brought into England in the mid-eighteenth century, and gradually replaced the harpsichord in both the parlour and the concert-hall. Cecilia orders 'a Piano Forte of Merlin's': *Cecilia*, p. 460 and note.

a composition of Haydn: still, at the time in which the novel is set, a modern composer. Haydn had spent two spectacularly successful seasons in London in 1791–2, and had returned to the capital in 1794.

116 *Boileau ... Pope ... Racine ... Shakespeare*: Ellis's reading proves her equal knowledge of French and English; she reads aloud from two classic poets of high neo-classicism in France and England, and from the most eminent dramatists of each nation. The reputation of Nicolas Boileau-Despreaux (1636–1711) was undergoing a decline in the Romantic age, which saw the satirist and theoretician as the arch-poet of rules. Keats rejects him; poor critics 'went about | Holding a poor decrepit standard out | Marked with the most flimsy mottoes, and in large | The name of one Boileau!' ('Sleep and Poetry', written in 1816, published in 1817, ll. 203–6). Pope with his heroic couplets is also rejected among those who 'swayed upon a rocking horse' (ibid., l. 186). The reputation of Alexander Pope (1688–1744) had been generally in decline in England since the 1750s; Burney in her plays

The Witlings (written 1779) and *The Woman-Hater* (written *c.*1800) seems to make fun of Lady Smatter's antiquated and culturally unfocused quotations of Pope. The reputation of the dramatist Jean Baptiste Racine (1639–99) was not as high as it was to be with the revival of his works in the French theatre of the 1830s, but his dramas of intense and inward passion were known to all major writers of the Romantic era. Shakespeare had, however, by this time been accepted as Europe's leading dramatist, and was widely discussed, quoted, and imitated. Burney's heroine, broadly speaking, displays 'understanding' in reading Boileau and Pope, and 'feeling' in reading Racine and Shakespeare.

117 *develope*: discover, detect.

"liquid lustre": from William Mason's 'Elegy on the Death of Lady Coventry'. See p. 766 and note.

futile . . . novels or poems: cf. Mary Wollstonecraft's *A Vindication of the Rights of Woman* (1792), ch. xiii, sect. ii. Wollstonecraft deprecates 'feminine weakness of character' instanced in 'a romantic twist of the mind . . . produced by a confined education', leading women to entertain themselves 'by the reveries of the stupid novelists, who, knowing little of human nature, work up stale tales, and describe meretricious scenes, all retailed in a sentimental jargon, which equally tend to corrupt the taste, and draw the heart aside from its daily duties' (Norton Critical Edition, p. 183).

131 *impertinent lampoons*: rude personal satires, especially in verse; the more 'impertinent' because, as Mrs Howel and Mrs Maple believe, the vulgar should not comment upon their betters. In *The Witlings*, Lady Smatter, who behaves to the heroine rather as Mrs Howel behaves to the Incognita, is forced into better conduct by the threat of lampoons.

137 *Gemini!*: since the Restoration, a euphemistic exclamation favoured particularly by ladies as a substitute for swear words; by the mid-eighteenth century, a vulgarism.

142 *think . . . for myself*: almost a refrain in Burney's works; cf. Belfield's arguments in *Cecilia*, vol. I, ch. ii, pp. 10–19.

152 *slough of despond*: from John Bunyan's *The Pilgrim's Progress* (1678). Christian and Pliable, encumbered by the burden of sin, fall into the Slough of Despond, which represents 'the descent whither the scum and filth that attends conviction for sin doth continually run'. Pliable flounces out and goes back home; Christian struggles through the mire and is pulled out by Help. See *The Pilgrim's Progress*, ed. Roger Sharrock (Oxford, 1960), p. 15.

dubiosity: doubtful matters, but here meaning the species of words expressing doubt.

the Rights of Man: a phrase often used in the period of the American and French Revolutions; the idea of universal human rights was new, although the English Revolution of the 1640s had seen the beginnings of the liberal ideology of rights. The phrase is the title of the best known book by Thomas Paine, *The Rights of Man* (1790; 1792). *The Rights of Man* was written as a response to Edmund Burke's *Reflections on the Revolution in France* (1790). Mary Wollstonecraft had written another such response, *A Vindication of the Rights of Men* (1790), before the better-known *Vindication of the Rights of Woman* (1792).

156 *Minerva*: who sprang full armed and full grown from the head of Jupiter.

157 *magnetize*: to attract as a magnet does, but probably with the sense of exerting the charm of 'animal magnetism', an early term for the power of hypnosis as practised by the Austrian physician Dr F. A. Mesmer (1734–1815).

willowed: wearing or being given the willow; to 'wear a willow' is to grieve the loss of a mate or to suffer from unrequited love. 'Willowed state' seems a half-pun on 'widowed state'.

162 *epithalamium—or a requiem!*: i.e. marriage or funeral. An epithalamium is a wedding song or poem praising and blessing the married pair. A *requiem* (from the accusative of *requies* or rest) is a funeral mass for the repose of the souls of the dead, in Catholic usage, hence generally the observation of a funeral or the repose of the grave; the word was popular among Romantic poets.

164 *egotist*: a word often used by Burney; cf. the Dedication to *Evelina*.

168 *wedding-garment ... or ... shroud*: the equivalent of epithalamium or requiem, above. This is another of Elinor's phrases that resembles the image vocabulary of the Romantic poets; cf. Coleridge's 'Dejection. An Ode' (1802), l. 49: 'Ours is her wedding-garment, ours her shroud'.

169 *shagrin case*: a case of chagrin or shagreen, untanned leather with a rough surface, from the skin of horse or ass, sometimes of shark or seal; frequently dyed green.

summer-house: another important scene in Burney's novels takes place in a summer-house, the reunion of Cecilia and Mortimer Delvile; see *Cecilia*, vol. IV, ch. iii, pp. 545–52.

171 *intellects*: the intellectual powers; the senses. *OED* cites this as an example.

173 *appendant*: attached to or consequent upon; *OED* cites this as an example.

175 *the Rights of woman*: a direct reference to the title of Wollstonecraft's book which best embodies the idea of woman's rights; Elinor is making her own 'vindication' ("my personal vindication, Harleigh!"). Elinor's quite impressive rhetoric on the 'Rights of human nature' seems close to Wollstonecraft's. Wollstonecraft, however, appeals constantly to God as Creator, whereas Elinor is able to acknowledge here only the power of 'equal Nature'. Elinor may also be influenced by *Les droits de la femme* by Marie Olympe de Gouge, published in Paris in 1791.

177 *look down upon the wife ... and upon the mother ... as upon mere sleepy, slavish, uninteresting automatons*: the ideas expressed here are similar to those found in Jean-Jacques Rousseau's *Emile ou de l'education* (1762), in which it is also lamented as unnatural that women should be raised as thoughtless and unknowing automata.

178 *"Lord of yourself, uncumber'd by a wife"*: John Dryden, 'Lord of yourself, uncumber'd with a Wife', from 'To my Honour'd Kinsman, John Driden', l. 18; first published in his *Fables Ancient and Modern* (1700); cf. *Camilla*, p. 402.

184 *ague-fit*: an attack of shivering in the cold fit brought on by malarial or other acute fever. (Ague is the Old French derivative of *acutus*, and an ague is any sharp fever with intervals of hot and cold sensations.) Cf. *Cecilia*, p. 200 and note.

VOLUME II

195 *"communed with her own heart"*: Cf. *The Book of Common Prayer*, Psalms 4: 4: 'Stand in awe, and sin not: commune with your own heart upon your bed, and be still'.

200 *M. Vinstreigle, a celebrated professor*: Vinstreigle is a music teacher (not a member of a university) and also a performer (just as Dr Charles Burney was both); he may be modelled on musicians in Charles Burney's circle.

204 *enthusiast*: a visionary rhapsodist, one who is deluded by fanatical notions, especially in religion.

208 *diletante*: corrected to *dilettante* in the second edition; an amateur, one who participates in artistic activity without making it a profession.

211 *coronet seal ... cypher*: Lady Aurora evidently has her own seal or seal-ring, with the device of a small crown (expressing noble rank) and her initials; she stamps this device on the red wax that seals her letters.

213 *gross and homely*: coarse and underbred: 'homely is a euphemism for wanting refinement or polish' (*OED*).

220 *Dans une position telle que la vôtre*: 'In a position such as yours'; this fragment of the opening sentence lets us know we are reading, in the rest of the letter, a translation from French.

superiour office of a governess: the position of governess had some shreds of gentility, and was higher in the social scale than a job requiring manual work (i.e. a 'laborious support').

221 *an humble companion*: a very specific phrase, referring to the position of a woman who is the paid companion of another woman, and is thus expected to be 'humble' and not give herself airs of equality, even if she is well-born and admitted by her employer to the drawing-room circles. The duties included sewing, care of pets, reading aloud, going over household accounts, and carrying about possessions and equipment for the mistress of the household. Cf. *Cecilia*, p. 11. Burney had complained that her superior at Court, Mrs Schwellenberg, had expected her to be 'her humble companion, at her own command!' (*Diary and Letters*, iii. 102).

224 *Good me!*: an unusual vulgarism, a form of 'Goodness me'; an unladylike exclamation, harking back to the assumed original 'God bless me!'

225 *begin his winter ... before May or June*: Miss Arbe's father cannot afford to go to London before May or June, when the fashionable season which lasts from the New Year to 4 June will be nearly over.

226 *benefit*: a play or concert, the profits of which were to be given to one well-known performer, or to the author or composer.

228 *dupery*: duped condition.

230 *hoyden*: more usually a noun; an inelegant, romping girl.

conformation: structure, organization.

The Ellis: Sir Marmaduke Crawley affectedly treats Ellis as if she were a well-known (and Continental) female professional performer.

231 *Vandals*: equivalent of 'Goths' in eighteenth-century speech, standing for everything that is uncivilized and crude.

"spirit, taste, and sense": Pope's *Epistle to Dr. Arbuthnot* (1735): 'Pains, reading, study, are their just pretence, | And all they want is spirit, taste, and sense', ll. 159–60.

virtuosi: (plural of virtuoso), collectors, connoisseurs, amateurs with an interest in the fine arts or sciences.

232 *dumpish*: inert or dejected; over-serious.

fogrum: see above, p. 70. The discussion of the word among the characters here may be a kind of answer on Burney's part to the critics of *Camilla* who had found fault not only with gallicisms and inversions but also with unusual or slangy words.

set of formals: a group of stuffy formal people; an unusual usage of the word 'formal' as a noun (*OED* records first use in 1605).

233 *gala dinners, and gala ornaments*: festive dinners and fine showy ornaments; *OED* gives first use of 'gala' as 1800.

234 *head-dress*: all ladies wore some form of lace-cap indoors. See Cunnington, *Handbook*, pp. 343–50.

239 *tudeling*: seems to be Tedman's own invention, a portmanteau word combining ideas of tutoring and tune-making. *OED* cites this instance as its example. The verb 'to tootle' did not come into the language until the mid-nineteenth century.

twiddle: to turn about with the fingers; to play with or upon in a trifling manner.

tudeler: again, Tedman's own word for one who plays at making tunes, and also tutors.

241 *blind Welsh harper*: the most famous blind Welsh harper was John Parry of Ruabon, a performer and a collector of folk-songs. Parry died in 1782, but other Welsh harpers made profitable expeditions to England, and the figure of the blind Welsh harper was to become an important Romantic image. Wollstonecraft presents a blind Welsh harper in Chapter xiv of her children's book, *Original Stories from Real Life* (1788).

242 *straitly*: should mean 'narrowly' or 'rigorously'; here, straightaway and in a straight line.

poke her way: potter or dawdle along.

side form: a backless bench at the side of the room.

244 *given dinner*: a dinner party.

put in case: say that, suppose that.

245 *boarding-school*: boarding schools for girls had existed in England since the late seventeenth century, and by the mid-eighteenth century were to be found throughout the country. For an account of their curricula, see Jill Grey's Introduction to Sarah Fielding's *The Governess* (1749) (Oxford, 1968).

a toss up: an unusual substantive, meaning a person who tosses the head in the upper echelons of society, though still with a hint of the condition of Miss Tedman, who has been tossed upward.

lauk adaisy: a vulgar exclamation, usually found only among the rural lower classes; an extension of 'lackaday' from 'alack-a-day': woe worth the day.

let the cat out of the bag: to let a guarded secret escape inadvertently. The expression is proverbial, and dates at least as far back as the mid-eighteenth century. See *Dictionary of Proverbs*, p. 457.

a so so hand at the agreeable: does but a mediocre job at making herself agreeable.

my particulars: my particular friends, my set.

246 *bang wang way*: in that noisy emphatic manner. Burney is fond of emphatic nonsense rhyme phrases: cf. '*pinky winky*' p. 314, and '*whisky frisky*', *Cecilia*, p. 784.

Queen David: Riley annotates himself by saying that Ellis is 'the finest harp-player ... on this side King David', p. 253. She is a female equivalent of King David, the Bible's most noted musician and song-writer, who in his youth was able to relieve Saul of the evil spirit by playing upon the harp; see 1 Samuel 16: 21–3.

uncurbing: from a rare transitive use of 'curb' as to bend or to curve: uncurving, unrolling.

247 *came hoydening up*: came prancing up in a boisterous unladylike manner; cf. 'hoyden', p. 230.

249 *rent-roll*: list of tenants and the annual rent paid, the source of a landed gentleman's income; cf. *Cecilia*, p. 96 and note.

250 *comical hand*: a strange person; cf. 'odd fish' in the same speech.

choused: cheated. A favourite word of Briggs in *Cecilia* ; see p. 119 and note.

place in the Diligence: her seat in the stage-coach; see p. 31.

252 *insignia of the order of fisty cuffs*: jocular; the tokens of honour (as from an order conferred by royalty) of having participated in a fist-fight—i.e. bruises.

A guinea to half a crown: Riley bets a guinea (21 shillings) against Ireton's suggested stake of half a crown (two shillings and sixpence)—a ratio of 42 to 5, or over 8 to 1—so sure is he of winning the bet.

253 *dowager*: strictly, a widow enjoying some property coming to her from her deceased husband. Mrs Maple may indeed be a dowager, but in speaking generally of those who would be anxious for the beauty-making recipe, Riley seems to be using the word in its more modern, vaguer sense, as an elderly woman of some dignity; the first instance of this usage is given in *OED* as 1870.

254 *white wine negus*: a drink invented by Colonel Francis Negus (d. 1732) composed of wine, hot water, and sugar, and flavoured with lemon and spice.

255 *most minimus*: least.

257 *rules the roast*: to be a master of everything (usually found as 'rules the roost').

liberty boy: 'a supporter of a freedom movement' (*OED*); the phrase dates back to the American Revolution, when it was first used as a nickname for Colonial Whigs.

of a fig: the worth of a fig; i.e. he would not care a bit how old you are.

258 *register*: parish register containing the dates of baptism, thus proving a person's age.

The man amongst your grand-dads: Riley's diatribe against class and descent resembles that of Briggs the city miser against the aristocratic Compton Delvile, *Cecilia*, pp. 455–6.

259 *qualmish*: queasy; here, seasick.

260 *pig-tail*: a queue wig; by the 1790s somewhat old-fashioned, and hardly to be seen in 1814. Tedman ornaments the end of the wig's tail with a black ribbon, as in the mode of the 1770s.

consort: concord of sound, then company of musicians and hence musical performance of any kind, a concert; 'consort' is really inappropriate to describe a solo harpist.

book-shop ... subscribe: circulating libraries functioned by subscription, usually quite expensive, at a guinea per subscriber; genteel visitors to watering places such as Bath, Tunbridge Wells, or Brighton became subscribers to the best library, usually conducted from a bookshop. Since the names of subscribers were published, people like Miss Tedman might think that appearing in the list registered one's claims to gentility. See *Camilla*, p. 99; cf. Jane Austen, *Sanditon* (Oxford World's Classics, 1980), pp. 344–5.

261 *mumbled*: chewed gently or nuzzled without using the teeth.

gilt head ... cane: gentlemen carried ornamental walking sticks, usually of malacca, with the knob in marble, amber, gold, or a precious metal; Tedman's is the cheap version.

263 *French plums*: bon-bons, especially dried fruits imported from France, and candied fruit such as apricots, chestnuts, dried plums *glacés*.

desert: the dessert course; not pudding but nuts, fruit or dried fruits, and sweetmeats.

265 *mechanics*: or mechanicals, artisans engaged in trades involving manual labour; Miss Arbe uses the term loosely for all middle-class people engaged in any form of trade.

266 *snap at*: snatch at, grab, 'make a quick or eager catch at a thing' (*OED*).

267 *fee ... pew-opener*: a pew-opener, often a female, collected fees from church-goers by opening for them the wooden doors to individual box pews. A pew-opener figures as a minor character in *Cecilia*; see *Cecilia*, p. 627 and note.

268 *out-topped*: overtopped, i.e. excelled, surpassed.

piping, and jiggetting: singing, or playing musical instruments, and hopping and skipping about.

our club: clubs proliferated in late eighteenth-century England, and the period of the French Revolution saw an efflorescence of different kinds of societies with different political interests. The London Corresponding Society admitted 'Tradesmen, Shopmen, and Mechanics' to discuss reform and particularly the universal Franchise. Corresponding societies flourished in various towns throughout England, but in 1794 the movement was harshly put down and the officers of the London society prosecuted for high treason (they were acquitted but the Society was outlawed). Gooch may belong to a branch of the Corresponding society, but it seems more likely that the young farmer belongs to a conservative group that endeavours (rather naïvely) to find out what is going on in France. Cf. *Cecilia*, p. 372 and note.

269 *rites practised ... Goddess of Reason*: the revolutionary government, in its endeavour to do away with the Christian religion as well as

the power of the Roman Catholic Church, not only introduced a new calendar and dispossessed the Church of its lands and authority, but also introduced a new mock religion in symbolic displacement of the other. As Anacharsis Clootz proclaimed, there should be one God only: 'Le Peuple'. In November 1793 Procureur Chaumette and other Parisian officials introduced the new formula of the worship of reason; in displacement of the Virgin Mary a young actress, costumed and bearing the accoutrements (a red liberty cap and pike) of the people, was escorted by members of the Convention and by Parisian citizens to Notre Dame, where she was placed on the altar. Other parishes throughout France took part in similar rituals of Adoration of Reason in November and December of 1793, and various young women were local 'Goddesses of Reason'. As Scope comments, the pagans represented Reason as a female, most particularly in the form of the goddess Minerva, but linguistically also; reason in Latin— *ratiocinatio* —is feminine and so is the French *la raison.*

coping: position of equality, able to cope with, prove a match or contend with an opponent; an odd usage, perhaps influenced by the architectural meaning of *coping* as the top course of masonry and by the *cope-stone* as the topmost stone; hence in an exalted or commanding position.

270 *pattens*: clogs to keep the feet from the wet, each consisting of a wooden sole mounted on an iron ring, elevating the wearer a few inches above the ground.

taken miff: taken offence at, become out of humour with.

271 *Indian slave*: Sir Lyell's information probably comes from materials imported from the orient and from ornamental motifs with Indian designs; high caste ladies in India are pictured being protected from the sun rather than the rain.

274 *adagio*: a piece of music, or movement in a piece, in slow time.

cadenza: a flourishing solo passage towards the close of a movement of a concerto, customarily brilliant and difficult of execution.

275 FEMALE . . . DIFFICULTIES: the locus of the novel's subtitle. The heroine of the radical Mary Hays's *The Victim of Prejudice* (1799) complains that prejudices about women's virtue and the mistreatment of women's sexuality make it virtually impossible for an unprotected woman to earn her own living honestly and acquire the dignity of independence.

276 *unhackneyed*: inexperienced in the good sense, not worn and staled by the use of the world.

articles which did not admit of trust: purchases which could not be made upon credit, e.g. foodstuffs.

280 *think of nothing less*: less than putting down the packet, or making excuses; i.e. think of it not at all.

absence: absent-mindedness.

284 *self-eulogium*: a eulogy delivered by the speaker in self-praise; this is perhaps Burney's coinage.

288 *theoretical ... science*: music theory, e.g. principles of harmony, counterpoint, musical composing, but also here principles of execution such as enable the teacher to help students around difficulties and make them sound better.

289 *premium*: the sum taken by a master or mistress in payment for keeping and instructing an apprentice; this could be a very large amount. Thomas Arne, in 1744, had wanted £100 to take Charles Burney as his apprentice, though he eventually agreed to take him for nothing.

290 *plain work*: plain sewing: basting, hemming, stitching seams.

teized: teased, disturbed by persistent annoyance. Miss Matson is plagued by requests to help find jobs for women, since female unemployment is high.

292 *common gear*: everyday wear, ordinary apparel; a somewhat archaic or provincial usage.

296 *eclat*: French (*éclat*) for brilliancy, dazzling effect, high renown.

297 *hardly*: with hardship, painfully.

flappers: In Swift's *Gulliver's Travels* (1726), Book III, ch. 2, Gulliver encounters the mathematically disposed and absent-minded Laputans. They are so taken up with intense speculations that no gentleman can attend to the common business of life without the assistance of a 'Flapper' who carries a bladder on a short stick with which to give 'a soft Flap' to the ears, eyes, or mouth of the abstracted employer when necessary (the ladies are sensuously active and do not require flappers). Burney used the term of herself in reference to her trying to rouse her mathematical and absent-minded son Alex to exert himself in working for a university degree; she had to act 'in the character of Flapper to Alexander' (*Journals and Letters*, ix. 231). Cf. also *Camilla*, p. 366 and note.

298 *virtuosa*: an unusual feminine form of virtuoso, a female with taste in the fine arts.

299 *gauzes*: thin transparent fabrics of silk, linen, or cotton.

300 *elegant toss*: an elegant action in throwing the body about.

303 *put in case*: italicized to show Giles Arbe is consciously quoting one of Tedman's favourite phrases.

305 *uniform for the lady-artists*: the ladies are to dress alike, in white with violet trim and accessories (see p. 314); these are also the colours which the lady dancers must wear to the nobleman's ball in *Camilla*: 'This uniform was to be clear fine lawn, with lilac plumes and ornaments', p. 690. Camilla is distressed at this dictate because she spends too much money in acquiring the costume; Ellis is distressed because she is crudely made to understand that she does not rank as a lady; she is to be garishly arrayed in bright pink to be stared at, in contrast to the symbolic modesty and chastity of the ladies in their elegant and apparently unpretending 'uniform'. When she does appear to perform, Ellis disdains the pink silk and appears in white satin (p. 358).

310 *"unstrung the lyre"*: Cf. Pope, *Odyssey*, VIII. 107: 'His golden lyre Demodocus unstrung'; cf. also William Whitehead's *Enthusiast*, XV: 'Enthusiast, go, unstring thy lyre'.

311 *bravissima*: superlative of feminine *brava* (masc. *bravo*), an Italian cheer meaning 'well done!' 'excellent!', imported to England and used chiefly in the Opera House for professional singers in public performance. Belfield applauds a speech by Cecilia with 'Brava!' in conversation (*Cecilia*, p. 19).

313 *gown*: not a dress fully made up, but material for a gown, a dress length of cloth.

sarcenet: or sarsenet, a fine soft silk material.

314 *body-lining*: a body is the part of the woman's dress above the waist, but here 1790s fashion and the too-soft nature of the sarcenet dictate that an entire inner shell of dress would need to be created, as well as a firm bodice; this will be more expensive and the ladies will need to find a 'cheap mantua maker', or inexpensive dressmaker, to make up the gown.

wax-doll: a child's doll, usually seven to fourteen inches high, the head, bust, and limbs of which were made of wax. Wax dolls imported from France with carefully sculpted faces cost anything from six to ten guineas, and were the most popular type of nursery doll by the end of the eighteenth century. See Magdalen King-Hall, *The Story of the Nursery* (London, 1958), pp. 146–7, 183.

315 *lessons*: studies (cf. 'études') and short pieces.

316 *"spirit-stirring praise"*: cf. Shakespeare, *Othello*, III. iii. 358: 'The spirit-stirring drum'; cf. also Thomas Gray, 'Agripinna', l. 122: 'spirit-stirring voice'.

their own line: their own appointed lot in life, but 'line' here seems more decidedly and overtly metaphorical, to indicate the line of partition that the gentlefolk mentally draw to keep others outside the pale.

least considerable: i.e. smallest in size.

319 *canvassed*: sought out and persuaded to give favours; now used mainly for the seeking of votes, but in the eighteenth century individuals were canvassed not only for votes but also for subscriptions and patronage.

322 *thrim thrum*: to thrum is to play unskilfully on a stringed instrument; Giles Arbe uses his own expressive nonsense intensifier, which seems to be Burney's nonce word; one of the jingling pairs of short words—onomatopoeic or pseudo-onomatopoeic—of which she is fond. Cf. *Camilla*, p. 946 and note.

323 *staff of life, as Solomon himself calls the loaf*: the Bible has numerous references to bread as a staff; e.g. 'when I have broken the staff of your bread', Leviticus 26: 26; cf. Psalms 105: 16; Isaiah 3: 11; Ezekiel 5: 16. The well-known expression 'Bread is the staff of life' occurs nowhere in the Bible, however, although Scope seems to think it is in the Book of Proverbs, which contains nothing close to it. There is no reason to expect pompous Mr Scope to make correct reference to the Bible or anything else. The saying is found in the speech of another pompous character, Peter in Swift's *A Tale of a Tub* (1704); 'Bread, says he *Dear Brothers, is the Staff of Life*', praising his own 'brown loaf', section iv.

figure: go through the figures or set of movements of a dance.

324 *quartern loaves*: loaves weighing four pounds each.

325 *gavots, and fandangos*: lively dances, imported respectively from France and Spain.

327 *scenas*: words and music of a scene, or a composition of a dramatic character for one or more voices, with accompaniment. Predates the earliest example (1819) in *OED*.

snug scrip-concert: a cosy concert arranged by subscription from among a select little coterie.

go to town: to London, for the season: see note to p. 225 above.

333 *burnt feathers*: feathers to be held under the nose as a remedy for faintness.

334 *patterns*: samples or swatches of material.

337 *conflicts*: a word most peculiarly Burney's, reserved in her diaries and letters, as well as her tragedies, for internal emotional disturbances and self-division.

349 *'hold its seat'*: *Hamlet*, I. v. 96–7: 'while memory holds a seat | In this distracted globe'.

356 *hôtel*: The French origin of the word is indicated, but the word in English already meant a superior sort of inn, as here, with public rooms.

slouched hat: i.e. a slouch hat; a soft felt hat, 'having a broad brim which hangs or laps down over the face' (*OED*).

357 *scarlet coat ... waistcoat of coloured and spangled embroidery*: men's waistcoats throughout the eighteenth century were typically embroidered, and often fringed or laced; spangles were small, glittering pieces of metal sewn to the vestment. See Cunnington, *Handbook*, pp. 203–11.

cravat: linen or silk kerchief worn round the neck by men; perfected by Beau Brummel, it was to dominate male fashion in the early nineteenth century.

foreign manufacture: either because of details in cut and workmanship (as in spangles), or because the whole is too showy and disproportioned; English fashion for gentlemen was becoming simpler and more subdued. Beau Brummel popularized the simple black-and-white look for males, although at a slightly later date than the time of the action of *The Wanderer*. If these clothes are 'foreign', they are probably German rather than French, as French fashion dictated a stark or revolutionary simplicity.

358 *style ... Grecian*: 'Grecian' style was very much in vogue in this period, and in women's looks it represented pleasing contours and a fine-cut profile; Emma Hart won the love and even the hand of Sir William Hamilton because she could adopt the postures of Greek figures from vases and sculptures. Goethe in 1787 described her attitudes in the Greek costume Sir William had made for her: 'In her he has found ... all the profiles of Sicilian

coins'; see John Buxton, *The Greek Taste: Literature in the Age of Neo-Classicism, 1740–1820* (London, 1978), p. 11. Ellis looks pale, pure, and noble, and thus beautiful in contrast to the eccentric, impassioned Elinor, who wishes to achieve the 'sublime'.

359 *phial of salts*: spirits of ammonia in a smelling bottle. See note above to p. 98.

360 *surgeon*: licensed to perform operations, unlike physicians, surgeons in the eighteenth century had developed in knowledge of anatomy, but were lower in the social scale than physicians, as they performed manual labour. Cf. *Cecilia*, p. 170 and note.

self-devoted enthusiast: one who is carried away by romantic notions to the point of devoting herself to destruction; Elinor is also 'self-devoted' in the sense of being selfishly devoted to herself.

361 *the hand of scorn*: see *Othello*, IV. ii. 54–5: 'A fixed figure for the time of scorn | To point his slow unmoving finger at'; cf. *Camilla*, p. 356.

364 *go one stage*: go by stages; here, go to the first posting stage where she might take a public coach; see note to p. 41.

365 *love of fame ... ruling passion*: see the title of Edward Young's series of seven satires *Love of Fame, The Universal Passion* (1725–8), as well as Pope's phrase: 'Search then the Ruling Passion', *Epistle to Cobham*, l. 174.

369 *interested*: self-interested or selfish.

371 *Cato's soliloquy*: The most famous speech in Joseph Addison's *Cato* (1713), v. i. Elinor slightly misquotes the speech, changing Addison's possessive 'her' ('favour her', 'her flight'), that makes both Nature and the soul feminine, into 'thee' and 'its', addressing Sleep (which does not appear in Cato's speech) and making her soul neutral. Elinor also sharply varies the ending, which in the original is 'take her flight, | Renew'd in all her strength, and fresh with life, | An offering fit for Heaven'.

peculiar to ... John Bull: John Bull, a name for the typical Englishman, originated with a series of pamphlets, *The History of John Bull*, published in 1712 by John Arbuthnot. The English had long been thought particularly given to suicide, a supposed fact blamed on their climate, their diet, or their religion.

372 *pop off*: now intransitive in the slang sense of 'to die', but here possibly transitive if 'more' is taken as an object rather than as part of the subject ('more of them pop off in a month'). The first use for 'to die' recorded in *OED* is 1764.

broadside: discharge of all the artillery on one side of a ship of war.

'spur my almost blunted purpose!': a misquotation of the Ghost's speech to Hamlet, *Hamlet*, III. iv. 111: 'to whet thy almost blunted purpose'.

approximation: close proximity.

376 *supine*: 'morally or mentally inactive, inert, or indolent' (*OED*).

adamant: sometimes diamond or lodestone, but generally a fabulous rock of impenetrable hardness.

'nauseous draught of life': not by Dryden as Burney's note asserts, but by John Wilmot, Earl of Rochester, from his 'Letter from Artemisia in the Town to Chloe in the Country' (1679), in which the female speaker says that love is 'That Cordial dropp Heav'n in our Cup has throwne, | To make the nauseous draught of life goe downe'. Perhaps Burney could not permit herself to remember that her character's quotation (suited to Elinor's libertinism) came from such an improper poet. See *The Poems of John Wilmot, Earl of Rochester*, ed. Keith Walker (Oxford, 1984), p. 83.

379 *chaise and four horses*: a light, open carriage drawn by four horses—one of the swiftest (and most expensive) modes of travel, and one fraught with possibilities of accident.

380 *litter*: a light bed or couch with a frame covered by curtains, capable of being carried on men's shoulders or placed on some steady vehicle drawn by animals; a slow method of travel.

cant: jargon, or stock-phrases of a profession or group.

VOLUME III

386 *Loin de toi ma malheureuse destinée*: may my unhappy fate be far different from yours. This sentence is omitted from Burney's English translation.

I had the bliss of possessing thee: expanded from the French 'je te possedois' (I possessed you).

pleurez vous: Gabriella's use of 'vous' marks her as of the *ancien régime*; the revolutionary government outlawed the use of 'vous', traditionally used in the singular as a sign of respect. When the young women, on recognizing each other, change to 'tu', it is an indication of their intimacy.

387 *Julie*: even when her real name is at last revealed, the heroine has two names, one French, one English. 'Julie' suggests Rousseau's

heroine in *La Nouvelle Héloïse* (1761), while Juliet suggests Shakespeare's heroine in *Romeo and Juliet.*

ma chère, ma tendre: my dear, my tender; but only 'my tender' in Burney's English translation.

un ange: an angel; but, more affectionately, a 'cherub' in Burney's English translation.

388 *a feeling of softness, nay of pleasure*: expanded from the French 'délice' (pleasure).

391 *suspensive*: kept in a state of suspense.

great name: this suggests that Gabriella belongs by marriage to one of the great French aristocratic families, and has to keep her surname a secret.

393 *pleurant sur*: weeping over, but only 'visiting' in Burney's English translation.

my darling boy: expanded from the French 'mon fils' (my son).

my dearest, best loved friend: expanded from the French 'mon amie' (my friend).

ashes: these ashes ('cendres') are not literally the residue of a cremation, but a classically based euphemism for bodily remains.

396 *studied how to die without torture*: perhaps by reading the anecdote related by Pliny of Arria, who encouraged her husband in his task of committing suicide by stabbing herself first. She then handed him the dagger, telling him 'it does not hurt' (*Letters*, iii. 16).

397 *like the man in the song ... could*: not identified.

398 *excommunicating scruples*: Elinor here implies that Juliet is a Catholic, fearful of being excommunicated from the Church; as would have been the case for an actress. Voltaire, as Elinor might be expected to have known, wrote a powerful poem, *La mort de mlle Lecouvreur* (1730), deploring the Church's treatment of the actress Adrienne Lecouvreur. Because of her profession she was automatically excommunicated, and thus refused consecrated burial; her body was 'thrown into quicklime on waste land' (Theodore Besterman, *Voltaire*, 3rd edn. (Chicago, 1976), p. 169). Elinor's false surmise about Juliet's putative Catholicism resembles that of other characters in the novel.

399 *making puddings and pies*: a cliché describing the work of women, often used seriously. Burney had made fun of the concept in the speech of Sir Roderick in *The Woman Hater*: 'What do they [women] know? And what ought they to know? Except to sew a Gown, & make a Pudding' (I. ix).

400 *toad-eater*: 'a humble friend or dependant; specifically, a female companion or attendant' (*OED*). The metaphor, deriving from the practice of charlatans' attendants being employed to eat (or pretend to eat) toads, is discussed at length in Sarah Fielding's *The Adventures of David Simple* (1744, Oxford World's Classics edition, 1987, p. 113). In *Evelina*, Mr Lovel describes the heroine as 'a kind of toad-eater' (p. 294).

rustic: rural; here in the sense of unfashionable and outdated.

402 *hydra-headed*: difficult to overcome, referring to the fabulous, many-headed water-snake inhabiting the marshes of Lerna. It was eventually killed by Hercules.

403 *Residing in ... Norbury Park*: the 'angelic beings' alluded to here are William and Frederica Locke, the owners of Norbury Hall in Sussex, who befriended a group of French émigrés, including Burney's future husband Alexandre d'Arblay, on their arrival in England in 1792, and Burney's beloved sister Susanna. With her husband Molesworth Phillips, Susanna had lived since 1784 in a cottage in Mickleham, close to Norbury Park, until their removal to London in July 1795 and subsequent move to Ireland in 1796. Susanna was brutally used by her husband, and her death in 1800 was Burney's sharpest sorrow. The inclusion of a secret tribute to her sister makes the author remember the last date (1795) when Susanna was living at the foot of Norbury Park, forgetting that the scheme of the novel demands a date of 1794. Frederica Locke is also praised for her 'kind zeal' in the Advertisement to *Camilla*.

balsamic: soothing, gently restorative.

405 *drug*: as in a drug on the market; something possessed in excess, which cannot be got rid of.

day-jobber: a piece-worker, hired for low wages by the day.

406 *paste for the hands*: such pastes, used as toilet accessories for women throughout the century, became especially popular during the last two decades. See Neil McKendrick's 'Commercialization and the Economy' in McKendrick, John Brewer, and J. H. Plumb, *The Birth of a Consumer Society* (London, 1982).

409 *better genius*: in the sense of a good angel or daemon; related to the idea of a genie, rather than to that of a fine intellect.

411 *Impship*: an unusual mock title for an Imp.

softness of the Dove's: echoing the *Song of Songs*: 'Behold, thou art fair, my love ... thou hast doves' eyes' (4: 1).

411 *whipt with nettles*: Sir Jaspar thinks in terms of punishments imposed by fairies in folklore and in Elizabethan and Jacobean literature.

412 *junket*: merrymaking and feasting; this passage is quoted as an example in *OED*.

413 *speak quite in the new manner*: Gooch's speech is characterized by colloquialisms which he imagines are fashionable, in contrast to the more formal language of the older generation.

slip of land: a narrow piece of land.

414 *mead*: a traditional alcoholic drink, made by fermenting a mixture of honey and water.

chay-cart: a vulgar corruption of 'chaise'; the passage is quoted as an example in *OED*.

lauk: like 'lack', 'lawk', 'lawks', etc., a corruption of 'Lord'. See also note to p. 712 below.

415 *hippish*: low-spirited, hypochondriacal; the passage is quoted as an example in *OED*.

419 *law*: indulgence, mercy.

gave me my swing: from the proverbial 'Youth will have its swing' (*Dictionary of Proverbs*, p. 929).

421 *portrait upon his snuff-box*: snuff-boxes, especially those made by French craftsmen, were valuable items, prized by collectors. Elegant snuff-boxes, such as Sir Jaspar's, would have portraits engraved on their lids.

423 *japan basket*: a basket varnished and adorned in the Japanese style. Japanese varnish is exceptionally hard.

426 *humours of a milliner's shop*: modes of characteristic behaviour, styles of action associated with the shop; also freaks, vagaries of the place. The phrase hints at Ben Jonson's influence on Burney's ideas of characterization.

cheapened: bargained for.

chaffering: bargaining, haggling.

skanes of netting silk: a quantity (skein) of silk used for needlework.

428 *the meaner ... sauntered away*: Burney had already observed this slighting treatment of less affluent customers. In Act One of *The Witlings*, set in a milliner's shop, a young woman asking for 'Ribands' is repeatedly put off. Eventually, she leaves without having been served.

429 *costume*: italicized to indicate the French term, used to signify fashionable, imported clothing.

431 *knight baronight*: i.e. a baronet, and hence of the same rank as Sir Jaspar Herrington.

432 *jessamy*: a colloquial term for jessamine or jasmine; a white or yellow flower prized for its beauty and fragrance.

433 *duennas*: elderly women, entrusted with the duties of chaperons.

435 *gala day*: a holiday.

436 *pommel*: or pummel, to hit and punch.

437 *upon my gig*: in a state of boisterous hilarity. *OED* quotes as an example a passage from Burney's diary for 1777.

438 *No ass so meek;—no mule so obstinate*: Pope's second *Moral Essay*, 'Of the Characters of Women' (1735), l. 102: 'No Ass so meek, no Ass so obstinate'.

quite a little goddess: as Flora is, in a sense, her name being that of a minor goddess, the deity of flowers.

441 *O my love ... dies for thee!*: not identified.

444 *a thing of alabaster*: smooth and white, alabaster is traditionally used as an image of sexual purity and chastity.

old Nick: *OED* gives the earliest use of this term for the devil as 1643, and states that 'the reason for the appellation is obscure'.

Crabs: sour, ill-tempered persons; so named from the tart, wild crab-apple.

à la mode of your vieille cour: fashionable in your old style of courtly behaviour.

445 *Statira ... Alexander*: Statira, daughter of the Persian king Darius III, married Alexander the Great in 324 BC, a year before his death. See Nathaniel Lee's play *The Rival Queens* (1677).

mantua-maker: a maker of mantuas, loose gowns worn by women in the seventeenth and eighteenth centuries; generally, a dressmaker.

452 *"Favourite has no friend"*: Thomas Gray, 'Ode on the Death of a Favourite Cat, Drowned in a Tub of Gold Fishes' (1747), l. 36: 'A fav'rite has no friend'.

454 *basting, running*: sewing together loosely, to hold a garment in place for the first time; sewing quickly, 'usually by taking a number of stitches on the needle at a time' (*OED*).

455 *bind herself ... as a journey-woman*: as a 'journey-woman', Juliet already has some experience and can work for another for a daily

wage. But by 'binding' herself to an employer as an apprentice, she could improve her skills and hope eventually to secure a better position.

456 *"If people won't follow advice, . . . 'tis a sign they are not much to be pitied"*: from the proverbial 'In vain he craves advice that will not follow it' (Morris Tilley, *A Dictionary of the Proverbs in England in the Sixteenth and Seventeenth Centuries* (Ann Arbor, Mich., 1950), p. 695).

positive engagements: fixed employment, working a set number of days and hours per week.

457 *return post-chaise*: a carriage hired by an individual for exclusive use, and hence a very expensive form of transport. The inexperienced Juliet, however, is unaware of the improbability of Mrs Pierson's hiring a carriage of this sort.

460 *huffed*: offended, put into a huff. *OED* quotes this passage as the earliest example of this usage.

461 *pig . . . well soaped*: in her journal for 19 August 1773, Burney describes a pig-catching contest. The 'poor animal had it's tale [*sic*] cut to within an Inch, & then that Inch was soaped:—it was then let loose, & made run' (*Early Journals*, i. 290).

462 *smoke*: suspect, get an inkling of.

top end: dialect for upper hand.

463 *pink*: a sweet-smelling flower, appropriately given to Juliet by 'Flora' Pierson.

464 *moped*: melancholy, low-spirited.

dowd: an unattractive, unfashionably dressed woman; this is the latest example quoted in *OED*.

465 *coz*: a familiar abbreviation of cousin.

chapman: here in the sense of purchaser or customer.

guiliotines: the notorious guillotine, used for beheading those condemned to death in France, was named after Dr Joseph-Ignace Guillotin, who first proposed its construction in 1789. It was used for mass executions at the height of the Terror, from 1792 to 1794. In the minds of Englishmen such as Gooch, it typified the worst excesses of the French Revolution.

staring: sensational.

466 *thof*: a dialect form of 'though'.

gudgeon: a small fish used for bait; hence a credulous, gullible person who will swallow anything.

peck: a great deal; a considerable number.

main: a dialect word for extremely, utterly.

roast beef and plum-pudding: Gooch names two quintessentially English dishes alien to the French palate. English contempt for French food, especially for frogs, already had a long tradition. See also note to p. 93 above.

stinted: a dialect form of 'stunted'.

467 *boggling*: bungling.

mounseers: an anglicized pronunciation of 'monsieur', indicating Gooch's contempt for the French.

Jack the Giant-killers: the popular fairy-tale *Jack the Giant Killer* dates in its modern form from the early eighteenth century. The Opies note that 'as the eighteenth century grew older Jack became a familiar character to all and sundry'; Fielding, Johnson, Boswell, and Cowper were among the story's admirers. See *Classic Fairy Tales*, pp. 47–50.

hop: a colloquial term for a dance.

468 *syllabub under the cow*: a dish made from milk, curdled by wine or cider and sweetened. The milk is drawn directly from the cow to ensure its freshness.

470 *phaeton*: a light, four-wheeled, open carriage, usually drawn by a pair of horses.

471 *got your ends*: had your way, accomplished your purpose.

473 *bowl or dagger*: alluding to Joseph Addison's *Rosamond: an Opera* (1707), in which Queen Elinor gives her rival, Rosamond, the choice of committing suicide by drinking poison or being stabbed with a dagger: 'Or quickly drain the fatal bowl, | Or this right hand performs its part, | And plants a dagger in thy heart' (II. vi). The same allusion is made on p. 585 above, and in *Cecilia*, p. 370.

477 *female fame ... suspected*: Julius Caesar divorced his second wife, Pompeia, because, according to Plutarch, 'Caesar's wife must be above suspicion' (*Lives*, Julius Caesar, x. 6). The phrase was proverbial from the late sixteenth century.

479 *charity school*: charity schools, established in England by the Society for the Promotion of Christian Knowledge in 1699, provided education and moral instruction at a low cost for children of the poor. 'They taught (boys and girls together) a straight and narrow curriculum, principally reading and Scripture' and emphasized discipline (Roy Porter, *English Society in the Eighteenth Century* (London, 1982), p. 182).

Mercer: a dealer in textile fabrics, such as silks, velvets, and other costly materials.

480 *spying glass*: a telescope or binoculars. Mrs Ireton calls for a 'spying glass' to emphasize Juliet's distance from her.

speaking trumpet: this device for making the voice carry further would normally be used to hail ships at sea.

481 *lavendar-water*: a perfume made from distilled flowers of lavender, alcohol, and ambergris.

482 *Mungo*: a type name for a black slave or servant, found in Isaac Bickerstaffe's comic opera *The Padlock* (1768).

483 *dish-clouts*: dish cloths; rags for doing the washing-up.

vestibule ... anti-chamber: synonymous terms for the entrance hall, normally used as a waiting-room for visitors.

work-house: initially set up in the seventeenth century, workhouses proliferated during the eighteenth century in towns and rural parishes. They provided food and shelter for the destitute, normally in return for long hours of hard labour. The death-rate of their inmates was notorious; see Porter, *English Society*, pp. 147–9.

485 *enamelling their own skin*: using preparations as a cosmetic process. This pre-dates the earliest example (1868) of the usage quoted in *OED*.

A wandering Jewess ... the old Jew: the Wandering Jew, a legendary figure, was condemned to wander around the world until Christ's second coming, for his ill-usage of Christ as Christ was carrying the Cross to Calvary. The legend was popular in the late eighteenth century, and its title lies behind that of Burney's novel. Mrs Ireton's references to the Jew's wife and mother are, as she admits, her own invention.

486 *grand climacterics*: the climacteric was held to be a critical moment in human life, occurring every seven years. The term 'grand climacteric' was generally applied to the sixty-third year of life (7 × 9). Mrs Ireton's sarcastic 'two or three grand climacterics' would thus make Juliet 126 or 189.

art of ingeniously tormenting: alluding to Jane Collier's *Essay on the Art of Ingeniously Tormenting* (1753), a bitterly ironic work with examples of taunting ridicule similar to those employed by Mrs Ireton. Cf. *Cecilia*, p. 113 and note; and see Doody, *Frances Burney*, p. 357.

494 *"it blesses those that give, and those that take"*: Portia's famous 'quality of mercy' speech in Shakespeare's *The Merchant of Venice*, IV. i. 184: 'It blesseth him that gives and him that takes'.

495 *Bijou*: French for jewel; a pleasantly inappropriate name for Mrs Ireton's disagreeable dog.

496 *breakfast ... about two o'clock*: an unusually late hour, but appropriate for the 'grand breakfast' that Mrs Ireton is giving. It has little resemblance to the normal breakfast, consisting only of tea and rolls or bread and butter; the 'traditional' English breakfast was a Victorian innovation.

Temple of the Sun: Mrs Ireton's pretentiously Druidic name for what seems to be an ordinary summer-house: a small, simple building in the grounds of a house, designed to provide shade and shelter.

497 *a cup and ball*: 'a toy consisting of a cup at the end of a stem to which a ball is attached by a string, the object being to toss the ball and catch it in the cup or on the spike end of the stem' (*OED*, which gives 1760 as the first use). For the wide range of games and toys available in the late eighteenth century, see J. H. Plumb's 'Commercialization and Society' in McKendrick, Brewer, and Plumb, *The Birth of a Consumer Society*.

mal à propos: inopportune, awkward, inappropriate.

parterre: a level space in a garden, used for flower-beds.

Loddard: this unusual name, apparently Burney's invention, could, like that of Ellis herself, be either a Christian or a surname.

498 *Mrs. Betty ... Mrs. Polly*: stock names for ladies' maids.

499 *flapping his hat*: pulling his hat down.

500 *children of a larger growth*: Dryden, *All for Love* (1678): 'Men are but children of a larger growth' (IV. i. 43).

501 *at Jericho*: the town in Palestine where David told his servants to tarry until their beards were grown; proverbial for a distant, out of the way place.

502 *Morpheus*: Sir Jaspar (and perhaps Burney) makes the common error of taking Morpheus, the Greek god of dreams, for his father Hypnos, the god of sleep.

Seven Sleepers: seven youths who, according to legend, were walled up in a cavern in AD 250, and slept for 187 years. On finally being liberated from their cave and awakening, they lived only a few days. See Edward Gibbon, *The Decline and Fall of the Roman Empire*, ch. xxxiii.

Sleeping beauty ... forty years: a fairy tale translated by Robert Samber in 1729, from Charles Perrault's 'La Belle au bois dormant' (1697). In Perrault's tale, Sleeping Beauty is awakened by the Prince after one hundred, not forty, years. See the Opies, *The Classic Fairy Tales*, pp. 81–3.

503 *mulberry leaves for silk-worms*: rearing silkworms was a hobby for the wealthy, rather than a practical means of producing raw silk. The efforts of James I and others to introduce silkworms into England on a large scale were unsuccessful.

recreative: 'tending to recreate or refresh in a pleasurable manner; amusing, diverting' (*OED*, which quotes this passage as an example).

504 *ball*: bullet.

"Sisters three": the Greek Fates: Clotho, who spun the thread of life; Lachesis, who drew it out; and Atropos, who cut it off. The daughters of Nyx (Night), they were represented as three old women. Cf. Shakespeare's *A Midsummer Night's Dream*, v. i. 323: 'O Sisters Three'.

505 *articled ... dowagers*: i.e. bequeathed his feelings, as well as his estate, to the widow of his late brother. Sir Jaspar's estate is entailed to Mrs Ireton (and after her death to her son), but the law cannot compel his affections. See above pp. 54, 531, 631.

To join the gentle to the rude!: James Thomson, 'Song': ['For ever, Fortune'] (1732), l. 12: 'And join the Gentle to the Rude'. See James Sambrook, ed., *Liberty, The Castle of Indolence and Other Poems* (Oxford, 1986), p. 290, and pp. 417–18.

Hymen: the Greek god of marriage, usually represented as a young man carrying a torch and a veil.

Madame de Maintenon ... amuse the unamuseable: Françoise d'Aubigné, marquise de Maintenon (1635–1719), married the poet Scarron and later Louis XIV. In 1805 Burney read *La vie de Madame de Maintenon* by Louis-Antoine Caraccioli, which made her 'appear to me a pattern of tried & principled virtue' (*Journals and Letters*, vi. 762). Burney also read a two-volume collection of her letters, published in 1752, in which the phrase 'amuse the unamuseable' is perhaps to be found.

507 *full many a lady ... best*: Ferdinand's speech in Shakespeare's *The Tempest*, III. i. 38–48: 'Full many a lady | I have ey'd with best regard... but you, O you | So perfect and so peerless, are created | Of every creature's best!'.

508 *second volume of the Guardian ... Addison*: the *Guardian*, the successor to Joseph Addison and Richard Steele's *Spectator*, first appeared in 175 numbers between 12 March and 1 October 1713. Founded and edited by Steele, it included fifty-three essays by Addison, as well as contributions from other writers. The 'second volume' mentioned here is probably that of a two-volume edition published by John Nichols in 1789. Almost all of Addison's fifty-three essays are to be found in this volume; John Stephens notes that 'of the last eighty essays he was responsible for fifty-one' (Introduction to *The Guardian* (Lexington, Kentucky, 1982), p. 19).

509 *poz*: a colloquial abbreviation for 'positively'.

510 *buckish*: vigorous, lively, or lascivious.

wight: person. The word was already archaic by the time of Johnson's *Dictionary* (1755).

512 *Will ye, nill ye*: willy-nilly; willingly or unwillingly.

514 *'maiden all forlorn' ... 'man all tattered and torn'*: two characters in 'This is the House that Jack Built', an immensely popular and much analysed nursery-rhyme, first printed in *Nurse Truelove's New-Years-Gift*, published by John Newbery in 1755. The verses are reprinted and discussed by Iona and Peter Opie in *The Oxford Book of Nursery Rhymes* (Oxford, 1952), pp. 29–32.

519 *the fates ... learning*: cf. *The Merchant of Venice*, II. ii. 57–8: 'Fates and Destinies and such odd sayings, the Sisters Three and such branches of learning'.

524 *merry-andrew*: a clown, buffoon.

527 *like Strife, in Spenser's Fairy Queen*: the varlet strife in Spenser's *Fairie Queene* (1590–6) tells Guyon that his Lord has sent him 'To seeke *Occasion*; where so she bee: | For he is all disposd to bloudy fight' (II. iv. 43, ll. 6–7).

528 *execution*: the seizure of the goods of a debtor in default of payment. The term is used repeatedly in *Cecilia*; see Doody, Introduction to *Cecilia*, pp. xvii–xviii.

530 *Minerva ... Juno*: Minerva, the Italian goddess of arts and trades, was later identified with the Greek goddess Athena and worshipped as a goddess of war and wisdom. Juno, wife of Jupiter, was the chief goddess of the Romans.

pin-money: an annual allowance settled upon a woman in marriage for her private expenditure (primarily on clothes), and not subject to her husband's control. See Susan Staves, 'Pin Money', *Studies in Eighteenth-Century Culture*, 14 (1985), 47–77.

532 *"buckled to"*: i.e. buckled down, girded himself; alluding to the fastening on of armour. The phrase occurs twice in the *Fairie Queene*.

533 *round*: large, considerable.

534 *Abigail*: a lady's maid, so named after the waiting gentlewoman in Beaumont and Fletcher's play *The Scornful Lady* (1610), and after the resourceful wife and 'handmaid' of King David (1 Samuel 25).

535 *bantling*: a depreciative term for a young child; a brat.

stores of Plutus: Plutus, the Greek god of wealth, was popularly represented in possession of vast riches.

536 *landau*: a four-wheeled carriage, with a top that could be opened.

537 *filliping*: flipping a finger against the thumb and releasing it, thus giving a sharp tap.

538 *bonbonniere*: French for a small, fancy box containing sweets. *OED* gives the earliest use in English as 1862.

543 *Will o' the Wisp*: something that deludes or misleads by means of mysterious appearances; an apparition.

Ænigma: an enigma, fancifully personified by Sir Jaspar.

Scylla to Charybdis: in Greek myth Scylla, a monstrous woman, lived in a cave in the Straits of Messina between Sicily and Italy, devouring sailors in passing ships. Opposite her cave was the whirlpool Charybdis, which also brought sailors to their deaths. To be between Scylla and Charybdis thus became proverbial for being in equal danger from two threats.

544 *Jupiter, Apollo ... secret progeny*: Jupiter, the chief Roman god, and Apollo, the Greek god of light, both fathered children outside marriage.

fortune ... capricious deity: Fortuna, the Italian goddess of fortune, was often represented with a revolving wheel, to indicate the uncertainty of fortune.

"vast abyss": Milton's *Paradise Lost* (1667), I. 21: 'Dove-like sat'st brooding on the vast abyss'.

caitiff: a base, mean wretch.

546 *Megara ... lower regions*: i.e. Megaera, one of the three Furies; in Greek myth spirits of punishment. See note to p. 872 below.

558 *delusory*: delusive. This is the latest example of the word quoted in *OED*.

560 *furred clogs*: overshoes lined with fur to protect the feet from damp and cold.

VOLUME IV

569 *made the tour*: the Grand Tour of Europe through France and Italy had formerly been taken by young men, normally on leaving the University, and lasted for a year or more. In 1794, however, France and Italy could no longer be safely visited; Lord Melbury would instead make a modified tour to such countries as Germany and Switzerland.

570 *peace-officer*: a constable, appointed to enforce the peace. They were poorly paid, ill-organized, and easily intimidated by well-connected members of society such as Mrs Howel.

573 *gold-purse*: a purse for gold coins: guineas and half-guineas.

580 *food only for worms*: echoing Hotspur's dying words in Shakespeare's *1 Henry IV*, v. iv. 84–6: 'No, Percy, thou art dust | And food for—' *Prince*. 'For worms, brave Percy'.

583 *pallet*: i.e. palette, a flat tablet of wood on which an artist mixes colours.

dodging: following stealthily; the passage is quoted as an example in *OED*.

588 *canonicals*: sacred books; i.e. works of Christian theology.

589 *LXIII*: this chapter is misnumbered XLIII in both the first and second editions.

603 *the music*: i.e. the members of the orchestra, instrumentalists.

takes: takes an interest in, or a liking to someone.

fleer: gibe, sneer, jeer.

605 *retrograded*: turned back.

le Moniteur: French for adviser, counsellor. Ireton mocks what he regards as Harleigh's hypocrisy.

611 *immense screen . . . winter*: a screen would normally be used in winter to ward off the heat of a fire. The hypochondriac Mrs Ireton uses it in summer too, to ward off draughts of air from open doors and windows.

617 *beautiful engravings of Sir Robert Strange*: Strange (1721–92), one of the leading English engravers of the eighteenth century, was a close friend of the Burney family. On his death in 1814 Dr Charles Burney possessed forty-two prints, 'most of them presents from my friend Sir Robert Strange'.

624 *"other times"*: a translation of 'autres temps' in the French proverb 'autres temps, autres mœurs'; customs change with the times.

band-box: a flimsy box made of cardboard or very thin wood, used for carrying hats, millinery, etc.

625 *drachm*: a small quantity.

queue, or for his shoe-strings: the queue of a wig, a plait of hair hanging down behind, was fastened with a length of ribbon. Shoe-strings came into vogue in the mid-1780s, replacing buckles which were 'uncommon after 1793' (Cunnington, *Handbook*, p. 228).

626 *'my mind's eye'*: Hamlet's phrase in *Hamlet*, I. ii. 185. Burney quotes the same words in *Camilla*, p. 845.

Philander of Arcadia: alluding to the hero of Beaumont and Fletcher's *Laws of Candy* (*c.*1619), who is 'passionately in love with Erota'. The word thus signifies a man hopelessly in love, rather than the modern 'philanderer' or male flirt.

'He jests at scars who never felt a wound': Romeo's words in *Romeo and Juliet*, II. ii. 1. Burney quotes the same line in *Cecilia*, p. 510.

627 *How's this, my dainty Ariel?*: alluding to Prospero's words in *The Tempest*, V. i. 95: 'Why, that's my dainty Ariel!'

the wayward sisters: the Fates; see note to p. 504.

628 *pink*: to pierce or stab with a pointed weapon.

629 *'the stars . . . fade away, the sun grow dim, and nature . . . sink in years'*: not identified.

the favourite attribute of our general mother: alluding to the desire for knowledge of Eve, 'our general mother', who ate fruit from the forbidden tree to gain wisdom (Genesis 3: 6).

632 *Venus attired by the Graces*: the Roman goddess of love, dressed by the three Graces, minor goddesses who personified grace and beauty.

634 *collaterally*: as opposed to lineally; not directly from his parents but from their families.

636 *'durance vile'*: Robert Burns, 'Fragment—Epistle from Esopus to Maria' (1794–5), l. 59: 'In durance vile here must I wake and weep'.

637 *Mercury*: the Roman god of trade, identified with the Greek god Hermes, noted for furtiveness and trickery. Hermes was said to have stolen fifty cows on the day of his birth.

641 *his sister's husband*: Lord Denmeath's sister was Lord Granville's second wife; see p. 645 above.

642 *Montpellier*: an ancient town in southern France, close to the Mediterranean. The Bishop's palace there was occupied by the medical school from 1795.

643 *Flanders*: divided between Belgium and France for much of the eighteenth century, until its annexation by France in 1795.

644 *la belle ... la sage petite Anglaise*: the beautiful ... the wise little Englishwoman.

646 *an earl's daughter*: as such, Aurora has the style of Lady Aurora Granville. Juliet, likewise, should be recognized as Lady Juliet Granville, rather than the Honourable Miss Granville; the latter would be correct only for the daughter of a Viscount or Baron.

647 *top-knot*: loops of ribbon of various colours, used to decorate the hair.

taper: tapering, slender.

648 *kennel*: a gutter, running along the side or the middle of a street. Their filth was proverbial; dead animals were left to decay in them.

"A fellow-feeling makes one wond'rous kind!": David Garrick, 'An Occasional Prologue on Quitting the Theatre' (1776). Garrick was a friend of the Burney family, and Frances Burney much admired his performances on stage.

651 *maundering*: wandering aimlessly, meandering.

c'est egal!: it's all the same.

652 *Newton ... angle*: Sir Isaac Newton (1642–1727) discovered the binomial theorem and invented the calculus while still in his early twenties. In 1774 the Burney family moved into his former house off Leicester Square.

'of the melting mood': Othello's words in Shakespeare's *Othello*, v. ii. 349: 'Albeit unused to the melting mood'.

655 *a cast*: a ride or 'lift' in a conveyance.

658 *Cicero or Demosthenes*: respectively, the greatest orators of ancient Rome and ancient Greece.

659 *petticoat*: not an undergarment but a skirt.

662 *advertised in the London news-papers*: such as the *Daily Advertiser*; in *Cecilia*, the heroine is 'advertised' in this paper by the woman who finds her during her madness (*Cecilia*, p. 901 and note).

665 *scouted*: dismissed scornfully, mocked, derided.

white chip: a small bonnet made from wood split into thin strips, and painted white; the style was popular in the late eighteenth century.

apron: worn as an accessory to women's dress, as well as for domestic wear, until the 1790s.

666 *higgler*: an itinerant dealer.

669 *salute*: a kiss.

the antique ballad of the children of the wood: the ballad, also known as 'The Babes in the Wood', which dates from 1595, is described by Addison in the *Spectator*, 7 June 1711, as 'one of the Darling Songs of the Common People'. It was included in Thomas Percy's *Reliques of Ancient English Poetry* (1765).

Nectar: the mythical drink of the gods, conferring immortality on mortals.

671 *ambrosia*: the mythical food of the gods, with the same properties as nectar.

Hebes and Ganymedes: Hebe, in Greek myth, daughter of Zeus, served nectar to the gods; Ganymede was their cupbearer.

Their little lips ... cried: this stanza from 'The Children of the Wood' follows the one described by Wordsworth in his Preface to *Lyrical Ballads* (1800) as 'one of the most justly admired stanzas of the "Babes in the Wood"'.

672 *like the apartment ... hall*: not identified.

674 *"Dull Incurious"*: James Thomson, *The Seasons* (1730); 'Spring', l. 227: 'With what the dull incurious weeds account'. Burney, like Thomson, uses 'incurious' here as a noun.

"God's Gallery": the Reverend Thomas Twining, a classical scholar and friend of the Burney family, was known as 'Aristotle' Twining after the publication of his celebrated edition of Aristotle's *Poetics* in 1789. The phrase quoted here has not been located.

675 *"wild fantastic roots"*: not identified.

"busy hum of man": Milton, 'L'Allegro' (1632), l. 117: 'And the busy hum of men'.

677 *va'nt*: a dialect form of 'warrant'.

wull: a dialect form of 'will'.

679 *chicky biddy*: a nonce-phrase, as the italics indicate; 'biddy' is dialect for a chicken. The children have been taught to call pheasant and partridge chicken because the game laws made it illegal to kill game birds. The severest penalties, however, were reserved for deer-poachers. See Douglas Hay, 'Poverty and the Game Laws on Cannock Chase', in Hay *et al.*, *Albion's Fatal Tree* (London, 1975).

681 *"Kind nature's soft restorer, balmy sleep"*: misquoting the first line of Edward Young's *Night Thoughts* (1742–4): 'Tir'd Nature's sweet restorer, balmy sleep!' The same line is quoted correctly in *Camilla*, p. 883.

690 *Addison, called an Hymn to the Divinity*: many of Addison's essays in the *Spectator* set out to demonstrate the presence of the Divinity. In No. 381, 17 May 1712, he describes an 'inward Chearfulness' as 'a secret Approbation of the Divine Will in his Conduct Towards Man'.

691 *wash*: swill.

692 *near*: stingy, mean.

693 *"mark or likelihood"*: the King's words in *1 Henry IV*, III. ii. 45: 'A fellow of no mark nor likelihood'.

695 *the right of strength*: in fact, 'the right of the strongest'. The French here is a variant of La Fontaine's maxim, 'La raison du plus fort est toujours la meilleure' (might is right).

697 *trials ... ballads*: trial reports, published in book form, provided sensational reading throughout the eighteenth century. The tracts on farriery, in contrast, were practical handbooks on the care of horses; while the 'dismal old ballads' were intended to entertain and edify children.

703 *Pollards*: trees, cut back to produce a thick growth of branches, forming a dense mass.

VOLUME V

711 *"business and bosoms"*: from the Epistle Dedicatory to the 1625 edition of Francis Bacon's *Essays*: 'I do now publish my Essays, which, of all my other works, have been most current; for that, as it seems, they come home to men's business and bosoms'. Burney uses the phrase frequently in her letters and journals.

712 *The La be good unto me!*: an obscure and slightly unusual dialectical corruption of 'La' for 'Lord' (i.e. 'The Lord be good unto me!'). The phrase is a favourite exclamatory expression of Sir Hugh Tyrold's in *Camilla*; see *Camilla*, pp. 548, 597.

'T be all blown, then ...: i.e. all will be betrayed, made public. Originally thieves' slang, 'to blow' meant to inform on someone, or to detect a criminal in the act of committing a crime. See *Camilla*, p. 205 and note.

717 *mislested*: i.e. molested; a dialectical corruption.

pretty ones: a familiar term of address for children, often shortened to 'my pretty' or 'my pretties'. Dame Fairfield is alluding to the Royal Family's journey through the New Forest, accompanied by Burney herself, in June 1789; see *Diary and Letters*, v. 28–32.

counterband merchandize: contraband goods. *OED* cites this example as an early variation on 'contraband'.

728 *her face that seemed bloodless with despair*: seem corrected to 'seemed' in the second edition. Cf. Pope's *Iliad*, xiii. 364–5: 'With chatt'ring teeth he stands, and stiff'ning hair, | And looks a bloodless image of despair!' See also *Evelina*, p. 182 and note.

734 *sal volatile*: ammonium carbonate; a volatile salt of strong pungent odour, consisting of three parts of carbonic acid and two parts of oxide of ammonium. Sal volatile, also called spirit of hartshorn, was frequently used to revive women who had fallen into fainting fits. See note to p. 98; cf. also *Camilla*, p. 326 and note.

737 *this Gallic Goliah*: i.e. this French Giant. Goliah is a variant of Goliath, the giant slain by David in 1 Samuel 17. Goliah or Goliath could be used to designate a tall 'giant' of an individual without particular reference to the biblical text.

753 *Joy, then, to great Caesar!*: Sir Jaspar refers to 'Joy to great Caesar', the beginning of Thomas D'Urfey's song 'The KING's Health: set to Farinel's Ground' (1681). D'Urfey's song was immensely popular in the late seventeenth century; in *The Guardian* 67, 28 May 1713, Addison comments that the song, a helpful piece of Tory propaganda, 'gave the Whigs such a Blow as they were not able to recover the whole Reign'. See *The Songs of Thomas D'Urfey*, ed. Cyrus L. Day (Cambridge, Mass., 1933), p. 47. Note also Pope's parody of D'Urfey's opening lines in *The Dunciad*, IV. 54.

"The little birds that fly, | With careless ease, from tree to tree": Burney quotes Thomas Parnell's *Song* ('My Days have been'). 'My Days have been so wondrous Free, | The little Birds that flie | With careless Ease from Tree to Tree, | Were but as bless'd as I'. Parnell's poem was first printed in Steele's *Poetical Miscellanies* (1714) and reprinted in Pope's 1722 edition. See *Collected Poems of Thomas Parnell*, ed. Claude Rawson and F. P. Lock (Newark, Del., 1989), pp. 113–14, 484.

755 *master of the whole planetary system . . . with Venus, in her choicest wiles, at its head*: with characteristic inventiveness, Sir Jaspar is playing on the two significations of Venus: as the Roman goddess of love and as the second planet from Earth in the planetary system. In *The*

Forgotten Sky (Oxford, 1984), J. C. Eade points out 'how often in literary reference Venus is presented as behaving in an impossible way' (p. 25). For Sir Jaspar's interest in astrology, see p. 541.

756 *alien-bill*: William Pitt's Aliens Bill, passed on 31 December 1792, granted the government summary powers to deport foreigners. See also note to p. 797 below.

759 *Cicerone*: an Italian term for a learned guide who would offer to show tourists and sight-seers ruins, estates, and works of art. On a visit to Plymouth Dock on 19 August 1789, Burney typically took advantage of this novel designation to coin the nonce-word 'cicerone-ing'. 'My constant Captain Duckworth', she wrote of her guardian on that occasion, 'kept me ... wholly to his Ciceroneing'. See *Diary and Letters*, v. 43.

"awake to tender strokes of art": from Pope's 'Prologue' to Addison's *Cato*, ll. 1–5: 'To wake the soul by tender strokes of art, | To raise the genius, and to mend the heart | ... For this the tragic muse first trod the stage'.

760 *alto and basso relievos*: from the Italian *rilevare*, 'to raise', relievos or reliefs are sculptures which project from a background surface. Alto or 'high' reliefs depict standing figures as substantially detached and almost distinct from their backgrounds. In basso or 'low' reliefs the projection is minimal, and the figures do not stand distinctly apart from the background surface. See *Camilla*, p. 602.

marbles, alabasters, spars, and lavers of all colours: marbles are any kind of hard, polished limestone. Alabaster is a soft, semi-transparent stone used for religious carvings and small retables or altarpieces. Spar is 'a general term for a number of crystalline minerals more or less lustrous in appearance' (*OED*); 'spars' are small ornaments made of such material. Lavers are large basins or bowls.

Æsculapius ... Mercury ... Minerva ... Venus: the baronet solicits those figures of classical mythology in some way featured in the tour of Wilton for their particular gifts. From Æsculapius, the god of medicine, he asks a prescription or restorative; from Mercury, who appears to be functioning here in his capacity as psychopomp as well as god of luck or good fortune, he rather amusingly asks an 'ordonnance' (i.e. a writ of passage) for Juliet's 'spirits'; from Minerva, patron deity of the art of war, he asks courage. Venus is also invoked for her beauty, and her power to create love.

Vandyke's children of Charles the First: the Flemish portrait painter Sir Anthony Van Dyck (1599–1641) was received in England by Charles I in 1632 and in the same year appointed 'Principal Painter in Ordinary to their Majesties at St. James's'. He was given a house in Blackfriars, and remained in England most of his life, painting many elegant portraits of the King and the royal family. His portrait (1635) of Charles I's children (an exact copy by Van Dyck of his own original, painted for the King at Windsor) hangs at Wilton in an elaborate frame over the chimney in the Double Cube room, an Italianate state room on the south side of the house; the room was included in Inigo Jones's reconstruction of Wilton in 1648–53 specifically to accommodate the family's collection of Van Dyck portraits. On a visit to the Double Cube room at Wilton in 1791, Burney commented that she there 'renewed my delight over the exquisite Vandykes ... which again I sighingly quitted, with a longing wish I might ever pass under that Roof time enough to see them more deliberately'. See *Journals and Letters*, i. 22.

an apartment which is presided by a noble picture of Salvator Rosa: Salvator Rosa (1615–73), a Neopolitan who lived and worked for much of his life in Rome, was famous as a painter of wild landscapes, marine views, and historical subjects. His 'Landscape with Figures', painted in the late 1630s, hangs at Wilton.

761 *to hang, henceforth, solely upon herself*: i.e. to rely, in future, upon herself alone. *OED* cites this example, but mistakenly gives the publication date of *The Wanderer* as 1817.

765 *"the beginning of things"*: not identified.

a bustard, or a wheat-ear: Burney is notably accurate in her description of the kind of fauna which naturally inhabited the great expanse of Salisbury plain. Bustards (now extinct in the British Isles) are large birds, related to cranes and plovers; the wheat-ear—also known as Fallow-finch—is a smaller bird, which inhabits rocky areas.

766 *"meditation even to madness"*: cf. Iago in Shakespeare's *Othello*, II. i. 305–6: 'practise upon his peace and quiet, | Even to madness'.

Gog and Magog: Sir Jaspar imagines Stonehenge to be a fittingly vast temple for the biblical giants Gog and Magog. The names 'Gog' and 'Magog' were also popular designations for the two wooden statues or 'giants' which stand on the Guildhall in London.

the 'liquid lustre of those eyes,—so brightly mutable, so sweetly wild!': from William Mason's 'Elegy on the Death of Lady Coventry', ll. 15–16. See p. 117 and note; cf. also Burney's description of Clermont Lynmere in *Camilla*, p. 569.

770 *turbently*: i.e. in agitation and turbulence; the coinage appears to be Burney's own.

le cher Epoux: the cherished husband. Cf. Mrs Elton's designation of her husband as her 'cara sposa' or 'caro sposa' in Jane Austen's *Emma* (1816).

as hang-dog a physiognomy as a Bow Street prowler: Bow Street, near Covent Garden, had long been the site of the principal police court in London. A 'hangdog physiognomy' is the face of 'a despicable or degraded fellow fit only to hang a dog, or to be hanged like a dog' (*OED*); Riley thus characterizes Juliet's 'husband' as looking like a common London criminal, an obvious reference to 'Bow-street Runners', who served as secret detectives and informants to the Middlesex magistrates.

771 *hocus pocus work*: the nonsense phrase 'hocus pocus' is traditionally but mistakenly derived from Protestant ridicule of the words of consecration in the Catholic mass (hoc est corpus meum); Riley's 'hocus pocus work' refers to Juliet's quick and unexpected transformations.

Hebe: see note to p. 671. Hebe, the handmaiden to the gods, was also the goddess of youth; hence Riley's reference to Juliet's 'Hebe face' calls attention to the virginal, unsullied bloom of youth.

that old Bang'em's concert: 'Bang'em's' seems to be Burney's own coinage. A man who 'came bang up to the mark' was one who performed with spirit, resolution, and commitment in a given enterprise, so Riley is perhaps complimenting the performer's enthusiasm.

Ovid ... Genii ... Mother Goose: impressed by Juliet's seeming metamorphosis, Riley invokes the authors popular for their fantastic tales of transformation. Ovid's *Metamorphoses* were popular throughout the eighteenth century. 'Eastern' or 'Oriental' tales had enjoyed a wide popularity in England since the appearance in translation of Antoine Galland's *Arabian Night's Entertainments* in the first decade of the eighteenth century; James Ridley's *Tales of the Genii* had been published in 1765. Mother Goose had since the mid-eighteenth century been associated with children's nursery rhymes. *Mother Goose's Melody*, a collection of nursery rhymes adapted from the French tales of Charles Perrault, was published by John Newbery in 1780 or earlier.

puppet-shew ... mummy: itinerant entertainments featuring the puppets 'Punch and Judy' were popular throughout the eighteenth century. Such 'puppet shews' commonly featured 'punchinello's' or 'Punch's' violent physical abuse of his wife and child, and the appearance of the devil—'old Nick' (see note to p. 444)—who attempts to carry Punch with him to hell. To 'pummel' something 'to a mummy' meant to beat it into a pulpy and unrecognizable mass. See *Evelina*, p. 150 and note, and *Camilla*, p. 493 and note.

skull-cap: a light, close-fitting cap for covering the head; skull caps could be made of silk, velvet, or linen.

781 *ecclesiastical court ... recantation*: ecclesiastical courts held authority in spiritual matters and affairs relating to the church. An ecclesiastical court would thus be the proper place for Elinor to renounce her disbelief in an after-life, could Harleigh convince her to do so.

783 *'this sensible, warm being,' will 'melt, thaw, and resolve itself into a dew'*: quoted in part from Shakespeare's *Hamlet*, I. ii. 129–30: 'O that this too too solid flesh would melt, | Thaw and resolve itself into a dew'.

786 *'how can we reason but from what we know'*: Pope, *An Essay on Man* (1733–4), i. 18: 'What can we reason, but from what we know?'. See also *Cecilia*, p. 576 and note.

787 *'we live, and move, and have our being'*: alluding to Acts 17: 28: 'For in him we live, and move, and have our being'.

790 *'that bourne whence no traveller returns'*: slightly misquoted from *Hamlet*, III, i. 79–80: 'The undiscover'd country, from whose bourn | No traveller returns'.

793 *'Lost and bewildered in my fruitless search'*: slightly misquoted from Portius's speech in Addison's *Cato* (1713), I. i. 52: 'Lost and bewildered in the fruitless search'. Burney had used lines from the same speech in her draft introduction to *Cecilia*: see *Cecilia*, p. 945 and note.

797 *advancing the postage*: throughout the eighteenth century postage on letters and posted packets was paid upon delivery by the addressee; the amount of postage on letters would be ascertained by weight, the number of sheets of paper, and the distance of

delivery. Perforated postage stamps did not come into general use until the mid-nineteenth century.

798 *double passport, for and from London*: after the Aliens Act received royal assent on 8 January 1793, foreigners landing in Britain 'had to register at the customs office on disembarking, give up any arms in their possession and then wait to be granted a passport by the Home Secretary or by a local magistrate'. Moreover, 'any alien who had landed since 1 January 1792 had to obtain a passport before changing his place of residence', and magistrates 'could require foreigners to reside in specific areas'. See Clive Emsley, *British Society and the French Wars 1793–1815* (London, 1979), pp. 20–1.

809 *a general-officer*: an officer of superior rank, 'one above the rank of colonel' (*OED*).

812 *standers-by see the most of the game*: alternatively, 'lookers-on see more than players'. The proverbial expression dates as far back as the early sixteenth century. See *Dictionary of Proverbs*, pp. 483–4.

813 *nearer the mark for falling to loggerheads*: i.e. any more in the right for coming to blows.

814 *cat-o'-nine-tails*: 'a whip of nine knotted lashes; till 1881 an authorized instrument of punishment in the British navy and army' (*OED*).

819 *insulated*: solitary, isolated.

822 *dial*: the face of a watch or clock.

828 *"like the baseless fabric of a vision"*: cf. Shakespeare, *The Tempest*, IV. i. 151–4: 'like the baseless fabric of this vision | The cloud-capp'd towers, the gorgeous palaces, | The solemn temples, the great Globe itself, | Yea, all which it inherit, shall dissolve'.

830 *flummery*: empty or insipid flattery. Flummery—sometimes called frumenty—was a child's pottage made of wheat or oatmeal steeped in water or boiled in milk. The resulting mixture could be exceptionally tastless and insipid; hence the extended meaning of the term.

832 *juggled*: cheated, imposed upon.

slabbering bibs: bibs which protected children's clothes from 'slabber' or slaver—the moisture from the mouth or lips. This use post-dates *OED*'s latest example, also credited to Burney, from *Cecilia* (1782). See *Cecilia*, p. 516 and note.

younkers: youngsters, youths; a dialectical corruption popular in the North and in Cornwall, used also by Admiral Croft in Jane Austen's *Persuasion* (1818).

836* *the company's service . . . East Indies*: the East India Company, originally chartered in 1600 as a trading company, was by the mid-eighteenth century granted joint sovereignty (with the Crown) of India. A young man entering the 'company's service' might look forward to a promising career in the territorial administration.

839 *post-captain*: a commissioned naval officer with the rank of captain; the term was used to distinguish a full grade captain who took command of a ship-of-war—i.e. 'took post'—from other officers, to whom the nominal title of 'captain' was often extended as a courtesy.

841 *rhino*: a slang term for money, especially a large sum of money. See *Camilla*, p. 91 and note.

the finish: the end, conclusion. *OED* cites this example.

842 *goust*: liking, taste; obscure form of 'gout'.

I should as lieve you had not tied such an ugly knot: i.e. I had rather you had not married such a man.

848 *bond-woman*: a female slave.

854 *wag*: 'move one's limbs' (*OED*).

chopfallen: i.e. chapfallen; literally 'down in the mouth', depressed.

855 *Dorchester ale, and Devonshire cyder*: Dorchester's fine pale ale had long enjoyed a high reputation, and the West country still produces celebrated 'hard' ciders. The Admiral's amusingly patriotic advancement of this peculiarly 'British' fare to the 'poor half-starved' Frenchmen is not entirely unfitting, as the embargo on French wines since the French wars of the early eighteenth century had in fact facilitated and encouraged the brewing and distribution of local liquors in areas such as Dorsetshire.

soup meagre: i.e. soup maigre, a thin vegetable soup.

858 *devizing*: imagining, conceiving; *OED* cites this example.

859 *ragouts and fricandos, made up of oil and grease*: a ragout is a highly seasoned dish of stewed meat and vegetables; fricandeaus—or 'fricandos' as the Admiral calls them here—are likewise stewed or roasted meat entrées, usually veal.

864 *bathing-machine*: an enclosed carriage which could be drawn into the sea by a horse, for the convenience and modesty of bathers. A detailed description is provided in Smollett's *Humphry Clinker* (1771) (Oxford World's Classics, 1984), ii. 178–9.

865 *Commodore*: 'an officer in command, ranking above a captain and below a rear-admiral' (*OED*).

the Gazette: i.e. the *London Gazette*, a bi-weekly newspaper in which were published news and notices of government appointments, honours, and promotions.

866 *sooner than call out Jack Robinson*: to 'say Jack Robinson' or 'call out Jack Robinson' meant to do something very quickly.

868 *she would have been . . . grandfather*: i.e. Juliet would have been styled Lady Juliet Granville, had her father recognized her in his lifetime. See note to p. 646.

871 *briefly*: soon.

872 *three ladies, whom he nominated the three Furies*: the Admiral designates Mrs Howel, Mrs Ireton, and Mrs Maple with reference to the 'Erinyes' or furies of classical mythology: Allecto, Megaera, and Tisiphone.

873 *a female Robinson Crusoe*: Burney likens the trials of her heroine to those of the hero of Defoe's *Robinson Crusoe* (1719). On the minor tradition of the 'female Robinson Crusoe' in the English fiction of the eighteenth century, see Doody, *Frances Burney*, p. 350 and note.

864 *bathing-machine*: an enclosed carriage which could be drawn into the sea by a horse, for the convenience and modesty of bathers. A detailed description is provided in Smollett's *Humphry Clinker* (1771) (Oxford World's Classics, 1984), ii. 178–9.

865 *Commodore*: an officer in command ranking above a captain and below a rear-admiral (*OED*).

the Gazette: i.e. the *London Gazette*, a biweekly newspaper in which were published news and notices of government appointments, honours, and promotions.

866 *sooner than call out Jack Robinson*: to 'say Jack Robinson' or 'call out Jack Robinson' meant to do something very quickly.

868 *she would have been a . . . grandfather*: i.e. Juliet would have been styled Lady Juliet Granville, had her father recognized her in his lifetime. See note to p. 646.

871 *by-the-by*: soon.

872 *furmaleers, whom he nominates the three Furies*: the Admiral designates Mrs Ireton, and Mrs Maple with reference to the 'Erinyes' or furies of classical mythology: Alecto, Megaera, and Tisiphone.

873 *a female Robinson Crusoe*: Burney likens the trials of her heroine to those of the hero of Defoe's *Robinson Crusoe* (1719). On the minor tradition of the 'female Robinson Crusoe' in the English fiction of the eighteenth century, see Doody, *Frances Burney*, p. 350 and notes.

THE WORLD'S CLASSICS

A Select List

SERGEI AKSAKOV: A Russian Gentleman
Translated by J. D. Duff
Edited by Edward Crankshaw

HANS ANDERSEN: Fairy Tales
Translated by L. W. Kingsland
Introduction by Naomi Lewis
Illustrated by Vilhelm Pedersen and Lorenz Frølich

JANE AUSTEN: Emma
Edited by James Kinsley and David Lodge

Mansfield Park
Edited by James Kinsley and John Lucas

ROBERT BAGE: Hermsprong
Edited by Peter Faulkner

WILLIAM BECKFORD: Vathek
Edited by Roger Lonsdale

CHARLOTTE BRONTË: Jane Eyre
Edited by Margaret Smith

THOMAS CARLYLE: The French Revolution
Edited by K. J. Fielding and David Sorensen

LEWIS CARROLL: Alice's Adventures in Wonderland
and Through the Looking Glass
Edited by Roger Lancelyn Green
Illustrated by John Tenniel

GEOFFREY CHAUCER: The Canterbury Tales
Translated by David Wright

ANTON CHEKHOV: The Russian Master and Other Stories
Translated by Ronald Hingley

Victory
Edited by John Batchelor
Introduction by Tony Tanner

CHARLES DICKENS: Christmas Books
Edited by Ruth Glancy

FËDOR DOSTOEVSKY: Crime and Punishment
Translated by Jessie Coulson
Introduction by John Jones

GEORGE ELIOT: Daniel Deronda
Edited by Graham Handley

SUSAN FERRIER: Marriage
Edited by Herbert Foltinek

SARAH FIELDING: The Adventures of David Simple
Edited by Malcolm Kelsall

ELIZABETH GASKELL: Cousin Phillis and Other Tales
Edited by Angus Easson

KENNETH GRAHAME: The Wind in the Willows
Edited by Peter Green

THOMAS HARDY: A Pair of Blue Eyes
Edited by Alan Manford

JAMES HOGG: The Private Memoirs and Confessions of a Justified Sinner
Edited by John Carey

THOMAS HUGHES: Tom Brown's Schooldays
Edited by Andrew Sanders

HENRIK IBSEN: An Enemy of the People, The Wild Duck, Rosmersholm
Edited and Translated by James McFarlane

HENRY JAMES: The Ambassadors
Edited by Christopher Butler

RICHARD JEFFERIES: After London or Wild England
Introduction by John Fowles

JOCELIN OF BRAKELOND:
Chronicle of the Abbey of Bury St. Edmunds
Translated by Diana Greenway and Jane Sayers

GWYN JONES (Transl.):
Eirik the Red and Other Icelandic Sagas

RUDYARD KIPLING: The Day's Work
Edited by Thomas Pinney

CHARLOTTE LENNOX: The Female Quixote
Edited by Margaret Dalziel
Introduction by Margaret Anne Doody

KATHERINE MANSFIELD: Selected Stories
Edited by D. M. Davin

HERMAN MELVILLE: The Confidence-Man
Edited by Tony Tanner

PROSPER MÉRIMÉE: Carmen and Other Stories
Translated by Nicholas Jotcham

MARGARET OLIPHANT:
A Beleaguered City and Other Stories
Edited by Merryn Williams

EDGAR ALLAN POE: Selected Tales
Edited by Julian Symons

PAUL SALZMAN (Ed.):
An Anthology of Elizabethan Prose Fiction

PERCY BYSSHE SHELLEY:
Zastrozzi *and* St. Irvyne
Edited by Stephen Behrendt

TOBIAS SMOLLETT: The Expedition of Humphry Clinker
Edited by Lewis M. Knapp
Revised by Paul-Gabriel Boucé

ROBERT LOUIS STEVENSON: Kidnapped and Catriona
Edited by Emma Letley

The Strange Case of Dr. Jekyll and Mr. Hyde
and Weir of Hermiston
Edited by Emma Letley

BRAM STOKER: Dracula
Edited by A. N. Wilson

WILLIAM MAKEPEACE THACKERAY: Barry Lyndon
Edited by Andrew Sanders

LEO TOLSTOY: Anna Karenina
Translated by Louise and Aylmer Maude
Introduction by John Bayley

ANTHONY TROLLOPE: The American Senator
Edited by John Halperin

Dr. Wortle's School
Edited by John Halperin

Orley Farm
Edited by David Skilton

VILLIERS DE L'ISLE-ADAM: Cruel Tales
Translated by Robert Baldick
Edited by A. W. Raitt

VIRGIL: The Aeneid
Translated by C. Day Lewis
Edited by Jasper Griffin

HORACE WALPOLE : The Castle of Otranto
Edited by W. S. Lewis

IZAAK WALTON and CHARLES COTTON:
The Compleat Angler
Edited by John Buxton
Introduction by John Buchan

OSCAR WILDE: Complete Shorter Fiction
Edited by Isobel Murray

The Picture of Dorian Gray
Edited by Isobel Murray

ÉMILE ZOLA:
The Attack on the Mill and other stories
Translated by Douglas Parmeé